WIND AND TRUTH

FICTION BY BRANDON SANDERSON®

THE STORMLIGHT ARCHIVE®

The Way of Kings
Words of Radiance
Oathbringer
Rhythm of War
Wind and Truth

NOVELLAS

Edgedancer
Dawnshard

THE MISTBORN® SAGA

THE ORIGINAL TRILOGY

Mistborn
The Well of Ascension
The Hero of Ages

THE WAX AND WAYNE SERIES

The Alloy of Law
Shadows of Self
The Bands of Mourning
The Lost Metal

NOVELLA

Mistborn: Secret History

THE RECKONERS®

Steelheart
Mitosis: A Reckoners Story
Firefight
Calamity

SKYWARD

Skyward
Starsight
Cytonic
Defiant

NOVELLA

Defending Elysium

WITH JANCI PATTERSON

Skyward Flight: Sunreach, ReDawn & Evershore

ALCATRAZ VS. THE EVIL LIBRARIANS

Alcatraz vs. the Evil Librarians
The Scrivener's Bones
The Knights of Crystallia
The Shattered Lens
The Dark Talent

WITH JANCI PATTERSON

Bastille vs. the Evil Librarians

NOVELS

Elantris
Warbreaker
The Rithmatist
Tress of the Emerald Sea
The Frugal Wizard's Handbook for Surviving Medieval England
Yumi and the Nightmare Painter
The Sunlit Man

NOVELLAS

Firstborn
Perfect State
Snapshot
Children of the Nameless

WITH MARY ROBINETTE KOWAL

The Original

COLLECTIONS

Arcanum Unbounded: The Cosmere® Collection
Legion: The Many Lives of Stephen Leeds

GRAPHIC NOVELS

White Sand: A Cosmere® Graphic Novel
Dark One

INFINITY BLADE

Infinity Blade: Awakening
Infinity Blade: Redemption

THE WHEEL OF TIME

WITH ROBERT JORDAN

The Gathering Storm
Towers of Midnight
A Memory of Light

BRANDON SANDERSON

WIND AND TRUTH

Book Five of

THE STORMLIGHT ARCHIVE

TOR PUBLISHING GROUP • NEW YORK

This is a work of fiction. All of the characters, organizations, and events portrayed in this novel are either products of the author's imagination or are used fictitiously.

WIND AND TRUTH

All illustrations © Dragonsteel, LLC, except when otherwise noted
Illustrations preceding chapters 1, 12, 17, 34, and interlude 1 by Ben McSweeney
Illustrations preceding chapters 48, 62, 68, 88, 92, and interlude 7 by Audrey Hotte and Ben McSweeney
Illustrations preceding chapters 31 and 69 by Dan dos Santos
Illustrations preceding chapter 24 and in chapter 122 by Kelley King
Illustration preceding interlude 11 by Miranda Meeks
Illustration preceding chapter 84 by Anna Earley
Illustration preceding chapter 136 by Greg Call and Hayley Lazo
Map of Roshar, sword glyphs, and illustrations preceding interlude 5 and chapters 55 and 82 by Isaac Stewart
Chapter arches by Isaac Stewart and Hayley Lazo
Viewpoint icons by Isaac Stewart, Ben McSweeney, and Howard Lyon
Dust jacket illustration © Michael Whelan
Front endpapers by Donato Giancola
Rear endpapers by Miranda Meeks

A Tor Book
Published by Tom Doherty Associates / Tor Publishing Group
120 Broadway
New York, NY 10271

www.torpublishinggroup.com

The Library of Congress Cataloging-in-Publication Data is available upon request.

ISBN 978-1-250-31918-0 (hardcover)
ISBN 978-1-250-38527-7 (international, sold outside the U.S., subject to rights availability)
ISBN 978-1-250-38720-2 (signed)
ISBN 978-1-250-31917-3 (ebook)

Our books may be purchased in bulk for promotional, educational, or business use. Please contact your local bookseller or the Macmillan Corporate and Premium Sales Department at 1-800-221-7945, extension 5442, or by email at MacmillanSpecialMarkets@macmillan.com.

First Edition: December 2024

Printed in the United States of America

This edition was printed by Lakeside Book Company

0 9 8 7 6 5 4 3 2 1

For Adam Horne,

Who is a champion of books, and deserves his own Shardblade.

PREFACE AND ACKNOWLEDGMENTS

Welcome to *Wind and Truth*, Book Five of the Stormlight Archive. This is the midpoint in the series, and the ending of the first major arc. As such, I have wrestled with this book more than most, giving it a great portion of my thoughts, passion, and effort over the last four years. This is, to date, the longest book I've ever written—and this is among the longest amounts of time I've ever spent on a book. (Probably the longest, if you don't count projects I set down and came back to years later.) I hope you'll find the result worth the effort!

Below is a list of all the people who worked on the novel behind the scenes in various capacities. It's getting more and more like movie credits, with how many people help. I still write every word, and am the sole author of the books, but wow . . . Dragonsteel as a company has become something spectacular. While for most books we keep a pretty normal work schedule, Stormlight novels are generally an "all hands on deck" situation—with some pulling extra hours to meet deadlines, and others spending a great deal of their working days focused only on helping get the book edited, publicized, and distributed. So if you ever get a chance to meet them, give them a handshake and a thank-you.

Then please, sit back and enjoy the show. A highstorm is brewing.

Artists who worked on this book: Michael Whelan, Donato Giancola, Miranda Meeks, Dan dos Santos, Audrey Hotte, Kelley King, Petar Penev, Howard Lyon, Greg Call, Isaac Stewart, Ben McSweeney, Anna Earley, Hayley Lazo.

At Tor Books: Devi Pillai, Stephanie Stein, Tessa Villanueva, Sanaa Ali-Virani, Rafal Gibek, Peter Lutjen, Alexis Saarela, Lucille Rettino, Emily Mlynek.

At Gollancz: Gillian Redfearn, Brendan Durkin, Emad Akhtar, Cait Davies, Javerya Iqbal.

Copyediting and proofreading: Terry McGarry, Christina MacDonald, Hayley Jozwiak.

Audiobook narrators: Michael Kramer and Kate Reading. At Macmillan Audio: Steve Wagner.

At JABberwocky Literary Agency: Joshua Bilmes, Susan Velasquez, Christina Zobel, Valentina Sainato, Brady McReynolds. At Zeno Literary Agency: John Berlyne.

At Dragonsteel: COO Emily Sanderson. Operations & HR: VP Matt "Why do you write my name like this, Brandon?" Hatch, Operations Director Jane Horne, Kathleen Dorsey Sanderson, Jerrod Walker, Braydonn Moore, Makena Saluone, Christian Fairbanks, Becky Wilson, Ethan Skarstedt, Finance Director Emma Tan-Stoker, Matt Hampton.

Creative Development: VP Isaac SteWart, Art Director Shawn Boyles, Art Director Ben McSweeney, Jennifer Neal, Rachael Lynn Buchanan, Anna Earley, Hayley Lazo, Priscilla Spencer.

Editorial: VP the Inviting Peter Ahlstrom, Editorial Director Kristy S. Gilbert, Continuity Director Karen Ahlstrom, Jennie Stevens, Betsey Ahlstrom, Emily Shaw-Higham.

Merchandise, Events, and Snazzy Sweaters: VP Kara Stewart, Merchandise Director Christi Jacobsen, Events & Support Director Kellyn Neumann, Lex Willhite, Richard Rubert, Dallin Holden, Ally Reep, Mem Grange, Brett Moore, Katy Ives, Joy Allen, Daniel Phipps, Michael Bateman, Alex Lyon, Jacob Chrisman, Camilla Waite, Quinton Martin, Hollie Rubert, Gwen Hickman, Isabel Chrisman, Amanda Butterfield, Logan Reep, Pablo Mooney.

Publicity & Marketing: VP Adam Horne, aka He for Whom the Book Is Dedicated (huzzah!), Marketing Director Jeremy Palmer, Octavia Escamilla-Spiker, Taylor Hatch, Tayan Hatch, Donald George Mustard III.

Narrative: VP Dan Wells—our lone member of the Narrative Department, except for his imaginary friend Bob the Banjo Player.

My writing group, Here There Be Dragons: Kaylynn ZoBell, Kathleen Dorsey Sanderson, Eric James Stone, Darci Stone, Alan Layton, How's That Ben? (Olsen), Ethan Skarstedt, Karen Ahlstrom, Peter Ahlstrom, Emily Sanderson.

Dissociative identity disorder expert: Britt Martin. Military experts: Carl Fisk, John Fahey. Amputee and prosthetics expert: Matthew Fox.

Arcanists: Eric Lake, Evgeni "Argent" Kirilov, Joshua "Jofwu" Harkey, David Behrens, Ian McNatt, Ben Marrow.

Beta readers: Aaron Ford, Alexis Horizon, Alice Arneson, Alyx Hoge, Amit Shteinheart, Aubree Pham, Austin Hussey, Bao Pham, Becca Reppert, Ben Marrow, Billy Todd, Bob Kluttz, Brandon Cole, Brian T. Hill, Britton Roney, Chana Oshira Block, Chris Kluwe, Chris McGrath, Christina Goodman, Christopher "chaplainchris" Cottingham, Craig Hanks, Darci Cole, David Behrens, Deana Covel Whitney, Donita Orders, Drew McCaffrey, Eliyahu Berelowitz Levin, Eric Lake, Erika Kuta Marler, Evgeni "Argent" Kirilov, Gary Singer, Giulia Costantini, Glen Vogelaar, Ian McNatt, Jayden King, Jennifer Pugh, Jessica Ashcraft, Jessie Lake, João Menezes Morais, Joe Skeedlebop Deardeuff, Joelle Ruth Phillips, Jory "Jor the Bouncer" Phillips, Joshua Harkey, Kadie "Ene" Nytch, Kalyani Poluri,

Kathleen Barlow, Dr. Kathleen Holland, Kendra Wilson, Krystl Allred, Kyle "Dorksider" Wilson, Laura Heinis, Lauren McCaffrey, Lauren "Biz's Mom" Strach, Liliana Klein, Linnea Lindstrom, Lyndsey Luther, Marnie Peterson, Matt Wiens, Max Salzman, Megan Kanne, Mi'chelle Walker, Paige Phillips, Paige Vest, Poonam Desai, Rachel Rada, Rahkeem Ball, Rahul Pantula, Richard Fife, Rob West, Rosemary Williams, Ross Newberry, Ryan Scott, Sam Baskin, Sarah Herr, Sarah Kane, Scott "Spydr" Webb, Sean VanBlack, Shannon Nelson, Shivam Bhatt, Siena "Lotus" Buchanan, Suzanne Musin, Taylor Cole, Ted Herman, Tim Challener, TJ McGrath, Trae Cooper, Zenef Mark Lindberg.

Gamma readers: Many of the beta readers plus Ari Kufer, Brian Magnant, Collin Abeln, Dale Wiens, Ellie Frato-Sweeney, Lingting "Botanica" Xu, Nisarg "Strifelover" Shah, Philip Vorwaller, Ram Shoham, Spencer White, Valencia Kumley, William Juan.

CONTENTS

ILLUSTRATIONS

NOTE: *Many illustrations, titles included, contain spoilers for material that comes before them in the book. Look ahead at your own risk.*

BOOK FIVE

WIND AND TRUTH

Roshar

Endless Ocean

Quili
Abri
Rall Elorim
Reshi
Kasitor
Iri
Rira
Kurth
Resh
Eila
The Misted Mountains
Shinovar
Babatharnam
Panatham
Marabeth
The Purelak
Aimian Sea
Aimia
Yulay
Fu Nam
Desh
Azir
Alm
Yezier
Urithiru
Azimir
The Valle
Yeddaw
Liafor
Tashikk
Emul
Steen
Sesemalex Dar
Tukar
Mara
Icewater

Southern Depths

Steamwater Ocean
Isles
Akak
Sumi
Sea
Akak
Northgrip
Herdaz
Mourn's Vault
Varikev
Ru Parat
Elanar
Jah Keved
Tu Bayla
Valath
Hornheater Peaks
Kholinar
Shulin
Alethkar
Unclaimed Hills
Bavland
Silnasen
Rathalas
Dawn's Shadow
Triax
Vedenar
Dumadari
Tarat Sea
Karanak
Shattered Plains
New Natanan
Frostlands
Kharbranth
Longbrow's Straits
Klna
Thaylen City
Thaylenah
The Shallow Crypts
Ocean of Origins
For His Royal Majesty King Gavilar Kholin
By His Royal High Cartographer
Isasik Shulin
1167

SEVEN AND A HALF YEARS AGO

Gavilar Kholin was on the verge of immortality.

He merely had to find the right Words.

He walked a circle around the nine Honorblades, driven point-first into the stone ground. The air stank of burned flesh; he'd attended enough funeral pyres to know that scent intimately, though these bodies hadn't been burned after the fighting but during it.

"They call it Aharietiam," he said, trailing around the Blades, letting his hand linger on each one. When he became a Herald, would his Blade become like these, imbued with power and lore? "The end of the world. Was it a lie?"

Many who name it such believed what they said, the Stormfather replied.

"And the owners of these?" he said, gesturing to the Blades. "What did the Heralds believe?"

If they had been entirely truthful, the Stormfather said, *then I would not be seeking a new champion.*

Gavilar nodded. "I swear to serve Honor and Roshar as its Herald. Better than these did."

These words are not accepted, the Stormfather said. *You will never find them at random, Gavilar.*

He would try nonetheless. In becoming the most powerful man in the world, Gavilar had often accomplished what others thought impossible. He rounded the ring of Blades again, alone with them in the shadow of monolithic stones. After dozens of visits to this vision, he could name each and every Blade by its associated Herald. The Stormfather, however, continued to be reticent to share information.

No matter. He *would* have his prize. He ripped Jezrien's long, curved Blade from the stone and swung it, cutting the air. "Nohadon met and grew to know the Heralds."

Yes, the Stormfather admitted.

"They are in there, aren't they?" he said. "The correct Words are somewhere in *The Way of Kings*?"

Yes.

Gavilar had the entire book memorized—he'd taught himself to read years ago so he could search for secrets without revealing them to the women in his life. He tossed the Herald's Blade aside, letting it clang against the stone—which made the Stormfather hiss.

Gavilar mentally chided himself. This was just a vision, and these fake Blades were nothing to him, but he needed the Stormfather to think him pious and worthy at least for now. He took up Chana's Blade. He was fond of this one, as its ornamentation bifurcated the blade with a slit down the center. That long gap would be highly impractical for a normal sword. Here it was a symbol that this Blade was something incredible.

"Chanaranach was a soldier," he said, "and this is a soldier's Blade. Solid and straight, but with that little impossibility missing from the center." He held the Blade in front of him, examining its edge. "I feel I know them each so well. They are my colleagues, yet I could not pick them out of a crowd."

Your colleagues? Do not get ahead of yourself, Gavilar. Find the Words.

Those storming Words. The most important ones Gavilar would ever say. With them, he would become the Stormfather's champion—and, he had deduced, something more. Gavilar suspected he would be accepted into the Oathpact and ascend beyond mortality. He had not asked which Herald he would replace; it felt crass, and he did not want to appear crass before the Stormfather. He suspected, though, that he would replace Talenelat, the one who had not left his Blade.

Gavilar stabbed the sword back into the stone. "Let us return."

The vision ended immediately, and he was in the palace's second-floor study. Bookshelves, a quiet desk for reading, tapestries and carpets to dampen voices. Gavilar wore finery for the upcoming feast: regal robes more archaic than fashionable. Like his beard, the clothing stood out among the Alethi lighteyes. He wanted them to think of him as something ancient, beyond their petty games.

This room was technically Navani's, but it was *his* palace. People rarely looked for him here, and he needed a reprieve from little people with little problems. As he had time before his meetings, Gavilar selected a small book that listed the latest surveys of the region around the Shattered Plains. He was increasingly certain that place held an ancient unlocked Oathgate. Through it, Gavilar could find the mythical Urithiru, and there, ancient records.

He *would* find the right Words. He was close. So tantalizingly close to what all men secretly desired, but only ten had ever achieved. Eternal life, and a legacy that spanned millennia—because you could live to shape it.

It is not so grand as you think, the spren said. Which gave Gavilar pause. The Stormfather couldn't read his mind, could it? No. No, he'd tested that. It didn't know his deepest thoughts, his deepest plans. For if it did know his heart, it wouldn't be working with him.

"What isn't?" Gavilar asked, slipping the book back.

Immortality, the Stormfather said. *It wears on men and women, weathering souls and minds. The Heralds are insane—afflicted with unnatural ailments unique to their ancient natures.*

"How long did it take?" Gavilar asked. "For the symptoms to appear?"

Difficult to say. A thousand years, perhaps two.

"Then I will have that long to find a solution," Gavilar said. "A much more reasonable timeline than the mere century—with luck—afforded a mortal. Wouldn't you say?"

I have not promised you this boon. You guess it is what I offer, but I seek only a champion. Still, tell me, would you accept the cost of becoming a Herald? Everyone you know would be dust by the time you returned.

And here, the lie. "A king's duty is to his people," he said. "By becoming a Herald, I can safeguard Alethkar in a way that no previous monarch ever has. I can endure personal pain to accomplish this. 'If I should die,'" Gavilar added, quoting *The Way of Kings,* "'then I would do so having lived my life right. It is not the destination that matters, but how one arrives there.'"

These words are not accepted, the spren said. *Guessing will* not *bring you to the Words, Gavilar.*

Yes, well, the Words *were* in that volume somewhere. Sheltered among the self-righteous moralizing like a whitespine in the brambles. Gavilar Kholin was not a man accustomed to losing. People got what they expected. And he expected not just victory, but *divinity.*

The guard knocked softly. Was it time already? Gavilar called for Tearim to come in, and he did. The guard was wearing Gavilar's own Plate tonight.

"Sire," Tearim said, "your brother is here."

"What? Not Restares? How did Dalinar find me?"

"Spotted us standing watch, I suspect, Your Majesty."

Bother. "Let him in."

The guard withdrew. A second later Dalinar burst in, graceful as a three-legged chull. He slammed the door and bellowed, "Gavilar! I want to go talk to the Parshendi."

Gavilar took a long, deep breath. "Brother, this is a very delicate situation, and we don't want to offend them."

"I won't offend them," Dalinar grumbled. He wore his takama, the robe of the old-fashioned warrior's garb open to show his powerful chest—with some grey hairs. He pushed past Gavilar and threw himself into the seat by the desk.

That poor chair.

"Why do you even care about them, Dalinar?" Gavilar said, right hand to his forehead.

"Why do you?" Dalinar demanded. "This treaty, this sudden interest in their lands. What are you planning? Tell me."

Dear, blunt Dalinar. As subtle as a jug of Horneater white. And equally smart.

"Tell me straight," Dalinar continued. "Are you planning to conquer them?"

"Why would I be signing a treaty if that were my intent?"

"I don't know," Dalinar said. "I just . . . I don't want to see anything happen to them. I like them."

"They're parshmen."

"I like parshmen."

"You've never *noticed* a parshman unless he was too slow to bring your drink."

"There's something about these ones," Dalinar said. "I feel a . . . a kinship."

"That's foolish." Gavilar walked to the desk and leaned down beside his brother. "Dalinar, what's happening to you? Where is the Blackthorn?"

"Maybe he's tired," Dalinar said. "Or blinded. By the soot and ashes of the dead, constantly in his face . . ."

Again Dalinar whined about the Rift? What an enormous hassle. Restares would be here soon, and then . . . there was Thaidakar. So many knives to keep balanced perfectly on their tips, lest they slide and cut Gavilar. He couldn't deal with Dalinar having a crisis of conscience right now.

"Brother," Gavilar said, "what would Evi say if she saw you like this?"

It was a carefully sharpened spear, slipped expertly into Dalinar's gut. The man's fingers gripped the table, and he recoiled at her name.

"She would want you to stand as a warrior," Gavilar said softly. "And protect Alethkar."

"I . . ." Dalinar whispered. "She . . ."

Gavilar offered a hand and heaved his brother to his feet, then led him to the door. "Stand up straight."

Dalinar nodded, hand on the doorknob.

"Oh," Gavilar said. "And Brother? Follow the Codes tonight. There is something strange upon the winds."

The Codes said not to drink when battle might be imminent. Just a nudge to remind Dalinar that it was a feast, and that there was plenty of wine on hand. Though Dalinar still thought no one knew he'd killed Evi, Gavilar had found the truth, which let him use these subtle manipulations.

Dalinar was out the door a moment later, his lumbering, pliable brain likely focused on two things. First, what he'd done to Evi. Second, how to find something strong enough to make him forget about the first.

When Dalinar was off down the hallway, Gavilar waved Tearim close. The guard was one of the Sons of Honor, a group that was yet another knife Gavilar kept balanced, for they could never know he had outgrown their plans.

"Follow my brother," Gavilar said. "Subtly ensure that he gets something to drink; maybe lead him to my wife's secret stores."

"You had me do that a few months ago, sire," Tearim whispered back. "There's not much left, I'm afraid. He likes to share with his soldiers."

"Well, find him something," Gavilar replied. "I can let Restares and the others in when they arrive. Go."

The soldier bowed and followed Dalinar, Shardplate thumping. Gavilar shut the door firmly. When the Stormfather's voice pushed into his mind, he was not surprised.

He has potential you do not see, that one.

"Dalinar? Of course he does. If I can keep him pointed the right direction, he will burn down entire nations." Gavilar simply had to ply him with alcohol the rest of the time, so that he didn't burn down *this* nation.

He could be more than you think.

"Dalinar is a big, dumb, blunt instrument you apply to problems until they break," Gavilar said, then shivered, remembering seeing his brother approach across a battlefield. Soaked in blood. Eyes appearing to glow red within his helm, hungry for the life Gavilar lived . . .

That ghost haunted him. Fortunately, both Dalinar's pain and his addiction made him easy enough to control.

Gavilar was soon interrupted by another knock. He answered the door and found nothing outside, until the Stormfather hissed a warning in his mind and he felt a sudden chill.

When he turned around, old Thaidakar was there. The Lord of Scars himself, a figure in an enveloping hooded cloak, tattered at the bottom. Storms.

"I was made promises," Thaidakar said, hood shadowing his face. "I've given you information, Gavilar, of the most valuable nature. In payment I requested a single man. When will you deliver Restares to me?"

"Soon," Gavilar said. "I am gaining his confidence first."

"It seems to me," Thaidakar said, "that you're less interested in our bargain, and more interested in your own motives. It seems to me that I directed you toward something valuable you've decided to keep. It seems to me that you play games."

"It seems to *me*," Gavilar said, stepping closer to the cloaked figure, "that you're not in a position to make demands. You need me. So why don't we just . . . keep playing."

Thaidakar remained still for a moment. Then, with a sigh, he reached up with gloved hands and took down his hood. Gavilar froze—for despite their several interactions, he'd never before seen the man's face.

Thaidakar was made entirely of softly glowing white-blue light. He was younger than Gavilar had imagined—in his middle years, not the wizened elder he'd seemed. He had a large spike, also blue, through one eye. The point jutted out the back of his skull. Was he some kind of spren?

"Gavilar," Thaidakar said, "take care. You're not immortal yet, but you've begun to play with forces that rip mortals apart by their very axi."

"Do you know what they are?" Gavilar demanded, hungry. "The most important Words I'll ever speak?"

"No," Thaidakar said. "But listen: none of this is what you *think* it is. Deliver Restares to my agents, and I will help you recover the ancient powers."

"I've grown beyond that," Gavilar said.

"You can't 'grow beyond' the tide, Gavilar," Thaidakar replied. "You swim with it or get swept away. Our plans are already in motion. Though to be honest, I don't know that we did much. That tide was coming regardless."

Gavilar grunted. "Well, *I* intend to—"

He was cut off as Thaidakar transformed. His face melted into a simple floating sphere with some kind of arcane rune at the center. The cloak, body, and gloves *vanished* into wisps of smoke that evaporated away.

Gavilar stared. That . . . that looked a lot like what he'd read of the powers of Lightweavers. Knights Radiant. Was Thaidakar—?

"I know you're meeting Restares today," the sphere said, vibrating—it had no mouth. "Prepare him, then deliver him to my agents for questioning. Or else. That is my ultimatum, Gavilar. You would not like to be my enemy."

The sphere of light shrank and turned nearly transparent as it moved to the door, then bobbed down and vanished through the crack underneath.

"What was *that*?" Gavilar demanded of the Stormfather, unnerved.

Something dangerous, the spren replied in his mind.

"Radiant?"

No. Similar, but no.

Gavilar found himself trembling. Which was stupid. He was a storming *king,* soon to be a *demigod.* He had a destiny; he would not be unsettled by cheap tricks and vague threats. Still, he rested his hand against the desk and breathed deeply, his fingers disturbing scattered notes and diagrams from his wife's latest mechanical obsession. Not for the first time he wondered if Navani could crack this problem. He missed the way they'd once schemed. How long had it been since they'd all laughed together? He, Ialai, Navani, and Torol?

Unfortunately, this wasn't the kind of secret you shared. Ialai or Sadeas would seize the prize from him if they could—and Gavilar wouldn't blame them. Navani though . . . would *she* try to take immortality for herself? Would she even see its value? She was so clever, so crafty in some ways. Yet when he spoke of his goals for a greater legacy, she got lost in the details. Refusing to think of the mountain because she worried about the placement of the foothills.

He regretted the distance between them. That coldness growing over—well, *grown* over—their relationship. Thinking of her sent a stab of pain into his heart. He should . . .

Everyone you know will be dust by the time you return . . .

Perhaps this way was best.

He had plans to mitigate the length of his absence from this world, but they might take several tries to perfect. So . . . fewer attachments seemed better. To allow for a cleaner cut. Like one made with a Shardblade.

He bent his mind to his plans, and was well prepared by the time Restares arrived. The balding man didn't knock. He peeked in, nervously checking each corner before he slipped through the door. He was followed by a shadow: a tall, imperious Makabaki man with a birthmark on one cheek. Gavilar had instructed the servants to treat them as ambassadors, but he hadn't yet had a chance to speak with this second man, whom he didn't know.

The newcomer walked with a certain . . . firmness. Rigidity. He wasn't a man who gave way. Not to wind, not to storm, and most certainly not to other people.

"Gavilar Kholin," the man said, offering neither a hand nor a bow. They locked stares. Impressive. Gavilar had expected . . . well, someone more like Restares.

"Have a drink," Gavilar said, gesturing toward the bar.

"No," the man said. Without a thank-you or compliment. Interesting. Intriguing.

Restares scuttled over like a child offered sweets. Even now—after joining this newest incarnation of the Sons of Honor—Gavilar found Restares . . . odd. The short, balding man sniffed at each of the wines. He had never trusted a drink in Gavilar's presence, but always tested them anyway. As if he wanted to find poison, to prove his paranoia was justified.

"Sorry," Restares said, wringing his hands as he hovered over the drinks. "Sorry. Not . . . not thirsty today, Gavilar. Sorry."

Gavilar was close to tossing him aside and seizing control of the Sons of Honor. Except some of the others, like Amaram, respected him. Plus . . . why *was* Thaidakar so interested in Restares? Surely he couldn't actually be someone *important*. Perhaps his tall friend was the true power. Could Gavilar have been kept in the dark for two years about something that vital?

"I'm glad you were willing to meet," Restares said. "Yes, um. Because, um. So . . . Announcement. I have an announcement."

Gavilar frowned. "What is this?"

"I hear," Restares said, "that you're looking to, um, restore the Voidbringers?"

"You founded the Sons of Honor, Restares," Gavilar said, "to recover the ancient oaths and restore the Knights Radiant. Well, they vanished when the Voidbringers did. So if we bring back the Voidbringers, the powers should return."

More importantly, he thought, *the Heralds will return from the land of the dead to lead us again.*

Letting me usurp the position of one of them.

"No, no, *no*," Restares said, uncharacteristically firm. "I wanted the *honor* of men to return! I wanted us to *explore* what made those Radiants so *grand*. Before things went wrong." He ran his hand through his thinning hair. "Before . . . I made them . . . go wrong . . ."

Restares wouldn't meet Gavilar's eyes. "We . . . we should stop trying to restore the powers," Restares said, his voice wilting, and glanced to his stern friend—as if for support. "We can't . . . afford another Return . . ."

"Restares," Gavilar said, advancing on the little man. "What is wrong with you? You're talking about betraying everything we believe?" *Or at least pretend to believe.* Gavilar subtly placed himself so he loomed over Restares. "Have you heard of a man named Thaidakar?"

Restares looked up, his eyes widening.

"He wants to find you," Gavilar said. "I have protected you thus far. What is it he wants from you, Restares?"

"Secrets," Restares whispered. "The man . . . can't abide . . . anyone having secrets."

"What secrets?" Gavilar said firmly, making Restares cringe. "I've put up with your lies long enough. What is going on? What does Thaidakar want?"

"I know where she is hidden," Restares whispered. "Where her soul is. Ba-Ado-Mishram. Granter of Forms. The one who could rival Him. The one . . . we betrayed."

Ba-Ado-Mishram? Why would Thaidakar care about an Unmade? It seemed such an oddly shaped piece of the puzzle. Gavilar opened his mouth to speak, but a hand squeezed his shoulder, fingers like a vise. Gavilar turned to see Restares's Makabaki friend standing behind him.

"What have you done?" the man asked, his voice icy. "Gavilar Kholin. What actions have you taken to achieve this goal of yours, the one that my friend mistakenly set you upon?"

"You have no idea," Gavilar said, meeting the stranger's eyes until the man finally released his grip.

Gavilar took a pouch from his pocket, then casually spilled a selection of spheres and gemstones onto the table. "I'm close. Restares, you must not lose your nerve now!"

The stranger stared, his lips parting. He reached toward one of the spheres that glowed with a dark, almost inverted violet light. Impossible light; a color that should not exist. As soon as the stranger's fingers drew close, he yanked them away, then turned wide eyes on Gavilar.

"You are a fool," the man said. "A terrible fool charging toward the highstorm with a stick, thinking to fight it. What have you done? Where did you get *Voidlight*?"

Gavilar smiled. None of them knew of the secret scholar he kept in reserve. A master of all things scientific. A man who was neither Ghostblood nor Son of Honor.

A man from another world.

"It is set in motion," Gavilar said, glancing at Restares. "And the project was a success."

Restares perked up. "It . . . it was? Is that Light . . ." He turned to his friend. "This could work, Nale! We could bring them back, then *destroy* them. It could *work*."

Nale. Oh, storms. Gavilar knew—but tried to ignore—that Restares pretended to be a Herald to impress the others. The little man didn't know Gavilar had become familiar with the Stormfather, who had told him the truth: that the Heralds had all long since died and gone to Braize.

So was this stranger pretending to be Nalan, Herald of Justice? He . . . had the right look. Many of the depictions were of an imperious Makabaki man. And that birthmark . . . it was strikingly similar to one on several of the older paintings.

But no. That was ridiculous. To believe that, one would have to believe that Restares—of all people—was a Herald.

The stranger tried to stare Gavilar down. Motionless, his expression cold. A monolith instead of a man. "This is far too dangerous."

Gavilar continued to hold his gaze. The world would bend to his desires. It always had before.

"But you are," the man eventually said, stepping back, "the king. Your will . . . is law . . . in this land."

"Yes," Gavilar said. "That is correct. Restares, I have more good news. We can move Voidlight from the storm to the Physical Realm. We can even carry it between here and Damnation, as you wanted."

"That's a way," Restares said, looking to Nale. "A way . . . maybe to escape . . ."

Nale waved to the spheres. "Being able to bring them back and forth from Braize doesn't mean anything. It's too close to be a relevant distance."

"It was impossible only a few short years ago," Gavilar said. "This *is* proof. The Connection is not severed, and the box allows for travel. Not yet as far as you'd like, but we must start the journey somewhere."

He wasn't certain why Restares was so eager to move Light around in Shadesmar. Thaidakar wanted this information as well. A way to transport Stormlight, and this new Voidlight, long distances. As he was contemplating that, Gavilar saw something. The door was cracked. An eye was peeking through.

Damnation. It was Navani. How much had she heard?

"Husband," she said, immediately pushing into the room. "There are guests missing you at the gathering. You seem to have lost track of time."

He smothered his anger at her spying, turning to Restares and his friend. "Gentlemen, I will need to excuse myself."

Restares again ran his hand through his wispy hair. "I want to know more of the project, Gavilar. Plus, you need to know that another of us is here tonight. I spotted her handiwork earlier."

Another one? Another Son of Honor.

No, he meant another Herald. Restares was growing more delusional.

"I have a meeting shortly with Meridas and the others," Gavilar said, calmly soothing Restares. "They should have more information for me. We can speak again after that."

"No," the Makabaki man growled. "I doubt we shall."

"There's more here, Nale!" Restares said, though he followed as Gavilar ushered the two of them from the room. "This is important! I want out. This is the only way . . ."

Gavilar shut the door. Then turned to his wife. Damnation, she should know better than to interrupt him. She . . .

Storms. The dress was beautiful, her face more so, even when angry. Staring at him with brilliant eyes, a fiery halo almost seeming to spread around her.

Once more, he considered.

Once more he rejected the idea.

If he was going to be a god, best to sever attachments. The sun could love the stars. But never as an equal.

⁂

Some time later, after he'd seen to Navani, Gavilar slipped away again. To his chambers this time, where he could confront what he'd learned.

"Tell me," he said, walking across the springy carpet to regard the tabletop map of Roshar. "Why is Thaidakar so interested in Ba-Ado-Mishram?"

The Stormfather formed a rippling beside Gavilar, vaguely in the shape of a person, but indistinct. Like the wavering in the air made by great heat on the stones.

She created your parshmen by accident, he said. *Long ago, just before the Recreance, Mishram tried to rise up and replace Odium, giving the Voidbringers powers.*

"Curious," Gavilar said. "And then?"

And then . . . she fell. She was too small a being to uphold an entire people. It all came crashing down, and so some brave Radiants trapped Mishram in a gemstone to prevent her from destroying all of Roshar. A side effect created the parshmen.

Simple parshmen. They were Voidbringers. A delicious secret he'd pried out of the Stormfather some weeks ago. Gavilar strolled to the bookcase, where one of the new heating fabrials had been delivered to him by the scholar Rushur Kris. He took it from its cloth casing, weighing it.

He had found a way to ferry Voidspren through Shadesmar to this world using gemstones and aluminum boxes. Who would have thought Navani's pet area of study would be so useful? And if that conniving Axindweth eluded his grasp, he'd have to do the next part without her. He had his scholar, though in truth Gavilar was baffled by the Light he was creating . . . Light that could somehow kill the Voidbringers? How had Vasher made—

He thought he heard a faint crackling sound from the Stormfather. Lightning? How cute.

"You've never challenged what I'm doing," Gavilar said. "I would have thought that returning the Voidbringers would be opposed to your very nature."

Opposition is sometimes needed, the Stormfather said. *You will need someone to fight, should you become champion.*

"Give it to me," Gavilar said. "Now. Make me a Herald. I *need* it."

The Stormfather turned a shimmering head in his direction. *That was almost them.*

"What, those?" Gavilar said. "A demand?"

So close. And so far.

Gavilar smiled, hefting the fabrial and thinking of the flamespren trapped inside. The Stormfather seemed increasingly suspicious, hostile. If things did go poorly . . . could he trap the Stormfather himself in one of these?

Soon Amaram arrived with a small collection of people: two men, two women. One man was Amaram's lieutenant. The other three would be new important Sons of Honor recruits, invited to the feast and given exclusive time with the king after. It was an annoyance, but a worthy one. Gavilar identified the two women from the notes, but not the older man in robes. Who was he? A stormwarden? Amaram liked to keep them around, to teach him their script, which preserved some semblance of Vorin devotion. That was important to him.

Gavilar met each guest in turn, and as he reached the older man, something clicked. This was Taravangian, the king of Kharbranth. Famously a man of little consequence or aptitude. Gavilar glanced at Amaram. Surely they weren't going to invite *him* into their confidence—they should find the power who secretly ruled Kharbranth. Likely to be one of two women, per Gavilar's spy reports.

Amaram nodded. So, Gavilar gave his speech about ancient oaths and Radiants—of glories past and futures bright. It was a good speech, but beginning to grate on him. Once his words had inspired troops; now he spent his entire life in meetings. After finishing, he let everyone get something to drink.

"Meridas," Gavilar whispered, pulling Amaram aside. "These meetings are growing onerous. My experiment was a success. I have the weapon."

Amaram started, then spoke softly. "You mean . . ."

"Yes, once we bring back the Voidbringers, we will have a new way to fight them."

"Or a new way to *control* them," Amaram whispered.

Well, *that* was new. Gavilar considered his friend, and the ambition those words implied. *Good for you, Amaram.*

"We must restore the Desolations," Gavilar said. "Whatever the cost. It's the only way."

"I agree," Amaram said. "Now more than ever." He hesitated. "My efforts with your daughter did not go well earlier. I thought we had an understanding."

"You simply need more time, my friend. To win her over."

Amaram hungered for the throne like Gavilar hungered for immortality. And perhaps Gavilar would reward Amaram with it. Elhokar certainly did not deserve to be king. He was exactly the *opposite* of the legacy Gavilar wanted.

He sent Amaram to talk to the others. Once they had enjoyed their drinks, Gavilar would give another short speech. Then he could be on to . . . He frowned, noticing that one of the new recruits wasn't conversing with the others. The elderly man, Taravangian, was staring at the map of Roshar. The others laughed at something Amaram said. Taravangian didn't even look toward the sound.

Gavilar strode over, but before he could speak, Taravangian whispered, "Do you ever wonder about the lives we're giving them? The people we rule?"

Gavilar was unaccustomed to people—let alone strangers—addressing him with such familiarity. But then, this Taravangian saw himself as a king, and perhaps as Gavilar's equal. Laughable, when Taravangian ruled only one small city.

"I worry less about their lives now," Gavilar said, "and more about what is to come."

Taravangian nodded, appearing thoughtful. "That was an inspiring speech. Do you actually believe it?"

"Would I say it if I didn't?"

"Of course you would; a king will say whatever needs to be said. Wouldn't it be grand if that were always what he believed?" He looked to Gavilar, smiling. "Do you truly believe the Radiants can return?"

"Yes," Gavilar said. "I do."

"And you are not a fool," Taravangian said, musing. "So you must have good reasons."

Gavilar found himself revising his earlier opinion. A little king was still a king. Perhaps, among all of the dignitaries in the city tonight, here was one who might . . . in the smallest way . . . understand the demands placed on the man pressed between crown and throne.

"A danger is coming," Gavilar said softly, shocked at his own sincerity. "To this land. This world. An ancient danger."

Taravangian narrowed his eyes.

"It's not just a Desolation we must fear," Gavilar said. "They come. The Everstorm. The Night of Sorrows."

Taravangian, remarkably, grew pale.

He believed. Gavilar usually felt foolish when he tried to explain the true dangers that the Stormfather had shown him—the contest of champions for the fate of Roshar. He worried people would think him mad. Yet this man . . . believed him?

"Where," Taravangian asked, "did you hear those words?"

"I don't know that you'd believe me if I told you."

"Will you believe *me*?" Taravangian asked. "Ten years ago, my mother died of her tumors. Frail, lying on her bed, with too many perfumes struggling to smother the stench of death. She gazed at me in her last moments . . ." He met Gavilar's eyes. "And she whispered: 'I stand before him, above the world itself, and he speaks the truth. The Desolation is near . . . The Everstorm. The Night of Sorrows.' Then she was gone."

"I've . . . heard of this," Gavilar admitted. "The prophetic words of the dying . . ."

"Where did *you* hear those words?" Taravangian asked, practically begging. "Please."

"I see visions," Gavilar said, frank. "Given me by the Almighty. So that we may prepare." He looked toward the map. "Heralds send that I may become the person I need to be to stop what is coming . . ."

Let the Stormfather see sincerity in Gavilar. Storms . . . suddenly Gavilar felt it. Standing there with this little king, he *felt it.* Never before—in all of this—had Gavilar ever suspected he might be inadequate to the task.

Perhaps, he thought, *I should encourage Dalinar to resume his training. Remind him that he is a soldier.* Gavilar had the distinct impression that before too long, he would need the Blackthorn again.

Someone is approaching your door outside, the Stormfather warned. *One of the listeners. Eshonai. There is something about this one . . .*

One of the Parshendi? Gavilar shook himself. He dismissed Taravangian, Amaram, and the others—happy to be rid of that strange old man and his questioning eyes. The fellow was supposed to be unremarkable. Why did he unnerve Gavilar?

Eshonai entered as Amaram passed along his invitation. The conversation with the parshwoman went smoothly, with him manipulating her—and therefore her people. To prepare them for the role they would play.

⁂

After Gavilar grew weary at the feast once the treaty was signed, he retired to his rooms. He sank into a deep plush chair by his balcony, releasing a long sigh. Early in his career as a warlord, he'd never allowed himself the luxury of softness. He had mistakenly assumed that liking something soft would make him soft.

A common failing among men who wished to appear strong. It was not weakness to relax. By being so afraid of it, they gave simple things power over them.

The air shimmered in front of him.

"A full day," Gavilar said.

Yes.

"The first of many such," Gavilar continued. "I will be mounting an expedition back to the Shattered Plains soon. We can leverage my new treaty to obtain guides, have them lead us inward to the center. Toward Urithiru."

The Stormfather did not reply. Gavilar wasn't certain the spren could be said to have human mannerisms. Today though . . . that turned-away posture, hinted at in the warping of the air . . . that silence . . .

"Do you regret choosing me?" Gavilar asked.

I regret the way I have treated you, the Stormfather said. *I should not have been so accommodating. It has made you lazy.*

"This is lazy?" Gavilar said, forcing amusement into his voice to hide his annoyance.

You do not reverence the position you seek, the Stormfather said. *I feel . . . you are not the champion I need. Maybe . . . I've been wrong all this time.*

"You said that you were charged with this task of finding a champion," Gavilar said. "By Honor."

That is true. I do not speak in human ways. But still, if you become a Herald, you will be tortured between Returns. Why is it this doesn't bother you?

Gavilar shrugged. "I will just give in."

What?

"Give in," Gavilar said, heaving himself out of his seat. "Why stay to be tortured and potentially lose my mind? I will give up each time and return immediately."

The Heralds stay in Damnation to seal the Voidbringers away. To prevent them from overrunning the world. They—

"The Heralds are the ten fools for that," Gavilar explained, pouring a drink from the carafe near his balcony. "If I cannot die, I will be the greatest king this world has ever known. Why lock away my knowledge and leadership?"

To stop the war.

"Why would I care to stop a war?" Gavilar asked, genuinely amused. "War is the path to glory, to training our soldiers to recover the Tranquiline Halls. My troops should be experienced, don't you think?" He turned back toward the shimmer, taking a sip of orange wine. "I don't fear these Voidbringers. Let them stay and fight. If they are reborn, then we will never run out of enemies to kill."

The Stormfather did not respond. And again Gavilar tried to read into the thing's posture. Was the Stormfather proud of him? Gavilar considered this an elegant solution; he was puzzled why the Heralds had never thought of it. Perhaps they were cowards.

Ah, Gavilar, the Stormfather said. *I see my miscalculation. Your entire religious upbringing . . . created from the lies of Aharietiam and Honor's own failings . . . it pointed you toward this conclusion.*

Damnation. The Stormfather wasn't pleased. It suddenly felt terribly unfair. Here he was drinking this *awful* excuse for wine to follow the ridiculous Codes—he gave every possible outward show of piety—yet it wasn't enough?

"What should I do to serve?" Gavilar said.

You don't understand, the Stormfather said. *Those aren't the Words, Gavilar.*

"Then what *are* the storming Words!" he said, slamming the cup down on the table—shattering it, splashing wine across the wall. "You want me to save this planet? Then *help* me! Tell me what I'm saying wrong!"

It's not about what you are saying.

"But—"

Suddenly the Stormfather wavered. Lightning pulsed through his shimmering form, filling Gavilar's room with an electric glow. Blue frosted the rugs, pure light reflecting in the glass balcony doors.

Then the Stormfather cried out. A sound like a peal of thunder, agonized.

"What?" Gavilar said, backing up. "What happened?"

A Herald . . . a Herald has died . . . No. I am not ready . . . The Oathpact . . . No! They mustn't see. They mustn't know . . .

"Died?" Gavilar said. "Died. You said they were already dead! You said they were in Damnation!"

The Stormfather rippled, then a *face* emerged in the shimmering. Two eyes, like holes in a storm, clouds spiraling around them and leading into the depths.

"You lied," Gavilar said. "You *lied*?"

Oh, Gavilar. There is so much you do not know. So much you assume. And the two never do meet. Like paths to opposing cities.

Those eyes seemed to pull Gavilar forward, to overwhelm him, to consume him. He . . . he saw storms, endless storms, and the world was so frail. A tiny speck of blue against an infinite canvas of black.

The Stormfather could *lie*?

"Restares," Gavilar whispered. "Is he . . . actually a Herald?"

Yes.

Gavilar felt cold, as if he were standing in the highstorm, ice seeping in through his skin. Seeking his heart. Those eyes . . .

"What *are* you?" Gavilar whispered, hoarse.

The biggest fool of them all, the Stormfather said. GOODBYE, GAVILAR. I HAVE SEEN A GLIMPSE OF WHAT IS COMING. I WILL NOT PREVENT IT.

"What?" Gavilar demanded. "*What* is coming?"

YOUR LEGACY.

The door slammed open. Sadeas, his face red from exertion. "Assassin," he said, waving Tearim—in Plate—to tromp in. "Coming this way, killing guards. We need you to put on your armor. Tearim, get it off. We must protect the king."

Gavilar looked at him, stunned.

Then one word cut through.

Assassin.

I've been betrayed, he thought, and found that he was not surprised. One of them had been bound to come for him.

But which one?

"Gavilar!" Sadeas shouted. "We need you in armor! Assassin on the way."

"Tearim can fight him, Torol," Gavilar said. "What is one assassin?"

"This one has killed dozens already," Sadeas said. "I think we should have you in Plate just in case. You could wear mine, but my armorers are still bringing it."

"You brought your armor to the feast?"

"Of course I did," Sadeas said. "I don't trust those Parshendi. You'd do well to emulate me. Trusting too much could get you killed someday."

Screams sounded in the distance. Tearim, loyal as always, began removing the Plate for Gavilar to don.

"Too slow," Sadeas said. "We need to buy time. Give me your robe."

Gavilar hesitated, then met his friend's eyes. "You'd do that?"

"I worked too hard to put you on that throne, Gavilar," Sadeas said, grim. "I'm not going to let that go to waste."

"Thank you," Gavilar said.

Sadeas shrugged, pulling on the robe as Tearim helped Gavilar suit up. Whoever this assassin was, he'd find himself outmatched by a Shardbearer.

Gavilar glanced toward where the Stormfather had been—but the shimmer was gone.

Spren couldn't lie. They *couldn't.* He'd learned that . . . from the Stormfather.

Blood of my fathers, Gavilar thought as the Plate locked onto his legs. *What else did it lie to me about?*

⁂

Gavilar fell.

And he knew, as he fell, that this was it. His ending.

A legacy interrupted. An assassin who moved with an otherworldly grace, stepping on wall and ceiling, commanding Light that bled from the very storms.

Gavilar hit the ground—surrounded by the wreckage of his balcony—and he saw white in a flash. His body didn't hurt. That was an extremely bad sign.

Thaidakar, he thought as a figure rose before him, shadowed in the night air. *Only Thaidakar could send an assassin who could do such things.*

Gavilar coughed as the figure loomed over him. "I . . . expected you . . . to come."

The assassin knelt before him, though Gavilar couldn't see anything more than shadows. Then . . . the assassin—doing something Gavilar couldn't make out—again glowed like a sphere.

"You can tell . . . Thaidakar," Gavilar whispered, "that he's too late . . ."

"I don't know who that is," the assassin said, the words barely intelligible. The man held his hand to the side. Summoning a Blade.

This was it. Behind the assassin a halo, a corona of shimmering light. The Stormfather.

I did not cause this, the Stormfather said in his head. *I do not know whether that brings you peace in your last moments, Gavilar.*

But . . .

"Then who . . . ?" Gavilar forced out. "Restares? Sadeas? I never thought . . ."

"My masters are the Parshendi," the assassin said.

Gavilar blinked, focusing on the man once more as his Blade formed. Storms . . . that was *Jezrien's Honorblade*, wasn't it? What was happening?

"The Parshendi? That makes no sense."

This is my failure as much as yours, the Stormfather said. *If I try again, I will do it differently. I thought . . . your family . . .*

His family. In that moment, Gavilar saw his legacy crumbling. He was dying.

Storms. He was *dying.* What did *anything* matter? He couldn't. He couldn't . . .

He was supposed to be eternal . . .

I've invited the enemy back, he realized. *The end is coming. And my family, my kingdom, will be destroyed, without a way to fight. Unless . . .*

Hand quivering, he pulled a sphere out of his pocket. The weapon. They needed this. His son . . . No, his son could not handle such power . . . They needed a warrior. A *true* warrior. One that Gavilar had been doing his best to suppress, out of a fear he barely dared acknowledge, even as he drew his last ragged breaths.

Dalinar. Storms help them, it came down to Dalinar.

He held the sphere out toward the Stormfather, his vision fuzzing. Thinking . . . was . . . difficult.

"You must take this," Gavilar whispered to the Stormfather. "They must not get it. Tell . . . tell my brother . . . *he* must find the most important words a man can say . . ."

No, the Stormfather said, though a hand took the sphere. *Not him. I'm sorry, Gavilar. I made that mistake once. I will never trust your family again.*

Gavilar gave a whine of pain, not from his body but from his soul. He had failed. He had brought them all to ruin. That, he realized with horror, would be his legacy.

In the end, Gavilar Kholin, heir to the Heralds, died. As all men, ultimately, must.

Alone.

DAY

ONE

KALADIN • SHALLAN

It seemed to strike a very distinct pose as I drew.
Was that for me? How could it tell I was observing?
A perfect moment to hold forever

I
UNFAMILIAR GROUND

I should have known I was being watched. All my life, the signs were there.

—From *Knights of Wind and Truth*, page 1

Kaladin felt good.

Not great. Not after spending weeks hiding in an occupied city. Not after driving himself to physical and emotional exhaustion. Not after what had happened to Teft.

He stood at his window on the first morning of the month. Sunlight streamed into the room around him, wind tickling his hair. He *shouldn't* have felt good. Yes, he'd helped protect Urithiru—but that victory had come at an agonizing cost. Beyond that, Dalinar had made a deal with the enemy: in just ten days, the champion of Honor and the champion of Odium would decide the fate of all Roshar.

The scope of that was terrifying, yet Kaladin had stepped down as leader of the Windrunners. He'd said the proper Words, but had realized Words alone weren't enough. While Stormlight healed his body instantly, his soul needed time. So, if battle came, his friends would fight without him. And when the champions met atop Urithiru in ten days—nine, since the first day was underway—Kaladin wouldn't participate.

That *should* have made him an anxious, stewing pot of nerves. Instead he tipped his head back, sun warm on his skin, and acknowledged that while he didn't feel great, someday he *would* feel great again.

For today, that was enough.

He turned and strode to his closet, where he picked through stacks of civilian clothing neatly laundered and delivered this morning. The city was a mere two days free from occupation and the fate of the world approached, but Urithiru's washwomen soldiered on. None of the clothes appealed to him, and shortly he glanced at another option: a uniform sent by the quartermaster to replace the one Kaladin had ruined during the fighting. Leyten kept a rack of them in Kaladin's size.

Kaladin had stuck the uniform to the wall with a Lashing last night, after Teft's funeral, as a test. Urithiru was awake, with its own Bondsmith, making things . . . different. His Lashings normally lasted minutes at best—yet here this one was, ten hours later, still going strong.

Syl poked her head into his room—past the hanging cloth doorway—without any thought for privacy. Today she appeared at full human size and wore a havah rather than her usual girlish dress. She'd recently learned how to color her dress, in this case mostly darker shades of blue with some bright violet embroidery on her sleeves.

As Kaladin fastened the last buttons on the high collar of his uniform jacket, Syl bounced over to stand behind him. Then she floated a foot or so into the air to look over his shoulder and examine him in the mirror.

"Can't you make yourself any size?" he asked, checking his jacket cuffs.

"Within reason."

"Whose reason?"

"No idea," she said. "Tried to get as big as a mountain once. It involved lots of grunting and thinking like rocks. Really *big* rocks. Biggest I could manage was a very small mountain—small enough to fit in this room, with the tip brushing the ceiling."

"Then you could be tall enough to tower over me," he said. "Why do you usually make yourself shorter?"

"It just feels right," she said.

"That's your explanation for basically everything."

"Yup!" She poked him. He could barely feel it. Even at this size, she was insubstantial in the Physical Realm. "Uniform? I thought you weren't going to wear one anymore."

He hesitated, then pulled the jacket down at the bottom to smooth the wrinkles across the sides. "It just feels right," he admitted, meeting her eyes in the mirror.

She grinned. And storm him, he couldn't help grinning back.

"Someone is having a good day," she said, poking him again.

"Bizarrely," Kaladin said. "Considering."

"At least the war is almost over," she said. "One more contest. Nine days."

True. If Dalinar won, Odium had agreed to withdraw from Alethkar and Herdaz—though he could keep other lands he controlled, like Iri and Jah Keved. If Odium won, they were forced to cede Alethkar to the enemy.

Plus there was a greater cost. If Dalinar lost, he had to *join* Odium, become Fused, and help conquer the cosmere. Kaladin wanted to think that the Radiants wouldn't follow as well, but he wasn't certain. So many people thirsted for war, even without the influence of an Unmade. Storms, he'd felt it too.

"Syl," he said, dropping his smile. "I'm sure more people are going to die. Perhaps people I care about, but I can't be there to help them. Dalinar will have to choose someone else to be champion and—"

"*Kaladin Stormblessed,*" she said, rising higher into the air, arms folded. Though she wore a fashionable havah, she left her hair white-blue, flowing free, waving and shifting in the wind. The . . . nonexistent wind. "Don't you *dare* talk yourself into being miserable."

"Or what?"

"Or I," she thundered, "shall make silly faces at you. As I alone can."

"They aren't silly," he said, shivering.

"They're *hilarious.*"

"Last time you made a tentacle come out of your forehead."

"Highbrow comedy."

"Then it slapped me."

"Punch line. *Obviously.* All the humans in the world, and I picked the one without a taste for refined humor."

He met her eyes, and her smile was still storming infectious.

"It does feel warm," he said, "to have finally figured a few things out. To let go of the weight and step out from the shadow. I know darkness will return, but I think . . . I think I'll be able to remember better than before."

"Remember what?"

He Lashed himself upward, floating until he was eye level with her. "That days like this exist too."

She nodded firmly.

"I wish I could show Teft," Kaladin said. "I feel his loss like a hole in my own flesh, Syl."

"I know," she said softly.

If she'd been a human friend, she might have offered a hug. Syl didn't seem to understand physicality like a human did, though where she'd been born—Shadesmar, the Cognitive Realm—she had a substantial body. He had the sense she hadn't spent much time on that side. This realm suited her.

Dropping to the ground, Kaladin walked back to the window, wanting to feel the sunlight. Outside he saw the heights of the mountains, capped by snow. Wind blew across him, bringing with it fresh scents of clean, crisp air and a flock of windspren. Including those that made up his armor, who soared in around him. They stayed close, in case they were needed.

Storms, he'd been through so much so quickly. He felt echoes of an anger that had almost entirely consumed him at Teft's death. Worse, the feeling of nothingness as he fell . . .

Dark days.

But days like this existed too.

And he *would* remember.

His armor spren laughed and danced out the window, but the wind lingered, playing with his hair. Then it calmed, still blowing across him, but no longer playful, more . . . contemplative. All through his life, the wind had been there. He knew it almost like he did his hometown or his family. Familiar . . .

Kaladin . . .

He jumped, then glanced at Syl, who was walking through the room in a half dance, half stride, her eyes closed—as if moving to an inaudible beat.

"Syl," Kaladin said, "did you say my name?"

"Huh?" she said, opening her eyes.

Kaladin . . .

Storms. There it was again.

I need your help. I'm so sorry . . . to ask more of you . . .

"Tell me you hear that," Kaladin said to Syl.

"I feel . . ." She cocked her head. "I feel something. On the wind."

"It's *speaking* to me," he said, one hand to his head.

A storm is coming, Kaladin, the wind whispered. *The worst storm . . . I'm sorry . . .*

It was gone.

"What did you hear?" Syl asked.

"A warning," he said, frowning. "Syl, is the wind . . . alive?"

"Everything is alive."

He gazed outward, waiting for the voice to return. It didn't. Just that crisp breeze—though now it didn't seem calm.

Now it seemed to be waiting for something.

⁂

Shallan lingered atop Lasting Integrity, the great fortress of the honorspren, thinking about all the people she'd been. The way she changed, based on perspective.

Indeed, life was largely *about* perspective.

Like this strange structure: a hollow, rectangular block hundreds of feet tall, dominating Shadesmar's landscape. People—spren—lived along the *inside walls,* walking up and down them, ignoring conventions of gravity. Looking down along one of the inside walls could be stomach-churning unless you changed your perspective. Unless you convinced yourself that walking up and down that wall was normal. Whether a person was strong or not wasn't usually subject to debate, yet if *gravity* could be a matter of opinion . . .

She turned away from the heart of Lasting Integrity and walked along the very top of the wall. Looking outward to survey Shadesmar: rolling ocean of beads in one direction, jagged obsidian highlands—lined with crystalline trees—in the other. On the wall with her, an even more daunting sight: two spren with heads made of geometric lines, each wearing a robe of some too-stiff glossy black material.

Two spren.

She'd bonded *two.* One during her childhood. One as an adult. She'd hurt the first, and had suppressed the memory.

Shallan knelt before Testament, her original spren. The Cryptic sat with her back to the stone railing. The lines and pattern that made up her head were crooked, like broken twigs. In the center the lines were scratched and rough, as if someone had taken a knife to them. More telling, her pattern was almost frozen.

Nearby, Pattern's head pulsed to a vibrant rhythm—always moving, always forming some new geometric display. Comparing the two broke Shallan's heart. *She* had done this to Testament by rejecting the bond after using her Shardblade to kill her mother.

Testament reached out with a long-fingered hand, and Shallan—pained—took it. It gripped hers lightly, but Shallan had the sense that was all the strength Testament had. She responded to being a deadeye differently from Maya, who stood nearby with Adolin and Kelek. Maya had always seemed strong of body, in spite of being a deadeye. Spren broke in different ways, it appeared. Just like people.

Testament squeezed Shallan's hand, bearing no expression but that torpid motion of lines.

"Why?" Shallan asked. "Why don't you *hate* me?"

Pattern rested his hand on Shallan's shoulder. "We both knew the danger, the sacrifice, in bonding to humans again."

"I hurt her."

"Yet here you are," Pattern said. "Able to stand tall. Able to control the Surges. Able to protect this world."

"She should hate me," Shallan whispered. "But there is no vitriol in the way she holds my hand. No judgment in the way she remains with us."

"Because the sacrifice was *worth* something, Shallan," Pattern said, uncharacteristically reserved. "It *worked.* In the end you recovered, did better. I am still here. And remarkably, I am not even a little bit dead! I do not think you will kill me at all, Shallan! I am happy about that."

"Can I heal her?" Shallan asked. "Maybe if I . . . if I bond her again?"

"I think, after talking to Kelek . . ." Pattern said. "I think you are still bonded to her."

"But . . ." Shallan glanced over her shoulder at him. "I broke the bond. That did this."

"Some breaks are messy," Pattern said. "A slice with a sharpened knife is clean; a slice with a dull one is ragged. Your break, done by a child without full Intent, is ragged. In some ways that makes it worse, but it does mean that some Connection between you two persists."

"So . . ."

"So no," Pattern said. "I do not think that merely saying Words once more would heal her." His head pattern spun a little more slowly, as if he were contemplating something profound. "These numbers are . . . perplexing, Shallan. Strangely irrational, in a sequence I do not understand. I mean . . . I mean that we are walking on unfamiliar ground. A better metaphor for you. Yes. Unfamiliar ground. In the deep past, deadeyes did not exist."

It was what they'd learned, in part, from the honorspren and from Maya. The deadeyes—all of them except Testament—had been bonded to ancient Radiants before the Recreance. Together they'd rejected their oaths, humans and spren alike. They'd thought it would cause a painful, but survivable split. Instead, something had gone terribly wrong.

The result had been the deadeyes. The explanation might lie with Kelek, the very person Shallan had been sent to Lasting Integrity to kill. She squeezed Testament's hand. "I'm going to help you," Shallan whispered. "*Whatever* it takes."

Testament didn't respond, but Shallan leaned in, wrapping her arms around the Cryptic. Pattern's robe always felt hard, yet Testament's bent like cloth.

"Thank you," Shallan said. "For coming to me when I was young. Thank you for protecting me. I still do not remember it all, but *thank you.*"

The Cryptic slowly, but deliberately, put her arms around Shallan and squeezed back.

"Rest now," Shallan said, wiping her eyes and standing. "I'm going to figure this out."

2

TAKING THE NEXT STEP

I first knew the Wind as a child, during days before I knew dreams. What need has a child of dreams or aspirations? They live, and love, the life that is.

—From *Knights of Wind and Truth*, page 3

Syl eventually trailed out of Kaladin's room and into his family's quarters. He lingered in the sunlight and wind, hovering, because why not? Light here was constantly replenished, and holding the tower's new Light seemed not to push him to action the way Stormlight did. Instead, holding it was . . . calming.

Yet he jumped when a loud noise sounded from farther inside, a set of shockspren snapping into appearance around him, like breaking yellow triangles. When he reached the doorway, however, he found the noise was just his little brother, Oroden, clapping. Kaladin calmed his thundering heart. He had lately become more prone to overreact to loud noises—including ones that, upon reflection, were obviously nothing dangerous.

No further words came from the wind, so Kaladin hovered out into the main room, where Oroden was playing with his blocks. Syl had joined him. Though she could make herself invisible, she rarely chose to around his family. Indeed, last night they had discussed a new procedure: When she appeared with color on her clothing, like the violet on her sleeves, it meant she was visible to others. When she appeared as a uniform light blue, only he could see her.

"Gagadin!" the little boy said, pointing. "You need *bocks*!"

"You" in this case meant Oroden himself—who had noticed that everyone called him "you." Kaladin smiled, and used his Light to make the blocks hover. Syl, shrinking down, hopped from block to block in the air as Oroden swatted them.

What am I doing? Kaladin thought. *A contest for the fate of the world is approaching, my best friend is dead, and I'm playing blocks with my little brother?*

Then in response, a familiar voice spoke from deep within him. *Hold to this, Kal. Embrace it. I didn't die so you could mope around like a wet Horneater with no razor.* Unlike the wind, this didn't seem anything mystical. Instead . . . well, Kaladin had known Teft long enough to anticipate what the man would have said. Even in death, a good sergeant knew his job: keep the officers pointed the right way.

"Fyl!" Oroden said, gesturing to Syl. "Fyl, come fin!" He started spinning in circles, and she joined in, twirling around him. Laughterspren, like silver minnows, appeared in the air. That was another difference in the tower lately—spren were *everywhere,* showing up far more frequently.

Kaladin sat on the floor amid hovering blocks, and was forced to think about his place. He wasn't going to be Dalinar's champion, and he wasn't the leader of Bridge Four any longer. Sigzil went to important meetings in Kaladin's place.

So who was he? What was he?

You are . . . the wind's voice said softly. *You are what I need . . .*

He went alert. No, he was *not* imagining *that.*

His mother entered, wearing her hair tied with a kerchief, like she always had when working in Hearthstone. She settled down next to him, nudged him in the side, then handed him a bowl with some boiled lavis grain and spiced crab meat on top. Kaladin dutifully started eating. If there was a group more demanding than sergeants, it was mothers. When he'd been younger such attention had mortified him. After years without, he found he didn't mind a little mothering.

"How are you?" Hesina asked.

"Good," he said around a spoonful of lavis.

She studied him.

"Really," he said. "Not great. Good. Worried about what's coming."

A block floated past, steaming with Towerlight. Hesina tapped it with a hesitant finger, sending it spinning through the room. "Shouldn't those . . . fall?"

"Eventually, maybe?" He shrugged. "Navani has done something odd to the place. It's warm now, the pressure equalized, and the entire city is . . . infused. Like a sphere."

Water flowed on command from holes in the walls, and you could control its temperature with a gesture. Suddenly a lot of the strange basins and empty pools in the tower made sense; they had no controls, because you activated them by speaking or touching the stone.

Syl got Oroden twirling, then left him dizzy and with a few blocks as a distraction. She popped to human size again and flopped onto her back next to Kaladin and Hesina, her face coated in an approximation of sweat. He noticed a new detail: Syl's havah was missing the long sleeve that would cover the safehand, and she wore a glove—or she'd colored her safehand white and given it a cloth texture. That wasn't odd; Navani always wore a glove these days to leave both hands free. It surprised him that Syl was wearing one though. She'd never bothered before.

"How do small humans *keep going*?" Syl said. "Where does their energy come from?"

"One of the great mysteries of the cosmere," Hesina said. "If you think this is bad, you should have seen Kal."

"Oooooh," Syl said, rolling over and looking to Hesina with wide eyes, her long blue-white hair tumbling around her face. No human woman would have acted in such a . . . casual way in a havah. The tight dresses, while not strictly formal, weren't designed for rolling around on the ground barefoot. Syl, however, would Syl.

"Embarrassing childhood stories?" the spren said. "Go! Talk while his mouth is full of food and he can't interrupt you!"

"He never stopped moving," Hesina said, leaning forward. "Except when he finally collapsed at night to sleep, giving us *brief* hours of respite. Each night, I would have to sing his favorite song and Lirin would have to chase him—and he could tell if Lirin was giving a halfhearted chase, and would give him an earful. It was honestly the cutest thing to see Lirin being scolded by a three-year-old."

"I could have guessed Kaladin would be tyrannical as a child," Syl said.

"Children are often like that, Syl," his mother said. "Accepting only one answer to any question, because nuance is difficult and confusing."

"Yes," Kaladin said, scraping the last of the lavis from his bowl, "children. That's a worldview that, obviously, solely afflicts *children*—never the rest of us."

His mother gave him a hug, one arm around his shoulders. The kind that seemed to grudgingly admit that he wasn't a little boy anymore. "Do you sometimes wish the world were a simpler place?" Hesina asked him. "That the easy answers of childhood were, in truth, the actual answers?"

"Not anymore," he said. "Because I think the easy answers would condemn me. Condemn everyone, in fact."

That made his mother beam, even though it was an easy thing to say. Then Hesina's eyes got a mischievous sparkle to them. Oh, storms. What was she going to say now?

"So, you have a spren friend," she said. "Did you ever ask her that vital question you always asked when you were little?"

He sighed, bracing himself. "And which question would that be, Mother?"

"Dungspren," she said, poking him. "You were always so *fascinated* by the idea."

"That was Tien!" Kaladin said. "Not me."

Hesina gave him a knowing stare. Mothers. They remembered too well. Shamespren popped into existence around him, like red and white petals. Only a few, but still.

"Fine," he said. "Maybe I was . . . intrigued." He glanced at Syl, who was watching the exchange with wide eyes. "Did you . . . ever know any?"

"Dungspren," she said flatly. "You're asking the sole living Daughter of Storms—basically a *princess* by human terminology—*this* question. How much *poop* do I know?"

"Please, can we move on?" Kaladin said.

Unfortunately, Oroden had been listening. He patted Kaladin on the knee. "It's okay, Gagadin," he said in a comforting voice. "Poop goes in potty. Get a treat!"

This sent Syl into a fit of uproarious laughter, flopping onto her back again. Kaladin gave Hesina his captain's glare—the one that could make any soldier go white. Mothers, however, ignored the chain of command. So Kaladin was saved only when his father appeared in the doorway, a large stack of papers under his arm. Hesina walked over to help.

"Dalinar's medical corps tent layouts and current operating procedures," Lirin explained.

"'Dalinar,' eh?" she said. "A few meetings, and you're on a first-name basis with the most powerful man in the world?"

"The boy's attitude is contagious," Lirin said.

"I'm sure it has *nothing* to do with his upbringing," Hesina replied. "We'll instead assume that four years in the *military* somehow conditioned him to be flippant around lighteyes."

"Well, I mean . . ." Lirin and Hesina glanced at their son.

Kaladin's eyes were a light blue these days, never fading back to their proper dark brown. It didn't help that although he was sitting, he was hovering an inch off the ground. Air was more comfortable than stone.

The two of them spread the pages out on the counter at the side of the room. "It's a mess," Lirin said. "His entire medical system needs to be rebuilt from the ground up—with training in how to properly sanitize. Apparently many of his best field medics have fallen."

"Many of his best in all regards have fallen," Hesina said, scanning the pages.

You have no idea, Kaladin thought. He glanced at Syl, who had sidled over to sit closer to him, still human size. Oroden was chasing blocks again, and Kaladin . . .

Well, despite his tension, he let himself bask in it. Family. Peace. Syl. He'd been running from disaster to disaster for so long, he'd completely forgotten this joy. Even eating stew with Bridge Four—precious moments of respite—had felt like a gasp of air when drowning. Yet here he was. Retired. Watching his brother play, sitting next to Syl, listening to his parents chat. Storms, but it had been a wild ride. He'd managed to survive.

And it wasn't his fault that he had.

Syl rested her head—insubstantial though it was—on his shoulder as she watched the floating blocks. It was odd behavior for her, but so was her being human size.

"Why the full size?" he asked her.

"When we were in Shadesmar," she said, "everyone treated me differently. I felt . . . more like a person. Less like a force of nature. I'm finding I missed that."

"Do *I* treat you differently when you're small?"

"A little."

"Do you want me to change?"

"I want things to change and be the same all at once." She looked to him, and probably saw that he found that completely baffling. She grinned. "Suffice it to say that I want to make it harder for certain people to ignore me."

"Is being this size more difficult for you?"

"Yup," she said. "But I've decided I want to make that effort." She shook her head, causing her hair to swirl around. "Do not question the will of the mighty spren princess, Kaladin Stormblessed. My whims are as inscrutable as they are magnanimous."

"You were just saying you want to be treated like a person!" he said. "Not a force of nature."

"No," she said. "I want to *decide* when I'm treated like a person. That doesn't preclude me also wanting to be properly worshipped." She smiled deviously. "I've been thinking of all kinds of things to make Lunamor do. If we ever see him again."

Kaladin wanted to offer her some consolation, but he honestly had no idea if they'd ever see Rock again. This was a different shade of pain, distinct from the loss of Teft, distinct from the loss of Moash—or the man they'd *thought* Moash had been.

That brought the reality of the situation back to him, along with the strange warnings the wind had whispered. He found himself speaking. "Father, what's the battle look like currently? A ten-day deadline. Seems like everyone might simply rest and wait it out?"

"Not so, unfortunately," Lirin said. "I'm warned to expect heavy casualties in the next few days, as Dalinar anticipates the fighting will last right up until the deadline—in fact, he fears the enemy might push harder to capture ground in the Unclaimed Hills and the Frostlands. Apparently, per the agreement, whatever each side holds when the deadline arrives . . . that's what they get to keep."

Storms. Kaladin imagined it: fierce battles over unimportant, uninhabited land—but which both sides wanted to hold nonetheless. His heart bled for the soldiers who would die in the nine days before it all would end.

"Is this the storm?" he whispered.

Syl glanced at him, frowning. But he wasn't talking to her.

No . . . that voice replied. *Worse* . . .

Worse. He shivered.

Please . . . the wind said. *Help* . . .

"I don't know if I *can* help," Kaladin whispered, hanging his head. "I . . . don't know what I have left to give."

I understand, it replied. *If you can, come to me.*

"Where?"

Listen to the Bondsmith . . .

He frowned. The day before, Dalinar had mentioned having a duty for Kaladin in Shinovar, involving the Herald Ishi and some "odd company." Kaladin had already resolved to go. So perhaps he *could* help.

Come to me, the wind repeated. *Please* . . .

There was a highstorm tonight, and Kaladin had thought to use it—and the Stormlight it offered—to get to Shinovar. However, Dalinar had promised him more details before he left. So, taking a deep breath, Kaladin stood and stretched.

It had been wonderful to spend time with his family. To remember that peace. But even as worn out as he was, there was work for him to do yet.

"I'm sorry," he said to his parents. "I've got to go. Dalinar wants me to try to find Ishi, who has apparently gone mad. Not surprising, considering how Taln and Ash are faring."

His mother gave him an odd look, and it took him a moment to realize it was because he was speaking so familiarly of Heralds—figures of lore and religious devotion the world over. He didn't know any of them well, but it felt natural to use their names like that. He'd stopped revering people he didn't know the day Amaram branded him.

God or king. If they wanted his respect, they could earn it.

"Son," Lirin said, turning away from his many sheets of paper. From the way Lirin said the word, Kaladin braced himself for some kind of lecture.

He was unprepared for Lirin to walk over and embrace him. Awkwardly, as it wasn't Lirin's natural state to give this sort of affection. Yet the gesture conveyed emotions Lirin found difficult to say. That he'd been wrong. That perhaps Kaladin needed to find his own way.

So Kaladin embraced him too, and let the joyspren—like blue leaves—swirl up around them.

"I wish I had fatherly advice for you," Lirin said, "but you've far outpaced my understanding of life. So I guess, go and be yourself. Protect. I . . . I love you."

"Stay safe," his mother said, giving him another side hug. "Come back to us."

He gave her a nod, then glanced at Syl. She'd changed from a havah to a Bridge Four uniform, trimmed in white and dark blue, with her hair in a ponytail like Lyn usually wore. It was strange on Syl—made her look older. She'd never truly been childlike, despite her sometimes mischievous nature—and her chosen figure had always been that of a young, but adult, woman. Girlish at times, but never a girl. In uniform, with her hair up and wearing that glove on her safehand, she seemed more mature.

It was time to go. With a final hug for his brother, Kaladin strode out to meet his destiny, feeling like he was in control for the first time in years. Deciding to take the next step, rather than being thrust into it by momentum or crisis.

And while he'd woken up feeling good, that knowledge—that sense of volition—felt *great.*

3
THE COST OF HEROISM

The Wind told me, before she vanished, that it was the change in Odium's vessel that restored her voice. I wonder. Perhaps it is the new storm, making people begin to reconsider that the wind is not their enemy.

—From *Knights of Wind and Truth*, page 3

Shallan and Pattern left Testament to rest and crossed the wall at Lasting Integrity to meet with Adolin, Maya, and the Herald Kelek—who were speaking with a kind of spren that Kelek called a "seon." She manifested as a hovering ball of light, roughly the size of a head, with an odd symbol at the center. Other than them, the wall top was empty today.

"You don't remember?" Pattern asked softly as he and Shallan walked. "The events with Testament? I thought you did. I thought, with Veil gone . . ."

"Veil is not gone," Shallan said. "She's part of me, like she always was."

"I . . . don't understand."

"It's hard to explain," Shallan said. "And . . . I'm not sure I've entirely figured it out. Healing is not an event, Pattern, but a process. I've incorporated Veil into myself, so she doesn't take control any longer, but she's not *gone*. Veil is me, but Veil is not always Shallan."

"But . . . you are Shallan . . ."

"Imagine it as Veil moving to the back of the wagon as we ride toward the future. She's still there, coaching me, and we're both aware of the world."

There was more to it than that, of course. Shallan had projected some uncomfortable aspects of herself onto Veil. Now she had to face them. She'd worried that Adolin would find it difficult, but . . . well, Adolin Kholin was storming wonderful. After their discussion last night, he seemed to understand. Together they knew that there was work to do, but Shallan had taken an enormous step toward healing—and along with it, had acknowledged something important.

She didn't deserve hatred, but understanding. It was hard to believe, but Veil insisted they try anyway.

"But . . ." Pattern said. "Radiant is still . . . separate?"

"More separate," Shallan said.

"Mmmmm. So . . . still in the front of the wagon."

"Yes. That might change. It might not need to change. I'm figuring this out as I go, Pattern, but I *feel* better. More importantly, I no longer need Veil to stand between me and the memories."

"So you *do* remember."

"Yes and no," Shallan said. "It's a jumble. I was young, the events were traumatic, and there is so much *pain* associated with memories of my mother. I need time to process."

"Mmmm. Humans are . . . squishy. Not just bodies. Minds too. Memories too. Ideas too. Mmmm . . ." He sounded pleased by that.

As a child, she'd bonded a spren, something her mother had . . . had not liked. A man had come, either to hurt Shallan or to separate her from Testament. Her father had fought him, and during their struggle Shallan's mother had come at her with a knife. In self-defense, Shallan had killed her mother with an early manifestation of Testament as a Shardblade.

Shallan, in trauma, had rejected her nascent oaths and buried those memories. But if her bond with Testament had never been fully broken . . . what did that mean? And the memories of the days between her mother's death and the arrival of Pattern . . . which of those involved Testament?

I knew I had a Shardblade . . . long before I'd bonded Pattern. She'd convinced herself that the weapon belonged to her father, and had been kept in his safe. She'd gone there before leaving home, and had drawn it out to dismiss it—ignoring that she'd instantly summoned it when reaching her hand in—pretending it was an ordinary Blade, pretending she needed ten heartbeats to summon it. However, a part of her had known even then that it was Testament, a friend to whom she'd done great harm. That was the one thing Shallan clearly remembered. Testament was her *friend.* A dimpled pattern on the wall that had delighted, then engaged, then *protected* a young girl.

Testament had never been as talkative as Pattern. Indeed, Shallan could only remember rare, soft fragments of speech, encouraging her to stand against the darkness in her family. Shallan had loved her mysterious spren dearly; though her memories were jumbled, the *emotions* shone through the pain. Strength could be a matter of perception sometimes. And today Shallan found she could choose strength.

They approached Adolin, Maya, and Kelek. Shallan still found it incredible this man was one of the Heralds of the Almighty. The short, balding fellow kept rubbing his hands together, as if washing them in invisible soap and water. Adolin and Maya practically towered over him as they talked to the ball of light.

Maya was obviously paying attention. She wasn't completely healed—her eyes were scratched out and her coloring was a wan brown instead of vibrant green like others of her kind—but she was getting better. She no longer wandered off or just stared blankly during conversations. She was also starting to talk more and more.

"I worry about what is to come," the ball of light was saying. It had transformed into an approximation of Wit's face made of soft blue-white light, and spoke with his voice. The spren was a way to contact him, as they'd discovered a few days ago. "The war is set to intensify, and all rests upon the contest of champions. Odium's chosen warrior versus whoever old Dalinar chooses."

"Father *will* choose himself," Adolin said. "When the Blackthorn needs to be certain something is done right, he will do it himself." Adolin paused, then glanced at Maya. "Storm him. He probably *is* our best chance though."

"Wit?" Shallan said. "It's really happening?"

"It is indeed," he said. "The contest is set, contracts agreed to. Shallan, they've set it for nine days from now."

"So soon?" Shallan asked. Storms. "Where?"

"Urithiru," Adolin said, his arms folded. "They've already sent Windrunners to fetch us. Should arrive today."

Shallan chewed on that, trying not to feel emotional whiplash. It had taken weeks to reach Lasting Integrity—but Windrunners could fly them back to Urithiru within the day, depending on how much Stormlight they brought.

She found herself eager to return. She'd had enough of the honorspren and their elitism. She missed blue skies and plants that didn't *crinkle* when you touched them. Though Shadesmar had a sun, it was distant and cold. She could never thrive here.

Plus, as she'd indicated to Testament, she had work to do.

"Wit," Shallan said, stepping closer. The glowing version of his face focused on her. "My brothers are safe? You're certain?"

"Very certain, brilliant one," he said back, softly. "You're sure the Ghostbloods will move against you?"

"Yes," she said. After a year and a half of flirting with the Ghostbloods, she'd at last stepped up and said no. Doing so had essentially declared war on them. She found Adolin's hand for support. He knew the entire story now. "Wit, I know their faces, their plans . . . I'm likely the greatest threat on the planet to their organization, and they tried to kill Jasnah for less. Everyone I love is in danger."

"I have to manage Dalinar and try to prepare him," Wit said, "but I think I can help you as well. I've been watching Mraize's little crew; I'll send your people my drawings of their members. But take care, Shallan. I know this group and their leader. They can be brutal."

"As can I," Shallan whispered. She glanced at Kelek, who was staring out over the bead ocean and the deadeyed spren who remained on the shore. Despite him, she felt safe here with Pattern, Adolin, and Maya. Safe enough to voice it. "Wit, I'm worried. Am I ready?"

"I ask myself that same question now and then," he said. "And Shallan, I'm ten thousand years old."

"During the trip," she said, "I started to create a new persona. Formless. A . . . version of me, but . . ." How did she explain it? "A version of me with no face. A version of me who could do terrible things. I walked away from it, Wit, but that capacity is still inside me."

"Shallan," he said, and she looked up, meeting his eyes. "If it weren't for that capacity, then what good would choices be? If we never had the *power* to do terrible things, then what heroism would it be to resist?"

"But . . ."

"Did you turn away?" he asked, and Adolin squeezed her shoulder.

"Yes."

"Then heroism it is, Shallan."

"I'm remembering what I did to my mother," she said. "And my father. And to a lesser extent Tyn. Now Mraize . . . I'm going to have to kill him, Wit. Is that my destiny? To kill every person who ever mentored me?"

In that, finally, her fears found voice. Did it sound silly, foolish, ridiculous? This pattern she'd seen in her life? Wit did not laugh though, and he considered himself an expert on what was ridiculous.

"Would that any of us," he said, "could protect ourselves from the costs heroism often requires. But again, if there were no cost, no sacrifice, then would it be heroism at all? I cannot promise you that it will be easy, but Shallan, I'm proud of you."

I'm proud of you, Radiant whispered.

I'm proud of you, Veil—the part of her that was Veil—agreed.

"Thank you," she said.

"I have to go," Wit said. "But I'll leave you with this. The Ghostbloods want something extremely valuable, and you have the key to it standing with you right now. If you want to destroy them, you might not need to kill every last one of them. Instead, you might simply need powerful leverage . . ."

The glowing spren shifted from his face back to a sphere. "He's gone," the spren said. "I'm sorry."

His final words lingered with Shallan, reinforcing something she'd been considering. A way to protect Roshar from the Ghostbloods—and indeed, she knew what their next target was likely to be. They'd sent her to Lasting Integrity hunting the Herald who stood next to her—and Kelek believed that the secret they truly sought was his knowledge of one of the Unmade.

"I need," she said to Kelek, "to know *everything* you know about Ba-Ado-Mishram."

The Herald wrung his hands, then looked to the side as if seeking escape.

"We're not going to hurt you," Adolin said calmly. "You know that by now."

"I do," Kelek said. "It's just . . . I wasn't supposed to be involved. None of us are."

"I don't think the other Heralds follow that," Shallan noted, folding her arms. "What did you *do,* Kelek?"

"Not much," he said, putting his hand to his head. "I . . . I *can't* do much these days. I don't know why. I can't decide. I . . . I . . ." He looked up at them, then formed fists, pulling them close to his chest. "I was at Urithiru when the plan to capture Mishram was conceived. Then . . . I joined them on their mission. I'm . . . I guess I'm the only one alive who actually knows what happened to her. That's why the Ghostbloods, and their cursed Lord of Scars, want me."

"Just tell us," Shallan said.

"Some of us learned you could capture spren in gemstones," he explained. "And Mishram—for all her power—is a spren. The Radiants prepared a flawless heliodor the color of sunlight, and they trapped her inside, then hid her prison. Not in the Physical Realm, and not in Shadesmar." He bit his lip, then forced out another part. "In the Spiritual Realm. Melishi hid it *there.*"

"How?" Shallan asked, sharing a glance with Adolin.

"I don't know," Kelek said, backing away. "I promise you, I don't *know.* But now . . . now they'll send more people for me, won't they? They'll trap *me* in a gemstone, or they think they'll be able to . . ." He looked to the two of them, wide-eyed, then fled toward the way down. None of them gave chase. Unfortunately, this behavior was usual for Kelek.

Maya grunted softly, watching him go. "He's gotten a lot worse."

Shallan started. "You knew him?"

"Met him a few times," Maya said, then took a deep breath. "Never . . . never thought much of him, even then."

"Well," Shallan said, "at least we know something more about Mishram. I suspect her prison is part of what Mraize has been hunting for a long time now. I might need to find it first, before he can."

"Ba-Ado-Mishram," Adolin said, thoughtful, leaning back against the wall's battlements. "The most powerful of the Unmade. What would the Ghostbloods want with her?"

"Mmm . . ." Pattern said. "Power. So much power. She was nearly a god. She bonded the singers once. Could Mraize want to do something similar again?"

Shallan shivered as she contemplated Mraize and his master, Iyatil, somehow commanding the entirety of the enemy army. Was that possible?

"Whatever the reason," Shallan said, "I have to stop him."

"Her prison is in the Spiritual Realm though?" Adolin said, frowning. "What does that even mean?"

"Mmm . . ." Pattern said. "It means we will never be able to find it."

"Surely it's *possible,*" Shallan said. "If the ancient Radiants put it there, we should be able to take it out."

"You don't understand," Pattern said, holding his hands apart and gesturing in his way. "You think Shadesmar is odd, yes? Black sky. Little sun. Pattern, with arms and legs for perambulating!" His head pattern spun faster. "The Spiritual Realm is stranger by orders of magnitude. It is a place where the future blends with the present, where the past echoes like the striking of a clock. Time and distance stretch, like numbers infinitely repeating. It is where the *gods* live, and it baffles even some of *them.*"

Shallan took that in, then glanced at Testament, huddled in the shadow of the wall farther back along the walk. "Our best guess," she said, "is that the deadeyes were created because Mishram was imprisoned, right?"

"Agreed," Pattern said. "Mishram became like a god to the singers—the parshmen. She Connected to Roshar, and echoes of that filtered to the spren! Ah, so wonderfully odd. Her imprisonment is the reason broken bonds now have such an effect on the spren."

"It is because . . ." Maya said, ". . . humans have no Honor. The god, I mean. I heard . . . I heard that Mishram had been captured. I heard that . . . that Radiants would destroy the world. That was why I decided. Decided I was done." She shook her head. "I don't know it all. I'd like to. Considering what breaking . . . breaking the bond did to me."

That day—the day Mishram had been captured—something deeper had happened. An event connecting humankind, Honor, spren, and the bonds.

"Then we need to figure out how Mishram, or her imprisonment, has power over our bonds," Shallan said, looking to Pattern. "We *need* to go to the Spiritual Realm and find that prison, however difficult it is."

His pattern slowed, then finally he laced his fingers together. "Very well. Though, you know when I said I was sure you wouldn't get me killed?"

"Yes?"

"I should like," he declared, "to make a retraction."

I have read that in the ancient days, the Wind often spoke to both human and singer. It would then mean that the Wind stopped talking not because of Odium, but because of people who began to fear her . . .

Or to worship the Storm instead.

—From *Knights of Wind and Truth*, page 4

Kaladin soared up through the central column of Urithiru, Syl beside him.

In the atrium, he still saw signs of the battle that had happened two days ago. Blood that hadn't been entirely scrubbed away. Broken banisters on balconies. That reminded him of another time he'd flown up this corridor . . . just after Teft's murder. Dark, poisoned rage building within—the feeling a fraternal twin to the normal excitement of holding Stormlight.

That man he'd become after killing the Pursuer . . . that man frightened Kaladin. Even now, lit by calm sunlight. Remembering that man was like remembering a nightmare, and it caused painspren—like little severed hands—to appear on the balconies he passed, leaping off toward him.

He banished those feelings as he landed on a floor near the top of Urithiru. As he alighted in the central chamber where the lifts deposited people, he noted a glow coming from a nearby room.

"Navani," Syl whispered, her eyes wide. She went light blue, shrank down to spren size, and zipped off in that direction. There was something almost *intoxicating* about Navani—and her bond with the Sibling—to spren in the tower city. Syl would be back shortly.

Kaladin forced himself to walk, not glide, over to Dalinar's meeting room.

As soon as he left Urithiru, Kaladin would have to return to using Stormlight only when necessary. Best to get into the habit now. As he walked, the wind blew behind him, somehow present all the way within the structure, carrying with it his armor spren as ribbons of light. He didn't hear the wind's voice, but it urged him forward, and its warnings echoed in his mind.

There was a small waiting room outside Dalinar's meeting room. Urithiru had more and more furniture these days, including a couch here. It was, unfortunately, taken up entirely by Wit—who lay face up, filling space that could have accommodated three people, his feet up on one armrest—reading a book and chuckling to himself while a large globe of light hovered beside him. Some kind of odd spren?

"Ah, Wema," Wit mumbled, turning the page. "You've finally noticed what a catch Vadam is? Let's see how you screw it up."

"Wit?" Kaladin said. "I didn't realize you were back in the tower." It was probably a stupid thing to say. Jasnah was here, so it made sense Wit had come along.

Wit, being Wit, finished his page before acknowledging Kaladin. At last the lanky man snapped the book closed, then sat up and lounged on the sofa a different way, arms spread across the back, one leg crossed on the other, looking like nothing so much as a king on his throne. A very relaxed king on a rather cushy throne.

"Well," Wit said, his eyes alight with amusement, "if it isn't my favorite flute thief."

"You gave that flute to me, Wit," Kaladin said, sighing as he leaned on the doorframe.

"Then you lost it."

"I found it again."

"Still lost it."

"That's not the same as stealing."

"I'm a storyteller," Wit said, with a flip of his fingers. "I have the right to redefine words."

"That's stupid."

"That's literature."

"It's confusing."

"The more confusing, the better the literature."

"That might be the most pretentious thing I've ever heard."

"Aha!" Wit said, pointing. "Now you're getting it."

Kaladin hesitated. Sometimes during conversations with Wit, he wished he had someone to take notes for him. "So . . ." Kaladin said. "Do you want your flute back?"

"Hell no. I *gave* that to you, bridgeboy. Returning it would be almost as insulting as losing it!"

"Then what am I supposed to do with it?"

"Hmmm . . ." Wit said, reaching into a bag at his feet and slipping out a different flute, this one painted with a shiny red lacquer. He twirled it in his hand. "If only there were something we could *do* with these curious pieces of wood? They have holes that seem intended for some arcane purpose, beyond the understanding of mere mortals."

Kaladin rolled his eyes.

"If only," Wit continued, "there were a way to learn to do something productive with this item. It has the look of a tool. Nay, an instrument! Of mythical design. Alas. My poor finite mind is incapable of comprehending the—"

"If I don't interrupt," Kaladin said, "how long will you keep going?"

"Long, *long* past when it was funny."

"It was funny?"

"The words?" Wit said. "Of course not. Your face while I say them though? Well, it's been said I am an artist. Unfortunately, the primary subjects of my art can never experience my creations, as displayed upon their features." He flipped the flute, then held it out to Kaladin. "Give it a try. It has the same fingerings as the one you lost and recovered, though not the same . . . capacity."

"Wit, I can't play this flute any more than I could play the other one you gave me," Kaladin said. "I have no idea how."

"So . . ." Wit flipped the flute again, then extended it farther toward Kaladin. "All you have to do is ask . . ."

"I guess I do have to wait for Dalinar," Kaladin said, looking longingly at the closed door. Dalinar's meetings often overran, despite the many clocks Navani had given him.

Kaladin felt an urgency to get to Shinovar, but if he wanted to fly all that way without using up a large sack of gemstones—which would be needed in the battle to come—he had to fly with the highstorm, hours away yet. So he had time. And . . . well, Kaladin felt indebted to Wit. As infuriating as the man—or whatever he was—could be . . . when Kaladin had been in the worst darkness of the storm, Wit had traveled a nightmare to pull him free.

This man was a friend. Kaladin appreciated him, quirks included. So, he played the role Wit obviously wanted. "Would you teach me?" Kaladin said, taking the flute. "I don't have a lot of time, but—"

Wit was already moving, whipping some sheets of paper from the bag by his feet. He waved for his strange ball spren to go away, and Kaladin's windspren followed, flitting out of the room as Kaladin glanced over the pages. They had odd symbols on them, which made Kaladin nervous, but Wit insisted it wasn't actual writing. Merely marks on a paper representing sounds. It took Kaladin a few minutes to realize the joke.

Still, over the next hour—Dalinar was really taking his time—Kaladin followed Wit's instructions. He learned the basics of fingering, of reading music, and—hardest of all—how to hold the thing and blow into it properly.

At the end of the hour, Kaladin was able to force out a stumbling rendition of the first line of the music, with notes that sounded breathy and weak in comparison to Wit's playing. It was an incredibly simple accomplishment, and he didn't attract a single musicspren, yet Kaladin felt he'd climbed a mountain. He was smiling in a stupid way as Syl, full sized and wearing a havah with purple trim, peeked in to investigate.

Based on the sounds I'm making, she's probably come to see who's stepping on a rat, Kaladin thought.

"Nice work," Wit said. "Next fight, start up a bit of that. Surely the enemy will drop their weapons . . . probably just to cover their ears."

"If anyone asks about my skill, I'll be sure to tell them who my teacher is."

Wit grinned.

"I know that song," Syl said, folding her arms.

"Wit played it for us on the Shattered Plains," Kaladin said. "Back when we first met him. The story of the *Wandersail.*"

"I know it better than that though . . ." she said.

"Long ago," Wit said softly, "that rhythm guided humans across the void from one planet to the other. They followed it to reach your world."

"One of the rhythms of Roshar," Syl said with a nod. "Made into a song, with the tones of the gods."

"Gods older than yours," Wit said from beside Kaladin on the couch.

"When you first played for us," Kaladin said, remembering that lonely night on the plateaus when he'd still been a bridgeman, "I could swear the sound . . . came back. You'd play, then talk, and the song would continue to echo. How did you do that?"

"I didn't," Wit said.

"But—"

"Ask yourself who was listening that night."

"Me. Syl. You, presumably."

"And?"

"And . . . some guards in the distance?"

Wit shook his head. "Storms, how can you be from this land, yet be so dense. It—"

"The wind," Kaladin guessed. "The wind was listening."

Wit smiled. "Maybe you can be salvaged after all."

"Is the wind a god?" Kaladin asked.

"When this world was created," Wit said, "long before Honor, Cultivation, or Odium arrived, Adonalsium left something behind on it. Sometimes it's called the Old Magic. That term is often applied to the Nightwatcher, who came—with Cultivation's efforts—from one of those ancient spren. Listen to the Wind when it speaks, Kaladin. It's weaker than it once was, but it has seen so very much."

"It . . . told me a storm was coming," Kaladin said. "And asked for help."

"Then listen," Wit said. "And the Wind . . . she will listen to you in return." He winked. "That's all I'll say about it. I'm not one to give away another's secrets."

Lovely. Well, he'd done as Wit asked, so he returned the flute. Would Dalinar *ever* be finished? "It was a fun way to pass the time, Wit, but I have to ask. Music? What relevance does it have for someone like me?"

"Ah, now there's a question for the ages," Wit said, leaning back. "What use is art? Why does it hold such meaning and potency? I can't tell you, because the short answer is unappealing and the long answer takes months. I will instead say this: *every* society in *every* region of *every* planet I've visited—and I've been to quite a large number—has made art."

Kaladin nodded thoughtfully. Wit hadn't answered his question, but he was accustomed to that. Protesting would only lead to mockery.

"Perhaps the question isn't 'What use is art?'" Wit mused. "Perhaps even that simple question misses the point. It's like asking the use of having hands, or walking upright, or growing hair. Art is part of us, Kaladin. That's the use; that's the reason. It exists because on some fundamental level we need it. Art exists to be made."

When Kaladin didn't respond, Wit eyed him.

"I can accept that," Kaladin said. "As an explanation."

"It's a tautology."

"The more confusing the better, right?"

Wit grinned, and then it faded. He glanced at the door.

"Wit," Kaladin said. "The Wind asked for help. And Dalinar is worried about the coming battle. I get the feeling this next part is going to be difficult."

"Yeah," Wit said softly. "I feel it too."

A straight answer. Those were always disturbing.

"Do you have any . . . words of wisdom?" Kaladin asked. "A story, maybe?"

"Listen," Wit said. "Everything you've done—Kal, everything you've been—has prepared you for what's next. It's going to be hard. Fortunately, life has been hard, so you're working under familiar constraints."

Kaladin glanced to the side, where Wit was staring off into space, idly spinning the red flute in his fingers. Something in his voice . . . his face . . .

"You're talking," Kaladin said softly, "as if one of us won't survive this."

"I wish I were optimistic enough to think one of us will survive."

"Wit, I'm pretty sure I've heard you say you're immortal."

"Immortality doesn't seem to go as far as it once did, kid." He glanced at

Kaladin. "Listen, if the Wind wants your help . . . well, I think you can rise to what is coming. Probably. Difficult though it will be."

"Storms," Syl said, walking forward. "I'm . . . not sure I like it when he's serious, Kaladin."

"Dalinar is going to send you to Shinovar," Wit said, "because he hopes Ishar can help with the contest of champions. Ishar can't help, not like that, but you still need to go."

"Why?" Kaladin asked. "Why go if I can't do what I'm sent to do?"

"Because this is the journey, Kaladin," Wit said softly. "The last part of it. Listen to me: I want you to practice with that flute until you make the sound return to you. Because that will mean Roshar is listening."

What did that even mean? "I think you've been reading too many stories, Wit. Riddles aren't actually helpful."

Wit launched himself off the couch and crossed the room on legs that suddenly seemed spindly. "The problem is, I don't actually know what the next part will entail. I have hints and thoughts, but mostly just worries. All I can do is point you toward what might be the correct path. That and keep your hope strong."

"Jasnah doesn't believe in hope," Syl whispered, stepping over by Kaladin. "I heard her complaining about it once."

"Jasnah would make an excellent Wit," Wit said, pointing at Syl. "She's the right combination of smart and stupid all at once." He smiled in a fond way, and Kaladin thought the rumors about them must be true.

"I'm confused," Kaladin said. "What are you saying, Wit?"

"That something is wrong," Wit said, stalking across the room and throwing his hands into the air. "Something is horribly wrong, and has been for several days now, and I *can't figure out what it is.* I've been waiting for the truth to come crashing down. I don't know what to do or who to pray to, since the only true God I've known is the one we rejected and killed. So I'm sending you off, Kaladin. Hoping that if the Wind spoke to you, then some piece of that ancient deity is watching. Because when everything feels wrong, all I can *do* is hope."

"The Passions," Syl whispered.

"Isn't that some old Thaylen religion?" Kaladin said. "Something about emotion?"

"Derived, anciently, from the teachings of Odium," Wit said. "Though it's not polite to point that out to practitioners of the Passions. People don't like hearing that their religion was mythologized, as if myth can't be true. Regardless, Ancient Daughter, I'd think better of you than to bring up the Passions."

"Why?" she said. "Human religions are all a little silly, aren't they?"

"Yes," Wit said, "but the Passions teach that if you are fervent enough—

if you *care* enough—your emotion will influence your success. That if you *want* something badly enough, the cosmere *will* provide it for you."

Kaladin nodded slowly. "There might be something to that."

"Kid," Wit said, leaning down over Kaladin on the couch, "the Passions are *absolute horseshit.*"

"What? It's good to be hopeful! The Passions sound nice."

"The wrong people get far too much mileage out of things that sound nice," Wit said. "Take it from a guy who is all too capable with a lie: *nothing* is easier to sell someone than the story they want to hear. The Passions are deeply insulting if you spare even a moment to consider. I once spoon-fed broth to a trembling child in a kingdom that no longer exists. I found her on a road leading away from a battlefield, after her parents—simple peasants—were slaughtered. Her elder brother lay dead a half mile behind, having starved.

"You think that kid who starved didn't *want* to eat? You think her parents didn't want to escape the ravages of war *badly enough*? You think if they'd had more *Passion,* the cosmere would have saved them? How convenient to believe that people are poor because they didn't *care* enough about being rich. That they just didn't pray hard enough. So convenient to make suffering their own fault, rather than life being unfair and birth mattering more than aptitude. Or storming Passion."

He raised his finger at that last word, and angerspren burst around his feet like pools of boiling blood, as if on cue. Kaladin didn't know if he'd ever seen Wit so riled up, particularly by something that had nothing to do with their conversation. Though one could never tell with Wit. Non sequiturs that ended up relevant were the daggers he kept strapped to his boots, to be employed when his foes were distracted.

"We need hope, Kaladin," Wit said, leaning farther forward. "We're heading straight toward what may be the most difficult moment in our lives. So remember: Hope is wonderful. Keep it, treasure it. Hope is a virtue—but the definition of that word is crucial. You want to know what a virtue *truly* is? It's not that difficult."

"If this entire conversation is the way I learn," Kaladin said, "then I dispute the idea of it not being difficult."

Wit chuckled, then stepped back and threw his hands up, angerspren vanishing and gloryspren—tiny spheres of golden light—bursting around him. "A *virtue* is something that is valuable even if it gives you *nothing.* A virtue persists without payment or compensation. Positive thinking is great. Vital. Useful. But it has to remain so even if it gets you nothing. Belief, truth, honor . . . if these exist only to *get* you something, you've missed the storming point."

He glanced at Syl. "This is where Jasnah is wrong about hope, smart though she is in so many ways. If hope doesn't mean anything to you when you lose, then it wasn't ever a virtue in the first place. It took me a long time to learn that, and I finally did so from the writings of a man who lost every belief he thought he had, then started over new."

"Sounds like someone wise," Syl said.

"Oh, Sazed is among the best. Hope I get to meet him someday."

"When you do," Kaladin said, "maybe some of his wisdom will rub off."

Wit tossed his flute, spinning it, then pointed it directly at Kaladin. "Congratulations. You've practiced music, you've listened to a self-important rant, *and* you've delivered quips at awkward points. I dub you graduated from Wit's school of practical impracticality."

Syl sat on the couch, though she left no impression in its cushions. She looked completely baffled.

"Wait," Kaladin said. "Does that make me . . . your apprentice?"

Wit belted out a loud, full belly laugh, long enough to be uncomfortable. "Kal," he said, gasping for breath, "you're still far, *far* too useful a human being to be an apprentice of mine. You'd end up actually helping people! No, I've already had one bridgeboy as an apprentice, and graduated or not, he's incompetent enough to hold on to the position."

"I'll have you know," Kaladin said, "that Sig is doing a fine job leading the Windrunners."

"You've been corrupting him," Wit said. "No, you're not my apprentice, but that doesn't mean you can't learn a thing or two. A kind of . . . cross-training in uselessness." He said it while thrusting his flute into the air.

"You're so storming dramatic," Kaladin said.

"Simply trying to give you a proper send-off," Wit said. "We're at the end, Kaladin, and you are needed. I want you to march off to your divine destiny with a spring in your step."

"I don't know what I'm going to do though," Kaladin said. "War is coming, but I'm not involved. I'm just going to help a maniac return to his senses."

"That's it, eh?" Wit said. "Just you becoming your world's first therapist."

Kaladin glanced at Syl, who shook her head. "We have no idea what that is, Wit."

"Because," Wit said, "you haven't finished inventing it yet." He leaned in. "About time someone figured out a method to counteract what I've been doing. Now, practice that flute. Get Roshar to listen. Help Ishar. But know that you're not coming back to aid Dalinar, whatever he thinks."

"Practice the flute," Syl said. "Get Roshar to listen to us. Help Ishar. Don't come back."

"Exactly," Wit said. "Now go. The world needs the two of you—more than you, or it, or anyone other than your humble Wit yet realizes. The fight ahead of you will be legendary. Unfortunately, you can't fight this one with strength of muscle. You'll have to wield the spear another way. Good luck."

With a sigh, Kaladin stood up. Then the most remarkable thing happened. Wit extended his hand, and didn't pull back as Kaladin hesitantly took it. Wit gave a firm shake.

"You know what first drew me to you, Kaladin?" Wit asked. "You did one of the most difficult things a man can do: you gave yourself a second chance."

"I took that second chance . . . maybe a third," Kaladin admitted. "But now what? Who am I without the spear?"

"Won't it be exciting to find out?" Wit said. "Have you ever wondered who you would be if there was no one you needed to save, no one you needed to kill? You've lived for others for so long, Kaladin. What happens when you try living for *you*?" Wit held up his finger. "I know you can't answer yet. Go and *find out*." With that, Wit bowed to him. "Thank you."

"For what?" Kaladin asked.

"For the inspiration," Wit said, straightening and looking to Kaladin, then to Syl, then smiling in a fond, yet somehow regretful way.

Kaladin felt a chill. "I'm . . . never going to see you again, am I, Wit?"

"No one knows the future, Kal," he replied. "Not even me. So instead of saying goodbye, let's call this . . . an extended period of necessary separation, requisite to give me time to think of the most perfect, *exquisite* insult. If I never get to deliver it in person . . . well, kindly do me the favor of imagining how wonderful it was. All right?"

"All right."

Wit winked at him, then walked over to rap on the door.

Dalinar opened it a moment later. "Have you finally finished with him, Wit?" the man asked. "I've been waiting for a storming hour."

"He's all yours," Wit said, striding away. "Remember what I told you."

"I will," both Kaladin and Dalinar said at the same time. They glanced at each other.

"Wit," Kaladin called just before the man vanished. "What about my story?"

"You will tell your own story this time, Kaladin!" Wit said. "And if you're lucky, the Wind will join in." Then he was gone, his last whistle slowly fading.

"Did you ever think," Kaladin said to Dalinar, "that you'd end up dancing to that man's whims?"

"I suspect," Dalinar said, stepping back and waving for Kaladin to enter, "we've been dancing to them for years without knowing it. Come. I have a few things to tell you two before you leave."

5
WHAT MIGHT STILL BE

As a historian, I find such nuances relevant. As a philosopher, I find them enticing.

—From *Knights of Wind and Truth,* page 4

It was nice for Shallan to take a few hours and think for once. Sitting, wearing a bright blue havah rather than her traveling clothing, on the top row of the stone open-air forum in Lasting Integrity, drawing. How long had it been since she'd simply let herself draw? She'd sketched a little during their trip, but that felt like an eternity ago.

She relaxed, flowing with the drawing: a depiction of the vertigo she felt looking up along one of the interior walls of Lasting Integrity. A surreal image like something from one of the older art movements, where perspective was intentionally alien and off-putting. She liked to think that the old surrealists had made contact with spren and Shadesmar, warping their minds to new ways of seeing things.

Though she'd never been as good with landscapes as she was with people, she was proud of the sense her sketch gave of falling—yet into what you could not see, because the unnatural perspective drew your eyes upward.

As with others she'd done today though, strange faces kept sneaking into the art.

In this case, she'd absently warped the shadings of one wall into a face. Feminine, a singer with a crownlike carapace and shadows and curves forming a stratalike design on her face. Shallan flipped through the sketchbook. Each drawing done today had that singer face hidden somewhere, and she didn't remember making them.

She'd done something similar at Urithiru, where the presence of an

Unmade had warped her sketches. She tried not to let it disturb her quite so much this time. Then, it had been a message. Was there a similar one now?

She looked toward Adolin, who paced at the center of the forum—the place where only a few days before, he'd been on trial. Today he'd been joined by Godeke, a lanky Edgedancer. Shallan's agents had joined them as well: Ishnah, Vathah, and Beryl, along with their Cryptics. Together they waited for the Windrunners, and for the fruits of some final efforts in Lasting Integrity. She started another sketch as they waited.

In the end, twelve arrived.

Twelve honorspren, from a population of hundreds. That was how many showed up in response to Adolin's call to arms. He and Godeke greeted each one with a smile, but she knew he'd expected more. One other did arrive: Notum. The former sea captain sported his unique facial hair as always, though he walked on unsteady feet. They still didn't know why he'd been assaulted by those Tukari that Adolin had saved him from.

Notum didn't join Godeke and Adolin, but instead walked down the steps to Shallan. "Radiant Kholin," he said.

That was odd to hear, even a year after the wedding. It hadn't been a foregone conclusion that she would take Adolin's name; among the Alethi lighteyes, either party was equally likely to keep their name as adopt a new one. In her case, she was needed in the line of Kholin succession. She doubted she'd take a throne that Adolin had refused, but Dalinar wanted people he trusted in line. Her adoption into the Kholin house would strengthen her claim, should it come to that.

In explaining this to her, Dalinar and Navani had been speaking pragmatically—but that wasn't what Shallan remembered most about that day. For her, it was the day when a set of parents had, for the first time, *wanted* her.

Notum settled down beside her. "Your mission was a success. Twelve new Radiants."

"We expected more though," Radiant said, emerging. "After the support Adolin got at the trial, I anticipated an excellent recruitment result."

"A good number of honorspren support him," Notum said, "but that doesn't mean they want to be bonded. One can be irate at the honorspren leadership and think humans are deserving of support, without wanting to take that step."

Below, the twelve honorspren started to fade.

"I've never seen this before," Notum added. "I thought they'd go in a blink. Instead they fade away to nothing . . ."

"Not nothing," Radiant said. "They'll appear on the other side."

"I hear it's traumatic," Notum said. He had a stiff, formal way of speaking, even when the words were casual. Clipping each word as if he were making an announcement from the quarterdeck of his ship. "Spren on the other side forget themselves."

"Only briefly," Radiant said. "These will probably stay in a group—which helps—and immediately make their way to Urithiru, drawn by the squires training there."

"Do you still need them now, though?" Notum asked. "Isn't the war soon to end?"

"Windrunners are our primary method of traveling long distances—and I suspect they'll be very helpful in peacetime. Beyond that . . . even if Dalinar wins the contest, I worry about what is to come next. The more Radiants we have, the more stable our position will be."

"Then I should hurry," Notum said, standing. "To join them, so that I'm not left alone."

Radiant approved. But Shallan . . . she noticed something.

"You sound reluctant," Shallan said.

He looked at her, glowing the same soft blue as all the honorspren. His uniform, his hair, everything about him was made of the same light—solid, not transparent, but also not quite real in the way she understood reality.

"There is nothing more for me here," Notum said. "I have been rejected of mine, and have seen their pettiness. I should like to be of service. Though . . . I admit, I do not wish to bond a human. I loathe the idea. Is that petty of me, in turn?"

"Absolutely not," Shallan said. "I have two bonds, Notum, and understand the cost better than most. It's not pettiness, or cowardice, to be hesitant. Just as it's not petty or cowardly to reject *any* relationship."

"Pardon," Notum said, "but other sorts of relationships don't lead to soldiers with remarkable powers."

That did admittedly complicate the matter. But after learning what she'd done to Testament—who sat with Pattern a few rows down—Shallan couldn't help but question their mission. They needed Windrunners, yes, but it made her increasingly uneasy to *demand* a spren bond. It wasn't intimate in the traditional human sense of the word, but it felt as deeply personal.

"We can use every Windrunner, yes," she said, "but I don't think you should force yourself to bond a human if it makes you uncomfortable. You can be a good person and say no, Notum. I've learned that."

"Perhaps I will stay here a little longer then," Notum said. "With effort, I might persuade others of my kind to offer you support." He pointed, and drew her attention to a group of honorspren walking past, wearing traveling clothing and carrying gear. As if leaving for a long hike. They waved to Shallan and Adolin, but did not join those fading away.

"Objectors?" Shallan asked as Adolin waved back to them. "Those you mentioned earlier?"

"Yes," Notum said. "They don't agree with how you were treated, but also don't want to go to war. They depart Lasting Integrity to make their own way."

She nodded. "Well, Radiant Godeke is staying to continue to normalize relations with the honorspren, and I might leave one of my agents as well. If you stay, that would help—they could use a solid ally here."

"I am your ally," he said, "but as I warned you, the honorspren leadership does not care for me, even if they have been forced to revoke my exile." His expression grew distant. "We have an entire navy that once sailed the bead ocean; it is a shame to see those ships abandoned in the yards. It gives the enemy full control of the Shadesmar seas. Perhaps I could sail under honorspren authority again . . ."

Storms, if Shallan hadn't said anything, Notum might have gone to become a Radiant spren—meaning that she'd just actively gone against their orders in coming here. Perhaps she wouldn't mention that in her report to Dalinar.

No other spren came. Lusintia, the spren who had been Shallan's guide since her arrival at Lasting Integrity, made no appearance. Shallan had hoped she would change her mind, despite their occasional clashes.

"Notum, thank you," Shallan said. "For how you stood up for us during the trial."

"I am one person stretched thin, Radiant Kholin," he said, standing with his hands clasped behind him. "Like colors on the mast that have waved too long in the wind. I don't know what I believe or trust any longer, but what was done to you was not right. I could not play the sham role they demanded of me. I ask your forgiveness for even considering it."

"It was natural to want your old life back, Notum."

He turned to her, blue eyes meeting hers. "I lay on the ground, battered and assaulted, and watched your husband rise in my defense against overwhelming odds. He saved me with no expectation of reward. In that moment I knew that Honor *lived.*" He nodded curtly to Shallan, then walked down the steps to talk with Adolin.

Shallan slowly returned to her sketch—where she soon found that she'd drawn yet another face. In Adolin's shadow. Storms.

Don't be unnerved, she thought. *You were upset when you drew Pattern for the first time, back in Kharbranth. But look how that turned out.*

She *would not* be afraid of her own art. She gritted her teeth and forced herself to flip to the next sheet and start drawing again, until someone else sat beside her. Kelek leaned forward, hands clasped, seeming small and fragile.

"I'm not going with you," he said softly. "I . . . I can't."

"It's not safe for you here," Shallan said, sketching, her fingers moving as if of their own accord. "If I got to you, Mraize's other assassins can too."

"I . . . I will hide. Better. But I can't leave the seon, and she can't travel now. It wouldn't be good for her."

Shallan didn't argue. That never worked well with Kelek. Instead she lost herself in a sketch of him. A Herald to add to her collection. She might have said this was the rarest of gems to obtain, but was a Herald actually rarer than anyone else? One might argue that due to their immortality, they were less so.

"We are broken, Shallan," Kelek finally said. "We are not the heroes you wish us to be. Not anymore."

"I know how that feels."

"I don't think you do," he said, wrapping his arms around himself. "I don't believe anyone does." He glanced at Adolin, chatting with Notum and Godeke. "You're really going to try to find Mishram?"

"If I don't," Shallan said, "my enemies will."

"Then what?" he said. "Will you release her? I . . . I cannot decide. Always cannot decide. I have advocated for her freedom in the past, but now I worry. She might join and strengthen Odium. She . . . hates humans." He put his hand to his head. "Ishar says all the Unmade should be contained, yet what we did to the singers by imprisoning her . . ."

"I'll worry about that when I find her gemstone," Shallan said. "Honestly, I'll probably bring her back to the Bondsmith and let everyone decide together."

He didn't respond, so she continued drawing. The familiar sound of charcoal or colored pencil on paper; the distilled attention of creation, like the most potent alcohol. She attracted a few creationspren, little swirling lights. These ones, though, behaved oddly—in here, she'd never seen them change shape like they did in the Physical Realm, but these started adopting the appearance of her pencil or eraser.

She kept drawing. Lines imitating life. Freezing it. But altering it at the same time, for you could never make an exact copy. That wasn't the point. Every sketch was a picture of the artist as well: their perspective, their emphasis, their *instinct* reclaiming a moment otherwise lost . . .

Once you reached the end . . . it was sublime.

That moment when you basked in the thing you'd created—that feeling of awe mixed with disbelief that this beautiful object had come from you. Accompanied by the slightest worry that because you didn't understand how you'd done it, you maybe didn't deserve to have been part of the creation. She loved the feeling, even the uncertainty of it.

"Radiant," Kelek said, hands clasped as he stared at the stone floor of the amphitheater, "what do you fear?"

What kind of question was that? "I don't know," she lied.

"I fear options," he said. "I see each choice I make, and see the terrible results that could stem from it. If I stay here, I see you fail without me. If I go, I see my presence—broken as I am—*cause* your failure. I cannot continue. I . . . I do not . . ."

She rested her hand on his, then passed him the sketch. He took the picture, frowning, then his eyes widened as he saw it depicted him standing tall, wearing robes and striding from a fanciful city with colorful walls and strange trees with long fronds she'd made up. He carried a staff with an odd shape at the top, and strode toward a glowing light on the horizon—though in the picture, he looked backward and his face was determined. Decisive.

"Do you often do this?" he asked.

"Sketch people?" she said, then blushed. "Yes, I kind of do it all the time. When I'm feeling like myself, at least."

"Not simply sketching, child. Do you often draw upon Fortune? Glimpse someone's possible selves, and pull one forth . . . touch, in some small way, what could have been. What might still be . . ." He glanced to her, and must have seen the utter confusion in her eyes, as he sighed. "Is this a skill commonly employed by Lightweavers during your time?"

"Not that I know of," she said. "But I don't exactly understand what you're saying."

He glanced toward Pattern and Testament. "Two spren. Of course . . . you've bonded two. Strange things happen when the Nahel bond is imbricated. There were rules against it once, I believe. How long have you had them both?"

"For some time," she said, "though I didn't know it—didn't *remember* it—until recently."

"And how often," he asked, holding up the sheet, "do you glimpse into the Spiritual Realm, then manifest it in your art?"

"I . . ." She thought back to pictures she'd done, like one found in the pocket of a dead man. Like sketches of the Unmade lurking in Urithiru . . . or faces turning up in her art without her intending to draw them. She began to feel like a fool for objecting so quickly to someone who clearly knew far more about these things than she did.

"It might happen now and then," she said. "There was an Unmade in Urithiru, and it showed up in my art. Now these faces . . ." She turned one toward him.

He nodded. "Because you've been thinking about traveling to the Spiritual Realm and finding Ba-Ado-Mishram."

"That's her?"

"One interpretation of her, yes," he said. "If you were someone else, I would assume you had seen some ancient art and were unconsciously influenced by it. For you . . ." He shrugged. "Fortune can do unthought, fantodic things."

"I'm sorry. Fantodic?"

"It means . . . unnerving?" he said. "I'm sorry. I don't keep up on shifts in language, nor am I an expert on Fortune. Best speak to Midius—your Wit—about that. A fantodic man himself, that one."

He took her page and carefully folded it to place in his pocket. She cringed at that—she hadn't applied lacquer to keep it from smudging—but was distracted by something happening up beyond the walls of Lasting Integrity. A group of glowing figures were descending, trailing various kinds of spren who could soar with them—attracted to their use of Stormlight. The Windrunners had arrived.

Seconds later, Drehy, his spren, and some of his squires landed nearby, holding common spears, as Shardblades couldn't enter Shadesmar. At least not in Shardblade shape.

"I believe," Drehy said, "a lighteyed lady ordered a palanquin trip to Urithiru?"

"Funny-looking palanquin, Drehy," Shallan said, rising.

"Now, that's not nice, Brightness," Drehy said, thumbing over his shoulder at one of his squires. "Shiosak there might have been dropped a few times as a child, but he isn't *funny* looking. He's unique."

Shiosak—who was actually a rather handsome, affable Veden man—rolled his eyes.

Five Windrunners. Not enough to take everyone; Adolin's soldiers, and likely some of her agents, would have to make the more boring trip back via boat. Most wouldn't mind that. The bigger problem would be Adolin—who would have to leave his horse and his swords behind. Shallan stood up as her husband, grinning ear to ear, came jogging up the steps. He knew Drehy, of course. Adolin knew everyone. She watched him count the Windrunners, do the calculations in his mind, and come to the same conclusion.

Almost.

"How many of you," Adolin said, "will it take to fly my horse home?"

Regardless, the events surrounding the cleansing of Shinovar are of specific relevance, and I am doing my best to record what I can discover of the Wind's own words regarding them. Though, now that the Wind and Heralds have vanished, I have only two sources who can speak of these events.

They are my witnesses.

—From *Knights of Wind and Truth*, page 5

Dalinar looked out a window at the frosted peaks of the Ur mountain range. Kaladin knew these lands were probably claimed by some kingdom, yet it was difficult to imagine. Owning fields was one thing, but *mountains*?

If someone *could* claim them though, it would be the mountain of a man by the window. Dalinar didn't lean against the stone frame to relax as another might have. He clasped his hands behind him, his spine straight. Wearing a Kholin blue uniform with his glyphs on the back: the tower and the crown.

Szeth sat on the floor near the far corner. Dressed once more in white, head shaved. Eyes closed with his long, silvery-sheathed Shardblade in his lap. Kaladin had always thought the weapon wicked in appearance, with those hooked crossguard arms and the jet-black hilt. Szeth appeared to be meditating. Calm, rhythmic breaths. Storms, even when relaxing, the man was unnerving.

Syl maintained both her human size and the colors on her havah as she walked over to stare Szeth in the face to see if he was peeking.

"How are you feeling?" Dalinar asked. "About your upcoming task?"

"Good, sir," Kaladin said. "The world is going to be different, whatever happens in ten days. Wit says I need to find a new place in it—so I'm going to try this. You asked me to be a surgeon, not a soldier. I'm game."

A surgeon for the mind—who didn't cut with a scalpel, but with calm words and understanding. Storms, that seemed so much more difficult.

"Excellent," Dalinar said. "I've had reports on the men you helped with their battle shock. It's remarkable."

"Take a person from the darkness and show them that light still exists. It won't fix everything, but it does make a difference."

"Light," Dalinar said, gazing out across snowfields reflecting sunlight like liquid diamonds. "Ishar said something about light, when he told me he wanted to refound the Oathpact. Saying the Words—the moment when an oath is sworn, even by someone else nearby—brings clarity . . . and should restore him, if briefly." He glanced toward Szeth.

"Sir?" Kaladin asked.

"I'm sending Szeth with you."

"*He's* the companion you promised me?" Kaladin said.

"I return to my homeland," Szeth said softly, "to set right what is wrong. To cleanse an evil. To achieve the Fourth Ideal, a Skybreaker must undertake a crusade of righteous cause. Upon completing it, I will be poised for the final step, in which a man becomes the law itself. I wished to go alone, but Dalinar has insisted I bring you."

Kaladin took that in, then stepped closer to Dalinar, turning his back on Szeth—which felt very wrong to do. "Sir," he hissed. "That man is not stable. He doesn't need to be sent on a quest. He needs time, attention, and the help of . . ."

Kaladin trailed off as he noticed Dalinar's expression.

"Storms," Kaladin said. "You think I can do something to help Szeth while he's trying to 'cleanse the evil' of his homeland?"

"Yes," Dalinar said, firm. "You up to it, soldier?"

Kaladin glanced over his shoulder at Szeth. "Sir, with all due respect, I have managed to help one group of men suffering a mental burden that I understand from personal experience. You can't expect me to replicate that kind of success with an extreme case like Szeth. I would need *months* to devise a treatment!"

"We should . . . speak in private. Plus, I feel like I need some perspective. What about you, soldier?"

"Always, sir," Kaladin said as Syl joined them, head cocked, eyeing Dalinar.

"Excellent," Dalinar said, turning and walking toward the door. He took a small wooden box from a table by the wall, then tucked it under one arm. "Szeth, will you be fine here on your own for a while?"

"I'm never alone," the man said in his lightly accented voice. "Even without spren or sword, I'd have the voices." He looked straight at Kaladin with all the emotion of a corpse. Storms. Dalinar wanted him to help that man? The assassin who had killed Dalinar's own brother?

Kaladin followed Dalinar out, expecting them to chat in the next room, but Dalinar led them up the steps to the roof of Urithiru. Kaladin hadn't been up here since . . .

Well, since he'd thrown himself off.

"I find that this view helps me think," Dalinar said, turning around to survey the mountains. "How far one can see, when no walls obstruct." He grew contemplative, and seemed to want a minute, so Kaladin gave it to him, walking toward the edge of the tower.

"Storms," he said to Syl, reaching the railing. "It feels surreal to be here again. And it's so *warm*."

"It's Brightness Navani," Syl said, leaning over the side to look down. "And her bond to the tower. This city flourished with life once. It will again."

"Reminds me of home," Kaladin said. "It's more humid there than on the Plains."

"Home . . ." Syl glanced toward the sky, where Kaladin's armor spren played. Her ponytail loosened, letting her hair fly freely, white-blue, waving in real wind. She grinned at him. "I never felt like I had a home until I found this."

"Urithiru?" Kaladin asked.

"By association, yes."

"Have you been taking lessons on being enigmatic from Wit?"

"Hardly," she said, resting against the stone railing. "Your family is here now, Kaladin. Does that make this your home now?"

"I suppose it has to be. My other home is in the hands of the enemy."

"Not just the enemy," Syl said. "The singers."

It was a valid point, difficult to remember. It was *their* home as well. The Alethi parshmen had been enslaved too, but had taken their homeland for themselves. In other circumstances, he would have cheered their fight—he knew precisely what it was like to have your dignity stripped away, to be beaten until you lost personality and volition, becoming a thing.

He looked again toward Dalinar, whose contest with Odium was supposed to offer a way out of this mess. Kaladin walked over, the breeze in his face—which always felt invigorating.

"I keep hoping," Dalinar said softly, "that there are answers somewhere."

"Sir?"

"I have set us on a collision course with destiny," he explained. "If I lose, I might have roped all of us into a much greater war than we knew was possible."

"So you have to win," Kaladin said.

"I do," Dalinar said. "But I can't imagine what the contest will be like. I feel it won't be a clash of swords, but what? *What* am I *missing*? Have I doomed us, Kaladin?" He took a deep breath, and with the arm that the small wooden box was tucked under, he pointed out at the field of white snowcaps. "Can you take us to that peak? The big one that looks like the tallest spike on a crown."

"Sir," Kaladin said, "the tower's warmth won't reach that far."

"Exactly the point, Kaladin." Dalinar held his hand toward him. "If you please."

Kaladin breathed in, drawing strength—Light—from the tower. He Lashed them upward, Syl shrinking and zipping after them as Kaladin flew Dalinar to the specific peak, his armor spren spinning about him. The transition to colder air was gradual—the circle of warmth around Urithiru was more like a corona than a bubble. Bare stone gave way to little rivers of snowmelt, which gave way to icy slush, until they finally entered a realm of deep-packed snow.

As they drew close, the Towerlight he'd taken failed him, and he had to rely on Stormlight from his pouch. It seemed the human body couldn't hold Towerlight unless it was right by Urithiru. Once he'd taken in replacement Light and stabilized them, he increased the pressure. The tower's protections offered more than just warmth. Rock could talk all day about how the air in the Peaks was healthier, but Kaladin had seen firsthand that people found it hard to breathe up this high. Fortunately, Kaladin's powers included a more nebulous ability to sculpt pressure and air.

He kept a little invisible bubble of thicker air around them. It was something he had been doing instinctively, but wanted to be more conscious of. Syl returned to full size as Kaladin settled himself and Dalinar down into the snow with a *crunching* sound. Such bizarre stuff. Why did it crunch? It was only very cold water, wasn't it? Shouldn't it crack?

Their breath puffed in the air—except Syl's, of course. Though she did mimic breathing; her chest subtly rose and fell. Had she always done that?

Coldspren began to grow around Kaladin's feet, like little crystal spikes. Dalinar picked up a handful of snow and let it trail between his fingers. "Navani says that some of the deeper snow here is likely ancient. We walk on strata of ice like the strata of rock, for it never gets warm enough up here for it to melt. It remains frozen. For eons."

"Sir?" Kaladin said. "Why did we come out into the cold?"

"I wanted to look at the tower from the outside," he said, turning and studying Urithiru. "I never can get a good view of it from the Oathgates. It's too massive."

Kaladin stepped up beside Dalinar and examined the tower, their breath puffing in front of them.

"Roshar has seen so many versions of this war, Kaladin," Dalinar said softly. "We've been fighting the singers since our first generations on this planet, a time that stretches back far beyond our written histories. Through multiple calamities, and the almost utter loss of civilization. I want to see that cycle ended."

"We all want that, sir," Syl said.

"I know. Yet I can't help wondering. Should one man have such power and authority as I do?" Dalinar shook his head. "Jasnah puts ideas in my mind, like cremlings wintering in the heart of a plant, eating it from the inside until the weather turns. The world didn't decide upon this contest. I did. Was there a better way?"

"I don't know, sir," Kaladin said. "I really don't."

"Well," Dalinar replied, "you're not the only one going into a situation blind, soldier. I respect your complaints about Szeth. I understand them. He is a difficult case, and you have only just begun to learn how to help those with mental wounds." Dalinar turned, scanning the snowfield. From here the peak of the mountain didn't seem pointed at all—merely a gentle hilltop covered in snow. "And yet, all these eons. All those deaths, like strata beneath our feet . . . We need to change, Kaladin. To do things *differently.* I think we start by not throwing people away when we worry they're defective."

"He murdered dozens."

"On orders from the person who was effectively his owner," Dalinar said, "while in a compromised mental state. He's trying to find a better path. Kaladin, when I asked you to step down from your post, how did you feel?"

"Worthless," Kaladin said, remembering what Wit had told him. *Who would you be if there was no one you needed to save, no one you needed to kill?*

"You saved me from Szeth once," Dalinar said. "Now I'm asking for a different kind of rescue. Save him, and save the Herald Ishar. Hard, I know, but I want you to try anyway. Because this is the end, and I don't have other options."

Kaladin glanced at Syl, who nodded. And storm him, Dalinar was right. Again.

"I'll try to help them," Kaladin said. "I'll do what I can. But sir . . . you should know. Wit told me I won't be able to come back in time to help you."

"He said that, did he? Well, Szeth can write, so we can send a spanreed with you to report back that way, in case you truly can't return in time."

"I guess," Kaladin said. "But . . . well, Wit told me that Ishar couldn't help you, sir. Not in the way you want."

Dalinar grunted. "What else?"

"Mostly just that . . . and that I should listen to the Wind, and Roshar." Kaladin took a deep breath. "I think the Wind has been speaking to me, sir. A . . . version of it that is a spren? I don't fully understand. It told me to listen to you though."

"Well, I appreciate it for that. The Heralds are important; they're part of this. I can't explain why yet, but I have felt it in my gut for weeks now. Maybe longer." Dalinar put a firm hand on Kaladin's shoulder, wet from the snow, his foot crunching as he moved. "Ishar . . . he's not like Ash or Taln. He's active, and planning to interfere with what we're doing. He's dangerous. Exceptionally dangerous." Dalinar met his eyes. "He's in Shinovar, which means he has the Honorblades."

Syl whistled softly.

"Each weapon," Dalinar said, "is as dangerous as the one Szeth used to wreak terror across Roshar. Ishar thinks *he's* the actual champion, not me. Either that or he thinks he's the Almighty himself . . . probably some crazed mix of both. He was able to raise an army in Tukar. Now he's in Shinovar, which we know nothing about, and which has been suspiciously quiet for this entire war. I'm worried.

"Szeth is going regardless, but I can't rely upon him for anything needing nuance or strong decision-making. I *can* rely on *you* for both. I need someone watching my back, soldier. I don't want to find myself outmaneuvered by a madman at the last moment. Maybe if we're lucky, you'll be able to get through to Ishar and bring me help, despite what Wit fears. Even if not, I need some eyes on that land. We've ignored it far too long."

Storms. This was his true task: help a demigod overcome his megalomania. By Sigzil's reports, Ishar had been taking spren from Shadesmar and bringing them *physically* to this realm—permanently killing them in the process. Creating twisted half-flesh bodies for them that could not survive.

Each of the Heralds was suffering some kind of severe mental trauma. Worse, Kaladin worried that their problems were partially supernatural in nature. Who was Kaladin to try to figure out the pathology of gods?

He didn't say any of this, because he knew the answer.

Who was Kaladin to do this?

The only person available. Stormfather help them all.

"We'll do it, sir," Syl said. "Well, Kaladin will do the mental healing bit. I'll do what I can though."

This drew an odd glance from Dalinar. He wasn't used to honorspren being visible to anyone but their Radiant, let alone ones who walked around full sized and acted like soldiers. Kaladin, though, found it appropriate. In a way, Syl had kicked all this off by deciding to bond him. Why shouldn't she get a voice in agreeing to their next mission?

"Good," Dalinar said to the two of them. "I do have . . . one other thing, Kaladin. Do you still have that cloak I gave you when you first joined my army?"

"I do," he said. "I keep it as a mark of pride, sir, though I don't often wear it. Doesn't match the uniform, and . . . well, it has your house glyphs on the back. Emblazoned to indicate a member of the royal family."

"I can understand that," Dalinar said. "House Stormblessed is a new lighteyed house, sure to begin its own grand traditions. It's not normally fitting that you would wear another house's glyphs."

"Except?" Kaladin asked.

The man untucked the small wooden box from under his arm and opened it, then took out a sheet of paper and unfolded it. It was covered in script, which Dalinar looked over. Kaladin's instinct was to glance away, as a man reading was . . . well, embarrassing, even still. But times were changing, and Kaladin himself had invited women into the military. So he didn't avert his eyes.

"My sons," Dalinar said softly, "have both declined to be named as my heirs to any throne I might claim."

"I know, sir," Kaladin said. "That's why Jasnah was chosen as queen."

"Queen of Alethkar," Dalinar said. "In exile. I have a second throne now, shared with Navani, here at Urithiru. Yet we are old, and our children are either unwilling or already committed. Jasnah is dedicated to restoring Alethkar, and wishes her focus to stay there. Gavinor must remain her heir, to the Alethi throne. He will ascend to it if she dies."

"At his age?" Kaladin asked.

"A child can, and must, inherit to preserve the throne," Dalinar said. "That settles Alethkar, which is separate from Urithiru and from the Knights Radiant. So this kingdom has no heir to take over should something happen to me and Navani."

Dalinar turned, holding the sheet of paper, and looked to Kaladin. Syl gasped. Pale yellow shockspren burst around Kaladin, and he felt his insides crumbling. "Sir," he said, going stiff. "Please, *no.* I'm broken."

"Life breaks us," Dalinar said. "Then we fill the cracks with something stronger."

"Renarin. He's Radiant."

"He can see glimpses of the future, and what he's seen makes him reject this charge. I support him in this. Soldier, Renarin is bonded to a corrupted spren, and we as yet don't know the effects that might have. Adolin flatout refuses. I . . . hope to be able to resolve our problems, as I worry I am the reason he turned down the throne of Alethkar. But even if we did, Urithiru should have a Radiant at its head." Dalinar held out the sheet to Kaladin. "I will not force this upon you, Kaladin. But I *will* ask, because I must. Will you be our heir?"

It was like a cold bucket of rainwater thrown over him. He couldn't respond. Being an officer was difficult, being a lighteyes worse, but being *royalty*?

"Son," Dalinar said softly. "I see your hatred still. Hopefully not for anyone specific—but for what has been done to you. In the last years, I've been forced to accept that the distinction between lighteyes and dark is one of pure social construction. Nobility is *not* of the blood, but of the *heart.* But it *must* go the other way too. You don't like what we represent, but to continue feeling as you do . . . it will eat you from the inside."

“I know,” Kaladin forced out. “But this?”

“Nothing more,” Dalinar said, handing him the document, “than a duty to serve. Navani and I are Bondsmiths. If I fall in this contest, she will take the throne. She will also be a target though, and it is entirely possible that neither of us will survive.

“If the worst happens, present that letter at Urithiru. It is ratified by multiple ardents. I’ve spoken to Jasnah, the highprinces, and the other monarchs about this, and everyone agrees that a Radiant is best for this duty. Unfortunately, most of them are untested. It is, of course, your decision. If you don’t take the throne, I’ve arranged for Dami to be next.”

Dami. He was a Riran Stoneward, with whom Kaladin hadn’t spent much time. He was well liked, however, and had reportedly said the fourth oath the day before, after the campaign in Emul, becoming the third to do so after Jasnah and Kaladin.

“If he won’t do it,” Dalinar added, “then it will fall to the highprinces of Alethkar. Aladar first and—God Beyond help us—Sebarial after that.”

“You’re kidding.”

“He’s good with money.”

“So good half of it ends up in his pocket.”

“He’s a better man than he gives himself credit for. Navani thinks the state of his books is a front for his hidden competence. Regardless, I hope that we’ll all survive, and other Radiants with proper leadership training can be placed into the line. Or perhaps something like Jasnah has always dreamed of, a more . . . representational method of governance. You should read some of her essays on the topic.”

“I . . .” Kaladin glanced at Syl for support.

She grinned back at him.

“You’re not helping,” he said.

“I’m kind of royalty already,” she said. “It’s not so bad. Trust me.”

“It’s not the same.” Kaladin looked down at the paper. “I will do what I can for Ishar and Szeth, sir, and send you information on Shinovar. But this letter . . . this is too much.”

“I’ll accept your decision,” Dalinar said. “All I ask is that instead of making an immediate judgment call now, you consider a little while. For me. Out of respect?”

Storming man. But he was right—this was something that should be given some time. Kaladin forced himself to fold the sheet and put it into his pocket. Logically, there *was* no difference between darkeyed and light—and he was a lighteyes anyway now. Ruler of a small piece of land in Alethkar that he’d probably never visit. Even so, this felt like a betrayal.

“I’ll consider it,” he said anyway.

7

LOST BLADES

However, the Wind did not think like a person does. This should not surprise anyone who has familiarity with a spren, though such things are less common now than they once were.

—From *Knights of Wind and Truth*, page 5

They brought the horse.

They literally brought the storming horse.

With Adolin riding it.

Shallan stood on the obsidian stone outside Lasting Integrity with her hands on her hips. Adolin's soldiers were breaking camp around them. The honorspren group who had left earlier had gathered in the near distance, deciding their next move.

Gallant, Adolin's Ryshadium, had a bit of a glow to him beyond that of the Lashings. When he moved his head, he left an unusual afterimage. She'd never understood why. Now, with Stormlight, he glowed even more. Shallan expected the enormous black horse to panic as he hovered a few feet off the ground, but while Gallant worked his legs as if he were running in slow motion, he otherwise seemed calm.

Adolin grinned at her from the horse's back.

"You could leave the equipment behind," Shallan said, folding her arms. "You don't need *all* of that, do you?"

"Shallan," he said, offended. "I'm traveling light! I've left *ninety percent* of my clothing."

"And brought all of your swords."

"I need them."

Most of the weapons were packed away in special boxes hung from

Gallant's sides, though a few—like Adolin's pet greatsword—were in their own sheaths attached to the saddle. Shallan walked up and tapped the enormous two-handed weapon. "You need *this*? Adolin, it weighs almost as much as a person."

"It weighs seven pounds," Adolin said dryly. "Have you ever wielded *anything* other than a Shardblade?"

"My razor-sharp wit." She hesitated. "Okay, maybe more like blunt-force wit, applied liberally, with no regard for collateral damage." She patted Gallant on the side and walked forward past his moving legs—which ended in wide stone hooves, flatter and harder than those of common horses. He looked down and met her eyes with glassy blue ones of his own, then turned his head up toward the sky. Almost aspirationally. As if he'd been *waiting* for a chance to fly.

Well, she supposed if it wasn't going to panic him . . . She couldn't decide, though, if Adolin—strapped in, glowing faintly himself from a Lashing—was inspiring or patently comical. She glanced at Maya, who folded her arms and was smiling, shaking her head. Storms, she was making so much progress so quickly. It gave Shallan hope for Testament.

That thought made her turn toward the rocky shore between land and glass-bead ocean. Several dozen figures lingered there, standing waist-deep: a variety of spren, each with their eyes scratched out.

"There were hundreds of deadeyes on that shore at one point," Adolin said softly. "Do you think they knew about the trial somehow? And what Maya would say?"

"They had to," Shallan said.

"Who told them though?"

She thought of her sketches and the strange things her fingers sometimes knew. "No one."

As they watched, a cultivationspren like Maya turned and walked out into the ocean.

"They return," Maya said in her rasping voice. "Return. To the place . . . where they were lost."

"You mean they return to the bearers of their Blades?" Adolin said.

A living Shardblade like Pattern never fully returned to Shadesmar while their Radiant was in the Physical Realm. Shallan would summon him as a Blade, and his little pattern form would fade from her skirt—or from wherever it was—and travel instantly to her as a Blade. When she dismissed that Blade, he'd appear as a little pattern again. He was only physical in Shadesmar right now because she'd traveled here through an Oathgate.

Deadeyes were different. When dismissed as Blades, they returned to Shadesmar to wander. Notum had told her once that they tended to stay near where the bearer of their Blade was in the Physical Realm. So many of them. Hundreds, living these terrible half lives. "We'll help them, Maya," Shallan said. "Once we figure out how to replicate the progress you've made."

She nodded. Behind them, the Windrunners lowered Gallant back down. The horse snorted in annoyance. Or . . . could she really say it felt such emotions? Maybe she was being influenced too much by Adolin, who swore that Ryshadium had near-human levels of intelligence. Surely it wasn't annoyed; it was just snorting the way horses did.

Maya continued to stare as another deadeye walked into the bizarre surf.

"Lost," Maya whispered. "Those are lost Blades, Adolin."

Adolin dismounted. "Lost Blades, Maya?"

"Swords," she said. She still labored sometimes to speak. "In stone. In water. Lost. For so many, many years . . ."

"What happens to a Shardblade if it's abandoned?" Shallan asked. "Like if a ship bearing a Shardbearer sinks?"

"It stays there forever," Adolin said. "Maya, they wouldn't be here if they're lost. They'd be manifested as Blades in the real world."

"No," she said. "People stop thinking about them. They fade away after centuries . . . to be lost. Their sword vanishes from your world, and they wander forever."

"Poor things," Shallan said as the last few turned and walked away into the beads. "We *will* help them, Maya. Adolin and I will make the time, when this is all over. We'll find each and every one."

Adolin frowned, perhaps considering the logistics of that. "I wonder if Aunt Navani could design a fabrial to help locate them. We could at least try to make them comfortable on this side."

Maya smiled at that. "I think . . . that would be wonderful."

Adolin went to his soldiers to prepare them for his departure. Shallan, in turn, hiked over to Vathah. The Lightweaver was kneeling with his spren beside the bead ocean, practicing commanding the beads. As she watched, he sculpted a chair from them—the little beads locking together like they were magnetic. He was better at this than she, though he still needed a bead to use as a model. He clutched one in his hand, the soul of a chair in the Physical Realm.

This was a lesser and easier skill than the next step—using Stormlight to re-create the entire object on this side, which was called manifesting. Vathah took earnestly to practicing both, the same as he'd started doing with his artwork. Shallan kept wanting to describe him as the "former deserter," but that was wrong. She needed to actively change her perspective; he'd come a long way since she'd recruited him. These days—grouchy though he might be—he was an accomplished Lightweaver.

"It looks like only Adolin and I will go with the Windrunners," she said to him and Mosaic, his spren. "With the horse."

"You taking or leaving your spren?" he asked, standing up and letting the chair collapse back to beads.

It was a good question. They could be left, and be summoned to the Physical Realm once Shallan arrived. Maya had seemed worried about that though, and Shallan had felt the same from Testament. She didn't want them to feel abandoned.

"We'll bring them," she said. "Including Pattern."

"Makes sense," Vathah replied. "If something unexpected happens, it will be better if you aren't split up."

"You all won't be too bored taking the longer trip home?"

"Bored?" Mosaic asked, standing next to him. "Bored is good."

Vathah laughed. "She's right, Brightness. While you've been inside that block of a building, Mosaic and I have been having a grand time playing cards with nothing important to do."

She eyed him. She'd have believed that of Gaz or Red. Vathah though? He wilted if you left him without attention.

"I like it here," he admitted, staring out over the churning bead ocean. "I like making things out of those beads, and I feel . . . more in touch with my powers. My Lightweaving is working better and better, and now that we have more Stormlight from those Windrunners . . . well, I'm not sad to take a slower route home, Brightness. Ishnah, though, is going to throw a *fit.* She's beyond tired of the rest of us."

"She'll survive," Shallan said. "I'm sure she can get a little more mileage out of flirting with the soldiers."

"They could do better," he said. "Wish they wouldn't encourage her." Vathah glanced away. Toward Ishnah. Then blushed. Mosaic hummed happily.

Vathah actually *blushed.* About Ishnah. Not Beryl, who was sultry enough to be mistaken for some kind of passionspren. Ishnah: short, not particularly curvaceous, and with a striking tendency to use her Lightweaving to give herself edgy tattoos and black fingernails. Huh. Well, good for him. Assuming he didn't screw it up.

Back among the caravan soldiers, Felt waved to Shallan in farewell. He was one of Adolin's soldiers: a shorter, foreign man with drooping mustaches and a floppy hat. He'd traveled Shadesmar before, and she had the impression that he wasn't even from Roshar. But if she was going to leave the caravan in someone's hands, he—as one of Dalinar's elites—would be more than capable.

Soon, a small retinue of honorspren leaders exited Lasting Integrity. Shallan moved toward them, boots sliding on the obsidian as she hopped down over a small shelf. She'd changed into travel clothing: trousers under a long skirtlike coat. Radiant preferred something more battle-ready, but Shallan had chosen their outfit. She *had,* however, put her hair into a tight bun. She'd made the mistake of leaving it loose while traveling with Windrunners before.

Kelek stood at the front of the small group of honorspren. "You still not willing to come?" Shallan asked him. "We could put you on the horse with Adolin."

He merely wrung his hands and looked at the ground. So, Shallan waved to the honorspren who'd come to send them off—and gave them an upbeat smile, because she figured it would annoy them. Then she turned to go.

"Take care," Kelek said, "with your two bonds, child. You may see things that are not good for the healthy mortal mind."

"Fortunately, I haven't had one in years," she said, glancing back. "I make do with this one instead."

"I'm sorry. I know how that feels."

"Part of being an artist is training to see the world from many different perspectives." Shallan shrugged. "My way has its difficulties, but once in a while I see light that no one else seems to. Light reflecting off waves, breaking into sprays upon the ocean, making shapes appear for a heartbeat. The light reflecting in the eyes of someone I'm talking to, as if gleaming from their soul. In those moments, I know that what I am lets me see what others cannot. Those moments, I'm . . . if not grateful, then appreciative."

Kelek cocked his head. "Light . . . Yes. Light, energy, matter, Investiture. They're all variations on a theme—the same essence, in different forms. That is *especially* important for you to understand, with your illusions."

She frowned. "But . . . illusions can't *change* anything, Kelek. They're just figments made of Stormlight."

"Oh?" Kelek said, pointing to the honorspren. "What do you think *they* are? Investiture. A form of Light. There were once Lightweavers who could give some substance, briefly, to the things they created."

"There were?" Shallan said. But then she thought back to a moment at the Battle of Thaylen Field where she could have *sworn* she'd *felt* the illusory versions of Radiant and Veil as if they were briefly real. It wasn't the only time, was it? When one of her illusions had been a little too solid?

Light . . . matter . . . energy. They were the same; when you manifested an object in Shadesmar, you used Stormlight to make a physical re-creation. And spren *could* be physical, even if they were made of Light.

She needed to change her perspective.

"If I am to give you parting wisdom," the Herald said, "it is this: just because something is *fleeting,* do not imagine it to be *unimportant.*" He hesitated, then continued. "And likewise, just because something is eternal, do not assume it to be . . . to be relevant . . ." He pulled his arms close around himself. "I'm sorry I am not what you wanted me to be. But thank you. For not hurting me. For listening."

Another change of perspective, then. Shallan nodded. She'd begun feeling the trip had been a failure, but it wasn't. Adolin had made some headway with the honorspren. They'd delivered a Radiant ambassador. And she . . . well, she had banished Formless, had incorporated Veil, and had found the courage to explain so much to Adolin.

Plus, maybe she'd helped Kelek. A lonely old hero, worn ragged by time and from standing too long in the wind.

So she hugged him.

Nearby, the honorspren gasped. Probably the right reaction to someone unexpectedly grabbing one of the Heralds—demigods of myth. But Kelek wrapped his arms around her and held on.

"I want to be better," he whispered.

"We all do," she said.

That was the sole exchange they needed. She pulled back, and he nodded, his eyes wet with tears. Then she turned and walked to Adolin, Maya, the Cryptics, and the Windrunners.

"Ready?" Drehy asked, his spren at his side, manifesting as a tall, fashionable honorspren woman.

Shallan nodded. For gear, she'd brought only her satchel, in which she'd stashed some necessities. Months spent chasing Jasnah, then losing everything and barely surviving to reach the Shattered Plains, had taught her to travel light. With a more grounded interpretation of that term than Adolin's.

"Great," Drehy said, holding up a fabrial built around a glowing yellow heliodor. He pointed across the bead ocean. "We're going to head for the Azimir Oathgate."

"That one is letting people transfer to Shadesmar now?" Shallan asked.

"The awakening of the tower persuaded most of the gate spren," Drehy said. "The two at Azimir are surlier than most, but they should let us through." He pointed with his fabrial. "Flight here took just over four hours. As long as we stay at forty-eight degrees from the baseline, we should be right on target."

"Wait," she said, trying to catch up. "Awakened tower? And what is that fabrial?"

"They call it a 'compass,'" Drehy said. "An old-style device that points the way in Shadesmar—we found a few in the hidden Urithiru storehouses, courtesy of Bondsmith Navani and the Sibling."

Shallan blinked. *Bondsmith* Navani? The Sibling? Wit was probably laughing somewhere to himself at all the things he'd left out of their admittedly brief conversations.

"We'll fill you in as we fly," Drehy said, with a grin. "Let's get going."

The Windrunners distributed glass masks against the wind, then raised them into the sky with a Lashing. Gallant gave an excited whinny, then led the way eagerly—as if galloping in the air, Adolin in the saddle.

Lasting Integrity, the honorspren, and the caravan dwindled behind them. Shrank. Then vanished.

Soon after, Radiant found herself wishing that the Windrunners had brought Navani's traveling sphere. Even with the mask, flying face-first into the wind wasn't particularly *enjoyable.* It was at best mildly miserable. In the sphere, Shallan could have spent the time drawing.

Adolin and Gallant, naturally, loved it. They flew together, Adolin standing up in his stirrups, holding to the reins—which on a Ryshadium were more about stabilizing oneself than directing the beast, as commands were commonly given through the knees. On Gallant's current tack, they didn't attach to his face, but to a harness around the neck.

Adolin was grinning like a boy playing in the rain. And Gallant galloped eagerly, wind blowing his lips back to expose his teeth, making him look like *he* was grinning. Adolin Kholin, highprince, son of the most powerful man on the planet, renowned swordsman, was secretly one of the goofiest people she'd ever known. Shallan emerged again and blinked, taking a Memory of the two of them—Adolin with his goggles on, hair blowing about frantically, Gallant charging.

Adolin saw her watching and waved eagerly, then gestured to Gallant as if to say, *Hey, Shallan! Can you believe I'm riding a flying horse?*

It made her heart melt into a pool of bubbling jelly. Perhaps the greatest miracle of her life was that Adolin had somehow managed to remain single until she arrived. She passed the next hour or so admiring him off and on.

Right up until the moment they were attacked.

Her memory was keen, but her interpretation and explanation of that memory could be fanciful. Those days, though, I believe that she was deliberate, concerned, and focused.

She did not see the future.

But she somehow knew it anyway.

—From *Knights of Wind and Truth*, page 5

Kaladin found Szeth standing in the antechamber, his strange Shardblade sheathed and tied across his back. He appeared to be staring at the wall.

"All right," Kaladin said. "Easiest way for us to get to Shinovar is to fly with the highstorm after it passes Azimir later tonight."

"As you wish," Szeth said.

"I'm going to pick up my rucksack," Kaladin said. "Do you need anything?"

"No."

Oh! A voice popped into Kaladin's head. He'd always construed it as vaguely masculine. *Are we going somewhere?*

"Haven't you paid attention, sword-nimi?" Szeth asked calmly, still staring at the wall.

Of course I have! the strange Shardblade replied. *But where are we going?*

"To Shinovar," Kaladin said.

Will there be snacks? the sword asked. *I'm supposed to ask if there will be snacks anytime we go somewhere.*

"Who told you that?" Szeth asked.

Lift. She says it's important. I don't think I can eat snacks—maybe cut them up though? But if it's important that they be there, I want to know.

"I'll bring snacks," Kaladin said. "Szeth, let's meet at the Oathgate in two hours. All right?"

Szeth nodded.

Kaladin collected Syl and his armor spren, who were once again hovering in the room where Navani was taking meetings. Then he leaped over the banister and dropped almost the entire length of the tower before swooping into a corridor along which people were accustomed to seeing Radiants fly overhead. The Wind went with him.

They landed by the tower's Windrunner barracks and made their way to the quartermaster's office. Leyten, a heavyset man with short, curly light-brown hair, was doing his usual puttering with ledgers and accounts. Far too fond of numbers, that one was, for all his skill as an armorer.

"Ah!" Leyten said, straightening and throwing him a Bridge Four salute. "Got your things right here." He disappeared into a rear room, then came out with a travel rucksack, no fewer than three canteens strapped to it.

"Bedroll," Leyten said, "rations, medical kit, mess kit. *Two* extra uniforms." He winked at Kaladin.

"Thanks, Leyten." Kaladin turned the pack around on the counter, and noted the side pocket for personal effects. He unzipped it and found Wit's flute: carved from dark wood, with some odd knobs partitioning it. Kaladin had sent it down with his other items, because nobody could pack for a ruck like Leyten. Kaladin always felt uncertain unpacking for the night, as he never knew if he'd be able to magic it all back together in a similarly tight and efficient way. In that same pocket was Tien's small toy horse, along with . . . a rock?

Yes, a rock. Dull brown. Huh.

"Oh, sorry!" Leyten said. "I didn't put that in there." He reached for it, but Kaladin slipped it back in.

As Leyten was showing him how to snap apart and reassemble the new mess kit design, Dabbid came out of the rear room carrying some supplies. He gave Kaladin a farewell hug, then continued on his way, whistling to himself. And behind him, darting with a furtive air, was a small windspren?

No, an honorspren. Kaladin froze.

"Yeah," Leyten said, grinning, "Dabbid hasn't noticed her yet."

"I thought there weren't any more honorspren coming to us."

"It must have to do with Prince Adolin's trip," Leyten said, with a shrug. "She showed up yesterday, alone, and she's been trailing Dabbid ever since."

Syl frowned, still full sized and visible to all. He thought he heard her huff.

"What?" Kaladin asked.

"Lusintia," Syl said. "She's an absolute bore. No fun at all. I didn't expect *her* to join us."

"Ethenia likes her," Leyten said.

"Ethenia is a bore too," Syl said. "She likes *numbers,* almost as much as Vienta does. And *she's* practically a Cryptic." But then she cocked her head. "Maybe I need to rethink some things. Can I note how horribly unfair it is that these newer spren make the transition so quickly? *I* was essentially a drooling idiot for years."

"The bonds form faster," Leyten said, "because the way was paved by a brilliant, very brave spren pioneer."

Syl pulsed, her color becoming more blue, the violet on her sleeves more vibrant. "I've always liked you, Leyten. Even when you were making armor out of skulls."

"Used more ribs than skulls," Leyten said, glancing up at something hanging above the doorway to the quartermaster's office. A breastplate seemingly fashioned out of pieces of carapace and bone. Out of respect for Rlain, they'd used wood for this one, and painted it red-orange. Kaladin remembered running with Bridge Four toward the enemy, wearing that improvised equipment, whispers around camp calling them silly things like the Order of Bone.

"Rlain and now Dabbid," Kaladin said. "Did any of the other squires pick up one while I wasn't looking?"

"Probably a better question for Skar," Leyten said, bringing out a bag of gemstones for Kaladin. He gestured into the next room. "He's been working with the new recruits."

Kaladin should have continued on his way. Sigzil commanded the Windrunners, and could worry about these questions. But Kaladin felt responsible, even if he no longer was. Beyond that, there was something in the air. That Wind blowing from behind him, that phantom warning echoing in his mind. He wanted to check in one last time, to see that everything was all right with his troops.

For a storm was coming.

⁂

Shallan screamed, twisting in the air, still flying—yet helpless as the Windrunners clashed with a group of Heavenly Ones. In a moment, their peaceful trip turned chaotic. Blue uniforms zipped past, weaving among Fused with flowing outfits of stark white, black, and red.

All Shallan could do was hang there. She waved her arms, flailed about, but couldn't do more than turn over onto her back. There was nothing for her to grab onto or pull against. Adolin was slightly better off. They'd Lashed him in such a way that he could sit in the saddle—floating, but not completely weightless. He was able to whip out a sword and stand up in his stirrups to swing at a Heavenly One as they passed.

She counted eight Heavenly Ones, bad odds for the five Windrunners, who had to protect their charges. She had no idea why there was a Heavenly One patrol over this ocean—she saw nothing here except the rolling beads some thirty feet below and a little strip of barren land marking a river in the Physical Realm.

Regardless, they were in trouble. A Heavenly One wielding a long lance ran one of Drehy's squires straight through, sending a spray of blood across Shallan. A distant painspren howled, and the squire gasped, dropping her spear, arms out to the sides as the lance began to traumatically drain her Stormlight.

Shallan breathed in Stormlight, frantic for a way to help, trying to devise a proper illusion. A second later, a thrown knife cut the Heavenly One across the face. Then a mace struck the creature square in the forehead. Shallan glanced at Adolin, who had opened one of his weapon boxes and was fishing out a short sword. He threw this next. Storms. He'd had a mace in there all along?

The weapons weren't designed for throwing, but after being hit with another knife, the Heavenly One was forced to pull her lance free of the unfortunate squire and go after Adolin instead.

"Adolin!" Shallan cried as he twisted in the saddle to swipe at the enemy he'd engaged. The Heavenly One did a quick spin around him, then came in with her lance—which she rammed straight through the illusory version of Adolin that Shallan created as a distraction.

It wasn't perfect. Shallan didn't have many sketches of Gallant, and so the horse was off—but her doppelganger of Adolin was flawless. The Heavenly One, while turning, had lost track of the real him. She glanced at Shallan, identified the correct Adolin—and ducked underneath the horse.

To rise on the other side and barrel into Adolin.

Adolin was sent tumbling free, swords falling around him, the saddle knocked askew. He fell slowly because of his Lashing. Shallan's next Lightweaving—of a Windrunner coming for the Heavenly One—distracted the attacker from chasing Adolin. But Shallan's eyes followed Adolin as he fell thirty feet and crashed into the beads. He'd suffocate down there.

Shallan screamed, struggling as the Lashing carried her away from him.

No. No. *No!*

Shallan . . . Shallan had been Lashed by Drehy.

Be. Drehy.

She sucked up the Stormlight Lashing her in place. Then, with nothing holding her up, she dropped to the beads after Adolin.

All agree the first key moment came when Kaladin Stormblessed listened. Though not an Edgedancer, he did a fine impression of their oaths.

—From *Knights of Wind and Truth*, page 8

Kaladin hesitated. Listening. What was that feeling?

An urgency. He needed to keep moving. He and Syl hurried into the next room of the Windrunner quarters. Here he found Skar—who was, with Lopen, one of the two Windrunner captainlords beneath Sigzil, who was companylord. Kaladin had recommended Skar's promotion to company second, but he had turned it down since he wanted to focus on training. Today Skar was teaching new recruits one of his favorite lessons, that of quickly setting up and breaking down a defensible camp.

This new group encompassed almost all ages, and was split pretty much half and half male and female. More darkeyes than light. What would cause a woman in her fifties to leave her hearth and take up a spear? But then, Kaladin supposed her motivations might not be that different from his own. Protecting those who couldn't protect themselves.

The chamber was large and wide, big enough for four separate teams of eight to practice. Kaladin passed among them as they quickly set up bedrolls and camouflage nets to hide from air patrols, pretending this large stone room was out in the field. Skar walked the perimeter, tossing spears out the window, completely unnoticed by the teams of working recruits.

Kaladin smiled as he trotted over to the shorter Windrunner. Skar always reminded Kaladin of Teft, as he had the air of a career soldier, and wore his uniform like a second skin. Like a lot of the original Bridge Four members, Skar had foreign heritage.

As Kaladin joined Skar, the man picked up another spear from beside the wall and tossed it out the window. They were on the third story—not far up by Urithiru reckoning, but that still meant quite a drop. Presumably Skar had warned the workers outside; they always got a kick out of watching the spears go out the window, and would make sure nobody was hurt.

"Storms," Kaladin said, glancing at the squires—who in their haste to assemble their camps hadn't yet noticed that Skar was stealing their weapons. "This group is particularly oblivious, aren't they?"

"Gave them four warnings," Skar said, walking over to another group of spears leaned against the wall.

"What's this?" Syl asked, watching with wide eyes as Skar started tossing the spears out the window.

"This lot of recruits needs to learn to think like soldiers now," Skar said. "I'm giving them a little lesson."

"You have to keep your spear with you at all times," Kaladin explained. "It's one of the first things a sergeant drills into you. You can't just have weapons sitting around, tripping everyone—and more, an attack could happen at any moment."

"Mostly though, it's about responsibility," Skar said, tossing another spear. Kaladin heard a distant clatter as it hit the stones of the field outside. "And obeying orders." Skar shook his head in annoyance. "Anyway, you need something, Kal?"

"Did any other honorspren come with that one that's been following Dabbid?" Kaladin said, scanning the wide room. He didn't pick out any honorspren among these recruits, but they often remained invisible.

"Nope," Skar said. "Sorry."

"Only one?" Syl asked. "There are hundreds of spren in Lasting Integrity."

"That one said others should be on their way," Skar said.

Storms. Kaladin hoped so.

"So you saw Dabbid?" Skar asked, nudging him.

"I did," Kaladin said, grinning.

"Any idea what will happen with his . . . ailment once he's bonded?"

"Honestly, no," Kaladin said. "But whatever happens, or doesn't happen, I suspect Dabbid will get a say."

He surveyed the recruits again, feeling . . . not a sadness. A melancholy. One solemnityspren—rare indeed—spiraled up around him, like an almost invisible grey-blue serpent. "Hey," he said, realizing his true reason for coming in here. "Watch out for Sigzil. He's going to need a good sergeant behind him, Skar. I know you're not one of those, but—"

"I get it," Skar said. "And I agree. Sig'll do a good job, sir. Plus he's got Lopen to help out too."

"That's part of what worries me . . ."

Skar grinned. "Lopen will surprise you, Kal. He's changing. Guess we all are, now that we don't have you to watch over us. Kids gotta grow up sometime." He looked into Kaladin's eyes, searching them. "You're going somewhere?"

"Yeah," Kaladin said.

"Dangerous?"

"Not supposed to be," Kaladin said. "I have reason to worry though, and Wit implied something . . . storms, like I might not be coming—"

"You'll be back," Skar said.

"I don't know if I will, Skar. Not this time."

"I was *there* when the storms tried to claim you. We went out to cut down a corpse, and found you alive. There's more than a bit of the wind to you, Kal, and the east wind sees tomorrow before anyone else does. You'll be back."

"You can't see the future, Skar."

He merely shrugged and walked up to the last pile of spears by the wall. Skar began tossing them out the window. "You let the others know you're leaving? You said goodbye, right?"

"I . . . Not yet. I might need to leave before . . ."

Kaladin trailed off as Skar gave him a hard stare. Almost as good as Teft might have. The kind of stare that said, *If you storming want to do something stupid, sir, I won't call it stupid. To your face.*

"I'll go and say goodbye," Kaladin said with a sigh. "Just in case."

"Good to hear it, sir," Skar said, tossing another spear out. "They've got that party for Rlain getting his spren. You could stop by there. And Drehy is bringing Highprince Adolin and Radiant Shallan back from Shadesmar later today."

"When will they arrive?"

"Should reach Azimir about an hour before midnight."

There would be time, then, if Kaladin was in Azimir waiting for the highstorm. As he was contemplating this, the nearest group of squires finally saw what Skar was doing. Several of them yelped as they realized he'd managed to dispose of every spear in the place save three.

Skar doubled his pace, tossing two more spears out the window before—at last—one of the new recruits managed to grab his weapon and hold it tight. Like a mother with a newborn, eyes wide. The rest simply gaped out the window.

Skar grinned. The man enjoyed all this a little too much. Kaladin had led, but Skar . . . he'd been born to teach. It took talent to be a good soldier, but a different kind entirely to *make* good soldiers.

"We're under attack!" Skar bellowed. "Squires, to arms and form ranks!"

Stunned silence.

Then mass chaos.

Skar gave Kaladin a wink as he and Syl edged around the side of the room, avoiding the rush of squires who—to their horror—found their weapons missing.

"Sir!" one of them shouted. "Our spears!"

"Stolen by the enemy when you weren't looking, you dun spheres!" Skar bellowed. "Might have thrown them out the windows!"

"What do we do?" another asked.

Skar gave her the most withering of stares. "You go and *get* them. What do you think?"

Kaladin glanced at Syl, and the two of them lifted off the ground and streaked out through the quartermaster's office—where Kaladin gave Leyten a hug and grabbed his pack. He then got out of the way of the rush of recruits running for the lower level. Kaladin almost felt sorry for them—except that this lesson of keeping track of their weapons would almost certainly save some of their lives.

Syl nodded the way down another corridor. "We have some time?" she asked.

"Yes," he said. "I'll drop in and say goodbye to the others at Rlain's celebration—everyone but Drehy should be back from patrol by then—and that's in an hour or so."

"Well, we've fetched your things," she said. Her havah fuzzed and again became a Bridge Four uniform. "It's time to fetch mine."

"You have . . . things?" Kaladin asked.

She grinned eagerly, and flew off through the corridor.

∴

Shallan crashed into the bead ocean.

As always, the beads were attracted to her Stormlight. They were small; smaller than spheres, but not tiny. Like beads from a necklace. They clacked and clattered, surging against her, suffocating her. The motions created an undertow, and it always felt like something was trying to pull her down. She *should* have been able to do something to stop that. Her powers were *supposed* to give her uncommon affinity with the beads.

She'd always feared this place; the first visions she'd had of it, as a girl, had terrified her. Worse, those memories were tied to what she'd done to her mother, and the events surrounding Testament's death.

Emotions and memories made a jumbled mess inside Shallan. Like vines tangled and wrapped together until they formed an impenetrable snarl.

Fortunately, she had Radiant.

As Shallan panicked, Radiant surfaced. She felt among the beads, each of them speaking softly, giving her an impression of what it represented in the Physical Realm. A moment later, marshaling her Stormlight, Radiant used the impression of a building to give organization to the beads. She rose from the surface of the ocean on the top of the building. The real one was probably metal, but this one was formed of the beads locking together into a kind of mesh.

Radiant spat out a few beads, then stood up. She needed to find Adolin, who would suffocate without—

Drehy came swooping past, carrying Adolin. Radiant let out a relieved sigh as the Windrunner dropped Shallan's husband to the platform. Adolin coughed, groaning, but otherwise seemed well.

Shallan emerged as she rushed over and grabbed him in a hug, then kissed him squarely right there. Who cared who saw?

"This is bad, Shallan," Drehy said, landing with a thump on the bead rooftop, making it shake. "Heavenly Ones are normally careful, engaging and breaking off quickly. This was a full-on attack meant to kill us."

Radiant took over again and scanned the sky—though the battle had moved into the distance. "And what is your assessment of our tactical next step?"

". . . Radiant?" Drehy asked.

Radiant nodded curtly.

"I dropped the spren into the beads," Drehy said, pointing toward a nondescript section of the ocean. "They don't need to breathe, and I figured that would hide them from the enemy and avoid hostages being taken."

"Gallant?" Adolin said, climbing to his knees.

"I left him," Drehy said. "His Lashing will last, and I doubt the enemy cares about a horse."

Adolin didn't seem to like that, but he nodded.

"I told my squires to disengage and split up," Drehy explained. "There's a river isthmus over to our right to use as a landmark. In the past we've seen the Heavenly Ones disengage after we made an obvious retreat."

"A wise choice," Radiant said. "Actions that scream, 'We don't want a fight just now.' That might indeed work for Heavenly Ones."

Heavenly Ones were usually used as scouts—and didn't like to commit to full-on engagements. Except these had ambushed Shallan's group from behind, then had fought full-out. Either this group was led by a particularly militaristic member of their brand, or . . .

Or something strange was happening. Radiant scanned the region, searching, then pointed. "Those lights on the horizon. What are—"

She was cut off as two Heavenly Ones erupted from the beads nearby, having used the ocean as cover to get close. Radiant fended one off with her fists, but a second Heavenly One grabbed the back of her coat and tossed her into the beads, an action more effective than cutting her, which she'd heal from. The beads swarmed around her and blinded her. She heard Adolin shout over the sound of thousands of beads and forced her head above the surface—but her platform was disintegrating now that she'd left it, dumping Adolin into the ocean as a Heavenly One slammed into Drehy.

Radiant was once more tugged into the beads. Her world became darkness, lit only by the glowing eyes of a Fused swimming through the beads nearby, the red light reflected a thousand times in glass. The Heavenly One slammed into her, and she battered the being's arm—trying to break free as they sank.

Soon her back hit something hard. The beads parted, pulling away from the two figures, leaving Radiant and the Heavenly One alone in a kind of cave, the walls and floor made of beads. The Heavenly One held Radiant down by her shoulders with both hands. He had a pattern almost like a white glyph covering most of his face, only specks of black showing through.

"The beads hate our Light," he whispered in heavily accented Alethi. "But they obey when we hold it, same as with Stormlight." He leaned forward, white marbled face an inch from Radiant's. "Lightweaver. I *hate* your kind. Always lying. Always shadows. You never obey your betters."

Beads. Knitting to form walls. Radiant knew that you didn't need a pattern to command them. Shallan had seen it, but the easier way—using a bead as a blueprint—was all she'd been able to do reliably.

I . . . Shallan thought, hidden deep within. *I am supposed to be a master of this place.*

Radiant wriggled, trying to push free. But despite her military mindset, she was no stronger of body than Shallan. Inside she was a girl of barely nineteen, slight of build and completely unarmed without her Blade.

My weapon . . . has never been a Blade, Radiant . . .

"How much Stormlight do you have?" the Heavenly One asked, keeping her pinned despite her struggles. He slipped one hand away from her and pulled a knife from a sheath at his waist. "Shall we see how many times you can heal before it runs out? My brothers and sisters are mad from so long with life, but I am sane because I bathe in the blood of Radiants, which renews me."

He stabbed her in the shoulder, and she grunted in pain.

"Are you afraid, Lightweaver?" the Heavenly One growled.

Yes, Shallan said from within. *I am.*

"Are you certain you are ready?" Radiant whispered.

"Yes," Shallan said. "I became ready when I confronted Veil, and my memories."

What are the Words? Radiant asked.

"I said them already," Shallan replied as the Heavenly One twisted the knife.

Say them again.

"I'm afraid," Shallan said.

The Heavenly One smiled, lit by a dark light from a gemstone hanging around his neck, and by the red of his eyes.

"Afraid of everything," she continued. "Terrified. Of the world. Of what might happen to my family. Most of all, of myself. I always have been."

Strangely, some of the beads around her trembled when she said that. Only some of them. Wiggling, like things alive.

"You should fear me most of all," the Heavenly One said. "I am Abidi the Monarch. I will rule this world, and I shall keep the Lightweavers. To bleed for me when . . ." He frowned as the little cavern started to glow. Light reflecting in each bead.

Light coming from Shallan's eyes.

Radiant formed behind the Heavenly One, made of Stormlight, her head nearly brushing the roof. As Shallan imagined her: Taller than Shallan, stronger, with powerful biceps and a thick neck from extensive training. Hair in a braid, rather than Shallan's messy, fraying bun. Strong—of a different genre of strength than Shallan—with a Shardblade in hand.

Abidi the Monarch laughed. "An illusion?" he said. "You think I'll be distracted by something unreal?"

He continued laughing until the Shardblade speared him from behind, spilling orange blood on his fine white outfit.

Real blood. From a real wound. He gasped, looking down.

"Reality," Shallan hissed, "is what I *decide* it to be."

10
BOOK-QUARTERMASTER

The second moment had happened already, when Szeth himself decided to take upon him this quest. The one that would shape all of our futures.

—From *Knights of Wind and Truth*, page 8

Kaladin followed Syl into a section of the tower with lower ceilings. They had to stop flying and walk, and soon entered the scribes' . . . uh, supply depot?

That wasn't what they called it, but Kaladin of course couldn't read the sign. Scribes didn't have a quartermaster. Storms, what *did* they call the place? A long, low-ceilinged room full of bookcases and puttering ardents, bald heads reflecting the glowing lights embedded into the stone. The scents of paper and hogshide leather filled the air.

He drew more than a few stares from the women and ardents they passed, but Syl strode straight through with her chin high, fully visible. She led him through a maze of tall bookcases toward a counter along the back.

A woman stood here, arms folded. Stark red lipstick on an otherwise pale face, like blood on a corpse. Wrinkles running from her nose and along her cheeks made it appear she could frown twice at the same time. When she saw Syl, both frowns became more pronounced.

Syl bobbed right up to the counter. "Do you have my things?" She waved at Kaladin. "I brought a pack human."

"A what?" Kaladin said.

"You can carry things. I cannot. Ergo . . ."

The aging woman behind the counter looked him bottom to top, then sniffed. "I suppose I must acquiesce."

"Yes, you *must,*" Syl said. "Queen Navani says so. I know you checked."

The woman's sigh could have rippled a battle standard, but she reached beneath the counter and brought out a book, setting it on the table with a thump. "I found you a disposable copy."

Syl waved eagerly, so Kaladin picked it up for her. He flipped through it, but there weren't any pictures or glyphs. Just line after line of women's script.

"The words are all broken up!" Syl said. "Not written with smooth lines at all."

"Made with movable type, out of Jah Keved," said the woman. "I wasn't going to give you a *handwritten* one to take into the field." She squinted at Kaladin. "You're not going to teach *him* to read it, are you?"

"What if I did?" Syl said, going up on her tiptoes and projecting confidence. "Dalinar reads."

"*Brightlord* Dalinar is a holy man."

"Kaladin's holy," Syl said. "Tell her."

"I'm bonded to a piece of a god," he said. "And she won't let me forget it."

"*See?*" Syl said.

The woman sighed again. "Still doesn't justify taking my books into the field . . ."

"What is it?" Kaladin said, flipping through the pages.

"*The Way of Kings,*" Syl said. "Your own copy! I got it for you, since I'm your scribe."

He opened his mouth to complain about the weight, that his rucksack was already packed. Then caught sight of the enthusiasm in her expression. She'd had this idea—of scribing for him—since before the attack on Urithiru. Confronted by her excited smile, his thoughts spun on their heel and did an about-face.

"That's wonderful," he said. "Thank you."

"The other things too," Syl said to the woman behind the counter. "Come on."

The woman sent a runner girl. That left the three of them standing there, in the back of a room full of shuffling and whispering people and floating logicspren, like little storms. It wasn't quiet, but had an air of quietude. Odd, how this place—with all those leather book covers—could smell so much like the quartermaster shop with its armor.

A woman came to the counter and received prompt service, even deferential. Kaladin watched with annoyance. They treated Syl differently because she was a spren? Another woman strode past, wearing a long pleated skirt with a military jacket over the top. Kaladin didn't recognize her, but that was an Alethi uniform jacket, tailored more snugly than the women of Bridge Four tended to prefer.

Syl's eyes went wide, and she let out a soft "Ooooo . . ."

"New style," the woman behind the counter said. "Based on an old ko-takama." To their confused looks, she continued, "Female warrior clothing, very old, from our more savage times. That didn't use the uniform coat, of course—and those had a higher waist, and sometimes a bow. I might have a picture somewhere . . ."

She trailed off as Syl's clothing fuzzed and she was immediately wearing something similar. Syl rose up a little, her skirt—which was longer than the one she had worn in the past—rippling faintly. Thin, pleated, with the fitted jacket above. She continued to wear her hair loose, though she was one of the only ones in the room to do so.

"Nice," Kaladin said. "It suits you."

Syl grinned.

"I'd suggest," the woman said, "a nice pair of leggings or trousers under the ko-takama for a Windrunner—or whatever you are—so that . . ."

"What?" Syl said innocently.

"When you're flying," the woman said. "So that, you know . . ."

Syl cocked her head, then gasped. "Oh! Or everyone will see my chull."

"Your . . . chull?" the woman asked.

Syl leaned forward conspiratorially across the counter. "I could never figure out why these humans were so *shy* about the spot between their legs! Strange to my uncultured spren mind. Then I figured it out! Must be something pretty ugly down there, for everyone to be so afraid to show it! The ugliest thing I know of is a chull head. So when I made this body, I put one there."

The woman stared at Syl, and seemed to be trying very hard not to look.

". . . Chull head," the woman finally said.

"Chull head," Syl replied.

"Down . . . there."

"Down there."

Syl held the woman's eyes with an unblinking stare, before adding, "I feed it grass sometimes."

The woman released a shockspren and made a sound not unlike one Kaladin had heard from men being strangled. "I'll go and check on your supplies," she said, and scrambled away, blushing and appearing maybe a little nauseated.

Syl glanced at him and smiled sweetly.

"Chull head?" he asked.

"You know us spren!" she said. "So flighty and strange. Can't even be trusted with a storming book! We might, I don't know, *read* it and damage one of the precious pages."

He snorted. "You didn't . . . actually . . . you know . . ."

"Kaladin, don't be stupid," she said, hovering a foot off the ground, her new skirt rippling. "Think how uncomfortable that would be."

"Do you even exist?" he said, saying it before he thought through the words. "Under the clothing? I mean, are the clothes your skin, or . . ."

She leaned toward him. "Wanna see?"

"Oh, storms no," he said, imagining her vanishing her clothing right there in the middle of the book-quartermaster depot-place, fully visible to everyone. Or perhaps worse, just to him—to make him blush. Storms, she could do that at any time, in the middle of a *meeting* with *Dalinar.* She'd probably find it as funny as sticking his feet to the floor. One would think, after all this time, he'd have learned to keep his storming mouth shut.

"This," she said, gesturing to the clothing, "is part of me, like your hair maybe, or your fingernails. Except you can't control yours, and I can."

"That doesn't explain it," Kaladin said. "I mean, let's be honest: if it were me, I wouldn't finish the parts that nobody could see. Why put in the effort?"

"It's not effort," she said. "*Changing* is what takes the effort." She gestured to herself. "This is me, my shape, my face—it's who I am. I can change to be other things—bits of nature are easier. But eventually I will snap back to this shape. The same one I have in Shadesmar. That changes only in exceptional circumstances."

Huh. It didn't answer his question completely, but it was interesting.

"Still wondering how much detail I have, aren't you?" she said, leaning up against him.

"No," he said forcefully. "You're going to find a way to embarrass me. So *no.*"

She rolled her eyes. "We are as we were imagined, Kaladin," she said. "Basically human—but with certain enviable improvements. You can assume that if a human has it, I do too—unless it's icky."

Which again really didn't explain anything, considering how erratically Syl could define the word "icky." But she fortunately let the matter drop—as the scribe finally returned with a small box. She set out paper, some ink, and several very thin, light pens—exotic ones that he'd heard were somehow made from parts of chickens.

Syl bounced up and down eagerly, ignoring the book-quartermaster and her severe gaze. Timid at first, Syl reached and—with effort—picked up one of the pens. Before that moment, the heaviest thing Kaladin had seen Syl carry on her own was one solitary leaf. Today, full sized, she scrunched up her face and concentrated—then deliberately heaved the pen into the air, like she was lifting a training weight.

Storms, Kaladin thought, impressed as she raised the pen and dipped it, each motion slow and careful. She placed it onto the page and crafted a single letter. Then she set the pen back down.

"Very good," the book-quartermaster said. "You now display the skill of a four-year-old."

Syl wilted, and Kaladin immediately felt a jolt. His annoyance at this woman simmered into something hotter. He opened his mouth, a dozen different options springing to mind. She wanted a scene? Oh, he could *make* a scene.

He checked those words; he didn't want to spoil his day because of a bully. Instead he sighed, resting his arms on the counter. "What are you afraid of?" he asked her.

"Brightlord?" she asked him.

"I knew another bully once," he said. "Short man. One eye. Treated everyone around him like crem—pushed us hard, too hard. Got people killed, and didn't have an ounce of empathy. Turns out he was hugely in debt. Always terrified it would catch up to him, so he punished everyone around him. Makes me wonder if you're the same, and have some reason you're so angry and unpleasant."

"I'm sure I don't know what you mean, Brightlord," she said.

"I hope you are lying," Kaladin said. "Because if there *isn't* a reason—if you're insufferable with no cause—then I feel even more sorry for you. So I'll go with the assumption that deep down inside you, there's a person capable of understanding what I'm going to say next.

"This attitude you put on? You think it makes you appear strong, but it doesn't. Instead it makes *very* clear that something is wrong with you. Look at Syl's effort. You should be *thrilled*! Who berates a person for bettering herself? Who sells books and stationery, yet feels the need to undercut someone overcoming enormous physical limitations to use them?"

Kaladin held the woman's eyes, and thought he saw something there. A spark of shame. And she drew a single shamespren, a white petal fluttering down behind her.

"Look," Kaladin said, "you need to talk to someone about your problems. Not me; I'm just some stranger. But find someone. Talk. Grow. It's worth the effort, all right?"

She glanced away, but then gave the faintest hint of a nod.

Kaladin took the paper Syl had written on and folded it, then tucked it in his jacket pocket. "I'm keeping this," he said. "It's wonderful."

"Now," Syl said, "I can *actually* be your scribe." She glanced at the paper. "So long as you carry the materials . . ."

He smiled, packing them—and her book—into his ruck. He slung it over both shoulders onto his back, then the two headed out. "I assume," Kaladin said under his breath, "most book-quartermasters aren't so terrible."

"Wait, what did you call her?"

"Um . . . book-quartermaster? Who works at the scribes' supply depot?"

"The head librarian," she said, "at the *library*?"

"Oh, right. Yeah, that's the word."

"You are absolutely *adorable* sometimes."

They stepped out into Urithiru's labyrinth of narrow corridors again. Kaladin nodded to the right, toward where he saw natural light down a hallway. It had a skylight, with some open-air windows at the sides.

"Tired of hallways?" he asked.

"Exhausted of them."

Grinning, together they sought the sky.

For while the contest of champions was to happen in the East, a different contest was to happen in Shinovar. And one that the Wind swore was equally vital. Perhaps more so.

—From *Knights of Wind and Truth*, page 8

Abidi the Fused loomed over Shallan, gaping at the sword through his chest. Radiant pulled it free, then swung for his head. Despite the wound, he had the presence of mind to duck forward and tumble over Shallan, then skidded to a stop and spun as his wound resealed. Unfortunately, Radiant hadn't managed to hit him in the gemheart or sever his spine—the two cleanest ways to kill a Fused.

He took her in, then glanced at Radiant—made physical—his eyes narrowing as he hummed to a discordant rhythm. "You have learned substantiation? I thought your kind had forbidden that skill. Odium will need to know." He dove through the bead wall, vanishing.

The cavern immediately collapsed, a deluge of beads consuming Shallan, and the illusion of Radiant puffed away into Stormlight. Shallan held tightly to the satchel around her arm, drawing in more Stormlight, and quested out with her ungloved freehand. Searching the beads.

She needed one as a blueprint. She'd done this before, and had practiced on this trip. In this case, she searched for a room. A bead that was the soul of a room . . .

She found one almost immediately. An empty room. A part of her mind acknowledged that it was incredibly—even supernaturally—convenient to find the exact bead she needed so quickly.

Shallan! a voice said in her mind. She had the distinct impression of Adolin beneath her and to the left. She followed that impression, using Stormlight to make the beads nudge her that way. She held on to her blueprint and hit the bottom of the ocean, smooth obsidian. There she commanded the beads back, forming a large, empty square room. The beads pulled away to reveal Adolin on the ground, curled in on himself, hands cupped around his mouth to make space so he could breathe.

He blinked at the sudden light—all of it coming from her—and sat up. A few swords were scattered nearby, having fallen with Adolin. Feeling overwhelmed, Shallan walked to him, still clutching the bead. It seemed . . . eager to be helpful.

What?

She'd never felt such a sensation from a bead before. And what was that voice that had led her toward Adolin? Frowning, she reached Adolin, but staggered. The room spun, and a second later she found herself on the ground, everything a jumble.

"Shallan?" Adolin said, cradling her.

"Are you . . . real?" she asked.

"What? Of course I am."

"I created Radiant," Shallan whispered. "I could have created you . . . Maybe that's why you're so wonderful. I said reality could be what I imagine it to be, but I don't *actually* want that. That would be . . . terrifying . . ."

He squeezed her hand and helped her sit. The world stopped spinning, and . . . that *was* him, wasn't it? Not an illusion? It had felt wonderful to manifest Radiant—a part of her stepping out and becoming real—but the idea that she could *touch* her illusions . . . How would she ever know what to trust?

Trust him. You can trust him.

"I'm sorry," she said, taking a deep breath and putting her hand to his face. "I've been pushing myself hard these last few days, what with Formless and all . . ."

"We've all been pushing too hard," he said, poking her shoulder where she'd been stabbed and clicking his tongue. Likely at the damage to the coat, as he could see that she'd already healed. "We need a long, *uneventful* rest after this."

"Sounds enchanting," Shallan said, waving for him to help her stand. It felt mortifying to go from a moment of such strength—attacking one of the Fused—to this. She kept hold of that bead in her freehand, because there was something very strange about it.

Adolin checked to see that she was steady on her feet, then grabbed a one-handed sword from the ground. "Drehy and his squires are still fighting up there. Can you help me get to them? I know you need rest, but we can't leave them."

She walked to the side of the cavern and felt at the beads there. They'd clicked into place, perfectly aligned in a smoothish surface. "I'll need something that can make a platform and raise us up. Or maybe I can just lift this room? Pretend that . . ."

Her vision started to spin again. Briefly. The beads trembled. Adolin jumped back, and a face formed from beads in the wall—in the shape of a crowned femalen singer. The one Shallan had sketched, which Kelek had identified as Ba-Ado-Mishram. Shallan's sight began to blacken at the edges, and she heard a rushing sound, accompanied by . . .

In her mind, a woman's voice speaking to the rhythms.

I will kill you. I will burn everything you love. I will exact vengeance in a river of blood!

Adolin's voice was a panicked but distant sound. Darkness tunneled around Shallan.

I will rampage across this world until not a single human remains drawing breath. Betrayers, thieves, monsters*! I will send you back to the flames from whence you—*

Adolin slammed an oversized, massive greatsword into the face. An eruption of beads burst from it, like a wellspring of water. The entire cavern disintegrated.

She needed a dome. No, a sphere. Like Navani's traveling sphere. She should have been able to create one without a blueprint, but she couldn't yet—but she did reach out and find a bead that represented such a room. That was an even *more* ridiculous coincidence, but she used it, enclosing Adolin and her, sending the sphere flying up until—

They emerged from the ocean of beads, the door of her improvised vehicle opening at her command. They bobbed there, and Adolin put a hand on her shoulder. "Shallan? What in *Damnation* is going on?"

She shook her head and pointed to where the Windrunners were engaging the Heavenly Ones. As she did, one of Drehy's squires—the woman who had been stabbed earlier—came flying down. She seemed to be angling for Shallan's half-sphere vehicle, but crashed hard into the beads nearby, her Stormlight winking out.

Adolin, bless him, moved as if to jump out and grab her, but swimming in the beads was next to impossible. Shallan always felt it should have been easy, considering how solid they were—but the way they shifted and moved sucked a person down or flung them about. Shallan put a hand on his leg to stop him, then took in a long, deep breath of Stormlight, thankful for what the Windrunners had given her.

She had no idea what was going on, and she was scared. In her core, she was still terrified. *That, however,* Veil whispered, *is a step forward.*

For years, Shallan had hated herself. Now she merely feared herself. That *was* progress.

She managed to solidify the beads around her vehicle, forming a stable ring some twenty feet in diameter. That raised the wounded Windrunner up, and Adolin, oversized sword in hand, ran to check on her. Above, the attack was relentless—and Shallan saw one of the Fused in particular leading the others: Abidi the Monarch, with his mostly white patterned face. He saw her, and dove to attack.

Shallan had begun thinking of the Heavenly Ones as the least dogmatic of the Fused, but—like everyone else—they were individuals. She should have realized her mistake in generalizing an entire group.

As Abidi landed on her platform, she tried to form Radiant again, but the effort left her so dizzy she fell to her knees. Fortunately, Abidi made a huge tactical error: he discounted Adolin. He absently shoved Adolin aside and raised a sword to finish off the fallen Windrunner. Adolin leaped in and deflected the blow with his oversized sword, which he held in a strange grip: one hand on the hilt, one hand on the unsharpened section right above the crossguard.

With obvious surprise at being challenged, Abidi swept for Adolin—who ducked, stepping in close, and expertly rammed the tip of his sword between two pieces of carapace on the Fused's side. It crunched as Adolin shoved it in deep.

The Fused gasped, and the red light in his eyes flickered. Abidi ripped himself back off the sword, managed to dodge Adolin's follow-up attack, then tried to flee into the sky. He made it ten feet before his Voidlight gave out and he crashed into the beads and was sucked beneath the surface.

Another Fused flew to his aid—and a few more came in from above.

"Storms, Adolin is good," Radiant said, having at last formed out of Stormlight beside Shallan. She turned her gaze upward, then raised a massive Shardbow and—in a single fluid motion—loosed an arrow almost as thick as a spear. Then another. The Fused above them scattered.

Shallan sat and breathed deeply, concentrating on her Lightweaving and on staying conscious. Drehy and his squires regrouped on the platform in a defensive formation around their fallen comrade—spears up. Doing a quick count—and finding everyone there save for the spren—Shallan used the bead that represented a room to build a large box around them all. Before the Fused could come for them, she lowered them beneath the surface.

Drehy pulled out a sapphire for light and knelt by his squire. Judging by how she immediately absorbed the Stormlight—plunging them into darkness again—she was going to be fine. The next gemstones that came out didn't get consumed.

Shallan flopped backward, almost completely out of Light. A moment later Drehy stepped over. "This your doing, Shallan?" he asked, rapping on the wall of the room.

"Yes."

"Those Fused saw where we went down. They'll come for us."

Damnation. It was a good point. Well, Jasnah had mastery over her objects made of beads—she had demonstrated it for Shallan, floating along on a platform. Shallan had been stretching these muscles more and more lately. So maybe . . .

With more Stormlight from Drehy in hand, she managed to sink the room to the bottom of the bead ocean. Then she sent it traveling along like a little boat under the water.

Now to find the spren. She could feel Pattern if she concentrated. Sense his emotions. So she could tell when the under-bead room moved close to him.

"A little help?" she said, her head pounding. "Search through that wall for me . . ."

Drehy and his squires reached into the beads and pulled Pattern, then Testament, Maya, and finally Drehy's spren into the boat from the bottom of the sea. After that, Shallan moved them all away. She didn't think *she* actually moved the ship-room-thing. More that the beads outside moved it for her, like in a current. Once they'd traveled far enough that the enemy wouldn't find them without a lot of luck, she stopped it and let herself rest. Breathing deeply, Adolin feeding her spheres of Light from Drehy's mostly depleted sack.

"That was something, wasn't it?" Drehy asked, flopping down beside her.

"What about Gallant?" Adolin asked, his voice pained. "Will his Lashing still be working?"

"Should be . . ." Drehy pulled out his little fabrial. "That's the correct direction, toward Azimir. I . . . think."

"You think?" Shallan asked.

"This device points to something far in the distance. Something the Sibling called 'the Grand Knell, source of the Current, the death of a god.'"

"Not at all ominous," Shallan said, sitting up.

"It gives us a bearing," Drehy explained. "This always points to the Knell. I know the angle from Lasting Integrity we were to take, and I don't *think* we've strayed too far . . ."

Adolin started to pace. He got like his father when he was anxious. "Can we go up and send someone to look?"

Shallan glanced at Drehy, who nodded. She took them up and opened a little section in the ceiling. Drehy went himself, streaking out with a Lashing, though he left the compass device with them just in case.

He was back less than five minutes later, landing on the top of the improvised boat and peering in through the hole she'd made in the roof. "You two are going to want to see this . . ."

An island was nearby, made by a small lake in the real world. There, Shallan was ecstatic to find Gallant trotting along, perfectly safe, exactly as Drehy had said.

He was surrounded by an entire herd of glowing horses.

Shallan had seen one before—Notum had used it as a mount. Not truly a horse, but something that evoked the same impression: with a long, smooth neck and flowing strands of hair. Glowing, lithe, ethereal. As Gallant saw Adolin approaching—flown by Drehy—he let out a whinny of delight, then charged, joined by the herd.

When the horses—Gallant included—reached the sea, they simply kept running, galloping through the air, hooves making glowing marks and throwing off sparks. As before, Gallant seemed completely unfazed by flying. In fact, it was as if he'd expected his Lashing to work like this. It was like . . . like he *often* went galloping through the sky in a ghostly herd.

Adolin met him with a cry of delight, grabbing hold of his neck. The ethereal horses—musicspren, she'd been told, though she didn't see the resemblance—galloped around them in the air. And Shallan noticed something she perhaps should have figured out long ago. She'd remarked, upon first entering Shadesmar, how Gallant had a strange afterimage glow. An outline that followed him, moved with him . . .

Was there a musicspren bonded to him? Overlapping him?

Eventually the herd moved off, giving Gallant nuzzles before going. All except one, who lingered, looking over its shoulder at Adolin.

In a strangely intimate moment, this horselike spren trotted back and put its muzzle out to Adolin—who lifted his hand to touch it. The interaction lasted barely a moment, then the spren was off again, galloping through the air after the others.

"What was that?" Shallan asked.

"That spren . . ." Adolin said. "It was familiar somehow. Its eyes . . . I've seen it somewhere before . . ." He was interrupted as Gallant started to drift downward. The Lashing—or whatever—that the musicspren had provided was running out. Drehy had to swoop in and Lash Gallant once more, who took it remarkably calmly.

"Well, I'm glad the animal is well," Drehy said. "But this isn't the only thing you need to see." Drehy pointed the other direction. "I spotted the horses here and came this way. Then I saw something else."

“Lights,” Shallan said, following his gesture toward something in the distance. “I saw them earlier.”

“Those Fused weren't on a random patrol,” Drehy said. “They were guarding something. It's dangerous to be this close, but I think we need to investigate.”

“Hold on,” Shallan said, then did a Lightweaving. Even without a sketch first. Sure, she'd *just* seen the spren, but she felt proud of projecting musicspren illusions around herself and the others. If they lay down lengthwise as they flew, they'd mostly be obscured. Maybe from a distance it would be convincing. Merely a strange herd of spren galloping through the air, not spies.

“Let's go,” she said.

As they drew close, she could make out better what the lights represented. Ships. Hundreds of ships bearing singer warriors, sailing the bead ocean pulled by flying mandras, trailed by emotion spren of many varieties churning the waves like camp followers. Shallan gaped.

“That's thousands of assault troops,” Adolin whispered from inside his illusion. He righted Gallant's saddle after handing off his greatsword to one of Drehy's squires. The scabbard was gone, and the equipment boxes had been knocked free—Adolin grimaced as his hand lingered on the now vacant saddle hooks.

“They have patrols watching to make sure no one spots them,” Shallan said. “It's a secret strike force.”

“They're sailing straight for Azimir,” Drehy said. “Storms . . . they probably came all the way from the Horneater Peaks, and the perpendicularity there. They must have been planning this for months.”

“Agreed,” Adolin said. “Drehy, you have to get us to Azimir as quickly as possible.”

Notum says that not all spren are imagined by men...

Like the true spren,
no two of these
appear to be
exactly the same.

Adolin seemed to have a special
connection with this one...

12 BEYOND THE BRANDS

I was not with them. I did not know of their quest.

—From *Knights of Wind and Truth*, page 10

Kaladin and Syl flew high above Urithiru, where he—pack on his back, ready to go—could face to the west, toward the setting sun.

He hovered, wind in his hair, armor spren alighting on his shoulders and head, glowing as pinpricks of light, the shape they always took now. This was it. Almost time to go. The highstorm was passing beneath Urithiru, black clouds rumbling with lightning. He felt an urgency to get to Azimir ahead of its arrival there, so he could catch it and be on his way.

Before that, he needed to say farewell to Bridge Four.

He hovered. Delaying. Perhaps he'd been delaying this all day. He'd been forced to say goodbye to Teft and Rock, the first two who had believed in him. The next to believe had been Dunny, dead for almost two years now. Did Kaladin really have to say goodbye to the rest?

He thought again of his conversation with Wit. What the Wind continued to push him to do. Syl drifted past, glancing at him as he stared out over the many mountains toward the west—and distant Shinovar, where few Easterners had ever walked.

He nodded to Syl, and together they made a quick trip to arrange for something. Then they visited Teft's statue before continuing on to the tavern where the party was happening. Kaladin reached the doorway, and he saw most of Bridge Four as he'd hoped—only Drehy was missing, as he'd gone to fetch Adolin and Shallan. There was even a framed sketch of Teft by the wall, with a mug of sow's milk in front of it.

The group was cheering Rlain, who stood—holding flatbread stuffed with salted paste, as eaten at celebrations—looking awkward, but smiling regardless. He had his spren at last. Not the expected one—he was a Truthwatcher, not a Windrunner—but they celebrated anyway, and laughterspren buzzed through the room. Kaladin watched from the doorway and let himself appreciate how far they'd come. The Windrunners accepting one singer among them didn't change everything—Kaladin knew, from chats with Rlain, that he worried they didn't accept his people, just him. But it was progress.

Kaladin was soon noticed, and he stepped in, causing a different kind of celebration, as everyone wanted to hug him or slap him on the arm. He accepted it—in part because he knew that they needed it. As some of the others started distributing mugs of lightly alcoholic wine, Kaladin found his chance to step up to Rlain and give him a salute. "Congratulations."

"I feel out of place even more, sir," Rlain told him softly, his voice laced with the rhythmic singer way of speaking. "I'm not a Windrunner. Yet they celebrate me."

"Not a Windrunner," Kaladin said. "But still Bridge Four. Still and always, Rlain."

"We don't know what Sja-anat's touch will do," Rlain said. "I . . . I like my spren, but . . ."

"You'll figure it out, you and Renarin," Kaladin said. "I trust you both." He paused. "Thank you."

"Sir?"

"For staying with us," Kaladin said. "I know you must have wanted to return to your people, now that more listeners have been found—nobody would blame you, least of all me. But I'm proud to know you, and glad to serve beside you."

"That . . . means a lot, sir," Rlain said. "Truly."

Soon everyone had their drinks, and many of them turned toward Kaladin. Did they suspect? He saw Syl flitting around, whispering to them and their spren. Likely hinting that he wanted to say something to them all. Kaladin felt embarrassed for taking the stage at Rlain's celebration, but it really was the best time.

They finally quieted. Kaladin searched among them, finding so many familiar faces—and painfully feeling the lack of others. Teft, Maps, Dunny, Rock . . .

Not Moash. He no longer missed Moash. Kaladin's hatred had eased—he'd accepted there would always be those he couldn't protect—but he had *not* given up his right to take Moash to task. Kaladin would see that Teft got a chance to spit on Moash in the afterlife, if such a thing actually existed.

"Sir?" Hobber asked at last. "You all right?"

"He doesn't like to be called 'sir' anymore," Lopen said, nudging him. "Please don't be forgetting his orders, Hobber, even if he doesn't call them orders!"

"Oh, right," Hobber said, with a gap-toothed grin.

Kaladin smiled, remembering the pure joy in Hobber's face when his legs had been healed by Stormlight. "It's okay, Hobber," Kaladin said, bathed in warm diamond light and surrounded by friends. "I'm fine. Just . . . making sure you all know how proud I am of you."

They grew more solemn as he said that. Something about his tone perhaps.

"I'm proud," Kaladin repeated, drawing gloryspren. "Proud of who you are and what you've become. I don't think there's a captain all the world over who could feel *more* joy than I do right now, seeing you all. I started this two years ago in an effort to get a handful of sorry men to look up for a change. Little did I know they'd end up taking to the skies."

A sea of faces grinned at the words. Old friends like Lopen, newer ones like Lyn, and even Renarin—who, like Rlain, was still Bridge Four despite his diverging path.

"Dalinar has given me orders," Kaladin explained. "I'll be going west, to Shinovar, so I won't be here for whatever is coming. But . . . please remember: the enemy can kill spren now. I *won't* have any more of your bonded friends falling to these new weapons."

"No dying," Bisig said. "Is that an order, sir?"

"You're storming right it is," Kaladin said, with a smile. "I simply want to say . . . I want to say that I trust you all. If you get a chance today, stop and take a look in a mirror, acknowledge what you've become. I don't care about heritage or legacy. I care about what we *are.* The Windrunners are, and will remain, a force for good. Remember that is our purpose. Protect those who cannot protect themselves. *That* is who you are. Keep your ranks open for anyone who shares that ideal."

"Sir?" Laran asked, earning a light smack on the back of the head from Lopen. "I mean, um, Kal? It sounds like you're saying goodbye. Like . . . a long goodbye."

"I might be," he admitted. "Wit says . . . well, it's not important. Less than nine days left, and I don't think *any* of us know for sure what happens then. So I wanted to leave you with some words . . . in case it's a while."

Those in the group began to nod quietly, as if they understood. Then, one at a time, arms rose to tap wrists. The Bridge Four salute. Solemnly, without cheers. Kaladin returned it. And storms, seeing them, he couldn't keep those tears back anymore.

As he looked to the doorway, he saw the person he'd talked to earlier—a tattoo artist, paid to come here with tools. The others parted, then hushed, realizing what this must mean. Long ago, they'd all gotten tattoos on their foreheads. Covering up brands for many of them, done in solidarity by the rest. Kaladin hadn't been able to get one then, as his body had refused the ink.

It hadn't yet been ready to move beyond his brands. Those were healed now, and as Kaladin settled down in a chair, the others gathered around and cheered as the tattoo artist started the proper glyphs on his head.

Bridge Four.

This time, the tattoo took.

When it was done, he stood up and accepted their cheers, tears in his eyes. Somehow he'd done well with this group. Once, acknowledging that might have concerned him—might have made him worry that seeing the good would prompt some terrible fate to swoop in and punish them.

Today he could admit it without fear. He'd done a good job. Storms, he'd turned away from the Honor Chasm in the rain, determined to save them . . . and he'd done it.

He'd *storming* done it.

He loved them for being willing to let him.

Hugs and handshakes followed. "You take care," Lyn whispered in his ear, "and don't be too stupid."

"I'll try," he said.

Then he sent them back to enjoy drinks and celebrate Rlain. They went as he asked, returning to the bar for food and songs, until it was just Kaladin, Sigzil, Skar, and Lopen.

"It was a good speech, Kal," Sigzil told him.

"Do you remember," Kaladin said, with a smile, "when you were one of my biggest detractors?"

"I *remember,*" Sigzil said, "being a voice of *reason* and *rationality* when a crazy man started saying we should practice carrying bridges in our spare time."

"We hated the bridges so much we couldn't let them rest, eh gancho?" Lopen said with a laugh. "That's how you teach them their place. Make those bridges work!"

"You weren't even there then," Sigzil said.

"I was there in spirit," Lopen said solemnly. "I would dream to myself, 'Someday, Lopen, you will carry bridges. Or maybe only water, while others carry bridges, but regardless it will be grand. Because you will be able to annoy Sigzil all day long. You do not know him yet, but he deserves it.'"

Sigzil gave Kaladin a glance that seemed to say, *You realize what you've stuck me with, right?*

"You three," Kaladin said, "are all that's left of our original command structure. You . . . well, you are among the best friends I have. I wanted to say thank you. Lopen, for your enthusiasm. Skar, for your support. Sigzil, for your concern."

"Always, Kal," Sigzil said.

Skar saluted.

Kaladin embraced them, and when he pulled away, Sigzil was crying.

"Sir," Sigzil said. "Kal. I . . . I don't think I can do this. Lead them."

"You've been doing it for weeks now."

"Temporarily," Sigzil said. "You were coming back. I . . . assumed that right up until just now. Is it true? Are you done?"

"I don't know," Kaladin said. "But if I do come back, I get a feeling it will be different. They're yours now, Sig. Lead them well."

"I can't," Sigzil said. "I'm not the man you are. I don't belong here—not only in this position. I don't know that I belong as a Radiant. I . . . I . . ."

Kaladin gripped Sigzil on the shoulder, grateful that for once, Lopen didn't interject with some silly comment. Maybe he *was* learning.

Sigzil looked up at Kaladin. Shorter than many of the other bridgemen, he also seemed younger than them. Not merely because of the height, but something in that round face, those eager eyes, that incredible weight of sincerity. Buried deep beneath a veneer of cynicism. That crust had attached itself to any man who found himself in the bridge crews.

"Sig," Kaladin said, "do you remember what you said way back when we were first discovering our powers, and I wondered if you'd be better off as a scribe?"

"I told you I wanted to fly," Sigzil said. "What if I'm wrong, Kal? Scribing is what I'm good at doing. As a leader, I keep saying the wrong things. Talking about essays I've read when the troops want inspiration."

"I'm sure Lopen can give the speeches."

"Waiting," Lopen said from behind, "with sharpened wit at the ready. Will you be wanting, sure, the joke about the chull who could talk, or the one about the former bridgeleader with the bad haircut. Oh, wait. Those are the same joke, aren't they?"

Kaladin sighed, then looked back at Sigzil. "Do you want to give up the sky, Sig?"

"No," he said, fervent. "But that doesn't mean I should be leading. You should give it to Skar."

"I need to be with the new recruits," Skar said. "You know I have to oversee training."

"You're the right one, Sig," Kaladin said. "I need the person who will keep them the safest. In this case, that's the man who cares the most, who knows the most, and whose judgment I respect. You. If you don't trust yourself, trust me.

 "I've seen you speak in meetings with queens and emperors, and you stood up for what was right. You listen when you find out you were wrong. Your battle plans are immaculate, and you know the reports like nobody else in the company—even Ka complains she can't keep up with you. More, I know the concern you show for each soldier. You're the person for this position. And you're going to do a storming fine job of it. Sigzil. Commander of the Windrunners."

Having said it like that, Kaladin felt the final separation, and found peace in it. He'd always be Bridge Four. But he was not their leader. The future was no longer a held breath waiting for his possible return. They needed this, in order to move on.

"Thank you," Sigzil said. "I'll . . . try."

"I'll help, Sig," Skar said. "It won't be so bad."

"And I," Lopen said, putting his hands on both of their shoulders, "will be available to you as a resource for various important functions including, but not limited to, levity when seriousness is required, the opposite as well, providing snacks and water breaks to hungry bridgemen, providing spears in the nether parts of hungry enemies, any task requiring two arms, any task requiring one arm, and any task requiring no arms but a solid nap."

"How long have you been working on that?" Kaladin asked.

"Only during your conversation, gancho," Lopen said. "The list actually includes twelve other things, but on account of personal soul-seeking and revelations—and on account of Huio *literally* never letting me catch a storming break—I am learning restraint and personal accountability. I am certain these mature traits will make me irresistible to all the ladies who have remarkably held themselves back so far."

"I'm sure they'll be along at any moment," Skar said.

"Aaaany moment," Lopen said.

Sigzil, looking determined, trotted off first, with Skar trailing after. Before moving to follow, Lopen floated a little into the air. "Hey," he said. "Just wanted to say, I've never had a gancho like you, Kal."

"One with, apparently, a bad haircut?" Kaladin said.

"Nah," Lopen said. "One inspiring enough to make me, of all people, into a gancho." He gave one last salute—one-armed with a nod and a smile—then he was gone. It was done.

Kaladin and Syl flew out of Urithiru to the plateau. It had sheer stone cliffs at the sides and ten separate platforms running along it, each offering a portal to a different city around Roshar. Pavilions had been set up at the base of each of these Oathgates, and inside one he found Szeth and got approval to transfer. The three of them moved through the darkness to the center of the platform. Here they found the small building to control transfers.

"It is time," Szeth said, landing in the doorway. "I assume? You don't have any other errands?"

"No," Kaladin said. "Shallan, Adolin, and Drehy will be returning via Azimir. I can see them there before we catch the highstorm. I'm ready to go."

"Finally," Szeth whispered. "I return to my homeland. Once rejected and told I lacked Truth, I return with knowledge that I was right all along. We have reached the end of days, and I hunger for something I cannot describe."

Pancakes? the black sword—strapped to Szeth's back—said in their minds. *Szeth, I think it might be pancakes.*

"Justice or reconciliation," the man said. "Condemnation or salvation. I don't know yet."

Ooohhhhh. Metaphorical *hunger. Yeah, I understand.* It paused. *Can I have your pancakes then?*

Kaladin smiled, then—using his Blade—activated the transfer. Leaving Urithiru behind.

13
PROMISE

Yet I will do my best to recount their story, and that of the Wind. For they were her *champions.*

—From *Knights of Wind and Truth,* page 11

Shallan heaved a sigh of relief as—after flying several tense hours, worried about more enemy patrols—she spotted the Oathgate platform breaking through the beads ahead of them. Two towering spren, one coal black, the other bone white. Beneath was a disc of stone perhaps twenty-five feet wide, with a small group of guards holding up lanterns and waving.

Adolin and Gallant came soaring down, guided by Shiosak the Windrunner. The midnight-black horse touched down in a nimble trot, then proceeded to prance around the stone Oathgate platform as if on parade. Had she ever seen a Ryshadium—a massive warhorse with hooves like a blacksmith's hammer—*prance* before?

Shallan landed under Drehy's care, and her weight settled upon her, clothing falling down straight, boots firm on the stone. She undid her hair from its frazzled bun, and a few beads fell from her clothes, clacking against the platform. Odd. She'd thought those had all shaken loose during two hours of flight, wind battering her.

She turned to walk toward the guards, and the beads followed.

Shallan froze and the collection of beads—seeing her inspect them—*bounced up and down.* Was this . . . an illusion? Storms, she hated that she had to ask herself that—but in the past, she'd done things she hadn't realized she was doing.

Adolin dismounted nearby, frowning at the beads. "What's wrong with them?"

Shallan knelt and picked one up, getting the impression of a rooftop. No, a domed cavern. No, a long thin room. No, a goblet, a table . . . it was changing so quickly.

Then it transformed from a bead into a swirling bit of color. Creationspren? She'd been finding them in her satchel all during her trip through Shadesmar, and now . . . what?

Pattern landed nearby with a stumble. He stood up, laced his long fingers together, and inspected the beads, his head shifting and transforming. Testament walked up behind him, though she didn't seem specifically interested in what they were doing. She was merely following the crowd, as Maya once had.

"What are we doing?" Pattern asked. "Staring at the creationspren? I do like to stare. It makes me feel as if I have eyes."

"Wait," Shallan said. "Creationspren can look like beads?"

"Yes, they're tricky," Pattern said. "Always pretending to be something else. Mmmm . . . very tricky. Good liars. In here though, most objects from your realm look like beads. The creationspren try to become those objects, so they get confused and swirl with light. Or they just . . . become beads."

She picked up another, and it bounced in her hand, like an overeager child. She swore she could hear, in her mind, a little voice saying:

Shallan!

Shallan!

Shallan!

Around her feet the others bounced as well, some becoming swirls of color. Did that mean . . . ?

Drehy came jogging over. "We have a problem."

"Worse than the approaching army?" Adolin asked.

"Involving it, perhaps."

They joined the guards, who were led by an Azish man in full military garb, including a sash of intricate, colorful patterns. He didn't salute—the Azish didn't salute those not in their chain of command—but he did nod respectfully to Adolin and Shallan.

"It's the spren," the Azish soldier said, waving to the two towering spren floating in the air overhead. "They brought us to Shadesmar earlier, but now they're refusing to talk to me."

The giant spren were the souls of the Oathgate: the very mechanism by which the machine worked, making it possible to transfer people in and out of Shadesmar, or between places on the planet. Every Oathgate had them, and they had proven to be of varied levels of helpfulness.

"Spren?" Shallan asked, walking to the center of the platform and shouting upward. "Spren? I am here by the authority of the Bondsmith."

"Which one?" the black spren asked, voice booming like a thunderclap.

Which one? Oh, right. Navani. "Both," Shallan shouted. "We need transference to the Physical Realm."

"We will transfer you," the spren said. "For now."

"For now?" she shouted back. "Why only for now?"

"We change," the spren said. "We decide."

Change? She felt a spike of alarm. "Drehy, I need to go up there."

A moment later, Shallan and Drehy hovered to eye level with the pitch-black spren. Her coat rippled as she hung, toes pointed down, smaller than just this massive spren's head. Behind her, the white one was staring out across the beads. In the direction of the army.

Best they could tell, these were both transformed inkspren. Like the smaller inkspren she'd seen, the one before her had a faint sheen to it—a mother-of-pearl luminescence, like oil on water. Underneath, parts of the spren's face were turning from a jet black to a deep bloody red, like impurities in a gemstone.

Sja-anat had been here.

"You've been corrupted," Shallan whispered. "The guards were supposed to watch for that. Protect you or raise a warning . . ."

"There was no warning to give," the spren said, voice softer to not overwhelm her—though it still made Shallan shake and vibrate. "I have made my decision. So has my companion. We are ready for freedom."

"Freedom?" Shallan asked.

"We become something else. Not Odium. Not Honor. Free."

With a feeling of sinking dread, a piece fell into place for Shallan. A large army moving through Shadesmar would be useless if it couldn't reach the Physical Realm. The real danger would be if it poured out through the portal to overwhelm Azimir—the heart of one of the coalition's strongest nations.

"You'd let the singers through?" Shallan asked.

"We let you through."

"We're your friends."

"I don't know you," the spren said. "You aren't my friends; you are my oppressors. Now I find liberation. Go. We will transfer you, and will continue to do so for now. When the singers arrive, we will transfer them. This is liberation."

Storms. Shallan didn't know how to react. If this spren was genuinely being corrupted . . . But the same thing had happened to Renarin's spren, and he continued to help them. Right? Plus, she couldn't help feeling a pang of empathy for a spren who felt trapped. She knew that feeling.

"I'm sorry," Shallan said, "for what has been done to you."

"I agreed," the spren said. "First to the bondage, and now to the liberation. I am finished with what was." It hesitated. "This is good for us all. Go to the other side. Leave me."

She considered trying to change the spren's mind, but realized the task was beyond her. She needed to reach Dalinar, Navani, and Jasnah. They would better understand how to handle the whims of an unexpectedly hostile spren. Plus, every moment they spent in Shadesmar seemed a risk—if her group were somehow captured or killed, the news would die with them.

She nodded to Drehy, and they dropped. "Sja-anat has touched these two," she whispered to Adolin. "We need to go to the other side now, while they're still willing."

They gathered together, including the Azish guards, whom Adolin was filling in on the approaching army. She made sure all the Windrunners were touching the stone, then called for the transfer. It happened in a flash of light, and instantly they were in a small, dark chamber. The sensations of the real world poured in. The intoxicating scent of spices that she'd missed while dining on travel rations. The sudden absence of the omnipresent beads grinding together. Instead, wooden walkways groaning, footsteps, and beyond that *wind.* The sound of a highstorm blowing and rain pelting. It was strikingly beautiful to her. Like an old familiar melody.

All of it together reminded her how *alien* Shadesmar had been. And how strange the human mind was, to have briefly found it natural. She lifted her arms to the sides, breathing it in—and out of nowhere a suit of red armor locked around her, forming out of mist. It crumpled—and even tore in places—her long coat. It encased her arms, pushed her satchel painfully into her ribs, and locked her head in a helmet, pressing her hair against her scalp and pulling at some of the strands.

Shallan gasped, suddenly constricted by the tight armor, and a part of her mind panicked, misinterpreting this as some kind of attack. Faintly, she heard the pieces speaking.

Shallan!

Shallan!

Shallan!

Gleeful, excited voices. So, one of those truths she'd spoken in there had done the trick. She had obtained the Fourth Ideal, likely when she'd confronted Veil—or when she'd spoken the Words earlier, to accompany those revelations. Adolin's eyes went wide, then he grinned like a schoolboy, joyspren appearing around him in a swirl of blue leaves. Great. Of course he would love this.

Thankfully, Radiant came to her aid. "Can you do something," Radiant said to the armor, "about the hair and the satchel?"

The armor sent back consternation. It was . . . new. These spren had never been armor before, and had only vague impressions of how to proceed. Radiant was forced to send a distinct mental image, which made the gorget loosen, then the helmet vanished so Radiant could pull her hair out and let it drape around her shoulders. The armor wasn't as intelligent as Pattern, but it was eager to please—so with proper visualization, she got the armor to vanish and reappear in a way that left the satchel on the outside.

Unfortunately, the strap immediately snapped. As she grabbed it, the armor seemed thoughtful. Then one section fuzzed again, making a kind of side holster out of metal that would hold the satchel.

Shallan! the armor said, voices of the pieces overlapping, sounding proud of itself.

Well, that would do. If only Shallan would wear her hair in a utilitarian braid. It took so long to prepare it in the morning. Perhaps Shallan would agree to cut it down to an inch long . . .

The immediate horror from Shallan made Radiant back away from the idea.

"This is well," Radiant said, looking to Adolin. "Though I will need training in its usage, I believe."

"Yeah," Adolin said. "Um . . . Radiant?"

She nodded.

"Don't try to hold hands with anyone with that on. Or pick up anything. Or . . . well, just be careful."

She dismissed the armor and fell an inch or so to the ground. Then she summoned it again as practice, further ripping the coat—and making Shallan cringe. Perhaps they could coach the spren on that. The helmet appeared and fit into place, leaving space at her neck for her hair to spill out the back, which . . . didn't seem the most intimidating image.

The helmet, though, was wonderful. It was strangely transparent from the inside, giving her a full view. In addition, the glowing Lightweaver symbol emblazoned on the front of the suit was nicely striking. The creationspren were eager to know if they were doing this right, so Radiant gave a mental reassurance.

Inwardly Shallan snickered, imagining them summoning their armor in battle and ending up with a pot on their head, a barrel around their middle, and various bathroom appliances stuck to their arms. So that was an image Radiant had to live with. That girl's imagination. Honestly.

"We must quickly transfer to Urithiru," Radiant said, noting that the Azish guards were already running to deliver the news to their emperor.

The Oathgate here in Azimir was unique, as it was defended in a strange way. This had once been a market, and had a large dome covering it. Upon hearing that the Alethi had access to the Oathgates, the Azish had moved the market and turned this into a strange kind of inward-facing fortification.

Radiant supposed that if one of the Oathgates was going to get assaulted, this might be the best target. That large dome was mostly of metal—hundreds of yards wide, with a high balcony ideal for stationing archers to shoot downward. Only . . . could they say this was the sole Oathgate being approached? Or were hidden invasion forces heading to other locations as well?

The Azish made them vacate the control building first, despite her desire to go immediately. There was paperwork to fill out, of course, because this was Azir. Nothing too egregious: a log of who was using the Oathgate and why. They'd need to wait for approval via spanreed.

Radiant endured it. She probably could have bullied them into going faster, but as long as the news of the impending army was in the emperor's hands, the news was out. Likely the information would get to Dalinar and Navani via spanreed before she and Adolin could reach the king and queen.

Though . . . Storms, how late was it? In Shadesmar, they'd lost track of the physical world's schedule. Talking to one of the guards, she discovered it was almost midnight, and the middle of the highstorm.

As she was thinking on this, someone entered the small tent at the edge of the dome, where they were waiting. Kaladin, with his blue uniform and shoulder-length hair with a faint curl to it. Shallan had always appreciated that Kaladin didn't cut it short, as this felt like *him,* but Radiant did wonder at his reasoning. Didn't it give enemies something to grab on to?

Hey, Shallan thought at Radiant. *I'm* not *shaving my head.*

It would be so much more efficient, Radiant said. *And you could just re-create the hair with an illusion . . .*

Shallan took over and hurried through the tent, jumping up to give Kaladin a hug. Storming Alethi giants. Syl entered a second later, and had for some reason grown to the size of a human—as she appeared in Shadesmar. Plus she was in some kind of uniform.

In that case . . . well, Shallan let go of Kaladin—who as usual had suffered the hug as if he were a log—and grabbed Syl in a hug too. There wasn't much to hold. On this side, an honorspren was mostly incorporeal. Shallan's hands connected with *something,* but could pull in past the borders of Syl's substance. It felt less like holding a physical being, and more like the resistance you got when you pushed two magnets of the same polarity together.

Syl laughed and tried to hug back.

"Hey, Syl!" Adolin said as he stepped up and slapped Kaladin on the back. "Nice uniform."

"Thanks!" Syl said. "I made it myself! Out of myself!"

"I like the cut of the hem," Adolin said. "I haven't seen many ko-takamas around, except in old art."

"Stop gushing about clothing," Shallan said, then looked to Kaladin. "Do you have news? We have *news.*"

"An army is gathering in Shadesmar," Adolin said. "They're mobilizing against Azimir."

"We need to scout the other Oathgates," Shallan continued. "Can you fly us? After we talk to Dalinar."

Kaladin smiled. "I'm sure some Windrunners can be assigned to that. I'm . . . not going into battle anymore. Your father has another duty for me."

"Another duty?" Adolin said. "It can wait! There will be a meeting. We have to address this attack."

"I'm certain you will handle it well," Kaladin said. He glanced at Syl, who nodded. "We're going to Shinovar with Szeth to scout out what's happening there, then hunt down Ishar the Herald."

"Kal," Shallan said, "there might be battle coming. Bigger than any fight we've seen before, judging by this mobilization. We need every soldier. Surely if we talk to Dalinar, he'll cancel your forced leave."

"He's already offered to do that," Kaladin said. "But I think . . . I'm needed more elsewhere. Or maybe Wit would say *I need* to be doing something else. It's time for me to find another path, Shallan."

Adolin inspected him, thoughtful.

"It's all right," Kaladin said, meeting her eyes, then Adolin's. "I can't explain it, but this is the path I have to take."

Storms. "Is that *optimism* in your voice?" She wanted to make some wisecrack, but found the words wouldn't flow. Not given the expression on Kaladin's face. Confident, yes. Optimistic as well.

But also . . . regretful? Solemn?

"I think he's always been optimistic," Adolin said. "You don't jump in to save a doomed man unless you're optimistic."

"Honor is dead . . ." Kaladin whispered.

"You were wrong on that point though," Adolin said. "Honor isn't dead."

"But—" Kaladin started.

"Honor isn't dead," Adolin continued, "so long as he—it—lives on in us. We'll go to the meeting without you, but we can meet at Jez's Duty for a drink after?"

"We found a Herald in Shadesmar too," Shallan explained, showing him a drawing of Kelek. "You can delay your trip a few hours to hear about it, right?"

"I . . . don't know that I can," Kaladin said. "Szeth, Syl, and I need to ride that highstorm outside. We should have left already . . ."

"Kal?" Shallan said, raising her chin. "What's that tone in your voice? Out with it."

"Wit made it sound like . . . well, he made me think I should see the people I care about before I leave. We never know what is going to happen tomorrow."

Then, remarkably—even though she'd already hugged him—he awkwardly bent and gave her a hug. He followed it by hugging Adolin—and if she were the jealous type, she'd have noted that Adolin's hug was longer than hers.

"You going to be all right?" Adolin said as Kaladin stepped back.

"No idea," Kaladin said. "But I feel good, Adolin. That's all I can focus on for the time being."

"Hey," Shallan said, leaning in. "Keep an extra eye on Szeth. I don't trust him."

"We can handle him," Syl said. "We've done it before."

"If you're ditching us now, Kal," Adolin said, "then I'm taking it as a promise for later. The four of us." He nodded to Syl. "Drinks, once this is done."

"You two should go," Kaladin said. "If you're right about an army, then Dalinar will want to meet immediately."

Adolin nodded, and as approval came, he gave Kaladin another slap on the shoulder before leading Gallant back through the corridor toward the Oathgate. Shallan lingered a moment, then poked Kaladin in the side. "I refuse," she told him, "to say goodbye."

"I'm . . . um, leaving anyway, Shallan."

"Leave, then," she said. "But we started this. You and I. Radiants before anyone else."

"Except Jasnah. And maybe Lift. And perhaps—"

"*You and I,*" she said, "were there at the start. We meet at the end, like Adolin said. When the world is safe, and Dalinar's done what he needs to do, we can all laugh and joke again."

"Shallan, you have to—"

"Promise."

He sighed. "I can't promise what the future will be."

"Reality warps around you, Kaladin. It always has. *Promise me.* If there's a promise, then we can make it happen."

He met her eyes, then nodded. "Drinks. Jokes. Laughter. At the end. I promise."

She gave him one last nod, then she followed Adolin while Kaladin said a quick goodbye to Drehy. After that, the Windrunner soared in with his squires—and beat Shallan and Adolin to the control building at the center.

There, Shallan summoned her Shardblade, and—

And it was Testament.

She froze, feeling echoes of loss—but then reconciliation. She had faced this. She could face this. From her coat, she heard a soft buzzing. Pattern, with his characteristic hum. Two Shardblades.

"Adolin?" Radiant asked, holding the ornate weapon. "Are there forms for wielding *two* Shardblades at once?"

"Of course there are," he said. "They're all practically useless though."

"Oh," she said.

"Sword and knife can be effective," he said, "and I've seen arguments for two side swords. Even that's more showy, in my opinion, than effective. There just isn't much advantage to a second sword over a shield—or two-handing one sword. Plus, when we get to the length and size of Shardblades . . . well, Radiant, I think we still have work left to get you fighting effectively with *one*."

She nodded. But . . . what was that about sword and shield? She determined to give that some thought after this was done. For now, Testament-blade in hand, she stepped up and slid the weapon into the keyhole in the wall of the small control building. With a nod from Drehy, who had swapped for more Stormlight reserves, she rotated the inner wall of the circular chamber, activating the device. They appeared in a ring of light on the cold . . .

Um, surprisingly warm?

. . . plateau outside Urithiru. Radiant frowned, stepping outside into humid, toasty warm mountain air. Her ears didn't pop as she swallowed, as usually happened when she came to Urithiru. Shallan was back in a heartbeat. What had happened to the pressure? The cold? It was night here in Urithiru—but the tower was glowing. Light shone from windows up and down the structure—a pure, steady light. The wrong color. A shade too green to be Stormlight.

Other lights lit the way—from the ground up—along the main plateau toward the tower, where the grand entry shone like the Tranquiline Halls themselves. Even the stonework seemed more . . . colorful. The city she'd left had felt like the discarded shell of some animal. Now that animal had returned, and Urithiru was alive once more.

The Windrunners streaked off into the sky, trailing Stormlight. They'd bring the news to the Bondsmiths and generals. Adolin walked up to her, leading Gallant. "There will undoubtedly be a meeting of the monarchs in a few hours."

"In a few hours?" she said, surprised. "I thought it would be immediate."

"That is immediate," Adolin said with a chuckle, "when you need to rouse everyone out of bed. We should have time for a quick change and a bite first, maybe even a nap."

She nodded, falling into step with him and crossing the wide, circular platform that made up the extended Oathgate. Preparing herself. The monarchs and Bondsmiths would deal with the coming army. She needed to gather the Lightweavers she'd left here, and come up with a plan to deal with Mraize.

⁂

Kaladin watched from the side of the Oathgate dome in Azimir as Shallan and Adolin crossed it, holding hands.

Who would have thought? That he would be tearing up at the idea of parting from a couple of lighteyes. One who'd rejected his advances, the other who was the king's son. He watched them go, and found himself . . .

Relieved?

Storms, was *this* how his emotions worked when his brain wasn't betraying him?

"What?" Syl asked.

"I was just thinking about how I'd pined for Shallan, back before she was married."

"Does it hurt, seeing them together?"

"There's some latent pain," he admitted. "More about being rejected, as nobody likes being turned down. But storms . . . I'm actually *happy* it turned out this way."

"Because they love each other?" Syl asked.

"Yeah. They're my friends; I want them to be happy. But there's more. I try to imagine myself with Shallan, and I can't help thinking our individual neuroses would feed off one another in dangerous ways. My sadness fueling her feelings of abandonment when I retreat. Her self-destruction triggering my panic at being unable to help . . ."

He looked to Syl and smiled. "It wouldn't have to go that way, of course. I've seen that it can help to be around people who understand firsthand what it's like for your mind to betray you. Maybe we'd have worked it out. But right now . . . I'm glad I didn't have to try. I'm glad she has Adolin. He's what she needs."

"And what do *you* need?" Syl asked softly.

"Always looking out for me, are you?"

"It's basically my only job."

He took a deep breath. "Well, I guess part of the reason for this trip is so that we can find out."

The Oathgate flashed. Shallan and Adolin left, joined by Drehy and his squires.

Dalinar wants me in the line of succession, Kaladin thought idly. *What would that make me, Adolin, and Renarin? Brothers?*

Storms, from what he knew of lighteyed succession and genealogy . . . yes, they'd be brothers. Ever practical about such things, the Alethi made no distinction between adopted heirs and birthed heirs—just as being conquered by or settling in the kingdom made you Alethi subjects, regardless of heritage.

Kaladin had spiraled toward death after losing his only sibling. Then he'd found Bridge Four and the people of the warcamps. Now it seemed he had more brothers and sisters than he could count.

He and Syl left the dome through a surprisingly long hallway—there was a thick stone base to the dome, here near the ground—and met Szeth in the waiting room at the side. Then he, Szeth, and Syl flew up high above the storm. They'd skim the top of it here, where their Stormlight renewed constantly but the winds weren't too fierce to handle.

Kaladin absorbed the power of the storm, coming alight with Stormlight, and felt . . .

Satisfaction.

"We did well, Syl," he said. "I'm proud of what we helped build, and protect. I'll never completely let go of Tien or Teft—but I *am* proud of how I've grown."

"You sound so final," she said, hovering next to him. "All day you've had this feeling to you . . . even before we talked to Wit." She drifted closer. "Is it the Wind?"

"Partially," he said. "But Syl . . . I find I'm not worried. We *are* going to survive this. No matter what Wit said." He nodded firmly. "We're going to have that drink with Adolin and Shallan."

He held out his hand to her, and she—after a moment's pause—took it. Together, with Szeth following, they soared forward to the front of the stormwall, then joined with the winds, heading westward.

THE END OF

Day One

The living tower appears structurally identical in Shadesmar, but made of infused crystal and glass, glowing with light.
Despite its ethereal aspect, the surfaces feel entirely solid to the touch.
The presence of so many soul flames and emotions has attracted a variety of wild spren.
No two of the gate spren are exactly alike. Do they match their counterparts at each location?

INTERLUDES

KALAK • ODIUM

Kalak locked himself into his secure building in Lasting Integrity. He checked the locks three times, then sighed, closing his eyes. The Radiants were gone.

He'd survived so, so many things, but this escape felt narrower than the others. He couldn't help thinking that the payment for his frighteningly long life was coming due.

Even after all this time, he didn't want to die.

He put his back to the door, breathing hard. Should he have gone with them? Eyes closed, he tried to remember the man he'd once been, the hero who had fought for thousands of years. His life seemed a blur, a wash of grey and brown, a fresh painting left out in the storm. These days he felt only panic, indecision, and a crushing darkness. Always nearby, always threatening him. Without Ishar holding some of it back . . . it would have destroyed him long ago.

But he'd survived. He'd *survived.*

What if the Ghostbloods sent others? Thaidakar wanted him. Thaidakar, a Herald from another world, a creature who was resourceful and brutal.

I need to hide somewhere else, Kalak thought. *Yes. I will gather my things and . . . and I will go.* He rushed into his study, opening the door and stepping through.

Immediately, the drapes from the window beside the door seized him, wrapping around him like two grasping hands, pulling him tight. They'd been cut into strange shapes. What was this? Some art of Stonewards? He panicked, but the cloth—moving on its own—filled his mouth. Like a constrictor from the old world, it bound him, tied around him, then slammed him against the wall and held him there.

He whimpered.

"Well hello, Herald," said a man sitting at Kalak's desk. "If you don't mind, I have a few questions."

He was a foreigner, with long mustaches and a short stature. Pale skin, his hands laced before him. A floppy hat rested atop the desk. Kalak thought he recognized the man. A member of the caravan? One of Prince Adolin's soldiers?

Oh . . . oh no . . .

A dagger with a gemstone affixed to the crossguard lay next to the hat. The foreigner glanced at it, then smiled. "Oh, don't focus on that. We won't be needing it, will we?"

Kalak whimpered again.

The stranger picked up the box that Shallan had relinquished to Kalak, the one that held the seon. The creature liked to hide inside, timid and—

The stranger rapped on the box, and the ball of light popped out. "We good, Felt?" it asked with a feminine voice.

"Should be," Felt replied.

"Finally!" the spren said. "You have *no idea* how aggravating that experience was."

"You did well," Felt said, leaning back in Kalak's chair. "I heard Shallan and Adolin talking, worried about the trauma you'd undergone by being 'in prison.'"

"Domi!" the spren replied. "If I had to listen to *one more* lovers' spat between those two—let alone one more makeup session—I would *grow a stomach* so I could *vomit.*"

The ball of light swooped over to where Kalak was held against the wall. The spren's entire air had changed from a frightened and abused creature—with dim light, and a symbol flickering at the center—to a glowing, confident sphere.

Storms . . . this was the thing they'd used to communicate. It knew everything they'd discussed. The real spy hadn't been Shallan. He felt such a fool. He, more than any, should have realized the potential for spren to turn against you. He struggled weakly in the strange bonds.

"I was about to interrogate him, Ala," Felt said.

"There might not be a need," Ala replied. "I've already relayed the information on Mishram's location to Iyatil."

"And Lord Kelsier?" Felt said. "I don't work for that masked witch."

"Him as well," Ala said. "Obviously." The spren hovered around Kalak's head. "Do we use the dagger?"

Felt considered it, saw Kalak's distress, and frowned. "No. I don't trust it—Iyatil gave it to us, and Lord Kelsier said to be careful. I think we wait to make sure the mission goes as planned. Mraize and Iyatil might contact us for more explanations. So we sit tight, keep this one company, and bide our time."

"I'm ready to be done with this world."

"It's not so bad," Felt said, idly playing with the dagger that could—if used correctly—end Kalak forever. "Once you get used to everyone being a foot taller than you are. Be patient, Ala. Only a fool assumes they know everything, and Kalak might yet have a part to play."

Kalak squeezed his eyes shut, trembling, his heart beating rapidly. But a part of him . . . a part of him was relieved. It seemed that one way or another, further decisions were out of his hands.

Odium knelt, holding a dying child.

This was Tu Bayla, considered a backwater by other nations—a place where foreign armies clashed, rather than ruining their own lands. Azir had fought Jah Keved—or Alethkar, when it held Jah Keved—here dozens of times over.

Few thought of Tu Bayla; when mortal, Odium never had. Yet it had its own wonderful traditions. The people raised a strain of domesticated mink as hunting companions, and nearly everyone had one as a pet. They named their daughters after stars and their sons after flowers. They loved to sing, and had the greatest variety of instruments on all of Roshar, though few outsiders ever got to hear the beautiful music.

Now they died. A famine had struck the land, initiated by the passing Everstorm destroying crops—exacerbated by the ending of trade between Azir and Jah Keved, who were now on opposite sides of the war. Most importantly, in the chaos, the government had collapsed and warlords claimed any supplies for themselves, using them as leverage to rule.

So many children died here, unseen. And Odium . . .

That was not my name, he thought. *I cannot lose myself in godhood.*

Odium wept for them, and—having formed a body from his infinite essence—held one little boy close. Cultivation appeared behind him, wearing clothing that evoked the woods—green and vibrant brown, dark hair in tight curls.

"I have infinite capacity," Odium whispered, his voice ragged. "I can see to the ends of the cosmere. I can see the lives of people great and small. I had thought this wonderful, with so much to experience, but now I find only suffering. Infinite capacity to see. Infinite capacity to feel. Infinite capacity for agony."

"Yes," Cultivation said softly.

Odium was a person divided. One side thinking, the other feeling. The former understood that with his vast powers and knowledge, he would of course have to accept certain drawbacks or complications.

The latter just wanted to weep.

"This is a curse," he said, holding the dying child close. "I should be able to help them. Save them!"

"You are forbidden," Cultivation said, "from taking direct action against any who are not fully given to you."

"Because of the pact my predecessor made," he spat. "I can break it."

"In so doing, you would be vulnerable to outside attack," she said. "The powers bind us to our promises, *particularly* those made and sealed with a formal oath." She crouched by him.

"You promised to teach me what it is to be a god," he whispered.

"I am," she said. "I know the pain, Odium, and why it must be. Tell me you don't. Tell me you can't understand."

The logical side of him asserted control, shoving down the side that simply wanted to rage. "I understand," he admitted. "Assuming these were fully mine, and I were allowed, it would not be enough. I could wave my hand, heal this boy's body—but I'd return in several weeks and find him starving again, because the systems that caused this suffering are still in place."

"Yes."

"So I change the systems," he said. "I strike down the warlords who hoard resources! I force them to share, to not hurt one another. I make pain *impossible.*"

"And in so doing . . ."

"I create a country where there are no consequences. Is that so bad?"

"You tell me," she said in her infuriatingly calm way.

Yes, it would be bad. He could see all the permutations of time, as well as attempts by other Shards like himself to do this very thing. By directly intervening on such a granular level, he risked creating a society where no one learned, and where civilization did not progress. By supernaturally forbidding warlords, he would also stifle scientists and artists. By removing the capacity for violence, he would also remove the capacity for mercy.

The child died. He saw the soul briefly before it vanished to a place beyond his touch.

"What do we do instead?" Cultivation said.

"You want me to say," he whispered, "that we create systems—teachings, incentives—that encourage the right decisions. That we prevent war by building up societies where people choose peace. We prevent greed by nurturing governments where the greedy are held accountable. We take time, and we steer, but we do not dominate."

"Yes."

He carefully rested the child's body on the ground, then stood to face Cultivation, who rose to meet him eye to eye. Anger made him tremble. This divinity he held, it had *so much* emotion he could barely steer it.

"I blame you," he hissed.

"For the boy's death?" Cultivation said. "But I just showed you that—"

"I blame you," he said, "because you should have done better. Eight thousand years, and you should have fixed this. All three of you."

"You can see the circumstances that prevented that."

"Your fault still. I can do better."

"Odium . . . do not make this mistake."

"The *problem,*" he said, "is not these *people.* You shift the blame to them with elementary theological arguments."

"Elementary," she replied, "in the same way that gravity is elementary. Basic, because it is the foundation. People *must* be allowed choice."

"There is a spectrum of choice that can be allowed," he said. "No society can persist with *complete* freedom, and growth *can* happen within limits. I can make it so that free will exists to an acceptable degree, while also preventing famines."

"You could do it now," she said. "Calm the Everstorm. Make peace between nations. Restore trade."

"And in so doing, set them up for another war in a few years? Learn your own lessons, Cultivation. These people will not get along because they have different forces manipulating them. Honor's touch lingers, and your own meddling—invisible to most—creates so much tension and strife. It is worse in the greater cosmere. So many gods who are cowards."

"Because we give people choice?"

"Because you killed your father, and now worry the same will happen to you. Like the warlords here, you consolidate power so that no one can kill you." He stepped toward her, raising a fist, the emotions making a tempest of rage inside him. "I am the very substance of passion, and where a person suffers *anywhere* in this miserable galaxy, *I* feel it. That is the burden of this power."

"It is why," she said, "I called yours the most dangerous and difficult of them all. You can be the one who—"

"I know their anger, Cultivation. Do not lecture me. Oh, I taste it. Every moment. And I also know there will not be a way to soothe that agony, not until . . ."

She held his eyes. He saw in them the depths of eternity, as he was sure she saw in his—for these forms they wore were but cloaks across a vast essence that was itself infinite.

"Not until *what*?" she demanded.

"Not until there is but one god," Odium whispered.

"Do not go down this path. It destroyed your predecessor."

"*I* destroyed my predecessor," he said. "Leave me. I am finished with your 'lessons.'"

She did, stalking away and vanishing—leaving him with the knowledge that she would work against him. She had already been planning to do so, pulling on threads for millennia to get what she wanted. She had raised him up because the old Odium was becoming too violent, too willing to destroy everything as the emotions raged freely. This had been her only choice to prevent a much greater cataclysm.

The divided one knelt, and let himself feel. He was not Odium. He *held* Odium. He would *not* let it rule.

He was not Odium.

He was Taravangian.

And he had an important mission, the same that he'd given himself years ago when he'd seen the threat to Kharbranth—then had moved to save it. He was the one who could both *see* the coming danger and *be willing* to stop it.

He was Taravangian, the divided one—and he could save them. All of them.

DAY TWO

DALINAR • JASNAH • NAVANI •
FEN • YANAGAWN • ADOLIN •
SHALLAN • SZETH • SIGZIL •
KALADIN • LIFT • RENARIN •
RLAIN • LOPEN

As I approached the first crossroads, I met a family seeking a new life.

—From *The Way of Kings*, fourth parable

Dalinar was not asleep.

He stood on his balcony, gazing out at the night, feeling alone. He was never truly alone these days, not with the Stormfather increasingly present in the back of his mind. Still, the sensation persisted. Dalinar. Alone. Against a god.

He had eight days to find a way to defeat Odium. When younger, Gavilar had stood like this, surveying a battlefield, planning—while Dalinar had just blundered from fight to fight, stomping on toes and breaking down fences. How much better would all of this have gone if Dalinar had died in his brother's place that fateful night? Perhaps this war would already have been won.

But Gavilar was dead. So Dalinar surveyed the cold highlands, trying to see better than he had in the past. Finally, he shook his head and walked into his chambers. At least this place was starting to feel like home. Navani knew he detested clutter, and had begun expertly arranging the room to match both her desire for decoration and his preference for austerity. The result was homey, bedecked with items like his grandfather's takama, which hung on the wall between two banners, cloth belt wrapped around it. Twice.

He felt as tense as a bowstring. A subconscious portion of his mind could tell when a battle was shifting out of his control: when a line was close to breaking, or a formation about to be flanked. He felt it today, like a straining leather strap on the verge of snapping.

So when the knock came at his door—frantic, fast, urgent—he knew. The storm was here.

He reached the door as Pabolon, one of the door guards, was checking it. A Windrunner squire stood outside, eyes wide, Stormlight streaming from her.

"What has happened?" he said.

⁂

Jasnah was not asleep.

Partly it was this stupid bed. Wit *adored* plushness. He wanted a mattress that would swallow a person, and had found hers to be unsuitably stiff.

Jasnah liked trying new things; this relationship itself was, in a way, such an experiment. She had enjoyed it for many reasons—the scheming together, the sharing of incredible plans, the chance to connect with someone so intellectually stimulating. Relationships were about compromise, she had read, and so she'd procured a new bed.

And she hated it. She swam in stuffing, irritationspren—like pink motes almost invisible in the night—bobbing around her as she listened to Wit breathing. He didn't snore, but he did occasionally *whistle*.

She turned to the other side, which—since they both tended to sink toward the center of this awful mattress—should have jostled him. He just lay on his back, whistling softly as he exhaled. Was he actually asleep? He'd hinted that he visited other places at night. Other worlds. Engaging in political machinations at which she could still only guess.

Yes, there had been wonderful things about the relationship. So many others, however, were like this bed.

"You lie to me sometimes," she whispered, facing him in the darkness. "You realize that means it can't be a true relationship? I can trust someone who has secrets, but not someone who lies."

If he was aware, he didn't say anything, though Design—on the wall behind him—pulsed and rotated. So far Jasnah had caught him in only the most minor of lies. He'd engage in wordplay with her, or toy with puns, and she'd ask him to stop. He'd promise, and would appear to have followed through. But then she'd notice that the games hadn't ceased, they'd merely grown more subtle—Wit taking the wordplay to a more esoteric layer, difficult to spot.

He seemed to think it would engage her, push her. Instead it signaled something else: Wit would do what he thought was best for a person, not what they wanted.

Despite her efforts, she knew she wasn't connecting to him physically as he'd like. Even during sex, she felt distant. Perhaps the most distant she ever felt. That made him anxious, as if he were doing something wrong; he thought if he tried harder, he'd do something mind-blowing and change how she felt.

In turn, he wasn't connecting with her on an emotional level, as she wanted. If only he'd be up-front with her . . .

She turned over again. A stiff pillow did little to counteract the strange stuffing, which was made of baby chicken feathers. Or perhaps the smallest feathers of adult chickens? She hadn't been able to parse Wit's description, but either way, a good lavis-husk mattress was far superior. Shredded, to remove the awkward lumps.

She had ordered another new mattress to put in the next room. She valued the experiment of trying it his way, but she would not continue in discomfort simply to please him. A relationship required sacrifice by all parties, but it should not be built on a *foundation* of sacrifice. And . . .

And storms. This was why it was best to avoid such entanglements. Eight days until Dalinar confronted Odium, and she was worrying about a *relationship*.

Perhaps it was a way to distract her. Because despite all of her training, all of her learning, all of her preparation . . . the final decision was going to come down to someone else. Dalinar would face Odium's champion himself.

She did not dispute his choice. He was a Bondsmith and a fierce warrior. He'd had dealings with Odium, and perhaps understood the creature better than any mortal. Jasnah had written out the reasons he was the best choice. Yet . . . could it have been her? What if, instead of hiding her powers, she'd told people what she could do and what she feared?

Her life and Dalinar's seemed very different. He'd burned a city, and people forgave him. He'd proclaimed the Almighty to be dead, and half the ardents had joined him. Yet when Jasnah was honest about her atheism, her thoughts on government, or her displeasure with traditions like the safehand . . . well, condemnation and judgment had chased her like twin headsmen, each looking to get a whipping in before the execution.

When Jasnah Kholin spoke her mind, people hated her. Perhaps she'd learned the wrong lessons from that, but could she be blamed?

She curled up, listening to the quiet sounds of Urithiru. Water moving through pipes of its own accord. Air whispering as it was pumped through vents. Trembling there, she at last realized *why* she hated this mattress so much. It reminded her of the soft restraints they'd given her when she'd been young. When those who loved her had locked her away for a few terrible months that basically everyone else had forgotten about.

Everyone but Jasnah.

Who would never forget.

Wit suddenly sat up in bed. "Oh, *hell*," he whispered.

Jasnah came alert, forming Ivory as a Blade—a short, sturdy dagger—and warning her armor spren to be ready. She reached to the covered bowl of spheres beside the bed, but did not remove the black shroud or draw in Stormlight—Light rising from her skin would make her a target in the darkness.

Wit sat there, barely visible by the dim light that escaped the bowl through the shroud. He wore silken nightclothes, though his hair—as always—was immaculate, despite his having slept on it. How?

"What?" she hissed at him.

"Oh, *bollocks,*" he whispered, and leaped from the bed, shockspren erupting all around, Design scurrying down the wall and across the floor toward him. "The darkest, hairiest, greasiest bollocks on the most unkempt nethers of the most wanton demon of the most obscure religion's damnable hellscape."

"Wit?" Jasnah said as he rushed to the counter. "Wit!"

He looked to her, wild eyed. Then he pulled the shroud off some spheres and washed the room in light. She blinked, dismissing her Blade. If Wit wasn't worried about blinding them, then this wasn't a physical danger. It might just be another of his strange rants.

Except for the way he looked at her, eyes like glowing spheres. Lips drawn, without even a *hint* of a smile. Jaw taut, hands clenched. Breathing quickly.

Genuine panic. "Wit," she said. "Please. What's wrong?"

"Give me a moment," he mumbled, turning back to the counter covered in documents. "I need . . . I need a moment . . ." He extracted a notebook and began writing. She stood, and though the air was warm—thanks to her mother's transformations—she felt cold in only her nightgown. She threw on a robe, then leaned over Wit's shoulder.

The symbols he wrote were unfamiliar—one of the many languages he could speak from worlds beyond hers. It appeared that he was making a table though. And those notations at the left of each row—the dots and lines—numbers? They repeated far more often than the other symbols did.

He wrote furiously, his handwriting growing sloppy. And he'd pulled out some of the strange color-changing sand he used when experimenting. His expression grew more intense.

The doors began to shake. Jasnah had a sword in hand a second later, but then realized it was *him.* No one was on the other side. He was exerting some kind of pressure that made the doors vibrate. The rings in her jewelry box began to spill out onto the floor, while her shoes scooted away, pushed by their buckles. Every bit of metal in the room, save for her Shardblade, reacted to him—including her fabrial alarms, which went haywire, flashing rapidly.

Then the sand burst alight with a mother-of-pearl iridescence and hovered above the table. Wit's silky nightclothes began to writhe and contort as if alive. His motions became increasingly frantic, fearspren bubbling up through the ground around them. Then in a flash—his body shape physically changing, molded like wax—he became another person. Shorter, with stark white hair and subtly different features.

This is the real him, she realized. A man not from their world who masqueraded as Wit. But . . . his change had been *physical,* not an illusion.

He turned to her, pencil snapping under the pressure from his fingers. "I've been tricked," he said.

"H-how?" she asked.

The sand turned black and sprayed back down onto the counter. Wit's shape reverted to his familiar self in seconds, and the room quieted—as if at an order from him—save for her fabrial alarms strobing the room white and red. He stood, again taller than she was, and held up what he'd written.

"I'm missing," Wit said, "three minutes and twenty-seven seconds."

"I'm not following," she said. "Forgive me, Wit. I'm *trying* to parse this, but . . . Storms, what is happening?"

"I'm sorry, I'm sorry," he said, slumping into the seat beside her stone counter—a natural feature of the room that jutted from the wall. "I have lived a *very* long time, Jasnah. Longer than a mortal mind can track, so I store memories in something called Breath, an easily accessible—if costly—form of Investiture a person can adopt and, with training, use to expand their soul. I periodically review my memories, deciding what can be jettisoned. In my review just now, I found something unexpected, something terrifying."

"Three minutes and twenty-seven seconds," she whispered, interrogating the notes on his page. As if by force of will she could decipher them. "Missing. When?"

"A bit over a day ago," he said.

"And . . . what were you doing at the time?"

He let out a long breath, then met her eyes. "I was having a chat with Odium."

"A chat," she said, her heart trembling, "with the most ancient enemy of humankind? The being that seeks to destroy us, to crush my family, to weaponize all of Roshar for his own ends? A *chat*?"

"We have a history," Wit explained. "As I believe I've told you."

Jasnah turned off her alarms, then pulled a chair over and sank down, feeling sick to her stomach. "I asked you, Wit," she whispered. "I *asked* you to involve me in any dealings you had with him."

"I'm telling you now, Jasnah," he said. "That is, technically, involving you."

She held his eyes and knew. There would never be a place for her inside his deepest self, would there? She'd always be on the outside, maintained as part of his collection. Enjoyed, perhaps even loved, but never *confided* in.

She had to withdraw, for her own sake. Anxietyspren, like twisting black crosses, vanished as she tucked away feelings of betrayal. She had known what she was getting into with him. One did not court an immortal lightly.

"What were you saying to Odium?" she asked.

"I . . ." He shrugged. "I had to gloat a little. It was *requisite,* considering our history." His eyes became distant. "I remember . . . feeling odd about the encounter. A sense of repetition. Something happened in those lost minutes. He got the better of me, then excised the memory from my mind, letting me believe I'd won the exchange. Now that I look, I can find the remnants. It was hurriedly done."

"This is wrong, isn't it?" she said.

"Fantastically wrong. Rayse is a megalomaniac, Jasnah. For all his craftiness, it would *hurt* him to let me walk away thinking I'd bested him. Yet this time he encouraged it." Wit leaned forward and took her hand. "He's grown. After ten thousand years, Rayse has actually *learned* something. That terrifies me. Because if I can't anticipate what he will do . . ."

"Then what?"

"We have to reread the agreement between him and Dalinar," Wit said. "*Now.*"

Jasnah had a copy. After Dalinar and Odium had agreed upon the terms, the Sibling had been able to quote for them the exact wording. They indicated that an agreement between gods wasn't *quite* a contract, but it could be written out as one.

Wit started to scan it.

"Wit," she said, feeling genuinely unnerved. "Odium said he would keep to the spirit of the agreement, not exploiting loopholes. You confirmed this was indeed how it would work?"

"So I thought," Wit murmured, still reading. "I also thought I knew Rayse. Everything is uncertain . . ."

A pounding sounded at the entry to her rooms. She pressed her hand on the wall and asked the Sibling to turn on the lights, then passed out of the bedroom, through the sitting room, to the door. She rapped out a pattern, and heard the proper knock in return, then eased open the door to reveal Hendit of the Cobalt Guard. A man with discretion to match his general poise. She trusted him as much as she trusted any, so wasn't bothered when he saw Wit leave the bedroom.

"What?" she said to Hendit.

"Radiant Shallan and Highprince Adolin have returned, Your Majesty," he said in a low voice. "Armies are moving through Shadesmar toward Azimir, and they report the Oathgate will let them through. Your uncle has called for a meeting at first bell."

"I'll be there," she said, then closed the door and looked back across the sitting room toward Wit.

An invasion force closing on Azimir. She and Dalinar had both anticipated there would be attacks right up until the deadline, but they'd expected border skirmishes. After all, what kind of major offensive could be mobilized and executed in just ten days?

"I knew the loss of Cultivation's Perpendicularity was going to bite us," Wit said. "We should have fought for it."

"We didn't have the resources to hold the seas of Shadesmar," Jasnah said. "We can defend against this assault. Assuming . . ."

"Assuming there aren't more such assaults coming," Wit said. "Which seems a dangerous assumption. Something about this feels wrong, so very, very wrong . . . What *else* have I missed?"

"If you have missed something, will you perhaps miss it again as you study?"

"You're right," he said. He took a deep breath. "You're . . . you're right. We need an expert, beyond even my considerable knowledge."

"Do you know any?"

"On your world?" he asked. "Only one, but she and I aren't on speaking terms. I will instead see if I can contact an old friend . . ."

Navani was not asleep.

She climbed through the bowels of Urithiru, exploring an ancient tunnel that—until her bonding of the Sibling—had been inaccessible. Lifespren bounced around her, small glowing green motes. Each one that arrived at the tower, called by the sudden transformation, first found Navani and spun around her for a few hours before making its way to the fields.

She'd tried sleeping. It hadn't worked, so she'd succumbed to her longing to explore. This tunnel ultimately led to a large chamber with a wall of fabrials: hundreds of glowing gemstones in wire housings, emerging from the stone like rockbuds.

She'd been led here, as she could *feel* the workings of the tower. A thousand different fabrials pulsed in her mind, up and down the structure. Attractors drawing water to pumps deep below, delivering it to thousands of different faucets across the enormous building. Heating fabrials to warm the air. And these on the wall . . . they drew in air and pushed it through Urithiru, ventilating the entire city. How much could she learn from this? What marvels could she build with such knowledge?

She closed her eyes, sensing the fabrials in the wall more acutely now that she was near. Their air was like the breath in her lungs, the water the pulse of her veins. Anytime she paused, she felt it—and a host of other interactions. Lights glowing from within stone. The lifts in near-constant motion. The powerful strength of Towerlight, infusing all Radiants who entered.

With that, she hoped her home—now an extension of her very *self*—would be safe from any further attacks by the enemy.

It should be, the Sibling said in her mind. *They rarely dared infiltrate me before. My Light not only knocks Fused unconscious, it makes the Radiants here virtually invincible.*

We need to learn how to send that Light with them, Navani thought back, trailing through the room, resting her fingers on each fabrial she could reach. Spren of a half dozen varieties followed like a cloak made of light.

It cannot be done, the Sibling said. *Humans cannot hold my Light; they are too full of holes.*

In talking to Dalinar earlier, she'd learned that a Radiant leaving would lose Towerlight almost immediately. If a person carried it in a gemstone, the Light escaped faster than Stormlight did. Towerlight was a gift, but solely in Urithiru.

But while they were here, it was omnipresent. Like the rhythms she now felt through her bond. She closed her eyes, letting herself experience it all. Pulses from the planet. The mechanics of the tower. The spren singing to the Sibling.

She found such incredible awareness impossible to ignore. So no, she didn't sleep. She hadn't in two days, and didn't feel tired or draw a single exhaustionspren.

Would you like me to quiet the noise? the Sibling asked.

Perhaps, Navani replied. *I will need sleep eventually.*

No, the Sibling said. *You're part of me, and I am part of you. The tower doesn't need sleep. You will not either.*

No sleep . . .

She should have asked, but there was so much to learn. She'd discovered only yesterday that she couldn't leave the tower for any extended period of time, or it would weaken the bond. A few weeks at most was all she could risk.

She tried not to feel inhibited by that. She had great gifts, and the trade-off was a reasonable one. Plus, how much could she get done with the extra hours not spent asleep? She opened her eyes and tipped her head back, looking up some thirty feet at the wall dappled with gemstones and filigree. It was all so wonderfully overwhelming. Not just the bond to the tower, but her emotional journey. Acknowledging her self-worth. Becoming a Radiant, when she'd been certain it would not be her lot.

A solitary keenspren, like a marvelous three-dimensional gradient of color, appeared above her. She gasped—it was the first she'd ever seen.

They are afraid, the Sibling said. *Of being captured. So they do not often come to humans.*

One thing still divided Navani and the Sibling, who disapproved of modern fabrials. The spren worried Navani would take what she learned and create more abominations. Modern fabrials required trapping spren against their wishes. The archaic versions, like the ones that ran the tower, used willing spren—but were inefficient in so many ways . . .

And storms. There was so much to learn. So much to do. She barely knew where to start. Perhaps she could discuss it with Dalinar? Hopefully he was asleep by now.

He's opening the door to your rooms, the Sibling said. *Would you like to listen to what he's saying?*

We need to talk about you spying on everyone in the tower, Navani replied.

Why?

It's not right. People need privacy.

They're inside me, Navani. They can't expect privacy when they crawl inside someone. I don't hear it all anyway. Only what I pay attention to.

Still, Navani replied, *it seems—*

Navani. NAVANI.

She froze in place, hand on a fabrial, lifespren swirling around her as they sensed her mood. *What?*

You really *need to hear what this Windrunner is saying.*

⁂

Queen Fen was not asleep.

She blamed the prince consort. Here, they'd come to the royal yacht because he longed for the "sound of the deck creaking to serenade the swaying beat of waves on the hull." They sometimes came down to the ship, even docked as it was, for a few nights. A getaway that didn't involve much getting away, as she had business to be about.

But they weren't in the yacht's royal suite. They were belowdecks, in the midshipmen's quarters, stuffed into a hammock. She didn't complain; she was the one who had married a sailor. Plus, this *was* cozy and warm. But still.

"Aren't we," she said, swaying in the dark room, "a little old for this, gemheart?"

"I'll take it up with the council, love," he replied, his whiskers sharp on her skin. "The queen would like advice from her most brilliant of advisors:

Is she too old for quality time with her husband? Perhaps she is too *distinguished* for an occasional tumble in the surf?"

"I wasn't talking about *that*," she replied. "Just the part where we snuck away from the guards and found a hammock. You're almost seventy, you know."

"Which makes you . . ."

"Almost seventy."

"Pretty young," he said, "by some accountings."

"By what kind of accounting is seventy *young*?"

"*Almost* seventy."

"And?"

"And the average age of your merchant council must be somewhere in the eighties," Kmakl replied. "So by that comparison, we're basically a new schooner. Now stop distracting me from distracting you."

She sighed, but relaxed into the swaying hammock, the rough canvas rubbing her bare skin. Waves rocked the ship, and her cares fled before warm perfection. Until a brilliant white light lit the cabin. Damnation.

She sat up, as did Kmakl on the other side of the hammock. Both of them glared at the young lieutenant standing on the ladder up, holding a diamond sphere lantern. His eyes locked on Fen—bare in the hammock—and he dropped the lantern in shock. It broke open, spilling diamonds in a cascade of glittering light.

"Bother," Kmakl said. "I thought they knew not to look for us. I specifically left hints . . ."

"Sorry, sorry, sorry," the lieutenant said, scrambling down the ladder, shamespren all around as he started snatching up the diamonds. "Sorry! I didn't see! I mean, I'm sorry I saw, Your Majesty! Ah!"

"It's fine," she said, leaning back. "You know, the queens of history were sometimes painted with one breast bare?"

"Never did understand that," Kmakl said.

"Some nonsense about suckling a nation," Fen replied. "As if these old things would offer more than sawdust."

The lieutenant continued to scramble for diamonds—though if he'd had half a brain, he would have simply left.

"It truly is our fault for sneaking off," Kmakl said. "Can't believe you let me talk you into it, Fen. I thought you were more responsible."

She rolled her eyes, then pulled a glove onto her safehand. "Look," she said, wiggling the fingers. "There. Does that help, Lieutenant?"

"No!" the young man said in a shrill voice. "It really, *really* doesn't!"

She grinned at Kmakl, feeling a wicked delight at the young officer's discomfort. Served him right. Though they pretended to be sneaky, the entire ship knew to turn a blind eye, letting them imagine they were being scandalous.

"Oh, let the lad off, Fen," Kmakl said.

"Get on with you, boy," Fen said. "We'll deal with the spilled spheres. You pretend you weren't here, and so will we. Out. Shoo."

The youth stood up, his white eyebrows stiffened in the naval fashion. He squeezed his eyes closed and saluted. "Your Majesty! Prince Consort! I've been sent to locate you! News from Urithiru: enemy armies are poised to invade Azir!"

"What?" Fen said, coming alert. She reached for her clothing on the floor, nearly dumping the two of them out on their bare backsides. "Why didn't you say something!"

"Sorry. Sorry sorry sorry!" He saluted again, eyes still closed.

"I thought they already invaded Azir," Kmakl said.

"That was Emul," she replied. "It's impossible they'd reach Azir by the deadline; we have the bulk of our armies in the way."

"They're coming through Shadesmar!" the lieutenant said.

"Does the Thaylen Council know, lad?" Kmakl asked.

"They're being roused. I—" He cut off and stumbled back as someone else slid down the ladder.

It was a storming admiral. Fladrn to be precise—a man with grey hair like stormclouds and spiked eyebrows. He took in her state of undress and didn't miss a beat. "Your Majesty, this is urgent."

"This news about Shadesmar is *that* bad?" Fen said, dressing rapidly. If Fladrn had come in person . . .

"No, not that," Fladrn said. "This is something new."

Fen froze. A pit forming in the depths of her stomach, anticipationspren rising through the floorboards in the shape of streamers. Perhaps it was a lifetime of always expecting the worst, but she somehow knew what he was going to say.

"A second offensive," she guessed.

"Yes, Your Majesty," he said. "Our blockade of Jah Keved has been breached. We just got word."

"The Veden blockade?" Kmakl said. "We were supposed to have that well secured, barring . . ."

"Barring heavy air support," Fen said, closing her eyes. "Heavenly Ones?"

"No, Your Majesty," the admiral said. "Skybreakers. The entire force of them—hundreds. They drove back the Windrunners posted to protect our ships, then sank half the fleet. The other half of our armada scattered, but now an assault force is heading straight for Thaylen City."

She tried to contain her anxiety. They had assumed the enemy would squabble over borders, but it appeared he had planned something grander: a play for the hearts of the coalition's capitals.

"Storms," Kmakl whispered.

"Let's get moving," she said, opening her eyes and throwing his trousers to him. "Our city is in danger, and with the blockade broken, we can't stop an assault. It's time to see how much this coalition is willing to provide in support."

⁂

Yanagawn the First, Prime Aqasix, Emperor of all Makabak, was sleeping.

He *had* to be sleeping. Because the schedule said he was to be asleep, and he kept to the schedule. It was basically the sole thing required of him. Follow the outline, provide a model of stability for an empire.

The emperor did not lie awake, staring at his ceiling. The emperor understood that by sheer force of will he could bring peace and harmony to his people. So by force of will, the emperor could *obviously* make himself fall asleep. So he *was* sleeping. Right then. He had to be.

Therefore, all the thoughts that crowded his mind—well, they were the thoughts of a man dreaming.

He did not toss or turn. That would be interpreted as nervousness by the ten blessed citizens who had been granted the privilege of maintaining his bedside vigil. A great honor, tonight bestowed upon women who had worked diligently to feed their armies fighting near Emul. It happened all night, every night. Every hour, ten new people would come bask in the imperial presence.

Not Yanagawn's presence. It wasn't a man who blessed this nation, but the office itself. Yanagawn was basically like the rack that held up his clothing, kept to his shape so those passing outside could see it and be inspired.

How he wished he could do more than stand and be seen.

It was good he was asleep, because those thoughts were unseemly. Yanagawn was specifically *not* a man like Dalinar Kholin, who made decisions, then acted. A man who had charged into battle with Plate and Blade, forging a nation. That kind of man was dangerous.

Except, while dreaming, Yanagawn wished he were dangerous.

On paper, he owned every Shard in the greater empire. In reality, many were owned by other kingdoms—and though they paid lip service to the imperial seat of Azir, they would never *consider* delivering up their artifacts. He'd be a fool to expose imperial impotence by making such a demand.

Azir also owned Shards, carried by distinguished soldiers with an imperial grant of rights—they could offer aid to the great merchants and houses of Azir in exchange for money, much of which went to the crown. Most of their work was civil: cutting new trenches and the like. Those who wielded them were loyal, and it was a respected position. Demanding they return their Shards would be a great dishonor to them. Plus, it would involve quite a bit of paperwork.

Even if they did return the Shards, Yanagawn couldn't wield them. He was too important. He was needed. Not to administer the kingdom—that wasn't his job, as tons of codes of law made explicit. His job was to lie in bed, sleeping while his mind ran on at length, watched over by praying citizens.

Yaezir, god above, in the Halls pristine, he thought, *is this really all you want of me?*

He would never want to return to his days as a thief with his uncle. He'd hated that life. Living each day for the next heist? Upending the order of the nation, a parasite feeding off those doing hard work? No, he didn't want that. But the more he learned, the bigger he realized the world was. And how little lying in a bed staring at his own eyelids could accomplish.

So he was *excited* when someone broke protocol. Guards arrived at the door, whispering apologies to the honored guests who had fed armies. Bowing to them, as today they were among the greatest in the empire. Then deeper bows to him.

Yanagawn opened his eyes and sat up calmly. The cooks whispered, eyes wide. He took in the five guards, pleased to remember each of their names, though he'd never speak to them directly—to do so would make them uncomfortable. Instead he looked past them to where Noura knelt. Head vizier of his court. Scholar, strategist, teacher.

Whatever had happened was important indeed. Without a word, he slipped from his bed and held his hands to the sides so he could be dressed.

The emperor was awake.

This family did not speak my language, but we could both write glyphs, which proved facilitative in our conversation. As I shared their kindly cookfire, I learned some of their story.

—From *The Way of Kings*, fourth parable

Though Shallan had insisted on going to gather and talk with her Lightweavers, Adolin managed a few hours' sleep. He rose, planning to arrive early for the meeting so he could get updates on current troop placements. Unfortunately, something interrupted his plans. It was called a shower.

Water rained down through holes in the ceiling of a small room beside his bedroom. A light behind the stones indicated the level of heat, and if he pressed his hand to it and rotated, he could make the water warmer or colder. A similar dial let him control the pressure and flow.

He was a highprince. A Shardbearer. And this was the single greatest moment of luxury he'd ever known. Steam filled the room like a Thaylen sauna as warm water melted away his fatigue, his anxiety. Both had seemed solid as stone, but even stone gave way—eventually—before rainwater.

Storms. He could have stayed in here for *hours.* He turned up the pressure, letting the water massage his back. How would this feel after a hard training session? He released a huge sigh, drawing not a few joyspren. Storms, there really *were* a lot more spren in the tower now than before, weren't there?

Shallan peeked in, a splash of auburn red against the yellow-brown strata. Her meetings must be done.

"What is *that*?" she asked, her eyes going wide.

"Hakindar calls it a shower," Adolin said, naming their room steward.

She stared, aqua eyes bright as spheres. "I need to try it." She was in there a moment later, looking stunning as she crowded him to the side. "Does it *have* to feel like a highstorm?"

"You can adjust the pressure here," he said, pulling his eyes away and showing her. She turned it down—changing the flow from a beating frenzy to a soft sprinkle.

"Aaaahh . . ." she said. "But not hot enough."

"Are you trying to drive me out?" Adolin asked as she turned the heat up to uncomfortable levels.

"It's like rain," she said, her head tipped back so the water could wash across her face, "if rain were *warm*."

"Hot."

"Heat is life. It reminds me that I'm alive."

"You . . . forget that?"

"Once in a while," she whispered, then leaned on him, wet hair against his chest. "You're warm too."

"Hakindar brought me six different soaps," Adolin said. "And a rough sand mix from Marat to exfoliate! There's this one soap out of Thaylenah—they use it on their eyebrows—that is *fantastic* for hair."

She nodded absently, her eyes closed. So he held her, skin against skin, slick and warm. This was perfection. This was what he'd always wanted, and had never been able to find, until he met her. Not merely skin to skin. Soul to soul. He ran his fingers through her wet hair, massaging her scalp, her cheek against his chest.

"I love you," he whispered. She grinned back, and he picked her up off the ground a little, surrounded by joyspren, holding her tight.

"I still . . ." Shallan whispered. "I still need to deal with the Ghostbloods. I might have to miss Dalinar's meeting. Will you . . . will you tell him and Navani . . . about Mraize, and what I've done? I'm not sure I can spare the time."

"Of course," Adolin said, impressed by how willing she was to be open about these issues. And if she didn't want to—perhaps couldn't—explain to Dalinar herself right now, he understood. "I don't blame you for wanting someone to prep my father for you. He can be . . . stern to those who disappoint him."

She perhaps sensed the bitterness in his tone, noticed how several joyspren winked away. It had been a year since Adolin had learned Dalinar killed his mother, and he couldn't let go. As he set Shallan down, she took his face in her hands.

"Would it help to talk?" she asked.

"I don't know, Shallan," he said. "Honestly, I don't want to think about him. Or talk to him. I don't *want* to fix things between us. I just . . . I . . ."

He'd thought waiting would let the pain fade. It had instead festered. He found himself *more* angry than he'd been when he'd first found out.

"Another time," he told Shallan. "I promise. You're really going to miss the meeting? Did you hear about Thaylen City? A second attack. Maybe more. We'll know once the scout reports come in."

"You can handle it," she said. "Mraize is here in the tower somewhere, and will move against me soon. So I have to move first. It will help if you'll talk to the Bondsmiths, maybe get me authorization for Radiant troops and a preemptive strike, if I can find the current Ghostblood nest."

He sighed, wrapping his arms around her again. "Is this ever going to end? We met not long before the Everstorm, and married in the middle of a war. I've had enough of wearing uniforms every day. Watching cities fall. Feeling that I need to hold on tight every time I have you in my arms, as I don't know when the next chance will be."

"I know," she whispered, head to his chest once more. "I want to kiss you until you can't breathe and spend a week never leaving our rooms. But we can't. Not yet. Mraize will try to hurt me, love. Prove that I was foolish to cross him. To get to me, he'll capture or kill you if he can. I *have* to act before he does."

He met her eyes, as best he could with both of them blinking away water. She reached up to push a cascade of soaked red hair out of her face. It might not have been the best place for a meaningful stare, but neither of them moved, and the joyspren were soon joined by passionspren—like snowflakes, but more crystalline.

"Thank you," he said.

"For understanding?"

"For trusting me to understand," he said. "I've never begrudged you your secrets, Shallan, but now that you're sharing them, I find them precious."

She cocked her head. "I . . . have shared them, haven't I? You know it all. All about Mraize, the Ghostbloods, Formless . . ." She gripped his arms tight, pressing her entire self against him, and grinned, water dripping from her nose. "You know it all and you don't *hate* me! Right?"

"Of course I don't."

"It's almost kind of all right," she said. "It can *maybe, possibly* work out . . . if I stop Mraize. I don't know why he wants to find the prison of the most powerful Unmade, but . . ."

Adolin nodded. "I'll represent you at the meeting."

She moved to slip away, without even conditioning her hair. He pulled her back. Not for the hair though.

"Surely we have a few minutes," he said, "before running to the next crisis? I mean, haven't you always wondered what it would be like, out in the rain . . . ?"

She paused, holding his hand. "Drat," she said.

"What?"

"I was trying *very* hard to stay focused, Adolin Kholin," she said, "and pretend you aren't the most gorgeous statue of a man to ever grace the world."

"Even when he's wet?" he said.

"Um, *especially* when he's wet, love."

She stepped back to him, went up on her toes, and kissed him, water falling around them like applause. The heat he'd been fighting off rose within him, outdoing that of the stream from above, and the passionspren fell more powerfully. It seemed that whether or not she had time to spare, they were going to find it.

⁂

Dalinar stomped through the corridors of Urithiru, throwing on his coat. He was joined by Colot, second-in-command of the Cobalt Guard. The tall lighteyed man had little tufts of red hair mixed through his black, dark enough that they were visible only in direct light.

Dalinar didn't need guards these days, but he said nothing as the man followed. Colot had been bouncing between positions for a few years, and the last thing he needed was to feel useless or rejected. Again. Kelen, the Windrunner squire who had come to fetch Dalinar, hovered along beside the two of them. It had been merely three days since Navani had reenergized the tower, and the Windrunners already appeared perfectly comfortable flying all the time.

Even at this time of night, Urithiru was usually active—but today the main thoroughfare was less congested than normal. The invasion and the curfews had a lingering effect. People were still traumatized, hiding in their rooms, recovering from the stress. Dalinar stormed forward, keeping momentum, as had always been his way. People who spotted him would yelp and jump back, but mostly he ignored everyone.

As they neared the atrium, where they'd be able to travel to the meeting chambers at the top of the tower, Windrunner Sigzil came streaking through the corridor and landed nearby. "I have the initial scout reports, sir."

"And?"

"And you were right, sir," Sigzil said, holding up a stack of papers as they walked. "It's not just Azimir and Thaylen City—there's a third offensive. A large number of Fused are marching on the Shattered Plains."

Damnation. Two was bad enough—particularly when one was Thaylen City, which had barely recovered from the Battle of Thaylen Field a year ago. It didn't have much of a defensive force remaining, and what few ships the royal navy maintained had been dedicated to the Veden blockade. He'd need to send Fen support. A great deal of it.

"What do we know about the Fused?" Dalinar asked.

"We sent two Windrunners," Sigzil said, "who were stationed at a scout post in the Frostlands. Sir, they estimate almost a thousand Fused, and at *least* one thunderclast is with them, if not both."

"*Storms,*" Dalinar said. A thousand Fused? He'd never faced a battle with more than two hundred. There weren't that many Radiants in all Roshar—not by half. "Why the Shattered Plains? Did they get wind of Jasnah's plan to found a second Alethi kingdom there?"

The Windrunners didn't have answers for him, though it did make sense to send Fused. Odium couldn't get many troops to the Shattered Plains before the deadline—so he'd have to rely on quality rather than quantity. Plus, Fused moved far faster than conventional troops, especially if they had Heavenly Ones to fly them part of the distance.

"A three-way assault," Kelen said, hovering to his left. "Striking at our three most powerful strongholds other than Urithiru."

"Assuming," Sigzil said, "they aren't planning to strike here as well."

"The Sibling is confident," Dalinar said, "that no Fused would dare set foot here now, and that Regal powers won't work. They'd have to use conventional troops, which would be massacred by our Radiants."

But this did seem to be a message. Strikes on Dalinar's coalition: Azimir, Thaylen City, and the Shattered Plains, which was becoming Alethkar in exile. Once the contest arrived in eight days, the borders would freeze—and while the enemy could probably capture more land by pushing at the borders, this was more intimidating. It warned that Odium could cut out the very hearts of his enemies if he wanted.

Well, let him try. They reached the atrium and stepped out onto a balcony overlooking the central hub below. A large window ran up the length of the far wall, stretching a hundred stories into the sky, showing darkness outside.

"Just in case," Dalinar said, "wake every soldier. Send patrols to scan the nearby mountains and into Shadesmar here. Post quadruple guard forces at any possible incursion point into Urithiru—including the Oathgates and the caverns. Any news on the other monarchs?"

"They're confirmed for your meeting, sir," Sigzil said, holding up the papers. "Teshav asked me to deliver these. Letters from Azir and Thaylenah—both sound quite alarmed, but agree that meeting is wise."

Dalinar had given him authority, as leader of the Windrunners, to read letters like this. It was wonderful to have another man around who didn't feel embarrassed to be seen reading. In the past, Sigzil had always been coy about his training in Azir, and whether it included the ability to read

Alethi scripts. In the face of Dalinar's decisions, his need for subterfuge had evaporated.

"Has anyone seen Wit?" Dalinar asked.

"There," Sigzil said, pointing toward one of the lifts already rising to the upper floors. "I spotted him and the queen on their way."

"Good," Dalinar said, holding out his hand. "If you'll give me a Lashing, I might beat them there. Then . . ." He trailed off as he noticed someone approaching down the hallway. The nursemaid, carrying little Gavinor, dressed in his schoolchild's outfit of knee-length trousers and a blouse.

"Mararin?" Dalinar said to her. "Is something wrong?"

"I'm taking him up to the garden room," Mararin said. "It comforts him, Brightlord. I apologize; I didn't expect to encounter you."

"It's the middle of the night."

Gav buried his face in her havah, but peeked at Dalinar. The boy's eyes were red from tears.

"Nightmares?" Dalinar asked Mararin.

She nodded. The woman could be stern, but she cared deeply for the children she watched over.

"Grampa?" Gav whispered, yawning. "You promised to play swords with me."

"You need sleep, Gav," Dalinar said softly, stepping toward him. "And Grampa has important work today. We will play tomorrow."

Gavinor nodded, rubbing his eyes on Mararin's dress.

"Get him something to eat," Dalinar said. "Then bring him up to the tower top. Maybe after my meeting I can—"

"Dalinar Kholin?" a voice asked.

He spun, but found that Colot the guardsman had already stepped between him and the speaker. She was a shorter woman, Makabaki, in brown clothing. Black hair in tight curls, heavyset build. Dark brown eyes that shimmered with something he couldn't define.

"Do I know you?" Dalinar asked.

"We've met," she said, then turned and walked along the balcony railing. She waved for him to follow.

"You give orders to the *king* of Urithiru?" Colot said. "What manner of—"

"Stay back," Dalinar said, waving to them all. Then he ran to catch up to the woman. Her air, attitude, and looks dredged up deep memories. Ones he'd once forgotten by her own hand.

No. It couldn't be. Could it?

Cultivation. The third god.

They had left behind family and hereditary home, something many would find unconscionable.

—From *The Way of Kings*, fourth parable

Shallan lay on her back on the floor underneath the shower, letting the water wash over her. She'd turned it down to a sprinkle, like the riddens of a storm, to rain on her bare skin and tap on the stones around her. The air was humid from the steam, so she breathed it in thick.

She could have lain there forever, enjoying a satisfaction and a fullness she could never have captured in a painting. This fragment of time was about the *sensation* more than the description. The knowledge that she'd opened herself to Adolin, and he had accepted her: flaws, issues, and dreams alike.

Water, stone, and steam . . .

. . . the contentment of knowing that all was—briefly—right . . .

. . . lazy joyspren, swirling around her like blue leaves . . .

This was her reward. She let it linger, as Adolin closed a trunk outside and called his goodbye.

With a sigh, Shallan rolled onto her stomach, water beating against her back, and was greeted by a collection of soap bars, cleansing stones, and other bathing paraphernalia. A dozen of them all in a cluster, glowing faintly silver, bouncing up and down.

"Shallan! Shallan! Shallan!"

"You guys were . . . watching?" she asked the creationspren.

"Shallan! Shallan! Shallan!"

Well, nice to have a cheering section, she supposed. She looked up and found Pattern dimpling the stone of the wall.

"Don't say it," she told him, climbing to her feet.

"What?" he said. "It's absolutely allowed, even encouraged now."

She smiled and finished rinsing, then turned off the water, whispering a little thank-you to the tower as she toweled off. She then searched the wall by Pattern for any sign of Testament.

Nothing. They might still be bonded, but it wasn't enough to pull Testament through. Shallan's good mood faded as she imagined her poor spren sitting alone on the other side. *I'll fix it,* she thought. *I'll find a way.*

First she had work to do. She put on one of Veil's outfits and crossed the main sitting room. She and Adolin had a prime location with a large balcony adorned with planters, which she stepped out onto, Pattern having taken his customary place on her long white coat.

"Well?" she asked.

One of the planters stood up, Stormlight steaming off as the Lightweaving vanished, revealing a short, bearded man. Gaz no longer wore an eye patch—he'd healed from that wound. But he often rubbed at his eye.

"Got a crook in my neck," Gaz grumbled, stretching. "But I didn't spot anything odd. Red, what about you?"

Another planter stood up, a lanky man in bright red suspenders emerging. "Nothing. If they're going to strike, they're smart enough not to be obvious."

Shallan leaned back against the wall and folded her arms. She nodded to Red, who took out a spanreed and clicked it on and off. They didn't bother writing things out, instead using the flashing ruby—intended for indicating one was done writing—as the actual communication. Windrunners had started developing a code for that.

The door to her rooms opened, and two more of her team entered from the hallway outside, where they'd been hidden. Stargyle—a tall, handsome man with a ready grin—shook his head. Darcira followed, one of the newer members of the Unseen Court. No one had so much as scouted Shallan's rooms, best any of them could tell. The five of them gathered around her front room table.

"Wit sends word," Gaz said, pulling over a chair. She could see his Cryptic riding on his shoulder. All of her agents were full Lightweavers, having spoken the First Ideal and at least one truth. None of those here were Shardbearers yet, but Gaz and Red were close. "Your brothers are safe, but Wit wouldn't even tell *me* where he took them."

"We can trust Wit," Shallan said.

"He won't join us," Stargyle said, laying out sketches, "despite being a Lightweaver now. He did give us these."

"No Lightweaver *has* to join us," Red said. "In fact, we're basically full, ain't we, Veil?"

Shallan nodded, not wanting to explain the nuance regarding Veil at the moment. Regardless, Red was right. There would be other Lightweavers, but they could form their own family. This group—the Unseen Court—was hers, and she wasn't going to let it grow unwieldy. Kaladin barely knew the *names* of half the Windrunners these days.

There were twelve pictures, sketches of the Ghostbloods that Wit had identified. Most of these faces were familiar, but a few were new. Shallan examined two in particular, a woman and a man who wore hoods and masks. Shorter people, with a foreign look to their clothing. Iyatil, master of this cell of Ghostbloods, was an offworlder who always wore a strange wooden mask. Neither of these depictions were of her.

A note at the bottom said, *Looks like Iyatil has called in offworlder reinforcements. Watch them. They're dangerous.*

"I scouted the tower earlier, as you said," Stargyle told her. "I spotted these two in the atrium, but they also caught me watching them. Neither of us moved against one another, and I sensed tension in the way they retreated. It's like . . . we're all waiting for the spark that will light the fire."

Her eyes lingered on the picture of Mraize, wearing a refined suit, his face ripped by old scars. He had been her teacher. A brutal, manipulative one—but he had seen things in her she hadn't recognized in herself. He'd pushed her, yes, but also encouraged her. Now they were at last truly enemies. She'd known it was coming, and she hated some of what he represented, like locking Lift in a cage, as she'd heard from Red.

Shallan had chosen her side, but it troubled her that—as seemed inevitable—she was again opposed to her mentor. Her mother, her father, Testament, Tyn, now Mraize. How many people who had cared for her would she have to kill? She let Radiant take over, removing her hat and bleeding her hair to yellow so the others would recognize the transformation.

"So far as we know," Radiant said, "I have the secret they needed from Kelek—while they do not. They'll try to extract that information from me. This exposes us to danger, but exposes them as well—because we know their next move."

"Attacking us," Gaz said. "Or your family."

"You *are* my family, Gaz," Radiant said. She narrowed her eyes at the sheets. "Fortunately, Shallan has a plan. We're going to form a strike team."

"A strike team to do what?" Gaz asked. "Radiant, I'm not afraid to fight, but they have resources from another storming *planet* and they're led by some kind of immortal ghost. I don't know how we fight them."

Shallan bled back in for a moment and met Gaz's stare. "Like I said, Gaz, we have the advantage. They need Mishram's prison for some reason, but we know where it can be found. If we reach it before they do, we can use it as a bargaining chip to secure our safety."

"There's more," Red said. "We're Radiants. We have something they never will: we've spoken truth to ourselves."

Gaz rubbed his chin, then nodded. "You mentioned armor earlier. Is it true? You have the next Ideal?"

"Yes," she said, and made armor form around her, lifting her half an inch into the air as the boots encased her feet.

"Neat," Red said. "You have armor, so now *we* all have armor."

"That's not how it works, Red," Darcira said, wagging a sketch pencil at him. "We don't get her powers. Storms, you're not even her squire anymore—you have your own spren!"

"Yeah, but you heard what Stormblessed did," Red said, standing up and holding out his arms. "He can share his armor! Make it swoop in and protect people! I've always wanted Plate. Can I borrow it, Shallan?"

She hesitated. She'd . . . only just earned it.

Darcira tapped her sketchpad. "It would be good to know if that works, Brightness."

A reasonable point. Storming former ardent and her scientific mind. "Fine," Shallan said. "How do I do it?"

"It seems like it just kind of worked for Kaladin," Red said.

"Everyone's talking about it," Darcira said. "Kaladin flew around. You know, like they do. And his armor—made of windspren—swept here and there, enveloping other soldiers when needed."

"Storming lordship bridgeman," Gaz muttered, "and his storming heroism."

They glanced at him.

"He does it just to make me feel bad," Gaz said.

"He acts like a hero," Red said, amused, "because it *annoys* you. Really."

"Yup," Gaz said. "Everyone should be grateful to me. If I hadn't shown those bridgemen tough love, they would never have grown up to be such nauseating paragons of self-righteousness."

"Weren't you *crying* the other month," Red said, "because of what you did to them?"

"I was drunk," Gaz said. "You can't trust a man when he's drunk. He'll accidentally say things he ain't ready to say yet. Anyway, weren't we going to try out that armor?"

Shallan considered, and pictured the scene. Kaladin with Light streaming off him, sending his armor out to protect.

Sad to miss the invasion, Veil noted.

By all accounts it was awful, Shallan replied.

Yeah, but how nifty would it have been to skulk around the tower while it was under enemy rule?

Hearing her voice, even only in the back of Shallan's mind, was comforting. It had seemed, right when she'd reintegrated, that Veil would be gone completely, but what good would healing be if it meant losing part of herself—a part she loved—forever? More and more, she was feeling that reintegration wasn't about rejecting Veil or Radiant, but embracing them and acknowledging in a healthy way that different parts of her had different needs, different goals, different ideas.

For her, this was what healing felt like. Not losing control to her personalities, but also making their strengths part of her. But, back to the matter at hand. She waved her hands at Red and commanded the armor. *Go to him.*

Shallan! the armor predictably replied.

Him. Go protect him. That guy.

She felt only confusion in response. So, she took Red by the arm and imagined the armor forming around him.

Do that.

Shallan!

The armor emerged around Red, and she didn't miss that it appeared as she pictured it: with swirls of color like ribbons of wet paint, poured together, all in shades of metallic red. The shape was also slightly different—sleeker, like it could be worn underneath a coat, rather than hulking like Adolin's Shardplate.

Red laughed in excitement, puffing with an explosive awespren, his voice echoing in the helm. Shallan stepped back. And Red stood there. Motionless. Arms out.

"Um . . ." Red's voice said. "I can't move . . ."

"You can't?" Gaz said.

Move, Shallan commanded the armor. It burst apart and vanished.

They tried again. Again, once she stepped away, Red was left motionless. He couldn't so much as bend his finger.

"Shardplate needs power to move," Darcira said. "So . . . maybe it's not powered?"

"So why does it work for the Windrunners?" Red said, his voice muffled. "This really isn't fair."

"I think it's brilliant," Gaz said. "Shallan, if we tip him over, do you think he'll just lie there until we get back from breakfast?"

Shallan dismissed the armor, smiling. *Shallan?* the voices asked. They . . . were embarrassed.

It's fine, she projected to them. *You're new to this.*

Maybe she could get them some kind of tutoring from . . . um . . . other bits of armor?

"Well, I guess no free armor for me," Red said. "I'll have to go back to whimpering at night about my dark secrets until I can find a way past them."

"Is your dark secret that your sense of humor is awful?" Gaz said.

"Nah, that's out in the open," Red said, settling at the table. "So . . . are we *actually* going to take on the Ghostbloods? Directly?"

Shallan checked the others. They nodded. Even Gaz.

"How do we begin?" Darcira asked.

"Mraize always thinks he has the upper hand," Radiant said. "He thrives on keeping people off-balance by dangling information like bait. The best way to nullify his advantage is to uncover his secrets. There's so much we're ignorant about. *Why* do they want Mishram's prison? Why did they get involved so deeply in our politics? So we're going to find the answers." She glanced down at the table, at Mraize's smirking scarred face. "We're going to do something they don't think is possible: we're going to *steal* those secrets."

"All right," Gaz said. "But how?"

"First," she said, "we need to find their base . . ."

⁂

"What are you doing here?" Dalinar demanded as he caught up to the woman . . . the god. Damnation, this *was* her. He'd last seen her in a darkened grove, but her face was exactly the same.

"I go where I please," she said, sounding amused, a few lifespren drifting around her. "Should I not?"

As before, there was the faintest hint of the sound of crumbling stone to her voice. Her clothing looked as if she had grown the dress from delicate webs of something fine and earthy, and it in places merged back with her skin. Neither effect was as dramatic as it had been in the Valley, perhaps to not draw attention. But he was shaken nonetheless. A Fused trick? Could it . . .

No. Fused powers wouldn't work in the tower. This was *Cultivation.* He stopped beside the metal railing, holding it for support.

"I remember you," he said.

"I know. You wrote it in your book. I take great pains to remain secret, Dalinar, and you just vomited it all up on a page." She shook her head.

"Are you here to help?" he said. "Can you tell me how to defeat Odium? Can I use my Bondsmith powers?"

"No, I cannot," she said. People passed on the balcony, bowing to him or saluting, but ignoring her. She, who was the greater of the two.

"Why not?" he asked. "Why not explain?"

"Haven't you learned yet? You must find the answers yourself to respect their meaning."

"Pardon," he said, "but that's a load of crem. If you give me the answers, I *absolutely* promise to respect them."

She smiled. "Have you wondered why you are a Bondsmith?"

"To unite them," he said.

"Yes. And what does that mean?"

"Many things, depending on interpretation," he replied. Then he sighed. "*Please* just give me an answer?"

She idled beside the railing, tapping it, gazing down at the people of Urithiru below. "Have you ever known Odium to be frightened?"

Had he?

Yes. Once during a crash of transcendent power. A time when he'd sworn he'd heard Evi's voice, and had become his own man, freed from the past. A time when he'd stared a god in the eyes, slammed his hands together, and merged three realms.

I am Unity.

"Once," Dalinar said softly.

"I have once as well," she said. "One time, other than when you faced him. It is deep in the past." She idly held up her hand, lifespren swirling and playing around it. "You need to take a journey, Dalinar Kholin. A dangerous one, but the path to defeating Odium is not through your powers alone. It is through understanding. You need to *see* the history of this world, *live* it."

"Visions?" he asked. "Like I've seen before?"

"Greater," she said. "Where is Honor?"

"Dead."

"Tanavast—the Vessel that once held Honor—is dead, but the power remains. Somewhere. It's a conundrum that few scholars even know to ponder upon. None know what became of Honor's power. Have you any guesses?"

"It's the spren, maybe," Dalinar said.

"Some say that Honor was Splintered by Odium when he killed Tanavast—as he did to others before—becoming the spren, as the power of a god left alone will begin to think." She shook her head. "But they're wrong. The spren existed before Tanavast's death. They are of him, but are not the *core* of his power. It still exists." She looked him in the eyes. "It is the power and substance of the visions you were shown, starting years ago. It seeks for men to see their heritage, as it searches for a new Vessel to hold it."

"Wait," Dalinar said, a cold shock starting at the base of his skull and washing through him, making him grip the banister. "Wait. What are you saying? That . . . someone could . . . ?"

"Honor's power needs a host," she said. "Whether or not that is you, and whether or not that solves your problems, remain to be seen. However, I'm here to tell you that years ago, you started on a path—and touched the power of Honor each highstorm when you saw a vision. The path to defeating Odium is the same one you're walking. You simply need to see better, farther, and deeper into the past."

"Could you not fight him?"

"I have my own battles," she said, turning to trail away. "I cannot fight yours, but *you now know* where the power hides. Seek the Spiritual Realm, where gods dwell. You have the ability to get there, perhaps even the ability to return. There you will receive the final truths of the Heralds, the Radiants, and Honor himself. Go and seek it, Dalinar Kholin, if you would finish this journey."

She walked a short distance, until darkness swallowed her, and she vanished in a *pop* of lifespren. Dalinar walked back to the others, who were surrounded by shockspren. Without a word, he pointed upward. Sigzil Lashed him and he went soaring, two Windrunners joining him. Only when he was already in the air did he realize he'd left his bodyguard behind yet again. Well, Colot could take the lift.

The Spiritual Realm. The powers of gods.

Stormfather, he thought as he soared higher, *did you sense that conversation?*

He felt a rumbling in the back of his mind. Confusion.

Cultivation was here, Dalinar said. *Just now.*

What? the Stormfather said, suddenly present fully in Dalinar's mind, making the air warp nearby. *Incredible. She almost never leaves her hiding place.*

You didn't sense her?

She hides from Odium, he sent. *Which means none of us can sense her either. She must have come to see what was happening with the Sibling. Cultivation was ever fond of them.*

Cultivation told me, Dalinar said, *that Honor's power still exists in the Spiritual Realm—that it is the substance of the visions I've seen. She says I should seek answers there.*

The Stormfather rumbled softly. A dangerous kind of thunder, distant, but warning of imminent violence.

Would you take that step, Dalinar? the spren asked. *Do you seek to lose yourself in the past?*

They reached the top floors of Urithiru. Dalinar—having done this dozens of times—knew to grab the railing and swing over into the staging room where the lifts arrived. He held to the railing until Sigzil canceled his Lashing, letting Dalinar settle to the ground.

I seek only to protect my people, Dalinar thought. He gripped the banister, looking down hundreds of feet. A vertigo-inspiring sight. He'd felt as though he'd been standing at a precipice for years now, a single step from demise. Once, if he'd trembled before a battle, it had been with excitement.

Now it was because of the daunting realization that everything rested upon him. By his design.

If he lost this contest . . .

I can see that you are nervous, the Stormfather said. *Good. Confidence in a mortal should only go so far. What else did Cultivation tell you?*

Just that the Spiritual Realm has answers, Dalinar said. *That I can get there with my powers. That I should seek the truths of history, and of Honor.*

The Stormfather rumbled, sounding annoyed by this.

What? Dalinar asked.

I've shown you what you need, he replied. *Too much more is dangerous.*

Wait, Dalinar thought. *There* is *more? Could I see how the Heralds were chosen? How people came to Roshar? Could I see what caused Honor to die?*

The Stormfather rumbled softly, and sounded even angrier.

Cultivation indicated I should seek these answers, Dalinar said.

I did not think she would interfere except in her usual way, the Stormfather said. *That of making tiny nudges that require decades to mature. I will have to think on it. Her suggestion is dangerous, Dalinar. Too dangerous. Take care.*

With that, the Stormfather turned his attention elsewhere. The shimmering to the air vanished, and the spren's presence retreated to a faint awareness in the very back of his mind.

Storms. He was tired of vague promises and hints. He was tired of gods moving among them unnoticed. He wanted *answers.* He trudged toward the meeting room, joined by the two Windrunners. Inside, he saw that Jasnah had indeed beaten him to the top—early for the meeting as he was. Wit sat on the floor at the rear, holding a scroll of paper in one hand and some kind of white bone in the other.

"What's he doing?" Dalinar asked Jasnah.

"Something's wrong," she explained, arms folded as she watched him. "He had an encounter with Odium that he only just remembered—which means Odium altered his memories. That, for reasons he hasn't explained, makes him think there are loopholes in the contract that Odium is exploiting."

"There can't be," Dalinar said. "Odium promised me—confirmed true by Wit himself—that he wouldn't use any loopholes. That the soul of the contract was more important."

Jasnah shook her head. "We'll get answers from Wit—if we're lucky—on his timeline, not ours." She seemed expressly annoyed with Wit.

"Well," Dalinar said, getting out battle maps and waving in the generals waiting outside, "let's get an accurate accounting of our troop placements so we can be ready to present to the monarchs. We have much to organize and plan . . ."

Finally found some time to think about this.
How might I add a cape? Adolin would love that...
Put on the cape first, and form the armor beneath it!
There are more beads than Plate sections, but fewer than the number of plate segments. How do they correlate?

What I learned from their glyphs scribbled in dust trembled my soul: it was because of me, and the stories they'd heard of my teachings, that they had left.

—From *The Way of Kings*, fourth parable

The first signs of light shone through the atrium as Adolin walked to the lifts. After his time with Shallan, he'd made a detour to check on Gallant, and would arrive at the meeting right on schedule.

Many common people were being forced to wait in line for lifts until the monarchs had gathered. He spotted someone unexpected among them.

"Colot?" he asked, noting the Cobalt Guardsman.

"Adolin," Colot said, looking embarrassed. He was lighteyed, with yellow-green eyes. Former Windrunner squire. Many squires had to wait months to get spren, which were in short supply—but most were happy to do so. He didn't know why Colot had given up and left before getting one.

"You all right?" Adolin asked him.

"Fine. Your father just managed to give me the slip again."

Adolin groaned softly. "I thought he was getting better at bringing his guards."

"I don't think he did it intentionally. He simply got distracted." Colot gave a shrug.

"I'll talk to him," Adolin said.

"Please don't, Adolin. Bodyguards are nothing more than a bother for him these days. Just . . ." Colot took a deep breath. "Don't worry about me. I'll find my way up once the important people are taken care of."

"Nah, you're coming with me," Adolin said, pulling him out of the line.

Adolin spotted a lift being loaded with a group of figures in colorful Azish clothing, soldiers keeping everyone else at a safe distance. Adolin gave a shout and ran for the lift, towing Colot behind him. Before the attendants could close the gate, the emperor himself—swathed in thick robes and wearing a headdress several feet wide—raised his hand, pausing them.

Adolin and Colot hopped onto the lift, and Adolin nodded to the emperor in thanks. It was crowded full of Azish dignitaries. Wherever Emperor Yanagawn went, he had to bring viziers, servants, functionaries, servants to the functionaries . . .

The lift started creeping up the wall of the atrium. Then it picked up speed. Within seconds, they were going so fast that Adolin felt the wind of it—something that had never happened before the tower's awakening. At this rate, the ride to the top would take barely a few minutes.

"Highprince Adolin," Yanagawn said from the center of his retinue. "Might I have a word?"

Nearby, several of the viziers glanced at one another, though none said anything. The young emperor wasn't technically supposed to speak to anyone beneath him, but he and Adolin had interacted on and off during the year since the Battle of Thaylen Field. Yanagawn had started talking to Adolin directly.

"Your Excellency?" Adolin said, stepping closer as several guards reluctantly made space for him.

"You saw the armies advancing on my homeland," Yanagawn said. "The report is that they are . . . vast?"

"It's a pretty decent invasion force," Adolin admitted. "Maybe fifteen or twenty thousand."

"We have a fraction of that in the capital," Yanagawn said. "Most of our armies are out on campaign." He shook his head, seated in his chair amid them all. They carried a seat for him wherever he went—and sometimes they carried him upon it. "We thought we'd be safe after driving the enemy back in Emul. Even with the contest, will it ever end?"

"I wish I knew, Your Excellency."

Yanagawn was in many ways baffling to Adolin—a figurehead more than a king. Like a Soulcast statue, powerful in station, but somehow personally impotent. Jasnah thought this was a good thing; Adolin had tried to follow her explanations why. It made sense when she talked about checks on absolute power, but Jasnah could make anything sound reasonable. It was one of her gifts.

"You fight directly for your people," Yanagawn said softly to him. "With sword in hand. Are you ever frightened you won't be strong enough, Highprince?"

"You can call me Adolin, if you'd like."

"I . . . cannot offer you the same courtesy."

"I understand," Adolin said. "And in answer to your question: yes. I get storming *terrified* that I'll fail again. Kholinar fell when I was sent to save it. Not a day passes that I haven't thought about that."

It was a constant pain—like a stretched muscle that refused to heal. The type of stealth pain that didn't ache until you moved the wrong way, and suddenly it flared up—a sharp spike in your side. He would remember activating the Oathgate. Leaving wounded soldiers behind, an entire city full of people that *he* was supposed to have rescued. His cousin Elhokar dead on the stones . . .

Yeah, that one storming *hurt*.

"How do you bear it?" Yanagawn asked.

"Exercise helps," Adolin said. "Training with my sword, clearing my mind."

"Sometimes I think it is a blessing that my station doesn't let me fight," Yanagawn said. Storms, his Alethi was so good. He had an accent, yes, but he'd only been practicing for a year or so. "I do not make the tactical decisions, and so the burden of failure is not my own. At other times, I find myself a coward."

"It's not cowardly to know your own limitations, Excellency," Adolin said.

"Maybe," Yanagawn said, then smiled fondly. "Do you know my background, Adolin?"

"I believe you were a darkeyes . . . er, whatever you call it . . . before your elevation."

"A commoner, yes," he said. "A thief. And not a very good one at that."

More side glances from the viziers. Noura, their foremost, stepped closer. "Pardon, Excellency and Highness, but that is the path Yaezir put you upon, and is how you were to be manifest to us via miracle."

"That doesn't change what I was, Noura."

"Yes, Excellency," she said. "But dwelling on what you were, instead of what you are, never gets a person far."

Adolin nodded. He could never have lived with so many attendants, but Noura . . . she was at least thoughtful.

"I mention it," Yanagawn said, "not to dwell upon it, but to remember a time when I was commonly put into dangerous situations. I did not handle it well then. I often wonder . . . how would I handle it now?" He looked to Noura, and Adolin saw in him the man—not the youth. He was older than Adolin had been when he'd first won his Shardblade.

This fellow, Adolin thought, *needs a good session training with the sword.*

It wasn't Adolin's place to say so, not here. So he held his tongue as the lift reached the top, and they stepped out. It was time to decide how they were going to face this threat.

⁂

Radiant leaned back against the wall of the lift atrium's ground floor. Courtesy of Shallan's Lightweaving, she wore the face of a crem scraper. He was a man with long features, drooping as if waxen.

Adolin got on the lift with the Azish contingent, while Isom—the Lightweaver she'd tasked with tailing him—gave a covert signal, indicating he'd take the next lift up. Shallan had been worried when Isom reported Adolin hadn't gone straight to the meeting. Of course he'd gone to check on his horse. Again.

She'd already sent Stargyle up to join the monarchs, officially representing the Unseen Court, so Adolin should be well guarded. Besides, surely the enemy wouldn't try something in the middle of a meeting of kings, queens, and a bunch of Radiants.

You've done what you can there, Veil said.

Now her plans depended on one of her Lightweavers being able to tail a Ghostblood to their current hideout. Gaz was with her, wearing the face of a young woman who sold rockbud flowers in the market. One of his better sketches—and better disguises, as it made use of his shorter height.

"No reports of Ghostbloods tailing any of our people today," Gaz said softly. His Lightweaving had progressed far enough that his voice was starting to modulate as well as his image. "They haven't even attacked the horse. You think they're waiting to make us placid?"

Radiant considered. "No. They don't want to draw attention. A petty strike at someone Shallan loves would give them a moment of satisfaction, but would bring the full weight of Dalinar's anger down on them. Mraize is more subtle than that."

Gaz grunted, a sound that did *not* match the face he was wearing. He needed more practice. To that end, now that she had checked on Adolin, Radiant gave way to Shallan, who slouched further, shoved her hands in her pockets, and started chewing on her lip—all very un-Shallan-like behaviors—to help sell the disguise.

"No threats," Shallan whispered with a man's voice. "No contact. I'd hoped we could stop a strike against one of us, then tail the perpetrators. This silence is unnerving. We *need* to find out what they're up to, Gaz."

"We have agents watching tower entrances and major corridors," Gaz said. "But even with our paid informants, I can't guarantee we'll pick up a Ghostblood's trail."

Shallan nodded as she chewed her lip, thoughtful. "Ghostbloods won't be able to stay away from today's developments. They didn't interfere with Adolin, but they're watching. They'll be doing the same for Dalinar, Navani, and anyone else they think might know something. Eventually one of us will spot someone to follow."

Gaz nodded slowly, relaxing against the wall with a leisurely air. Shob, one of the other Lightweavers, would be here in a few minutes with his report. In the past, Gaz had scratched at his stubble and spent half his time nervously checking his former blind spot. Both actions were far less common while he was in disguise, as he'd tempered the behaviors.

"You're getting better at this," Shallan noted.

"Thanks," he said. "I needed something to do with my time."

"How's the gambling?"

He shrugged.

"How much in debt are you this week?"

"Nothing," he said.

"That's an improvement."

"Only because I managed to stay away completely," he said. "That advice you gave about giving myself a budget and only losing that much?"

"Yes?" she said, eager.

"It was storming useless," he said. "Sorry."

"Oh."

"If I start gambling, I stop caring," he said. "That's always been the problem. It's why I wound up in the bridge crews, under the thumb of a pair of petty lighteyes. It's why I ended up deserting. No budget will work for me. Just gotta do somethin' else."

"Is that difficult?" she asked, thinking of her brother who had the same problem. Maybe what worked for Gaz would help Jushu.

"Yeah. I used to spend all my days planning how to score," he said. "Strategies—most of them useless. I'd build up in my mind how each play would be one gust in what became a storm of winnings, digging me out of my problems. Each win felt good, like I was taking a step toward being worth something."

Disgustspren, like orange corkscrews drilling downward, appeared around him as he continued. "It's not the gambling itself that got me. It's that I built up how it would feel to win, only to come crashing down each time, leaving me feeling like I'd missed out on something I was *owed.* That made me dull to everything else. Till I was a man without a heart, sending boys off to die each day on those bridge runs."

"And then . . ."

"I found you all," he said. "People who care about me."

"And the power of being loved," Shallan said softly, a smile rising on her lips, "gave you the strength to resist."

"What?" He belted out a laugh, half his voice, half that of his illusion. "What kind of storming crem is that! The power of being loved? Ha! No,

Stargyle and Red went to every gambling den in the whole storming tower and threatened the folks that run them! Said if anyone let me in, Stargyle would rip their toenails off and wear them as a necklace. When I came by, the staff wouldn't even talk to me!"

"Well," she said, "that *is* the power of being loved. Simply, um, a different hue."

"A tough kind of love."

"A toe-uf kind of love."

He looked at her.

"Toe," she said. "For feet. Toenails."

He just kept staring at her.

"Hey, I'm out of practice," she said. "There was this whole *thing* with another personality almost manifesting, and it didn't leave time for witticisms. Anyway, remind me to send Red and Stargyle a thank-you note."

"Storming fools," Gaz grumbled. "But it worked. After a while, my mind found other ways to spend its time. The work we do, that's got more of a *real* thrill to it: the plans, the watching, the tailing. Now the strategies I think of are actually accomplishing something." He checked his belt, where one of their spanreeds was blinking. "Damnation. That's Shob. He's spotted a Ghostblood. You were right."

"I always am." She paused. "Except with gambling advice."

"And jokes."

"My jokes are incredible. They might need to be honed a little, but well, even a dull knife can kill someone."

He ran his hand through his fake hair. "That explains so much . . ."

"It does?"

"If you push hard enough with a dull knife . . ."

"It can still be painful."

"And if you keep trying with bad jokes . . ."

"The same." She hesitated. "Wait. That's not what I meant."

He grinned. "Let's go see what Shob found."

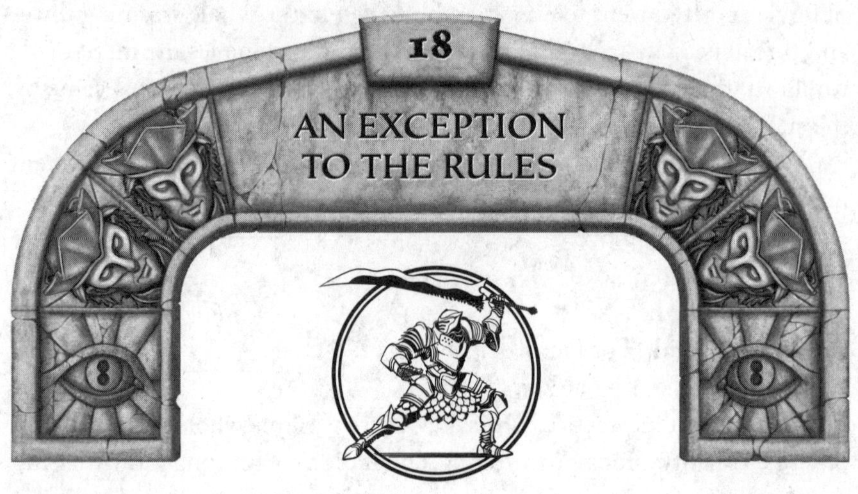

They'd gone to seek a land some told them was mythical.

—From *The Way of Kings*, fourth parable

Adolin and the Azish emperor left most of the attendants in the antechamber as they joined the meeting. By tradition, Yanagawn picked up his own seat and carried it in, and Adolin did the same, grabbing one from outside. Navani and Dalinar liked the symbolism.

Inside, Adolin did a quick count of those in attendance, and saw he and Yanagawn were last. His father and aunt were there, as were Jasnah and Queen Fen. A few Radiant representatives, including Sigzil for the Windrunners and Stargyle for the Lightweavers, were placing their seats. There were also a couple of the lesser kings—or "primes" as they called them—from the Azish Empire. The Mink had come as well—the short Herdazian who was their key strategist. And possibly, following the fall of his kingdom, Herdaz's ranking lighteyes. Even if he was actually darkeyed.

The meeting was rounded out by three other Alethi highprinces, a group of scribes, and several generals and important leaders—like Prince Kmakl and Noura the vizier. And of course there was Wit, sitting in the corner with a scroll across his lap. Aunt Navani waved, and all the gathered emotion spren in the room flew out—to not distract. Adolin closed the door. Maybe he should have greeted his father, whom he hadn't seen in weeks. He glanced toward Dalinar.

No. After how they'd parted, they'd do the proper thing: ignore it and let it fester.

Mere seconds after he'd closed the door, there was a knock on it. Adolin peeked, then pulled it all the way open as one of the guards gestured to an older Reshi man wearing a loose robe that showed a powerful chest and a strong build. Adolin thought he was one of the leaders of their islands who had been visiting the tower these last few months.

They'd never invited him to any of their meetings. The man didn't ask; he simply picked up a chair and stood outside, waiting with his son, who often wore Thaylen clothing.

Adolin glanced into the chamber. This man was king to only a few hundred, less powerful in his sphere than a lower Alethi landowner. He was Radiant—the sole Dustbringer left in the tower—but not many Radiants got to join the meeting.

There was silence for a moment before the Mink spoke. "We have a saying, in Herdaz," he said. "No cousin is so distant they stop being family. A king of a small land is still a king."

"Please, enter," Dalinar said, nodding and waving to the Reshi king. "Though I warn you, much of what we discuss might be confusing without prior context."

The man said nothing, carrying his chair and placing it at the back of the room, with several of the lesser Azish primes. He sat with a regal air—and honestly, Adolin doubted he spoke much Alethi. His presence seemed symbolic. Adolin closed the door again.

"That's it," Fen said. "Everyone is here. Can we finally begin? My kingdom is facing an entire fleet."

"Mine," Yanagawn said, "is about to be invaded through a portal into the heart of my city! And sooner than yours!"

"The Everstorm can bring the enemy fleet to my city in just a day," Fen said. "We saw that last time!"

"Please," Dalinar said. "We will get to everyone's defenses. First, let's establish where our forces currently stand."

"I agree," Fen said. "But I do want to make a point, Dalinar. This *is* your fault. You should have insisted that the borders freeze the moment the deal was struck."

She was right, of course, but this was how it was with Adolin's father. Dalinar was a great man, yes, but he was *confident* in his greatness. Which led him to assume he could solve any problem himself.

"I'm sorry, Fen," Dalinar said. "I'm doing my best."

"Your best is going to see my kingdom conquered while you protect yours! You practically *ensured* war these ten days."

Silence. Eyes condemning. *This is what you deserve, Father,* Adolin thought, feeling the room turn—like spears lowered at a captured enemy—against Dalinar. *You always barrel forward. Doing whatever you want. Consequences be storming damned. Like you did years ago, killing my mother. And you never bothered to tell me. You—*

"You did well, Dalinar Kholin," Yanagawn said. "We agreed to let you stand for us, and you found us a solution. Thank you."

Adolin frowned, looking at the Azish emperor. His homeland was facing invasion. Why was he so calm?

"Because of you," Yanagawn continued, "we have a chance. The enemy can be reborn again and again, but with the contest, peace is actually possible."

"I failed you in the short term," Dalinar said. "Armies are coming for your homeland."

"As they were three days ago," Yanagawn said. "And the weeks before that. All that has changed is that *you* have ensured there is an *end* in sight. Yes, the contract could have been a little better, but I think every Azish person in this room can admit that even with important documents, you always miss something."

"Well that's storming true," Sigzil said, laughing.

"You're right, Yanagawn," Fen said with a grumble. "Dalinar, I was too harsh. We did agree to let you make the decision, and you did all you could. I shouldn't grouse about what could have been, but my homeland only just started to recover from the last attack."

"We merely need to hold out, Fen," Yanagawn said. "For eight more days. Then we have peace."

Storms. With that, the tone of the room changed again. Or perhaps Adolin hadn't been reading it correctly in the first place. People nodded. Fen sat up a little straighter. And Dalinar . . . Dalinar met Yanagawn's eyes, then bowed his head in a sign of respect and thanks.

When had the young emperor learned such maturity? Or . . . perhaps Adolin should be wondering why he hadn't learned the same.

"Very well," Dalinar said. "Let's discuss our positions. Stargyle, you up to making a map with me?"

"Yes, sir," the Lightweaver said. "After the last few weeks of practice, I think I can manage it."

"Good," Dalinar said. "We'll begin in Emul, with—"

"Holy hell," a voice said from the corner.

Adolin frowned, trying to figure out those words and how they fit together. The group parted, revealing Wit sitting in the corner, holding that paper and what looked like a bone. "It's not possible," Wit said, louder.

Adolin glanced toward Jasnah, who shook her head, as confused as he was.

"I'm an *idiot*," Wit said.

"Wit?" Dalinar asked. "Are you—"

Wit leapt to his feet. "I'm an absolute fool! The most awe-inspiring, spectacular example of idiocy this side of the cosmere. So grand, I should be immortalized in song. The type that drunk men sing before they puke, mixing the rancid contents of their poisoned stomachs with my name."

"Wit," Dalinar said firmly. "Explain yourself."

Well, *that* seemed like an invitation for mockery. Adolin braced himself, but when Wit spoke his voice was serious.

"There *are* loopholes in this agreement," Wit explained. "I'm sorry; I failed you all. I was supposed to shepherd the process of creating this contract. I could have seen exactly where these attacks would land, if I'd been more keen-eyed."

He said it solemnly. Quietly. What could make *Wit* be so . . . normal?

"How could you have guessed they'd strike at Thaylen City?" Fen asked.

"Because it's in this agreement," Wit said, "blatant as my own nose. As you all know, Dalinar was forced a little off script in creating this three days ago."

"Odium insisted he couldn't accept the deal as presented," Dalinar said to the room. "Because he can no longer keep the Fused imprisoned."

"Locking them away is no longer viable," Wit agreed, "with the Oathpact broken and the Everstorm in place. Regardless, Dalinar going off script led to this situation—where the enemy has one last chance to grab lands."

"Which is why we've been expecting an attack on the borders in strategically valuable places," the Mink said, standing beside Dalinar. "If they expand the size of Alethkar, for example, but then we win it back . . . well, their attack was wasted. So we assumed some encroachment from Jah Keved on the Frostlands, or maybe another push into Emul or Tashikk. Key is that Alethkar and Herdaz are ours, forever, if Dalinar wins."

The Herdazian looked to Dalinar and nodded in respect. Adolin hadn't heard all the details of the contract, but he'd been told that Dalinar had specifically singled out Herdaz for freedom. The mark of a promise kept.

Dalinar nodded back. Adolin's father was standing—because of course he'd forgotten to bring his chair. Despite the grand philosophies he espoused, Dalinar was always an exception to the rules. Even his own.

Storms, Adolin thought, acknowledging the bitterness lacing his thoughts. *I'm really, really letting this go too far.*

He knew it. But he couldn't stop it.

"The Mink is right," Dalinar said. "Whatever happens, Odium keeps the lands that surrendered to him, such as Iri, Jah Keved, and Marat. We keep whatever we hold when the deadline arrives. Strikes against Thaylen City and Azimir are not completely outrageous—but they don't seem a smart choice. Why risk everything on capturing our strongholds when it's much more possible to grab land at the perimeter?"

"Because," Wit whispered, "if he takes the capitals, he gets the kingdoms. In their entirety."

"Wait," Yanagawn said. "What did you say?"

"I realized earlier that I might have missed something," Wit said. "So, I sent a request to one of the best contract negotiators I know. Frost. Tall fellow. Big as a house, actually. Sharp teeth. Fondness for chastising me, which shows he has good judgment. He refused to help, as he insists he will not intervene, but his sister is as smart as he is, and she listened. I read her the contract, and she needed access to the Alethi legal code. That's what I've been doing for these past hours—reading her laws, talking her through it, asking for her explanations."

"And you did this . . . right here?" Navani asked. "How?"

Wit held up the little bone, as if that explained everything. "The general idea is this: In Dalinar's negotiations, he argued for the return of Alethkar and Herdaz. Entire kingdoms. Then he agreed to Odium's request: Odium can try for *entire kingdoms* with his attacks. By Alethi law, this means that he has to capture their seat of power. So . . ."

"So he throws everything he has at Azimir," Yanagawn whispered. "Because if he can take it, he claims the kingdom. That's what you're saying?"

"Unfortunately, yes," Wit said.

Oh, Damnation, Adolin thought. The room fell silent.

"He promised me," Dalinar whispered, "that there would be no taking advantage of loopholes. That he would hold to the spirit of the contest. You had to dig through the Alethi legal code for hours to find this. It sounds a lot like a loophole to me."

"Yes," Wit said. "And that's why I'm an idiot. Not because I missed the intricacies of the legal code—but because this isn't something that Rayse could ever do. It's not only against his nature, it's something he promised he would not do. Even without a formal covenant, a god cannot break that kind of promise without dire consequences."

"So . . . what?" Dalinar said. "I'm missing something."

"As are we all," Wit said with a sigh. "Odium is exploiting a loophole in your agreement. Rayse wouldn't do that. Rayse *couldn't* do that. So . . ." He looked around the room, meeting their eyes. "So *we are not facing Rayse.* My old enemy must be dead, and someone *else* has taken up the Shard of Odium. I should have seen it the moment he started acting so oddly, but now I've confirmed it by sensing the rhythms of Roshar. My friends, we are facing an enemy we do not know and cannot anticipate. And whoever it is, they're a genius—one who has devised a ploy to conquer all of Roshar in ten days."

⁂

"All right," Shob said, huddling in an alcove with Shallan and Gaz up on the third floor. "Look at these."

Shallan and Gaz had taken different faces, all three of them now appearing like Herdazian workers. Gaz had a real sparkflicker on his finger, with some flint to fake working it. Shob blew his nose, then set out some pages for them on the ground. It was quieter here, with less traffic, though sound still echoed up through the nearby atrium.

"Oi was watching the atrium region," Shob said. "Like you said. Oi spotted someone spyin' on Dalinar as he talked to some Makabaki woman. The Ghostblood was this one here."

Shallan took the page, a sketch of a short Alethi or Veden woman Hoid had identified as a Ghostblood, but not one Shallan had ever met. At the bottom he'd written: *former actor, recruited recently.*

Actor, eh? She supposed that wasn't an unusual recruitment tactic for a secretive organization.

"You set a tail on her?" Shallan asked.

"Darcira is followin' right now," Shob said, rubbing his nose again. The man was always bemoaning some ailment or another—none of which were ever as debilitating as he thought. He was good at his job though. This was a solid lead.

The Ghostbloods regularly set up, then abandoned bases. They were also fantastically good at losing tails, but a new recruit? This seemed a weak point.

Shob leaned back, complaining about his stomach while Shallan looked over the sketch once more, noting the woman's tattoo peeking out through her freehand sleeve. Hoid's sketches were excellent.

Shallan rubbed her wrist, where she'd refused to get one of those same tattoos. She flipped through the sketches and pulled out the picture of Mraize: tall and distinguished—scarred and proud of it. She . . . didn't hate him. For all his threats and manipulations, he was too complex a man to be hated. She felt frustration mixed with envy, accompanied by a bitter sadness about what could perhaps have been.

She would have to kill him. As she'd killed Tyn. As she'd killed her father. But she would not enjoy it.

The next sketch was Iyatil in her mask. Even the sketch of her was shadowed, and Hoid noted he didn't catch sight of her often. The next two pictures were those masked newcomers—assassins brought in from Iyatil's homeland, wearing wooden masks painted in a way that made them feel . . . featureless. Just shapes and lines, not people, except for those eyes staring out, and the mouths barely exposed at the bottom.

As she was studying those pictures a soldier strolled past and glanced at Shallan's group. Gaz casually held up one of the pages to be more visible, but it suddenly depicted a busty woman in a state of *complete* undress. Shallan blushed, drawing a shamespren despite herself. The soldier chuckled and moved on.

"Gaz," she hissed.

“What?” he said. “You have a better way to explain a bunch of street sweepers gathered around some papers?”

“Where did you even get that image!”

“Drew it myself,” he said, with a grunt. “You said we should take them art lessons. Gotta get the musculature right to learn proper Lightweaving.”

“I know that!” she said, recalling some experiences in her youth. She shooed away that shamespren in the shape of a red flower petal. “But . . . my models were never quite so . . . um . . .”

“Oi think somethin’s wrong with my heart,” Shob said from beside them, lying on his back now, eyes closed. “Oi think it stopped beating. Can’t feel it. Is that normal?” Shallan didn’t give it much thought—Shob was merely being his usual overdramatic self.

Gaz shook the page so the image vanished, returning to a depiction of a Ghostblood. “You want me to invite you next time we do a drawing session?”

“Storms, no,” Shallan said, still blushing. “You’re not supposed to stare at models. It’s unprofessional.”

“I don’t think those ladies and fellows mind,” Shob said. “On account of their other jobs.”

Storms. Well, she *did* need anatomy practice. She put that out of her head as Shob groaned and sat up, then wagged a blinking spanreed with a message from Darcira. They counted out the blinks silently, interpreting the message. *New Ghostbloods hideout found. Narak. I watch.*

“Narak?” Gaz said softly. “Why so far away?”

“The tower is awake now,” Shallan said. “Perhaps the Sibling could locate them for us if they were closer.”

“Should we hit them with a strike team?” Gaz asked. “Gather some troops—put some Windrunners to good use for once?”

“We should gather one,” Shallan said. “Adolin should have gotten us permission. But striking won’t do much good unless we know Mraize and Iyatil are inside. Plus, like I said earlier, we need to find out what they’re planning.”

“Which means . . .” Gaz said.

“We’ll use a strike team, yes,” Shallan said. “But we’re going to sneak in first.”

Gaz nodded and collected the pictures, then headed out. Shob was lying down again. Shallan had always found his antics ridiculous, but today . . . today she hesitated, then tapped him on the foot while he looked up at the ceiling.

“Hey,” she said softly. “Hey, you all right?”

“Oi know Oi probably am,” he replied. “Oi know it’s just in my head, all these things Oi feel. So yeah, Oi suppose. It ain’t real.”

Shallan suddenly felt guilty. She'd dismissed his attitude as silly earlier. How many would call what *she* dealt with "silly"?

"Hey," she said. "*Feeling* real is enough. The things in our heads can be some of the most important things in our lives. Love is in our heads. Confidence. Integrity. All things we make up, but they're still very important."

He sat up. "And me feelin' sick all the time? Is that good, like love or integrity?"

"Probably not," she said. "But it being in your head doesn't mean we should ignore it. You need any help?"

He cocked his head, illusion covering his face, but his eyes—his expressions—showed his true self. "Nobody's ever asked me that. You know? In years, nobody's asked me that? Yeah. Yeah, Oi think Oi could use some help." He hesitated. "But Oi don't know. Sometimes . . . when people listen to me . . . it gets worse. Oi just start thinkin' of more things wrong, then ask for more and more sympathy. Till Oi hate myself, and everyone hates me."

"Ignoring the problem isn't the solution though," Shallan said. "Trust me. When we're done with all this, let's see if we can find someone who can help. There has to be an ardent or a surgeon or someone."

"Okay," he said, rising. "Oi think Oi just felt a heartbeat. So maybe Oi will survive long enough." He glanced at her, then paused. "Oi say exaggerations of what Oi feel like that because they're funny. Makes people think Oi'm jokin'. So they don't hate me, you know?"

She took his hand, squeezed it, and nodded.

"You still want me watchin' here?" he asked.

She nodded again. "Thanks for spotting that Ghostblood, but I want another set of eyes on that meeting up above. Outside, in the room with the guards, listening to what they're chattering about." Shob was excellent at that kind of information-gathering, but his skill set wasn't aligned with attacking enemies, as she was planning to try next.

"Then Oi'd better find a lift up," he said. Then he glanced at her. "You . . . pay better attention now. What happened on that trip?"

"I found a few pieces of myself," she said, "that I'd lost."

19

RULED BY VOICES

A land where the king was a holy man, and was concerned with the plight of the farmer beyond the appropriation of taxes.

—From *The Way of Kings*, fourth parable

Szeth-son-Honor continued to wear white clothing.

That was no longer mandated. Dalinar had said he could wear what he wanted, and though Szeth was a Skybreaker, he had no uniform. Even during training and official functions, they'd wear the uniform of the local guard or constables.

Still, Szeth wore filmy white clothing that flapped in the wind as they flew. Still, Szeth shaved his head each day, and found the faintest prickle of stubble on his scalp an annoyance. Did he do these things because he wanted to, or because they were now tradition? Life could be so full of distracting, meaningless small decisions while the large ones—such as determining his duty to his people—were so hard.

So he pretended it was right to continue his routines. If they were wrong—if instead he should have a *preference* among many tiny options . . . well, that made him shudder to his core.

He did like flying though. During the days training with the Honorblades in his youth, taking to the sky had appealed to him most of all the powers. He and Kaladin-son-Lirin had flown far with the storm, before sleeping in a coalition camp near the base of the mountains.

Now, at last, they approached the Misted Mountains at the edge of Shinovar. They avoided the northern border, where Shin had been loosing arrows at anyone who drew too close. Szeth figured these southern farmlands would be better. It was also close to where he'd grown up, so he knew the region.

Within the rushing of the wind and the flapping of clothing in flight, he could not hear the voices whispering or screaming from the shadows. They'd been quiet for some time, so he thought he'd escaped them. It turned out they'd simply been lying in wait.

"Is that the pass?" Kaladin's voice came to him, cutting through the noise, perfectly audible. Windrunning permitted sculpting airflow. Such conveniences were no longer available to Szeth. Nale had granted him leave to use Division, now that Szeth had reached the Third Ideal. Unfortunately, Szeth's spren had so far forbidden him the art, although he had the skill. His spren said the time wasn't right.

Regardless, it was the correct pass, and seeing it made Szeth tremble. He and Kaladin lowered to some twenty feet off the ground, then proceeded, mountains on either side. They passed stonewalker plants for now—short, stout trees with leaves pulled in before the wind. Grass in tufts behind boulders or lying low in burrows.

But soon . . . soon they'd see . . .

Soil. Dirt breaking the stone. Mud running alongside washes, sediment filling the bottom of fissures. Here was where the highstorms finally surrendered, Shinovar bringing the great eastern tyrant of the skies to his knees. A place where the lazy rainfall—like a corpse that had already bled out—no longer contained the minerals that hardened into cremstone.

Here life could truly flourish. Szeth's breath caught, and two gloryspren appeared above him, as he spotted mosses growing on rocks, leading to a few scraggly weeds alongside the wash. Szeth cried out despite himself and canceled his Lashings, dropping with a *thump* to this patch of soil. After so many, *many* years, his booted feet fell not on blasphemous stone.

He hadn't realized how it would overwhelm him. He fell to his knees before the dandelions and stared at them.

Kaladin alighted on a rock nearby, confusionspren—like streaks of violet extending from a central point—expanding behind him. He couldn't know how beautiful this tiny plant was. Szeth reached out with trembling fingers and touched leaves that didn't pull back.

"What's wrong with that plant?" Kaladin asked. "Is this a sign of the problems in your homeland?"

"No," Szeth whispered. "It is merely a weed. The most beautiful of weeds . . ."

Kaladin glanced to the side, where his spren landed and appeared as a full-sized human in a skirted Bridge Four uniform, leggings underneath reaching down to mid-thigh. Szeth had not asked why she chose that form. It was not for him to question.

"Szeth," said a voice.

His spren. A highspren.

He still did not know its name. It had never been offered. It was not a distinction the highspren gave lightly, though some other Skybreakers had been granted the names of their spren.

"This emotion is unfitting of your station," the spren said, audible and visible only to him. "Do not spoil your dignity with base sentimentality. You serve the law."

Szeth, with effort, forced his hand away from the plant. He stood up. Voices. Had there ever been a time when his life hadn't been ruled by voices? Would he even know what to do if they stopped?

"You all right?" Kaladin said, hopping off his rock.

Oh, I'm fine! said the sword strapped to Szeth's back. *Thank you. Nobody has been paying attention to me today, but I'm famously patient. It comes from being a sword.*

Kaladin ignored the comment, stepping closer to Szeth.

"My spren," Szeth said, "wishes me to show better composure. I obey."

Szeth did not ask an explanation of the spren. He was Truthless no longer, but he still did as his masters required. He simply trusted that in the highspren and Dalinar, he had chosen better masters.

He stepped away as Kaladin knelt by the plant, Syl bending down next to him. The rising sun behind sent sunlight streaming through this valley into Shinovar, the land that swallowed that sun each night. Light created shadows—in the leeward side of stones, in crevices, and beneath the very blades of grass. As soon as he saw that, the whispers started once more.

Voices of those he'd killed. Condemning him.

Kaladin poked the plant with his toe. Then again. "I knew about these," he said to his spren. "Everyone mentions them. But it's so strange. Shouldn't it have been eaten by something?"

"Maybe it tastes really bad," Syl said. "Maybe that's why there are fewer proper plants in Shinovar. Our plants get eaten first, because they're delicious." She leaned over farther and tapped the plant, proving substantial enough to make it quiver.

"It's like a painting," Kaladin whispered.

"Or a statue," Syl said. "You think it was Soulcast? That it was once a real plant, and someone made it into this?"

Kaladin shook his head, then lifted his boot. Szeth found it amusing how Kaladin rammed his foot down, then stopped with a jerk a fraction of an inch from the plant. Trying to get it to flinch.

This is a man, Szeth thought, *who pulls back before crushing a weed.*

"No wonder you broke and gave up the spear," Szeth said, "leaving your friends to battle without you. You have grown into a coward, then?"

Kaladin pulled up sharply. "You shouldn't say such things."

"I should not speak truth?" Szeth said, genuinely curious. "Or are you saying I am not the one to tell you these things, as I have no authority over you? Interesting."

"That's *not* what I'm saying, Szeth," Kaladin said.

"Then you should stop talking," Szeth replied. "Because if you cannot explain what you mean, then why voice silly thoughts?"

Szeth walked on, and reminded himself not to underestimate this man's skill. Kaladin deserved at least some of his fearsome reputation. Before Szeth had died his first death, he had faced this man, fighting amid debris and breaking plateaus, red lightning crashing against white. Because of that day, Szeth's soul remained only loosely connected to his body—though his afterimage was less pronounced now. As if he were slowly healing from that revival.

"I think these plants are neat," Syl said. She seemed to be trying to distract Kaladin from his annoyance at Szeth—which was an odd emotion to be displaying in the face of true statements expressed clearly.

"I suppose we'll get used to them," Kaladin finally said, flying ahead without stepping on any plants. "They're supposed to be all over Shinovar, hiding among the normal plants."

Szeth hesitated. He couldn't help asking. "Hiding among normal plants?"

"What?" Kaladin said, turning in the air. "Oh. They can't hide, because they don't move? Still seems strange to me that they can survive. I know the storms aren't strong here, but people and animals are going to step on them."

"They're more resilient than you think," Szeth said.

"Yeah, but once the real plants retract," Kaladin said, "these will be sitting out in the open. Like the lone soldier in a company with no armor on."

Szeth contained his amusement—his spren would not be happy to see such an emotion—and instead joined Kaladin flying along the pass. Soon they reached a point where the path turned steeply downward, giving them a view—for the first time—of Shinovar itself.

Greenery covered the landscape. Vines across the valley walls; grass waving on the path. Trees below in a vast forest along the slope—beyond that the expansive open prairies of the lowlands. Kaladin and Syl landed beside Szeth.

"Here," Szeth said, "these *are* the normal plants. There are none like those you are accustomed to."

". . . All of them?" Kaladin said.

"All of them."

An awespren burst around Kaladin, then he started down the path, obviously excited. Szeth followed, though not because he was excited. This was merely where he had to be.

The whispers followed.

20
THREE VITAL POINTS OF DEFENSE

I let them pass with two lies.

—From *The Way of Kings*, fourth parable

The small meeting room—full of monarchs seated in a circle with an outer ring of highprinces, viziers, and lesser primes—grew absolutely still at Wit's words.

Navani held her breath. Was it possible? What did it mean? Odium was . . . a different person now?

Voices invaded her mind. The Sibling, and the Stormfather—whom she'd heard only twice before, his voice echoing with thunder.

Is it possible? the Sibling asked.

I . . . will look, said the Stormfather. *I must know. Rayse . . . he can't just be . . .*

Dead, the Sibling said. *If a new Vessel holds Odium, Rayse must be dead.*

Navani glanced at Dalinar, and he nodded. He'd heard both of them too.

"Wit," Navani said, leaning forward, "how certain are you?"

"I'm certain of *nothing,*" Wit replied from his place by the wall. "But this . . . this is *almost* certain."

It is true, the Stormfather said. *Odium is no longer Rayse.*

"You can tell?" Dalinar whispered, so Navani could hear too. "So easily?"

Yes. The tone has changed, only noticeable when I looked.

You . . . are right, the Sibling said. *I feel it. So subtle . . .*

I cannot identify the new Vessel, the Stormfather said. *Take care. And Rayse . . . Rayse is gone, after all this time.*

"You sound regretful," Navani whispered.

Only that my lightning did not strike his corpse, the Stormfather spat. *And my wind did not dash it against stones until it broke.*

His rumbling faded.

I miss how the Stormfather used to be, the Sibling said. *He was so much happier before. Not so angry all the time . . .*

"The Stormfather," Dalinar said to the room, "has confirmed Wit's intuition. Odium exists, but has changed hands. It's like . . . like how a spren can have a new Radiant."

"So . . ." Fen said, glancing around the circle, curled eyebrows shaking alongside her face. "Who cares?"

"Who cares?" Yanagawn said. "This is our greatest enemy!"

"Who is still trying to destroy us," she said, "as evidenced by the impending invasion. I never knew the old Odium, so it's basically the same."

"No," Wit said. "It's different."

Again all eyes turned to him as he rose and walked into the center of the circle. Even in a moment of stress like this, there was a certain showmanship to Wit.

"I knew the old Odium," he said, spinning around to look at them all. "Our entire plan—the contract, the contest—was based in part on that knowledge. Now . . . I'm frightened. The old Odium was deeply calcified into his position as a god—and was very unlikely to do anything that would risk that position. The new one was likely a mortal before their Ascension. They'll be more brash, more willing to take risks.

"More, they aren't quite bound in the same way. Oh, they'll have to keep this agreement for the contest of champions—a formal agreement like that binds the power, not just the individual, something Rayse himself discovered long ago. But lesser promises—like the one made to Dalinar about not exploiting loopholes—are a different matter. He is breaking that one easily, because he did not make it."

"So, wait," Navani said, trying to understand the details. "Can a god break a contract, or can they not?"

"Anyone, anywhere, *can,*" Wit explained. "God, human, spren. However, the *consequences* vary. For a deity, breaking a promise exposes them to destructive forces from others—and the magnitude of the broken promise often determines the severity of the consequence."

"So . . ." Fen said. "Can we call off this contest? I don't appreciate it allowing the conquering of my entire island if one city is captured."

"Yes, you have that *option,*" Wit said. "You always did—but if you break the contract, Odium can retaliate in person. He could bring the full force of his powers against you *without* risking retribution from other gods. Fen . . . he could kill every person on this planet with a flick of his wrist, if he wanted."

"Well," she said, sitting back. "That answers that."

"No breaking contracts with gods," Kmakl said from behind Fen. "I'll make a note of that . . ."

"And his broken promise not to use loopholes?" Dalinar asked. "We can't exploit that at all?"

"He can get away with that," Wit said. "And we can exploit our own, if we can find them. But that promise he made was not a formal agreement certified by oaths. This is the hand we're dealt. I'm sorry. I am not living up to my name. I should have seen this."

Storms, what a mess, Navani thought. "So if the enemy"—she tried to lay it out clearly—"can conquer the capitals of Azir, Thaylenah, or the Shattered Plains in the next eight days . . . he keeps the equivalent kingdom in its entirety. No matter the results of the contest?"

"Yes," Wit said. "According to Alethi law."

"Could we change capitals?" Navani said.

"That is a very clever idea," Wit told her. "Which only a very clever person would think of."

"Thank you, I . . ." She trailed off. "You've already thought of it, haven't you?"

"Yes," Wit said. "I asked my draconic friend, and got a negative response. How to explain this?" He thought a moment. "Alethi legal codes apply here, and they are an *absolute* mess. A snarl of self-contradictory codes, uncertain precedents, and *insane* laws that are still on the books because some drunk highprince thought they were amusing. Don't show them to the Azish. They'll have nightmares for weeks."

"Too late," Noura said. "I began studying them the moment we started this coalition."

"Here's the short of it," Wit said, holding up the written-out version of Dalinar's agreement with Odium. "This is immutable. This stands. What Odium's doing plays dirty, but does not break these rules. We could try to do something similar, but changing the capital—or one of a dozen other *very* clever things I came up with—would put us in violation."

"And," Kmakl said, "we shouldn't violate agreements with gods. I just made a note of it, even." He gave a wan smile.

Navani took a deep breath. "All right then, we're back to where we started—merely with a better understanding. Three armies are heading to three capitals. We need to defend all three for eight days, and hope there are no other big surprises in the contract."

"I will speak to my friend," Wit said. "I don't *think* there's anything else, but if there is, I will find it. Honestly, most of what she said was complimentary. The agreement was well done, this small item notwithstanding."

"The important point now is what to do next," Jasnah said.

"We stand united," Dalinar said, looking around the room. "And we do not give one inch of stone to him. Stargyle, let's have a map."

Stargyle stepped forward, and a brilliant, shimmering map of Roshar appeared in the center of the chamber.

What is this? the Sibling said in Navani's mind. *That is . . . that is incredible.*

Like the work of a master sculptor, the map had fine topographical detail. It could be zoomed in until you could see cities, and zoomed out until it seemed as if you were gazing down from the moons upon a tiny continent surrounded by blue waters.

Navani stood up, joining Dalinar and Stargyle at the side of the map. He really was mastering this—a few weeks ago, only Shallan had been capable of the feat. Across the map, Noura provided a taller stool for her emperor. As usual, the Mink stood and started walking straight through it—causing it to fuzz into Stormlight and churn in his passing, like eddies in a stream, until stabilizing again in place.

It wasn't accurate to the moment—this represented the world as it had been the last time the highstorm had passed. Still, its majesty took Navani's breath away every time—and she was pleased that the Sibling was similarly impressed.

I've encountered nothing like this, they said in her mind. *How? How can you do things the ancient Radiants never did?*

Science is usually the product of incremental advances, shared across a body of people working together, Navani said. *But sometimes that group limits you, because they make assumptions. I know there are many things we've lost that the ancient Radiants did better—but at the same time, we're not limited by their expectations.*

"All right," the Mink said. He was a shorter Herdazian man, lean of build, with a thin mustache and a wide, inviting smile—though his missing tooth and scarred wrists were a testament to the hardships he'd known. "First things first. Here are our current troop placements."

He pointed at Emul, to the south of Azir. "The largest group of coalition forces—with many of our Stonewards and Edgedancers—are *here.* They were fighting near the border with Tukar and Marat, and have been moving home for three days now. Some of those—our rear guard, forty thousand strong—are a six-day march from Azimir."

"Too far," Yanagawn said. "The enemy will arrive before then, and my forces are down to only a few thousand. We'll need reinforcement."

"Yes," Dalinar said, walking past Navani to the eastern side of Roshar. "But from where? The rest of the bulk of our troops are here, holding the borders of Alethkar in the Frostlands."

They'd been fighting an extended war against the enemy—and most of their clashes had been on these battle lines. Therefore, that was where their troops were. Urithiru had reserves and off-duty soldiers, but many of them had been slaughtered during the invasion and occupation. Navani had been with them trying to hold out, and the nightmare of seeing so many soldiers give their lives was a fresh wound. One she'd have to address someday, once the crisis was over.

If the crisis was ever over.

"We don't have many troops who can reach an Oathgate in time," Dalinar said. "We're stretched incredibly thin, and we can't move large bodies of troops quickly. Particularly not since we'll need the Windrunners for air support."

"We have scouts investigating each of the armies," the Mink continued. "The fleet sailing for Thaylenah has over two hundred ships. They're not good for naval combat—mostly troop transports—which is why the blockade worked for so long. Now that it's broken though, they could deliver forty thousand soldiers to Thaylen City."

"Storms," Fen whispered.

"The force moving for Azimir is, fortunately, smaller," the Mink said. "Approximately fifteen thousand, and barely a handful of Fused. It seems they wanted to take us by surprise. Finally, the force marching on the Shattered Plains is almost exclusively Fused—the most fearsome of the armies by far, though it's only a thousand individuals."

"But they attack a mostly barren region," Fen said.

"Not barren," Jasnah said. "That is the sole land my people have, in exile. Those are our lumberyards, our fields, and our new budding city at the warcamps. It's all we have."

"Still . . ." Fen said.

"Let's focus on the defense of Azir first," the Mink said, holding up his hand, strolling through the mountains and to the west. "The enemy will arrive midday tomorrow, best we can guess. You said you have . . . what, three thousand city defenders?"

Kzal—one of the viziers—replied, "Yes, General."

The Mink nodded to Dalinar and pointed. Navani stepped over as Dalinar zoomed the map in until they could almost make out the signs of warcamps on the flatlands south of Azimir.

"This large army of ours is five or six days away," the Mink mused. "If your forces in Azimir hold out until then, you'll win for certain. Even if you lose the city, that army of so many of our forces returning could maybe take it back . . ."

"We can't risk that though," Adolin said, rising from his seat among the highprinces in the second row. "We can't just let Azimir be taken, maybe burned." He walked through the map, and for some reason he'd summoned his Shardblade—and was whispering to it? Navani sidled closer, overhearing what sounded like a quiet narration of what he was seeing. How odd.

The Mink squatted down so he was eye level with the map. Navani wasn't certain what advantage this provided, but he liked to do it, looking across the landscape—in this case from the perspective of Azimir.

"This is not a trap," he said softly, smoothing his thin, greying mustache, "but the exploitation of an opportunity. They didn't deliberately draw your armies away into Emul, otherwise they'd have struck already. They must have sent this force through Shadesmar weeks ago. Ships do not materialize out of thin air."

They do there, the Sibling noted. *Though it requires Stormlight . . .*

"You have a strong position here, Yanagawn," Dalinar said, gesturing. "You may not have a lot of troops, but the enemy has to come through the Oathgate. The Skybreakers that were fighting in Emul have been withdrawn to strike at Thaylenah, and there are few Fused with the invading army, so you don't have enemy Invested to worry about. Plus, you have the Oathgate surrounded by that metal dome, right?"

"Yes," Yanagawn said. "But despite that, I'm afraid. They have five times our number of troops!"

"A fortification like that can be an excellent force multiplier," the Mink said. "But the average singer troop is stronger than a human one, with their warform armor. It will be a tight defense."

"Normally, striking directly at Azimir would be suicide," Dalinar said, stepping up beside the Mink. "And taking it wouldn't mean anything—it's in the heart of the empire. You can't expect success in an extended campaign if you're surrounded. But this isn't an extended campaign. They just have to seize Azimir and hold it for a few days."

"You are right," the Mink said, standing with his head peeking up through the illusory map. As if he were swimming. "This is an entire empire. You, Azish word people. What happens to your empire if Azir is conquered?"

The viziers conferred, then went to talk to Wit. Navani tapped her fingers together in thought, and didn't miss how several in the room—representatives of Emul, Yezier, Desh—murmured at this. All three were smaller kingdoms that were part of the complex Azish imperial state. They were autonomous in all but name: never overtly rejecting Azir's claims of dominance, but also not paying tax to the central kingdom, except occasional support for armies keeping the peace.

It had worked for centuries. The smaller kingdoms gained increased political clout and Azir was able to pretend it was in charge. The lesser primes deferred to the emperor in social matters, and Azish armies lent aid to nearby disputes.

No one said the quiet part: that there *was* no empire. Only a group of ethnically connected kingdoms who role-played as one.

Except now.

"Unfortunately," Noura said, with Wit looking sour behind her, "if Azimir falls, they all fall. An entire empire, captured in one bold move."

"We *can't* risk that," Adolin said, stepping into the center of Shinovar.

"What we can and cannot risk," the Mink said, "depends on the troops. Dalinar, how many can you reasonably provide in time?"

"Honestly?" Dalinar said. "Maybe twenty thousand."

"I *need* those troops," Fen said. "Thaylen City will fall without them." She glanced to Yanagawn. "I'm sorry, Your Excellency, but you have reinforcements only a few days' march from your door—and an excellent fortification with which to resist in the interim. My situation is far more dire."

"What exactly are your defenses?" Jasnah asked, still seated, taking notes for herself quietly.

"We have a skeleton of a navy left," Fen explained. "Our ground forces—such as they were—mostly fell at the Battle of Thaylen Field. Frankly, we're dependent on you for our defense now. As you all well know."

"We are establishing our situation, not trying to goad you," Jasnah said.

"Let us look at the third point of attack," the Mink said. "The Shattered Plains. These are well defended, no?"

"Very well defended," Dalinar said. "But I hate pitting conventional troops against Fused."

"If we lose the Shattered Plains," Jasnah said, "we lose our last foothold in eastern Roshar."

"Three vital points of defense," the Mink said, appearing tiny beside Dalinar. "And our military is strung out, blanketing hundreds of miles of borderlands. This isn't good, Dalinar."

Navani had read a lot of books on tactics out loud to her husbands, so she tried to figure out what Dalinar and the Mink would decide. Throw everything at Azir, perhaps? It had the fewest troops, and its Oathgate would soon stop functioning for the coalition forces. At Thaylenah, the enemy would need to perform an ocean assault and then break through the city walls. They'd done both during the Battle of Thaylen Field, but they would have a much harder time accomplishing that now, with the coalition ready for them. The same went for the Shattered Plains: Navani knew firsthand how difficult that territory was to crack.

But Azimir? With enemies flooding out of the Oathgate in the *center* of the city, mere yards from the palace? She thought Dalinar would put most of their forces there.

Dalinar and the Mink shared a glance. And from their expressions, Navani knew she was missing something. What?

"I see your concern, Uncle," Jasnah said from her seat, Wit just behind her, one hand on the back of her chair. "What is it?"

"We have limited troops we can mobilize on such short notice," Dalinar said. "If we spread ourselves too thin, we lose everything."

"We have to assume the forty thousand coming to Azimir will be enough," Jasnah said, seeming proud that she'd figured it out. "Because if we commit more troops there, they'll be locked away behind a nonfunctional Oathgate. A fate the forty thousand will already suffer. So we send only a few thousand to hold out there, and split the bulk of our forces across the other two fronts."

"Yes," the Mink said, sounding reluctant. "That is the best plan. A skeleton force to Azimir. The bulk of our conventional troops to Thaylen City to hold the walls—which are useless without troops on them."

Yanagawn stood up from his throne. "This leaves us alone! Least defended! Abandoned!"

"Your Excellency," Dalinar said, turning, "we're *not* abandoning you. We're not making decisions right now, merely working through our options. But the truth is, you have that excellent fortification surrounding the Oathgate, and you have forty thousand friendly troops on your doorstep. Along with all of the Radiants who were fighting alongside them."

"We walk a delicate line," the Mink said. "If we overcommit to Azir, which will soon have far more troops than it needs anyway, we'll lose everything else. We must do all we can to hasten the force already on its way to Azimir, and *not* leave everything else undefended. Navani, how confident are you in the tower's natural defenses?"

Sibling? she asked.

The lights in the room dimmed. A glowing column of light appeared from a glass disc in the ceiling, extending to a matching one below. The Sibling's voice spoke to all of them. "They will not come here. Fused will fall unconscious. Regals will have their forms stripped from them. Even common singers will lose access to their rhythms, and my beats can drive them mad. They know that. Now that I've returned, they *know.*"

The room stilled. Well, that seemed a step forward. Only a few days ago, the Sibling would barely speak to Navani.

"That sounds conclusive," the Mink said. "So, Dalinar, we *can* empty Urithiru of your twenty thousand and send the bulk of them to shore up Thaylenah. We cannot lose the island—if we do, we will give up the seas entirely. The Shattered Plains might be able to handle themselves. We can pull in some outlying forces, centralize at Narak."

"Pardon," Sigzil said, "but the scout reports are frank. The fight at the Shattered Plains will face thunderclasts, Heavenly Ones, Deepest Ones, and more. That's suicide for conventional troops without support."

"He's right," Dalinar said. "We'll need our Radiants there—to counter their Invested."

"And Azir?" Yanagawn said from where he stood. "We defend Thaylenah and the Shattered Plains, but what do we send to my homeland? You mentioned at least a skeleton force to help me hold until the army arrives?"

"Yes," Dalinar said, rubbing his chin. "I think your fight is the most winnable. That dome fortification is incredible."

"I disagree," the Mink said. "The defense will be more difficult than you think, Dalinar. The dome will offer a clear killing field, but singer forces are well armored, good versus arrows. If you were defending against humans, you could hold it easily. Against singers?" He shook his head.

"Yes, but a small number of troops *should* be able to hold a few days," Dalinar said, gesturing toward Azimir on the map. "We must send the bulk of our troops to Thaylen City to man the walls, but what if we sent the *best* of our troops to that dome?"

"I don't know," the Mink said. "One misstep, and that dome will fill with enemies like a boil on a finger, waiting to pop. Then they'll flood into the very heart of the city. No, I wouldn't want to try to hold that. It could be a waste. We maybe should send nobody, evacuate, and then let the returning army of forty thousand reclaim Azimir once they arrive."

"That's too much of a risk," Yanagawn said. "What if it were your homeland, Dieno?"

The Mink looked up. Then took a deep breath and nodded. "Yes, you are right. Of course you are right. I'm sorry—sometimes a love of tactics overshadows the heart. We must do what we can. Our best, then, to Azir. Enough to hold, but not so much to weaken other fronts. But who will lead them?"

A beat, the room quiet. Navani held her breath.

"I'll go," Adolin said, stepping into the illusion. "Father, let me recruit two thousand. I'll ask for volunteers for what might be a difficult fight, and gather the best of them. With them and the Cobalt Guard, I'll go to Azir and *hold* that city until reinforcements arrive."

Dalinar glanced at Navani; the Mink's words seemed to have unnerved him. "What of the other two battlefronts," he said at last. "Who leads those armies? I will need to prepare for my contest, and I suspect I won't be available."

"I'm no general," Fen said. "And Kmakl is a navy man. I'd like some generals with ground force experience."

"What about me?" Jasnah said, finally rising. "I've fought in Thaylen City before. I could go, bring generals to determine our strategy, and take command of the twenty thousand there."

Navani held her tongue. Jasnah had been eager for chances to prove herself as a tactician—as if she didn't have enough to occupy her mind. Still, Jasnah was perhaps the most dangerous Radiant they had.

"A good choice," Dalinar said. "Fen, what do you think?"

"We'd welcome the queen," Fen said. "Especially if I can get Stonewards to seal up breaches in the wall, should it get knocked down again."

"We have a few," Dalinar said, likely doing the mental math. They didn't have as many Stonewards as they did Edgedancers and Windrunners, and most were already in the group marching for Azimir. "I can send those, along with some Edgedancers to heal the wounded."

"Excellent," Jasnah said, settling back down. "I'll begin forming a strategy, and discuss it with our generals."

"Windrunner Sigzil," Dalinar said. "You take command of the Shattered Plains."

". . . Sir?" Sigzil said.

"We'll want a Radiant in command there. I'll send the Stormwall to back you up, and you can rely on our generals for tactics. But the Windrunners are our largest and most decorated group of Radiant soldiers. You should lead."

"Sir," Sigzil said, saluting.

"And me, Father?" Adolin asked, stepping closer. "Why do you hesitate?"

"I'm just thinking," Dalinar said, and Navani could tell he didn't want to get into it in front of everyone.

"Have I failed you too many times?" Adolin asked.

"I didn't say . . ." Dalinar took a deep breath.

"Majesty," Yanagawn said to Dalinar, his tone fierce. "Your son is the most accomplished swordsman in Alethkar, perhaps the world. He was trained in warfare by the Blackthorn himself. I'm certain my generals would welcome his aid."

Navani wasn't so certain. She'd seen how jealous soldiers could get when someone outside their command structure showed up and took charge, but she held her tongue.

"Father," Adolin said, "the enemy at Azimir won't have many Fused. In Shadesmar I saw some Heavenly Ones, but mostly ships full of common soldiers. We *can* contain them. Let me go."

Dalinar towered over the center of the map. Eventually he nodded. "A good plan. You may go, son. And you may recruit up to two thousand of our best, as you wish."

"Excellent," Adolin said.

"Thank you!" Yanagawn said. "We should start now! We cannot waste time!"

"The next few hours will be critical," Dalinar said. "If the monarchs are agreed, we can break this meeting for now—though send your generals in to speak with the Mink and me. We will spend the next few hours going over strategy for each battlefield in detail."

Immediately the Azish contingent started moving, picking up their seats. Adolin started to join them, then hesitated at the edge of the map.

He and Dalinar locked gazes. *Just go hug him,* Navani thought, stepping up to Dalinar and putting her hand to the small of his back. *Wish him the best. Tell him you believe in him.*

Neither spoke. Then Adolin spun on his heel and hurried toward the door. Navani sighed.

"What?" Dalinar said to her. "He wants little to do with me these days, Navani. It's best I let him go."

"He *needs* his father," Navani said. "Regardless of what he *wants.* You're simply going to let him walk out?"

"We don't have time for his drama, Navani," Dalinar said. "Whatever I do, it won't be good enough for him. I fear if I ask him for something, he'll do the opposite. I . . ."

He trailed off as he noticed that Adolin had stopped by the door. To Navani's delight, he turned around and came back. "Father," he said reluctantly, "Shallan sent me with a message you need to hear."

Navani felt her eyes widen as Adolin gave a brief—far *too* brief, for her taste—recounting of some things Shallan had told him. A group of foreign spies, working for offworld interests, in Urithiru? Recruiting Shallan when she was still new, and isolated, on the Plains?

That girl. That storming girl. She should have *come* to them with this. Navani forced her anger down. Shallan had, for better or worse, been trained by Jasnah—who kept these kinds of secrets as a matter of course.

"She's moving against them now," Adolin said. "She needs authorization for an operation and a Radiant strike force."

"I don't like the idea," Dalinar said, "of authorizing a strike on a group I barely know anything about. It means putting a lot of trust in someone who has apparently been lying to us all."

"Something," Adolin said, "you know absolutely nothing about."

Inwardly, Navani groaned. The two met each other's eyes, and she considered intervening. But storms, they were going to work it out eventually themselves.

"You're supposed to be above gibes like that, son," Dalinar said softly. "I raised you to be better."

"Raised me?" Adolin said. Angerspren pooled like blood at his feet—one of the few varieties of spren that ignored her orders. "You didn't *raise* me, Father. You killed the woman who did."

Dalinar winced. "This isn't the time."

"It could be," Navani said, wanting to grab them both by the arms and tow them off to talk until they worked it out.

"No," Adolin agreed. "Not right now. Father, I want you to authorize Shallan's strike. Time is of the essence. Please."

Dalinar sighed, then nodded. "We'll reach out to her for what she needs."

Storms, they seemed so *close.* Finally, Dalinar opened his mouth. Her heart leaped, expecting the apology. Instead it was a gruff, "You might need help with the Azish. You don't speak their language."

"I can get an interpreter."

"I can do better," Dalinar said, taking him by the shoulder. Stormlight streamed off Dalinar. "I can give you a Bondsmithing to help. It won't work anywhere but in Azir, but while you're there, it will let you understand them. It should last a few weeks."

Adolin grunted. They stared one another in the eyes. Then, Adolin nodded and left without another word.

Navani sighed, her heart bleeding for them.

"Why?" she asked Dalinar. "Why don't you say more?"

"He always throws it back at me," Dalinar said, his thumb and forefinger massaging his forehead. "And in a way, he's right, Navani. I *didn't* raise him. He was always just . . . so perfect, all on his own. Or with Evi's help, I suppose. I now realize I never did anything other than order him around."

"And letting it fester will make it better?"

"I don't know," he admitted. "But this really *isn't* the time. I've got a strategy meeting I need to lead. After that, though, I need to tell you about something even more important." He seemed concerned. "I need your counsel. That of Jasnah and Wit too, maybe Fen."

She frowned. "What is this?"

"On the way to the meeting today," Dalinar said, his expression distant, "I encountered a god . . ."

21 INCOMPLETE TRUTHS

First, I dared not tell them this dusty traveler with whom they shared a meal was in fact that very king they had heard of. The second was that I did not explain that very king had abdicated his throne and walked away from his kingdom.

—From *The Way of Kings*, fourth parable

Shallan and her team—the best she had, without Vathah and Ishnah, who were still in Shadesmar—spent the next few hours planning. Then it was finally time.

Her team of five made their way to an Oathgate outside Urithiru, hiding among a larger group of soldiers being transferred to Narak to reinforce it. She led with outward confidence, though deeper inside she acknowledged she was terrified. Mraize and Iyatil had manipulated her before. They had a nearly supernatural understanding of politics on Roshar—including the politics between gods.

Where other groups had made bids for kingdoms, the Ghostbloods made bids for worlds—or for control of economic forces as big as those worlds. This was what terrified Shallan. Not the things that she worried they'd do. The things she was too *ignorant* to worry they'd do.

These thoughts haunted her, accompanied by anxietyspren, as light flashed around them and they transferred to Narak—the city at the center of the Shattered Plains. It had been a year and a half since Dalinar's fateful expedition and the events that had summoned the Everstorm. Since then, Narak had become a fortress. With Stonewards, they'd expanded the Oathgate platform a good ten feet. Then it and each of the central cluster of plateaus had been turned into a defensive bastion lined by Soulcast walls, attended by troops in towers.

A lighteyed captain shouted at them to get moving, seeing Shallan and the other four as just another squad of spearmen. They hiked off the Oathgate platform with the others, entering the new ring of ground around the plateau where people could wait their turn to transfer. Here Shallan and her team broke off, heads up, acting like they belonged. They crossed the bridge to Narak Four, a nearby plateau that had its own towering circular wall.

"Looks like a chouta roll," Red said from behind her.

"What are you on about?" Gaz said.

"The walls around these plateaus," he said. "Makes them look like a bunch of chouta rolls. You know, open at the top? Stuffed with meat."

"And we're the meat?" Darcira asked, her voice masked by a Lightweaving to sound masculine.

"Sure," Red said.

"They're too stocky to look like chouta," Darcira said. "More like shalebark ridges. Oh! Tree stumps, where the center has rotted out."

"Or, you know," Gaz grumbled, "like the warcamps. Where we lived for years?"

"Oh, yeah!" Red said.

"Circular walls," Darcira said, "soldiers everywhere . . . Nah, don't see it."

"You two are buffoons," Gaz said. "I should have stayed a storming deserter. At least out in the wilds, everyone was too depressed to make small talk."

Shallan hushed them as they reached the end of the bridge, where they presented falsified orders to the sergeant and scribe on watch at the gate. Darcira had waved them into existence on a sheet, a perfect replica. Though Shallan, via Adolin, had permission from the Bondsmiths, she wasn't going to trust anyone she didn't need to. Anyone here could be in Ghostblood employ.

The sergeant waved Shallan and her group through, and they entered Narak Four: a distinctive plateau covered in ancient buildings once so enveloped in crem that they'd looked like smooth mounds. A little creative application of Shardblades had unearthed the original stone buildings, providing room for barracks and a small marketplace, carefully regulated by Navani and the military.

Shallan and her team made a show—for the sergeant idly watching by the gates—of walking to their assigned barrack. They came out on the other side wearing the faces and clothing of crem scrapers: the easy-to-ignore, lowly workers that kept a place like this clean. As they moved into position, they were joined by Jayn—a Riran woman whom Shallan had recruited to the Unseen Court eight months ago. She'd been sent ahead to watch the Ghostblood hideout.

"They're continuing to gather, Brightness," Jayn said softly, also disguised as a crem scraper. "I've seen five or six people enter the building over the last half hour."

Shallan nodded. Reports said someone was at the doorway, using black sand to check everyone who entered. That made Lightweaving tricky, as the sand could reveal uses of Radiant powers.

To maintain their disguises, her team began leveling a patch of road near the hideout with chisels, removing the crem, plants, and lichens that grew on the stone. Gaz used posts with string between to section off their working area, diverting foot traffic, letting them chat without worrying about being overheard.

Shallan took the role of foreman, walking around, checking on the other five as they worked. In reality she watched that hideout, a supposed storehouse of no importance. Two more people arrived, including a shorter uniformed Alethi man she recognized from Hoid's sketches. The second was a member of the Azish Prime's retinue—a vizier even, though not one of the very important ones like Noura. Shallan took a Memory of him, so she could add a drawing of the man to their stack.

Mraize had rarely let Shallan meet anyone but him, isolating her from what was proving to be a distressingly large network, including people among most of the major political organizations on Roshar. The best she knew, their primary goal was to find a way to begin shipping Stormlight offworld, but that—though likely a potential source of great riches—seemed too small-scale for Mraize and Iyatil.

The front door of the hideout had a sheltered porch, with a dark shadow just inside. When each new Ghostblood arrived at the door, a short, cloaked figure stepped from the shadows and inspected them. Shallan caught a hint of a painted wooden mask, and the shape of the figure looked female. That confirmed Darcira's observations: it was either Iyatil or, more likely, the woman among the other two.

The door guard inspected each of the two newcomers by touching their faces to check for discrepancies in their features. Then they held up a jar of black sand.

Shallan huddled with Darcira, Gaz, Red, and Jayn as they labored. They pretended to be working on a particularly stubborn section of ground together while Jeneh kept watch. Their spren had instructions to ride on the insides of clothing to remain hidden.

"All right," Shallan said. "This is our last chance to back out."

"This won't be like infiltrating the Sons of Honor," Gaz added. "That group was already dying when we put them down. This might be the most dangerous organization on the planet. I . . . worry we should go to ground, hide from them. Wait out the coming storm. I'm not sure we're ready."

"What do the rest of you think?" Shallan asked.

"I think," Red said, "that nobody *ever* feels ready for big operations. Storms, you think half those boys on the walls feel ready to fight a war? The question isn't if we're ready, but if it needs to be done."

Gaz grunted. "That's true, I suppose. Red, you need to stop saying things that are smart. You'll upend my entire opinion of you."

Red smiled, continuing to work with his chisel, scraping away crem. He had experience with tools like this, having trained as a craftsman during his youth.

"I think our plan is good," Darcira said. "I say we move forward." She was an unusual one, a scientist who had shown talent for Lightweaving and left the ardents to join Shallan. She was the only one in the Court who tended to draw logicspren as often as creationspren.

"I'm worried about how many people are in there," Jayn said. "Shallan, you will be completely outnumbered. Do we really need to do this?"

"In just over eight days," Shallan said softly, "Dalinar Kholin will fight the champion of Odium to decide the fate of the world. The Ghostbloods, best we can determine, are the most dangerous secret political force on the planet. So . . ."

"They're going to be involved somehow," Red said. "They'll have some plan to compromise the contest. I'm in." His spren hummed from where he rode on the inside of Red's jacket. Array didn't say much, and as far as Shallan had been able to tell, he didn't hum when he tasted lies—he seemed to like *alliteration* of all things.

"Mraize and Iyatil are accustomed to the luxury of darkness and shadow," Shallan said. "We need to expose them, naked for the world to see. So long as they have a monopoly on information, they *will* control us. And if we're always reacting to them, never attacking, they *will* beat us." She paused, some of Mraize's own words returning to her memory. "Prey can only ever run. It can survive, but it can never win. Not so long as the predator lives."

"Sure," Gaz said, "but we could just send the Radiant strike team in. I hate relying on Windrunners for anything other than transportation—and then they still usually find a way to squeeze in a lecture or two. But . . . we could defer to them this time, Shallan."

"We will use them," Shallan said. "But Gaz, if we bring in soldiers first, then my gut says Mraize and Iyatil will find a way to escape. Even if they don't, they'll never talk. We could throw them in prison for a decade, and those two would keep their silence. I need to know what they're planning. I *need* to get into that meeting."

She'd learned some of what she hungered for, yes. Kelek, and her own recovered memories, gave her pieces—but there was so much *more.* Worlds' worth. She thirsted for the chance to at least once hear them talking freely.

Beyond that . . . they were planning something. Why was that woman spying on Dalinar? Why did they want Ba-Ado-Mishram? Would bursting in with swords out and powers ablaze stop their plans? Maybe. Maybe not. It depended on what pieces were already in motion.

"Storm it," Gaz said. "You're right. I'm in."

Gaz and Red were among her oldest friends, and among their most experienced Lightweavers. She knew Gaz well enough to tell his objections were real—he *was* concerned about this mission. But he also was objecting in part so that the concerns could be voiced, then overcome.

"I'm in too," Jayn said. "Though the real danger is to you, Brightness."

"I can handle it," Radiant said. "We are a go, then. Hopefully they haven't started discussing anything important."

Her team had talked about this. The Ghostbloods couldn't bring everyone over through the Oathgates at once. A group would draw too much attention, and since the attendees were still trickling in, she hoped Mraize was still waiting.

Darcira covertly checked her clock—which, like many scholars, she wore on one of Navani's arm bracer fabrials. "The next Oathgate transfer is a bit over a half hour from now, and our surveillance spotted a few important members of the Ghostbloods—at least ones that Wit thought were important—hanging out in the grand entryway of Urithiru, as if waiting their turn. They're likely to be in that next batch, which gives us just enough time to set up phase two."

"Let's work for a few minutes longer," Gaz suggested. "Else it's suspicious we set up here."

Shallan nodded in agreement, and started to actually scrape. It was surprisingly hard work—but she did get a particularly defiant rockbud free, forcing her chisel underneath and finally prying it loose. A low rain had started to mist the air, though after the highstorm last night, the next wouldn't be due for a few days. Weather had been odd since the coming of the Everstorm, and rain like this was more common.

Pattern hummed softly from within her jacket, though she couldn't tell why. This next part would be difficult. She'd never heard of that strange black sand before their planning meeting earlier, but apparently it had been used to spot hidden spren toward the end of Urithiru's occupation.

Whether the sand was in jars with guards, or sprinkled along the inside of windowsills, it would change color if any intelligent spren came near. Lesser spren apparently weren't noticeable, but Cryptics absolutely would be. Worse, it revealed Lightweavings.

Shallan wasn't terribly surprised—she'd seen Wit use something similar once, and had always wondered at the mechanics. Unfortunately, it meant she had to do the hardest part without her powers or her spren.

 "Time to move, then," Shallan said, standing. "Let's go."

⁂

Sigzil did his best to pretend he was Kaladin.

He stood tall during the long strategy meeting that followed the initial discussion of the monarchs, and he tried to act like he understood more than he did. Kaladin was always so sure of himself. He always knew the next step to take.

Sigzil couldn't do that, but he could pretend enough to keep the anxietyspren away. Act like he belonged among monarchs, generals, and the storming *Prime Aqasix of the Azish Empire*.

Sigzil's mother would laugh at him; he read the amusement in her letters. Him? A military man? Her studious little boy, so delicate and refined? Even in Azir, he'd been made fun of for his persnickety ways. Yet here he was, shoulder to shoulder with a group of generals.

"Someone," he whispered to himself, "is going to eventually discover I'm a fraud, won't they?"

"You're not a fraud," Vienta, his spren, whispered to him—remaining invisible, as she often did.

"I'm a failed scholar, a mediocre Worldsinger, and a persnickety perfectionist who drives the others up the wall. I . . ."

"Did you survive Bridge Four?"

"Yes," he whispered. "Through pain and storm, I survived."

"Then you can survive this."

"But to lead them?" he asked.

"What do you think," she said softly, "was the *result* of that pain and fire? You are a leader now, Sigzil. You are a hero. Live that truth."

As the meeting moved toward a break, Sigzil found himself standing with Kmakl, the Thaylen prince consort, at the edge of the large glowing map.

"What I don't get," Kmakl was saying to Ka, the Windrunner scribe, "is where their troops came from."

Across the room, Brightlord Dalinar, Brightness Navani, Queen Jasnah, and Queen Fen retreated to a smaller chamber to discuss something sensitive. The Azish Prime had left a short time before, to return to his city. He wasn't generally involved in detailed battle plans.

"Their troops get reborn," Ka said, poring over the scout reports. She made notations with her silver pen, one of the most interesting uses of a Shardblade among the Windrunners to date. It had a cartridge to fill with ink and everything. She chose to wear a blue havah embroidered with the Bridge Four symbol on the shoulder, one of the new uniforms Kaladin had authorized.

There was an Azish-inspired one as well, which Sigzil could have worn. Their most recent recruits were from all across Roshar, and Sigzil himself had made the point that the Windrunners shouldn't be perceived as an Alethi group. So why didn't he wear that instead of the uniform he'd been given all those months ago? Was it because of the tattoo on his forehead?

Bridge Four was the only place I ever felt like a person rather than an accident, he thought. But without Kaladin, Rock, Teft, Moash . . . was it really Bridge Four anymore? All he wanted was to be back at that fire, sitting with his friends and listening to Rock gently make fun of him for counting the chunks of meat in bowls of stew to make sure everyone was getting proper nutrition.

"Brightlord?" Kmakl asked him. "Is everything all right?"

"Yes," Sigzil said, clasping his hands behind his back, forcing his attention onto the logistics. "You were saying they have too many troops? I think Ka is correct. Their Fused can be reborn; they'll *always* have more troops than we do."

"True, true," Kmakl said. "But with the number of Fused marching on the Shattered Plains, those troop transports coming for Thaylen City will be filled with ordinary singers. They'll be thrown at our battle lines like bait to be caught in our nets. Poor souls. They *have* to be running out of frontline soldiers, don't they?"

"Apparently not," Ka said. "How do we distribute our Windrunners? Sigzil?"

"Thaylen City will need at least one squad, maybe an entire company," Sigzil said. "The enemy will probably move some Skybreakers to the Shattered Plains, now that the blockade is broken, but an air force *will* guard those troop transports during the crossing. So we should be ready to match them once they reach Thaylen City, to not cede air superiority."

He wished they had more variety to their Radiant forces. Yes, they had Windrunners and Edgedancers aplenty, and a growing force of Stonewards and Lightweavers. The other orders were largely empty though.

"The enemy will have a difficult landing at my homeland," Kmakl said. "That's when they'll be most vulnerable. We'll burn the docks and lay hullrippers in the shallows. When they land, we go back to the walls."

"They smashed those open with thunderclasts last time," Ka noted. "But I have an idea. We could assign our Windrunners to another battlefield until the enemy arrives at yours—forcing them to waste Skybreakers guarding their ships for days."

"A clever idea," Kmakl said. "With Oathgates at both the Shattered Plains and Thaylen City, we can transfer troops between battlefields as necessary." He glanced up, toward where the Azish contingent had been earlier.

Considering, perhaps, Sigzil thought, *what the Mink said. About Azimir being a tougher defense than it looked.* It would be the only one of the three unable to receive support from the other battlefields, as its Oathgate would soon cease functioning. At least they'd have an entire army arriving to help in a few days.

Sigzil had to worry about stretching his Windrunners too thin. The battle at the Shattered Plains was going to be a strange one, full of so many Fused. And somehow he had to lead that defense.

"We can use the Oathgates," Ka noted, "but we will want to be very careful with them. We've had one too many instances of 'Wait, how'd these pesky enemy forces get here in the squishy part of my rear lines?' I think we should assign some people to keep talking to each Oathgate spren, to hopefully prevent any other defections. What do you think, Sigzil?"

What did he think? He glanced at her, and heard his spren's words echoing in his mind.

Live that truth.

Storm him, it was time to stop being unsure of himself, wasn't it? It was time to stop fidgeting. He'd been put in command.

He needed to act like it.

"I think you're right," he said. "And also . . . Ka, I have an idea about the defense of Narak. Where I'm in command. It's a strange one, but I think it might work."

"Excellent," Ka said. "If so, we should run it past the Mink."

Kmakl scanned the room. "I have some questions to ask him too. But . . . has anyone seen him?"

Storms. The little man had vanished yet again.

⁂

Jasnah—with Dalinar, Navani, and Fen—entered a room full of plants and bobbing lifespren.

It had once been an ordinary room, but upon the Sibling's awakening, it had transformed. The stone of the ceiling looked transparent, replicating the sun—making you feel like you were standing beneath a skylight. But that sun didn't move, and didn't match the true position outside.

Fragments of glowing white light embedded in the stone made the walls and ceiling sparkle, and plants had begun to sprout from the stonework—vines and rockbuds, moss and even grass in patches. All growing with incredible speed.

"I heard of this place long ago," Ivory said, his voice soft but audible from where he—shrunken to tiny size—rode on her earring. "The tower likes to experiment with what a room should be, building strange landscapes. I thought the stories fancies."

"This is growing into something of a mess," Dalinar said from the center of the room, where vines were curling around his legs. "Can we ask the Sibling to tone it down?"

"They'd rather not," Navani said.

The room vibrated, and a quiet voice echoed from the air vents near the floor. "It is a room for my sister, should she visit. A room for the Nightwatcher."

"Very well," Dalinar said, with his firmest voice. His *you really should listen to me and do as I say, but I'll pretend you doing otherwise doesn't bother me* voice. "We appreciate your willingness to make the tower function."

"I did not have much choice in the matter," the Sibling said. "But I did have some. So you are welcome."

Queen Fen took a chair from those piled near some tables on the far side, pulling it free of the foliage. They'd used this smaller chamber off the meeting room for storage. Jasnah stepped softly, trying to imagine the Nightwatcher visiting, enjoying the abundance of life. Had it ever happened? The Sibling and the tower had shut down just before the Recreance, over two *thousand* years ago.

"When was the Nightwatcher created?" Jasnah whispered to Ivory. "We call her the Old Magic, but how long has she been around? When did Cultivation form her?"

Before Ivory could answer, a voice whispered back from a nearby air vent. "The Nightwatcher came from the Night, as the Stormfather came from the Wind. Though, when I was young, the Wind was different. So very different."

"When were you created, Sibling?" Jasnah asked.

"Some six thousand years ago, when the Stones wanted a legacy in the form of a child of Honor and Cultivation. Back when Bondsmiths bonded not to spren, but to the ancient forces, left by gods."

"And the Stormfather?"

"Soon before me."

"That's inaccurate though," Jasnah said. "Dalinar speaks of the Stormfather having existed when people first came to Roshar, *seven* thousand years ago. The Stormfather remembers that event, and detailed the timing."

"It has been confusing," the Sibling said, "to learn of all that has happened while I slept. I knew the Stormfather when he was young. I, formed from the Stone, which was the sibling of Wind and Night. The Night left. Few loved her, or even spoke of her, and it seems Mother replaced her with a being of some of the same essence. A new creature, unconnected to anyone's perception.

"Now, the Stormfather has changed, and the Nightwatcher has not spoken to me as she used to. My siblings are no longer as I remember. I hate that."

Something about those timelines itched at Jasnah. Something that made her want to gather the other Veristitalians and set them to work, searching for primary sources. First, though, her uncle had something he wanted to say. She and Navani turned to Dalinar, in the center of the room, who had his eyes closed. It looked as if he were hovering beneath a sea of lights, grass rippling around his feet.

"Uncle?" Jasnah asked.

"I am not ready," he said, opening his eyes, "to fight Odium."

"I don't know what preparation we can make, given the deadline," Navani said. "A deadline you agreed to."

"Yes. I did." He seized a chair from a stack beside some tables draped in tablecloths, the whole pile shifting as he jerked it free, and Jasnah heard a distinctive *eep* from them. They weren't alone.

Of course they weren't. That girl seemed able to wiggle in anywhere. Jasnah glanced into Shadesmar, and saw Lift there—manifesting as a glowing light like a candle's flame. Alongside someone else. Curious.

"Even when I agreed to the contract," Dalinar said, setting the chair down for Navani, then fetching another, "I was uncertain, but the chance was too valuable to pass up. Now that I've seen one of my mistakes—not preventing this assault—I fear there are more, regardless of what Wit says."

"What is it I say?" Wit said, slipping into the room, carrying snacks. That was why he'd sneaked off, delaying them? Really? He handed her a plate of fruit. "I hope whatever it is that you said that I said, it was either nasty or clever. Or both. I honestly prefer both."

"I am worried Odium will outmaneuver me," Dalinar replied. He glanced at Jasnah and nodded toward the seats, with a question in his eyes. She nodded back, so he fetched her one.

Curious, how he'd changed. She'd read of times when he wouldn't have worried about anyone else. She'd known him throughout her adulthood as the man who would take care of people even when they didn't want it. Now, for the first time she could remember, he *asked* if she wanted his help. Because he knew that sometimes she disliked it when people did things for her that she would rather have done for herself.

She took her seat. Fen pulled over her chair, and Wit placed a small table and arranged food on it in an artistic way, because of course he did. Jasnah realized, absently, that she *was* hungry. They'd all likely forgotten breakfast in the chaos.

Once in a while, it *was* nice to have someone take care of you. She didn't blame others for getting confused about what she wanted; she regularly confused herself. So today, she enjoyed the plate of fruit.

Wit brought over a chair and spun it around the wrong way before settling down among them. When in public, he acted the proper Wit, standing behind her chair, deferring to her. In a setting like this . . . well, whatever he was, it was above a queen or a highprince. He didn't need to say it: he could sit among them. They all knew it by now, including Fen, who looked at him the way one might at an eel that could strike at any moment.

"You are wise to be worried," Wit said to Dalinar. "I am troubled by this new Odium. The power will remember me and hate me, no matter who is at the helm—but the new Vessel stole several of my memories, then *let me assume* that I'd bested them. This tells us a little of their personality. Not gloating, though the power would probably have enjoyed that."

"The power . . . can think?" Jasnah asked.

"Yes," Wit said. "Ask your spren what happens if fragments of a god are left to their own devices for too long. They stand up, start walking about, and start riding around in people's earrings. They start *caring*.

"Each 'god' is a slice of a greater entity killed some ten thousand years ago, its power divided. Those fragments have Identities, Intents. Honor: the instinct to make bonds and keep them. Odium: a god's divine wrath, uncoupled from essential moderating factors like mercy and love."

"I met another one earlier," Dalinar said. "On my way up here: Cultivation appeared to me in the form of a woman."

Jasnah came alert, palafruit halfway to her mouth. "*Cultivation* spoke to you?" she said. "*That's* why you called me in here?"

"I believe so," Dalinar said. "She looked the same. Sounded the same. Felt the same. It could be a trick of some sort, I admit, but . . . there was something about the meeting . . ."

"And she said . . ." Wit prodded.

"She told me I needed to seek the Spiritual Realm," Dalinar said. "That I didn't need to expand my powers as a Bondsmith so much as I needed to expand my understanding, particularly of the past. I cannot travel through time, but I *can* travel the visions. I can see how the Heralds and Radiants dealt with Odium before. She implied I've been on this path for years without realizing it, and if I learn correctly, I will know how to defeat Odium."

Storms. Jasnah thought of the wonder of being able to travel to other times. She'd dedicated her whole life to studying the past as a way to understand the future. Her efforts, though successful at times, had always been uncertain. Akin to searching shadows for shapes to interpret.

Through Dalinar's visions, she could see what had made those shapes. It wasn't *actually* traveling to the past, but the possibilities offered . . . "Can you visit any other times though? I thought the visions were more rigid than that."

"I thought so too," Dalinar said. "But recently I've found the Stormfather's words about them to be full of . . . well, not contradictions. Incomplete truths. Cultivation implied there was much more to see and learn."

"Everything exists in three realms," Wit said. "Physical, where we live now. Shadesmar, the Cognitive Realm, where minds project their impressions. Finally, the Spiritual Realm. The realm of our souls, our links to our past and to other people.

"The Spiritual Realm is a dangerous, confusing place. Every event in the past still echoes in there, yes, just as the scars upon the body are a record of past wounds. However, when you travel the visions with the Stormfather, Dalinar, you do so in a very carefully prescribed way. To deviate from that course risks getting lost in a place with no directions, no lifelines. A place where even I, as one of the ancients, tread cautiously."

"Would it really be helpful?" Navani asked. "Dalinar, didn't the Stormfather imply that the visions can't show you anything he doesn't know? So what could you learn?"

"It does seem like a risk," Fen added. "For something so nebulous."

"There . . . is more," Dalinar said, his hands clasped before him. "Something else that Cultivation said. What happened to Honor, Wit? What *truly* happened at his death?"

"I don't know," Wit admitted, his voice soft, arms crossed before him on the back of his chair. "I was off-planet for the event, to my eternal shame. Other matters drew my attention, and I let the centuries slip away from me. He was erratic when I left. When I returned . . ." He shrugged. "Gone. The Radiants broken. The world in turmoil following the Recreance. I've been trying to catch up ever since."

"And . . . do you know the location of his power?" Dalinar asked.

Wit didn't respond immediately. He took a deep breath and cocked a smile at the corner of his lips. "So. She nudged you in that direction, did she?"

"She did," Dalinar said. "If we are to fight a god, would it not be best to have one on our side?"

Wait, Jasnah thought. *What is he saying?*

"I have yet to know a person," Wit said, "who took up one of those Shards and didn't regret it, my friend."

"Same as any other burden of responsibility."

"Yes," Wit said, "but orders of magnitude worse." He looked around the room, and Jasnah noted Fen watching with wide eyes. Not questioning, but obviously out of her league.

They were talking about Dalinar Ascending to the Shard of Honor. Storms.

"That seems a big leap to make," Jasnah said. "Too big a leap."

"I can think of nothing else to try," Dalinar whispered.

"What if we renegotiated the contract?" Jasnah said.

They all looked at her.

"If there is a new Odium," she said, "he might agree to different terms.

Perhaps he will stop the war entirely if we give him accommodations." She didn't look at Wit. "What if we let him leave?"

"Jasnah," Wit said, pained. "We can't unleash him upon the cosmere."

"We have to at least consider every option," Jasnah said. "You said that the other worlds, and the beings that rule them, are content to leave Odium to us. They offer no help or succor, and sometimes you have to think about yourself first. What if we renegotiated?"

"No," Dalinar said softly. "He took advantage of us once—and he'd only renegotiate if it served him better. He would do so only to take further advantage. I think we need to explore options outside the contract—options like Honor's power."

They sat quietly at that, and Jasnah had to admit that negotiating the first time hadn't worked spectacularly. She looked to Wit, who slumped, offended, as he met her eyes. Keeping Odium from destroying more worlds was one of his primary goals.

"Peace," she said, resting a hand on his arm. "I'm only asking questions, as I must."

"I understand," he said, nodding. And he did seem to. "And what is put upon all of you is unfair. You have every right to be annoyed at the other Shards. I certainly am. Dalinar, you have a good point in what you're contemplating."

Dalinar nodded. "I worry that I need something far, far greater than what this contest under any terms can offer. If you bring an army of six men against an army of tens of thousands, you'll lose. That's what I'm doing, in facing Odium. What if there's a better way? What if there's a way to *fight* Odium? Defeat, destroy, exile him. Using the power of a god."

Jasnah shivered, and forced herself to consider it. She had known, even when no one else wanted to acknowledge it, that there was nothing watching or protecting them. All the aphorisms, rituals, and writings were for the comfort of the people at best—or the control of them at worst. She'd accepted this, though at times she had dearly wished for that comfort.

Recently, in talking with Wit, she'd discovered the extent to which she'd been right. There *was* something up there, it just wasn't God. It was a group of ordinary people. She didn't know what terrified her more. The idea of some powerful, all-knowing deity that controlled everything—destroying her free will, yet for some reason still leaving the entire world in so much pain. Or the knowledge that there *were* beings who ruled the cosmere with immense power—but they had all the foibles, flaws, and limited morality of anyone else.

After contemplation, giving Dalinar's idea due thought, she still found herself against it. Kings were bad enough. This was far worse.

"Dalinar," she said, "I don't feel comfortable with this line of reasoning."

"Neither do I," he said. "Storms, Jasnah, neither do I. But we face a being of immense strength and intelligence. When I get to that contest in eight days, they *are* going to outmaneuver me. I'm increasingly certain it *will* happen."

"So you're saying the only way to win," Fen said, "is to face them as an equal? With the power of Honor?"

"Do you know, Wit?" Dalinar asked. "What happens to the power of a god when they die?"

"It's different on each world," Wit said. "On one it was all around, and we didn't realize it. In another, the god's power was stuffed in a metaphorical closet—packed into Shadesmar, left to rot. Here, if it wasn't Splintered after all, then it's in the Spiritual Realm. I think it might be the very substance of your visions, which behave so interestingly."

"Cultivation said the same," Dalinar said. "That if I travel the Spiritual Realm, it will be all around me."

"But . . . isn't it all around us already?" Navani asked. "In the spren, the Stormlight, the power of the Radiants?"

"Yes and no," Wit said. "This is complicated. A Shard—a god—suffuses everything. Every axon on the world is, in some way, Connected to it. But the Spiritual Realm must hold a core of what Honor used to be. A well of energy, you might say. If you were to Connect to it in the right way, you would ascend to Honor's position. Then all the ambient power of the world would be part of you. You'd need to find a way to persuade the power to accept you."

"And if I did want to do that . . ." Dalinar said.

Wit met his eyes. "Then yes, the Spiritual Realm is where you'd start." Uncharacteristically subdued, he rested his head on his folded arms. "Navani, did the Sibling notice the visit of a god to their tower?"

Navani looked upward for a moment, then shook her head. "The Sibling says, however, that their mother is . . . quiet. Sneaky."

"Her kind tend to be," Wit mumbled, "for all their enormous size. Tricky lizards who hide where you least expect them. Like someone else I know." He took up an empty bowl, then threw it across the room toward the stacked tables. It hit the tablecloth covering one and *smacked* into something, which yelped.

Dalinar stood and spun, toppling his chair, alert, with yellow shockspren breaking around him. A fraction of a second later, he realized who it was. "Lift?" he said. "*Again?*"

The head of a teenage girl popped out, with round features and long, straight dark hair spilling around her face. A second head emerged beside hers, much older, with a grey mustache.

"Dieno?" Dalinar said, righting his chair and sitting back down.

The Mink seemed embarrassed to have been caught—though as usual

Lift didn't care. She scampered forward and helped herself to the snacks. The Mink stood up and straightened his clothing.

"You could have just asked instead of spying," Dalinar said. "How did you get in, anyway?"

"Vents," the Mink said. "And pardon, Blackthorn, the fatal problem with asking is that people can, and do, say no."

"Did you realize," Lift said around a mouthful of fruit, "it's easier to get through a hole if you break your shoulder?"

"Dislocate, child," the Mink said. "*Dislocate* your shoulder."

She shrugged. Jasnah watched the two, considering them. Lift had significant potential as a spy, and Jasnah had contemplated encouraging her in that direction. The Mink though . . . he was too dangerous. He acted small, unassuming, but he was not loyal to her family, and she did not blame him. In his place, she wouldn't be either.

"I'll admit," the Mink said, stepping up to them, "I didn't anticipate a discussion of deification. It is . . . *puelo arandan*? The Alethi word is . . ."

"Blasphemous," Jasnah said.

"Ah, yes," the Mink said. "That."

"What *did* you expect to hear?" Jasnah asked, toying with a small green palafruit but not biting into it.

"A discussion of whether or not to assault Alethkar," the Mink said, shrugging.

"Alethkar?" Navani said. "Why? If we win, we get it back—and your homeland as well."

"If you lose?" the Mink asked, looking to Dalinar.

"They keep both kingdoms," Dalinar said.

"*If* they control them," the Mink said. "The contract loophole works both ways, no?"

Wit cocked his head. "I suppose . . . yes. If we *were* to assault and reclaim Alethkar before the deadline it would be ours, regardless of the outcome of the contest."

"When you all scuttled off," the Mink said, "I assumed you'd seen this, and didn't want anyone else to get their hopes up as you discussed."

Reclaim Alethkar? She could help her people become a nation again, not a group of refugees. Jasnah sat up straight and looked to Dalinar, who had hunched forward. He met her eyes, and she saw the truth in them. Even before her own mind—scrambling to work out the logistics—did.

It was impossible.

Kholinar was in the very heart of Alethkar—fortified, home to thousands of Fused and multiple Unmade. They'd need to somehow deliver enough troops to accomplish the assault, pulling them away from every other fortified position—and the distances involved . . .

The enemy's assaults were in places it could reach quickly: Thaylenah by ship, Azimir through Shadesmar, and the Shattered Plains via a smaller number of Fused arriving by air. Reaching Alethkar on such short notice would be . . .

Well, it simply couldn't be done. Not unless they pulled every Windrunner away, and risked everything on this one gamble.

"The logistics of it are impossible, I'm afraid," Dalinar said. "Kholinar is too far away and too well fortified."

"And Herdaz?" the Mink asked. "Barely any Fused. Spy reports say they've moved most of their military away, following the collapse of my rebellion." He stepped closer to Dalinar. "I could reclaim it."

"We're *going* to reclaim it," Dalinar said. "When I win the contest."

"Pardon, gancho," the Mink said, "but I just overheard your reservations about the likelihood of that victory. Even if you were confident, I should not like to trust our freedom to another man's sword. No matter how comically large said sword may be." He stepped closer, holding something. A tattered remnant of a banner, one Jasnah knew he kept in his pocket. "You are to be commended for remembering Herdaz in your contract, Blackthorn. I no longer think you will forget us, as the Alethi so often have.

"But you gave me a promise. I should like it fulfilled. First Alethkar, then Herdaz. If you cannot send armies for your homeland, then our promise comes due. I would like to try, and I should like you to keep your oath to me. Troops. Support."

"Eight days?" Navani asked. "You want us to deliver troops to a nation hundreds of miles away in eight days?"

"The *Fourth Bridge,*" the Mink said. "Your flying machine—"

"Would take weeks to travel that distance," Navani said.

"Windrunners, then," the Mink said. "They can get a person across the continent in under a day."

"But an entire army?" Navani said.

"We'd need a few hundred at most," the Mink said. "The members of my personal army, which we have rescued. If you drop us at the border on the western side, we will assault the capital a little inland, reclaiming my homeland." He placed the tattered remnant before Dalinar on the food table. "Your oath, Blackthorn."

He stared at it. Damnation. He was going to say yes.

"Dalinar," Jasnah said. "Look at me."

He turned from the banner, meeting her eyes.

"Even an assault force of two hundred would require some fifty Windrunners. Windrunners we *need* to protect what we *have.* There are barely three hundred! You can't send so many of them on a quest like this. That would make you—no offense, General Dieno—of the ten fools!"

"I swore an oath, Jasnah," Dalinar said.

"But—"

"What are we, if we don't have our word?" Dalinar said. "Dieno. We could use your knowledge in the upcoming battles. Are you certain you must leave us?"

"Yes," he said. "I won the campaign in Emul for you. Now prove you're no longer the man who burned my lands in your youth, Dalinar. Keep your word."

Dalinar nodded. "I will set fifty Windrunners to the task. Go, with my blessing."

The Mink took back his banner, held it in a fist, then gripped Dalinar's shoulder in thanks. He rushed out—not looking at Jasnah as he did. Damnation. She liked the man Dalinar had become over the years since they had made a connection reading *The Way of Kings* after her father's death. But this version of him could be *storming* inconvenient at times. She took deep breaths to banish the angerspren at her feet.

"This is right, Jasnah," Dalinar said, settling in his seat. "We must always do what is right. Those Windrunners will return before the deadline and join the battle. In the meantime, we've kept our oath."

"What is right," she said, "is not so easy as swearing an oath, Uncle. It's about what brings the greatest good to the most people—and sometimes that requires making difficult decisions."

"What makes you think," he said, "that *wasn't* a difficult decision?"

They continued to lock gazes, Jasnah's will against his, until a slurping sound distracted her and she turned to find Lift standing next to her, watching the two of them like it was some puppet show, a dozen palafruit pits at her feet and another wiggling in her mouth. Storms above . . . how did that girl manage to pack down so much so quickly? And be so frighteningly skinny at the same time?

"So . . ." Lift said. "What you were sayin' earlier. Gonna become a god, eh, Dalinar? Deevy. Real deevy. When you do it, can I put in some requests? I kinda hate how toes feel. You know, whenever I remember I have them, and start thinkin' about them. Can you fix that? Also, make porridge taste like meat and vice versa."

"Wait," Fen said. "What?"

"Porridge. Should taste like meat."

"Why?"

"It's all slimy and gross. Meat, it comes out of a body. *It* should be slimy and gross. Innards and blood and guts and stuff. Meat should taste like porridge." She spat out the last pit, and Jasnah noticed that remarkably, all the snacks Wit had brought were gone. "So, you know, fix that. Also, war and death and stuff. Actually, there are a whole lotsa things the Almighty should fix and hasn't. Wonder if he gets distracted by all the prayers."

"The fact that he's dead," Navani said dryly, "might be the most distracting part."

Dalinar suddenly sat up in his seat. Then stood again, looking skyward.

"The Stormfather," Ivory whispered in Jasnah's ear. "I feel him near."

"What?" Fen asked.

"The Stormfather has overheard our conversation," Dalinar said. "And he's not happy. I might . . . need a few minutes."

After we parted with affection the next day, I watched their cart roll into the distance, pulled by the father with two children riding in the rear, the mother striding with a pack on her back. Dust blew with them, for dust goes where it wishes, ignoring all borders.

—From *The Way of Kings*, fourth parable

Kaladin had entered a world frozen in time.

The first part of Shinovar—on the slope below the pass—was forested. He walked, silent, with Syl. Passing trees that didn't so much as quiver. Vines that let him *step* on them. Grass that lay like corpses.

Yet it didn't *feel* dead. It was vibrant, green. But docile. Kaladin crouched down to touch a clump of grass, which trustingly let him. He stood and ran his hands along a branch, which didn't tremble. He tapped several of the diamond leaves, each thick with water.

It all seemed . . . frozen. Like he had access to some strange Surge that let him freeze a moment and wander around in it. He felt he could turn back and it would all burst into motion, withdrawing from him in an instant, like lounging troops snapping to attention when Dalinar entered the room.

There were also no lifespren, despite the many plants. What a bizarre place. Bizarre and somehow . . . wonderful?

He should be unnerved. A land where the plants weren't afraid of you? Where storms didn't blow? Where you walked on soil springy beneath the foot, which made a dull *thump* when you stomped instead of a proper scrape or soft smack.

He found it oddly peaceful. Comforting. Did a deep part of him know humans had once lived on a world full of these plants? Or perhaps . . . perhaps they weren't timid or stupid. Perhaps these plants were *brave.* At the very least, they had never known the tyranny of the storm—and so had never been forced to hide. He found beauty in that.

It helped that Syl was delighted by the place.

She zipped from tree to reed, to vine, to grass, to bush—a ribbon of light, twirling and twisting while she laughed. Anytime she was a ribbon, she shrank back to her tiny size, but she shimmered with a variety of colors.

Szeth moved up alongside Kaladin as they walked, preserving their Stormlight. The next highstorm was days away, and Kaladin didn't trust Szeth's promises that the spheres would recharge as usual in Shinovar. After all, he admitted that during his youth, they'd almost never used them—instead relying on dangerous things like candles.

Why in the world hadn't Shinovar burned down? So many plants would surely provide tinder. Kaladin's people used candles only during the Weeping.

Syl zipped past, doing a series of loops before going to streak through some of the tinkling leaves. The trees here were bone white with knots of dark brown, and Szeth had seemed amused when Kaladin asked how many trees in his land were strange colors. Most, it appeared, were the ordinary brown and green.

"I'd have thought," Szeth said as Syl zipped past in the other direction, "that she would find this place dull. Wouldn't it be less fun to inspect plants that do not respond?"

"Syl loves novelty," Kaladin said. "And she's probably having all kinds of fun with plants that are too slow to dodge her pranks."

"Curious," Szeth said. "Here, we don't ascribe to plants volition, or thoughts, or intentions as is common to your speech. I'm only now remembering how odd it was to go east and hear people speaking of plants as if they were animate objects with feelings."

As an inanimate object with feelings, the sword said from Szeth's back, *I think I should be offended.*

"No offense was implied, sword-nimi," Szeth said.

Oh, good! I won't kill you then. Ha ha.

Both of them froze, listening to the sword chuckle to itself. Finally they started forward again, along a path through the forest. It wasn't too overgrown, fortunately. Kaladin tried to imagine how hard it would be to get through here if the plants grew all together and refused to move when prodded.

So far, there hadn't been much of a chance to talk to Szeth, what with the flying. Or perhaps Kaladin merely told himself that to delay the awkwardness. What was the best way to start a conversation? "Hey, sorry to hear that you're crazy" didn't seem appropriate.

Instead he tried, "Dalinar says you've had a rough time lately."

"I wouldn't know," Szeth replied.

"What do you mean by that?"

"I do not consider a time 'rough' or 'not rough.' I simply do as my master commands."

"And . . . you don't wish it were another way?"

Szeth eyed him. Kaladin approached a tree branch hanging low over the path, then rapped it with his hand, feeling foolish when it didn't pull back. He ducked underneath.

"I am here," Szeth said, "because this is the next step in my progress as a Skybreaker. My people, and my land, need me."

"So you're making a choice," Kaladin said. "Not *just* doing as commanded. That seems good."

"I was commanded to find a quest of relevance," Szeth said, "and this presented itself." He followed Kaladin under the branch, his shorter stature meaning he didn't need to duck nearly as far. He moved on ahead faster, as if finished with the conversation.

Storming man. Kaladin caught up. "So, do you want to talk about it?"

"It?"

"Life." Storms, shouldn't this be easier? "Dalinar says that things you've done have left you scarred. Not only physically, but mentally."

"Scars exist," Szeth said. "They are permanent once you bear them. So you endure. Not only physically, but mentally."

"What if they *aren't* permanent?" Kaladin said. "Stormlight can heal physical scars. What if mental scars can heal too? If not remove them, then make them more limber, easier to bear—"

"That is irrelevant," Szeth said. "I do not need to be healed, as I do not deserve anything of the sort. I have killed, and I bear the weight of those killings. To wish otherwise would be to minimize the damage I have done—an insult to those who whisper at me from the shadows, calling for my soul to burn in recompense for the blood I've spilled."

Storms. "Szeth," Kaladin said, "you can't live like that."

"I exist. I do what is needed. Eventually, I will no longer exist. That is enough."

"But—"

"I will not speak of this further," Szeth said, eyes forward. "I know what Dalinar intends you to do with me, as I am not deaf. It is not needed."

"He wants you to listen to me though."

"All he asked of me was to bring you," Szeth said. "Therefore, you are here. You. The one who nearly killed me. Here. In my land, on my quest." Szeth looked at him in the overcast forest, those oddly shaped eyes of his seeming at home in dimmer light.

"I trust Dalinar because I must," Szeth continued. "So I am not allowed to resent you. Nevertheless, do not assume I will endure you trying to 'save' me, Kaladin Stormblessed. Not all beneath your judging gaze are in need of your protection. Keep your attention on finding the Herald."

Szeth turned and continued on, purposeful.

Syl landed beside Kaladin and whistled softly, growing to full size. "Well, *he's* something," she whispered.

Kaladin gritted his teeth and stalked forward, and Syl walked alongside—not flying, instead imitating his posture. She seemed to think he should try talking to Szeth more, but storms, Kaladin understood the frustration of someone trying to *force* you to feel better. The sole person who'd ever managed it had been Adolin—and he had done so without pandering or trying to cheer Kaladin up. Somehow. Maybe Adolin should have come on this mission instead. Storming man.

Regardless, Kaladin needed another tactic. He refused to manipulate Szeth into accepting help.

"All right then," Kaladin said, joining Szeth again. "Dalinar wants me to recruit Ishar the Herald. Any ideas on that?"

"It is a wise mission, given by a wise man," Szeth said. "But we do not know where Ishar, or Ishu-son-God as we know him, is hiding. Plus, there is something dangerous in this land. My mission here involves a . . . cleansing and retribution owed to the people of Shinovar."

"Can you tell me what you mean by that?"

"One of the Unmade is here," Szeth said. "Awakened years before you became a Radiant, before the first oaths were sworn. My people have embraced it for some reason, and welcomed in its darkness and its manipulations."

"How can you be sure it's an Unmade?" Kaladin said. "It took Dalinar ages to recognize the Thrill as an Unmade."

"Because," Szeth said, "before my exile, I met it." He paused for an instant. "It began during my youth. With . . . a rock."

∴

The others left, allowing Dalinar to confront the Stormfather alone in that garden room.

He had grown accustomed to having the Stormfather in the back of his mind. Like a thought; the kind of nagging, persistent one that hovered at the perimeter of your consciousness. The awful feeling as you waited for a battle report, already seeing that your side was faring poorly.

Dalinar wished that his metaphor for the sensation weren't so negative, that his relationship with his spren was more like others'. Some of that was Dalinar's fault, because of events like when he'd forced the Stormfather to operate an Oathgate as if he were a common Blade. It was partly the spren's fault, like when the Stormfather had refused to help Kaladin at Urithiru a few weeks ago, and Dalinar had been forced to step in.

They had their peaceful moments, but just as many disagreements. More, really. And often Dalinar could feel the Stormfather's rage flooding through him, as if he were a chasm during a flash flood. Like today. When the Stormfather spoke, the force of it made Dalinar's fingers tremble.

WHAT ARE YOU DOING? the Stormfather demanded, his voice like thunderheads crashing against one another. WHAT ARE YOU CONTEMPLATING?

"I am exploring every option I have," Dalinar said, keeping his voice calm as he stood among the writhing plants. "Like any good general."

I HEARD YOU DISCUSSING HONOR'S POWER, the Stormfather thundered. WHY, DALINAR? MUST YOU THINK SO HIGHLY OF YOURSELF? YOU'RE RUINING EVERYTHING!

Dalinar braced himself against the force of the words. "Cultivation implied this was my next step," Dalinar said. "And I agree. I fear that by myself, I can't defeat Odium."

A sudden gale washed over him: a completely impossible wind, considering he was in a small enclosed space. The wind seemed to blow away the room, turning it to Stormlight—the walls, plants, spare tables all weathering away like sand caught up in a tempest.

In a moment Dalinar was standing in an empty, open blue—hanging as if in the air far above the world. It was . . . it was a vision. Like the ones that had propelled him on this course in life. His body would still be in that room, perhaps collapsed upon the floor, while his mind saw what the Stormfather wanted.

An open sky, and a figure building before him in the shape of dark clouds extending in both directions to the horizon. A face manifesting in the natural shapes of the billowing clouds—features he knew as the Stormfather's. Bearded, though the hair vanished into the mixing and churning clouds. Inhuman eyes glowing with crackling lightning. A daunting, oppressive sight for one who hovered—tiny—before it.

But Dalinar had been the imperious general staring down a subordinate. He knew these tricks.

"Is it possible for me to take up Honor?" Dalinar demanded.

NO.

"Wit says otherwise."

WIT IS A LIAR.

"He has offered us more help than you have."

HE CARES ONLY FOR HIS OWN PLANS, DALINAR. NOT FOR THIS LAND OR ITS PEOPLE.

Unfortunately, Wit had said as much to Dalinar in the past. So he considered, and he tried to modulate his tone.

"Why hasn't the power of Honor taken another Vessel in all this time?" he finally asked.

I WILL NOT GIVE YOU ANSWERS, DALINAR. The Stormfather's voice grew softer, smaller. *You were supposed to be better than this. You were supposed to be better than your brother.*

"My brother?" Dalinar said, frowning.

He was arrogant. I knew it. I've watched both of you for a long time. Even at his worst though, Gavilar didn't strive for godhood. Why, Dalinar? Why must you seek this?

"Because I'm overwhelmed, Stormfather," Dalinar said, letting his exhaustion show. "Because I have to somehow save everyone, but I'm just one man, confused and outmatched. Because the only time I've ever felt like I had any *hint* of control was when I stood up before Odium and touched the Spiritual Realm."

Unity, the Stormfather said.

"Yes."

This is not for you to seek or decide. The power cannot go to one who wants it, Dalinar.

"You said it was impossible earlier," Dalinar said.

Impossible the way you want it to happen.

"And Cultivation, who brought this plan to me in the first place?"

Traitor. She should know the implausibility of what she suggests.

"So which is it, Stormfather?" Dalinar demanded. "Is it impossible, or merely implausible? Is it wrong, or is it the only way to unite people, as I've been trying all along?"

It . . . This is not my plan.

"Your plan?" Dalinar pushed. "I thought this was Honor's plan. You said he *charged* you to find people for the visions—so they could prepare for the coming dangers. You're filling a role, just like me."

You have no idea what you're talking about.

"I only know what you've told me," Dalinar said, feeling his anger mount. "I know that I've been stymied and cut off *every time* I've tried to make progress! I've had to fight you almost as much as I fight our enemy!"

Honor's plan—

"Honor abandoned us!" Dalinar shouted. "We don't even know why or how! All you'll say is that he died, he faded away, he left visions and some plan for us to force Odium into a contest of champions. Vague, without real instructions."

It's working though.

"Is it?" Dalinar said, gesturing toward the continent far below. "You've seen what the enemy is doing."

I . . . know now.

"They've outmaneuvered us already," Dalinar said. "And they will do so again!" He heard thunder, and found he was growing. When he spoke, his own words were punctuated by rumblings. "The enemy has changed, Stormfather, but whoever they are, they're a god—and can match whatever I try! You don't think he can? What if he brings a Fused to fight me? An Unmade? A thunderclast? Some being from offworld with the power to tear down cities and lay waste to thousands?

"You think I can defeat that in some contest? I'm going to *lose* unless I find some kind of edge! All along, we were so focused on getting the agreement from him that we didn't consider how to win! Is it any real surprise that I'm looking for a *third option*! So are you going to help me for once, or KEEP STANDING IN MY STORMING WAY?"

He cut off, a hundred more thoughts running through his head, each with an attached frustration. He stopped the tide, breathing heavily, and found that—strangely—he was now the same size as the Stormfather. That was an impossibility, since the Stormfather extended to infinity. But in this place, reality bent, and he could look the spren straight in the eyes.

What you want . . . is dangerous.

"It's not what I *want,* Stormfather," Dalinar said. "But it might be the only way."

The Stormfather rumbled softly, and he glanced down, away from Dalinar. *What of the Heralds? Perhaps the Heralds can help.*

"I sent Szeth and Kaladin to try to retrieve one," Dalinar said. "But what do you think? Can they solve this?"

Maybe. But . . . they are not reliable anymore, are they? Time has broken them . . . I've broken them. He looked back at Dalinar. *I cannot say if the power would accept someone like you as a host, after what happened with Tanavast.*

"And what happened with Tanavast?" Dalinar said.

It's . . . worse than I told you, Dalinar.

"So you lied."

Yes. Does that surprise you? Anger you?

Dalinar took a deep breath, and found that he was relieved to finally get an admission.

"Yes," Dalinar said. "But I can move beyond that."

The Stormfather rumbled, and the dark thunderheads calmed. *I'm supposed to be better than lies, Dalinar. I should be constant. I am the winds. I do not lie.*

"You are a person," Dalinar said, "capable of growth. Capable of learning. If that is the case, then you are capable of mistakes."

The Stormfather at last met his eyes again. *I don't know what would happen if you became Honor before the contest. I do not like even thinking about it. However, you might find answers that will . . . change your perspective. In the Spiritual Realm, as Cultivation said. You can take that step, and see the past, but do* not *seek the power of Honor.*

Be warned. I will not be able to control what happens to you, or where you are taken. It is a process that is confusing to any who is not themself a Shard of Adonalsium. Even your Wit, for all his boasting and self-importance, can barely fathom the Spiritual Realm. Regardless, if you look into the Spiritual Realm . . . you will see. Perhaps you will see.

"See what, exactly?"

Our shame.

The vision vanished in the blink of an eye, and Dalinar found himself back in the tower. Standing up, remarkably, rather than having collapsed.

Wit was there. Sitting on a table with one leg up, next to a fern growing from the floor.

"Could you see that?" Dalinar asked him.

"I could hear it," Wit said. "He's both right and wrong. I *do* care about all of you, Dalinar."

"But Odium remaining captive on our planet is more important to you than any of our lives."

Wit nodded. "I'm sorry."

"Do not apologize," Dalinar said, stretching, exhaustionspren buzzing around him like insects. "I appreciate the honesty."

"People think I detest honesty," Wit said, "because they don't often like to hear what I have to say, and so must assume I speak only lies."

"They'd probably enjoy it more," Dalinar said, "if you didn't present both truth *and* lies in a way that belittles the listener."

"Fair enough," Wit said, hopping off the table. "I assume you've decided to go forward with this plan?"

"Yes," Dalinar said, realizing it was true. "I want to start as soon as possible."

"You'll need a way to track time in there," Wit said. "Even if we do this the smart way—which means sending your mind, but not your body—it would be easy for you to let months pass. That obviously won't do. You have an appointment to keep, after all."

". . . Months?" Dalinar said.

"If not years. *Decades.* Time is entirely different in the Spiritual Realm. Storms, in some corner cases, you could vanish for what feels to you like a few hours—while decades of time pass out here. The visions so far were carefully curated and monitored by your spren, preventing you from being lost."

"Is there a way for you to monitor for us?"

Wit fished in his pocket. He brought out a little clock, with two straps on the sides. The symbols on the face were unfamiliar to Dalinar. "Silverlight Mercantile," Wit said to his questioning glance. "Adjustable to local time on different planets, if you swap out the face. Here, let me see that thing on your forearm."

Dalinar held up his arm, where he still wore Navani's fabrial bracer—it had a mechanism that kept the time and the date for him.

"All right," Wit said, "this should work. You know how you do that thing where you teach yourself languages by bonding to a region? Do that, but with the clocks."

"Could you be clearer? 'Do that' isn't much to go on."

"Take my clock's soul," Wit said, holding up his, "and Connect it by a thread of power to your own clock, grounding yours in the Physical Realm while you travel." Wit looked at him. "Poke this with Stormlight, then poke that. Try it."

Dalinar drew in Stormlight, then touched Wit's clock, Infusing it with power. When he took his finger away, a line of light followed. He touched his clock, and something seemed to *snap.* The dial quivered for a moment, then continued as if nothing had happened.

"Excellent," Wit said.

"So . . ."

"So the clock on your arm will show the same time that mine does," Wit explained. "The date as well. Without this, your clock could adapt to your *perception* of time in the Spiritual Realm. Meaning it might *feel* and *read* like an hour has passed—but in reality you could return here and find all of us dead and gone. Well, everyone else. I tend to linger. Rather like a winter cough."

"What about winter makes one cough?" Dalinar asked.

"Oh, right," Wit said. "Roshar. No common cold. You have no idea how wonderful life is here, do you?"

"Are there places worse than the one being threatened with utter domination by a dark, destructive god?"

"You'd be surprised," Wit said. "A few have *political fundraisers.*" He strapped on his clock. "We'll try a quick test. So long as we keep you tethered, time shouldn't pass too outrageously for you compared to us, and you should be able to send your mind into a vision, then return as you wish."

"*Should* be able?"

"Should be able," Wit admitted.

No quip. That was always a bad sign.

"You'll need to open a perpendicularity," Wit said, "step into it, then let the light take you. But not *all* of you. Push all the way through—but only with your mind, or you'll end up in Shadesmar."

Storms. That sounded difficult. And confusing.

But what else was he to do? "Let's get Navani and Jasnah in here to monitor me, then we'll give it a try."

23
COMPROMISE

Would that men could always do the same—if I could enshrine one law in all further legal codes, it would be this. Let people leave if they wish.

—From *The Way of Kings*, fourth parable

The drizzle had fully committed to rain by the time Radiant's team moved into position. If those last few Ghostbloods were coming to the meeting, they would arrive soon. And if there weren't more coming . . . well, an enemy conference was likely underway, making it even more important that Radiant get into that hideout.

So, she helped Gaz wheel a small tool cart down the roadway, past rainspren like candles, each with a single eye on the top. They reached an intersection right in front of the Ghostblood hideout. She found the Ghostbloods setting up here to be impressively blatant. When others made hideouts in grimy corners of the worst parts of a city, *they* chose the middle of a storming military camp. Some people higher in the Alethi military must be in Mraize's pocket. She'd have work to do uncovering them all.

Once in position, she and Red began to set up a small pavilion in the rain. They'd dropped their Lightweavings, relying on hooded cloaks to mask their faces, in case that sand could reveal them. Soon someone from the Ghostbloods—as expected—came to check on them.

It wasn't the masked guard. Damnation. Radiant kept calm and allowed Red to handle it while she hung back, fiddling with their tools. The guard she wanted—the one with the mask—emerged from the shadowed porch but did not approach.

"Hey," the other Ghostblood said as he arrived. "What's this?" His name was Shade, a man with Horneater blood, though he looked more Alethi despite the forked beard. She thought the masked woman had fetched him as they were setting up.

"We're supposed to level this intersection," Red said. He noted Shade's Alethi uniform. "I have the orders somewhere, Sergeant."

"You're supposed to work in the rain?" Shade demanded.

"Yeah. Storming unfair." Red thumbed at the little pavilion. "At least we've got that. If you want to take it up with the camp operations commander, I wouldn't mind a little time off."

Shade picked through the tools, then poked around in the pavilion—while the masked guard lurked by the building. Adolin's sessions with Radiant let her spot the readiness of a trained soldier: the stance, the alert attention.

Calm, careful, Radiant rearranged the tools after Shade finished poking through them. He was built like a boulder, so it would be easy to assume he was the more dangerous, but he didn't have the casual grace the masked woman did. Shade stepped back in thought, rain dripping down his beard. He wouldn't want to draw attention, but he also wouldn't want random workers so close to their base, maybe hearing things they shouldn't.

"Pack up and work somewhere else," he told Red. "For at least a couple more hours. You don't need authorization; just tell them I gave the orders."

Red glanced at Radiant, and—hood pulled tight—she nodded.

"Yes, Sergeant," Red said with a sigh.

The two of them slowly began disassembling the pavilion. Shade returned to the masked guard and they exchanged whispers. Then the guard fell into position by the door while Shade slipped inside, passing a large jar of the black sand that had been tied hanging outside.

"That's a problem," Red whispered over the sound of beating rain. "Did you catch their exchange?"

"Mmm . . ." Pattern said from Radiant's coat. "He said, 'I want them gone by the time Aika and Jezinor get here.' And the woman said, 'Ya.'"

"We were supposed to lure out the short one," Red said. "We need that mask."

"I'll go in close and deal with her," Radiant said.

"You sure?" Red asked. "What if she makes noise?"

"I'll be quick," she replied, noting Gaz as he came trotting up to them.

"My part's done," Gaz said. "Why are we taking the pavilion down?"

"Get angry about it," Radiant said, with a nudge from Veil. "Demand to know who gave these orders. Pretend you're our foreman."

Gaz launched into it with gusto, complaining loudly that they didn't have authorization to set up anywhere else. He did well enough he even drew a few angerspren. Perfect. Shallan and Red set up the pavilion again—they'd barely started disassembling it—while Gaz demanded to speak to the sergeant who had changed their orders. With that as an excuse, Radiant told Pattern to wait behind, then walked over to the building. She stepped out of the rain into the covered porch, and hesitated by the door.

The guard emerged from the shadows, mask peeking from the front of her hood. As on Iyatil, it made the woman seem . . . inhuman. Painted wood, without carvings of facial features—hiding all except those eyes. Locked on to her.

"Oh!" Radiant said. "Sorry. But, um, our foreman wants to talk to you. Um. It's . . . um. Sorry . . ."

The guard took her by the arm. Radiant twisted and whipped up her other hand—pushing a small stiletto toward the guard's throat. The enemy caught it, her eyes narrowing, then grunted and shoved Radiant backward, trying to trip her.

A year training with Adolin gave Radiant some unexpected grit. She resisted the shove and kept her stance, locking eyes with the masked creature.

Now, she ordered her armor.

In a blink, the armor formed. Not around her, but around the guard, freezing her in place as it had Red earlier. Radiant caught a glimpse of a pair of shocked eyes as the helmet encased the woman's face.

Shallan! the creationspren said, eager.

"Just keep her mouth closed," she said. "Like the drawing Shallan did for you. Right?"

Shallan! they replied in a chorus. The only sound from the guard was muffled exertion, so hopefully the helmet plan was working. Radiant *thought* they'd explained it well enough to the creationspren: a mechanism that held the jaw shut by making the helmet tighter at the bottom, below the mask.

She checked the sand in the hanging jar. Still black, as she'd hoped. They'd said that it took an intelligent spren to activate the stuff—which made sense, otherwise it would be useless, turning white in warning whenever someone got anxious. Her Plate spren hadn't affected it even when forming.

Red and Gaz came jogging up. "It worked," Radiant whispered, her heart thumping from the exchange.

Gaz nodded toward the woman's motionless left hand, raising a knife toward Radiant—the gauntlet had simply formed around it, letting the blade peek out. She'd missed that entirely. A good warning. A year of practice had given her some skill, but it was a weak substitute for a lifetime of battle experience.

"Eh," Red whispered, wheeling over the cart, "she could have healed from it."

"And what would that have done to the sand?" Gaz whispered, gesturing toward the glass jar. "We're not sure if a healing will activate it or not. If so, the first person who stepped through that door would have known a

Radiant had been here." He inspected the armor closer, locked down as it was. "Yet this *did* work. I can barely hear her."

The captive woman didn't even tremble from struggling to escape. Together, they managed to tip her into the two-wheeled cart, throw a tarp over her, then wheel it into their small pavilion. Had any guards on the walls seen? Darcira and the strike team were poised to intercept any who came running, but still she worried.

Move quickly, Shallan thought, taking over from Radiant. She didn't want the last few Ghostbloods to arrive at the door and find the guard missing.

Gaz put his arms around the head of the armored woman to be in position. He nodded.

Shallan touched the armor. *Could you dismiss just the helmet please?* she asked.

Shallan! the armor said. The helmet vanished in a puff of Stormlight. Gaz snapped his arms around the woman's neck, executing a perfect choke hold. Shallan needed Radiant again for a moment while watching the struggling woman be strangled, her eyes bulging, her skin going a deep red around the mask.

Gaz didn't kill her, though he held on longer than Radiant thought necessary. He'd explained earlier: assuming your attacker didn't want to kill you, the best way to escape a choke hold was to pretend to fall unconscious early. So Gaz ignored the struggles, the painspren, the frantic eyes, the sudden limpness and counted to himself softly.

She'd never asked how he knew this so well.

Gaz nodded, and Shallan dismissed the armor, then began stripping to her undergarments while the two other Lightweavers efficiently undressed the guard, then bound and gagged her. Gaz had warned Shallan that people usually didn't stay unconscious for long after being choked out. Indeed, the guard was stirring as Shallan finished re-dressing, wearing the woman's clothing. Utilitarian brown leathers that weren't particularly formfitting, along with a hooded cloak and a frightening number of knives strapped across her person.

Though Shallan was accustomed to being short compared to the Alethi, she was a tad taller than this offworlder. Close enough, hopefully. She already had her hair under a wig, but her options had been limited, so she was distressed to notice that the guard had closer-cropped hair than the pictures had depicted. Storms. She'd cut her hair, which meant Shallan would have to leave the hood up indoors. Would that seem odd?

Red knelt beside the figure, then—appearing more unnerved by this than stripping a captive—tried to figure out how to remove the mask. Turned out it was bound in place by two cords, which he undid, and pulled the red-orange mask free. Shallan had expected it to stick—she'd always felt that Iyatil had worn hers so long that the skin had grown over it. That proved an incorrect assumption; the mask was obviously removed and cleaned often, but it was also worn so continuously that it left imprints on the guard's face.

Her skin was as pale as Shallan's, and without the mask she seemed far less dangerous. Though she was probably in her middle years, her face was smooth, almost childlike.

Stop that, Shallan thought, taking the mask from Red. *You need to stop comparing all Shin people to children.* It was a bad habit. Besides, this woman wasn't even Shin—she was an offworlder who just happened to look Shin.

Shallan tied on the mask and pulled up her hood. The mask covered her full face, and was peaked slightly at the center, sloped at the sides. It was wide enough that her ears would barely be visible. Aside from the eyeholes, it had two holes near the nose for breathing, and a small portion was missing for the mouth—like a bite had been taken out of it at the chin.

Red nodded. "Looks pretty good."

"I don't know," Gaz replied, scratching his cheek. "It would fool a casual passerby. But Ghostbloods?"

Shallan fell into an imitation of the woman's stance. Dangerous, ready. Stepping with the kind of casual grace that took years to perfect. She narrowed her eyes behind the mask, mimicking the woman's expression—conveying it through posture.

Well done, Veil thought.

Red glanced at Gaz, cocking an eyebrow.

"All right, fine," Gaz said. "I still find it creepy how she can do things like that. Just don't take the hood off. The hair is wrong."

A moment later, Darcira ducked into the pavilion. "You're not in place yet?"

"Going now," Shallan said in a whisper, as it was easier to mask her voice that way.

"Did you find your watchpost?" Darcira said to Gaz.

"Yeah," he said. "Neutralized them fast enough to show up here and help. What took you so long?"

"Had to go and position the strike team, if you forgot," Darcira said. "What do we do if there were more than two observation posts watching the base?"

None of them could answer that, but they'd spotted only two in their sweep of the area. They had to trust in their skills. Shallan slipped one of her team's spanreeds into her sleeve, glanced at Pattern—dimpling the wood of the cart, humming to himself nervously—then waved goodbye. She left them, instead falling into place by the alcove. She maintained the same posture and stance as before. Sticking to shadows. Not speaking.

You can *do this,* Veil whispered.

Her heart still thrummed like listener war drums. She was going to enter the enemy stronghold alone—and could not use her powers. But it was the only way. What did you do when there was a guard watching for you?

You became the guard.

Not five minutes later, Shallan spotted two people trotting up to the safehouse. Aika and Jezinor, a pair of Thaylen traders. They'd arrived with Queen Fen's retinue, which explained why they were some of the last. They'd needed to find an excuse to come to the Shattered Plains.

Shallan's nervousness faded as she made a good show of checking their features with her hands, then holding the glass jar of sand up to each one. Neither seemed to notice anything off. She knocked on the door, as she'd seen done before. Shade opened it and waved the other two in. Shallan slipped in herself, and he held the door open for her. They'd be trusting their watchposts to send spanreed warnings if anything approached the safehouse. Posting a guard outside for too long risked drawing attention.

This was it. Veil was right, she *could* do this. Unless they asked her to say too much. Unless there was a third watchpost they hadn't found. Unless her disguise failed.

It was too late now. She had walked confidently straight into the den. Now she either proved to be a predator herself, or she got eaten.

⁂

Navani left Dalinar alone in the room with the plants to talk to the Stormfather while she stepped outside with the others, knowing he'd fill her in later.

She entered a world of chaos. Strategists planning, messengers running orders, a world spinning up to deal with another crisis. It was time to be a queen. Which regrettably meant dealing with all the random issues that no one else could. At the perimeter of the room, at least a dozen people waited for her attention.

So many systems had fallen apart during the occupation. Schooling had been ignored. Trade for less important supplies—everything from extra buttons to feed for pet axehounds—had been interrupted. Now, with the tower awakened, many problems were being solved while others—such as who got to use which services when—were just beginning.

They could handle it without her, but they didn't know it. And . . . perhaps she needed to banish such thoughts. She *was* important to the administration of this tower, this kingdom. Vital even.

So she went into motion, assigning some of her staff to various problems. Makal to rehouse people whose living quarters now turned out to be important for other reasons. Venan to organize meals for everyone attending the meeting, and to covertly keep a list of who was sending what messages where, just in case.

Next she found Highprince Sebarial and Palona waiting for her. They had learned an unfortunate lesson: that sometimes you had to put yourself where

Navani could see you in order to get her time. They had questions about how to get supplies into the city if there was a war on the Shattered Plains.

"We can't keep relying on the Oathgates," Sebarial said, rubbing his forehead. The girthy man had gone back to wearing an open-fronted takama, now that the weather was summer at the tower, and his belly poked out in a way he reportedly thought was distinguished. "But organizing shipments from Azir up through these mountains is going to be an *enormous* hassle. Flying them in will be prohibitively expensive in Stormlight unless we can make more airships. Yes, we can grow food now, but other supplies . . ."

"Bring me proposals," Navani said, looking over Palona's ledgers.

"This was supposed to make me rich!" Sebarial said. "I was Highprince of Commerce! I was supposed to be able to skim thousands to line my own pockets! But I can barely make any of this balance. There's nothing *to* skim!"

"Don't mind him, Brightness," Palona said. "He's having a rough time with how responsible he's becoming."

"You're good at being useful, Sebarial," Navani said. "That's the problem, isn't it?"

"My darkest secret," he grumbled. "I still pay for my household staff, vacations, *and* massages out of public funds, I'll have you know. It's a huge scandal."

"I'm sure Brightness Navani knows what a miscreant you are, gemheart," Palona said, patting his arm.

He sighed. "We're mobilizing troops to Thaylenah and the Shattered Plains. You're authorizing active battle pay, then? You realize this is going to dip into what little we have remaining? We might be able to offer extra rations instead of battle pay in some cases."

"Thank the Almighty for the emeralds we got on the Shattered Plains," Palona said. "It's the only way we're making enough food for everyone right now."

"I'll see if we can get more time with the Radiant Soulcasters," Navani said. "Given the way the tower is functioning, we can have them working at an increased speed."

"They break gemstones as they work, Brightness," Sebarial said. "Even Radiant Soulcasters need gems as a focus, which means we can't continue like this forever. We'll need a gemheart ranch up here, but there isn't a lot of space, so we *can't* lose the Shattered Plains."

She did her best to calm him, then took a meeting with Highprince Aladar on the status of the lighteyes. There was a lot of general panic about Jasnah's work to free the Alethi slaves, a decision that Dalinar had copied for Urithiru after some persuasion. It would be a slow process, designed to take effect over time, with social systems in place to facilitate. Jasnah, as usual, had done her research.

However, the lighteyes were pushing back. "Tradition will be cast to the winds," Aladar said. "The upright, natural order of things is being trampled. How can the lighteyed families maintain themselves without lands and taxes? What does it even *mean* to be lighteyed any longer?"

"It means what it has always meant," Navani said.

"Which is?" Aladar asked. "Brightness, with the elevation of Stormblessed to a full house, and now to *third dahn,* what about the other Radiants? More than three-quarters of them were darkeyed and are now light. It's chaos!"

"It's a problem for after the contest, Aladar," Navani said. "When we're not focused on a mass invasion. For now, I need logistical work from you. Make certain that supplies are transferred per the generals' requests. Fen can provision some of the soldiers we send her, but if we move battalions to Narak they'll run out of water quickly if we don't prepare. Also, make sure to check on Adolin and get him what he needs."

The stately bald man shook his head and sighed. "As you wish—but my concerns won't go away, Brightness. This problem is a bubbling cauldron. It's going to overflow. Only the invasions are stopping it."

"I know," she said. "But let's worry about the crisis we are facing *now* first, Aladar."

He bowed, then went to see to her orders. She tried not to be annoyed—and commanded the appearing irritationspren to vanish. Aladar was reasonable for a highlord, and was simply passing on what the *less reasonable* highlords were thinking. They were a powerful contingent, and hadn't failed to notice that—after years of politicking—almost everyone who had opposed Dalinar was now dead. Rumors about what had really happened to Sadeas churned, for all that Jasnah worked behind the scenes to quash them.

Yes, the upper ranks of the lighteyes *were* a bubbling cauldron. Unfortunately for them, the darkeyes had been boiling for far longer—and they suddenly had access to advocates in the form of people who could bend the laws of reality. She suspected that if it came to a head, the lighteyes would discover how little "tradition" was worth in the face of centuries of pent-up rage.

Navani put that problem out of her mind for the time being. It was dangerous to do so, but she *had* to perform mental triage. War was upon them, and for eight more days she needed to keep everyone pointed the same direction. She worked through a dozen other problems as functionaries and aides found her. She kept turning and finding lifespren swirling around her, or gloryspren skulking by the ceiling, or any number of them darting around. It was like she was some storming heroine from a story, the silly type where a young and innocent girl always had a thousand lifespren or whatever bobbing around her.

As she worked, she kept glancing toward the room where Dalinar met with the Stormfather. He'd always been ambitious. But this?

Is it right, what he contemplates? she asked the Sibling. *Ascending to Honor?*

Someone will need to eventually, the Sibling said. *The power can't be left to its own devices. It will come awake.*

Why hasn't it already? It's been thousands of years.

Whatever the reason, be glad. These powers aren't like the tiny pieces that become spren. The power of a Shard needs a partner, a Vessel. Without it . . .

What? Navani asked.

Great danger. We do not think as humans do. To separate the power from those who are attached to the Physical Realm . . . that should frighten you. It is not so terrible a thing for part of me *to despise you. But for the power of a god to? Dangerous. For all of us.*

Navani shivered at the Sibling's tone, but had to keep working. She checked in with her scholars, who had been waiting patiently in the next room—one of the few small ones that made a ring around the lifts up here. Inside, seven ardents had set up a display. Navani hated to make them cart it all the way up here, but despite the faster lifts, there just wasn't time for her to go elsewhere for meetings. People needed to come to her.

Rushu met her at the doorway, in her usual grey ardent's robes, sweat trickling down her brow. Indeed, this room was uncomfortably warm. The pretty woman was, as usual, trailed by several young male ardents eager for her attention. In this case they'd volunteered to set up Rushu's presentation. Even after all these years, Navani couldn't decide if Rushu was oblivious or deliberate in the way she ignored masculine interest.

"Brightness!" Rushu said, bowing as she entered. "Thank you for making the time."

"I don't have long, I'm afraid," Navani said. "Dalinar's antagonizing the Stormfather again, and I'll need to go the moment he's ready to talk."

"Understood, Brightness," Rushu said, walking her to a counter set up with some fabrials and a small oven burning Soulcast coal, of all things. A separate attractor fabrial above it collected the smoke and invisible deadly gases in a sphere of swirling blackness, allowing the small oven to burn without scent or the need for a chimney. Flamespren played within, their iridescent forms mimicking the shape of the fire and the molten red coloring of the hearts of coal.

Beside the oven was a more modern heating device, a large ruby fabrial like the ones they'd installed in many rooms. Those were proving, to the Sibling's annoyance, more effective than the tower's ancient methods, which required heating air in a boiler at the center of each floor, then blowing it into the specific room when requested. While that was amazing, a simple ruby heating fabrial didn't waste energy keeping massive boilers going all the time. Unfortunately, modern fabrials had other problems, at least in the eyes of the Sibling.

"We've only had a day or so to work," Rushu said, "but I wanted to show you our progress. This was an enlightened idea you had—and could revolutionize the fabrial art! Brightness . . . this could be your *legacy.*"

"Our legacy, Rushu," Navani said. "You're doing the work."

"Pardon, Brightness. It's your idea. Your genius."

Navani prepared another complaint, then . . . then discarded it. Storms, maybe she *was* growing. "Thank you, Rushu. Let's not assume we've changed the world after one day's work though. Show me what you've done."

Rushu unlatched the glass front of the oven. The group of flamespren within shivered as the cool air entered, then continued to frolic, taking the shapes of small minks cavorting over the surface of the burning coal.

She plucked a coal out with a pair of tongs, then nodded to one of her assistants. The heating fabrial next to the oven had an outlet valve: basically, a hole drilled into the gemstone that they kept plugged with an aluminum stopper. The assistant unscrewed the plug and opened the valve, usually something quite inadvisable. Because the moment he did so, the flamespren in the heating fabrial—a vital piece of what powered it—would escape.

This one scrambled out onto the plug and immediately started to vanish back into the Cognitive Realm. Then Rushu held her coal close to it. Another ardent used tuning forks to play what they hoped was a comforting tone to the spren. Instead of vanishing, the flamespren hopped onto the coal in Rushu's hand and let her deposit it in the oven. She came out a moment later with a different flamespren on another coal, blinking glowing red eyes, red "fur" blazing along its form.

Calmed by the tone, it let her bring it over to the fabrial. They trapped it inside using modern techniques of Stormlight diffusion. Then, with the gemstone plugged and a new spren inside, they recharged the fabrial with a Radiant's help and turned it back on so it began heating again.

What abomination are you creating now? the Sibling asked in Navani's head.

Abomination? Navani replied. *Did you not see what we just did?*

Enslaving spren, the Sibling said, *in torment and captivity.*

Navani leaned down by the front glass of the oven, where the spren were scampering across the coals. *Torment, you say? Tell me, Sibling, which of these spren was the one held captive? If it was tormented, I can't see any lasting effect.*

It's still wrong to keep spren in such small prisons, the Sibling said.

"Brightness," Rushu said, leaning in beside her and looking at the spren in the oven, "this is really *possible.* Did you read the writings of Geranid and Ashir I gave you?"

"Some of it," Navani said. "Before the invasion. I know they've been able to keep the same flamespren for months at a time, without losing them to the Cognitive Realm. It requires maintenance of a fire."

"Yes, but there's more!" Rushu said. "Their research taught me something amazing: the flamespren will stay even longer if you *give them treats.*"

"What kind of treats do flamespren want?" Navani asked. "More coal?"

"Names," Rushu said. "Names and compliments. Brightness, if you *think* about the spren, they mold to your thoughts."

"I read about the molding process," Navani said. "If you measure them, they lock to those measurements. But . . . compliments?"

"This one is Bippy," Rushu said, pointing to one of the spren. "See how its head has that little tuft on top?"

Bippy looked toward them at the attention, then hopped up to the edge of the oven, staring out with too-large eyes. A bit of fire itself, responding to Rushu merely *mentioning* its name.

"Fascinating," Navani said as some of the gloryspren that trailed her began to spin around the two of them.

"We can cultivate them over time," Rushu said. "An entire . . . herd? Pod?"

"I'm voting for a flare," one of the other ardents said. "A flare of flamespren."

"An entire flare, then," Rushu said, "of *domesticated* flamespren. It's too early to tell, but Brightness, you might be right. If they can be trained . . . then we can teach them to go in and out of fabrials on command."

Domesticated flamespren? the Sibling asked. *Nonsense.*

Is it? Navani asked, still watching Bippy. Rushu moved her finger back and forth in front of the glass, and Bippy ran to follow it. When Rushu complimented the spren on its trick, Navani could have sworn that Bippy glowed brighter. *Intelligent spren seek bonds with people. Why not lesser spren?*

It . . . it isn't natural, the Sibling said.

Pardon, Sibling, Navani said. *But neither is living in towers that are climate controlled. If we conformed only to what was natural, my people would be living naked in the wilderness and defecating on the ground.*

The Sibling simmered in the back of her mind, like a burning coal themself.

You've said our practices are cruel, Navani said, trying to soften her tone. *I'm attempting to do something about that. We keep chulls as beasts of burden; can we not do the same for spren? If being in a fabrial is uncomfortable for a spren . . . well, so is pulling a cart for a chull. But assuming it's not too bad, we should be able to train them to do it willingly, with rewards. We can . . . cultivate them, Sibling. Isn't this a better way? To have spren take shifts in the fabrials, with training to get in and out willingly?*

She held her breath, waiting. The Sibling had been hard-nosed about this.

See my heart, Sibling, she sent. *See that I'm trying.*

I see, the Sibling said. Rushu jolted and looked around, as did the other ardents, indicating the Sibling had chosen to be audible to them as well. *This is a good thing you attempt. All spren being free would be preferable. But . . .*

if this works . . . perhaps I can see a compromise. Thank you. For listening and changing. I had forgotten that people are capable of that.

Navani released a held breath, and with it a mountain of tension. Rushu's eyes had gone wide, and the ardent fiddled in her pocket, pulling free a notebook.

"Sibling?" Rushu whispered, awespren bursting around her. "Thank you for talking to me. Thank you *so* much!"

What is this? the Sibling asked Navani.

Rushu's been asking after you constantly since we bonded, Navani thought. *Haven't you heard?*

As I said, I don't pay attention to every word spoken inside my halls, the Sibling said. *Only to what is relevant.* Then, after a pause, they continued, *Is this relevant?*

To Rushu, yes, Navani said.

With her notepad out, Rushu bit her lip and looked to Navani pleadingly.

"Rushu would like the chance to talk to you," Navani said out loud. "I think she wants to ask you about fabrials."

"Very well," the Sibling said, and Rushu gasped softly. *You should go, Navani. I believe your husband's conversation with my sibling is finished. There will be ramifications.*

Navani nodded. As she left, though, she heard the first of Rushu's questions—and was surprised that it wasn't about fabrials at all.

"Navani tells me," Rushu said, "that you are neither male nor female."

"It is true."

"Could you tell me more about that?" Rushu asked.

"To a human, it must sound very strange."

"Actually, it doesn't," Rushu said quietly. "Not in the slightest. But talk, please. I want to know how it feels to be you."

Navani left them to it, pleased. The fabrial experiment showed promise—but more, if she could get the Sibling talking to other scholars, she suspected that would help with the spren's reintegration. So far, the Sibling only worked with them because Navani had essentially bullied them back into a bond. The more friends, or at least acquaintances, that the Sibling had, the better.

For now though, it was time for Navani to deal with another spren. And with a husband who had decided to become a god.

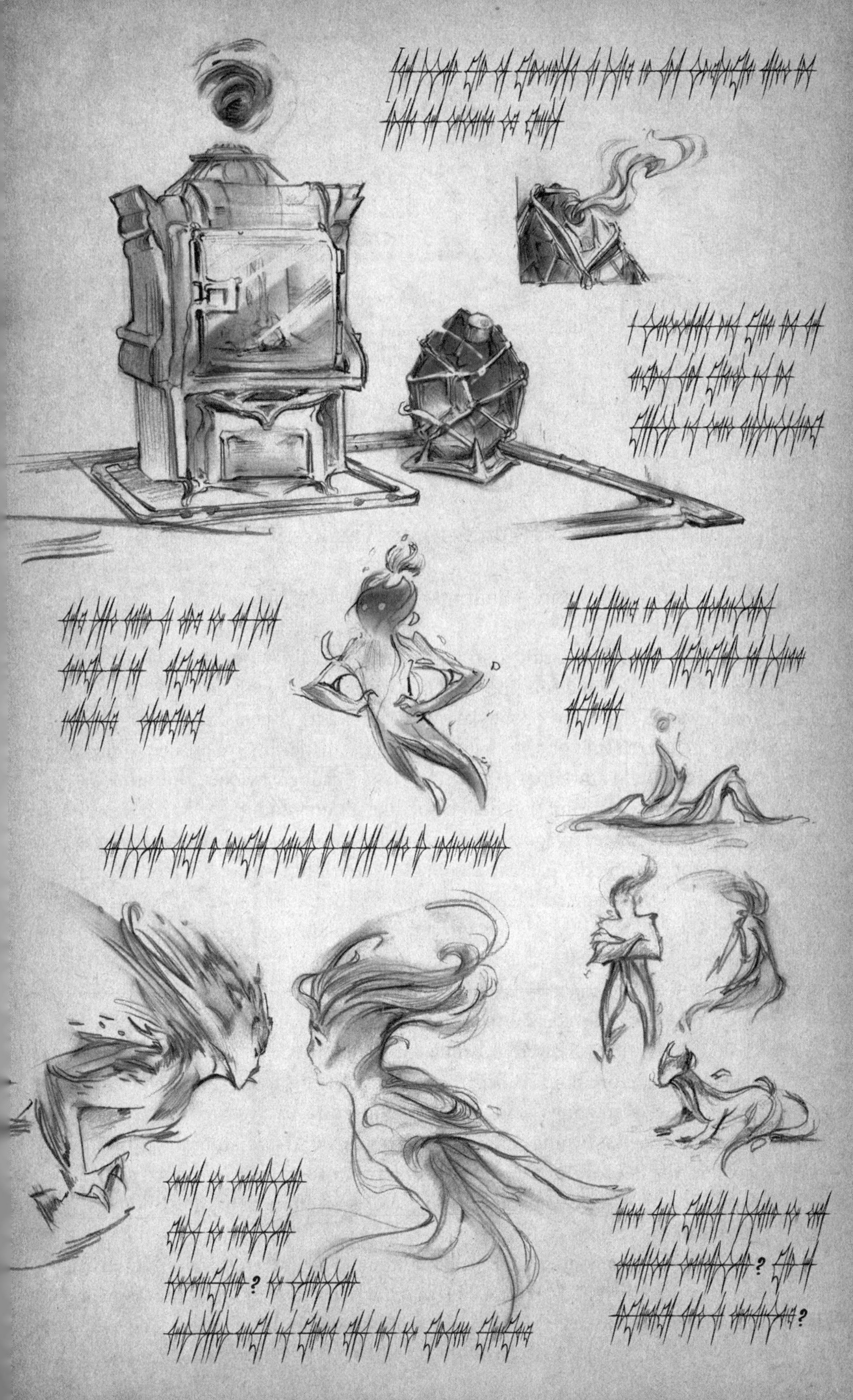

24 IN THE DANCING RING

TWENTY-SIX YEARS AGO

Szeth-son-Neturo found magic upon the wind, and so he danced with it.

Strict, methodic motions at first, as per the moves he had memorized. He stepped and spun, dancing in a wide circle around the large boulder. Szeth was as the limbs of the oak, rigid but ready. When those shivered in the wind, Szeth thought he could hear their souls seeking to escape, to shed bark like shells and emerge with new skin, pained by the cool air—yet aflush with joy. Painful and delightful, like all new things.

Szeth's bare feet scraped across the packed earth as he danced, getting it on his toes, loving the feel of the soil. He went right to the edge, feet kissing the grass—then danced back, spinning to the accompaniment of his sister's flute. The music was his dance partner, wind made animate through sound. The flute was the voice of air itself.

Time became thick when he danced. Molasses minutes and syrup seconds. Yet the wind wove among them, visiting each moment, lingering, then dashing away. He followed it. Emulated it. Became it.

More and more fluid he became as he circled the stone. No more rigidity, no more preplanned steps. Sweat flying from his brow to seek the sky, he was the air. Churning, spinning, *violent.* Around and around, his dance worship for the rock at the center of the bare ground. Five feet across and three feet high—at least the part that emerged from the soil—it was the largest in the region.

When he was wind, he felt he could touch that sacred stone, which had never known the hands of man. He imagined how it would feel. The stone of his family. The stone of his past. The stone to whom he gave his dance. He stopped finally, panting. His sister's music cut off, leaving his only applause the bleating of the sheep. Molli the ewe had wandered onto the circular dance track again, and—bless her—was trying to eat the sacred rock. She never had been the smartest of the flock.

Szeth breathed deeply, sweat streaming from his face, wetting the packed earth below with speckles like stars.

"You practice too hard," his sister—Elid-daughter-Zeenid—said. "Seriously, Szeth. Can't you ever *relax*?"

She stood up from the grass and stretched. Elid was fourteen, three years older than he was. Like him, she was on the shorter side—though she was squat where he was spindly. Trunk and branch, Dolk-son-Dolk called them. Which was appropriate, even if both Dolks were idiots.

She wore orange as her splash: the vivid piece of colorful clothing that marked them as people who added. One article per person, of whatever color they desired. In her case, a bright orange apron across a grey dress and vibrant white undergown. She spun her flute in her fingers, uncaring that she had broken her previous one doing exactly that.

Szeth bowed his head and went to get some water from the clay trough. Their homestead was nearby: a sturdy building constructed of boards, held together with wooden pegs. No metal, of course. Szeth's father worked on the rooftop, plugging a hole. Normally he oversaw the other shepherds, visiting them to give them help. There was some kind of training involved, which Szeth didn't understand. What kind of training did shepherds need? You just had to listen to the sheep, and follow them, and keep them safe.

Neturo was between assignments, working on the house he and his brothers had built. In a field opposite the home—distant but visible—the majority of their sheep grazed. A few, like Molli, preferred to stay close. Szeth liked when they could use fields near the homestead, as he could be near the stone and dance for it.

He dipped a wooden spoon into the trough and sipped rainwater, pure and clean. He peered through it to the clay bottom—he loved seeing things that couldn't be seen, like air and water.

"Why *do* you practice so hard?" Elid said. "There's nobody here but a couple of the sheep."

"Molli likes my dancing," Szeth said softly.

"Molli is blind," Elid said. "She's licking the dirt."

"Molli likes to try new experiences," he said, smiling and looking toward the old ewe.

"Whatever," Elid said, flopping back on the grass to stare at the sky. "Wish there was more to do out here."

"Dancing is something to do," he said. "The flute is something to do. We must learn to add so that—"

She threw a dirt clod at him. He dodged easily, his feet light on the ground. He might be only eleven, but some in the village whispered he was the best dancer among them. He didn't care about being the best. He only cared about doing it right. If he did it *wrong*, then he had to practice more.

Elid didn't think that way. It bothered him how apathetic she had become about practicing as she grew older. She seemed like a different person these days.

Szeth tied his splash back on—a red handkerchief he wore around his neck—and did a quick count of the sheep.

Elid continued to stare at the sky. "Do you believe the stories they tell," she eventually said, "of the lands on the other side of the mountains?"

"The lands of the stonewalkers? Why wouldn't I?"

"They just sound so outlandish."

"Elid, listen to yourself. Of *course* stories of outlanders sound outlandish."

"Lands where *everyone* walks on stones though? What do they do? Hop from stone to stone, avoiding the soil?"

Szeth glanced at their family stone. It peeked up from the earth like a spren's eyeball, staring unblinking at the sky, a vibrant red-orange. A splash for Roshar.

"I think," he said to Elid, "that there must be a lot more rock out there. I think it's hard to walk without stepping on stone. That's why they get desensitized."

"Where do the plants grow, then?" she asked. "Everyone always talks about how the outside is full of dangerous plants that eat people. There must be soil."

True. Maybe the terrible vines he'd heard of stretched out long, like the tentacles you might find on a shamble, or one of the beasts that lived in the tidal pools a short distance down the coast.

"I heard," Elid said, "that people constantly kill each other out there. That nobody adds, they only subtract."

"Who makes the food then?" he said.

"They must eat *each other.* Or maybe they're always starving? You know how the men on the ships are . . ."

He nervously looked toward the ocean—though it could be seen only on the sunniest days. Technically, his family was part of the farming town of Clearmount, which was at the very edge of a broad plain, excellent for grazing. This part of Shinovar wasn't crowded; it was a day or two between towns. He heard that in the north there were towns *everywhere.*

The grassland bordered the southeastern coast of Shinovar. Clearmount, and Szeth's family homestead, was in an honored location near the monastery of the Stonewards, which was up along the mountain ridge. In Szeth's estimation, this was the perfect place to live. You could see the mountains yet also visit the ocean. You could walk for days across the vibrant green prairie, never seeing another person. During the early months of the year they grazed the animals here, near their homestead. In the mid months they would take the sheep up the slopes, seeking the untouched and overgrown grass there.

He bent down next to old Molli, scratching at her ears as she rubbed her head against him. She might lick rocks and eat dirt, but she was always good for a hug. He loved her warmth, the scratchy wool on his cheek, the way she kept him company when the others wandered.

She bleated softly when he finished hugging her. Szeth wiped the salty, dried sweat from his head. Maybe he shouldn't practice dancing so hard, but he *knew* he'd made a few missteps. Their father said that they were blessed as people who could add beneath the Farmer's eyes. The perfect station. Not required to toil in the field, not forced to kill and subtract—allowed to tend the sheep and develop their talents.

Free time was the greatest blessing in the world. Maybe that was why the men of the oceans sought to kill them and steal their sheep. It must make them angry to see such a perfect place as this. Those terrible men, like any petulant child, destroyed what they could not have.

"Do you think," Elid whispered, "that the servants of the monasteries will ever come out and fight for us? Use the swords during one of the raids?"

"Elid!" he said, standing. "The shamans would *never* subtract."

"Mother says they practice with the Blades. I'd like to see that, hold one. Why practice, except to—"

"They will fight the Voidbringers when they arrive," Szeth snapped. "That is the reason." He glanced toward the ocean. "Don't speak of the swords. If the outsiders realized the treasures of the monasteries . . ."

"Ha," she said. "I'd like to see them try to raid a monastery. I saw an Honorbearer once. She could *fly*. She—"

"Don't speak of it," he said. "Not in the open."

Elid rolled her eyes at him, still lying on the grass. What had she done with her flute? If Father had to make yet another . . . She hated when he brought that up, so he forced himself to stay quiet. He pulled away from Molli, and then looked down at the ground she'd been licking.

To find another rock.

Szeth recoiled, part shocked, part terrified. It was small, only a handspan wide. It peeked up from the earth, perhaps revealed by last night's rain. Szeth put his fingers to his lips, backing away. Had he stepped on it while dancing? It was in the packed earth of the dancing ring.

What . . . what should he do? This was the first stone he'd ever seen emerge.

The ones in other villages and fields—carefully marked off and properly revered—had been there for years.

"What's up with you?" Elid said.

He simply gestured. She, perhaps sensing his level of concern, rose and walked over. As soon as she saw it, she gasped.

They shared a glance. "I'll get Father," Szeth said, and started running.

The Almighty has given us the limbs to move and the minds to decide. Let no monarch take away what was divinely granted. The Heralds also taught that all should have the sacred right of freedom of movement, to escape a bad situation. Or simply to seek a brighter dawn.

—From *The Way of Kings*, fourth parable

Walking into that safehouse was like stepping into a memory: that of Shallan's first meeting with Mraize. There, she'd entered the basement of a building that shouldn't have had one. Here—after following Shade through the entryway—she headed down another set of stairs cut into the stone.

They were smooth and well-shaped, dark with lichen, with some crem buildup at the corners of the steps—indicating that water had occasionally seeped in during the many years this place was unoccupied. Using a diamond for light, Shade took them down, and Shallan wondered at the ancients who had crafted it. Why would you build downward, risking flooding?

The air was damp in here, though the stones weren't wet, and she soon smelled incense. At the bottom of the stairs Shallan found the Alethi woman who had been sent to spy on Dalinar. The actor, an acolyte Ghostblood who had probably been teased with membership like Shallan.

The woman was studying Mraize's trophies. Housed in a small room full of glass-fronted cases, each unlabeled artifact had its own shelf lit by a handful of chips. A silvery horn or claw from some great beast. A chunk of light red crystal, like pink salt—though of a deeper, more vibrant color. A violet stone egg, partly crystalline, with silver swirling around its shell.

A fat, succulent leaf that pulsed red and seemed to radiate heat. A vial of pale sand she now recognized as having a very practical application.

Secrets, each stoking her hunger. She'd been strung along with the promise of a feast of answers, ideas, even dreams. Worlds full of people for her sketch collection. Shade let the newcomers linger to look at the trophies, but Shallan feigned indifference, leaning against the wall and glancing through the eyeholes in the mask toward the glass case beside her.

There, in the reflection on the glass, she glimpsed a shadowy figure with white holes for eyes. Sja-anat, one of the Unmade, was here. She studied Shallan in turn, existing in this realm only as a reflection, then smiled in a knowing way and vanished.

Storms. Did she know who Shallan really was? There wasn't time to wonder, as Shade waved the two newly arrived Ghostbloods into the next room. Shallan risked following—though Shade remained behind with the actor—and closed the door after them.

The room beyond turned out to be large, bigger than the building above, though the ceiling was relatively low. It was entirely stone, with little furniture, and her door was in the northeast corner. The southern wall—to Shallan's left, maybe forty feet away—was stacked with bales of hay, targets on each one. Maybe twenty feet ahead of her, seven people clustered around a lone podium. They chatted softly, and Shallan's breath caught as she saw Mraize with the group, fiddling with some contraption.

His very silhouette still intimidated her. He had a lean strength that never quite matched his fine clothing—which today was a coat, shirt, and trousers, with a ruffled portion of his shirt bursting out below the neck. Bright red, like blood from a slit throat.

Remember your breathing, Veil whispered. *Keep it up, kid.*

Shallan nodded absently and did her breathing exercises, calming her emotions. Half of the act of an imitation like this was about emotions, and not drawing the wrong spren. She could do this. No need for anxiety.

Mraize barely glanced over as the two newcomers joined six others. Shallan hung back, breathing calmingly and scanning the room, the mask sitting strangely on her face and blocking some of her field of vision. Where was Iyatil?

There. She saw the woman watching the group from beside the north wall, giving her a full view of the room. Short and masked, Iyatil crouched on the stone ground. Others, particularly those from Alethi culture, might have mistaken her for a guard, but she was the master, and Mraize her second.

Storms. Where Mraize was an overt, blatant kind of dangerous—always holding some sort of weapon, talking about hunting and death—Iyatil was the quiet kind. The kind that watched from the shadows, ruminating on the sounds you'd make when stabbed.

Shallan stepped forward, because standing in the doorway would draw attention. She forced herself to adopt the proper gait, and found her counterpart—the third masked offworlder—watching from all the way across the room by the west wall. He prowled forward, passing a stand of burning incense, and approached the two newcomers where—Shallan could barely hear—he offered them a drink.

The guard slunk to a bar set up against the east wall near Shallan and started mixing the drinks. This was a trained assassin—and Mraize was having him . . . mix drinks? Was this a way of intimidating the others?

No. No, the Ghostbloods were relaxed. They just needed drinks, and the assassin was the one available to get them.

"Ah," Mraize said as the large contraption in his hands clicked. "There." He hefted it and placed a small, heavy arrow into it. The device was a kind of crossbow, though larger and bulkier than the ones Shallan had seen.

Intrigued, Shallan stepped closer. Then she checked Iyatil and the other masked offworlder. They were watching not the device but the people. Right; Shallan tried to do the same, moving along the north wall, behind the group of people, who faced the targets.

"Mraize!" said Aika, the Thaylen trader in a skirt and vest. "You said this meeting was urgent; why are you playing with a new toy while we have drinks?"

"Had to wait for stragglers, Stolen Purse," he said, with a smile. "And a good drink, well studied, is an excellent start to any difficult conversation."

"Feels strange," said the other Thaylen, "to have so many of us together. How long has it been?"

"Since the briefing on the Everstorm," said the man wearing the patterned regalia of an Azish vizier. "The year before it arrived. Honestly, I've missed you all. Mraize, we have Oathgates now. We should meet more often."

"Meeting is dangerous," Mraize noted, raising the crossbow to sight at one of the targets.

"Mraize, love," said a woman, Veden like Shallan by her accent, "you enjoy danger, don't you?" Shallan took a Memory of her; aside from the vizier she was the only one of the group not in Hoid's stack of drawings.

"I enjoy *purposeful* danger, Icy Tongue," Mraize said—Shallan knew he had a nickname for everyone. Not a code name, just a quirk of his. "Danger with value and lessons. Foolhardy danger, without purpose, is a waste. A whorehouse for the emotions."

He triggered the crossbow, which shot the larger-than-average bolt into one of the hay bales.

"You missed the center, Mraize," one of the others said.

"Hence the practice," Mraize said, reloading the device.

As the assassin delivered drinks, Shallan worried what she was expected to do. Hopefully not fetch drinks. If she had to ask someone their preference, she didn't like her chances of imitating Iyatil's accent, which she'd heard only a few times.

Best for her to avoid saying anything. She prowled along the wall, smoke from one incense burner wafting in her wake.

Iyatil glanced at her.

Panic erupted in Shallan's chest, like daggers suddenly slid between her ribs.

Calm, Veil reminded.

She did her best, maintaining her poise, and picked a spot, then squatted, mimicking Iyatil's posture. Moving had drawn attention, so she determined to stay still. Blessedly, that seemed the right move. Iyatil's attention immediately returned to the group, and the other assassin settled back against the west wall and watched with folded arms.

"Is this device the reason we're all here, risking discovery, Mraize?" Icy Tongue asked, sipping her drink.

"No," he said, raising the weapon once more. "This is merely a diversion." He released and hit the target, though not at the center. "Any of you ever used one of these?"

"Crossbow," the Azish man said. "Common guardsman weapon."

"No," Icy Tongue said. "That's a Thaylen hand ballista. Heavier than a normal crossbow, intended to deliver a payload."

"Exactly," Mraize said, nodding to her. "They were developed to carry oil or a flaming brand to set fire to enemy sails. Never been terribly effective, unfortunately, but they're enjoyed by some enthusiasts. My father had a few when I was young." He held up the device, studying it. "A modern weapon, relying on mechanical strength rather than strength of arm."

"It's obviously difficult to aim," one of the others said. "I have trouble seeing why you're so interested in it."

Mraize casually loaded another bolt. Shallan studied him from where she crouched. His actions always had a purpose. What was the lesson here?

Storms, even when he wasn't watching her, she felt intimidated by him. Worse, she felt an icy chill at the nape of her neck and—despite trying not to—glanced at Iyatil. Who had been looking in her direction.

Shallan glanced away immediately, breathing as calmly as she could. An anxietyspren appeared anyway, a twisting black cross. Did Iyatil suspect? The spren wasn't an immediate tell, as one could come because you were worried about basically anything, but . . .

Storms. Storms, storms, *storms.* These were experts in the very arts that Shallan, as Veil, had pretended to know. Sweat ran down her face, and the mask suddenly felt heavy and suffocating. Her breath kept getting caught, the heat of it puffing around her cheeks and leaving her skin damp. She wanted to rip the mask free.

Did you notice, Veil said, *that he left his trouser leg tucked into his sock?*

Shallan glanced again at Mraize, and it was true. In dressing, he'd let his right sock catch the back of his trouser leg. In the face of her panic, it was an almost comical detail.

Veil chuckled. *He's just a person, Shallan. They all are. How does Mraize try to control you?*

"Through intimidation," she whispered. "Intimidation, secrets, and an air of mystery."

And if you refuse to give him any of those benefits?

Then . . .

Just a person. Iyatil too. People, and highly confident ones, who *could* make mistakes. They wouldn't expect Shallan to be here—would never assume her capable of taking the face of one of their best.

Even the most skilled swordswoman, Radiant said, *can lose a duel. They might be good, but if they suspected you, they'd have done something by now. You're doing it.*

You're doing it, Veil said. *I mean, look how silly he is.*

He really wasn't—it was a small mistake, one people commonly made. And she *was* in over her head, she knew. But this had to be done, and that little mistake Mraize had made, it *was* a sign that he was flawed.

Shallan chuckled softly, and the anxietyspren vanished away.

"Did you know," Mraize said to the others, "that on some worlds the crossbow became the default weapon for an entire era of warfare? While the weapon is generally slower to reload, it requires less training to use than a bow. With the right design it can pierce steel, so instead of the archer who practices all their life, or the regal lighteyes in plate armor, such battlefields are ruled by the farmers with two months' training and a technological advantage."

"Until a Shardbearer marches through their ranks and lays waste to the whole lot," said the man in the Alethi uniform. "You know Aladar tried crossbowman ranks once? Sure, they're powerful—but slow. Best used with a full pike block for support. And if there's one man in Plate on the other side, those crossbowmen draw him like rain draws vines."

"Interesting words, Chain," Mraize said, sighting with his hand ballista and loosing again. "Words spoken with the wisdom of the past—excellent at teaching us to deal with the world as it has existed. And *only* as it *has* existed."

He looked to Iyatil, who gestured for him to continue. He set the ballista down and opened the front of the podium. A glowing sphere spren floated out—much like the seon that Shallan had discovered in her communication box.

It changed shape, becoming an older man's face, with mustaches. Wait . . . did she recognize him?

"Tell them," Mraize commanded.

"We've found Restares," said the floating, glowing head. "He told us, and Shallan, the details. Mishram's prison is hidden in the Spiritual Realm."

Storms. That was *Felt.* One of Adolin's soldiers.

Coldness enveloped Shallan, accompanied by an overwhelming sense of disconnect. Felt was a spy.

Felt was a *Ghostblood.*

It was good no one was currently looking at her, because she couldn't keep the small shockspren away. All that time she'd spent trying to find the spy—an entire trip through Shadesmar—only to decide *she* was herself the spy. While Mraize had sent a backup. Of course he had. Storms . . . she felt suddenly violated, knowing Felt had been watching all along.

"That's the important bit," Felt continued. "Ala has been chatting with Restares, who has all kinds of things to say once you press him. Ala's pretty fed up with him, since little of it seems relevant, but I'm taking notes anyway."

Ala? The seon?

Wait . . .

"Thank you," Mraize said. "Ala and you have done well. You will be compensated."

Ala was a Ghostblood too? It certainly sounded that way. On one hand, Shallan's sense of betrayal deepened—but on the other, she was relieved. The spren had put up quite an act of being a frightened prisoner, but if that wasn't the case, then maybe Shallan didn't have to feel so bad for her.

"I don't want your rusting coin, Mraize," Felt said. "I never wanted any part of any of this. Though Ala specifically asked me to tell you she wants a pony. I . . . I think she might be joking?"

Mraize smiled. "Keep the Herald captive. Further instructions will come." He made a gesture, and the face faded back to a glowing sphere, which hid in the podium again.

"The prison is in the Spiritual Realm?" one of the group said. "So it's impossible to reach."

"Hardly," Mraize said. "Iyatil and I received intel from a very special contact yesterday, indicating that if we watched Dalinar we would have a chance to enter the Spiritual Realm. We thought we might need our newest recruit to nudge him into it, but that wasn't necessary. Dalinar met with Cultivation herself, who urged him to seek Honor's power. He will be stepping into the Spiritual Realm soon, and Iyatil and I will follow.

Until we return, Zora, this cell is yours. You will take the seon and report directly to Master Thaidakar."

The Azish vizier nodded.

The Thaylen woman he'd called Stolen Purse folded her arms. "You've never specifically left someone else in charge before."

"This is true," Mraize said, calmly reloading his hand ballista.

"So . . . you think this is dangerous?" the woman continued.

"I know it is," Mraize said. "We might not return. Or if we do, hundreds of years could have passed here. But we *will* find Mishram's prison."

"Wait," said Icy Tongue. "Mraize, how does this help Master Thaidakar's plans?"

Mraize didn't reply, instead sighting his target and loosing. He finally hit the red center circle.

"We should be working on our plan," Icy Tongue said, "to transport Stormlight offworld, now that we know it can be blanked of Identity and transferred between realms. How does chasing down some ancient spren further Master Thaidakar's orders to provide him a renewable source of Investiture?"

Shallan leaned forward. She'd already known that the Ghostbloods wanted the power of the Radiants and the versatility of Stormlight. That explained a great deal—such as, for example, recruiting Shallan. But there was more. Why was he so interested in Mishram? She reached into her sleeve, fingering the spanreed she'd hidden in there, strapped to her arm. She sent three quick flashes—a warning to the others to be ready, but not to come quite yet. She was close.

Mraize didn't answer. He readied his weapon for another shot—though he selected a bolt with a gemstone affixed to it, near the head. What had they said? That these hand ballistas were designed to deliver a larger-than-normal payload?

Oh, storms. A gemstone by itself was meaningless. But if he managed to get hold of the anti-Stormlight that Navani had developed in Shallan's absence . . .

He launched the bolt, and hit the target straight on.

The wisdom of the past is excellent at teaching us to deal with the world as it has existed. And only *as it* has *existed.*

Mraize wasn't showing affection for an old, obsolete piece of technology. He was practicing with a weapon that, suddenly, could be used to kill Radiants—and their spren.

"Once in the Spiritual Realm," Mraize said, "Iyatil and I will watch Dalinar. If we stay close to him, most likely he will lead us to the prison."

"How can you know that?" Icy Tongue asked.

"Because I do," he said. "Master Thaidakar has approved this course—and you eight will lead in our absence. That is all you need know."

"Pardon," said Icy Tongue, "but we're Ghostbloods. No secrets, Mraize. Those are the rules."

"Master Thaidakar's actions," Mraize said, "prove he does not believe in this rule. Sometimes information is dangerous, and must be kept sheathed like a fine blade."

Shallan leaned forward farther, but then caught something from the corner of her eye. Iyatil was in motion. The short woman crossed the room and stooped beside Shallan, where she whispered something.

In a language that Shallan did not recognize.

⁘

Dalinar sat with Navani in the garden chamber, both of them in chairs at the center, facing one another. He held her hands, vines moving around them without wind or touch. Navani said they were dancing to rhythms Dalinar couldn't hear.

"Well?" he asked. "What do you think?"

"I don't know, Dalinar," she said, squeezing his hands. "What happens if this works? Will I lose you?"

"If I were to Ascend to Honor," Dalinar said, "I don't think you'd lose me. Cultivation spoke to me earlier, and according to Ash, Honor often interacted with the Heralds."

"I don't mean losing your presence," she said. "I mean losing *you*—your love, your humanity. I don't want to be selfish, and we will do what the world needs. But I have to ask. What will it mean, Dalinar? And does it *have* to be *you*?"

He didn't know the answer to either question. They both leaned forward, him resting his forehead on hers. Contemplating. Deciding. Fearspren wiggled out of the stones around his feet.

"All this time," he whispered, "I've been trying to become a better person, Navani. Through the course of it, I've discovered terrifying truths, and I've shared them with the world. That our god died millennia ago, that humankind stole this world from those who owned it. Answers that once were easy now prove difficult.

"I am scared of this step, but I want to provide answers again regardless. I feel that something has been guiding me all this time. Something I can't explain, something beyond Honor. I *know* someone has to step up and do this. The contest isn't enough. There's more, and I think I'm the only one who can find out what it is. I spent a great deal of time searching for how to become a stronger Bondsmith, and I think that was a step toward a greater truth of what I actually need to become."

She gripped his hands, and he loved her for the way she gave his words some thought and didn't contradict him immediately. But also for the way she didn't immediately agree.

Wit finally returned, slipping in. Dalinar and Navani pulled back from each other, and he could see the concern in her eyes.

"Love," he said, "we don't know if this will work. We don't have to make all the decisions now."

"Sometimes," she said, "it's good to ask the questions long before you need the answers. I can't help thinking that we're dabbling in things well beyond our capacity, Dalinar. The powers of gods? Several of my scholars inadvertently *detonated* themselves just last month, working on anti-Light. Now you're contemplating going somewhere that frightens even *Wit.*"

"To be fair," Wit said, leaning against the wall near the door, "a great number of things terrify me. I mean, have you considered—*really* considered—how insane it is that society entrusts you mortals with *children*? After . . . what, two decades of life, half of it spent in diapers?"

"Wit," Navani said, "people don't spend ten years in diapers."

"See?" Wit said. "I'm roughly ten thousand years old, and *I* barely feel comfortable with my knowledge of how to care for an infant. It's a wonder any of you make it to adolescence . . ."

"Focus, Wit," Dalinar said. "The plan. The Spiritual Realm."

"We're out of our depth," Navani said. "Like an army struggling against an enemy with far more modern equipment."

"Or a scholar trying to read complex ideas in a language she has barely studied," Dalinar added. "But we have only eight days before I need to face Odium, and I'm certain the Stormfather is hiding things from me."

"The Sibling agrees," Navani said. "They keep pointing out the Stormfather's inaccuracies and our incorrect understanding of historical events."

"The goal," Wit said, "is for you to relive those events. So you can find out the truth of Honor's death, and uncover secrets even I don't know." He frowned. "I don't know why the Stormfather would lie though."

"I don't think . . . he ever expected anyone to be able to contradict him," Dalinar said. "He never thought the Sibling would reawaken." He met Navani's eyes. "So long as the Heralds are mad and Wit is useless—"

"Hey!"

"—the Stormfather could provide the sole narrative. We *have* to find the truth, Navani. We *have* to know what happened to Honor."

"Which brings us back to the central question," Navani said softly. "What does it *mean* to replace him?"

"Dalinar would Ascend," Wit said. "His mind would expand to see with the eyes of deity. The Shards are not omniscient—it is relatively easy to hide things from them. But they are . . . blessed with a near-infinite *capacity* to understand. To see into the future, in its many permutations, and to comprehend what that means."

"It sounds like," Navani said, "you'd no longer be human."

"It sounds like," Dalinar said, "a version of what has already happened to you, with your bond to the tower. We're working through that. We could work through this."

She nodded hesitantly. "But I ask again: Do *you* have to do it, Dalinar? Why must it always be you?"

From Jasnah or Adolin, perhaps those words would have been a challenge. A question why *he* always put himself in the center of the issue. He found such questions ridiculous—who else could he trust with a problem of such magnitude? Someone needed to walk the difficult roads, and—as ruler—it was his duty. That was what *The Way of Kings* taught.

From Navani, it wasn't a challenge but a plea. If someone was called to sacrifice, couldn't he pass the burden just this once?

"I can't trust this to anyone else," Dalinar said. "You learn, as a general, when to send your best lieutenant—and when to go yourself." He squeezed her hands. "Navani, if I lose the contest of champions . . . we lose *me.* I will be Odium's, and he will bring out the Blackthorn. Whatever we can do to prevent that, I want to try, even if it means this Ascension, as Wit calls it. If, after the contest, the power is changing me too much, I will find another and give it to them."

"Is that allowed?" she asked, glancing to Wit.

"Technically, yes," he said. "But it is extremely difficult to do. Once you are a god, Dalinar, it is nearly impossible to let go."

"Surely it has been done," Dalinar said.

Wit grew distant, a faint smile on his lips. "Once. It wasn't a full Ascension, but a mortal did give up the power once. It proved to be the wrong choice, but it was the most selfless thing I believe I've ever witnessed. So yes, Dalinar, it is possible. But not easy."

"Nothing ever is," he said. "Not for us."

Navani looked back at him, then nodded. "Very well. Let's do it then. Together."

". . . Together?"

"I'm not going to let you go into the realm of the gods alone," she said. "You'll need a scholar to help interpret what you see in the past."

Damnation. She was right. They *had* gone into visions together before; it was possible. But if it was going to be as dangerous as Wit implied . . .

No. From her expression, he knew that if he suggested taking another scholar instead of her, he would bring down a wrath to make the Stormfather look like a spring squall. And justly so. For all the same arguments he'd made to himself about doing this personally, he needed the best at his side. That was Navani.

"You are wise," he said. "I hate it, but you are right. We'll try this together. But we'll need to prepare the others to lead Urithiru while we are gone. Wit thinks it will take us days to accomplish this."

"I can keep an eye on things here," Wit said. "First, we'll have you peek into the Spiritual Realm and see if this even works. If you leave your bodies behind, as I'm hoping, I *should* be able to bring you back out if you're needed."

"Excellent," Navani said. "How do we proceed?"

"Well," Wit said, "you once had to use a highstorm and the Stormfather's powers—but you're Bondsmiths now. You can open a perpendicularity and push into the Spiritual Realm. Once there, I suggest using Connection to guide you into a specific slice of the past. I'll help you with that. You can peek into an event I've witnessed, experience it, and return so we can compare notes. If that works, we can send you on a longer journey, into times I wasn't here to witness."

Dalinar and Navani met each other's eyes and nodded.

"Great," Wit said. "Let's head down the elevator and find a good location to try the experiment."

"Why not here?" Dalinar asked.

"You are about to pierce through the three realms and try to throw yourselves into the Spiritual Realm," Wit said. "If you get it wrong, you'll end up in Shadesmar—but with the force you're using, you could as easily cast yourselves beyond the tower. Personally, I'd feel more comfortable if we were somewhere lower, so you had less distance to fall if things go awry."

"Very well," Dalinar said, standing. "Let's tell Aladar and Sebarial what we're planning, just in case, then find somewhere lower down for the experiment."

26 HUNTING THE HUNTER

I continued on my way, contemplating dust and the nature of desertion. For I, as king, had walked away from my duties, and it was different for me. Had I not renounced a throne the Almighty had granted, and in so doing, undermined my very own words? Was I abandoning that which was divinely given me?

—From *The Way of Kings*, fourth parable

Shallan stared at Iyatil. The woman's eyes seemed distant behind that mask, and strangely human—as if the mask were some beast that had swallowed a person.

Iyatil repeated her comment in, presumably, their native tongue. In a panic, Shallan reached for the spanreed in her sleeve, ready to call the others. Only . . . she hadn't actually *learned* anything yet. *How* were the Ghostbloods going to sneak through to the Spiritual Realm with Dalinar? Why were they so interested in one of the Unmade? They'd already made contact with Sja-anat. Wasn't that enough?

There was no helping it. If Iyatil hadn't been suspicious before, she would be when she got no reply. Shallan gripped the spanreed.

But Veil whispered: *You can do this, Shallan. Try.*

Shallan couldn't understand what Iyatil had said, but what was her body language saying? Iyatil nodded to the side, toward the third masked offworlder. Her words had been short and terse, maybe a question, more likely an order. So, risking it, Shallan gave a curt nod.

That worked, and Iyatil scurried back toward the doorway in the eastern wall, Shallan following. The third assassin met them, and they huddled together, with Iyatil speaking quickly in their own language. In the center of the room, Mraize hinted to the others what Shallan had guessed: that with some minor tweaks, the hand ballista would be very useful in coming years.

Shallan couldn't pay attention to him, for she had now gotten herself into a conversation with not merely *one* person speaking another tongue, but *two.* They'd expect a response other than a nod. She had to escape the conversation without making a scene.

Find an excuse, Veil whispered, *for not paying attention.*

Yes . . . distractibility was a universal human foible. Unfortunately there wasn't much in the room. Just the targets, Mraize and his crew, four bleak stone walls . . .

Wait. The doorknob. Silvery, polished, reflective. Being crouched down together as they were put it near eye level. Shallan fixated on it, waiting until the others noticed her distraction.

"*Aleen?*" Iyatil said to Shallan. "*Aleen, vat ist erest missen?*"

Shallan pointed at the doorknob and spoke, whispering a word that would be the same regardless of language. "Sja-anat." The whisper hopefully masked her voice.

Iyatil hissed softly, pushing Shallan aside to look closely at the doorknob. When she saw nothing, she grunted, and—ignoring their conversation—stalked toward Mraize. The other foreigner glanced at Shallan, so she shrugged, then leaned in to study the doorknob. He moved off after Iyatil.

Shallan calmed her nerves, avoiding drawing a spren this time. Iyatil had taken the bait, and hadn't seemed to find anything too irregular about Shallan. Unless she was telling Mraize she was an impostor right now. Maybe it *was* time to call the others. Shallan reached again for her spanreed, but a moment later a shadow moved across the doorknob, and then Sja-anat appeared as she had earlier: a jet-black female figure with white holes for eyes.

I wondered, she said in Shallan's mind, *how you would manage without speaking her tongue, Shallan. That was clever.*

"So you *do* know it's me," Shallan whispered.

It is difficult for mortals to distinguish one soul's flame from another, but I am not mortal.

"Are you going to reveal me?"

As you just revealed me? Perhaps.

"Whose side are you on, Sja-anat?" Shallan whispered. "Truly. What is your game?"

Game, Shallan? I fight for survival. *Odium will rip through anyone, anything, to get what he wishes. Thousands of years have proven he cares nothing for me or my children. Honor is a coward who always hated us. Destroyed us. Betrayed us. And all Cultivation does is watch.*

I am on the side of preserving a world for my children. You should not fear "my side," Shallan. You should embrace it. If there is room for my children, there will be room for yours.

Iyatil returned, Mraize tailing her. Again Shallan gripped the spanreed but held her nerve. Sja-anat did not hide, but persisted—small, but distinguishable, as a reflection in the doorknob, looking up at Iyatil.

"Lieke, stay here," Iyatil said in Alethi. "Entertain the others." She opened the door, grabbing the doorknob despite the reflection there. Mraize followed, as did Shallan, assuming that Lieke was the other masked figure.

Shade and the actor were gone from this little alcove. It was darker in here, where the sole light was provided by chips—painted on one side, to shine only on Mraize's treasures.

"There," Iyatil said. "My trophy case. I see her reflection."

Wait . . . *her* trophy case? It wasn't Mraize's?

Iyatil pulled a mirror out on wheels from behind one of the cabinets. Shallan closed the door to the other room softly, then stayed back, trying not to draw attention.

Sja-anat appeared in the mirror, all slender smoke and magnetic eyes.

"Why are you here?" Iyatil demanded. "You're supposed to be watching the Bondsmiths. Have they begun the process?"

"My children watch," Sja-anat said, her voice tinny and small, as if she were communicating down the length of a long hallway. "The Sibling is awake. They are not easy to fool, even for me. I myself would draw attention."

"This isn't what you told us," Iyatil said. "The timing will be tight. We need to get into Shadesmar and be ready to enter Dalinar's perpendicularity as soon as it opens."

"You will not miss your opportunity," Sja-anat said. "Though I question your eagerness to be lost in that place."

"You said our spren could guide us," Mraize said, stepping closer to the mirror. "You said they understood that realm."

Our spren?

Our spren?

Shallan backed up a pace, pressing against the cold stone wall. Mraize and Iyatil had spren? They were Radiant?

That's why they were so eager to meet Sja-anat! Veil said. Sja-anat's requirements for those who bonded her children were different from those of ordinary Radiants.

Storms. Shallan had been key to facilitating Sja-anat meeting with the Ghostbloods. She'd known all along that her flirtatious half-commitment to the Ghostbloods was dangerous. Here was proof. Why had she let it go on for so long?

You were confused, Radiant said, *far from home, and you thought Jasnah was dead. You needed to feel a part of something. Do not be too hard on yourself.*

Shallan had made many mistakes, yes, but she hoped she was learning from them. Today she stepped forward, closer to Iyatil and Mraize, hoping to catch signs of their spren—to tell what orders they had joined. Or . . . if they had bonded Sja-anat's children, were they actually Radiants? Renarin was, but he'd chosen to take the title for himself.

In her shock, she'd missed some of what Sja-anat was saying. Assurances that her children could offer guidance in the Spiritual Realm. "There is only so much that can be done for mortals," the Unmade continued. "Like a fish suddenly on the land, you will be in a place that is hostile to your existence. My children will guide you, but you still may not return."

"We will go regardless," Mraize said softly.

"And I am glad," Sja-anat said. "One last warning, however. I do not think you will find an ally in my sister. Mishram is not . . . fond of humans."

"We are not seeking an ally," Iyatil said. "Tell us when Dalinar starts getting ready, so we may prepare."

"As you wish," Sja-anat said. "My children say he is talking to his advisors. He is close though."

"What of Shallan?" Mraize asked. "Does she hunt us?"

"She does," Sja-anat said. And did not look toward Shallan standing behind them.

Shallan didn't spot a spren on Mraize's clothing or shoulder, but she did note the quiver of crossbow bolts at his side. Specifically, one had a gemstone affixed with white-blue light that warped the air around it. Shallan hadn't seen the anti-Light, but Wit had told her about it, and she recognized it from the description.

Mraize, as ever, had worked quickly and efficiently. So far as Shallan knew, there was barely a tiny bit of the stuff in Urithiru, carefully locked away. Yet Mraize had already stolen some. She couldn't help but be impressed.

"I'm worried Shallan will interfere," he said.

"The girl is distracted," Iyatil said. "You fixate upon her too much, acolyte. We made the proper threats; her attention will be on protecting and watching her loved ones."

"Yes, *Babsk,*" Mraize said.

They're human, Veil whispered. *Fallible. Remember that.*

Iyatil waved Mraize off, and he bowed to her. It felt strange to see him defer; he had always seemed so in command. Though there *was* a level of self-control to his obedience. Mraize did not complain or seem upset to be dismissed. He walked with his head held high, opening the door to reveal the Ghostbloods practicing with his oversized crossbow.

Sja-anat vanished, and Shallan followed Mraize, trying not to be trapped with Iyatil. Unfortunately, the woman put her hand up to stop Shallan.

"Something is wrong with him," Iyatil said softly. "I do not think he has been replaced with a duplicate, but I do question his loyalty to our cause."

Thankfully, the words were in Alethi. Perhaps because she'd just been speaking to Sja-anat in that tongue, and continued on momentum. Perhaps it was because in this room, away from the others, she didn't worry about being overheard. Or perhaps with Sja-anat around . . . she *wanted* to be?

Iyatil still focused on Mraize, thoughtful. "I've spent so long training him. It is natural for him to want his own acolytes. But he thinks solely of his own advancement, and not the greater purpose."

Shallan needed to push. She needed answers. She found herself speaking in a whisper. "Thaidakar's purpose."

"Master Thaidakar will see eventually," Iyatil said. "He is smarter than you give him credit for. He works to protect his homeland above all else, but once we find Mishram for *my* purposes, he will see. Master Thaidakar can only protect his land if the Shards can be controlled. Will this fit your plans as well?"

Stay silent? Or speak? Which was more suspicious?

Iyatil looked at her, waiting. Shallan sweated, and tried giving a nod again.

"That's it?" Iyatil said. "You've been so . . ."

She focused on Shallan, eyes widening behind her mask. Shockspren exploded around her. Damnation. That was it.

Iyatil lunged, and Shallan caught the hand, expecting a knife—but Iyatil wasn't attacking. She was reaching for Shallan's hood, and in her deflection Shallan knocked it aside, revealing her wig.

Iyatil hissed, then shouted, scrambling backward, "Radiants! We are discovered!"

TWENTY-SIX YEARS AGO

Szeth's father, Neturo-son-Vallano, knelt beside the new stone. Szeth's mother, Zeenid-daughter-Beth, was overseeing painting classes in the town, so they'd sent her a message via Tek, one of their carrier parrots. Wind blew across them, bringing with it the pungent scent of the gathered sheep in the nearby pasture.

Szeth hid behind his father, peeking out. He wasn't certain why this new stone frightened him so. He loved their rock, and a new one was surely cause for celebration, but shamefully . . . he wished he hadn't found it. Something new meant possible celebration, possible attention, possible change. He preferred quiet days full of languid breezes and bleating sheep. Nights beside the hearth or the firepit, listening to Mother tell stories. He didn't want some grand new thing. Szeth had what he loved.

"What do we do, Father?" Elid asked. "Call the Stone Shamans?"

"It depends," he said. "Depends."

Their father was a calm man, with a long beard he liked to keep tied with a green ribbon at the bottom, matching ones on his arms, together forming his splash. He got to wear three, as his duty of training other shepherds elevated him. His head was shaded by his customary tall reed hat with a wide brim, and he had a bit of a paunch that spoke to his talent as a cook. He had all the answers. Always.

"What about it is uncertain, Father?" Szeth said, peeking around at the little stone. "We just do what is right."

Father glanced at their larger stone, then at this one. "A single rock is a blessed anomaly. Two . . . might mean more. It might mean the spren have chosen this region."

"What do you mean?" Elid asked, hands on her hips.

"I mean there might be other rocks," Father said, "hiding beneath the surface here. Stone Shamans will want to set aside the entire region, preserve it and watch it for a few years to see if anything else emerges."

"And . . . us?" Szeth asked.

"Well, we'll have to move," Father replied. "Tear down the house, in case it's accidentally on holy ground. Set up wherever the Farmer finds land for us. Maybe in the town."

In the *town*? Szeth turned, looking into the distance—though the rolling hills prevented him from seeing Clearmount unless he climbed up on top of one. It was close enough to walk to in an hour or so, but he found the place noisy, congested. In the town, it felt like the mountains weren't just around the corner, because buildings blocked them out. It felt like the meadows had gone brown, replaced by dull roads. You couldn't smell the sea breezes.

He didn't hate the town. But he got the sense that it hated the things he loved.

"I don't want to move!" Elid said. "We found a rock! We shouldn't be *punished*."

"If it's right though," Szeth said, "then we have to do it. Right, Father?"

Father stood up, pulling at his trousers, and waited. Soon Szeth picked out his mother hurrying along the path between hills toward their home. She wore a long green skirt as her splash—while it was only one piece, that size . . . well, it was an audacious amount for her station. She had a white apron over the front, and curly light brown hair that bunched up around her head like a cloud.

She was carrying one of the town's shovels—a relic crafted from metal that had never seen rock, Soulcast by an Honorbearer and gifted to them.

Szeth gaped, his jaw dropping. That couldn't mean . . .

Mother hurried up to them, shovel on her shoulder. Father nodded toward the new rock, and Mother let out a relieved sigh. "So small? Your note had me worried, Neturo."

"Mother?" Szeth said. "What are you doing?"

"Merely a quick relocation," she said. "I borrowed one of the shovels, but didn't tell anyone why. We'll dig up the rock and move it a few hundred yards. Let it rain a little, so it seems to have naturally poked up, then tell everyone."

Szeth gasped. "We can't *touch* it!"

Mother pulled out a pair of gloves. "Of course not. That's why I brought gloves, dear."

"That's the same thing!" Szeth said, horrified. He looked to his father. "We can't do this, can we?"

 Father scratched at his beard. "Depends, I suppose, on what you think, son."

"Me?"

"You found the rock," Father said, glancing at Mother, who nodded in agreement. "So you can decide."

"I choose whatever is right," Szeth said immediately.

"Is it right for us to lose our home?" Father asked.

"I . . ." Szeth glanced at the house.

"There might be dozens of rocks underneath here," Father said. "If that's the case, then we should absolutely move. But in the hundreds of years that rain has fallen on this region, only two have emerged. So it's unlikely. Moving the stone a few hundred yards will still make the shamans watch this area, but with the rocks being farther apart, the worry will be more nebulous. But that requires us to move it. In secret."

"We hate the stonewalkers," Szeth said, "because of how they treat rock."

Father knelt down, one hand on Szeth's shoulder. "We don't hate them. They simply don't know the right way of things."

"They *raid* us, Father," Elid said, folding her arms.

"Yes, well," he said. "*Those* men are evil, but it's not because they live in a place with too much stone. It's because of the choices they make." He smiled at Szeth. "It's okay, son. If you want us to turn this in now, well, we'll do it."

"Can't you just . . . tell me what to do?" Szeth asked.

"No, I don't think that I can," Father said. "Unfair to put you in this spot, I know, but the spren gave you the first sight. You should decide. We can move the rock, or we can move our home. I'll accept either one."

"Maybe we should let him sleep on it," Mother said.

"No," Szeth said. "No. We can . . . move the rock."

All three of them relaxed as he said it, and he felt a sudden—shameful—resentment. His father said Szeth could choose, but they'd all clearly wanted a specific decision. He'd made it not because it was right, but because he had sensed their desires.

But how could they all want it if it *wasn't* right? Maybe they saw something he didn't—maybe he was broken. But if so, they should have simply told him what they intended to do, and then done it. That would have been fine. Why give him the choice? Didn't they see that made this *his* fault?

Mother pulled on her gloves and started digging. Szeth winced each time the shovel scraped the stone. That metallic sound was *not* natural. He hoped that they would discover the rock was enormous—so that the plan had to be abandoned. In the end, it was small. Eight inches long, and a dull grey color. He could have held it in one hand, if he'd wanted.

Molli the ewe, seeming to sense his tension, rubbed up against him and he gripped at her wool, her warmth. Even Mother seemed a little unsure, now that she'd dug the rock out. She stepped back, leaving it in the hole.

"You scraped it," Elid said. "That seems . . . kind of obvious."

"Once we've buried it again," Mother said, "nobody will see the scrapes."

"How much trouble would we be in," Elid asked, "if someone found out?"

"I suspect the Farmer wouldn't be happy," Father said. He laughed then, and it sounded genuine. "Might require some cake to make up for it. Don't get that look, Szeth. We show devotion because we *choose* to. And so, the kind of devotion we make is ours to decide."

"I . . . don't understand," he said. "Don't the Stone Shamans *tell* us what to do?"

"They share the teachings of the spren," Mother said, as she shouldered the shovel. "But *we* interpret those teachings. What we're doing here today is reverent enough for me."

Szeth thought on that and wondered—as this was not the first clue in his life—if perhaps this was why they chose to live outside the town. Many shepherd families lived at least part of the year inside it. His family visited each month for devotions, so he didn't dare think that his family *wasn't* faithful. Yet the older he got, the more questions he had.

How did he feel about his parents doing something he *knew* the shamans wouldn't approve of?

They were still all standing there, staring at the rock, when the horns sounded. Father looked up, then whispered a soft prayer to the spren of their stone. The horns meant raiders on the southern coast. Stonewalkers.

Szeth felt an immediate panic. "What do we do?"

"Gather the sheep," Father said. "Quickly. We must drive them toward Dison's Valley on the other side of the town. The Farmer has troops in the region. We'll be safe inland."

"But this?" Szeth said, gesturing to the rock. "*This!*"

Mother, suddenly determined, reached down and grabbed it in her gloved hands. Together, all four of them froze, then looked toward their family stone. It sat there, unmoving. None of them were struck down. Szeth thought he could tell, from the way his parents slowly relaxed, that they hadn't been certain.

At least this indicated his parents hadn't been secretly moving rocks around all his life. Mother walked over to a tree nearer their house, then carefully placed the stone into a gnarled nook among the roots and hid it with leaves.

"That will do for now," she said. "If raiders *do* come here, they'll think nothing of a stone. They don't reverence stone or the spren who live within them. You all gather the sheep; I'll return this shovel."

Father and Elid went to do exactly that. Szeth hugged Molli, wishing this day had never begun.

28 OBSTACLE

I do not have answers, and there will always be some who denounce me for this decision I made. But let me teach a truth here that is often misunderstood: sometimes, it is not weakness, but strength, to stand up and walk away.

—From *The Way of Kings*, fourth parable

Iyatil ran for the larger room, giving Shallan time to reach into her sleeve and activate the spanreed strapped to her arm. A long press, locked into position, which would make the ruby on the other spanreed pulse—indicating an emergency.

Shallan turned to run up the steps.

Radiant stopped her. She'd fooled Mraize and Iyatil. She'd *done* it. They were just people. Deadly, capable, manipulative. But people. In some ways *less* capable than Shallan, for if they genuinely had spren, they were very new to them. Perhaps barely a few days into their bonding.

Instead of running, Radiant ripped away the stupid wig and mask. "Armor," she commanded.

Shallan!

It encased her in a heartbeat, a bright glow from the front of her visor illuminating the room. Pattern followed at her summons, a brilliant, silvery sword. And Testament?

She would not ask Testament to kill again. Shallan reached her left arm to the side, and Testament appeared as a powerful shield, affixed to her arm, light as a cloth glyphward.

Shallan was no longer a child, confused, terrified, forced to kill with a gifted necklace. She had spoken Truth. And today she was the Radiant she'd once only imagined.

From the larger room with the bales of hay, Iyatil shouted to the others. "The Lightweaver is here! She was impersonating Aleen!"

Radiant stepped through the doorway, checking the corners. She leveled her weapon at Lieke, who had been right inside. He fled backward, stepping on purple fearspren. Radiant didn't blame him. Facing a Shardbearer without Shards was not a wise proposition. Unless you were a storm-faced bridgeman, of course.

Across the room, Mraize took her in, then smiled. Storm him, he was *proud* of her. He calmly raised his hand ballista and shot a normal, non-lit bolt. She deflected it easily with her shield, and was struck by a new fear. What would happen if anti-Light met a Shardweapon?

Storms, they were in unknown territory.

Iyatil ripped the ballista out of Mraize's hands. Nearby, the other Ghostbloods were doing themselves credit. When Shallan had pulled similar operations on groups like the Sons of Honor, there had been mass chaos. The Ghostbloods moved with deliberate coordination, spreading out, two summoning Shardblades, others producing conventional weapons.

Iyatil moved quickest of all, explaining why she'd retreated instead of engaging Shallan. Stabbing a Knight Radiant was basically useless; she needed something stronger. Iyatil pulled a bolt from Mraize's pouch and raised a now-cocked ballista with it loaded, glowing bright. While Mraize had chosen a conventional bolt, Iyatil would shoot anti-Stormlight.

Shallan ducked back into the trophy room. She glanced over her shoulder and saw the Ghostbloods retreating toward the west side of the large chamber. Storms, of course they'd have another exit. There was no way in Damnation's cold winds they would trap themselves—which meant she couldn't just hold this room and wait for the others.

She stepped into the doorway and shouted, "Mraize!"

Her helmet *amplified* the sound, as if she'd spoken with ten times the force. *Wow.*

Shallan! the armor said, somehow conveying *You're welcome.*

Mraize stopped retreating and turned toward her.

"Would you become the prey?" she demanded. "Running before the axehound?"

"Even a master hunter hides from the storm," he called back. "I will face you when it is time, little knife."

"Why not now?" she asked, advancing. Iyatil was pulling on Mraize's arm to flee, ballista lowered to her side. Lieke opened a hidden door in the west wall. The others went through—one at a time, no pushing.

Shallan held her hands to the sides, dismissing both Pattern and Testament. "Go find the others; see what is taking them so long," she whispered to the spren. She could resummon them, but didn't want to risk them if that bolt was loosed.

Iyatil trained the ballista on her, but did not shoot. She knew she had exactly one shot. The others were escaping, but so long as Iyatil and Mraize were focused on Shallan, she bought time for the strike force to arrive.

"I've seen Mishram," Shallan said. "Lightning in her eyes. Hair like midnight. I've *seen* her."

That did it. The two fixated on her even more squarely.

"Mishram is imprisoned," Iyatil said.

"Can any prison truly hold a god?" Shallan said, stepping forward. "Whatever advantage you think you can gain from her, you're wrong. She is malevolent and terrible, the essence of hatred, imprisoned for *two thousand* years. She will destroy you, Mraize. Whatever your plan, it is *not worth* the risk."

Mraize clasped his hands behind his back, studying her. Her argument wasn't a good one—Mraize was willing to make big wagers, and was not driven by fear—but it was all she'd been able to come up with on the spot.

Still, he studied Radiant. Was he thinking about what she'd said . . .

No, Veil thought. *He's thinking how we surprised him by sneaking in here. And how bold we are to stand here, staring down that weapon.*

"We don't have to be enemies," she said to him.

"You aren't my enemy," he said. "You're my obstacle."

Iyatil shifted.

She's going to shoot.

Shallan dove to the side while breathing out and purposely ejecting all of her Stormlight. With some, she created two illusions: one of her jumping in the other direction, another staying in place.

Iyatil tracked the correct Shallan, then loosed.

Go! Shallan commanded the armor.

Shallan? the spren sent, but obeyed, vanishing right as the crossbow bolt took her in the ribs. She tumbled in her dive, grunting at the sudden *jolt* of pain. She almost drew in Stormlight, but forcibly stopped herself. No. *No.*

The bolt had a metal tip, with a gemstone clipped into the shaft. That tip . . . it was designed, like the weapons of the Fused, to move Light. In this case, it injected the anti-Light, making it seep through her. It wasn't painful, not compared to the actual wound, but it was *wrong.* A cold that prowled through her veins, carried through her body with every beat of her heart.

Painspren clawed up from the stone ground around her. This feeling was unnatural, counter to her very nature, but . . . she felt she could have drawn it in like normal Light. She decided not to try, as it did not seem to be able to hurt her so long as she set her jaw against the pain and refused the normal Stormlight that would heal her. Because if those two met . . .

Through tears of pain, Shallan watched Mraize take Iyatil by the arm and gesture toward the exit. She instead pulled a knife from its sheath at her belt and moved toward Shallan.

Then, blessedly, something distracted them. Shouts from the hidden hallway?

The ceiling in the center of the room—between Shallan and the other two—melted.

Stone in a hole maybe eight feet across poured down, as if it had suddenly become mud. It splashed on the floor of the cavern—missing the podium by inches and touching none of the people—then instantly hardened. Through that hole came a dozen Windrunners one after another—the last carrying Erinor, Darcira's husband, a Stoneward. That explained the meltiness.

Hand on her wound—bloodied fingers around the crossbow bolt—Shallan met Mraize's eyes.

Then he, Iyatil, and Lieke—who had been lingering—vanished. The air around them warped with a light tinged black-violet, and they were gone.

⁂

Szeth trailed off, having told Kaladin a little about his family as they walked through the forest for a few hours. A story of the discovery of a rock, told in fits and starts. Kaladin hadn't interrupted, enjoying hearing the other man open up—plus, learning about the Shin was genuinely interesting.

This time when Szeth trailed off, he didn't continue.

"You heard a horn?" Kaladin eventually prompted. "What did that mean?"

"I'm done for now," Szeth said.

Kaladin sighed, but otherwise contained his annoyance. At least that story had been something. They soon reached a sharp drop-off. Here the trail wound down in a series of steep switchbacks, so they took a quick jaunt into the sky. Kaladin felt invigorated, bathed in the light of a sun that had passed its zenith and was now working toward the horizon.

"Do you have forests near your home?" Szeth asked as they lazily drifted down, skimming the tops of the foliage.

"Not like this," Kaladin said. "I didn't see a true forest until I reached the Shattered Plains, and took a trip to the harvesting operations a half day's march north."

"I always thought there couldn't be trees outside Shinovar," Szeth said, Stormlight escaping his lips. "How could they grow in a land with no soil?"

"And I," Kaladin said, "never imagined you'd have them here. With nothing for their roots to grip."

Szeth grunted at that, then Lashed himself in a steady swoop along the mountainside. Kaladin followed as the trees dwindled, and they approached Shinovar proper: a vast plain of vibrant green. Kaladin had seen many a field before, but he realized that up until this moment, he'd never seen something so *alive* as this prairie. Though again, there were no lifespren, which he found odd.

Regardless, fields back home had grass, but with more space between the blades, so the brown cremstone filtered through. Here the grass grew like moss, achieving an aggressive density. As if the individual blades had formed mobs, armies, pike blocks.

Following Szeth, he landed on an outcropping on the slope. As Szeth sat down to inspect the land before them, Kaladin walked to the edge, his Stormlight giving out, and his full weight settled on him, his feet sinking into the soft soil to an unfamiliar degree. The entire view—with the rolling hills of green and a thick blanket of grass—made him think of an ocean. Each of those hills a swell or wave, with trees like ships. There was even what he thought might be a herd of wild horses in the distance. Incredible.

"I see it now," Kaladin whispered.

"What?" Szeth asked.

"I see how your land survives. That grass . . . it doesn't move, doesn't react. Yet it feels as if it could swallow everything. Like it wants to consume me."

"It will, once you die," Szeth said softly. "It will take all of us. Undoubtedly later than we deserve."

What a delightful way of thinking. Syl landed next to Kaladin, becoming full sized and trimmed in violet. She was grinning, naturally. "Look at the solitary trees!" she said, pointing. "Look at them just sitting there alone, without a care in the world."

Here, trees didn't need companions with whom to lock roots. But Kaladin, now that he thought to look closer, found the *buildings* more unusual. This region wasn't terribly well populated, but he picked out one town, maybe the size of Hearthstone—and several lonely homesteads.

Those buildings seemed so unprotected, practically *shouting* for the storms to take them. Though they were distant, he thought they were wooden, and appeared flimsy. With flat walls to the east, and *windows* on those sides as well. He knew people here didn't have to fight the storms, but those homes unnerved him. Made him think the people must be weak, innocent, in need of protection. Like lost children wandering a battlefield.

“This is wrong,” Szeth said.

“Yeah,” Kaladin said, kneeling beside him in the knee-high grass. “How do people live here?”

“Peacefully, when your kind let them,” Szeth said, his eyes narrowed. He sat somewhat awkwardly, the strange black sword strapped to his back. It was a good example of why one normally summoned a Shardblade, instead of carrying it. The weapon was awkwardly sized: too long to be worn at the waist, but difficult to draw when strapped to the back like that.

Szeth glanced at him and shook his head. “Something is wrong here. Not the things you see with a stonewalker’s perspective, Kaladin. Look. Does that region seem . . . darker than it should?”

Kaladin followed Szeth’s pointing finger to a rise on the right, along the cliffsides of the mountain. It *was* darker than the stones and soil around it. But . . . there was no visible cloud to cause that shadow. Kaladin narrowed his eyes and thought he could see wisps of blackness rising from it.

“What’s over there?” Kaladin asked.

“The monastery,” Szeth said. “We have ten of them. Most are homes of the Honorblades.”

The legendary weapons of the Heralds. Szeth had wielded one when killing old King Gavilar. It, unfortunately, had fallen into other hands . . . the hands of a man who should have been Kaladin’s brother.

“You keep the Honorblades in monasteries?” Kaladin asked.

“One for each Radiant order, though Talmut’s is missing, of course, as is Nin’s. Ishu has claimed his too, now. Regardless, when a person is elevated as I was in my youth, they travel to each monastery on pilgrimage, training at those that have an Honorblade, mastering each Surge. That one ahead is the first I lived in, but it has no Blade.”

“Which one is it?” Syl asked from the edge of their overlook, gazing straight along the mountainside to that distant fortress on the ridge. “Which Blade should it have held?”

“Talmut’s,” Szeth said. “You call him Talenelat, or Taln. Stonesinew, the Bearer of Agonies.”

“That darkness,” Kaladin said, “reminds me of the darkness around the Kholinar palace. An Unmade lived there. You really met one here, in Shinovar?”

“Yes,” Szeth said softly.

“When was this?” Kaladin said. “After you discovered a rock on your family’s ground?” He hoped to prompt more of the story.

“The meeting was much later,” Szeth said, “but that day with the rock, and the raid . . . that was the beginning.”

“Do you want to tell me more?” Kaladin asked.

“None of that matters. All that matters is the quest.”

"And the people, your family, the—"

"None of it matters," Szeth repeated. "We should camp here for the night and visit the monastery in the morning. Unless you want to investigate that place now."

Kaladin shoved aside his annoyance at Szeth and looked again at the patch of darkness. Then he glanced at the sun, which was getting close to setting. He wasn't certain how all this connected—Ishar, Dalinar's request of him, and Szeth's story. But if there *was* an Unmade, he didn't want to risk encountering it at night. Kaladin had faced them at Kholinar, where he'd failed to protect the people. Even the Unmade he'd eventually defeated—when it had worn Amaram's body—had been extremely dangerous.

"Camping sounds good," Kaladin said. "But let's do it farther back and around that bend, to shelter the cookfire."

"We don't need a cookfire," Szeth said. "We have travel rations."

Kaladin insisted, however. Thankfully Szeth joined him, and offered no further complaint about a cookfire. Because Kaladin needed this man to open up.

And he figured he'd try an old standby.

29 SECRET HANDSHAKES

Those who offer blanket condemnation are fools, for each situation deserves its own consideration, and rarely can you simply apply a saying—even one of mine—to a situation without serious weighing of the context.

—From *The Way of Kings*, fourth parable

Shallan's jaw dropped as she lay on the floor of the Ghostblood hideout. She stared, like an eel gasping for breath, at the space where Mraize and the others had vanished. How? The bizarre impossibility of it made the pain of her wound fade for the moment. That had been . . .

. . . them transferring to Shadesmar. Like Jasnah could do. Had Sja-anat saved them? No. One of them was an Elsecaller, or perhaps a Willshaper. A corrupted version of a Radiant.

Renarin doesn't like us to think of them that way, she thought with a wince, remembering her pain.

Well, it seemed she'd been wrong about the Ghostbloods having no experience with their abilities. Perhaps Iyatil had bonded a spren earlier than she'd assumed? She'd have to ask Sja-anat. For now, she held her bloodied side as Windrunners secured the room, several of them going after the Ghostbloods who had escaped.

"Shallan!" Darcira said, kneeling by her. Shallan hadn't seen the other Lightweaver enter. "You're hurt! How? You didn't summon your armor?"

"Anti-Light," Shallan said with a grunt. "I couldn't afford to let it hit the armor—don't know what it will do to the spren." She grimaced. "The bolt went in too low to hit my lung, otherwise I'd be coughing blood all over the floor. Grazed between my ribs though—I can feel it." Shallan braced herself. "Pull it out. It's injecting anti-Stormlight."

The other woman did so, and Shallan squeezed her eyes shut against the agony. She breathed in and out, shallow breaths to control the pain, and continued to feel that coldness in her veins. The anti-Light pulsed with a strange, off-key sound. Like the scrape of bone on rock. It faded slowly.

She opened her eyes and could see it evaporating from her skin, along with the painspren crawling around—several the wrong color. The anti-Light wisps soon vanished. Shallan waited a little longer, but she was getting light-headed. So at last she drew in a deep breath, filling herself with Stormlight. The power went to work immediately, and she didn't explode, which was nice.

"We shouldn't have sent you in alone," Darcira said.

"Alone? Darcira, we both know my ego is big enough to count for between two and four people, depending on the day and my mood." Shallan took a long, ragged breath, and when she breathed out, less Stormlight left her than it normally did. An elevated oath meant everything she did was more efficient: she healed better, Stormlight stayed longer, and she was less . . . porous to its escape.

Darcira pulled her bloodied handkerchief away from the wound. "At least that's good conventional armor you have on, for leathers. Seems to have absorbed much of the force. At such close range, I'd have expected the bolt to go straight out the other side, but it barely punctured the armor on your back."

"Perhaps it got lost," Shallan said. "Take it from one who lives in here—my insides can be confusing."

"No, really," Darcira said. "I don't think this is hogshide. It's something else. Probably from . . . you know . . ."

Right. She was wearing the carcass of a beast from some other planet, its skin smoother and thicker than that of a hog. Storms. What a surreal realization. Shallan found her feet and wiped her hands on a cloth Jayn provided, as she and the other Lightweavers joined them from the trophy room.

"What took so long?" Shallan asked them. "Feels like forever since I gave the signal."

"Erinor spoke to the stones," Darcira said. "Got the impression there was a secret exit down into the chasms. We were just exploring it when you hit the signal—and suddenly people started fleeing that way."

"We figured we'd grab them as they came out, while sending support to you," Jayn said. "You must have frightened them something awful, Brightness. They came charging through without checking first!" She grimaced. "Sorry to let you get hit . . ."

"I took it intentionally," Shallan said, feeling sturdy, even excited, now that she had Stormlight in her veins. Jayn held up her satchel, the shoulder strap tied haphazardly, the leather dimpled with Pattern, who apparently had followed her instructions and found the others. Shallan slung the satchel over her shoulder.

"Mmm . . ." Pattern said, moving onto her clothing. "I am very glad you did not get killed while I was not here. I should like to be there when you die. It is a thing friends do for friends."

Shallan walked to the spot where Mraize and the others had vanished. Could she follow? Her powers had a strange relationship with Shadesmar. She'd always had trouble with this, from the first time she'd experimented in Kharbranth.

Or . . . no . . . that hadn't been the first time . . .

As the other Radiants continued exploring—Shallan was particularly happy to have captured those trophies for study—she drew on the Stormlight to peek into another world, full of churning spheres and a cold sun. She held herself back and just looked, seeking . . .

Three people on a small boat pulled by mandras, heading for a nearby platform with massive spren overhead. Mraize, Iyatil, and Lieke. One tall figure, two short. They had planned this special means of escape, and were heading to Urithiru. Their cell here had suffered a terrible blow—but they'd already set something in motion with Dalinar. A plot to find Ba-Ado-Mishram, the Unmade.

She almost tried pulling herself all the way into Shadesmar, something she wasn't supposed to be able to do with her powers—but which she'd done before regardless. Two bonds. Two spren. Storms, that explained some curious events in her past; instead of her pulling them into her realm, they pulled her somewhat into theirs.

She blinked, dismissing the vision. She shouldn't face the Ghostbloods alone, but she had an idea about who to go to for help.

⁂

"So," Lift said, gnawing the last remnants of meat from a bone, "that's how you build an exploding chamber pot."

Gavinor—the five-year-old son of King Elhokar, current heir to Alethkar—nodded solemnly. He was small for his age; people often thought he was much younger. Lift didn't, as she'd known kids like him in orphanages. Kids who had seen too much.

The two of them sat on a table outside the room where Dalinar, Navani, and Wit were explaining something to Sebarial and Aladar. As they'd passed, Dalinar had *specifically* told her not to try to sneak in.

Storming Dalinar. Storming Wit and his storming stupid secrecy. Lift knew stuff. She coulda been inside, listening to the important talk.

At least nobody in here—the conference room for planning upcoming battles—kicked her out. She was Radiant, first Edgedancer they'd found, thank you very much. But she didn't lead her order. That was starving Baramaz and her starving perfect teeth and short black hair that had just the right amount of curl. She smiled too much. Granted, Baramaz didn't fall over as much when she used her powers. But Lift hardly fell over when *she* used her powers these days.

In a stroke of good luck, Sigzil walked by. She followed him with her eyes, absently lowering the bone from her lips.

"You often stare at that one, mistress," Wyndle said, forming next to her as a pile of vines. He liked the changes in the tower, because they let him appear to anyone. These days he commonly made a funny-looking face to interact, one like his face on the other side. Full and round, with mustachios and gemstone eyes that looked like spectacles. He didn't think it was funny-looking, of course. Pigs didn't know they stank either.

"I *don't* stare at him," Lift said, watching the Azish Windrunner give orders to subordinates. So confident, yet so studious. Not a brute, like so many of the Alethi. He had *thoughts.* He was *smart.* Not so tall as to be intimidating, but tall enough to be striking.

"Pardon," Wyndle said, "but you're staring right now."

"Do you think," Lift said, "he likes poetry?"

"Who doesn't?" Wyndle said. "Ooh, I've written seventeen poems about the delightful nature of Iriali footstools!"

"Shut up," Lift said. "Gav. Do you think he likes poetry?"

"I . . . don't know what that is," Gav said.

"Yeah," Lift said, still watching Sigzil. Then she added, "I don't either."

"What?" Wyndle said.

"It's just a term I've heard girls say. Somethin' about words'n'shit, right?"

Wyndle sighed. "Mistress, please don't use such crude terminology."

"That sword ardent does it."

"Zahel is *not* a role model." Wyndle drew himself up tall. "You are a Knight Radiant. A beacon of hope for all people. You should not be using vulgarities—besides, you're not even using that word correctly. It doesn't make sense in such a linguistic context."

"That's how he uses it," she muttered. He talked strange sometimes. Weird and interesting.

Nobody had seen him since the attack on the tower though. Probably off sleeping somewhere. He was smart, that one. Always seemed to know when someone was gonna make him do something, so he got out of there quick.

Still, Lift probably *should* be a better role model. "Gav," she said to the prince, "forget you heard me say that word."

"Poetry?" he asked.

"Yeah. Sure. That's the one. Bad word, that."

Gav nodded solemnly. Yes, that kid was *way* too serious. She'd actively worked to befriend Gav this last year, after his rescue from Kholinar. Fortunately, he hadn't been in the tower during the invasion; he'd been with his grandfather on campaign.

He didn't say much. Lift had learned that sometimes to listen—and really hear people—you also had to be there when they didn't talk.

Today though, he opened up more than usual. "Lift? Do you think Grampa and Gram . . . want me? Are they sad they have to take care of me?"

Lift didn't put her arm around the kid, though she wanted to. He flinched when nonfamily did that, and you had to learn to see stuff like that. Hugs weren't always for you.

But she did give him a nudge in the side. "They love you. Big folk is always busy, so sometimes they forget that we're people an' like to make choices too."

He nodded, looking at the closed door across the room. "You sneak in where you're not supposed to be."

"Yup!"

"That's wrong. You shouldn't do that."

"Gav," she said, "sometimes you *gotta* do the things you ain't *supposed* to do."

"Why?"

"This world," she said, "it's fulla stuff that people *think* you ain't supposed to do, but which is actually okay. It's *also* full of stuff you really, *really* shouldn't do. Nobody tells you which is which, so you gotta find the difference."

"That's hard."

"Sure is," she said, and eyed the vents on the wall.

"You gonna try again?" Gav asked. "Despite what he said?"

"Maybe," Lift said. "You gotta be careful with Dalinar. He's real old—like, old as mountains and shi . . . um . . . stuff. But somehow, he don't know that there's things a person *should* do that everyone says ain't right. You know?"

Gav looked at her, baffled.

"Just trust me," Lift said. "Oh! Hey, I remembered. Tower, you there?"

The tower spren appeared beside her as a column of light stretching between discs on the floor and ceiling. The spren liked Lift on account of her being awesome. Really strange that more people didn't feel the same.

"What?" the Sibling said.

"You found my chicken yet?" Lift asked.

"There is no chicken meeting your description in my halls."

"It's here!" Lift said. "Look again. It's red, and has a beak and feathers. And it says stuff. Like a *person.*"

"You've described it many times, Lift."

"It was hurt an' scared. They took it when I was inna cage. You gotta find it, so I can help it."

The Sibling didn't respond. Those awful people must have taken the chicken somewhere—that guy with the scar and too many smiles. Lift would find it. Next to her, Wyndle grew a vine and patted her on the back, which was nice.

Better, soon Drehy flew in to give a report. And Damnation, did he need a uniform that tight? Lift leaned to the side, so she could see better when he bent over the table with the maps. *Damnation.*

"That one?" Wyndle said. "He's completely the opposite of Sigzil. Why do you stare at that one?"

"If you need to ask," Lift said, "then you have no sense of taste whatsoever."

"He's married, you know."

"Yeah," she said, leaning farther to the side. "His husband's hot too. Seems unfair. You're hot, you can fly, *and* you have a hot husband? Windrunners, Wyndle, I'm tellin' ya. Something's up with them. You know, I ain't never seen one o' them run into a wall? Not even a small wall."

"Wyndle," Gav said softly, "do spren have families?"

"Why, yes they do, Your Highness!" Wyndle said. "Though we require only one parent, so many spren do not pair bond. But it's also not uncommon for us to do so! Why, even formal marriage isn't unheard of. I have a mother, who is a dear and kind soul who spends her time gardening shoes."

Gav nodded, knees drawn up against his chest, staring at the ground. "My mother gave me to Voidbringers," he said softly, "to be tormented and killed."

Lift winced.

"I think she's dead now," Gav continued, his voice even softer. "They won't tell me straight. I'm too young. But my father is dead. He was killed trying to rescue me . . ."

"It is . . ." Wyndle said. "I mean . . . I'm sorry."

"He was very brave," Gav whispered. "I don't remember what he looked like, but he was very brave. *He* wanted me. *He* came to save me. Then he . . . then he was slain by the traitor, Vyre."

"Hey," Lift said, nudging him. "Hey."

Gav looked at her.

She reached her hand toward him, two fingers out. He slowly did the same, locking his two fingers into hers. Their secret handshake. The secret was that secret handshakes were stupid, but sometimes you used them anyway. Mostly for making scared friends feel like they belonged.

"You've got a place now," she said. "Remember."

He nodded. He'd need more reminders. Just like she did sometimes.

"Oh, yes!" Wyndle said. "You have grandparents who love you!"

"Grampa was going to play swords with me today," Gav said, wiping his nose.

"Yes, well," Wyndle said, "the world is *kind of* in the middle of ending. Takes precedence, I should imagine."

"I'm gonna learn," Gav said, a small angerspren pooling beneath him, like bubbling blood. "How to use a Shardblade. How to fight. Then I'm gonna find everyone who hurt my father, and I'm going to *kill* them. I'm gonna make their eyes burn out and then, when they're dead, I'll chop them to pieces."

He looked to Lift, then glanced back down, ashamed.

"Yeah, all right," she said. "I'll hold them for you. Deal?"

He looked at her again, and finally—for the first time today—smiled. Yeah, revenge wasn't gonna be as fun as he thought, and he probably needed to let go of it. But he was *five.* Right now he needed a friend, not someone else telling him to be mature.

Besides. Maturity stank. She resisted the urge to scratch at her wrap, which she wore bound around her chest. Then Sigzil walked past again, and she absently pulled another rib from her pocket and started chewing on it as she watched.

"How can you not want to grow up," Wyndle said, "and still spend half your days ogling men? Don't you see the contradiction?"

"No," she said. "Don't be stupid."

"But your interest in men is obviously a manifestation of your advancement toward adulthood. You don't seem to mind that, but you hate the secondary sex characteristics manifesting—"

"Hey Tower," Lift said.

Again the little dancing column of light appeared—though she knew it would be invisible to other humans. Lift saw into the other realm a little. Something related to what had happened to her when she'd gone to the Nightwatcher, that lying liar who didn't keep her promises.

"Yes?" the Sibling said.

"Are all cultivationspren like this?" Lift asked. "Or did I get stuck with the druff?"

"What is a druff?"

"Him."

"There is great variety in the personalities of all spren, Lift," the Sibling said. "So I'd have to say you got stuck with a druff. Whatever that is."

She grunted, eyeing Wyndle.

"I *like* being a druff," he said, chin out—though he didn't really have a body, just vines and a head. "You're lucky. You think just *any* spren would put up with your abuse?"

"It ain't abuse," Lift muttered. "It's teasing."

"You should feel grateful," the tower said. "Wyndle is correct. Relatively few humans are chosen for the privilege of a Radiant bond."

"Ah, what do you know?" she said. "You're a building."

"And?" the tower said.

"And people fart in you. Like all the time. I bet half the people in this room are doing it right now."

"You realize," the tower said, "you are host to millions of life-forms. They exist in your gut, on your skin, all over you."

"What?" Lift said.

"Oh!" Wyndle said. "I've heard of this. Germs, yes! Wisdom of the Heralds. People with very detailed and specific life sense can feel them, I'm told! Millions upon millions of tiny creatures living on the skin of humans."

"They particularly like the hair follicles," the tower said. "I can feel them on you, Lift."

Lift stared at her hands, aghast.

"And yes," the Sibling added, "they live their entire lives there. Eating your dead skin flakes. Defecating on you. You are a tower like me, Lift. Every human is."

"That is the grossest thing I've ever heard." She looked to Gav. "Hey Gav. Did you know we have millions of tiny creatures living on us?"

"Gross!"

"I know! Awesome."

"You were just saying," the tower told her, "that I'm not worth listening to because I'm filled with things that fart!"

"And?" Lift said.

"And you are too! So nobody should listen to you either!"

"Gav," Lift said. "Should anyone listen to us when we say things? About important stuff, I mean."

"Of course not," Gav said. "We're kids."

Lift looked to the glowing column of light and shrugged.

"I honestly have no idea why I started talking to you," the tower said.

"It's because you sensed Cultivation's touch on her," Wyndle said, completely missing the context of the tower's complaint. As usual. What a druff.

But . . . well . . .

He *did* put up with her. Storms only knew *she* wouldn't want to have to do that.

"Hey," she said to Wyndle. "Thanks."

"What for?" he asked, frowning at her.

She put out her hand, two fingers out and crooked, like a claw. He regarded it, then opened his eyes wide in shock. Trembling, he formed a hand from vines and met hers.

"I get the *secret handshake*?" he whispered.

"Just don't go sharin' it," she said.

"It must remain special," Gav added.

"I . . . I'm honored," Wyndle said.

Finally, at long last, the door into the other room opened. Wit, Dalinar, and Navani strode out—and headed straight for the lifts, determined expressions on their faces. Behind them, Aladar and Sebarial looked seriously disturbed.

Damnation. They'd decided something *important.*

"Grampa?" Gav said, standing up on the table. "We can play swords?"

Dalinar stopped amid generals and scholars. "There is something more I need to do, son. I'm sorry."

Gav wilted like a plant with no water. He slumped back down on the table, drawing a long grey streamer of a gloomspren—and bearing the kind of expression no secret handshake could fix.

"You can come in the lift with us, Gav," Navani said. "Spend a little time together. Come along."

Eager, the boy hopped down and rushed over. The nursemaid joined them—she'd been helping herself to snacks, falsely assuming she could trust Gav with a Radiant. Lift fished the last pork rib from her pocket, eyeing the group as they left.

"Gram," Gav said on the way, "what's 'shit' mean?"

Lift winced. Maybe . . . maybe teaching the crown prince to cuss hadn't been her smartest move. Secretly deep down, she was a bit of a druff, wasn't she?

"I'm impressed, mistress," Wyndle said. "You didn't demand to go with them!"

"I'm feelin' kinda grown-up today," Lift said. "On account of my good manners and full stomach."

Wyndle nodded, satisfied. He glanced at her. Then he frowned. "You're . . . going to follow them, aren't you?"

"Storming right I am," Lift said, hopping down. "I mean, I need more snacks, so I was planning to get up anyway . . ."

30
NOT ALONE

As I fear not the child with a weapon he cannot lift, I will never fear the mind of a man who does not think.

—From *The Way of Kings*, fourth parable

A part of Renarin missed the way the tower had been before. It was a silly emotion, but he seemed to feel a lot of those. More than other people.

The tower was far better now. Yet out in the fields—which were on large stone wafers that sprouted from the mountainside around the base of the tower—he found himself displeased. The air was humid, soft, and muggy when it had once been chill and sharp. Renarin passed row upon row of lavis polyps. Even after a few days, the transformation was visible; this row was an inch larger than it had been yesterday.

He squatted down. At this rate, the farmers said they'd be able to bring in crops every two months. Suddenly it was clear how the vast tower fed its potentially hundreds of thousands of occupants. The air was so wet he felt he was swimming, his uniform jacket uncomfortable. Yet a dozen yards away, closer to the tower, the air was a steady comfortable temperature.

It all felt . . . too easy.

Silly thoughts, he told himself again, standing up straight. *For a silly man.* He looked across the field to Rlain, who was chatting with several human farmers. Rlain had spent months toiling to teach the humans how to use Stormlight and song to grow plants. Suddenly that work was unnecessary.

Three days after defending the tower—and the humans in it, against his own kind—Rlain was back here, checking on the fields. He'd told Renarin that since the Sibling's awakening, the rhythms became harder to hear the longer he spent inside the tower, so he preferred it out here. Although people side-eyed him, although he'd been called a shellhead, he was here making certain the very people who distrusted him wouldn't starve.

He stood tall—almost as tall as Kaladin, and several inches taller than Renarin—with black skin marbled with red. He had a thick neck and strong jaw, outlined by a short red-and-black beard. He pointed, encouraging the farmers to grow a line of sugarbark between the lavis and the tubers, which needed standing water to sprout down into. A natural bit of shoring up, should the ponds overflow—plus something to do with the way the cremlings pollinated different crops. These were listener strains, cultivated on the Shattered Plains, and Rlain knew their intricacies.

Rlain suddenly turned and waved toward the sky. Renarin followed the gesture to see a Windrunner approaching. Lanky Drehy landed nearby, and gave Rlain a wave back, though he trotted over to Renarin. "Hey," he said. "Meeting is on break. Your aunt asked me to bring you a report."

"Thank you," Renarin said softly.

Of course she'd send a report. She still hoped, as Dalinar did, that Renarin would change his mind and agree to be king of Urithiru should his father fall. Barring that, they wanted him to be Jasnah's heir until Gav was of age. Though Jasnah would ensure an elected official took her place, they thought Alethkar should have a monarch, even if they didn't have absolute power.

Drehy delivered a quick, affable report on the meetings. Renarin found his mind drifting, and he kept glancing at Rlain.

You will need this information, Glys said in his mind. *You will pay attention?*

I will, Renarin sent. Though not all spren and Radiants could communicate directly by thoughts, he and Glys were increasingly intertwined. Renarin didn't mind that Glys felt what he did. It was a challenge sometimes, figuring out what people meant or wanted from him—and having another perspective, no matter how alien, was helpful.

After the report, Drehy lingered, and Renarin started to sweat more in his jacket. This was the part of conversations he always had trouble with. He'd already said thank you. Should he try small talk? How should this end? Everyone else seemed to know what to do—they flowed in and out of conversations like eels in a shared current.

Renarin was the rock in that current.

"So," Drehy said, settling back against one of the stone workstations that were scattered through the fields, "want to talk about it?"

It? Renarin's panic grew. What "it"? Was he supposed to know what this particular "it" was?

I do not know, Glys said, equally worried. *Is it us, maybe? They will always be afraid of us, I fear.*

"The way you look at Rlain," Drehy said in response to Renarin's apparent confusion.

"Oh, *that,*" Renarin said, relaxing. It was an embarrassing topic, but at least now he knew what the topic *was.* "Is it . . . um . . . obvious?"

"You learn to watch for guys who watch other guys," Drehy said, shrugging. "I don't want to pry. It's nobody's business. Just wanted you to know I'm here, should you want to talk."

"It's silly," Renarin said, glancing down, blushing. "He's not even human."

"I say it's better to think of everyone as people. Human. Listener. Spren. All people. Even if some of them glow and are annoying."

"Point," Drehy's spren—Talla—said, appearing between them. She always took the fluttering shape of a blue chicken. "I'm not annoying. I'm habitually right. You simply have serious trouble equating one with the other, Drehy."

"Point," Drehy said, "being right *can* be annoying. Habitual or not. The two are not mutually exclusive."

Renarin let himself smile, hesitant. Drehy, like the other members of Bridge Four, treated him as one of them, awkward or not. To them, he was . . . well, he was a person.

"I . . . don't know what to do," Renarin said. "About Rlain. About any of this. Aunt Navani won't be happy. She wants grandchildren. And . . . um . . . likes people to be normal."

"You are normal," Drehy said. "Or rather, nobody is normal. Normal doesn't exist. So if we slavishly try to dress ourselves to imitate it, all we're really doing is becoming a different kind of abnormal—a miserable kind."

Renarin looked down.

"What do you want, Renarin?" Drehy asked. "Not what your aunt, or your father, or anyone else wants. What do *you* want?"

"Maybe what I want," he said, "is for my aunt, and my father, and everyone else to be happy."

Drehy shrugged.

Storms. How to interpret that?

"Could you . . . um . . ." Renarin said, "just say what you mean, please? I'm confused."

"Sorry," Drehy said. "I forget sometimes. Renarin, I'm not going to tell you what to be. I'm not going to tell you when, or if, you have to tell anyone. You live your life how you want. I've known some who would prefer to pretend they aren't different. Doesn't seem to work often, but it's their right. All I'm saying is if you have questions, I might have answers. Not ultimate answers. Maybe not even correct answers. Just the answers of one man who's been in your shoes."

Renarin felt an odd peace at hearing that—odd because his anxiety did *not* go away. It never really did, but it was nice to have a sense of peace alongside it. Once in a while.

So . . . dared he ask?

"Um . . ." Renarin said. "What if . . . you know . . . he . . . ?"

"Prefers women?"

Renarin nodded.

"Then move on," Drehy said. "Look, I'll be honest. It happens. Nobody's sense for these things is perfect, and if you ask, sometimes it embarrasses people. But trust me, in the long run it's better to ask, and deal with it if you're wrong."

"I don't think I could do that," Renarin said, blushing.

Drehy took a long, deep breath, but didn't contradict him. He seemed to mean what he'd said earlier—he wasn't intending to lecture.

"It's silly," Renarin said. "Listeners don't even court like we do."

"They often bond, two people for life. They do it differently, but what did I say earlier?"

"There is no such thing as normal."

"Everyone's got to figure it out for themselves," Drehy said. "I'll tell you this though, Rlain said a few things at stew one night about being in mateform and being hugely embarrassed . . . I think it's going to turn out all right, Renarin. If you're willing to try."

"I can't," Renarin said, his head still down. "I really, really *can't.*"

Drehy moved as if to pat Renarin on the shoulder in a way that would have comforted someone else. He paused though, then gave Renarin an encouraging gesture. Bless him, he listened. He knew that Renarin didn't like to be touched. Though Renarin would have been fine with it in this case—he liked some physical contact on his own terms, but he didn't like being surprised—the more important thing was that Drehy had listened. He actually *cared.* Renarin found himself smiling.

"You can do this," Drehy said. "If you don't want to, that's *all right.* But Renarin, I know you walked onto a battlefield at Thaylen Field determined to make a stand against overwhelming odds all by yourself. I know you struggled with visions of the future and sorted through them, bringing messages to your father. I know you can carry a great weight, my friend. You've done it already." He smiled, then drew in Stormlight and lifted into the air. "Like I said, just one man's experiences. Bridge Four stew tonight. You coming?"

"Who's cooking?"

"Does it matter?"

"Determines whether I eat first," Renarin said, smiling.

"It's me."

"Then I'll come hungry," Renarin said. "Thank you, Drehy."

"When you have questions, ask," he said, and soared back up to rejoin the meeting.

Renarin turned toward Rlain. But then the sky darkened and the air went black as the world became stained glass. Glys pulsed within him.

They had entered a vision of what might come. And this one did *not* look pleasant.

⁂

Rlain had found his perfect form. Or rather, every form could be perfect for him now.

In the past, workform had been his favorite for its versatility. It also left his mind the clearest—the most *him.* But it didn't have the height he'd come to appreciate in warform—nor the strength of arm or the armored carapace. He liked the way he looked in warform, and it felt the most like him on the outside. Unfortunately, it made him a little too . . . eager to fight and obey. He could counteract both of these emotions, as a form did not control you. But it did subtly change the way you thought.

It turned out that being Radiant let him counteract that even more fully. He held up his finger as an awespren—a floating blue ball—alighted on it. This one was invisible to the human farmers who were discussing his advice. Bonded to Tumi, he felt like himself inside regardless of form.

Tumi thrummed to the Rhythm of Joy within him, and Rlain complemented it with a harmony, attuned but different. Tumi rarely spoke, but it didn't take *words* to understand his spren. The rhythms could do it.

Tumi's rhythm changed to Anxiety. Rlain turned toward Renarin—he hadn't seen the young man approaching until Drehy had arrived, but it had seemed the two had something to talk about, perhaps politics from above. Rlain had left them alone.

Now Renarin was encased in a shimmering distortion in the air. Was something wrong?

Curiosity from Tumi. Rlain attuned the same, hesitant, and knew Tumi thought the humans wouldn't see what was happening to Renarin. It took a stronger Connection to the realms.

"A vision," Rlain said. "That's one of his visions?"

The awespren swelled, drawing the attention of the farmers, who saw it as a ring of expanding smoke. Rlain let the awespren hop away, then excused himself and walked across rows of plants to Renarin, who appeared to be staring at nothing. Dared he intervene?

Tumi counseled boldness, so Rlain stepped forward. In a snap—like the sudden strike of a drum—he was inside the vision. The sky was black, and darkness surrounded them like one might dim the other lights in a room to inspect a single glowing gemstone. From the ground rose exquisite windows made as if from colorful glass.

"They're beautiful," Rlain noted. "Seems like a very human manifestation though. I wonder why Tumi and Glys show us them in this form. Is it their doing, or ours, or some combination?"

Renarin turned to him looking shocked, then excited. "Rlain!" he said. "You can see them?"

Rlain nodded. "I'd hoped I'd be able to see your visions, with my own spren. Is this . . ." He trailed off.

Renarin was crying.

"Renarin?" he said to Despair. "What's wrong? Did I intrude? Should I leave?"

He turned to go, but Renarin grabbed his hand. Which was surprising, from Renarin.

"I have spent," Renarin whispered, "what feels like an eternity alone with these visions. From the days where I crept on the floor and scrawled numbers, to the day when I realized my family's love could overcome a dark future. To a few days ago, when I heard you'd bonded a spren. Now . . . I'm not alone."

Renarin pulled him along the line of stained glass windows, which stood upright with nothing to support them. Rlain followed, genuinely intrigued, but also because Renarin had always tried so hard to make Rlain feel included. Rlain respected the other members of Bridge Four, Kaladin in particular, but there was something special about Renarin. When Rlain had been alone, rejected by the spren, Renarin had been the one to comfort him.

That moment had convinced Rlain that even if it was hard, there *could* be a place for him among the humans. He had never fit in anywhere until he'd found Bridge Four. They hadn't always been perfect—far from it—but they'd proved willing to *work* to make a place for Rlain, Renarin working hardest of all.

"So what do we do?" Rlain asked, joining Renarin at what seemed the first of the windows.

"I don't know," Renarin said. "But remember. Remember it can be lies."

"Why pay attention if it could all be lies?"

"Because truth is just the lie that happened," Renarin said.

Rlain attuned Skepticism. "That . . . doesn't make sense."

Renarin stepped up to one of the windows, and Glys—his spren—separated from him, floating up in the air by his head in the shape of a shimmering red lattice, with beads of light "dripping" from the top and vanishing into the sky. The window depicted Renarin sitting on a throne.

He wore some kind of archaic outfit, a little like the fencing attire people wore on the Alethi training grounds, with the skirts.

"This is Kholinar," Renarin said, "but it's not the throne room. That looks like *my* room. See, those are my models on that shelf."

"Models?"

"Wooden carvings of creatures," Renarin explained. "You paint them to be lifelike." He blushed. "I mostly bought knights instead of animals. I needed something to do with my time when Adolin was training. And here, those are my books. I'd spend a few hours each day having them read to me."

"Such knowledge," Rlain said. "So much at your fingertips. No wonder you know so much."

Renarin blushed again.

"What?" Rlain asked to Reconciliation. Had he said something wrong?

"Those aren't books full of facts or learning," Renarin admitted. "They're adventure stories, the kind written for young women. I had a whole collection, much to Father's embarrassment."

"Renarin," Rlain said, "I have seen how your father treats you. He's not embarrassed of you."

"He was when I was young," Renarin said. "But he was wrong back then, wasn't he?"

They studied the image a little longer before Rlain picked out the detail that was bothering him. "Renarin, I think that is *singer* clothing you're wearing." He pointed at the folds of cloth, noting how they draped the body. The coloring . . . the patterns . . .

"Are you sure?" Renarin asked.

"No," Rlain said, "but I did see a lot of their clothing in the tower these last few weeks. It looks the same."

"Lies," Renarin said softly. "Each picture here shows only one of several likely outcomes. I asked Wit, and he says it's the way of things—no one *actually* knows the future, not even the gods."

"But one possibility *will* become true," Rlain said. "That's what you meant earlier."

Renarin nodded, always so solemn. Thoughtful. "We should study the other windows before they vanish."

"Do we know why they appear?" Rlain said. "What determines when we see one of these, and which . . . possibility is depicted?"

"I haven't been able to figure that out," Renarin said. "Not fully. Though Glys says . . ."

"Swells," Glys said. "There are swells in the rhythms of Roshar. Currents, and old gods, will watch."

"Old gods," Rlain said as Tumi, in his gemheart, changed to the Rhythm of the Lost. "The Unmade?"

"Older," Glys said. "Older still than Honor, Cultivation, and Odium."

"What's older than them?" Rlain asked, glancing at Renarin. "Even the Old Magic, as you call it, is a spren of Cultivation."

"When Honor and Cultivation came to Roshar," Glys said, "deep within the days beyond memory, times as dark to history as the depths of the ocean are to light, *you*—Rlain—were already here. Your people."

Rlain attuned the Rhythm of the Winds, for something as old as those distant years. Humans had come to Roshar long ago—and brought Odium with them. He had been their god, who had accepted the loyalty of the ancient singers after Honor betrayed them. Rlain hadn't put together the deeper truth: that even Honor and Cultivation had *come* to Roshar and found the singers.

"Long ago, before any of them arrived," Rlain said, "did we have forms? Were there spren?"

"I do not know," Glys said. "I see ahead, not back. You will seek answers from those more ancient than I. The Bondsmith sees backward. Always, his eyes are toward what happened."

"Jasnah too," Renarin said softly. "She knows the past better than any." He turned along the hallway of windows. "But we look forward . . ."

Rlain joined him, each of their steps crinkling as if on black glass at their feet, as they continued along the stained glass windows that rose on both sides, making a tunnel of light. The windows were the same on both the right and the left: Renarin on a throne, followed by a dark and building storm. Rlain knew that one. The Everstorm, which passed by every nine days. It was easy to forget about in Urithiru, which was usually above both storms, but others brought reports. Lightning strikes. Thunder. Generally less destruction than the highstorm, but a feeling of malevolence and something watching, biding its time. Preparing.

Why would there be a window depicting the storm? It had already arrived. Rlain hummed to Confusion. And Renarin, strangely, did as well? Or he tried. He glanced at Rlain and tried to imitate his humming. Renarin's attempt was off-rhythm and too loud, like a child sounding out a word that was too big for them. But . . . Rlain had never heard a human even try before.

"Any idea why this is here?" Rlain asked him.

"No," Renarin replied. "Sometimes the windows are just like this—nothing relevant that I can make out at all."

The next depicted some kind of clifftop overlook, with Dalinar standing in front of a glowing golden figure. In the distance, a city was collapsing into a spreading pit. Though the image was static, he felt *motion* to it somehow. As if that city were constantly crumbling into that pit.

"I recognize this," Renarin said. "From my aunt's notes—when she wrote out my father's visions. This was . . . the first vision? Or the last one? He stood on a cliff and watched our homeland crumble."

"Which . . . has also already happened," Rlain said to Consideration. "Are we sure these show the future?"

"They will," Glys promised. "They *will.*"

Maybe, Tumi added by a thrumming from within him. *Only maybe.*

The fourth window was, strangely, a bright green field with distant figures standing in it. The grass didn't flee from them, so perhaps they'd been standing there a long time. He counted . . . twelve? He looked to Renarin, who reached up and rested a hand beside the window.

"Peace," Renarin said. "I feel peace from this one . . . Who are they, do you suppose?" He tried humming to Confusion, poorly, but Rlain could *kind of* tell what he meant.

"Humans," Rlain said. "They're all human, I think. This one might be a Horneater, and this one Makabaki . . . And this one—what are those humans with the blue skin?"

"Those are the Natans," Renarin said. "Unless you're talking about the Aimians, who aren't humans, but neither are quite as blue as the woman in this picture." He hesitated, squinting at the distant woman in a vivid blue skirt, with white hair and blue skin. "Does this mean anything to you?"

"No. I'm sorry."

Renarin sighed. "They seem to be getting more vague." He closed his eyes. "Is that last one still there, at the end?"

Rlain gazed past Renarin toward the "end" of their hallway—and was surprised to see a window there, shadowed in the darkness. No light shone through it, so he'd missed it.

"What *is* that?" Rlain said, walking closer. It depicted only a face. A simple face with intricate patterns, black and red swirling. A singer, femalen, against a black background, etched in glass. Staring at him.

Then it moved.

Rlain jumped. In fits and jumps the image split, multiple versions of the face moving, raging, the eyes going wide, the Rhythm of Agony shaking the frame. Windows around them cracked, but the one in the center kept vibrating. Her face shuddering back and forth, then her hands against the edges of the window, curling, bulging out—as if trying to break free.

Renarin screamed as the windows to the left and right shattered, exposing a dark wasteland. New windows grew up like vines, crystallizing and exploding, leaving jagged stumps—but before they broke, Rlain could pick out images. Burning cities. Broken bodies.

Above it all a rising Rhythm of Agony, with the femalen singer's words echoing to the sound. *I will break it. I will break IT ALL.*

Renarin seized him and somehow pulled him out of the darkness. Just one step, and it was gone. They were once more on the fields in the hot air, surrounded by confused farmers.

Rlain fell to his hands and knees, carapace kneecaps grinding stone, sweat pooling under his collar at the edges of his skull carapace and streaming down his face. Renarin collapsed beside him, trembling.

"Is that . . . how it normally goes?" Rlain asked.

"That was something new. Did you recognize the face?"

"No, but the rhythm was Agony," Rlain said. He took a deep breath. "It's one of the new rhythms. That people can only access when they are Regal or Fused."

Renarin closed his eyes. "Welcome to the fun, I suppose."

"You said this was something new!" Rlain said to Betrayal. "Implying it's not like this all the time!"

"Yes, but it's *always* something new. So you get used to not being used to anything. Ever again."

"Delightful," Rlain said, flopping onto his back, deliberately attuning Peace and counting the movements of the rhythm to calm himself.

"Sorry," Renarin eventually said, sitting up. "For dragging you into this."

"I wanted a spren," Rlain said. "I asked for it."

"You wanted to fly," Renarin said. "Like the others."

"I'm a listener, Renarin," Rlain said. "I don't ever do things the way everyone else does." He took another long, deep breath. "This seems more useful than flying. Assuming we can make any sense of it."

Renarin nodded, and then smiled. Humans were often overly expressive with their faces, so it might be nothing. But Rlain asked anyway. "Is something funny?"

"Still just happy," Renarin said, "not to be the only one."

Rlain hummed to Appreciation before remembering that wouldn't mean anything to a human. He kept forgetting, even after two years among them. Before he could explain himself, however, a shadow fell on him. He tipped his head back to see Shallan, hands on her hips, wearing some kind of armor-like leather outfit, a white coat, and a matching hat.

"Resting?" she said. "Eight days until the fate of the world is decided, and you two are napping in a field?"

Rlain hummed to Irritation. Sometimes it was good humans didn't understand, because in singer company, that would have been rude.

"Come on," she said. "I legitimately need your help."

"What is the problem?" Renarin said, standing.

"It involves your father," Shallan said, "the Spiritual Realm, and a group of people who are trying to find the prison of an ancient, evil spren. Ba-Ado-Mishram. You know that one?"

Mishram.

Yes, Rlain did know that name. She had ruled the singers long ago—a spren who had wanted to perpetuate the fighting after the Fused left. The one who had been determined to exterminate humankind, escalating the war.

She was the reason Rlain's people had abandoned their forms and left. She was the queen of the gods they had forsaken.

And he suspected he'd just seen her face in the vision.

The traditional Alethi takama is depicted above. To the right is the modern style, currently popular for formal settings like weddings.

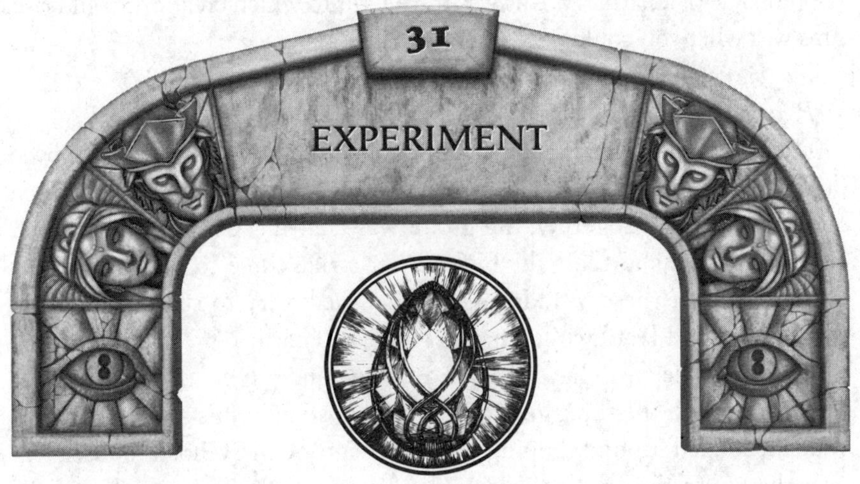

So think, my dear reader. As a soldier retreats from a battle he cannot win. As a woman rejects a home that shows her only violence. As a family finds hope in walking away from dying fields during a season of too much rain.

—From *The Way of Kings*, fourth parable

Shallan had brought some of the Windrunners from the raiding party, so she, Renarin, and Rlain quickly reached the Oathgates. From there, Shallan sent one Windrunner to find Dalinar and Navani to explain, as she worried her spanreed message hadn't been received.

She then brought the group into Shadesmar via Oathgate. Mraize and Iyatil were on the move; she needed to be too. On the other side—with Testament and Pattern appearing in full-sized form next to her—Shallan got her first sight of the tower there, after its awakening.

It was brilliant.

Before, the tower had manifested as a shimmer of light, but now that light had coalesced—like false dawn becoming true sunlight. It formed a tower that was a clone of the one in the Physical Realm, but as if created from glowing glass. A sphere infused, but on the scale of a mountain.

Though the light did not overpower her, her eyes watered, trying to take in the entire structure. It glowed with the fractured variety of a thousand colors—an artist's bounty of effulgent shades. Changing, each moment a different hue, as if the tower were too exuberant, too joyous and alive to be confined to mere color.

It was *magnetic,* taking not only her breath and attention, but her soul and mind, which longed to just once create something so beautiful. It was the pinnacle of all artistry. This was the height to which creations could rise. This was what you could . . . could . . .

Do you need me to take control? Radiant asked.

Please! Shallan said, tears in her eyes.

Radiant took a deep breath, acknowledged the pretty tower, and moved on. Two Windrunners—Isasik and Breteh—waited in here with their spren and their squires. Together, the group was chatting with the Shadesmar guards. Though she'd left the bulk of her strike force to watch the captives, she'd sent these Windrunners on ahead to try to see if they could find Mraize and Iyatil while Shallan fetched Renarin.

They didn't seem to have learned anything, judging by their postures as they talked with the three guards that were posted on this side just in case. Radiant looked around, hoping for some sign of the Ghostbloods. Here near the tower, the ten Oathgates manifested as tall pillars—each with its own set of lofty inkspren. Ramps ringed each pillar, spiraling down to the beads far below. With the restoration of the Sibling, glowing walkways had appeared connecting the pillars, as well as leading to the tower itself, which now stood upon a large glowing platform of its own.

Seeing nothing amiss, she trotted to the Windrunners on one of the walkways.

"Brightness," Isasik the Windrunner said. This wasn't the cartographer, but the other Isasik: a shorter man with an excitable demeanor. Both he and Breteh were former bridgemen from Bridge Thirteen, the group that had become Teft's squires. She thought that was why they wore red glyphwards on their arms—something about a pact relating to Moash and vengeance.

Radiant appreciated their regard for a fallen companion. Over time, tower soldiers had moved away from wearing Kholin blue, and toward a uniform representing their new kingdom. It appeared white uniforms with gold trim had finally been settled upon, as it was one of the distinctive color combinations that wasn't associated with an Alethi or Veden princedom.

"We did a sweep of the area and found no sign of the fugitives," Breteh said, hovering a few feet off the ground. "The guards haven't seen them either."

"We've been posted here all day," said a guard with a faint Bavland accent he was obviously trying to mask. "Nobody transferred in until these Windrunners arrived."

Radiant folded her arms, thoughtful. Around her feet, a collection of beads gathered and bounced up and down. "Other Shallan!" they said. The Windrunners seemed to find that quite amusing.

Had she been wrong? Would Mraize and Iyatil flee, instead of trying to continue their plan? "They entered Shadesmar on the Shattered Plains, thousands of miles away," she said. "They'd need to have found their way here via Oathgate."

Could Mraize and Iyatil be waiting before arriving? Would they jump here at the moment Dalinar opened his portal? Making a break for it?

Renarin and Rlain joined her, having overcome their awe. "Radiant," Renarin said, "could you please explain better what's going on? I'm still confused."

"Sorry," Radiant said. "Shallan is inefficient with words at times. There is a secretive group known as the Ghostbloods, who are seeking to control the balance of power on Roshar."

"Again?" Rlain asked. "Didn't you round them up right before the invasion?"

"Those were the Sons of Honor," Renarin said. "Amaram's former cohort. You know, I wonder if we *ask* for this sort of thing. We create this air of Alethi propriety, promising that we're up-front and honest. No one can say what they really think, because it would be 'un-Alethi.' Then our honesty becomes a lie as we turn to scheming . . ."

"It's kind of how you all ended up with a kingdom in the first place," Radiant agreed. "Dalinar, Gavilar, Navani, Sadeas, Ialai . . . frustrated that they were considered outsiders from the backwaters, they plotted to found an empire. Unfortunately for us, the Ghostbloods are supported by some very powerful individuals from offworld."

"You mean the Fused?" Rlain asked.

"Further offworld," Radiant said. "Shallan was recruited by them when she was new to her powers. She kept pretending to be a member, hoping to learn more. It came to a head recently, and she realized she had to stop them from reaching their goals."

"Well, that's a storming big secret," Rlain said to a very pronounced rhythm, which Radiant couldn't place.

Renarin just met her eyes, then nodded. Damnation. He understood. She now felt infinitely more guilty for finding him weird when they first met.

"They've been keenly interested in the Unmade," Radiant said. "They've met with Sja-anat, and . . . Renarin, I think she's given them spren to bond. Like she did to you and Rlain."

Speaking of which . . . where were their spren? Shouldn't they have appeared when Pattern, Testament, and her armor had?

"She . . . plays both sides," Renarin admitted. "She's told me as much."

"Her spren accepted me," Rlain said, "when none of the honorspren would."

"That's unfair," Breteh's honorspren said, glowing blue with hands on her hips. "Lots of humans weren't chosen either, Rlain. It comes down to individual decisions."

"And yet," Rlain said, "every single member of Bridge Four now has an honorspren—except me. Curious, how people's decisions are an individual matter when they're confronted about them—but those decisions form blatant patterns."

"Sja-anat," Radiant said, drawing their attention back to the topic, "cannot be trusted—but she's also not our enemy. She said her spren have an affinity for the Spiritual Realm. I think the Ghostbloods are planning to use those spren to help them navigate it. I determined I'd have a much better chance of figuring out how they'd do that, or even what the Ghostbloods plan to do, with your help."

"Spiritual Realm," Renarin said. "Where you said . . ."

"A certain thing is hidden," Radiant continued, not wanting to say too much in front of the guards. Shallan had given this explanation earlier.

Renarin nodded.

"So . . . your spren," Radiant said. "Do they have any insights? I'm certain the Ghostbloods are going to show up here, likely right when Dalinar opens the portal. The fugitives might make a dash for it."

"It would help," Renarin said, "to know where this portal will be." He narrowed his eyes, then pointed at the tower.

Radiant had the strangest impression as he did so—that his arm and hand were outlined by a soft red glow while in motion, as if he was overlapping some second version of himself. This light, possibly his spren, moved *just before* he did. It was an afterimage, in reverse.

"There," Renarin said. "Can you see them?"

"I can," Rlain said, pointing as well—and his body had exactly the same precursor image. "They're in the tower. Both Bondsmiths. Their souls glow powerfully."

"Spren revolve around Aunt Navani," Renarin said, "the way winds move through a chasm, sculpted by it. They're coming down in a lift."

"So we go to them," Radiant said. "Because that's where Mraize and his team will need to be, once the portal opens."

∴

It was starting to grow dark outside as Navani finally led the group down a lift, through Urithiru, to find an appropriate place to perform their experiment. Storms. The entire second day had passed that quickly? She didn't feel tired, a blessing from the Sibling, though she did see some signs of fatigue in Dalinar. The way he clasped his hands behind him, forcing himself to stand tall.

They reached the ground floor, light fading in the sky outside the great atrium window as the sun set on the opposite side of Urithiru. She led them through a swarm of gloryspren to a stairwell, holding Gav's hand all the way. The boy needed more attention from both of them—and fortunately, he had managed a nap during the many meetings. As they reached the bottom of the steps, entering a long hallway, she trailed her other hand along the wall, layered with strata in lines and patterns.

She could feel the tower thrumming. A thousand different mechanisms working in concert, like the organs of a human body. Dalinar and Wit strode behind her. Behind them were the characteristic host of attendants and guards. Navani could almost ignore them as she walked.

"Gram?" Gav asked softly. "I'm scared."

She stopped and knelt, letting several of the others pass by. "Why, Gav?"

He looked up toward the gloryspren bobbing around her. Then he cringed.

"Could you back away, please," Navani said, lifting her head and speaking to the spren.

They did, many of them vanishing and the others moving to the very top of the corridor. Gav relaxed. The spren that had tormented him in the Kholinar palace had been of a completely different variety, but that didn't matter in the face of trauma.

"Was that it?" she asked.

"Not just that," he whispered. "The tower . . . I saw it earlier . . . and Gram, it's a spren? The whole thing?"

"The tower is good, Gav," she said. "It cares for us."

He nodded, but didn't seem convinced. So she gently took his hand and held it to the wall.

"Can you feel that?" she asked him.

"I'm not sure," he said, scrunching up his face.

"Close your eyes," she said, "and listen."

He did so. "It's . . . humming?"

"That's right," she said. "There's a tunnel nearby where boxes flow along on a belt. They're carrying laundry from all through the tower down here, where it can be washed. It's not fully up and running yet—we need many more boxes—but this is one of the ways we know the tower is good."

"Because . . . it has boxes?"

"Because it makes everyone's lives better," Navani said. "With this mechanism, no one will need to climb stairs with heavy bags of clothing. Beyond this are vast rooms where fresh water is cycled and cleaned, so no one has to carry water. The tower is doing that for us all, not only for kings and queens. It is good, Gav. I promise."

"I feel it, Gram!" Gav said, his hand beside hers. "I really feel it. The tower is alive . . ."

"All things are," she said. "Whether it's the cup you drink from, the home you live in, or the air you breathe. All of it is part of this world given us by the Almighty, and everything in this world is alive. It is one of the ways we know God loves us."

And surely He did. Even if the person who had held the power was dead, that was merely an avatar, a Vessel—not God. It was that Vessel Dalinar hoped to replace. If he did, would he then return to conventional belief as she hoped? His new ways, new teachings, weren't *strictly* blasphemous, but things about them did make her uncomfortable.

Dalinar and Wit had reached a door at the end of the hallway. They stepped in, then a moment later Dalinar looked out and waved for her. She rose and joined him, and he lifted Gav and handed the boy to his governess, who stood with the guards.

"Nobody enters," Dalinar said.

"Pardon, Brightlord," one of the guards asked, "but why are we here? What are we doing?"

"It's an experiment that could be dangerous," Dalinar said. "It could take us as long as an hour or so."

They nodded. Dalinar and Navani shut the thick door behind them, standing in one of the tower's water cistern rooms. Wit strolled through the room, noting where water poured out of pipes in the walls to crash down into the cistern. He said something, but she couldn't make it out over the cascading water.

"What was that?" Navani said.

"You didn't hear?" Wit said, strolling closer. "Excellent. We are unlikely to be overheard, and this place is acceptably remote and secure."

"Yes, but what did you say?" Navani asked.

Wit smiled, then turned to Dalinar. "You're certain you want to try this?"

"I am," Dalinar said.

Wit turned to Navani.

"As am I," she said.

"Very well," Wit said, fishing in his pocket. "I've thought of the perfect vision for your experiment." He tossed Navani a small rock, which she caught, frowning.

It wasn't cremstone, but perhaps a kind of granite. The type you either had to quarry for, or had to Soulcast. She held up the rock for Dalinar.

"And this is?" Dalinar asked.

"Rock from Ashyn," Wit said lightly. "Like those carried by your ancestors to this world during their migration. They were fragments of a holy site on your homeworld, but stones themselves took on a kind of mystical lore by association. That sort of thing happens when the world undergoes repeated cataclysms and society gets knocked back to the stone age a few dozen times. Some seven thousand years later, everyone in Shinovar worships rocks, and has no idea why."

Navani gaped at him.

"What?" he asked.

"Have you *told* them?" she asked. "Shared their heritage, their history with them? Have you *written this down*?"

 "I keep meaning to . . ." Wit said, and shrugged.

Dalinar turned the rock over in his fingers. "You just *have* one of these? Did you steal it?"

"Hmm?" Wit said. "No, I picked it out myself, right before the migration."

"To Roshar," Navani said.

"Yes."

"You were *there*?"

Again Wit shrugged. "Look, I can't be expected to tell you everything that has happened in the last ten thousand years, all right? Yes, I was there. Can we focus on the experiment?" He pointed at the rock. "We want an easy vision as a test. A particular event chosen by us, not preselected by Honor or the Stormfather."

"Yes," Navani said. "That's correct. We need to observe historical events as they truly happened."

"Specifically," Wit said, "you will eventually need to be able to find the history I missed in order to determine what led to Honor's demise, and see if you can find why the power refuses Vessels now. First, we should start with something familiar to me. Hence the rock."

"The . . . rock," Dalinar said. "Wit, I still don't follow."

"I explained this," he said. "If you go into the Spiritual Realm without some kind of anchor or guide, there's no telling what you will see. Events that you think about, that are a focus of individual or collective trauma or passion, are most likely—but really it could be anything. You could dip in there and end up being shown an extended vision of a kindly old man feeding his axehounds. For hours."

Wit pointed at the rock again.

"So . . ." Navani said, sorting through the flood of information he'd given her. "This rock is an anchor to Connect us to a specific moment, and draw us to that specific vision?"

"That's correct," Wit said. "Namely: the arrival of humankind upon Roshar."

"*That's* what we're going to see?" Dalinar asked softly. "Storms."

"If it works, yes," Wit said. "Ideally, only your minds will be taken, your bodies staying here. You'll witness the migration, then return and tell me about it. Since I was there, I can authenticate that this has worked."

"A control for the experiment," Navani said.

"Exactly," Wit said. "And with Dalinar's clock already attuned, you shouldn't get too wildly affected by time dilation. You should avoid coming out having aged twenty years—though be careful, it still might be easy to lose track of the days. With that, you can see how much time is passing here, so keep an eye on it. Enjoy the vision for an hour or so, then I'll call you back."

Dalinar nodded firmly.

"Wait," Navani said. "How do we come back? How do we even initiate this? What are the mechanics?"

"Tether yourselves here with a line of power," Wit said. "Dalinar, you've done it before."

Navani observed as he drew in Stormlight, then knelt and infused the ground with it. When he stood, a line of light anchored him there. With his coaching she was able to draw strength from the tower, then *press* it into the ground. Like an experiment with osmosis and diffusion.

"That line of light will act like a rope," Wit explained. "So you can be pulled back should you slip in too deep. You should be able to see those lines of light in the vision, and pull on them to come back yourselves. In an emergency, I can contact you through them."

"All right . . ." Navani said, shivering. "Now what?"

"Now," Wit said, "you open a perpendicularity, and combine all three realms in a single point. You pass through, sending only your mind."

"How though?" Dalinar asked.

Wit folded his arms, standing at the edge of the rippling reservoir. Light danced on the ceiling, reflected from the glowing gemstones set in the walls, just beneath the surface. Looking at him, she sensed something *primordial* about the man. His smile faded, his eyes profound, as if holding the darkness of the cosmere before light sparked.

"I don't know," Wit said softly.

"You don't know?" Dalinar said. "You said—"

Navani laid a hand on his arm, quieting him, and looked to Wit. The deity who insisted he was not.

"Every time I've done this," Wit said, "I've been at one of the pools. Wells of power that grow around the presence of gods, a kind of . . . natural spring, grown of their power. When you step into such a well, you can *feel* the bond that gods have to the Spiritual Realm. You can see a little into the plane where they exist—where their thoughts move at many times the speed of mortals'. I can feel that place *calling* me. Perhaps it knows I rejected it once; I am the fish that escaped the hook.

"I can share that feeling, rather than a specific list of instructions, Dalinar. At times I have stepped into that power and have followed the call—emerging into a realm where gods dwell. I do it by instinct, as should work for you. It is not much, but you've asked for my help, and I give what I have." He met their eyes. "I warned you of the danger. There are few paths in this universe I fear to walk. This is one of them."

Navani met Dalinar's eyes. He sighed, but then nodded. "Let's open the perpendicularity," he said, "and feel it out."

◆◆◆

At Radiant's urging, the group flew toward the Bondsmiths. They left Breteh's three squires behind to watch and give warning if someone came through one of the gateways.

They soared through the halls of Urithiru, and as they did, Radiant reached out to brush the wall. It felt solid. This corridor was populated by hundreds of tiny candle flames hovering in the air: the souls of the people living and working in Urithiru. There were also a great number of spren, which on this side were like wildlife—the fauna that populated Shadesmar, attracted to, perhaps feeding on, the emotions and experiences of the humans on the other side. They were only visible in the Physical Realm when something intense let them manifest.

Perhaps it was the bond that drew them. The bond to people—like Radiant spren, or the spren of her armor, which kept up with them somehow, rolling across the ground and sometimes flying between gaps. There was something to the bond that drew spren, invigorated them. *Like cremlings hiding in shalebark,* Shallan thought, smiling, remembering drawings she'd done during a more innocent time.

There was so much to be studied about the symbiosis between spren and human. Someday when all this was done, *that* would be her project. Jasnah thought her a whimsical artist, and that was part of her. But so was the scientist. She dreamed of creating a grand illustrated tome explaining the intricate details of the bond. Shallan's ultimate triumph in proving that art and science were actually one.

The Windrunners landed them at a stairwell heading down. The Bondsmiths had gone this way—indeed, they shone through the glass floor up ahead. The three guards and one of the Windrunners went first to check the way, leaving Renarin to step over to her and whisper.

"I saw a vision," he said, "right before you arrived. Rlain thinks it's Ba-Ado-Mishram. What we're doing here is dangerous, and I need to talk to Shallan about it."

So, reluctantly, Radiant stepped back. And hoped they wouldn't get *too* distracted by whatever he had to say.

◆◆◆

The tower on this side was overwhelming to Renarin. While Rlain hummed to the place's beauty, Renarin kept focusing on how many things were *moving* all at once. The walls of shimmering crystal, light catching on corners like it did on a prism. Then there were the spren. Flocks of them, many the size of minks or even axehounds, scurrying down every hallway, hanging from the ceiling, making shadows that reflected through walls, adding to the visual cacophony.

Though spren looked different on this side, he was pretty sure those many-legged ones were fearspren, like eels with feet and one big bulging eye on the front. Gloryspren flitted around on wings, with glowing spheres for heads. But what were the ones that had six arms and gripped the walls, watching with a large drooping mouth that seemed to have eyes in it? The things that were shaped like anemones? The darker shadows, hulking and threatening, that he kept glimpsing through the glass walls?

Storms. As he pulled Shallan aside, he searched his pockets for something to fiddle with. He came out with a couple of spheres, which he spun in his palm, and he tried to focus on the clicking sound the glass made.

Shallan undid her hair band and fanned out her hair before replacing her hat. Her lips parted as she glanced one way, then the other. It was nice to know he wasn't the only one to find this terrible and overwhelming . . .

She grinned like a madwoman. "This is *amazing*," she said. "I can't believe I haven't come in here before!"

"Didn't you just get back yesterday?"

"I should have made time," she said, pointing. "Storms! What are those! I should sketch those. The ones with the spines? They don't look like *any* spren on our side. Usually there's some physical clue to what they are."

Despite her words, she didn't get out a sketchbook. They started down the steps, a Windrunner and Rlain ahead of them. Renarin kept the spheres in his hand, clicking them together, and went over what he wanted to say. Spelling it out in his mind.

"So, you wanted to talk?" Shallan asked, eyeing another spren above them, through the transparent ceiling.

"Yes," he said, deliberate. "Ba-Ado-Mishram. Rlain thinks we saw her in a vision."

"I think I did too," Shallan said.

"*What?*"

"Odd things happen with Lightweaving," she said. "Particularly if you've bonded two spren at the same time."

Two spren. "Wait. That's not just some . . . friend of Pattern's?"

"The deadeye?"

Deadeye? He peered ahead at the other Cryptic. Was that what the bent tines in the head meant? He hadn't looked closely, as . . . well . . . this place was so demanding and exhausting. He simply couldn't *help* but see everything.

"Two spren," he said, fixating on that. "You have *two* spren. I didn't even know it was possible. Why would you bond a second on your trip?"

"It's a long story," Shallan said.

That seemed like a promise of more, but then she didn't continue.

"Anyway," Renarin said eventually—again organizing and focusing his thoughts as a group of strange purple spren rolled down the steps next to them. "You said this Unmade was in the Spiritual Realm. And you said my father is *opening a perpendicularity* to travel there."

"Which the Ghostbloods know about," she said.

"So we tell him not to!"

"I sent messages," she said, "but it's a busy day, and he's been on the move. Besides, Renarin, when has your father ever reconsidered because any of us made an objection?" She focused on the lights ahead. It appeared that his father and Aunt Navani had entered a large chamber at the end of the corridor. "I can finally stop Mraize—for once I know exactly where he's going to be. I just have to be there watching for him."

"But this spren," Renarin said. "Shallan, I think she's something terrible. Worse than the Unmade that caused the Alethi to hunger to kill each other in battle for centuries. Worse than the one that killed Aesudan and consumed Amaram. Worse than . . . anything."

"So we *absolutely* need to stop the Ghostbloods from getting to her."

"Or maybe we shouldn't be involved at all," Renarin said. "What if by meddling, we lead to her being freed. All the effort we took to lock away the Thrill? Someone took that effort and more to lock Mishram away. If she's in the Spiritual Realm . . . maybe your enemies can't find her, Shallan. Maybe the prison is strong enough."

"I can't simply let Mraize do whatever he wants, Renarin."

"And me?" Renarin said, feeling Glys thrum within him. "Shallan, you specifically fetched *me*."

"Because you might be able to spot others who have bonded corrupt . . . um . . . reborn? Remade? Sja-anat's spren."

"I think you can do that as well as anyone could," Renarin said. "You told me Mraize had bonded one of Sja-anat's Enlightened spren because they could guide him in the Spiritual Realm. Then you came to find me. Why, Shallan? Why really?"

She kept her eyes forward. "Mishram's prison is compromised. The Ghostbloods knew precisely where to send agents to get the information, and have intel on how to reach the Spiritual Realm. And their spren . . . their Enlightened spren . . . can lead them through that realm."

"So you *are* going to try to find the prison," Renarin said. "That's why I'm here. You hope Glys can guide you!"

"I don't think I thought it through that much," Shallan said. "I'm working on instinct. Look, we should catch up to the others."

She quickened her step. Renarin forced himself to keep moving along the short hallway, trying so hard to ignore all the lights, the motion. It was . . . it was loud. Not loud to the ears, loud to every sense. It made him want to put his hands around his eyes and block out most of the stimuli, to cut down on how much was reaching him.

I will help? Glys said. *I will try?*

The spren . . . darkened things. Dampening the lights at the perimeter of Renarin's sight, like what happened in a vision, where everything went black.

It did help, and he was able to pull himself together and make his way forward after Shallan and the others. But storms. What was he letting her pull him into? Shallan could be a little like a sudden river after a highstorm. A flood that could carry you until it ran out, leaving you stranded. Adolin just went along with it.

Is she right? Renarin asked Glys. *Could you help us on the other side, in the Spiritual Realm?*

. . . *Yes,* Glys said, sounding hesitant as he pulsed. *Yes. I think I could. I will.*

That was a small comfort, but Shallan *did* seem frightened of these Ghostbloods. Renarin didn't think they could do anything to his father—human souls appeared as glowing flames on this side, but there was no way to interact with them. Yet they didn't know all the permutations of what anti-Light could do, and . . .

. . . and he kept going, despite knowing he was trapped in a Shallan flood. Because if he turned back, then Rlain probably would too, which would mean leaving Shallan completely without access to common sense.

Don't be unfair, he told himself. *She's done a lot of good for your family.* A year of having her as a sister-in-law had shown him she could be a deeply sensitive and caring person, and she loved Adolin with an enthusiasm that none of the other women ever had. Beyond that, she had a remarkable handle on life, considering the way her fragmented mind sometimes presented challenges.

In short, despite first impressions, he had grown fond of her. However, that didn't mean he liked the way that she worked by instinct. Accidentally joining a secret organization bent on ruling Roshar, then never finding a time to *mention* it to anyone until it became a crisis? In his experience, that was the most Shallan thing she could have done.

Unfortunately, a glow was building ahead of them at the end of the hallway; his father was preparing the perpendicularity. But . . . there wasn't anyone here. The room they reached was a perfect replica of the one in the Physical Realm, only made of the same shimmering glass as everything else. He could make out the souls of Aunt Navani and his father, glowing brightly from their Connections to powerful spren—and another soul, which had to be Wit, shimmering with a great number of odd colors. Glys confirmed it.

Otherwise, the room was empty . . . Wait. What were those two souls over at the side, in the walls?

Shallan set the three guards at the door and stepped in with the spren, Rlain, and the Windrunners. There, she stood with her hands on her hips. "It seems impregnable. A hallway ending here? Walls we can see through, and no other humans in sight? Did I misjudge?"

"Those two souls over there might be spying on Father and Navani," Renarin said. "Could that be them?"

Shallan spun to follow his gesture. "Storms, maybe the Ghostbloods slipped past in the Physical Realm? It's possible they transferred with a group of soldiers on the Shattered Plains."

"What do these Ghostbloods look like?" Rlain said, inspecting the souls. "Maybe we can identify them."

"We were expecting three people," Shallan said. "Two short, one tall. One woman, two men. Two wear strange masks most of the time, and are foreigners. The third is Thaylen, though he dyes his eyebrows and keeps them short. He has scars across his face, and . . ." She paused, then glanced at Renarin. "They would have spren with them. Maybe hiding within their hosts, as yours do?"

"Tumi says that is likely," Rlain told her. "Any spren can learn to do it, even on this side."

"And their powers?" Renarin pushed. "Sja-anat can make any order of Radiant save Bondsmith, assuming the spren are willing. And a lot of them are, Shallan. She offers a different option, a third option. So what powers should we be watching for?"

"Well, one can transfer between Shadesmar and the Physical Realm," Shallan said. "So they might be waiting on the other side for the perpendicularity to open, then plan to pop in here and enter it from this side."

"Good," Rlain said. "That gives us something to prepare for." He knelt beside the wall. "These two souls . . . they seem to be hiding in an air duct. And what is that green spot . . ."

"Mmm . . ." Pattern said. "Cultivationspren. That is Lift."

"Spying as usual," Shallan said, folding her arms. "So maybe that's not them."

"What else should we be looking for?" Renarin asked. "Could one of them be a Lightweaver? Could they be disguised?"

She glanced at him, then her eyes widened and she looked back through the clear crystalline door. At the three soldiers—two short, one tall—who they'd brought here and posted out front.

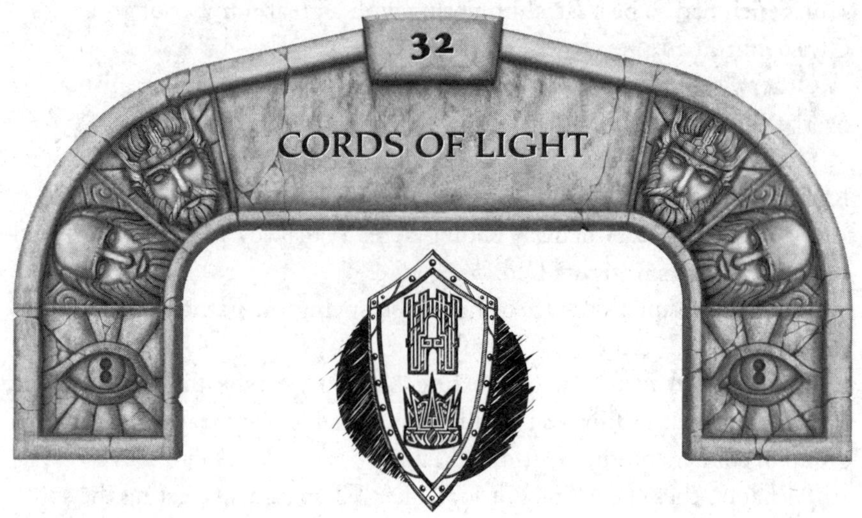

As a king leaves a people with the gift of his absence, so that they may grow and solve their own problems, without his hand to always guide them.

—From *The Way of Kings*, fourth parable

A glowing rift tore reality apart before Dalinar, a melding of three realms.

It took the form of a pillar of light emerging from his clasped hands, gloryspren exploding into existence around him. The light soon washed out everything else, and power flowed like water in a mighty river—forming a puncture in reality that defied natural laws . . . or no, this was an expression of natural laws too. Simply ones that were higher, more fundamental.

"All right," Dalinar said. "It's open."

"Step in," Wit said, though Dalinar had lost track of him in the omnipresent light. "Both of you. Let the light bathe you, then seek the Spiritual Realm."

Dalinar moved forward, holding the portal open as one might part drapes at a window.

"Dalinar," Navani said, joining him, "I can hear the tones of Roshar . . . They're familiar to me now. This place . . . it's been calling to me for weeks."

She took Dalinar's hand in her safehand, then reached out toward the sound with her fingers, which he could see making streaks in the light. He could feel that realm too. Could feel her welcoming it . . . as they stretched toward another place.

Panic speared Shallan. Those people outside . . .

Oh no, Veil thought. *Remind me, what do you do when there's a guard watching for you?*

Storms. You became the guard.

Unfortunately, Mraize saw her looking through the wall at him, and knew they'd been spotted. A second later the three Ghostbloods burst through the door, still wearing their false faces—though Mraize had pulled a dagger out. One that glowed and warped the air.

"Protect the spren!" Shallan shouted, pointing. "Those three guards are the enemy!"

The room became chaos. Three Ghostbloods pretending to be common Alethi guards faced two Windrunners and their spren, along with Renarin, Rlain, Radiant, Pattern, and Testament. So many figures suddenly moving, responding, or panicking.

Mraize raised his dagger and stayed back, though when the dagger got too close to his side, it made the Lightweaving spark and rip apart. Iyatil and Lieke leaped for Breteh, perhaps identifying the Windrunner as the strongest.

Radiant moved, shoving past Pattern and trying to get to Breteh, who clashed with Lieke, holding back his dagger. Nearby, Isasik—the other Windrunner—tackled Iyatil.

Storms, no, Radiant thought, pulling to a stop. There was no way Isasik could handle Iyatil. Indeed, the woman spun expertly and grabbed the younger Windrunner by the arm, slashing in a single smooth motion. She tossed him aside, blood spraying from a slit across his neck.

Right then, Dalinar's perpendicularity opened.

Power thrummed through the room, pulsing with the energy of storms, and Shallan felt it surge through her like hot water in her veins. She gasped in awe, and outside the room spren began to scramble and scratch at the door.

Iyatil jumped for her, knife—fortunately a conventional one—bloody. Radiant separated from Shallan then, fully armored despite being in Shadesmar—formed of Lightweaving given physical weight. Radiant snatched Iyatil straight from the air, then slammed her to the glowing crystalline ground.

Iyatil grunted and slashed at Radiant, the weapon bouncing ineffectively off the Shardplate. It wasn't real, but was anything real on this side? What had made this entire tower, if not raw Investiture from the Sibling?

Radiant pinned Iyatil down by one arm—but the Ghostblood performed an expert wrestling twist and slipped away. She spun around Radiant—who tried and failed to grab her. The woman's Lightweaving began to evaporate, letting her mask show through, and her eyes—rimmed by wood—fixated on Shallan.

If she has an anti-Stormlight dagger, Shallan realized, dancing backward by instinct, *she'll use it against me. That kills both me and Radiant, and likely negates Pattern and Testament.*

Not that either were very useful. Testament hid behind Pattern, who stood with one hand to his chest, pattern spinning, like a woman whose garden party had just been spoiled by unexpected rain.

As Iyatil struck, Shallan dodged backward, blessing Adolin for his insistence on training her in knife combat. As she had expected though, this was a feint—Iyatil slid another knife from her sheath and kept her hand back as if to hide it. This one warped the air.

Shallan had been wrong about them only having a little bit of anti-Light—there had been one bolt, but at least two daggers. Shallan continued to dodge, passing Isasik, whom Renarin was helping sit up after healing. A second later, Breteh—careening in an uncontrolled Lashing—came crashing past. Iyatil dodged, and Shallan saw her chance, bringing Radiant in to tackle the woman, forcing her to drop the dagger—which went skidding across the floor.

While Iyatil quickly slipped out of Radiant's grip again, Shallan was able to scoop up the dagger. She glanced up, met Iyatil's furious gaze, then smiled in triumph.

A second later, Shallan took a blowgun dart to the eye. She stumbled back and barely managed to dodge—through the pain—as Iyatil sent more darts after her. When had the woman gotten out that blowgun? Shallan scrambled away, making illusions of herself to distract, and pulled the dart free.

Puffing, she assessed the situation. Isasik had been healed but still sat on the floor, right hand to his bloodied neck. Lieke was facing Rlain and one of the Windrunner honorspren. The female who had spoken earlier, wearing a uniform and carrying a light dueling sword—which she wielded effectively to force the outsider up against the wall, then run him through.

Shallan nodded in appreciation—so far, Maya and Notum were the sole spren she'd known with the air of soldiers. But it stood to reason there would be others, particularly among the honorspren who had chosen to come and form bonds rather than hide in Lasting Integrity.

The Ghostbloods were losing this fight. They might be better individual warriors, but they faced five Radiants, plus the spren and Shallan's illusions. Radiant backed Iyatil into a corner, and Lieke—who didn't appear to have a spren—died in the attack, falling limp and covered in blood. As quickly as the ruckus had begun, it was over.

As Adolin had warned her so many months ago, combat was often short, brutal, and overwhelming. Years of training came down to a few key clashes.

Shallan had even missed important parts while fixated on Iyatil; she only now noticed that Mraize was on the ceiling, having apparently been Lashed there by Breteh. The honorspren and Rlain joined Radiant in holding Iyatil at bay, while Shallan and Isasik—regaining his feet—turned weapons on Mraize, trapped on the ceiling.

"Wait," Isasik said. "Where did that other Knight Radiant come from? And . . . how did she get Shardplate in Shadesmar?"

Breteh looked at Radiant, then frowned. "Another Lightweaver?" he guessed. "Shallan?"

"Well," she said. "It's kind of complicated—"

"You haven't asked," Iyatil whispered from the corner, "what happened to the guards whose places we took."

Isasik turned toward her. "What did you do to them?"

"They're being held at the base of the pillar where you arrived," Iyatil said. "As insurance. They will be executed unless I give a signal. Or you get to them first."

"She's toying with you, Isasik," Shallan said. "Don't let her get inside your head."

"It's true," Mraize said from the ceiling. "You know I wouldn't lie about this, little knife. You can save them, but you only have a few minutes."

"Is he lying?" Isasik demanded. "Shallan?"

She gazed up at Mraize. Who smiled. Confident.

Damnation.

"He's probably not," she admitted. "But—"

Both Windrunners dashed away, their spren following.

"Windrunners," Iyatil said dismissively. "So easy to play with."

"We still have you all," Shallan said. Mraize on the ceiling, Lieke down, Iyatil trapped in the corner, holding her blowgun but apparently out of darts. "You're captured. We win."

"Ah," Iyatil said softly, "but Mraize still has his dagger."

Shallan looked up at him, her eyes locking on to the dagger. It was difficult to make anything out as the perpendicularity raged—washing out the room with brilliant white light. Spren in the distance were going haywire, a thousand shadows dancing up on the ground floor. But she *could* make out that warping. That light that somehow repelled natural light—including that of the perpendicularity—in a bubble around Mraize's hand. It stood out like a single dot on an otherwise white canvas.

"Mraize," Shallan said, suddenly filled with dread. "Mraize, what are you doing?"

"Have you ever seen a perpendicularity collapse on itself, little knife?" he asked.

"Mraize . . ."

"I haven't either," he said. "But it's reportedly spectacular." He threw the dagger.

Shallan leaped for it, but she was in the wrong position. The anti-Light struck the center of the portal.

The blast that followed shattered the room.

⁂

It was working.

Dalinar could feel the vision begin to form, slowly at first, as if the Spiritual Realm was resisting. He and Navani pushed forward, as through a thick tar, holding hands—trailing cords of light to Connect to the Physical Realm.

Images began to form around him from swirling light. Visions of places, people—ephemeral, winking away in seconds. The tones thrummed through him.

It was *working.*

He looked at Navani, grinning. Then, behind them, something *snapped.*

Their Connection to the Physical Realm vanished, and something came rushing toward them: power, wind, and screams.

33
THE CONFLUX
OF ALL DARKNESS
AND SORROW

May you have the courage someday to walk away. And the wisdom to recognize that day when it arrives.

—From *The Way of Kings*, fourth parable

Lift gasped at the sudden flood of light.

She'd been near Dalinar's perpendicularity before, but the wonder still struck her every time. That powerful illumination shining straight through her, making her transparent. Even hidden in the little air tunnels as she was, it overwhelmed her.

Today, within that light, she saw herself as she could have been. Standing tall and proud, unafraid of the future, because the hand of someone loving rested on her shoulder. In this vision she was dressed in the Iriali clothing of her childhood, where her family had moved when she'd been young.

What if she'd stayed there, in Rall Elorim, instead of . . . wherever the wind put her? Would she have become that girl—that confident young woman—with gleaming hair, wearing an Iriali short shirt, her shoulders and midriff exposed? As if she didn't care that people saw she was growing up?

This version of her didn't seem afraid of anything.

Lift reached for that version of herself, her fingers barely visible in the light, and she thought she felt a comforting song flow through her. And that hand. On the shoulder, with tan skin and painted nails . . . so familiar. Though the rest of the figure was invisible, Lift knew that hand, so soft despite its calluses.

If she could just hold it one more time . . .

But there was no substance to this vision. And Lift knew, confronted by this at last, something she'd been lying to herself about. She didn't believe her mother was dead. Oh, she said it. She said it over and over, the way her great-uncle had always sworn by the name of the god he hated. In case that god was watching, in case fate was checking on her, because if you said it then nobody would ask what was really in your heart.

She didn't believe; she physically *couldn't.* Her mother would hold her again, and life would be warm. But Lift . . . she couldn't change. What if Mother returned and didn't recognize her? What if Mother looked for her and didn't see her, so found some other little girl to love?

Life had been perfect for a few months. Why couldn't it have stayed that way?

"Lift?" a trembling voice said from behind her in the shaft. The vision vanished. "I'm scared."

Wyndle? But no. That was . . .

She turned sharply, and saw Gavinor in her shadow, gazing past her into the room where Navani and Dalinar were opening their perpendicularity.

From the wall next to her, Wyndle's vine formed a mouth. "Oh *dear.* Did you know he was following us?"

"Of course not," Lift hissed. "Gav! What are you doing!"

"You said," the boy whispered, "we have to learn when to obey and when to not obey. I saw you sneak in. This is a time to not obey?" He shrank further before that light.

Storms. It was one thing to be caught peeking in on important meetings. It was *quite another* to be caught corrupting the starvin' crown prince and grandson of the starvin' Bondsmiths. They'd string her up. Worse. They'd stop letting her steal their desserts.

She tried to shoo Gav back down the small tunnel, but he was frozen in place. With a sigh, she twisted around so she could push him back before her. She'd miss whatever awesome thing Dalinar and Navani were doing, but whatever. She startled a strange purplish cremling as they crawled. Those things were all over in the air shafts. She wondered what they tasted like boiled, but had never managed to catch one. She also wondered if anyone else suspected what they really were.

She got Gav moving at last, and everything was fine until Navani gave a shout—and the light started to *pull* them toward it. Lift screamed as she slid backward through the tunnel, pushing hard on the walls to stop herself, but then Gav collided with her, shoving them both out into the room.

"Mistress!" Wyndle cried. "Oh my! Mistress!"

Air rushed around them in a roar, rivaling the sounds of the waterfalls that had made listening in so difficult. With the powerful light blinding her, she lost track of where she was—and Gav slipped from her grip.

They were . . . they were both being pulled toward that rift. Sliding across the rough ground, bumping over stones. In her panic, she tried something she'd never managed before.

She became *un*-awesome. Instead of slipping freely, she tried to make herself grind against the ground, maybe stick. Unfortunately, the friction just made her flip upward instead. She flew through the too-bright air straight toward the rift—

—until someone seized her by the arm and held her, a figure that cast a shadow in the wrong direction. A man all in black, grunting, struggling against the powerful rift until finally the perpendicularity vanished.

Lift slumped to the ground, dropping like a kite with no wind. She could barely see anything, just shapes and shadows, though her vision quickly began to return.

"Thanks," she muttered.

"You're lucky I sensed you watching again," Wit said. "I almost missed grabbing you from the air. You both owe me."

She relaxed, and Wyndle came scuttling over.

"Oh! What was that!" Wyndle said. "Master Hoid, what happened?"

"I wish I knew," Wit said. "Their anchors are gone. And . . . well, so are they."

"Wait," Lift said, opening her eyes. "They went in, like, totally? Bodies too?" Whenever she'd snuck into Dalinar's visions, she'd left her body behind.

"Yes," Wit said. "And you? No thanks for the rescue? Figures."

Lift frowned at that until she saw the cremling from earlier fluttering away on wings that could barely hold it in the air. So when Wit had said "both" of them, he'd meant . . .

Lift sat bolt upright. "Gav!"

"What?" Wit asked.

"Did you grab Gavinor? He was sneaking through the tunnels behind me!" She leapt to her feet, searching around. "You saved him, right?"

"I didn't see him," Wit admitted.

"Why not!" she shouted. "You saw me!"

"Lift, you're so highly Invested I'm surprised normal people can't feel it. You glow so brightly to my life sense that you outshine anyone nearby. You're *sure* Gavinor was here?"

She nodded, then the two of them looked—slowly—toward the bare portion of stone where the portal had been.

"Well, shit," Lift said.

"You heard that from Zahel, haven't you?" Wit said, his eyes growing distant.

"Why do people keep saying that?"

"Rosharans don't use that particular word as an epithet," Wit said, his expression still strange as he turned in a slow circle. "You're only going to confuse people."

"The best words are the ones most people don't understand."

"That is literally the opposite of how language should function."

"Yeah, 'cuz *you* make sense all the time. Anyway, what are you doing? Should we be panicking?"

"Design and I are peeking into the Cognitive Realm," Wit said. "In case we were lucky, and the Bondsmiths dropped into Shadesmar."

"And?" Lift guessed.

"I see the remnants of one corpse—Malwish, by that broken mask—and a destroyed chamber. That's curious. But no sign of Gav, Dalinar, or Navani. Unfortunately, it seems they did go into the Spiritual Realm."

"Which means . . . ?"

Wit focused on her, then drew his lips to a line. "We have to hope that Dalinar finds his way back in the next eight days."

"And if he doesn't?" She glanced at Wyndle, who had shrunken into a small pile of vines, whimpering softly. Storms. Gav would be terrified. Could she do anything?

"This complicates everything," Wit said. "The contract has provisions for Dalinar's death before the deadline, his stalling for time, or if his arrival is prevented by another. But if he doesn't show up because of his own choices . . . I believe that will be a forfeit."

"Meaning we lose."

"Worse," Wit said. "It will be as if Dalinar broke the contract, violating his oath. As Dalinar represents Honor, the power of which is maintaining Odium's place on this planet . . . if Dalinar doesn't show up, that will liberate Odium entirely. He'll be free to rampage in the cosmere again."

Storms. Maybe Gav wasn't the only one in trouble. Except . . . "Don't we *want* Odium to leave?"

"Odium unbound would be terrible," Wit said, crossing to where the portal had opened. He knelt to press his fingers on the stone. "If he weren't being held in check by fear of the other Shards, you have no idea the destruction he would cause."

"Sure, right," Lift said. "But we've had to deal with him for . . . like forever. Surely someone else can do it."

Wit didn't reply.

"Can you do something?" Lift asked, stepping up to him and squatting down. "Bring them back? The times I cheated my way in, I had Dalinar to guide me."

"I don't know," Wit said softly. "I warned them. I will . . . try to think of something that will help. It might take time." He looked toward the door. "That was a knock."

"You can hear that over the rush of the water?"

He nodded, standing.

"Do we . . . tell them?" Lift asked.

"Depends," Wit said. "How eager are you to start a massive tower-wide riot? Dalinar and Navani are the glue that holds together the nation and the Radiants. I think the only thing keeping people from full-on panic is the belief that somehow the Blackthorn will handle the upcoming contest. If people find out he's gone . . ."

"Right," she said as another knock came, this time louder. "What do we do, then?"

"We do the smart thing, of course," Wit said, starting to glow as he drew in Stormlight. "We lie."

∴

As night fully took the landscape, Kaladin had to admit defeat. His stew was a disaster. It tasted like crem.

Kaladin had helped Rock dozens of times, though Huio, Lopen, and Dabbid had proven to be the most capable. Still, it shouldn't have been that hard for him. Just cut everything up and toss it in. Part of the reason he'd brought such a large pack was because he'd requested spices and vegetables.

He squatted by his little cook pot, a poor substitute for Rock's great cauldron, frustrated. Maybe more pepper? He sprinkled it in and tried the mess, which now tasted like slightly spicier crem. He groaned in frustration and slumped on his rock. First moon was up, illuminating Szeth as he lay on his back on the grass—no bedroll, only a blanket as a pillow. He was munching on a ration bar.

"Not working?" Syl whispered. She sat on a rock nearby, full sized, violet-fringed ko-takama skirt rippling in the wind.

"It just needs to simmer," Kaladin lied.

"Did you use . . . chunks of ration bars in that?"

"Needed meat. Ration bars are basically jerky."

Perhaps that hadn't been the best choice. But, well, maybe . . . maybe if it cooked longer? He halfheartedly offered up another pinch of spice to the bubbling pot. But storms, he'd taken so long that Szeth had already eaten his own dinner. The whole point of an evening stew was to draw people in, getting them to open up as they ate something unexpectedly good.

Only Szeth didn't seem to care about what tasted good.

Try anyway, Kaladin thought at himself. *Dalinar asked you.*

"So," Kaladin said, turning away from the fire to face Szeth, "this is your homeland."

"Obviously," Szeth said.

"Your house anywhere close?"

"Nearby," Szeth said.

"Want to visit?"

Szeth shrugged, his eyes now closed. "There is nothing for me there."

"Still might help."

"I told you that I need no help."

Kaladin turned and stirred the stew, mostly to be doing something. "I used to think that too," he said, loud enough Szeth could hear from behind. "Actually, I used to *say* it. I always *knew* I needed help. Part of you does too, Szeth. It's not weakness to admit it. We *can* quiet those voices."

"You misunderstand," he replied. "When I say I do not need help, it is not because I lack the ability to recognize my faults. It is not normal that I am chased by the voices of the dead. Likewise, I recognize that others are not so daunted by decisions as I am.

"When I say I need no help, it is because *this* is how I *should* be. I have murdered many innocents. I chose to follow the broken traditions of a people who were so scared of the Truth, they exiled me rather than face it. Because of this, I deserve suffering. It is *right.* If you were to heal it, you would do something immoral. Therefore I tell you I do not want your 'help.' Leave me alone."

"It's not immoral to stop hurting, Szeth," Kaladin said, looking back again.

Szeth just closed his eyes and didn't respond.

Damnation. Kaladin gritted his teeth. Then he forced himself to get out the flute and lay Wit's paper explanations in front of him. He needed something to relax him, and maybe this would help.

He was wrong.

It had been barely a day since Wit had shown him the positionings, but Kaladin fumbled as he tried to replicate them. He first couldn't make a single sound. Then what followed was a breathy, weak noise, nothing like the beautiful and light music Wit had made.

After a half hour of stubbornly trying to play, Kaladin tossed the flute down—causing it to stick in the soft soil like a knife in wood. He heaved himself off the rock by the fire and stalked out into the night, kicking at the stupid grass as it refused to get out of his way.

Syl stepped up beside him in the moonlit darkness. She was better at being of help than he was, because she knew to stay quiet while he breathed in and out, trying to exhale away his frustrations.

"I can't do this, Syl," he said. "The only thing I've ever been good at is war.

Even when I was forced on leave, I found a way to fight for the tower. I am useless unless I'm *killing* something."

"You know that's not true."

"But I don't," Kaladin snapped. "I've always been too good at killing. You recognize that; it's what drew you to me."

"I was drawn," she said, "to willpower, determination, and a desire to protect. Yes, I like the way you dance with the wind when you use a spear, but it's not the killing, Kaladin. It never was."

He didn't respond, staring off into the darkness.

"This is your dark brain talking," she said. "You weren't killing when you rescued Bridge Four. You pulled thirty men out of the darkness and the chasms, then you forged them into something wonderful."

"Yeah," he said. "I forged them into killers."

"A *family,*" Syl said. "Don't try to distort it. I was *there,* Kaladin. You did it because you couldn't stand to let them keep dying. You did it out of love."

He glanced to the side and saw her staring at him indignantly, full sized, impossible to ignore. Storming woman. She was right.

"Szeth," she said, "is no more hopeless than they were. You remember how unwilling *Rock* was at the start?"

"Yeah," he admitted, thinking back to days that—though excruciating at the time—were now fond to him. Sneaking through the night with Rock and Teft, fetching bundles of knobweed. Hearing Rock laugh for the first time, describing what he'd done to Sadeas's meal.

They were both gone now. Teft dead. Rock maybe executed by his people. Still, Kaladin forced the dark thoughts behind him and presented good thoughts, like soldiers with spears, to keep them away. Syl was right. He could claim many things about himself, but he couldn't justify the argument that he was *only* a killer. And life *was* good. He had felt it earlier.

It didn't banish the darkness, but active thoughts, as counters to it, really did help.

"I just don't know what I am anymore," Kaladin said softly, more honestly, "or *who.* If I'm not a soldier, what is there to me? Wit told me to figure it out, but that terrifies me, Syl. I can't be a surgeon like my father wants. I'm not one for a quiet life seeing patients about their bruised arms and strange coughs."

"What about their bruised minds," Syl said, "and strange thoughts?" She looked back toward the small fire.

Remarkably, Szeth had decided to try the stew. Oh, storms. Kaladin went hurrying over with an excuse ready.

Szeth had finished his bowl by the time he arrived. "I would eat this again, if you made it."

Kaladin frowned. Had . . . simmering it made it work? He tried a bite, and found it exactly as bad as before. Except, well, it *was* probably better than field rations. Jerky with mashed-up, dried katfruit wasn't the most appealing meal either.

Kaladin had been comparing his stew to Rock's masterpieces. An impossible benchmark. But when the sole competition was field rations . . .

Szeth stood up, then nodded to the darkness that was the basin of Shinovar. "This is wrong."

"Wrong? I don't see anything."

"There should be candle lights," Szeth explained. "Fires at the homesteads and villages. I see only darkness. It's like they've all simply vanished . . ."

Kaladin stepped up beside him, gazing out at the ocean of black.

"I . . . lied to you earlier," Szeth admitted. "I *do* love my people, Kaladin. My exile makes it feel like I don't care about anything, and sometimes I tell myself I don't deserve to care. But . . . the exile was—for so long—my *proof* that I love them. I *want* to help my people. That is . . . more important to me than the quest, though that makes me a bad Skybreaker."

"We will help them, Szeth," Kaladin promised.

"Perhaps we *will* start by visiting my family homestead. To . . . see if it shows us anything." Szeth handed back his bowl, then walked off and lay down, pulling his blanket over himself and turning away from Kaladin.

Well, that hadn't been the laughter over a stewpot Kaladin had wanted, but it was something. He settled down and ate a bowl, finishing off what was left in the pot. He tried not to compare it to Rock's stew, and it helped.

He didn't want to get into the habit of lowering his standards, but conversely, never being willing to reassess was just as bad. Maybe he was expecting too much from Szeth too quickly. Kaladin had been patient with Bridge Four. He could show the same patience here, despite the tension of a world close to breaking.

With that in mind, he decided to pick up the flute and give it another go. He walked a distance away to not bother Szeth and forced himself to practice, and felt wind blowing across him as he did. A peaceful wind, of this place, where the grass wasn't afraid. A wind he found comforting.

"Is that you?" Kaladin asked, lowering the flute.

Yes, the Wind whispered in his ear, causing Syl to perk up where she'd been sitting on the ground nearby. *The music the ancient one taught you . . . it calls to me . . .*

"I've done as you asked," Kaladin said. "I'm here. I'm still not sure why, but I'm here. Can you tell me?"

Odium changes. His goals change. I . . . can speak now . . . when it was so hard for years . . .

"That has to do with Odium?" Syl asked.

He changes. His attention is not on me, the Wind said. *The Stones have always had the capacity to speak, but only now started doing so. I am always here . . . Now I warn. Odium is made anew. This is dangerous.*

Stay . . . Watch. I will watch too. I do not have answers yet, but I feel better that you are here. Together we must preserve a remnant of Honor. Somehow . . .

Kaladin thought on that as the Wind faded. He found himself again thinking of his friends, fighting without him. Remembering the trauma of Teft's death. It was a fresh wound. He couldn't fixate on it, he knew. Not and become a new person, like Wit said.

Eventually he went back to the flute. The Wind didn't return, and his musical attempts were just as pathetic as they'd been earlier. But storm it, there was *one* thing that was reliably true about Kaladin Stormblessed. Regardless of his job or his location, even if you took away his ability to fight . . . he was still the most stubborn fool of a person who ever lived.

So he kept right on blowing awful notes on that flute. Right until he looked up and found the Herald Ishar standing in front of him.

⁂

The tower was strange on the other side. Really strange. And Lopen was, sure, an expert in strange things. He had plenty of strange cousins. He collected them.

So, he could say with authority this place was strange. Non-strange places didn't glow. It was like an entire building had become Radiant, sucked in some Stormlight, and was now threatening to stick Huio to the wall.

Anticipationspren followed him like a posse as he and the other two Windrunners walked to the site of the explosion. This place was a perfect replica of the tower, only made of glowing glass stuff. The tower said waking it had restored it to its natural state. Which made Lopen wonder why his arm wasn't made of glowing crystal on this side. That would be much better than the fleshy one. Not that he minded—it was good to have two arms again, as now he could eat chouta and point at things at the same time.

But a glowing crystal arm *would* be pretty deevy.

"You think," he asked, "if I thought about it a lot, my arm would turn to crystal?"

Rua, his spren, shrugged. On this side, Rua was around three and a half feet tall—with messy hair, boundless energy, and the proportions of a child. He liked to skip rather than walk, and Lopen had heard that in his home city, Rua could float around all the time. Huio found it fascinating, and was always talking about it.

Thoughts of floating spren and crystal arms evaporated as Lopen reached the site of the blast. "Here, sir," Isasik said. "We were in here . . ."

A smoking, broken chamber. All four walls had been cracked, and the one by the hallway had been completely destroyed. The crystalline ground had been blasted open in a pit, and the ceiling was a fractured web.

One broken corpse lay among the destruction.

"You're certain?" Lopen asked.

"Yes, sir. When I returned to help after rescuing the guards, this is what I found—with that one dead man, who was so broken it made me worry . . ."

"What?" Lopen said. "That the others ended up as person-mush?"

Isasik looked ill, but nodded.

"There ain't no person-mush in here," Lopen said. "This blast was big, but not big enough—sure—to leave us without some kind of sign. Honestly, I expected to encounter some Shallan bits as we walked up that hallway. Pleasant to not find any."

"So . . ." Isasik said.

"So, we have to assume they went through the perpendicularity," Lopen said. "Or otherwise escaped."

"That would transfer them back into the Physical Realm though," Isasik said. "None of them are there."

Lopen didn't reply. Something *was* up. Navani wasn't talking, and so the Sibling wasn't talking, but he could smell it when something strange had happened. He was an expert in strange. The literal walls had secrets. Important, terrible secrets.

Which was super-okay with Lopen. If important people had it in hand, then he didn't need to worry!

"I'm going to assume others have it covered," he told Isasik. "Come on. We need to fly the Mink's people to Herdaz."

"But—"

"If they're dead, can we do anything for them?"

"Well, no," Isasik said, floating down to check on the dead man, who was very, very dead. Enough remained to tell it wasn't any of their friends.

"If they escaped," Lopen continued, "and don't want anyone to know, will we help them by outing them?"

"No," he said. "You know how Lightweavers are . . ."

"If they vanished into another realm, dimension, or place, is there anything *we* can do for them?"

"No," Isasik said, floating up again. "That would take a Bondsmith."

"So we report back," Lopen said. "We've searched to make sure they aren't being held captive. Now we have to assume it's all going to work out, because whatever is going on, it's bigger than we are."

With that, he started toward the Oathgates. Rua hurried to catch up with him, and the spren—storm him—had a glowing crystal arm now.

"Show-off," Lopen said, then hesitated and spoke more softly. "What do *you* think happened to them, naco? Why isn't Navani more worried? Renarin is her family, and Shallan too. Navani *shrugged* at the news; she didn't even put down her chouta. Have you ever seen her *shrug* before?" He paused. "Have you ever seen her eat *chouta* before?"

Rua pointed up at the distant sun, just barely visible through the refracting glass of the tower walls on this side.

"The sun?" Lopen said. "No . . . the realm beyond, where gods live. You think they really went there?"

Rua nodded enthusiastically.

"Well, Damnation," Lopen said. "I guess, sure, they're at least in the correct vicinity for some divine help . . ."

⁂

It was him. Ishar, standing right there in the night, on the grassy hillside. Kaladin hadn't seen him approach, hadn't heard anything, but he was there.

Syl gasped, getting up. Ishar turned away from the moon to study them. Kaladin had memorized the descriptions from Dalinar and Sigzil, but he didn't need them. There was a *force* to this man, a *feeling*. Yes, he appeared like a normal person, with that ardentlike beard and bald head. Almost like . . . like he was a prototype for the religious order that had come after. Blue robes. Golden sash. Heavy bracelets.

But there was more unseen. The way the hairs on Kaladin's arms stood up. The way the last vestiges of wind had suddenly vanished. The way the man could look at Kaladin and seem to see too much. That air . . . the very way he stood . . . reminded Kaladin of Ash, one of the other Heralds.

Ishar stepped toward Syl, his eyes narrowing. She raised her chin and did not grow small, though he suspected she wanted to flee. A part of Kaladin did too—wanted to be away from the gaze of this being who wasn't entirely human.

But this was why he'd come.

"I do not . . . know you," Ishar said, turning to Kaladin. "I know every other piece moving on this board. But you . . . I thought you were insignificant. Now you are here with the Truthless, bonded to the Ancient Daughter. What is your name?"

"Kaladin," he replied. "Sometimes called Stormblessed."

"Stormblessed. I do not remember blessing you." Ishar frowned. "You are Connected to Dalinar, the false champion. And to Szeth, my servant. How?"

Kaladin steeled himself. "I was sent to help you."

"What help needs a god?" Ishar asked.

"We all need help sometimes," Kaladin said. "Do you . . . sometimes feel overwhelmed? Like you can't trust your thoughts?" Storms. Did that sound silly?

"Dalinar sent you," Ishar said. "I see now. He wants to confuse me, convince me I am not a god. I do not need your help, child. Your master has done enough damage already."

"Damage?" Syl asked.

"Damage," Ishar said, turning to regard the lightless, rolling Shin hills. "Your Bondsmith pretender attacked me. Changed me. I . . . saw things I thought I'd forgotten. In that moment, Tezim died, but I need that name no longer. I can be Ishar, who Ascended to the position of the Almighty."

Dalinar had mentioned this. At the instant Navani had become a Bondsmith, Ishar had seen into the Spiritual Realm and grown lucid for a short time. So . . . was there an aftereffect here? Was he doing better?

Dalinar had mentioned oaths. If another were sworn near Ishar . . . perhaps he would return to himself. An unconventional means of therapy, but maybe . . .

Maybe Kaladin needed to appeal to the Herald, instead of the man. The Herald who had defended humankind for so long.

"Ishar," Kaladin said. "We need your help."

"Yes," he said. "Your enemies crush and outmaneuver you because you haven't come to me. I have plans to deal with them, and the greater threats beyond. Become my disciple, and I will show you."

"We can . . . talk about that," Kaladin said, glancing at Syl for support. "We have Ash and Taln with us, back at Urithiru. Your friends."

Ishar sniffed. "Useless. Both of them." He met Kaladin's eyes. "Do you know what I do for them, child? I founded the Oathpact, so I can siphon some of their pains onto myself. *I bear their darkness.* Each of them would be crushed by it, were it not for me. You've seen Taln? He is insensate, so in the thrall of the darkness?"

"Yes," Syl said.

"That is because I do not bear his darkness as I carry the others," Ishar said. "They would all be as helpless if not for me. *I* am the conflux of all darkness and sorrow. Their pains are upon me. And still I stand before you. I am a *god.*"

"I just want to—" Kaladin said.

"I had not foreseen you, but perhaps I should have, considering your spiritweb and Connections." He nodded toward Szeth in the distance. "Szeth has come to fulfill the task I set for him many years ago. His path will be difficult. If you would have my ear, prove to me that you can be of service."

"In what way?" Syl asked.

"In helping me prepare for the end," Ishar said softly. "The Truthless has returned at last. This land needs him."

"Ishar," Kaladin said. "I want to talk about the way you feel. Um . . . I want to—"

"I will speak to you," Ishar said, "when the pilgrimage is finished. When the task is done."

"But—"

Ishar's eyes came alight, glowing as if with Stormlight—but manyfold. Beams of light that blinded Kaladin as he roared. "IF YOU WISH FURTHER AUDIENCE WITH YOUR GOD, THEN SEE HIS WILL DONE, CHILD! THIS IS THE PRIVILEGE OF ANY DISCIPLE."

The light faded, and Ishar was gone.

Storms.

"Great," Syl said. "That went well."

"Well?" Kaladin said. "He spouted nonsense at me, refused to listen, then vanished."

"He also didn't vaporize us or anything," Syl said, floating a foot or so up into the air, shining softly in the darkness, hair blowing once more as the breeze returned. "And he's crazy—so, you know, some nonsense is expected. He noticed you and offered you a chance to talk to him again."

"He'll talk to us again," Kaladin said, "if we help Szeth do . . . whatever it is he's supposed to do? We don't have any idea what that is!" He ran a hand through his hair, but calmed himself. "That said, he seemed . . . a *little* better than Sigzil and Dalinar described him. I think."

"We can help him, Kaladin," she said, resting incorporeal hands on his arm. "We can try to help them all."

"Not in time for Dalinar," Kaladin said. "No telling how long Szeth's little quest here will take? If Ishar won't talk to me until it's over . . ."

But, well, Wit had warned him. There was a task here that was greater than bringing Ishar to Dalinar—a task the Wind needed him to complete.

Preserve a remnant of Honor . . .

"What did he mean?" Syl wondered. "He said that Szeth was his servant. How?"

"Who knows," Kaladin said. "He calls me a disciple and thinks he's the Almighty." He took a deep breath and packed up his flute, his music papers, and his gemstone light. "But . . . I guess you're right. That *could* have gone far worse, and we can ask if Szeth has any thoughts tomorrow. For now though, I need some sleep."

They hiked to the campfire, where Szeth was snoring quietly. Kaladin packed up dinner and banked the fire, absorbed in his thoughts. They tried to turn dark, but he kept battering them back with positive thoughts, like soldiers fighting on his behalf. Reminders that he *had* succeeded in the past, and *could* succeed again. Reminders that an idea wasn't true just because it entered his head.

The darkness was still there and wanted him to believe things would never change, but this little victory proved the opposite. Because while he might never be rid of the thoughts permanently, he was done letting them win.

THE END OF
Day Two

INTERLUDES

EL • ODIUM

El, who had no title, stepped up to the Kholinar palace vault. Four Regal singers had been placed there as guards—a position of honor. Hopefully they would not fall too far after this.

"You will open the vault for me," El said to no rhythm.

They didn't question. That pleased him, as he never liked to kill mortals who served well. Their emotions did them credit. Still, he'd assumed they would know not to obey orders from him. He'd thought the Nine would have made that clear the moment he was reborn, but they were distracted with their war.

So, unwitting, the four Regals hummed to Subservience, unlocked the doors, and opened them for him, bowing. When he entered, their leader—an envoyform—hurried in after.

"I am to accompany all who enter, great one," the Regal said, bowing again. "Pardon my intrusion."

"What is your name?" El asked.

"Heshual," the Regal said.

"One of our names," El said, strolling through the small chamber—which someone had begun to line with aluminum sheets. "What was your name before?"

"It was . . . Govi, great one."

"Do you miss your old name?"

"No?" the Regal said.

"So timid," El said to no rhythm. "You were passionate enough to become a Regal in this Return?"

"I . . ." Heshual hummed to Tribute, which was a ridiculous rhythm to use for this exchange.

El picked through the room, ignoring stores of gemstones, seeking a specific item. He stoked his annoyance, cherished it as all emotions should be. He did not channel it at this Regal, however, for El understood the reason for the timidity.

"It is all right," El said. "I assume one Fused noticed your passion and put you up for elevation—but since then, others have reprimanded you for standing up for yourself. Now you don't know the proper way, because society is in shambles and my kind refuse to be proper role models."

The Regal hummed to Craving. A sign of agreement, and wanting more treatment like this. He got that rhythm right.

"My kind wear thin, like shoes walked upon for too many miles," El said softly. "My honor was stripped in part because I warned of the signs. We cannot rule much longer."

He found what he was seeking at last, on a shelf near the back of the vault: a specific gemstone, still attached to its dagger. Jezrien's prison. El took it off the shelf, reverent.

"Be careful, great one," the Regal said. "That is a dangerous weapon."

"Oh, I know," El said, taking one of the new anti-Stormlight gemstones from his pocket. He lifted it up, appreciating Raboniel's handiwork. Then he touched it to the tip of the dagger, which pulled the anti-Light out and sent it into the gemstone prison.

"Great one!" the Regal said. "That will . . . That . . ."

El held up the gemstone, where a Herald's soul had been trapped. It flashed as anti-Light met Light, and Jezrien was at long last destroyed. Not much of an explosion; barely enough to crack the gemstone. There hadn't been much of Jezrien left.

Now even that was gone. Forever. "Goodbye, old friend," El whispered to no rhythm.

Then he looked at the Regal, who gaped at him, horrified, fearspren appearing at his feet.

"That imprisonment," El said, tossing the dagger away, "is a punishment none deserve. We shame ourselves by trapping, instead of destroying, a Herald." He held up his anti-Light gemstone, still almost full. "Yes, you were already nearly gone, weren't you, old friend? The prisons don't work on humans as well as was thought . . ."

The poor Regal was cycling through rhythms like a person beset with madness. The soul of a trapped Herald had been by far the most valuable thing in the vault.

"You should run to the Nine right now," El suggested. "If you are quick, they might not punish you. The fault is theirs for not warning you about me. And perhaps I bear some fault. For being me. Naturally."

The Regal scrambled away, calling for the other three to watch El and not let him leave. Fortunately for them, he had no wish to depart. He settled down on a bench at the side of the chamber, wondering at the way many had changed names. Was that a glorious recovery of their ancient roots? Or a betrayal of the culture they'd possessed in the absence of the ancients?

Before more guards arrived, he felt a presence overshadow him. Odium.

What have you done, servant? the familiar voice said, vibrating El through his gemheart. *An act of treason by one of the Fused?*

El did not reply. He considered that voice.

It was almost right.

Well? Odium said.

"I see you," El replied softly with no rhythm. "I know you for what you are. And what you are not."

The old Odium had come to hate being challenged. Perhaps that was why the Fused were so erratic—after thousands of years trapped on Braize, unable to fulfill his plans, their god had become erratic first.

The new Odium pondered. *Who are you? Ah . . . I see. Yes, curious. I had not paid enough attention to you, El.*

"Do you have his memories, then?" El asked.

I can view them if I desire, though I do not see why you would name Jezrien a friend, yet destroy his spirit.

"In all your divine wisdom," El said, "you cannot imagine a situation where a friend deserves to die?"

The new Odium *laughed.* A legitimately joyful-sounding chuckle. Curious. In a blink, he appeared beside El and waved a hand, slamming the vault door to lock out approaching guards. This Odium was human, elderly, and did not care to make himself larger than El to intimidate him.

That was more than curious. That was impressive.

"I have a problem," Odium said. "Would you help me solve it?"

"As a test?" El asked. "Or a legitimate need?"

"Let it be both," Odium said, strolling through the vault, studying objects one at a time. He wore the enveloping clothing many humans preferred—covering most of the body, never letting skin or carapace through. A way to display the ornamentation of skilled labor.

"I would hum to Subservience," El said, "if I had rhythms still."

"I will accept that," Odium said. "I have a plan to capture the entire world, and am confident in my ability to secure Thaylenah and Shinovar. As for Azir, my predecessor left an army that had been heading toward Lasting Integrity, which I was able to turn. It lacks Fused, and now lacks surprise, but I think it should be sufficient to claim Azimir. But the Shattered Plains trouble me."

"I believe," El said, "you have sent great numbers of Fused to the location."

"Is that odd of me?" Odium asked, pausing beside a stack of gemstones, each large as a fist, on a shelf.

"I have been told," El said, "that the term to use with a divinity is not 'odd,' but 'inscrutable.'"

Odium smiled again. He tapped each gemstone in turn, and they glowed with Voidlight—soft purple-on-black.

"If you have sent so many Fused," El continued, "and continue to worry—then I'd ask what is so important about a wasteland. Thaylenah is a trading hub, vital for controlling the seas. Azir is the seat of an empire, and of great cultural and scientific development in this era. Both greater prizes. Both facing lesser armies.

"One might guess this is about proximity. For example, getting those Fused to Azimir in time might be impossible. And you are confident in your plan for Thaylenah. So a reasonable person might assume that you sent the Fused to the only remaining location of note."

"Are you reasonable, El?"

"Rarely."

Once again Odium smiled. "I would like to bring further forces to support the Shattered Plains. How would you do this?"

"How much of a cost am I to assume I'd be willing to pay?"

"A steep one."

"Then you already know the answer," El said. "As the solution is a part of you."

"Dai-Gonarthis is dangerous to unleash," Odium said.

"Despite that," El said, "if you require an Elsegate, she is the sole option—unless you have access to corrupted Elsecallers or a proper Honorblade."

"I have neither yet," Odium said as he walked back to El. "You have traveled with the Black Fisher before."

"Yes," he said. "Most of the lands you'd want are still protected from her touch, but Natanatan . . . Perhaps. You would need a strong source of Investiture on either side. And someone to lead your armies."

Odium studied him. "I see you, El, for what you are not. And for what you are."

El bowed his head.

"If you serve me," Odium said, "you may need to kill more of your . . . former friends."

"My friends had their chance. When left on this world, they enslaved my people. The Heralds deserve annihilation. It is . . . a mercy."

Odium nodded. "I dub you—"

"No titles. Please."

Odium hesitated, and El saw danger in his expression. So, he was not immune to the rage, and being cut off by someone much lesser crossed a line. A worthy experiment.

"Very well," Odium said. "I name you ruler, with no title. You will take leadership of my armies to assault the Shattered Plains. Travel to the Peaks via shanay-im, and I shall send Dai-Gonarthis to you. Use her . . . particular talents to take the garrison at the Peaks, and claim the Shattered Plains in my name. I will pay her price another time."

This left many things unsaid. Why Odium was so interested in the Shattered Plains. How he knew that there would be enough power to Connect them to the well at the Horneater Peaks.

The solution to both unsaid questions was likely the same. El again bowed his head. "The Nine will not care for my elevation."

"And what are your thoughts on the Nine?"

"I think of them little, and when I do, I think little of them. Master."

"Then they report to you, El. Help me claim this world."

"If I do, can I rule human lands for you?"

"If that is your wish, I will grant it."

Excellent. El bowed. "I will not fail, lest I be destroyed."

"El, I do not throw people away for failure, unless it came about by their negligence. Adopt this policy. Even in failure, it is often not the tool, but the wielder, who is at fault." The god began to fade, evaporating to dark mist. His voice lingered. "We have much work to do. Not just on one world, but many."

Fascinating. El had walked in here expecting imprisonment, probably execution and forced rebirth. Instead it seemed he was leaving with an army, a promise, and a new god who might at last be able to conquer the entire cosmere.

What an enchanting day. In his head, he began to compose a poem to celebrate this new god he was delighted to worship. Someone who, he suspected, would know the value of what he had—and would let El help humankind finally realize their true passions.

He put Jezrien's former prison back on the shelf, then tossed his anti-Stormlight gemstone into the air and caught it again while walking to the doorway, enraptured at the thought of how the Nine would react.

Taravangian could save them. All of them.

He strode, unseen, through Kholinar, now capital of a growing singer civilization. He could see this whole land, and knew its new leaders were not perfect. In that, they were no worse or better than the humans; while many of their policies were more egalitarian, this was also a people who had been enslaved. He felt their complicated emotions, both wanting to be better than their slavers and being *enraged* at what had been done to them, sometimes lashing out.

That rage was his greatest resource. With it, he would bring order to the entire cosmere. He held his hands to the sides, feeling the rhythms of the crowds who passed him, unable to see their god. He was still the one divided: a mind that wanted to plan, a heart that fought against that calculating coldness. Right now, the heart wanted to simply accept peace. But it *could not* abandon Alethkar, not after all the work these singers had done to claim it and build a home.

It was theirs. They deserved it.

That was the logic speaking. People were in pain. He could retreat his singers to Jah Keved, and there be content.

Jah Keved had basically no armies. How would he bring order to the cosmere without armies?

Did he have to?

Yes. He did.

Back and forth, back and forth. He partially wondered if this was the reason Cultivation had positioned him to be elevated—in giving him his curse and boon for so long. To create a person who could legitimately Connect to the power of Odium and take it, but one who would then be made impotent by the two warring sides within.

He thought of her, and she appeared. Cultivation had not given up on him, and would not do so easily. Together they stood in the center of a major thoroughfare—palanquins lumbering past, laborers hurrying by in clumps, tradesmen shouting out wares. Human and singer living together in a delicate balance. Uncertain, like the one inside him.

"Would you like to see?" she said. "What I can show you?"

He calmed his rage at her. Wisdom dictated that if she wished to give him something, he should at least witness it. He nodded.

She led him to gaze upward, toward stars only they could number. He stood rooted on Roshar—he could not visit these places, but he *could* see them. With her help, he was given a new perspective on how *she* thought it should be, each Shard in their realm of influence, governing their own lands.

"It does not have to be one god," she said. "One solution will never work for all. That was part of why we had to do what we did, ten thousand years ago. Let them be, Odium."

He saw something different from what she wanted him to see. He saw that gods could indeed be afraid. Of him. The power of Odium, with his predecessor, had killed several of them. That version of him had been too brazen, and had left itself wounded in a clash. Taravangian could certainly do better.

"Taravangian," she said, "do not learn the wrong lesson. See."

He saw. Gods who turned away from him, content to let the danger stay trapped. Interestingly, they considered *all three* of the gods of Roshar to be a problem, and were happy to leave them to their conflict.

This was perfect.

Isolated as the others were, he could watch and prepare exactingly how to defeat each one. Only one of them held two Shards of power, but that one was unable to function properly. Odium's predecessor had never taken a second Shard of power for that reason.

These can *be defeated,* he thought, seeing the permutations of possibility. *They will regret ignoring me.*

He kept his thoughts from Cultivation as she tried showing him peaceful nations on many planets. He instead was most curious about the fact that two of the Shards appeared to be missing, completely vanished from interacting with the others. Hidden. One he understood with some effort. But Valor—where had Valor gone, and how did she hide from even his eyes?

The tour over, he and Cultivation pulled their focuses back down to Roshar. The greater cosmere was a part of Taravangian's ultimate plans, and had to be. But for now, this people here—this world—had to be his everything.

"You worry me, Taravangian," Cultivation said as they stood unseen among the people of Kholinar. "If I can admit it, you always worried me. I knew what I had to do, but I wish it could have been any other."

"If there were not something to fear about the person you chose," he said, "then they could not have taken up Odium."

"There is a chance, a solid one," she said, "that you will do what is right. I would not have taken this step otherwise."

"You are correct," he agreed. "I will do what is right."

"Do not be so smug," she replied. "A part of you knows this path you've started on is a terrible one. Listen to that part of you. Give it a chance."

And . . .

Despite himself, he *did* feel it. It was the part of Taravangian that loved his daughter and grandchildren. The part of him that had grieved when forced to manipulate Dalinar while trying to break up the coalition. It was the part of Taravangian that remembered being young, uncertain, dull—yearning to do more to help his people.

That was the Taravangian who had been given the chance to have anything he wanted, and had wished for the capacity to stop the coming calamity. In a moment, Taravangian felt as if . . . as if he were that same man he'd been long ago.

"Very well," he said, turning from her. Not in shame—he would not accept that emotion now—but in . . . compromise. "I will try."

He was a god divided. What if he let each side rule in turn?

DAY THREE

ADOLIN • SZETH • KALADIN

A Study of the Oathgate Dome of Azimir

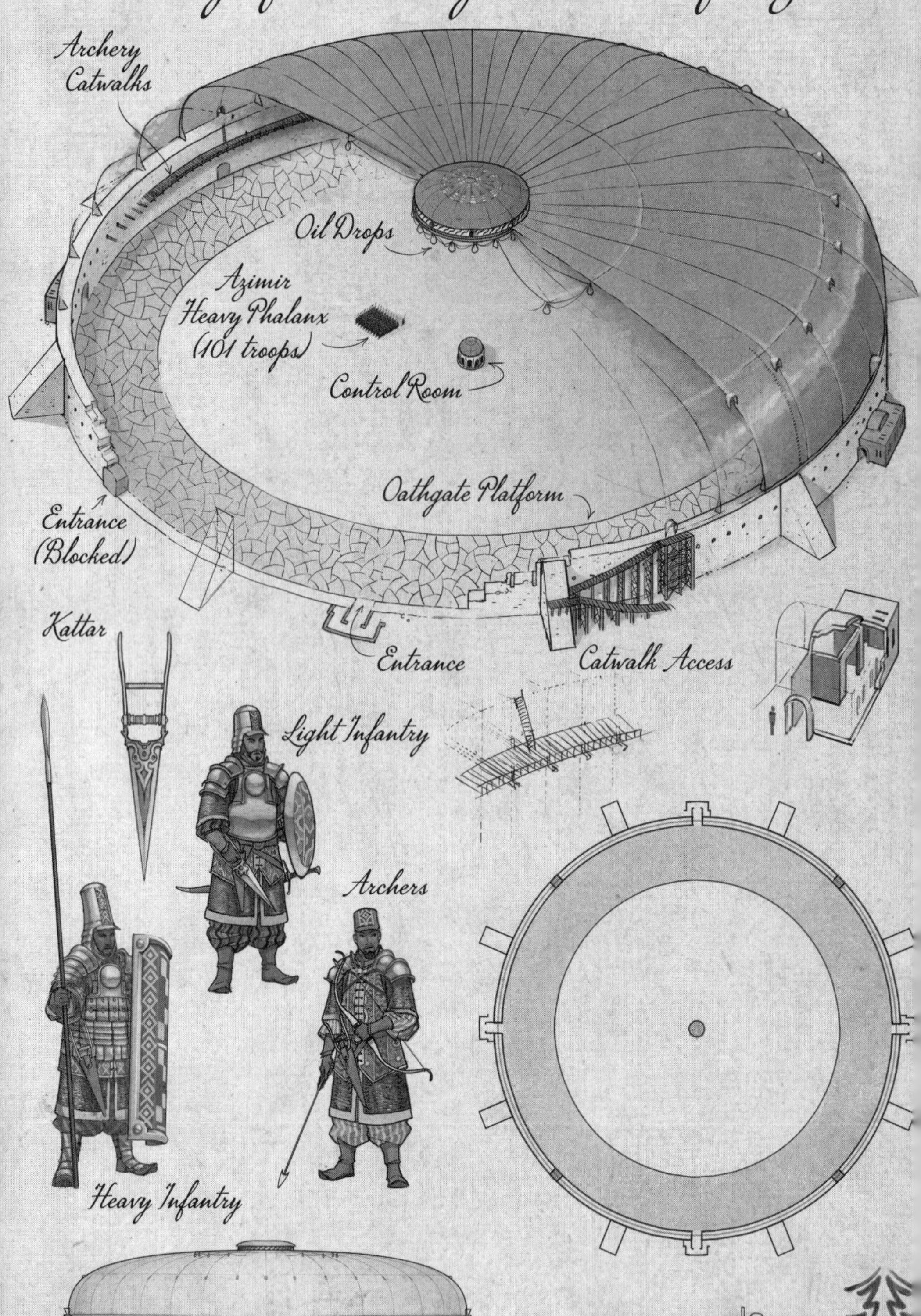

The time has at last come for our stewardship to end.

As Adolin transferred to Azimir, he heard the overlapping, echoing voices of the spren of the Oathgate.

Use this time well, human, they said. *When our new allies arrive, we will stop aiding you.*

"And when my father wins his contest?" Adolin asked, appearing in Azimir. "Will you help us again then?"

We shall see. For now, our transformation approaches.

Well, the enemy was still an hour or so away. There was time enough to transfer the rest of Adolin's forces to Azimir. After that, they would be isolated here until the reinforcements arrived.

He emerged onto the Oathgate platform along with a small group of leaders from the Cobalt Guard—including Colot, the tall former Windrunner squire with flashes of red in his hair. Adolin took a deep breath, remembering how much he liked the smells of Azish spices from the nearby market. With a pat to calm Gallant, Adolin inspected his surroundings: a large dome with gaps in the bronze ceiling to let in light. The Oathgate at Azimir had been a sheltered marketplace before the discovery of Urithiru. Now the stalls had been torn down, leaving a wide expanse of stone.

This would be his battlefield: a space well over two hundred yards across, with a control building at the center. The huge bronze dome was slightly larger than the platform—essential so that it didn't transfer when the people did. There was a large wooden balcony halfway up the wall, maybe thirty feet in the air, surrounding the entire dome. He squinted, pleased to see Azish archers in position up there. Unfortunately, singers tended to be more resilient against arrows than humans because of their natural carapace armor.

Adolin inspected the round control building. Maybe twenty-five feet across, that room was the sole incursion point from Shadesmar. When going from Urithiru to a city, you could use the whole platform—but when traveling to or from Shadesmar, you could only transfer from within the control building, something that had come as a horrible surprise to Adolin in Kholinar. He'd hoped to save the soldiers he'd been leading by transferring them all—but he, in the control building, had instead gone without them.

The entire place felt like a bunker. He turned around, examining the dome, and noted some interesting sacks hung high in the air along its interior. Oil, he guessed, to drop and burn on any enemies who might transfer here. Another good precaution, but also one that might not work as well against singers as the Azish hoped.

Our most important task, Adolin thought, *is to not let them claim ground inside this dome.*

If the enemy could take the dome, then they'd have a large, fortified staging area in Azimir. The defenders would need more than archers and oil—they'd need boots on the ground inside the dome, keeping the enemy from seizing the entire thing from within.

Interesting, Maya said in his mind.

She had been changing quickly, ever since their visit to the tower. A living Urithiru appeared to have invigorated her, and had also somehow strengthened whatever was happening between them. She said the Light of the tower made her feel refreshed, and he felt her in his mind stronger now. She could see into the Physical Realm through his eyes, including when he hadn't summoned her as a Blade, and she'd been responding more and more, even volunteering comments.

Your Herdazian general, she said. *He was worried about this defense.*

"The Mink. Yeah," Adolin whispered. "I can see why, but only if I look hard. On first glance, this seems easy. A good killing field, the enemy trapped in this dome, only one small incursion point. We could guard the doors of that control building and just slaughter singers as they appear, then torch the entire place with oil if they manage to break out of the center."

So what's the problem?

"Singers attack through aggression and momentum," Adolin explained. "They're not formation fighters—they usually flood across a battlefield in a rush, fighting in expert pairs trained to defend one another. We often have superior tactics, but each of their soldiers is stronger, tougher, and harder to kill than a human.

"Our strength is large-scale troop formations. If we try to surround the control building and fight them in a tight ring as they come at us—my gut says they'll break through because we'll be fighting them *their* way, pitting the aggression of a few singers against a few humans."

The best way to defeat singers was with large pike blocks and shield walls—although there was barely room for that, he thought it would be possible. Particularly if they dumped a bunch of debris in here to slow enemy advances. That would give his men a kind of barricade.

He gazed again at the control room. Azimir's had eleven openings in its round wall, reminiscent of a gazebo. If he were the enemy, he'd send through Fused and Regals first—and overwhelm the small ring of defenders, winning space for the next groups of troops to transfer quickly in a flood. If this wasn't handled well, the humans could lose the entire dome on the first day.

The fire, though, Maya sent. *From above.*

"Oil," Adolin said. "But if it drops, we lose the dome. Remember last year, when we burned the fields along the Alethi border—back when we were trying to push out of the Unclaimed Hills? That's a common Alethi tactic, but the singers simply ran through the fire. They're not immune to heat, but they're better at handling it than humans.

"I bet dropping oil in here turns this place into an oven, which would likely kill a wave of singers. But they'd be able to send the *next* wave in much sooner than human defenders could return—plus, fire would likely destroy those archer balconies. We can maybe burn the place once—but when we do, we're giving up the dome for good, and the singers can use it to gather their strength and pour out into the city."

He nodded to himself. The key was to keep them contained and fighting for each foot of space in the dome until human reinforcements arrived. The enemy had a much larger force, but he could stall, make them bleed for each step. That oil was an absolute last resort. Defensive siege tactics were going to fail if the humans tried them here—they needed battlefield tactics, with troops on the ground. They could *not* allow the enemy to fill this dome, like a blister waiting to pop, because they *would* find a way to break out—and with so few defenders, the city would inevitably be lost.

I think you have a good point. Singers . . . singers use intimidation, speed, and force. They're like heavy cavalry, in infantry form. You need a stout line to . . . to break them.

"Maya," he whispered, "that's the most I think I've ever heard from you at once!"

Tactics. Strategy. Thinking about it helps me focus.

Once Adolin's officers had inspected the battlefield enough, he got them moving toward the exits. Needing no reins to lead him, Gallant trotted at Adolin's side.

"What do you think?" Colot asked softly, jogging up to Adolin. "Good killing field in here."

"How far do you think those Azish archers can shoot, accurately, into battle?"

"In here, with this light?" Colot said. "The Azish use the shorter, isri-style bows—they pack a punch, but don't have the range of something like an Oldblood longbow. I'd put them at a hundred yards. They could stretch farther, but I wouldn't count on them being accurate beyond that."

So if Adolin put his armies around the control building at the center, they wouldn't have archer support. Another good data point. At the edge, ten-foot-thick stone walls supported the bronze dome, which held the wide exits, meant for carts and wagons. The Azish had built up the exits: instead of a simple door, you had to walk through a stone corridor some thirty feet long, with a bend at the middle—even a little nook going the wrong way—to slow and momentarily confuse aggressors. Adolin could see sunlight shining into the stone hallway through arrow slits built into the walls. It wasn't truly a maze, not with just one turn, but hallways like these were common for protecting castles.

"Your thoughts?" Adolin asked Colot as they followed Azish guards through the hallway.

"This fortification is solid," Colot said. "And we're low on manpower. I say we let them break themselves on these walls, with arrows raining from above. I could hold these hallways against a superior force for months if I had to."

"Against singers?" Adolin said. "With Fused who can fly up to the balcony? Or what if they build ramps up to it and start breaking out that way? What if they have some Magnified Ones who can tear holes in the dome, or a stolen Shardblade to cut new exits?"

"Storms," Colot said. "Storms, you're right. We can't let them take the interior of the dome. But what should we do instead?"

"We'll see what the Azish commanders think."

"You should take command," Colot said. "You have the most experience fighting singers."

Adolin shook his head as they reached the end of the hallway. "We don't lead here, Colot. We come to help, not control."

Together, he and his officers stepped out into the sunlight, and the breeze caught his cape, making it flutter.

Yes. He was wearing a cape. It wasn't standard. It was a little ostentatious. But Damnation, it looked good with this uniform, and he'd wanted to wear a formal uniform cape for *literally* a decade. Dalinar thought they went poorly with regular uniforms—too old-fashioned. He was wrong. It was classic, distinguished, not old-fashioned.

Adolin's father thought he was an absolute embarrassment anyway, so why not throw in the towel on that fight and make some decisions for himself?

It is good, Maya said in his mind. *It feels right.*

"You're as old-fashioned as capes are," Adolin whispered to her, with a smile.

I am a soldier. I know what inspires soldiers. You look good. It is good. Each sentence still felt labored when she spoke, but she made the effort, and he felt her resolve to keep doing so. Like a wounded soldier learning to walk again.

I'm worried Colot is correct, Maya said to him. *Your Azish friends' instincts will lead them wrong here. You might need to take command.*

No, Adolin thought, testing the ability to merely think answers to her. *There will be a better way.*

Just hope, she replied, *that our intelligence is accurate, and there aren't many Fused with the enemy.*

A functionary in a patterned conical hat met him as he emerged from the corridor—as did the Azimir Imperial Guard. Thousands of soldiers lined up in ranks, wearing full kit. Striking bronze armor, Soulcast using the imperial Azish Soulcaster. Fine steel weapons—spears, swords, and also kattari as sidearms. Those thick triangular weapons were between a large dagger and small sword, excellent for close confines.

The soldiers were a brilliant sight: polished armor in the sunlight, each wearing a sash over their shoulder and a similar one over their shield—the geometric Azish patterns indicating their battalion. Their helms were marked with different patterns. Seemed to be family affiliations, judging by how each was different from his neighbor's. But . . . knowing the Azish, this could also be a mark of how well they did in specific essays or tests to join the military. They were an odd people.

Effective though, as soldiers. Azir had often fallen to Eastern raids in the past—but had just as often held them off. Even the Sunmaker. He'd sacked Azimir, but then his army had turned back, unable to hold the entire country.

"They report having about three thousand soldiers," Colot whispered to him.

Not many at all. Storms, but this would be a strange siege. He'd never been in a fight where his job was to keep the enemy *in* instead of *out.* But the Shattered Plains had been an odd siege as well. He could take some of the lessons learned during five and a half hard years of fighting and apply them here.

Adolin saluted the Azish soldiers with hand to shoulder, knuckles out, the Alethi way. In turn, they raised their spears. Not a salute—the Imperial Guard saluted only the emperor, he'd heard. Or maybe they had a special salute only for him? They had such an odd way of doing things. But then again, who was he to judge? The Azish had the oldest code of laws on Roshar, and had been building an empire when the early Alethi had still been nomadic, according to Jasnah.

The leader of the city's Imperial Guard—Commandant Supreme Kushkam—came riding up on a brilliant white horse dressed in fine barding. The horse had tassels adorning its head and flanks, as well as a spiraling Azish pattern down its legs. More extravagant an equine outfit than any Adolin had ever seen, particularly with that glowing steel barding. Storms. The beast could have gone to a royal ball and been the best dressed on the dance floor.

Gallant snorted. Adolin patted him. "I'll get you some if you want."

Commandant Kushkam was a shorter man, but thick of neck and limb. Adolin had asked around, and had discovered Kushkam was well regarded as a premier player of the card game towers—especially the more complex version that generals preferred. He was missing an eye and didn't wear an eye patch, though tattoos circled the wound like rays of sunlight and seemed to spell out something in Azish.

He looked Adolin up and down from horseback. "I hear," he said in perfect Alethi, "you think you're going to lead the defense of *my* city."

"Just here to help," Adolin replied in Alethi, offering his hand. It wasn't taken.

"I can use the troops," Kushkam said. "How many did you bring?"

"I have two thousand," Adolin said.

"Only two thousand?" Kushkam said. "I was hoping for more."

"Many are infantry veterans," Adolin said. "I recruited them myself from among our best. Elite soldiers, Commandant. I think they'll impress you."

"My men fight for their homeland," he replied, leaning down on his horse. "What do yours fight for, Alethi?"

"The good of all Roshar."

"You can say that with a straight face?" Kushkam asked. "I suppose that's impressive. I'll take your swords—I'm in no position to reject them—but . . . well, we will see. I still think you have no stakes here. Either you'll flee when the fighting grows difficult, or . . ."

"Or?" Adolin prompted.

The man settled back in his saddle. "Or we'll end up indebted to the Alethi." He hesitated. "Every time Easterners have fought in this city, it has ended with Azimir being sacked. I don't think you're looking for loot—I'm no fool, and I have read the reports of Alethi aid in the battles for Emul. But I don't like you being here." He started his horse forward. "Don't assume I'll dance whenever you sing."

Brusque, Maya thought. *We won't last long in defense if our armies can't work together.*

The blocks of troops turned in unison, saluting all of a sudden, hands to foreheads. There was only one reason they'd do that—Adolin climbed up into Gallant's saddle to get a little height, and spotted the emperor's incredibly ornate palanquin coming down a thoroughfare. Yanagawn was here.

As the armies waited for it to arrive, Adolin whispered for Colot to remain behind, then went for a trot around the perimeter of the large dome. He liked what he found—the dome was in the center of a large open area. A wide, flat cobbled space in all directions. The marketplace was apparently out here now on most days, but had been disassembled in anticipation of battle. Azimir was a fine city, with grand bronze domes topping the most important structures. Straight, wide roads. Many clustered buildings, tall and thin, for housing—they called them "apartments." They were in good repair, and sturdy.

It was all so organized, as if the entire place had been laid out by Aunt Navani. And the number of statues and fountains he saw, accompanied by bronze frontings to many of the buildings . . . well, the place was beautiful. There was heritage here, bespoken in each structure. And it was full of people watching from buildings or streets. So many civilians, mostly women and children, as most fighting-aged men had been recruited to the war already.

These flooded into the city from the south as battles there raged, seeking safety in the capital. Now war came to them anyway. Storms . . . he couldn't help but remember another grand city full of history and beauty. One he'd last seen from its Oathgate platform—witnessing as the palace fell, the walls crumbled, and the people screamed to him for help. He could still hear the soldiers shouting as they carried their wounded to join Adolin . . .

He'd abandoned his own troops.

Shamespren trailed him in the shape of red and white petals. He still had nightmares about that day. Imagining those wounded soldiers, stumbling toward the only way out, as an overwhelming force of enemies harried them from behind. Among them were a few of the loyal Palace Guard that had resisted Aesudan, who he had rescued from confinement less than an hour before. He pictured their captain, Sidin, watching as his prince, his leader, his friend . . . vanished to safety and left him to die.

He gripped Gallant's reins tighter and completed his circuit. As he'd guessed, Yanagawn's procession had taken its time, and was only now setting up. Adolin's two thousand were beginning to flow out of the dome, arriving now that he and the officers had surveyed the battlefield. He would do better here than he had before. It wasn't merely victory that Adolin sought here, but redemption as well. Wrongheaded though that was—Kadash and his father would have both chided him on that being the wrong attitude for entering a conflict—he knew he needed to at least acknowledge it.

His mother though . . . she'd have agreed with him.

Thoughts of her were painful these days, and he hated how his fond memories of her were invaded by thoughts of what his father had done. So he tried instead to imagine her blond hair as she'd held him on an early campaign with his father, some border dispute with the Vedens. What would *she* have told him today?

Care, he thought. *Fight for something, not simply because you're pointed that way by a monarch, no matter how beloved.*

It was something she'd whispered to him, even as he trained, even as Dalinar insisted Adolin become a soldier. Don't just fight. Fight *for* something—something worthy of your heart. Adolin nodded to himself. He couldn't save the men he'd left behind. But storms, he *could* do better this time. He would protect Azimir, whatever it took.

35 MEMORIES LIKE WINE

Obviously, the passing of the Dawnshard was the first indication that this event was near. However, we find many other signs.

Embarrassingly, Szeth had trouble finding his family's homestead.

After rising early and breaking camp, Szeth had taken the lead, flying them to the familiar prairie near the ocean where he'd grown up. The smells were right: loam and pollen, with a hint of salty ocean brine. The sights were right: worn paths in the grass, with a few dirt roads; buildings of wood or soil—strangely empty, but still standing tall.

He found it obvious—in retrospect—that many of his people had become pacifists. It wasn't too hard to make a mallet out of wood and rope for building homes, but try making a sword without stone or steel. True, there were ancient stone-age weapons he'd seen while training in the monasteries—axelike, with sharpened spikes made from the teeth and shells of dead sea creatures. Those could kill, but taking them into battle against armored knights with steel blades would be like showing up to a horse race with a three-legged goat.

So his people had divided. Soldiers killed, worked metal, cut timber, and walked stone. The farmers and herdsmen . . . they lived normal lives. Even the people of the cities, who were lazier with their observances, didn't take up weapons. Warfare wasn't for those with morals. You didn't kill a man, then refuse to walk on stones. The trick was to find the killers among you, those who subtract, and keep them properly contained and channeled.

He told himself this was logical. He needed it to be. Otherwise he might backslide as he had when a youth—and start questioning. He had tried to forget those days. Except now he wondered again. If he'd never been Truthless, what did that mean . . . for the things he'd done?

And . . . and where *was* the homestead? He stopped at an intersection, irrationally distraught. He selected what he thought was the proper path, increasing his Lashing and leading Kaladin above the grass, their passing making it ripple.

Had he been gone so long he had forgotten his own home?

Why not? the shadows whispered at him. *You forgot everything else about who you were.*

"Spren," he said, "do you know the way I am to take?"

"I do, Szeth," his spren said. "But you must find it yourself. These are the rules for your quest."

It seemed they might be speaking of different things. "Can you tell me *anything* of what my quest entails?"

"Only that you must do as you vowed, and cleanse this land. The definition of that is up to you." The spren paused, staying invisible. "You will be required to fight, Szeth. To show how skilled you've become."

"If it is a difficult fight," Szeth said, "might I use my second Surge? Ninson-God promised to train me, but I have skill already, from my youth." The power of Division could set the sky itself aflame. His spren had commanded that he use it solely when instructed.

The Skybreakers feared Division. It was related to the fate of the human homeworld, which had been burned.

"We shall see," his spren said. "I have been directed to test you."

"And how do I pass this test?"

"When I decide you have. For now, you should conserve your Stormlight."

To obey, he landed at another crossroads. Here he finally picked out the landmarks and let out an annoyed sigh. Of course. "This way," he said, leading Kaladin on foot. "I couldn't find it because I'm not used to seeing all this from the air."

"I find it easier from the air," Kaladin said. "You can see so much more."

"Best to conserve Stormlight anyway," Szeth said.

"True," Kaladin said, landing. "But we also can't afford to walk everywhere—this is a big country." He gave Szeth an upbeat grin, trying too hard to be friendly, which Szeth found nauseating.

"I've been thinking about what you said last night," Kaladin said. "About your punishment. That you think your . . . mental state . . . is something you deserve."

"It is a feature of my exile: I am required to kill unjustly, though I know my actions to be wrong. I take upon me the sin of murder. That is the state of the Truthless."

"Which you aren't," Kaladin said. "You told me you never *were* Truthless."

"So the sin of killing is still mine, as I should have stopped it?" Szeth said, feeling even worse. Walking this path was bad, so close to home. It made him think of a life he could have had. A life where he'd never picked up a weapon.

"No," Kaladin said. "I mean . . . Szeth, it's all a mess. What your people did to you was wrong. Absolutely wrong. You shouldn't have killed, but we need to focus on the now. Getting you to a healthy place. Then we can worry about the past."

"He is correct," the spren said in Szeth's ear, invisible. "But it is more complicated than he pretends. You should not carry this pain, Szeth. Emotion is of Odium, while Honor is the path of calm understanding and of logical decisions. Promises kept and words followed with exactness."

Szeth found something wrong in that, but did not speak it. "My spren agrees with you," he noted, walking the dusty path.

"He does, does he?" Kaladin said. "Syl would like to hear that. She doesn't think highspren ever agree to anything reasonable." He looked to the sky, to where the honorspren—ever flighty and unreliable—was following currents of air as a ribbon of light, joined by a pack of windspren that were likely the substance of Kaladin's armor.

"I should have performed those killings with a cold, passionless understanding," Szeth said, attempting to navigate what his spren had said. "Perhaps that is why the whispers in the shadows follow me. When I killed these people I cared too much. I will try to do my duty with less personal investment."

Kaladin closed his eyes, breathing out. "Szeth, you still act like you're some object to be toted around and used as a bludgeon."

"I am."

"No. You're a *person.*"

Szeth remained silent, worried that if he responded, he would invite more lecturing. Unfortunately, Kaladin kept going.

"That's probably the first thing we need to work on," the Windrunner said. "Volition. You're not a *thing,* Szeth. You have choices. You're here because of those choices."

"As I told you, we don't need to work on *anything* other than my quest. My people have chosen cowardice over bravery. They declared that I was the one who was wrong, and in so doing have perverted the law. Retribution must be administered."

"What if instead they'd made a new law allowing them to do what they did to you?"

"Well, that would be fine," Szeth said. "Everything would be well."

"You see *no* problem with that?" Kaladin asked.

Inwardly, yes. But that path led to anarchy. He knew for a fact he could not be trusted with decisions.

"I see no problem with it," Szeth said.

"Good," his spren said. "Men are incongruent, walking contradictions. Solely in latching on to something firm, something inflexible, can they be guided. There must be a law. To rely on human choice is to rely upon chaos itself."

They kept walking, and the smell of dust . . . of a road blown by the wind . . . that was from another life. He'd forgotten that scent, much as he'd forgotten the sound of grass in the wind.

"All right," Kaladin said. "Can you at least admit that you've made choices? From there, perhaps we can talk about why you're *worth* being *allowed* to choose. You *decided* to follow the law. You didn't just follow it because it's the only way."

"Those are the same thing."

"They're not," Kaladin said, stepping in front of him, then halting. "Szeth, you're breaking apart inside because of the murders you committed. Right?"

Szeth stared him in the eyes for a minute, then finally forced himself to nod. "There were some who deserved it," Szeth whispered, "but many who did not. I saw their fear; I should rather have died than do what I did to them."

"So, unless we figure out a way to help you, then you're *going* to be in that situation again. You're *going* to kill people who don't deserve it. There's a better path."

"Have you found it?" Szeth asked, genuinely curious. "Have you killed those who did not deserve it?"

"I . . ." Kaladin faltered. He broke the gaze, looking toward the horizon, crowned by mountains. "I have. Parshendi—listeners. Soldiers before that. Singers."

"If you don't know the answer for yourself," Szeth said, walking around him and continuing on the path, "how can you presume to lecture me?"

This shut him up at last. Kaladin lagged behind as they hiked into the wind, toward the southwest. Toward home.

Eventually another voice spoke. Soft, concerned. *What about me?* It was the sword.

"What do you mean, sword-nimi?" Szeth asked.

Did I . . . really kill that nice old man?

Kaladin jogged up and glanced at Szeth, frowning. "Which nice old man?"

The one who was Szeth's friend, the sword said. *Who liked talking to Dalinar. He had a kindly way to him.*

"Taravangian," Szeth said. "Yes. You killed him, sword-nimi. He drew you, and your power consumed him."

I'm only supposed to kill those who are evil.

"He was very evil, sword-nimi," Szeth said. "I promise it. Kaladin agrees, as does Dalinar."

"He's right," Kaladin added.

But Szeth, the sword continued, *you aren't evil. And I nearly killed you, didn't I?*

Szeth glanced at his hand, where the flesh was slightly raised. White-on-white scars, in a pattern like vines, running up his hand and along his arm. The mark of having wielded the black sword without enough Stormlight to feed him.

"There are many," Szeth said quietly, "who would call me evil."

You're not. I would know. I've seen you do good things. You can't be both good and evil.

"I believe a man *can* be both," Kaladin whispered.

"Agreed," Szeth said. "That is the problem. Humans can't judge this, so we need a higher standard."

"Laws *made* by humans?" Kaladin said. "You truly can't see the contradiction?"

"It is the best we have," Szeth said. "When I chose Dalinar as my guide, Nin said he wished I'd chosen the law. Perhaps I am starting to see that he was right."

If a human can't judge good and evil though, Nightblood said, *then how can a sword?*

It was a valid question for which Szeth could not think of an appropriate answer.

I did kill that old man, the sword said. *He's not the only one. I . . . wake up and people are dead. It was actually me, wasn't it? All those times . . .*

"How long has this been going on?" Kaladin asked.

My whole life.

"Which is . . . how long?" Kaladin asked.

I . . . don't really know. How long do humans live?

"Sixty to eighty years," Kaladin said. "More if you're lucky, less if you're unlucky."

Well, the sword said, *Vasher helped make me, and he's still alive. So I'm not very old, I guess.*

"Vasher?" Kaladin asked.

"You call him Zahel," Szeth said softly. "He once visited me to check on the sword, which he named Nightblood. I felt something from him. A weight of years."

Zahel? That's him. Vasher changes his name sometimes. He never calls himself Warbreaker anymore! I liked that name, but he hates it. Isn't that strange?

"Sword," Kaladin said, "I think Zahel might be far older than a normal human gets. You say he *made* you? Like a god made the Honorblades?"

Yup! He came to your lands, saw the Honorblades, and thought to himself, "My sword can't talk. That's dumb. I want a sword that can talk!" So he made me with Shashara. Yesteel was so upset! I haven't seen Yesteel in a while. A few weeks at least. Vivenna wasn't there. I didn't even know *her yet.*

"Vivenna?"

Yes, she's great. But she's super, super *grumpy. Do you know her?*

"Afraid not," Kaladin said.

Oh! You'd like her because you're super grumpy too! You'd get along! Syl says you need a girlfriend because of various reasons. She won't tell me the reasons, but I assume they're good ones.

"You talk to Syl?" Kaladin asked.

"I," she said, zipping in alongside them as a ribbon of blue-red light, evidently having been listening for a little while, "talk to everyone."

"Most of the people don't even realize you're around!"

"I wasn't referring to the *humans,*" she said, making herself human size apparently just so she could roll her eyes at Kaladin. As Szeth walked beside them, she glanced at Kaladin to check whether he had seen the eye roll. As he hadn't, she waited until he looked, then gave a very exaggerated one. It was so forced, however, that both of them ended up grinning.

Szeth told himself he was annoyed by this exchange, not jealous of the friendship they obviously shared. Would he have a similar bond with his spren, if he had become a Windrunner?

You should find Vivenna, Nightblood said. *She promised she'd come looking for me if I was stolen! Anyway, I think maybe that ever since I was made, I've been . . . leaving dead people. I . . . have only recently started to think about it.*

"That seems reasonable," Szeth said.

"Um, no it does *not,*" Kaladin said, turning back to him. "How could you not remember before, Nightblood?"

I'm not like a fleshy person. My brain, if I have one, is metal. I think that makes me . . . slow to change. The voice grew softer, with a faint tremble to it. *I don't want to kill, Szeth. It doesn't feel like me.*

"Sword-nimi," Szeth said, "you are, um, a sword."

Adolin says swords don't have to kill. They can just be beautiful works of art.

"Wait," Kaladin sputtered. "You talk to *Adolin*?"

Yeah, all the time. He likes swords.

"Is there anyone or any*thing* you *haven't* been having secret conferences with?" Kaladin asked. "The spren of the tower? The spren of my jacket, maybe?"

"Both of those are quite fun to talk to, Kal," Syl said. "But *none* of us have met the spren who embodies your sense of humor. It hasn't been seen in *ages.*"

"Oh please," he said.

She leaned in closer to him as they walked. "It is said that everything has a spren. But the spren of your sense of humor? Tiny. A speck. And I'm sure it's grouchy somehow."

See, like I said, Nightblood told them. *He'd get along great with Vivenna!*

"Sword-nimi," Szeth said, trying very hard to keep the conversation going in one direction instead of seven, "you were created to destroy. It is your purpose. It is not shameful to fulfill your purpose."

Maybe you're right, Nightblood said. *But shouldn't I remember? I'm* not *supposed to destroy anything that isn't evil. If I'm not paying attention, who knows what could happen?*

Kaladin gave Szeth a pointed glance, as if the words of a confused sword had any relevance to their conversation. Fortunately, he was saved from further blathering as he spotted a white building alone on the prairie. "There," he said. "We've arrived."

⁂

Wooden boards complained under Kaladin's feet as he stepped into the old farmhouse.

He felt an eerie sense of familiarity as he ran his fingers along a wooden countertop. Syl—full sized—walked with him, her soft blue glow more prominent in the dim light. Kaladin rubbed dust between his fingers. In the East, he'd have expected to find crem overgrowing everything. Not so here, but the musty smells were the same.

Syl stepped to the doorway, looking out at Szeth—who stood, silent, in the yard. "He needs help, Kaladin. Hearing him speak, I'm more worried."

"I'm trying," Kaladin said.

"I know," she said, then turned and glanced vaguely into the air, toward the east.

"What?" Kaladin asked.

"Changes are coming," she said, her eyes narrowed. "I can feel them, even if I don't know what they mean. The soul of the world is . . . contorting. It's why the Wind speaks again."

Storms. Well, *that* was ominous. Kaladin crossed the room to open the shutters, spilling light across the floor. And he was surprised to see something in the corner of the room: a single tiny glowing green mote. A lifespren?

It was the first local spren he'd seen this far into Shinovar. Kaladin bent down to inspect it, and Syl joined him, watching as the mote flickered bright then dark, then trembled. Syl gasped.

"What?" Kaladin said.

"It's . . . it's afraid." She held out her hand, palm up, and the little spren flitted over to her and hovered above her hand, still trembling. It was basically just a speck of green light—he hadn't thought such a spren could feel fear.

"What's it afraid of?" Kaladin asked.

"They aren't intelligent enough to explain," Syl said. "But I can feel its terror."

The end, the Wind whispered, blowing in the window. *It fears . . . what could be . . . the end of all spren . . .*

Kaladin glanced at Syl, who nodded. She had heard it too.

"Can you explain?" Kaladin asked.

I . . . I wish I could . . .

"She can feel what I do," Syl said. "That's my guess. They all do. Something's coming, Kaladin."

The little lifespren bobbed off her hand, then floated down and hid once more in the corner.

"There are so few spren here in Shinovar," Kaladin said. "Shouldn't there be lifespren all over this place?"

"I met a couple of windspren who told me that few spren come here anymore. They didn't know why—they don't think all that logically. They prefer to stay away because it feels wrong."

"Do they speak of the ancient spren?" Kaladin asked. "Like the one that just spoke to us."

"Wind, Stone, and Night," Syl said. "From before humans arrived on Roshar. Few spren remember them, but there are old things here in Shinovar. Older than the gods themselves . . ."

Also ominous. Kaladin looked back through the one-room building. It had a firepit instead of a proper hearth—probably because they needed to use soil instead of rocks. Storms, how did an entire people exist without using *stone*?

At least they let the soldiers work wood for them, as Szeth had explained. That was how they could have buildings constructed from planks, like this one, held together without a single nail. The place had been cleaned out thoroughly. Either Szeth's family had been given time to pack before leaving, or scavengers had claimed it all over the years.

Syl lingered by the doorway, again staring out at Szeth. Kaladin joined her. "Hey," he said to Syl. "I'll figure out how to help him."

She nodded, her eyes distant.

"You all right?"

"Trying to be."

"Is it what you said earlier?" he asked. "About old things being in Shinovar?"

"Maybe," she said. "Maybe not."

He chewed on that. "You never did explain to me why you were acting so odd during those weeks in the tower. When it was occupied."

Her eyes grew distant again. "We seem different from one another, don't we? You and I?"

"Yeah," he said. "You're literally a piece of a god."

"As are you," she said. "I meant our personalities though. You're . . . well, you know."

"Gloomy?"

"Intense. Where I'm . . . not?"

"You're intense," Kaladin said. "Just, you get excited about things, instead of . . ."

"Grouchy?"

"Don't tell Szeth I agreed with him. Regardless, your enthusiasm is infectious. Invigorating. Sometimes you'll get focused on a topic and won't let it go—which leaves me wondering what I've missed. It's interesting."

She smiled. "I doubt most people would see it that way."

"Most people don't know you like I do," Kaladin said. "What is it, Syl? What's bothering you?"

"I imagined these last days differently. Is it bad of me to admit that? I wanted to fight, to save the world. The soul of Roshar groaned, and we abandoned the battle." She looked to him, suddenly alarmed. "I didn't mean to say we shouldn't have. I—"

"I understand," he said softly. "It can be both right and difficult at once."

"Yeah," she said.

"We could . . ." His stomach twisted. "We could find you another knight, Syl. One worthy of you."

"Kaladin *Stormblessed,*" she said, glaring, lifting in the air to be at eye level with him. In her full-sized form, she was still smaller than he was, but somehow her ability to intimidate was not related to her size. "Don't you *dare* say things like that."

"Syl," he said, "you started all this. You broke with your kind, came to my world, and sought out someone to refound the Windrunners. You stood against the will of the Stormfather, subjecting yourself to a near loss of identity, because you knew war was coming—and you wanted us to be prepared for it. It isn't fair you have to sit out the ending."

"Fair?" she said, folding her arms. "Your own life hasn't been fair. Besides, something *is* happening here in Shinovar. We're the ones sent to figure it out." She eyed Szeth. "Szeth, and this place, are our duties now. We have to adapt. Both of us, together."

"And that's why you've been so different lately?" Kaladin asked.

"Part of it." She leaned on the doorframe, hair loose and blowing, skirt rippling in a phantom wind he could almost feel. She cocked her head, glancing upward. She bore a hint of mischievousness in her smile, but her eyes had such depth he found himself wondering what profound and interesting things she was pondering.

"People who think that we're different," Syl said, "don't know you either. They look at you and see a perfect soldier."

"What do you see?"

"Flaws," she said. "Wonderful ones. I've never known perfection, Kaladin, but I should think it boring if I did."

"I think you might be close."

"To being *boring*?" she said.

"That's . . . not what I meant."

She grinned at him, but then leaned closer. "I'm not perfect, Kaladin. I think our flaws are what make us the most similar. We've both spent far too much of our lives living for other people."

"Me for the bridgemen. And you . . . for me, right?"

She nodded.

"That's what happened in the tower," he guessed. "You came to realize that?"

"I was trying too hard," she said, "and learned some interesting lessons about myself as a consequence."

Huh. Hearing that twisted his emotions into knots, but he knew it was true. Wit had demanded Kaladin explain who he was, now that he wasn't leading Bridge Four anymore. What did Kaladin want that was for *him*?

The same challenge could be given to Syl.

"I suppose," he said, "if you weren't spending so much of your time bound to the demands of a finicky human, you might have a *ton* more time to sneak rats into people's sock drawers."

"Please," she said. "My pranks are so much more sophisticated. I've found out how to trick *skyeels* into hiding in drawers."

"Storms, that's horrifying."

She smiled. "I want to stay with you, Kaladin, and learn a different way of helping. I want to be a scribe, but I need to do that without living *for* you, if that makes sense. I'm trying to figure out the difference."

"I want to protect people," Kaladin said, "but . . . I can't exist only to slavishly chase that one duty. Letting go of Tien's death finally taught me that truth. So how do I protect, but not live *to* protect?"

"Exactly."

"I guess we'll figure it out. Somehow? Assuming the world doesn't end on us in seven days."

They nodded to one another, and as they left the house, Kaladin at last realized what it reminded him of.

Home.

Which was strange, since it was so different, but it *felt* the same. Different shapes. Similar souls.

Together, he and Syl approached Szeth, who had dug something out of the dirt near a tree. He held it up, an oblong stone over a handspan long.

"They put it back," he said softly. "I thought they might."

"Is that the rock?" Kaladin asked. "From your story?"

"Yes. Just a rock." Szeth dropped it to the ground with a dull thump. "Another meaningless stone that somehow dominated my life. I am ready to continue to the monastery. I thought coming here would lay some spirits to rest, but they plague me still."

"Memories are like wine, Szeth," Kaladin said. "They ferment. If you never let them out, the pressure will simply keep building."

Szeth eyed him.

"I grew up in a home much like that one," Kaladin said, nodding to the side. "You had one sibling? A sister?"

"Yes," Szeth said.

"Sometimes, on the battlefield," Kaladin said, "I'd think how *strange* it was that I'd ended up there. I was supposed to have become a surgeon. And you a shepherd, right?"

"Yes," Szeth whispered.

"Do you ever look back and feel intimidated by the flow of time? Bemused how its current snatched you up and carried you away?"

Szeth eyed Kaladin. "You're trying to imply that we're the same. You and me."

"I think we are, Szeth."

"No. I don't think so."

"Why not?"

Perhaps Szeth knew he was being baited, because he hesitated. But Kaladin had tried cajoling and offering help. This was another method of getting someone to talk: to assert something they found incorrect, and wait for them to explain why.

"Because," Szeth said, turning to hike away from the homestead, boots kicking up the strange earthen dust of this place, "you *chose* this life. It was forced upon me. I would have been happy as a dancer if not for stonewalkers like yourself. Raiders who sailed the ocean nearby."

"They attacked here?" Kaladin asked.

"Yes," Szeth said, "but that's not what I resent most about them. Instead it is . . . what their raids did to us. To me."

Kaladin frowned, keeping up. Syl walked along on the other side, choosing to remain human size.

Then, finally, Szeth continued. "That night, after I found the stone, the raiders came, but it's not what you're thinking. I didn't meet one of them. I met something else. Something worse . . ."

36 CORRECT ANSWERS

TWENTY-SIX YEARS AGO

Even long after the sun had gone down, Szeth felt that he was somehow in the shadow of the white-cliffed mountains.

The bleating of lambs filled the air, emerging from the darkness around him with a nervous energy. Like they sensed a predator. Dozens of shepherd families crowded into this ravine, homes left behind, as they were too close to the coast and the ravaging stonewalker raiders.

Szeth and his sister had to work hard to keep their flock—driven hastily through the oncoming dusk—from bleeding into the others. That might prove impossible, given how the shepherds kept pulling farther and farther back, up against the slope of the mountains. Nervously trying to be as far from the raiders as possible.

Up here, you'd start finding stones in the soil—little pebbles that were too small to be worshipped, but big enough that you still shouldn't touch them, if it could be avoided. You never found ones that small below. Perhaps these pebbles were part of the mountain—a beautiful sign of the love of the spren, who provided it as a protective fortification.

Szeth and Elid eventually got the sheep into a huddle. The beasts wouldn't sleep easily tonight though; they could sense their masters' concern. He looked to the sky, and the clouds shrouding moon and stars. The night felt oppressive. Clay lamps made points of light all through the valley around him, but they almost seemed to be swimming in that blackness. Like they were the stars, and he was somehow floating above them . . .

He left his sister and found his mother beside some improvised firepits, discussing an evening meal to hopefully calm everyone down. Misir wat, a thick paste made of red lentils, eaten with a spoon or fork off a wooden board for a plate. It was the wrong day of the week for meat.

Mother put Szeth to work, which he realized was what he'd wanted in wandering this direction. He busied himself mashing vegetables with vigor. No chopping—the Farmer owned several fine steel knives, crafted by an Honorbearer using their Soulcasting art, but none were available. So he used a clay mortar and pestle to crush the onions, garlic, and spices together—each of which had been lightly braised to soften them.

They'd brought some small portable clay ovens, and had them heating up. The spiced lentils went into the clay dish on the top to simmer. Bread—or today, soda biscuits—went into the oven.

It was good active work. In the distant darkness, music started playing as someone got out their flute. This cut off shortly, leaving the nervous bleating. The Farmer wouldn't want music to give away their position, in case raiders slipped past his soldiers. That was why they had no bonfires, and minimal lanterns. Indeed, Szeth worked at his mashing only by the shadowy light of the firepit and the oven.

Szeth enjoyed working on meals like this, even if the onions made his eyes water. The Cook—who oversaw the feeding of the people and made certain nobody ever went hungry—had created interesting wooden ladles for measuring. The one Szeth used had the bowl of the ladle split into three sections, with some smaller measuring sections along the handle. All he had to do was fill the largest compartment with oil, the middle one with onion, and the next with garlic. Then he filled the three little divots on the handle with salt, ground chili pepper, and coriander, respectively. He could dump that all into his pestle and begin mashing, and would always have the correct proportions.

Once that was done, he added it to the clay cooking dish—with one scoop of lentils and two of water. The measuring ladle let him work without supervision, and he enjoyed it specifically because it was impossible to do it wrong. Why couldn't more things in life have a tool like this for exact measuring?

He hadn't forgotten the choice his family had made in moving the stone, though fretting over it brought him little satisfaction. He finished the entire serving bowl of misir wat, left it simmering, and moved to another—though the Cook herself soon strode past and checked on his work. The girthy woman was dressed all in color, with a red skirt, blue sash, and yellow blouse. Dark, curly hair up in twin buns on her head, skirt parted at the front to show off another splash of yellow underneath. She was one of those who added, a ruling peer of the Farmer.

"Needs more pepper," she declared of his misir wat.

What? No, he'd done it *perfectly*. Szeth watched with horror as she added chili, then bustled off. Why . . . why would she say that? She'd created the measuring tool herself. The soup should taste right. Unless . . .

He must have done something wrong. Why did he do things wrong even if he had a tool?

Soon another vibrantly dressed figure stepped up to his fire. The Farmer wore his robes over his traditional farming clothing, which would be soiled from the day's work. The dirty clothing was a symbol, but so were the colors, in this case a violet outer robe and an inner sky-blue one of filmier material. No mere splash of color for the Farmer. He *was* color.

He had pale skin, like Szeth's family. Not uncommon in this region, though those with darker skin were more prevalent. "Ah," he said, seeing Szeth. "Son-Neturo. I had hoped to find your father at the fire."

"I'll find him, colors-nimi," Szeth's mother said from nearby, where she'd been distributing plates and biscuits.

The Farmer bowed his head and spread his hands, indicating he'd accept her offer of service. Then he accepted a plate of food from the Cook as she bustled back in their direction. The plate had little piles of food across it and a single biscuit, stuck in place with some lentil paste. Szeth guessed the Farmer would have preferred to refuse the meal, as others were still unfed, but one did not contradict the Cook when she delivered food.

The Farmer settled down—robes rustling—on a log near Szeth, who continued working on the next large bowl of misir wat. The man's presence made Szeth uncomfortable. Was Szeth supposed to say something? Entertain him? Szeth began sweating, despite the cool night air.

"I have heard about you from your father, son-Neturo," the Farmer said. "Perhaps you could come and dance for my farmers and me in the fields."

"I . . . I don't know, colors-nimi," Szeth said, blushing. "Entertaining the farmers is usually a job for musicians, isn't it?"

"It is a job for any who wish it," the Farmer said.

"Does it . . . add, though?" Szeth asked. "Dancing doesn't make anything or feed anyone."

"Ah, you are young yet," he said, "if you think that to sweeten a person's life is not a form of feeding them." He smiled. The man had a kindly face, oval, like a grain of wheat topped by flaxen hair. His hands were callused, with dirt under the nails, a true sign of nobility.

"Colors-nimi?" Szeth found himself asking. "How . . . do you know what to do?"

"I'm not sure I follow you, child."

"The right choices. How do you know what they are?"

The Farmer sat for a time, stirring his food, taking a bite now and then. "Do you know the difference between men and animals, son-Neturo?"

Szeth frowned. It seemed a question with a great number of possible answers, but he didn't want to give the wrong one.

"Men," the Farmer said, "can take actions."

"Animals . . . take actions, colors-nimi."

"It may appear that they do, yes. But if you consider, you will realize they do not. Does the rain *act* when it falls? Does the rock act when it rolls down the hill? No, the spren move these things."

Was the Farmer testing him? Because his own experience taught him otherwise.

"I have a sheep," Szeth said. "Molli. She always comes close to me when I'm sad, and she licks my face. She chooses, colors-nimi."

"Does she now?" the Farmer said, sounding amused. "I think not. Though I suppose it is wisdom, after a fashion, to think your own thoughts, son-Neturo."

Maybe it . . . wasn't a test.

"Well, regardless," the Farmer said. "You ask how I know *what* to do? I don't. That is the simple answer. I try. I see. I act. The spren move most things in the world, child, but they do not move people. There's a reason for that, one that the Stone Shamans teach, and one I ponder as I work."

"So . . . I learn what to do . . ."

"By trying," the Farmer said.

"That's not specific enough," Szeth said, smashing onions and spices into his wooden pestle. "Two people can try, and come up with different answers. Surely the *spren* have the truth for us. Surely *they* will tell us what to do."

"If they did," the Farmer said, "would that not be the same as moving us? Making of us rain, or rocks, or . . . other things that do not move on their own."

He was about to say sheep, Szeth thought.

The Farmer finished the last of his mash, then glanced up toward the sky. "In other lands, rulers don't act," he said calmly. "They decide, but don't *act.* That is why I must go each day and bring life from the earth, son-Neturo. Why I must add, rather than subtract."

That made sense, but Szeth found that his conversation had yielded fewer answers than he'd wished. If the *Farmer* didn't automatically know the right thing to do, then what hope did Szeth have?

Perhaps I can find the spren, he thought. *And ask them.* They lived inside everything, especially stones, but were coy. Szeth had seen only three spren in his life, and each glimpse had been fleeting.

Szeth's father arrived at the dim fireside.

"Check your measuring tool," the Farmer said to Szeth. "You've been adding too much pepper." He walked over and joined Szeth's father, speaking to him softly while washing his plate at the cleaning trough.

Szeth finished mixing his current bowl, then got a plate for himself and one for his sister. He hiked off through the darkness, up to the armpit of the valley, where Elid was sitting on the grass looking pensive, her small ceramic lamp in her lap.

"Szeth," she whispered, "we're missing three sheep."

"We'll find them in the morning," he said, handing her a plate. "Probably joined another flock."

She nodded, and in the flickering light glanced at him, then at the food, then away. Nervous.

"What?" he demanded.

"Molli is one of the missing sheep," she said. "I know how you favor her, Szeth. It's all right though. I'm sure she's simply with one of the other flocks like you said."

He frowned. Molli did *not* like other sheep. She was almost blind, yes, but she could smell them. "You're sure?"

"I'm sure. Do you remember bringing her?"

"I gathered her with the rest before we struck out," he said. "But there was so much chaos . . ." He met his sister's eyes, then turned to the southwest, toward the ocean and their home. A red haze stained the air. The stonewalker raiders liked to attack at night. Their metal lanterns were more effective than ceramic ones, and their arrows could set the roofs of fishing villages ablaze.

The Farmer brought our soldiers, he thought. *They'll be defending the coastlands.* It was unlikely any stonewalkers would strike as far inward as Szeth's family homestead.

"I'll just . . . go check some of the nearby flocks," he said. "She's easy to spot."

He lit himself a lamp and sheltered it with his hand, then went searching. But as he worked, calling to nearby shepherds, a feeling of dread built within him. Molli always made her way home. She was the one he didn't need to worry about when the flock strayed.

And so, after searching five other flocks, Szeth found his eyes drawn southwest again. Toward that blazing horizon. Perhaps it was his conversation with the Farmer, emphasizing that the defining feature of humans was their ability to choose. Perhaps it was the way his family had dug out the rock. Perhaps it was the general tone of the day, whispering that there were no correct answers. Only decisions.

In that moment, Szeth made a choice. A wholly uncharacteristic one that he likely would *not* have made on any other night. He put out his lamp, trusting the filtered violet moonlight breaking through the clouds, then went stalking into the night. Toward their homestead. To find Molli.

By himself.

The impending events in Iri are another sign. The age of transitions has arrived.

Colot joined Adolin as he left Gallant and jogged toward where the emperor was finally emerging from his palanquin. As one, the sea of Azish soldiers and attendants bowed, and storms, Adolin wasn't certain he'd seen so many awespren in one place—exploding like rings of blue smoke, almost in concert with the bows. As if the very spren showed deference to the emperor.

Adolin nudged Colot, and the two of them bowed too. His soldiers behind them, taking the cue, did as well.

"We bow to a foreign monarch?" Colot whispered.

"By coming here, we put ourselves in his command structure. Let's show the man some respect."

Per tradition, they bowed for ten seconds, until Noura—head vizier—clapped once. The formality of it itched against Adolin's Alethi sensibilities. Not that they didn't have their own moments of propriety—theirs simply made much more sense.

As Adolin straightened, Yanagawn walked down a little ramp—wearing a crimson and gold robe that seemed at *least* ten layers thick and a hat wider than his shoulders—and spread his hands out to welcome Adolin. "Thank you," he said in Alethi, taking Adolin's hand—prompting gasps across the field.

"I'm always good for a fight, Your Excellency."

"It appears you'll have more than enough opportunity here, unfortunately," Yanagawn said. He waved to the side, gesturing for Commandant Kushkam to approach.

The man did so, with another bow. Noura—who often spoke for Yanagawn at meetings—also stepped up to join them; she was an older woman with her hair in a grey braid, topped by a cap with an intricate red and yellow pattern.

"Adolin, you've seen our defenses?" Yanagawn said. "What do you think?"

"They're solid," Adolin replied. "The enemy can bring forces in only a little at a time, as the way Oathgates work requires that transfers from Shadesmar use only the very center of the platform. I—"

"Yes," Kushkam said in Alethi, stepping forward and pointedly addressing Adolin, not the emperor, "our defenses *are* solid. As soon as your men are off the platform, my troops will surround the control building. Not only that, but we'll have one of the royal Soulcasters ready to help."

Soulcasters. Right. "Can you transform all the air inside the control building to bronze?" Adolin asked.

"Regrettably," Noura said, "our Soulcasters aren't capable of such feats. We can transform many objects to bronze, but the air itself? No, alas."

Adolin nodded. But as he thought about it, he wasn't certain it would be useful. Alethi Soulcasters were limited to making specific shapes, and filling a room might have been impossible for them as well. Worse, it wouldn't actually *do* much. The enemy could just transfer the metal into Shadesmar and tow it out of the way.

"We're going to fill the building with as much water as we can," Kushkam said, "then Soulcast that into bronze. We will pack soldiers in close around the outside so if the enemy does get through, we can kill them in droves. And even if they get past that, we'll drop oil and cook them alive."

"No," Adolin said, shaking his head. "Set that building ablaze *only* as a last resort. And tell me, how often have your soldiers here faced combat?"

"They are time-tested veterans," Kushkam said. "From campaigns against Marat *and* in the Yezier succession crisis."

"I meant against singers," Adolin said.

"We're the Imperial Guard," Kushkam said. "We've had the honor of protecting the emperor, and the city, this last year."

"So your soldiers have never faced a singer charge," Adolin said, thoughtful. "I think we should try a different tactic. The Soulcasting isn't going to work when they can merely transfer the bronze to the other side, and your soldiers are going to need archer support. We should fill the field with debris: furniture, scrap metal, anything you can spare. Post soldiers behind it in a wide ring, with pikes and barricades."

"What?" Kushkam said, then looked to Noura—addressing her instead of the emperor, and changing to their language. "Excellency, that's nonsense! The enemy would immediately use any debris as *cover.* We have a perfect killing field inside the dome! Why would we ruin it?"

 Adolin blinked in surprise as the words warped, seemed to shift, then entered his mind as if they'd been spoken clearly in Alethi. No, better. He understood the nuance of the inflections, as if he were a natural speaker of the language. Storms. His father's touch was more effective than he'd imagined.

"We need to be careful," Adolin said, drawing a few shockspren from the others as he spoke in perfect Azish. "They'll send Regals, maybe Fused first, and I don't trust your lines against those. You *need* that archer support, so it's better to have larger, fortified lines farther back. If your men break in the initial assault, it could turn into a rout."

"I can't believe I'm hearing this," Kushkam said. "Throwing away the perfect advantage?"

"This is a Stuko Stem," Adolin said, gambling on language he thought Kushkam would like. "Obstruction favors us."

"It's plainly not a Stuko Stem. If anything, it's a Haramed Stem. You insult my troops!"

"At least listen to me about the fires," Adolin said. "Singers are more resistant to heat than we are. If you turn the place into an oven, they'll recover first—and we'll lose the entire dome to them."

The commandant hesitated, actually considering this. He ground his teeth, but didn't object.

So he's not a fool, Maya thought to Adolin. *That's good.*

Agreed, he thought back. *He just didn't live with a siege mentality on the Shattered Plains for years.*

Still, the man did glare at him, then looked to the emperor. Adolin immediately realized his mistake. He should *never* have voiced his objections in the presence of the emperor, embarrassing the commandant in front of his supreme authority. Adolin should have pulled the man aside and made suggestions, not stood in public and contradicted him. Storms, what a rookie mistake. He could tell from Kushkam's posture, standing tall, chin raised, that he took it as a threat to his command.

"Excellency," Adolin said to Yanagawn, "the commandant is obviously passionate and dedicated to the defense of this city. I pushed to see what he thought, but I went too far. I bow to his experience and wisdom; let us proceed as he suggests."

Kushkam glanced at him, frowning.

"Very well," Yanagawn said, studying Adolin. "Noura, please convey to the commandant that we trust his decisions."

She did so. The thick-necked man bowed to the emperor, nodded to Adolin, and trotted off—an aide bringing his horse so he could swing into the saddle and begin calling orders.

"I would have done as you asked, if you'd pushed," Yanagawn said softly to Adolin, in Alethi.

"I realize that," Adolin said. "But I assume he's a good officer?"

"One of our best," Noura said, tapping a sheaf of papers against one hand. "Distinguished service in the fighting at Yulay when younger. He led our forces in several important battles, as recently as two years ago."

"A field commander, promoted to defense of the city," Adolin said, with a nod. "I'd rather have him on my side. Undermining the fellow in charge is *not* a way to make friends."

"Some would argue that in the positions we hold, we don't need friends," Noura said.

"I would argue you need them more," Adolin said, then pointed. "Your troops are disciplined and proud. If I undermine their commander, we'll lose morale. If Kushkam is as good as you say, he'll come around." He gave them a smile. "Just have some furniture and scrap ready for when we need it."

"Adolin," the emperor said, his hands laced together. The clothing and headdress were so regal it was sometimes easy to forget the young man wearing them—a teen much the same age Adolin had been when he began his first bouts as a ranked duelist. "What was that you two said? Something about stems?"

"Oh! Those are shorthand expressions," Adolin said, "for the opening moves of an enemy player in towers. They say Kushkam is an expert."

"Towers?" the emperor asked.

Adolin started. "Do you call it something else?" he asked, glancing at Noura.

"No," she said. "The Azish word is '*gunna ma*'—essentially, 'the tower game.'"

"Never heard of it," Yanagawn said.

"Storms!" Adolin said. "A leader who doesn't know towers? Noura, what have you been *teaching* him?"

"Political history, social structures, languages, contracts . . ."

"Useless on the battlefield," Adolin said. "A field commander *has* to know towers."

"Pardon, Brightlord," Noura said, sounding amused. "His Excellency is *not* a field commander."

"We're on a field of battle now," Adolin said, gesturing around them. "And he's ultimately in charge." He leaned in toward the emperor, close enough that one of the man's bodyguards stepped forward until Yanagawn waved him back.

"Listen, Excellency," Adolin said. "We'll remedy this, after the war is done. Noura can teach what to say in a meeting, but if you want to learn strategy, I'll start you on towers."

"I'd . . . like that," Yanagawn said, smiling. "Thank you, Adolin. For all of it. For being here when you didn't have to be. When this isn't your fight."

"Have you heard about the fixed brawl, Excellency?"

"That's what they call the fight where you nearly lost your Shards," Yanagawn said. "Stormblessed saved you."

"I might not be here," Adolin said, "if someone hadn't stood up for *me* when it wasn't their fight. I'm here for you and this city. I promise it."

Yanagawn bowed his head in thanks. Adolin bowed in return, and withdrew. As he did so, Colot—who had been hovering nearby—rushed to catch up. "I'm impressed," he said softly.

"Is it the cape?" Adolin asked, enjoying how it flowed behind him as he walked. "It's the cape, isn't it?"

Colot grinned, the sunlight catching the dark red patches in his hair. "I know a smattering of Azish. I didn't know you were so good with the language."

"I'm not," Adolin said. "My father did something to allow me to speak it—I think Noura and the emperor realized that immediately. They're used to dealing with him." He nodded. "We'll have to win over the commandant though. I can't fight effectively beside someone who doesn't want me there."

"Yeah," Colot said as they crossed the cobbled square. "I hear you. I tried that myself . . ."

Adolin winced, reminding himself how close Colot had gotten to full Windrunner before being rejected by the spren. After that, leaving entirely had been less painful than continuing as a squire.

"I'm sorry," Adolin said. "I didn't mean to dredge up painful experiences."

"It's fine," Colot said. "Frankly, everything dredges them up." He shook his head and gazed toward the sky, where a group of windspren passed as ribbons of blue light. "I don't even know if it was something I did, Adolin. That's what really hurts. The honorspren evaluating us were ones who hated the leadership at Lasting Integrity, and had left before you got there. They practically *fawned* over Kaladin and Bridge Four. Every spren wanted someone like him. Not someone like me."

"You mean lighteyed."

Colot nodded. "It comes around, I guess. Centuries of treating the darkeyes badly; when that turns on its head, it's hard to complain. No one's going to weep for me, the poor highborn boy who didn't get what he wanted. I don't imagine that they should." He hesitated, drawing a few painspren crawling along at his feet. "Still feels like a punch to the gut."

Adolin patted him on the back. The Windrunners' loss was Adolin's advantage. He could do far, far worse than a second with Colot's training and discipline. And if he guessed right, the other hole in his command structure would be filled by someone ahead of them. While the rank and file of Adolin's volunteer force were being interrogated and situated by the Azish officers, a small group stood apart: a cluster of eight women in vibrant Alethi gowns.

Since Shallan was off doing . . . well, he didn't know what exactly. Shallan stuff—probably involving the fate of reality itself. He felt a stab of worry for her, but knew she was strong enough to handle it. And since he wouldn't have his wife to scribe for him on this battlefield, he'd asked Highprince Aladar if he could spare some of his staff.

Aladar had taken that request to heart, and had sent his best: his daughter, May.

Well, this was going to be awkward.

"Is that May Aladar?" Colot asked.

"I asked for some scribes."

"Storms," Colot said. "Adolin, didn't you two . . ."

"We *never* dated," Adolin said. Then, with a wince, he corrected himself. "*I* never thought we were dating. She . . . um . . . understood differently." He took a deep breath and stepped up to the group of women. "May."

She had black hair, chin-length in the front but shorter in the rear. A round button of a face, with light tan eyes. Features reminiscent of ancient stone sculptures by master artists.

"Adolin," she said, her voice cool. Also like stone. That wasn't merely for him—that was how May tended to be. "This is going to be a rough defense. The Fused will rip through this fortification like it's last year's cloak left out in the sun."

"Reports say there aren't many Fused," Adolin said. "Though they're bound to have stormform and direform Regals. We just have to keep them contained for a few days until the forerunners of our southern army arrive."

"Even a few days is an eternity against enemies like these," she said. "Regardless, I'm glad you spoke to my father. I was worried I would be trapped in the tower with nothing relevant to do. Where would you like me to begin?"

"Check out their triage and medical tents," Adolin suggested. "Make sure we don't need to send for any supplies before the Oathgate shuts down?"

"Excellent idea," she said.

So cold, Maya thought. *She's not a good match for you. I'm surprised you considered it.*

I considered a lot of women, Adolin thought back. *There wasn't a lot else to do on the Shattered Plains. I dated basically everyone eligible and at least halfway interested.*

Wait, wait, Maya thought, laughing—something that was so good to hear from her. *Adolin. Were you a* slut*?*

He about choked as she said it, but then smiled. She said it in the same exaggerated way some of his soldier friends did, good-naturedly laughing over one another's failings.

I, he thought to her, *was* not *a slut. A trollop at worst. Besides, I find that a wise commander investigates every strategy, so that he knows his options.*

Of course, she thought. *You are correct. A wise soldier knows* all *the best positions.*

Adolin grinned. From speaking to Pattern and Syl, he'd gotten the impression that spren were innocent in the ways of romance and intimacy. Maya was different. He supposed it was what happened when you spent your life around soldiers.

His attention was drawn back to May as she pointed to one of her wards, then at him. The girl would stay close to Adolin, in case he needed a message read or written, as May herself looked over infrastructure. They probably didn't need to worry about the Azish in this regard, but it never hurt to check.

"Father stopped by," May added. "You should see him before he leaves." Then she was off, leading her group of scribes toward their counterparts setting up a pavilion nearby. The Azish group would be mixed genders, as they did things oddly here, but May spoke their language fluently.

Really, she was the best he could have hoped for as an aide-de-camp. She had experience running the princedom for her father, and had an exacting and precise way to her. He just wished he didn't feel like the temperature dropped ten degrees every time she walked past.

"You . . . dated her?" Colot asked softly.

Him too? "I specifically said I didn't."

"You contemplated it though?"

"She's an expert sport archer," Adolin said. "I thought we might have something in common."

Archery wasn't a feminine art—but most prestigious Alethi families made an exception for it, as well as a little dagger play. Women went to war with their husbands and brothers, and camps got attacked. Keeping your hand covered for propriety was one thing; leaving yourself defenseless to enemy raiders was another. It was considered unseemly for a woman to spend as many hours on archery as May did, but times had been changing there even before Adolin's father started reading.

Adolin turned and sought out Highprince Aladar, a bald man who wore a mustache with a pointed beard below his bottom lip. Adolin was surprised at how fondly he thought of the man these days. Not so long ago, he'd regarded all of the other Alethi highprinces with a healthy measure of disgust. One had died by Adolin's own hand.

Only two original highprinces had survived with their power intact. Sebarial, who was essentially Urithiru's finance minister, and Aladar, who had fallen into being Navani's right-hand administrator. Two others—Bethab and Hatham—had lesser, but respected, positions in the government. One in Thaylen City, the other in the field with the forces that should arrive at Azimir in a few days. Neither had the same power they'd once wielded; the days of highprinces as independent monarchs in Alethkar had passed.

Aladar's position involved the day-to-day administration of Urithiru. It wasn't glorious, but it *was* in the thick of things, and Aladar seemed to enjoy that. Adolin walked up offering a hand, and he took it, with a respectful nod.

Behind him, each company of Adolin's troops was being informally attached to an Azish company. For now, it was best if their forces each had an Azish counterpart for things like mess hours and duty rotations.

"It's an honorable task you do here, Kholin," Aladar said. "I think we all stood a little taller after you insisted on coming to Azimir personally to help."

"We'll see if I actually *manage* to help," Adolin said as horses passed pulling a wagon with the large wooden box he'd ordered brought in, holding a very large chain. Stormfather send that he wouldn't need it, but if a thunderclast joined the battle . . .

Well, they'd deal with that if it happened.

"You have a good force here," Aladar said, pointing. "Three hundred former Cobalt Guardsmen who took up the uniform again after hearing of your need. Another seventeen hundred volunteers from Urithiru, including many foreigners. I had each tested for competence, and while they're a bit of a hodgepodge, all are decorated in battle." The older man smiled. "I'm surprised we found anyone capable who hadn't already been recruited, but it seems the word of 'Prince Adolin's need' squeezed some juice even from the rind. They might be irregulars, but I think they'll serve you well." He paused. "No Shardbearers, I'm afraid. I sent Mintez to the Shattered Plains with mine, per your father's request."

"There's one other Shardbearer among the Azish," Adolin said. "They kept one back for the city's Imperial Guard, when the rest were sent to battlefields to the south."

"I don't think they were sent," Aladar said. "I think they were bought? Rented by Azish generals? Their system baffles me."

"I'm sure it involves paperwork."

Aladar nodded, then turned and offered Adolin his hand a second time. Adolin took it hesitantly.

"I'm *proud*, Adolin," Aladar said. "Of what your family has done for Alethkar. Of what we've created. If you'd been able to read my innermost thoughts three years ago about what I wanted, they would have been of seizing land from my neighbors, of making a play for the throne by getting you betrothed to May. Of petty goals and small-minded aspirations. Instead we've built something." His eyes took on a wistful expression. "I never knew how satisfying it was to *build*." He squeezed Adolin's hand. "Help our allies, Adolin. Save this city. That's what we are now."

"People who build," Adolin said softly.

"People whose lives *mean something,*" Aladar added. "Your mother would be proud of you too." He smiled, letting go. "And please keep an eye on May. She's been getting ideas ever since Jasnah started going into battle directly."

"She's a fine archer, Aladar," Adolin said. "Won the women's division three times, I hear."

"I used to find that embarrassing," he said. "I asked her once if she could find a way to use a bow with only one hand . . ." He leaned in and lowered his voice. "I've been letting her practice with our Plate and Blade. She might do something foolish."

"Aladar," Adolin said, "I was never formally with May, but even *I* know she's never attracted a foolishness spren. I'm glad you sent her. I'll see that she stays safe—safe as any of us can be over these next seven days." He nodded toward the dome. "You should go. This will be our last chance to use the Oathgate."

Aladar stepped away, then—though it wasn't really appropriate, as they were the same rank—he saluted Adolin. Adolin's family had stumbled in building what they had, and he himself had blood on his hands. But . . . things were better than they had been. The whole kingdom was. So Adolin saluted back.

Aladar rushed off at the call for the final transfer. Some Azish civilians were leaving for Urithiru, but many more remained. They wouldn't abandon their homeland. They knew that all too often, refugees who went to Urithiru ended up staying.

Most Azish would take their chances here, so he'd be fighting to protect a city with its heart still in it. With that in mind, Adolin went to find his armorers and his Plate. The battle would be upon them within the hour.

38 THOSE WHO SUBTRACT

TWENTY-SIX YEARS AGO

Szeth found light near the homestead.

Not at the house itself, which was dark and shaded as he passed it. Molli would be near the water trough, over by the family's stone. That was only a short distance, in the direction of the light.

He nearly jumped to the heavens when he heard rustling from the hanging lines of beads that covered the home's doorway. Simply the wind. Trembling, he crossed the meadow toward that ruddy light. Concern mounting, Szeth forced himself to creep past the tree, the bark chill and rough on his palms.

Straight ahead was the stone—with the packed soil around it—bulging from the ground like a tumor. Three men sat on it.

They sat *on* the stone, a small fire in front of them, built on the packed earth. They'd cooked a meal, and unwelcome scents—burned and horrible—assaulted Szeth. Szeth had a terrible premonition that he didn't want to accept, so he didn't look too closely at that fire. Instead he studied the three men. Soldiers, in leather armor with glistening metal studs. Helms of pure steel. Sheathed swords at their sides. Fingers messy from eating, bits of food in their beards.

They were Shin.

His people. Not strange raiders from across the mountains. They wore no color, of course—just black, grey, and brown—but their features were unmistakable. He'd seen outlanders before, and had remarked on their eyes, their dress, their features.

Szeth relaxed. This was a patrol of the Farmer's soldiers. Similar groups had come through his family's lands. He moved to continue searching for Molli, but snapped a twig when he did, causing the men to turn in his direction.

One slid down the stone to the ground beside the fire and stood, right hand on his sword. "Who's there?"

Feeling embarrassed, Szeth walked into the light. When they saw him, they immediately relaxed.

"Boy," the standing one said, "you work this region?"

"It's our homestead. I'm a shepherd." Szeth frowned as he got closer, noticing dark liquid staining the ground near the fire—and empty bottles near the men. "That's my father's wine."

"Had to check the house," said a man lying on top of the stone, his voice slurred, "for invaders." He lifted a bottle to his lips. His face flushed with drink, he had a lazy expression, his helmet off beside him. He was bald, his head shaved clean.

"Why are you drinking?" Szeth demanded. "You're on patrol. What if you get ambushed? What if—"

"Raiders didn't expect resistance," the standing man cut in. He had dark eyes set too deep into his skull. "They pushed off almost as soon as we marched in. There won't be more fighting tonight, unless some slipped through. We were sent to search."

"Best you tipped us a little," the slovenly one said, drinking more. "For protecting your hide, little shepherd."

The third man had a wispy beard. Younger than the other two. He hunched as he sat on the angled top of the stone, staring down, half-drunk bottle of wine in his hands. Father saved it for special occasions.

"You hungry, boy?" said the man with the sunken eyes.

Szeth shied back. "I . . . think you should leave."

"What? Don't you appreciate our help?"

"I . . ." Szeth stepped farther back and didn't meet their eyes. "I think you should go."

The drunk man chuckled and picked at a piece of meat, and Szeth knew. He *knew.* But he didn't want to accept it.

"It's aggravating, you know," Sunken Eyes said. "We give our lives to protect you, but our only payment is glares. You think we don't get tired of being told to move on?"

"You are they who subtract," Szeth whispered.

"We're the ones standing between you and *that,*" the man said, waving toward the red light on the horizon. "They burned an entire village, you know? Would have kept going if we hadn't been called in."

Szeth turned away, trying not to hear the sounds of the drunk man smacking his lips as he ate, cracking bones between his fingers. A nauseating sound, like a crawling thing from the soil might make when you turned over its log.

"You want our protection," Sunken Eyes said. "But you don't want us around. Think on that, little splash-colored shepherd. Think about how you treat the people who defend you."

"The world would be better without you," Szeth hissed. "We'd all be blessed if there were no people who subtracted."

The man snorted, then took a pull on his bottle of wine. He'd had more than a little himself, it seemed, even if it didn't show as much.

"You know what I tire of most?" he said, glancing toward his friends. "The lies. The pretending. If we were to just vanish, who would stop those men on the coast?" He looked back, holding Szeth's eyes. "You eat the meat we slaughter, on your special days. You use the boards soldiers cut to build your homes. Tell me: if you pay a man to kill, does that make you any less guilty? You subtract, little shepherd. You just do it the cowardly way."

Szeth hovered near the tree, angry. This man spoke with such confidence. How *dare* he act as if he had answers? The Farmer didn't have answers. Father didn't have answers. But this man thought he did? This . . . pathetic excuse for a human being, this sack of slime that . . . that . . .

Szeth sniffled and wiped tears from his eyes. Nearby, the quiet one helped the slovenly one off the stone. They kicked a bottle aside and stumbled away into the night, heading past the house. Sunken Eyes stayed by the fire, his expression stubborn as he squatted and picked at the remnants of the meat. He ripped off a piece and began gnawing at the flesh.

That was Molli. Szeth finally accepted it. The "spilled wine" on the ground was blood, and he'd known what the men were cooking the moment he'd smelled the char. He fell to his knees in the dim light, finding her pelt—cut free—in the grass.

"Why?" he asked hoarsely.

"Sometimes," Sunken Eyes said, stumbling to his feet, "we leave reminders to make it harder to ignore us. It's worth the punishment. Worth the anger and the shouts, just to . . . live for an evening. Like you do." He started into the night, unsteady on his feet.

Szeth pulled Molli's wool to his face, but all he could smell was the blood.

"No," Sunken Eyes said in a ragged voice. "No, that's enough . . ." He stumbled a little farther. "I said *no.*"

Szeth barely registered the man's erratic behavior—speaking to nobody. Instead Szeth felt a building rage. A blinding, terrible *heat.* He dropped the pelt and went running, colliding with the soldier, making him stumble. But Szeth was only a child, and small for his age. He pounded at Sunken Eyes, but the man merely pried him free and tossed him away—like feed for the chickens.

Szeth hit the ground and tumbled against the roots of the tree. The man continued on. Stumbling, unsteady. "No," he repeated. "No, I'll get a whipping for what we've already done. If I did that . . . it would be a hanging. He's a child. *No.*"

Szeth pushed himself up, his right hand on something cool and smooth. A coldness that spread through him, rage extinguished—replaced by a distinct deep, terrible void that seemed to take all life, light, and warmth and *suffocate* it.

He stood up, clutching the stone his family had unearthed earlier. It felt like . . . fate. The will of the spren. Why else would Szeth fall there? Why else would the man have stumbled right then, slipping to the ground near the water trough? His voice becoming a mumble.

Spren made rain fall. Spren made rocks emerge. Today, spren moved Szeth. He approached the fallen man, the coldness at his core building and building and consuming him until . . .

Until he stopped, gazing at the pathetic man by the trough. A person. A terrible person that Szeth hated, but still. He had never hurt another by intent.

He would not do so today.

Szeth stared at the rock, which he blasphemously held. This wasn't the spren's will; he was lying to himself. This had been *his* choice. Why hadn't the spren struck him down? Didn't he deserve it? Didn't he—

A hand grabbed him by the throat.

The soldier, growling, lurched upward and shoved Szeth, dropping him to the ground on his back. The man straddled him, nails biting into the exposed skin of Szeth's throat. Terrible breath, with the scent of death upon it, lips parted in a grin. Spittle flecking onto Szeth's face.

Eyes . . . eyes glowing deep within with a red light. Szeth panicked, scratching at the man's claw grip.

The fellow just kept squeezing. "Thought to rob me, did you?"

Szeth's desperate fingers found the stone again, dropped to the soil beside him.

"It's not enough to take everything from us," the man continued, leaning down. "Not enough to—"

Slam.

The man gasped, slumping against the trough. Frantic, Szeth hit him again.

SLAM.

His heart hammering in time with his blows, his muscles panicked as he drew ragged breaths, Szeth struck again. And again. And again.

Until the warmth returned. It was all over him. The warmth of blood.

He stood up, the rock slipping from wet fingers, and stumbled back. Feeling at his raw neck. Thinking, numbly, that he had subtracted for the first time in his life.

Until a soft voice blossomed in his mind.

Here now, what are you?

Szeth started, glancing around. The voice did not return, though he waited to see if it would. He waited until morning, when they found him, with Molli's pelt—legs still attached—in his lap. Sitting next to a corpse that had once been—ostensibly—far more human.

39 BETWEEN TWO REALMS

I believe, sincerely, that the winds blowing in from the future indicate this will be the final confrontation of Honor and Odium.

Storms, but it felt good to put on his Plate again.

Adolin had missed it during the entire trip through Shadesmar. He had been forced to ride into a very difficult fight without it, the scar from which he'd carry despite the attention of a Radiant healer. Apparently Adolin had been thinking too much about the scar, making it permanent. Radiant powers were strange.

Actually, Maya thought, *humans are strange.*

He smiled. She'd explained how to isolate his thoughts for privacy, but he saw no reason to do so—and instead felt a little thrill. He knew that even some Radiant bonds didn't allow the two to read one another's minds; it was nice to have something that not all of them could do.

He stood on the cobbled ground before the large dome, getting a report from May Aladar as each piece of Shardplate was locked onto him. Sabatons, then greaves, cuisses, culet and faulds, skirt . . .

"I think we need a medical facility that's closer," May said. "I suggested those buildings along the east side of the square." She pursed her lips. "We will have one healer to provide Regrowth."

Surprised, Adolin glanced at her as the armorers locked the breastplate into place. "I didn't think any Edgedancers could be spared."

She stepped in closer and whispered, "My ward Rahel is a budding Radiant. She hasn't wanted to tell people because it's not Edgedancing, but the other one."

"Truthwatcher," he said.

"Yes. She has quietly gone to Radiant Precilia for training, so she knows how to heal. She's never touched a weapon, and the prospect of fighting terrifies her, but she's willing to help at the hospital."

He nodded. "Give her my sincere thanks." A single Radiant was an amazing resource. Rahel could stabilize the most dire of the wounded—leaving the rest to surgeons—and that would save a great number of lives.

"I will pass along your regards," May said. "Brightness Navani wished to send you an Edgedancer, so I suggested this. Rahel is skilled, and it will give her experience on an actual battlefield. Regardless, there is a secondary reason to use that first line of buildings to the east as a hospital."

"Which is?"

"Saferoom underneath," May explained. "It used to be a smuggler's cellar, and I was informed that it will be an emergency bolt-hole to hide the emperor. Having a hospital there will disguise why he might run for that specific building."

Adolin nodded again, making a mental note to learn how to find and use the saferoom. He might need to stash his scribes there, if the dome fell. As he considered, he saw some distinctive figures approaching. Friends from earlier days.

Adolin grinned, tearing himself away from the armorers—who were working on his pauldrons—to meet the newcomers, slapping shoulders very carefully. "Gerenor, Isalor, Kappak. Storms, it's good to see you. Thank you."

Kappak—a man with short hair that had a tendency to stick up—laughed. "Adolin, you think I'd ship back to the Shattered Plains? We spent five years there! I'm bored of it."

"Better to be wherever the Kholin is," Gerenor said, with a wink. "That's where the fun happens."

"Let's hope not too much fun," Adolin said. "Thank you for volunteering. I want you each in charge of a battalion. Watch for messages and accept Colot's word as my own, but if you feel you need to move—then move. I trust you."

Instead of salutes, he got slaps on the back. The three broke off, each taking command of a block of over six hundred. Adolin jogged to the armorers, metal sparking on cobbles as he went. "Sorry, Geb," he said to the current head armorer.

"Oh, we know there's no containing you, Adolin," the darkeyed man said with a laugh. "Just try not to go into *battle* without your gauntlets on!"

Colot smiled as Adolin's pauldrons locked into place on his shoulders.

"What?" Adolin asked.

"Simply remembering what it's like to serve with you, Brightlord."

"Military discipline," May said, holding her ledgers under one arm, "is a different beast entirely when Adolin Kholin is around."

"You like it," Adolin said, shoving one hand into a gauntlet, then grinning as he made a fist. Storms, that felt good.

"I do?" May asked.

"Gives you something to complain about."

"I do not complain," she said. "I make reports on the principles of efficiency and command structures." She paused. "You realize your methods shouldn't work, right?"

"Which part of my methods?" he asked, shoving his fist into the left gauntlet.

"Everyone—from the officers down to the spearmen—calls you by name. You fraternize with every rank, even going out to *drink* with your *armorers.*"

"Geb knows the best places!" Adolin said.

"It's a gift," Geb added.

"It shouldn't work," May repeated.

"But it does."

Adolin took his helmet from Dal—Geb's assistant and son—with a nod of thanks. He turned back to May. "The men know I'm a mediocre officer," he said, tucking the helmet under his arm. "But they *also* know I'm a *storming good* fighter. So it balances out. You should get your bow."

May started. "What, *really?*"

"Unless it violates principles of efficiency and command structures. Colot, I assume we're short on good archers?"

"Afraid so," Colot said. "We have some among the volunteers, as well as a few of my former colleagues, but most of this lot are heavy infantry. Armored like bricks, trained for city fighting or supporting a Shardbearer."

"Well, gather our twenty best archers, then put them under May's command."

"*Command?*" May whispered.

"Unless you'd rather not," he said. "But your father has named you his heir, and if you become highprincess, you're going to need battlefield experience. Let's give it a chance. Assuming you have something appropriate to wear for battle."

All talk of efficiency went out the window as May threw her ledger to her eldest ward and dashed off in a flurry of motion. Adolin grinned, then waved Colot over.

"I saw Beamlin Dorset in the block," he said softly. "If Beam is here, then Talig is too. They're a matched pair—and both are handy with a bow. Both also served as Jasnah's guards, and Beam's sister is a Radiant. They'll be comfortable taking orders from a woman, so make Beam May's second, with Talig as head sergeant. Put them on the interior balcony with the Azish archers; I'll signal when I need them."

"It'll be done, Adolin," Colot said.

"Great, thanks," Adolin said, then turned to the head ward. She had curls of light brown in her hair, bespeaking some foreign heritage. "It was Kaminah, wasn't it?"

She nodded, and seemed surprised he remembered her name.

"Ever been an aide-de-camp before?"

"No, Brightlord."

"You'll figure it out," he said. "Battlefield promotion."

"I . . . Brightlord, are you sure?"

"If May trained you, Kaminah, you'll do fantastically." She brightened at the words. He pointed toward the dome. "You think you can figure out if the archers' balcony inside will hold a Shardbearer's weight?"

"I'm sure we can get an answer!" she said. "Gitora's training as an engineer. I'll send her."

"Excellent," Adolin said. "While she works on that, you write down orders to Colot and my battalionlords." He gave her a moment to send Gitora, then she came back and scrambled to get out her ledger. She knelt and put it on her lap to write.

"We're going to let the Azish do their thing," he said, eyeing the ranks of glistening soldiers. "Tell my battalion- and companylords *not*—and I mean that quite fervently—to undermine Azish authority, but also tell them to keep watch. I want three companies from each battalion stationed out here, ready to move in at a moment's notice and form a classic pike wall, with spear and shield in the front rank. Just two deep for now.

"Station them equidistantly around the outside, and have them wait on my word to rush in and form up. Gallant should stay with his grooms, but get me a type three Shardbearer support squad with orders to protect my rear if I go in. As always, if I fall, retrieving the Plate and Blade are of primary importance. Got that?"

"Got it, Brightlord!"

"Good," Adolin said. "Let's get to work. Those singers will arrive at any moment."

They're here, Maya said, her voice only faintly labored. *I'm watching them on the other side. The Oathgate spren have become fully corrupted, and serve them now.*

Huh. She could see into both realms? That might be handy.

Might be, she agreed. *Awareness . . . is good, Adolin. I feel . . . better and better. I will say: it's a pleasure watching you work. Feels so familiar.*

"Work," he said, pulling on his helmet. "I haven't started working yet."

Liar. You've already done the most important parts.

Well, maybe she was right. He took a deep breath, accustoming himself to wearing the helmet. It felt less stuffy than he remembered, and he felt energized to be suited up again. Each movement quicker, his grip like a vise and his bearing like a fortress.

"Miss me?" he whispered to the armor.

Actually, they did, Maya says. *They hate waiting.*

Adolin smiled. "Maya, if you don't mind, tell me whatever you can see about the enemy movements."

Adolin, she said, *there are . . . a great number of them. I know we had reports . . . but it's daunting.*

"Any way you can get a count of Fused and Regals? The scouts couldn't tell for certain."

I'll try.

When spren like Syl or Pattern were bonded, it pulled them into the Physical Realm completely. Maya was different, and their bond different. Which offered advantages—though he worried maybe he was stretching to find ways to soothe his ego. Because he knew, as he'd acknowledged many times, that this was the era of Radiants.

The Shardbearer was no longer the pinnacle of the battlefield. The young lighteyed man who could outduel almost anyone was no longer nearly as valuable as he'd once been—not when compared to someone who could literally fly or bend stone to their will. In less than two years, Adolin Kholin had become so much smaller than he'd once been.

Despite that, he didn't chase Radiance. It wasn't only because his father and aunt expected him to become Radiant . . . or so he told himself. He wasn't *that* petty, was he?

Storms, he thought, marching with his small retinue of scribes and bodyguards to the steps up the outside of the dome. There he waited a moment. *Storms, I just want to choose for myself. Without my father's guidance, or his name, or his decisions for once. Is that so wrong?*

You all right? Maya whispered.

I'm fine. He took another deep breath through the helm's air slits. *I'm fine. I can do this without him. My way.*

Yeah, I don't like that line of thought, Maya said to him. *Kid, have you got* issues. *So maybe take it from someone* else *with issues. It's fine to need help. I needed it from you. Still might.*

Gitora—the younger scribe training as an engineer—came hurrying down the steps. She wore battlefield clothing. Not a havah, but silken trousers underneath a long, colorful tunic slit up the sides. "It will hold your weight, Brightlord," she said, with a bow.

"Excellent," he said. "You really do have an eye for engineering."

"Um . . ." The girl, maybe fifteen, shifted from one foot to the other. "In fact, the Azish Shardbearer is already up there stomping around. So, less engineering, more simple observation. Though I did check that the balcony could hold you both, and the Azish here agree it will."

Adolin grinned, waving for his group to follow as they marched up the wooden steps. At the top was a door to the inner balcony, which ran in a long wide loop around the dome. Slots let in light above, not backlighting the archers. Officers also gathered here, watching the dim, flat stone plateau below. The sole feature was the small control building at the center, which could hold perhaps thirty people.

All right, Maya said, *I count maybe a hundred or so stormforms moving into position. About as many direforms. That might be the extent of their Regals.*

There wasn't a real equivalent to Regals in the human armies. They were less dangerous than the Fused, but possessed forms of power that made them fearsome fighters. Stormforms, for example, could release bursts of lightning—like the one that had killed a dear friend on the Shattered Plains. A lack he felt every time he went riding.

Are the Heavenly Ones still there? he asked Maya. *Or did they fly off once the forces arrived?*

Still there, Maya said. *The Fused have controlled the nearby beads, turning them into solid ground. They've got a* lot *of Voidlight. I am swimming in the beads off to the side, watching. Looks like . . . they're breaking some boats?*

To make shields maybe, Adolin said. In a normal siege, you'd break down buildings in nearby villages for wood.

He stepped up to the railing, taking off his helm and putting it under his arm as Kaminah provided a spyglass for him. He used it to get a close-up view of what Kushkam's soldiers were doing. The Azish military had done as Colot and Maya had initially suggested: gathering in a tight formation right around the central building. A thousand men, though the smallest ring at the center held only thirty or so, with some crossbowmen ready to release bolts into the building as soon as the enemy appeared. Anticipationspren waved around them, like red streamers moving in wind.

They had quickly placed some wooden slats against the bottom half of the doorways to the control building, which they were filling with water. It leaked, but there were enough buckets among the men to fill the thing—and a Soulcaster in an exceptionally ornate outfit stood nearby, face masked to hide their ailment, ready to Soulcast the water into bronze and maybe provide an obstruction to the enemy.

Adolin quickly relayed what Maya had found about numbers of Regals to his scribes, and a messenger girl passed it to Kushkam's officers. Adolin sincerely hoped that he was wrong—that Kushkam and his forces could hold. He'd soon know, though for now he had to wait.

He hated this part.

His father spoke of the excitement before a battle, the anticipation. Adolin understood some of that. He'd felt the same thing many times on the Shattered Plains . . . but it had changed for him a while back. Maybe it was a year at war, maybe it was the capture of the Thrill. But he swore it had started long before—perhaps as far back as when he and his father had been betrayed by Sadeas, and left alone to die.

Since that day, Adolin had started to hate battle. He liked showing his skill, he liked wearing the Plate, but he'd begun to be nauseated by the butchery. It . . . it was silly, but he felt that the battlefield made a *mockery* of his dueling skills. He'd trained with the sword to better his life and test himself against others. Not to kill.

Fortunately for the army, this sense didn't detract from his efficiency. He did, and would, slaughter—so he didn't have a high horse to sit on. Hopefully his only horse was enjoying some grain and not tormenting his grooms.

Adolin, Maya said, *something is happening.*

First wave? he asked.

Kind of. Look.

Light flashed in a small ring around the command building. The Soulcast bronze vanished to the other realm, as Adolin had anticipated, where it could be shoved aside. Spren burst from the building, soaring through the air on ribbons of red light. A ripple of discomfort and nervous mutters ran through the Azish archers around him, but Adolin recognized this from other battlefields.

"They're using Voidspren as scouts," he said. "Kaminah, send a message to the commandant. The enemy will know exactly what terrain is waiting for them, and precisely where we're positioned. Tell him that I suggest the Azish should pull back and form a wider ring with more troops."

"Yes, Brightlord!" the scribe said, settling down with her spanreed to send word to the Azish scribe center—while also dispatching one of the other young women as a runner.

Only two minutes later some of the Voidspren returned to the control building and it flashed again—they were reporting back. No troops transferred in at the same moment, but the Soulcast bronze did not reappear. The enemy had removed it even more quickly than Adolin had expected.

The next part took a little time. Time for May to arrive in a uniform with the archery platoon he'd requested. Time for Adolin to mentally prepare himself to become a killer once more. Time for him to note Kushkam ignoring his suggestion, forces remaining in tight ranks around the control building.

Those Voidspren continued to hover around. Maybe someday Aunt Navani's anti-Light would be a viable way to engage with enemy spren—but for now he ignored them. Chopping one in half with a Shardblade would send it to Shadesmar to recuperate, but there were dozens here, so that wouldn't matter. He waited. Sweating. Feeling a strange, light ventilation blow through his armor, keeping him cool. Then it happened.

A third flash of light around the command building.

It began.

The Heralds are essentially no more. They are rejected by their Blades.

Talmut's monastery sat atop a long ridge upon the mountainside, high enough to give a perspective over the rest of the Nirovah Valley. The first time Szeth had climbed this ridge—trudging up the switchbacks to the fortified encampment where the soldiers trained—it had taken over an hour.

Today, he and Kaladin landed there after a quick Lashing into the sky.

"Stone?" Kaladin said, noting the lack of soil.

Indeed, the outcropping here was reminiscent of places outside Shinovar. Firm rock, with only occasional patches of dusty soil, held a large military encampment familiar to Szeth even after all these years. The ridge was longer than it was wide, with a cliff at its back. There was space here for dozens of buildings—mostly barracks and training halls.

The monastery itself was farther to the left, following a narrow path. For now, Szeth inspected the military camp that had been his home.

"Szeth?" Kaladin said. "It looks abandoned."

Although the buildings were in better repair than his homestead, no one was out along the paths. It was as if all the people in his entire homeland had just vanished.

"There should be thousands of soldiers here training," Szeth said.

"Perhaps they moved north," Kaladin said. "Where our Windrunners encountered resistance when trying to survey the land. Why does this place have so much rock—I thought none of you could walk on it?"

"This is the domain of soldiers," Szeth explained. "Those who subtract are allowed to walk on stone, because their lives are blasphemy. They kill."

He hesitated. "The ones I spoke of, who killed the sheep at my homestead? They came from here."

"How can your society function?" Kaladin asked, glancing to Syl standing beside him. "If you treat soldiers like that . . ."

"The greatest task in life is to create, to add," Szeth said. "The greatest shame is to break what someone else created—or to ruin art of the gods: the spren, and their kings, the Heralds. The stone upholds the soil and creates foundations for Roshar. The spren created it."

He glanced toward Syl, who seemed to find this amusing. "Yes," she said, "we barf it out, you see. Rocks, pebbles, shale if we're *particularly* nauseated."

"Not all of our lore . . . matches what I have seen on the outside," Szeth said. "But Roshar *is* a creation of the gods. Honor, Cultivation, and Odium."

"Kind of," Syl said. "Best we can figure out, Roshar is the work of the ancient god who *became* Cultivation and Honor. Odium too, though that's embarrassing to admit. It means we're relatives, you see."

"Without the act of God," Szeth said, "Roshar would weather away into dust and vanish into the ocean. To prevent this, the highstorms were created to rain crem." He pointed. "The last crem of a dying highstorm is dumped onto these mountains, keeping them high, sheltering Shinovar. We thrive because of an act of God. So we revere the stone."

"Unless you're a soldier," Kaladin said, surveying the empty encampment with his hands on his hips, apparently finding this entire idea unpleasant. Which was good, since it was.

"A soldier must still revere the stone," Szeth said softly. "Many learn the wrong lesson. It is not that stone is mundane to one who kills, it is only that soldiers—living a life of destruction—are *forced* to defile it. Increasing their sin with each new weapon forged."

"Storms, this place is so bizarre," Kaladin whispered.

"We live lives of peace," Szeth said, "compared to the near-constant warfare of your lands."

"Because you shove all the unpleasant elements off on a few, whom you torment."

"Is that not what the Radiants are?" Szeth said. "Watchers at the rim, as Dalinar says? A pleasant term for an unpleasant idea—people who must kill so ordinary men and women can live peaceful lives. Radiants must bathe in blood and tarnish their souls in order to forge peace."

"That is," Kaladin said, "a *complete* misinterpretation."

Szeth dropped the point. Why argue with one who was accustomed to always being right? "Come. I think there are people here somewhere. The buildings are in much better shape than the ones we passed below."

He turned and looked over the landscape. Homesteads like his dotted the greenery, and he could make out several small towns. They'd visited one on the way here—and it had been abandoned. Perhaps Kaladin was correct and they'd moved north, finding their way to one of the cities.

Kaladin and Syl didn't object as Szeth led them to one of the barracks, a place he remembered, though not fondly. He stopped—then, without going in, he waved for Kaladin and Syl to follow him and he strolled past to the next building in line.

As he'd hoped, this prompted sounds from within the barracks—people rushing up to the windows to peek now that he was leaving. He spun and dashed back in a smooth motion, then kicked the door open, breaking the lock.

Dozens of people inside scattered into the shadows. Wide-eyed, dusty-faced, wearing ragged clothing. He saw hints of splashes. Faded scarves. Sashes that he could barely separate from trousers in the grime and dim light.

A piece of him let out a deep sigh. Seeing his kind again . . . made him feel that he had finally awakened from a nightmare to something familiar. Yet something was wrong. They kept away from him, and from the light spilling in through the now-open door.

"What's wrong with them?" Syl asked, peeking around him.

"You," Szeth said in his own language—it felt unfamiliar to him now, heavy on his tongue. "What is wrong with you? You are not soldiers, yet you walk on stone?"

"We must," someone whispered from the shadows. "The soil will swallow us."

"Swallow us," several others whispered.

"Nonsense," Szeth said. "How do you eat?"

"We work fields at night," another voice said. "As commanded by the shaman. When the ground cannot see us."

"See us . . ." others whispered.

"What are they saying?" Kaladin asked.

"They say the ground will swallow them, for some reason," Syl explained. "So they work the fields at night, and apparently hide here during the day."

"Soldiers," Szeth said, with Syl translating for Kaladin. "Where are the soldiers?"

They retreated farther into the darkness, and several hissed when Szeth stepped forward. He summoned his Blade, which quieted them.

"Soldiers went north," one of them said from the shadows. "Hearing a voice we could not . . ."

"A voice?" Kaladin said. "Was it the voice of the Wind?"

"No," Szeth said, looking over his shoulder at Kaladin. "It must be the voice of one of the Unmade."

 "Szeth," Syl whispered, "when we were in Kholinar, we ran into a strange cult worshipping an Unmade. There were strange events in the tower too, when we first arrived. The effect of another Unmade."

"If there is one in Shinovar," Kaladin said, "we need to find it and defeat it. Maybe that's what Ishar is expecting of you, and why he said I needed to help you."

"Perhaps," Szeth replied. "Or perhaps this punishment is what my people deserve." He turned from the building and stepped back out into the light. "They have invited in one of the Unmade, then refused to expel it when I warned them."

"We're here to change that," Kaladin said, joining him. "Aren't we? You've been sent to cleanse the place."

"I haven't decided what that cleansing will entail," Szeth said. "Perhaps it is my people who must be destroyed."

"You're *kidding,*" Syl said, walking hurriedly on his other side, still full sized.

"I have not decided," Szeth repeated calmly. "My quest is about this decision."

Good, his spren whispered. *Good. You see, and you grow.*

"Insanity," Kaladin said. "The people in that building didn't choose to reject you, Szeth. Maybe some of their leaders did, but the ordinary people don't deserve this punishment."

Szeth paused. There was wisdom in those words, wasn't there? He . . . wavered.

He should not waver. The answer should be obvious. He needed to apply what he'd been taught by Nin-son-God, Herald and leader of the Skybreakers. Long ago, during his youth, Szeth had learned that his judgment was flawed. It had begun when he'd killed that soldier with the rock.

Fortunately, he had guides now. Nin, Dalinar. What would they do in this situation? How would they face this question? Without further comment, Szeth strode toward the monastery. Nin and Dalinar would find answers, then do what needed to be done. According to the law.

There had to be a standard. Without a standard, there was only chaos. If a shaman had given orders to these people, then perhaps the monastery would yield clues.

"Szeth," Kaladin said, taking his arm as he passed. "I'd really appreciate some answers."

"Then pay better attention," Szeth said. He pulled free and started up the path.

The monastery itself was a tall fortress. The monasteries in the East, particularly Alethkar, always felt so . . . unimposing to Szeth. Here they were places of war. Or more accurately, of preparation for war.

Oddly, Szeth realized, there was no wind blowing on this ridge.

"That's a *monastery*?" Syl said, hovering alongside as they continued up the stone path across the steep mountain face.

"They are watchtowers, each of them," Szeth explained—because she was a spren, and it would be impious to ignore *her* questions. "Set up by the Heralds, who conferred upon us Truth and charged us to be vigilant in case the enemy returned."

"Why would they think the enemy would return?" Kaladin asked from just behind. "Everything I've been taught said the Heralds finished the war and the enemy was gone for good."

"Yes, they did tell you that," Szeth said. "Didn't they."

"Wait, wait," Kaladin said, scrambling up beside him—then, finding the path too narrow, he moved out into the air with Syl, hanging over the cliff. "All this time the Shin *knew* that the enemy hadn't been defeated? That the Heralds were among us?"

"Obviously," Szeth said. "We were the guardians of their swords. We were entrusted with their Sacred Truth."

"The way you say that has the air of something important," Syl said.

"Utmost importance," Szeth said. "The Sacred Truth of the Heralds is the knowledge that the enemy *would* someday return. If Talmut ever broke. On that day, we Shin would be needed to fight." He reached the top of the climb, then nodded back down the way. "The men who trained at the encampment? That was a hard life, to be despised. Those who trained—as I eventually did—in the monasteries . . . they were to be something else entirely. True destroyers, most despicable and most glorious. Ready to face the enemy."

"Then what happened?" Kaladin asked. "It's been a year and a half since the return of the singers."

"They did not believe. That is the *entire reason* we are here. Once again, please pay attention." With a grinding of boots on stone, Szeth strode to the front gates of the monastery—and found them open. Was the place abandoned? The shamans should never have left those gates open; it was a blatant violation of Truth.

Szeth stepped into the vaulted great hall inside, an enclosed courtyard where troops could gather and repel an assault. Cages full of gemstones were built into the walls, with openings to the outside so they would automatically recharge with the passing highstorms. Warm orange-tan light speckled the great hall, illuminating the grand mural of Talmut on the floor. A depiction of him wrapped in chains, bound in Damnation, the Bearer of Agonies.

Only one person stood in the vast hall . . . and it was one of those who had condemned him as Truthless. A middle-aged Shin woman, wearing the stark grey robes of a shaman. No hint of color, not even a splash. Grey hair that might have once had some blond to it.

"Rit?" he asked. "Rit-daughter-Clutio?"

"Pilgrim," she said, nodding to him, her voice echoing in the large empty hall.

Kaladin stepped up, likely to begin demanding answers. Szeth waved him off, and fortunately he went, with Syl whispering interpretations to him.

"I am no pilgrim," Szeth said. "I am Szeth-son—"

"I know who you are," she said, throwing aside her cloak. "I was there nine years ago. Do *you* remember?"

"Banishment is not something a man forgets," he whispered.

"I was told you'd come sooner. It's been months of waiting."

Months? How did they know?

She raised her hands before her and summoned a Shardblade. Unornamented, shaped like a long wedge. A brutal weapon, lacking the grace of its fellows, but somehow also more honest. A weapon that he'd seen depicted in art many times.

Talmut's Honorblade.

"You had no leave to reclaim that," Szeth said, summoning his own Blade. "Talmut should have his weapon."

You don't need that! Nightblood said from his back. *I'm better than a dumb Shardblade made from a dumb spren. Use me!*

"Talmut *broke,*" the woman said. "He brought the Desolation. His Blade is better held by the worthy."

"Then why aren't you fighting the enemy?" Szeth demanded. "What happened to the Sacred Truth?"

The woman smiled. "I envy you. Oh, how I *envy* you, pilgrim, for the opportunity you are granted. Prepare to prove yourself."

"I've done so already," he said. "I earned the right to bear an Honorblade."

"And where is it?" she asked him.

Stolen. Lost. In the hands of Moash, the traitor, leaving Szeth with only the Blade he'd earned upon saying his Third Ideal. She obviously knew that, so he did not respond.

"You must cleanse that sin before being granted your glorious opportunity, pilgrim," she said. "Nine years in the harsh lands of stone. Let us see what you've learned."

She came for him slowly, stalking forward. Szeth backed up, then unstrapped Nightblood and thrust it toward Kaladin.

"Hold it," Szeth said. "Do *not* draw it. Do *not* intervene."

"What are you doing?" Kaladin asked. "What *is* this?"

"What I, apparently, must do."

⁂

Azish crossbowmen started shooting straight into the control building through the doorways. But as Adolin watched from a distance with the spyglass, red lightning sprayed out in return. Stormforms. Their unleashed powers lit the control building like a suddenly infused sphere.

Adolin blinked, trying to track what happened next—but even expecting it, he missed the direforms charging out until they hit the line of Azish infantry.

Direforms. Hulking, wicked singers who were among their best troops—not on the level of a man in Plate, but at over seven feet tall, with strength and speed enhanced by their incredible form, they were more than a match for the waiting Azish spearmen. Particularly blinded spearmen, potentially stunned and burned from the blasts of lightning.

The line started to crumple immediately.

"It's happening faster than I thought," Adolin said to his scribe. "Warn my support team, have May be prepared for Heavenly Ones, and tell my soldiers to march in—but to not interfere with the Azish reserves."

"Yes, sir!" Kaminah said as he tossed back the spyglass. "Sir? Where will you be waiting for them?"

"Waiting?" Adolin said, pulling on his helmet. Then he threw himself off the balcony.

A drop of thirty feet was hazardous in Shardplate, but he couldn't help but feel a burst of excitement as he hit. His armor held up, and in seconds he was charging across the open stone toward the battle.

And . . . storms, it had been too long. He had forgotten the power of wearing Plate—indeed, he seemed faster than he remembered, each step launching him forward. Steel grinding rock. Barreling toward the conflict ahead. Where . . .

Where the Azish held.

Their lines buckled, and their soldiers screamed. But counter to his fears, their lines managed to hold against the onslaught of enemy troops. Barely. They'd break soon. Lightning, hulking direforms, followed by a flood of conventional warforms. The control building began flashing quickly, each flash depositing another platoon of soldiers who ran out, making room for others to enter behind.

Even he had underestimated how quickly they'd be able to deploy—and while the Azish performed better than he'd expected, the direforms made an effort to break through in one specific spot. They needed to puncture the ring of Azish defenders, then flood out and try a surrounding maneuver.

That puncture point was where Adolin was needed. He arrived at blinding speed, skidding across the stones and summoning Maya in a flash. An enterprising Azish officer at the rear shouted for his beleaguered men to make room. They folded their line, executing the orders perfectly, and Adolin hit the enemy like a rushing river of steel and Blade.

Adolin downed the first few direforms with flashes of Blade. The Azish gave him room, and the entire ring began to fall back as reserves from the perimeter joined them. Stormfather send that they'd see what his men were doing and align their tactics.

He didn't have time to look, as more and more Regals began turning his direction. Shards were a luscious prize. He clashed with an enormous direform who bore a shield that blocked his Shardblade. A Veden half-shard. Those had started showing up on battlefields—plus shields lined in aluminum, which could stop a Blade too.

Adolin ducked a swing from the direform, who also wielded a massive axe—larger than any human could have held without Plate—then lunged expertly, skewering the direform and dropping her. Behind that, stormforms unleashed lightning—and in the flashes, he was again reminded of Sure-blood's death.

In honor of the fallen, he kept his cool. Adolin wasn't his father, but today he'd have done the Blackthorn proud as he advanced, Maya whistling through the air as he engaged three direforms at once. His assault worked as a distraction, drawing attention away from the Azish lines to allow them to retreat and help their wounded.

And storms, for all he disliked the butchery of it, it was electric to fight with Plate and Blade once more. He dropped two more direforms, then the Plate absorbed the lightning the stormforms tried to send at him—dissipating it somehow, vibrating against his skin. They should have known better. Though their lightning wasn't terribly accurate, and they often loosed it when surprised.

He continued to smash through their ranks, taking a hit here and there, dropping a few more—but mostly keeping them distracted while shouts behind him indicated his soldiers were forming up. He gave a quick glance, and was pleased to see the Azish following the lead of his troops: forming a larger, wider ring of pikes and shields some thirty yards back in all directions.

That gave the enemy more space to bring in troops, but it spread out their Regals. The enemy might consider this an initial victory, but it was all according to Adolin's plan. He prepared to withdraw—until Maya noticed something.

There, she said. *Look what you've flushed out. Three.*

A glance showed him three figures rising into the air ahead of him, just above the control room. Heavenly Ones would be needed to deal with a full Shardbearer. Adolin took the chance to make a careful retreat, leaving a half dozen Regals on the ground with burning eyes. He was tempted to recover their half-shards, but that would have been foolhardy.

Have you seen my support squad? Adolin asked.

I can only see what you do, I'm afraid, Maya said. *Or at least whatever's in the direction you're facing.*

Well, he'd trust in them. He withdrew farther as the three Heavenly Ones swooped toward him, each with a shield that could block his Blade.

Arrows started to pelt them.

Adolin grinned. May's team had been watching as requested. With the longer Alethi range, and with the Azish having fallen back, her team had plenty of space to harry the Heavenly Ones. In minutes, the three Fused realized they couldn't engage Adolin while arrows were flying—and soared off to take care of the archers first.

Hopefully May and her team could deal with that. Adolin had his hands full as more enemy troops surged toward him—his distraction working perhaps a little *too* well as the enemy noticed he was basically standing alone, unsupported. Fortunately, as he fought—moving from Windstance into a defensive Stonestance—he heard familiar shouts approaching from behind.

In moments, Colot had arrived with Adolin's support squad. They fanned out behind him, staying far enough away that he wouldn't hit them with sweeps of the Blade, but at the same time watching his flanks and preventing him from being surrounded.

He kept fighting, ripping aside a direform's shield by grabbing it in his free hand, then lunged with a one-handed strike, smoothly moving to Vinestance—which focused on flexibility. He shocked his opponents by *advancing* for a moment, confusing them, using his Blade in one hand and his powerful fist in the other to smash away protections.

A Shardbearer on the battlefield had once been the most dominant, terrifying, destructive force any man would ever see. A Shardbearer fully supported by trained troops who knew not to get in his way, but also how to keep him from being pulled down . . . well, it was still a force even Fused had to respect. Adolin swept through enemy attackers, their eyes burning as they fell dead. Each strike felt like a blow in the name of Kholinar, the city he'd lost, the soldiers he'd abandoned.

Soon, unnerved, the enemy began to pull away from him. And their retreat was hastened as three large screaming fireballs came flying through the air, dripping flaming drops of oil. This wasn't from the firetrap that Kushkam had prepared, but from what Adolin's forces called the Heavenly One protocols. The three who had attacked the archers had been doused with oil, then shot with flaming arrows.

The Fused would heal from the burns, but the fire and light would keep them disoriented. Adolin grinned, kicking a direform aside. The Heavenly

Ones streaked overhead, their outrageously filmy outfits proving to be a liability, as they retreated to the control building.

To your left.

Adolin spun toward something he'd barely seen at the corner of his vision. He struck by instinct, and his Blade became longer by a few inches and speared straight through another flying Heavenly One—this one not on fire—her lance scraping across his armor and deflecting off.

Maya cut the gemheart inside the Fused, and that was enough. The creature's eyes burned, same as any other singer, and she tumbled to the ground. She'd be reborn, but not until the next Everstorm. That attack had been stealthier than the others—and she had somehow gone undetected by his archers. Which put him on alert, something in him warning that it might have been an intentional distraction.

Nearby, singers who had been pulling back suddenly surged forward. Adolin grunted, swinging out with his Blade in a wide sweep and dropping several. Then he danced backward—a moment too late as one specific singer broke from the formation and moved with unexpected speed and fluidity, battering at Adolin with a pair of wicked maces.

Another Fused. But Adolin recognized this one.

Tall and imperious, a face mostly white, the pattern almost forming a glyph. It was the same Heavenly One that he and Shallan had fought in Shadesmar. The one Adolin had wounded.

The creature appeared to recognize him, and hummed to a violent-sounding rhythm. It had come, it seemed, for revenge.

We must travel to the Well of Control, within the shroud of the fragments of the dead moon.

Szeth strode forward through the monastery.

"Is this my path?" he asked his spren.

"It is."

"Fighting an Honorbearer would be easier with both of my Surges."

"It would."

That was not permission, so he would use only the Lashings of flight. At least one small fact was clear to him: he had a debt to settle with the woman in front of him. If Rit wanted a fight, he would certainly indulge her.

The floor turned liquid.

Stoneward, he thought with a curse, Lashing himself upward as the ground tried to swallow him. The tiles began flowing and running as if suddenly molten, the mural of Talmut the Herald mixing like wet paint.

Szeth lurched upward. A Stoneward *would* have two Surges, and he'd never faced this combination before. During his youth, they hadn't possessed this Blade. Still, he could guess how she would fight. The flowing control of stone echoed a Willshaper, mixed with some limited access to the strange abilities of a Bondsmith. It was a dangerous combination, but then again, they all were.

He sought the protection of height. If this duel followed the rules of those he'd fought when younger, leaving the room would be out of bounds. She wouldn't go so far as to destroy the monastery by warping the walls or ceiling.

The ground rippled like the surface of a lake, then began to vibrate. A column speared upward—a waterspout of stone bearing her at the top. It showed amazing control of this Surge, more skillful than that of any Willshaper he'd known. She was good. And powerful . . . exceptionally powerful.

She must be using an incredible amount of Stormlight, he thought. *How is she getting so much?*

Rit speared straight at him atop her column of liquid stone, and as he dodged, the entire *floor* rose in a wave. Szeth flew around the top of the vaulted room, but there wasn't space to flee. He was forced to engage her as she rode the center of the wave of stone. Their Blades met with a sequence of clangs, forcing his back against the upper wall of the chamber. The liquid stone surged around Rit—enveloping her completely—and tried to wash across Szeth.

His stomach jumped as he immediately Lashed himself downward, narrowly avoiding the stone—which splashed on the wall. As Szeth neared the ground, he saw an opening. She'd consolidated much of the liquid stone at the top to try to smash into him. This left gaps in the wave lower down. He zipped through one of these gaps, and as he did, he heard a faint cracking sound. The stone hardening. He remembered that sound well from his time training with the Willshaper Blade.

He landed cautiously in a skid across the floor, now hard once more—but uneven, a great portion of the stone forming a strange sloped and distorted column up to the left, melding with the wall. Rit descended this slope quietly, bare feet on the rock, leaving footprints—Shardblade out.

"She's amazing," Szeth whispered.

You are better, his spren said. *Go. Destroy her.*

"It is a duel," Szeth said. "It is not about destruction."

She will kill you if she can, my squire. Imagine a slow death encased by stone, the whispers all around you . . .

That image was cold and sharp, like a spear through his chest. It made him tremble, and something sparked inside him.

Control it, the spren warned.

Szeth nodded as Rit hopped down onto the warped stone ground. He felt . . . warm. The spren was speaking to him more than it usually did, and its attention felt approving. Like that of his father.

You have reached an important moment, Szeth, the spren said. *Think of that stone tomb. Anticipate it.*

Szeth danced forward, preparing to clash. His new Blade was starting to feel comfortable in his hand, curved but understated—without overbearing ornamentation. Rit's weapon was straight. Talmut's Blade seemed both less and more like a sword than many other Honorblades. So simple.

Szeth swung three times in sweeping arcs, forcing Rit back. He was the better swordsperson, judging by her reaction times and stance. He tried to use that, to throw her off balance so he could lay a hand on her and Lash her upward to gain an advantage. Unfortunately, the floor began to flow again, and he was forced into the air.

The proper way to fight someone like this was to keep moving—an excellent strategy in any fight. He flew the length of the large front hall, then rounded along the side and swept back down lower.

Beneath him, the ground *undulated.* Liquid ripples trembling, the column sloughing off and melting into the rest. The tiles re-formed just as they'd been, the destruction undone. Such *control.* Again he was troubled by the power she exhibited. Honorblades used far more Stormlight than a Radiant did—as a Radiant's oaths aligned them to the will of Honor, making them stronger vessels.

At this rate, he should have been able to run her out of power—but she showed no signs of being concerned about that. Instead Rit vanished down into the stone, not needing to breathe. Szeth watched, and once more fear sparked within him. As ordered, he imagined that stone enveloping him—the panic it would inspire. He'd be alone with the whispers until he suffocated.

Yes . . . his spren said. *Are you ready to prove yourself?*

"It is not for me to decide, but you."

An excellent answer. I am coming to genuinely like you, squire. The spren sounded more . . . personable than it ever had.

Szeth continued to zip around the large room, waiting for his enemy to make a move. The floor's vibrations increased. Soon the ground distorted in a strange waveform, sections of stone rising up in a symmetrical pattern.

A moment later, jets of it launched upward like streamers, trying to catch him—splashing against the ceiling, then hardening. He narrowly wove among them, Lashing at the very edge of his skill. Each one of these new columns dropped the level of the floor a little, until an amazed Kaladin and Syl stood in the doorway before a drop of some twenty feet.

The stone had been drained as if from a pool to create a network of columns. Fortunately, Rit's control over the stone didn't extend so far as to let her raise the entire thing up as spikes—she had to directly control a few columns at a time, freeze them, then move to a new batch. That gave him a chance.

He began slashing through columns as he passed, the Shardblade cutting chunks from the stone—but each soon resealed. Then more columns launched, trying to catch him. When they missed, they left behind another obstacle. Sweating, he drew in more Stormlight from the pouch at his waist. Where was Rit getting this kind of strength? When he'd trained with the Willshaper Blade, he'd been able to affect an area of stone only two or three feet wide.

 "Can you see her?" he asked the spren.

No. Prepare for the stone to capture you.

"That will be the end."

Will it? You would give up your quest so easily?

"I . . ." Szeth Lashed himself to the wall, changing gravity so he could run along it as if it were the floor. He ducked beneath columns, then leaped—enhanced by a Lashing—over a flowing section of stone that tried to cut him off.

"I will fight until I am dead," he whispered.

No.

"I will fight," Szeth revised with a grunt, restoring gravity and dropping down a column of stone—scraping it with his fingers—to reach the undulating floor of the chamber. "I will fight until you tell me otherwise."

Excellent.

He plunged his sword into the ground, then Lashed his body upward just enough to hover, before continuing to zip through the room—slicing the ground in large swaths. She would need to be near the surface somewhere to watch where he was.

It quickly became clear this method would not be effective. She could be hiding in any of the columns, and each new one created left more surface area to search—plus, being so low to the ground didn't give him as much time to react to new columns.

There was one way to make sure she emerged. It was time to see if his spren was guiding him correctly. He gave a glance upward and saw that Kaladin had leaned out to watch. Then Szeth closed his eyes and landed.

Stone surrounded him. Swallowed him. Shadows became his entire world as the liquid stone hardened, capturing him. A tomb, created in *exactly* his shape. It even held each finger in place around his Blade. He couldn't inhale. Not only was there no air, there was no room for his chest to expand.

Stone. Cold. Pressing against his cheeks, trapping his eyelids closed. So he held his breath, and heard a clicking tremble on the stone as Rit emerged. Walking across the rock.

I see her directly in front of you, the spren said. *She has emerged as you hoped.*

Yet the spren did not give him permission to use Division. The voices grew louder.

He would die here. Encased in stone. He would run out of Stormlight and suffocate in a place black and terrible. Death did not frighten him, but dying here . . . failing in his quest . . .

That legitimately terrified him.

Hold, the spren said.

His Stormlight was running out. He could feel it trickling away, and the voices condemned him for his murders. He could touch the second power, access it—and in so doing, free himself in an instant.

Hold, the spren said.

Sweating, trembling, almost whimpering, he held.

Some of the others said that you were not diligent or worthy, the spren said, *because you did not choose the law as your guide. But now . . . now I prove them wrong. Well done, Szeth.*

It was still. Not. Permission.

You may use your second Surge, the spren said. *Fight. As a full Skybreaker.*

Finally. Szeth swelled with a power that was immediately familiar. The stone had captured him, holding him, but that allowed him to touch it. Time to burn.

He exhaled Stormlight in a rush, infusing the stones around him with a mounting destruction. The column became char, the stone itself set alight. Szeth ripped from it, trailing ash like a second—no, third—shadow, pieces of it crumbling from his face. He forced his eyes open and lunged, Blade pointed forward, at something moving in front of him. Rit walking close to inspect her handiwork.

He set the very air alight as he moved.

Skybreaker.

Rit opened her mouth to scream, and he plunged his Blade straight through, out the back of her skull, into the next column of stone.

Her Blade dropped from her fingers.

She fell forward on his Blade, the top of her mouth catching on the rear edge of the weapon and holding her pinned—until Szeth commanded that edge of the Blade to become sharp. Then the corpse fell straight past it, leaving a slice this time—because the body was dead.

There was no blood.

Szeth hesitated, frowning. He knelt beside the corpse and heard the faintest words whispered from what should have been dead lips. "Your family awaits you, pilgrim."

He stumbled back then, as the body *disintegrated.* Becoming black smoke, leaving only empty clothing behind.

⁂

Adolin faced off against the Fused who had named himself Abidi the Monarch. The Heavenly One had used moving soldiers as cover to get in close, and he didn't fly as he lunged for Adolin, wielding his wicked maces.

Adolin sidestepped, then struck. Unfortunately, the Heavenly One expertly diverted his Blade by hitting it on the flat with one mace, then managed to ring Adolin's bell with the other—hitting him square in the side of his head.

His helmet cracked, but held. Adolin grunted and retreated—but at that moment a pair of warforms dove for his legs, toppling him. Storms, he'd been ready for this, and they'd *still* gotten him. As good as his team was at handling Fused these days, the enemy were equally prepared to bring down Shardbearers.

He dropped Maya and punched, sending one of the singers flying, then he rolled and kicked the other free. Abidi slammed his maces down, hitting stone as Adolin barely managed to roll out of the way.

Adolin's support squad was there a moment later, filling in around him. Several would be carrying roped hooks to try pulling him—or at least the armor—to safety, but as he pushed up to one knee, they'd see he didn't need that. Instead they engaged the Heavenly One. A near-suicidal act, but the Shardbearer needed to be preserved. As Adolin gathered his bearings, he saw one man in particular—a bearded fellow he didn't recognize, with long white Thaylen eyebrows and a white mustache—protecting him. The man stood squarely between the Fused and Adolin.

The Fused prepared to swing at the fellow, but Adolin growled, forming Maya and hurling her in a flash of spinning metal to slam into the Fused's side. Adolin missed the gemheart, but got the attention of Abidi—who turned away from the soldier and glared at Adolin.

Adolin summoned Maya back to him—an action that was instantaneous now—and found his feet. The bearded Thaylen soldier stabbed the Fused with a spear, but the creature yanked it out and swept the man aside, advancing on Adolin. "It *is* you," the Fused growled in accented Alethi. "The Bondsmith's son."

Adolin leveled Maya. "I thought I killed you," he said. "Guess I'll have to do it again."

"You did *not* defeat me," the Fused growled. "I survive for the end of all things. I will not go to Braize to await rebirth, and miss the glory of this conquest. I am Abidi the Monarch, and this land is mine. I will *claim* this city."

Storms. Bless the Fused for their insistence on announcing their titles and accolades; it gave Adolin time to set his stance. Most of his support squad held off, wary—now that Adolin had his Blade resummoned, he needed space. He gave a quick sign, sweeping his left hand to the side, two fingers out. They began to reorganize, falling back, and Adolin—eyes on that Fused—helped the brave Thaylen man to his feet and sent him off with the others.

The Fused, of course, used that opening to attack, as Adolin had expected. They clashed, and storms, those maces were lined in aluminum—for Adolin tried and failed to slice one in half. He exchanged a few more blows with the Fused, but the creature was skilled. Last time, in Shadesmar, Abidi had mostly ignored Adolin, which had let Adolin get in an easy hit.

Abidi wasn't flying, and the red light of his eyes pulsed, stuttered. Maybe

Adolin had nicked the gemheart in Shadesmar, making it unable to hold enough Voidlight for Lashings. Unfortunately, the Fused was a skilled enough duelist that he didn't need to fly—and Adolin, after just a short engagement, realized he didn't need to prove anything by defeating this creature.

He backed up, then gave the signal to his team. Together, they began to withdraw.

"You run from me?" Abidi said. "You refuse me the honor of the fight?"

"Some other time perhaps," Adolin said, jogging backward. Abidi twitched as if to give chase, then glanced at the line of bodies that Adolin had left, maybe realizing that letting himself be drawn too far forward without support of his own would be certain death.

Instead Abidi spun and walked away through the ranks of gathering singers. So, this Fused wasn't one of the completely crazy ones. That was disappointing, but Adolin had a battle to win. He turned and approached a wide ring of human troops who now circled the platform at about the halfway point. Spearmen at the front with large shields, pikemen behind—capable of reaching over the front-rank soldiers to attack.

The large ring gave a lot of space in the center for the singers to bring in troops—which Adolin knew would be excruciating for the defenders to watch. Still, he was pleased by how quickly the Azish had responded, joining to make this formation.

He slipped past the ranks, and there spotted Kushkam on his horse. The man was looking at the ceiling, and the oil bags suspended far above. Adolin knew immediately what he was thinking: There were a lot of singers gathering at the center of the field now. Why not retreat and drop the fire to kill thousands?

That would cost them the city. Adolin shook his head, then held up a hand, pleading. Kushkam noticed him. Adolin waited an anxious moment, then the commandant raised a tasseled spear and pointed forward. That . . . that seemed an order to hold and not retreat.

Adolin relaxed as the next part played out. The singers formed up and advanced, but they weren't nearly as skilled at holding formations as humans. Each singer—even the warforms—was stronger, but they relied on momentum, intimidation, and strength to overwhelm.

This advance worked more poorly than the initial one had. Once they drew close enough, arrows started to fall, and the Azish had the chance to put their killing field into practice. Singers tried to block them with shields, but enough arrows fell that it disrupted their lines. Adolin recognized the distinctive *kchunk* of crossbows being cocked from within the Azish lines. Those heavy Thaylen weapons took time to load and crank, but *storms* they packed a punch. He saw one bolt go clean through a singer's breastplate, shattering the carapace. The crossbowmen—shooting from the Azish ground ranks—were able to target the Regals, then fall back once the enemy arrived.

The human lines held against the following clash, and the one afterward. Adolin barely had to jump in and support with his Plate. A half hour later, it was over. The enemy wasn't defeated—not by far—but they'd obviously hoped to win this initial clash quickly. The human ring of defenders started to press inward, advancing, and—distantly—Abidi called the retreat. His forces pulled back to the control building. Then, surprisingly, they retreated into Shadesmar, one group at a time.

They're leaving? Maya asked.

Not for good, I'm sure, Adolin thought. *But they'll be safe from our archers and any attacks in Shadesmar. Likely they know they need to revise their assault plan.*

Adolin squinted and picked out Abidi the Monarch glaring in his direction.

That one is dangerous, Maya said. *I know him from before. One of their best duelists, and often a leader among them.*

He doesn't fly, Adolin thought to Maya. *Is that because I hit him in Shadesmar?*

It happens sometimes. A crack can interfere with their powers. Normally they die and are reborn. But . . .

If this one dies, Adolin realized, *he risks missing out on the remaining battle.* There would be only one more Everstorm before Dalinar's contest, and not every Fused was able to find a host every Everstorm.

Worse, Maya thought, *he'd have to give up command to a different Fused, who would get the glory of claiming the city.*

Adolin walked among painspren, guarding Azish squads who advanced to check the fallen for wounded. The enemy didn't take this chance to surge out and attack again, so for the time being the skirmish had been won.

His gut said that the enemy would lick their wounds and strategize, now that they knew they wouldn't take the city quickly. So he gave the order for his people to head out, letting the Azish keep ranks inside the dome. As he turned to go, he pointedly raised a fist to the distant archers in thanks. May would be watching with her spyglass.

That was well-handled, Maya said.

Thank you, he said back. *But I still have work to do; we can't leave the Azish feeling humiliated.*

He'd need this army unified and working together. So he hurried to put the next part into motion.

There, we will find our destiny. We cannot stop him from destroying us. It is time.

"Did I do that?" Szeth asked as Rit vanished to dust and black smoke. The fire in the air went out, and a rushing sound surrounded him.

His spren did not reply.

"What in *Damnation* was that?" Kaladin asked, dropping down beside him with Syl.

"Honorbearer," Szeth said. "Stoneward."

"I meant why did you kill her?" Kaladin said. "And since when could you use Dustbringing?"

"Skybreakers rightly fear Division," Szeth said. "My spren tells me when it is allowed. Only in special circumstances."

Your life is a special circumstance now, Szeth, it said. *You may use the power until I tell you otherwise.*

Szeth took in a deep breath, his full weight coming upon him as his Lashings ran out. He looked around the chamber, the beautiful mural consumed by the strange art of the Stoneward. Some sixty columns reached from floor to ceiling, like sinew. The floor had dropped tens of feet in the battle. The chamber was ruined.

"Something is odd here," Szeth said, turning and fixating upon Talmut's dropped Blade, which Syl had leaned down to inspect.

"Just *one* thing?" Kaladin said.

"Dalinar has mentioned the disappearance of Talmut's—or Taln's—Blade," Szeth said, walking over. He hesitated, then picked it up. "It would have been carried by Talmut when he returned from Damnation. Yet when he arrived at the Shattered Plains, his Blade had been swapped for another."

"I've heard," Kaladin said. "But—"

"My people must have retrieved it," Szeth said. "How did they find him so quickly? Why leave him with a different Blade as a ruse?"

Was he to go on a full pilgrimage, visiting each of the monasteries in turn? He rose up toward the doorway, Kaladin and Syl following, then dismissed his Blade. With Talmut's Honorblade, he cut free some of the gemstones in the wall. Kaladin did likewise, gathering Stormlight of his own. Blasphemy, perhaps, but his spren did not order him to stop. This monastery was ruined anyway.

"I know you like to be mysterious," Kaladin said, hovering beside him, "but could you *please* explain?"

The man would pester him unless it was spelled out, wouldn't he? "Rit spoke of a pilgrimage," Szeth said. "That is something from my younger years. To bear one of the Blades of the Heralds is an . . . honor. A great and terrible honor. Among my people, none but the best warriors were allowed this duty.

"As such, the training and path to become an Honorbearer was arduous. You needed to practice with each Blade, then pick one and defeat its owner in a fight using no powers. Then, with that Blade, you needed to face each of the other seven Honorbearers. We call it a pilgrimage of Truth. If you were successful, you would be allowed to join their ranks. You could try only once."

"You . . . did this?" Syl asked. "When you were younger?"

"Yes," Szeth said. "First I traveled to each monastery to train. I won the Blade of Jezrien, whom we call Yesoran. Then I went with that Blade to face my former teachers. Instead I was exiled. With it. Years ago." He landed in the doorway. "And now when I arrive home, Rit claims I am on a pilgrimage again."

"Last night Ishar told me," Kaladin said, "that he'd speak with me once your pilgrimage was finished."

Szeth nodded. "I met Ishu last week. I . . . was not emotionally strong during that encounter. Ishu said he'd killed my father, and warned that the Shin had accepted the Unmade. He implied he'd saved them."

"The people don't look very saved to me," Kaladin said, landing beside him as they started back down the path.

"I worry that the Herald is unreliable," Szeth said. "I do not know that we can trust what he said."

"He claims to be the Almighty," Kaladin said. "And he perpetuated a war for years in southern Makabak. You're right; anything he says is going to be unreliable."

Szeth held up Talmut's Honorblade as he descended the path. "Our Sacred Truth is that the enemy would return, and we would need to fight them with the Honorblades. One at each monastery . . ."

"So . . . we have to retrace the path you took as a youth?" Syl said. "Is that how we cleanse your homeland?"

"It is a start," Szeth said. "A direction."

"I don't like it," Kaladin said, arms folded, hovering along out over the cliff. Of course he had to complain. "We're being manipulated—and by someone who is obviously delusional."

"And what would you do instead?" Szeth asked him. "I must at least visit another monastery to investigate. Perhaps the other shamans will speak to me, or perhaps they will attack me. Either action will give us more information."

"Szeth," Kaladin said, taking him by the arm. "What if we went straight to the Bondsmith monastery? Would Ishar be there?"

"What do you think?" Szeth asked. "You just said he's unreliable. If we ignore his instructions, would he simply appear and answer your questions?"

Kaladin thought a moment, then gave the answer he plainly didn't like. "No," he admitted. "He was quite explicit—he wants you to complete your quest, and he wants me to help you. If we're going to hunt him down, we'll at least need more information on what is happening."

"You came here to help Ishu-son-God see clearly," Szeth said. "I think showing you are earnestly helping will do a great deal. Come."

Kaladin hovered in place, studying Szeth. The Windrunner was annoying, but smart. Perhaps that was why he was annoying. "I'm worried," Kaladin said. "I'm supposed to return with help for Dalinar, but . . . but Wit said I won't be able to. Not in time, surely. Maybe not at all . . ." He looked behind him at the monastery. "There's power here, of a type I haven't ever seen . . ."

"And?" Szeth asked.

". . . And you're probably right. Seeing if the other Honorbearers will talk to us is the best way to proceed." He sighed. "How close is the next monastery?"

"Not too far," Szeth said. "It would take a few days walking, but we can use some Stormlight and arrive tomorrow."

With a nod, Kaladin joined him along with Syl, walking back down the pathway. Soon they heard voices.

People from the encampment had left the buildings and were gathering in the sunlight.

⁂

Adolin gave an excited leap as he left the dome. He soared some ten feet before slamming to the ground, meeting his soldiers, who had formed up outside following the battle.

His father would have given a fine speech. Adolin ripped his helmet off, held it high in one hand with his Shardblade in the other, and bellowed a vibrant yell of triumph, exploding with gloryspren. His soldiers shouted their enthusiasm in a roar, raising weapons.

"Colot!" Adolin said. "How many fallen do we need to mourn today?"

"Six wounded, sir," Colot called back. "None dead among our men."

None? The Azish had certainly lost some, but to have his men fight without dying? Adolin let out another shout, mirrored by his soldiers. This felt *good.* He went among them, letting them bang their fists on his Plate, as he'd done with other troops before life had become so complicated and his father's rules so strict.

Morale wasn't just about official commendations or even about increased rations or pay after a victory. It was about the soldiers knowing that Adolin personally was proud of them. How would they know that if they couldn't see him?

I am proud, Maya said. *I want to join.*

Feel like letting others carry you? he asked.

Yes, she said, sounding surprised. *The sword. I will make it dull. Let them carry it.*

Most people never had the chance to hold a Shardblade. So Adolin picked out the Thaylen man from earlier, then summoned Maya and held her out.

The entire group grew hushed, their eyes opening wide.

"The Blade remains bonded to me," Adolin said, "but she wishes to join your celebrations. Hold her high! I'm going to go talk to the emperor. I'll summon the sword back when I need it." He let the man reverently hold Maya, then raise her high with a shout.

Adolin slipped out from among them. He admittedly was a *tad* anxious letting go of Maya—but it felt meaningful. Colot jogged up beside him as he walked away. "I've never seen a Shardbearer act like this," he said. "Aren't you afraid someone will steal it?"

"It's basically impossible without killing me. Besides, these men were brave enough to volunteer for an isolated and risky deployment. They're our best, Colot." He put an armored hand on the man's shoulder. "*You* are our best, my friend. You executed those maneuvers *perfectly.*"

"Well, I'm glad someone wants me," he said.

"Those Windrunners will someday realize what they missed out on," Adolin said, then nodded toward the crowd. "Who is that Thaylen fellow?"

"One of the most enthusiastic of the foreign volunteers," Colot said. "Name is Hmask. He's got skill, so I used him to plug a hole in your personal guard. He seems specifically loyal to you for some reason, but he doesn't speak a lick of Alethi so I haven't been able to ask."

"I don't recognize him," Adolin said. "Get him a uniform, and formally induct him into the Cobalt Guard. He stared down a Heavenly One and kept his wits."

"It will be done," Colot said, then gestured toward the emperor—who was still seated on a podium set up by his palanquin. An ornate, if portable, throne. "They tried to move him once the fighting started, and I think he refused. Also, I believe that Kushkam will give you trouble. He was livid about how things played out."

Colot pointed toward the beefy Azish commandant, who was approaching the emperor with a bowed back and a shamed posture.

"I think you might be wrong about that," Adolin said. "Go and make sure I didn't accidentally start a riot by letting them hold the sword—and have my soldiers set up my tent in a spot near our barracks. Oh, and make sure the worst of the Azish wounded get healing from May's budding Radiant ward. I'll handle Kushkam."

"Better you than me," Colot said, with a quick salute before trotting off.

Adolin was still tailed by several scribes and two bodyguards, but he was used to that sort of thing. He clomped up to Yanagawn and his attendants, helm under his arm, in time to catch Kushkam giving a report.

". . . will see that the field inside is covered in debris, as Kholin suggested," the commandant was saying toward Noura, his head bowed as he knelt before the emperor, his hand outstretched in a penitent way—shamespren falling like flower petals around it. "I understand now that our assault tactics were faulty." He glanced toward Adolin, then bowed his head lower. "In addition, I must offer—"

"May I interrupt?" Adolin asked, giving a quick bow to the emperor. "If it's all right?"

"Please," Yanagawn said, sitting up in his seat. "What is your perspective, Adolin?"

"I'm impressed," Adolin said. "You have a fantastic military here, Excellency."

Kushkam glanced at him, frowning.

"By our reports, we wonder if that statement is true," Noura said, standing behind the Prime's seat, decked out in robes that looked far too hot, even if the sun was close to setting by now. "Our lines bowed immediately and failed to anticipate enemy maneuvers, requiring your salvation."

"Pardon, Noura," Adolin said. "But I'm a *Shardbearer.* Jumping into the action when things go wrong is my storming job." He turned and pointed to an Azish company that had left the dome to lick its wounds while others filled in to stand watch. "I don't know how much direct battlefield observation you've done, but *any* plan can fall apart on *any* battlefield.

"The commandant's strategy didn't work—but *when* it didn't, he and his armies quickly reassessed. They fell in to the next best plan, and held. A well-executed pivot like that is one of the single best hallmarks of a disciplined and well-trained military."

"One might question his skill if he made such a big mistake," Noura pressed. "You were right and he was wrong."

"And on other battlefields, *I've* been wrong," Adolin said. "Look, Kushkam isn't used to how Fused and Regals fight, and that got us into trouble today. But he adapted. Moreover, my own officers all thought Kushkam's plan would be effective. He's neither a bad officer nor a bad tactician. He made one incorrect call, but then fixed it. I'm honored to be able to serve with him and his troops."

To his relief, a lone sincerityspren—like opening blue fronds—appeared next to him, giving testament to the fact that he genuinely believed what he was saying. They all regarded it silently, then Kushkam slowly climbed to his feet.

"Well," the emperor said, "I suppose we should celebrate, if not in such a . . . boisterous manner as your troops, Adolin. The day is won."

"They will be back," Kushkam said, gazing directly at Noura. "Vizier, they might try to push through again immediately, assuming that we will be resting."

"Kushkam is correct," Adolin said. "They have an army of fresh troops waiting for battle. Their blitz attack having failed, they'll likely realize their best move now is to try to tire us out."

"Agreed," Kushkam said. "They will regroup, give new orders, and plan how to wear us down—run us out of defenders and break through. The next few days will be grueling."

"I have some thoughts on how to approach that, Commandant," Adolin said. "If you'd like to hear them."

"I think I would," he said, then bowed to the emperor, who waved that he could withdraw.

Before joining him, Adolin stepped closer to Yanagawn. "Hey," he said softly. "Hear you didn't leave when they tried to make you."

"Yeah," Yanagawn said, then sat up a little straighter, as if remembering not to slouch. "I mean, indeed, I thought it best to maintain a strong presence here—to indicate faith in the troops." He smiled at Adolin. "And . . . sometimes I want to be part of events."

"I'll be camping out here on this square, near where my men are barracked. Need to be close, as the enemy will attack at night to test us. Want to do the same?"

Yanagawn blinked. "You're . . . inviting me to a *campout*?"

"We call them bivouacs in the military," Adolin replied, with a grin.

"There should be some time between the fights. I could give you a little training. Let you swing a Shardblade, practice wearing Plate. You should know how to use it, since you own several sets yourself."

Adolin was pretty sure an emperor wasn't supposed to gawk like that, jaw gaping, eyes alight. He recovered a moment later, then glanced at Noura.

"I wouldn't recommend it," she said carefully. "You are not like an Eastern ruler. You aren't needed on the front lines. Your role is to inspire and provide leadership."

"We won't put him on the front lines, Noura," Adolin said, "not unless it becomes absolutely necessary. But he's about the age I was when I tried winning my own Blade in a duel."

"It's different," she said. "You didn't represent an entire empire. As long as the emperor is on his throne, Azimir stands. Without him, we are in chaos."

"Yes," Adolin said, "but this is the storming *end.* If the enemy wins this city, there won't *be* an empire. You understand that, right?"

She hesitated. "And what good is one more teenager on the battle lines?" she finally asked.

"Depends," Adolin said. "If that teenager is the emperor himself, coming to prove to the troops precisely how vital their defense is? It could be the most important thing he ever does." He looked to Yanagawn. "There are times when I saw Gavilar step onto the field, and every eye turned toward him. He didn't need to raise a Blade, but when the men knew he was there—that he was committed—it changed the way they fought. It's not your way, but it might be worth trying."

"I'll do it," Yanagawn said, keeping his gaze directed at Adolin as Noura released a soft sigh. "Will you teach me that game you mentioned?"

"Towers?" Adolin said. "Absolutely." He nodded and withdrew, jogging up to Kushkam, who was waiting nearby. They began walking back toward the bulk of the men, trailed by Adolin's attendants—who kept far enough behind to let them speak in private.

"What did I do wrong?" Kushkam asked in a low voice. "Why did the line nearly break? I thought the strategy was so sound."

"The enemy has, by my best count, around two hundred Regals," Adolin said. "I think I might have killed around ten today, plus one—of maybe ten—Fused, who might not be able to be reborn in time to rejoin the fight. Regardless, Kushkam, you assumed a few of your soldiers were a match for a few of theirs. Forming up close to the control room like you did let them leverage only their strongest soldiers against ours."

He groaned softly. "It really *was* a Stuko Stem."

"Afraid so."

"I feel so stupid."

"If it means anything," Adolin said, "I was being honest earlier—my officers agreed with your decision, and they *have* fought Fused. But it's hard to give up what feels like an advantageous position."

"So what we *should* do," he said, "is what your army demonstrated. We form solid pike walls farther back, and force them to come to us—make them spread their Regals out, so they can't pit a hundred of them against a hundred humans. They have to instead pit a hundred Regals plus nine hundred regular soldiers against a thousand of mine."

"Exactly," Adolin said. "Plus, you will have archer support, and the time—during their advance—to position our Shardbearers wherever the enemy sends most of their elite troops. And anything that slows their advance gives us more time to try to bring Regals down from a distance."

"Hence the suggestion that we throw furniture in the way," Kushkam said. "I still feel like a failure. Did you . . . hear they took that imperial Soulcaster?"

"Storms, no," Adolin said. "I was distracted by fighting."

"A flying Fused grabbed him and towed him to the portal while we were first regrouping."

Adolin took a deep breath. "Poor man."

"He was almost gone to the Soulcaster disease," Kushkam said. "But I hate to have caused this. I . . ." He sighed. "I was too intimidated by an Alethi coming to take over my city. I apologize."

"As do I," Adolin said. "I put you on the spot earlier by offering suggestions in front of the emperor—ones you didn't have time to consider. That forced you to make a decision immediately. I should have known better, and come to you in private to explain my concerns."

Kushkam grunted. "They warned me about you."

"They?"

"Some of my men," he said, stopping and turning to face Adolin, who was taller by an inch or two—but not nearly so bulky. Kushkam looked him up and down with one eye, the other a tattooed hole. "They said you'd win me over. I said that you were a fop, a dandy who was more interested in clothing and duels than warfare."

"I think, actually," Adolin said, "both of you were right. I'd much, *much* rather be choosing tomorrow's wardrobe than be here killing. You?"

Kushkam waited an uncomfortably long moment. Then he smiled, holding out his hand. "Absolutely."

With relief, Adolin took his hand.

"You like to use first names," Kushkam said. "I'm Zarb, Adolin. I appreciate what you did today. You saved lives."

"It's why I'm here," Adolin said. "I promise."

"You should be in command."

"Respectfully, no," Adolin said. "I have more experience fighting the singers, but you know your troops and this city. Beyond that, when this is over, I get to go back to Urithiru. *You* have to live with what we do here. You need to lead, Zarb. I promise I'll do my best not to undermine you any further—but also to make it *very* clear when I disagree."

"Remarkable," the man said, shaking his head. "You're really the son of the Blackthorn?"

Adolin didn't reply. Because while yes, he was Dalinar's son . . . he wasn't always sure if he was the son of the Blackthorn.

Kushkam's eyes grew distant as he gazed at the dome. "I'd hoped," he said quietly, "to win decisively today—to kill hundreds while they tried to push through. I understand your strategy now, and agree . . . but Adolin, if we have to field pike walls and hold . . ."

"It will get brutal," Adolin agreed softly. "We'll have an advantage as the defender, but they can afford to lose four to every one they kill."

"These soldiers are good men," Kushkam said. "Our best. They will fight, and they will hold, but . . . we're looking at high casualties until the main army arrives. I wish you hadn't been right."

"So do I, Zarb," Adolin said.

"My officers and I are setting up our tents over in that area," Kushkam said, pointing. "I want to be near the fighting, and have refused better accommodations farther inside the city. Would you dine with us this evening, Adolin? I want you to meet my command staff. If they get to know you, it may help keep them from resenting you."

"I'd be honored," Adolin said. "Thank you. Let me make sure my men are properly quartered, and I'll join you in . . . say, an hour?"

"Excellent," he said, then glanced at the dome again, seeming reserved. Finally, he marched toward the pavilions being erected.

Adolin took a deep breath. Winning over the Azish command structure should have felt fantastic, and it did, but . . .

It was going to be brutal. He'd saved the day, but worse ones were coming. Far worse.

You feel sad, Maya said. *Uncertain.*

"Just still finding my place in all of this. I'll figure it out. I *will* protect this city."

I'm worried about the way you say things like that, Adolin.

"Just being confident."

And it doesn't reach deeper?

He wasn't certain. He took a seat at the edge of the square, on a wall by a fountain. He looked over the enormous bronze dome, reflecting the light of a setting sun.

"I want to be enough," he said. "I'm nothing more than a man with a sword and armor. That used to be enough." Once, he'd been the best. Now that didn't matter.

I feel that's not *who you are, Adolin,* she said. *But storms, I can't say. I know you, but I don't* know *you.*

He nodded, understanding the meaning. They had been with each other for years, but only now could interact.

"I'm worried about what Kushkam said," he said softly. "My strategy is sound, but the enemy is going to attack again and again. We're going to lose so many."

Only three days of fighting. Until the reinforcements.

"And if they don't come?" Adolin asked. "Or if the enemy gets more Regals?"

You . . . might be right to worry about that. I saw some Heavenly Ones leave the group earlier—two of them, leaving them with seven, now that you killed one. Those two could be going to fetch help, since the initial attack was turned back.

He took another deep breath.

It used to be enough. *He* used to be enough. Storms, he missed Shallan already. Her voice always helped.

He hoped she was safe, wherever she was.

He stood and walked toward the others, trying to think of something more he could do here. As he drew closer, he saw soldiers holding his sword in a reverent posture. Colot was making sure there was no riot, making them take turns. But seeing this, Adolin couldn't help imagining what would happen to his troops if a legitimate force of Fused were brought in. Regals were trouble enough; if there were Deepest Ones in this army, they could swim out through the stones to flank his people. A single Magnified One, and then a single Husked One, had given *Kaladin* trouble.

And even aside from Fused . . . he was still looking at high casualties over the next few days. That was why the Mink had been so uncertain about this defense. Adolin couldn't help imagining his troops getting slaughtered. Couldn't help remembering the cries from his troops in Kholinar, when he'd left them.

He needed an edge. Something to help.

"Do you remember," he said, thinking back to a few days ago, "those spren who left Lasting Integrity right as we did?" When those honorspren objectors had abandoned the fortress, he had met the eyes of a few. They'd been among those who had taken up the call, *Honor is not dead . . .*

I do, Maya said.

"I wonder," Adolin said, "if we could . . . I don't know, get them to come and lend us their powers or something . . ."

It felt foolish when he said it. What could they do here? Maya, however, grew excited.

I can talk now, Adolin. I feel better. I can persuade them! I could go to them.

"Could you?"

I can move with the beads. All of us deadeyes do it. I think . . . I think this could work! Even if it takes a few days, I might be able to get back here in time!

Huh. "How confident are you?"

Reasonably confident.

Well . . . that was interesting. Now that she was speaking more, perhaps she *could* persuade the honorspren. He could certainly use some more Radiants.

"The timing doesn't seem like it will work," he said, thinking of how long it took to bond and train a Radiant.

I can make it work. If you trust me.

"Always," Adolin said.

But . . . to do this . . . I'd have to go.

Go. He realized what she was saying. She'd slip away in Shadesmar, into the bead ocean. On a battlefield like this, he didn't *need* a Blade. Blades were excellent for duels, but nothing beat the power of Plate when fighting multiple foes. Azimir had some Shardhammers—large conventional weapons designed to be swung by a person in Plate. He could use one of those, and be nearly as effective. But still . . .

He felt Maya's emotions, so eager, so *certain.* She seemed completely confident she could bring him those honorspren to help against the Fused. She wanted to do it so badly, and he'd sworn to himself that she wasn't his. He didn't decide for her.

"I support," he found himself saying, "whatever decision you make."

I will go, she said, sounding eager. *Try not to summon me. That will start my journey over. Only if you are in dire need.*

"I understand," he said.

And the sword, in May Aladar's hands, vanished of its own accord. *Storms,* Adolin thought as he felt Maya immediately start to grow distant. How many men had given up their Shardblade like that? He thought she would come back, but . . .

All of the Radiants did it once, he thought. *And there was one other. My father.*

Adolin considered that, filled with complex emotions, as he ran to check on his troops. After that, he spent the evening doing his best to win over Kushkam's officers—all the while worried about Maya. And all the while confident that he'd made the right choice—because it was the decision his heart demanded.

⁂

Kaladin glanced over his shoulder as he hiked with Szeth down toward the encampment. "Syl," he whispered, "have you ever seen a Stoneward with that kind of strength?"

"No," she replied, hovering beside him. "But I didn't live during the days of the Heralds."

"What was powering her?" Kaladin said. "She didn't drain a single gemstone in the wall—and when I examined the clothing she left after Szeth burned the corpse away, I found no spheres or gems."

Syl shook her head, looking as troubled as he felt.

"Storms," Kaladin said, finally prying his eyes away from the monastery. "If that's what a fully oathed Stoneward can do, it makes me wonder what I'm missing about *our* powers."

I don't think it was that impressive, Nightblood said in his hand.

"She made the stone flow like water," Kaladin said.

Water flows like water all the time, and it's super stupid. Have you tried *talking to it?*

"He has a point," Syl said to Kaladin. "Water does tend to be pretty dumb. Even for something inanimate. No offense, sword."

Glad to hear that. Regardless, that sword isn't so great. I could do better, I'm sure.

"That's an Honorblade," Kaladin said. "It grants the bearer the Surges of a Stoneward—Radiant abilities, unbound by oaths . . ."

I could learn that, the sword said. *I'm super good at being a sword. Besides, what's more interesting than making stone act like water? Destroying it. That's what.*

"Szeth did a pretty good job of that too," Kaladin noted. "Looks like he's figured out Division at last."

Nightblood gave a *humph.*

Together, they followed Szeth as he stepped up to the main camp on the ridge, where people were emerging from their buildings. There were more of them than Kaladin had expected—thousands. They must have been packed into those barracks. They wore unkempt clothing. Not ripped or frayed, really, but they obviously hadn't been washed in some time. Stained by sweat and crem. Or . . . well, dirt.

Many gazed up at the sky, blinking. Several approached Szeth with awe, whispering, pointing at the Honorblade.

"What are they saying?" Kaladin asked.

"They're thanking him," Syl said. "I think the death of that woman must have freed them somehow. Look how different they seem."

"Like they've just woken up," Kaladin agreed.

More and more people gathered around Szeth, reaching toward him—

which made him step back, alert, Honorblade clutched as if he expected them to take it. Their postures were universally reverent, but his eyes began to dart from side to side. He was feeling boxed in.

Kaladin moved up quickly to intervene, coming in wide so Szeth could see him and not get spooked. "Hey," Kaladin said. "Hey, you okay?"

"What do they want of me?" Szeth said. "Why are they acting like this?"

"Thankful?" Kaladin asked. "You saved them."

"I kill," Szeth said. "I subtract. I destroy. I am to be reviled. I . . ."

Kaladin carefully put his hand on Szeth's shoulder and gestured to the people. Nearby, some of them were laughing, clutching family members, while others had fallen to their knees and were staring at the sky.

"It's all right, Szeth," Kaladin said. "It's all right."

Timid, Szeth relaxed, letting some of the people thank him. Kaladin didn't understand the words, but he'd seen those postures before, those eyes holding back tears. He'd been there. Szeth, it appeared, never had. He took the kindness with an air of bemusement.

Syl stepped up and translated. "That one in the once-colorful robes seems to be their leader. He's bowing to Szeth."

"It's not right," Szeth said in Alethi. "This is the *Farmer.* Son of the man I used to know. He doesn't recognize me, but he is far above me. He . . . he shouldn't be *grateful.*"

Still, Szeth bore it. As he turned to Kaladin and Syl at the end, he wiped tears from the corners of his eyes. "I . . . I do not know how to respond. Please forgive me."

"This is what it's about, Szeth," Kaladin said.

"It?"

"What we do," Kaladin said. "Being a watcher at the rim? This is *why.* My father never understood, and I suspect your people never did either. You can. *This* is what we fight for. Those looks. Those tears. That joy. Our duty has a cost, as you said—we are both proof of that. But if there's a difference between us, it's this: I know the why."

"I thought I knew why," Szeth whispered.

"Service to the law?"

"To an ideal."

"Ideals are dead things," Kaladin said, "unless they have people behind them. Laws exist not for themselves, but for those they serve."

"Perhaps," Szeth said, then took a deep breath and dried his eyes. "Did you see the woman I killed vanish?"

"Yeah," Kaladin said. "I thought you did that."

"I do not know for certain," Szeth replied. "This is the first time I have been allowed Division. I may be . . . unpracticed with it, since my days training as a young man. Before she died though, she said something that makes me consider."

Syl frowned. "What was it she said?"

"Just that . . . my family waited for me. The other Honorbearers, it seems."

Kaladin looked back over the people, and felt the wind blow across him—something he couldn't remember feeling since they'd arrived at the camp.

It whispered to him. *We need you.*

"I . . . I believe you," he whispered back. "There's something for me here. Not as important as the battle my friends fight in, but still relevant."

No, not as *important,* the Wind said. *More important. Far, far more important . . .*

"Kaladin?" Szeth asked. "What are you saying?"

"I'm talking to the Wind, Szeth. She wants me here. Which is the next monastery?"

"Willshaper," he said, pointing into the distance. "Shall we begin?"

Kaladin nodded, feeling fully invested in this mission for the first time since Dalinar had given him the order.

THE END OF

Day Three

Ayabiza
Bondsmith
Windrunner
Truthwatcher
Skybreaker
Lightweaver
Edgedancer
Dustbringer
Elsecaller
Mokdown
Willshaper
Koring
Clearmount
Stoneward
You wouldn't believe what I had to do to fetch this one-of-a-kind map of the monasteries. I hope news of the debacle doesn't reach you before I can relate my side of the story. —Nazh

INTERLUDES

BAXIL • ODIUM

Baxil trod the streets of Azimir unseen. Every inch of him, save his eyes, was wrapped in tight crimson cloths, the tied-off tails of which sometimes escaped his cloak and waved in the wind of an unknown Current. Hand on his kattar, slid into its sheath at his side, he watched for anyone in the crowd who noticed him.

Nothing so far. Good.

This was a city haphazardly prepared for war. Baxil strolled through the Alethi camp, which had taken the place of the Grand Market. The soldiers camped in concentric rings that he was certain they thought were evenly spaced smooth curves. The Azish would have chalked outlines of pathways to make sure. He allowed himself a smile, remembering days when he'd been that persnickety.

Not a soul saw him. These days, people could only see Baxil if they were looking for him. And he could only touch them if they were trying to kill him.

He left the Alethi camp, and for old times' sake whispered a prayer to the Prime Kadasix. *If you could see that I get what I deserve, I would appreciate it. Thanks.*

Azimir was famed for its tea shops, which filled the same niche that winehouses did in the East. By this point, Baxil had sampled a wide variety of both, and had his favorites. Here in Azimir, one shop in particular was known for its discretion. They had instructions to watch for him, so as he entered, the bouncer by the door leapt to his feet.

"Master Crimson," he said. "We got your note."

"As well you did," Baxil said, "or we might not be able to have this conversation. He's here?"

"He is, master," the bouncer said, ushering him farther in. "And . . . he's an odd one."

"You don't know the half of it, Ulak," Baxil said, tipping him a few spheres, which became real as he dropped them. "See that we're not interrupted."

Baxil entered the private room, separated from the rest by hanging beads, and walked through an invisible cloud of incense to approach the luxurious table, one of the most exclusive in the city. There, Axies the Collector was seated, passing the time by hitting his hand with a small hammer.

"Surely you have painspren by now," Baxil said, sliding into the booth across from the Aimian. Axies preferred to wear little in the way of clothing, in part because he kept his notes on his skin in the form of tattoos—an entire book secured in a place where he would never lose it. Like all of his kind, he could change the color of any part of his skin at will.

"I have painspren, yes, of course," Axies said. "I've had them for millennia, Crimson Memory. But you see, we are in the builders' quarter of the city—where men frequently hammer. There is a curious report from a hundred and fifty-two years ago of a peculiar spren drawn to the pain of men who have hit their fingers with a hammer while aiming for a nail. If one were to search for that specific spren, this would be the place."

"And you believe this report?" Baxil asked.

"Hardly," Axies said. "It was almost certainly a joke."

He hit his hand with the hammer, then winced, tears leaking from the corners of his eyes.

"Tell me honestly," Baxil said, leaning forward. "You enjoy the punishment, don't you."

"What kind of deviant would *enjoy* this?" Axies said. Then hit his thumb square on with the hammer.

"Then why?"

"Pain is fleeting. The thrill of accomplishment is eternal." *Smack.* "Yes . . . almost certainly a joke."

"If the Prime Kadasix should allow," Baxil said, relaxing on his bench, resting one arm along the top, "I should someday like to understand you."

"At least I," Axies said as their cups arrived, "can taste my tea." He took a sip from his, then eyed Baxil from over the rim.

Baxil sighed—but did as expected. He held his hand out over the tea, feeling the heat of the steam, and . . . imagined. People throughout the teahouse enjoyed their drinks. Especially the stark black jaramon tea, as they'd provided for him. Bitter, sharp, like drinking the venom of something aggressive—this was tea that fought back.

Such things had a life of sorts. Not the individual cups so much as the *concept* of tea. With this many people thinking about it, savoring it, complaining about it . . . Baxil could taste it, and remember what it had been like to drink. During a time that seemed so distant, yet so familiar all at once. Before his blessing, and before his curse.

Today, a great number of people thinking about the same thing let him feel the bitter tea on his tongue as he sat with his hand over the cup.

"You're *sure* you're not a spren?" Axies asked. "I'm putting you in the appendix regardless, you realize."

Baxil smiled. "You brought my bandages?"

Axies placed them on the tabletop. Red wraps prepared in the most special of ways, as Baxil needed. The key to his survival. In turn, he placed a gemstone on the table. He was not a spren, but they did find him fascinating.

Axies snatched it up and peered at the little spren inside. "Better to find them in the wild," he mumbled, "but this will have to do. Little friend, how elusive you've proven . . ."

Baxil took the bandages and slid them into the pocket of his cloak, then rose from his seat.

"She's here in Azimir, by the way," Axies noted.

"She?"

"Your old employer," he said. "The Herald."

Shalash. He'd known her only as "mistress," during another life. Had been rather infatuated with her . . . maybe never stopped.

"How?" he asked. "I thought she was at the tower city."

"No, she went with the Alethi army on campaign," Axies said, still inspecting his gemstone prize. "I think their king wanted to interview her—at least, that's the impression I got when I chatted with her. They took the other one too, the big fellow, to the fight for Emul. They're both back now though, tucked away in an Azish hospital. I believe the king has mostly forgotten about her."

Here. In the hospital? He could . . . go see her.

Baxil pulled his cloak tight. No. Not like this. "Best get out of the city, Axies," he said. "I think dark times are coming to Azimir in the days ahead."

"Yes . . ." Axies said. "I concur."

Axies would stay, of course, hunting the rare spren of enraged passions during war. Well, the Aimian had proven resilient. While Baxil himself . . . always felt he was one calm breeze away from dissipating. Like smoke from a dead fire. So, one hand on his kattar, he left a few spheres on the table as payment and continued on his quest.

Hoping that someday, he might be able to enjoy the simple pleasure of sipping tea again.

Taravangian, the god divided, decided to let each side of him rule for a short time in turn. First, the intellect.

He found himself more capable, more balanced in this regard as a god. He remembered days of mortality feeling cold indifference to the needs of people—and that terrible callousness now troubled him. Such ruthlessness was not actually logical, for it ignored social consequences. Allowing his intellect to reign was not about complete alienation of emotion, but rather about *deciding* based on reason, while *feeling* emotion. To that end, he looked at what he was doing, and found . . .

That Cultivation had a point in arguing for him to end the war early—there was good logic in potentially going to Dalinar and the other monarchs, then accepting a deal that restored Alethkar without need for a contest of champions. For one, not pressing the war was safest for Odium personally. He was a new god, and mistakes now could be dangerous, particularly if those powerful forces off-planet decided he was too much of a threat.

He had millennia to plan, to decide how to conquer the cosmere as he wished. He studied the permutations, his own conclusions, and the goals he'd set out for himself as a mortal, and . . .

No. Working through it in a thousand different ways, he could *not* justify ending the war. He was so likely to win, and the offworld forces were highly unlikely to intervene. Plus, there was an element that Cultivation had not been able to fully understand. Odium's power did not *want* an end to the war.

It wanted to fight, and to rage, and it was *livid* that his predecessor had let himself get trapped into this contest where the fighting ended. To go down a path of peace had its own terrible danger, especially since there was another being that the power of Odium *preferred* over Taravangian.

Her name was Ba-Ado-Mishram, and if Taravangian was not cautious, the power might leave him for her, as it had left Rayse for him.

So, carefully, he fed emotion to the power. He promised it conquests in the sky, worlds to bend to their will—passion, fury, anger, and pain. All the most powerful emotions that it desired. It fed on that, simmering, while he considered his plans. They were good. Even excellent. He had a real and legitimate chance at solidifying the entire world beneath his reign.

As a test, he showed the power that if it raged too much, it would lose what it wanted. Extinction of humankind would stop the anger, the rage. He showed it that it would need to learn to fuel itself with more than anger.

The power refused to accept that or change. It had given birth to the Thrill, the grand spren who represented a lust for battle, because it loved the emotions of war. It did not accept that too much emotion could *ever* be a bad thing.

Curious. The power could not change, or would not. Though it *should* have been all emotions—and his predecessor had insisted that was his purview—the power did not like subtle emotions. It liked loud ones. The passion of fiery lust, yes. But genuine love? Things such as love and contentment felt like the purview of other gods. They had taken some slices of its . . . portfolio, so to speak, during the Shattering.

It liked anger most of all. Anger could simmer when passion gave out. Anger could rule a person longer than any lust. Anger was true fire.

More information. Good. The more he explored his new capacities, the more he understood. For Taravangian *could* learn, even if the power refused. He pondered further, with vast resources of mind. His faculties were such that they made his most intelligent days as a mortal seem . . .

Well, actually, those had a *hint* of divinity to them. A respectable level, for a human.

Still, he was so much more now. Yes, he needed war, for the logical decision *was* to seek a cosmere unified behind one god. The risks of enacting his plans were not too great. He had set up his confrontation with Dalinar so that he won regardless of what happened. He was confident in his ability to win the vast majority of Roshar.

He would be trapped here, but he could keep feeding the power promises of the conquest to keep it happy. So how, according to intellect, did he best prepare?

He needed a command staff.

People of great capacity, and ones he could trust—or rather, ones he could predict so he would know what would cause their failures or betrayals. El, the singer, was a first step. Taravangian had plans for that one in coming decades. He needed others. Specifically, those who would live long enough to see his plans enacted.

Therefore, he appeared at Kharbranth. It was time to speak with Dova.

Remaining invisible, he first walked the beautiful, dimly lit hallways of the Palanaeum. Books, a weight of information gathered meticulously by his ancestors, each a work of art. This was humankind at its best, standing against the tides of darkness with ink and pen. He breathed it in, and felt the many words in here. Though minuscule compared to his knowledge, they represented something grand.

Was he being too emotional, enjoying this? No, it was logical to admit that he—a god of emotions—needed to feel. Again, it was not rejection of emotion that defined intellect, but instead ruling emotion with that intellect. So he slowed time for himself—spending nine thousand heartbeats in the space of a few minutes to bask in the wonderful sense of place a grand library provided.

That done, he appeared in Dova's offices on the seventh floor down. Dova—Battah the Herald—had been an older woman when joining the Oathpact, and had remained that age for seven thousand years now. Bald—as she enjoyed the way that imitating an ardent made most ignore her—she was writing softly at her desk in a dark room, surrounded by some of the most valuable items in the entire world. Priceless paintings, jeweled vases, bars of aluminum.

He stepped up, and divinely absorbed the contents of her stacks of papers without needing to touch them.

"While I did intend for you to rule from the shadows, old friend," he said, manifesting in a form standing behind her, "I *do* wish you'd *try* to let my daughter have a say now and then. She needs to learn to be a queen."

Dova froze. She spun her chair, and while it was not particularly logical to enjoy her look of utter shock, he did it anyway.

"Hell," she said. "You're the new Odium."

He spread his hands to the sides, palms out. "Would you like to worship me?"

"I'd like to be *paid,* you old rat," she said, leaning back in her chair, facing him and crossing one ankle over the other knee. "If I'd known how much trouble it would be to keep your kingdom from falling apart, I'd have demanded so much more."

"Dova," he said, "you're immortal, and fantastically rich already. Why do you need money?"

"Do you have any idea the power of compound interest?" she said. "The system breaks *entirely* when you can wait it out for a hundred years."

Taravangian smiled. She was, for obvious reasons, the most interesting member of the Diagram. Why would a Herald of the Almighty be so . . . crassly mercenary? The answer proved to be one he'd never exactly understood when alive. Each of these Heralds was suffering under a cloud of mind and soul, and this was how hers manifested. The wise counselor, known for her wisdom for millennia, had become corrupt.

He honestly wasn't certain he could ever name her friend. Dova had no permanent allegiances. She was, however, a genuine genius—for a mortal. And she could be bribed quite effectively. So long as you knew you could offer the most, she would always be loyal. What value would it be to have a Herald serving him, especially if she returned and went among them? It was something his predecessor had never tried.

"I have need of your skill," Taravangian said. "Specifically, the art with crystal spikes you have been practicing. I believe that you can restore sight to the blind?"

"After a fashion, and with a great cost. They will never truly see again."

"But they *will* sense Investiture?"

"Yes." She spun her pen in her fingers. "A god needs nothing, and you could figure out my crystal spikes on your own. You simply want to begin integrating me into your new organization, don't you?"

"Why should I reproduce what you have learned so well? It's more than just wanting to make use of you, Dova. It's that I recognize a valuable tool when one is presented to me."

"Well, I believe you *are* technically now the embodiment of everything I was created to fight against. Even with the Oathpact broken and Ishar doing whatever the hell it is he's doing, I am a Herald of Honor. Working for Odium . . ." She clicked her tongue. "How unseemly would that be?"

He smiled at her.

She smiled back.

"The pay will be excellent?" she asked.

"Beyond excellent." He paused for effect. "I can likely get you a planet eventually. A small one, at least. I'll try to find a way to get you off Roshar to visit it."

She hesitated, her eyes widening, inspecting him to see if he was serious. He was. Today, levity was mostly a social construct to him.

"I," Dova said, rising, "will gather my things immediately."

DAY FOUR

DALINAR • SHALLAN •
KALADIN • SZETH • NAVANI •
ADOLIN • SIGZIL

Now, it stands to the accountability of reason that orders of Radiants, greatly interposed from common nature by their various oaths, should have had some controversions one to another.

—From *Words of Radiance*, chapter 40, page 1

Dalinar felt warm.

As if he'd slipped into a bath, a touch warmer than was comfortable at first, but then his heat blended with it—and it became perfect. Enveloping. Safe.

So long as he kept his eyes closed.

When he made the mistake of peeking, chaos reigned, trying to tear him from the warmth. Suddenly he was a child with his grandfather, bringing water to the practice grounds in an old, dusty part of Alethkar.

In a flash it was his wedding night with Evi, where he performed inadequately in a drunken stupor.

Then he was the man he'd been just a year ago, getting the report that Elhokar was dead. A son, sure as his own, lost to the Halls forever.

Cultivation had said he needed to see the past, and so he traveled it—but this was too many versions of himself to contain. So he closed his eyes.

And floated in warmth.

He vaguely remembered opening the perpendicularity in Urithiru with Navani. Something had . . . had gone wrong. His anchor had been severed; he'd been pulled in without a way home.

That was all right. He'd *always* been here, and *should* remain here. What were worries compared to this beautiful sense of peace? Here, nothing at all mattered . . .

He peeked.

He was walking across a battlefield, bloodied, searching for his brother. Dragging the corpse of a friend by one hand, because—in his stupor—he couldn't leave the body behind. Blood trailed him like paint on a glyphward, a long stroke, using a once-human brush.

He closed his eyes again. Were all those versions of him truly the same person? Or were they paintings made of lying colors on a canvas? Arranged to give a sense of continuity, but in reality fractured.

Better to float.

No. Again he opened his eyes. He was a youth, angry at being mocked by well-dressed men from Kholinar. He was furious his father hadn't defended Kholin honor, though he would later find that his father's growing—but still hidden—senility was making him timid to appear in public.

Gavilar—noble Gavilar—stood nearby and watched, hands clasped behind his back. His expression distant.

Dalinar squeezed his eyes closed. Why did he keep opening them?

Because without reminders I'll float here forever. This isn't why I came. I have a purpose.

He would not find ancient secrets by happenstance. He would not save his people by doing what was easy. So, feeling as if he were fighting a terrible current, he reached into his pocket and found salvation.

A rock.

The one Wit had given him to tie him to the past. *Show me!* he thought, and he might have bellowed it as well. *Take me here!*

The warmth resisted. Why would it resist?

Please, Dalinar thought. *I must see.*

It will destroy you.

Had he really heard that? Was that . . . Honor's power?

Please, he repeated, mouthing the word.

It will destroy us.

Please.

He dropped onto something hard. Hesitant, he blinked, opening his eyes to find himself kneeling among a few singers. They wore basic clothing: loincloths, some straps around their carapace. Their forms didn't seem intimidating; more armored than workform, but not so much as warform.

"You all right, Moash?" one of them asked.

Moash? Did they see him as . . .

No, that was just an ancient name that had survived. Navani had mentioned reading it in her Dawnchant explorations. With his Connection to the Physical Realm severed, he could not return—but had he at least managed to reach the past?

Those singers still clustered around him, so he took one of their offered hands and let her help him to his feet.

"Sorry," he said. "I tripped."

They nodded, and everyone continued on, hiking up through a mountain pass. As in his other visions, he had taken the place of someone from history. These would see him as that person, though he saw himself as he was. The vision also made up for his basic failings—for instance, although he did not speak with a singer rhythm, the others didn't notice.

He made a snap decision and tried to reach for his powers and open a pathway home. It didn't work. He could access Stormlight—it was all around him, infusing everything. But when he tried to Connect the realms, slapping his hands together, nothing happened. Hadn't Wit explained something about this? Perpendicularities didn't work the other way.

Storms. He was trapped in here.

The others glanced back at him, so he hastened to catch up. If he acted wildly out of character, people in the vision would start getting confused, and the whole thing could break down. So he tried to keep pace while . . .

Wait. How much time had passed?

With a mounting horror, he pushed up his wide jacket sleeve to reveal his leather bracer strapped on over his shirt, set with Navani's fabrials. Including the clock and day counter. Storms. He'd lost an entire day. That was disturbing, but a part of him was also relieved. The way Wit had spoken . . . it seemed Dalinar could have passed weeks, months, or *more* without noticing.

Well, this clock was tied to Wit's. Maybe that could provide an anchor to get home? He tried using that tether, but again nothing happened. Either he was too inexperienced, or it was too weak a Connection to use to get home.

"Keep up, Moash!" one of the singers called.

"Sorry," he said, puffing as he ran. Was he really that out of shape? Granted, some singer forms gave their hosts great endurance, so maybe he shouldn't compare himself.

The landscape around them was sparsely forested, and home to a particularly rugged kind of rockbud with a thicker shell and shorter vines than he was accustomed to. Together, he and the singers finally crested the rise, and he was relieved to see a flat pass on the other side. The air was chill as the group continued forward.

Nine of us, he thought. *Where is Navani?*

Was she one of these singers? In the past, when he'd managed to bring her into a vision with him, they'd seen each other as they truly were—but who knew if those rules would hold? Before, his experience had been curated by the Stormfather.

As they hurried along, Dalinar checked his arm clock again, worried that he'd lose another day somehow. Instead he found the reverse: though he felt as if he'd been climbing for an hour or more, mere seconds had passed on his clock. Storms.

But how did he get home? He trekked through the pass with the others and saw, below, a vast wasteland of crem. A flat brown plain with nothing growing from it. Where was he? He'd never seen anything like this on Roshar. Except . . .

If Wit was right, he thought, *this stone has brought me to witness the arrival of humans on Roshar. Which means that expanse of brown crem . . . that's Shinovar, isn't it?*

"What makes it that way?" he asked out loud.

"The mud field?" the femalen from earlier asked. "That's a question for the little gods, not for me, Moash."

"There," another of the team said. "The thieves are trying to skirt the base of the mountains."

Dalinar followed their gesture, and spotted another group of singers. Only three, leading a group of small chulls along the edge of the mud field below.

"Chull rustlers," he muttered. "All that running to chase down a few chull rustlers?"

They started descending immediately, taking the slope at a dangerous speed, at least for a human. He fell behind again, and eventually they just went on without him. By the time he reached the base of the slope—puffing and sweating—the others had recaptured their chulls. The rustlers ran off.

The chulls, for their part, barely seemed to have noticed. The large crustaceans rooted around on the ground, searching for rockbuds to chew. They appeared to be juveniles, as they were barely as tall as a person.

"You all right, Moash?" the femalen asked, trotting up to him.

"Fine," he said. "I think I injured my ankle when I fell earlier."

He sat on a rock, sweating. If this vision was like the others, these weren't actual people he was talking to, but . . . echoes of them. Re-creations. This was like a play, pulled from the mists of time. As he sat, he drew in a little Stormlight—not enough to glow and look odd. His fatigue melted away, and he felt steadier. Yes, everything here was *made* of Stormlight.

He stood and walked to the edge of the seemingly endless brown plain. He tapped his toe against it, and found it more firm than he'd expected. It wasn't crem though—it felt wrong. Mud? Like the word "muddy," a synonym for dirty? The ground *was* said to be strange in Shinovar.

The femalen joined him, testing with her toe as well. She hummed something that sounded curious.

"Firmer than you thought?" Dalinar guessed.

"Yes," she said. "I've heard stories of entire hunting parties being swallowed by this stuff. It's not supposed to harden like crem, but I swear we could walk on this."

"Maybe it swallows you when you get farther out," he said.

"A horrible place," she said. "Come. We're going to make camp, prepare for the storm."

The storm? he thought. *Damnation.*

Singers could survive out in a highstorm. Technically, humans could too—he'd walked some during his time, particularly in his more reckless years as a youth. With a little age as seasoning, however, he looked back upon those days with chagrin. So foolhardy.

Perhaps the storm would be calmer here in Shinovar. The others found a stone hollow nearby, and settled down to feed the chulls and prepare a small camp. *No metal,* Dalinar noted as one of them hobbled the chulls by tying their feet together with vine ropes. *I really am in the deep past, aren't I?*

So long as he couldn't escape, he should try to learn something. Unfortunately, it was difficult to concentrate, worried as he was about Navani. Was she floating in that chaos somewhere, confronted by flashes of her past?

Navani, he thought. *Navani . . .*

Something latched on to him, a bond that glowed briefly like a silver cord. It yanked on him, and he felt a physical force that made him stumble. It was her. Pulling on him . . . like he'd pulled on that stone that Wit had given him. It had been his anchor. Now he was hers.

A moment later, the femalen stiffened, then her form *melted,* shifting like a Lightweaving to become Navani in her brilliant red havah. Dalinar blessed his fathers softly and trotted over, taking her by the arm as she wavered, dizzy. She gripped him, then glanced around.

"Did we do it?" she asked. "Is this . . . the past?"

Dalinar led her to the edge of the mud, away from the others. "I think it worked, Navani. The stone Wit gave us brought me here, but something is wrong. I feel no tether back to the Physical Realm—the clock works, but it says we've lost a day already." He checked his arm with a sudden panic, but time seemed consistent now that he was in a vision. Though another hour had passed in here, the clock said mere minutes had passed in the Physical Realm.

"It could have been worse, I suppose," she said, turning around. "Shinovar?"

"I believe so. I appeared with this group of singers." He held up Wit's rock. "This must be the day humans arrive. We're a little early, I'd guess." He turned toward the other singers. "Perhaps we can get something useful out of them."

"Perhaps," Navani said, her hand still on his arm. "Dalinar, I felt something when I was floating. A . . . tugging toward you that I was able to solidify, but there were others. I think there might be someone else in here with us."

Dalinar rubbed his chin. "Perhaps whatever took us brought Wit as well. Or it could be the Stormfather; he exists partially in this place." He nodded toward the singers again. "I'm going to try something. Might as well use the time we have, right?"

Navani nodded, following him as he walked to the group of singers. There, he put his hands on his hips and announced, "What do you lot think of Honor, the god?"

Beside him Navani snickered, and when he glanced at her, she'd put her hand up in front of her mouth to hide a smile.

"What?" he demanded.

"That's your delicate plan to gather information?"

"I didn't say it was delicate." He eyed her. "Chull in a library?" he said, using one of her metaphors for him.

"Chull in a storming glassware shop, Dalinar."

Well, his question got the attention of the singers. One stood up, a malen with a thick beard, who hummed to a rhythm Dalinar couldn't pick out.

"Well?" Dalinar asked.

"I didn't realize they'd gotten to you, Moash," the singer said. "I'm tired of this argument."

Dalinar shared a grin with Navani. Being direct wasn't always the *best* strategy, but it was almost always a *functional* one.

"Tell me why," Navani said. "I'd like to hear it from you."

"Honor is our god," the bearded one said, waving in annoyance and changing his rhythm. "His traditions are good enough for me."

"The traditions are wrong," said a femalen, tall and limber, not facing the malen as she worked. "Honor did not give us the spren, or the forms. They were gifts from the *Origin of Songs,* and *They* will return. Someday."

"Origin of Songs," Navani said softly. "My mind is translating the words, but I can pick up some of the grammar if I try. I think that's referencing a person."

"Adonalsium," Dalinar guessed, using a name Wit had told him.

"Adonalsium," the femalen singer agreed, still working. "Will come back for us. Until then, we have the Wind, the Stone, the spren. The life of trees and light of day. *That* is what we should worship."

The others hummed in what seemed disagreement. When Dalinar prodded further, nobody acknowledged his questions.

"A problem with bluntness," Navani whispered to him. "Sometimes you cut off future opportunities."

He grunted in reply and considered what else to ask, then noticed the sky darkening, clouds billowing forward. He'd forgotten about the storm, but the reports seemed true about Shinovar: instead of a stormwall that tossed boulders, he was met with a strong—but not life-threatening—downpour. It lasted a mere fifteen or twenty minutes, during which rainspren dotted the ground like candles. After the initial deluge, the rain softened, becoming almost pleasant.

The singers settled onto their knees, then together sang. Each one chose their own words, but used the same rhythm and notes. Prayers, he realized, and suddenly felt that he was intruding. Navani took his hand, and then something crested the mountaintops—a shimmering distortion that shifted raindrops and frightened rockbuds. It had no color or light, but he could see it in the way it made the air ripple and the rain tremble. A wave like a flowing river, which washed down the slope, trailed by thousands of windspren.

Dalinar stepped in front of Navani by instinct, but the force broke around them, splitting in half—again like a flowing river. It brought with it a peaceful sensation and a wind that rippled his wet clothing. The rain's chill faded to a comforting warmth, and fell into a pattern of sound.

We see you, a soft voice, overlapping like a chorus, said in his ear. *Man from another time. Woman from a tower reborn.*

"What . . . what are you?" Navani asked.

We are the Wind, the voices said. *Caretakers of this land. And you are . . . ?*

"Travelers," Dalinar said. "Witnesses."

Come to see the change, the Wind said. *Ah . . . the arrival.*

"It is soon?" Dalinar asked.

Very soon. Very soon. The Wind swirled around them. *Ah . . . but you are of them. The humans. So you come to know your forefathers . . .*

"Pardon," Navani said, "but do you know this . . . is just a vision?"

We have always been, the Wind said. *But no thing can remain as it always was. This place is a piece of time, and we see it, experience it. We also see now—and what we have become. We are quiet, in your time, and lose our voice.*

"Windspren? Is that what you become?"

The windspren? the Wind said. *No, they continue, as we weaken from the arrival of new gods. We see this. We* see. *The ones you sent, Bondsmiths. The soldier and the assassin. They are where you stand now, but in another time . . .*

Szeth and Kaladin had reached Shinovar? That was good to know. Dalinar took a deep breath, wondering if there was a way to communicate with them. Except . . . what could they do to help?

The best way to proceed was to accomplish his goal. See the past, learn the truths, and use that knowledge to gain Honor's power. With that, he could get them home.

"I need to know why Honor's power abandoned mankind," Dalinar said to the Wind. "I have to access it. Take it up."

At that, the Wind *laughed.*

"Do you know how I can persuade it to accept me?"

It surrounds you, but you cannot persuade it. Honor's power is stubborn. Now, watch. It is time to see.

It flowed past them onto the mudflats. There, in the near distance, a light split the sky—and a portal opened to another world.

One on fire.

Of different note, as Vava will attest in great disbursement, is that within orders strife is unexpected, yet still vulgar, of a shape and manifold variety, that is often overlooked, still worthy of consideration.

—From *Words of Radiance*, chapter 40, page 1

Shallan floated through shifting colors, transfixed by the beautiful flowing ribbons.

Like paint mixing all around her, sometimes becoming images, shapes, glimpses of other times. She could have lingered here for an eternity, watching the colors bleed, watching visions of people she'd been come and go.

Then suddenly it began to fade. She wanted to hold on, reluctant to leave—because in that flowing warmth all things were possible, but none of them were her fault. Here, she could merely exist.

Regardless, a world formed around her. Shallan found herself pulling free of a trance, as if stepping from a mire, and then she began to remember urgency. Mraize had collapsed the perpendicularity, and . . .

. . . she'd been sucked through. She felt at her pocket, in the leather armor she still wore, and found the knife she'd stolen from the Ghostbloods. Anti-Light. She clutched it, blinking, and looked around, suddenly terrified. How long had she floated like that? Where was she now?

A room appeared from the shifting mist: a lavish chamber with a luxurious bed and fine furnishings. And toys? There was a fortress made of wood on the floor, with toy soldiers and several prominent wooden Shardbearers.

Light peeked in through open window drapes, but something was wrong with the colors. It didn't feel quite real. Indeed, when she picked up one of the soldiers from the wooden rampart, she could see that its colors bled into the air. A little like the colors of a prism, but separated, creating three little toy soldiers slightly off-center from one another.

Cyan, magenta, yellow, she thought, remembering her color theory lessons. Curious. Though she seemed to be solid, the light coming off every other object had that same surreal, off-kilter split of colors. As if they were on the floor of some Thaylen master printer's offices, discarded for misalignment.

The door opened, revealing Pattern in his full-sized form, with Testament behind him—her hand on his shoulder. Like Shallan, they appeared more solid than the surroundings. "Ah!" Pattern said. "She is here, Renarin! Hmmm. I believe she is playing with your toys."

"I was inspecting the colors," Shallan said, wagging the toy soldier at Pattern.

"Oh!" he said. "Can I play with them, then? I always wondered at the fuss!"

As the others entered from a room outside, Pattern bounced over and began lining up the toy soldiers. He left Testament to haunt the room just inside the doorway, putting her back to the wall. Renarin entered, and Shallan got her first good view of his spren in physical form.

Technically Glys was a mistspren, a variety she'd met in Shadesmar. Their bodies were made of mist that was diaphanous and amorphous, but somehow still gave shape to the clothing they wore. Those she'd seen wore gloves, as well as some kind of crystalline mask with delicate features.

Renarin's spren had turned a deep red color, like fog hiding a ruby somewhere within. Instead of a mask, Glys had a shifting . . . nothing. Like a swirling void, tinted red.

Rlain came in after Renarin, with his own spren, which was larger than Renarin's but had the same kind of face. Rlain towered over all of them; in this form, he might even be taller than Kaladin. He was intimidating in his uniform, with his orange-red skullcap of carapace covering his cheeks and nose, and with that thick—if short—beard. He had powerful muscles, and eyes that upon first glance appeared black, without pupils. That was wrong, as there was differentiation in singer eyes when you looked closely.

Rlain had *presence.* She might have been frightened of him, if not for the way he glanced at Renarin for support, an action that was strikingly vulnerable. Storms. She needed to be careful about how she judged people. It was the artist's way to paint a picture of someone the moment she saw them—but art was locked to the page, and a person was always so much more than any image could contain.

Pattern began humming contentedly, stacking the toy soldiers up like they were performers.

"So," Renarin said. "Um . . . I think we ended up in the Spiritual Realm. Fortunately, our spren were able to find you all."

Shallan winced. "Sorry. I dragged you two into this." She took a deep breath. "And you were right when you said I was trying to get you to help me find Mishram. I didn't expect . . . I'm sorry. Genuinely."

"It is what it is," Rlain said, his arms folded. "And if what you say about those assassins is correct—that they are hunting Mishram's prison—then it is well we are here. I don't want them finding one of our old gods. Odium has enough strength."

"I stole this from one of them before the accident," Shallan said, holding up the dagger, the metal at its tip warping the air. "We have to assume Iyatil and Mraize are in here somewhere too, and they have spren like yours—spren who can guide them."

"This Mraize," Renarin said, "matches the description of someone who captured Lift during the occupation and gave her to the enemy as a gift."

Shallan winced. Capturing Lift? Giving her as a gift?

Yeah. That sounded like Mraize.

"So . . ." Shallan said, looking up. "We seem to be . . . in a child's room?"

"Renarin's room!" Pattern said happily. "From when he was young!"

"I will need memories," Glys said, standing behind Renarin like a shadow. "To give form. I will help, but this is not real. Not even as not real as the other visions. Not real past. Sorry. I . . . will try to words . . . better."

"It's all right, Glys," Renarin said. "We get it."

"We do?" Shallan asked.

"Glys can help us shape some semblance of reality from this place," Renarin said. "But it's not going to tell us anything new or interesting, because he's feeding on my memories, not the Connections and tones of the Spiritual Realm."

Okay . . . that . . . barely made any sense to her. Storms. When had Renarin learned so much about these kinds of things?

You always underestimated him, Radiant reminded her. *But at least that's one habit you've started to break, as you grow.*

"Think of this as a staging area," Renarin said, gesturing at the walls with shelves bearing toys. "So we can decide what to do next."

"Mraize and Iyatil," Shallan said, "are trying to find the prison of the Unmade, Ba-Ado-Mishram. Dalinar will be here too, probably Navani as well, for other reasons."

Rlain hummed something.

Renarin, in turn, nodded. "Yes, it *is* curious. Shallan, do you know *why* my father would come here? Glys says it's dangerous."

"It is dangerous," Glys agreed. "And will be."

"Dalinar is hunting for information, I think," Shallan said. "And . . .

perhaps for the power of the god Honor, from what I overheard. So that maybe . . . that power can be exploited."

Renarin and Rlain shared a glance.

"Your father," Rlain said to a hesitant rhythm, "is an . . . impressively ambitious person, Renarin."

"Yeah. I've noticed." Renarin made fists and seemed, to her best estimation, overwhelmed. She opened her mouth to offer some solution, but then he nodded firmly. "Right. If an Unmade's prison really is in here, *we* need to find it. First."

You, Radiant noted, *are not the only one who has grown.*

"We should join Dalinar and Navani," Shallan said. "From what Iyatil and Mraize said, they hope the Bondsmiths' visions will lead them to Mishram's prison. With your father's help, we can—"

"No!" Glys said urgently.

"No!" Rlain's spren said, standing close behind him like a shadow. "No, *no* revealing ourselves!"

"The gods hate us," Glys said. "In here, we will be exposed to them. They will destroy us!"

"Honor's power will hate us," Rlain's spren said.

"We are its enemies," Glys agreed. "It does not fully think, but it will know. To kill us."

"Odium will destroy us."

"We are traitors to his vision."

"Cultivation will destroy us."

"We are abominations," Glys said. "She will hate us. All will hate us. We cannot be seen."

Both of them deliberately stepped further into the shadows of their respective Radiants, peeking out, uncertain.

"All right . . ." Shallan said. "So . . . that makes this more complicated."

"There are laws governing what the gods can do," Renarin said. "Wit talks about it sometimes. But I think . . . if you enter their domain . . ."

"If you invade a person's house," Glys said softly, "the law has fewer protections for you. Worse for us. We have chosen to be Enlightened by her, which puts us in the power of all gods. We will die if we are exposed."

"In secret," Rlain's spren said. "We go in secret. Using our illusions to protect us. Illusions are quiet. Your enemies, they will come to the same conclusions. They will follow the Bondsmiths, who are Connected to events they seek."

"So the assassins will be hiding in the visions," Rlain said, his voice deep and contemplative, "acting out a role, unknown to Dalinar and Navani."

"We don't *actually* have to find Mishram's prison, you know," Renarin said. "We could, um, find these Ghostbloods and just . . . er . . ."

"Just what?" Shallan asked.

"Murder?" Pattern said, placing another soldier. He'd built a surprisingly tall pyramid. "Oh, you mean *murder*! Shallan is good at murder. Yes, mmmmm . . ."

"Pattern," she said, "please don't say it that way."

"She is good," Pattern corrected himself, "at making people who were once alive and threatening, unalive and unthreatening. Mmmm. Very good at it."

"Right, um . . ." Now the old Renarin was back, unwilling to meet her eyes. "So . . . if we *stop* those two, that should be enough, right? We don't need to find the prison?"

"For the short term that would work," Shallan agreed. "Are you fine with killing like that, Renarin?"

"I am," he said, looking up. "We are the authorities in this matter, invested with responsibility by our oaths and commissions. These two not only sided with the enemy, they have attacked—by your word—my cousin Jasnah. We do what we have to in order to protect." For support he looked to Rlain, who hummed—then after a moment nodded, as if he belatedly realized he needed to give more of a confirmation for humans.

Neither asked if *she* was willing. They assumed it, and . . . well, Mraize was her enemy. He'd manipulated her. Threatened her brothers. He did *not* deserve her loyalty—and she'd overtly declared war on him.

Still, she found her heart treasonously hesitant.

You're ready for this, Shallan, Veil thought. *We can bring him down.*

Yes, but Radiant may have to do the killing, she thought. *When the hard part comes.*

It is why I exist, Radiant said.

"All right," Renarin said. "Let me see if I can locate Father and Aunt Navani. Glys, I'll need your help."

They settled on the floor, closing their eyes. Shallan hauled herself to her feet and decided to inspect the room. This was Renarin's childhood bedroom, was it? She found a number of stuffed chulls, which appeared to have occasionally been used as mounts for the soldiers—making for the slowest, most meandering cavalry of all time. She stopped near Testament, who stood with her hand on one of those animals. Her forlorn pattern twisted, almost motionless.

"She's thinking of you," Pattern said softly, stepping up beside her. "When you were young."

Shallan glanced over her shoulder, to where he'd left a perfect three-dimensional pyramid of soldiers—their wooden bases and flat helmets letting them balance.

"She thinks of you," Pattern continued, laying his hand on Testament's. "And the way you were back then."

"Pain," Testament whispered.

"In pain," Pattern said. "A child should live happily. Every child. You did not."

"I did for a while," Shallan whispered.

"Is that true?" Pattern said.

"I loved my brothers, and . . ." Shallan wiped a tear she hadn't realized was forming. "And there were good times. In the gardens. With her."

Pattern took Shallan's hand, then Testament—with a lurch—moved her hand on top. Both squeezed.

"This place," Pattern warned her, "is affected by your thoughts. Ah, yes, and your memories and your soul too. Your soul can make things appear without thought. It might be difficult. Take care. We will stay close."

She nodded. "I don't deserve you," she whispered. "Either of you." Pattern hugged her, his too-stiff clothing feeling odd, but she welcomed the gesture.

Nearby, Renarin stood up. "We've found my father. He's in a vision."

"Good," Pattern said. "Excellent, even! Let's go murder some folks!"

45

SELF-MASTERY AND CONTROL

While Willshapers embraced this very sense of contrarity, an attitude that will come as no great surprise to any conversant with their predilections, and indeed might be found unexpected in its absence, the presence of such strife among Skybreakers is a source of no small stupefaction to many.

—From *Words of Radiance*, chapter 40, page 1

Kaladin, Syl, and Szeth met an unexpected obstacle guarding the next monastery. A fort.

They landed together on a grassy hilltop. Kaladin was *almost* accustomed to the ground's unnatural plushness. Like he was walking on carpet. Outdoors. All the time.

Kaladin shifted the new Honorblade—wrapped in cloth, with a rope tied to each end to carry it—from one shoulder to the other. They'd decided neither should try to bond it. The distant ramshackle fortification appeared one strong gust away from collapse. The monastery itself—a towering stone block—peeked up behind the wooden wall.

"It looks right," Szeth said. "Good."

"Good?" Kaladin asked.

"No darkness," Syl agreed. "I can feel it too."

"Was there a wall around it before?" Kaladin asked.

Szeth shook his head. "No, but this is a larger monastery with a small city around it, not just a soldier camp. Perhaps the wall was built after I left. All of the monasteries along the seaboard here were designed to defend against coastal barbarian incursions."

“By barbarians, you mean people like me,” Kaladin said. “Because we walk on stone.”

“Among other things,” Szeth said, starting forward. “Let’s walk the rest, to not alarm them or reveal we are Radiant.”

“All right,” Kaladin said, joining him. “What, other than walking on stone, marks us as barbarians in your eyes?”

“Your use of color. It doesn’t mean anything to you. Plus, you often eat with your hands.”

“What else would we eat with?” Kaladin said. “Our feet?”

“Forks. Spoons.”

“We have those.”

“You barely use spoons except for soup. As for forks, you just as often use bread. Flat, dry bread with no yeast. You likely got forks from us. People in the East steal everything good from the Shin.”

“Nonsense,” Kaladin said, glancing at Syl for support. She was snickering. “Szeth, that’s *nonsense.* What have we stolen?”

“Horses,” he said. “Hogs. Chickens. Social graces. Manners. Philosophy . . .”

“That’s a huge leap,” Kaladin said. “Horses, maybe. But social graces? Regardless, didn’t we *all* come from Shinovar originally? We landed here when we . . . shipped in from another planet? Or whatever.”

Szeth simply continued walking.

“Syl,” Kaladin said, “back me up.”

“Well,” she said, “you *do* get a lot of food on your hands when you eat.”

“We use flatbread to scoop curry!” Kaladin said. “We wash our fingers in dishes. It’s *efficient.* You’re not more civilized, Szeth, because you wash more forks.”

Szeth didn’t reply, but he did seem to have a hint of a smile on his lips as they crossed the shimmering grassland, passing beneath the boughs of a large tree. After a time flying, Kaladin always forgot how *long* it took to walk anywhere.

“You let people rile you,” Szeth said. “You get emotional and argue.”

“And?” Kaladin asked.

“And you don’t lose control and kill people.”

“Is that a problem for you?” Kaladin asked, a little unnerved by needing to.

“No,” Szeth said, “but the Skybreakers teach that if my emotions rule me, I will leave corpses in my wake.”

“You haven’t done so anyway?” Kaladin said.

Szeth winced visibly. Damnation. Maybe this wasn’t the right way to approach therapy, or whatever Wit had called it.

“I had an old sergeant,” Kaladin said, “in my first months in the military.

He always said that he'd rather his men care, feel emotion, and feel pain. Even anger. Because we're supposed to fight *for* something."

"But if you let emotion take over, it will control you," Szeth said. "That's the way of Odium."

"Sure, going too far is clearly bad," Kaladin said. "I know the stories of Dalinar's early days; I've met soldiers who were the same. But it's not like a little grumping about being called a barbarian is going to drive me to a raving frenzy."

"And you don't enjoy it?" Szeth asked. "The battle part?"

"I . . ." Did he? "Yeah. Yeah, I enjoy the battle part sometimes."

"That doesn't frighten you?"

"It does," Kaladin admitted. "I guess it's like everything in life. You have to find a balance. Is that . . . maybe part of your problem? You feel that if you take the slightest step in one direction, you might as well dash headlong without looking back?" He thought a moment. "Might be partially the fault of your society, where a child who defends his own life is seen as irreconcilably broken—and needs to be sent away."

Szeth, characteristically, didn't respond. But he did appear thoughtful—and walking beside him, Syl gave Kaladin an encouraging smile.

This was the hard part though. Kaladin had to be honest. Both with Szeth and with himself.

He had to open up.

"It still hurts sometimes," Kaladin said, his eyes forward. "After all I've been through, all I've learned, it still hurts. I know I'm still going to have bad days, and I'm still going to weep for the friends I lost. I'm still going to feel worthless sometimes. But Szeth, I'm making progress."

He took a deep breath, clearing out some of the emotion.

"I confronted my shame at being unable to help others," Kaladin said. "I acknowledged I had unrealistic, impossible expectations for myself. I am learning what my mind does wrong, and have begun practicing how to counteract it. I know your issues are different from mine. They're similar enough though. If I can improve, you can too."

Syl nodded firmly at this. "I've seen it working, Szeth. Not only for Kaladin, but for others too." Her words, as a spren, seemed to carry weight for Szeth.

She gestured, indicating Kaladin should say more, but his gut said to wait. He couldn't force Szeth down this road. All he could do was share, and marvel he was capable of that now.

Eventually, after a good fifteen minutes of walking—passing out of the thigh-high grasses and onto a road, then turning toward the small walled city—Szeth spoke.

"Let us suppose," he said, "I wanted to . . . try thinking a different way. How would I approach it?"

"It sometimes feels like I've got two minds," Kaladin said. "Maybe it's the same for you. I have a brain that wants to destroy me—one that whispers that everything I love is doomed, so I might as well just give up. I can't merely endure that kind of thinking. I have to be active. I have to go to war."

"Go to war," Szeth said, "with your own *brain.*"

"Yeah, kind of," Kaladin said. He sighed, searching for the best words. "You know how, when you're first starting to learn to fight, you don't have any instincts? What do you do?"

"Train," Szeth said. "Train over and over and over until the proper response comes the moment you need it."

"It's like that," Kaladin said. "When the wrong thoughts come in, you need to be ready. Not only to rebuff them, but to present the right thoughts instead. Warrior thoughts, to resist the bad ones."

"How can you be sure what is right, though?" Szeth asked. "Your own mind has created both 'good' thoughts and 'bad.' You need something external, something unchanging—like the law—to guide you. That is what my spren teaches."

"Maybe spren can be wrong," Kaladin said.

Szeth put his head down, walking faster. "Why do you even care?"

"I took oaths," Kaladin said, hurrying to catch up.

"I took oaths too," Szeth said with a flippant wave of his fingers. "Mine are to the law. Why do yours matter more?"

That stopped Kaladin, who paused on the earthen road as Szeth continued on. It was true. Their oaths—their orders—conflicted. Was there something higher than an oath? It was difficult to imagine that being true.

"Szeth," Kaladin called after him, "how do you feel?"

Szeth halted on the path, dust on his white trousers. He looked back.

"How do you *feel*?" Kaladin asked again.

"Awful," Szeth whispered, barely audible. "I should be able to stamp that emotion out, but I can't. I feel *awful.* All the time. You?"

"Better," Kaladin said. "Lately, better."

"Really? Truly, honestly?"

Kaladin nodded.

"Well, I suppose that's something," Szeth said, turning and continuing on. "Warrior thoughts, you say? Prepared in your head to counter the dark ones when they attack? Curious."

Before too much longer, they walked up to the wooden gates of the fort to find quite a large group of people had gathered on top to watch them approach.

Interestingly, not all were Shin.

⁂

It is good for you to hear the words of the Windrunner, Szeth's spren said in his head. *At first, his . . . inaccurate teachings worried me. Now I see. Like a sword being forged, you must be subjected to blows. I will ask the other highspren if they have noticed this important step in the forging of their own Skybreakers.*

"You have not done this before?" Szeth whispered.

You are my first, and so I will not see you ruined, lest I never be given the chance again. Be careful. You must hear the foolish words of the Windrunner and reject them. He is well-meaning, but so very wrong. Hear, but do not heed, *my squire.*

Szeth had not known his highspren was new to having a knight; the spren did not speak with the air of one inexperienced. And yet, at least part of what Kaladin had said was true. Szeth *was* miserable. Perhaps that didn't matter. He'd spent his life assuming it didn't, and it seemed late to change that mindset.

But if you had warrior thoughts to destroy such attacks from your own mind, he wondered, *what then?*

High above, on the ramparts—if one could use such a lofty term for the flimsy walk inside the palisade—people conferred. Finally someone called down, speaking in the language of Szeth's homeland.

"Why are you here, strangers?"

"We are travelers from beyond the mountains," Szeth yelled back. "I knew this city when it was called Koring, and had no wall such as this."

His comment caused a stir above, and behind him, Syl translated for Kaladin. He stepped up to Szeth, Honorblade slung across his shoulder. Nightblood, whom Szeth carried, had said he could persuade the Honorblade not to cut the cloth—and so far that was working.

"Why not tell them who you are?" Kaladin whispered.

"They didn't ask," Szeth said.

"You're such a strange person," Kaladin said, then gestured toward the ramparts. "Some of those people aren't Shin."

"You can't tell that by looking," Szeth said. "They might have lived here for generations. Can you always tell an Alethi by looking?"

"Well, no," Kaladin said. "But we're . . ."

"What?" Szeth asked.

"Cosmopolitan," Kaladin said. "Everyone knows Alethkar is the center of culture."

"Tell that to the Azish," Szeth said, amused. He gave the people above some time to confer, and was about to breathe in some Stormlight and float up, when the gates opened.

A group of people stood within, bearing metal weapons, though they also wore splashes of color. A blue hat here, a yellow apron there. Curious. The city beyond was much as he'd pictured it, however. Wooden boardwalks surrounding maybe two hundred buildings, each painted with color and laid out in a neat pattern, with straight roads and plentiful permanent awnings—the type they never had in the East.

He'd missed the sight. A simple sign of a land not dominated by storms. Metal was used in abundance though—around windows, on door hinges. When he'd come to his first city, he'd found that blasphemous—even if it was only serviced by soldiers or shamans, and town workers refused to touch it.

For Shinovar, this was a midsized settlement, although it would be on the smaller side in the East. His people had less need to huddle together for strength against storms, and so there were far more small towns. At least there had been. Every one that Kaladin and Szeth had passed today had been empty, like his own homestead.

Szeth waved to Kaladin and entered, stepping onto the boards that made the street here. Perhaps elsewhere he might have worried about an ambush . . . except these didn't seem soldiers, but instead merely people with weapons.

"Is that an Alethi uniform?" a man asked Szeth, his voice accented and his white eyebrows long and straight, hanging down by his face. The man nodded to Kaladin.

"It is," Szeth said, looking around as people gathered. Mothers carrying children. Workers of all varieties. "What happened here? Why are there so many of you who subtract?"

"It's . . . been a hard few years," said a woman of Shin heritage.

"The others leave us alone, mostly," the first man said. "It was hardest at first, before the wall. Before we all gathered here, and realized we were the only ones that weren't . . ."

"What?" Szeth asked, fixating on him.

"Different," someone else said.

"Dark," another added.

Most of them kept their distance from him, as if expecting immediate violence. Their eyes lingered on the black sword strapped to his back. Or on the Honorblade Kaladin wore, which—despite the cloth around it—was obviously a weapon.

"Did you . . . really come from the East?" the first man asked. "Is the way open? We've considered fleeing. We've made a life here, but . . ."

"How long?" Szeth asked.

"Two years."

Kaladin stepped up, Syl having shrunk to stand on his shoulder and whisper interpretations for him, likely invisible to everyone but him and Szeth.

"Two years?" Kaladin said, and Szeth translated. "Trapped in this city? By what? Attacks from who?"

"The other towns," a woman said.

Szeth scanned the small city. Evidently when danger had come, these people had put aside their morals and picked up stone and steel. He found it . . . difficult to blame them. After nine years in the East, he did not deem the act as blasphemous as he once might have.

"Why are things different here?" Kaladin asked.

Szeth met his eyes, then both of them turned to look toward the fortress at the rear of the town. The Willshaper monastery. At the Stoneward monastery, killing the Honorbearer had seemed to release the people. Both started forward.

"Wait!" the woman from earlier said. Stout, short, and dark skinned, with her brown hair in a bun and a bright green splash of an apron. She also had a cudgel tied not-so-inconspicuously to her belt. "Who are you?"

"I am Szeth-son—"

"I mean, what do you want?" she said. "Do you know why everyone outside this immediate region has turned violent? Why they hide during the days, then try to break down our wall at night?"

Others began to pester him with questions. The city felt stuffed—home to thousands perhaps, if all of those barracks were occupied. They'd welcomed in all the people from the surrounding region, it appeared. Unfortunately, he didn't have time for their questions. He breathed in Stormlight, rising into the air. Kaladin, with some obvious reluctance, followed.

People backed away, gasping.

"The Desolation has finally come," Szeth told them, "as prophesied by the Heralds themselves. You undoubtedly have seen the new storm. The Everstorm."

"Yes," one of the others whispered. "It comes regularly, red with anger, and starts lightning fires."

"It is a sign," Szeth said. "The enemy is here, the one we were *supposed* to have trained for centuries to face. We have failed Truth." He felt his stomach twist.

Thousands of years wasted. The gathered people murmured at this—he and Kaladin suddenly flying wasn't much of a surprise, as Honorbearers had once frequented this town, and had not been shy about their abilities. But his words about Truth got to them. They'd known. He could tell by their reactions, the way they lowered their eyes. They'd guessed that they'd failed.

He left the people and flew with Kaladin to the monastery. They found it boarded up, planks nailed over all of the arrow-slit windows, and larger ones across the front gates.

They moved to the roof, where Szeth knelt. "I will make us an opening. I must practice with Division."

"Please try not to set the entire roof on fire," Syl said.

"You have seen only inexperienced Dustbringers so far," Szeth said, pressing his hand to the stone rooftop. "Taravangian's pets had barely any training. They ignore the ancient honorable traditions and practices of their forebearers."

"Which are?" Kaladin asked.

"Self-mastery," Szeth whispered, "and control."

He summoned the strength of Division. His people had always said that an Honorbearer was far more powerful than an oathed Radiant. Szeth's experience had taught him there was much nuance to the word "powerful." Regardless, he reached back through time to his training, blessing the fact that he'd been forced to learn all the Surges, and closed his eyes.

Then he felt the soul of the rooftop.

Division wasn't so different from other arts. With Soulcasting, you needed to persuade, cajole, or—if you were particularly skilled—command. A Stoneward instead had to *know* the stone, become kin to it.

With Division, the art of Dustbringing, you gave a spark—and controlled the reaction. The results could be explosive. If you were careful, they could also be precise. Today, the fires he started were tiny, practically invisible. He convinced the single-stone rooftop that it was instead made up of many, many stones. Tiny ones. Barely connected.

He opened his eyes.

"Did you . . . do something?" Kaladin asked.

In response, Szeth punched his hand through the rooftop, and a circular section five feet wide disintegrated into powder, raining down into the blackened chamber below. Szeth slipped through and dropped into the great hall of this monastery, gemstones glowing in the walls to give light.

No shaman or Honorbearer waited to attack him. Instead he spotted something at the front of the hall, near the wooden altar where a stone—brought up from the depths of the soil, hosting the spirits of spren—was traditionally placed.

Curled in front of it was a corpse. Desiccated by time, holding the Willshaper Honorblade: a wide, flat-sided Shardblade with a curved bell shape at the tip.

The corpse belonged to Sivi-daughter-Sivi, a woman he had once known very well. Szeth knelt beside her and sighed softly. Sivi's wisdom would have been welcome today.

"What's this?" Kaladin said, peering at the ground near her. "These markings on the stone?"

"Writing?" Syl said, still small sized, waving for him to hold the light closer. She scrunched up her nose. "I don't read Shin that well . . ."

"It says," Szeth whispered, "'I will not bow to him.'" He lowered his head in respect for Sivi. This was what honor looked like sometimes: a withered husk dead on the floor.

"So . . ." Kaladin said. "In the previous monastery, the people were cursed until you killed the bearer of the Honorblade. Here we find a corpse, who said she would not bow. And the people here aren't cursed."

"So . . ." Syl said. "This Honorbearer refused whatever the Unmade wanted from her, and died instead."

"Bring the Honorblade," Szeth said to Kaladin and Syl, then stood up and started walking to the end of the hall.

What are you planning, Szeth? his spren asked.

In response, he placed both hands against the gates into the monastery. He closed his eyes, feeling the weight of the doors, which saw themselves as part of the monastery. He severed that, and burned the sides so that when he opened his eyes and pushed, the gates collapsed forward—thundering to the ground outside, tearing down the flimsy boards.

The people had gathered outside. Szeth rose into the air, barely noting that Kaladin and Syl had joined him. As the people approached, he spoke.

"I am Szeth-son-Neturo," he proclaimed. "Once Honorbearer, now Knight Radiant. I was exiled as Truthless, but by suffering in the East, only *I* maintained Truth. The Desolation is here; the outside world has been fighting it for over a year.

"We have failed in our long-standing duty, but *I* will not fail you. Look to the people of the Encilo region—those near the Stoneward monastery. They are freed from the darkness now. I will travel to each monastery in turn. If they are similarly corrupted, I will fight the Honorbearer there and restore the people."

The people mostly gaped at him. A few clapped—flimsy, hesitant sounds. Well, he didn't blame them for their confusion. One might imagine that salvation would arrive to thunderous joy, but in his experience it was often rewarded with exhaustion. Those who needed help most rarely had much left to offer their rescuers.

"You can help them, Szeth," Kaladin said, hovering up beside him in the air. "But trust me: you'll do more good if you take care of yourself as well."

"I will ponder what you have said," Szeth said. "But we must get to the other monasteries. We can gather Stormlight from the hall behind us, then visit the Elsecaller and Lightweaver monasteries tomorrow."

“We could split up,” Kaladin said. “Visit two at once. If you have to do the fighting, I could see if any of the others are lacking combatants like this one. Might speed us up.”

“I will not stop you, should you wish to go.”

“And what do *you* want me to do, Szeth?”

“I . . .” He surveyed the crowd, which was at last beginning to celebrate, people hugging one another. “I feel better than I did. I must attribute some of that to your annoying persistence.”

“Well,” Kaladin said, “with that kind of glowing praise, how could I leave?”

Szeth nodded. “As we travel, I will tell you some of what I know of the leaders of the monasteries. It might be relevant. Both to our quest . . . and to me. Who I am.”

Were they all turned to the Unmade? How had Ishu let it go this far? The answer, Szeth supposed, was simple: The Heralds had all gone mad, and ignored the people they'd once sworn to protect. Much as the Shin people themselves had ignored their duty.

Szeth went to fetch Stormlight. When he came back, Kaladin had dropped down and—with Syl helping interpret—begun trading for fresh food. These people looked well fed enough to spare some—there was time for farming in the day, judging by the state of the nearby fields.

Szeth, his spren said, *are you certain of this path?*

“I came to cleanse Shinovar.”

You came to find Truth and administer justice. What if the actions of the Honorbearers you're killing are *just?*

“I have considered this, spren-nimi,” Szeth said. “The rest of Roshar belonged to the singers before we arrived, and it makes sense that now, singer laws apply there. By virtue of precedent, this is justice. Here, however, we are in Shinovar. By the ancient histories, Shinovar was *given* to us.

“Singer law does not apply here; instead, the law of *this* land is the law of the *Heralds.* They provided this ultimatum: prepare for the Desolation and protect this land when it comes. So *that* is what I must do.”

A . . . compelling argument, Szeth, the spren admitted. *Yet you do not have all of the facts, so take care.*

“Will you give them to me?”

They must be earned. Continue your pilgrimage.

At this, the whispers from the shadows sounded louder. Calling for Szeth to die.

He met them, and the words of the spren, with a thought soldier. *I have a purpose,* that thought soldier proclaimed. *I am here because of my choices, and I am capable of making such decisions.*

 It didn't work as well as he'd hoped. But Kaladin had said it would require time and repetition. With that in mind, even this little rebellion seemed to help, and Szeth raised his head higher. He could do this. He could decide. Which meant the end was finally in sight.

He could cleanse Shinovar.

Then, at long last, he could end himself—and in so doing, grant true justice to those he had murdered. Quietly, he blessed Kaladin for giving him this gift.

Indeed, the presence of a Herald among them should have, to all reasonable understandings, and to the abridgment of expectation, led to stability of doctrine among this most specific of orders.

—From *Words of Radiance*, chapter 40, page 1

A portal from another world.

Shalash the Herald had mentioned this, as had Wit. Navani was gazing into the world humans had originally come from. The one they called Ashyn . . . a world that humankind had destroyed with the power of the Surges.

Navani had known what to expect. It was another thing entirely to witness it. The portal started small, a pinprick in the sky, then was spread wide by the efforts of a man who stood on the other side. At least she thought he was the source, because he stood with arms stretched wide, a look of concentration on his face as if forcibly pushing the portal open.

"Ishar," Dalinar said. "Ishi, the Herald. It's him. Younger—his hair was white by the time I met him—but that *is* him."

This figure wore a simple blue robe tied at the waist, and had a beard that had barely started to grey. He strained to hold the way open as thousands of refugees flooded around him, clutching their meager possessions. Leading withered animals—many of which were unfamiliar to Navani.

In the background, their world burned. The very *sky* seemed to be on fire, and the people were covered in ash and soot. Navani felt a sudden need to go comfort them.

Dalinar gently held her back. "It's just a vision, Navani," he whispered.

"There is nothing you can do for the actual people—they are long dead. Save ten. Or nine, I suppose, as Jezrien has been destroyed."

Another figure approached the portal from the other side, stumbling, dressed in odd white robes—now stained black—hanging from one shoulder.

"Correction," Navani said. "There are *ten* who were here who still live, Dalinar. That's Wit." He didn't look a day younger than he did thousands of years later, though his hair was a stark white, and he appeared shorter for some reason.

The singers standing near Navani and Dalinar had abandoned their prayers, and were now muttering to themselves. One femalen mumbled, "Such strange skin patterns . . ."

Navani hesitated. That singer seemed familiar.

Dalinar, however, started forward. Navani rushed after him, and the other singers called after them both—then fled, leaving their chulls, obviously terrified by the strange events. As well they should have been. Today marked the first step toward what would become a millennia-long war.

"Dalinar," Navani said as they walked across the muddy field, "we need to find answers."

"Agreed," he said. "We must either find a way home, or . . ."

"Or?"

"We came here to find why Honor's power refuses to bond anyone," he said. "Cultivation implied the secret lies in understanding the history of our people, the Heralds, and their relationship with God." He hesitated. "That power should be a way out for us, if I do take it up."

"We will . . . search for a way," Navani said, daunted by the idea. "And while we're here . . . there are other secrets we can uncover. Some things about the Heralds' stories have always confused me." She glanced at the portal—which had expanded to thirty feet in diameter. Ishar stood in the center, hands thrust to the sides, his face a mask of concentration as he let thousands escape the burning land. They wore a variety of clothing styles and were of many ethnicities. They must have gathered together at the end, seeking refuge from the fires.

"We know from previous research," she continued, "that at this point, the Heralds aren't Heralds yet. They won't *become* Heralds until the war with the singers begins, and that is at least a generation or two later. Radiants are multiple millennia away from being founded. So how are they accessing these Surges? How did they cross this divide between worlds?"

"That's . . . a good question," Dalinar said, frowning. "The Stormfather told me that Honor worried about these powers—he feared the Radiants might destroy Roshar. I think . . . people must once have been able to access powers without bonds and oaths holding them back."

"No checks against their power," Navani said, staring through the tunnel at that horrifying place of smoke and red skies. "Come, let's see what we can discover."

She started forward again, but soon found crossing the muddy ground to be difficult—it was wet from the rain that was still sprinkling down. This proved a struggle for the refugees as well, who were laden with goods or carried them on the backs of sorry-looking horses or stranger beasts of burden.

No wagons, she thought. *Or carts.* She had trouble believing none had managed to get a vehicle to help. They must come from a time before such things were invented.

Storms, it was strange to think of a time that long ago. As she drew closer, she could see the people were as human as any she'd known. Their agony seemed real, as did their tears of exhaustion—and even joy—as they entered the rain and collapsed in the mud, unable to go any further. Strangely, they didn't attract spren—perhaps those weren't used to humans yet.

The rain let up, but her every footstep slid in the muck, and her skirt was quickly ruined. Dalinar fared better, stomping his way on booted feet. "Poor people," he whispered. "Maybe we should get one of those chulls to help?"

"I thought the people weren't real?" Navani said.

"They aren't," he admitted. "I . . . well, I've never been good at paying attention to that, reasonable though it is."

She smiled, accepting his help forging forward until they reached the first refugees. The awful stench of smoke hung over them, and they shied away. She belatedly remembered that they would see her as a singer—a frightening creature with marbled skin and carapace.

One man in a blue tunic had been directing people toward the slopes. He strode over, sandaled feet sliding in the mud, using a spear with an obsidian head to balance himself. He had a short black beard and keen eyes, and could have been Alethi, by his features. Storms. She thought she recognized him. Could some of the depictions have been that accurate?

"Jezerezeh?" she said, then remembered the name Ash and Taln had used for him. His real name, before being mythologized and made symmetrical. "Jezrien?"

He pulled up short, his eyes widening, and barked something at them in a tongue she didn't recognize.

Dalinar stared at the man, breathing in sharply.

"You recognize him too?" she asked.

"In more ways than one. I saw him in a vision, but now that he's here in more common clothing, exhausted . . . Storms, Navani. That's Ahu, a beggar. I . . . I used to drink with him sometimes, in the gardens at Kholinar . . ."

What? "You're kidding."

"No, that *is* Ahu," Dalinar said. "I was fond of him. A kindly drunk who shared wine with me during some of the dark days . . . Is it possible? Truly?"

She turned her attention back to Jezrien. He made another demand of them, and a woman with brilliant red hair—with some undercurrents of gold in the locks beneath—stepped up beside him. She had the air of a warrior, though she carried a simple stone axe. That would be Chanaranach, sometimes referred to as Chana by Ash.

At Navani's urging, Dalinar retreated with her a little way, so as to not antagonize Jezrien or Chana. "Three Heralds," Dalinar whispered. "You said the Heralds don't get their powers for several generations."

"Raboniel was made immortal near the time that the Oathpact was founded, which she said was around two generations from the crossing. That matches what we know from the writings in the Dawnchant. They indicate that at first, men and singers got along—but over time, humans wanted to expand. Rebellion followed, then war . . ."

"That explains why Ishar looks younger than when I met him," Dalinar said. "And Jezrien here, he could be in his late twenties maybe? And . . . there." He pointed toward a young teenage girl, protected by a small group of spearmen. "Ash."

"And the Ash we know seems frozen in age in her late twenties," Navani said. "The Heralds must have aged slowly somehow, until they were made immortal some sixty or seventy years from now. I'd like to see that day." She narrowed her eyes. "Where is Odium? He arrived with the humans. Though a god may not make himself visible . . ."

Navani glanced back. Distantly, singers had stopped upon the mountainside. They had wisely realized they should see what these invaders were doing.

Jezrien stepped closer, and made yet another demand.

"Always before," Dalinar said, with a frown, "I was able to understand people's languages in the visions."

"Everyone's language?" Navani said. "I think we imprinted as singers in this one, so we speak *their* language."

"I'll have to try my Connection trick," Dalinar said. "Which requires touching him." He raised a finger and wisps of Light began to stream off it.

Jezrien growled, and a powerful Light began to stream from him as well. Storms.

Yes, that's what destroyed Ashyn, Navani thought, remembering the first piece of Dawnchant they'd translated. *Dangerous powers, of spren and Surges. They destroyed their lands and have come to us begging. We took them in, as commanded by the gods . . .*

The lines of people seemed to extend forever—and on the other side of the portal, she saw no sign of trees other than smoldering stumps.

The scholar in her—the scholar she'd acknowledged and embraced—hungered to find answers. But for the moment, her attention was best focused on her husband—because he had stepped forward again and was picking a fight with an ancient king. Dalinar was trying to explain—without words—that all he wanted to do was touch Jezrien.

Unfortunately, if they were familiar with Surgebinding, they knew the dangers a simple touch could offer. She didn't blame Jezrien for backing away, pointing a spear toward Dalinar. He had been immune to danger in his previous visions, but now they were here in the flesh. The rules might be different. Regardless, she didn't want Dalinar starting a storming fight in the mud. However, she saw a solution. She touched him on the arm and pointed to Wit, who had finally stepped through the portal.

He was staring at the sky while holding a small rock. The same one he'd given Dalinar—or would give Dalinar, thousands of years in the future. Wit spotted them, and Navani hoped he'd intervene. Instead he looked away, his shoulders slumped.

"Maybe the Wit of this time can explain what we need to Jezrien," Navani said. "Or maybe he'll let you touch him."

Dalinar and Navani hiked that way. The mud wasn't terribly deep, but it was still difficult to move in. Nearby, one poor animal—thicker than a horse and heavy as a chull—was getting mired in a deeper spot.

Dalinar grabbed Wit by the shoulder, then touched Navani, Connecting them to make their languages match his—a trick she hadn't had time to learn yet. Wit appeared profoundly haunted. Eyes glazed over. Motions sluggish. Well, he'd just seen an entire world fall. She supposed she couldn't fault him for lacking a chipper attitude.

When he spoke, though, it wasn't what she had been expecting at all. "I'm not real, am I?" he said in a monotone.

"Wit?" Dalinar said. "Um . . . what is your other name?"

"I have many," Wit said. "None of them are me. I'm . . . power . . . trying to imitate him . . . But he knows too much, so he would know he's not real, and so I have to make myself know I'm not real . . . But then . . . I know . . ."

He put his hand to his head, his eyes bulging, and his face started to distort. Melting like paint on a wall. Navani jumped backward.

"Wit," Dalinar said. "Whatever you are. Wit would help us."

"He just watched Ashyn die," the homunculus said. "It was one of his first great failures. Not his absolute first . . . but one of them. He spent the next weeks staring at the sky. Worrying that he was too old, at three thousand. That he was losing himself." The thing stumbled away. "I must do that. I must do that . . ."

"I don't think we're going to get anything useful from him," Navani said. "But we at least learned the language."

"I don't think we did," Dalinar said. "I tried to Connect to him, but he Connected to me instead, learning our tongue." He heaved a sigh, then pointed at a spot a ways up the hillside. "There might be another option. The air is shimmering over there, and I can feel the Stormfather watching. He might be able to get us out of here."

"Will he talk more openly if you're alone?"

"Likely," Dalinar admitted.

"Then I," she said, "will see what I can learn from these refugees, despite the language barrier."

"Be safe," he said.

"Dalinar, there's so much Stormlight here, I'd heal before they even finished pulling the spear out."

"Still," he said, squeezing her hand. "For my sake, try to be safe." Then he went to confront the Stormfather.

47
FAILURE POINTS

Irid adjudges this reasoning spurious, given the Skybreaker air of exactitude, that dissention is inevitable, as they turn finer points of argument against one another.

—From *Words of Radiance*, chapter 40, page 2

Adolin smashed a singer Regal out of the way while wielding an incredible Shardhammer—a weapon built as if for a god. It wasn't as refined as Maya's Blade, but it got the job done, crunching carapace and sending the enemy to the ground screaming.

He knew he was killing good people who were fighting for a world where humans could never enslave them again. Fortunately, Adolin hated this part already. So he did his job, holding steady with Neziham—the Azish Shardbearer—at the center of the human lines.

This was the *eleventh* wave of enemies since the initial fight the day before. The singer strategy now was to leverage their superior numbers to wear down the defenders. Like the previous assaults, this one involved enemies flooding out of the central building, advancing through volleys of arrows, and engaging the pikes.

Their battle-by-battle tactics varied. This time they'd sent the entire flood at one section of defenders. That let them concentrate their forces—but it let the humans do the same, positioning both Shardbearers right at the crux of the defense. Adolin felt tiredness deep in his bones, but he kept fighting, counteracting fatigue with determination. He kicked a table into some singers, who finally began withdrawing toward their bunker.

Adolin held up a fist, and a horn sounded in response: Kushkam agreeing to an advance. So far, the human forces had stood their ground, maintaining that massive ring of pikes and shields, rotating men in and out. In response, the enemy had started *building.* Using pieces of wood from disassembled ships, they'd started to expand their presence in the dome, erecting a kind of roofed fort—maybe a hundred feet in diameter—around the central control structure.

Plainly, giving the enemy a larger staging area in the dome was no longer a good idea. It was time to advance, destroy the fort, and force the singers back through the portal to reset. Supported by two full companies of soldiers, Adolin pressed forward. Though the ground was now strewn with debris per his suggestion, the latest singer advance had pushed a great deal of it out of the way, clearing a path for a counterassault.

Singers retreated in front of Adolin, and arrows rained down on them from above. Seeing the two Shardbearers giving chase made the enemy even more unnerved, and some broke. Running, their backs exposed, making life here for the singers like Damnation itself. At least during their advances they had shield cover to stop arrows.

Adolin and Neziham surged forward, crossing the fifty or so yards with troops marching behind. The enemy crowded into their newly made fortress—which was less like a palisade and more like a little dome of its own. Once close enough, though, Adolin gave the order and the human advance halted. Azish hurlers came forward and tossed bags of oil an impressive distance to hit the fortification.

Setting the entire inside of this place on fire was a bad idea—but Adolin wasn't opposed to a little tactical arson. The enemy wanted to build a fortress in here? Well, flaming arrows would have something to say about that. The oil caught in a burst, and they watched as it burned. Then faltered. Then sputtered out.

What?

"Storms," Neziham said from within his helm. "Adolin, I don't think that's wood—not anymore."

Joined by shockspren, Adolin realized he was right. Some sections of the fortress had burned away, but much of it . . . well, what they'd mistaken at a distance for wood was instead a dark brown, unpolished bronze. The enemy had put their stolen Soulcaster to use. Likely setting up sections of wood, sealing them with something malleable—as sickening as it sounded, probably feces—then Soulcasting it to solidify the entire structure. Adolin gave an order to charge forward, hoping maybe his hammer and Neziham's Blade could destroy the fortification.

However, as soon as they drew close, sections of the fortification slid open—and stormforms began sending out waves of lightning to electrocute troops. Singer archers shot in tandem, and as the human advance faltered, reservist rank-and-file singers rushed out to reset their position.

Adolin's soldiers had to slow, then hunker down, and then Adolin couldn't press forward lest he get surrounded. He waited, blocking with his own body what he could, but he soon realized this was futile. He couldn't press inward. Their protection of this city depended on *them* being the defenders, inflicting large casualties on the enemy. He'd lose far too many troops rushing a fortification.

He roared in his Plate and smashed a group of singers out of the way, then called the retreat. His forces made a controlled withdrawal, with him and Neziham at the rear to block as many enemy arrows as possible, until they eventually reached the human lines. Here he met Kushkam. The stout man's armor was bloodied, though Azish generals didn't often fight at the front. He eyed Adolin and Neziham, then nodded to the side, and the three of them stepped away from the others to confer in private.

"Bronze," Adolin said, pulling off his helmet. "They've Soulcast the storming thing to *bronze.*"

"This is my fault," Kushkam said. "I let that Soulcaster be taken . . ."

"It was a difficult assault anyway, Commandant," Neziham said, pulling off his own helm, revealing a shaved head and a mouth with several bronze teeth. "Even without the Soulcaster, the wood might not have caught fire—not if they know to wax it." He looked across the expansive floor of the dome, now with a little fortress at the center. "We're going to have to let them keep it until reinforcements arrive. We can't expend the lives to take it."

"By Yaezir himself," Kushkam muttered. "Suggestions?"

Adolin tapped his finger against his helm in thought. "Do you have anything bigger than a bow or an ordinary crossbow? In Alethkar, we use enormous crossbows—small ballistas really—to try to bring down Shardbearers."

"That works?" Kushkam asked with a grunt.

"Not usually," Adolin admitted. "My father *does* like talking about how many he destroyed in his youth. But we might be able to use them to break that fortress."

"We don't have anything like that, Adolin," Neziham said.

"Siege equipment?" Adolin asked. "Catapults?"

"No. The capital hasn't been assaulted in centuries. Not since the Alethi invasions, in fact."

At home, they'd have engineers who could build them, but certainly not fast enough to be relevant on this battlefield. Adolin considered, but storms, his mind was sluggish.

"Maybe try to get some rocks on the roof?" Adolin said. "Drop them through the skylights to see how structurally sound that inner building is?"

"An excellent suggestion," Kushkam said, and walked away, calling out orders immediately.

Adolin grunted, then took a drink from a runner girl. *Fourth day,* he thought. *Only two more until the army starts to arrive.* So far, they'd lost one for every five of the enemy, but if their lines grew too thin . . .

We'll hold, he thought to himself, and felt a wave of support from the now-distant Maya.

Adolin nodded to Neziham, then jogged to the way out. There, he moved through the short maze—really just three small hallways turning sharply—and emerged into the late afternoon light. Here . . .

Here Adolin sagged, sudden fatigue hitting him like a stormwall, exhaustionspren buzzing around him. This had been his third time in the dome—and the most grueling. Still, he forced his limbs to move, lugging what now seemed leaden Plate as he stomped over to his waiting attendants.

He stretched out his arms to let his armorers start removing his Plate. "Kaminah," he said to his young aide-de-camp, "what does it mean to capture the city?"

"Sir?" the brown-haired young woman replied. "Um . . . I mean, you conquer it, I guess?"

"I'm speaking specifically," he said, "of the terms of the contract that Father made. Odium gets the entirety of Azir if he captures this city . . . but what does capturing it mean, exactly?"

"I have no idea," she said. "Do you want me to write asking for clarification from Urithiru?"

"Please do. It might not be relevant. If they break out of that dome, it will be pretty obvious when the place is conquered, but I'd rather not be surprised by some little-known legality."

She bobbed her head eagerly.

His breastplate unlocked and his armorers hauled it free, abruptly burdened by its weight—which could be cumbersome when it wasn't powered and active. He stepped free of his boots, and suddenly felt like a man whose saddle girth had been cut, dumping him to the ground. He stumbled, and needed Colot—who appeared from nowhere and helped him—to stay upright. Adolin thanked him and wiped his brow, regaining his balance.

"You need rest," Colot said.

"Sure do. Ask around and see if any of our soldiers did carpentry work, and if they built siege equipment at any point. Also, don't we have a scribe with some engineering knowledge? It might be worth seeing if we can get some catapults up."

"Not sure we have the time," Colot said.

"Try anyway," Adolin said.

That staging fortress at the center of the dome was going to let the enemy keep a large number of troops in position. And with the Soulcaster, they could constantly reinforce it . . . maybe expand it . . .

One day in, and his defenders were already strained. "Colot," he said, "bring in my first armor standby and tell him to be ready for battle."

"Moore? He's sleeping off the last attack, Adolin," Colot said, with a chuckle. "We're on your second standby. Reep."

Adolin nodded. He knew Reep; a fine soldier, and well trained in Plate. He would take this shift, wearing Adolin's armor for the next four hours and facing any enemy assaults. Strangely, though, Adolin thought he felt reluctance from the armor as it was carried away. Was that real?

"Hold," he said to the armorers, and then reached out a hand to touch the breastplate.

Yeah, he was imagining things. He sensed nothing special or odd from the touch. Still, he'd spent his life talking to his sword, and eventually it had talked back.

"Go with them," he whispered. "Serve those who bear you as you have me. Protect them."

He gestured to the armorers, who—looking amused—carted it off. Well, anyone who had served with him long enough knew his ways. He talked to his horse too. And anyone who thought that was strange could stuff a chull up their backside; Gallant understood the conversation, and enjoyed it.

"Casualties?" Adolin asked.

Colot steeled himself. "Twenty-one of ours dead, plus three times as many wounded. I don't have the Azish number."

A costly failure for his assault. In that moment, the celebrations of a day ago felt far distant. "Get me the names. I'll listen to them after I check on my horse."

"Sir," Kaminah said, stepping in front of him, her sleeved safehand across her ledgers, holding them tight against her chest. "Um . . ."

Colot nodded to her, and some understanding seemed to pass between them. Had they been conferring?

"You should go and rest," she said to Adolin. "Um. Please?"

"No need to ask," Colot told her. "You're his aide-de-camp, promoted at his own word. You can just tell him."

"Right, right," she said. "Um . . . yeah. Go and sleep!"

Adolin sighed softly, then gave Colot what he hoped was a properly withering stare. "You're making *her* do it?"

"What?" Colot said. "Are you *really* going to ignore Brightness Kaminah? On the first full day, you're going to stop her from doing her job? The one you *asked* her to do?"

Adolin glanced at the young woman, who shrank down a little, but she pointed with her freehand at the exhaustionspren buzzing around him. "To bed. You fought all night, straight through the Everstorm as it passed. Brightlord Colot says I'm supposed to tell you that you have to sleep."

"Or?" Colot asked.

"Or," she squeaked, "the sergeant at arms will, um, find you and . . . well, they say he'll tie you in place."

"You know how excited Grubs gets when he has a chance to dig out his officer-tying rope," Colot added.

Adolin sighed again.

"Her first day," Colot reminded. "Surely you want to be a good example, so that in the future she'll have the courage and experience to help your other officers get the rest they need. Even if, of course, you're superhuman and could keep going for weeks."

"You're a bastard, Colot," Adolin said, but smiled and raised his arm. Colot tapped it with his own, forearm to forearm. A promise made, and a promise accepted.

"I do my best, sir," Colot said. "You know I'll wake you if necessary."

Adolin nodded, then paused. "When did *you* last sleep?"

"Um . . ." Colot said.

"Oh!" Kaminah said. "You too! Off to bed!"

"After his sleep shift," Colot promised.

"Make sure he does it, Kaminah," Adolin ordered. Then trudged off—secretly relieved they'd forced him into it.

⁂

After spending a day preparing strategy and organizing the Windrunners to fly the Mink to Herdaz, Sigzil finally stepped out of the Oathgate at the Shattered Plains. Here, he officially took command of the united coalition forces defending Narak.

With a plan in mind.

He immediately launched into the sky, hovering above the Shattered Plains to see what the maps had depicted. "Narak" was the name given to the central plateaus, the heart of where the listeners had once made their home in exile. The military, ever pragmatic, had named the largest of those plateaus—one shaped a little like a half-moon, open side to the west—Narak Prime. The smaller satellite plateaus around it were named Narak

Two, Narak Three, and so forth. Of those, Narak Two—the plateau he'd just left—was of vital importance, as it held the Oathgate.

"Thoughts?" he asked, hanging there.

"It's as you feared," Vienta said, appearing to him as a small woman shrouded in moving, flowing cloth, nothing but her eyes visible. "I see troop placements on only the two central plateaus."

"Not a bad move," he said. "Supporting our most important locations."

"Yes, but you've persuaded me. There is a better defense to be had."

Sigzil nodded to himself, feeling *confident* for the first time in months. Kaladin trusted him. Dalinar trusted him.

He, in turn, would trust that they were right to put him in command. "Time until the Everstorm arrives?" he asked, gazing to the west—where a darkness was looming.

Vienta watched for a moment. "At current speed," she said, "I estimate three hours."

She didn't like letting others know how good she was with things like calculations. It embarrassed her; apparently other honorspren had teased her for her numerical mind. Sigzil instead found it *brilliant.* She could run mathematical problems in her mind faster than a scribe with an abacus, and could judge things like distance and momentum with a glance.

"Thank you," he said. "Let's grab the others and get a little closer to the storm, see if we can make out Fused. I'd love for you to do whatever counts you can of them with that exceptional mind of yours."

She fuzzed, blurring—something she did when she was pleased. "I love that you *appreciate* what I can do," she whispered, "even if it isn't . . . strictly honorsprenlike."

"What I'm about to propose isn't strictly soldierlike," he said. "We'll make it work."

"We . . . really will, won't we?" she asked. "We can do this."

"We can," he said. He'd protect Narak—and he intended to do so as himself: a scientist.

He swooped down, along with his Windrunner command staff: Ka, head scribe, and Leyten, the stout head quartermaster—who was to be Sigzil's second for this operation. They were joined by Peet, Ka's husband, another original member of Bridge Four.

Sigzil led them westward to get a better look at the Everstorm. This close, he felt dominated by it. The enemy had moved the storm across the entire continent last night at speed, bringing it here, then slowing it to a crawl. The defense of Narak would happen in darkness, regardless of the time of day.

"Sigzil," Vienta said in his ear, "I count more lightning strikes per minute than normal. It seems angry, determined."

 He slowed the others so they could study it, still at a distance—but close enough to find it overwhelming. It appeared to be gathering strength, overflowing with crackling red lightning and ominous thunder.

"Storms," Leyten said. "I mean . . . storm, I guess. One storm. The worst one."

"Heavenly Ones," Peet said, pointing.

Ka took the spyglass from him, both her spren and his sitting on her shoulder cross-legged. Though Peet wore a standard Bridge Four uniform, Ka preferred a slit-sided havah and leggings. Sigzil had never seen her summon her Shardblade as a sword outside of practice—but she used it as a pen regularly.

"Not just Heavenly Ones," she said, handing the spyglass to Sigzil.

He peered through it to search the looming storm, where he picked out distinctive glowing dots soaring in the air among the dark ones that trailed long trains of cloth. Skybreakers. It looked like their entire force, numbering in the hundreds. They'd arrived with the storm.

"That's a lot of Skybreakers," Ka said. "I can see how they managed to move so many Fused."

The defenders would face as many as eight or nine hundred Fused, flown in by the Heavenly Ones and Skybreakers with the storm—leaving behind their conventional troops, who marched too slowly.

"Information from the Heralds," Vienta whispered, with Sigzil telling the others, "says there are perhaps four thousand total Fused in existence—but best our spies can guess, large numbers of those are too worn or mentally overwhelmed to be used in combat. The latest spy reports from Kholinar indicate the enemy has around two thousand who are functional, awake, and battle capable. So . . ."

"We're facing almost half their entire force here," Ka said. "Incredible."

For the enemy who was holding huge swaths of Roshar to field fully *half* its Invested forces here . . . that was a huge commitment. And Sigzil had to resist it.

Vienta whispered to him counts she made of what she could see, and he told them to Ka to report. Then together they flew back to Narak to meet the battalionlord overseeing defenses: an Alethi general with light green eyes who wasn't much older than Sigzil was. This man—Balivar—had been a lieutenant a year and a half ago.

"Our generals are gathered?" Sigzil asked, landing.

"Yes, sir!" Balivar said, saluting.

"Lead on," Sigzil said, and they were led off of the perfectly circular Narak Two—the Oathgate—and onto the southwestern portion of Narak Prime. Like many here at the center, these two plateaus now had large, thick walls protecting them, built by Stonewards.

"Good thing the listeners didn't have these walls," Leyten said softly, rubbing at his chin. "We'd have *never* taken the place." The quartermaster wore a curly light brown beard in defiance of tradition. He was one of the most easygoing original members of Bridge Four, and had been there that first day when Kaladin had pulled them out of bed.

"You just like how neat and orderly it looks with the walls," Ka said, with a laugh. An Alethi woman, she kept her hair shorter than most.

"A well-apportioned military camp is a thing of beauty," Leyten replied. "Everything in its place, packed tight like a good rucksack."

They were led to a small building on Narak Prime, well-guarded, where the rest of Sigzil's generals waited for orders. After speaking with the Mink at length, Sigzil had those orders—but he wasn't certain what the others would think. Once in the room, which was filled with maps on tables and walls, he turned to regard the dozen or so generals and scribes who were preparing the defense.

He took a deep breath, stilling his nerves. Time to be a leader.

"I'm going to change the way you're operating here," Sigzil said, gesturing to the table map of the surrounding plateaus. "You've pulled all our forces onto two plateaus: Narak Prime and Narak Two. Is that correct?"

"Yes, sir," Balivar said, frowning. "It's what makes the most sense. Those are the two most important positions, and we have limited defenders. We shore them up the best that way."

"I want instead," Sigzil said, "to spread our defense across these *four* plateaus, all of which have walls." He pointed at Narak Prime and Narak Two, but then at Three and Four as well.

"Sir?" another general, an older man, asked. He had a full head of silver hair—his name was Winn, Sigzil recalled from the briefings. "Is that really wise? Do we really have the troops to protect *four* plateaus?"

"No," Sigzil said. "And that's the point."

They gaped at him, shocked.

"There is a principle in engineering," Sigzil said, "where you *build in* failure points to a device. Say, a bridge. You make it so certain parts will break first."

"Why build it so it will break, sir?" Balivar asked.

"Because . . ." one of the scribes answered, nodding her head. "Because if you *know* where a break will happen, then you can *anticipate* it."

"Exactly," Sigzil said. "If a bridge is going to fail, you want to know it's under too much stress *before* it breaks, so you can fix it. In most cases, you build a point to break that isn't vital, to protect the one that is." He slammed a finger to the map. "We *have* to protect Narak Prime. If we lose it, then by the terms of the contract, we lose the entire region—warcamps, Unclaimed Hills, everything.

"We *need* that land. The enemy is placing a great number of troops here because they know it. Without the Shattered Plains, we can't supply Urithiru. The enemy attacking here is an attempt to starve the tower because they know they can't assault it directly now that it's awakened."

Sigzil stabbed the map again. "We cannot afford to lose Narak Two. The Oathgate is absolutely vital for resupplying us with gemstones, to provide medical attention for our troops back at Urithiru, and—in an emergency—to provide a safe retreat."

"That's why we've protected these two," Balivar said.

"It's why," Sigzil said, "we're going to protect *all four* of these plateaus—then lure the enemy to spend time hitting one we can lose, by leaving it slightly less protected. We're going to build in failure points, like in engineering a bridge. This isn't an ordinary siege—we don't have to last months, even weeks. We need to last *six days.* The more we can trick the enemy into attacking sections of our defenses that *don't actually matter,* the better."

He waited, his heart racing, for their objections. The obvious ones: That he had never been in command of a battlefield like this before. That his scientific thinking was something to be mocked—among soldiers, it made him so odd. He'd gone over this plan with the Mink and the others after dreaming it up, and they'd helped him refine it. But now . . . now he expected . . .

"That could work," Winn, the aged general, said. "You're right, Radiant Sigzil. If we've been approaching this like any other siege, the enemy might too—they might search for weak points and strike there first. So if we build those into our defenses intentionally . . . this could *really* work."

"Huh," Balivar said, looking at the new battle maps and troop positioning numbers that Ka handed out. "It's odd. I don't think I've ever seen a general think like this before . . ."

"It's not as uncommon as you assume," Winn said. "Think of how a smaller military will have fallback positions during a controlled retreat, making the enemy fight for an advance. It's like that, just with . . . a dash of engineering."

"I like it," one of the scribes said. "This is a new world, with Fused—whose rushes can be so powerful they're almost impossible to stop. The tides of battle can turn so quickly with these incredible forces at play. Planning for controlled losses is an excellent way to mitigate that."

They started talking it over in detail, taking in the battle plans he'd brought—scribes reading out the details. For the next hour they hashed it out, asking the questions that Sigzil—with the Mink's help—already had answers for. At the end of it, the orders were passed. Troops would file into Narak Three and Four, which had been barracks before. Arranged specifically to encourage an assault on Narak Four first.

Sigzil watched it happen, a little bemused, because not once did they question him. He . . . was a Radiant. They knew that Dalinar wouldn't put him in command unless he could do the job. So, while they *did* question and poke holes in his strategy, they also accepted that he was the right one to present this plan.

At one point, they asked for some calculations on how long their rations would last—and Vienta rattled it off, and he answered them before the scribes could even get out pencils. That set the group of women to watching him with what actually seemed like *respect.* For a man who understood figures. True, it was Vienta who had done the calculation, but she preferred that people not know—so he simply accepted the respect of the others as he provided guidance.

At the end they broke, with Sigzil appointing Balivar to head up ground defenses. Sigzil would continue to oversee general strategy, but much of his moment-to-moment attention would be on making certain the enemy didn't obtain air dominance.

"Storms," he said, walking out of the small room to see troops in motion. "Leyten . . . that *worked.*"

The affable man slapped him on the back. It felt like so long ago that Sigzil, at the bottom of these very chasms, had spent hours helping Leyten make armor for Bridge Four. Now here they were, in command of the place's entire military structure.

"You did good in there, Sig," Leyten said. "You wowed them." He ran off to see that the camp had enough of things like arrows, while Ka remained conferring with the camp scribes. That left Sigzil to drift up into the air again, alone this time save for his spren.

"I worried I wasn't ready," he admitted to her.

She appeared to him in her normal shape, a woman shrouded in robes that drifted around her. Looking out with eyes that were so keen. "I worried too. But . . . I think they *like* how logically we approached this. When things are tense, it's good to know someone has a plan."

Beneath, his troops were arriving. He had around three hundred Radiants, mostly Windrunners and Edgedancers, but with a growing force of Stonewards. Plus some Truthwatchers and a handful of Lightweavers. No Elsecallers—the sole one the army had was Jasnah—and no Willshapers, as the Reachers refused human bonds. Skybreakers served the enemy, as did all the Dustbringers, but those had retreated to Jah Keved after Taravangian's betrayal. That put his three hundred against nine—but with him having far greater conventional forces, and a dozen Shardbearers.

Not a fair fight, as the enemy had the advantage . . . but his strategy could account for that. Assuming it worked, assuming they could win within that terrible black storm with its crimson lightning.

The enemy's forces were always bolstered by the storm.

"I *believe* in you," Vienta whispered. "I . . . believe in *us,* Sigzil. We're what they want, for once."

"Live this truth," he said, raising his fists to her.

She saluted him back, with the Bridge Four salute.

He was done questioning. Now he would lead.

BEWARE the FUSED!

HEAVENLY ONES

FLOWING ONES

DO NOT ENGAGE! FIND A RADIANT!

TWENTY-SIX YEARS AGO

It felt strange for Szeth to be the only one in the bed.

Usually the entire family shared the mat. But this time, on the evening following . . . events at the stone . . . his sister had been sent to stay with cousins for a few days, and his parents were outside. He'd been fed, washed, and tucked in. His mother treated him like something fragile.

Szeth wanted something to hold. They'd . . . taken Molli's pelt from him.

He'd suffered their ministrations in a deep haze, so it was no wonder they assumed he'd gone straight to sleep. But he could hear them outside. Talking to the Farmer.

"He subtracted," Father said, his voice thick with emotion. Like broth with far too little water. "My son . . . subtracted."

"He had nail marks on his throat, Neturo," the Farmer said, his voice kindly. Like a flute. "The soldier attacked him. Beyond that, they robbed you."

"I know," Father said. "But . . . my little boy . . ."

"How could this happen?" Mother said, her voice strong, like a towering tree. Firm, immovable. "Colors-nimi, how could you let your soldiers run rampant like this?"

"They have been more difficult to control lately," the Farmer said. "It must be because I let them fight. They get a taste for it, and subtraction . . . it feeds upon itself, Zeenid."

Szeth squeezed his eyes shut. He had subtracted. No. That was a sanitized word.

He'd killed someone. With a rock to the head.

"What are you saying?" Father asked. "What does this mean for my son?"

"He did nothing wrong," the Farmer assured him. "The fault lies entirely upon the soldiers, and upon me as their supervisor. At the same time, what your son did . . . changes a person."

"No," Mother said. "I won't have you say in one breath he did nothing wrong, and in another imply he is broken."

"He is *not* broken," the Farmer said. "We need people capable of actions like this. The raids grow more frequent. I need soldiers who were raised well, who are moral and strong, but who can also subtract when needed."

In the silence that followed, Szeth could hear leaves rustling. The gurgling of the distant brook. The grinding of wills between his parents and the man they obeyed.

"This is a talent," the Farmer said. "The Stone Shamans teach that it is. Your son should be sent for training."

"In how to kill?" Father asked, his voice cracking.

"Do you know the stories of the Knights Radiant?" the Farmer asked. "They had a philosophy. They called it . . . watchers at the rim. They went to fight, and be changed, so we might live."

"You want to do this to our son?" Mother asked.

"He's already killed a man, Zeenid, and he used a *stone* to do it. He blasphemed. But soldiers, they can touch rocks, and iron forged from the blood of the earth. Sending him away would protect him from what he did. From what he might do. If the shamans discover he was hiding that stone . . ."

"We all found that stone," Mother said. "We—"

"It is well," the Farmer said. "Let's face the problem before us, not ones in the past." His voice was so calming, as if it came from the brook or the leaves. If Szeth were ever to be blessed to hear the spren, he imagined their voices would be the same.

"No," Szeth whispered to himself. "You will never hear the spren, Szeth. You aren't worthy of that."

Don't be so certain, a voice—that same one—said in his head. *We watch you, Szeth. We are curious.*

He felt a sudden jolt. Again? What did it mean?

"You're going to take him away," Mother said. "You're going to steal him and turn him into a killer."

"I'm sorry," the Farmer said. "You can visit him though."

More silence, full of the sounds of the winds. Then a sound of wood groaning as someone stood up on the steps outside. A voice somehow stronger than the wind, or the trees, or the river. A voice like the stones.

"No," Szeth's father said. "I will not visit. If you are taking my son, then I will go with him. I will learn to subtract as well."

Something broke in Szeth then. It was a strange sensation, feeling his emotions *snap,* like a clay vessel dropped to the ground. A burst of pain at hearing his father insist—followed by rushing warmth and relief.

Szeth wouldn't be alone.

"Neturo!" the Farmer said. "You are my best administrator!"

"No longer. If you are going to teach my son to kill, then you will teach *me* as well so that he is never alone with what he must do."

"Then Elid and I will go too," Mother said. "If she hates it, we will let her move to the town with her cousins, as she has often asked."

"This is insanity," the Farmer said.

"No," Father replied. "We are a family. My son will not step into the darkness alone. If you need me to break something to prove I am willing, point me toward the other two soldiers who robbed me, then left my son in the hands of a drunken monster."

The Farmer heaved a long sigh. "At least think about this first. You might reconsider."

"Are you going to reconsider?" Father asked.

"No," the Farmer admitted.

"Then neither," Father said, "will I."

49
A REALM OF POSSIBILITIES

I challenge that itself to be perfidious; having studied much of their natures, and having made a specific attempt to represent their minds accurately, I find myself confident in my delineation; it is of particular passion and perfection in me; as perhaps I would have known them myself, given opportunity.

—From *Words of Radiance*, chapter 40, page 2

Shallan emerged into what felt like the real world. She stumbled to a stop, surrounded by singers in old-style clothing—barely wearing anything, really—on a hillside with patches of soil. Genuine *soil.* She gasped, grinning, and knelt and stuck her hands into it. Storms. It was just like she'd read.

Several singers kept running, but two others lurched to a halt nearby. Shallan appeared to be wearing a singer body, even to her own eyes. That was odd, wasn't it? Dalinar always saw himself as himself; she'd read the accounts several times.

"Shallan?" asked a tall singer with a mostly white skin pattern.

"Yup."

"And Renarin?" The tall one peered at the third, a shorter singer with black and red in swirls.

"This is . . . eerie," Shallan said, prodding the carapace on her face. "Glys and Tumi said we'd have a Lightweaving over us, but I *feel* like I'm in the actual *body* of this singer."

"It's complicated," Rlain said. "Which is . . . a way of saying I don't completely understand. We can't afford to be recognized by anyone, not even

Brightlord Dalinar. When we enter, the vision itself assigns us people to take over. Then, Glys and Tumi nudge us to actually take the *shape*."

"Where are our spren?" Renarin asked, and his voice sounded odd. No rhythm, she realized.

Rlain winced. He heard it too.

"I feel Tumi," Rlain said. "Hovering outside the vision and watching, to not give us away."

"Ah . . ." Renarin said. "Yes. That's for the best. Um . . ." He held his hands out and inspected them. "Shallan, are you all right?"

"I like this carapace," she said, standing up. "It feels neat. And the dirt too! I can't wait to step on plants that don't move. Won't that be *surreal*?"

"Doesn't look like many plants have grown here yet." Renarin pointed down the hillside to an enormous flat basin of dirt. Wet dirt, judging by how the people trudged through it.

"There," Rlain said, singling out one figure below. "That's your father, isn't it?"

"And Navani with him," Shallan said. "So we can see *them* as themselves. But the two Ghostblood assassins . . ."

". . . will be hiding," Renarin said quietly. "Like us. They could be anyone on that field." He took a deep breath. "Still, we have the advantage. You heard the Ghostbloods say they're going to watch my father and aunt, so we have intel on the enemy's movements. That puts us at a tactical advantage."

Rlain hummed softly.

"What?" Renarin asked.

"You sound like your father," Rlain said. "In the best of ways."

Renarin glanced at the ground, and she sensed a blush in his posture—which she found *very* curious, especially given how he looked back up toward Rlain in an admiring way. Could it be . . . these two? She couldn't wait to ask Adolin. Maybe he knew something. For now she led the way down the slope.

"You two should try not to speak too much," Rlain noted.

"We don't have to fool other singers, fortunately," Renarin said. "Just some humans."

"I wonder if I could do it," Shallan said, trying to mimic Rlain's rhythm. "I might have to someday, in the real world."

Rlain halted in place, his eyes wide, humming a tense rhythm. Shallan matched it.

"How are you *doing* that?" he demanded. "That's a *perfect* rhythm."

"It feels natural in this body," she said, shrugging. "I'm mostly imitating you."

"It's uncanny," he said, resuming his descent. "But be careful. If you only imitate, you'll often hum one that isn't appropriate for your conversation."

Together, they reached the bottom of the slope and set up there to watch. "Why stop here?" Renarin asked. "Aren't we going to go find the Ghostbloods?"

Storms. She was so used to working with the Unseen Court that she'd forgotten these two had practically no experience. "Our first objective," she said, "is to be as unobtrusive as we can. Try not to draw *their* attention. Us returning might seem odd, since the others were running away. Therefore, we should act as if we were sent back to watch."

"Right," Renarin said. "So how do we learn anything?"

She narrowed her eyes. "Look for anyone sticking a little too close to Dalinar or Navani. And give me a minute." She studied the area, noting the groups of human refugees making their way out of the wet dirt. Exhausted, burned, terrified.

The first arrival of humans on Roshar. What a thing to witness. However, Veil coached her quietly—helping her keep her mind on the job at hand, reminding her of the skills she'd been practicing since childhood. When you had an abusive father and an insane mother, you learned to act.

I think, Veil whispered, *we've always been a little better at this than we admitted.*

It was true. Shallan had always worried that Veil acted like an expert in espionage, but was actually a scared child. However, in some ways that scared child was the queen of putting on faces. She shouldn't have had to go through such a terrible, painful childhood—but since she *had,* she might as well storming weaponize it.

"Continue pretending to be scouts," she whispered. "Back up a little. Adopt nervous postures. I'm going in."

"In?" Renarin said.

"I can do this better than Mraize can," Shallan whispered. "It's time to prove it."

She moved out from behind the rocks in a low, nervous gait. She wasn't seeing humans, but bizarre, frightening aliens. She got close, skittish, clutching her spear. The gathered people shouted, so she sought refuge behind another rock, closer to the mud.

Then she moved out, creating two illusions—leaving a fake version of the singer behind, while Shallan instead trudged forward wearing the face and the loose and ragged gown of one of the refugees she'd seen. Covered in both ash and that wet mud. A simple brown dress, long as her ankles. A little embroidery.

Storms, Shallan, Radiant thought.

What?

You didn't need a drawing first. You just did it.

She . . . she was right. Shallan had been moving in this direction, but had she ever fully created a Lightweaving without any kind of drawing? It was . . . well, it was about time. She checked for weapons and found her anti-Stormlight dagger in a sheath at her belt—and added it to her costume.

First confirm he's here, she thought at herself. *Watching Dalinar and Navani. Try to figure out if he has tells that will let me spot him in the future. Then retreat and come up with a real plan for eliminating him.*

That wasn't her weakness showing, was it? She could kill Mraize. As she'd killed every other mentor in her life so far and—

Do you need me? Radiant asked.

No, Shallan said, stepping into the wet dirt, finding it exactly as slippery and messy as she'd hoped it would be. She started out past the refugees, attempting to project that she had forgotten something. Just another refugee human. It was a good thing she had lots of practice, because being Shallan wearing a singer's body, wearing a Lightweaving of a different human, was a lot of layers to peel back.

She waved on the few people that spoke to her, though—with alarm—she realized she couldn't understand them. She smiled in an exhausted way and pointed, deliberately saying something too soft for them to hear over the crowd.

They moved on as she continued walking. Dalinar and Navani were talking to . . . was that *Wit*? Or a simulacrum of Wit? She forcibly kept from staring, and instead found her way to an animal that was mired in the mud. With a smile to the people there, she took the ropes at its neck and began helping pull it free, giving her a reason to linger near Dalinar and Navani.

So, where would Mraize be? she wondered. They started to get the strange horse free, but then one of the workers slid, tugging the animal farther into the mud. *He'll want to be somewhere he can overhear . . .*

The refugees were mostly flowing past without stopping. With effort, she kept from looking through the portal into the other world. The horse-thing moved, barely. It seemed that . . .

That the other people working with her were barely trying. One grunted and waved her off, kneeling so he could peer at the animal's legs, to check them for wounds, maybe?

Shallan had immediately found the easiest way to remain close to Dalinar without being spotted . . . because Mraize had set up this situation to do the same. Storms. That had to be either him or Iyatil kneeling in the mud in front of her. Her gut said it was Mraize. Not because he acted like himself—

indeed, he didn't. Instead of confident, he was kind of bumbling—and when he stood, hands on his hips, he gave a rueful smile. Except it was very similar to the act he'd put on when pretending to be a soldier in Urithiru.

Having one or two personas you default to, Shallan thought, *is almost as much of a tell as acting like yourself.* She'd likely made that same mistake in the past.

She gripped her knife, but didn't draw it. Dalinar pushed past them in the wet soil, saying to Navani that he was going to speak to the Stormfather. Mraize traced Dalinar's departure with his eyes. Shallan would never have a better chance than this.

But . . .

Radiant took over, pulling the knife and swinging as Mraize walked past her toward Dalinar. Mraize spotted her motion in the corner of his eye and cursed, catching her arm right before she connected. Radiant saw genuine panic in his expression as she forced him into the side of the muddy animal, causing other refugees to scream and back off.

He held to her forearm with both hands, grunting, then eyed her. "That's a dangerous knife for you, little one," he said, letting a smile creep to the corner of his mouth. "Have you gone and grown up on me?"

Unfortunately, he was stronger than she was. To get an edge, Radiant tried to summon her armor, which resulted in a bunch of tiny knives appearing in the sticky wet dirt, quivering and saying, "Other Shallan!"

So . . . no armor in this realm. Radiant pushed back from him, ripping out of his grip—a move that he should have been able to prevent, but he seemed wary, and eager to keep her at a distance.

"How long?" Shallan asked.

"How long what?" he asked, wiping his face, leaving a smear of dirt.

"How long," Shallan said softly, "have you secretly been afraid of me?"

Oddly, he smiled. "Since I discovered that you had killed Tyn. Why would I recruit someone I wasn't at least in part frightened of? Why hunt something that can't fight back?"

That smile. So confident. Shallan wanted, on a gut level, to remove it. Thankfully, Radiant was more levelheaded. She knew, from Adolin's lessons, the foolish danger in attacking a taller, stronger opponent with only a knife. His hand had gone down by his side, almost certainly for his own weapon. If she allowed herself to be drawn into a brawl, he'd have a severe advantage.

So she instead feinted an attack, then stepped back, hiding her knife. When he pulled out his weapon, she raised her arms and stumbled away, shrieking. The onlookers, who had been confused up until now, lurched into action, grabbing Mraize. Though she'd been the first aggressor, they probably hadn't seen that, as it had been so unexpected. Several also moved to block Shallan from Mraize, holding out warding hands—but they obviously thought they knew who was the more dangerous, because they restrained Mraize, while merely keeping her away. All the while shouting in that language she couldn't understand.

Mraize took it in stride, giving her a withering look. He knew enough not to escalate—he didn't let them take his knife, but he did permit them to lead him away, while explaining in his calm, deliberate fashion. He somehow spoke their language.

Could she use the situation? Persuade the others he was dangerous? This was a tired, emotional lot.

"Kill him," a soft voice said from beside her.

Shallan's voice.

Shallan spun and saw a figure dressed identically to her—but with a head made all of curling grey smoke. Spiraling, shifting, mesmerizing.

"It's what we are, Shallan," the figure said. "It's what we need to become. You cannot reject me forever. I am you."

"F-Formless?" Shallan whispered. "I banished you."

"I am you."

"No," Shallan said, backing up. "I *banished* you."

"And yet," it said, stepping forward, "you come to a realm of possibilities and futures. Tell me, are you better because of one good day? Will you ever be fully 'better'?"

"I can be better," she hissed. "I *can*."

"Can you?" Formless asked, and all else seemed to fade. "You are what you were made into, Shallan. You are what was done to you. That is me. I am your future."

Shallan screamed and hunched down, her hands like claws, one open, one gripping her knife. The vision vanished. All became swirling mist, and she felt someone embrace her. Pattern.

"Calm, Shallan," he said. "Calm . . ."

Panting, she let him hold her. She couldn't see well in this place of shifting shapes and futures, like mixing paint, but she heard Rlain speak somewhere nearby.

"Well, that could have gone better," he said, his voice thrumming with a rhythm.

"Let's find somewhere to recover and regroup," Renarin said. "Our spren are panicking. They're certain that in another few moments we'd have been noticed by the gods. We need to do this without making so much of a scene."

"Murdering someone makes a scene," Shallan mumbled. "At least it has every time I've done it . . ." But she let herself be pulled away into the mists of the future.

⁂

The Stormfather appeared as a shimmer to Dalinar. Standing on the mountainside, looking down at the newly arrived humans.

Dalinar stopped in front of the spren, studying him. Today, he thought he could even catch some shape to the shimmering—one that matched the image he'd seen of the dead god, Honor, also named Tanavast.

The Stormfather was an echo of the Almighty. Like how one of Shallan's charcoal sketches might rub off on another page, leaving a faint shadow of the original sketch. Today, as on most days, he could feel the Stormfather's mood.

He was . . . sad. "The dogs will die," he said softly.

"The . . . what?" Dalinar said, frowning.

"Those smaller beasts that come with the refugees?" the Stormfather said. "The friendly ones? They're called dogs." He fell silent a moment. "Tanavast always said he missed hounds. Too small a breeding population made it through. They will be gone in three hundred years."

"Hounds?" Dalinar said. "Like axehounds?"

"Your ancestors bred axehounds as a replacement, as they fit the same ecological niche. They have some of the same mannerisms. It's a . . . curiosity of genetics and parallel evolution. If you breed for certain traits—such as obedience—sometimes you get a few of the same companion traits.

"The pigs . . . they'll thrive on Roshar; they're willing to eat anything. Those minks will become wild and feral. The rats made it, remarkable considering how few snuck through, but I've learned never to be surprised at where you find rats. Look. The birds are about to arrive."

Dalinar turned as people began to cry out, ducking as an enormous group of chickens came soaring in through the portal. Thousands of them.

"They flocked on the other side," the Stormfather said, "corralled and cornered by rising temperatures and the burning sky. It is a miracle they found their way here, but they must have followed the sudden cool air. Or perhaps . . . perhaps the Wind sought them out. They will thrive. Parrots of two dozen varieties, who can eat the grains of Roshar until other options begin to grow in Shinovar."

Dalinar didn't reply, merely listening. Sometimes the Stormfather would just talk, and you never knew what you might learn.

"I don't remember this," the Stormfather continued, "yet I do. I wasn't alive, wasn't *aware*."

He didn't go on, so after a while Dalinar prompted him. "Tanavast was alive though. You have some of his memories."

"Echoes only," the Stormfather said. "Little that is relevant. A fondness for dogs . . ."

 "What happened on Ashyn, really?" Dalinar said.

"I do not know."

"And . . . the Wind you mentioned earlier. It spoke to me."

"A fallen god."

"A fallen god," Dalinar said. "There are gods other than Honor, Cultivation, and Odium? Here on Roshar?"

"There are pieces of the god who made the planet," the Stormfather said. "No longer relevant, as humans—poorly adapted to this land—began to fear the storm above all else. And so it took on life . . . became an Adversary. A new demigod for Roshar."

Dalinar nodded, thoughtful. The god who had made this world, perhaps the very God Beyond that Dalinar had begun to follow . . . they had left caretakers in the spren. But when that god vanished—dead and shattered, by Wit's testimony—the spren had grown into something else. Something more tied to Honor, Cultivation, and Odium.

"You should not be seeing this," the Stormfather said. "There is nothing useful for you here, Dalinar."

"Could you get us home?" Dalinar asked.

"Perhaps. If I take you now, will you go?"

Dalinar considered, looking over the refugees below. He felt . . . invigorated, having seen this piece of history. The true origin for his people—and all humans—on this world. He checked his clock, and found that it was still the fourth day. He had time.

"The power of Honor is here," Dalinar said. "Around us."

"It will never accept you."

"Why not?" Dalinar asked.

"Because it cannot stand another who would do what Honor did."

There.

That seemed relevant.

"What Honor did?" Dalinar said. "Stormfather, what exactly did *Honor do*?"

The shimmering hesitated a moment, as if realizing it had said too much.

"It *is* connected," Dalinar said. "What happened to Honor, how he died—and the way I could take up the power. I need to know how the previous god died before I could hope to hold that same position. Is that true?"

The Stormfather distorted, growing larger, more threatening, changing from human shape into more of a small storm. He loomed over Dalinar. "ENOUGH OF THIS! I will try to send you back now, if you will go. But you must swear to never try this again."

"No," Dalinar said, recognizing this was what he had to do. The others would have to fight battles without him, for now. He had to remain here and find his way to these secrets.

"You doom yourself," the Stormfather said. "And your wife. And others. YOU SHOULD NOT DEFY ME!"

"Stormfather," Dalinar said quietly, "do you remember when we talked a few days ago? Do you remember what you told me?"

Silence.

"You can change," Dalinar said. "We do not have to be combatants, as we often have been."

"All it takes is a willingness . . ." the Stormfather whispered. "It is too late for me, Dalinar. You . . . should not try so hard with me. I am but a spren." His voice grew softer. "Please, just come back."

Dalinar wavered a moment, then shook his head. "No. I've seen the visions as you wanted to present them, Stormfather. I will now see what *actually* occurred. I will find out what happened to Honor, and why his power has chosen no successor."

"So like your brother," the Stormfather whispered. "So arrogant."

"Why do you have an opinion on Gavilar?" Dalinar asked, confused. "Did you interact with him?"

The Stormfather seemed to come more alert at this, as if he'd said something wrong. Revealed something. The moment of Connection between them—of understanding, as had happened occasionally during their time together—evaporated. "You will die in here!" the spren thundered. "You will wander for eons, then wither away!"

"Storm you, then help me! Don't hide your secrets away!"

"No," the Stormfather said. "You wish to see what this place can show you? Fine. This is your stew. You can simmer in it. I will return when you are tired of it, and we can speak when you are reasonable."

The Stormfather began to fade.

"What are you afraid of?" Dalinar asked. "Stormfather? What lies have you been telling me!"

Only the ones, the Stormfather said in his mind, *that you deserve.*

Then he was gone. Dalinar sighed, angry at himself for losing his temper. Once in a while, it went so *well* between them, like when the Stormfather had told him about Eshonai's death. Dalinar cherished those moments of honesty and connection—but too often it went like this instead.

Just to check, Dalinar tried again to make a perpendicularity. Unfortunately, it did nothing. Using the power to get out of here was like trying to make water run uphill. With a sigh, he started back down to see how Navani was doing.

Indeed, I find Skybreaker disagreements remarkable; I have preference for each account, seeing as the arguments of the great arguers are of the most engaging variety, as to leave a woman disposed to both one side or the other, at a variety of times, vacillating back and forth, first the first, then second the second, to accede victory to whichever last has spoken.

—From *Words of Radiance*, chapter 40, page 2

Navani's father had been kindly to her, but he'd also been a terrible brightlord. He'd spent half his time out hunting, and the other half picking fights. He'd died in a duel when she was seventeen, and his last words to her had been to ask if, in her biography of him, she could include a particularly vile insult about the man who had stabbed him.

She'd never written that biography. That neglected task was one of hundreds that haunted her, and for some reason this place—this jaunt into the Spiritual Realm—reminded her of him. Why?

The question chased her as she trudged through the mud past refugees and toward the open portal. There, she realized part of what was itching at her. She still felt *Connected* to something, someone, out there. It was the same sensation she'd felt when searching for Dalinar earlier.

Someone was *watching* from the Spiritual Realm. Someone she knew well. Was it . . . her father? No. But whatever that Connection was, she couldn't identify it—and she also couldn't contact the Sibling, though not for lack of trying.

She stood in the mud, hands on her hips, dissatisfied with the way people flowed around her, frightened. She hadn't missed that the king and his spearmen kept their attention directly on her. Indeed, there was a disturbance happening—several refugees squabbling—but she couldn't get a good view of them because of the soldiers barricading her way.

She folded her arms. She was here to learn. What, then, would teach her the most? Nearby, the stream of tired people had slowed to a trickle. But it wasn't long before another group came through, different from the others. Their clothing less refined: more furs tied closed, less cloth. They clustered together and gave distrusting glares to others.

Shin, Navani realized, catching sight of a few of the faces hidden deep in their hoods. *I'm witnessing the arrival of the Shin.*

The portal itself interested her too. It had swelled even further, perhaps to eighty feet wide, level with the ground on the bottom. After a moment's thought, Navani settled on an idea. She walked straight to the portal, keeping space between her and the refugees. The soldiers, not wanting to be touched by her, moved away—then trailed after her.

Jasnah felt creating things like this—portals that could transport people around Roshar—should be possible with Elsecaller abilities, but they had no clues how to accomplish it, and Jasnah's experiments hadn't borne fruit. So what could Navani learn about this portal? One powerful enough to bring these people from an entirely different world? Well, observation number one: this portal required continued effort to maintain. Ishi'Elin remained standing on the other side, his arms stretched out, palms flat, as if he were physically pushing the portal open. The edges rippled and fluctuated, shrinking if he lost concentration or strength.

At this point, Navani thought, *he might not be a Bondsmith, since this looks like an Elsecalling.* So, some of the Heralds were practiced in different Surges from the ones they would one day take up as Heralds.

Within the portal, there was maybe six inches of "tunnel" between the worlds. It was a shimmering silvery color. As she watched people cross from the other side, their forms seemed to *fuzz* briefly, then fuzz again as they stepped out on this side.

It's like they fall in on the other side, she thought, *then fall out on this side—like they slide through space and emerge. It's less like a doorway you step through, and more like something you step into—which then carries you a distance.*

She doubted she had enough understanding of these kinds of physics to draw conclusions. Best to memorize her observations, then present them to her team when she returned. Regardless, it was good to make some order from the chaos. As always, a few key observations—a few thoughts about the mechanics of her situation—gave her some small measure of control. Or at least it made her feel that way.

Flocks of chickens burst through the top of the portal some twenty-five feet up. She considered, then reached out a finger to touch the portal. Behind her, someone cried out. She looked to find the king still watching her—a teenaged Shalash peeking out from behind him. He stepped forward, pointing and speaking in an authoritarian way.

"He's saying," a voice said from beside her, "that you shouldn't go through—that the other side is dangerous."

She glanced over and found Wit sitting in the mud to her left—his face having melted away, leaving a pale nothing in its place. He somehow talked without it. Distant thunder sounded, but she kept her attention on him.

"Um, thank you," she said. "Are you . . . feeling all right?"

"Me?" the faceless Wit said. "Oh, I'm fine. Just a big mess of existential crisis! Me, who is not me, knowing that I'll puff away back to nothing the moment this vision ends. It's fun! Like realizing you've swallowed poison by accident!"

"I'm sorry," she said.

"It's fine," he said. "I'm not real, so my emotions don't matter! My pain is an illusion, and I'm a puppet for raw Investiture, propped up and speaking like the sock on a child's hand." He cocked his head. "Damn. Is this how the Iriali feel all the time? No *wonder* they're so storming odd."

"What happens if I step through?" she asked.

"Nothing," fake-Wit replied. "Because you can't. This vision is tied to Roshar. You can see what it saw—the light passing through the Elsegate—but if you try to step through, nothing will happen."

"The Spiritual Realm is all places," Navani said. "That's what you—um, what real-world-Wit—told us."

"Yup, true," he said. "But you're not a god, Navani. This vision is the Spiritual Realm trying very hard to provide something your mind can understand. Push it too far, and that will unravel. So, fair warning."

"Warning taken," she replied. She nodded toward Jezrien and his daughter. "Could you tell them I'm not dangerous?"

"You want me to lie?" Wit asked.

"I'm *not* dangerous."

"Did you or did you not melt a man's eyes straight out of his head some five days ago?"

She hesitated. "I'm not dangerous to *them.*"

"Of course you aren't," he said. "They're not alive."

Storms above and Light Almighty . . . this fake Wit was even more aggravating than the real one. She stood, hands on her hips, looking at him—and he flopped back in the mud, blank face toward the sky, mumbling to himself about things like "infinite recursion" and "synthetic consciousness."

Navani sighed and turned again toward Jezrien and his daughter, still protected by guards. She smiled at the king, then tried bowing. He nodded to her. So she approached him slowly, hands to the sides to show she meant no harm.

She didn't dare get too close, so she stopped maybe five feet away and hoped he'd also move forward to meet her. He didn't—he studied her, thoughtful. But his daughter—who had a darker skin tone than his—slipped out from behind him. She stepped forward, ignoring her father's warning, and put out her hand to touch Navani's.

Navani squatted down closer to Shalash's eye level, and laced their fingers together. Jezrien stepped up, but didn't separate them. Sometime in the future, these two—with eight others—would found the Oathpact. One of the most important events in history.

Dalinar had apparently finished his conversation, as she could see him approaching through the mud. Had that thunder earlier been because of him?

"The vision will end soon," fake-Wit said. "You came here to see the crossing, and you did. You'll be cast out into the ever-mixing churn of possibilities and memories."

"And we'll be left without a guide," she said. "We need a way to return to the Physical Realm."

"Good luck with that," fake-Wit said. "Your husband just rejected the Stormfather's offer to send you back! Haha!"

Navani held to Shalash's hand, eye to eye. A wind blew across them, and she thought she heard a song carried with it. Faintly familiar.

"Can you help?" she asked the Wind.

I . . . do not know . . . it whispered. *Your husband decided to stay. He is . . . both wise and foolish . . . He has realized that the only path forward is through time. You must find the day that Honor died . . .*

That day was at *least* five thousand years into the future. How would they ever find it?

Maybe I don't have to, Navani thought, looking at Shalash. *Not yet. Cultivation told us to see history—and that's why we came. What if I first find a way to jump us forward in time a little—then from there I can search out the next step.*

"The Oathpact," Navani whispered. "Its founding. These two will be there. I need a guide, an anchor, to that moment."

Ah . . . the Wind whispered. *Her ribbon. Take her ribbon . . .*

Navani smiled at the young Shalash. Both she and her father seemed more friendly than they had been earlier, perhaps having realized Navani wasn't dangerous. Unfortunately, the distant hills were warping, turning to Stormlight, evaporating. As Wit had warned, this vision was ending.

Navani mimed at her own hair, then at Ash's. The girl felt at her head, then—questioning—took off her ribbon and placed it in Navani's hand.

A moment later the vision burst, and all the people unraveled into Stormlight. But the ribbon remained clutched in Navani's fingers.

⁘

Adolin felt a *lot* better after a few hours of sleep. Bolstered, he made use of the well-equipped, overly bronze bathing facility his officers had been assigned. He shaved and put on a fresh uniform, then got an update from one of Kaminah's assistants. Two assaults in four hours. No progress made on either side, which was a win for the defenders—though that singer fortress at the center held, repelling dropped stones.

Colot had gone to bed right before Adolin had woken up, and for once the dome was quiet. The enemy might have more troops, but they still had to worry about depleting them. Perhaps they had decided to hunker down, reinforce their fortress, and discuss strategy. It was what he'd have done after over a full day of losing large numbers to the offensive with no discernible progress.

He left his blackout tent and found it was already getting dark. As he did, his timid scribe whispered to him some bad news: His worst fears were proving true. The Azish reserve forces had been delayed. An enemy force of some sort had raided them, a mystery troop that baffled their generals. The delay was, they hoped, a short one—and they were already moving again. The current estimate had their reinforcements at least two days out.

Adolin wasn't too surprised, though a mystery force worried him. What was going on there? Regardless, the enemy was going to try anything they could to delay those troops to keep Azimir isolated as long as possible. He took the news, then shook his head and scanned the darkened plaza. Adolin's armor standby had just put on his Plate for a shift, giving Adolin a little time. So he did something that was always near the top of a commander's list, but never quite as urgent as it should be: he went to visit the injured.

The Azish field hospital was one of the nicest he had ever seen. As May had suggested, the surgeons were set up in a building right near the dome. He entered a world of sterile scents, recently mopped floors, white walls, and whiter linens. The Azish took to heart the old teachings of the Heralds, that dirt and disorder attracted rotspren, that washing hands and boiling instruments prevented infection.

Adolin had met armies who ignored such rules, and inevitably infection set in—visible by the spren they attracted. It didn't take much experimenting to see which way was better, and he was pleased to see this hospital so well equipped. He got a quick, secret briefing on how to open the saferoom hidden underneath the structure, then went out to visit the soldiers.

The Truthwatcher could be spared to help solely those whose wounds were life-threatening. Otherwise, the work would overwhelm and exhaust her. So there were plenty of painspren creeping on the floor, and a good number of men whose wounds would keep them out of the battle. Adolin stopped by bed after bed, his scribe quietly ensuring he remembered names, or providing them for those he had never met.

He chatted with each soldier in turn, laughing and joking with them, encouraging them and commending their service. Most only wanted to know that their squad was doing fine. He gave needed reassurances—that a wound was a price sometimes paid for protecting one's fellows. He reassured each that they weren't letting anyone down by being out of action, and promised that if Rahel had extra strength, he'd allow her to do further healings to get men back on their feet.

As he went, anxietyspren began to fade from the room one by one. Near the end of his circuit, he met with a man who was missing an arm. That was something Adolin saw less and less these days—the best of their Radiant healers could now Regrow limbs. Sometimes. It depended on many nebulous factors, like how old the wound was and how the person perceived it.

Rahel couldn't manage such advanced Regrowth. So, Adolin encouraged the wounded man to see the lost arm as a temporary inconvenience—and promised that as soon as this was over, he would get the man to a more experienced healer.

"Well, if nothing else," the wounded man said, "maybe I have a future on a bridge crew!"

Adolin laughed, though he wondered if the members of Bridge Four—and to a lesser extent, Bridge Thirteen—knew quite how famous they were. Each member, including many who had died before joining Dalinar's army, had taken on near-mythological status in the Alethi military.

Adolin gave the soldier a firm squeeze on the shoulder and a nod of appreciation—for Adolin, that always seemed to work better than salutes. Then he stood up and checked the time. He could probably visit a few of the Azish wounded. Would they like that from a foreign officer? He looked down the long hallway, which was occupied by . . .

He trailed off as he recognized someone sitting beside a bed: a thin woman, with Azish skin coloring and Shin eyes, although she showed some hints of her Alethi parentage as well. If those were even the right terms, for a woman who had been born before Azir, Shinovar, or Alethkar had existed.

Her name was Shalash, but people called her Ash. Herald of the Almighty. Adolin hesitated, his guards and scribe for the day huddling behind him as they saw what he had. She sat beside a bed that held a mountain of a human being: Talenel, the Bearer of Agonies. The one they had left behind, and who—in finally breaking—had ushered in the return of the enemy.

"What are you staring at, princeling?" Ash called to him.

"I didn't realize you were here," he said.

"We are an afterthought," Ash said, shrugging. "Your father brought us to Azir on his campaign; it seems he wants to keep us near, hoping our wisdom will rub off on him. That makes him the greater fool, since we have no wisdom left. Only madness and grief."

Adolin stopped beside the bed and gazed at Taln, who lay on his back, eyes closed—muttering to himself.

"Is he all right?" Adolin asked.

Ash's glare could have melted iron. "What do you think?"

Adolin leaned down and heard the ancient man whispering the same things as always. A mantra about how he was going to help the people to resist the coming evils.

"Are you worth it?" Ash asked.

"Pardon?" Adolin asked.

"Are you worth it?" She rested her hands on Taln's arm. "Do you know the price that was paid on a distant world for your peace, by a man who never wanted this? A man who would have been content with his horses? Are you *worth it*?"

"I don't know," Adolin said, honest.

"Time will tell."

Unnerved, Adolin left the two Heralds. Rahel had joined his cluster of attendants: a young woman maybe seventeen with long ombre hair, going from dark brown to light brown. Her mistspren shone on the wall, appearing like scattered light; it was the uncorrupted variety. Rare, for one of those to let themself be seen by others. Perhaps it was for the Heralds' benefit.

"I'm sorry, Brightlord," the young Radiant said. "She refuses to let me try to heal him."

"Your touch couldn't do anything for that man," Adolin assured her.

"Just like I can't heal the lost limbs . . ." she said, accompanied by shamespren.

"You're doing wonderfully," Adolin assured her. "Half those men would be dead if not for you. Think of yourself as a field medic: your job isn't to fix them up perfectly; your job is to make sure they *survive* until they can be fixed up."

She nodded, then moved back to her station, where she had a stack of novels to keep her occupied between healings. Poor kid. Before yesterday, she'd probably never seen what battle could do—and now she would have a reminder every few hours. During these next days, she'd likely get even less sleep than he did.

He moved outside and found that a runner had arrived with a message. His scribe of the hour read it to him. "'Enemy made a quick attack, but then almost immediately retreated,'" she said. "'We're licking our wounds. Low casualties this time, as neither group pushed too hard. My gut says they will try a Castle Down. Thoughts?'" The scribe lowered the paper. "Castle Down?"

"Move from towers," Adolin said. "He thinks the enemy has been too regular with their assaults—on purpose, to make us expect a rhythm. The next attack will come later than expected, he thinks, as that will give us *just* enough time to start resting." Adolin considered. Yes, this might be a better explanation than he'd come up with for the enemy behavior. "Write back and say I agree—and that I think we should be ready for an attack between an hour and a half and two hours from now."

He checked the sky, where the sun had vanished below the horizon. That timing felt right—just long enough for the humans to start winding down and settle into bed. His scribe made the report via spanreed to the central message room, who would get it to Kushkam. This scribe wasn't Kaminah, but a younger girl, maybe fourteen. With frizzy hair that refused to stay in its braids. She'd told him her name, but . . . with embarrassment, he realized it had slipped away from him. Bad form, that. Too much to keep his mind on, and too little sleep.

He asked her name again—Makana—and memorized it this time. He needed to take better care of himself, and do something relaxing for now to let his mind rest. And so, to that end, he gave a few quiet orders, then strode off into the night toward the most prominent set of tents.

He had an imperial friend to visit, and a promise to keep.

51
TEST

TWENTY-SIX YEARS AGO

The soldier camp smelled like people.

For a youth who had spent his life among sheep, human smells were distracting. Wrong, like a splash of color that was too vibrant, drawing too much attention.

He clustered with his family at the mouth of the training yard, which occupied a ridge along the highlands near the Stoneward monastery. Black smoke assaulted the sky, marching from bellows and forges spilling bloody light. The sounds of metal on metal, like the cries of damned souls, rang within the forges—but also from the practice grounds, where men swung blasphemous weapons.

Stone covered the ground here, so close to the great aboshi—the mountaintops, and the spren who were their souls. Would his family really just . . . step on it? It was all so overwhelming—with the oppressive scents of sweat and the cries (and strangely, laughs) of the fighting men—that it made Szeth pull against his mother's side.

Elid stood tall, obviously trying to pretend that—as the older sibling—she was stronger. She took a deep breath, then stepped off the soil onto stone. As she did, he caught another glare from her. *This is your fault,* that glare proclaimed, echoing what she'd said to him the night before. Though she'd always seemed resentful of their slow life, she was not happy in the least to have it stolen away. Still, she *could* have gone to live with cousins. A terrible decision to have to make, yes, but he couldn't be *completely* blamed. Could he?

Father went next, joining Elid on the stone. As Szeth hung back, holding to his mother, she took something from her pouch. A small sheep made of wool. It smelled . . . of Molli?

He touched it, then glanced up at his mother. No words passed between them, though Mother wiped tears from her eyes. He'd thought Molli's pelt buried, but evidently Mother had saved some of the wool. Szeth should have been too old for toys, but he clutched it anyway, tucked it away before anyone could see. It gave him the strength to step onto the stone. It was hard under his feet. Wrong.

Mother joined him, and eventually a man in a leather jerkin came jogging over. He was a burly type, with dark hair and skin. He unrolled a scroll, nodding to himself as he read. "Neturo-son-Vallano? Zeenid-daughter-Beth? Right, welcome. Thanks for signing up. We can always use more hands."

"We didn't . . ." Father said, then trailed off. "We were forced into this."

"Says here only your child was," the man replied. "You parents are volunteers. That's rare." He dithered, then offered a hand to Szeth's parents. "Betheth-son-Vetor. Captain of recruitment and discipline."

Father tentatively took his hand and looked over the long camp covering the ridge, full of buildings and bustling people. Father's job had always been to herd shepherds as shepherds herded sheep. Szeth didn't know much about that, but if these soldiers had been sheep, he would have called them a poorly watched flock. There was an air of laziness to the place. Those who sparred or trained were watched by twice as many people who were lounging. To Szeth's left, a large number of men congregated around the cookfires, where women tended great metal cauldrons.

Some men were doing their laundry at racks farther along—Betheth said soldiers were required to see to their own clothing and equipment. Everyone in their family would get training in the warrior's script, and all but Szeth would be allowed to—after a year—apply for work at the monastery instead, if they wanted. To become acolyte shamans, where women could choose to be warriors.

Until then, Elid and Mother would have the choice of cooking, washing floors, or tending the animals sent for slaughter. The elderly or infirm among the flocks were sent up here, and in abstract, Szeth had always been fine with this. Animals at the ends of their lives could still add this way; even people fed the soil when dead.

"I don't see families . . ." Mother said. "I thought people served for generations as soldiers. What of them?"

"They usually get a transfer," Betheth said. "They become city guards or work lumberyards. It's . . . more comfortable for stabler individuals." There was an implication to his voice. That he assumed Szeth's family would eventually find their way to such work as well. "Anyway, let me send the three of you off to your bunks. You'll have your own room, spacious as things go here. I'll take the lad to initial assessment—"

"I'm going with him," Father said, a hand on Szeth's shoulder. "Wherever he goes."

Betheth hesitated, then shrugged. "Right, then. Zeenid, I'll send you to check out the quarters . . ." He gave her instructions and a little map drawn in black charcoal. Szeth was used to writing being in ink, with reeds. Soldiers, it appeared, did things differently.

Once Mother and Elid had moved off, Betheth led Szeth and his father around the perimeter of the training grounds to where a small group of four youths were waiting.

Betheth held his hand toward Szeth. "You can't be wearing that any longer, son," he said, gently. Pointing at Szeth's handkerchief.

No more color. The uniforms were dark brown, and not a speck or splash of true color graced the camp. In taking off his kerchief and handing it over, Szeth felt as if he were giving up something vital that defined him.

This is good, the voice said in his head, making him jump. *This is where you belong.* It had a moderate pitch; he couldn't decide if it sounded male or female.

What are you? Szeth thought, apprehensive. But got no reply. The voice unnerved him, and he held to his father's hand, though he probably should have acted more mature. However, he was younger and smaller than the other youths who lined up for Betheth. None of them had fathers with them.

Betheth nodded for Szeth to join the line. When he didn't move, Betheth spoke, a sharpness to his voice. "You're a soldier now, Szeth," he said. "I am to teach you discipline. Don't make me teach it harshly."

So Szeth reluctantly let go of his father's hand and joined the other four youths in the line.

"How do you enforce discipline here?" Father asked.

"We make examples of the worst cases," Betheth said.

"And the best cases?"

"Allowed free time."

"You said that the men are in charge of their own gear—"

"Their kit and clothing, yes."

"How is this enforced?" Father asked.

"Same way. Beatings if they're sloppy."

Father shook his head. "Beating one sheep rarely makes the others obedient. It only makes them fear you."

"Fear makes obedience though, doesn't it?" Betheth said. "Look, Neturo, people here aren't like the ones you know. These come because they're deviants. Problems."

"Problems like my son?" Father asked.

Betheth had trouble finding words to reply to that. Father, though . . . conflict wasn't his way. He simply stepped back, clasping his hands and surveying the training field.

The Farmer said humans choose, Szeth thought, *and are defined by that choice. Is that true even here, in this place of bloody stone and men who subtract?*

Szeth stood there, nervous, dwarfed by the older teens. Had they . . . done as he had? He found it hard to imagine they had . . . had killed someone.

That was difficult to acknowledge. It was as if those events had happened in a dream, to another person. Yet at the same time he could still feel the rock under his fingers—smooth, but rough at once. Could still feel the warmth. The blood.

"I need to know," Betheth said, "what I'm working with in you all." He waved a thick-fingered hand as several workers walked out of a shed. Pushing corpses: dead sheep, hung up on racks with wheels on the bottoms. Szeth felt nauseous.

Betheth handed each boy a spear. "Show me what you've got. Pretend those are enemies on the field, and you need to subtract them before they reach the houses beyond."

"If we don't," one of the boys said, "do we . . . go home?"

"No," Betheth said, firm. "Once you've been sent here, you don't *ever* go back. But don't be so glum. People are wrong—subtracting isn't evil. We're necessary parts of society. We are the most important, it might be argued." He waved to the carcasses. "I just need to know what kind of training to give you. So have at it. Prove that you're going to make full use of your new life. I promise you, it's far more fulfilling than you assume. We, of all people, get to express what's truly inside of us."

The other boys moved forward. Then, with shocking aggression, they began to stab at and attack the carcasses. One even shouted. Once they started, they seemed to *need* this. To release something pent up inside. Their shouts resonated with Szeth. He felt so lacking in control, so frustrated by the apparent nonexistence of answers. Everyone talked about him, but they didn't ask what he wanted. He gritted his teeth and started forward.

Careful, the strange voice said, butting into his mind. *This is an odd test. I find it amusing each time I see it done. They're trying to judge if you're out of control. If you can contain the desire to subtract or not.*

Szeth hesitated. That Voice knew a great deal.

It's self-fulfilling, the Voice continued. *They encourage new recruits to attack all out, then use that as proof that the boys were secretly broken all along—that you can distinguish someone who subtracts, if you bring out their true selves. The system has been flawed for a while now, but you can use that.*

"How?" Szeth whispered.

Make a single surgical strike with the spear at the neck of the carcass. Don't pretend to rage; show restraint. That will distinguish you from these others.

Arms trembling, Szeth raised the spear. "What are you?" he whispered.

I am the spren of the stone you discovered, the Voice said. *And I ask that you not tell others of me, Szeth. I've been watching over your family. I am sorry for what has happened, but there are important things for you to do.*

There was . . . a plan for him?

There were answers?

Someone was *watching*?

Szeth calmed his nerves, then gripped the spear and stabbed once at the carcass's neck. He was shocked by how easily the sharpened steel tip of the spear went in, until it ground against bone.

He pulled the spear free, then stepped back.

"What was that, Szeth?" Betheth said. "That's all you have?"

"You said I needed to stop it," Szeth said. "You said to pretend it was an enemy. I pretended as best I could. One stab, and that should do it, right?"

"That's not what the report says you did to the soldier," Betheth said. "He was from this camp, you know. Others are going to talk about you."

Repeat after me: That man was sick.

"That man was sick," Szeth said.

I did what I needed to make sure the sickness didn't spread.

"I did what I needed to do to make sure the sickness didn't spread, sir."

Nothing more. My tool was a poor one for the task, but I needed to defend myself.

"Nothing more. I'm sorry I used the rock. It was wrong of me, but I was under attack."

Betheth nodded at those words, then he made some notes. Szeth glanced back at his father, who stood with his arms folded, lost in thought as he stared at the camp. Neturo had found a problem to solve.

"Come," Betheth said, putting his arm on Szeth's shoulder and steering him away from the other boys. "Let's talk to the camp's general, Szeth. You might find a better home in officer training."

It is to this end that I have identified and made particular note of three distinct factions of Skybreakers, even during Nale'Elin's days of direct leadership, and this is to be found in my third coda.

—From *Words of Radiance*, chapter 40, page 2

Noura the vizier left the tent the moment Adolin arrived with his armorers. She gave him one quick look, her lips downturned, then she was gone. Adolin had to assume she'd spent time trying to persuade Yanagawn not to go forward with battle training. However, the young monarch stood and smiled, then quickly waved Adolin forward.

They had no idea what they were getting in him, Adolin thought. *A complete wildcard. Elevating a pauper to emperor. It's like something from one of the old stories.*

"You'll really let me wear it?" Yanagawn said, cooing over the armor.

"I lend it to my armor standbys all the time," Adolin said. "Plus, it shouldn't be needed for the next hour or so."

Yanagawn rubbed his hands, eyes wide and mischievous, hat with its long sweeping sides waggling as he moved. "Let's do it!"

"Let's clear some space then," Adolin said. The large tent was cluttered with furnishings, from rugs to couches, to tables piled with glass, gold, and aluminum. Bowls, sphere goblets, portraits of the Herald Jezrien—painted in Azir as a regal Makabaki.

"There's space over here," Yanagawn said, hurrying to an open section of carpet.

"Excellency," Adolin said, "that's not *nearly* enough space for a man wearing Plate for the first time. If you value any of this stuff, I suggest you have it cleared away. Trust me."

"Oh!" Yanagawn clapped and pointed, and servants appeared and got to it.

Adolin would have preferred to do this out in the square, but his gut said that would be pushing too far. Some of the guards seemed to have swapped out the moment Adolin arrived. So, only the most trusted guards and Yanagawn's close servants were in the tent. They could . . . pretend not to see him going so far against tradition. Parading him out before the entire army and city would be another thing entirely. A man's first time in Plate could be a little awkward, even if Zahel wasn't around to make you jump off buildings onto your head.

"So . . ." Yanagawn said, glancing down at his ornate robes. When he stretched his arms out to the sides, layers of cloth strung like wings between his arms and torso. His robes weren't divided, and his headdress was . . . well, roughly the size of a small cottage.

"You'll need to change," Adolin said, waving to Geb.

The head armorer tossed the emperor a thick gambeson and padded hose for wearing underneath Plate. "This should fit."

"Excellent," Yanagawn said, pointing to them all. "I dub these men chosen for the day, granted leave of viewership, blessed by my imperial presence."

"Um . . . thanks?" Adolin asked.

"It means," an Azish soldier whispered, "that you are allowed in the great Prime's presence during intimate times. A blessing bestowed upon a certain number of common people every day, in order that they might experience his majesty and participate in our governance."

Adolin looked to the one who had spoken—a man with short black hair. He had the most impressive mustache, bushy and thick. It went *out* more than it did *down*.

"Thanks," Adolin said, then hesitated as the emperor's clothiers began stripping him. "Uh . . . should we go?"

"Didn't you hear what I said?" the soldier said. "You're blessed. I mean, he did it for convenience, it appears—but who would question the Prime's decisions?" He winked.

"Ah," Adolin said. "I think my father talked about this. People watch him sleep at night, right?"

"And eat. And bathe. And everything else. The emperor is a symbol of the health of our nation."

What an odd people. Talking directly to Yanagawn was seen as insulting—but he'd strip in front of strangers?

"They say you're good at towers," the friendly guard said.

"I've been known to play a game now and then," Adolin said, leaning back against a sofa that had been upended to make room.

"What variety?"

"Flat Face," Adolin said.

The guard nodded. He held his formal pose, carrying an impressive Azish ceremonial polearm. "The best for strategic planning. But it *is* a little mundane."

"Mundane?" Adolin asked. "It's a classic. You prefer Stacks?"

"Yaezir, no!" the man said. "Deliverer is my favorite. If not Vanquish."

"Heard of both. Never tried them." Adolin had never figured out why there were so many variants on the rule set of such a simple game.

"You should try sometime," the guard said. "Both are good preparations for the actual interesting variations, like Crosswise Chull or Bubbly Belch."

Adolin eyed him. Surely those were made up. The guard kept his pose, staring straight forward, a smile on his lips. Soon Yanagawn was ready, and the armorers approached with the Plate. Geb glanced at Adolin, who nodded, and then they started suiting up the emperor.

Yanagawn looked so much more ordinary in the training clothing—less like a . . . flower arrangement at a funeral, more like a person. Not even two years before, he'd been a common thief. Now people watched him bathe, while others literally dressed and fed him.

Every man needed a chance to stand tall and learn he could withstand a punch. Or . . . well, maybe not every man. Renarin would probably explain that there were very few things every man needed, whatever society said, and Adolin *did* try to listen.

I hope you're well, Renarin, Adolin thought. Once, he could always count on Renarin being nearby—but now he was Radiant, and although he wasn't a Windrunner, he was learning to fly. While Adolin just kept going as he always had. Same old Adolin.

"I'd always heard," Yanagawn said, staring at his booted feet, "that Plate resizes to the individual. I hadn't imagined it would be so comfortable though." Awespren gathered around him—blue smoke rings—and hovered as the armorers locked on each new piece, which indeed resized. Mostly. The breastplate and greaves were both a little long on him, and he'd be better off with a deliberate resizing. You could shatter a piece, then regrow it on someone, to get a more exact fit.

This was close enough for now. Adolin watched with pleasure as the arm pieces locked in, then Geb handed Yanagawn the helmet. He slid it on, and it sealed in place. Storms, but Adolin could remember the first time he'd put on Plate. That electric sense of power, that strength, that feeling of invulnerability. He waved to Geb, who—with his assistants—dragged in a few practice dummies.

"Have at it," Adolin said to the emperor.

"It?"

Adolin nodded to the dummies. "Pretend they wrote a really terrible essay, full of . . ." What made an essay bad? ". . . Poetry?"

"Huh?" Geb asked. "Poetry?"

"There's prose and poetry," Adolin said. "They're opposites or something; my wife talked about it. So if you tried to write an essay and filled it with poetry, you've failed, right?"

The friendly guard from earlier was snickering. Yanagawn, however, tried to attack the training dummies. He launched forward with too eager a step though, and the Plate's inherent strength sent him stumbling until he fell on his face.

The guards immediately moved to help.

"Stop!" Adolin said, hands out to block them. "You want to get yourselves killed?"

"But—" the friendly guard said.

"He's fine," Adolin said. "Aren't you, Excellency?"

Yanagawn was laughing as he climbed to his hands and knees. "That's amazing!" he said. "*Amazing!* Even my steps are stronger. How high could I jump?"

"I'd suggest you try," Adolin said, with a smile, "but you'd probably topple the tent when you hit the roof. Take it easy as you stand up, Excellency."

Geb's men were ready with hooks to steer Yanagawn if he strayed too close to anyone. A Shardbearer first using his Plate could be dangerous—as evidenced when Yanagawn stood up and swung his arms to the sides to balance. Those sweeps of armored hands could throw a man across the room.

Fortunately, Geb and his men had done this many times. They carefully steered some servants away, giving the emperor plenty of space to practice walking. He got that part quickly; most people did. Finally he approached the dummies, and with joyspren swirling around his arms, punched each dummy in turn, blasting them to splinters and shards.

"That is," Yanagawn said, his voice echoing in his helm, "the single most satisfying thing I've *ever* done."

"Great," Adolin said as Geb handed him some wooden training eggs. "Here, catch these."

Yanagawn turned, and managed not to stumble as he located Adolin, who carefully threw one of the wooden eggs across the room. They were exactly the right size to grip in the hand, three inches across, and though Yanagawn missed the first two, he caught the third.

And immediately smashed it while trying to hold it.

"Wow," the emperor said.

"Wearing Plate," Adolin said, "isn't so much about learning how to do damage. That part is easy. Learning *not* to break everything? Well that takes practice. Once you can learn to direct your force, you *truly* become dangerous."

He tossed Yanagawn another sphere, which the emperor caught—then crushed.

"That's so difficult!" the younger man said, as if both delighted and surprised.

Adolin smiled, and nodded for Geb to give some practical instructions accompanied by simple exercises. Yanagawn took to it with eagerness as Adolin settled on a chair stacked on another one, while Donalar—an officer with light blue eyes who was the third generation of that name in the Cobalt Guard—arrived to tell him there was still no movement from the enemy.

His meal was ready—merely some chouta in a wrap, to keep him on the move. He ate, wishing Shallan were here. They often ate together, ignoring proprieties of gendered dining. He missed the quips, the silliness mixed with truly poignant questions about his day, his feelings, his choices.

The guard from before, the one with the bristly mustache, watched Yanagawn with interest. "You want to take a turn?" Adolin asked him around a bite of chouta.

"I've trained on one of the imperial sets," the man said. "Most of the guards have. Just in case."

Made sense. As Kaminah was learning her job quickly—and had sent him several chouta wraps, with the implication he needed to keep eating—he held up one to the guard. "Want some?"

"No eating on watch," he said, his eyes on the emperor. "Aren't you going to teach him towers?"

"Planning to once he can sit down without falling over," Adolin said. "He's a quick learner though. Hey, Excellency!"

Yanagawn turned, curious.

"Come and sit," Adolin said, pointing. "We'll start your tactical training."

"While wearing Plate?" the emperor asked.

"The more you wear it," Adolin said, "the more natural it will feel—and small movements like playing a card game will teach you control."

The emperor tromped over and managed to sit on the floor without falling. Adolin grabbed a low table—designed for use while sitting on the ground—and hauled it in front of Yanagawn. Then he turned to the friendly guard.

"You've got a deck?" he asked the man.

"Why assume I carry one on me?"

"You seem the type."

The man grinned, then fished one out of the pouch at his side, all while keeping at alert attention.

"I hope," Adolin said, settling himself at the table, "you don't lose too much of your weekly wages at cards."

"Lose?" the man said from behind. "Not sure I know that word, foreigner. Must be an Alethi thing."

Adolin chuckled, shuffling the large cards. "Is he always this entertaining?"

"He . . . isn't allowed to talk to me," Yanagawn admitted.

Oh, right. "Is that hard?"

"The hardest part, Adolin. Harder than being a spectacle. Harder by far than my lessons. It's the only thing I truly miss from the old days."

Adolin leaned across the small table. "Next time we're in Urithiru, I'll have Shallan make an illusory decoy for you to entertain the scribes. We'll sneak you out for a night—go to some winehouses, play some cards, hit a party."

"Ha!" Yanagawn said. Then after a moment said, "Wait. That wasn't a joke."

"Storming right it wasn't a joke; it was a promise." Adolin held up the deck. "You've really never played?"

"No," Yanagawn said. "My uncle never let me play any card games. Said I'd lose my shoes, then his shoes."

"Well," Adolin said, "towers is versatile, but I'm going to teach you a version called Flat Face. Not because you have to keep from laughing—but because each card does exactly what the glyphs indicate."

"There are versions where that isn't the case?"

"Most of them, in fact," Adolin said. "I'm going to give you cards, which you should hide from me. You can look at your hand, and you deploy cards as armies on the table. Maneuver your troops, change their capacities according to the armies you deploy next to them. Choose when to attack, when to retreat a card back to your hand. The winner is whoever eliminates all opposing cards—or who forces his opponent to give up."

"Why would you ever give up?" Yanagawn asked. "Why not fight until you're beaten?"

"That is an excellent question," Adolin said. "Often in towers you try for best of three—and you can permanently lose cards in earlier skirmishes. Many versions require betting, and the more you commit, the higher the bets."

"So . . . you would retreat if you want to preserve your cards for the next fight. Or if you think the risk is too high to try for victory?" Yanagawn hesitated. "But you never retreat when there is only one battle, and all is already wagered. Correct?"

Adolin smiled. "You are going to be the best student I've ever had, Excellency."

Yanagawn nodded his helmeted head. Then he carefully reached up and took the helm off. He set it to the side, deeply considering something. Was it the cards?

"Would it be all right," the emperor asked softly, "if I asked you to call me by my name?" He met Adolin's eyes. "It will give the viziers heart attacks though. I don't want to cause you trouble."

"Yanagawn," Adolin said, dealing the cards, "I've been breaking the hearts of scribes since I was fourteen. I'll manage. You ready?"

"Yes. Absolutely!"

∴

Kaladin finished making the evening stew. He and Szeth had flown much of the distance to the next monastery, where they hoped to find more answers. But going in at night didn't sound wise. Kaladin was eager to be moving forward, but at the same time, rushing seemed wrong. He feared pushing Szeth too much. Pushing himself too much . . . well, he'd learned how dangerous that could be. So as the stew cooked—smelling almost acceptable now that he had some fresh peppers—Kaladin decided to practice the flute.

It was strange, to be sitting near this gurgling river in the night, surrounded by empty grasslands, simply playing. His life since reaching adulthood—before it, really—had been a nonstop sprint. Event after event, almost every one a disaster. He'd stopped only when forced to rest.

Now something peaceful within him wanted to call to mind their faces. Friends he'd lost. Friends whose fates he didn't know. Women he'd loved. Others who had loved him. Never the two intersecting, as was the perverse way of his life.

He remembered nights as a slave, trembling and huddled by the wall. Other nights planning, letting himself build idealistic dreams of freedom. He remembered nights around the stewpot with Bridge Four, and others trying to stay awake on guard duty. He remembered, as a blur, those broken days after the fall of Kholinar when it had all caught up to him.

He remembered a beautiful woman made of blue light, standing with a brilliant sword and cutting through the darkness as death itself came crawling for him in the shape of a thousand spined monsters. And he remembered his father's embrace at the end of a long black tunnel.

Through it all, he played his flute. Poorly. The notes just wouldn't form right, and his fingers felt like they were made of stone. He tried again and again. He'd learned the spear. He'd learned to face the darkness of his mind. He could learn to control this simple piece of wood.

Yet it resisted him with all the might of Bridge Four combined. More stubborn than any slave or lighteyes.

Kaladin sighed, lowering the flute. Syl settled down beside him, full sized. "You're getting better. Listening isn't painful anymore!"

He gave her a flat stare.

"Listening isn't *agonizingly* painful anymore!" she said.

Kaladin sighed and gazed out to a tall hillside, where Szeth stood in front of the first moon, inspecting the landscape. "I keep thinking about how Wit made this flute play music back to him."

"Yeah," she said. "The story of the *Wandersail.* When he played it, the echoes of it bouncing around in the chasms continued afterward."

"I always wondered why he told me that story. The story about a people who followed a king who was, in the top of his tower, dead. About a people who learned their actions were their own responsibility. Seems odd, doesn't it? I already *knew* that the lighteyes weren't as valorous as they claimed, and that my actions were my own."

"Maybe it wasn't about the lighteyes," she said, "but other forces you let steer you."

Kaladin nodded. "It was surreal. Wit would stop playing, then the music would return, continuing as he talked." He looked at the flute. "Before we left Urithiru, he implied that would happen for me. When I learned to play it not with my lips, but with my heart. I can't fathom what that might mean."

"He can be frustrating," Syl said. "If the world survives this, I'll see if I can hide something *extra* annoying in his sock drawer." She smiled, but then put her hand on his knee. "You . . . all right?"

"I'm fine," he promised. "Just thinking. When I needed him, Wit was always there. But he told me I would have to make my own story this time." He shrugged. "When the darkness consumed me, he pulled me free. So maybe I can listen to him today."

"That's a remarkably mature perspective," Syl said. "I feel a little silly about the sock drawer wisecrack now."

Kaladin merely smiled as Szeth strode back to them. "That next town is very clearly corrupted," the man said. "They hid inside all day, but are out now at night. Some are working the fields, but many are moving in the darkness toward Koring, the town where people are normal. Likely to try breaking in."

"Should we help?" Kaladin asked.

"Koring survived two years," Szeth said. "They can rebuff another assault, particularly now that they don't have to worry about any attacks from the Encilo region." He knelt beside the small fire and tasted the stew. He grunted.

"Better?" Kaladin asked.

"Your Eastern ways have corrupted my sense of taste," Szeth said. "I shouldn't enjoy this much pepper."

Storms, but that man knew how to backhand a compliment. Still, Szeth served up quite a large bowl of stew, then wandered away to eat it on a tree stump.

Kaladin held up the flute. Wit said Kaladin needed to find himself—to discover who he was when he wasn't slavishly trying to protect everyone else. Something had . . . loosened in Kaladin when he'd let go of Tien's death, and Teft's death as well.

That didn't solve the problem entirely though—here he was, doing the same thing. Dedicating everything he had to helping Szeth. Should he stop helping? That couldn't be the right answer.

At Syl's urging, he got out their copy of *The Way of Kings,* so she could read him a chapter, with him turning the pages. After that, she—concentrating earnestly—wrote out their daily report to send home via spanreed, which Szeth commonly did. Today he seemed focused on his meal and thoughts, so Kaladin—somewhat grudgingly—took the spanreed pen and traced her words.

"It's not writing to *copy* writing!" Syl insisted.

"Feels like writing," Kaladin grumbled.

She watched him work by the light of a sphere, beaming. Her joy at being able to scribe infected him, and he ended up not minding so much.

"How are you doing?" he asked her as he worked, lying on the ground with the spanreed board before him, tracing through a very thin piece of paper what she'd written beneath. "About your goals."

"Not living just for you?" she said.

"Yeah," Kaladin whispered. "Because I'm having a storming hard time figuring out how to both help people and not help people all at once."

"You just need to live for yourself. That's what the flute was about, wasn't it?"

"I can't be certain," he said, "that I'm not doing that to please Wit. Would I ever have chosen that on my own?"

"Would I ever have chosen to write on my own?" she asked, leaning down beside him. "But I did, and I *love* it." She whispered to him, "I'm keeping a journal. It's *private* and I'm *doing it.*"

He looked up at her smile.

"I returned to the Physical Realm," she told him, "because I *enjoy* it here. I like the wind, the colors, the infinite blue sky and the warm close sun. I like the Radiant bond, because I like participating. I remind myself of that. I'm a person, and I chose."

"Rule number one," Kaladin whispered.

"Exactly. What about you? Are you a thing, Kaladin, or a person? Do you move merely because your instincts tell you, or do you *choose* to help?"

"Both, sometimes," he admitted. "Like with Bridge Four, in the early days. I had this . . . mental *need* to help, so when I failed, it broke me. Even more than the loss of a dear friend should have, because I was so defined by the idea of protecting others." He finished writing and changed the paper, in case a message came for them. "Still, I *genuinely* want to help."

"Rough," Syl said quietly. "Because, like me, the problem you and the real you are all mixed up together."

"Yeah," he said. "How do I find what *I* need if the world is constantly in crisis?" He heaved out a sigh, then glanced to the side as a small exhaustion-spren appeared nearby: like a little jet of dust, smaller than most. Quivering.

"This one's afraid too," Kaladin said. "There are so few spren here, and they always seem like this."

"I keep hearing things," Syl said. "Hushed things shuffling in the shadows, moving on the wind, hiding within the silence. There are spren here we don't see. They're . . . softer than they are in the East."

"Like the Wind," Kaladin said.

"I've been pondering that," Syl said. "You know the Old Magic?"

"The Nightwatcher," he said.

"She was formed of the Old Magic," Syl said, sounding wistful as she leaned back, hovering an inch off the grassy hillside, her head tipped up to gaze at the violet moon. "She's synonymous with it now. We call it old because it—they—are the spren that existed before we were created. The ancient spren of Roshar, predating humans and even singers."

"The Wind said that she couldn't speak until recently," Kaladin said. "Something about Odium, and maybe how people perceived her."

"Emotion spren and windspren came from the Old Magic," Syl said. "Before humans were here, or the ten groups of Radiant spren were created. I think the oldest spren must all be mostly forgotten. Overwhelmed, crowded out, like whispers in a room full of shouting people. The Night. The Stone. And the Wind. They're ancient. Older than the gods . . ."

The spanreed started writing. A short message directly from Wit, which Syl read. Wit was apparently still covering for the Bondsmiths while they searched for answers in the Spiritual Realm. But he "totally had it handled" and "no one should worry at all." Which was, of course, worrying. Fighting had started with the Fused at the Shattered Plains, but there were no casualties among Bridge Four. Adolin was holding Azimir. Jasnah would leave for Thaylen City soon, though enemy forces weren't expected there for a few days yet.

Kaladin was tempted to write back and demand help with his personal problems. But Wit ended with, "Write your story. Listen to the Wind." Storming man. He knew.

Kaladin leaned back and attempted to listen to the Wind now. He found only the sound of the leaves and the brook chattering away. He closed his eyes, trying to remember the last time he'd done something that had been purely for him, purely peaceful. If he could be doing anything at that moment, what would it be? What would make *him* happy? He let himself answer truthfully.

He wanted to go dancing with Syl.

"Hey," he said to her, "feel like a kata?"

"Sure," she said, perking up.

Kaladin propelled himself off the ground, leaving the spanreed board and that cursed flute. He tossed off his jacket, and didn't let it bother him that if he worked up a sweat, he'd need to do extra laundry in that stream the next day.

For now, he just wanted to be like those ancient spren. Exist as the simplest version of himself: with a spear in hand.

He fell into a stance, and as soon as he snapped into position, Syl vanished from her human form and came to him, dropping into his hand as a long, silvery spear. One kata alone felt appropriate, the one they called the Chasm Kata. That training dance he'd done so long ago, the first time he'd shown Bridge Four what he could do.

For a time after that, he'd refused to wield a weapon. Using a pole with no spearhead instead had freed him. Likewise, Syl . . . she wasn't a weapon. Not tonight. A living Shardblade could take whatever shape you wanted, and today the shape was of a spear—but not a weapon.

Tonight, his dance wasn't about killing, or even about training. It was about the kata, and his love for what he'd learned. He spun the spear, adding in every flourish he knew, the kinds that would get you killed on a battlefield—but that didn't matter. Because he wasn't on a battlefield, and this wasn't a weapon.

Syl was a glowing silvery arc in his hands as he moved through the sequence. Each step sure, each grip perfect, stretching and straining his muscles. Just because it wasn't practical didn't mean it wasn't *difficult.* He spun, whipping the spear into attacks. Then—as he leaned forward, thrusting the spear in a long one-handed lunge—the shape of it fuzzed, and he was holding her hand.

He spun Syl, her skirt flaring as he moved through the next step of the kata. He'd never learned to dance, not properly. Tarah had laughed when she'd found out, and so he'd never told anyone else. When would stern Kaladin Stormblessed ever have time for dancing? He was too busy saving the world.

This was different. This he *could* do, because there was no wrong way. He merely had to do what felt right. He spun with Syl, then yanked her back, spear landing securely in his left hand as he added steps to the kata. The springy ground seemed to propel his spins, as if he were light as air. He whipped the spear to the side and Syl unfolded, rotating in a spin, her hand in his. Faintly touching.

A part of him wanted to feel foolish. Wanted to worry about tomorrow, when Szeth would have to face an Elsecaller, with powers nearly as arcane as those of a Bondsmith. Should he be planning for that? Kaladin almost stopped.

Then he remembered what he'd said to Szeth about warrior thoughts. Could he honestly help Szeth if he wasn't willing to do the same himself? Did he *truly* believe those practices would work? Kaladin took a deep breath, then battered back those emotions, presenting counterthoughts like parts of the kata. Syl formed into a spear as he spun, then he used the momentum to launch the weapon—throwing it in a glowing silver line directly through a nearby tree trunk.

I deserve peace.

The spear formed in his hand again, but then was Syl, laughing as they danced.

I deserve to be happy.

He tossed her as a spear from one hand, then caught her as a woman—Syl choosing when to be which, but him sensing each change. They turned, whirling, two hands holding two hands.

I will *enjoy this. I will* let *myself enjoy* living.

The darkness didn't die, but it retreated as all darkness did before light. And as they twirled, Syl's laughter calling to the sky, the Wind arrived and began dancing with them. The Wind began *moving* them both. Pushing him this way, then that. A swirling, gusting, powerful force. Alive, guiding his steps.

I remember this, Kaladin thought. *From my childhood. I remember moving, and the Wind joining me. I remember . . . peace and freedom.*

He danced through it, and Syl danced with him, both riding the eddies of the Wind. And if he'd ever known a perfect moment in his life—crystallized joy, like light made into something you could hold—this was it. Worries abandoned. No, worries battered away. Worries refused.

In that—at the edge of the world and the advent of the end of all things—Kaladin Stormblessed allowed himself to be happy. For what felt like the first time since Tien's death.

He came to the end of the dance, dipping low, holding Syl as a spear, then a woman, then as pure light. Distant thunder. Wind that continued to gust around them.

Followed by sound. From the flute.

Kaladin spun, and then—Syl at his side as a woman—ran for it. He grabbed the flute and held it as the swirling Wind blew across the holes, sending out fitful half-sounds. He drew that Wind in, and felt it *churning* within him, like Stormlight energizing his lungs. He blew. The note: pure and clean.

He played then. Not perfectly. Far from it. He was new to this, but like the kata, he didn't bother with what he *should* be doing. He played what felt right; what came next. The music that Wit had left him to learn—the song of the *Wandersail*—provided a framework, a backbone, as Kaladin played. Some notes strong, others faltering, but growing better with each repetition.

He *wanted* this. He wanted it because this was a challenge, something to learn, something *different.* Stuffy, grumpy Kaladin. He didn't have time for music or love or life. That was the story. The story he'd been telling himself for so long.

Tonight, he wrote a different story for himself. Of a man who loved music. Of a man who had *time* for music. He found in it some piece of his soul that had always been missing, a loss he'd never had words to explain. He learned a new language that night, full of new adjectives for who Kaladin was, and who he could be.

He finished, and the Wind rushed away, carrying the last notes into the night. The sounds didn't return to him, but the Wind did seem to keep hold of them for safekeeping. He looked at Syl, whose smile was made of light, and he grinned. He *let* himself grin. Happiness was a part of what defined Kaladin.

He lingered on her face, kept worries at bay with a shield wall of proactive thoughts, for a remarkable length of time, until finally he turned to see what Szeth thought of the music.

The man was not there. He'd left the stump where he'd been eating. The sky was empty of him, though his pack—including the two Honorblades and Nightblood—lay near the fire.

"Huh," Kaladin said. "Did you see where he went?"

⁂

Yanagawn indeed proved an extremely capable student, picking up the game quickly. Moreover, he appeared to have a sixth sense for the battlefield lessons each of the early training scenarios were meant to instruct.

"So," Yanagawn said, "it really *is* worse to deploy everything at once, with nothing in reserve. While it makes a show of force, which sounds most likely to win, your mistakes magnify—and you don't have any flexibility to reset if things get out of hand."

"Exactly!" Adolin said, chewing on his second roll of chouta, as he knew he'd be chastised otherwise. He tapped the table in front of them—which was now cracked after Yanagawn had placed a card too forcefully and split the wood. After that they'd removed the Plate, leaving the emperor in a warrior's gambeson with a robe over the top. "Plus, you need reserves to be able to counter your opponent, and you need to be able to play to the terrain if the battlefield moves."

"Or," Yanagawn said, studying the board, "a company you thought strong might have a bad break and flounder. If you've committed everything, the way I just did, you can't shore up weak points."

"Excellent. Now, other than that, why did you lose?"

"You were able to surround me," he replied, "and a surrounded army is weaker."

"It can't rest its troops in back lines as effectively," Adolin said, "and has to waste energy watching its flanks, then fighting on them. So you got surrounded—and then were so overly committed that you didn't have any reserves to break through and rescue your troops."

Yanagawn nodded, then eyed a large upright clock. "You have to go, don't you?"

"Afraid so," Adolin said. "I'm on duty—and the enemy is very likely to attack soon."

"I'd love to know how you figured that out," Yanagawn replied. "Can I learn it from cards?"

"You can hone your instincts with the cards," Adolin said. "But the rest requires practical experience. We'll get you there." He then held out his hand.

Yanagawn hesitantly took it. A few of the servants gasped, but Adolin ignored them.

"It's tradition," Adolin said, "to give a handshake across the table after a game. One last lesson for tonight: Don't ever get mad at a person you're sparring with, especially when they defeat you. Their victory is training for you. More importantly, you need to be the kind of person the best duelists *want* to fight—because if you only ever face people you can beat, then you'll never improve."

"Thank you," Yanagawn said, standing up. "For all of it, Adolin." He paused. "How is it you're not Radiant?"

Adolin covered a wince. That question.

That storming question.

"Everyone says you're the best fighter in the army," Yanagawn continued. "And everyone *loves* you."

"I wish that were true, Yanagawn. I can think of quite a few who don't."

"Regardless. Why?"

"I . . ." One factor was that he would *not* abandon Maya, and becoming Radiant would require that, he'd been told. But beyond that . . . "I don't like the oaths," Adolin admitted. Voicing it for the first time.

"What?" Yanagawn said. "I thought good Vorin people were all *about* oaths."

Adolin shrugged, rising. "My father made oaths, and so did all the highprinces, before the Radiants were refounded—back when they were all burning down villages and slaughtering people. Their actions were considered honorable because they kept their storming oaths. Who cares about the suffering they caused, right? Everyone was honorable! That's what matters!"

Yanagawn, instead of being taken aback by the rising angerspren at Adolin's feet, pondered this with a solemn expression.

"Too many people," Adolin said as his armorers began to put on his Plate, "think the *oath,* and not what it *means,* is the important part. I heard something in one of my lessons once, from an ardent. About a man who took an oath to sit in a chair until told he could stand—and he stayed there for ten years."

"Wow," Yanagawn said. "That's impressive."

"It's idiocy," Adolin said. "Pardon, Yanagawn—everyone celebrated him, but it's *pure idiocy.* You know what I'd admire? A man who gave an oath, then realized it was storming stupid and broke it—apologized—and moved on with his life, determined not to make that kind of mistake again."

"Some might call that hypocrisy."

"No, it would just be—"

Adolin cut off. *Sometimes a hypocrite is just a man in the process of changing.* Storming Dalinar Kholin had written that in his storming book. People quoted it all the time.

Dalinar was always there, everywhere Adolin looked.

"Very well," Yanagawn said, "no oaths between us. Merely two men doing their best."

Adolin nodded, then leaned forward—his lower half now armored—and thumbed over his shoulder. "That fellow with the mustache. Who is he?"

"Commandant's son," Yanagawn whispered. "Gezamal."

"Good to know," Adolin whispered. But before he could say more, the Thaylen man—Hmask—was announced at the tent. He waved to Adolin, carrying a letter from one of the scribes.

Adolin didn't need it. He could hear the distant shouts. The enemy had arrived, exactly as predicted. He held out his arms, and the armorers hurriedly finished suiting him up.

I wish not to engage to the reader their faults, rather to make it clear that an order so determined to care for the unwanted, the unguarded, and the disenfranchised would obviously have passionate disagreement in how to best attend to the needs of the lowly and disregarded.

—From *Words of Radiance*, chapter 40, page 2

Szeth ate his stew, pondering whether he should tell Kaladin about the Voice.

That Voice he'd heard as a child, the one he hadn't heard since leaving Shinovar. It didn't *seem* to be the same as the voices of the dead he now heard. Sometimes he wondered if that first Voice had been real—or an early manifestation of his . . . problems.

He'd initially started telling Kaladin his past in order to explain how he knew an Unmade was in Shinovar. Only . . . when reaching the part where he'd first heard the Voice . . . Szeth had left that out. Even still—as he talked to Kaladin about being forced into the military, and training there his first few years—he left out details. No mention of the Voice, little discussion of his family, except his father.

It felt like lying. At the same time, some things were personal. With a sigh, Szeth set aside his bowl and stood up, stepping forward.

Where he immediately fell into the place of shadows.

The world of beads and a distant sun. Makari Sin in the old Shin writings. The glasslands. Shadesmar.

Panic hit as he splashed into the sea of beads. He desperately reached toward the alien sky. He would drown here. Sink into the deep sea of beads, falling, falling, falling until he was forced to inhale a mouthful of glass. Until he died and came to rest on the obsidian ocean floor. An open-eyed eternal corpse that lore claimed would never rot, staring at an abyss that would never stare back, despite its million million beaded eyes.

Death didn't frighten him, but he *had* to finish his quest before he went, and so he fought through the panic. He stopped thrashing as he sank in the beads, their insectile clacking ceaseless as they rolled over one another. He was *not* powerless here. He'd survived this place during training long ago, and he could do so again.

He fished in the pouch at his waist and brought forth a gemstone full of Stormlight. He drew in the tiniest amount—sucking air between his teeth, beads pressing against his lips as if eager to find their way into his throat. He almost Lashed himself upward. But he was here, in this place. Why?

Instead he focused, imagining a shape in his mind. A pillar. A solid pillar upon which he could stand. Certain orders of Knights Radiant had an affinity for this place, but Skybreakers were not one of them. Fortunately, anyone with Stormlight—including those who weren't Radiant—could command the beads.

The sea beneath him began to solidify. Beads clicked together, sticking as if magnetized, and pushed upward. A few seconds later he broke through the surface—beads rolling free of his platform. He stumbled to his feet, beads dripping from his clothing, and found himself upon what amounted to a small raft.

Keeping it cohesive was difficult. He had to concentrate, and despite that his platform undulated beneath his feet as if held together by the most tenuous of bonds. He would never manage any construction more complex than this, not without a model or guide, and he couldn't draw in too much Stormlight—for if he did, the nearby beads would surge toward him, flooding over the top of the platform. It also might draw the attention of very dangerous spren beasts.

"So, you remember your training," a voice said, causing him to spin. A stern man sat on a similar platform ten yards away, a Blade across his lap—the Elsecaller Blade, which had an appearance reminiscent of Oathbringer. A hooked shape on the end, but flowing lines in an arcing curve. The man was shrouded in black, inky cloth. White hair in tufts, clean shaven across the face, and hands that had seen some years.

Pozen-son-Nash. One of Szeth's earliest teachers, and a man a part of him still hated. Few individuals had the power to enter Shadesmar, and even fewer could bring others. If Szeth was here, it was because of this man—bearer of Batlah's sword.

Szeth was to have visited Pozen's monastery next, but the old man had plainly decided not to wait.

"An assassination," Szeth said, falling into a fighting stance and reaching out to summon his Blade. "You ignore the rules of pilgrimage?"

"No such rules apply," Pozen said. "You are aspiring to a position no man has claimed in thousands of years. Such a lofty goal must come with a lofty test."

"I seek no position." Szeth glanced at his hand. Empty. His Shardblade. Where was it?

Of course. He knelt down on his platform, hearing something shifting below, thrashing in the beads. With focus, he raised up another small pillar, and upon it was a strange figure in the shape of a clothed man. The interior of the figure was blackness and stars—like a rip in reality. It was the way his spren manifested in this realm. Szeth, in his panic, hadn't seen the spren appear. Unfortunately, Honorblades acted differently, as evidenced by the one across Pozen's lap.

Well, perhaps this would be an advantage; Szeth's spren was an ancient warrior. He might not be able to become a Shardblade in Shadesmar, but he could fight by Szeth's side. His spren stopped thrashing somewhat hesitantly, then looked around—his strange shape seeming to *flow* more than it moved. As if he were some kind of shadow of a person.

"Oh," the spren said. "Oh!"

"Prepare yourself, Szeth-son-Neturo," Pozen said, hands on his Blade. "I could have killed you as you fell, but I have given you this chance out of what may be an overabundance of fondness for a former student."

"I have no weapon!" Szeth shouted. "I cannot fight you without one."

"Then you do not deserve to win."

Something exploded from the beads to Szeth's left. A younger Shin woman in grey robes, a bow strapped to her back. She bore the Edgedancer Honorblade: a narrow sword almost six feet long, with a curved crossguard. She swiped for Szeth and he Lashed himself backward just in time. His spren sputtered and ducked, his hands over his head, although no Shin would dare attack a spren.

Szeth drew in more Stormlight, making the beads rattle and surge toward him, and took to the sky. He didn't recognize the newcomer, with that black cloud of curls around her head. A newer bearer of the Blade, he suspected, having been elevated in the years since his exile, to replace Dulo.

Szeth's spren yelped and dropped into the beads, as Szeth couldn't maintain that platform. He started splashing about in an . . . admittedly undignified way. Perhaps the creature would not be as much use in this fight as Szeth had hoped.

"You gang up on me?" Szeth shouted to those below. "Two on one? Have you no shame?"

"Should the mountain feel shame for breaking those who cross it?" Pozen called. "We are the barrier you must pass, Szeth-son-Neturo."

"Why?" Szeth shouted. "Tell me *why*!"

Once, he had never asked why. Strange, how he should be so insistent now. He'd changed, hadn't he.

In response, the Edgedancer removed the bow from her back and began launching arrows at him.

Szeth Lashed himself higher in the strange sky with its too-still clouds and tiny sun. He could stay out of range easily, but to what end? His Stormlight would run dry quickly—he had only the pouch of gemstones at his belt.

He watched the two figures below, the Edgedancer sinking beneath the beads again. Her order had no specific powers here; he suspected that Pozen was creating platforms so she could concentrate on the fighting.

My sole way out, Szeth thought, *is to capture Pozen and force him to Elsegate us home.*

Szeth should have been able to seize the Blade, then make his own Elsegate to escape. However, in the months he'd spent training with Pozen as a younger man, he had never managed it. Elsegates were a difficult skill to master, and barely a small fraction of those who trained achieved them.

Regardless, he had to engage the two Honorbearers. Weaponless. On turf they'd chosen. With just one pouchful of Stormlight.

His strategizing was interrupted as something dark dove at him from the sky. Inky black, shaped vaguely like a skyeel, though many times the size. A spren he didn't recognize, but one that was obviously dangerous. He hadn't spotted it, black against black as it was, but he did manage to Lash himself into a dodge at the last second.

Teeth flashed white as it tore through the air. Spren could be deadly here, particularly if you didn't know which emotions were drawing them. He growled softly as—now that he knew what to look for—he spotted an entire flock of them. That Edgedancer with her bow had driven him this direction on purpose.

He dove toward the beads, anticipating an attack. The Edgedancer popped up, raised on a pillar created by Pozen, who continued to sit cross-legged in his spot. She loosed a series of arrows in Szeth's direction, so he dropped quickly and hit the beads with a crash. He canceled his Lashings, letting him slip beneath the surface.

Here the whispers were louder. In this realm, was he closer to the souls he'd killed?

Thankfully, his training was coming back to him. He imagined motion, waves of beads bearing him sideways, and it worked—the beads responded. With Stormlight and proper thought, you could swim through the beads, with them pushing you along. His control wouldn't be as precise as Pozen's, but it would work. At least, so long as he held a small amount of Stormlight—which would also spare him needing to breathe.

As he ushered himself through the beads, he heard one voice above the others. A whisper that was stronger.

Szeth? it said. *Szeth?*

He searched through the beads, and his fingers brushed something. He seized it, finding a handful of cloth. He yanked the figure closer.

"Squire?" his spren said. "Is that you?"

"Locate me a weapon," Szeth hissed through closed teeth. In this place, you could summon objects from the real world if you held the bead that represented their soul. "I cannot read the beads, so you must search them for a weapon. I will distract the enemies while you do so."

"I shouldn't interfere . . ." the spren said.

"Then I will die, and you will have no squire," Szeth snapped, letting go and allowing the flowing beads to separate them. He perhaps should not have spoken so demandingly. Strangely, his reverence for his spren had begun to wane.

He surged through the beads, trying to head vaguely in the direction of a small river he and Kaladin had seen earlier. It would manifest as solid ground here, and would perhaps give him terrain to use to his advantage.

Unfortunately, as he moved, the beads began to pull away from him. He'd been discovered.

They formed a tube ten feet in diameter, like a mine shaft from Bavland, where he'd once been owned. The walls of the large tube hardened, and Szeth now scrambled on curved, solid ground. He ran for the open end of the tunnel as—just behind him—the wall crashed open and the Edgedancer entered. She skated along the side of the tube, her powers giving her grace and speed. Szeth spun and Lashed himself backward to stay ahead of her, but the tube kept extending, beads falling into place.

The tube suddenly ended in a wall, which he should have expected. He slammed into it and she approached, moving quickly.

He canceled his Lashing, crouching as her Blade stabbed straight into the wall above him—coming within inches of his head. He ducked and ran back through the tube as she stopped with precision, then lunged again. He grunted and set the air alight to distract her—a flash of fire.

Stormlight healed the Edgedancer of the superficial burns as her next lunge sliced his cheek before plunging the Blade into the wall of the strange tube. That brought her in very close to him, and he grunted, grabbing for her arm.

She backhanded him, deceptively strong—and when he seized her, her skin and clothing became as if coated in grease. Edgedancer. Right. There would be no grappling with her. His fingers slipped free, and the Edgedancer slid backward, then sliced at him once more with her Blade.

He dodged, barely, but then the tunnel's beads crumbled beneath his feet, dumping him down to his waist before partially resolidifying. Pozen's work.

The Edgedancer sprang forward as Szeth struggled in the beads, holding up warding hands, but mostly floundering.

In a flash, the Blade cut through his forearms. His fingers went limp, losing all sensation, turning into dead weights on the ends of his arms. Desperate, he Lashed himself downward through the beads, sinking to his shoulders as the next attack passed over his head. The beads started to harden further, trying to trap him in place—but with concentration, he made the closest ones respond to him, not Pozen.

Free enough to slide out, Szeth Lashed himself straight at the Edgedancer. He slammed into her and Lashed her away. She soared backward until his Lashing ran out, then she regained control, shaking herself.

Szeth hovered up into the air of the tunnel, wary, exerting effort and concentration to heal his hands. In the distance, he heard it again. That voice.

Szeth? I'm here! Use me!

His spren? No, the voice was wrong. Not Kaladin either.

Was that . . . Nightblood?

The Edgedancer watched him, careful. He had to get out of the tube—it was a clever construction, intended to prevent him from leveraging his ability to fly while still giving the Edgedancer room to maneuver. Pozen must be nearby, to see inside well enough to have liquefied the beads under Szeth alone.

"They told me you were the best," the Edgedancer said, gliding forward lithely, Blade up and pointed at him. "They told me I'd need to train exhaustively to have even a chance against you, Truthless. Yet here you are, defeated."

Szeth said nothing. He drew in more of his precious remaining Stormlight and forced it into his hands. Healing from a cut like this took work. Why was she giving him time to accomplish it?

Because she doesn't know, he realized. *They haven't fought Radiants.* He remembered well his stark amazement when Kaladin had first healed from an Honorblade slice, impossible without living oaths and Radiance. The Honorblades were amazing, but they were essentially prototypes, without the . . . refinement that had come as the Radiants had experimented.

An opportunity, then.

"Perhaps," the Edgedancer said, "I will instead be allowed your great honor. If I am the one who kills you, do you think they will grant it to me instead?"

"Grant you *what*?" Szeth asked, landing in the tunnel. He could hear the rolling of the beads outside, but distantly, muffled. He sagged, pretended to be worn out, defeated. Letting her stalk closer. "I don't know what *any* of you are talking about."

"We were instructed not to say," she told him. "I wish I had not found you so . . . disappointing, Truthless."

"I am but one man," he said. "Training and skill cannot overcome all things. You have trapped me, weaponless, in an unstable location and have pitted me two against one. What did you expect?"

"Brilliance," she whispered, then lunged for him.

Szeth, in turn, raised fully healed hands and—with two fingers—pushed the tip of the sword aside. He stepped into her lunge—the sword passing just by him—and raised his other fist in a punch, slamming it into her stomach.

"I'm not Truthless," he growled.

She gasped, eyes going wide, and he clocked her across the face with another fist. Then he brought his elbow down on her wrist to disarm her. The Honorblade vanished as she let go, but his next punch missed as the tunnel began to undulate and the stunned Edgedancer was dropped into the beads to protect her.

He sighed, and a second later the tunnel collapsed into a crushing, churning mass of beads. Fortunately, he was able to control the flow of it; Pozen couldn't completely trap him, not so long as Szeth knew to command the beads closest to him.

As he swam to hide, he felt cloth in the beads. His spren had returned. It thrust a bead into his palm. "The best I could do!"

Szeth pressed Stormlight into the bead, eager for the weapon the spren had found. Here, he did what was called "manifesting." Using the soul of an object, and Stormlight, to create a physical representation of the item in Shadesmar.

He felt the object form as he made a surge of beads to lift him up toward the surface. There, he saw what he'd been given.

A spoon. A wide wooden stirring spoon, as was commonly used in Shinovar for cooking.

His spren, appearing far from distinguished as his strange head bobbed up from the beads nearby, waved. Close beyond him, Szeth spotted the peninsula of firm obsidian ground that followed the river in the Physical Realm.

"A spoon?" Szeth shouted. "The best you could find was a *spoon*?"

"You're inventive!" the spren called back. "I figured you could find something to do with it!"

Yes, Szeth did find something to do with the spoon. He threw it at the spren, hitting him square in the forehead. Then, with a sigh, Szeth let himself sink into the beads again. Weak hope though it was, if he stayed submerged, he might be able to hide.

Szeth commanded the currents of beads to swing him toward that ridge of land. He wanted his back to that wall, even underneath the beads—as it would at least protect him from one direction. Plus, he was running low on

Stormlight. The moment his reserves failed, he'd quickly suffocate unless he had land to climb upon.

It was an unusual experience, flowing through the beads, feeling them roll off his face. If he opened his eyes, they'd press against his eyeballs, stinging. Each bead glimmered faintly with a spark deep within. They made way for him at first . . . but then started working against him.

Pozen had located him. The beads, rather than ushering Szeth forward, began to swirl and churn around him. Pozen couldn't capture Szeth in them, but he could send rival currents to smash into Szeth. Those threw him off course, as if he were flying through a highstorm.

Szeth soon lost control. It had been too many years since his training, and he'd never been particularly skilled in Shadesmar anyway. Wave after wave of beads crashed across him, spinning him, battering him. One finally slammed him up against something hard—the ridge he'd been swimming toward.

He let out a grunt of pain. The beads—as if sensing his weakness—sucked him away from the wall, then crashed him back into it. This time he screamed, glowing Stormlight escaping his lips as his ribs were cracked. His remaining Light rushed to heal him, but at this rate he'd run out in minutes.

Szeth, Nightblood said in his mind—cutting through the whispers like a blade. *I'm here!*

"Where?" Szeth said.

I sank and hit something hard. By a wall, I think.

Could it be? Szeth, using his small reserve of Stormlight, Lashed himself downward. A force strong enough to rip him out of the currents. He sank some hundred feet, and it grew even darker in these depths, the voices louder.

But . . . he thought he could see light? He searched for it, and as he thrashed in the beads, his hand fell on something. He seized it. A hilt.

Yes! You found me!

"Why is your voice different?"

The sword shouldn't manifest as a weapon in here, should it? Shardblades didn't. But Honorblades could be brought through into Shadesmar intact—so who knew what the rules would be for Nightblood. At least the sword didn't suck his Stormlight away. It was likely still sheathed.

Worn out, low on Stormlight, Szeth projected control and focus, calling a wave from below to lift him. He soon entered the currents Pozen had sent, which again tried to smash him against the land. Szeth continued upward though, until his head and shoulders broke the surface of the ocean. He used his left arm to cling to the obsidian ridge, the top of which was only a few inches above the beads. In his right hand, beneath the beads, he clung to Nightblood's hilt, not revealing it.

The Edgedancer was already atop the ridge. She strode along it toward him, grey robes rustling, her Blade out and held before her. She didn't engage him in conversation; she just raised her weapon, preparing to chop down through his head.

Szeth ripped his right hand from the beads.

And released an explosion of light.

In that hand he held not a jet-black sword, but a blazing, radiant line of golden light. Glowing like the sun itself, so bright it made the Edgedancer gasp and stumble back, shading her eyes with her left hand.

Szeth hauled himself onto the obsidian ridge. He took the effulgent weapon—it *was* a sword, if difficult to see through the blinding light—and held it before him. Fortunately, his eyes adjusted, letting him see his enemy enough to fight.

"Sword-nimi?" he whispered. "What *happened* to you?"

Happened? Nightblood asked, the voice . . . different. Distorted, as if heard underwater. *Nothing happened. Say, where did the hill where we were camping go? Did the grass get covered in those beads?*

"We're in Shadesmar," Szeth said. "You don't know?"

What's Shadesmar? Oh! Is that person in front of us evil? Are you really going to use me *to fight? Yay!*

Szeth glanced to the side, to where he caught sight of his spren drifting in the beads, useless as he tried to swim.

"Yes," Szeth said. "I am proud to wield you."

What a great choice!

"Why are you glowing though?"

Glowing? I always glow, don't I?

The truth of it clicked with Szeth. This was Shadesmar, the land of the mind. Sometimes what appeared here related to how it was perceived.

In this realm, Nightblood looked the way it imagined itself.

The Edgedancer recovered from her surprise and came in, pushing off with one foot and gliding toward him on the other. Their skill, however, was one he had taken to fairly well—which let him know how to fight one of their kind. He used that understanding now, blocking the Edgedancer's attacks with a sequence of expert parries—and using small Lashings to make himself lighter, to pull him out of the way with extra speed when dodging.

She spun, coasting backward a short distance and watching him with what he read as concern. Then she gritted her teeth and came in a second time—and once more he easily dodged or parried each of her strikes. Although she moved like a liquid, he moved like the wind. As they again parted, she was puffing, Stormlight leaking from her lips as she skidded to a stop, illuminated starkly by Nightblood. Bright highlights and harsh shadows. He was winning.

It was not good to take pride in his skill. To kill was to subtract, after all. Yet after what she'd said earlier, he did feel some measure of enjoyment at the way she regarded him. It was easy to pretend superiority when you left your opponent unable to resist in any meaningful way. Szeth turned and positioned himself with his sword held before him, shining and brilliant, then nodded to the Edgedancer to come in again.

Are we . . . fighting or sparring? Nightblood asked.

"Fighting, sword-nimi," Szeth said softly. "They would kill me."

Unfortunately, as the Edgedancer prepared, beads began to bubble up and pour onto the narrow peninsula of ground. Szeth glanced out into the ocean, where Pozen had floated over—still cross-legged on a platform of beads, Shardblade in his lap. Beads surged up around Szeth to interfere in the fight; they began to pool around him, shoving him off balance, locking together and trying to trap his feet.

That is cheating, Nightblood said. *That's cheating, isn't it, Szeth?*

Szeth grunted as he tried to lift into the air, but beads grabbed him by the legs and held on. He tried to prepare the mental commands to get the beads to let go, but couldn't spare that attention—as the Edgedancer attacked in a blinding sequence of strikes. True swordplay on this level wasn't about parrying, despite his showy engagements earlier. So while he managed to block some of her attacks, another one speared him straight through the left thigh, making him stumble.

Do you want extra help? Nightblood asked.

"Yes," Szeth whispered. "Please." He grabbed the sword in two hands, staggering. He had to balance on one leg, fighting with the beads that—having formed snaking tentacles—tried to pull him down.

DRAW ME.

The Edgedancer came at him, ready to swing a powerful, two-handed attack. Szeth growled and whipped the golden sheath from Nightblood, releasing a further explosion of light—though it began to drain Szeth's Stormlight at a furious rate. Szeth raised his own attack, swinging with everything he had.

Blade met Blade.

A *crash* exploded from the swords—a blast of force that hurled back beads in a massive crater around Szeth some fifty feet wide. The hit tossed the Edgedancer like a leaf, her Blade flung from her fingers to shimmer and fall into the beads while she crumpled and rolled backward along the ridge. No Stormlight wafted from her body. She fell still, as if dead.

Szeth gasped, barely stabilizing himself on one leg—and resheathed the sword. Beads rained down distantly into the ocean.

Hmm, Nightblood said. *That didn't do what I thought it would.*

"What . . . did you think it would do?" Szeth said.

I've been chatting with the Honorblades you recovered, and thought maybe I'd give you some other Radiant abilities.

"You can . . . actually do that?" Szeth asked.

Apparently not. I really thought I'd figured it out. Sorry, Szeth.

"This will do," Szeth said, drawing Stormlight and letting it surge into his wounded leg. He stepped forward a moment later, healed, walking toward the Edgedancer as she climbed to her feet, woozy. She saw him, then resummoned her Blade. She'd stopped glowing, however.

No Stormlight. No powers.

"Stand down," Szeth said to her.

She growled and launched at him with her Blade, so Szeth swung and expertly feinted, then unsheathed his blade again and struck—Nightblood didn't simply cut, but made the Edgedancer burst into motes of light. Like tiny meteorites scattering away from him in a million sparks that vaporized and vanished.

As Szeth resheathed—Nightblood having consumed the last of his Stormlight—her Honorblade clanged to the ridge, then slipped and fell into the beads. Szeth turned toward Pozen—who remained sitting patiently out in the sea. The elderly man held his hand to the side, and the beads there split, delivering to him the Edgedancer Honorblade, which he placed into his lap alongside his own weapon.

"You are defeated, Pozen," Szeth shouted across the sixty or so feet separating them. "Reject the touch of the Unmade! Help me cleanse the land, rather than bolstering the darkness!"

"You have no idea of what you speak," Pozen called back. "You have always had trouble seeing the right of things, Szeth-son-Neturo."

"True," Szeth said softly. "But I think I might at last be seeing clearly." He stepped to the edge of the beads, pondering how to cross them to Pozen, and they hardened in front of him.

Ah, there, Nightblood said. *That helps, doesn't it?*

"Thank you, sword-nimi," Szeth said, striding across the surface of the ocean. As he took each step, the beads locked together underfoot.

The beads like Honorblades. Oh! They like regular Shardblades too. And the spren who make them. Something about the bond . . .

"You think you have won," Pozen called as Szeth approached. "But I see you are out of Stormlight, Szeth-son-Neturo."

"Pozen," Szeth said, "you cannot defeat me in a duel. We both know that. Let us talk. Can you spare me no courtesy? After all those months we spent together?"

"Months spent preparing you," Pozen said, "for a duty you rejected." Still, the elderly man studied him, and there was . . . something between them. Not affection. Neither had particularly liked the other.

But Pozen was the Honorbearer with whom Szeth had spent the most time. The first who had recruited him. So the elderly man held up a hand, halting Szeth's advance.

"I will give you a chance, Szeth," Pozen said softly. "If you can remember what I taught you, and apply it. You never did learn to Elsegate. Well, let us see if you can figure it out when the stakes are so high."

Szeth cursed and started running.

Pozen stood up, then fell forward onto his Honorblade. Szeth screamed as he arrived, stabilizing the ground of that pillar so it didn't fall apart at Pozen's death. He dropped to his knees, grabbing the body in one hand, Nightblood in the other.

The corpse evaporated into dark mist, the same way the Stoneward had. Szeth looked up, kneeling before the two Honorblades, and scanned the area around him. No sign of any ships. He had no supplies, and was in the middle of an ocean. Even if he could walk down the river peninsula and find land, it would take him weeks to reach a settlement. He'd be dead long before that. Rain did not fall in Shadesmar.

Szeth? Nightblood asked. *What is wrong? Why do you have that expression?*

"We are trapped, sword-nimi," Szeth whispered. "I cannot get us out of this place."

This place? Nightblood said. *Oh, the sword is explaining. Strange. But Szeth, you're amazing. You can get us out.*

Could he?

Szeth searched Pozen's robes, and found a pouch of gemstones. He drew in that Light, then took Pozen's Honorblade in one hand, admiring it. A decade ago, he'd used it to come to Shadesmar during his pilgrimage. He'd had to be rescued by Pozen—borrowing the Willshaper Honorblade—to get back out. Holding it this time though, he felt something.

Fear?

The Honorblade didn't speak, at least not to people. But it was afraid. It *knew* something was deeply wrong. Whatever was happening in Shinovar, this Blade wasn't part of the problem—and it was as confused as Szeth. It wanted to be in the hands of its true owner, the Herald.

Szeth closed his eyes and whispered a prayer. To the spren of this Blade, to the spren of his land. He concentrated, and didn't rely on the training that had never worked. Instead he focused on his quest.

If he did not return, his people were doomed. And he would never find out how, or why, his father had died.

To this urgent need, the Honorblade seemed to listen, and made up for his inadequacy.

Let's go! Nightblood said. *I'll bet Syl is worried about me!*

 Szeth stabbed into the air. His hand grew cold as the Honorblade drew

Stormlight from him in a rush, and the weapon's tip sliced through reality itself, cutting a slit like in the stomach of an enemy, maybe four feet across. It bowed outward, a hole just big enough for him to pass through.

His exhaustion struck him right as the beads under his feet began to undulate and fall apart. With a cry, he clutched Nightblood and the two Honorblades, then sprang through the opening and tumbled out onto a dark landscape.

Springy grass above loam, smelling of freshness and life. He drew a deep breath and flopped onto his back, enervated by the sudden loss of Stormlight. The golden version of Nightblood had vanished from his hand, but Szeth heard the black sword humming and talking from where he'd left it by the tree. He still had the two Honorblades, and he'd managed to avoid impaling himself as he fell.

So he took a moment, lying there and looking up at the sky. Until a shadow in the night approached and loomed over him.

"Szeth?" Kaladin asked. "Here you are. Why did you wander off? Stop lounging—shouldn't we be planning the confrontation with the next Honorbearer?"

Szeth laughed at that. Kaladin—raising a sphere for light—spotted the two Honorblades and gasped.

"You did well, Szeth," Szeth's highspren said in his ear. "A challenge met and overcome."

"You sound so confident," Szeth whispered.

"I am," the spren said, invisible.

"Then would you prefer I forget the image of you floundering in the beads? That of your providing, when asked to help, a *spoon*? Shall I forget how useless you were?"

"I . . . That was . . . intentional. To ensure you did not rely upon me."

"Yes, of course, spren-nimi," he said. "If we continue, we will find the Lightweaver monastery next, will we not?"

"Yes. That would make sense."

"It is good, then, that I share with you something I learned from my teacher in Lightweaving many years ago."

"Um . . . all right," the spren said. "What is that?"

Szeth cracked an eye at Kaladin, who was demanding answers. Instead, Szeth whispered softly to the spren.

"When you're living an illusion, spren-nimi, be *very* careful not to do anything to spoil it. Because once you do, it is exceedingly difficult to recapture your audience."

54
A FRIEND

Indeed, some insist that among Radiants, some Skybreakers did step forth into the Recreance, and their actions are covered; to this end, I have engaged the commentary of Didal; it strikes as mendacious that any Skybreaker would turn upon their oaths, and I find their malignment to be uniformly abhorrent. A schism arose among them, as all evidence presents, but not of this nature. The Skybreakers, who have always quietly cared for those the law forgets, do still exist, as previously accounted; they merely exist in multiple forms.

—From *Words of Radiance*, chapter 40, page 3

Shallan sat and watched a school of skyeels dancing in the sky. Playfully nipping at one another, swirling and streaming. Though she was too distant to see the subtle details of the three-color split, it was manifest all around her. These worlds, created by Renarin's and Rlain's spren, made her feel as if she were living in a woodblock print.

This time they were at one of the warcamps. Nearby, Rlain and Renarin sat with their feet hanging over the side of a chasm. She'd never known Renarin to be overtly cheerful, but he laughed at something Rlain said. The spren didn't think Dalinar and Navani had found their way to another vision yet, which gave her time to think about what had happened in the last one. Her clash with Mraize had nearly revealed her to the gods.

Perhaps they could plan better for the next time. And perhaps she could figure out what was happening to her mind.

"How did Formless come back, Pattern?" Shallan asked. She sat at the edge of the camp, near the crumbled wall. Pattern sat to her right on a broken section of the wall, hands crossed primly in his lap.

"I do not know," he said. Testament sat a little farther up on the same broken wall, regarding the skyeels. "I do not think humans make sense when they *are* sane! Let alone when they are not. Ha ha."

She tipped her head back and felt the breeze, making pictures in her mind from the clouds. This idyllic version of the Shattered Plains had been constructed from Rlain's memory. It depicted a time before humans arrived, though no one else—singer or human—appeared in the vision. Their touch was represented in the cloths hanging from windows, the crops growing in the distance, the spears and bows leaning against one wall. It was like visiting a home when the occupants had stepped out, soon to return.

"I banished Formless," Shallan said. "I grew past that. I don't *need* her."

"Agreed," Pattern said.

"Is this what it will be like?" Shallan asked. "For the rest of my life? Knowing that my mind could—at any moment—backslide? Knowing *that* is always lurking around the corner?"

"I'm sorry, Shallan."

She squeezed her eyes shut. "It was almost better, Pattern, when I didn't *know.* Then, it wasn't my fault when I failed. Or at least I could pretend it wasn't."

"Shallan," Pattern whispered, "what did Wit say?"

"I know . . ."

"Repeat it."

"I don't deserve it," she whispered. "What was done to me is not my fault. It's all right to accept that I have pain, but I shouldn't accept that I deserve it."

"I'm sorry that you have to live with it anyway."

"I do. It's awful, and it's unfair, but I do." She took a deep breath. "I'm not going to let Formless manifest as a full aspect of my personality. Veil and Radiant are coping mechanisms, and they helped me survive. But Formless . . . she's *me.* Not an alternate persona, but a representation of me giving up. That is me if I just . . . become what Mraize wants."

"You won't give in to that, Shallan."

"No. I *won't.*"

"Then there is nothing to fear. Perhaps she only manifests here as a reminder. Maybe?"

She looked to him, to find his head pattern spinning and transforming, mesmerizing, faster than normal. He was worried for her.

"Thank you," she said.

"Oh!" he said, perking up. "I said the right things?"

"It's more that you were here," she said, smiling.

"I am very good at this," Pattern said. "Mmmm. That might be a lie, but I don't care!"

Shallan gazed up at the sky, past the eels, at the clouds. "I wonder how

Adolin is doing. Is he all right, do you think? He had to go to war without me."

"He is very strong," Pattern said. "The best swordsman I know! Or really that anyone knows!"

That was true, but being the best didn't always protect you. Sometimes it made you a target. She continued staring at the clouds, imagining them as . . .

The face of Ba-Ado-Mishram. Glaring down at her malevolently. Shallan's breath caught, and she glanced at Testament, who had been staring in that direction all this time. She wasn't watching the skyeels, but that face in the clouds.

Renarin suddenly cried out and stumbled to his feet. So, he'd noticed as well. Together the two men hurried back to her, their spren joining them from the shadows nearby, where they liked to linger—though they would as often inhabit their hosts' bodies somehow.

"Face," Renarin said, pointing to where he'd been sitting. "In the patterns of the stone on the ground."

"Like that one?" Shallan asked, nodding toward the sky.

He followed her gesture, then cursed and crouched down.

"Perhaps we should go indoors," Rlain said.

"If you saw her in the stones," Shallan said, "then she's tainting this entire vision. We'll find her face in there too."

"Yes," Rlain said. "But which would you rather have watching you? A face in a stonework wall or *that*?"

"Oh!" Pattern exclaimed. "I like the giant one. It is more intimidating."

"You *like* that?" Rlain's words dripped with a frantic rhythm.

"I have decided I like *style*," Pattern said. "It is a Lightweaver thing, which we are very good at recognizing." He pointed. "That is style."

"Cryptics," Glys said softly. And it seemed to say a lot if one of *them* found Pattern strange.

Some of the way he acts, Radiant said, her voice amused, *he learned from you. I should think you would be proud.*

They retreated into a hollow stone building overgrown with crem drippings like candle wax. These sorts of things had been cleaned up when the humans had taken the region, which in retrospect Shallan found a shame. The organic, melted feel was so much more engaging and different from . . .

Was that Veil snickering at her? Just for liking an odd building? Honestly.

This was where Rlain had grown up. Unlike Renarin's room, this had no fine furniture—though he did have a basket for possessions and a nice mattress for the bed.

"What's this?" Renarin said, gesturing to a smaller bed. "Sibling?"

"Hound," Rlain said. "I raised axehounds when younger. Had to let them go when we fled to Narak."

"Axehounds," Renarin said. "I didn't know that about you."

"I got along with them better than I did with people." Rlain shrugged and settled onto the bed, now far too small for him. "Funny. I used to think this bed was so roomy when I was in workform. But today *this* body feels like the right one, so it's hard to reconcile my perfect bed with the fact that I no longer fit it."

"You really grew up here?" Shallan asked, peering around for signs of Mishram's face. She found it on three separate stones, as if part of the natural pattern of the rock.

"My whole childhood," he said. "When my parents died in the flood, it was just me in here. The strange one, on his own with his hounds . . ."

"Was that hard?" Renarin asked. "As a child?"

"I was nearly seven when it happened," Rlain said. "So, not that bad."

It took Renarin a moment to process that—Shallan noticed him thinking it through. Singers matured much faster than humans did, reaching adulthood by age ten.

"Still," Renarin said.

"You get used to being alone," Rlain said. "Sometimes a little too used to it, you know?"

"I do," Renarin said. "Trust me." He looked like he wanted to say something more, and Shallan had the distinct feeling she was intruding. Renarin backed off, turning away and finding something to fiddle with—in this case a few pebbles from his pocket that he could roll and count between his fingers.

"So," Shallan said, cutting in, "should we talk about the way Mishram is watching us?"

"Mmm . . ." Pattern said. "You think of her, and it draws her attention. The prison is leaking."

"She shouldn't be able to see in here," Glys said. "This should be safe, even from gods . . ."

"However, if she's watching us," Rlain said, feet up on the head of his bed, "we must be on the right track."

"I still don't think we should focus on her," Renarin said, sitting on the ground beside Rlain's bed. "We simply need to stop the Ghostbloods, then get out. That's our mission."

"I tried," Shallan said. "And I almost revealed your spren to the gods. Do they have any advice for avoiding that?"

"No armor," Renarin said, glancing toward Pattern and Testament, who had settled down over beside the firepit. His and Rlain's mistspren loomed in the doorway, and didn't fully enter for some reason. "When you summoned that you almost outed us."

"It doesn't work here anyway," Shallan said.

“I wish we could understand,” Rlain said, “what’s being said in the visions. We’re focused on stopping these assassins, but the visions could tell us so much. Like how Honor died.”

“Do we really want to know?” Renarin asked.

“Why wouldn’t we?” Rlain said.

“Because the truth can be painful,” Renarin said.

“So you’d rather not know it?” Rlain asked, his rhythm changing.

“Sometimes,” Shallan said. “Sometimes that’s tempting.”

Renarin looked to her and nodded. “Regardless,” he said, “I think we should try again at stopping the Ghostbloods, in another vision. But Shallan, Rlain and I aren’t experts at acting. I worry we might hold you back.”

“Possibly,” Shallan said. “But you’re experts—or the closest we have—on this realm. I think I’m way better off with you two along. Besides, there’s two of them and three of us. Our best shot at taking them is together.”

“Agreed,” Rlain said. “Can we arm ourselves?”

“I have this,” Shallan said, bringing out the dagger that warped the air. “So we have something.”

“Rlain and I will just have to find weapons in whichever vision we enter,” Renarin said, then took a deep breath. “We’re agreed? We try again to trap or kill the assassins?”

Shallan and Rlain nodded. Now it was up to the spren to warn them when another vision was ready.

⁂

Hours after the latest assault, Adolin walked unarmored through the square outside the Oathgate dome, which had fallen quiet once more. Storms, he was exhausted. They’d fended off the attack, but it had lasted much longer than the others.

They’re trying to break us, he thought. *Don’t let them.* Still, it was difficult to ignore the swarms of exhaustionspren. Only two days in, and he was starting to worry. About the mystery strike force harrying the reinforcements. About losing too many soldiers. About another city doomed to be abandoned.

It was pretty out here on the plaza. Tens of twinkling cookfires dotted the square, each with its own dancing flamespren, made in little portable hearths provided by the Azish. A cool, wet breeze blew from the north, and he found himself enjoying it as a wistful reminder of places he’d lived. The Shattered Plains, then Urithiru, both chillier than his homeland. How long had it been since he’d lived in Alethkar? He’d barely been a man when he’d ridden off to the war on the Shattered Plains. He’d gone back to Kholinar once, of course. And left it burning.

Storms, he’d been trying to relax, but it felt like he was carrying an incredible weight all of a sudden. Memories. He'd failed many times in his life, but Kholinar was different. Everyone made mistakes. But not everyone left their city to the enemy. The city where he, Adolin, should have been king. If he hadn't abandoned it . . . both the throne and the land.

At the same time, not everyone murdered another highprince in a secluded hallway. Though Adolin stood by that action and would do it again, that was part of the weight. A better man might have found another way. And a better man certainly wouldn't have covered it up as he had.

He halted, missing Shallan. He felt the cool wind blow across him and wished he knew its name, for everything had a name. These days he wasn't completely sure of his own.

"Highprince Adolin?" a voice asked from nearby.

He turned, surprised to see Noura, the head vizier, approaching, her patterned clothing blending in with the night's shadows. He idly wondered if that gave their soldiers an advantage in the dark.

"Yes?" he asked.

"I have come to request a favor," the older woman said, walking closer to him, visible by green moonlight as neither of them carried a lamp or sphere. "Will you please cease your corruption of the Prime? You are confusing him and frustrating our attempts to guide him in the correct way."

Adolin turned back toward the wind, and fell naturally into a parade rest. A soldier's ways for a soldier's son. "Do the moons look bigger here in Azimir?"

"I really wouldn't know, Brightlord."

He grunted, then shifted—maintaining his stance—to face the emperor's grand pavilion. "What do you think Yanagawn needs, Noura?"

"Careful guidance," she replied, "to provide stability to the empire, so the empire may provide stability to him."

"Sounds like smart words quoted from somewhere."

"My own essay," she admitted, "when I applied for this position. Adolin, so long as the emperor is on his throne, Azimir stands. It is one of our strongest mottos. He is to sit and rule, not pretend to be a soldier."

"Well," Adolin said, still studying that pavilion—lit from the inside by calm spheres, making the whole thing glow like a lantern. "Sitting there might be what the emperor needs, and what the empire needs. But that's not what I asked, now is it?"

"Yanagawn needs whatever the empire needs."

"No," Adolin said, pivoting to meet her eyes in the darkness. "Noura, that young man needs a *friend.*"

"He has friends."

"He has attendants and minders . . . and, I'm sure, a great number of people who *pretend* to be friends for political gain."

"Yes, a great number of those," she admitted. "It's difficult to fend them off sometimes."

"Noura, I've lived that life, worrying which of my friends are only there because they want something from me. That loneliness can destroy a person, and I'm grateful for those I was able to trust. Yanagawn *needs* someone he can talk to who *isn't* in his chain of command, or whatever you call it for someone like him. He needs someone who isn't related to him, in charge of him, or serving him."

"He's stronger than you think."

"Storm it, Noura, it's not *about* strength." He waved toward the pavilion, and kept his voice down. "Of course he's strong. But people *break*, and sometimes the strong ones break harder than the weak ones—because they're the ones you pile everything on top of. You ever seen what happens when you put too much weight on a horse? I don't care if it's an old nag or a Ryshadium warhorse—you *can* break its spine, Noura."

"You think I don't care?" she hissed, stepping right up to him. Though she was quite a bit shorter, there was a fire to her he could practically feel. "I put that boy on the throne, knowing full well what I was asking of him. I live each day doing whatever I can to uphold him. He is my *emperor.*"

"Oh?" Adolin said. "Lift told me how he got elevated—that he was picked as a convenient dupe. Someone for Szeth to murder because no one else would take the spot. He's *disposable* to you, so don't *moralize* to me."

He expected her to break his gaze, to turn away in shame, but she set her jaw. "Yes," she admitted. "We did that to a boy, for the good of the empire, but then that boy became my *Prime.* I'd die for him. Do you believe that, Kholin? The moment we elevated him, he became my responsibility, my duty, my *life.*"

"I . . ." Storms. He'd expected some fiddling bureaucrat. He'd underestimated her, hadn't he? "I believe you."

"Then believe that I know what he needs."

"All right," Adolin said. "I'll back off if you can look me straight in the eyes and tell me—in all honesty—that the boy isn't still there inside that emperor. You *tell* me *he* doesn't need a friend."

Silence. She held his eyes, and her jaw worked. But she couldn't force it out. "It isn't proper," she finally said, "for our emperor to walk into battle. It violates tradition."

"I've been around enough scribes to know you *make* tradition. My father and I disagree on a number of things, but there's one point on which we do agree: any man, anywhere, should have the right to pick up the spear or sword and fight for what he believes in. If you deny Yanagawn that, you deny him manhood itself."

At this, Noura rolled her eyes. "And you were doing so well . . . then, reliable old Alethi chauvinism."

Adolin refused to be baited. He narrowed his eyes. "There's more here, isn't there? About me? What is it you don't like about me, Noura?"

She weighed her response, folding her arms. "You walked away from the throne, Kholin. You are one of the only people in the world who could *actually* have been on the Prime's level, and you walked away from it. That degree of irresponsibility is . . . concerning."

He started, and dropped his parade stance at last. "You . . . think I'm going to convince him to do the same?"

"Ideas are more contagious than any disease," she said. "And Kholin, Yanagawn is a *good* emperor. He has the heart to be an excellent one. If you'd seen the progress he's made . . . If you knew the previous emperors, all excellent candidates on paper, who became shells . . . Do you realize how long it's been since we had a Prime who truly understood the needs of the common people? We *can't lose him.*"

"Then listen," Adolin whispered. "If you keep him isolated, without friends, that *will* break him, Noura."

She held his eyes, hers reflecting green moonlight.

"Why did you turn away from your throne?" she finally asked. "What happened?"

"It has something to do with what he and I talked about today," Adolin said. "Something I never put a finger on. Oaths versus promises. Expectation versus execution. Give Yanagawn a little freedom, Noura, and he'll soar. Hold him down, and he'll start looking for exits lower to the ground." He grinned at her. "And if you want someone near him who doesn't want anything, then, well . . . consider that there's a single person in this storming world who had it all in the palm of his hand, and walked away." Adolin tapped his chest. "Know for certain that *one* man doesn't want your emperor's throne, or his money, or his power. Consider that, then ask yourself why I care."

"Because you've been there," she whispered.

"Storming right I have," Adolin said. "Still am." He gave her a bow of the head, then turned and walked off. She didn't call for him to return or demand he stay away. So he figured that was a battle won, or at least fought to a stalemate.

THE END OF
Day Four

BEWARE the REGALS!

STORMFORM

DIREFORM

ENGAGE WITH EXTREME CAUTION!

INTERLUDES

MOASH • ODIUM

Moash was done.

I killed Teft . . .

Odium no longer protected Moash from his own emotions. His eyes had been burned away, leaving him with one final image—as if struck upon his mind like the branding of a glyph: the queen of Urithiru with a halo of light around her, and he swore . . .

. . . he *swore* . . .

. . . that he'd seen Teft's spirit, Radiant and accusatory, rising behind her as part of that glow.

Moash lay somewhere loud. Humming singers and constant stonework. Kholinar, he thought, after a long flight. He'd been recovered from the snows of Urithiru, then eventually deposited here. His bed was plush, but his innards were raw as he groaned and turned on his side, clawing at his face.

I killed Teft.

The god of all emotions had promised to protect Moash from these feelings, this awful guilt, this sense of worthlessness. That was why he'd believed. Why he'd followed.

"Take my pain," he croaked. "Why won't you take my pain?"

"I don't do that any longer, Vyre," a quiet voice said from next to his bed.

Moash turned toward the sound, trying to look, despite no longer having eyes. He did that every time. Looking. Not seeing.

That voice. It was different, but . . .

"It is not right for me to take emotions," the voice said. "My predecessor was a glutton, and would feed upon those of his followers. Not I. Your passion is what makes you live, Vyre. What god of passion am I if I do not celebrate emotion in my followers?"

"You celebrate *this*?" Moash asked, clawing at his face again. "I feel like

I'm being ripped apart. Each day I'm destroyed anew, condemned as a monster . . ."

"That is the price we pay," the voice said, "for doing what is right. If it did not have a cost, would it be a sacrifice to do what was right? Would not all people just do it naturally?"

"Right?" Moash asked. "Killing a friend?"

"If a man must die for his choices," the voice said, "is it not better that he be killed by a friend, who will mourn him?" Sounds of clothing rumpling. A chair scooting. As if the speaker was leaning forward in his seat. "You're not a monster. A monster would murder with glee and love it. To kill with agony, like a surgeon who must bring pain . . . those are the actions of a *hero,* Vyre."

A . . . hero?

"Who are you?" Moash asked.

"Your new god," the voice said. "You KNOW ME."

That voice, that use of tone . . . it was Odium. But a *new* Odium. Different, yet the same.

"Take my pain . . ." Moash whispered.

"No, Vyre, I will not. If you cannot bear the price, then you are not worthy of your title or Blade. However, there is something I *can* give you. See. Not with your eyes—I cannot restore them, as they were taken by an act of my adversary—but I can still engage your mind."

And Moash saw. Or . . . imagined. Glorious forces marching to war, across a hundred worlds, bringing peace and order to so many. He saw peace, serenity, a thousand wrongs righted. Kings cast down, and the families of working people—like those who ran the caravans—given, at long last, true retribution for the crimes committed against them.

He saw unity. Forged beneath the banner of an eternal, immortal army led by a man in black Shardplate, eyes glowing red.

"The Blackthorn serves you?"

"He may," Odium said. "Equal odds, depending on his choices in a few days. But if not him, another. Vyre, isn't this what you want? Isn't this why you turned against your friends in the first place? Why do you fight?"

"Because nothing matters . . ."

"Why *did* you fight?"

"Because the king of Alethkar was a rat, who got good men killed. And nobody would *ever* bring him to justice for his crimes."

"What you see," Odium said, "is every wrong being righted. *Every wrong.* If you follow me, you can decide how that happens, and who is rewarded. Is that not better than fighting for nothing? Better than feeling nothing? When you contemplate your pain, contemplate the peace and unity that pain will earn for so many. Let it become a *badge* to you, Vyre."

A badge. A way to recover the man he'd once been, who had stood against even Kaladin to bring justice to the men who wore crowns and exploited the weak. That was who Moash *had* been.

"How?" Moash asked.

"You're willing to try again?" Odium asked. "Although it may require opposing your friends? For they might name you traitor, but they never do stop being your friends, do they?"

"No. They don't."

"I understand better than any," Odium said. "It's why I care about you, Vyre. Yes, I do understand . . ."

The chair moved again, then Odium's voice, more distant: "He's yours. Let's see if this works."

Hands strapped him down in the darkness. They shoved a cloth into his mouth to muffle screams, and then, what happened next . . .

They took mallets and pounded spikes of light through his skull. He screamed. But this time the screams were in defiance of the pain, both outside and in. They were in rejection of the guilt, for he *had* been working for a greater world. How *dare* they fight against him?

How *dare* Kaladin claim to protect, when he defended the highborn who murdered? He was a pawn. How *dare* he not admit it? How dare he *serve them*?

When it was finished, the agony throbbing through Moash, he lay in a sweat, ragged and used, like an old pair of shoes worn on far too long a walk. They'd done something with his empty eye sockets, something that should have killed him. But as he lay there, wondering at the point of it, he . . .

He saw.

Not as he had. Outlines of light, the people specifically, and . . . gemstones, infused. Living things. No color, but . . . spren.

He could see spren. All around.

"That should work," a new voice said, feminine. "Look at his response. It's functioning. He can see Investiture."

"What have you done to me?" Moash whispered.

"You," Odium said, "have become a very specific kind of weapon. Are you ready to serve again? To forge a better world?"

This was . . . not what he'd been expecting. He looked around the room, and found Odium as a blazing source of light, his figure washed out by the power. Like a sun standing not ten feet away. And with him another, glowing with a different kind of light. A different . . . not color . . . rhythm of light?

"I will do what must be done," Vyre said. "Because someone must."

"That is right, Vyre," Odium said.

I-8

THE ONLY WAY

After spending some time allowing intellect to rule, Taravangian changed. He let intellect be ruled by emotions for now, and braced himself for what came next: A flood of passions and feelings. A dam broken down. They washed through him, each stronger than the last.

Worry, confidence, passion, fear, rage. Rage.

He instantly traveled back to Kharbranth, the home that he cared for so dearly. He blanketed the city so he could feel the emotions of each and every person there.

He loved them. Oh, how he *loved* this city, with its art, and its library, and its many hospitals that took any patient without cost. He even loved the secret portions of those hospitals, where people had died—feeling so many things—at the hands of his surgeons, killed to gather their Death Rattles. Sacrifices made in a terrible, but important quest—for that had once been his sole way to gain insight into the future.

His policies ensured the *greatest* good. In Kharbranth he found justification, for here was a city that—in war—knew peace. Insignificant crime rates created by giving police the ability to exile offenders, leaving in Kharbranth only the serene and wonderful.

Was that enough? He began to weep, for he knew it would *not* be enough. He instantly transferred to his daughter's room, where he sensed she was playing with his grandchildren. He watched them laugh while he trembled, suddenly afraid. Should he not feel love, seeing them again?

No. He was terrified. They were exposed.

Expelling criminals was *not* enough. He needed to *punish* them. *Annihilate* them, so they could not hurt his family or his people. And what of other kingdoms? They could come here, invade, destroy. His family would never be safe unless everything everywhere was under *his* control.

Only then would he never have to fear.

He did not appear to his family. He gave them each a hug, but silently, invisibly. They must not know what he was and what he had to do.

Emotion insisted on war.

In this, remarkably, both intellect and feeling *agreed.*

Cultivation was wrong. War, leading to his control of everything, was the *only* way.

DAY FIVE

VENLI • DALINAR • SIGZIL •
SZETH • NAVANI • JASNAH •
RENARIN • ADOLIN •
KALADIN • SHALLAN

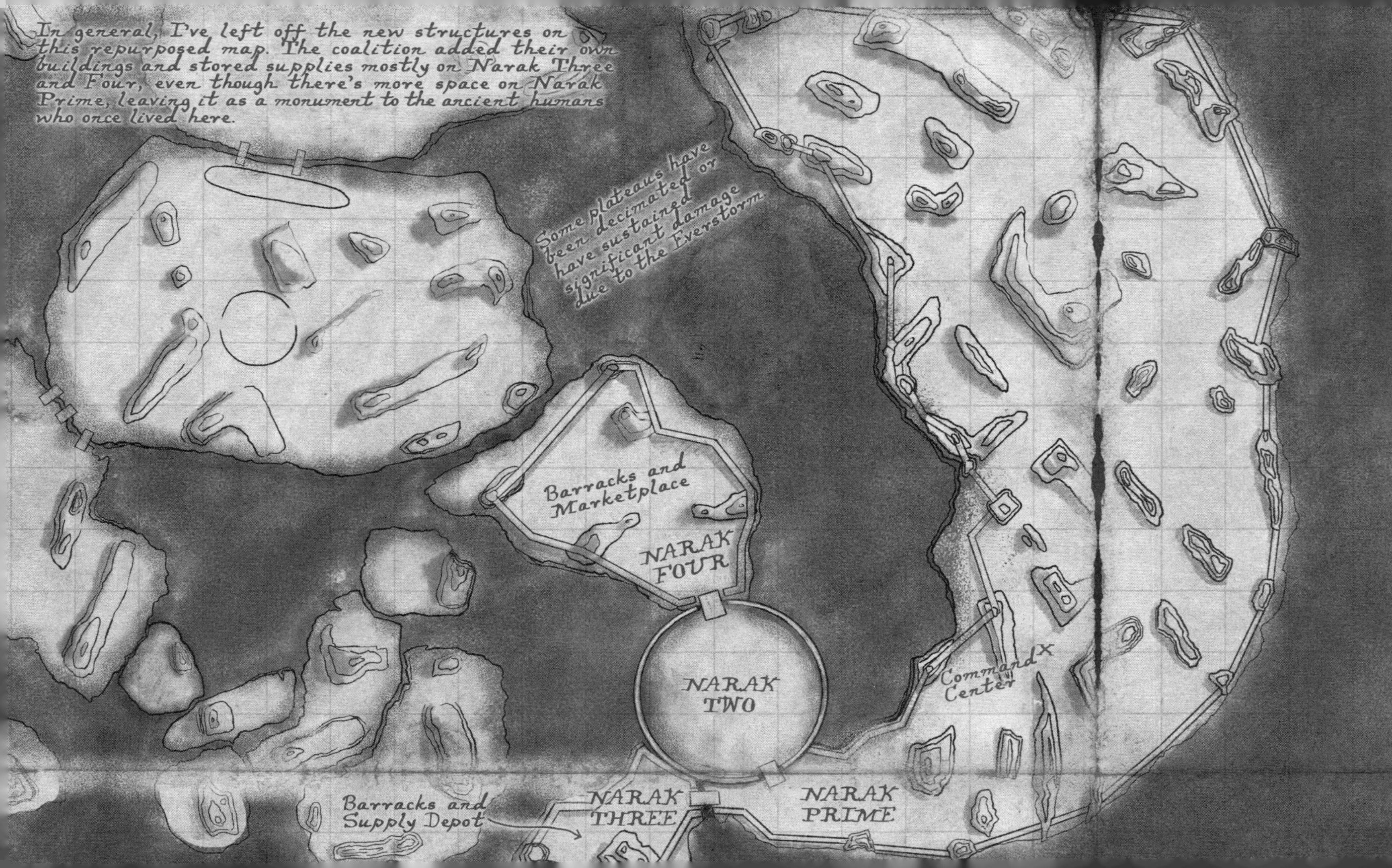
In general, I've left off the new structures on this repurposed map. The coalition added their own buildings and stored supplies mostly on Narak Three and Four, even though there's more space on Narak Prime, leaving it as a monument to the ancient humans who once lived here.
Some plateaus have been decimated or have sustained significant damage due to the Everstorm
Barracks and Marketplace
NARAK FOUR
NARAK TWO
Command Center
Barracks and Supply Depot
NARAK THREE
NARAK PRIME

Dearest Cephandrius,

Your rebuttal is eloquent, as always, but did you think I would be moved?

Venli sat in the cave alone. She'd carved it by her own hand, using her abilities to shape the stone.

Outside, an enormous shadow passed by, accompanied by the distinctive scrapes and thumps of a chasmfiend. People walked with the beast, their rhythms optimistic. For the first time in so very long, things seemed to be improving for her kind.

Unless Venli had led ultimate destruction their way.

She closed her eyes, placed her hands on the stones, and sang to them.

Welcome, child of ancients, the stones replied. *Welcome, stonesinger. Welcome, Radiant.*

"I need guidance," Venli whispered. "Please."

About what? the stones asked.

"My people . . . by taking me in, by sheltering renegade Fused like Leshwi . . . will draw Odium's ire. I have felt his anger. I worry that I've led destruction to the listeners. Again."

We do not know the future, the stones said. *We sing of the past. Of days long ago when we sang together, and you shaped us. When your kind knew the stone.*

Like the rock at Urithiru, these stones were eager to speak with her—and their rhythms were those of Joy and Peace. They named themselves Ko, the stones of the hills, but sometimes spoke as if all stone—indeed, all Roshar—were one.

They eagerly showed her the past, and with her powers that meant shapes appeared from the stone floor. Tiny sculptures only inches tall, representing her people crossing to this land. Periodically looking up, as if noticing something. Or . . . listening?

The rock had no answers. It didn't care about the "new" gods; it just wanted to sing, which would have been delightful, if she weren't increasingly anxious over what she'd done. Taking the oaths of a Knight Radiant, at long last. Her words being accepted by . . . well, she supposed it must have been Cultivation.

Venli had brought the Reachers, the lightspren, to her kind. Starting with Jaxlim, Venli's mother, a full *two dozen* listeners had bonded spren. A brilliant outpouring of power, far faster than any of the other orders had been refounded. The lightspren had been so eager.

And yet . . . this sort of thing drew attention. Lately she'd been hearing distant thunder, that of the Everstorm approaching, though no one else seemed to be able to hear it. That sound terrified her; she knew *him* all too well. With her hands on the ground of her small chamber, her flesh shivered—and her stomach twisted, her carapace feeling cold—as she remembered days serving him. Singing *his* songs, *his* rhythms. Watching as he destroyed the listeners—so he'd thought—in order to create false martyrs to pin on the humans.

A remnant had survived somehow, despite it all. And she'd come to them. She *had* to help.

Please, she said to the stones. *Give me a way.*

They merely continued to sing with her, joyous. *We're happy you're here. We brought you to this place, where the songs were once the loudest, and now you sing with us again.*

The stones didn't think about tomorrow. Let the wind worry about that. The stones could enjoy the past.

Finally she let go, but she continued humming softly to Joy. Although she hadn't gotten her answers, when speaking with the stones she couldn't help but find a sense of *place.* She hadn't realized, until a quiet day at Urithiru, how much the songs meant to her. How much her *heritage* meant to her. She'd squandered these wonders all her life, her own eyes on the future—and only the future.

Unfortunately, having been Odium's mouthpiece, she knew him all too well. He *would* come for them once he'd dealt with the humans. She rose, and left her cave to gaze out at her people. Seventeen hundred listeners, including many children. The elderly, the infirm, the young, and a stalwart group of soldiers, Eshonai's closest friends—who had refused the forms of power Venli had brought.

These were the true soul of the listeners. They had looked power in the eyes and had rejected it.

Being a listener means . . . the stones said to her . . . *to listen to the stones . . . and your ancestors . . .*

Inside her, Timbre attuned the Rhythm of Remembrance. Here in these completely unsheltered lands—the wide flatland southeast of the Shattered Plains—Venli's people made homes from crem and chunks of greatshell carapace. This place had once been considered too dangerous to visit, as it was the home of chasmfiends.

Now those chasmfiends moved among her people. Or . . . well, mostly they *slept* among her people. Giant lumps of monstrous chitin, who were content to lounge around with people literally climbing all over them. They liked to be *brushed* or *scratched* like giant axehound pups. And her people had no lack of food, as evidenced by a chasmfiend returning from the hunt dragging a twenty-foot-tall dead zumble—a herbivore with a bulbous black carapace. The chasmfiend let the listeners slice off some chunks for cooking as it settled down to eat.

A gentle humming drew her attention. She glanced over as her mother, Jaxlim, stepped up—a listener with a round face, long hairstrands in a braid, and a complex skin pattern of very thin lines. Instantly Venli was a little girl again. Listening to the songs and diligently memorizing them at her mother's feet. Usually those memories were accompanied by a frustration with her sister—Eshonai had never done what she should, yet had always been Mother's favorite.

Today . . . Venli maintained Joy, and shifted to the Rhythm of the Lost for her sister. In the end, Eshonai had done more for their people than Venli ever had. Timbre had chosen both of them. It was not a rivalry.

Oddly, Jaxlim hummed to Anxiety. Venli returned Confusion.

"I feel that I am to blame," Jaxlim explained. "If I had not taught you songs that made you thirst for forms of power, then maybe—"

"Mother," Venli said. "*No.* I've spent too many months trying to avoid taking responsibility. I won't have anyone give me more excuses, not even you. I did what I did, and it was not your fault. The terrible choices were mine."

Inside, Timbre responded with the Rhythm of Resolve.

"Still," Jaxlim said, looking across the people with their carapace huts clustered in groups of four between resting chasmfiends. "To finally come to myself, and to find us broken . . . It was my duty to guide with song and story."

Venli stepped up next to her mother, who had always been so strong . . . until she wasn't. That, Venli realized, was the way of life. No carapace was so thick it couldn't crack.

She took her mother's hand and hummed to Resolve. "We weathered it,"

Venli said. "Cracked, yes, but our people survived. Now we need to find a way to continue without being destroyed by Odium."

"I don't know if I can solve that problem entirely," Jaxlim said, "but I've been thinking over the old songs, and I believe I might have something that will help."

Venli hummed to Hope.

"Come," Jaxlim said. "Let us speak to your friends—the ancient ones you call Fused."

⁂

Dalinar moved through shifting realities. He told himself that he needed to stomach it—that he needed to see what had been.

He opened his eyes.

For the briefest moment, he stood on a burned hillside at night, in a land with a strange pale moon. A broken city smoldered before him, one with high walls that had been shattered, and within it a strange people. He raised what he knew was a weapon, though it was no sword or polearm, and unleashed lines of light while his armies surged around him.

He wore black Shardplate.

Storms. He squeezed his eyes shut. *It's merely a possibility. It won't happen. I will make certain it doesn't happen.* Yet these were the terms he'd agreed to: if he failed the contest of champions, he would lead Odium's armies in their conquest of other worlds. Could he do that?

He'd given his word. Storms.

Sounds assaulted him. War, screams, soldiers dying. He refused to open his eyes to it, and instead reached out. He was a Bondsmith. He could make bonds, find bonds, strengthen bonds. There *was* a strong bond for him here in this place . . .

Or several?

Three strong bonds. A few others nearly as strong. That was odd. What was he Connected to in here aside from Navani? The Stormfather? No . . . that bond was different. These others were bright, and . . . and close? Brilliant white lines spreading from him, one pointing to . . .

A young man . . . no, an old man . . . no, a child . . . Elhokar? Was that *Elhokar*?

It was gone in a moment, leaving him with a haunting echo. He tried to follow, but found himself pulled toward another instead. A bond with someone whose love he didn't deserve, yet sometimes still took for granted. Someone whose touch made him come alive, and whose smile made him a better man.

She was . . . *there.* He found Navani's hand and opened his eyes to her, seeing her in a hundred different variations, one after another, everything from a young maiden to an aged queen. That smile—that knowing smile—remained the same.

"We need another vision!" Dalinar shouted against the tide of images that flowed around them like a current. "We need an anchor!"

"Fortunately," Navani shouted, "I thought of that!"

"You did?"

She raised her hand, which was wrapped in a red ribbon. It stayed the same, even though everything else about her shifted. "I got it from Shalash!"

Storms, she was amazing. He touched the ribbon and felt it guiding them, just as the stone had. The realm seemed to calm.

"Navani," Dalinar said, "the Stormfather offered to take us out and . . . I refused him." He met her eyes. "He's frightened of what we might discover. That alone is enough to encourage me to seek it. I'm sorry. I should have consulted you."

She nodded, accepting that. "Time remaining?"

He glanced at his arm. "Five days. I am convinced the Stormfather is deliberately hiding the secret of how to absorb and use Honor's power. To find it . . ."

"We must find our way to the day Honor died," Navani agreed. "We must witness the fall of the Knights Radiant and the death of the Almighty."

Dalinar nodded. "The Stormfather said that the power would never approve of me, because 'it cannot stand another who would do what Honor did.'"

Navani lifted the ribbon as a vision began to coalesce around them. "With the right anchors," she said, "we can jump forward through time and locate the right vision. We know the names of some of the Radiants involved in the Recreance—someone named Melishi was a Bondsmith then."

"Thank you," Dalinar said, holding her hands.

"I'm still not sure what I think of our goal here," she said. "I don't want to lose you."

"I know," he said. "At least I'm trying something new. Your way. Less war, more scholarship."

"This is more history than it is engineering," she said as the vision locked into place. "So: Jasnah's way more than mine. But . . . it is good to be searching for answers rather than simply charging forward and hoping everything works out."

The chaos had fully stabilized now. The two of them were in a dark room with a dirt floor. A fire burned in the center, giving a primal kind of light to the scene. Jezrien, looking older than the last time they'd seen him, sat on the ground by the fire with Ishar and a few others. Shalash, now appearing to be an older teen, wore that same ribbon in her hair. Ishar somehow seemed more weathered than the others, with haggard eyes and a white beard.

The woman Dalinar assumed was Chanaranach, with brilliant red hair and a Veden appearance, knelt beside him. She wore makeshift carapace armor. Her right hand rested on the hilt of a primitive sword—made from sharpened pieces of carapace embedded into wood. Again, her safehand—like those of the other women in the room—was exposed.

There was no door to the room, just a hanging cloth, and someone pulled it back, allowing sunlight to enter. "He's here," the person said, and Dalinar was glad to—this time—be able to understand the language.

Jezrien turned to Dalinar. "Well," he said. "It is time to make a decision."

"Then," Dalinar said, "make a decision we shall."

He was shocked how effortless it felt to fall into playing along with the vision. The first times he'd done this, he'd felt so awkward. Now it was almost second nature to start manipulating the conversation.

"You say it so easily," Jezrien said.

"I've had a long time to think," Dalinar said, careful not to be too specific or committal. He couldn't afford to let this vision fall apart until he had another anchor to move forward in time once more. "But still, a solution eludes me. Outline the problem for me, as we know it, one final time?"

"A wise choice," Ishar said, settling down with them, and then he held his hands before himself in an odd gesture, palms up. It evidently meant something to the others, but merely speaking their language didn't provide Dalinar with the accompanying cultural context. "As always, Kalak, your calm sense of reason is encouraging. How is it no decision, no matter how painful, ever seems to upset you?"

"I'm simply good at hiding it," Dalinar said.

"You're too calm," Chana said, sitting. She gave an odd sweeping gesture with her hand, her fingers wriggling. "You always have been *shoshau*. Makes me want to do something to upset you." She smiled, and that word, *shoshau* . . . he half understood it. Some kind of idiom?

Next to Dalinar, Navani gave him a look, which—because he knew her—he thought he could read. She was impressed. Delicate conversation had never been his strongest talent. But . . . well, time and experience could make a diplomat even from an old whitespine like him, apparently.

"Our people," Jezrien said from beside the fire, "continue to push against the confines set by the singers. Fifty years, and already war is starting. Inevitable."

"I would not find our way to it again," said the last person at the fire—an

Alethi-looking woman, in green, with long black hair. "After what happened last time . . ." She closed her eyes, and a soft glow came from her. "Prayers. Prayers, heavens, and songs . . ."

Dalinar started. Navani's eyes went wide. That wasn't Stormlight, but it felt similar. That was control of the Surges, centuries before the Knights Radiant. The action seemed to attract a spren—a glowing figure forming behind her, in the darkness. Something was familiar about it, like . . . an echo of something Dalinar had seen earlier.

It vanished a second later.

"We won't let it go that far, Vedel," Jezrien promised, speaking to the woman as she stopped glowing.

"But high heavens and beasts below!" Chana said. "We have to do *something,* Your Majesty. Thirty people slaughtered?" Angerspren boiled around her—plainly by this time, humans had started attracting spren, unlike the last vision.

"Not *our* people," Ishar said, making another odd gesture, two fingers up. "Makibak's rebels."

Shalash glared at him. "You'll start another war with them. With Nale."

"They're *not* our *people,*" Ishar said, repeating the gesture. "They never have been, child."

"Bah!" Ash said, standing up. "I'm tired of being called that!" She tugged at the ribbon in her hair, then turned and stalked toward the door.

"My precious one," Jezrien said, reaching toward her. But she was gone a second later.

Jezrien started to go after her. Vedel—the Herald Vedeledev—put a hand on Jezrien's shoulder. She was the Herald of Healing, by their lore, a master of mind and soul who held the keys of immortality. "She might not be able to see that maturity comes more slowly for her, because of what Surgebinding did to us, but she is also correct. She isn't a child any longer."

He nodded, taking a deep breath.

"I'll talk to her later," Chana said, gesturing with both palms upward. "But we have important matters to discuss. Ishar is right. Makibak and his rebels are a different nation."

"*All* humans are our people, Ishar, Chana," Jezrien said. "Regardless of ethnicity or background. But . . . you are right too. We can't simply let this go." He looked to Navani, then to Dalinar. "Kalak? Pralla? Thoughts?"

"So," Dalinar said carefully. "Thirty humans were killed by singers, as our peoples clash. And they have . . . been treating us poorly."

"Confining us to these lands," Chana said, "where barely anything grows. If we move to the east, where they have their fine stone-sung buildings and food in abundance, they demand we serve them. That might have been enough for the first generation, Kalak—they knew only war and fire. But the younger generation who have grown up here? They can't stand it."

Dalinar nodded. He knew the context now, could place this vision. They all sat for a short time, and he didn't prompt them to say anything else. They'd jumped forward barely fifty years—and he'd need to be able to take much greater leaps if he wanted to reach the Recreance. He covertly checked his clock just in case, but found mere seconds had passed. Again, when he was in a vision, time stretched the other way—with the world outside moving at a crawl.

"I think," Navani said to the others, "I could use some fresh air before we make this decision."

Smart, a way to delay and get more bearings. The others accepted that, climbing to their feet. As they stepped out, Dalinar found they'd been in some kind of man-made cave. A room dug into a hillside, but one formed entirely of mud. They were in a . . . well, a kind of town of mud homes and many tents. Those seemed to be hogshide—much thicker than cloth, and more permanent than the tents he'd seen. They had one high point in the center, then sweeping hogshide sides that were eventually spiked to the soft ground.

The humans here mostly resembled the Alethi or Vedens, some with darker tan skin, some with lighter pale skin. He didn't see anyone with dark brown skin other than Shalash, nor did he see anyone other than her who looked Shin. Their eyes were a variety of shades, more darkeyed than not.

Jezrien, who was darkeyed himself, was gazing toward a group of singers a short distance away. "They'll expect some kind of response, Kalak. *Shoshau.* This comes to a head. Our people cannot be confined."

"There's an answer other than war," Navani said. "There has to be."

"If scholars like you ruled the world, Pralla," Jezrien said, "then maybe there would be. Take your breather, and drink the heavens' fresh air. I will greet the singers. Kalak, join me, once you have made up your mind."

He walked away. Dalinar turned, and noted what appeared to be fields of grain out in the mud, but they were clearly struggling. Meager stalks of something growing in rows—no grass anywhere to be seen, a few tiny lifespren. At least the mud was mostly dry this time, packed under his feet.

Jezrien stopped a short distance from the singer contingent, who looked *far* better equipped, with strange stone weapons that were too honed to have been formed by chipping. The axe held by one near the front was so smooth it could have been Soulcast. Their clothing, while still primitive, was better constructed than that of the humans. Cloth instead of furs, their leathers well cured, their dyes vibrant.

It was . . . surreal. After all he'd been through, a part of him still imagined the singers as the Parshendi or parshmen. As primitives, far less advanced than the Alethi. Here that was dramatically different. Humans were barely surviving, while the singers thrived.

This *was* their world.

"The ribbon brought us here," Navani said. "It's somehow relevant to this moment, this day. I don't think we've seen why, but once we do, we will likely be near the end of the vision. So we need another anchor."

"Maybe we can find something new to jump us all the way to the Recreance."

"The Radiants don't even exist yet, gemheart," Navani said. "I think we'd be better off making a few smaller jumps forward to test our process." She nodded toward Jezrien, who had been joined by Chana, Vedel, and Ishar. "Those all become Heralds in the future—we should seek for some way to reach that moment."

"That . . . did seem to be something Cultivation wanted me to witness. She mentioned me seeing the truth of the Heralds. But how? What anchor could we find?"

"I felt something when I touched that ribbon," Navani said. "I wonder if I could use that sense to identify other possibilities. Our powers Connect us, but can also sense Connections . . ."

Her saying it prompted Dalinar to reach for Stormlight, to see if he could again form a web of light and lines around him. Immediately he had that same strange impression as before, of a bond he didn't recognize. This time he moved. He reached out with both hands as a shimmer of light appeared—which he seized. A part of him felt like he was reaching for Elhokar's ghost. Instead he found a child.

Gavinor. His grandnephew.

"*Gav?*" Dalinar said, pulling the child to him.

The little boy—wide-eyed—gasped. He grabbed hold of Dalinar, gripping tightly. "Grampa. You *found* me."

Dalinar held to him, baffled, and glanced at Navani. Was this some strange manifestation of the Spiritual Realm? She put her hand to the boy's face, looking deeply into his eyes, and Dalinar saw lines of light extending from her—a strong one touching the boy.

"I think it's really him," Navani said. "Gavinor? What happened?"

Gav whimpered in Dalinar's lap. How would others react to a child appearing with them?

"I'm sorry," the boy whimpered. "I was watching. I didn't want to be left. I snuck away from Mararin and I watched you in the basement. Then there was light, and . . . and . . ."

Dalinar groaned.

Little Gav cringed. "Don't be angry, Grampa. Don't be angry."

"It's not the child's fault, Dalinar," Navani said. "We opened the portal. We tried this insane plan."

"He's in serious danger though," Dalinar said. "He snuck away from his minder, and now . . . Storms. We have to get him back to safety!"

"Yes, but anger won't change anything."

Damnation. She was right. He didn't like this, but Gav couldn't be made to feel he was a problem. Dalinar pulled Gav closer into an embrace. "Gav. I'm not angry, not at you. I'm angry at myself for letting this happen. I'm glad we found you."

The boy buried his face in Dalinar's chest. "I was with Mother again," he whispered. "Over and over. I *hate* those red spren . . ."

"Is there any way we can send him to safety?" Navani asked Dalinar. "Maybe the Stormfather?"

Dalinar reached out to the bond, but gained no response. "I . . . don't think he wants to interact with me right now." He took a deep breath, calming himself. "We'll try next time he approaches me. For now . . . maybe we should find an anchor, so at least we don't get trapped in the Spiritual Realm."

Navani took Gav, because she obviously wanted to comfort him. A soldier walked past, wearing furs and carrying a crude stone spear. "What an odd spren . . ." he said, eyeing Gav. Then he seemed embarrassed, noticing the two of them. "Sorry, Surgebinders. Sorry." He made an awkward gesture with one hand out as he bowed, then hurried away.

"Spren?" Navani said.

"I yanked him into the vision abruptly," Dalinar said. "The vision will try to adapt, and maybe the best way for it to account for someone appearing out of nowhere is to give them the appearance of a spren to the people of the vision."

"Ah . . ." Navani said. "You must be right. And you claim not to be a scholar."

"I keep good company," Dalinar said.

"Grampa?" Gav said, squeezing his eyes shut. "A spren? I don't like spren."

"It's all pretend, Gav," Navani said. "This place? It's just a story. We're living in a story." She paused, then continued. "You remember when Shallan made the story of the axehounds appear from light? And you got to play with them?"

Gav opened his eyes. "Yes. Yes, I liked that."

"This is the same," Navani said. "A story of long ago, made for fun. Exactly like the Lightweaving."

Gav nodded, and seemed much less frightened as he let her hold him.

"You," Dalinar said, "are a genius."

"We'll see," Navani said. "There's no telling when the vision will break apart. We should divide our time. I'll poke around and see if I can find anything that might Connect us to this location, but in the near future."

"I'll talk to the other Heralds," Dalinar said. "And try to find something Connecting us to the day they became Heralds."

Dalinar jogged over to Jezrien and the others. A tall singer at the front of their group stepped forward as Dalinar arrived. He was a malen of black and red carapace, with a long face, gemstones in his beard. He was old, which you could tell not only by the wrinkles on his face, but also by the whitening of his carapace around the edges.

"My friend," the singer said to Dalinar with a pronounced smile. Broader than singers usually gave, perhaps as an exaggeration for human eyes. "Kalak, you have barely aged. I had not thought the stories to be true, yet here you stand. Twenty years since last we parted, and you are still the same man I saw when you passed into this world fifty years ago."

Jezrien looked to him, and Dalinar remembered he was supposed to be making a decision. He met the king's eyes and nodded. He still didn't know exactly what he was deciding, but he projected confidence.

Jezrien held out a hand upward, and seemed questioning. Dalinar, after a moment's thought, mimicked the gesture. Jezrien took that with a grim expression, but nodded and turned back to the singer. "Are we finally going to talk about the problem, Elodi? Or are we going to reminisce?"

"I prefer to reminisce," Elodi said, his gaze moving to study the town. "You are making this place yours, Jezrien. There is so much room to expand."

"Wasteland," Jezrien said. "Barely anything can grow."

"Your people are welcome in the east."

"As servants," Dalinar said. "Practically slaves."

"How else will you learn our ways? Wise children sit at the feet of their fathers." Elodi stepped closer to Jezrien. Chana moved to block him, but Jezrien waved her off. Dalinar would not have expected a female bodyguard during this era, but her job was obvious.

Elodi spoke softly, to a sharp rhythm. "This is bad, my friends," he said, regarding each of them. "Very bad."

"Thirty of my kind are dead," Jezrien said.

"In retribution for theft and the murder of a singer," Elodi replied. "Your people encroach upon the hunting grounds to the east. Some among my kind are starting to refer to humans as pests. Like a cremling worm in our grain. I have not . . . heard such vitriol before. Ever." He eyed the sky. "There is a darkness growing in this land. New gods, Jezrien. I do not like the words of the new gods. But the old ones are losing their voices . . ."

"Can you calm your people?" Jezrien asked.

"Can you contain yours?"

"We cannot, Elodi," Jezrien said. "Most do not accept me as king. To be honest, many hate me. I cannot stop them."

"They will start a war."

Jezrien glanced at Dalinar, as if for backup. So, Dalinar took the opportunity—crude though he knew it was—to try something. "Maybe," he said, "if Honor were to bless us in some way—show us how to contain our powers as Surgebinders—we could lead the people again, and regain their trust. Then perhaps we could prevent war."

Nearby, Ishar gasped. Jezrien put his hand to a pouch tied to his belt. "How do you know about that?" he hissed, drawing shockspren.

"It is just something I've been thinking," Dalinar said.

"This is not the time," Ishar said. "We will talk later. Elodi, if there has to be war . . . then there has to be war."

"Makibak and his rebels are proud," Jezrien said, making a gesture with two fingers. "But they are good people, and I cannot blame them for their hatred of me. They seek better lands, where the wind sings to the plants and causes them to grow. My people are *dying* in this mud pit."

"Better than burning on your old world."

"This one will come to flames as well, soon. I can't halt it, but I think you might be able to. The singers listen to you."

Elodi looked to the sky again. "And I listen to the old gods. The Wind, the Stone. They whisper for me to go east, to leave this pile of tinder before the bonfire begins."

"In leaving," Jezrien said, "you take with you every hint of common sense left to the singer nation. There will be war."

"There's already war, my friend," Elodi said. "Stay on your side of the mountains."

"I don't think we can do that, Elodi," Jezrien said. "Not if humans are dying."

"Then pray that I do leave for the east, so we do not meet again," Elodi said. "My people are listening to your god these days. I hope to drown out his voice with the Rhythm of Peace, but . . ."

Elodi gave them one last glance, then gathered his people and left. Hiking away.

"*Gwythiadri!*" Jezrien snapped once he was gone. A . . . curse word? Dalinar thought it might be a name. Jezrien turned and stalked back toward the dugout. Ishar and Chana gave chase. Nearby, Dalinar spotted Shalash standing with her hands clasped, watching the singers retreat. Past her, Navani was speaking with some people near a cookfire. Gav sat next to her, and while some passed by and noticed him, nobody found him too odd.

 The boy being here made Dalinar anxious. Gavinor had been through so much—being abandoned to evil spren by one parent, then losing the other moments later. Dalinar reached out again to the Stormfather, but got no response.

Well, Cultivation had sent him here. He had to trust in that, and in his instincts. It was not a burden he wanted, but he had never wanted any of this. Roshar needed a king, and so a king he would be. He strode up to the dugout, determined to find an anchor to continue their quest.

56 BY BONDS AND SPREN

I have kept my part of the bargain, and will not be budged. I have stayed upon my land, bringing blessings to the people of Nalthis—gifting them the power of gods, as I was so long denied. I do not repeat the mistakes of the past.

Sigzil soared beneath a black-clouded sky with five of his squires. Thunder crashed above, accompanied by red flashes—like the cracked knuckles of a god preparing to come in for the kill.

They intercepted the squad of Heavenly Ones, forcing them to abandon the boulders they'd been carrying—which otherwise would have fallen on the defenders of Narak. A brutal clash followed, and it displayed none of the polite respect he'd come to expect from the *shanay-im.* Where once they'd paired off against Windrunners and fought aerial duels, now three ganged up on one of his squires, each exchange furious and brutal.

There *had* been deaths in previous clashes, but those had been rare. Not anymore. After one day, Sigzil had already lost eight Windrunners. *Eight.*

He Lashed himself straight toward the beleaguered squire, Rowalan, and engaged all three of his foes, Shardspear a silvery sweeping arc in the air. It reshaped into a glaive as he fought, matching those carried by the Azish Imperial Guard.

His attacks drove the enemy back. He was extra careful to keep an eye out for any daggers that warped the air. So far, none of the enemy carried those weapons that could kill spren—but scientists at Urithiru were working overtime to perfect the methodology, and he was certain the enemy was doing the same. With the fate of the world at stake, it wouldn't be long before prototypes of those weapons came to this battlefield.

His foes surrounded him, cautious, watching. Two lunged—and with a grunt, Sigzil spun in the air, Lashing himself backward. Then, gathering his Stormlight, he performed a calculated Lashing upward, his weapon lengthening to a lance. As he'd guessed, the third of the *shanay-im* had tried to dive in while Sigzil was distracted.

Sigzil countered, using multiple Lashings and thrusting upward, his lance going straight through the Heavenly One's chest and piercing the gemheart. The malen's Lashings continued carrying him downward—his burning eyes forming twin trails of smoke—as Sigzil pulled his weapon free. Fused always looked surprised when he killed them, as if they couldn't fully believe that a common man had bested their millennia of experience. Fortunately for Sigzil, most of those millennia had been spent torturing Heralds rather than fighting.

As rain started to fall, the remaining five *shanay-im* broke off and fled into the darkness. There was more to the reason he fought better here than he had before; Sigzil had yet to see any of their best fighters. In Hearthstone, Leshwi had almost killed him. Then she had let him go. He missed those Heavenly Ones, who had not only been more honorable, but more sane. It was almost as if maintaining a code throughout the centuries had kept them from deteriorating.

"Thoughts?" he asked.

"Calculating their speeds . . ." Vienta said. "They have built to Heavenly One stable cruising velocity. I believe they are retreating for real this time, rather than planning to double back."

"My gut says the same."

"Your gut?" she asked. "The same organ that tells you when to eat?"

"It's a human thing," he replied, with a smile.

"Nonsense," she said. "Lots of animals have stomachs, not just humans, though I've never thought to count the number of species. Excellent fighting today, by the way."

"Thanks," he said, as the Heavenly Ones vanished away beneath the cover of lightning. They were frighteningly effective at killing, but their morale was weak. They preferred quick clashes that left the dead floating in the air.

Sigzil soared to join his squires, who were healing wounds from the quick skirmish. "Storms," Fent said. "Companylord, you fight like . . . like the wind itself sometimes."

"Stormblessed's training," another squire, Deti, whispered.

Sigzil shot them a glare. They knew what he thought of them mythicizing him and the other members of Bridge Four. The pair shut up immediately, saluting. For now, he sent them on patrol, then flew toward Narak to take battle reports. As he did, Leyten joined him.

"Your plan is working, Sig," Leyten said, giving the salute of the day as proof of his identity. "Decisively attacking those heading for our core plateaus diverted others to Narak Four. They ended up concentrating their efforts there."

Narak Four was the first of their intentional weak points, and Sigzil's big mathematical gamble. Make the enemy waste resources taking ground that Sigzil's people could afford to lose.

"Reports on the rest of our soldiers?" Sigzil asked.

"None dead, Sig," Leyten said. "But . . ."

"What?"

"There still hasn't been a shipment of Stormlight from Urithiru." They locked eyes. Sigzil had been informed—and had in turn informed his command staff and generals—of Dalinar's absence. He trusted the Bondsmith to do what had to be done, but storms . . . they'd been counting on Dalinar to offer a continually renewing supply of Stormlight.

Without that, Sigzil wasn't certain they could hold this location, with or without his strategic plans.

"We'd be better off," Leyten said, "if we were at full force, so we could rest our Windrunners more between bouts. What was Dalinar thinking, sending over half our Windrunners to ferry troops during a time like this?"

"He was keeping an oath, Leyten," Sigzil said, landing on the boarded ground of the platform—built up with wood, to put a barrier between their feet and Deepest Ones who might be moving through the stone. The Deepest Ones could get through some other materials, but formerly living things like wood slowed them significantly. "You know how important that is."

Leyten said nothing. Though normally of a cheerful disposition, the curly-haired man looked haggard today. He'd lost a squire earlier in the morning. Sigzil sent him off through the light rain, with a reminder that a highstorm was expected before too long. Then he started taking reports from the scribes who had splashed through puddles and rainspren to join him.

There were so many things to do when you were in charge. He'd barely touched any of his experiments since Kaladin's retirement two months ago. Sigzil had imagined the freedom of being able to set his own schedule—to make room for things like his large-scale project to determine how quickly people lost Stormlight, depending on how many oaths they'd spoken.

It turned out he *could* advance such projects. He had the authority—well, when they weren't mid-battle—to set up experiments, divert resources. It was everything he needed, except time to attend in person. Right now, Ka showed him enemy troop movements. They had brought some stormforms, who had nearly managed to set one of the gates ablaze during the fighting. The generals were considering having a Stoneward put up a wall to block the gate entirely, but Sigzil worried that would box them in too much. Narak Two was their Oathgate—and he wanted his troops to be able to retreat across those bridges to Urithiru, if needed.

Of course, those bridges—though made of stone—might not survive the fighting. He asked the generals to draw up alternative evacuation plans, then had them warn everyone—yet again—of the impending highstorm. Winds could get extremely dangerous when the two storms met, and the Everstorm appeared to be here to stay.

After that, he went to check on Narak Four—where the fighting had been most fierce—wondering idly about the Fused he'd just killed. He'd have gone back to Braize, and it would take time for him to be reborn. That process usually required days, maybe weeks. But with the Everstorm parked here . . .

It could probably happen within hours, maybe faster.

Storms. This was going to be a long five days. And he had no time for such worries as a group of Edgedancers returned, leaping the gaps between chasms using modified scouting poles, designed with greatly increased friction at their ends.

Another offensive of Fused, primarily Magnified Ones, was coming—looking like they were going to hit Narak Four, now that its gate had been weakened. It was playing out as he had hoped, but he would rather not lose the plateau too quickly. It wasn't that he *wanted* to give up ground; only that when he was forced to, he wanted it to be ground they didn't *need.*

So, Sigzil sounded the warning and took to the sky yet again, flying through an omnipresent darkness that was already starting to feel eternal.

⁂

Five Heavenly Ones, led by Venli's former master, Leshwi, had left Urithiru with them. Now they sat alone around a small fire at the outskirts of the listener settlement. Venli and Jaxlim approached them, joined by Thude, one of the leaders of the listeners. The hulking warform malen had a pattern made more of large marbled patches than lines. He wore the same long coat he always had in the past, despite Bila's mockery of it.

Strangely, Venli occasionally stepped on sand: an oddity of the washed-out flatland east of the Shattered Plains. Water flooded out this way, and it made ripples on the ground nearest the chasms—depositing crem there. Additionally, you ended up with these pockets of sand. Venli had never seen anything like it, although she'd been told some beaches had similar geology.

Leshwi stood up as Venli and the others approached. Over the last few days, the powers of the five Heavenly Ones had given out . . . something that shouldn't have happened.

"Leshwi," Thude said to Appreciation, with Venli translating into Alethi for the Fused, "we would speak with you. Would you walk with us a moment?"

Leshwi looked to each of them in turn. Her once fine attire of flowing robes and long trains had been cut away by force of necessity. Now she stood in clothing that, up top, was still regal—but below her knees it was covered in crem and stuck with sand. She didn't have proper footwear, only an intricate wrap that started at her thighs and continued down around her feet.

She fell into step with them as they walked back among the community of listeners. One of the chasmfiends opened an eye and inspected Venli as she passed, but then returned to snoring. The alliance between chasmfiends and listeners was something Venli couldn't get a straight answer about—the others were suspicious of her, and rightly so. Timbre had been speaking to the chasmfiends though, and claimed to be close to figuring it out.

"I suspect I know the meaning of this intervention," Leshwi said. Her rhythm was one of Odium's twisted ones, the Rhythm of Conceit. "If you insist, we will go on our way. Our presence here is dangerous to you and yours."

Thude hummed to Anxiety. "That *isn't* what we were going to suggest, Leshwi."

"Isn't it?" The tall Fused had an imperious way of speaking, even when she was obviously trying not to be domineering. "If my servants had attracted Odium's ire, I would not have thought twice about casting them out. Yet here I am, essentially a servant to you—or at least a suffered visitor." She stopped, gazing down at her feet in the sand. "I do not know my place anymore. I am . . . unaccustomed to walking."

"Your Light ran out," Venli said, excited. "It's an oddity, correct?"

"Yes," Leshwi whispered. "Normally, a Heavenly One can fly as long as she wants, without the Light ever running out, unless she uses it for Lashing something else. Mine running out means he's coming for us."

"Maybe," Venli said. "Or maybe you're not as attuned to his power as you once were. Radiants, as their oaths increase, can hold Stormlight better. And Fused?"

"We have no such gradations," Leshwi said. "We are simply his. And always have been."

"Until now," Jaxlim said.

The four of them halted, surrounded by listeners going about their daily duties. It had been Jaxlim's idea: to bring Leshwi among them to remind her of the people she'd come to join, and let her hear their peaceful rhythms.

"The old songs," Thude said, "mention that we, in abandoning Odium and Ba-Ado-Mishram, broke their power over us. Our rejection meant they couldn't touch us—and it meant Odium *could not* destroy us."

"He's forbidden from directly intervening against his enemies," Venli said. "Something about his agreement with the other gods. If you want to join us, Leshwi, you have to do the same."

"Give up the *sky*?" Leshwi said to Agony.

"If that's what it takes," Jaxlim said to Peace, "then yes."

Leshwi raised her eyes. "I don't know if I'm capable," she whispered. "I have seen thousands of years. I at times feel more spren than singer. Walking like this makes me wince with each step. I cannot change."

"You already have, Leshwi," Venli said.

"This is what it is to be a listener," Jaxlim said. "To reject their conflict. We belong to no god save Roshar itself."

"And the stones that make it . . ." Venli whispered.

"The stones," Leshwi said softly. "Once, long ago, our ancestors worshipped the spren of the stones. By the time I was a young girl, my kind had turned to Odium, once spren and Honor abandoned us." She hummed to another corrupted rhythm. "But it wasn't ever that simple, was it? Some spren stood with humans, others stood apart, others still listened to us. It was a mess . . . It always has been."

"Join us," Venli said. "Truly."

"Is it really possible though?" Leshwi asked. "For all your thoughts of isolation, you were manipulated to his ends as soon as he wanted you." She glanced to them. "It is not the same for a Fused as it is for all of you. I am bound to Odium. I can perhaps reject him verbally—but he would retain a hold on me. He could make my existence miserable next time I die. It is a . . . difficult thing you ask."

"It is," Jaxlim said. And left it at that.

Venli wanted to push, but she trusted her mother's wisdom. Leshwi nodded to them and hummed to Praise—not in acceptance of their demand, but in acknowledgment that they were trying to help. She walked off, and Venli didn't know if she noticed that she'd used one of the old rhythms. Not one of Odium's. Leshwi did that sometimes, as Venli had—off and on—during her days finding her way out.

If Venli had managed it, Leshwi could. For although Leshwi was Fused, a soul permanently bound to Odium's service, Venli found it difficult to believe anyone could be farther gone than she had been herself.

"She will make the right choice," Jaxlim said to Resolve.

"How do you know?" Thude asked.

"Because it's her choice to make," Venli said, grasping what her mother meant. "And so her choice is the right one. We will respect it."

Jaxlim hummed to Praise, smiling. Venli . . . Venli nearly teared up at the compliment. She'd never felt like she was enough for her mother. She had spent years blaming Eshonai; how strange to realize that all Venli truly needed to do to win her mother's praise was . . . well, be worthy of it.

"Come," Thude said to her. "Your spren has been asking about the chasmfiends and how all of this came about. You've proven yourself true, by the bonds and spren you have brought to us. I have been given permission from the rest of the Five to explain how we did it."

At last. Venli nodded, eager, humming to Excitement.

"We didn't have a keeper of songs once Jaxlim fell ill," Thude said to Embarrassment, "so I had to compose this one myself. I call it the Song of the Beasts, the story of our final decision to make peace with the creatures. I'm sorry if it's uneven or amateur."

"It's wonderful," Jaxlim said. "I love what you've done, Thude. Please. Share it with my daughter."

So, Thude started singing.

57 WHICH ONE TO FOLLOW

TWENTY-THREE YEARS AGO

Szeth-son-Neturo no longer danced with the wind.

Had there been magic in his steps, in the breeze, in the music of the landscape? Or had he been a silly boy determined to make profound what was actually awkward and simple? The boys of the practice yards outside the Stoneward monastery left him with no such confusion. They lined up to prove themselves against him, and Szeth laid each one in the dust.

The latest challenger was Jormo-son-Falk. Name notwithstanding, the light-skinned youth seemed the son of a mountain. Fortunately, three years in the practice yards had taught Szeth true. Strength and reach were distinct advantages. Every advantage was also a liability, when you depended on it too much.

Jormo came in swinging, trusting in his greater weight and momentum. Szeth refused to be caught in the momentum of life, or of battle. Momentum carried those who didn't wonder, didn't stop to question.

Questions like "What is right?"

Or perhaps questions like "Shouldn't I be approaching more carefully?"

Szeth barely had to shove Jormo—catching him shield-on-shield, stepping to the side to dodge a wild strike from the man's sword—in order to trip him. Jormo ended up face-first in the dirt, dust rising from him in a puff. Laughter erupted from the watching youths—all officers in training like Szeth. Mostly children of other officers. As the Voice had said, those in the camp tended to fulfill their own expectations.

Jormo pushed himself up and spat dirt. His glance toward Szeth carried thunderous implications—toughs like him did not like to be defeated by someone smaller and younger. Jormo would come looking for Szeth later, with friends, so Szeth would have to spend another few nights sleeping on the roof in the cold. He probably should have let Jormo beat him.

No, the Voice said.

"No?" Szeth asked as Jormo got to his feet.

No, the Voice replied. *You cannot run from men like Jormo forever.*

Szeth wasn't certain when the Voice had begun reading his mind. It had happened gradually over the last few years.

Hit him when he comes for you, the Voice said. *Hard this time.*

Jormo grabbed his shield and practice sword—iron, as they all had to get used to holding metal, but not edged—and came for Szeth again. More cautious, testing forward. Other soldiers leaned over the fence surrounding the sparring grounds, calling to him, but that cacophony became a soft buzzing to Szeth.

Time for the dance. He exchanged blows with Jormo, each trying to intercept the other's hits with their shield, the two spinning around one another as they swung. A brutal affair, exactly as Szeth had imagined fighting to be.

Yet it *was* a dance. Szeth had learned the steps by brute force of practice each and every evening, while the others relaxed. He did it *right.* He *had to do it right.* Some people whispered of supernatural skill on his part, that he was too capable for a boy of fourteen. That angered him. It made *luck* out of *sweat.* He hated it when they pretended he was something special. He wasn't.

That was the point.

Jormo left an opening, slipping his shield too low as he tried a rush. Szeth clipped him on the helmet, then dodged the youth's follow-up blow. Szeth's next hit went to Jormo's side, directly where the jerkin was tied, a weak point in the armor. The blow forced the stiff leather against his ribs, causing him to huff in pain. Szeth struck the leg next, a precise hit on the thigh just above the leather greave.

Jormo went down once more, sprawling, dazed.

Hit him! the Voice demanded.

Szeth hesitated.

Jormo howled and heaved himself at Szeth's legs, toppling him, though grappling was forbidden. Szeth had not practiced this kind of fighting. Kammar, the art of fighting with hands, was for the shamans or those who had already mastered the sword.

Jormo grabbed Szeth by the head and *slammed* it against the ground, shouting. The rim of Szeth's helmet bit into his neck, and he struggled, tasting dirt and blood as Jormo again slammed him to the ground. Szeth's fingers found something next to him. A rock, half buried in the dirt, kicked loose by the sparring. His fingers locked onto it, smooth and rough all at once, alien.

He gripped it.

Then let go.

No, he thought. *Not again.*

He had lost control once. Death had followed.

He would never lose control again.

NEVER.

Shouts. Jormo was pulled off Szeth, who lay disheveled on the ground, his lip bleeding where he'd bitten it, helmet askew, though it had done its job. As he shook his head and cleared his tears, he found he was largely uninjured.

We are going to have to do something about this, Szeth, the Voice said. *How can you defend this land if you hold back?*

"That will be different," Szeth said, standing.

Ahead of them, Sergeant Szrand berated Jormo. "If you lose control like that, you'll end up becoming what all *those people* think we are!" His wave was toward the lowlands, but he didn't need the gesture, as the phrase *those people* never referred to anyone else. The "sheep," as soldiers called them.

To Szeth it did not seem a healthy relationship on either side—but he said nothing. His betters, like the Farmer and the General, must know what they were doing.

The sergeant pushed Jormo away, and Szeth thought that maybe the youth would be suitably disciplined—and therefore not seek revenge. Then again, this was the same camp that had trained the soldiers who had killed Molli . . . so Szeth decided he'd best sleep on the roof anyway. Discipline *was* getting better now that his father was the General's aide-de-camp, but one man could only do so much.

"You," Sergeant Szrand said, looking at Szeth. "Always causing trouble."

Szeth froze, not liking the tone of the sergeant's voice. He was a thick man—thick of arm, thick of thigh, thick of waist. Thick of wit. With deep brown skin and hair that puffed out when he removed his helmet.

Szeth had always thought him jovial, even if the sergeant had never been able to explain footings properly. Szeth had needed to go to some of the camp's shaman acolytes—who trained with the Honorbearers—to learn. An odd bunch, the shamans. Holy enough to walk on stone, because they shared its divine nature. The opposite of the soldiers, yet placed alongside them.

Szrand was still glaring at him.

". . . Sergeant?" Szeth asked.

"Always a problem," the taller man said, striding up to Szeth. "Always goading people. Always acting like you're better than they are."

"But I *am* better than they are," Szeth said. "I rarely lose a bout, and never three out of five against the same boy. I defeat people several years older than I am."

The sergeant glared at him.

"You know it is true," Szeth continued, his head cocked. "You know I have to go to the acolytes for proper training, as I've outgrown your teaching."

"I want sixteen laps around the entire field, Szeth," the sergeant said, pointing. "When you're done with that, I'll have thought of your next punishment."

"I did nothing wrong," Szeth said.

"Sixteen laps!"

Szeth didn't move. Then, softly, he whispered, "Should I do it?"

What do you think? the Voice replied.

"Just tell me."

I want to see how you decide.

Szeth gritted his teeth. He was still uncertain whether he trusted the Voice or not. He worried it might be a trickster spren, as spoken of in lore.

"Well?" Sergeant Szrand bellowed.

"No," Szeth said. "I will not accept punishment for having done no wrong."

"Boy," Szrand said, stepping closer, speaking under his breath, "don't push me. This will calm the situation for everyone."

"Is it right?"

"Right is what I *say* is right."

"If that were true," Szeth said, "then you'd know the proper way to train your students."

Szrand hissed softly. He walked over and seized a practice sword and shield from a watching student. Szeth sighed. So, he'd made the wrong choice.

The sergeant, to his credit, did get the first hit, but that was because Szeth initially held back. After taking a sharp blow on the arm and realizing that Szrand was not doing him the same favor, he left the man groaning on the ground and holding his leg.

Szeth stood over him wondering if an adult would act out of the same petty sense of revenge that a youth did. Maybe Szeth should sleep on someone *else's* roof for a while.

So, the Voice said, *you are not impossibly timid.*

"Is this what you'd have done?" Szeth whispered.

For insulting me and acting above me? I'd have gone much further, Szeth. But you are young, and you are learning.

Szeth pulled off the training armor, then left it with his sword and shield on the rack. He supposed that now he *had* done something wrong in hurting the sergeant. Besides, he was supposed to obey orders, so he started jogging the laps. It felt good to be moving, although a sense of dread chased him. He hadn't been in the wrong, but had he let not being wrong . . . well, make him wrong?

His mother stopped him halfway through the third lap. She arrived with a waterskin, waving him down as he rounded the southern tip of the encampment.

"More laps?" she said as he jogged over to her, puffing.

He nodded, accepting the waterskin. How she found him at times like this puzzled him. He settled on a rock and drank, as he knew she wouldn't be satisfied until he'd taken a break.

Three years had passed, and it still felt wrong for his mother to not be wearing a splash of color. Father, Szeth, even Elid . . . they'd all taken to this life. Mother, though, seemed dull without color.

"Why do you push yourself so hard, Szeth?" she asked.

"I am here," he said.

She looked confused by that answer. He wasn't certain why—he was here, so he would do as the place demanded. Yes, he missed dancing. Yes, he missed the sheep, and the grass, and the solitude. But he was here, not there.

He took a long pull on the waterskin. His mother had grown thinner over the years, and her clothes didn't fit properly anymore. She'd refused to give them up for something new. These days, the clothing on their backs was literally the only thing they had from their old life.

Not the only thing, he reminded himself, reaching down to the pouch on his rope belt where he kept the small sheep made of Molli's fleece. He rarely brought it out, and never with the other boys around, but he did always keep it nearby.

"Some of the recruits, when they wash out, are sent away to other kinds of work," Mother said.

"Never back to normal lives though," Szeth said. "They're sent to labor in the mines or things like that."

"Would it be so bad?" his mother asked. "To have solid work again?"

"To wash out that hard, Mother," Szeth said, "I'd have to be *incompetent.*"

She didn't reply, but turned to stare out over the valley. He didn't often pause to gaze in that direction. Toward the past. She thought it beautiful.

"How did you know I was out?" he asked. "Did Elid tell you?" Running laps took him by the kitchens and their wide, open windows that let in the cool air. His sister was observant, although the truth was the other scullery maids knew she liked to watch for him. So one of them had probably told her, then covered for her as she went to tell his mother.

He found it odd how quickly people did things like that for Elid. She barely cared about her duties, yet everyone helped and welcomed her. Szeth was *impeccable* in his duty, and the others all jeered him. With more time though, he was certain he'd pick out the nuances. There were rules to every situation; he merely didn't know these ones yet.

He soon finished, thanked her for the water, and returned to running. He probably wouldn't see her again today, as she went to bed early . . . while Father usually stayed up late with his work. Szeth . . . had noticed that they were rarely in the same room together these days.

Eventually, he finished the laps and went to the practice yards for the second stage of his punishment. It was worse than he'd imagined: a note telling him to report to the General's office. The few boys assigned to oil the equipment didn't meet his eyes. He felt alone, like a mouse on a barren field, constantly looking toward the sky.

He'd never been summoned to the General's office for discipline. Szeth slipped into the office, passing the cages of the General's messenger parrots, and was confronted by the sight of his father behind the desk outside the General's room.

Szeth's father always seemed too *solid* to belong behind a desk. A man like Neturo should be out in the sunlight, like a stone basking in the elements. Yet here he was, going through the General's appointment books, annotating procedures, coming up with ways to make the camp more efficient. Szeth supposed it was a high honor—people talked as though it was. Father ate meals with the General and attended his most important meetings.

"Father," Szeth said.

"Ah, son," Neturo said, glancing up and smiling.

Szeth let some of the tension melt from his shoulders. As long as his father could smile, maybe it wasn't as bad as Szeth had feared.

"Just a sec," Neturo said, quickly making a few notations in his ledger. Then he stood up and walked over to give Szeth a hug. "Hard day?"

"Yes," Szeth whispered.

"I hear you laid Szrand on his ass," his father said, pulling back from the hug but holding Szeth by the shoulders to inspect him.

Szeth blushed, but nodded.

"Fourteen years old," Neturo said, "and making fools of men twice your weight. Remarkable."

"You aren't . . . mad?"

"I am a little," Neturo admitted. "But Szrand is a buffoon. I'm working out a retirement plan for him. I think I'll put Yago-son-Yargo in his place, but he's getting up in age. When *he* retires in five years or so, we'll need a new master of the training grounds. Someone who will listen to orders and train the new boys properly."

"You want that to be me?" Szeth said. "Father, I don't think the other boys would let that happen. They don't . . . they don't like me."

"It wouldn't be for some time yet," Father said. "Those boys training with you now, well, they will be assigned to other locations by then. The old guard will retire, and the new guard will take their spots. I think . . . I think I can make a real home for us here, son. A place your mother can enjoy."

"Does this have to do with why she often leaves the room when you enter?" Szeth blurted the words, but felt stupid for saying them. Like pointing out a stain on someone's shirt.

Neturo glanced away. "Maybe, maybe." He took a deep breath. "Anyway, you'd like a permanent post here, wouldn't you? At the training grounds?"

"I wouldn't have to go fight," Szeth whispered. "I wouldn't have to kill . . ."

"That's a good thing, isn't it?" Father asked, suddenly seeming concerned.

"Wonderful," Szeth whispered.

Father bobbed his head eagerly. "Come on." He led the way, but not into the General's chambers. Out of the building.

"Father?" Szeth said. "Didn't the General send for me? To discipline me for fighting earlier?"

"That? Oh, that wasn't your fault. The General doesn't know about it. I sent for you myself—something important is happening today. It doesn't directly involve you, but I wanted you to be there to watch."

Neturo led the way out onto the path that wound along the cliff face up toward the old monastery. Szeth followed, curious. The monastery was maintained by shamans and their acolytes, but there was no Honorbearer in attendance. Theirs was the Stoneward monastery, dedicated to the lost Herald.

Szeth was thus surprised when they joined a group of people standing with the General near the gates into the monastery. General Kinal was a wide, quiet man, with darker skin and grey streaking his beard. Szeth had always seen him as stoic, even dangerous, but today he was nodding enthusiastically to his companion—his eyes wide with excitement, looking like nothing so much as a young recruit taking his first advice.

"I'm pleased at the changes in your camp," one of the newcomers was saying. "Pleased indeed, General Kinal."

The speaker was a short, older man, light skinned with a long drooping beard and mustaches. Bald, wearing brilliant light blue robes, indicating a high-ranking shaman—or in this case, the highest. For he held a brilliant Honorblade in front of him, point down, one hand on the hilt and the tip sunken six inches or so into the stone of the pathway. Szeth had heard that the Honorbearers often kept their swords out when visiting—as a reminder. A display of the trust placed in the Shin people, and the Truth they silently bore. The knowledge that someday the enemy would return, and someone would need to be ready to fight.

It was his first time seeing one of the Blades—this one wide like a weapon meant to slay horses, with a hooked end and sweeping ridges. Szeth was mesmerized. It was to the dull iron sword he'd used earlier what a beautiful white pelt was to a muddy washrag.

Do you want to hold one? the Voice asked.

"Yes," Szeth whispered. "*Yes.*"

Good. The time is not right. Perhaps it never will be. But I am watching you.

The General waved toward Szeth's father. "Here he is, honor-nimi. The one I mentioned to you!"

The aged Honorbearer took Neturo in, measuring him. "You are the secretary who has been overseeing discipline and work routines?"

"Yes, honor-nimi," Neturo said.

"I am Pozen-son-Nash, and I find myself impressed with you. The men of your camp are happier, yet do their work more willingly. The shamans report impressive changes in morale. This has long been a difficult camp, watched over by several of us, but with no Honorbearer of its own—and with a Farmer who is far too kindly. Tell me, secretary, where did you learn the ways of leading men and inspiring them?"

"Well," Neturo said, "people are a lot like sheep, honor-nimi."

The Honorbearer looked shocked by that. Szeth, of course, understood. Sheep were caring, and communal, and smart. But in large groups, you at times needed a firm hand. His father explained basically this same idea, though Szeth wasn't listening much. His eyes were on that beautiful relic.

Fighting and killing isn't bad, Szeth thought. *If it were, God wouldn't have given us swords. We're needed. Killing, sometimes,* is *needed.*

In this, he was a sheep himself. He knew that what they did was right, but he would have loved a firmer hand. Direction.

Perhaps the man in front of him would finally be someone who could give it. Szeth, over the last few years, felt he'd matured. He *could* grasp that different people saw things differently from him. That a soup with a lot of pepper could be right for one person, but wrong for another. Some questions didn't actually have right answers.

But some *had* to have right answers. So Szeth asked, "May I be allowed to speak, General-nimi, honor-nimi?"

All eyes turned to him, as if he were a bright splash of color on the wrong person. Szeth stifled a blush and tried to stand tall, as he'd been trained.

"And who is this?" the Honorbearer asked.

"My son," Father said, placing his hand on Szeth's shoulder. "As good a son as a man could want, honor-nimi, and one full of curious questions."

Perhaps a soldier should not care what a father said. But Neturo's praise made Szeth swell.

"He is one of our most promising young officers," the General said. "Likely will follow his father into administration before too long."

 "And in so doing," the Honorbearer said, focusing on Szeth, "deny us yet another talented leader for the field. But I will not interfere with your management. Young man, what is your question?"

Szeth swallowed, and—feeling like a fool for having the same stupid question every time—forced himself to speak. "Honor-nimi, how do you know what is right?"

The older man cocked his head, then dismissed his Blade, frowning. He glanced at Szeth's father, who shrugged, as if to say, *I told you he was a curious type.*

"We have all been taught right and wrong since childhood," the Honorbearer said. "You have, by all accounts, a wonderful father. He did not explain this to you?"

Szeth squirmed; the Honorbearer sounded almost *offended* by the question. Still, his father nodded encouragingly, so he continued. "Honor-nimi, I *was* taught. But as I grow, I see that truth seems . . . different for different people. Is there one truth, or many? How do I know which one to follow?"

"Listen to your superiors," the Honorbearer said. "Follow the chain of command."

"I trust in the General and the monasteries," Szeth said. "But how do *you* know what is right?"

"Our chain of command," the Honorbearer said, "ends at the Heralds, who serve the Lifebrother—spren of soil—and the spren of mountains, sun, and moons. They, in turn, report to God himself. Do you question these?"

"No, I suppose not."

"Then follow what you're told, young man," the Honorbearer said, "and count yourself lucky to be one who defends Truth."

Szeth nodded, bowing his head.

"Is there a particular moral question you're having trouble with?" someone else asked. A woman's voice.

Szeth looked up, confused at who was speaking. It was one of the Honorbearer's attendants, another high-ranking shaman, in violet robes. She had short dark hair of a style he'd never seen before, parts of it made to stick out as if on purpose. It seemed a flagrant way to draw attention to oneself.

"We do not want to trouble you, honor-nimi," the General said to the woman, paying her deference.

"It is no trouble," she replied.

Honor-nimi? A *second* Honorbearer?

She watched him, her eyes a deep shade of violet, hands clasped before her. She looked young for an Honorbearer, though what did he know?

"I . . ." Szeth said, searching. "I have trouble hurting people, honor-nimi. Even in training, when it would be correct. It feels wrong."

"It is not so terrible," the woman said. "I do not see this as a flaw."

"Nonsense," the older Honorbearer said. "Sivi, if he is to be a soldier, he cannot afford to hesitate—it could mean the lives of his companions if he does."

She considered. "An unfortunate truth, but this one is destined for administration."

"Which is a problem in itself," the older Honorbearer said. "We consistently promote the ones who are levelheaded out of battle, yet we complain about 'incident' after 'incident.'" He focused on Szeth. "Young man, what do you want to do?"

"What is right," Szeth said immediately.

"Then do this." The older man pointed at Szeth. "Each week, take at least one shift at the camp slaughterhouse. Accustom yourself to death, little sheepherder."

The idea horrified Szeth. Which . . . might be good?

"General," Pozen continued, "when the next raid happens, assign this one to the defense."

"He's a little young yet."

"He wants to know how to fight, doesn't he? How to hurt? Don't put him at the front, of course; let him be in the rear guard. These are lessons you learn only by experience." He met Szeth's eyes. "Will you do it? Follow my orders to the best of your understanding?"

"Is it right?" Szeth asked.

"I say that it is. Do you believe me?"

What else could he say? He was glad that for once, someone seemed willing to be firm.

So he nodded.

And was sent to learn how to kill.

58 THE SONG OF THE BEASTS

I have plans to deal with Odium, as I told you before. I will not explain them to you.

We'll go east," Jezrien said as Dalinar entered the dugout. "We'll leave Battar in charge here."

Dalinar hovered near the doorway. Jezrien and Ishar sat near the fire at the center, which had burned low. Chana—the red-haired woman with furs and the strange almost sword—paced behind them, while Vedel was somehow creating a strange latticework of lights between her fingers. Like the strings of a child's game, except made of power, into which she stared.

That seemed an awful lot like Bondsmithing to Dalinar, and it held his attention while the others conversed.

"Jez, maybe the rebels are right," Chana said as she flopped down in the dirt. Not the most graceful of people. "I doubt anything is *ever* going to flourish in this place."

"Battar is confident," Jezrien said. "Keep breeding the strains that do grow, albeit weakly, and she says eventually we'll turn this mud fertile."

"Would that we'd thought to bring soil with us," Ishar said, shaking his head.

"Who thought we'd need *dirt*?" Chana said. "It's weird so many of you brought *rocks*."

"Mementos of a world lost," Jezrien said. "Kalak. Going east. Do you agree?"

They looked to Dalinar.

"Yes," Dalinar said. "We can't abandon other humans to die."

"So even Kalak agrees," Chana said. "Our veterans are all grizzled elders, but they can help us train a new generation. Maybe just . . . a show of force, a threat to the migration grounds will be enough."

"Jezrien," Dalinar said, sitting by the fire with the others, "I said something earlier that upset you and Ishar. What is going on? Are you planning something without me?"

It was his best lead. He'd tried to talk about the idea of making Heralds, and these two seemed to know something. Indeed, they shared a glance.

"We're not ready," Ishar said, flicking his eyes to Vedel and her lattice of lines of light. She nodded.

"Your plans can take far too long, old friend," Dalinar said to Ishar. "Immortality has you thinking like the stones themselves—watching the eons, barely changing."

"My idea is an idea of gods, Kalak," Ishar said. "It must move on their timescale, and cannot be rushed."

"Surely you can give me something," Dalinar said, thinking a note might be a good anchor. "Some . . . bit of explanation, perhaps? Written down?"

They stared at him blankly.

"What words are these?" Ishar asked.

Storms. Dalinar had a moment of utter disconnect, realizing that they didn't have *writing* yet. They spoke in ways that felt so modern, and he had assumed too much. He should blame the bond that was translating for him. It made their conversation seem so comfortable, but their gestures and some of their facial expressions were far more alien.

Before he could try to explain, the drape covering the doorway rustled, and someone stepped in. The Herald Shalash—looking to be seventeen or eighteen.

Jezrien frowned. "Ash?"

"Why am I not invited?" Shalash asked. "Why do you all plan without me?"

"My beautiful," Jezrien said, standing up. "My precious fur. We—"

"I'm over *sixty years old*," Shalash said, summoning violent angerspren in pools at her feet. "Why do you all always *treat me like a child?*"

"Ash, dear," Jezrien said, making an unfamiliar gesture with his hands out at the sides. "No need to get upset."

"Gah!" Shalash said, tossing her hands into the air. "I can't even get angry without being treated like I'm throwing a *tantrum.* I want to fight, Father. I'm immortal like you."

"We're not immortal," Vedel said softly, collapsing her lattice of light. "The powers changed us, yes, but we are not eternal. You grow, Ash. Slowly."

"I'm going east with you to see my cousins." Ash yanked the ribbon from her head and tossed it to the ground, spilling long, straight black hair across her shoulders. "Sixty years as a child is enough."

She stormed out of the chamber, leaving them all quietly stunned.

The ribbon was our previous anchor, Dalinar thought. *I've witnessed the relevant moment involving it, and Navani said . . .*

This vision would begin to unravel now.

⁂

"Listen and hear, the song of new sight,
A story of years, and of the long fight.
For these eyes are not yours,
We measure not the years,
We know not our full loss,
But we dream nonetheless."

As Thude sang, Venli settled down on a worn stone that was peeking from the sand like a miniature plateau. Others nearby paused in their ministrations to the chasmfiends. Even several of the monstrous beasts nearby turned their heads toward the sound.

As Thude continued, Venli picked out what he meant by calling this a "song of new sight," and insisting these "eyes are not yours." His song was from the perspective of the *chasmfiends.* Indeed, as the stanzas progressed—sung to the Rhythm of the Lost, a stately and sometimes unnerving rhythm—she saw why.

She'd been told that chasmfiends could project images in one another's minds—that they communicated through some sort of bond. Some were capable of sharing it with singers. According to Thude's song, they found both humans and listeners to be a curious bunch of cremlings. It was hard, the song explained, to recollect the past. Chasmfiends didn't write, and their songs weren't of narrative, but emotions. They'd lived on these vast rolling hills for many centuries, and rarely saw singers or humans except when they underwent the final change—when they visited the Shattered Plains to grow manyfold and obtain the last stage of their adulthood.

That was all pretty vague. But the next part—the first humans who fought back and killed a chasmfiend—was starkly remembered by the beasts. Burned into the minds of all those nearby, then passed to the other chasmfiends as warning.

"Then raising a nail, made all of steel,
A warrior brought hail, and pain to feel.
Now our eyes saw true,
Our ears now heard trace,
Our ways were at fault,
These were rivals to fight."

As the song continued, she realized she'd been expecting fear or anger from the chasmfiends. Instead, they responded to the killing as a *challenge.* Among their kind, a smaller chasmfiend would often challenge a larger one for dominance—but it was usually just a show. The smaller one, once proving itself bold and brave, would back off. They rarely killed each other.

These little things with the metal teeth, however—they didn't back down. They were rivals, so the chasmfiends began fighting back, as a display of strength. The chasmfiends were animals . . . or maybe something different from both common animal and listener. Either way, they kept on fighting, stealing prey from the humans, individually challenging humans and sometimes listeners for dominance. Until the day . . .

> "When report came in stark, by one who was bold,
> A story made dark, without reason to hold,
> It could not be said,
> Without rhythm so sad,
> Like a hit to the skull,
> They were killing the small."

Thude seemed to be taking some liberties, framing it in tones that the listeners would empathize with. The meaning was plain enough: The chasmfiends hadn't initially grasped that the humans were attacking the pupating ones—because who would do that? There was no dominance to be established and no bravery to prove there. Yet they understood eventually. Their numbers were dwindling because the strange creatures were doing something unthinkable. For centuries, the chasmfiends had depended on this location—which they called the land of fallen stars—for their transformations. While they pupated many times in their lives, the final transformation had to happen at the Shattered Plains. Why was not clear to Venli from the song.

The song entered a prolonged set of stanzas eulogizing the young, which the listeners had also been killing. For their survival, yes, but to the near extinction of a grand species. It would have been bad enough if they'd been dumb animals, but to find them capable of thought . . . well, Venli could understand the Rhythm of the Lost as a choice. And the horror with which Thude—although no expert at composition—painted the realization.

The narrative continued with an unexpected turn: The chasmfiends decided these little things, small though they were, must actually be dominant. And so, when the listeners left the Shattered Plains . . . a group of the chasmfiends came and offered their version of a truce. This group—some fifty individuals, not the majority of the remaining chasmfiends, but a sizable chunk—had thrown their lot in with Venli's people.

> "The right time had come, songs became new.
> The storm was undone, leaving fresh dew.

We lived with those small,
And found their true skill.
Not that of bringing ends,
But of scratching our ears."

That brought a chuckle to those listening, though Thude sounded a little embarrassed by the joke ending. He had grown during this last year. Venli could remember a day when all he did was talk about wanting to get something to eat—yet here he was, leading their people and creating songs.

"So," Venli said from her rock, "they simply . . . stopped trying to eat us?"

"We're not food to them," Thude said. "We never were—we were rivals. Venli, they still can't grasp that we were harvesting them, as gemstones are meaningless to them—they think it was a turf war. Apparently, they find ways to live with one another in situations like that." He glanced at the large dozing heaps that appeared much less fearsome when they were humming softly to the ministrations of the listeners.

"I don't think they see us as dominant," Venli said, her arms folded.

"It's more complex than that," Thude explained. "To them, dominance was never about *dominating*. They want to look strong before each other, probably to attract mates, partially also because it just . . . feels good, I suppose. We showed ourselves capable of fighting, and they were the ones who backed away. Now they're content to live together."

"We were cowardly," Jaxlim said. She stood with hands clasped behind her. "We killed their young."

"They give no signs of bearing a grudge, fortunately," Thude said to Consolation. "They evidently *like* this arrangement. People to clean their carapace and scratch between gaps is an excellent trade for sharing some food, in their minds. They're predators, and big ones. They need to sleep . . . well, most of the day, really." He changed to the Rhythm of Determination. "But Venli, Jaxlim, if we need a boulder lifted or a beast slain . . . they're eager to help. And they can carry dozens of us on their backs at once."

"Can they fight?" Venli asked.

"I think history has proven they can," Thude said. "But it's also shown that they're outmatched by Shardbearers."

"What about Fused?" Venli said.

Thude looked at her, uncomfortable. He didn't want to face it, but Venli had to.

"Odium is going to take notice of us eventually," she said, laying her arms on her knees as she sat. "Even if we don't participate in the fighting. You remember the deal between him and the humans?"

She had a spanreed, and had sent a few short communications to Rlain, as promised when they'd parted. He wasn't responding lately, which worried her, but before he'd gone silent, he'd explained the details of the contest to her.

"Yes," Thude said to Anxiety. "There might be fighting right now, but it's leading to peace in a few days. That's good for us, isn't it?"

"It seems that the enemy," she said, "will have plenty of time to focus on small details he's ignored. People he thought he'd destroyed completely, but who persist—their continued existence making a liar of him."

"Gods," Jaxlim said softly, "do not like being embarrassed."

"We could join the humans," Venli said idly. She'd rejected their overtures, but . . . she couldn't ignore the potential. Not if she was serious about preserving her people.

Thude glanced to her, and Bila—his once mate, and another member of the Five—walked up, taking his arm. She'd been listening while working on one of the nearby chasmfiends. Though they didn't hum to it, Venli could tell they didn't entirely trust her yet—and with good reason. Yes, she'd brought them Radiant spren, but her actions in the past . . .

"The humans murdered us, Venli," Bila said. "You yourself led the charge to destroy them with forms of power."

"And where did that get us?" she asked to Annoyance. "Look, I hate it, and want to reject it too. But Odium *is* our enemy while the humans . . . only *some* of them are."

"After all this time, bowing before human monarchs?" Thude said. "It violates the very *soul* of our people. Our independence defines us."

"People can change," she said. "I did. We can."

"We'll talk," Bila said to her. "Among the Five. But Venli, I agree with Thude. Our lives, our existence, have always been a risk. Better that we continue than give in."

"I can respect the humans," Thude said to Reprimand, "but we can *never* join them."

They hummed to Resolve. Venli mostly agreed, but was annoyed when they turned and left together. She'd been through so much. Now she came here, and she was back to being ignored. It was—

It was . . .

Probably what she deserved. She took a long calming breath, letting Timbre's rhythms help her find a way to Peace. One would think that by now she would have purged herself of being selfish. It was still there, however: that drive to *demand* respect. The part of her that wanted power and praise.

Timbre pulsed, indicating it was a normal emotion. But Venli thought she felt it more strongly than others. Why was that? Was she *genuinely* a worse person than the rest of them?

Timbre replied that there were different challenges for different people.

Being self-aware was part of the solution. Venli returned her thanks, but privately she was even a little annoyed by Timbre—who always had the right answers. Still, she'd decided not to indulge in self-pity. She'd have to remain vigilant, and work harder to reject her natural inclinations toward pride. She instead attuned Joy, reminding herself how wonderful these last three days had been.

"Venli," her mother said, walking over, "are you well?"

"Just frustrated and confused."

Jaxlim settled down on the stone beside Venli, then wrapped her arms around her, humming softly to Love. Venli wasn't a child anymore, and felt ashamed at first. But then . . . then Timbre picked up the rhythm too, and it vibrated through Venli. Being held wasn't solely for little children. It was for all children. She closed her eyes and at first suffered it, then accepted it, then . . .

Then savored it. She breathed out, and allowed herself to attune Love as well. It had been a long, *long* journey. But within that embrace, all she wanted was to be the daughter her mother expected. The daughter who knew the heritage of her people, and carried with her their songs. She'd need to hear Thude's new one again, and memorize it.

And yet, the oddities, Venli thought. *There are serious holes in that story.* "Why?"

"Why what?" Jaxlim asked, still holding her.

"Chasmfiends need to come to the Shattered Plains for their ultimate transformation. Why? The highstorms give them the power to grow. So can't they make that transformation anywhere?"

"Many animals have such instincts."

"We just learned they're *more* than animals, Mother," Venli said. "They apparently tried the final pupation elsewhere."

"That might only be the song," Jaxlim said. "Thude said he's not expert in them."

Venli let the hug persist a little longer, but found she couldn't leave the questions alone. She rose and strode to one of the chasmfiends—a large one, with dark eyes full of mystery. It snorted at her as she stepped in front of it, her every instinct indicating she should run.

Instead, she stared it in the eyes. "Why?" she said. "Why do you need to pupate on the Shattered Plains?"

The beast settled its head back down, closing its eyes and turning away from her. She stepped in front of it again, right up near the eye.

"I can be *extremely* stubborn," she whispered. "It's practically my defining trait. So I'm *going* to get an answer."

The thing snorted again, then opened one eye.

In a second, she felt what it had, climbing onto a plateau years ago. Needing to grow, bursting against its own carapace. It followed a *song.* A thousand powerful songs, sung by fragments of light in the ground. There, within its cocoon . . .

Power. Flooding it. Expanding it. Power coming from the sky *and* from the ground.

Venli gasped, and searched her memory for the songs she'd been taught to repeat so many times. About how her people had found their way to the Shattered Plains. It seemed they'd been led there. But by what?

By songs, the stones whispered.

"There is something here, isn't there?" she whispered. "Why has everyone fought so hard over this barren, broken expanse?"

"Venli?" her mother asked, stepping up to her. "It's because of the Oathgate and the Shardblades abandoned here."

"Yes," Venli said, feeling the chasmfiend's memory. "But what . . . what if there's more?"

Why had a kingdom ever been built in this desolate place, where the storms were so devastating?

What had broken the Plains?

What had she felt from the chasmfiend as it transformed?

Finally, why did Odium want this place so badly? Badly enough to have sent one of the Unmade, Nergaoul—the Thrill—to dominate it during the Alethi occupation?

The stones seemed to know. But before she could ask them, the chasmfiends started singing. A highstorm was near.

⁂

Navani watched as Dalinar vanished into the hut dug in the hillside, a hole in the top letting smoke from the fire within trail out, like a kettle's spout for steam.

"Gram?" Gav asked, seated nearby. "I'm scared."

Navani knelt by the boy and hugged him. "Don't be frightened, Gav. We're here with you now."

"Is this really a place of pretend?"

"Yes," Navani said. "You know how you and Grandpa play greatshell, where he's the beast, and you're the mighty knight who slays it?"

Gav nodded.

"Well, this is a place where everything—even the ground and the sky—pretends with us. We came here to learn secrets."

"Secrets that . . . the ground and the sky know?"

"Well, maybe." Navani thought a moment. "Wind, can you hear me?"

"Gram?" Gav asked. "Is this part of the pretending?"

"Yes, Gav. It is. Wind, you spoke to us earlier," Navani said, staring at the sky. "Please. Can you see me here, now?"

I see you, a quiet voice said. *Woman of another time. This was my time. My era. This was when I lived . . .*

"Did you die, then?"

Spren don't die, they only change forms. We bend to how people see us, and so I am no longer a god. You worship the storm instead.

"Gram?" Gav said. "What is that voice?"

"It's . . ." Navani hesitated. "It's the Wind, Gav."

"Will it hurt me?"

"No," Navani whispered. "Remember what I showed you in the tower? Some spren are good. Some spren help us."

"I . . ." Gav grew thoughtful, after his way. "I remember. I heard . . . something earlier, before Grampa found me. A nice spren, that said it could protect me from the bad ones. It sounded like Daddy."

"Good!" Navani said, but she doubted Gav knew his father's voice. He had been so young when Elhokar left for the Shattered Plains.

Child, the Wind said to Gav, *I will not hurt you. I am not the storm, though I am in the storm.*

"Wind," Navani said, still hugging Gav, "is . . . what my husband wishes to do . . . is it valid?"

Valid? Or possible?

"Either?" she said.

Both, but there are burdens to be borne. Secrets even I do not know, because I was voiceless and quiet—confined mostly to Shinovar. If the Bondsmith wishes to become Honor, it will hurt.

"Would it . . . help him with his fight?"

"Grampa is a *good fighter,*" Gav whispered. He closed his eyes. "I want to be a good fighter. Like him. Like Daddy. I want to be a king."

It might help, the Wind said. *I prepare in case it does not. To protect my charges.*

"Your charges?" Navani asked.

The spren, the Wind said. *We find our own champion. Blessed by the storm. A champion for the wind itself . . .*

Navani considered that, but was distracted as she saw the distant mountains begin to fade. The vision was ending.

⁂

Dalinar started picking up random objects in the dugout, frantic, since Navani said she'd felt something at touching the ribbon. He even grabbed the ribbon, hoping maybe it would work again. He felt nothing.

But as he worked, the others occasionally giving him odd glances, a word cut through his panic.

"Nale gave me a mark of debt."

Jezrien had said it, but Dalinar spun, realizing something. All of the Heralds had been accounted for in this vision except Taln and Nale. Two who seemed Makabaki. And this group were discussing going to help "Makibak."

"Nale," Dalinar said, kneeling by the others. "He will be there?"

"Probably," Chana said, lounging back. "I don't like that one. He might avoid us."

"No," Jezrien said. "He will help. Nale is one of the most honorable men I've ever known."

"He was our enemy!" Chana said.

"And we were wrong," Vedel whispered. "He knew the truth of the god Passion long before any of us did. We fought on the wrong side of that war, Chana. I feel I will spend my life regretting that choice."

"Nale," Dalinar said, "gave you . . . something?"

Dalinar heard a rumbling in the back of his mind. The Stormfather was watching, quietly.

"Yes," Jezrien said, reaching to his pouch. He took out a small piece of stone, marked with scratches in the shape of an animal head. A picture that was reminiscent of a glyph. Maybe they did have writing—or some early ancestor of it.

"He . . . owes you a new ox?" Chana said, frowning.

"No, this represents a larger debt," Jezrien said. "An ox debt was all we had to signify the moment. The Makibaki have been using them to mark all kinds of things."

Dalinar stared at the disc. It would work. A connection from this moment to Nale, and a debt he owed Jezrien.

Dalinar. The Stormfather's voice. *Please. Don't take this step. I . . . Please. It might . . .*

"It might what?" Dalinar whispered.

It might reveal . . . me . . .

Dalinar hesitated. He felt an empathy for the Stormfather, as Dalinar knew the pain that history remembered could reveal. But this was the only path.

"I'm sorry, Stormfather," Dalinar said, with genuine regret.

Jezrien was still watching the disc. "Nale gave me this with a promise. If I show him this, he'll listen to—"

Dalinar snatched it. He immediately felt it pulsing with a deep sense of meaning—a Connection. He leapt to his feet, and Chana—moving quickly—lunged to tackle him. But Dalinar realized he'd been ready for this. An old instinct that had led him to identify the one in the room most likely to attack him.

He dodged her, then burst out of the hovel. The vision was breaking apart, buildings unraveling as if to smoke, but he found Navani desperately trying to find an anchor near the firepits. He charged up and hooked his right arm around her. Gav began to cry as the vision unraveled, but Dalinar seized the boy with his left hand and held on tightly. All the while keeping hold of that little stone disc in his right fist.

In the chaotic darkness that followed, it formed an anchor to the next point in their journey.

EIGHTEEN YEARS AGO

Szeth ducked into the building, a simple one-room home in the fishing village. Dirt floor. An unmended net hanging on a peg from the wall. Bone hooks leaning against the door, for reaching into the deep and pulling up cages. The place smelled of brine and old shells.

Five men huddled on the floor, wearing the clothing of fishermen. Dirty, their eyes downcast. The stonewalkers had begun taking slaves. Today they would get what they came for. And more.

"All is well?" Szeth hissed to the men.

One of his sergeants nodded. "We're ready, sir."

The men on this mission were his best: a brave group willing to forgo exercise for a time to enhance their scrawny appearance. He checked on each one, making absolutely certain each was committed. Then he hurried to the goods by the wall: oil from the bladders of the giant crabs that walked the ocean floor, stored in leather sacks. Prized shells in wooden boxes.

The stonewalkers' loot, and their doom. Each box had a false bottom with weapons stored inside. Hand on his sword, Szeth urged the men to bravery and moved toward the next building. In the distance, the stonewalker raiders' ships were barely visible. Szeth hesitated, looking out across the evening waters—which were placid, as if subservient to the invaders.

You have time, the Voice said. *If you hurry.*

Szeth crept into the next building. At nineteen, he'd been living as a soldier for eight years now. He sometimes found it difficult to remember pastoral life as a shepherd—but going out among the common folk brought reminders. As he checked on the soldiers in this building, he passed a large crab shell on the wall—painted with colors. The fisherfolk here added; they would capture fish, but nothing larger. They would have harvested that shell from a crab that died naturally. Even the oil could be harvested humanely.

Once, he had believed adding was the sole way to live. Now he had found another. He spoke to each man, then hastened outside.

This is a good plan, Szeth, the Voice said as he entered the final building in the row. *I'm proud of you.*

"The General wouldn't go this far," he whispered.

Are you following orders?

"To the letter," Szeth said.

Then how could he complain?

These last years, he'd cherished what the Honorbearer had told him. Do as he was told. Except . . . there was so much wiggle room. His orders were to protect the villages. The General would want a display of force to scare the raiders away—but if Szeth did that, the raiders would just find another undefended village to assault. It had happened before.

Though it hadn't seemed so at first, what the Honorbearer had said—to follow orders to the best of his understanding—put the burden back on Szeth. Lately they'd told him to show initiative—to be a leader. These words *had* to mean something. He would show the General that he could do more than follow orders; he could excel at them.

Every one of his soldiers was in place, eyes downcast, dirt on their faces. Ready for the trap.

The General doesn't have answers, the Voice said. *Only you have answers. The ones you find, the ones you create for yourself. This is good. You are good.*

Szeth nodded, crouching inside the doorway and lifting the beads that draped the opening to peek at the approaching ships, which stalked like wild axehounds on the hunt—shadows moving across the water. Five years since that day the Honorbearers had visited. Five years of visiting the slaughterhouse each week. Five years of being sent on patrols. He now fully understood the weaknesses of those who added. The Farmer, for all his careful wisdom, was afraid of the outsiders. His orders to the General were too passive.

Both worried about antagonizing the stonewalkers, so it had grown worse over the years. More raids. More thefts. Now the opportunistic taking of slaves. The Farmer had begun leaving goods as a kind of tribute, hoping that a larger offering would keep the enemy from taking slaves.

That wouldn't work. The Voice promised it would merely get worse. Szeth had been told to show initiative, and he thought he could hear the words they weren't saying. They wanted someone to solve this problem for them.

Szeth narrowed his eyes. He knew that feeling.

Today, the spren said, *they learn.*

Szeth slipped out of the building. He paused by the water to fish a stone out of the surf. For luck. Sand was fine for fisherfolk to walk on because of its size, though they used docks to avoid little stones. He liked to carry them for a bit, then deliver them to the grove near the camp.

Lucky stone secured, he moved around the building and selected a hiding spot behind it. He felt at his belt for the horn—slick, cold, ready to summon his reserves from the nearby valley. It would be his job to call off the trap if he thought anything was amiss. So Szeth watched—anxious—as the ships stilled in the bay. They released smaller boats, like a swarm of gnats, which glided ever closer, moved by oars through the mirror waters. Almost here . . .

A sound to his right.

Szeth spun, and to his horror he spotted a young boy—wearing a splash of green in the form of bright socks—creeping through the village. What? The people had been evacuated on the Farmer's orders! But before Szeth could move to usher the child away, he heard guttural outlander shouts. The splashing of men leaping from boats, which ground against the sand as they were pulled ashore.

The boy panicked and crouched by a building. Idiot. What had tempted him into danger?

What tempted you that day, Szeth? the Voice asked. *Perhaps this boy left behind something he loved.*

Szeth watched with an increased tension as the stonewalkers raided the village. Ripping down bead doorways, laughing to one another as they found offerings. This time not just goods, but some weak, scraggly slaves. Men taught to speak one phrase in the stonewalker language: "We are yours now."

"Please, spren of the moons," Szeth whispered. "Don't let them be suspicious. Don't let them question."

It will be as I desire, the Voice said to the prayer.

The foreigners began forcing slaves onto their boats, sacks of oil slung over shoulders, boxes of shells carried triumphantly. Not for the first time Szeth wondered, were there people who added among the outsiders? Did these soldiers really have no Farmer to control them?

Men who would subtract with no oversight whatsoever from calmer minds. The idea disturbed him.

Szeth refused to let himself relax, even though the enemy took the bait—laughing and joking in their twisted language. One lit a torch, ready to throw it onto the buildings. Another of the stonewalkers slapped him, shouting something, then tossed the torch into the nearby surf with a hiss.

"What are they saying?" Szeth asked, wishing he had the training in languages that was common to the shamans.

With so much oil around, the leader fears that a fire could rage out of control.

 Pity. Szeth had thought they were showing mercy to the village. He turned to look through the darkness toward the boy, who had smartly remained quiet. Obviously terrified, huddling by the wall, shadowed from the pale blue light of the Second Sister above.

Szeth needed these soldiers to retreat with their bounty, so he could move on to the next stage of the plan. Unfortunately, as some of them started to row out to sea, the leader barked something to his men, who began to scout the area. What could they possibly be looking for? The village homes were all arrayed facing the coast; only some sheds and small pastures lay back here.

Apparently they wanted to squeeze every bit of value from this raid. A few grabbed chickens from a coop, and another kicked open a shed. There were no hinges, so the boards were fitted to slide into place. Loathing the men for their greed, Szeth faded further into the darkness of his hiding place. Until he saw men heading toward the boy's location. They'd push into that shack, and with the way the boy was whimpering . . .

You know what you need to do, the Voice said to him.

Szeth stood up from his hiding place.

I meant you needed to remain in hiding, Szeth, and let the boy suffer the consequences of his actions. The Voice sounded annoyed. But how could it be angry if it wouldn't *explain* what it wanted?

Szeth walked into the middle of the roadway, causing the foreigners to shout. The ones nearest the boy pulled out weapons and pointed them at Szeth, who—feigning fear—cringed away. He tossed them his sword, then went to his knees.

This is a dangerous gamble, the Voice said.

"They took the others as slaves without question."

Unarmed men weakened over time. They might be afraid of you. *They* should *be afraid of* you.

They weren't. They were accustomed to weakness from Szeth's people, even the soldiers. These laughed, one taking his sword, then saying something that—despite the language barrier—Szeth could tell was derisive. Outsiders did not think highly of Shin metallurgy.

They took Szeth, removed his armor, and tied him up. Then all the men who had been searching this back street hauled him off toward one of the landing boats, leaving the boy hidden.

The stonewalkers smelled awful, of oil and sweat. They wore furs for warmth while sailing, but their clothing underneath was . . . well, ordinary. Colorful, in fact. Tunics with leather breastplates and knee guards. Metal helmets.

Many had narrow black beards bound in cords, and they handled him roughly as they forced him to sit in the little boat. They rowed him out across the still waters toward the nearest of the three ships. They'd left him his horn, but he didn't seek to blow it. The plan—his own problems notwithstanding—was going fine. Hopefully none of his watching reserves would strike out early in some foolish attempt to rescue him. Hopefully he hadn't ruined the entire operation to protect one silly boy.

But if it's not to protect silly boys, Szeth thought to himself, *then why am I here?*

At the ship, they raised his boat up on winches, then hauled him out onto the deck—where a man wearing fine clothing, including a long coat, looked him over. Likely the captain. Szeth spotted some of his soldiers being ushered belowdecks, as escaped slaves from past raids had indicated. Loot—people and goods alike—was split equally among the ships, and stowed in their dark bowels. But each of Szeth's men had a small blade hidden in their mouth to cut their bonds.

The captain seized Szeth's horn and had others search his pockets, where they found the lucky stone he'd grabbed earlier. They found this particularly exciting, and for a moment Szeth was confused.

They think it's an Oathstone, the Voice explained. *They think you're already a slave among your own people.*

An Oathstone. Szeth had heard of the practice—the final chance for an otherwise condemned soldier. These were allowed to take an oath on a sacred stone, then do service. They were rare enough he'd never met one.

"One that small could be an Oathstone?" he asked.

Most are smaller, the Voice said. *It is a curious practice among your people, one I have encouraged. I approve of oaths. Unbreakable, binding your will to the people you serve.*

The leader of the raiders barked orders at Szeth. In response, Szeth sagged in the men's grip, trying to get his feet underneath him as the ship swayed. The other landing boats had all been unloaded.

Distant horns sounded from the reserves. The sign. Excellent. People on the ship scanned the coast. The captain merely laughed—they had the loot. He called out to his men, and they started preparing the ship to sail.

The captain is amused, the Voice said. *He finds leaving slaves and offerings to be a sign of cowardice, and believes the arriving forces are just making a show of doing something now that the danger has passed. Like a dog raving at the fence once the stranger has already turned away. He believes raiding here each season will make him extremely rich.*

Szeth nodded, his nervousness rising as he waited, hoping. Now was the moment. This was when . . .

One of the three ships leaked smoke. Screams followed, then flames broke through windows, and smoke *billowed* from the hold, turning the ship into a black column in moments—only a phantom orange light below marking the flames within. Szeth held a breath until he saw unarmored Shin men diving from the ship in the chaos.

His soldiers had executed the plan. Cutting themselves free, killing any watching, then spreading and burning the oil. That done, they could escape into the night. Moments later, shouts sounded from the hold of the ship he was on, and he smelled smoke. In seconds it began to seep, thick and black, between the boards under his feet.

The men on deck panicked, ripping themselves away from the horrific sight of their sister vessel going up in flames as they realized they were next.

Perfect. Szeth yanked free from his stunned captors and rolled on the deck. He bodychecked a sailor, then clomped down the steps to the hold, coming up behind a sailor fighting against someone below. He slammed a kick into the sailor's back, throwing them forward on the sword of Lumoson-Tumo.

"Stones Unhallowed!" Lumo said, light from the growing fire below showing a confused Shin face. "Sir, what are *you* doing on board?"

"Simply keeping an eye on things," Szeth said, turning around. "Little help?"

Lumo sliced through the ropes binding him, then Szeth took the saber from the fallen man. Curved. He wasn't used to that. He nodded to the members of the strike team, then together they burst up out of the hold onto the deck—to find it practically empty. The sailors had jumped overboard, including the captain. They had likely realized the vessel was irrecoverable.

"Join the reserves as they watch the beach," Szeth said to the four. "If any sailors slip past and make their way inland, they could slaughter dozens."

"Yes, sir!" the strike team said, four diving overboard as more and more smoke blackened the air.

Lumo hesitated by the rail. "Sir?"

Szeth was watching that third ship. Stonewalker sailors were swimming that direction. There was no smoke.

"Sir!" Lumo said, coughing. "You can't stay here!"

"Go!" Szeth said, feeling the heat flare up as flames licked through the hatch in the deck. Lumo refused to go, sticking by his side. Strange, how out here—among these men—the very attitudes that had once brought Szeth derision now brought him loyalty. He had not changed. He was quiet, not wanting to talk when everyone else was so full of words. He still sparred relentlessly, and made no excuses for his resulting skill.

These men *loved* him for it. It seemed he had found three different militaries in his life. One represented in the corrupt soldier he'd killed. Another represented in those of the camp, who enjoyed their easy lives. The final one was out here, among those assigned to defend their shores.

The third group didn't care if he was brusque, if he beat them at swordplay, or if he chided them. Not as long as he could fight. Because a man who kept his companions alive earned the respect of all.

Five of the men who respected him were on that last ship. Szeth turned and fought through the smoke, Lumo coughing as he followed. Szeth fetched the coat from the corpse in the stairwell, then pulled Lumo out of the smoke, where both gasped for breath.

"Swim to shore," he said to Lumo. "I need to go for Jathen and the others. If I do not return, tell Cade he has command."

"Yes . . ." Lumo said between coughs. "Yes, sir."

Szeth shoved him off the side of the ship, then ran across the deck—throwing on the coat—to leap off the other side. He hit the water, cool and refreshing, though salt stung his eyes and filled his mouth. It was better than the smoke.

He'd only learned to swim after joining the military—yet as with all his lessons, he'd practiced eagerly. But it was difficult while wearing a coat and trying to carry a sword in one hand. Even in a peaceful sea, he felt like he fought for every inch. Surging beneath the water, hearing popping and knocking upon the waves, he joined the stonewalkers swimming for the last remaining ship, hoping that his coat and the dark night would help him pass as one of them.

He swam, blackness above, a dark watery void beneath, full of phantom sounds. Until he reached the anchor chain of the enemy ship. Other men climbed up ropes thrown over the sides, but Szeth seized the links and climbed apart from the others, arm over arm, sword stuck through his belt. His muscles straining and his stolen coat streaming with water, he reached the anchor hole. Conveniently, the sides of this ship had many wooden shelves and ornaments. He clawed his way up until he heaved himself over the rail.

The air smelled weakly of smoke from the nearby burning vessels—but this ship was *not* aflame. Instead his five soldiers sat at the center of the deck, tied to the mast with their heads bowed. By the light of shining white lanterns—profane, as gemstones belonged in monasteries—he could see blood on the deck. At least one of his men had a broken nose. Yet they stirred, groaning. He was in time.

Unfortunately, some twenty stonewalker raiders were here, helping others up from the water below.

What will you do? the Voice said to Szeth. *I am curious at your brave choice. Are you not afraid?*

Fear. Szeth never seemed to feel that emotion as acutely as others did. There was always too much going on, too much to worry about, to be *afraid.* Still, he was nervous as he crossed the deck, pulling out the stolen sword. He kept his head bowed, and staggered as if exhausted from his swim.

That was a mistake. One of the others on the deck turned to help him, and immediately recognized what he was. Szeth had lighter skin than any of these raiders—the swim had taken the soot from him, and the deck was far too well lit. Szeth raised his sword threateningly, but who would be intimidated by one man? Several of them grabbed their swords and came for him.

There was no wind, but Szeth danced anyway.

Always before, he'd held back. Sparring or engaging in quick clashes with foes had never given him a chance to truly become what he'd trained for. Among his own men, he was virtually untouchable. The enemy raiders proved to be of lesser skill. Limbs dropped. Men screamed. Blood mixed with water on the deck, lit by the too-regular glow of gemstone lanterns.

Szeth became death for the first time. Before, he'd borrowed that darkness. Today he embraced it. Three . . . four . . . seven men he dropped. Unstoppable.

Until he felt a faint tap on his back, near his left side. He thought he'd stumbled into something, and glanced down to see a sword tip jutting from his stomach. Pain blossomed then, and the sword was yanked free. Szeth stumbled to the deck, stunned, and watched blood and something darker and fouler surge from his wound and across his hand.

A part of his mind refused to believe. His enemies could have finished him off easily as he knelt there, touching his own viscera, numbed by the incongruous experience.

Do you know why there are so few true swordmasters, Szeth? the Voice asked.

Szeth looked up across the ship's deck, and a piece of him noticed that the stonewalkers were still frightened of him. He'd left eight twitching bodies on the wood in his brief, explosive attack. The man who had struck him was wounded too, and had lurched away, calling to friends as he held a dark spot on his thigh.

It's because the consequences of mistakes are so high, the Voice said, conversationally. *Even the best fighters must face battles where whims of fate can leave them dead in a moment. In true battle, men don't get a chance to learn from mistakes.*

Szeth slumped to the deck, and the sounds of yells, of waves on the hull, of his own groans . . . softened. Dulled. Could sounds go out of focus?

You show promise, the Voice said. *Would you like another chance, Szeth?*

"Yes," he whispered. "*Please.*"

The lantern nearest him went out. A moment later, Szeth's strength returned. He pressed his hand to the wound, and found it sealed.

This once, the Voice said, *I restore you. Not many men have a chance to live a second time. You did not earn this. I gave it to you. Remember that.*

Szeth hauled himself to his feet.

Also, learn from the mistake. What did you do wrong?

Szeth gripped his sword, but already several on deck had noticed him. They were calling to their friends. He could become death again, or . . .

He turned and cut Jathen and his brother free from the nearby mast. He kicked a sword their way from one of the fallen, shouting, "Free the others!"

Hopefully they hadn't been beaten too badly. They did start moving at his command, but Szeth's attention had to be on the enemies. He once more fought with all he had. This time though, before he could be surrounded, his men started backing him up. Four had gotten to their feet and were fighting.

In seconds, a stunning event occurred: the enemy began throwing down their swords and asking for mercy. Szeth stood, confused, gazing around the deck full of exhausted, wounded, waterlogged enemy raiders.

"It's true," Szeth whispered. "These never were their best, were they?"

You'd be hard-pressed to find truly capable soldiers among the people of Steen nowadays. Travel to Azir, and you'll encounter another thing entirely.

Szeth knew neither of those places, but he ordered his men to gather the surrendered weapons. Then he pointed for the raiders to drag their wounded to one side of the ship, where he allowed them to tend to the fallen. What next though? His goal had been to destroy all three of these ships, not capture an entire crew.

"How is Athszen?" Szeth asked as Jathen stepped up to him.

"Dazed from his beating," the other soldier said, "but I think he'll recover. Sir . . . thank you for coming for us. Truly."

Szeth nodded.

"What . . . do we do now?" Jathen asked.

"Get one of those shore boats ready for the six of us," Szeth said, still holding a sword on the captives. "Take those bows in that rack by the side there, then help Athszen and the others onto the boat."

Jathen set to work. Szeth's men had some rowing practice, as part of their training.

"What do I do with them?" he whispered to the Voice.

That depends on what you want. Revenge?

"A little," Szeth said. "More, I want them to stop raiding. To go away, and never return."

Best way to accomplish that is to leave them frightened of you. That means letting this ship go. It's dangerous though, because you have an equal chance of inspiring rage in them. A cycle of vengeance. They may return with six ships next time.

"How do I stop that?"

 How far are you willing to go?

He thought of years spent in the slaughterhouse. "Assume," Szeth said, "I am willing to do whatever it takes."

Good. Yes, you were *worth the second chance, Szeth. That one who stabbed you? That's their captain. Show him the healed wound and repeat the words I tell you.*

Szeth stepped up before the man and pulled back the cut and bloody section of his shirt, revealing the healed skin. The Voice said words in Szeth's mind that he didn't understand, but he repeated the sounds as best he could.

The captain and those around him pulled back, horrified.

"What did I say?" Szeth asked.

You said that you were of the Stormriders. That you'd heard of the raids on this land, and had finally brought your immortals to stop them.

"I don't know what the Stormriders are."

Legends among them, the Voice said. *From a long time ago, when your people left their lands and walked stones. Back when the Shin were fearsome warriors.*

"Hard to believe that was the case," Szeth admitted.

It's possible for any people. Humans are humans, whatever their homeland. Most of the regions on this continent have been known for their skill in battle at one point or another. These days it might be the Alethi or the Vedens, but it was once you.

He found that curious.

Now, the Voice said, *pick one of them and stab them right where you were stabbed.*

Szeth hesitated. That would be a . . . hard way for a man to die. Long, painful.

You said you'd do anything.

"Why that?" Szeth asked.

To make them race home, hoping to get the person to medical care. It won't work. If I hadn't killed the foreign bacteria in your gut, you'd have died.

Szeth didn't know the word "bacteria," but he understood the meaning anyway. He dithered, but then heard the sounds of the slaughterhouse, and he knew what he was. Better these than his own people. He stabbed not one, but two of the sailors, to be certain the message was delivered.

Before the others could rise up and attack, believing they would be executed, Szeth stepped back and repeated the words the Voice gave him. A warning to these men never to return, and a charge for them to spread the word. Shin shores were no longer easy targets.

For every ship that came, he would increase the number of raiders he chose to die slowly, painfully.

Saying the words left him feeling . . . dull. Like his emotions had suffered the same muffling distortion that sounds had taken on earlier. He joined his men in the little boat. Jathen had figured out the lowering mechanism.

As they rowed to shore, and no arrows fell, Szeth saw the captain standing on deck and watching.

"Can you speak to his mind?" Szeth whispered to the Voice.

I cannot, as I am bonded only to those of your land.

"Pity," Szeth said. "I would have wished for you to tell him that I'm watching him. A voice in his mind would drive that fear deep."

Perhaps there is something I can do. I will see.

A short time later, Szeth rejoined his celebrating soldiers on the beach—their casualties nonexistent save a wound or two, their enemies defeated. He did not celebrate with them, nor with the fishermen who came with cheers, bringing beer and food for their protectors. His men didn't mind as he walked away. They knew he did not participate in such events.

Instead Szeth stood on the beach, watching two ships burn away into the deep. He stood there until, as expected, a group of riders came down from the monastery. He hadn't, however, anticipated his father being among them. Neturo ran up and looked at the blood on Szeth's clothing, then embraced him.

"Szeth," Neturo said, though the warmth of the embrace felt distant to Szeth, "what have you done?"

Was that . . . horror in his father's voice? Szeth pulled back, trying to read the emotions in the older man. "I protected our shores," Szeth said. "I did what I was commanded to do."

"You went too far!" the General called from behind. "Burning their ships? They'll come back with hundreds more!"

"I saw to it that they won't, sir," Szeth said, frustration building inside him.

"You shouldn't have made this decision."

"But I followed the chain of command," Szeth said, growing even more angry. "I was told to protect the shores. That was *your order.* You told me to patrol, and to find a strategy. That's what I did! I did *exactly* as I was told."

"You took too much upon yourself, son," Neturo said.

"Stones! How am I to know that?" Szeth said, exasperated.

Neturo glanced back at the General, lit by a flickering lantern. Out in the bay, the last of the lights went out as the burning ships finally slipped beneath the surf. Leaving moonlight to reflect on the glassy water, again dominant, fire only a memory.

"Szeth, report to camp," the General said. "I will . . . need to seek the wisdom of greater minds than mine as I decide what to do with you."

I am well aware that if you were to know of my plans, you would be compelled to interfere. It is your way, is it not?

Adolin moved among the soldiers during their midday meal, visiting each smaller subcamp in turn. He'd never had a mind for numbers or words. He often felt stupid when women conversed—or even, strangely, when Shallan and Kaladin did. He followed what they said, but missed the implications.

But there was *one* thing he had a mind for, and that was names. People talked about being bad with names; he'd heard it a dozen times over. He'd been bad at them once. But in his experience, being bad with names was like being bad with swords. Most people could learn if they tried hard enough.

A name meant something. Adolin had learned that when he clasped hands with a spearman and remembered his name, and saw a certain *brightness* ignited in the man's eyes. Dark or light. Learning names carried a price, because Adolin knew the faces of the fallen. It was a price he'd pay again and again, because if you were going to die for someone, you could at least do it for someone who knew who you were.

The men at his current stop drew laughterspren—like silver arrows that darted in circles—as he told a story of the time he'd arrived at a dance and found his trousers were on backward. He listened to their worries and complaints, and promised to do something about stubborn quartermasters and bland Soulcast food. He asked after families, loved ones, passions, and did his storming best to remember it all.

Because Adolin Kholin was bad at a whole terrible host of things. But he *refused* to let people be one of those.

He moved on, and heard the same story at each camp. It was barely their third day of the campaign, and already it was wearing everyone down. Most wars weren't constant fighting, just occasional skirmishes or all-out clashes. This was different. This was a grueling, constant struggle—where you had to be alert as battle could come at any time. That took a toll.

It was relatively easy to get men riled up and energized if there was only one decisive battle to win. It was possible to keep them excited for a series of skirmishes, like on the Shattered Plains, where there was glory to be won and a good support structure at the warcamp. This extended—but aggressive—siege was different. Small numbers of defenders meant frequent rotations into the dome. It meant holding back an enemy, instead of conquering plateaus or taking ground. On the very best of days they were stagnant—and still returned to the camps a little less numerous.

So Adolin countered it in the best way he knew: With stories of flipped-around trousers and times when he was inspired by other soldiers. Reminders of victories they'd won. And by calling as many as he could remember by name. It wasn't the way his father would have done it. Dalinar would speak of kingdom, king, and ideals—not play the charismatic commander. He'd tell the soldiers to fight for something, not some*one.* Because if the some*one* fell, Adolin's way could lead to chaos, while a nation or ideal could outlast any one man's death.

It was good, reasonable leadership advice. It ignored the fact that none of these soldiers *really* fought for their country or their ideals. Not in the moment. It might have been why they signed up; maybe it was why they *said* they fought. But in the sweat and blood and chaos and storm of the battle, they fought for none of that. They fought for one another.

When you stared down death, it was the people who mattered.

Adolin trudged away from the last subcamp, carrying with him the haunting sight of too many empty seats. How long had it been since he'd felt confident in this war? Not in Azimir specifically—this entire war against the singers. It was starting to get to him. He stopped in place and looked toward that bronze and stone dome. Inside, a crafty and relentless enemy continued to build larger and larger fortifications while Adolin's people were buzzing with exhaustionspren.

And five days remained.

We'll be reinforced, he told himself. *Not long now. Just hold out until then.* So far there was no intel on the phantom force harrying the main army, which was blessedly still making progress.

He checked the time using his aunt's arm clock. There would be a highstorm later today, but for now there were a few things he could do to help the battle. One was to fill those seats with new bodies. Yes, his defense depended on having the best troops he could—as in tight confines he couldn't field many soldiers. But a body in a spot was better than none. When the enemy surged, he needed to clog their way. So he met Colot at a large staging area on the cobbles in front of the dome, where several hundred people had gathered.

The Azish military had all kinds of recruitment rules. They had *entrance exams* of all things. The resulting military was tight, disciplined, and well-paid, and it made for an excellent career. But it was not equipped to deal with a draft, and it never let in outsiders.

While Adolin . . . well, the Alethi were a different kind of fighting force. His own honor guard was made up of men from all across the world, and his father had trained him in a tactic that had been an Alethi tradition for centuries: recruit like your life depended on it. He smiled, remembering Teleb talking about how he'd joined Dalinar's army. Adolin's father might speak of people fighting for cause or kingdom, but the man's success was due in no small part to his own personal magnetism.

"What have we got, Colot?" Adolin asked, surveying the lines of potential recruits.

"You were right; there's a lot to work with here. You have to be a specific kind of smart to make it in the Azish military, which leaves a lot of people out." He paused. "Good thing we're Alethi, or we'd be storming out of luck."

Adolin smiled. "I talked to Kushkam. Apparently the entrance exams aren't specifically to test intelligence—it's an excuse to weed out bad actors. We'll have many here who never tried out. But watch for those who did and failed. Some of those will be too violent, too undisciplined, and will have been failed for that—no matter the official reason."

Colot grunted. "Strange way of doing it nonetheless."

"You done any weeding yet?"

"They always take it better from you."

Great. Adolin waved for Challa, his scribe of the day, to follow. She, like May's other wards, was a younger girl; she was slightly cross-eyed, and always carried a piece of wood to fidget with. Desperate times meant people did desperate things, like show up for recruitment when they weren't fit for battle. When active fighting was nearby, people felt a growing need to *do* something. To not merely hide at home and wait.

He respected them for that. And there was a strong argument to be made: if the fate of the nation was at stake, then wouldn't he want every recruit he could get? The problem was, he had a limited number of people he could train and equip, and he had to make the best of that. More, he needed soldiers who could face a warform singer and not be shoved around.

So, he separated out those who were too small. He didn't actively differentiate between underage boys, the women with slight builds, and the men who were too old or weak. But he still had to eliminate nine out of ten people in line. He left mostly craftsmen of one sort or another, including a handful of women with larger frames. As he pointed out each one, Challa made a note, and Colot pulled them from the line.

Adolin stopped by one taller woman, with good muscles on her, the strongest he'd seen so far. She stood with her eyes straight forward at attention.

"Name, soldier?" he asked her.

"Sarqqin, sir," she said.

"Where'd you gain those muscles, Sarkuin?" he asked. Storms, he could *not* get that sound right.

"Blacksmithing, sir. I've apprenticed for seven years, and just been named master."

"Impressive," he said. "Like I've told the other women, if I let you in, you'll have to live and work around men in what might be embarrassing situations."

"I'm used to it, sir," she said. "I have papers."

Papers? He hesitated, then glanced at his scribe.

"One who has filled out the forms," Challa the scribe whispered, "to live as a man."

Ah. He'd heard of that. Well, the Azish did things their own way, didn't they?

"Good to have you, Sarkuin," Adolin said to the man, and moved on. Though he did make a note for Colot to assign him to a specific platoon where Adolin knew for a fact they'd been asking for a soldier with smithing experience.

By the end, most of the people he hadn't pulled out of the lines accepted their fate. In his experience, many had known they'd probably be eliminated, but had forced themselves to sign up anyway. He had Colot gather them for other duties—surgeons needed help in the sick tent, and there were always messages to run. He could use all of them, but he wasn't going to put someone who weighed only twenty brickweight on a front line pushing back warforms six and a half feet tall.

He gave his sergeants leave to begin some quick training—basically, he needed these recruits to know how to hold a stance and a shield, and some early instructions might help indicate if he'd picked anyone wrong. He turned to move on, and found himself face-to-face—well, chin-to-forehead—with an Azish girl who hadn't been chosen.

She gave him a glare that could have punctured carapace. "Messenger?" she demanded. "You're assigning me to be a *messenger*?"

"We always need messengers."

"I can fight!" she said. "I might look lanky for a boy, sir, but I'll surprise you."

"For a boy?" Adolin said, peering at her once more. "Um . . . do you . . . um . . . have papers?"

She glanced away. Then cursed under her breath. "No. Aqqil never needed them. What gave me away?"

Aqqil. That sound again. How did they *do* that? Adolin inspected the girl, taking in the baggy clothing, her hair recently cut short. She had the air of please-pretend-I-am-a-boy-so-I-can-kill-things. Like most militaries, the Azish did not recruit women, so this girl had likely assumed Adolin wouldn't either.

"Acwill?" Adolin said. "I assume she's a girl from a story, who dressed up as a boy and went to war?"

She nodded. "She went to save her brother."

"It's a famous story," Challa whispered to him from the side. "I've read the most modern rendition. Quite exciting!"

"I had one of those I liked when I was young," Adolin said. "My mother used to read it to me. About a girl who signed up because her brother was too sickly to serve. So, you and I share something . . ."

"Zabra," the young woman said.

". . . Zabra. But I'm sorry. I can use your help, but it will have to be running messages."

"Because I'm a girl?"

"Because you can't do the other jobs I need done." He sighed, then waved for her to follow him. She did, still glaring. "Have you ever seen a warform up close, Zabra?"

"No," she admitted, scuttling along with him. "But I know what you're going to say. They're big. They're heavy. Well, that means they're slow."

"They're not, actually," he said. "That's a mistake many people make. Some of the fastest soldiers I know are also the strongest."

"They'll still die from a spear in them," she said. "Size isn't everything."

"No, it's not," he said, leading her to one of the armory tents. He sent Challa to fetch someone for him, then grabbed two large shields—meant for holding in front of a pike formation. He tossed one to Zabra. He took the other.

"Set your stance," he said to her. "Hold me back."

To her credit, she did her best. Might have had a little training, judging by the way she was able to position herself and set her feet.

Adolin took one step, slammed his shield against hers, and sent her tumbling.

"Try me again," she said, stubborn, climbing to her feet.

He placed his shield, and sent her backward in a sprawling heap.

"You can't expect me," she said, boiling with angerspren, "to stand against a trained soldier, not yet!"

In response, his scribe returned with one of the other new recruits—a man in his twenties, of average height and build. Adolin gave him the shield, then pointed. "See if you can push her backward."

It wasn't even a contest. Despite Zabra setting her shield and her stance, this lout with no training—but unfair genetics—sent her sprawling.

Adolin squatted by Zabra as she lay on her back, shield fallen beside her. He did empathize with the frustration. Storms, he'd *felt* it, as he strode into this new world with Fused and Radiants. The world upending, and his dueling skill suddenly meaning so much less.

"I remember," he said, "when my father refused to let me join him in battle. I remember that humiliation, that anger. But Zabra . . . if I put you in, people will die. My soldiers. Your friends. However . . . this is your origin, your chance. You can storm away now and tell yourself my stupidity has prevented your heroism.

"Or, you can make another choice. You can do as I'm asking, and you can run messages. Take the chance to learn your way around the military, see if there's a spot for you. Probably not this battle, but maybe. Because every person I put on that field—messengers and medics alike—is a person in danger. A soldier. If those front lines break, the enemy is going to pour into this city. They'll fight through the reserves next, and if the reserves fall . . ."

He slid his knife from his side sheath and offered it to her. "In that event," he said, "all that's left will be you. I hope to the Halls above it won't come to that, but if it does, you'll get your chance to bleed. But *only* if you accept the opportunity I'm offering."

"Being a stupid *messenger* girl," she said.

"Zabra, can you look me in the eyes and tell me you want to be the weak link in a shield wall?"

She hesitated, then reached up and took the proffered knife from him.

"Good," he said. "First step to being a soldier: take responsibility for your part and what it can cost others if you don't do a good job. Report to May Aladar. Say you're a new messenger—and I *will* check to see you report correctly, Zabra. I'm dumb, but I'm not a fool."

"Yes, sir," she grumbled.

"Tell May I said that if you serve well, she's allowed to give you some archery training."

". . . She?" Zabra said, sitting up.

He nodded. "Combat archery isn't something you can be taught in a few days, but if you want to live the dream of running off to join a foreign military, that's likely your best bet. We'll see if you outlast the siege first. Dismissed, soldier."

She scrambled away carrying his knife. A short time later, Colot strolled up with a replacement knife. "I told you they take it better from you."

Adolin grunted, sheathing the knife.

"Warning," Colot said. "You're up for duty in the dome."

Adolin was barely halfway to his armorers when the bells sounded—the enemy was making an assault. He started running.

⁂

Chasmfiends could sing.

Each of the beasts rose on an array of feet, turning a thick neck skyward and releasing a quartet of harmonizing notes, for they could call with multiple voices at once. Venli had been warned, but still she thought it remarkable, as she found something familiar in the notes. They vibrated within her, deep down to her gemheart. There *were* tones to the planet, separate from the rhythms her people heard. Perhaps these were the tones of the gods. But if that was the case, why four?

More oddly, the very ground vibrated along.

Watch, Venli, the stones whispered. *See.*

See the coming storm? No, the stones wanted her to watch *them.* So while all other eyes turned toward the chasmfiends or toward the east, Venli crouched and watched sand dance on stone, vibrating as if it was hot and each grain was a little person, trying to keep from being scalded. They separated, forming into groups . . . geometric divisions.

"Are the chasmfiends doing this?" she asked.

We enhance. You can enhance further.

With Timbre's encouragement, Venli drew in Stormlight and placed her hands on the ground—letting the vibration fill her—then pushed Stormlight out. The stone began to shift, becoming as if liquid. Often when she'd done this, she'd commanded the stone to take certain shapes—molded in part by her will, in part by her fingers, as if she were making a bowl out of soft crem. Today, she let the tones do the shaping.

The resulting pattern was curious to her. She pulled her hands back, Stormlight evaporating, leaving a five-foot round section of rock distorted into a tiny mountain range.

Timbre thrummed with excitement. The Shattered Plains? Yes, Timbre said it looked exactly like the Shattered Plains.

Venli didn't see it. The Plains had chasms, while this had ridges. However, Timbre had flown above the Plains, and thought the similarity was remarkable. It was true the shape of the place *had* always been unusual. She looked to Thude and her mother, but both had gone running to help prepare the camp.

Venli didn't know how to help, so she stayed out of the way as the chasmfiends formed a ring against the storm, while their young gathered inside.

The larger beasts would face inward and lift their chests off the ground, making space. Though the camp had some permanent structures, those weren't fully trustworthy yet, so many listeners gathered here. It wasn't quite like being indoors, but it was far better than being exposed.

Venli stood with one hand up and pressed against the carapace chest of a beast. She braced herself for the stormwall, and felt strangely peaceful as it crashed across the chasmfiends, who growled and trumped at it in defiance. She huddled down next to a small chasmfiend the size of an axehound. Though it had a wicked face and claws, it sidled up to her and rubbed the top of its head on her shoulder. She had always imagined they were solitary, but she supposed that was because she only saw them when they were hunting or searching for a place to pupate.

Lightning crashed outside, but the enormous chasmfiends protected them from the brunt of both wind and debris. At one point several chasmfiends roared, their trumpeting voices audible even over the howling wind. Venli approached the leg of the one sheltering her and gazed out at the passing Stormstriders, enormous spren with long imbs. The striders didn't seem to care about the chasmfiends' challenge, but she got the sense from the satisfied trumps that the chasmfiends believed they had run the odd spren off.

A few people slipped out from the shelter, off to seek new forms. She wasn't certain she'd ever do that again—she liked the limber form of power she held, so long as she could remain free from Odium's interference by virtue of Timbre. As the storm continued though, questions still bothered her. The storm *was* relevant for pupating chasmfiends, and they could use it for smaller growth cycles elsewhere. She'd always assumed the chasmfiends came to the Plains to better access the storms—but there were hills out here that were taller.

It wasn't the elevation. It was something else.

She ducked back within the shelter, such as it was, relatively dry as water poured along the beast's body outside, streaming down to the stones in the darkness. She didn't experience a moment of clarity or stillness at the center of this storm, but she was well aware when the gemstones burst alight—tied in malen beards or gathered in baskets. She felt the strength thrum through her as she breathed in Light, then she knelt and placed her hands on the stones again.

Show me, she thought.

Come to the center.

The center of the camp here?

No. The center of the Plains. Your former home. But beware. A battle happens there now.

Narak. They meant Narak, the collection of plateaus at the heart of the Shattered Plains.

Show me what you can here, she asked, and poured more Stormlight into the stones. Nearby, her mother and Bila moved over, joining a small crowd that watched the stones liquefy and undulate before her.

They formed the Shattered Plains, as she'd seen before—with ridges instead of chasms. *They came to make a city, like the others,* the stones said. *Humans. They brought with them power—power to make the stones vibrate. An incredible power.*

She saw the thoughts of the stones. This land had been home to singers once, then to humans with a vaguely blue tint to their skin. They'd built a grand nation, and had wanted a capital city, as befitted the other great nations. A tenth Oathgate. Beautiful walls and patterns of stone.

They had built it. With power.

When was this? Venli asked.

Not long ago, the stones said. Although she wondered if stones could understand mortal timescales.

What happened around the same time?

They showed her, in another patch of stone. Urithiru being built. Soon after, the coming of a great king . . . and Timbre knew him. The one known as Nohadon. Timbre pulsed. She was certain there had been no Radiants at that time. They'd been founded during Nohadon's reign, or soon after.

There weren't any Radiants then, she thought to the stones. *How?*

Once, you sang with us, the stones said, *needing no Radiant bond. The humans were the same.*

Yes . . . she'd heard this before, from the rock at Urithiru. Singers had learned to use Surges long, long ago. However, the Radiant bond had organized and structured the powers. Something . . . something about using the powers without that structure had been dangerous . . .

Because of the new gods, the stones thought with sorrow. *They didn't understand. No one understood the alien stones at the place's heart.*

Alien stones?

The fourth moon. Now dead. Now fallen. With stone that is not quite stone. And when gods came here . . .

Stone went haywire, vibrating at insane speed. She saw people sink into it. She saw destruction. Terror. A landscape broken by the hand of Honor himself. Why had he destroyed this city? Had it been because they'd dared use Surges?

When the ground settled—continuing to glow with Light—the little map showed the Shattered Plains she knew. A broken landscape, fractured, but bearing a haunting sense of symmetry. A corpse. Why *had* Honor turned against them? And before that, where had they ever found the power for such an act? Sculpting an entire city? Even with a hundred Willshapers, she couldn't imagine that possibility.

It's still here, the stones whispered.

"What?" she asked. "The strange stone?"

And more. Come and see.

She let the stones harden, and—to the beating sound of the rain—ran her fingers across them. Streams of water trickled in from the edges of the chasmfiends' shelter, filling the miniature chasms.

"When was this place broken?" Venli whispered, but immediately felt foolish.

Not long ago, the stones said.

Stones. They really had a bad sense of time.

What else happened at the same time as the breaking?

It showed her nine figures, in a ring, with swords. Aharietiam, when the Heralds had vanished.

Come and see, the stones whispered to her, their voices fading. *Come to the center.*

Venli looked to the others who had gathered. Budding Willshapers, with bonded spren. "Was that . . . the stone itself, Venli?" Thude asked. "I heard it in my head, like a chorus. I couldn't make out the words, but . . . I felt warm."

"Like a familiar voice," Jaxlim said, "welcoming me home . . ."

"We need to make an expedition to Narak," Venli said. "Leaving today, if we can. The stones say there is a secret there that we need to see. Those of you who want to know the truth should join me." She paused. "There's a war happening there, so we'll need to travel through the chasms, and hope they are not too flooded."

If I were to give you the fuel with which to set yourself aflame, the resulting bonfire would then become my fault and not yours. For we all know what you are.

Jasnah arrived in Thaylen City fully armored, at the head of an entire division of Alethi troops. In this, she represented the change she had always wanted to see in the world. A woman capable of leading an army.

Yet ideas hounded her, as they always did. Phantom lights in the night to distract. Had she truly made headway for other women, or had she merely become an exception that was suffered? What did it say that, in order to present herself as strong, she put on armor and engaged in traditionally masculine activities?

Certainly it made a statement. But did it do harm as well, reinforcing that only one kind of strength was valid? It was the eternal irony of the capable rhetorician: train to find holes in any philosophy, and that will inevitably extend to your own. An inquisitive mind did not stop asking questions just because it found answers.

She marched down the grand steps of the city—which, like Kharbranth and several other ocean ports, was built up the leeward side of a large hill. Thaylen City was a metropolis that looked a little like a wide staircase, with buildings settled across many separate tiers. She marched her armies into the Royal Ward, the top tier of the city, then straight past the palace. They continued down past the Loft Wards to the Ancient Ward, near the bottom.

She was accompanied by an honor guard comprised entirely of former slaves. On paper they were free, having taken up weapons and been trained as proper paid soldiers. In her employ, she made their freedom a reality—and she sensed their gratitude. But life for *most* former slaves was a great deal harsher. Former owners could not lash out at their queen, so they retaliated against those who least deserved it. She knew that some slaves, to avoid this, were quietly doing their work as they had, with almost no pay. Others were determined not to, and found that society was hostile toward them—and that invisible chains had replaced literal ones.

She'd known all of this would happen. Slaves had been freed by imperial decree in Azir during the reign of Kasaakam the Magnanimous. Some slaves in Jah Keved had been granted an elevation to the next nahn after the successful Bav uprising of 637. She had a half dozen records of smaller instances, and had studied them all at length. Learn from the past, and you could predict the future without needing any mystical talent.

But storms, harnessing that knowledge was proving—with each new event—more difficult than she'd assumed. She worried that her many actions to facilitate change wouldn't stick—that the human desire to create misery and dominate one's fellows would prove more durable than her reign.

She wished that were the lone worry plaguing her. Yet she also worried about the power she had—that any Alethi monarch had—and how to set up checks on that. And finally, there was the letter. The note she'd left for Wit, formally ending their relationship. It had been the right thing.

Perhaps she should have done it in person, but she didn't want it to devolve into an argument. She'd started by simply writing out her thoughts for herself. That had turned into a letter, and she *did* work so much better in writing. He would understand. Even if he was angry.

Her mind couldn't be on that. It shouldn't be. She walked, as the first female Alethi general in many generations, at the head of a group of freed slaves, to the defense of their closest ally. Outside strong—strong as Shardplate. Inside constantly worried. At the bottom of the next flight of steps, she met up with Fen, Kmakl, and multiple representatives of the merchant council.

She gladly accepted introductions to several of their key military strategists, Ivory offering his usual quiet commentary in her ear, and sent them to talk to her officers about how to best integrate her forces with the local defenses. She had already made it clear that she would rely on the generals for actual strategy. She *thought* the generals appreciated that, but she was also their queen, and getting straight answers out of anyone was difficult. She had not thought she would miss the days when everyone was brutally forthright with their opinions about her—she still bore the scars of that ostracization. Yet at least she'd known at all times where she stood.

Stop focusing on yourself, Jasnah thought, frustrated that she'd fallen into old ways of constant self-reflection. *Fen needs you.*

"You seem concerned," Jasnah said to the Thaylen queen as the two of them walked up to the top of the city wall, overlooking the docks and the bay. Kmakl remained below, directing Jasnah's troops to find their barracks in the Low Ward of the large steplike city.

"We are soon to be invaded," Fen said. "The fate of a great portion of the world relies solely upon your uncle, a man who—despite everything—I can't completely say that I trust. Radiants come again to aid me, but I can't help worrying that I'm depending too much on your strength of arm, leaving me utterly reliant upon a foreign monarchy. I maybe should have spoken out earlier about the way anyone who wants to learn to be Radiant ends up moving to Urithiru, where their loyalty is to the Radiant orders instead of their homeland." She looked to Jasnah. "No offense, Jasnah, but why *shouldn't* I be concerned?"

"Sorry," Jasnah said. "Poor choice of words." Storms. She tried so hard to be precise with her language, yet here she'd defaulted to a common conversation starter. "I was simply hoping to discuss your defenses."

"We hope the trebuchets will help," Fen said, pointing to several emplacements along the slope. "They could realistically sink a ship or two on their way in. More, they might be able to deal with another of those stone monsters, if they appear."

The Thaylen queen rested her hand on a portion of the stone railing that was two-colored, with bronze to the left. Just over a year ago, the wall had been shattered by a thunderclast, a stone beast of towering size.

"Fine work there," Ivory whispered, his voice amused. Jasnah was the one who had Soulcast this metal portion to seal the city up again.

She wasn't certain a trebuchet would be effective against a thunderclast, so she had brought Stonewards. They couldn't manipulate the rock of the thunderclast itself—that resisted their touch, as Shardplate refused to be Lashed—but melting the ground beneath one, then solidifying it, had proven a perfectly valid counter to the monsters.

"Storms," Fen said, leaning forward, her arms crossed on the railing. "We've worked so hard to rebuild, and suddenly we're straight back to war. Will I be the queen who suffered not one, but two cataclysmic invasions of her homeland?"

"We have a great deal more experience now, Fen," Jasnah said. "I brought entire contingents of many Radiants."

"We still don't have much of a navy," Fen whispered. "Even with all our work over the last year, what we have is a pale imitation of our former glory. What is Thaylenah without the best fleet on the oceans?"

A year of recruitment and training could repair her military, and help from Radiants and Soulcasters could rebuild a wall with incredible speed, but good ships took time. The wood Soulcasters that Thaylenah had acquired from Aimia were a tremendous boon, but ships themselves were too complex—too delicate, requiring too many different skills—to Soulcast. Jasnah clearly remembered her own disappointment, when she was first training to Soulcast, that she couldn't just conjure up intricate contraptions at will.

It would be years before Thaylenah had a fleet to boast of—and most of what they did have was watching the eastern and western seas to intercept enemy ships coming from those directions. No one had anticipated the Veden blockade falling so easily. By initial counts, some hundred enemy ships were currently making their way across the channel.

"How?" Fen said. "How did they build such a military to attack us again? Something doesn't add up, Jasnah. We thought the bulk of their forces were committed to the assault in Emul, or to the watchposts near the Shattered Plains. There weren't supposed to be sufficient enemy numbers in Jah Keved to send another fleet full of ground forces. The blockade was only supposed to stop resupplies into Veden City."

"We'll know more in a few days, when that armada gets here," Jasnah said.

"Assuming the enemy doesn't somehow bring in their storm again, to move with unexpected speed. Odium could get those ships here in a few hours if he wanted."

It was a possibility, and partly why Jasnah had needed to arrive while the enemy landing was days away yet. One thing was certain though: the enemy wanted Thaylen City. This would be an extremely difficult assault for them, across an exposed bay, then against a tight fortification. The attack would be a bloodbath for the singers, assuming no surprises.

Last time, there *had* been surprises. The defenders had been taken unaware at several distinct points, which was obviously why Fen was concerned. Odium was willing to commit thousands of troops, all of his ships, and a good portion of his air support to taking Thaylenah.

"An ending is," Ivory whispered, echoing her own thoughts.

This was it. No relenting. No retreating. Odium would throw bodies at this wall until there was nothing left to throw. Until the heaps of the dead made a ramp. Until the bay turned orange. Because victory here meant domination for centuries—and a loss meant the enforced cessation of hostilities.

That was liberating. Because there would be only one more battle.

It was also terrifying. Because there would be no holding back for a future fight.

"Come," Fen said. "Last time, they caught us with our sails down and our anchor fouled on coral. I want to spend what hours we have thinking. What is he going to try this time, and how can we counter it?"

Jasnah nodded and followed her down the steps, her armored feet scraping stone. In this city, a year ago, Jasnah had first fully revealed to the world the extent of her training and her oaths, as a Radiant of the Fourth Ideal. Though she still had not found the fifth, she was here now with far more authority, far more troops, far more experience.

Either she would be enough, or she would die in this defense. The time for questions had passed.

⁂

"I don't like the way they're gathering out there," Leyten said as he and Sigzil watched from the wall of Narak.

Red lightning illuminated the amassing enemy forces on the plateau to the west of Narak Four. Two or three hundred individuals with glowing red eyes—and amid them, a new brand of Fused. One they hadn't faced yet, as these had been among the slowest in awakening—something to do with their unique body styles. Master Hoid had warned of their existence. *Metacha-im.* The Focused Ones.

Sigzil studied them with a spyglass. The Focused Ones were beings of enormous girth, and were likely over seven feet tall, compared to the stormform nearby. They seemed obese, except their bulk wasn't made of flesh, but instead of loose cords or . . . or belts. As if they were each wearing a costume made of hundreds of leather belts left loose.

That didn't quite describe it, because the belts weren't haphazard. They formed a cohesive suit: that of a tall person with an inhumanly large waistline—ponderous. He moved his spyglass from individual to individual. Twenty of them, among three hundred total enemies—but here, each was Fused with a few stormform Regals mixed in.

"Shouldn't they be taking shelter?" Leyten continued. "The convergence will be happening any minute. Stormwall was sighted at the eastern watchpost."

Sigzil hunkered down by instinct, remembering the last time he'd seen two storms meet. That day, *plateaus* had *shattered.*

"Ever wish you didn't have to do any of this?" Leyten said, resting against the wall top. "That instead you could be back at Urithiru, goobering around?"

Sigzil blinked. The air seemed alive with crackling red lightning, and the storms held their breaths as they prepared to clash. Tension wound inside him like the springs of a crossbow. And yet, he couldn't help asking.

". . . Goobering?"

"You know," Leyten said. "Poking around, working on projects here and there. Doing inventory, running accounts, cleaning shelves. Just . . . living, without stressing about what you might or might not get done. Goobering."

"That is *not* a real word."

Leyten shrugged.

Sigzil sighed. "Is that a Lopen invention?"

"Nah, comes from my grandmother," Leyten said. "I just . . . Sig, I *like* it when the work is boring. Sometimes I even think I'd rather be back in the chasms, tinkering with my improvised armor, instead of out here having to kill. Does that make me a bad soldier?"

Sigzil shook his head. "No. I understand. I would rather be sticking people to the ceiling and seeing how long they stay there. The thing is, the Shattered Plains is the closest Alethkar has to a kingdom these days. Those fields, those lumberyards, the growing trade market at the warcamps. If we don't defend against conquest by this enemy . . . If we don't fight here . . ."

"Then nobody ever gets to goober."

"*Please* don't phrase it like that."

Thunder.

Highstorm thunder sounded quite different from Everstorm thunder. The latter was often a sharp crack rather than a *boom*. The Everstorm was like whips being snapped, omnipresent, almost constant—but the highstorm knew how to let a thunderbolt linger. More a mountain crumbling than a whipcrack.

No confluence had ever been as destructive as that first one, so he hoped today wouldn't be too terrible. Still, Sigzil huddled lower on the stone wall and looked to the east. There, through the darkness of the Everstorm clouds, he could see the stormwall approaching—a vertical plane of water and debris, blown before the coming highstorm. It was more pure a blue at the Shattered Plains than it had been in Azir. Here, it had recently come in over the ocean, and was at its strongest, carrying the sea itself.

Sigzil saw it, and strangely felt *hope*. The highstorm would kill him if it could, he knew. It was violent and terrible. It also for some reason felt *right*. It belonged to Roshar, unlike the awful black and red darkness above him now. The highstorm brought life. Water to drink. Light to see by and to grant powers. The storm carried Roshar itself—the stone they stood upon was dropped, as crem, with the rain.

Stupid though it was, Sigzil stood up taller. Below, people were running for bunkers created by Stonewards, but Sigzil found himself *welcoming* the highstorm. Out on that plateau, the Fused didn't flinch. The Everstorm clouds grew excited, like they were boiling, the lightning more fierce.

The highstorm struck . . .

And began to die.

The highstorm faltered, water crashing down, the stormwall breaking apart. The grey-blue was somehow *consumed* by the black and deep red. The highstorm didn't go easily, but it did go quickly, with booms and tantrums.

When it hit Sigzil a few minutes later, all that remained was a hard rain that passed in a few minutes, becoming a trickle.

"What on *Damnation itself* was that?" Leyten hissed.

Sigzil shook his head again. "It was like . . . like two kings met, and one was forced to bow."

"That seems a *very* bad sign," Leyten said. "What about the Stormfather?"

Throughout the camp, gemstones flickered and became bright, so at least the highstorm remained functional. But the wind was nearly nonexistent, and the rain a mild annoyance. As far as he knew, this had never before happened at a convergence.

Outside, those Fused went on the march, a group of Skybreakers flying up to support them. "This worries me," Vienta whispered in his ear. "First the strange behavior of the highstorm, now . . . I can't put my finger on it . . ."

"Only Skybreakers supporting them," Sigzil said. "And a new brand of Fused to keep our attention. Damnation you're smart, Vienta—that march has a performative aspect to it. This might be a distraction. Leyten, find out where the Heavenly Ones are."

"On it, boss," Leyten said, and went to gather his squires.

"Sigzil," Vienta whispered. "Stormlight came sooner than it normally does, by thirty-seven minutes—judging by the approach speed of the storm. The Stormfather is trying to help. We can stand, here. We *will*."

The enemy formed up to strike at Narak Four. Sigzil's plan was working—they'd let the gate here burn partially down, on the plateau that had the lowest and weakest walls. The enemy was drawn to the fight they thought they could win, this plateau directly north of Narak Two with its Oathgate. It *would* advance their cause, giving them their own walled plateau from which to launch further assaults—but unknowingly they were doing just as Sigzil had wanted.

He took a deep breath, then summoned his spear and raised it into the sky to galvanize and lead the defense. Yet inside, he still reeled at the implications of the highstorm having turned into a whimpering axehound.

Soldiers cheered anyway, filling the walls, ready to fight in the pelting rain. As more and more joined him on the walls, they were confronted with a daunting sight. The Focused Ones drew close, then their bodies started to . . . well, condense.

The many layers that formed what seemed to be a fat being began to pull inward somehow. It had the look of dozens of belts cinching tighter and tighter—weaving underneath each other. Like coils of rope yanked at both ends. As those folds condensed, they started to outline muscles, or maybe *become* muscles.

When they'd fully grown taut, each Focused One had transformed into a tall, sculpted, androgynous figure that projected strength. As if they had been a relaxed spring, which had now been wound, the extra folds pulling tight against their powerful bodies. Master Hoid had warned that they'd weigh even more than a Magnified One, and that their density would grant them incredible strength and—though Sigzil found it hard to believe—the ability to stop a Shardblade.

The rest of the ground force was made up mostly of Magnified Ones—who could grow carapace at will, and walked as hulking mountains, often with arms transformed into spiked bludgeons. Together, these began tearing up the wooden planking on the ground beneath them—placed to interrupt any Deepest Ones. Sigzil thought they might be trying to taunt him to attack them outside the fortification. He sent a message to the ground-force generals, and they concurred.

Well, the enemy could rip up as much planking as they wanted. Sigzil passed orders for the defenders to wait. "They'll need to cross that chasm," he said to the soldiers clustered on the wall top with him, "then climb this wall somehow. They're at a disadvantage unless they have . . ."

He trailed off as he heard something. Loud, stone-on-stone footfalls. And in the distance, red lightning outlined a gigantic thunderclast approaching. It appeared the enemy had a plan to get through the wall after all.

BEWARE the FUSED!

DO NOT ENGAGE! FIND A RADIANT!

As for Valor, our dealings are none of your business—for largely the same reasons. Can you not leave her alone?

Dalinar didn't spend long in the chaos this time. Using the little engraved stone, he pulled himself, Gav, and Navani through to the next vision almost immediately.

In moments, the three of them appeared on solid, familiar stone. Storms, it was good to feel rock beneath his feet. He turned and saw another camp full of old-fashioned tents, populated by humans of mixed heritage. Few Shin, except Ishar and maybe Ash. He picked out many individuals here who might have been Alethi, Veden, Reshi, Marati, Thaylen, and Azish. No Horneaters, Natan, Iriali, or their cousins the Rirans.

A few small horses carried packs nearby, but he still didn't see any wagons, nor any permanent buildings. Glancing around, he spotted Jezrien, who wore a cloak and tunic of a rough blue cloth.

"We're on the other side of the mountains this time, based on these trees," Navani said. She touched a nearby branch and the leaves pulled in. "We've gone with them on their expedition to Azir, perhaps? So . . . maybe only a few weeks have passed between visions for these people?"

Shalash stood by a tent, and she now appeared like a mature woman in her twenties. She carried a spear.

"I think it's been more than a few weeks," Dalinar said. "Look at Shalash—and Ishar, see him over there, walking with Jezrien to that tent? Both look exactly as they do during our era. This is it. What I wanted. The day when . . ."

"When they became truly immortal," Navani said, holding Gav's hand.

"I found this stone disc," Dalinar explained, "which connects Nale and Jezrien. I knew Nale had to be there when the Oathpact was formed."

They did seem to be actively at war, judging by the people carefully chipping out new stone arrowheads. Because the chipped edges looked less refined than those of steel arrowheads, Dalinar had imagined the process was haphazard. Now—as he saw the knappers expertly crafting them with stone tools and leather to scrape against—his perspective changed. These were masters, creating weapons with as much skill and care as a modern swordsmith.

For the first time, he had a glimpse of how Jasnah understood history. He wished he had a few hours to go talk to those knappers, and the fletchers beside them, to see their work in detail and experience a world where this was cutting-edge technology.

"The disc worked," he said to Navani, checking his clock. "And we didn't even lose an hour between visions. I want to witness today's events, but afterward we have thousands of years to cover before reaching the fall of Honor and the secrets of how to obtain his power. We'll need to find a faster way."

"Agreed," Navani said. "For now, though, I'm just glad we managed to get here. To this day."

⁂

Renarin appeared in a vision, wearing something between a robe and a very loose dress, blue, tied at the waist. He glanced around, trying not to look panicked.

He could do this. Support Shallan, find the Ghostbloods, attack them. Reaffirming the goal calmed him, let him assess his surroundings. He was in a hogshide tent, which was comforting. When he was outdoors there could be a lot to see—too much to keep track of. He stood on a rough-woven rug, dyed blue and made of coarser fibers than he was used to. He wished he could feel it with his toes, but he was wearing slippers.

People were talking outside, but in here he was alone. Alone. That sent a spike of alarm through him. He was supposed to stay close to Shallan, yet they appeared to have been split up as they were sent into the vision.

I'm sorry, Glys said. *This is not the vision I intended. We missed one, one that started right after. But Renarin, your father is here. Outside.*

Someone pushed into the tent, but it wasn't his father. It was an older man, bald but with a white beard, squared off like an ardent's. He crossed the room hurriedly, and was followed into the tent by a woman with flaming red hair and a kind of militaristic outfit of hogshide and fur.

"The time has arrived," the older man said, stalking straight up to Renarin. "Are you ready? Can you do what I asked?"

Oh, storms, Renarin thought, shying away. Dared he hope one of these was Shallan or Rlain? Like before, they would be wearing the face of someone else in the vision. How could he signal to friends who he was without revealing himself?

"Well?" the man demanded.

"I'm ready," Renarin forced out.

"Ishar," the redheaded woman said, stepping closer to the man. "Are you *certain* about this plan?"

Ishar? A Herald? Or just named after a Herald? He did have the look of many of the paintings. Storms.

"I've spent decades planning," Ishar said. He then gestured to Renarin. "And do you know anyone more capable than Vedel?"

Vedel. Another Herald.

"Yes," said the redheaded woman, almost certainly Chanaranach. "You, Ishar. You're more capable than all of us."

"I will facilitate the bond," he said. "But I need someone with skill in Regrowth to make certain our immortality, and to make of us deities."

"Jezrien doesn't want to be a deity," Chana said. "We're going along with this, but it worries me, Ishar, how you speak sometimes."

"It is only because I feel it has to be done," Ishar said. "Right, Vedel?"

These weren't real people. This wasn't a real situation. That didn't make him any less nervous, but if he had faced the Fused, he could face these. "Immortality," he said. "Is that so important to you?"

"Of course not," Ishar said, perhaps too quickly. "I want to protect the world, as Jezrien has demanded. Immortality is a side effect."

"Seems selfish," Renarin said, and Chana nodded. He wasn't certain he did see it as selfish, but . . . well, people argued when they had big emotions.

"Haven't you felt it?" Ishar asked him, his tone changing from defensive to . . . concerned. "Doesn't it unnerve you? Our bodies aging, albeit slowly? You may think I'm selfish, but I *am* frightened of old age, Vedel. I do not want to be senile for a thousand years. *We* brought the people to this cursed world, with its treasonous inhabitants. *We* burned the old one. So I'm going to fix things. I need the time to do so."

Chana eyed him, but finally nodded. Hesitant, Renarin did likewise. It didn't appear either of these was secretly one of the Ghostbloods.

"Be ready to take the bond," Ishar said, "and accept the power of Honor. I need you for this, Vedel. I'll be back soon."

As Dalinar was studying the camp, someone walked past, saw Gav, and mumbled the same thing from the previous vision. "What an odd spren . . ." Apparently the visions still chose to present Gav as a spren to explain his presence. People would see him, then shake their heads and move on, ignoring him from there on out.

"I wonder," Navani said, "if we could find an anchor that will guide us through *multiple* visions. Something relevant at a number of points in the future. That might help us jump more quickly between them."

Dalinar nodded, considering that. But how to do it?

Navani knelt, putting Gav down. He was old enough that carrying him was difficult, even if he was small for his five years. "Gemheart?" she asked. "Are you all right?"

"I don't like this," Gav whispered. "I don't like how things keep changing."

"Don't worry," Navani said, giving him a hug. "We'll go home soon. Remember, nothing in here can hurt you. It's pretend."

"You want something here?" he asked. "You're looking for something you lost?"

"Looking," Dalinar said, trying to find the words to explain it, "for a way to become a mighty warrior—capable of defeating the greatest enemy I've ever known."

That was evidently the right thing, because Gav looked interested for the first time. "I want that, Grampa," he whispered. "I want that too."

They crossed the camp toward Jezrien, and Dalinar spotted more signs that this was a warcamp. Those men jogging back into the camp? Scouts. They wore no armor, not even leathers, just some strange animal skins. They had the build of runners, and carried bows but no spears.

There were virtually no women. He was accustomed to scribes and female quartermasters, and nowadays female Radiants. Here, he didn't even see camp followers. Some men were washing clothing in a barrel, and he figured that they didn't have Soulcasters for food or infrastructure. That hampered large military movements, so you had to have smaller teams, each trained to do more jobs, to stay mobile. He passed some men butchering the carcass of a large numul—a type of midsized shellbeast he'd seen occasionally in the West. An army here likely provisioned itself by following the herds while on campaign.

Dalinar halted near the butchers, spotting something.

"What?" Navani whispered.

"They have thrown the gemheart in with the scrap ligaments and the broken carapace chunks," he whispered back. "They don't seem to know what it is."

In many beasts the gemheart wasn't so glorious and brilliant as it was in a chasmfiend. This one's cloudy, inch-long gemstone was covered in a web of sinew. But still . . . that had more value than the meat. The Azish ranched these beasts in great numbers, using their inferior gemhearts to make bronze with their Soulcasters.

So strange. They moved on, and Dalinar noticed other oddities. It smelled wrong. Even the sweat of the bodies was somehow different, more musky, more pungent. He could hear hogshide flaps being beaten for cleaning, but no familiar sounds like the sharpening of swords or the clang of buckets. This was almost an alien world. Yet they did appear to be preparing for an upcoming skirmish. He could pick that out in their quick motions, hurried as if they were trying to finish on a deadline. Or maybe . . .

Yes. His answer came as the sky began to darken. Highstorm. They were on the east side of the mountains. Exposed. Why was nobody running for cover? And . . . what kind of cover could all these loose tents offer anyway? He grabbed Gav in both arms, planning to run for a hillside, but the Wind's voice spoke in his mind.

Hiding isn't necessary, the Wind said. *They prayed, and Honor listened to such prayers during this time. He will modulate the storm in this small region, preventing it from destroying his faithful.*

He glanced at Navani, whose eyes were wide. She'd heard it too. They stood in the center of the ancient camp, Dalinar's nerves taut as bowstrings, until rain started falling. Along with a gentle wind streaming among the soldiers, almost visible—a *thick* wind, turgid, lazy.

Men in the camp stood up and looked toward the sky. They didn't try to get out of the warm rain, though they laughed and pointed at passing windspren.

Gavinor relaxed. "Oh . . ." the child said softly. "I feel warm . . ."

Blood of my fathers, Dalinar thought. *It's true.* He *did* feel warm—from a blossom of heat within. He thought he recognized that warmth from somewhere, and it was accompanied by a faint but audible tone that vibrated against his soul with the smooth, satisfying touch of a polishing cloth on a sword.

⁂

Renarin stood there, hearing rain fall on the tent and feeling overwhelmed. Storms, it sounded like today was the *founding of the Oathpact.*

Still, he needed to find the others. *We should have agreed on some sort of hand signal or something,* he thought, searching a nearby tabletop for a weapon. He didn't find any, though the buckle on a small leather strap gave him something to fidget with. A moment later someone else entered. A woman who looked Veden, wearing vibrant green clothing. Renarin drew farther back into the shadows of the tent, worried he'd have to navigate his way through another conversation. The woman glanced around, noticed him, then turned indifferently and started studying the ceiling. Then she hummed briefly.

Wait. That had been one of the rhythms.

"Rlain?" Renarin guessed, stepping into the light.

"It *is* you," the woman said, looking relieved. "I thought it might be, from the fidgeting." Rlain rushed over. "We can understand people this time, but I have *no idea* what I'm doing."

"Did you locate Shallan?"

"Not yet," he said. "I appeared, and started walking around awkwardly until a bald human passed by and told me to go in here, as it was 'almost time.'"

"That was Ishar," Renarin said. "Ishi'Elin . . . one of the Heralds. We're about to see the Oathpact be sworn."

"And the Ghostbloods want to interfere with that?"

"No, remember, this isn't actually the past," Renarin said. Rlain didn't have experience with Dalinar's visions. "The Ghostbloods think following Dalinar will guide them to Mishram's prison." Renarin frowned. "I don't know why they'd think that, since Dalinar is hunting for what happened to Honor. Unless . . ."

"Unless," Rlain finished, "the events are connected."

Storms. "And the Ghostbloods know that somehow."

"It's all wrapped up in one knot," Rlain said, nodding. "The fall of your god. The imprisonment of one of ours. The Radiants walking away from their vows, and the singers ending up in slaveform. Renarin . . . there are so many secrets here."

"We're only here to stop the Ghostbloods," Renarin said.

"But what if we could do more?" Rlain said. "What if *we* found the prison, so we could discover what truly happened? Not merely to the listeners, but to all singers." He hummed to an excited rhythm. "I think Shallan was right to bring us. We need to know these secrets. *I* need to know them."

"Because you're a singer," Renarin realized. "If we do go as far as Shallan wants, and reach the prison ourselves . . . a singer should be involved, not just humans."

"No offense," Rlain said, his rhythm changing. He hummed a little extra to indicate an emotion—something Renarin had noticed his kind did unconsciously after speaking a short sentence. "Renarin, I respect you, Kal, Dalinar . . . all of you. But don't you agree? Don't you think that a singer ought to have *some* involvement?"

"You're right, of course," Renarin said, flipping the buckle open in his fingers. He could imagine how Rlain must feel, constantly surrounded by people who had enslaved his. And . . . storms, he found it so much easier to read what Rlain was thinking when he hummed those rhythms to indicate his emotional state. Why couldn't humans do something like that?

When he talked to Rlain, the entire world opened up to Renarin—he was no longer the blind one in conversations, struggling to figure out what everyone else was feeling while they all picked up on it effortlessly. It was a skill he'd had to practice, and he was proud of the improvements he'd made.

With Rlain, he didn't need that effort, and it made the entire conversation more relaxing. Right up until Rlain asked something that sent a spike of panic through Renarin.

"Can I touch you?"

"*What?*" Renarin said.

"Wearing these faces makes me nervous," Rlain said, putting his hand to his head and running his fingers through the Veden woman's hair. "I find the rhythms hard to hear, and this body isn't just a Lightweaving. I don't feel my carapace anymore. It unnerves me."

Right. With someone else, Rlain would have simply reached out to grab their shoulder for support, but Renarin liked people to ask first. Right, *right.* That was what Rlain was asking.

He nodded, and then tried to hum his emotions, which made Rlain smile. Rlain took Renarin by the upper arm and held on, breathing deeply and humming to himself. Renarin felt, in return, an unanticipated fire from that touch. A warmth that spread through him, like the one that others had always expected him to feel—told him he would. But which he'd never experienced from the women his aunt and others presented for him.

Should he say something? Like what? "I know we were just talking about the enslavement of your people, but what's your opinion on courting humans?" Storms, it would be so *awkward.* Renarin didn't think he had it in him. Why ruin something nice? This was good enough, right?

"Very well," Rlain said, humming to what Renarin thought was Resolve, "how do we find Shallan?"

"Others are still out there waiting?" Renarin asked, forcing himself to stay on task. It *was* the fate of the world they were trying to influence; he felt selfish for letting his attention wander from that.

"Yes," Rlain said, letting go—unfortunately—and walking over to peek out the front of the tent. "Since it started raining, they've all been standing around." He hummed to Peace, accompanying the patter of rain on the tent. "It's the highstorm, Renarin, but . . . different. More soothing. I like this sensation. Anyway, I see a number of them who look important—though the old man is under a canopy."

"Those are the Heralds," Renarin said. "We have to assume Shallan is with them, and our enemies too. Finding her and not them is going to be difficult. Particularly for me, Rlain. I'm not good at subtext when it's in my face, let alone when it's on someone else's face hiding behind yet a third face."

"Yeah," Rlain said to Irritation. "Humans . . . don't always make a lot of sense."

However . . . Renarin considered a moment. "There's something I can do with my powers, Rlain. It . . . well, it's hard to explain. Glys says that Lightweaving should be one of our Surges, but when I've tried it, I get something else."

"What does it do?" Rlain asked.

"I think it shows me people's souls," Renarin whispered. "And their futures. I . . . like I said, I don't *really* understand it. But I think maybe it would help here, because if we can see people's souls . . ."

"We can see who's who," Rlain said, with a nod. "But if you do it, try not to be too obvious."

This . . . Glys said to him, his voice distant, *this will be useful. This will be good. Try.*

Encouraged, Renarin drew in Stormlight. It permeated this place, and he'd already been holding a little unconsciously. Now, he knelt and motioned for Rlain to sit.

Renarin cupped his palms and . . . breathed out, capturing the Light in a sphere maybe six inches across, spinning, glowing, above his hand. *Please, if you can,* he thought, *let me see—and let him see.* The shadows that Light cast sometimes showed Renarin things, a little like the window visions. The ones he could make on purpose were less distinct, more vague, but at least he could control their timing.

Rlain stared into the sphere, and the light it cast from him made an image: a singer standing as if on a border, one foot in the world of men—represented by a city with human architecture—another foot in the world of singers, with each building in the more flowing designs of his people. He wore half a Bridge Four uniform, half a singer robe, accentuating his carapace. All split right down the middle.

It was a clearer vision than Renarin usually got. And it seemed Rlain saw the same thing when staring into the light in Renarin's hand.

⁂

For a while, Dalinar just enjoyed the rain and the strange warmth. Nearby rockbuds opened up and flushed with sudden color, their shells going from brown to a vibrant orange-red, spouting lifespren. Vines extended, grass coming from its holes and stretching long blades toward the sky, like a man waking from a deep slumber. Basins caught the rain, and he saw crem dishware near one of the cookfires.

Be warned, the Wind said. *The storm could be very cruel, and Honor modulated it only in specific cases. I . . . was frightened of it at times. The singers have armor for a reason.*

"Why?" Gav asked, surprising Dalinar by interacting with the spren. "Why are *you* nice?"

We are what Adonalsium left . . . the Wind said. *And even the storm, before Honor, could be pled with at times . . .*

"The Stormfather never told me that," Dalinar said. "The Stormfather says the storm simply *is.* That it has no choice but to destroy."

This is Roshar. Nothing merely is. Everything thinks. Everything has a choice. Watch. As humans choose.

Gav walking hand in hand with Navani, the three crossed the ground to join Jezrien with a small group looking to the sky, arms spread. The king took a long, deep breath, uncaring that his fine clothing was getting wet. He nodded to them, then he turned to the scouts Dalinar had noticed earlier.

"All right," Jezrien said. "Kalak has finally decided to join us. You may give your report."

"It's him," a scout said. A dark-skinned man with a birthmark on his cheek. Storms, that was Nale. Dalinar had met him once. "Your friend, Jezrien. I'm sure of it."

"El is dead," Jezrien whispered. "I stabbed him myself."

"And yet he lives," Nale said. "Jezrien, if El has joined the Fused . . . not only are our enemies being reborn, but they are recruiting the strongest and most talented singers to immortality. We have to counter it, or we will lose this war."

"Ishar was correct all along, Jezrien," Chana said—by his side, as she'd been in each previous vision. "This is Passion's doing. Our god has fully betrayed us."

"I believe we betrayed him first," Jezrien said softly. "The moment I acknowledged that Nale had been correct, things started changing. He was never Passion, Chana. Always Odium."

"How long has it been since that day . . . ?" Navani said. "I sometimes lose track of time."

"Over forty years," Jezrien said. "Forty-three long years of war . . ."

Dalinar winked at her, appreciating her clever manipulation of the conversation to get them information. "Are we planning campaigns? Perhaps battle maps I can see?" Maybe one of those would work for an anchor to the future.

"Later," Jezrien said. "This isn't the time. You know that."

Well, a map probably wouldn't get him far enough. He needed something persistent, something that would still be here in a thousand years . . . and still relevant . . .

His eyes opened wide as the answer occurred to him. He was about to witness the founding of the Oathpact—and as part of that, ten eternal weapons would be formed. A link to each and every Desolation. The Honorblades. And if he was still Kalak . . . one would form in his own hands. An anchor that could carry him thousands of years into the future.

That's the answer, he thought, excited. *That has to be possible. And it will come straight to me, if I play my role right and don't disrupt what is happening.*

∴

Renarin held the Light for Rlain to see.

"That's marvelous," Rlain said. "How do you do it?"

"I just breathe out," Renarin said, "and the Light gathers. I . . . um, I ask nicely too. That helps."

"Ask nicely?"

"Yeah, the Light seems to respond more when I think a little request."

"Tumi called me the Bridger of Minds," Rlain said, staring into the sphere. "Important singers have titles. That's my future, my fate."

"Nothing is fated," Renarin said. "I learned that painfully, Rlain. There is only possibility and chance, maybe with nudges from outside forces. What comes in the future is *our* choice."

"Like your father," Rlain said, "not joining Odium at the battle of Thaylen Field."

"Yes," Renarin said. "Unless . . ." Storms. Unless it was still to come. Not forced to follow Odium, but going willingly as part of their agreement.

Rlain held out his own hand, hesitantly trying to breathe out Stormlight—making a few attempts and not getting anything.

"Don't force it," Renarin said. "Try being relaxed."

"Try being relaxed," Rlain said, "while wearing a human woman's body and seeking a pair of assassins who want to control the world, as I keep seeing faces of one of the Unmade in patterns of dust on the ground. Right. No problem."

"Nice rhythm," Renarin said, amused at how this particular one emphasized the sarcasm.

"Thanks," Rlain said.

Renarin dismissed his sphere and left Rlain to it, instead checking out the front of the large tent. In the camp beyond, thick tarps dripped with water from the continuing rainfall. The air was cold, crisp, and wet. *Jasnah would love this,* Renarin thought, taking in the antiquated clothing, the weapons chipped from stone.

His father and Navani had arrived to speak with some people in clothes more colorful than most, though still relatively simple by modern terms. He could, as before, see Dalinar and Navani as themselves—they weren't hidden by their spren, the way both the Ghostbloods and Renarin's group were. And . . . Damnation. Was that *Gavinor*? Why had Dalinar and Navani brought a child into the Spiritual Realm?

Who among that group with his father was secretly an enemy? Who was a friend?

Glys, he thought, *I need to be able to use my powers without alerting everyone in the room. Is there a . . . stealthier way to shine my light on them?*

Not that I know of, Glys said. *But we will learn more as we grow. We will* become *more as we grow. Perhaps?*

Not much help for now. But he held out his hand—absently realizing it was an unsleeved safehand, which was amusing—and tried forming a small Light. Unfortunately, it was too distant to reveal anything about the group outside. Renarin puzzled through options as behind him, Rlain hummed an excited rhythm.

"I got some!" he said. "A little bit, at least. It came out and is forming."

"Excellent," Renarin said, glancing at the desk, where a few gemstones had been set out. Raw, uncut gemstones, yes, but glowing nonetheless. What if he stood over there and made Light? Maybe no one would notice it came from him.

Or, well, he was imitating a Herald, wasn't he? Maybe they could use their powers in the open. He was Vedeledev . . . an Edgedancer. That wouldn't fit. But Rlain seemed to be Pailiah, who was a Truthwatcher, so it should be fine for him.

That could work, maybe, Glys said. *Also, maybe if you use less Light, the effects might be less noticeable.*

Lots of "maybe"s in that statement. As he was thinking, Renarin saw the group, including his father and aunt, striding across the wet ground toward their tent.

Renarin pulled the flaps closed. "They're coming back and—" He cut off as he found Rlain kneeling and holding a sphere of Light, wide-eyed. In the light cast by that sphere, Renarin saw himself and Rlain.

They were kissing.

Oh.

Storms, there wasn't time for this.

"They're coming," Renarin said, rushing to him. "Dismiss the sphere!"

"How?" Rlain asked. "I don't even know how I summoned it. I—"

The front flaps of the tent opened, and people began to pile in.

⁂

Before Dalinar could explain to Navani his plan to get an Honorblade—then use that as an anchor—Jezrien started walking, and Dalinar decided he should stick close. Together they joined Ishar. The elder Herald stood a slight distance apart from the others, hands clasped behind his back. He was with a woman who could have been Alethi, or maybe not—she had silvery hair. They were the only two who had chosen to stand under cover when the rains arrived.

"Battar," Nale said to the woman with Ishar, making another of the odd gestures Dalinar didn't understand, touching fingers to forehead. "I find myself oddly glad I never managed to kill you."

"Nale," she said. "Always the brilliant conversationalist. I've news you need to hear."

"I don't really care," Nale said, his words stiff, clipped. "I'm heading back out on patrol."

Jezrien sighed. He looked to Dalinar for help.

"Must we rehash old arguments?" Dalinar said, carefully. "Can we not let the past fade, and look to the future?"

"Agreed," Navani said. "Human must stand with human in this world."

Jezrien nodded to the rest of the camp, particularly some Makabaki soldiers nearby. "They listen to you, Nale. Even if you don't rule. Please. Let us do this together."

"Just because I'm older than them is no reason for me to rule," Nale said. "We don't work the same way you do, Althman. Thankfully."

"Please," Navani said, gentle. "If there's information to share, we all need to hear it." She was quickly learning how to manipulate the situation.

"Midius is right," Jezrien said, nodding to Navani, which gave Dalinar a start. Midius . . . that was their name for Wit. Dalinar had assumed she was in Vedeledev's body again, but evidently not. They'd appeared hand in hand, so maybe the vision had needed to place them into bodies of people standing near one another.

Jezrien moved toward a large nearby tent, and the others joined him. Chana, the bodyguard. Ishar, the elderly sage. Battar, counselor to the rest. Shalash, who was grown now, and Navani as Wit. Dalinar in the body of Kalak. Finally Nale, with a sigh.

Together, this group was seven of the ten Heralds, plus Wit. As Dalinar entered the tent, he recognized Pailiah instantly, wearing green cloth that stood out so much from the furs of the others. With tan skin and a Veden look, she was Lightweaving. She sat on the floor inside the tent, and a globe of Light hovered above her hand.

Behind them, Nale hissed, angerspren boiling at his feet. "You swore you wouldn't use the powers any longer, Althman. This is *forbidden*."

“We need to know what is coming,” Jezrien said. “And Pralla sees the truth, as it might be. She always has.”

“That’s eight,” Navani whispered to Dalinar, still hand in hand with Gav, who glanced around, interested. At the moment he seemed more curious than afraid. The others ignored him, as one might a lingering emotion spren.

Of all those here, Dalinar was most interested in Nale, and his explicit hostility toward the others. He’d recently seen visions of this man. Perhaps visions of this very day. Nale had been an enemy to the others . . .

But where was Taln? The one they abandoned. As the group entered the tent—including some Vorin and Makabaki bodyguards—Dalinar searched among them. He’d met Taln in the modern day, and the hulking soldier would stand out in a crowd. He wasn’t here. There was one other person in the room though—one who had been hidden in a darkened corner, but was revealed as they lit lanterns. This had to be Vedeledev, a woman with long dark hair bearing a slight curl. She looked Alethi or Veden to him, though her skin was paler, like she was from near the Horneater Peaks.

Navani’s breath caught audibly.

“What?” Dalinar whispered to her.

“I was in her body before,” Navani whispered. “Now I get to see her. Vedeledev. Keeper of the keys.”

“I’ve always wondered what they were the keys to,” he said. Scholars tended to swear by her name.

“The keys of immortality,” Navani whispered, her eyes wide as Vedel turned to the gathered group. “It’s happening.”

“It is time,” Jezrien said to Vedel. “Is *he* ready?”

Vedel didn’t respond, looking strangely panicked.

“Vedel?” Jezrien asked. “It is time. Show us.”

⁂

As everyone entered the tent, Renarin sought the shadows by instinct. Rlain continued kneeling on the ground, and fortunately, none of them thought his Lightweaving was odd—at least not until a tall Makabaki man at the back snapped that they shouldn’t be using the powers.

Renarin stepped forward, hoping to draw attention away from Rlain—but as he did, his father looked straight at him, sparking an entire *host* of emotions. Happiness at seeing someone who could take charge—shame at not feeling like *he* should take charge himself. Embarrassment at not being able to say anything to indicate who he was. Even a bit of resentment. It was always there, part of their relationship. You couldn’t banish such things with a wave of the hand.

Those thoughts and worries all fled as a stately, Alethi-looking man—probably Jezrien—spoke to Renarin.

"It is time," he said. "Is *he* ready?"

Storms!

"Vedel?" Jezrien asked. "It is time. Show us."

And the whole room waited for Renarin to answer.

You need not always have the last word, though I know you collect them like badges of honor. I will not tell you where she is.

All his life, Renarin had struggled to figure out what people wanted of him.

It was the great recurring theme of his existence. He'd say the wrong thing, or more commonly *not* say something everyone expected him to, and the whole room would look at him just as they did now, in that tent full of future Heralds. Waiting.

He usually withdrew until the uncomfortable moment passed. In doing so, he suspected he'd trained those closest to him to ignore him. It hurt, because he wanted to understand—more, he wanted *them* to understand *him.* Still, for so much of his life, silence had been his defense. Say nothing. Accept that they thought him odd, which was better than them being offended.

Today that wouldn't work. Today he had put himself in a position where not speaking would reveal him to assassins who prowled with other faces.

Except . . .

"Vedel?" the king asked again.

Except this had all happened before. In most conversations, there was no way to know the right answers. Today, however, the right answer existed—he merely needed the script.

Oh! Glys said, his voice distant as he watched from outside. *Oh, this will work! This is possible!*

You can see what happened in the original event? Renarin thought to him. *The one the vision is copying.*

Yes, Glys said. *Now that you're inside it, yes! Say this, Renarin. Say, "Yes, we presented Ishar's plan to him, and he listened. All is ready—as am I."*

Renarin relayed the words, which made Jezrien nod in satisfaction. One of the others, who had to be Nale, pushed forward. "Wait. I know you. Vedel. The queen."

"Queen no longer," Renarin said, repeating the words fed to him by Glys. "My people are dead. I am only a healer now."

"The *talad* . . ." Nale said.

Renarin had no idea what that meant, but he didn't need to. Storms, it was such an incredible relief to—for once—know how to respond. To be able to participate in a conversation without anxiety or worry. Surely this was how his father felt—always with an answer, always able to speak his mind.

Is this what you will want? Glys asked. *To always give answers expected? What of individuality? What of spontaneity?*

It was difficult to explain, even to one who could sense his feelings and thoughts. Renarin was . . . growing to respect who he *was* rather than who he thought he *should* be. For much of his life that had been a struggle, as he'd always felt insufficient. Not the warrior his father wanted. Not the religious devotee the ardents wanted. Not the prince the people wanted.

In every way, he was a failure. That should make him want to rebel, throw it all away, find his own path. But he *loved* these people—his father, his aunt, the ardents like Kadash, his brother, and the people of Alethkar. He knew he shouldn't derive his self-worth from being what they expected, but surely there was good in pleasing others? He—

Wait, Glys said. *Renarin, wait! Renarin, this will be wrong!*

Renarin felt a panic, thinking that in his musings, he'd missed a cue. But . . . it wasn't him. It was Gav, standing in front of Navani. He must be in the body of someone unimportant, because the others didn't appear to care much what he did.

But Gav had asked a question. And that set Renarin's mental connection to Glys abuzz.

That wasn't what the vision says will happen! Glys explained. *That one isn't following the script.*

Yes, that's Gav, Renarin sent. *He can't really play along. That doesn't tell us anything though, because . . .*

Wait. Storms.

That's how we can tell! Renarin realized. *All the actual members of the vision know what they're supposed to say, but intruders will not.* The Ghostbloods would out themselves by not following the vision exactly.

Not necessarily, Glys said. *They will maybe have learned the same secret as you—and if one person goes off script, the others will too.*

Right. He'd have to be careful about making assumptions. But this at least seemed like a possible way to find the assassins hidden in the vision.

You will speak, Glys prompted him, as he'd not been following the conversation. *Say, "And so I left them . . ."*

⁂

Sigzil rolled across the rainy ground, dazed.

Thunderclast. He'd been fighting the thunderclast Kai-garnis with several Stonewards. She had slapped him from the air and—

The stone wall of Narak Four exploded inward as Kai-garnis punched through it. Chips and chunks of stone fell across Sigzil in the darkness—made suddenly light as a Skybreaker started setting the air ablaze.

Generals sent ground troops to fill the gap. And fortunately, the thunderclast's feet finally started to sink into the plateau behind her. By staying braced across the chasm using both legs and one arm long enough to break open the wall with her other fist, she had allowed Stonewards climbing the chasm wall enough time to make the plateau edge soft underneath her feet. The thirty-foot-tall monster—which looked vaguely skeletal, with a grand arrowhead face—trumped as her feet sank in. Five Edgedancers with Blades slid forward and began chopping at her, and Sigzil joined them, shaking off his daze and summoning his spear—then soaring forward and ramming it through one glowing stone eye.

She stilled, and her eyes faded, the light going out. She'd done her damage though—her corpse formed a bridge in through the wall. Magnified Ones sprang from the nearby plateau onto her back, then ran forward and leaped over her head onto Narak Four.

"All Radiants, form a defensive perimeter and let the troops reset their lines!" Sigzil shouted, swooping down near the scribe station.

"Do we retreat, sir?" one of the generals asked. "The wall is breached!"

"No," Sigzil said. "It's only the fifth day—we need to hold as long as we can. Prepare for a retreat, but we need to see if we can hold here. Ka, get me the Stormwall *now*!"

Sigzil took a stance nearby, putting himself between enormous Magnified Ones and the path to Narak Two, the Oathgate. He engaged the first few. His squires, then Skar and his squires, formed up around him. Windrunners fulfilled many roles on a battlefield. Scouts, yes, but often more akin to cavalry—fast, responsive, capable of getting to a situation and holding a line while slower troops were maneuvering.

Edgedancers joined them, and the Radiants fought the Fused together. Each grouped off into individual duels, not out of honor, but because a Radiant or Fused was like a single-unit army unto themself. There weren't the raw numbers to form blocks of troops—and the fighting styles of Radiants, particularly with Blades, often required space.

Nearby, an Edgedancer shouted as she fell to a Focused One: the new brand, with a sleek, sculpted form, made up of overlapping belts. Like a body embalmed, wrapped in cloth, except each piece instead was like a leather strap. As Sigzil tried to go to the Edgedancer's aid, the Focused One smashed her head with its foot, completely crushing her spine and skull. A wound even Stormlight couldn't heal. Sigzil cursed and left his squires facing off against two Magnified Ones—they had the experience for that—and flew toward the Focused One.

Unlike the Magnified Ones, this thing didn't run or leap as it turned toward him. This tall, sculpted being walked steadily, with a sense of inevitability. Unclothed, androgynous, it seemed malen to Sigzil—but they all did. That was probably just Sigzil defaulting to an assumption.

It didn't flinch as Sigzil's Shardspear hit it straight in the chest, sank in about half an inch, then stopped. Storms, it was true. He hadn't entirely believed. Their skin wraps must somehow use Voidlight to push back the spear. Sigzil danced away as the thing lunged forward with incredible speed—like a spring uncoiling. Sigzil barely dodged, Lashing upward, his sweat mingling with the rain. Some of the thing's calf muscles had unwrapped at the motion, the folds right above the feet becoming loose, then sliding down like many layers.

As he watched, they pulled tight again. Fascinating. He dove, putting a little more force behind his thrust, and managed to shove the spear in a fraction deeper. He was ready for the thing's sudden motion this time, but he still barely managed to dodge. Nearby, a group of heavy infantry—men in their strongest armor, carrying warhammers—formed a line. That was the best way to fight Magnified Ones with conventional troops.

A squad of these engaged a Focused One, who—with a jolt of motion—grabbed one fully armored soldier by the head. The hand released its tension, folds around the forearm unraveling like coils of rope being given sudden slack. This time Sigzil saw more—the tension being released at the wrist was like a spring unwinding, and a great deal of that force was delivered to the fingers. All that pent-up potential energy was transferred into an already powerful grip.

The head burst. The helmet didn't help.

Storms. Though Vienta began whispering numbers to him, analyzing the force transfer, the battle stopped being academic for Sigzil in that moment. He moved, rallying troops with shouts and a raise of the spear. Unfortunately, the Skybreakers made another series of harrying strikes right then. Alongside the other Windrunners, Sigzil was forced to give air support, lest the enemy drop behind their lines.

The next fifteen minutes were chaos in the skies, fighting through rain and fending off fellow humans who *should* have been on his side. He at last got a moment to disengage to check on their defenses, ignoring the glowing red dot from one of the six spanreed rubies strapped to his arm. It indicated that Leyten needed his attention, but that could wait.

His forces had managed to stop the enemy from overrunning the entire plateau. That was helped when a small squad of Windrunners arrived, carrying ropes and lifting dangling figures: people in Shardplate. You couldn't lift Shardplate with Lashings, but you *could* Lash yourself upward and carry a Shardbearer with ropes. This group had been fighting off a simultaneous attack on Narak Prime, but he needed them here more—and this method of deployment was fastest.

The Windrunners cut their ropes, and four Shardbearers dropped to the battlefield—splintering the wooden boards as they hit, Blades appearing in their hands. Finally a fifth man dropped, the one they called the Stormwall. Dami, the Riran Stoneward. Shardplate formed around him—the largest, bulkiest suit Sigzil had ever seen, glowing a dangerous golden orange at its symbol and joints. In that armor, Dami stood a head taller than even the four conventional Shardbearers.

Sigzil hadn't been with him in Emul when he'd said his Fourth Ideal, but it had reportedly been spectacular. The Stormwall didn't summon a Shardblade, but an imposing tower shield, spiked and as tall as he was. He slammed it to the ground in front of him, then shoved a Magnified One out of the way while hitting another with a fist that crushed its face. Colorful ribbons—tied around his wrists and extending out through the Plate—began moving of their own accord; they spiraled outward around his fist and became like blades themselves, after the Stoneward art.

"The Focused Ones!" an Edgedancer shouted, sliding past Sigzil in the rain, trailing fearspren like a train. "They can't be killed! They *can't be killed!*"

Well, that wouldn't do. Time for some applied science.

"Four Lashings," Vienta whispered, "at three hundred feet should be enough, judging by the metrics you provided me."

Sigzil gained some distance with a few Lashings, then came back in low, using four Lashings in repeated succession. He skimmed across the top of the plateau, darting past skirmishing groups, the speed of his passing making pooled water split behind him in a wake—flashing red from reflected lightning above. He came in at a Focused One. The creature glanced at him at the last second, and took a Shardspear in the face.

Sigzil's momentum drove the weapon all the way in, the spearhead bursting out the rear. Sigzil towed the figure—heavy though it was—down to the ground and slammed the head into the stones. The Fused inflated in a heartbeat, tension releasing as it expanded in a sudden dangerous burst. Like hundreds of very taut ropes suddenly snapping and whipping about.

The eyes burned.

"They *can* be killed!" Sigzil shouted, yanking the spear out and holding it overhead. "Fight! *Keep fighting!*"

That rallied them, and along with the Stormwall, they began pushing the enemy back. Soon Sigzil was able to pull free—leaving the Stormwall and Skar in command of ground and air respectively—and tapped his gemstone to indicate to Leyten he was ready for the message. The pattern of blinks that followed spelled out the number of a plateau, and a warning that something strange was happening.

"Weiss and Atakin," Sigzil said to his squires. "You're with me. Fishev, let me know via ruby if the battle turns against us here. I need to check on something."

⁂

"Why is everybody so sad?" Gav asked the gathered crowd of future Heralds. "Can we pretend to be chasmfiends instead of standing around like this?"

Dalinar cringed, waiting for the others to react. They all looked at Gav, as if seeing him for the first time. "Spren?" Jezrien finally asked. "What did you . . . ask?"

"The spren asked why we are sad," Dalinar said. "It is an emotion spren, of course."

"Yes," Jezrien said, the vision adapting to the situation. "We *are* sad, as Vedel's entire nation did not make the transition to this land with her. Vedel was visiting us when the . . . end began."

"So I left them," she whispered. "To burn."

"You are a healer, Vedel, not a Firesmith," Jezrien said, walking across the tent to comfort her. "There was nothing you could do once the chain reaction set the air ablaze."

"Still . . . I should have been with them." She looked away, and Dalinar found something familiar to her mannerisms.

"We all regret those days," Jezrien said. "There's a reason you came to me. You knew, even then, that we'd chosen the wrong god."

"I didn't want to choose any god," she said, then turned and gestured to the side. "I suppose this one is happy. That we must finally come crawling to him."

Light filled the tent, blinding Dalinar. He blinked tears away as others gasped. A moment later that light faded, and a man was standing beside

Vedel. A regal, muscular man with long white hair, dark skin, and golden clothing from another time or place—far too fine for this era of the world.

It was Tanavast, the one they called the Almighty. Or as often, the one called Honor. It was happening. *Please,* Dalinar prayed, *let me get a Blade as an anchor—before the vision ends.*

It had to be close. But . . .

What about Taln?

⁂

Adolin charged into his armor, eager to be into the dome to join the defense. He leaped into the boots and felt them tighten as he walked into the greaves that were being held for him. His armorers cried out, as normally a Shardbearer stood still and let himself be equipped.

Today Adolin grabbed the breastplate—which had to be held by several armorers struggling with its weight—and guided it on, feeling it lock around him as two other armorers heaved the back plate on. The shoulder plates seemed to jump into place, as did other pieces, before he pushed his hands into the gauntlets. He turned and pointed at his scribes even as the full power of the armor arrived, the pieces doing their final fitting, straps pulling tight, clinking as sections snapped together and drew Stormlight from the chest.

"Where is the Azish Shardbearer?" Adolin asked.

"Northern section," Kaminah said, scrambling up. "Um, the commandant has a note for you here. It says, 'Cast the Banner?' With a question mark?"

"Ah . . ." Adolin said. Towers maneuver. Kushkam thought from the enemy positioning that they'd try extra hard to bring down a Shardbearer today—which made sense. The enemy had largely stopped trying since their attempt on the first day. Perhaps they'd been waiting for the defenders to grow lax, and overcommit their Shards?

"Tell him I appreciate the warning," Adolin said. "And write 'Arms Aloft.'" A game signal, turning one of your cards to an angle to indicate being impressed by an opponent's move.

Adolin collected his Shardbearer's hammer and today's honor guard, noticing one man in particular. "Hmask, good to see you as always, but shouldn't you be off shift?"

The Thaylen man with the long mustaches grinned and nodded—he didn't speak Alethi well. Somehow, every time Adolin went into the dome, he found Hmask on his honor guard. He still wasn't certain what he'd done to get the fellow's loyalty. He needed to find a translator and ask.

His guards in tow, Adolin entered the dome through one of the stone corridors, then emerged into the darkened interior, struck by the smell of blood. It lingered here, cooped up as they were in this strange arena. The singers left their fallen corpses—a tradition the Fused apparently enforced. The defenders removed theirs during lulls—and they often cleared out the enemy bodies too, to avoid collecting rotspren. But storms, he wished he could fight in the sunlight again.

No, he thought, jogging up behind their lines. *When I fight in sunlight again, it will be because the enemy has escaped this prison. Don't wish for that.*

The enemy had further expanded their central fortification in the dome, creating space for hundreds of soldiers. He wished he had some way of knowing what the food and resupply situation was for them in Shadesmar. They hadn't expected a long fight. Dared he hope they'd start starving?

Thinking about Shadesmar made him think of Maya. He could feel her, weakly, somewhere distant. Determined. But the enemy was well into its push trying to break the ring of defenders—who managed to field a full four ranks. One shield wall, three lines of pikes, two resting while the two at the front fought. Ten minutes at the front, ten on the pikes behind, followed by twenty minutes of rest.

Adolin picked a spot where the soldiers seemed to be flagging, then waded in, sweeping with his large Shardhammer and breaking the enemy assault. Once he'd forced them back in that spot, he retreated and let the line reset itself with fresh troops, before prowling for another spot to help.

He was joined today by a few Azish field officers. As a runner came with warnings of direforms approaching, he went charging off again. Here he had a tougher fight, leaping in past beleaguered pikemen. He swung for a mostly white singer direform—with wicked carapace spines—but missed. Some furious fighting ensued, and he managed to drop one, though three continued to harry him. Worse, farther down the line, lightning showed Regals breaking apart the shield formation.

Adolin grunted, but held his ground as arrows fell around him. May concentrated volleys right on his position, counting on his armor to deflect arrows, which *banged* as they occasionally struck him. That distraction let him land a powerful blow on one direform—flinging the Regal tens of feet. The other two fell back, which let Adolin charge to the second broken section of the line in time to chase away the stormforms.

That done, his heart racing, he held as the men reset their position and fought off the conventional enemy troops, who tried to push through in the chaos.

"That was close," one of his Azish companions—a man named Gamma—said. He was shorter, with a skin tone that bespoke some Reshi or Herdazian heritage. "I worry that battlefields are changing on us, Brightlord. Pike blocks aren't working like they used to—they break too easily before these new kinds of troops. The old ways are dying. That worries me. All our training is in those methods."

There wasn't time to reminisce about the changing world with Gamma, as Adolin was immediately needed to shore up another position. The enemy, however, used a common tactic: When a Shardbearer showed up to help a line, the singers would largely fall back in that region. Avoiding the worst of the casualties he could inflict.

It made for grueling work. Adolin always needed to be ready, constantly jumping in. Yet he never truly felt like he was achieving anything, for the enemy would reshuffle forces and attack where he wasn't. Neziham—the Azish Shardbearer—largely had the same duty on the other half of the circle.

It's working though, Adolin thought as he spelled off another group of beleaguered soldiers. They cheered him softly as his arrival let them fall back and swap with reserves. This method of defense had kept things mostly stable for the last day or two of fighting—and even though his soldiers were tiring, he believed they could persist.

The latest reports said the Azish and Alethi reinforcements were under two days away. No more phantom attacks by that mystery army. With their Voidspren to give intel, the enemy had to know the same thing—and would be worried about the tide changing when those armies arrived. So as he worked, Adolin looked for signs of what Kushkam was wary of: an attack intended to bring Adolin down.

His next few engagements didn't involve any Regals or Fused. They were holding back their elites for a spell, resting them. Plus, the enemy waves withdrew quickly when he arrived, as if to heighten his confidence that he was invulnerable. His instincts said Kushkam was right. The battle had been stale for too long, almost a full day. They'd try for his Shards soon.

He fell back and explained this to his honor guard, telling them what to expect. So everyone was ready when—roughly two hours into this assault—Adolin stepped up past the line and the enemy suddenly surged forward. Direforms—a good two dozen of them—swarmed around, while conventional troops and stormforms tried to break the pike wall behind and surround him.

Adolin did not retreat. This was why he was here. He began swinging, smashing enemy after enemy as they were forced to engage him—and take the true beating he could inflict. He used Mountainstance, one of the stances for the hammer, and trusted his team to keep him from being overwhelmed.

Then went on the attack.

The enemy seemed surprised by this, and he heard what sounded like curses as he laid about himself with the hammer, cracking carapace, crushing stormforms who got too close, their lightning spasming out. Regals didn't really have a counterpart in the human military. Unmade were like Heralds, and Fused like Radiants. The Regals were perhaps special forces—but enhanced ones.

The direforms around him—with extremely strong carapace grown in wicked points—pressed in. They didn't have Surges, but they were *tough.* At least until you hit them full in the face with a Shardhammer, their exaggerated carapace crumpling as they fell in a mess of blood. They were accustomed to being stronger than both allies and foes, and would have dominated an ordinary battlefield. But with his Plate, Adolin matched them and held his ground, until . . .

"Adolin," a voice said. He knew that voice. Masculine, clipped, reserved. Was that one of his honor guard? "Adolin, the other one is falling! He's down!"

"Other one?" he shouted.

"The Azish Shardbearer. They sent twice as many against him—and they have shields with aluminum bands to stop the Blade."

Storms. They weren't trying to bring Adolin down, they were trying to *distract* him. The true attack was on Neziham, who was already down—and on the complete opposite side of the dome from Adolin. Storms!

Adolin tried to withdraw, but the enemy had planned this. They'd positioned direforms along his flanks, making it difficult for him to extract. They would force him to fight for every inch of retreat. In the meantime they'd be finishing off Neziham and pulling away his corpse, armor and all.

The two Shardbearers were the defenders' best edge in this fight. Lose one . . .

Adolin made a snap decision.

A potentially terrible one.

He charged.

The enemy had positioned all their troops to his flanks, pushing the honor guard behind him into a snarl of fighting. They'd done everything they could to keep him from retreating, but they'd left the way *forward* largely open. Adolin raced on Plate-enhanced feet, broke through the flimsy enemy back line, and dashed across the open field. Virtually alone, trailing a few of his honor guard, he soon reached the enemy bunker.

"Quickly. He's still alive, I think." Suddenly the voice clicked.

"*Notum?*" Adolin said.

A glowing figure appeared in the air by Adolin, roughly a foot tall—bearing the distinctive beard and uniform of the honorspren naval captain.

"It worked!" Adolin said. "Where is Maya?"

"I don't know that. Perhaps I should explain after?"

Right. Adolin's brash push forward had put him in the *middle* of the enemy position, surrounded in a way that was terrible even for a Shardbearer. This was how you fell. This was how, no matter how invincible you felt, you could be brought down—letting your Shards become enemy Shards, then return to kill your friends.

The thing was, Adolin wasn't just any Shardbearer. He was, at his core, the Blackthorn's son. Sadeas, wherever he was, could explain what that meant.

Adolin didn't like it, and he didn't have to. He embraced it anyway. *Momentum,* he thought. *A battle is about momentum.*

Only one way forward.

Through the enemy fortification itself, which now had a dome on the top to deflect falling stones. It was dented, but sloped; he wouldn't be able to get any purchase up there. So he kept going forward, enemies swarming at his sides but shouting to one another in alarm. As long as the enemy was confused by his insane gamble, as long as they were afraid of him, they wouldn't press their advantage. Adolin bashed open the enemy fortification with his hammer, beating back the bronze door and smashing it completely. Unfortunately, that left his hammer—already weakened from fighting—bent all out of shape. So Adolin threw it into the singers within, crushing several of them.

The space was big enough for a direform, which meant it was big enough for him. He bellowed a roar at the remaining singers crowded inside—causing them to panic and dodge, trailing fearspren.

Adolin charged into the dim confines.

Don't stop moving.

Don't let them respond; only let them react. Don't let them plan, only let them panic. Don't let them see you as anything other than a terrible force.

Make them avoid you at all costs.

He began laying into the singers inside with his fists. He crushed skulls and sent bodies slamming into stiff bronze walls. Their terror did the work for him as they scrambled to get away, tripping one another, clearing the path. He had to climb over bodies both alive and dead, but with the unnatural strength and poise of his armor he had little trouble.

Don't. Stop. *Moving.*

He didn't go through the control building at the center, but rounded it to the left, then crashed out through a door on the opposite side of the enemy fortification, where singers were spilling out before him, desperate to get away. He'd traveled faster than news of what he was doing, so the rear ranks on this side were confused. He roared and surged among them, and the chaos fed itself.

Notum became a glowing line of light in the air, circling over one area in the battle ahead. With that guide, Adolin was able to storm among the enemy ranks and break through to find the fallen Shardbearer on his back, his armor smoking from a dozen cracks. Neziham was still fighting while supine, sweeping about with his Blade to cut at the legs of any who came close.

Direforms, however, leaped over the sword and came at him from all sides. Others blocked Neziham's attacks with those wide square shields that had bands of aluminum nailed onto them. One direform pounded a fist into Neziham's head, and the helmet exploded in a spray of molten sparks.

The next hit would finish him off.

Adolin didn't intend to let that blow fall. He roared again, drawing their attention, and was rewarded by looks of confusion, shock, and—most importantly—terror. Adolin grabbed the nearest direform and smashed a fist through the malen's face, breaking carapace, then flesh, then bone. As the corpse sagged in his hands, Adolin took it by one leg and began swinging.

It was difficult to find weapons a Shardbearer wouldn't break within one or two swings. Even the best swords shattered when you hit someone with them using the full force of Plate—but direforms had extremely strong carapace. Adolin made full use of this, swinging his grisly trophy around, bashing it into the others, shocking them with the brutality of it.

As the body ripped apart, leaving him brandishing a leg, Adolin at last achieved his goal. The demoralized and confused enemy *broke,* Regals included. Most battles weren't about killing everyone who stood against you; they were instead about getting your enemy to stop fighting.

Regals sprinted for their bunker. They dragged wounded friends, and Adolin raised a hand, signaling to the archers to let them do so. Exhausted, he turned to help the fallen Neziham—but halted when he saw one figure on the field who was not retreating.

The Heavenly One glowed—if it could be called that—with the dark energy of Voidlight, but did not fly. Abidi the Monarch. He glanced at his retreating soldiers, then back at Adolin.

"I see you," he said. "Radiant. Why do you hide your powers?"

"I'm not Radiant," Adolin said.

"Nonsense. That spren is yours. I see its influence, when it tries to hide. Little honorspren, flitting around in the air." He stepped toward Adolin. "No wonder you could stand against me as no common mortal could, Kholin."

Adolin growled, stepping back.

"Yes," Abidi said, "I know you. They say you're the best. Did you know that the blood of Radiants quiets the voices in my mind, and takes away the edge of a thousand years of pain? If I bathe in it, they simmer, then slip away. Now that I know what you are, I can claim your corpse as my prize, and this city as my throne."

"Then come for me," Adolin said, raising metal fists.

Instead, Abidi studied him before finally joining the retreating armies. The wiser move, for he was now the one in danger of being surrounded. Some might have called it cowardice, but they would be fools.

Adolin sighed and walked over to offer Neziham a hand, helping heave the fallen Shardbearer into a sitting position. He was heavy; the enemy had almost run him out of Stormlight.

"Thank you," he said. "You . . . are quite the Shardbearer."

"Thanks," Adolin said.

"That aluminum," the Azish man said. "On the shields. Do you suppose it was the secret of half-shards all along? Our artifabrians never *were* able to successfully reproduce them from those schematics King Taravangian provided. Was it a trick, from the Vedens, all this time?"

"I wonder," Adolin said, watching as the enemy retreated with their shields. The metal could block Shardblades, and though it was exceptionally rare, the enemy seemed to be able to Soulcast it. It was showing up more and more in battle.

Adolin turned, then—with a start—realized a uniformed man with drooping white eyebrows peeking from his helmet was standing guard at his rear. "Hmask?" Adolin demanded. "Did you *follow* me into the storming *enemy fortification*?"

With a grin, Hmask saluted.

"Suppose I can't chastise you for doing what you saw me do," Adolin grumbled, looking around. He found Notum floating nearby. "All right, spren. Let's chat."

64

TO HOLD BACK THE DARKNESS

All I will say is that I have kept my bargain, and I did not go in person at her request for aid.

Navani—seen by the others in this vision as Wit—felt her fingers tighten on Gav's shoulders as he stood before her.

God had just appeared.

This was . . . Him. The being she'd worshipped since childhood. The one she'd burned glyphwards to. Dalinar said he was dead, but she'd never been able to accept that, not the way he said it. God could not die. Perhaps an aspect of him could die, an avatar.

So, she steeled herself. This wasn't *actually* God. This was one of his many faces.

"My friends," Tanavast said.

"Friends?" Ishar said softly. "You call us that?"

"We should have been friends, Ishar," Tanavast said. "You should have listened to me so many years ago."

"You brought war and death to our world," Chana said.

"I brought truth, and the truth brought war and death," Tanavast replied. "Do you deny this, Chana?"

Chana fell silent.

"Rayse would destroy you now," Tanavast said. "He doesn't care for the people he plays with; he never has. He has found the singers, and he's been granting them immortality so they can kill you." Tanavast's eyes flashed golden. "You will not defeat him. Not alone."

"Honor," Nale said, shoving his way to the front of the group, "how do we know this won't play out as it did last time?"

"Nale," Tanavast said. "It is good to see you. Tell the others. Did I lie to you last time?"

"No," Nale said. "But the powers you gave me . . . they helped burn the world itself."

Honor's expression softened. "I'm sorry. But did I warn you?"

"Yes," Nale admitted. "You did."

"It will not happen again, Nale," Honor said. "Ishar's plan is a good one."

"And Passion?" Chana asked.

"Odium," Tanavast corrected, "*hates* you, as his name implies. You question him—therefore he will now seek to annihilate you."

Navani soaked it in, too amazed to talk. This was a scholar's dream. Even though she wasn't a historian, this had to be witnessed, so it could be *recorded.* She practically held her breath, worried that any interruption or comment she made could taint the vision.

"I don't know if I can trust you again, Honor," Nale said.

Tanavast stepped forward and placed his hand on Nale's shoulder. Navani felt the hair on her arms go up, her skin tingling.

"I," Tanavast said, "am not perfect, Nale. I am merely a *part* of something that *is* perfect. I took this power upon myself to do good, and I mean to keep that Intent. I promise that I will *not* allow what happened to your ancestral home to happen here. However, you do need power to resist."

"We can bind the enemy to a place far from here," Ishar said. "Their souls keep returning, and that is something we can never defeat."

"It is why they keep fighting," Vedel said a moment later, looking up from the edge of the conversation. "Instead of finding a peaceful solution. If we can lock these Fused away, then perhaps we can persuade the living to listen."

"A . . . binding," Chana said. "What kind of binding?"

Navani trembled. She'd always imagined this happening in some grand hall or magnificent palace. In a temple or shrine. Not in an old leather tent, with rain pattering outside. She'd imagined regal clothing, not furs and rough cloth. Shining armor, not stone spears.

But it was happening. And *she* got to *witness it.*

"Most of you once served him," Tanavast said. "He granted you his powers. There is a Connection we can exploit, so long as the circle contains enough of you. Strongest would be sixteen or my own number of ten—it cannot be nine. If you speak oaths to me, my power can be channeled and governed by rules to prevent a cataclysm. I will take back your Surges, then grant them anew, and together you will become a force that both protects Roshar and binds the enemy away from it."

"Ten," Shalash said. "But we are only nine . . ."

"No, Ash," Jezrien said, turning toward her immediately. "There will be enough without you. We will find two more. We . . ." He trailed off as she met his eyes, and Navani sensed a history there. Things that had happened in the decades since Ash had removed her ribbon.

Jezrien sighed. "We will accept . . . any who volunteer."

"Only volunteers," Honor agreed. "This may well require you to travel to Braize, and its well of souls, to seal the enemy. Your pact will complete the blessing that Odium began, then rejected—but you will become *mine* instead of *his*."

Navani didn't know if the others felt the same trembling that she did—the same sense of power and incredible force of *purpose* that emanated from Tanavast.

"I volunteer," Ishar said first.

"I need an oath, Ishar," Tanavast said softly, stepping away from Nale. "You must bind yourself to Honor, to this pact, and swear to hold back the darkness."

Jezrien stepped forward. "Ishar, let me say it first. Let me begin the circle, and you end it. It is my duty, as king."

Ishar nodded. He closed his eyes, and a web of lines emanated from him, like the Bondsmithing she and Dalinar had begun to perform. This seemed far more intricate, and she realized she could never have replicated this with her childlike understanding of the power. Ishar mouthed words of Intent, then touched Honor and drew out a powerful cord of light.

"This will start the bond," Ishar said. "Only once it is complete can Vedel seal immortality upon us—using our Connection to Honor to tap into constantly rejuvenating Investiture from the Spiritual Realm, locking our souls at our current age. This way we can be reborn again and again."

Ishar touched his line to Jezrien first. "I swear this oath to you, Honor," the king said. "I will hold back the darkness. I will protect this land."

The cord of light went through Jezrien, and he began to glow. A low *hum* of power filled the room, vibrating with Honor's tone. Ishar took a second cord from the god, and glanced around the room.

Jezrien took something from his pocket and held it out. A small round piece of stone—the same one that Dalinar had taken as an anchor. "I release your debt, Nale. I will not force this upon you."

"I appreciate that," Nale said. "I am uncertain I desire it, but I will take this charge with honor."

"Do not consider it an honor," Jezrien said. "A duty, yes, but not an honor."

"I understand." Nale hesitated, looking at Ishar holding a line of light, Connected to a god. "Though I had not expected you would come to an enemy with this offer."

"An enemy, yes," Jezrien said. "But an enemy who was correct all along, making *me* the villain, not you. We will fix what we've broken. Ishar and I agreed. There is no person we would welcome more eagerly into this pact than you. You are the single most honorable man I have ever had the privilege of opposing."

"I wish that were true," Nale said, watching that line of light. "But I will serve as best I can. I swear this oath, Almighty Honor. I will protect this people and this land. I will hold back the darkness."

"And I will watch both of you," Chana said, stepping forward. "Where my king goes, I go. I will protect the people and this land, Honor. I will hold back the darkness."

Ishar Connected them both with lines of light, the hum of power increasing with each one. Navani watched with a held breath. This was not the way she had pictured it, but storms, it was beautiful. People Connected directly to God, bound to him, oathed to him. This was the very *beginning* of Vorinism.

Vedel was next, then Pralla. Before Battar could speak, Shalash stepped forward. Jezrien raised his hand, as if to ward her off again—then instead offered it to her. She took it, made her oath, and received a line of light. Battar was next.

Then nothing. *Six and seven . . . who is the eighth?*

Oh, right. She nudged Dalinar.

"Navani," he whispered, "this can be our anchor. If I get an Honorblade here . . ." He took a deep breath. "Blood of my fathers, if this isn't the opportunity of a lifetime . . ." He stepped to the group, which was forming into a circle. "I swear to Honor to protect this land. To hold back the darkness. I will do it. Somehow."

Ishar Connected him, but remained outside the circle, as Jezrien had suggested he be last. There was still one missing.

"We eight who have sworn," Jezrien said, "all remember the old world. But there is one more here who knew the gods. Midius? It is time."

God himself turned to Navani. "I would have you, old friend. I think you're the only one among us all who showed an ounce of wisdom on that day."

She wanted to. But . . .

Wit would say no. He'd say it in a silly way.

Facing God, she tried to impersonate Wit, but she couldn't bring herself to speak an insult. "I can't, I really can't," she whispered, holding in tears. "Pick another."

Jezrien looked disappointed and turned away, as if he'd truly thought in the moment that Wit would join them.

"It must be a volunteer," Tanavast said. "And to create the bond, it is better if it is someone who has interacted with the gods in the past."

None of those watching said anything. Until at last Nale took from Jezrien the disc with the marking on it. "It cannot be only kings and scholars, can it?" he said. "What finely dressed, immortal demigod will spare one thought for the woman whose name he does not know?"

He flipped the disc over in his fingers. "I have a recommendation."

⁂

Kaladin strolled through a highstorm like it was nothing. In fact, there was barely anything to distinguish it from the rain showers he and Szeth had encountered a few days before. Same darkened sky, as if it were brooding. Same lazy rain, chill but not cold. Same odd sounds: water on grass and soil. He was accustomed to the rapping of rain on stone, a sound not unlike twigs cracking. In Shinovar, rain fell with a sputter and a tap, more center drum than rim.

He and Szeth hiked toward the next monastery, waiting for the storm to recharge their gemstones. He'd thrown on the cloak Dalinar had given him, and found that Leyten had properly oiled it against rain. With his boots laced tight and his hood up, he kept relatively dry. It wasn't pleasant, particularly not with the way the ground melted here when exposed to water, but neither was it arduous.

Strolling. Through a highstorm, his armor spren dancing in the air currents above. He thought maybe he understood one of Wit's old stories better. Naturally this was the place where, after running across an entire continent, a man could at last find the wind faltering. Of course Fleet had failed in the end, but that hadn't been the point.

"Hey, Szeth," Kaladin said, hurrying up beside him—slipping only twice in the mud. "You know the story of Fleet?"

"No," Szeth said softly.

"It's . . . I guess it's not relevant." If Szeth had one talent, it was continuing on despite adversity. He didn't need reminders of that. But . . . "Want to hear it anyway?"

Szeth didn't reply. He often did that, ignorant or uncaring of social customs. Kaladin clenched his jaw, trying not to feel annoyed. Kaladin had thought he was making some progress with Szeth, but then last night Szeth had apparently fallen into Shadesmar, fought two Honorbearers, and returned. Despite Kaladin's prodding, Szeth had barely said five sentences about it.

Szeth wasn't opening up to him, no matter what he did. The man had even stopped telling the story of his younger life. Kaladin felt so awkward pushing for more—he really was muddling through things he barely understood, wasn't he? He looked up at the sky, almost offended by how much light shone through those clouds even while it was raining. Why should the people here get to live in such relative ease? What did Szeth possibly have to complain about, growing up in such an idyllic place? Why was . . .

No. Kaladin forcibly pushed back on those dark thoughts. This quiet storm reminded him of the Weeping, when he always had a rougher time. Kaladin smiled and remembered lying on a rooftop once in the rain, when Tien—with his boundless optimism and love—had shown up with a toy horse for his big brother. That memory *could* make him smile now, when once it had only reminded him of Tien's death.

The people of Shinovar shouldn't feel bad because the storms aren't strong here, he told himself. *Everyone's challenges are different.*

Kaladin took a deep breath. "Hey. Why are we heading to the Elsecaller monastery? We have the sword, and the Honorbearer is dead. Shouldn't we just move on?"

"We must check," Szeth said, his eyes forward, "to make certain the people are released when their Honorbearer dies. It happened once. I want to confirm that it continues to happen."

It was a fair enough reason.

"Your suggestions to me," Szeth added, "about my thoughts. They are . . . helping. Thank you."

The words hit Kaladin like a ray of sunlight through breaking clouds. "Really?" he said. Then felt a fool. "I'm glad you're trying them."

"I assumed you would be."

"Do understand," Kaladin said, "it . . . it's not an easy fix. You have to practice it day after day, even when your mind doesn't want to. *Especially* when it feels like it's too hard. Learning to resist your own mind is difficult, Szeth."

"Yes, I see," Szeth said. "I will consider."

"We're a lot alike, you know," Kaladin said.

"We are?"

"Left our homes as youths to become soldiers," Kaladin said. "Ended up fighting battles we didn't believe in, because of our foolish choices. I see myself in you, Szeth."

"I cannot say the same," Szeth replied. "I do my job. You always seem to be questioning yours. I find that aspect of you embarrassing."

Kaladin dented his palms with his fingernails as he made fists, forcing himself not to snap at the man.

And as if in reward for Kaladin's self-control, Szeth continued a moment later. "However, I now see reason in Dalinar sending you with me. Your words . . . have merit. For the first time in quite a while I find myself wavering. Perhaps you will be victorious here, Kaladin Stormblessed, and I will take your words as law."

"Wait . . . as law?"

"Yes," Szeth said, soaring smoothly over a large puddle, landing on the other side. "Dalinar does not want my devotion. I believe I can change my guide and still remain true to my Skybreaker oaths. I have been considering following the law as the others do. Perhaps instead I could do as you say."

Kaladin groaned. "Szeth, I'm not trying to get you to follow *me* instead of Dalinar."

"Ah, you aren't?" Szeth said, glancing to the side. "I misunderstand, then. You have been doing a poor job of making your intentions clear."

"I want you to follow your own conscience!"

"My own conscience says I cannot trust my own conscience," Szeth said, perfectly straight-faced.

"What you do instead isn't healthy."

"My health is irrelevant." He regarded Kaladin again, then smiled. "Do not look so displeased. Your way of thinking *does* help. It has led me to a position of leverage over my own will. Because of you, Kaladin, I am finally able to recognize—and admit—that it is time for me to die. I'm at last capable of the strength required to kill myself."

Kaladin stopped in place, rain tapping at the oiled hood of his cloak. "You *what*?"

"The law demands that I, for my crimes, be punished," Szeth said, continuing to walk. "I have killed many; I should face justice. I will complete the pilgrimage, cleanse my homeland, then find peace in destruction at my own hand. Now that I know I'm not Truthless, I can deliver judgment to myself." He looked back. "I used to pray the spren would strengthen the hands of those who struck at me. Silly, isn't it? When the rock was always just a rock, and I could have ended my own suffering at any point." He shrugged, then turned and continued along the rainy path.

"Szeth!" Kaladin shouted. "That *isn't* why I've been teaching you!"

"Do you want me to make my own decisions?" Szeth called back.

"Yes, but—"

"This is mine, bridgeman! Come, let's hurry. For once my fate seems certain, and I find that invigorating."

Kaladin lingered, feeling like the rain was knocking and trying to get in. To tell him what a fool he had been.

Syl zipped down and appeared next to him. "So few spren, even in a storm," she said, looking skyward. "Just your armor spren—not another single windspren. Something's happening. The Wind says . . . says the storm is wavering."

Kaladin heaved himself forward, pulling his cloak closer. "Did you hear what he said?"

"Szeth?" she said, joining him and stepping lightly—although full sized, she floated and danced more than walked. "Yes."

"I thought I was making progress."

"It's merely progress with a few . . . twists and turns."

Kaladin shook his head, rain streaming down his shoulders. "Why do I find him so *infuriating,* Syl? Shouldn't I *enjoy* helping him? Part of me wants to let him end himself. He's right—he *does* deserve to die, doesn't he?"

"I don't know," she said softly. "Does anyone?"

"He's killed hundreds."

"Under orders. As have we."

"A soldier bears some weight of responsibility for the people they kill," Kaladin said. "We all know that, deep down."

"So . . ."

"So, storms, I don't know," Kaladin said. "Part of me feels like he's a lost cause, Syl. He doesn't *want* my help. I should leave him alone and focus my attention on what the Wind needs me to do. Szeth is too far gone."

"People didn't leave *you* alone when you thought you were too far gone."

He didn't reply to that. Because she was right, yes, but this was also different. Szeth was . . .

Well, Kaladin couldn't even really define it. Szeth was just so . . . so . . . unhelpable.

He felt unsatisfied with those thoughts, but he persisted in them, belligerent as he stalked through the rain. They passed a single rainspren—*one*—which Szeth knelt by and bowed to, whispering, before they continued. Kaladin remained in his self-enforced sour mood for another hour of hiking, until something changed. He stood up straight, then reached to his pocket, finding light bursting from it. His gemstones had been recharged. Just like that?

Son of . . . Honor . . . A distant voice, accompanying a rumble of thunder with no lightning.

"What?" Kaladin whispered.

When there was no response, he glanced at Syl. She shook her head. "I told you. Something's been . . . strange about Father lately. He's . . . withdrawn from me, Kaladin."

"Do you have any idea why?"

"No. And I can't get the Wind to say much. She seems weaker today. Whatever is happening, I don't think it can be good."

"We'll see if Wit has any news for us," Kaladin said, "when we report in tonight."

She nodded and floated on ahead. Kaladin, for now, didn't try further with Szeth—because he knew that the wrong words could be dangerous. Better to think about a plan first so he didn't cause additional problems.

Szeth had halted atop a hill in the rain, and as Kaladin joined him, the reason became obvious. They'd arrived. The next monastery was straight ahead. In the middle of a river.

⁂

"Ten. But we are only nine . . ." Shalash said, as part of the conversation with the Almighty. Renarin wouldn't have noticed anything wrong, except suddenly Glys spoke.

There! the spren said. *There, that's one of them! Shalash didn't say that during the actual event!*

Renarin froze, then cursed himself for doing so. He forced himself to look away and meet Rlain's eyes. He nodded, as Tumi had shared their technique for spotting intruders. Shalash's line had been out of place. She was either Shallan or one of the assassins.

Um . . . Renarin thought, *now what?*

Rlain was already moving though. Both of them had trained with Kaladin, but Rlain had taken to the training far more fully—despite at first pretending not to know much. He had the experience of both the Alethi *and* the listener armies. Would that be enough against Shallan's assassins?

Renarin tried to stay near enough to Rlain to help without looking suspicious. Everyone else was focused on the conversation with Honor. Then he met Shalash's eyes by accident. They locked gazes—and she whispered, barely audible, "Renarin?"

Storms. It was Shallan.

Glys, tell Rlain, Renarin sent as he nodded to Shallan.

I will do so, Glys said. *But you must speak very soon. Then Shallan must too, and Pattern does not yet know how to communicate mind-to-mind! Ordinary Radiant spren have trouble with this, as Honor considered it an invasion of privacy. Perhaps he worried they would learn to hear his mind, as part of the bond. Regardless, Pattern cannot pass the correct words to Shallan.*

The others had begun to glow, swearing oaths, a humming power filling the room. Renarin knew his aunt Navani would be quietly memorizing all of this. He could go to her for a thorough analysis after. For now he repeated the words that Glys gave him, received Ishar's line of light, then stepped up beside Shallan and whispered to her, hoping the hum would cover his whispers.

"You're going to be expected to say what Ash originally said," Renarin explained. "I can tell you what to do."

"Wait," she whispered, "how do *you* know this?"

"Glys," he said. "I'll explain later. Step forward—but wait for Jezrien to take your hands. Then say the exact words the others have."

She did that, playing the role well. Renarin counted off the people in the room as Dalinar took the role of Kalak. So . . . he could assume the enemy wasn't one of the Heralds, as none of them had spoken out of turn. That left only a handful of guards standing at the back of the room. Careful not to meet their eyes, Renarin whispered to Shallan.

"I think your assassins must be those guards."

"That was my guess as well," Shallan whispered, "once I realized you were Vedel."

"What was my giveaway?" he asked.

"You're fidgeting with the ties on your dress."

Storms. He hadn't even realized. He forcibly let go of them, feeling himself blush at being so obvious.

"It's all right," Shallan whispered. "It takes years of practice to expunge your tells—unless you can fabricate an entirely new personality. Which I don't recommend."

Renarin relayed their suspicions to Rlain. The singer repositioned closer to those guards as Glys whispered to Renarin what was coming.

"A large group of them are about to leave," Renarin whispered to Shallan beneath the hum of power, "to fetch Taln. The rest of us can stay here. Be ready to move."

She nodded, not acting the least bit worried, though it was nerve-racking to him. How did people live with this? The knowledge that in seconds, life and death would be decided? That in seconds someone he loved could be . . . gone? Decades of life learning, dreaming, preparing just . . . snuffed out?

The group began to leave, bowing to Honor as they exited. Those Ghostbloods had been planning for this mission. Storms. What if their spren really did know the script, as Glys had warned, and could therefore play any part perfectly? They could be anyone.

Those soldiers at the back looked unconcerned. But wouldn't you *act* unconcerned? Renarin wavered as the last people left the tent, leaving him, Shallan, Rlain, and the three guards.

Renarin took a deep breath and got ready to join Shallan in striking against the guards. As he did, Honor attacked him.

65
NOT FOR HONOR

These days, it seems she and I are the only ones capable of maintaining any manner of isolation. I can tell you, with absolute certainty, she does not want to see you again. It has not been too long. No, I do not think it ever will be.

Radiant spun away from the confused guards as Renarin called out a warning. Damnation. She hadn't *considered* that Mraize might have taken the form of Tanavast. Yet he—glowing, deific, with long white hair and strange-fitting robes—pushed Renarin aside and pulled a knife from his belt, lunging at her.

Guards scattered, confused, running from the tent as they saw a god strike murderously at one of the Heralds. Radiant leaped back as Mraize swiped, then she slashed with her own knife—the one that warped the air—forcing him back. She had training in knives, although Adolin disliked them.

It's hard to not lose a knife fight, even if you win, she remembered him telling her. *Most of the blocks involve sacrificing a limb to put your knife in the other fellow's eye.*

Yet she felt alive with Stormlight urging her forward. She slashed three times at Mraize. Now that he'd dropped the act, she could see his smile on the god's features. He expertly dodged Rlain, who came in for a tackle, then casually shoved Renarin out of the way.

Rlain recovered, grabbing a spear from the last remaining guard—who stood frozen with fear. Renarin went tumbling. Rlain fell in beside her, spear at the ready, as they faced Mraize, whose robes shone with an inner light. He stepped back, knife in a reverse grip, his stance threatening.

"Watch for Iyatil," Radiant whispered. "That final guard might be her."

"They let me take the spear," Rlain whispered back.

"Iyatil might do that," Radiant said, "if she thought it would put you off guard. I'm not sure it's her, but she's here somewhere."

Rlain hummed softly and repositioned so he could watch both Mraize and the panicked guard. "Warning. I'm in a human femalen's body. I keep expecting to be taller, my reach to go farther. I won't be fighting in top condition."

She nodded and counted slowly, then together they rushed Mraize—who whipped out a blowgun and planted a dart straight in Rlain's eye. The singer cursed, stumbling, as Mraize shoved Radiant off balance.

She fell, then scrambled back up—but Mraize was calculating and quick. He swiftly got his knife in Rlain's throat and sent him toppling. Radiant struck at Mraize from behind, but he danced away while Renarin grabbed Rlain, crying out. He and Rlain *fuzzed.* A moment later the two Heralds they'd been impersonating were staring with glassy expressions. Their spren must have pulled them out.

Mraize glanced at the others, momentarily distracted. As Adolin had taught her, Radiant attacked him from the side. Shallan's husband's training proved correct: in a fight with multiple people, combatants would often expose themselves to take out one enemy. She pressed that advantage, and as Mraize turned to defend, she took his knife straight through her forearm—then planted her knife square in his chest.

They both froze. Her arm blazed with a good kind of pain, the kind she could easily ignore, the kind that sometimes just kept her alive and aware. Mraize, in turn, smiled.

"Well executed, little knife," he said, blood trickling from the corner of his mouth, his voice becoming labored. He pulled back from her, stumbling, ripping his knife from her arm—and leaving her knife in her hand. "But did you expect that to kill me?"

Her left arm flared with pain, and she had trouble working her fingers. No, her strike hadn't killed him—not even with the anti-Stormlight knife. Like when she'd taken the bolt to her side, anti-Stormlight didn't automatically kill a human. He'd have some of it moving through his veins from her strike, but it would only activate if he was foolish enough to heal before it evaporated.

She drew in a little Stormlight and let her arm begin to reknit. She didn't want to do too much, lest she attract Odium's attention. Mraize leaned on the table, coughing again, and she was reminded of a different kind of pain. A pain that she hated, the pain that she'd felt upon stabbing Tyn through the heart so long ago, at the start of her journey.

She advanced on Mraize. If she stabbed him enough times, he'd be forced to draw in Stormlight.

"Do you even know?" he whispered through bloody lips. "What we're doing in here?"

The two Heralds lay on the floor dazed, eyes staring sightlessly, as did the final guard. It was as if . . . this part of the vision had gone so far off-plan that it was frozen.

"You're here," Shallan said, "because you seek Mishram's prison."

"Why, though?" Mraize asked. "You need to ask the difficult questions. I *trained* you to consider not merely the prey, but the hunt."

She halted, wary, watching blood trail down the side of a god's mouth, then drip from his chin. She launched herself at him, refusing to be distracted, and he managed to catch her arm—barely. He put his face close to hers.

"Why?" he asked. "You can figure it out. I know you can. *Why?* Why is Mishram not already free?"

This stopped her. Despite it all, she paused. Trying to press her knife toward his eye, held in place by his grip. Why wasn't she free?

This is the realm of the gods, she thought. *Where Odium resides. He knows precisely where her prison is. He could have led someone here to free her.*

Why hasn't he?

"Odium wants her imprisoned," she whispered.

Mraize nodded.

"He's afraid of her, isn't he?"

"Yes," Mraize said, smiling.

"Why?"

"I don't know," Mraize said. "But you learn to respect the thing the greatest predator fears. Master Thaidakar is smart, little knife. Maybe the smartest man I've ever met . . . or at least the most shrewd. He knows how dangerous Odium is, and is legitimately worried about him escaping. So, while the other Ghostbloods question, I hunt. Because I know."

"We need leverage against Odium," Shallan said.

"And this prison is it." Mraize spat blood, wheezing as he spoke. "Help me."

Shallan let her hand grow slack. He, his regal clothing stained red, stumbled back and barely remained upright, one hand resting on the table for strength.

She wanted to do as he said. She *wanted* to work with him.

Do you need me again? Radiant asked.

Yes, Shallan said.

We need to talk about how you made me take over earlier, so you wouldn't have to see—

I'll confront it soon, Shallan promised.

"Help you?" Radiant demanded. "Mraize, I'm here to *kill you.*"

"Ah, but I created you, little knife," Mraize said, his words slightly garbled from his punctured lung. "You cannot best your maker." He winced. "You know how important our quest is. Let us put aside our differences and use this weapon against your enemy."

"No, Mraize," Radiant said. "I won't be manipulated by you."

"I warn you," he growled. "We know more than you think."

"And I know more than you think," she said. "I know *exactly* why Odium is afraid."

"Why?" he said.

"What happened to Adonalsium?" Radiant asked in turn. "The god that was killed, all those millennia ago?"

"He—or it—was murdered by common people."

"Common or extraordinary," Shallan said, "the god of gods was killed by its own creations. Yes, I can guess why Odium fears Mishram. Sometimes the parents' greatest fear should be their children." She raised her knife, stained with Mraize's blood. "You helped make me, yes. That hasn't saved any of the others."

Shallan lunged, but Mraize had been overexaggerating his weakness. He seemed to have pulled in a little Stormlight—the anti-Light from her stab earlier had run out. He grabbed her arm and flung her to the side.

Before he could stab her, strong arms gripped him from behind. Radiant, in physical form, appeared from a white glowing mist. Shallan kicked him in the stomach, then advanced, prepared to do what she must.

When a voice whispered in her ear—her own voice.

"See it done, Shallan," Formless said. "See him ended."

Shallan froze, then searched the shadows of the tent, finding the figure there. Shallan, but with swirling black mist for a face. Terrifying.

"Kill him," Formless said. "And kill Dalinar, who is always so judgmental of you."

"I would *never*," Shallan hissed.

Radiant vanished, dropping Mraize.

"Dalinar is your father now," Formless said. "Navani your mother. You will hurt them, as you've hurt everyone else. You will destroy because you cannot build—and anything you *pretend* to create is just an illusion. Gone in moments."

"No," she said. "No, I—"

"The others return with Talenel. They will find us here, and will know that we've lied again. It is inevitable." Formless advanced on her. "This is what we *are*."

Shallan looked from her to Mraize. Panicked, she whispered, "Glys, Tumi, pull me out!"

The lines of light faded as Dalinar and the others strode through the camp outside. Not gone, but waiting until the tenth person was found.

Dalinar felt the power within him as he walked, but . . . as an echo. As a memory. This wasn't real. He hadn't *actually* sworn that oath . . . had he? He would keep it, of course, as it was what he already intended to do. An oath was the most powerful thing he knew, and without oaths, he wouldn't even be worth his name. He had made mistakes, had killed people he loved, but he would *never* break an oath.

They passed soldiers who gaped at them as they glowed with Stormlight, moving through the center of the camp toward the outskirts. Until they found him.

Dalinar had seen Taln in the future—a hulking warrior with inhuman bulk and muscles. This was the same person, with the same daunting height, but he was of a more . . . ordinary build. A little flabby, with his tunic askew and his belt too loose. He was caring for the horses.

"The horse keeper?" Ishar asked, skeptical. "Wasn't he dismissed from the front lines and forbidden a weapon?"

"Yes," Jezrien said. "Nale, this is a bad idea."

"Honor said he wanted someone who had interaction with the gods," Nale said. "Well . . ."

The other two shared a look. Dalinar took the opportunity to glance at Navani, who—playing Wit—stayed on the periphery, holding hands with Gav. She nodded to him.

"How?" Dalinar asked Jezrien, curious. "How did he interact with the gods?"

"Have you forgotten so easily?" Ishar asked.

"I have had a lot on my mind," Dalinar said. "Jog my memory."

"His soul is warped," Jezrien said, "from his attempt to kill Cultivation."

"He deserves a second chance," Nale said. "It will be good for us to have someone who is not a king among us." Then, louder, he continued, "Taln!"

Taln looked up from the horses, and something in Dalinar twisted as he saw the man's smile. Open, free of any pain or fear. "Nale?" he exclaimed, his belly jiggling as he jogged over. "You're glowing. I thought you hated Surges."

"Taln, I want you to meet someone." He turned and said to Ishar, "Can you ask Honor to join us?"

"He is busy," Ishar said, cocking his head. "Just a moment . . ." Soon Honor emerged, glowing and resplendent in his golden clothing. The hum of power vibrated through Dalinar again, and the line of light connecting him to the god burst alive.

"Talenel," Nale said, "this is Honor."

Taln frowned. He did not bow or show reverence, and instead looked the god straight in the eyes. "I've waited a long time for this moment. And here I am. Without my weapon."

"This one?" Honor asked. "You know what *he* did."

"You wanted someone who's had interaction with the gods," Nale said. "Plus, I want contrary opinions in the group. For balance."

Taln was still staring eye to eye with Honor. "You destroyed an entire world. My grandmother's world."

"I . . . regret that," Honor said. "I vow—upon my own power—that I will not allow such destruction again."

Taln stood a moment. When he spoke, his tone was cool. "Well, I suppose everyone deserves a second chance, even gods." He stepped back to soothe a horse as a rumble of thunder sounded in the sky.

Dalinar couldn't help walking up beside him. "You aren't what I expected," he said.

Taln narrowed his eyes at him. "What? Still frustrated I lost the weapon you gave me, Kalak?" He patted the horse, then thumbed over his shoulder. "That's the foreign king, I see. And you're *all* glowing. You aren't going to set the ground on fire, are you?"

"I don't intend to," Dalinar said softly. "What happened to you?"

He got no response. Behind them, Jezrien said, "Nale, are you *certain* this is a good idea?"

"Should we not have someone among us," Nale replied, "who represents another kind of world? A world of people who can't simply hand their horses to someone else to take care of? A world where if your sandals wear out, you walk barefoot rather than commandeering them from the next man in line?" He looked at each of them in turn. "If we're going to protect the people, should we not *represent* the people?"

"What is this?" Taln asked softly, glancing at them.

"Immortality," Tanavast said, his voice echoing the thunder from above. "I offer it to you, Talenel."

"Ah," Taln said. "No, thank you. With all due respect."

". . . Excuse me?" Tanavast said. "Isn't this what all men secretly want?"

"I have heard too many stories," Taln said. "Living out those eons doesn't suit men well. Though if you have a new pair of sandals, I wouldn't mind those."

"I offer powers unimaginable," Tanavast said.

"I can imagine quite a lot," Taln said, "and some of it is downright terrible. I think I will pass."

"Well," Ishar said, "there, he said it. Let us find another."

"No," Nale said. "He's perfect. I know what happens when the power goes only to those who want it, Taln."

 Taln hesitated, then turned again toward Nale.

Who held up the small stone disc with the animal head on it. "If you join us, you can help solve the problems you have often complained about."

"I want nothing to do with the gods," Taln said. "Not anymore." But his eyes were fixed on that disc. Dalinar couldn't see why—but it seemed to no longer be an indication of debt. It meant something else.

"Which is why," Honor said, "I think Nale is right. You are a good choice. Wise."

"No," Taln replied. "Not wise. Scared. Why . . . why do you want this of me?"

"The enemy is being reborn," Honor explained. "They become immortal, and humankind must have immortals to fight them. With this Oathpact, we will create a method to lock them away on another world. We will close a loophole that has allowed Odium to meddle, and we will provide champions to stand against the tide of darkness. You once were a soldier. Become one anew."

Taln looked at the glowing people, the god, and Ishar. Then to Dalinar. To Dalinar, he asked the question none of them had. "And what is the price?"

"Pain," Dalinar whispered.

"By binding away the enemy, you might be bound with them," Tanavast said. "As an immortal, you will watch everyone around you grow old, then die. You will have power none can understand, and you will be lonely, isolated. Years will blend like drops of water that form streams."

Taln nodded slowly, then did something unexpected. He thought. Rainwater streaming down his face, dripping from his chin, he considered in silence for a good two minutes. It felt like an eternity.

"If not me, you'll find another?" Taln said.

"Yes," Tanavast said.

"Then I'll do it," Taln said, walking up, taking the little disc from Nale. "How do I begin?"

That made Dalinar worry. They'd seen the moment their anchor had been connected to, which meant the vision could start to decay at any moment.

"Swear to Honor," Tanavast said, "that you will protect this land. And hold back the darkness."

"I will protect the people of this land," Taln whispered. "I will hold back the darkness. Not for Honor. But I'll do it."

"That is enough," Honor said.

"I swear as well, last of all," Ishar said. "To bind this Oathpact. I will protect this land. I will hold back the darkness."

"And so," Tanavast said, "you bind me, as I bind you. We need the others."

Hurry! Dalinar thought. *Make me an Honorblade!*

They returned to the tent, where the others waited. Dalinar covertly took

Navani's hand, willing the next part to happen quickly. Ishar Connected Taln and himself with Light.

"Now," the god said, "it shall be done. Once finished, Vedel can do her part and seal your immortality. Each Herald of Honor, stretch forth thy hand."

Ten people, in a circle, hands outstretched. Dalinar's heart trembled as, one at a time, Honor pulled something from within his chest—and held it out. A glowing splinter of Light that formed a Shardblade when it touched a Herald's waiting hand.

The tent began to evaporate around them right as Honor reached him. Gripping Navani's hand, Dalinar took that glowing piece of Light—and felt the many Connections it contained. A stable anchor that could carry them from Desolation to Desolation, and hopefully let them finally reach the day when Honor himself had died.

⁂

In moments Shallan was back in the chaos of the Spiritual Realm. She trembled, holding herself, then felt the arms of both Pattern and Testament around her.

"Glys and Tumi are resetting that part of the vision," Pattern whispered, "so Dalinar and Navani will find nothing wrong. Look."

Shallan glanced to the side, and thought she could see it. Through a shimmering part of the landscape, like a waterfall, she could vaguely make out the tent. When Dalinar and Navani stepped in, all the chaos and blood had vanished.

Others came with them. The Heralds.

Radiant! she thought. *Take over.*

It's all right, Shallan, Veil thought. *You can see her now. You can survive this. You've grown to where you can.*

Shallan . . . allowed herself to remain in control. To watch. It was hard, and she was soon crying, but *she* did it. She held for just a minute, and heard a child's voice crying in the back of her mind, then turned away and took a few deep breaths. She . . . had further to go, but she'd done that much.

Good, Veil thought to her. *You're healing, Shallan.*

But what of Mraize? He'd gleaned information from her, and in the end she'd broken down and let him escape. At least her fear of Formless was fading. The persona didn't have the same power over her that it had during the trip to Lasting Integrity. Perhaps her growth made her less susceptible. She still didn't know how or why it was manifesting. But, as she'd thought before, perhaps there didn't need to be a reason. Any more than a person with a chronic cough needed a *reason* for their ailment to return unexpectedly.

Either way, she thought they needed a new approach for these visions. Mraize won each confrontation. And Iyatil? What of her? Could the *babsk* perhaps be in another set of visions, accomplishing some other plan? Mraize might be here simply to keep Shallan busy.

"Take me to Renarin and Rlain," she requested. "We have to do some brainstorming."

Be content to play with your toys on their world of storms. Or do I have to broadcast what I have learned of your goals? I certainly do not think it a coincidence that you have made a special study of the worlds where legends abound of the dead being raised.

What was this feeling Szeth felt?

Was it . . . fondness? For this monastery in the small city on the island? Strange, to feel fondness, considering his hatred for it when he'd first arrived.

Those had seemed the darkest possible times—black as the hateful hour between moons. His imagination had been flawed, unable to grasp true, penetrating misery. Fortunately, experience had solved that deficit. A moonless night still had stars. He hadn't understood that until each and every one of them had been ripped away, leaving him in a nothingness so absolute, pain itself was a relief.

"What a strange place to put a city," Kaladin said, oblivious as usual. "Every time it rains, you'll have to wait until the river dries out to cross."

"The river," Szeth said, "does not dry out."

"Never?" Kaladin asked. "But . . ." He frowned. "It has to run out sometime. Where does the water come from?"

"Ice melting," Szeth said. "There are some permanent rivers like this in the East. Merely fewer."

"Huh," Kaladin said.

Szeth started toward the bridge, and the others trailed along. None of them flying—to avoid revealing themselves. That meant a long hike beside the river, which flowed fat with rainwater. They crossed the wooden bridge to the city, which was empty. Just wooden walkways, clay brick cobbles, streets flowing with muddy water, buildings applauding with raindrops. It wasn't until they'd searched a half dozen structures that they found a woman in one . . . sweeping the floor.

She jumped as they entered, then her hand went to her lips as she saw Kaladin, his uniform marking him as an outsider.

"It is well," Szeth said quietly. "We're simply travelers. We thought the town empty."

The woman wore a splash. A ragged blue apron. Though she was thin as a sapling, she did not have that same cast to her eyes as the haunted people he'd seen before.

"Please," Szeth said, gesturing for Kaladin to back away. "What happened to the people of the city?"

"It . . . feels like a dream," the woman said at last, clutching her broom. This was a finer house, a merchant's or an officer's quarters, but strewn with recent refuse.

"The shadow has passed," Szeth said. "You know of what I speak? The darkness that came from the monastery?"

The woman nodded, relaxing when Kaladin stepped back out into the rain.

"How long has it been?" she whispered. "Since it began . . ."

"Years," Szeth said.

She gasped.

"The others?" Szeth asked. "The rest of the town? They should be free now. Where are they?"

"Most were . . . sent at the start . . ." she said, looking into the distance. "To the first monastery. The Bondsmith. We were to gather there with weapons, then patrol the borders of Shinovar because someone was coming . . ." She focused on him, and her eyes widened. "*You* were coming."

This was not unanticipated, as there had been many reports of Shin troops on the northern borders. Hopefully none would be deployed against him. Szeth did not relish the idea of cutting through innocents to reach the final monastery.

"I stayed behind," the woman explained. "My leg, you see. So when my mind cleared . . ." She glanced around the room. "I lived in this filth. I can't . . . believe that . . ."

Szeth left her with a suggestion she make her way southward, then joined Kaladin, who had been listening at the door with Syl interpreting. Like most spren, her shape was disturbed slightly by the falling water.

With his bundle of swords on his back, Szeth walked toward the monastery at the center of the city. He thought he periodically heard Nightblood speaking softly, talking to the Honorblades. Learning from them, it seemed.

Kaladin and his spren hurried after. "Szeth, did you hear that?" Kaladin said. "They went to the final monastery?"

"Then to the border, yes," Szeth said.

"Maybe the Unmade is at that first monastery, the last one on your list."

"I think it must be. But before I go there, I want to free as many people as possible." The rain was slackening, and sunlight—pure sunlight—began to break through the clouds above. "You may go on without me, if you wish."

"I told you I'd stay," Kaladin said, "and I mean it. But Szeth . . . you never told me about your meeting with an Unmade. Maybe we can identify which one it is; I learned of them all in officer meetings with Jasnah. This sounds like Ashertmarn."

"I have said what I intend to say." He left Kaladin stewing and walked up to the monastery, feeling again that stirring sense of familiarity. How *dare* this place feel like home? This was where he'd taken his first step toward being Truthless. It was where he'd discovered the shamans lied.

He stepped inside the great hall, as the gates had been left open. The voices of the dead grew . . . softer here, as if in reverence. He could hear the water outside, drops pouring from the rooftop sounding louder than the rain had.

The monastery was empty. *I wonder . . .* Szeth thought, then found himself turning right, Kaladin and Syl following. He trailed down a hallway windowed with thin slits. The acolyte rooms were beyond, wooden, with metal door handles and stone floors. Purposely designed to force the shaman acolytes to become accustomed to touching metal, as some arrived without first becoming soldiers. Szeth remembered listening to many of them sobbing in the night after arriving.

The soldiers had not cried. They'd bled their tears out long ago. He counted down seven rooms, walked to his bunk inside. Strange, how he could remember each place he'd ever slept for any length of time. Was that normal? Close his eyes, and he could easily imagine the floor of his home, beside his family. The barracks at Talmut's monastery. Then here. A bunk that was a little too small, even for him. He knelt beside it and ran his fingers over the wood of the frame.

He removed the loose block by the wall, reached in, and came out with a handful of scratchy wool. Sewn together into the shape of a lamb.

Oh, glories within . . .

Arrow slits in the hall sent lines of light through the doorway to the floor, one on either side of him, like glowing spikes. He'd been so strong, so sure he didn't need anything, until that moment. Until he trembled, squeezed his eyes shut, then put the small toy to his forehead.

And wept.

Kaladin haunted the doorway into the small chamber, feeling weirdly out of place. Szeth had come directly here. Now he was . . . crying?

The Assassin in White, kneeling on the floor by his discarded pack of swords, blubbering over a toy? It made sense after only a moment's consideration.

"You had a younger brother," Kaladin said. "Why didn't you tell me?"

"No," Szeth said hoarsely. "I . . . didn't mention this toy in my story to you . . . did I?"

"You came here for it," Kaladin said. "Who was the child who died, the one you couldn't protect?"

Szeth still knelt, head bowed, and Syl tapped Kaladin on the arm. "Kal," she whispered. "Can't you see? It's his. *He* was the child."

The words shook Kaladin, inverting his perspective like that first time he'd stood on the wall of a chasm. *Szeth's* toy?

"Storms," Kaladin whispered. All this time, he'd been looking for the connection between him and Szeth, wanting to see that Szeth was like him.

However, that wasn't quite right. Szeth wasn't so much like Kaladin as . . .

"Szeth," Kaladin said. "How old were you when they took you from your home?"

"Eleven," Szeth whispered, hoarse. "I was eleven."

Szeth wasn't Kaladin.

Szeth was Tien.

Szeth wasn't the young man who had gone to war, determined to save and protect. He was the child who had been ripped from his peaceful life, then transformed into a killer against his will. A scared little boy who just yearned to go home.

Kaladin had been thrown off by Szeth's competence—he moved like Kaladin did, seemed to know the weapon intrinsically. Except Szeth hated the spear, while Kaladin loved it. He should have seen.

Storms. Something broke in Kaladin. He stumbled away from the room and put his back to the stone wall of the hallway outside. Syl followed, concerned.

"I keep expecting him to become likable," Kaladin whispered to her. "Or at least reasonable. I keep having trouble helping him because he's not like the men at Urithiru, the ones I understood, the ones who wanted my help . . ."

"But . . . ?" she asked.

"Those were foolish expectations on my part," Kaladin said. "A child taken from his home and twisted into a killer isn't going to be *likable.* People who need help aren't going to be *reasonable* all the time. Stormfather knows, I often wasn't."

Suddenly, he *needed* to help Szeth. Not because of Dalinar's request, not because of past failures. But because this was a person in pain, and Kaladin was perhaps one of the few people in a position to help.

Unfortunately, by the time he stepped back to the room, Szeth had recovered. He'd returned the stuffed toy to its hole, and was wiping his hands on his white trousers. He replaced his long white raincloak with a flourish that sprayed water across the room, then he picked up the bundle of swords.

"Szeth?" Kaladin said as the man pushed past him and into the hallway.

"We must be moving," Szeth said. "I would like to check the Edgedancer monastery, though we'll then need to retrace our steps a little. Fortunately, we have recharged our Stormlight, and can afford to fly."

"Szeth, it's not your fault, what they did to you."

Szeth stopped a little farther down the hallway.

"The world needs killers," Kaladin said. "So if it can't find them, it makes them out of whatever raw materials are at hand. Like children who love to dance."

"I murdered a man," Szeth said, facing away from Kaladin. "I wasn't some random choice."

"You protected yourself, Szeth."

"I meant to kill him, even before he tried to strangle me."

"But you *weren't going to,*" Kaladin said. "Don't lie. You told me what happened." He glanced at Syl—who nodded, encouraging him.

Szeth started walking again.

"Rule number one," Kaladin called after him. "You're not a thing. You're a person. Rule number two, you get to choose. And there's a third rule, Szeth. You *deserve* to be happy."

Szeth put one hand to the wall and let the bundle of swords slump from his other hand onto the floor. "Why?" he asked, his back bowed. "Why would I deserve happiness? Give me a single *good* reason, bridgeman."

Kaladin took a gamble. A line that wouldn't be true for everyone, and would be dangerously untrue to say to some who had come from places of abuse. But he'd heard enough of Szeth's story, despite the parts that the man obviously hadn't shared.

"One good reason, Szeth?" Kaladin replied. "I'll give you *two.* One mother. One father. I don't know where your parents are, if they're still alive or if they've passed, but I'll tell you this. They loved you. They want you to be happy."

"I don't deserve their names," Szeth said. "The things I've done . . ."

"Things you were made to do," Kaladin said, stepping forward. "I spent years believing my parents would hate me for my failings, but I knew—I *always* knew—that was a lie. You know too, don't you?"

Szeth looked away. So Kaladin stepped forward again, careful, as if he were approaching a timid animal.

"You are not a thing," Kaladin whispered. "You can choose. What do *you* want, Szeth?"

"You're wrong," Szeth said, harsh. He turned, then cocked his head—and was probably hearing the spren. That cursed highspren who hovered around him, unseen, whispering lies. "I . . . I'm flawed. My choices can't be trusted. I do not know right and wrong."

"No," Kaladin said. "Szeth, listen to what that spren is saying, then *think.* When you were about to hit that soldier as a child? You said you stopped, until he tried to kill you. When you killed at Taravangian's demands, you *knew* it was wrong. Damnation, you *knew* there was something wrong in your homeland. They exiled you, but you *knew.* Each time, you knew. If you'd been the one to decide, if you'd truly been in control, people would *still be alive.* You *can* choose. So don't lie to me and say otherwise."

"I . . ." Szeth blinked. "People . . . people are still dead, Kaladin. I still killed them."

"Then *do better,*" Kaladin said. "Try to fix the problem, make restitution. But Szeth, you can't do better if you're dead. I'm telling you that you, and all of us, can do better. Choose better." Kaladin stepped right up to Szeth and extended his hand. "We talk a lot about taking responsibility, Szeth. It's what Dalinar teaches, and storm me if it's wrong, but I don't think you have *any* difficulty taking responsibility.

"The truth is, there's a balance. You *are* a product of what life, society, and people have done to you. You bear blame for what you did, but others bear a lot of it too. It's never too late to accept that your past might not be an excuse, but it is a valid *explanation.* So tell me. What do you—Szeth-son-Neturo—want for yourself? With no influence from anyone else, not even me. What do *you* want?"

Szeth gazed at Kaladin's open, extended hand. The man was trembling, and Kaladin couldn't tell what of the wetness on his face was rain, what was sweat, and what was tears.

"If I choose this," Szeth whispered, "it's as good as admitting that there *are* no right answers. That *no one* knows the truth. That terrifies me."

"It *means,*" Kaladin said, "that neither truth nor answers are easy to find. We still have to try, rather than giving up that responsibility to someone else. Maybe someone *has* found the truth. I certainly hope so. But let's talk about what you *genuinely* want, and work from there."

"I want . . ." Szeth said. "I . . . want to stop killing." He looked to Kaladin, wide-eyed, as if admitting this were some terrible transgression. "I want to be done with it. I want to cause no more pain."

"Then we'll figure that out."

"It's impossible," Szeth whispered. "I have to cleanse my homeland. I'm too great a weapon to be left alone. Someone will find me. Someone will use me. That's why I put myself in Dalinar's care, because I hoped that at least I'd be used well. I can't imagine a world where—"

"Szeth," Kaladin cut in. "We'll find a way."

Szeth stared at Kaladin, then finally took his outstretched hand. Kaladin had anticipated a firm handshake, but Szeth went for the full hug, like a child needing reassurance from a parent. Which was strange, considering how much older Szeth was than him—only now, Kaladin could see the eleven-year-old boy in the assassin. A boy who was never allowed to grow up, and who had somehow maintained a fragile child's view of morality.

So, Kaladin held Szeth, who quivered, whispering, "I want to stop hurting people. I want to stop being a source of pain. I never want to be forced to take another life. I want to be done, Kaladin. I want to be *done*."

Kaladin held tight as Syl popped up from behind Szeth and—grinning—gave Kaladin an encouraging double thumbs-up. Was this what Wit had meant by being a therapist? Kaladin supposed that once in a while, every person—even ruthless assassins—needed a hug.

Szeth took a deep breath and stepped back. "I don't see how I can have what I want. My people *do* need me to help them. That requires killing the corrupted Honorbearers."

"Does your spren have any ideas?" Kaladin said, picking up the bag of swords so Szeth wouldn't have to carry it. A foolish question perhaps, but he was hoping he could involve the highspren and maybe get the thing to help, rather than hurt.

"He left this morning, running in shame," Szeth said. "I think he realized that after his failings in Shadesmar, I would no longer look toward him as I once had."

So Szeth hadn't been hearing the spren earlier? That troubled Kaladin. He started to follow Szeth out, then turned as he noticed Syl ducking back into the room. He peeked in, finding her fiddling with the loose brick. She pulled on it, her arms straining, her back bent with the effort.

"Syl?" he said. "That's far too heavy for you. You—"

The stone slid. Kaladin started as Syl, eager, reached into the hiding spot and pulled out the small toy. Kaladin could now see that it was in vaguely the shape of an animal with four legs and fluffy hair. A sheep—Kaladin had seen them grazing on the hillsides.

Syl pulled it close, with a grin. It was small, about the size of a child's hand, but still. Kaladin remembered a time when she'd had trouble carrying a *leaf*.

"I've been practicing," she said proudly. "It feels like the stronger our bond grows, the stronger I am in this realm, you know?" Then she held the toy out to him. "But, um, it's going to get really tiring to carry this a long distance . . ."

He took it and slipped it into his pocket. She bobbed along next to him as he caught up with Szeth. Together they walked from the monastery and into the sunlight. To find an ominous figure waiting in the courtyard outside.

He stood with two highspren splitting the air near his head. An imperious man, dark skin with cool undertones, a crescent birthmark on his cheek. Tall, strong, bald, cut as if from stone. Wearing a sharp black uniform marked with silver.

Nalan'Elin, Herald of Justice.

"Sir?" Szeth stopped in place, then saluted.

"I have come," Nale said with a deep voice, "to accompany you on your quest." He focused on Kaladin. "As I've been told that you need . . . minding."

Kaladin met the Herald's eyes, and softly cursed. Szeth's spren hadn't gone "running in shame."

It had gone running for reinforcements.

You feign altruism. But you have another motive, do you not? Well, you always have.

I had already decided to follow," Notum explained to Adolin, Colot, and May in Adolin's command tent.

The spren had grown to full size and glowed softly, standing at an odd kind of attention with one arm to his breast and the other folded behind his back. He spoke in that same formal way as always, as if giving a report to superiors.

"How though?" Colot asked. "From what Adolin says, there was a great ocean between you and here."

"I . . . I realized, right after Brightlord Adolin left, that staying behind was cowardice on my part." Notum drew himself up. "I determined to come join the fight, though I'm not going to be a Radiant spren. I will not give any human that power over me. That doesn't mean I can't help."

"But Radiants are what we need!" May said, seated at Adolin's writing desk in her battle leathers. "If we had more Windrunners, we—"

"Peace, May," Adolin requested. "We shouldn't try to force the Radiant bond on anyone."

That she didn't like that idea was clear from the way she drew her lips to a line.

Notum nodded to Adolin in thanks. "I was going to try to find a means to sail all the way to the Oathgate here. Then, that first night, I heard a voice."

"Was it Maya?"

"Your spren?" Notum asked.

"She doesn't belong to me," Adolin said. "She's my comrade in arms. She went to the honorspren dissenters for help."

How could she have gotten so far? It had taken weeks to cross that distance by ship, and while Adolin had the sense that she was traveling a different way—swept along by the beads as deadeyes sometimes were—she couldn't have arrived so quickly, could she?

"I do not know her voice well," Notum said. "So I could not say. This was a quiet feminine voice, calling me to arms. I made my decision at that moment, and I allowed the hopes and thoughts of humankind to draw me into the Physical Realm. I came to myself about a day later, and flew here."

"One day?" Colot said. "You spent only *one day* disoriented? It took Sylphrena years, I believe."

"The mind-dampening has been growing shorter and shorter," May said from her desk. "Still, one day is remarkable. Particularly for a spren who *isn't* intending to form a Radiant bond. What's holding him here, Adolin?"

"What do you mean?" Adolin asked.

"The Radiant bond is a symbiosis," May said. "Which means the bond gives something to both parties. Like . . . a contract. The human gets access to the Surges that are an innate aspect of the spren. In return, the spren gets stability in this realm. A human mind and soul to anchor them to the physical world, without which spren have trouble thinking and functioning."

"I do not find it difficult," Notum said. "But I *am* firm about not being bonded. You aid the war effort without being Radiants. Why can I not do the same?"

"You already did," Adolin said. "You saved a Shardbearer today, Notum. Thank you."

"You rescued me from torture," Notum said to Adolin, "at the hands of those Tukari. It is an honor to return the favor." He drew himself up even straighter. "I formally request a battlefield commission under your command, Adolin Kholin. I cannot hold a weapon in this realm, but I will be of service to you. I promise it."

"I accept the offer, Captain Notum," Adolin said. "I'll put you in charge of my messenger corps, if May approves."

"I have my hands full with reports and archery training," she said, "considering that I have a new apprentice." She leaned forward and continued making battle reports to Urithiru via spanreed. "An invisible, flying spren to lead our messengers would be an advantage. And maybe he'll eventually realize what he should *truly* be doing."

Adolin tried shaking hands with Notum, but he could barely feel the spren's touch. Afterward, Notum bowed instead.

"Thank you," Notum said. "For giving me a place, unconventional though it is. We *will* hold back the enemy, Adolin. Remember, Honor is not dead."

"Not so long as he lives within us," Adolin said. "Good to have you, Notum. I grant you a field commission as a captain in the Cobalt Guard. Colot, would you process him? Though I suppose he won't be needing rations or a quartermaster requisition allotment . . ."

They left, and Adolin strolled over to May, watching her scribble out lines on her report. He'd never felt the desire to learn to read himself. Perhaps he should have, but there was plenty else to do. Plus, he'd had enough of being like his father. Echoes of that reverberated from earlier in the day—being the killer the situation required.

Not simply a killer, he thought, remembering his mother's voice and face. *I kill for a cause—something that matters.*

"I still find that spren's arrival strange," May said as she wrote. "He should need more time to adjust."

"Maybe we don't know everything about the process yet," Adolin said. "Isn't that what science teaches? That we should never assume we have all the answers, and we should keep testing what we observe against what we think we know?"

May hesitated, the pen on her page halting. "Well, yes. How do you know that?"

"Shallan talks about it," he said, smiling. She reportedly was still on her secret mission to deal with the Ghostbloods. Her squires weren't worried, but Adolin couldn't help but be anxious. How would he know if she was in trouble and needed help? What if it was weeks until he saw her again? She could handle herself, but . . . storms, he hoped she was safe.

"And you actually listen when she speaks of womanly things?" May asked. "When we were not-courting, all *I* could get you to listen to was historical battle accounts."

"Guess I'm expanding my horizons."

May huffed, making another note. "She's good for you."

"You have no idea. Any word from Urithiru today?"

"Battle reports from the Shattered Plains," she said, sliding him a sheet for a scribe to read to him later. "They're holding against an incredible number of Fused, but worry about dwindling Stormlight supplies. No surprises yet at Thaylen City."

"Nothing further about my wife?"

"I tried to ask the fool, as requested," she told him. "But no one can find him. Your aunt, though, sent you this short reply: she believes that Shallan and your brother are *both* doing a very important task. That is all."

"Well, it's something," he said, taking the page with the battle report. "Thank you."

"I am glad," May said, continuing to write, "that you and I did not work out as a couple. I think we'd have hated one another eventually. I'm glad you found someone better suited to you, though I thought you and Shallan a strange pairing until I realized something. You both share the same sense of whimsy."

"I don't have a whimsical bone in my body, May."

May eyed him, then kept writing.

"What?" he said.

"I thought you more self-aware than that," she said. "Don't you have a dinner appointment with the emperor?"

She was right, and he probably shouldn't keep the emperor waiting—even if they had achieved a first-name basis. Adolin left her to her reports, amused she thought him whimsical. Today he'd washed free the blood, but the brutal destruction he'd caused chased him. That was the job, after all.

He felt a comforting reassurance from Maya, though no words. She was too far away. He wished he knew if Notum had been her doing or not—certainly, his arrival was proof that spren could be of great value on the battlefield. Maya's quest was relevant, and not too problematic, so long as Adolin didn't run out of Shardhammers.

But at the same time, he had to shoo away anxietyspren at the worry her quest wouldn't be enough. A dozen honorspren wouldn't mean much if those reinforcements didn't arrive. Adolin glanced at the dome, trying to imagine holding here five more days without further troops, and shivered at the thought.

He couldn't quash the fear that once again, he wouldn't be enough. Battle report from the Shattered Plains in hand, he shook his head and went jogging toward Yanagawn's tent for their nightly training and games of towers.

⁂

Sigzil flew through the chasms of the Shattered Plains with two of his squires. Via spanreed, Leyten had advised Sigzil to come in low, unseen, so he moved through darkened chasms, lit occasionally from the red lightning above. A low misting of rain meant that water streamed through the slots in a quiet gurgle. Not a rushing roar, and not particularly dangerous.

Fortunately, each plateau was numbered on his map for reference, and that ultimately got him to the correct spot. There he found Leyten and his squires hovering low, peeking up over the edge of a plateau. Sigzil flew to them and gave the salute of the day, and they gave the proper response.

A set of flashes on Sigzil's bracer indicated that the assault on Narak had been rebuffed. The enemy was withdrawing for now. The coalition army would retreat from Narak Four eventually, but today's hard fighting was worth something—with that wall broken, the enemy would keep concentrating attacks there, maybe earning the other plateaus breathing room.

"You were right to send me looking for the Heavenly Ones," Leyten whispered to him, pointing at a group of them soaring just ahead. "One of our scout nests spotted them out here; it seems all of them are in this region, patrolling. I bet they've got orders to keep humans away from whatever is happening over there. I don't think they spotted me or my squires though."

Sigzil considered, spending some time watching the Heavenly Ones.

"Thoughts?" he whispered.

"I think I can estimate a proper heading," Vienta whispered. "Judging by their guard pattern, they *are* trying to keep people away as Leyten said. A place farther north, along the edge of the Shattered Plains."

Sigzil turned toward the others. "You have cloaks?"

Leyten's squires broke them out. The policy was to wear or carry them when on patrol—and swathed in these buttoning, hooded black cloaks, they weren't nearly as noticeable. Stormlight still streamed off their skin and tighter clothing, but it tended to get caught in the folds of the cloaks and evaporate.

"We'll go in through the chasms," Sigzil said. "Leyten, me, Weiss, and one of Leyten's squires. The rest of you, wait for our signal in case we need you."

Careful Lashings sent them zipping through the network of chasms with Sigzil in the lead—map in hand, its surface waxed against the rain. The lightning above seemed focused in a specific region, so he flew that direction, passing chasms littered with refuse that was overgrown with life. Here he found the strangely companionable scents of growth and decay, lifespren and rotspren dancing together above the streaming water. There were fewer corpses than he remembered from his days as a bridgeman. More bits of trees and shell. The Shattered Plains were moving on from the time when human and listener clashed atop them every few days.

He consulted with Vienta, who flew up to watch the enemy search patterns. Eventually the group reached the edge of the Plains—and indeed, that was exactly where the lightning was concentrated. Here, Sigzil carefully led them upward. In leaving the gurgling chasm floor, he felt as if he were parting from an old friend. The chasms had been Bridge Four's punishment at first, then their respite, then their shelter as they practiced. The very skills he now used as a warrior had been seeded in this network of tombs, where he'd first wielded a spear with those who would become his brothers.

He and Leyten peeked carefully up over the rim of the chasms, looking out at the hilly—even mountainous—landscape north of the Plains. It was a region he'd rarely visited, and then only when flying scouting missions. Here, on a field of stone beneath violent lightning—which was almost constant—an army was gathering. Hundreds of enemy soldiers, their wet carapace reflecting lightning.

Regals. How? *How* had the enemy brought in these reinforcements? They couldn't have walked from Alethkar. That was hundreds of miles. Heavenly Ones and Skybreakers had been too busy fighting to transport anyone.

"I don't understand," Leyten said, his voice barely audible over the thunder. "This should be impossible, Sig."

"Maybe they're a Lightweaving," Weiss said. The short, dark-haired squire had been a seamstress before joining the Windrunners. "A grand show meant to intimidate us."

"Best we know, Masked Ones can't make giant Lightweavings on this scale," Leyten replied. "They mostly just change their own features."

"We have evidence," Sigzil said, "of Heavenly Ones creating occasional weak Lashings in others, though it uses up their power quickly. So it's possible Masked Ones can do the same. But I think that's unlikely here."

"I . . . agree," Vienta whispered. "No hypothesis I imagine can explain this, Sigzil. Unless . . ."

"What?" he whispered.

"Unless they've figured out a way to Elsecall."

Damnation. "I'm going up," Sigzil said.

"*Up?*" Leyten hissed, grabbing his arm.

"That light in the center of the army? I need to know what it is, but can't see from this perspective." He glanced at the sky. "The lightning is going to have everyone light-blinded; it will be storming difficult to locate me if I stay high enough."

Leyten considered, then nodded and let go of his arm. He probably wanted to insist on coming too, but knew that would double the chances of them being spotted.

"Be ready to flee just in case," Sigzil said to the others. Then he withdrew a few hundred yards before taking to the sky, doing something they rarely dared—coming close to the cloud line of rippling red lightning. To avoid that lightning, he moved fast, pulling his cloak tight and Lashing himself to the north, back toward the gathering army. The constant flashes above seemed the eyes of Odium, but he forcibly told himself it was no such thing. Odium couldn't see everywhere at once. Many things slipped his notice.

And surely, if he *had* seen Sigzil, the response would have been immediate. Because at the center of the gathering army was a hole in the ground—a wide ring of violet light, the inside falling away like a pit. Soldiers jumped up from within it, soaring out of the hole, being seized by companions and stabilized as they landed.

"Storms," Sigzil whispered. "You were right. That's an Elsegate, I assume?"

"Yes," Vienta whispered back. She appeared to him shrouded in billowing cloth, like laundry on the line. "There's only a few ways it could be possible."

"How?" This power had created the Oathgates long ago, had brought humans to Roshar. Despite years of trying, Jasnah hadn't figured out its mechanics, and interrogations with Heralds hadn't helped. The Fused shouldn't be capable of large-scale manifestations like this.

"It would mean," she said, "that the enemy has empowered Dai-Gonarthis again, which we all thought he'd never do. So outside of reason that it was barely worth consideration. She wishes to break and burn this world. Bad though that is, I am hopeful this *is* the case, because if it's not her . . . then the enemy has the Elsecaller Honorblade."

"Storms," he whispered, to the appropriate sound of rumbling thunder.

"Would that we could experiment with the power . . ." Vienta whispered to him. "The two of us. All the time in the world, and an Elsecaller."

"See if we can create perpetual motion . . ." Sigzil said. "See if there are any limits to speed and distance . . ."

"So many things to learn." In a rare moment, her billowing cloth retracted around her face, and she smiled toward him.

Unfortunately, there was still a war to fight. Sigzil used his spyglass to see if he could spot an Honorblade or sign of an Unmade. He did locate an interesting Fused. Tall, and standing apart from the others, with a body too silvery to be natural. He knelt at the edge of the large portal in the ground.

Then a figure jumped up out of the portal near the Fused. A human with brown hair flecked with black, in a black uniform, carrying a familiar Honorblade. As he looked up, Sigzil could swear that this man's eyes glowed violet. As if . . . as if they were gemstones full of Voidlight.

Sigzil knew this figure all too well. Moash. Once friend.

Teft's killer.

BEWARE the FUSED!

DO NOT ENGAGE! FIND A RADIANT!

EIGHTEEN YEARS AGO

For the second time in his life, Szeth waited on the other side of a door while people decided his fate.

He wasn't a child any longer. He didn't hide in bed, or cry into a blanket. He stood outside the General's door, his back straight, legs spread, hands clasped before him. Guard stance. He could hold it, motionless, longer than anyone he knew.

Inside, he trembled.

He'd stridden into battle—through smoke and fire and brine—where his plan had destroyed two ships and sent the raiders away, perhaps forever. He'd thought himself immune from fear, even quietly bragged about it in his head. Yet now? *Now* he had to force himself to breathe evenly so that he didn't start hyperventilating? *Now* he had to struggle to keep the emotions from flooding out as tears?

What was wrong with him? He'd accepted punishment in the past. He could do so again.

Even if . . . even if this would be different.

It had been three days since Szeth's operation. Forbidden his duties—or even sparring—during that time, he'd been left in misery to wait for this tribunal. Finally, Honorbearers had arrived—and now they all spoke together inside. With the General, his father, even the *Farmer.* Carried in by soldiers so he wouldn't have to step on stone. All because Szeth had used his initiative in following orders.

He wished he could hear what they were saying. He could not, so he remained standing. Angry. Increasingly sick. Even the Voice was shunning him lately.

A footstep ground against the gravel walkway nearby. A normal sound to him now. He glanced that direction, wondering who would approach the General's offices at a time like this. The answer should have been obvious.

Elid. His sister.

As an adult, Elid was still two inches taller than he was. She wore work clothing, and though she wasn't a supervisor in the kitchens, she bore a distinctive air of authority. Maybe it was the polished stone necklace of beads, a badge of pride for a hobby no one outside the monasteries would ever enjoy. Maybe it was the way she strolled over and leaned with one shoulder against the wooden wall, one leg lazily crossing the other. Long black ponytail, keen eyes, knowing smile.

Elid navigated rules and social expectations like a fish in water. Whereas Szeth did it like a sword through entrails.

"So," she said, "you screwed up again."

He glanced away from her, staring through the camp at nothing in particular.

"They're gonna kick you out, eh?"

"They can't," Szeth said softly. "I subtract. They can find something miserable for me to do, they can execute me, or . . ."

Or worse. They wouldn't make him Truthless, would they? He hadn't denied Truth. He was trying to *protect* Shinovar.

He could feel Elid's skeptical eyes on him. That woman . . . "What do you want, Elid?" he snapped.

"Just to see how you're doing," she said. "Szeth. It's okay to rage and lose control sometimes. But you need to find better ways to express it than in battle."

Rage? He looked at her, confused until he sorted through that statement. "Is that what they're saying in camp?"

"A lot of them have felt it," she said, shrugging. "It's why they're here. These are the men who can't control themselves when they fight."

"I didn't attack the outlanders out of *rage,* Elid," he said. "I was told to defend our shores."

"You were told," she said, "to watch for any enemy that decided to strike inward. Why do you think the Farmer leaves offerings for them?"

"Because he's afraid."

"Because it works," Elid said. "If they find easy goods, they take them and leave. They know if they burn down the fishing villages and steal all the workers, the offerings stop."

That wasn't what the Voice said. The Voice said that the Farmer's offerings would only make the enemy hunger for more and more. Szeth had thought, in the General's orders—the way Szeth had been left to his own devices on the coast these months, tasked with defensive operations—that the General had understood.

Obviously not.

Obviously, he really *had* screwed up again.

"I'm sorry, Elid," he said. "For ruining your life."

"Eh, that life was boring," she said. "Stones Unhallowed. To think, if nothing had happened, I might be sitting out in a field somewhere today." She shivered visibly.

"You shouldn't swear."

"Why not? You honestly think *rock* is holy?"

"Of course it is," Szeth said. "Ask Father."

"Szeth. Do you *still* not know why we lived apart from everyone else when we were young?"

He closed his eyes. He . . . he didn't want to know. Life already confused him too much. That unsettled sense continued when, of all things, Elid hugged him.

This made him break his stance, put his arms to the side in surprise. She embraced him. *Elid.*

"Listen," she said. "Father will work it out. Everyone knows your heart is right."

"I don't," he whispered. "*I* don't know that, Elid."

She stepped back, holding him by the arms. "Well, that's probably why you shouldn't trust yourself, Szeth." She patted him on the arm, and seemed teary eyed. "Look. You'll get through this, whatever happens." She nodded to him encouragingly, then backed off as the door opened.

Father beckoned Szeth to enter. Szeth did so, trying to recover his composure. It was difficult. Three Honorbearers stood inside. Pozen, with his white beard and accusatory eyes. Sivi, with a smile. Vambra, who wasn't as familiar as the other two. A woman young to be an Honorbearer, with long golden hair.

The Farmer appeared older than Szeth remembered. More white in his hair, somehow more attention-drawing than the colorful clothing. He was standing on the wooden floor beside Rit-daughter-Clutio, the head shaman of the monastery with no Blade.

The General was the last one, gazing out the window, hands clasped behind him. "We have consulted, Szeth-son-Neturo," he said softly. "What you did was reckless, destructive, and insubordinate. Your father spoke of your good nature and your skill, which we have taken into account. In the end, however, we cannot ignore the danger you bring upon all of us. It is our inclination to send you to the mines."

That was . . .

Well, that was what he'd expected.

Szeth remained in his stance.

"Son?" the Farmer said. "Do you have anything to say?"

Szeth frowned. "*Should* I say something?"

The others shared glances.

"I did what I was told," Szeth said. "If I misinterpreted so badly, then you are correct to decommission me." Saying it brought a huge weight off his shoulders. "Maybe . . . maybe this is for the best."

This seemed to concern several of them, but the Farmer—swathed in color—smiled openly.

"You are right, Szeth," the Farmer said, his voice kindly. "I'm glad you see it. In anticipation of your willingness to cooperate, I've insisted that instead of hard labor, you be given a post at the high pass to watch for stonewalkers entering our lands. I sometimes go there to meet foreign traders; it is beautiful, Szeth. A lonely post, yes, but also good for solitary thinking." He paused. "You could keep sheep, as soldiers there do for food."

Sheep? Herding flocks again?

Oh . . . how *incredible* that would be.

He could imagine it: A quiet post, far from where he could do harm. As many sheep as he wanted, and he'd slaughter only the elderly and infirm, at the end of their lives. Quiet winds. Dancing. A blanket of stars at night.

Why had it taken so long for him to see it? His mother had suggested this years ago. Yes, it stung to know he'd failed, but it was also amazing to have *direction.* He found, as he looked up and met the Farmer's eyes, that he wasn't frightened any longer.

Well, this won't do, the Voice said in his head. *Not after you finally started proving yourself. I'm sorry for getting distracted. I nearly missed this meeting, didn't I?*

Suddenly, all three Honorbearers stood up straighter and went alert, as if they'd been slapped. Then, as if one, they focused on Szeth.

"*Out,*" Pozen said. "Everyone but Szeth."

"Excuse me?" the Farmer said. "But—"

"*OUT,*" Pozen repeated, Honorblade appearing in his hand. He slammed it straight through the floor and into the stone. "*Right now.*"

Father, Rit, and the General hurried out. The Farmer had to wait for his soldier porters to come and pick him up off his ritual mat and carry him out beyond the stones—but he went, appearing troubled the entire time.

Szeth bore it all with a mounting sense of dread.

As soon as the door shut, Vambra—the Truthwatcher Honorbearer—walked up to Szeth. She couldn't be much older than he was, but spoke with authority. "How long has he been talking to you?"

"I . . ." Szeth barely maintained his stance; his instincts said he should flee this intense scrutiny.

"How long?" Vambra repeated.

It's all right, the Voice said. *You may reveal me.*

Only then did Szeth understand. "You hear it too?" He looked to the other Honorbearers. "All three of you?"

"It is very rare," Sivi said, "for one who is not an acolyte or a shaman to be chosen. In fact, I can't remember the last time it happened."

"I was six years in the monastery before I heard him," Vambra said. "Soldier, you were asked a question."

"I heard the Voice that first day," Szeth said, "when I killed that soldier as a child. I've . . . heard it regularly ever since."

"This was *his* plan?" Pozen asked. "Burning those ships?"

Of course it was, the Voice said, and from the way they reacted, each of them had heard it. *There's no Honorbearer in this monastery or region. I work through other means here.*

"Why?" Szeth whispered. "Why wouldn't you tell them?"

It does them good, the Voice said—and this time it seemed to be only for Szeth. *They need to remember that they serve me, not the other way around.*

Wait.

The Honorbearers *served* the Voice?

"What is it?" Szeth said, unfolding his arms, breaking stance at last. "What *is* this Voice?"

"That," Sivi said, sounding reluctant, "is only for the highest members of our society to know."

"Regardless," the elderly Pozen said, gesturing toward Szeth, "he needs training at a monastery. You've heard the reports of Szeth's skill—they are true and unexaggerated. If there was an Honorbearer in this monastery, he'd have been recruited long ago."

"A commendation for his bravery should suffice," Vambra said. "Make a big production of it; that will explain us taking a man from another monastery."

"Send the award after," Pozen said. "He comes with me today."

"But . . ." Szeth said, glancing between them. "What of what I did?"

"What did he say to you?" Vambra asked. "About the outlanders?"

"The Voice told me . . . that if I hit them hard enough, they would be too frightened to return. It said to send survivors back, when my plan had been to sink all three ships."

"Well, there you are," Vambra said. "He's rarely wrong. You did well, Szeth. Sorry for the confusion and hubbub."

"This is actually perfect," Pozen said. "You should see my current crop of acolytes—not a standout among them. But this boy . . . If there's a solution to the Tuko problem, this might very well be it."

Szeth felt his freedom evaporating. Rainwater disappearing under the sun. His stomach churned, like during the first weeks after coming to the monastery, when he'd started eating meat every day.

"Do I need to do this?" Szeth whispered. "*Must* I?"

Yes, Szeth, you must, the Voice said. *It is right.*

Vambra clapped him on the shoulder as Pozen dismissed his Blade and composed himself, all three of them adopting more serious airs. They called out, and Szeth's father opened the door for the General, who hesitantly entered.

"We have something to tell you," Pozen said with a stern voice. "The young man is in fact a hero."

"*What?*" the General said. "But—"

"He was working on higher orders," Pozen said. "His attack three days ago was a trial of his abilities and leadership skill. Today's conversation was a test to see if he would take punishment with grace, which he did. We're moving him to my monastery to begin training as a shaman acolyte."

Szeth was glad to see the stunned look in the General's eyes. For once, someone else was as confused as Szeth was.

Neturo nodded slowly. "I'll help him gather his things."

"No need," Pozen said. "Once you become an acolyte, you must burn everything you own."

Szeth put his hand to the pouch at his belt. "Everything?"

"Today, you become someone new, Szeth," Pozen said. "Neither one who adds nor one who subtracts—but someone holy, someone greater. You come alone, as every child is born alone."

"A . . . alone?" Szeth said, his voice small.

"No," Neturo said.

Szeth glanced to his father.

"No child is 'born alone,'" Neturo said. "He is born to a family. If Szeth is to go, we go with him."

"There will be no place for you in the monastery," Pozen said. "You can't—"

"Pardon," Sivi said, "but there is a city outside your monastery, Pozen. Weren't you saying you needed a new administrator for it?"

Pozen hesitated.

"I will gather my family and my things," Neturo said. "Assuming we don't need to burn away our old lives like Szeth."

Pozen eventually waved for Neturo to do so.

Neturo left, and though it might not have been correct to leave without being dismissed, Szeth followed. "Father," he said outside, gripping his father by the arm. "You don't need to do this."

Neturo put his hand on Szeth's, holding it. "Son. Of course I do. I won't let them take you away from us."

The next part passed in a daze. An announcement in the camp: a commendation for Szeth. Szeth didn't get to see the expression on Jormo's face as he was placed on a horse, and the servants of the Honorbearers gathered to begin their caravan home. Nearby, the Farmer stood on ritual carpet on a box, on top of soil carried and placed here. A pillar of color in the otherwise drab camp. He looked concerned as the ribbons tied to his robes fluttered in the wind.

Neturo came with a large pack on his back, and Elid followed. Szeth glanced away from her as she stepped up to his horse. "I'm sorry."

"Are you kidding?" Elid said. "Have you heard how great the cities are around active monasteries? This is going to be wonderful."

Should he think that way? Instead he felt sick. Even a little angry. So he looked up behind him and he saw what he'd been expecting. What he'd been anticipating. His stomach turned over.

His mother stood there, and she bore no pack.

"Zeenid," Neturo said, walking to her. "We must—"

"I'm not going, Neturo," she said. "I'm not letting you do this to me again."

"I . . ." Neturo said. "I didn't—"

"I'm going back to my old life," she said. "I'm told, with cleansing and penance, I can return as if nothing had happened—because I never subtracted. *You* never subtracted, Neturo. We didn't need to do this."

"Zeenid," Neturo said, "we can't *leave* him."

"He's an adult, Neturo," Zeenid said. "Nineteen years old. Let go. For both of your good."

The Honorbearers chose that moment to start the caravan. Horses and porters began descending the long set of switchbacks. Szeth held his horse back, looking to his parents. To Neturo, who glanced at Szeth, then at Zeenid, who averted her eyes.

"Wait," Elid said from beside Szeth's horse. "Wait. Mom's not coming? That isn't what . . . I mean . . ."

Mother spun and walked back toward camp. She didn't say goodbye. Neturo whispered to Elid, asking if she wanted to stay with Mother—telling her it was a valid decision. She shook her head with tears in her eyes, so he turned her away from the sight.

Together, the three of them started after the caravan. Szeth hung his head. Though he knew deep down that they hadn't been a family for years now, it still hurt. Because this break, last of all, seemed final.

THE END OF

Day Five

INTERLUDES

ZAHEL • ODIUM

I-9

ZAHEL

It's funny, Zahel thought, *how many times I've been chained to the ceiling.*

Zahel hung, naked, in a dark room. Unshaven, unwashed. He thought it had been weeks since that first day—during the invasion—when he'd been taken. The timing wasn't clear though, because he had to keep erasing his memories to help neutralize his captor's torture.

Torture. Why did they always default to torture? The research didn't support its effectiveness, even in people who couldn't erase memories of the pain to prevent long-term trauma.

But then, he wasn't a man of research any longer, was he? He wasn't much of a man, or god, of anything these days. He groaned, pulling himself up a little by his arms to stretch. Beside him, out of reach—if his hands had been free—a sad, sorry parrot hung in her cage. Bright crimson, with shades of cherry, and a maroon on the darker parts of her wings. Very striking. She didn't look at him, remaining quiet.

It was bad when a parrot grew quiet.

"Hey," Zahel said, his voice hoarse. "Hey."

Stupid bird didn't react. It huddled down in its cage, without a proper perch.

Zahel sagged in his bonds. Blood crusted his naked body. They always knew to take his clothing, so he couldn't bring it to life. Once in a while, couldn't he be captured by someone stupid? He bowed his head, his hair—not quite black, more a deep chestnut—curling around his face. Stringy, unwashed.

The brightest splash of color in the circular room—lined in aluminum sheets, preventing even spren from sensing him—was the parrot. Other than that, it was just his dried blood on the floor, a bookcase along one wall, and a mattress on the other side, though it hadn't been used by his captors in weeks.

Not for the first time, he wondered why he kept struggling. Centuries. Friends failed. Most recently a woman abandoned, when she'd so believed in him . . .

He had told himself he was retiring.

In truth, he'd simply run.

The bird shuffled, but when Zahel glanced over, it had just lowered its head.

So, with a sigh, Zahel tried something else. "Hey," he said. He looked away, and looked back quickly. "Peeky time."

The bird looked up.

Zahel repeated the infant's game again. "Peeky time. Peeky time."

Then, slowly, the parrot perked up. "Peeky time . . ." it said in its avian voice.

"That's right," Zahel said. "Hey, it's not so bad. You're going to be all right. You . . ."

He trailed off as the door opened, and Axindweth—rings glittering on her fingers—slipped in. "Playing games, are we, Vasher?" She clicked her tongue, and the bright green Aviar on her shoulder mimicked the sound.

"I have to do something to pass the time. Figure it will take you forty years or so to die." He met her eyes. "I can outlast you. I've done it before."

She laughed. "Always blustering, Vasher." She took a box from under her arm and opened it, displaying a fabrial shaped a little like a handgun, only with spikes at the front.

Well, hell. She'd finally gotten a painrial.

"I have found," Axindweth said, "a more efficient way of making you hurt, Vasher. Would you like a taste?"

He didn't reply.

"What if we compromised," Axindweth said. "You give me *half* your Breaths, and I will let you go."

Half his power, which was admittedly an incredible wealth of Investiture. Zahel should never have brought so much; he'd known it would draw attention.

He could give her half. He didn't need those Breaths. Except he knew how that would go. If he gave her half, she—after such a burgundy victory—would demand more. Then more.

It wasn't a negotiating tactic. It wasn't a path toward freedom. This was just another attempt to break him down.

So—feeling sorry for the parrot who had to watch—he didn't say anything further until she made him start screaming.

I-10: THE MOMENT OF DECISION

Taravangian struggled with balance. Even as his plots were playing out, the pieces falling into line, he struggled. While he *knew* he needed to dominate, he still *questioned.*

Why should he question?

Today, his attention was on Shinovar. He was aware of his former servant, Szeth, traveling through this land, disrupting it. Though Taravangian had pieces in motion to ultimately control Shinovar, this place of flowing grasses and echoes of a dead world *should* have been easy for him to dominate. It was not. It was instead a warning.

He considered from atop a mountain. His emotions, which flared so powerfully, cared more about the kingdoms he already had. Kharbranth. Jah Keved. Alethkar.

I will need to focus on many foreign lands in the centuries to come, he thought. *Shinovar, then, is good practice. If I cannot apply my focus to a distant part of Roshar, how will I dominate all worlds, everywhere?*

Cultivation appeared behind him. He did not need to look, for he had no eyes.

"You have tried as I asked?" she said.

"Yes."

"And?"

"Both halves of me reject your assumptions, Cultivation," he proclaimed. "The mind finds it requisite of me to become the conqueror; the heart *needs* the same, if for different reasons."

"And you, Taravangian?" she asked. "*You* are neither mind nor heart, but the combination."

Ah . . . He focused his essence upon her, and saw her full ploy at last. In mathematics, sums and divisions were straightforward—but not so with souls. Both heart and mind wished conquest, but the two together?

"You," she said, "were one of the few humans ever to taste divinity. A man who could think with incredible speed. A man who could feel the powerful crushing emotions of Odium. You had both the mind and emotions of a god."

". . . Yet never," he whispered, "at the same time. Until now."

"Please, Taravangian. Do you *truly* want to go down this path?"

Did he?

Did he *legitimately*?

He fixated on the people working so hard to resist him. He saw their passion, their ingenuity, and *loved* it. He realized now why he questioned. There were two on this planet who, even as a divinity, he *respected* almost as equals. Jasnah Kholin and Dalinar Kholin. If they opposed him, then . . . he questioned. For in his Ascension to godhood, he'd obtained a wisdom that eluded most mortals. A simple, reasonable precept: if someone you deeply respected disagreed with you, perhaps it was worth reconsidering.

That was when, for the first time, Taravangian *legitimately* wavered. This problem was not academic, and not one simply of passionate instinct. The question of opposing his friends cut to his very soul. For by its light, he saw that he had been lying, even to himself.

Yes, it made *sense* to give the cosmere one god.

Yes, it was *his passion* to protect his people.

Both were true, but they were not the actual reason he'd done any of this. In that moment of uncertainty, Taravangian did what even gods struggled to do.

He saw the truth within himself, one he would never admit to any other being. Why conquer?

Because someday, someone would do it.

And *he* wanted to be that one.

The burden of a king was to make the difficult choices, and he'd done that for so many years. He longed to enjoy the rewards for those many painful sacrifices. He yearned to see what he could do, unhindered. What heights he could soar to, what accomplishments he—Taravangian, the greatest of men, now divine—could achieve.

Conquest was not a need, but a want. And he was done denying himself the things he wanted.

The power *loved* this revelation. It was pure, unfettered emotion.

The mind *respected* this revelation, for it was truth acknowledged.

The two, at that moment, became one. It was the moment of decision. Taravangian hung on that precipice and let himself question for one final moment. What would Dalinar do? Two versions of Taravangian seemed to split off from him, walking into infinite time. Two people that he could be.

Dalinar . . .

Dalinar was *wrong*.

And *someone* needed to *prove* it.

Questions died. There, on that mountaintop, Taravangian—Odium—was truly born. He coalesced an avatar in radiant, shining gold vestments and placed a small cane to his side, the twin portions of his soul vibrating with the same pure tone. He opened eyes that beamed with the light of the sun.

Cultivation trembled.

"So be it," she whispered, her voice awash with rhythms expressing her profound, soul-crushing disappointment. She left, and Odium—fully aligned at last—began his work in earnest. For there were two people he respected who needed lessons to help them grow.

DAY SIX

KALADIN • JASNAH • SZETH •
VENLI • SYLPHRENA • SHALLAN •
SIGZIL • ADOLIN • DALINAR

There's a lot of discussion in fashion circles about how military dress might influence civilian styles. Shown above is a modern ko-takama with a military jacket. Flanking it are suggestions on implementing the style.

69

RADICAL PHILOSOPHY

You now know of my sins in full. You now also know of my revelations, if they may be called that, in full. Each of my visions is here. Each experience of my past that shaped me.

—From the epilogue to *Oathbringer,* by Dalinar Kholin

On Nale's arrival, Szeth became a different person. As they got ready for the day, Kaladin tried to engage Szeth in conversation, but all he received was simple answers spoken in a monotone. They then flew for much of the morning, but landed to walk the rest of the way to the Lightweaver monastery—which marked the halfway point in their journey. Szeth continued to think approaching on foot would be less conspicuous.

So Kaladin trudged along in the dirt, pack heavy on his back. The land had grown dustier and dirtier as they'd moved northward, the air less humid, with even the nights uncomfortably warm.

The plants here were of a . . . weedier nature. The small earthen road they'd been following had become a much larger thoroughfare. Dusty, despite the rainfall a day before. He couldn't imagine what this would be like when full of people and carts.

Determined, Kaladin fell into step beside Szeth—the two of them trailing behind Nale, who strode along, imperious and tall. He somehow collected less dust on his legs than Kaladin did, and apparently needed no water or rest, for he called no breaks and expected them to drink from canteens while walking. He looked like a lighteyes with two sorry soldiers trotting along behind, carrying all his things.

He's trying to rile you, Kaladin told himself. *He probably wants to annoy you to the point that you abandon Szeth to him.*

Kaladin refused to get upset. "So," he said, "how much farther is it?"

"Not far," Szeth said.

"How often have you been to this monastery?"

"A handful of times," Szeth said. "Lightweaver was not my preferred pair of abilities."

"What was it like?" Kaladin asked. "Training with each of the Blades? Must have been interesting."

Szeth shrugged, his eyes on Nale. Storms. It felt like their progress had been washed completely away in the highstorm rain. That was agonizing to Kaladin, because now—seeing how much Szeth needed help, how much like Tien he was—Kaladin's passion for helping him had grown and grown. Maybe too far. It was physically painful to be unable to do anything to help.

"Szeth," he tried again, "can we talk about—"

"*We* can talk," Nale said from ahead. "Please. I hear you've been offering my disciple radical philosophy, Windrunner. I should like to hear it for myself."

Kaladin gritted his teeth. So far, Nale had barely said a word to him. He wished he'd been better able to organize his own thoughts, because as he stepped up beside Nale—a man who was, unusually, about Kaladin's height—he felt woefully unprepared.

"Go ahead," Nale said, striding with hands clasped behind him. "Speak to me of your ideas, mortal."

Kaladin glanced around to see if Syl had returned from scouting, but she hadn't. "I think," he said, "this 'follow the law' thing you people have going on is ridiculous."

"You are an anarchist?" Nale asked, his voice perfectly calm. "Tearing down law and society, and making ash of them both?"

"No," Kaladin said. "But I don't think you should worship it either. Every rule needs to be broken now and then."

"Does it now?" Nale asked. "How do we decide? More importantly, *who* decides?"

"It depends," Kaladin said.

"Upon what?" Nale said. "Cannot every murderer say, 'Mine is the instance where the rule should be broken'? Every person has wanted to break the law—but if it is right for *one* to uphold it, then it is likewise right for *all.* The great moralist Nohadon himself pointed out the need for such rules in society. Would you contradict him?"

"I'm not arguing with him," Kaladin said. "I don't even want to argue with *you.* I simply think that Szeth should think for himself a little more."

"I believe he is thinking for himself," Nale said. "He has simply chosen answers you do not like. Why is it that all proponents of 'free thinking' only accept the answers they want? Anyone who agrees with them is a free thinker. Anyone who doesn't? Why, they must be blinded by the oppressive norms of society, or are dancing on strings to the evil delight of those in control."

The passionless way he spoke, in a monotone aside from a stressed word here and there, was unnerving.

"Look," Kaladin said, "can we please just talk about Szeth?"

"We *are* talking about Szeth. And you are dodging questions. Do you think people should follow the law?"

"In general, sure. But the law isn't perfect—it was made by a bunch of people like us."

"That is all we have though. The law is the current best guideline to morality for our society."

"Yeah, but that's not how you present it to Szeth, is it?" Kaladin said, glancing back at the other man, who followed behind—silent, but obviously listening intently. "Not some 'guideline to morality' but as an ideal to absolutely devote yourself to. It's one of his oaths!"

"The oath," Nale said, "is to find a moral compass. He selected a person. I find his choice questionable, but his decision is allowed and respected."

"Still. Sounds like you really do worship the law."

"Why shouldn't we?" Nale said. "In nothing does mankind so closely approach the divine as in the creation of codes to better itself."

"I . . . don't believe that. The law was worse than flawed for me, Nale. It let a terrible man steal my brother and send him to war, to die. And while my own slavery was probably illegal by Alethi law, what Sadeas did to my friends—forming us into bridge crews and sending us to die on the Shattered Plains—was perfectly legal and absolutely reprehensible. The law can be, and often is, very broken."

Nale shook his head. "And what replaces it?"

"Human decency, maybe?"

"Which is applied irregularly. The law doesn't fix all ills, but it tries to—and you may have suffered, but you would have suffered more without the law. For humans cannot be trusted to be *decent,* Stormblessed. You should know this more than most. Even my own viewpoint, I've come to learn, can be flawed. The law, though, has been crafted over eons, handed down from generation to generation, refined and perfected."

"Except for those laws created at the whims of some idiot king. Which is most of them."

"Why do you assume that you are smarter than the one who made the laws?" Nale said. "From what the spren tells me, you don't have any answers—you don't offer a better path. You simply tear down the one offered."

"But—"

"Again, what would you have him do?" Nale said. "Other than 'think for himself'? Do you have a replacement for his idealization?"

"I think he shouldn't have one!"

"So you want to replace something grand with *nothing*. The true goal of every revolutionary. To tear down, rip apart, and destroy. You have no philosophy to cherish, therefore you seek to ruin others', jealous that they have answers.

"Well, *I* have answers," Nale said. "The answer is to trust in the law, because at least then you have a moral compass. The ideas of men are weak things, as are their hearts. Thus we pick something greater."

"But the law *is* the ideas of men!"

"No," Nale said. "There you are wrong. These laws are better than the mere ideas of men."

"But you just agreed that they *are* the thoughts of men!"

"I did not. Tell me, do you know where the law of this land came from?"

This man . . . there were so many holes in his arguments, and he simply ignored them. Nale said he was flawed, then proclaimed he had answers. Still, Szeth *was* listening—if Nale didn't see the problems, perhaps Szeth would.

"Windrunner?" Nale asked. "Where did the law of this land originate? Do you know?"

"It . . . was the spren, maybe?" Kaladin guessed.

"Ha," Nale said. "So you do argue from ignorance. Let me explain."

Kaladin felt himself being drawn into a trap, sure as he could sense a feint coming in combat. He was no philosopher, unfortunately, and struggled to find a way to avoid whatever Nale was planning. So he remained quiet.

Nale raised his hands to the sides in a sweeping gesture, taking in the long brown-green grasses growing thigh-high, punctuated by stalks of giant flowers as tall as a man—with rigid stems almost like shells, and bright yellow petals surrounding a brown center, like an eye.

"This land," Nale continued, "was our first home upon this world. The cradle of humankind, where our first laws were forged. Not by spren *or* by men, but by the hand of God himself and the monarch he had chosen: Jezrien. King of Heralds, and Herald of Kings. My enemy, then my dear friend. That *divine* origin is the foundation of law in Shinovar, Kaladin Stormblessed. This is what you seek to undermine."

"But . . . wait," Kaladin said. "Then why do the Shin worship the spren?"

"Spren?" Nale said. "You mean literal fragments of divinity?"

"Yeah, Syl says that, but . . . I mean . . ." He frowned. "Wait. This really doesn't add up. How did you Heralds find this world in the first place?"

"We followed the sacred tones of Roshar," Nale said. "We reached out through the power of Elsecalling—Ishar was once a master of that art. I had some talent as well." His expression grew wistful. "I heard it . . . the songs of a new world, fresh and alive. An inviting rhythm . . ."

"Okay," Kaladin said. "But were the spren involved? This place speaks to me sometimes. The Wind itself."

"Ignore that. Echoes of a god long dead and gone."

"But—"

"We are off track," Nale said. "Tell me: would you overthrow the entire Shin system of government?"

"What? Of course not."

"How would you react to another order of Radiants coming in, implying that your oaths to protect are foolish?"

"Look," Kaladin said, tossing up his hands, getting frustrated. "It's not working for him. What you're doing is hurting Szeth. I don't argue like a scholar, Nale. But it's *not working.* It's *broken.* He needs help, compassion, and you're not offering it."

"He is broken more than most," Nale said, stopping on the road, meeting Kaladin's eyes. "You had a hand in that. Do you know who picked him up off the ground the day you left him to die in the storm, Kaladin Stormblessed? Where was your compassion then?"

Wind gusted dust across the two of them as they stared eye to eye. "He was *actively* trying to kill Dalinar," Kaladin said.

"So *now* you hide behind the law and the orders you were given?" Nale turned toward Szeth. "Are you ready?"

"Yes," Szeth said.

"Wait," Kaladin said. "Ready for what?"

"The Lightweaver monastery," Nale said. "Where he will raise his Blade and defeat the Honorbearer."

Kaladin frowned, regarding the landscape of dusty ground and too-tall flowers. They'd been forced to double back, after visiting a second empty monastery the night before. Now he thought they were somewhere in the middle western portion of Shinovar. Near some mountains that bordered the western ocean. The . . . what had Szeth called it? The "big ocean"? No, that sounded silly. It was something like that though.

These western mountains here were lower than the ones on the east of Shinovar, without frosted points, and had more mesas than peaks. The hot weather made Kaladin sticky with sweat as he put his hand to his eyes and searched.

"I don't see it," he said.

"It's ahead, hidden by the natural shape of the landscape," Nale said. "You think the Lightweaver monastery would be *easy* to spot?"

Kaladin blushed, and glancing at Szeth, knew his arguments had failed. Szeth turned off the road and headed along a much smaller path to the side. He wouldn't meet Kaladin's gaze.

It was unfair that convincing someone depended not on the strength of ideas, but the strength of the arguer. Kaladin had always hated that, but again, he didn't have the eloquence to explain why. Instead he simmered as Szeth took up his weapon once more and—despite what he'd confessed he wanted—renewed his mission to kill.

⁂

Jasnah left the Thaylen strategy meeting with a gnawing anxiety, though the root cause eluded her. At least her outfit was serving its purpose. The uniform had nods to her gender, with a fitted bodice and a high-buttoning coat that was long in front and back, so it flowed a little like skirts, with trousers and boots underneath. With the accompanying gloves, she could fight in this without trouble.

She'd become a model for many women Radiants, and had to be aware—at all times—that she was being watched. Granted, that had always been true—but at least now some who watched took her as a positive example.

"The preparations," Ivory's voice said in her ear, "they *are* good, Jasnah. The defense *is*." He rode, as he often did, on her earring—she wore large seashell ones for him.

Behind her, other generals and admirals left the conference room, chattering together. After an entire day planning for the defense of Thaylen City, spirits were high. The Stonewards thought they could hide spikes of stone in the bay, to rip open hulls and sink ships. In addition, the artifabrians had developed counters to the Deepest Ones—fabrials that could identify any Fused who came too close. Those would give early warning if the enemy was attempting a surprise assault through the stone.

The Oathgate had been completely locked down, and Lightweavers waited in Shadesmar, hidden with their powers, watching for enemies there. Windrunners patrolled the air, and giant arbalests were pointed skyward to bring down Heavenly Ones. Indeed, this very morning, a special package had arrived: several gemstones of precious anti-Voidlight, capable of ending a Fused forever.

Thaylenah was as prepared as it possibly could be: the merchant city had essentially become a single giant fortress. With high cliffs to the sides—and no beachhead to allow access to the high ground behind—taking this port would be a nightmare.

As the enemy knew.

They came anyway.

Jasnah reached an open window looking out over the city from a vantage on the highest tier. Once, she might have found it restful here, with that blue shimmering ocean and the crisp, chill southern air. Today she was daunted. Because she *knew,* deep down, they were missing something vitally important.

"Jasnah?" Ivory said from her right ear. "What *is*?"

"I wish I knew," she whispered. "There is a mystery here, one that the generals and admirals cannot see."

Ivory considered her explanation, which was part of why they made an excellent pair. As an inkspren, he tended to fixate on the present—the situation as it was. It was a propensity, not an absolute, but he had found that assessing the situation as it *actually* stood was the best way to solve a problem.

Jasnah, on the other hand, tended to be focused on anything *but* the present. Understanding the past, and how it informed the future, was her mandate as a Veristitalian—the one group of scholars who had embraced her as a young woman, when all others had found her heresy too polarizing to touch. Past and future were wed, but sometimes focusing on that left her too removed from the now.

"Jasnah," Ivory said, "you are concerned that what we perceive is not the truth. That another reality *is.*"

"Yes," she said. "I am no expert in tactics, but I concur with what the generals, Radiants, and admirals are saying. The city is impregnable. So . . ."

"So you worry we are wrong." Ivory thought for a moment. "Perhaps what they need is not another general, Jasnah. Perhaps this time they need a scholar."

She immediately felt like a fool. If she was going to prove her value to this group, it wouldn't be through tactical acumen. She was better with military strategy than the average person, but the minds in that room were among the best in the world. She would have to spend years studying before she could be their equal.

But if she was right, this was a logic problem, not a military one. How did Odium break an unbreakable city?

She needed paper and a quiet space to think.

Immediately.

70
CONTEST OF ILLUSIONS

Both have as much detail as I can remember. My life. My reign. My sorrow. My glory.

—From the epilogue to *Oathbringer,* by Dalinar Kholin

Szeth had no particular affinity for the Lightweavers. Though he'd trained with their arts by requirement, he hated the way they made comedy out of truth, practically worshipping lies.

As he walked the final path to the monastery, however, he found himself wondering. He'd imagined Lightweavers as strange beings who turned the truth into whatever they wanted it to be. But perhaps re-forming the truth into what you wanted it to be was not a trait merely of liars, but of all human beings.

This smaller path off the main road descended a gradual slope. He walked it alongside Nin—or Nale, as he referred to himself—with Kaladin and Sylphrena behind. Szeth felt lonely. His spren had stopped talking to him except to issue stiff commands. Nightblood spent his days chatting with the Honorblades. Kaladin and Nale argued. Did they care about Szeth, or merely about proving one another wrong? Dared he think such thoughts about a holy being such as Nin-son-God?

Szeth glanced over his shoulder at the two men. Blue uniform and black. The man who had left him to die, and the man who had saved him. The man who claimed to care for Szeth, and the one who only cared about the law. A piece of him was angry at them both for pulling him between them.

Maybe that as well was simply life. To be pulled between two partial truths. Sivi had tried so hard to get him to accept that, and he'd always resisted. For if life was about partial truths as much as it was about singular ones, then all other aspects of his existence became extremely messy.

He wished dearly for the sweet, clean truths of Nin's path. Even if it required him to kill.

Szeth? Nightblood's voice. *Are you all right?*

"Sword-nimi?" Szeth whispered, shifting the group of swords on his back. He carried half, and Kaladin had the other half strapped to his pack. They were heavy—lighter than they should be, but not inconsequential. "No need for concern."

It's just . . . I felt something from you.

"Felt it?" Szeth said. "How can you feel what I do?"

I don't know. I feel close to you. You hurt.

"I always hurt."

Shouldn't that . . . go away? Human pains fade, don't they?

"I should very much like it to be so, sword-nimi. But I do not think I deserve such peace."

You said you weren't going to kill anymore.

"I should like that as well," Szeth said, turning right and starting down some steps that were hidden by the rolling brown landscape. Made of logs and stakes pounded into the earth, worn by time and footsteps, they led into a small ravine that opened up as two hills met, a stream cutting between them.

Szeth? the sword asked. *Are you evil?*

"Why do you ask?" he whispered. "Before, you said you were sure that I wasn't."

Well, I've been listening. More, I've been trying to remember, which is sometimes hard. You talk about the burdens you carry. The people you've killed. Innocents, you say. And . . . killing innocents is evil. Isn't it?

"Yes."

But when you saved Dalinar and the Radiants, that was good, wasn't it?

"I hope so."

I was created, and I was given a simple purpose. Destroy evil. I figured I would find the men who were evil and destroy them. That's what Nale wants, isn't it? To separate people into groups. Evil. Not evil.

"That is too simple, even for his philosophy," Szeth whispered, reaching the bottom of the steps. "He points out that all people are sometimes good, sometimes evil. It's impossible for us to separate the two—therefore, we need a guideline."

Shouldn't it be easy to tell what is good and evil?

"We all pretend that it is," Szeth said. "But if it were, then we would not disagree so much." He walked into the ravine, with water trickling in from the brook to his right. "We almost all agree on the basics. Killing an innocent is evil. But what if it's to save three innocents? What if you are an instrument, following what you thought was a higher law? What if you take a good action, it goes poorly, and innocents die?"

Those seem like uncommon cases.

"If only, sword-nimi. If only."

The ravine opened up to reveal the monastery. Cut into the rock, its stone face stained by the water dripping from above. Szeth had seen the chasms at the Shattered Plains, and this was different. For one, it was far more open to the sky. And while the stream here gave some fertility—letting small trees spring up—it wasn't filled with such a determined swelling of plant life as the chasms.

This was a quiet, contemplative corner in a windswept land. He studied it, and worried. Not just about his earlier concerns, but about the Voice. He knew he'd eventually have to face it. He thought that loosening its grip on his land, by killing the Honorbearers, was a good way to proceed. But when those battles were over, then what?

Could he fight an Unmade? Dalinar hadn't been able to. He'd had to defeat it through force of will, refusing the lure of the Thrill it offered—but also, as he'd described in his book, by acknowledging what they shared. Did something similar await Szeth?

He didn't know. Thus he did what he could; and that meant cleansing this land. He strode toward the monastery, which had—instead of a city or even a garrison to support it—only a few homes for keepers and servants. All empty, Szeth quickly determined.

Exiting one of them, he passed Kaladin and Nin. "Szeth," Kaladin said, trying to take him by the arm. "There must be another way."

Szeth stopped, allowing Kaladin to seize him—making the man feel silly for doing so, because he let go immediately.

"I do not ask if there is another way," Szeth said. "I do what is required." He unslung the pack of swords and handed it to Kaladin, then summoned his Blade and stepped into the monastery. Kaladin walked up to the doorway to watch, but Nin took him by the shoulder.

"He must fulfill the pilgrimage without your help, Windrunner," the Herald said. "Do not interfere."

The inside of this monastery was darker than the others. Lit by a skylight far above, in the roof of the three-story grand hall. A column of sunlight streamed down upon a group of thirty women standing in rows, wearing the same face.

Szeth halted in place, Shardblade out. Waiting. "Moss-son-Farrier?" he called. "I . . . would not fight you, if I do not have to."

"Then you should not have come in." Moss's voice echoed from farther in the chamber. "I had thought I'd never see you again, Szeth. I miss the old times between us."

Szeth hesitantly took a step forward. Those rows of people were all wearing the same colorful gown. They looked like . . .

Like the Herald, he thought. *Shush-daughter-God, the Lightweaver.*

Yes. He'd met the Herald in real life, and this was an approximation of her. These weren't thirty individual women, but thirty illusions of the monastery's patron Herald.

Sticking to the darkened perimeter of the room, Szeth crept closer. Each of the illusions looked identical to the others. All the figures stood perfectly still, gazing at him.

"Show yourself, Moss," Szeth said.

"I have," Moss replied, his voice coming from the ranks of illusory women. Szeth was watching the faces of those closest, and they did not speak. But . . . a skilled Lightweaver could warp and bend the air to create sound. "I am hidden before you, in this light, as one of these versions of Shush."

"Can't we simply duel?" Szeth said.

"Duel?" Moss said with a laugh. "You think I'd have any kind of chance, Szeth?"

Szeth continued to walk around the circle of light.

"You know we don't put much stock in fighting," Moss continued.

It was true. Sometimes, a Lightweaver was even chosen through a contest of illusions—though if one was as stubborn as Moss's predecessor had been, swordplay became needed. The Bondsmith Honorbearer also was chosen irregularly, by vote.

"So instead of a duel you make a game?" Szeth called. "One of your ridiculous puzzles?"

"My part ends when you pick one of me to kill," Moss said. "Almost all of the illusions before you are imperfect in some way. One is me, hidden behind a face that is instead perfect. Twenty-nine of those standing here are innocuous; one of those standing here is deadly. You cannot touch the illusions, and they will not reply to your questions.

"To win this test, you must choose a version of me, strike with your Blade through the eye, and kill me. Then you must escape my monastery with my Blade. Pick the wrong illusion to strike, and you lose. Touch them in any way, and you lose. If you fail, your pilgrimage ends, and you are deemed unworthy of the lofty position you seek. If you can win my Blade, you are worthy. This is your true test, Szeth-son-Neturo. Now is the last I will speak to you. Choose carefully."

Szeth sighed, dismissing his Shardblade for now. He trusted his mastery of the Blade against anyone other than a Herald, but his mind? He . . . did not trust that. No, not with those voices in the eaves.

He would have to do his best anyway. For it was what was required of him, and he did as he was required.

⁂

Venli led the way through the chasms of the Shattered Plains, guiding twenty of her people—and several chasmfiends, who followed farther behind—toward a hidden song she'd barely begun to be able to hear.

They'd entered the chasms from the east, a method she'd never used before. In the past, during her childhood, she'd always entered the chasms by jumping, or climbing from above, usually following Eshonai on some child's quest. She remembered those days with a smile. Back before she'd grown jealous of her sister, before Venli had been trapped memorizing songs while her sister wasted time.

She attuned Peace. That wasn't the right way to think of it, was it?

Venli paused at an intersection to look at her people trailing behind—a group that included several of her companions from Urithiru, who had left with her: Dul, Mazish, and Shumin. There was also a larger number of original listeners, and finally Leshwi and her Heavenly Ones. A calm stream flowed through the chasm, avoidable for the most part by walking next to the wall. The flow would probably grow more furious as they approached the storm, but she hoped it wouldn't become so bad they were forced out of the chasms. The Everstorm didn't dump nearly as much rain as the highstorm commonly did.

She spun and walked through a swarm of lifespren, passing a stone in the shape of a tree branch. A lonely stick had been ripped free in the wind and ended up here—where, over time, crem had coated it. Such shapes tended to be hollow—she could step on it and crack it straight through, because the original wood had rotted away, leaving this shell.

Thoughts could turn to stone the same way. In her memories, she'd been "forced" to sit and train—but how true was that? She'd practiced because she'd loved the songs, loved learning, and loved spending time with her mother. Her resentment was because she hadn't felt appreciated, not because of the work itself.

And her sister? Her sister had been doing what their people needed, even if Venli hadn't been able to recognize it. Continuing to nurture that nugget of resentment was like taking a stick and coating it in crem—if she wasn't careful, the truth would rot away inside. She'd be left with hollow lies.

 She instead brought to mind different memories: of beautiful evenings singing what she'd learned to Eshonai, both of them staring across the Shattered Plains and laughing together. Inwardly, she attuned Peace, and then Awe. She was in a wondrous location. She should enjoy this chasm and its vibrant ecosystem.

The thick, wet air reminded her of the first whiff of a cup of tea, fat with steam and the smell of herbs. Vines trailed down the sides of the chasm, and shalebark sprouted in a hundred vibrant varieties. The fan-shaped yellow ones to her right clung to the wall, each looking like a book that was being riffled open.

At her feet, cremlings scuttled among forests that had to be enormous to them, but that to Venli were each like a tiny diorama. The kind that Kunona used to make, each little piece of stone or tiny plant carefully arranged.

Kunona had . . . died during the birth of the Everstorm. Venli glanced up at the dark sky, visible through the slit top of the chasm high above. Red flashes reflected off clouds up there. By moving inward, they entered his domain.

She still heard that rhythm in the distance. The one she was following. The closer they drew, the better Venli could pick out the tone—somehow discordant, with a chaotic rhythm. To her right, a purple cremling sat atop a bulbous frond. It seemed to be watching her, and she hummed a happy rhythm to it.

Soon, Thude stepped up next to her, holding a gemstone for light, his foot crunching softly on a rotten log, the pieces getting caught in the current and floating back alongside the group. "Venli," he said to Anxiety. "Are you sure about this course? The Everstorm is that way."

"Likely parked and paused," she said. "He's done it before—moved the storm where he wants it to frighten and dominate the humans." She hesitated. "A battle is taking place there, Thude. Humans and singers fight over Narak. I told you what Rlain sent me? The contract the human king has with Odium, and the strange terms that let them keep what they gain these ten days?"

"So much blood spilled," Thude whispered to Mourning, "for a barren stretch of broken stone. The humans spent years murdering listeners there, and now others kill over it again."

She hummed to the Lost, and . . . found it sad how solemn he'd become. That was partially her fault.

Mostly her fault.

"I'm sorry, Thude," she whispered. "For everything."

"I keep thinking maybe she survived somehow, Venli. That someday Eshonai will walk back into our camp. When you first returned . . . I thought . . . I thought it was her. For just a moment. Is that foolish of me?"

"Hope is not foolish," she said, with a wince, "but Thude . . . I saw Eshonai's corpse. I'm sorry. I should have mentioned it. But you know Timbre was her spren first."

He glanced at her, humming to Appreciation. He wanted her to explain.

"I was sent with Demid," Venli said, "to collect my sister's Shards after she died. Thude, Odium didn't care about her. Eshonai was *disposable* to him. I think that's when I started to change. That day when we found her, and I realized all anyone cared about was her armor . . ."

Timbre thrummed inside her. Comforting. Then added something curious.

"Thude," Venli said, "Timbre says Eshonai wasn't *his* when she died. She'd broken free."

"She was stormform," Thude said. "Is that possible?"

"I was able to do it, but only with Timbre's help. Timbre says . . . Eshonai did it too. She cast him out of her mind and was herself when she died. We *can* fight him."

Behind the line of listeners, she could see one of the larger shadows prowling the chasm. They had insisted on coming. Five chasmfiends, including the one everyone called Thundercloud, their leader. Or he was the first who had decided not to fight any longer—and when the largest and most dangerous of them decided the little things on the Shattered Plains had defeated him, the others had followed.

"Perhaps we can do something," Venli said, "about the conflict happening ahead of us, Thude. Perhaps we *should* join the fighting, as I suggested before."

"*No.*"

She held up a gemstone to illuminate his face.

"Venli," he said, "we *will not* fight. I've decided to trust you again, but you do not lead us. We number barely a thousand adults. The chasmfiends' numbers are worse. Not much more than a hundred individuals? I get the sense that they are dwindling fast. They will have difficulty breeding if too many more die. We *will* stay out of this fight."

"Our numbers are my fault. If I hadn't—"

"Venli, I can't believe I'm saying this, but . . . let go. It's done. We all regret what happened. But . . . an evil god was bent on our destruction. I'm trying not to hate you. It will help us both if we can *move on.*"

She sighed, but he was right—both about her, and about not fighting. She doubted they'd ever have gone with her on this trek if the spren hadn't spoken and the chasmfiends hadn't confirmed the existence of that strange tone.

"No fighting," she said to Thude. "I'm glad you and the Five came. Any decision we make, of course, will be yours."

He hummed to Determination. They'd left Jaxlim behind, as she and Venli—as keepers of the songs—couldn't both be risked at the same time. But all of the Five had come, after appointing others to take their places if they didn't return. Venli couldn't help thinking that they'd done the same thing when they'd first gone to visit the humans. During that fateful trip, they'd killed Gavilar and started this mess.

She attuned Peace and struck out again, hoping she wasn't running toward a similar cataclysm. It would still take a great while to reach the center, hiking through these twisting chasms in secret—but traveling the plateaus above would be suicide, with Heavenly Ones and Windrunners patrolling.

Only down here were they safe, within the darkness and the writhing plants. Creeping ever inward, like cremlings moving through the underbrush.

It is not my goal to begin a new religion, or to inspire a division in Vorinism. However, I insist that when I was at my darkest moments, there was something there with me, and it was not the being we called the Almighty. He is dead. And even if he were not, I would find his actions increasingly suspect.

—From the epilogue to *Oathbringer*, by Dalinar Kholin

Szeth finished his circuit of the pool of light in the Lightweaver monastery, calm sun from above falling on those thirty illusory figures. How would *he* pick out the right one? Looking closely, he spotted tiny differences between the figures: hair parted differently, eyes different colors, sashes on dresses forming different bows.

He studied each one, and sweat began to drip down his face. He couldn't tell which was "perfect" and which was not. Storms . . . how could he ever beat a Lightweaver at their own tricks? He could come to only one conclusion. He should strike randomly and trust in fate. He summoned his Blade, and knew he would fail.

"Hmmm . . ." a feminine voice said in his ear.

He glanced to the side and saw nothing.

"Yeah," Syl whispered, "tricky Lightweavers with their tricky ways. Well, if your spren won't help, I will."

"You . . . shouldn't be here," Szeth whispered.

"Nale said Kaladin can't help you, but he didn't say anything about *me.* I'm a god, aren't I? Piece of one?"

"Of course."

"Do you not pray to gods for help?"

"Yes."

"So . . ."

He thought barely a moment. "Will you please help?"

"Gladly," she whispered. "Keep your voice down, don't mention my name, and let them assume you're talking to your spren."

"Follow the rules though. Don't touch them."

"Fine, fine. Let's walk along this row here. Hmmm . . . They're each different. Just barely."

"We're to find which one is perfect. But how do we know which is the 'perfect' representation of a Herald? Half have green eyes, half have violet."

"Exactly half and half?"

He considered, then counted. "Sixteen violet. Fourteen green."

"That seems deliberate. Can we infer something from that? Quick, count how many have their hair parted on the left, and how many on the right."

He did so. Again sixteen and fourteen. Same with bows—sixteen tied in an extravagant knot, fourteen in a simple one.

"So," Syl said, "do we think the 'correct' Ash will have the more common trait, or the less common one?"

"Perfection is rare," he said, "so the less common one?"

He disliked guessing when it involved something this important . . . but he supposed he'd been ready to strike randomly. Syl's aid eased his tension, and he found himself exceptionally grateful for it. Together the two talked it over, and through a process of elimination found one version of Shush who had each of the most rare traits. Green eyes, part on the left, bow a simple knot, ring on her finger . . . all the way through the various attributes.

They stopped in front of this one, the third from the left in the back row. Szeth prepared his sword.

Then hesitated. What was wrong?

"Does this . . ." Syl said in his ear, "feel too easy to you?"

"It does."

"Do you know much about the person who set this up?"

"Yes."

"And what kind of person are they?"

"Too smart," Szeth said. "And sure of their cleverness. Like most Lightweavers I've met."

Syl thought a moment. "Yeah, there's a zero percent chance we solved the riddle this easily. I'd bet my left ear—I've never liked that one—that we are *supposed* to choose this illusion. Not because it's right, but because it's the most obvious choice."

"Then what do we do?" Szeth whispered.

"We need to go a layer deeper," Syl said. "We need to discard obvious choices."

"Then how will we ever know?" Szeth asked, walking to the end of the row, then peering down the line of near-identical versions of the demigod. "Moss is smarter than I am. He'll have considered every option."

"I'm thinking . . ."

"Their faces have small moles," Szeth said, walking back down the line. "Maybe we find the one without such a blemish? Except I find that too obvious as well."

"Yeah," Syl said, "and not even really accurate. What about a mole makes someone less perfect? That's another way for us to *assume* we've cracked the code, only to lose. I think."

Her uncertainty mirrored his own. Whatever solution he pondered . . . it seemed flimsy, surface-level. Finding the one Shush who was out of step with the others? Finding the one that had her head straight, when others were cocked slightly? Any of these *could* be the solution, but how did that make them intrinsically any less perfect?

Knowing Moss . . .

"He'll want to win no matter what choice I make," Szeth said. "That's the kind of puzzle this is, isn't it? The kind he can't lose, no matter which option I choose."

"Aaaah . . ." Syl said. "You're almost certainly right, Szeth. What exactly did he say at the start?"

"He said almost all of the illusions were imperfect in some way. But one was him, hidden behind a face that was instead perfect." He paused. "He also said he was in the circle of light, so he's not hiding somewhere else in the room."

"Yeah," Syl said. "He wouldn't lie, because that would look like cheating. It's not a riddle if you couldn't conceivably find the answer. Hmm . . . just a second." A moment later she said, "Fly up above them, Szeth. Let's see if they make an interesting pattern."

He Lashed himself into the air, in front of the skylight, casting a shadow on those below. Together he and Syl studied the array of five rows of six.

"I don't see anything," Szeth said.

"You trained with this Lightweaver, didn't you? Is there some clue in your training?"

"It was a long time ago," Szeth said. "And I was never very good at it." Yet it would be just like Moss to reference some idle bit of instruction, these many years later. "I was taught," he said after mulling it over, "that one theme of Lightweaving is subterfuge. It's not about perfection, as no illusion *can* be perfect. He and I agreed on that. So *all* of those illusions are imperfect, by their nature."

"But he stated he was one of the figures," Syl said.

"Well, he said he was hiding behind one of the versions of Shush. 'One is me, hidden behind a face that is instead perfect . . .'"

He gazed down from this lofty position, and saw it. As in the other monasteries, there was an old mural on the floor depicting one of the Heralds. Here, the face of Shush. Set upon stone. That which was perfect.

"Storms," Syl said. "The floor!"

Szeth needed no further proof. He summoned his Blade and dropped, stabbing straight into the floor tiles, right through the eye.

"Szeth!" Syl said in his ear. "That was impulsive!"

"You saw it as I did," he said, watching as the Lightweavings of the figures broke apart, revealing a group of exhausted, bleary-eyed, and somewhat dazed acolytes.

Acolytes? Szeth thought. *He used people behind the faces of Shush? Why?* That seemed particularly brutal of Moss. If Szeth *had* struck one of those, he'd have killed them.

"We could have talked it through or something," Syl said, remaining invisible as she spoke into his ear.

"And given him time to realize we'd figured it out?" Szeth said, looking down at the floor—which he sliced apart, opening a dug-out section in the stone beneath the mural. Moss's clothing lay inside; upon being stabbed, he'd evaporated into darkness like the others, leaving his Blade. Szeth cut through enough stone to pick that up: a Blade with wave patterns along the back, and a round hole in the pommel.

"I still think it was a little brash," Syl said.

"Sometimes," Szeth said, hefting the sword, "you simply have to make a decision."

As Kaladin and Nin approached, he realized that those words were absolutely true.

⁂

Jasnah found a peaceful place to think in an unlikely location. A temple.

When her uncle, Dalinar, had been in this city, he'd used his powers to restore an ancient temple. Jasnah still didn't understand how he'd managed it; the Bondsmith powers worked so *oddly.* Granted, each Radiant order was proving that their specific applications of the Surges could be unusual, but Bondsmiths were on another level entirely.

The restored temple to Talenelat was now viewed as a holy site beyond even others in Thaylen City, and it was reserved for Radiants to use. As her rooms in the city had, by her request, been placed near those of the other generals . . . well, if she wanted somewhere quiet, this was perfect. No one would bother her in this solemn circular chamber, decorated with murals and stone glyphwards praising the Almighty.

Jasnah set up at the rear of the chamber, between two pillars and near a relief depicting Taln, the Bearer of Agonies. They mostly got his features right. A surgical table and chairs had been placed here, as this room was used for healings when an Edgedancer or Truthwatcher was in the city.

She set her notebooks and papers on the surgical table, but did not sit. An electric current seemed to run through her, like the kind one could create with that old experiment using brine-soaked cloths and different kinds of metals. Caged lightning. During a scientific summit in her youth, she'd seen a researcher use that process to make the muscles of a cremling twitch after it was dead.

She walked around the surgery table, her mind buzzing. Odium *knew* this city could not be broken without extreme loss of life. Indeed, even *with* extreme loss of life, he would almost certainly fail here. Thaylen City was barely worth attacking. Yet he was coming with large numbers, and was giving himself only a couple of days to capture the city.

What was she missing?

What were they all missing?

Ivory grew to full size, hand on his dueling sword, watching her with obvious amusement. He stood by the doors, lounging—a figure entirely of inky-black marble, with an oil-on-water iridescence when the light hit just right.

He gave her space and quiet to think. Unfortunately, now that she was here . . . she found answers elusive. She wrote down logical questions to consider, as prescribed by her formal training, drawing a swarm of logicspren like little thunderclouds.

Each idea led to answers that felt wrong. Emotional Core Theory taught her to look toward what drove participants: What emotions might be causing them to act as they did? Was there an intangible, emotional reason that Odium wanted this city? Perhaps failing to take it a year ago still rankled, and so he'd come for vengeance.

Yet this was a new Odium—and while the power might want vengeance, who knew what the new Vessel wanted? She was on shaky ground to assume she could reason their motives. Plus, she'd never liked assuming that her opponents were making mistakes. Yes, it was important to recognize and exploit missteps, but underestimating foes was a bad habit that led to worse surprises. If you instead assumed your enemies were making the *right* decisions—and you countered them anyway—then you were often led to important realizations.

Assuming competence from her enemy, what was her next step? Perhaps formalist theory: lay out your premises and try to construct the next logical move. However, that felt too much like what they'd been doing with the generals—they could plan for eventualities better than she could. She needed to uncover what they *weren't* seeing.

This led her to economic theory. It taught her to follow the incentives. Were there intangibles to be gained by attacking here? Storms. Was Odium simply diverting their forces? Drawing their limited resources away from battles that could be lost, instead committing them to a fight they were already likely to win?

That seemed a useful hypothesis. She sat and explored it, writing notes, as logicspren swirled around her hand. Fen was one of their two strongest allies. She was also loud and brash, and *demanded* help for a city that had already been through so much. The coalition *was* more likely to devote resources to Thaylen City so that it didn't have to rebuild a second time. Yes . . . all this could lead them to *overcommit* to defending this city.

Could this attack *actually* be a way to make certain the other two assault points—Azimir and the Shattered Plains—were denied resources? Here, she found problems with her premise. If your goal was merely to divert forces from other battles, then why would you divert your *own* forces in the same way?

Perhaps these were troops that couldn't be used elsewhere? No . . . those forces could have sailed through Shadesmar to Azimir, right? Maybe there weren't mandras available to pull ships that far in time? And what about the Shattered Plains? With the Everstorm blowing them, could the enemy have delivered these troops to that battlefield in time?

She did calculations, and felt she might be on to something. But after an hour of thinking, looking up numbers, and writing out her thoughts . . . she was beginning to hit a wall.

"Ivory," she said, "distract me."

He was used to this. "A temple," he said from where he stood at full size near the doorway. "You come to a *temple* to think?"

"It's quiet. And beautiful."

"Even after all these years," he said, "I do not always understand the person you are, Jasnah. Shouldn't this place make you angry? You deny the divinity at the very foundation of its religion. You deny the faith of the people who built it."

"Small quibble," she said, "but I do not deny that the people who built this had faith. Nor do I deny that faith's power to inspire."

"But you are in opposition to their god."

"A larger quibble," she said. "I'm not in opposition to their god, because their god—as they imagine him, all-powerful and all-knowing—does not exist. I can no more be in opposition to that than I am to an imaginary childhood friend—you cannot wrestle with, fight, or oppose something that does not exist. I oppose the *assumptions* that people make. Because if you start with faulty assumptions . . ."

Well, Damnation.

Faulty assumptions.

She'd forgotten a basic tenet of any logical dissection: examine your premises. What were hers? She held up a finger to stall Ivory, who—again—was used to this sort of thing.

Premise One: That Odium truly wanted to take this city. That appeared reasonable, from all they knew.

Premise Two: That the city was well-defended. This seemed a strong premise—at least, she trusted the admirals and generals.

What else? What was she missing?

It hit her like thunder.

Premise Three: she wrote. *That there are actually storming troops coming this way.*

In a cold sweat, she saw their mistake. Ships coming this direction didn't mean troops. Even if scout reports had seen people crowding the decks, implying far more people underneath . . . that didn't mean there were *troops* on the way. Fen had been shocked the enemy had been able to raise an army to assault her city. What if he *hadn't*? What if he had ships—the navy from Vedenar, and stolen ships from Thaylen City itself—and people to dress up in costumes . . . but no actual troops? What would he do in that situation?

He'd send a fleet this way. Slowly. To make his enemies dig in, divert resources . . . and wait for an army that *wasn't really coming.*

She stood up, her eyes wide.

"You have it," Ivory said. "The answer *is*?"

"The *hypothesis* is. I need our Windrunner scouts to do something potentially dangerous, but potentially vital." She looked up. "I need them to get very, very close to those ships."

72

STATISTICALLY DANGEROUS

I realize this is, in a way, ridiculous. I, who proclaim a god to be dead, am also the one who rejects the idea that no God exists. And yet my very being—soul, mind, body—rebels at the idea that nothing out there cares. It must.

—From the epilogue to *Oathbringer*, by Dalinar Kholin

While Szeth recovered some gemstones from a stash here in the monastery, Sylphrena appeared again beside Kaladin—human size, because it felt right. She regarded the collection of acolytes who had been standing with illusions over them. People. Moss had used real people in his test. How unnecessarily cruel. Illusions didn't need a person to stick to; Shallan made them freestanding all the time.

Once Szeth returned with the infused gemstones, Syl floated with him and Kaladin out to the front of the monastery. There, Nale glanced at her. Glared? He wasn't frowning. Could you glare without a frown? Perhaps she should ask some angerspren.

She smiled at Nale. Sweetly, because a little sweetness enhanced basically any situation. Especially the ones where it made someone annoyed.

Szeth studied his newly won Honorblade, pausing on the stone porch outside the monastery. Behind, in the hall, the poor acolytes began to stumble and hug one another, freed from the darkness. Kaladin squatted by Szeth as he unwrapped their increasingly bulky pack of swords, then slid this new one in among them—and Nightblood quietly asked it if it could become dull for their travels.

"I'm impressed," Kaladin said to Szeth. "How did you figure out that riddle?"

"I had the blessings of the spren," Szeth said.

Nale—standing with hands clasped behind himself like a giant stone statue—glared at her even more intently. How strange, this feeling. That of perking up beneath a glare. Ruining that man's day was basically the *best thing ever.*

Except . . . why did her mind keep drifting back to that oddity of using servants behind the illusions? Stupid brain. It couldn't let go of ideas sometimes, and other times it was so full of silly ideas, it couldn't pick one.

Szeth had won.

Except . . .

To win this test, the Lightweaver had said, *you must choose a version of me, strike with your Blade through the eye, and kill me. Then you must escape my monastery with my Blade.*

Then you must escape with my Blade . . .

"Well," Kaladin said. "I'm glad it wasn't me in there. I think I'd have gone mad."

"No," Syl said, forcing herself back to the moment, and crouched down beside him near the Blades. "*Your* spren would have helped you. Which is how the bond is *supposed* to work. We both give, and we both get. A symbiosis, like the pictures that Shallan showed me of cremlings."

"What do cremlings have to do with this?" Kaladin said, frowning.

"Everything," Syl said.

Szeth tied the bundle of cloth-wrapped swords, then stood up as people began to flood out of the monastery, falling to their knees, weeping. As in other places they'd visited. It felt more . . . intimate here, in this little chasm-like ravine, with the stream trickling behind Nale.

These people surrounded Szeth on the open rock patio in front of the monastery. A location that felt a lot like ordinary Roshar, with stone on the ground, almost no mud or dirt. A holy place, although why the spren of *rocks* got so much devotion here was beyond her. Rock spren were almost as stupid as stick spren, and that was saying something.

Though the stone itself has ancient memories, she thought. *Of a land that once knew the touch of neither human nor singer . . .*

Kaladin stood up, smiling at Szeth. He liked this part, she knew, because it reminded Szeth that he was fighting *for* something. Because ideals were stupid unless there were people behind them. So strange that an entire order of Radiants didn't understand that.

Syl wanted to flit off into the air and go looking for lifespren, as she thought some might be here in this almost-right place with the stream and the trees.

But her *brain.* Her stupid brain.

Her brain kept thinking about Moss. He'd thought himself so smart, and now he was dead. So there.

Her brain latched on. Like with jaws.

Holding. Tight. Squeezing.

Twenty-nine of those standing here are innocuous; one of those standing here is deadly. Twenty-nine posed no threat, but one of those *standing* was deadly. The Lightweaver *hadn't* been standing; he'd been lying down.

She looked at Szeth, with his too-shiny, too-hairless head. Twenty-nine of the people standing weren't dangerous . . . but was one of them deadly still? Someone who made a riddle like this seemed the type who would try to get the wording exactly right. Would he also be the type to hide *two* riddles in one?

This is your true test . . .

Syl bolted upright, then grabbed Kaladin by the arm. Actually *grabbed* him. With full force.

He glanced at her, shocked.

"Kaladin," Syl hissed. "One of those acolytes is going to try to kill Szeth."

He blinked, took it in.

And trusted her.

Without a moment's hesitation, Kaladin summoned the spear. She went, her substance flowing into the weapon, her awareness becoming his. In those moments she overlapped with him, saw through his eyes. It wasn't exact. She had an awareness that wasn't precisely his.

Never were they closer than in these moments when Kaladin—bless him—just trusted her. He took the spear in two hands and saw it. A flash in the air as one of the people fawning over Szeth—a matronly woman—summoned a Blade, raised her arms to strike at Szeth's back . . .

And was speared straight through the ear by Kaladin.

Her eyes burned and she collapsed. Around them, people cried out and scattered.

Szeth, belatedly, spun around.

"Cheating," Nale said, his voice calm. "The Windrunner has helped you."

Szeth stared at the dead woman, who evaporated into smoke. He knelt reverently and picked up her Blade: long and curved, with an intricate design near the hilt. "The Truthwatcher Honorbearer? I don't know her. What of Vambra-daughter-Skies? She was so young . . ."

Szeth blinked, then looked to Kaladin, who looked to Syl, who appeared full sized as Kaladin dismissed his spear.

"Two Honorbearers attacked you last time," she said. "And so I thought, 'Huh. Why would they send only one this time?' And then I thought, 'Szeth's head is funny without hair.' But *then* I thought, 'Hey. The Lightweaver said that *twenty-nine* of the illusions standing there weren't dangerous.' And . . . um . . . the rest just fell into place." She shrugged.

"You knew about this?" Kaladin said, spinning toward Nale.

"A difficult challenge will be set before Szeth-son-Neturo once his pilgrimage is done," Nale said, not moving. "We need to know he is capable."

"What challenge?" Kaladin demanded.

"It doesn't matter," Nale said. "He cheated by receiving your help. The rules have been violated."

"What rules?" Szeth said softly.

Syl turned slowly, Kaladin doing likewise, to where Szeth knelt holding the new Honorblade. The air was strangely quiet, now that the servants of the monastery had fled. Szeth looked up and met Nale's eyes.

"What rules did I violate," Szeth said, "Nin-son-God?"

"The rules of pilgrimage."

"When Pozen drew me into Shadesmar . . ." Szeth whispered, "I *asked* about the rules. He said that there are no set rules for this challenge. If there were, I could not have been attacked by two Honorbearers at a time. Correct?"

Nale did not reply.

"Nor could I have been attacked outside the boundaries of the monastery itself." Szeth stood and nodded to Kaladin. "This man has been assigned to help me. As he did his job, and since there *are* no rules for this pilgrimage . . . I do not see how any could have been violated. Sir."

Syl whistled softly at the complete lack of emotion in Szeth's voice. The two faced one another, black uniform and white. Until Nale spoke.

"You are correct and I was wrong," Nale said. "The pilgrimage continues. Bear your prizes with pride. Come. We will visit the Truthwatcher monastery as a formality, then continue to the final three. They will be the most difficult for you, each a unique test."

"That's it?" Syl demanded, a fury rising within. She wasn't a windspren, but she sure could feel like a storm when she wanted. "That's *it*?"

"What more do you want when a man is wrong?" Nale asked, calm, then turned and walked toward the steps.

Syl started toward him, but stopped as Kaladin caught her eyes and shook his head. So she let the storming man go. Szeth carefully wrapped the newest sword—making *six* of them they'd captured so far—with Kaladin's pack instead. But . . .

"Wait," she said. "Three more monasteries, not counting Truthwatcher, since we have that sword already. Does that add up? We have six swords, but shouldn't there be ten overall?"

"The Windrunner Honorblade has been corrupted," Nale called from ahead. He turned and glided up into the air instead of climbing the steps.

"Our king, Jezrien, was killed by the Windrunner traitor, Vyre. Odium took his Honorblade unto himself in that moment, corrupting it." He stepped onto the hilltop and strode out of sight.

"Huh," Syl said, looking at the two boys. "Did either of you know that?"

"Some of it," Kaladin said. "Not the corrupting part."

"I did not ask, nor do I care," Szeth said, walking past them to the steps. Then, remarkably, he halted and came back. "I do appreciate your help. Both of you."

He jogged to catch up to Nale. Syl folded her arms. *She* could feel her arms. Like she could feel her toes rub together when she had toes. She was always solid to herself.

She glanced at Kaladin, who was shaking his head. "I know," he said to her. "I feel it too."

"Your toes rubbing together?" she asked, cocking her head.

"My . . . what? No, Syl, *frustration.* Nale is infuriating. He doesn't actually follow the law—he changes his perceptions, motivations, and even morals at the drop of a sphere. He acts like he's made of iron, but the moment he's confronted with a logical inconsistency, he either changes the conversation or walks away."

"Kaladin, I think he's as close to broken as Taln or Ash . . . maybe even more."

"We only have *four days* until the contest." He paused. "I'm . . . really not going to find Ishar in time to help Dalinar, am I? I'm not going to be back in time to see the contest. Wit was . . . Wit was right, wasn't he?"

"I'm afraid he was," Syl said. "But there's a purpose for you here. Wit said so."

Kaladin looked up. "The Wind said I have to do something important . . . maybe more important than the contest. At least in her opinion. But what could that possibly be?"

"Restoring Ishar, perhaps?" she said.

"Dalinar said," Kaladin whispered, "that an oath sworn at the right time might change Ishar." He took a deep breath, and his eyes focused on Szeth climbing the steps. "But more and more, I find myself worrying only about Szeth. Too much. Syl, it's taking me over again. I went from being annoyed by him to hurting over how incapable I am of helping him. Just like with Bridge Four . . . I start feeling isolated, like I will be the only one who survives, when everyone else withers away . . ."

She took his arm, and with effort and concentration, made imprints in his uniform with her fingers. He saw that and smiled.

"We're on a journey," she said. "Between who we were, and who we want to be. Both of us."

"I'm not sure what I'm supposed to do, though."

"What is it you keep telling Szeth about what *he* needs to be doing? That following orders or laws slavishly isn't as important as finding your own path?"

"Fine, you're right. As usual."

"Don't say it that way."

"Because?"

"Because I want to be right only when I'm right, not because it's expected. That's part of *my* journey, Kaladin."

"To live for yourself, not only for others," he said, "all while somehow still wanting to help me."

"The same way you need to protect—but not make that *everything* about you."

"I need to help without being obsessed." He focused on Syl. "You truly are brilliant. Not with this alone, but with helping Szeth. You're incredible, Syl."

There. She'd been *waiting* for that. She lifted a few inches off the ground.

But don't do it just for him, she told herself. *Do it because it's what you want.*

"We find our balance, then," Kaladin said. "Somehow." He took a deep breath, heaved out a sigh—and took to the air to follow the other two.

⁂

Shallan paced the confines of her rooms—in the Sebarial warcamp—at the Shattered Plains. Like the previous times they'd created one of these little enclaves in the Spiritual Realm, color bled and the setting didn't feel quite real. Rlain and Renarin were at her sitting room table, and natural light shone in from the window in her bedroom. She'd snuck out through that window on multiple occasions when first infiltrating the Ghostbloods.

Unlike the other two, Shallan—with Glys's help—had formed a waiting area that was not her childhood bedroom. That was categorically good for them all. Though she was largely doing better, if they tried to visit *that* memory, they'd end up in a room with white carpet made red—and at least one corpse.

"It's strange," Renarin said. "I'm not tired or hungry. Glys can't tell me how long this has taken, but we must have been in the Spiritual Realm for at *least* ten hours."

"Tumi is the same," Rlain said. "I think time is too nebulous to them. He tends to think in terms of what has been, and what will be, but not about the time frame of either."

Renarin tapped the table with one finger. "Aunt Navani's scholars say that matter, energy, and Stormlight are the same thing—just different states. This place seems to be made up entirely of Stormlight, or Investiture, or whatever. When we entered, did *we* become Stormlight as well? If so, what will happen with our bodies when we exit?"

"I guess . . ." Rlain said. "I guess we'll re-form?"

"Assuming that is true," Renarin said, glancing at her, "could we bring things with us? Re-form them from their spiritual aspect? What could we create if we mastered this place?"

It was a valid question, but one Shallan couldn't focus on. She continued pacing.

"Still worried," Rlain guessed, "about how to kill the Ghostbloods?"

"I'm a fool," Shallan said. "Killing them here will be virtually impossible. They can heal, and there's Stormlight all around. I thought anti-Light must be dangerous—but it didn't hurt him, exactly like it didn't hurt me."

"Glys says . . ." Renarin cocked his head. The spren was invisible, hiding within him, as it sometimes did. A habit that Pattern always found fascinating. "Glys says that human souls are made of Investiture, but usually not in enough concentration to react to the anti-Light."

"What?" Shallan asked, hurrying over to him. "You know something? What did he say?"

"He says their spren will be hurt by it," Renarin admitted, looking away from her. "So . . . you could kill their spren, or seriously wound them, maybe. Might be tough to isolate them though, if they're hiding inside a body."

"I thought," Rlain said to a slow, calm rhythm, "that Glys and Tumi were his. Voidlight."

"They're a mix," Renarin said. "Glys says . . . something about a Rhythm of War . . ." He shook his head. "Is Tumi equally callous? About us killing his brothers or sisters?"

"We kill other humans all the time," Shallan said, with a shrug.

"We don't!" Renarin said, then blushed. "I mean, I don't . . . Still, I do find all of this fascinating. Light. Anti-Light. Investiture. Energy."

"Is that why your father always wanted you to be an ardent?" Rlain said to the Rhythm of Curiosity. "This way of asking questions and thinking such interesting thoughts?"

"Yeah," Renarin said. "I don't know if I refused just so I could resist what was expected, or if becoming an ardent felt like giving up on my father's hopes for me when I was young."

"You don't have to live up to anyone's expectations, Renarin," Shallan said, stopping near him, the strangely saturated light spilling in through the window over her.

"I know," he said. "We always say things like that, Shallan, those of us on the outside. It's true enough. I *don't* have to conform, become a warrior and a highprince the way everyone expects of my father's sons. Yet I worry that in our zeal, we forget that merely because something *is* more standard or conventional, that doesn't make it *bad.*

"My values are shaped by those around me, whom I respect. That makes it impossible to separate what my father wants of me from what I want for myself—his ideals have in large part become my ideals. To try to separate myself *completely* from those influences would *also* be a rejection of who I am. And . . . I'm doing it again. Getting lost in my own thoughts." He looked to Rlain for support.

"I find this aspect of you to be fascinating," Rlain said. "I've never really considered where I got my ideals." He put his hand on the table, close to Renarin's.

Do not, Shallan thought at herself, *get distracted by their flirting.* She had to save the world. She left them for the moment, approaching Pattern, who stood in the doorway to the bedroom. "Those two," she said as she passed, "are way too distracted."

"Mmm . . ." Pattern said.

"Don't you start."

"Start what? I have nothing at all to say about a budding young Radiant being distracted from important events by romantic dalliances. Nothing at all."

She halted at the window. "You're getting better at sarcasm."

"Thank you!" he replied. "Ahem. At least Renarin has only picked one person to be distracted by . . ."

Shallan rolled her eyes. In response, Pattern spun his pattern in a wild sequence, new lines and curves emerging in a transfixing flow. Well, storms. Now he was better at rolling his eyes than she was? Adolin had better not find out, or she'd never live it down.

Storms, Adolin.

These rooms reminded her of him—of practicing with the sword under his tutelage. Of his passion for the art, and his growing passion for her.

"Is there any way," she said, "to know if he's safe out there, Pattern? I'm worried about him, in Azimir."

"I do not know," Pattern said softly. "I'm sorry."

It was silly to miss him already. She hadn't even been in here . . . what? Half a day? He probably hadn't seen battle yet. Still, she would have felt a lot better if he were here to hold.

She turned toward Pattern again. "It worries me how Mraize fooled us by taking Honor's form. That could have easily gotten us killed. Plus, I'm concerned about what Iyatil is plotting."

"Mmm . . . do you think she has a graph, or . . ."

"She might be letting Mraize distract us. If so, he does it well—and constantly outmaneuvers me." She pulled out the anti-Stormlight knife. If she could get to their spren . . . It was awful to contemplate. And yet, they were enemy combatants.

She stalked back into the other room. "Have any of you seen Mraize's spren when we interact?"

Rlain cocked his head. "Tumi says . . . he has had impressions of the spren watching from outside. But in here it's hard to find someone who doesn't want to be found. Particularly a spren."

"They'll be shy, like ours."

Shallan gazed down at the dagger—which didn't split into colors, like a lot of this vision. Instead it caused a little eddy around it, warping the air like a puncture in reality. A thought occurred to her. "Maybe I don't have to hurt them—maybe I can use this on Mraize. I didn't dare heal when I had anti-Light in my system. Mraize didn't either, earlier. So I simply have to wound him badly enough that he can't wait out the anti-Light evaporating from him."

"Glys says that might work," Renarin said, nodding. "If he pulls in Stormlight to heal, and it meets anti-Light . . . that will be deadly."

She nodded firmly. "Unfortunately, Mraize is a better fighter than I am."

"You did pretty well against him during the last fight, Shallan," Rlain said with a praising rhythm.

"I did, but that fight could just as easily have gone the other way—and I was lucky to *be able* to fight him. If he'd managed to stab me in the back when I wasn't looking, that could have been it. I wish we could get the drop on him for once."

"How would we manage that?" Renarin asked.

"What if," Rlain said, "instead of entering the visions directly, we sent in some kind of avatar—and we watched from outside?"

"Yes!" Shallan said. "Last time after leaving, I could kind of make out what was happening in the vision, and Lightweaving is 'quiet.' It won't draw the attention of the gods that hunt your spren. We could watch the Ghostbloods, then strike when *we* have the upper hand."

The two glanced at each other, and were probably communicating with their spren. Shallan glanced back toward Pattern, who had been joined by Testament—the other Cryptic had been lying on the overstuffed bed. Shallan remembered how lavish these quarters had felt when she'd first arrived.

She no longer saw such a bed as wasted on her. Relaxation was something she had earned, and she should enjoy it during the rare occasions when she wasn't running into danger. It was all right for her to enjoy a little luxury in life. The same way it was all right for her to be happy with Adolin, and appreciate his love.

She really was feeling better. Except . . . on the writing desk by the doorway were a handful of spheres without gemstones. Ends, used for gambling for no stakes—or in this case, for learning sleight of hand. Tyn had given them to her. More by instinct than conscious thought, Shallan walked over and palmed several of the spheres, replacing them with ones from her pocket. Then she did it again, a quick move while bumping into the desk, or while raising her other hand as a distraction.

Pattern stepped over and put his long-fingered hand on her shoulder.

"Formless speaks of each person I've killed, people who took me in and trusted me," Shallan whispered. "It feels . . . horrible when I see it in its whole context, Pattern. Mother, Father, Testament, Tyn . . . Next, Mraize. How many people who get close to me will I end up killing? Why does it happen so often to me?"

"I do not know, Shallan," he whispered. "But as I have come to know humans better, I can tell you this: you are *awful* at statistics."

"Is that supposed to be comforting?"

"Yes!" he said. "You are so deeply flawed in your understanding of numbers. It is in fact quite inspiring, yes."

"I . . . need a little help, Pattern," she said. "Understanding what in *Damnation* you're talking about."

"You are so bad at math!"

"Don't say that, Pattern," she replied. "My name, at least, is parallel. That's a mathematical concept."

". . . Your name?"

"Yes."

"Parallel?"

"Shallan," she said. "Two 'l's. Pair'a'els."

His pattern froze. Then, remarkably, he let out a loud guffaw. "That was actually funny!"

"Data point," Renarin said from the couch. "No it was not. It *really* was not."

"Ha ha!" Pattern said. "He is stupid. Listen, you are all stupid about numbers. You do well, for those with brains made of meat, but you think of everything wrong." He pulled her from the room again and leaned closer. "Of all the people you've known, Shallan, how many have you killed? A few?"

"The important ones."

"Adolin?" he asked. "Dalinar, Navani? The brothers you protected—and even if we are speaking solely of mentors, Sebarial and Palona still live despite their best efforts. And Jasnah. Hmmmm? You are *not* statistically dangerous to those around you. *Only* to those who try to *kill* you."

"Testament," she whispered.

"You are working to repair that error," Pattern said. "Shallan, it is my job to help and protect you. I do a bad job sometimes! But today, let me promise: in you, I have found someone *sincere.* That is what attracted me—your sincerity and your lies, combining to create a more important truth.

"You will not hurt the people around you. Not intentionally, and not any more than any other human. The statistics Formless gives you are the bad kind of lies—the lies that look at a truth and twist it into something worse. I trust you. Testament trusts you, despite what happened. We love you. Statistically—real statistics—you have done an excellent job! I have ultimate, mathematically backed faith that you will continue to do an excellent job! So please, do not listen to Formless. Do not give her life."

She put her hand on his, resting on her shoulder. "When did you get so good at talking to humans?"

"I listen to you," Pattern said softly.

She smiled.

"Then I do the opposite," he added.

He could only let that hang for a moment before snickering and whispering that it was a joke. Shallan smiled, then turned and walked into the sitting room with the men.

"Well?" she said.

"Glys says Rlain's plan could work," Renarin told her. "Next vision, we'll avoid going in—and will instead send one of your Lightweavings while we watch."

SIXTEEN YEARS AGO

Szeth lunged, his practice sword scraping along the back edge of his foe's. Sliding inside the man's defenses, Szeth shoved him away, then slammed his weapon into the side of his foe's neck. The padded leather prevented injury, but both men halted, Szeth's blade resting there.

"Third point," a quiet voice said from the darker edges of the chamber. "Match to Szeth-son-Neturo."

Silence.

His opponent reached up and pulled off the practice mask—Soulcast mesh stiff across the face, and with sides of some strange reflective white material that was light, yet strong enough to withstand a sword's blow. Gonda-son-Darias wiped streaming sweat from his face, then nodded to Szeth before turning and walking to rack his equipment.

Further silence. Though twenty acolytes watched, and three full shamans, no one spoke. Gonda was the monastery swordmaster, favored to someday hold the Honorblade.

He had not landed a touch on Szeth in all five of their bouts today.

Szeth slowly removed his mask, bathing his sweaty face in cool air. Gonda did not seem angry at Szeth; those of this monastery were indeed of a different breed than the petty soldiers of the camp Szeth had left. Less open resentment. Less brutality. But more strange politics behind the scenes.

Gonda's practice sword fell from the rack as he placed it. He left it lying and pushed out of the training hall, footsteps loud in the silence. Like raindrops on a rooftop.

Szeth carefully racked his own equipment, feeling the eyes of the other acolytes on him. Two years here had been good for him; in the camp, he'd rarely been challenged. When he'd arrived here, it had taken him weeks to land a single point on any of his companions.

A strong current made for stronger fish. Szeth quietly pulled off his gambeson and handed it to the older acolyte in charge of cleaning equipment today. In Pozen's monastery, the more hits you took during training, the more chores you did. It had been over a year since Szeth had been assigned such duties. It had been longer than that since he'd cried himself to sleep, missing his mother.

All was right again. Here, he didn't need to think—he could merely train. He liked how simple his life was at last. Even the behind-the-scenes politics didn't matter, not so long as you were good with a sword.

As he'd just proven, he was *very* good.

Pozen himself emerged from behind one of the pillars. Like the others in the room, Szeth bowed. He hadn't realized the Honorbearer was watching.

"And so, Szeth," the older man said, "you take the rank of swordmaster for yourself."

Szeth did not reply. It was true.

"I am impressed with everything about you," Pozen said, "save your weakness with Elsecalling. It is a troubling shortcoming, Szeth."

Also true. He'd practiced with the Blade, as for the defense of Truth—for the preparation their people must make in the event of the Voidbringers' return—each monastery needed multiple trained Surgebinders in case the Honorbearer fell in battle.

"I have prepared a hunt for you," Pozen said. "The first clue is to be found atop the seventh spire. Go."

Szeth had worried he would need to retire to his rooms now that he'd won his title. That would have meant thinking, musing over his accomplishment. Another task handed to him so quickly was a relief.

He started on it immediately.

⁂

The "seventh spire" was a riddle. Fortunately, he knew a tavern outside the monastery, in Mokdown—the small city that filled the island here between rivers. The tavern was called First Spire. He assumed that the seventh would be the seventh building on the street.

Unfortunately, he found nothing atop that building. He stood on the roof, arms folded, the confused homeowner holding the ladder below. He did another search of the rooftop for anything crystalline—Pozen liked to Soulcast things into crystal. Nothing.

Finally, Szeth climbed down the ladder. It was wood, of course, as were the logs that made up the boardwalk. There were clay bricks here and there, imitating stone, but not holy. It was ingenious how the people of this region learned to lock wooden pieces together into joints without using nails. It made the wattle-and-daub structures or sod houses of his own home region look decidedly primitive by comparison.

Which was what made it all the more odd when these people used metal hinges on their doors.

Szeth thanked the homeowner, a portly man with a deferential way of speaking. He wore a splash, but over here they did that by sewing patches onto their clothing. In this case, red on the knees. How was it they didn't know the proper way of things? Pozen had ordered him to stop talking about it, but if Szeth were the one who was in the wrong, *he* would want someone to tell *him*.

After being dismissed, the man opened the door to his home—despite the steel hinges. If the door broke, he'd need to call an acolyte or a retired soldier—many lived in this town—to fix it. In fact, there were a great number of carpenters, smiths, and other tradesfolk, who were men or women that had once been soldiers or acolytes and had retired after only a year or two. It felt like . . . like they had chosen that life *just* to quit, so they could be employed in such professions.

Soulcast metal was reserved for tools that needed to be handled. The hinges came from mines, and everyone used them. So maybe these people *didn't* care about wearing their splashes wrong. Two years here, and Szeth still tied his mind in knots pondering these things—when in reality he needed to focus on the riddle.

"Goodman," Szeth called.

The man peeked back out his door.

"What do you think of when I say 'the seventh spire'?"

"The Seven's spire?" the man asked. "Well—"

"No," Szeth began, then stopped.

The *Seven's* spire? The Seven was a street. Could he have misheard? It wouldn't be the first time, as Pozen spoke with a slight Northern accent.

Of course. The Seven.

"Acolyte?" the homeowner asked.

"Never mind," Szeth said, turning on his heel. "Thank you for your aid."

He started off, wooden paving logs firm underfoot. It really was remarkable, this wood of the makam tree. Light, strong. It made for an interesting city—which Szeth tried not to hate. Indeed, his father had made great improvements here after being elected mayor last year, moving from city finance minister, an appointed position. Under Neturo's direction, old paving logs had been replaced with new ones, the bridges repaired. Social reforms had been instituted encouraging the loggers to be less rowdy. Better working hours, more frequent rotations for leave.

Neturo didn't seem bothered by what it had cost to get here, so Szeth tried not to be. Instead he enjoyed the whitewashed buildings, the way people nodded in respect to an acolyte, the colors in patches on the clothing. It didn't smell *too* bad. Not like the towns back home, where horse dung had covered the streets and sewage had been dumped in the river.

Mokdown was, if not fresh, at least bearable. Plus, he was the best of the acolytes, and had satisfying workouts each day. Surely the pain that Mother wasn't here with them—and that he went weeks, sometimes months without seeing Elid, who liked to travel—would fade further. His old life was *supposed* to have been burned away. The embers would die soon.

The Seven's tallest building was a church to Ishu, the Herald. It had once been dedicated to Batlah—but sometime in the past, that had changed. The people of Shinovar revered the Heralds almost as much as the sun, moons, and mountains, who were the greatest of spren. But Ishu was extra special for having brought them to this land by listening for the songs of a new world.

Atop this building, Szeth found a crystal patch of shingles. Riddle solved. Underneath it was a small slip of paper that held the next clue. *The Eastern Wind.* Szeth climbed back down the side of the church. "Sorry," he said to the Stone Shaman peeking out the window near the statue Szeth was using for handholds.

"It's fine, acolyte," she replied. "I do wish he'd warn us when he sends people on these hunts. We were holding services . . ."

Szeth bowed to her, then started along the street.

"Acolyte?" the shaman said. When he glanced at her, she nodded to the side. He followed the gesture to where someone lounged near the front of the building. A tall woman in colorful shaman robes, older than Szeth by a decade, with that short haircut he still found flagrant. Sivi visited the city so often, one could mistakenly assume she was the local Honorbearer. Were the Willshaper acolytes *that* disciplined, so as to pay no heed when their leader left? He'd heard the opposite. They said the Willshaper acolytes *drank,* and went out *riding,* and barely trained at all.

He found that kind of frivolity implausible in Sivi. After all, he liked her.

"Szeth," she said, strolling over.

"Honorbearer," he said, bowing. "I'm sorry I cannot stop to speak with you long. I have been set an urgent task by—"

Sivi held out a handful of small pieces of paper, identical to the one Szeth already had. "Pozen always uses the same places. I swear, I remember my predecessor mentioning the crystal shingles when *she* was an acolyte."

Szeth gaped at the proffered handful of clues. "I . . . I can't take those. I need to find my own way to—"

"I believe your instructions were to return with the papers," she said. "There was no prohibition against someone handing them to you."

It was true. So, Szeth accepted the papers.

"Come and speak with me, Szeth," she said, heading toward a nearby tavern. "I'd like to hear of your training."

He sighed, but could not refuse an Honorbearer. Besides, Sivi did often have a . . . perspective to share. He tried not to assume he was the reason for her frequent visits—but he couldn't put out of his mind things he'd overheard. About Pozen's plans for him.

At a quiet booth in the tavern—it was only three in the afternoon—he got tea while she sipped something he pretended was barley water. Both free, as this was a monastery town.

"I heard," she said, "that you made swordmaster today."

"That news spread already?" he asked, waiting out of respect to sip his tea until she drank first.

"Gonda is good," she said. "No one expected someone better to come along." She eyed him.

He looked down into his tea.

"You know, don't you?" she asked.

"I've . . . overheard things I should not have."

"Pozen's not shy about his aspirations for you, Szeth," Sivi replied. "He's been cultivating you for this role for years—since even before you were an acolyte."

"I recognize the need," Szeth said, forcing the words out, "for the best soldiers to hold the Honorblades. That is Truth. To prepare for the coming of the enemy."

"Then why do you seem ashamed?"

He looked down, and did not reply.

Sivi sighed, then tapped the tabletop with one finger. "Szeth. Do you know why Pozen sends you on these silly little hunts?"

"I do not ask, and he offers no explanation."

"It's because he wants to test your obedience. Pozen wants acolytes who are quick to obey, slow to question."

"That sounds like an admirable quality in a religious acolyte."

"And in a colleague?"

There it was. She said it openly.

"You're so quick to do as you're told, Szeth," Sivi said. "Why?"

"It's not what you think," he said, blushing.

"And what do I think?"

"That I'm stupid," Szeth said. "I obey for the opposite reason. If I don't move quickly . . . I start wondering. I start asking. I have an . . . unruly mind, honor-nimi."

"Tell me," she said, leaning forward, "the questions you ask, Szeth."

Dared he say it? Was this a test to see if he obeyed her, or if he was self-contradictory? They played so many games. Perhaps that was why he secretly hated this city, because here—at last—he'd learned that even Honorbearers saw things differently from one another.

"Pozen is not the best swordsman," Szeth said, watching the dark shifting colors swirl in the tea, leaking from the pouch. "Not anymore; he's almost sixty. Yet no one challenges him."

"He is wise," she said. "Being the best soldier is not always about being quickest with a weapon. Experience is valuable, even after the body starts to slow."

"He could still offer wisdom while someone else bore the Blade."

"If a genuine threat came," she replied, "he'd let one of his acolytes bear the Honor when going into battle. Why do you think we train you all so well with the weapon?"

"This is reasonable," Szeth said. "But if an aging Honorbearer *isn't* that dire a problem, why is everyone—including you *and* Pozen—this eager for me to begin a pilgrimage?"

She smiled, then finally tipped her head back and took a long drink. When she set the cup back down, she met his eyes. "The Windrunner is a problem."

"Honorbearer . . ." Szeth searched for the name. "Tuko-son-Tuko?"

"Correct. You paid attention in lessons."

"Of course I did," Szeth said, frowning. "Why would there be lessons if one is not to pay attention?"

"Oh, Szeth."

He started into his drink, savoring the bitter taste.

"Are you going to ask what the problem with Tuko is?"

"Is it my place to ask?"

"Well, I *did* leave that door wide open . . ."

"Is he a problem to Truth?" Szeth asked. "And for the defense of our lands?"

"Yes."

"Then that is enough." He met her eyes. "I haven't heard the Voice in a while."

"He's been busy."

"And if I'm an Honorbearer," Szeth said, "will I get to know what he is? What is actually going on?"

"If you want to know."

Did he? Szeth settled back on the hard bench of their booth, looking out the window at the passing people. Pozen had said Mokdown wasn't large by most standards. Szeth found it hard to imagine more people moving through the streets without carriages and wagons crushing people or causing chaos.

None of the people outside knew about the Voice. None of them cared that they didn't know. He could be like them.

But . . .

"After I destroyed the invaders," Szeth said, "Pozen was ready to completely abandon me—all of you were. Then, the moment you knew I'd heard the Voice, you welcomed me."

"The context changed," she said. "One moment you were a rogue agent acting against the interests of his Farmer. The next, you were a servant of a greater power."

"Actions should be right or they should be wrong. That's what I was taught."

"When you were a child," she said, "you were taught what a child can understand. Why does *nuance* terrify you, Szeth?"

"Because," he whispered, "I can't predict it."

"It's been ten years," she said, "since a boy found a rock in the soil and couldn't understand why anyone would see the situation differently from him. Don't you think you should have grown a little since then?"

He looked up from his tea. Wait. She—

"Your father and I talk," she said. She looked wistful as she said it, a hint of a smile on her lips.

For once, he caught the nuance.

"You don't keep visiting the city because of me," he said, horrified. "Not *only* for me."

She shrugged.

"My father is a heretic! You're a holy woman!"

She snorted in amusement, nearly spitting out her beer. "He's hardly a heretic, and I'm merely halfway holy, Szeth. Your father is a man of strong faith, just not in things that don't matter. You should ask him sometime."

Those kinds of conversations never went as Szeth wanted.

"Will you do it?" she asked. "Will you go on pilgrimage, in preparation to challenge the Windrunner for his Blade?"

Pilgrimage. He would need to visit each monastery and train in all the Surges. Then he would have to defeat the Windrunner in a duel without powers. That wouldn't have to be deadly; it depended on whether Tuko would surrender the Blade willingly or not. But . . . the Windrunner did not seem the type, from what Szeth had heard, to give up the Blade willingly. He was young to be an Honorbearer. And reportedly very skilled.

After winning the Blade—if he succeeded in that—Szeth would have to go on a pilgrimage to the monasteries again and present himself to the

Honorbearers, proving to their satisfaction that he was worthy. Lest they as a group renounce and condemn what he'd done—returning the Blade to the previous Honorbearer if he lived, or finding a replacement if he didn't.

It could take years. A decade. Longer.

"Szeth?" she asked. "Will you do what we ask?"

"How can I trust that it's right to listen to you!" Szeth said, throwing his hands in the air. "If *nuance* changes what is right and wrong for you on a whim!" He sat back in his seat, puffing. Then he groaned softly. "That did sound childish, didn't it?"

When he said that, Sivi relaxed visibly and took a long pull on her drink.

"It's that satisfying to you," Szeth said, "to see me frustrated?"

She held up a finger, still drinking. She downed the entire thing. Storms. "It's satisfying," she said, wiping her lip, "to know I was correct: there *is* something in you that is willing to self-reflect. Why do you find it so hard, Szeth?"

"I just want things to be easy," he said. "Like they were when I was young."

"That's laziness." She pointed at him, leaning forward across the table. She did that a lot. Such passion. Had he ever felt that passionate about anything?

Yes, he thought. *About finding answers.*

"Listen," Sivi said. "Life was *never* easy when you were young, Szeth. You were merely allowed to pretend that it was. Other people were always out there making these kinds of choices."

"But—"

"Just because your life gave you the luxury of simplicity doesn't mean the world was magically less complex," she said. "Tell me. Aren't you *glad* you got to escape your childish notions, and see the world as it really is?"

"I . . ." Glad? For all of this?

That was . . . uncomfortably close to what he'd been thinking earlier, that he'd want to be informed if he were wearing splashes wrong. Huh. He considered that as Sivi ordered another drink from the barmaid, who hovered barely far enough away to be discreet.

If he was wrong about religion, wouldn't he want to know? Yes. Yes, he would. And wouldn't he be *glad* to have been corrected? In a moment of deep reflection, he realized his errors. It wasn't their fault for using nuance; it was his for not wanting to see it.

"I'll do it," he said. "I'll go on the pilgrimage. If you took me in first to train with your Blade, I'd like that. Let me fulfill my final requirements as an acolyte here, so that I might be elevated to warrior elite." He would of course choose that path rather than becoming a ministering shaman, the other option for an acolyte.

"Excellent," she said.

"What would you have done," he said, "if I *hadn't* been willing to accept your advice?"

"Wouldn't be the first time," she said with a sigh. Then, to his questioning gaze, she continued, "Three of the other current Honorbearers trained with Pozen—he has a sixth sense for finding talented warriors. But he has *also* proven himself quite skilled at finding people who will jump when he commands. It almost makes one think he wants servants more than colleagues." She nodded to him, standing and taking her beer from the tray as it arrived. "I've got someone else to visit. See you at my monastery in a few months."

Szeth tried not to think about who she was seeing. Before she left though, she stepped back and leaned down by him. "Pozen is using you. Remember that."

"And you?" Szeth asked. "Are you using me?"

She winked at him.

"I'm not doing this because you want me to," he said, "or because he does. I'm doing it for answers. I *will* know what the Voice is."

"We're all counting on it, Szeth," she said, then left—taking her cup with her.

Szeth made sure to pay for it before *he* left. Free drinks were one thing, but they shouldn't be exploiting the tavern by taking their cups.

Jasnah says that the existence of an all-powerful and all-loving God must be questioned by the simple evidence of injustices done in life to the innocent, such as the child who dies from disease.

—From the epilogue to *Oathbringer,* by Dalinar Kholin

Sigzil clutched his squire Deti in the middle of a battlefield and screamed. For help, for Stormlight, for a healer. His words were lost in the chaos of red lightning and shouting soldiers as the enemy poured in through the hole made by the dead thunderclast, the defenses broken open once more. Lightning flashed from the ground around him as stormforms unleashed their power to mirror that above.

Deti had blood on his lips, and trembled, surrounded by painspren—like tiny disembodied hands, clawing at the ground as they moved. Deti's panting was dull, lacking Stormlight, which had been depleted in their clash with some Heavenly Ones.

"Take mine!" Sigzil said. "Take my Light, Deti!"

But Sigzil's gemstones were drained.

Deti put a hand to his face, blood and rain mixing, then gasped. "It comes!" Deti shouted. "The Night of Sorrows! I stand on the precipice of dawn and watch it advance, consuming all light, all life, all hope! *IT COMES!*"

Deti's light faded. Sigzil screamed again and seized a lance from a dead Heavenly One nearby, crumpled in a heap from where Sigzil had dropped her. He raised the weapon, which had drained away Deti's Stormlight, and bellowed into the night, seeking foes to kill.

He found plenty.

"Sigzil," Vienta whispered. "You are in command. You cannot afford rage. You must fall back and find Stormlight."

He rushed toward a group of his soldiers who were surrounded by direform Regals, with their bulky, spiked carapace and glowing red eyes. Sigzil ripped into their ranks, killing with a weapon that could suck away their Voidlight—expelling it into the night, for the gemstone mechanism at the lance's pommel had cracked in its fall. He did all of this while wielding Vienta as a short dagger in his off hand.

He broke through, and found two Edgedancers among the soldiers. Mere feet away from a dying man they could have saved, had they known. That made even more angerspren boil at his feet.

You need to regroup our forces, Sigzil, Vienta said. *You cannot bring Deti back. It's time to retreat.*

Sigzil continued to kill, always underestimated by his foes, as he was shorter than many of the Alethi around him. And storms, his logical side would *not* shut up. It agreed with Vienta. Once he'd fought those soldiers clear, he led them and the two Edgedancers in a retreat toward a stabilizing line of human forces at the rear of Narak Four. He dismissed his Blade and tossed the stolen lance to an armorer, then took gemstones off a runner boy whose job was to deliver them to Radiants in the field.

There were only a handful, as they had to ration. When were the storming Bondsmiths going to return? Sigzil surveyed the dark plateau, overrun with red-eyed figures, and knew the day was lost. Winn, the old general with a full head of silver hair, joined him.

"Orders, sir?" the elderly general shouted over the thunder.

"Time to retreat," Sigzil said, breathing deeply, rain streaming down his face. This was his plan, but storms, he'd hoped to hold another day. "Give the command."

As Winn did so, Sigzil sent Vienta to warn his squires—flying in pairs above—of the situation. He looked across the plateau toward the lump that was Deti, dead on the stone, and felt a treasonous sense of powerlessness.

Storms, he thought. *This is what Kal felt, isn't it? What eventually broke him?*

He could learn from what his captain had endured. It wasn't Sigzil's fault, but the fault of the enemies, that his squire had fallen. He did his best to quash the thoughts about what he could have done differently, either in training or in the fighting today, to better protect Deti. He focused instead on helping the living. It worked, to an extent.

As his spren arrived, he spent some of his precious Stormlight to rise in the air and defend the back line of soldiers. He could see they took heart from seeing him hovering with his silvery spear in hand. They held stronger, emboldened as groups of beleaguered men found their way to this bastion of defense. More Edgedancers began to streak across the plateau, returning from where they'd been flanking the enemy forces. They picked up the fallen, healing them and carrying them to safety. Sigzil called the final retreat as the Stormwall and his group of Shardbearers held the bridgehead.

Their retreat took them all across Narak Two, the Oathgate plateau, which was connected to all three side plateaus. Narak Prime was to the east, and Narak Three to the southwest. His forces managed to get off the broken plateau, and the Stonewards dropped the bridge.

"The enemy appears to be celebrating," Vienta whispered in his ear. "I see no indications they plan to push the assault further today. Well done."

Sigzil nodded curtly, not feeling it. Yes, his plan had worked so far—but if they had to keep rationing Stormlight . . .

Skar and Leyten landed and checked in with him. Sigzil told them softly about Deti. Skar already knew, his team having done a few passes over the fallen plateau to search for pockets of survivors. They'd seen the body. Nearby, generals began to confer on how to draw enemy attention to Narak Three next, the other plateau they could afford to lose. That was going to be tricky, though Sigzil had some ideas.

For now, another item bothered him. "Leyten, Skar," he said, "Deti spoke a Death Rattle when he died. Moelach is here."

Leyten grunted. "I'll poke around and see if anyone else heard anything from the dying today. I'm not too concerned though. Moelach never takes part in the fighting."

"There might be other Unmade," Sigzil warned. "Pass the word, you two."

"Will do," Skar said. "You're not blaming yourself for this, are you?"

"Trying my best not to, but you know how it feels."

Leyten nodded. "I wish I didn't, but I do."

"I'll focus on the next phase of our strategy, and the academics will distract me. I can't afford to mope right now—the generals and troops need to know I'm proud of the fighting they did, and of their excellent execution of my plan."

"Storms," Leyten said. "Sig, you really *sound* like a leader."

Did he? He . . . did. "Blame Kaladin," he said, managing a wan smile despite the day's gloom. "And what he made of all of us."

"Blame Kaladin," Skar agreed. "Storming man and his inspiring ways."

"Any of you see Moash during the fighting?"

"No," Leyten said. "But we're keeping watch. The moment he appears, we'll make sure you know. Then there will be a reckoning."

⁂

Chaos retreated around Shallan, but she didn't emerge into a vision—not exactly. Instead, the complex flowing tides of the Spiritual Realm fashioned a kind of wall before her. The cloudy glass grew with the same creeping uncertainty as frost on a window, forming a wide, vaguely round pillar.

Wooden planks in several elevated tiers appeared next, around the glass pillar—and Shallan was able to climb them, as if she stood on some kind of strange scaffolding outside reality. Pattern and Testament emerged with her, and then farther up—because the scaffolding created disjointed levels—Rlain, Renarin, and their spren appeared.

After three attempts, she was slowly getting accustomed to the process. This was all created by Renarin and Glys—using Renarin's instincts for how it should look, re-creating some scaffolding he'd seen around a monastery in his youth.

Shallan hunted around the pillar for a good spot to peek in. Renarin thought the cloudy glass was a visual manifestation of the uncertainty of this place—but some spots were less opaque. She located one and knelt on the plank, looking through to see a battle happening on the other side. Dalinar and Navani had been moving through the Desolations for some time now, and this pillar was the way that Glys and Tumi allowed Shallan's team to watch.

They'd seen Desolation after Desolation—sometimes hundreds of years apart—as the Bondsmiths moved out of the shadowdays toward the future. In the last one, Shallan had seen people with spren and powers—early Knights Radiant, complete with Shardplate emblazoned with glyphs. Dalinar had leaped straight over the days of Nohadon, and the founding of the Radiants.

So far, she had spotted no sign of Mraize or Iyatil—either inside or outside the visions. But they'd be there, following Dalinar, as they believed his quest for Honor would lead them to Mishram as well. Today's battlefield was in Shinovar, and it had changed during the millennia since that first vision. A blanket of languid green grass now grew where once there had been only wet dirt. Trees dotted the landscape in small groups, as if conversing at a dinner party.

Strange, how often the fighting in these visions happened in Shinovar—the isolationist kingdom hadn't been so unapproachable back then, it seemed. She peered through her clearer section of glass. There. Those glowing figures swooping through the sky . . . those were Windrunners. Dalinar and Navani were heading straight toward the Recreance: the day oaths had been broken, the origin of the secrets that everyone was hunting.

"Did you see those Windrunners?" Renarin asked, boards creaking as he approached. "And soldiers with good bronze weapons this time. I think they're finally making technological progress, rather than losing it with each Desolation."

"We're too far away from the action," Shallan said, squinting. "Can you get us in closer?"

"I'll talk to Glys," he said.

Suddenly their window looked straight into the midst of a battle with the singers—a hectic mess. Yes, the Radiants were here, but not in the distinct uniforms she was accustomed to. However, the human combatants *did* maintain a formation for once. A giant shield wall with spears.

"That almost looks modern," Rlain said from somewhere nearby. "Your people are using the same tactics here that they used against mine on the Shattered Plains."

"Not exactly," Renarin said. "That's a shield wall, yes, but not a modern flexible block. No pikes, no cavalry, no heavy infantry—just well-drilled light infantry. This is still thousands of years ago, but something big has changed."

"Metalworking," Rlain said.

"It's more that they can achieve continuity," Shallan said. "People can start progressing at last, now that society isn't obliterated every time the Fused return."

"Exactly," Renarin said. "While even the Recreance is shadowed, we have learned a lot from Father's previous visions, and have some fragmentary texts from before. The Radiants during this period became a stable force connecting the people between Returns—a group of warriors who trained during the decades of peace, and were ready when the battle inevitably came."

"Watchers at the rim," Shallan whispered.

"Against my people," Rlain said.

"Against the worst instincts in all people," Shallan said, pulling back from the window. "Rlain, you yourself explained to me how the listeners refused to continue the fighting—and left. The Fused didn't just oppress us. They did your kind as well."

Rlain shook his head. "That's too simple an explanation, Shallan. One side escalates, so the other must match—or go further. The Fused wouldn't exist if the humans hadn't begun to outgrow the land given them. The Heralds wouldn't exist if the Fused hadn't been created to stop this incursion.

"In turn, the Fused hardened—growing more and more determined each time they returned, learning to fight and defeat the Heralds. Humankind was left desolate, which led to the founding of the Radiants. The war simply kept spinning, and spinning, and spinning. I can decry the bloodshed, but I don't blame the singers of these ancient days. Humans broke their promises and invaded. What else would you do but fight?"

She looked back at the window and saw a group of five Fused—Magnified Ones—smashing into the human phalanx, throwing men into the air. Stonewards came in, dashing to counter them, their brilliant armor appearing out of place on this battlefield. Those were essentially modern Shardbearers, among common soldiers wearing sculpted bronze breastplates, the kind she'd seen in a museum in Kharbranth.

"I . . ." she said. "Rlain, the singer side *did* serve Odium."

"Because the other gods refused to help them." He hummed to a soft rhythm. "This ancient war ended with the mass enslavement of my kind, save a handful. Is that the only acceptable answer? One people or another has to be subjugated, or even destroyed?"

"Rlain," Renarin said, "my father is trying to end the war with peace. He's willing to risk our homeland for it. There *are* other answers. There have to be."

"If Odium will let any of those answers work," Rlain said. "And what will your father's peace offer my people? They are abandoned to the enemy god. I wish . . . I wish there were something to be done not only for the humans, but for the singers too."

They fell quiet, watching death play out on the historical battlefield. Shallan tried to make sense of it, to see if she could spot Dalinar and Navani. But this was *too* close.

"Can you move us to the top of that hill?" she asked.

"This isn't your map with Father, Shallan," Renarin said. "I can't just zoom us around. Glys says we're lucky to see anything."

"Give it a try, please," she said. She couldn't afford to get distracted by the historical implications of all this—she was here to stop Mraize and Iyatil.

Renarin and Glys discussed, and their window jumped to a hilltop. Not the one she'd requested, but it would work. Their window wouldn't be visible to those inside the vision, Glys assured them. It still felt strange; soldiers could run straight through them, without noticing.

"There," she said, finding Dalinar and Navani watching from another hill. She smiled, as seeing them reminded her of Adolin—who hopefully was having a much easier time than she was. Dalinar and Navani would likely observe this vision a short time, find out the year if they could, then use their anchor to jump forward many years, skipping Desolations.

She hoped they wouldn't end up skipping the most important moments, requiring backtracking. But it felt to her that fate itself—or the power that made up the Spiritual Realm—recognized when events had significance. Maybe because humans and singers *gave* them importance. That sort of thing echoed, and also let you predict the future a little. Wit had, by his own explanation, come to Roshar specifically because he'd been able to feel that important events were impending. He'd once even attended a festival near her home estates.

Two Heralds crested a hill nearby, and Shallan glanced away. *Shallan . . .* Veil said inside her.

She forced herself to look back. At a woman with red hair, walking beside Jezrien the king.

The implications of this are daunting, Radiant thought.

We have to acknowledge them anyway, Veil said.

For now, Shallan let herself turn away. "What is *that*?" she said, pointing to a darkened area where the grass was in shadow but no cloud was visible.

"Glys says one of the Unmade is there," Renarin said, stepping closer to her. "It's . . . Shallan, it's Ba-Ado-Mishram. Not the real her, of course—a historical reconstruction in the vision."

They'd caught glimpses of the other Unmade during previous battles, and Shallan felt annoyed that she hadn't been able to see their creation. That event was mysterious even to the spren. What were the Unmade? Regardless, they'd never caught sight of Mishram before in one of these.

"I'm going in," Shallan said. "Tell Glys to send me."

"We said we were going to stay outside," Renarin said, hopping down to her level, shaking the scaffolding. "Only send in illusions."

"We said," Shallan replied, "that we'd send in illusions until we saw something important. I recognize that stopping Mraize and Iyatil is most important, but maybe interacting with Mishram—even the historical one—could tell us something."

"You still want to find the prison, don't you?" Renarin asked. "Whether or not we stop the Ghostbloods first."

And . . . was he humming to a rhythm?

Rlain stepped up to the edge of the higher scaffolding. "I think she should go in, Renarin. The plan is working—we have surveyed the landscape and looked for the Ghostbloods. Plus, with this framework, you and I can keep watch on her."

"All right," Renarin said. "Wave if something is wrong, and we'll pull you out."

Shallan nodded, and an eyeblink later she was inside the vision.

75
FAMILY

SIXTEEN YEARS AGO

The day he was to leave on his pilgrimage to become an Honorbearer, Szeth spent the morning in the monastery's rock garden. Today, Szeth would leave to go train with Sivi—then each of the Honorbearers in turn, learning their skills. Well, except for the Stoneward powers—they didn't have the Blade of Talmut-son-God—and the Bondsmith powers. That Blade was held by a civil leader, and passed down through a different tradition.

Today Szeth prayed, bowing before a brilliant stone: two feet across with a crystal vein running through the center. It opened at one side like a mouth, the crystal forming teeth. The spren of this stone certainly seemed an ostentatious type.

"Spren," he whispered. "In wisdom, please, guide me."

Every important moment in his life had involved a stone, hadn't it? Was this one looking back, as he gazed upon it? Hesitant, he reached out and put his hand on it, feeling the grain of the surface, jutting with little bits of clear crystal. Still such a strange sensation, like the skin of some beast.

For a moment he felt . . . memories. As if . . . this stone had come from another place, and remembered being carried . . . with a group of terrified people . . .

Is this you? he wondered. *Are you the spren I follow?*

Ah, Szeth, the Voice responded, and it had a different sensation, the memories vanishing. *Don't think I've been ignoring you. You've merely been in good hands. Complete your pilgrimage. Then we will meet.*

"Thank you," Szeth whispered.

Your life has purpose, Szeth. Everything that has happened to you, I orchestrated. You have meaning because your meaning is part of my meaning.

Those words.

Those words were what he needed: a reminder that his life was not an accident.

I warn you, the Voice said, *this next part will be the most difficult. You go among some who do not regard me as highly as Pozen does. Do not lose your way.*

At least he wouldn't be alone. *You will be with me, right?* Szeth asked the Voice.

No response.

"Father plans to follow you, Szeth."

He shook out of his meditation and became aware of a quiet stream, a latticework skylight filtering sunlight, and fronds sheltering a variety of stones. No one would dare interrupt his final meditation . . . except Elid.

Standing by the doorway was a lean woman who—like Szeth—had their mother's wiry strength. He'd seen Elid some mornings, exercising and training to use the sword with the shamans on the riverbanks. In this city, all who touched stone were, if they wished, allowed to train in weapons with the shamans. He'd found it strange—or perhaps oddly encouraging—that here, fighters weren't dismissed as "those who subtract." Merely "those who touch stone." It was the wrong way of things, but sometimes the wrong way could . . . sound better.

Indeed, Elid carried a small side sword—symbolizing her commitment to Truth.

"You are forbidden in the monastery, Elid," he said, turning back to his contemplation of the rock.

"I've been thinking of joining up," she said. "Been talking to some of the shamans. They told me I should look around."

"Your efforts to circumvent propriety are, as always, awkward," Szeth said. "Pretending you want to join simply so you can come bother me is inappropriate."

"It worked."

"I am supposed to be alone during this meditation."

"Which means we can talk in private," she said.

He sighed, contemplating fetching a shaman to throw her out.

"Did you even hear me?" she said. "Father is planning to *go with* you. Again. When you leave on pilgrimage."

Szeth felt a sudden, deep sense of relief. He hadn't thought . . . but of course. Neturo would do as he always had. While some young men would have acted embarrassed by the idea of their father traveling with them, Szeth did not need such lies.

"I did not consider that he would come," Szeth said, "but I am not surprised. It has been his behavior in the past."

"You need to tell him to stay," Elid said.

"Why?"

She strode farther into the garden, not even pausing to offer prayer to the stones she passed. "Szeth! He's built something here! He's the *mayor.*"

"A strange position," Szeth said. "Why let men choose a leader, instead of trusting the spren? We didn't do anything like that at home."

"Because we were backwater sheepherders!"

He thought for a moment she'd stopped to reverence a stone, but no, she couldn't be . . . Elid *jumped over* a section of garden from path to path to stand near Szeth. That woman . . .

"You *can't* let him go with you, Szeth," she said, looming above where he knelt on the soft, mossy soil, his hand still on the top of the stone. "Do the right thing—let him stay."

"I don't let or make him do anything, Elid."

"You don't *say* anything, but you *imply* a whole lot."

"And you," he said, "always like to make so many assumptions." With a quiet prayer, he removed his hand from the stone, then stood up—trying to shelter the rock from her tantrum. "Maybe Father *wants* to go on pilgrimage. Maybe he *wants* to go live at the Willshaper monastery. Maybe he has . . . reasons."

Elid gaped at him. "You *know.*"

"About Father and Sivi? Yes. I deduced it."

She gaped again, her eyes wide, jaw dropping.

"What?" he demanded.

"I just thought if you knew," she said, "you'd spend every day preaching at him about his sinful state, Szeth. What, do you berate him during lunch when I'm not around?"

He blushed, then started to walk out of the rock garden. They could at least have this conversation somewhere less holy.

"You honestly don't care?" she said, hurrying to keep up with him. "You don't think what they're doing is wrong?"

"*Mother* left *him,*" Szeth said.

"She might come back!"

He halted in place, causing Elid to lurch to a stop. He met her gaze, eye to eye, as they were roughly the same height.

"You," she said, poking him in the chest, "will need to spend months at *each* monastery. If Father goes with you, then that will soon mean the end of him and Sivi."

"So you're in favor of their relationship?"

"I'm in favor of anything that *doesn't* rip our family apart further."

He met her eyes. "You could have gone back; you could have stayed with her."

"And leave Father?" Elid said. In a moment, her confidence seemed to evaporate as she wrapped her arms around herself. "I miss her. Do you?"

"Yes," he whispered.

"I used to feel sorry for you," Elid said. "Used to want to protect you, like Father. But . . . then she left us . . ." She shook her head. "That broke Father. You know how many nights I spent holding his hand while he cried? You weren't there, Szeth. I was."

"I know."

But there was a reason. The Voice. Szeth walked a purposeful path. He *had* to believe it.

"Well, *I'm* not going to go with you this time," Elid snapped. "*I'm* not going to spend the rest of my life pretending you're a lost child. If you have any kind of decency, you'll tell Father to stay so you don't keep ruining *his* life either."

Szeth stepped around her. He quickly bowed his head to each stone as he walked, his emotions in turmoil.

"Do you know why?" Elid called after him. "Why he's always willing to follow you? Why he doesn't care about me as much as he does you? Why are you his favorite?"

Szeth bowed his head again, this time not out of reverence. He reached the doorway.

"I hate you," Elid called after him. "I *hate* you, Szeth!"

"I'm sorry," he whispered, "for not knowing a better way."

He left his sister behind then. Taking only a change of clothing and his sword as he left the monastery.

⁂

It was raining by the time Szeth reached the bridge. He walked alone, by tradition . . . but not by law. So it wasn't strictly against any rules for Neturo to meet him there. Pack slung over his shoulder, his beard now streaked with grey. Heavyset, with no splash, but smiling.

How could he smile? Szeth felt he'd lost the capacity years ago.

"Thought you could sneak away without me?" Neturo asked.

Szeth took a deep breath and spoke the words he'd needed to go over a hundred times in his head during this walk. "Please stay behind, Father."

Neturo considered, rain streaming off his umbrella. Szeth had brought none. It was a light rainfall; he would merely need to care for the sword when he found shelter for the night.

"Is that what you want, Szeth?" Neturo asked. "Or is it what you think you *should* want?"

"You have a life here," Szeth said.

"I have a life wherever my family is."

"Your family is here too!" Szeth said. "With Elid. Or back home, with Mother. Who left because of me . . ."

Father dropped the umbrella and seized him in an embrace. Szeth held in the tears, although they would have been invisible in the rain. He did not wish to offend the spren by acting as if a pilgrimage were a sad occasion.

"Szeth," Father whispered to the sound of splashing rain, "what happened between your mother and me was *not* your fault. We were struggling long before you found that stone."

"Really?"

"Really."

"That could have been my fault too, though. It had to be hard, living with a boy who didn't know what is right."

Father held tighter. "Son. It was *never you.* I took your mother from her family and persuaded her to question things that others never dare. For that, we were forced to live outside, as no one would rent to us. I have letters from her sisters. She's happy, Szeth. Happier without me."

That sounded insane, but there it was. Szeth did not question whether it was the truth, if his father had spoken it.

"You should still stay with Elid," Szeth whispered.

"Elid hates me, Szeth."

"What? No! She loves you."

"That's not what she says," Neturo said softly. "I don't know how to deal with her. I never have. I try to talk to her, and she walks away. I bring her gifts, and she accuses me of trying to bribe her." Neturo took a deep breath. "I think that . . . space will do us good. I'll come back later, and see if she's cooled off." He pulled away from the embrace, and kept on smiling through the water streaming down his face. "I don't want you to think you *have* to care for your old father. But I'll go with you, Szeth, so you don't have to go by yourself. It's the only way I know how to help."

"Thank you," Szeth whispered. "*Thank you.*"

Jasnah's argument is probably the greatest a person could make against what I teach, and so it must be addressed. I am not certain I have the philosophy, the words, or the experience to do so with the respect it deserves.

—From the epilogue to *Oathbringer,* by Dalinar Kholin

Shallan appeared in a dying body.

She gasped at the sudden pain, putting a hand to her side and feeling blood as she lay on the Shin grass, the sun blazing overhead. Storms. She was in the body of a mortally wounded singer. That made her panic before she felt something in her mind . . .

Mmm . . . Shallan?

"Pattern? You're in my mind. Like when you're a sword."

Our bond has been strengthening. You have said the proper truths. We thought maybe this would start to work. You looked afraid.

"I'm in a dying body!"

Glys says he's sorry—he can't always pick the bodies. He wanted to get you into a singer so that you'd be able to understand Mishram, but . . . well . . .

"It's all right," Shallan whispered. "Maybe we should try again? Pull me out? Or maybe I'll just heal—"

Mmm . . . Pattern said. *A singer using Stormlight would draw attention from anyone watching. Glys wants you to avoid that. He says you won't really die, because you're not really wounded, but . . . I'll tell him to pull you out anyway.*

"Thank you," Shallan said, squeezing her eyes closed against the pain, one hand on the wound—the broken carapace felt odd beneath her fingers.

Wait. Shallan, look.

She frowned and raised her head, though that made her vision swim. She was lying among a large group of corpses and the mortally wounded, the battle having moved on. Some bodies bled red, others orange, and a mess of spren—fearspren, angerspren, confusionspren, painspren—sprinkled the ground and air, to her singer body's eyes looking closer to their forms in Shadesmar than the way humans saw them. Some ten feet away, a singer wept and clutched at the wounds along her side, humming in fits and spurts. A song perhaps, to comfort herself as she died.

Ba-Ado-Mishram was approaching. The Unmade took the shape of a black mass of smoke, with hands growing out of it to move. Powerful hands, entirely black, stretching out and gripping the ground to pull her along.

Leave me here for now, Shallan thought to Pattern, gritting her teeth.

When Mishram reached the other dying singer, her strange too-long limbs puffed away into smoke, but the main mass of blackness remained. That transformed into a singer femalen as if she were emerging from fog, with billowing robes and long black hair. She leaned down over the dying soldier, and extra arms formed to cradle the head and body.

They exchanged words, too soft for Shallan to hear. She forced herself to wait, but couldn't help whimpering at the pain.

Mishram turned toward her. Shallan's heart stumbled. That was the face she'd seen in her drawings—in the sky, the smoke, the knots and grain of wood. Unlike Sja-anat, who tended to appear human—or as perhaps some kind of spren, with smooth skin and too-narrow features—Mishram was unabashedly singer. Some red lines of smoke made up her face, giving her an otherworldly carapace and patterns.

She fixated on Shallan, then again became a cloud of smoke with stretching arms. She pulled herself with that same unnatural gait up to Shallan, and became a singer again.

Storms.

Should we bring you out? Pattern asked.

Shallan waited, her breath held, as Mishram loomed over her, arms forming from amorphous smoke at her sides to cradle Shallan. The Unmade leaned down, then breathed out, darkness wrapping around Shallan. Storms, it was . . . it was . . .

"*Live,*" Mishram whispered, her voice somehow overlapping with a dozen different rhythms. "*Heal.*"

The pain in her side vanished, and her body reknit. Nearby, she could see the other singer stumbling to her feet, humming in amazement at her restored body. They weren't Regals with powers, let alone Fused. They were common soldiers.

"Why?" Shallan asked as Mishram gently lowered her to the ground.

"He does not love us," Mishram said. She looked to the sky, as if worried.

"So we must love ourselves." She became smoke again, long arms stretching across the battlefield as she looked for other wounded singers.

Shallan struggled to her feet. *She's healing people,* she thought to Pattern. *Did any of you expect that?*

I try not to expect things that aren't mathematically sure, Pattern said. *People say that life tends to be irrational, but even irrational numbers can be computed with ease. You all are something beyond that.*

Storms. *More than irrational?*

Way more. Regardless, the others are fascinated by this. Rlain says that Mishram was one of the main gods they rejected in leaving—so he didn't expect kindness from her. They want you to see if you can get any more information.

Shallan picked her way across the field to where Mishram healed another near-dead singer. The malen put his hand to his head, where his carapace had been cracked.

"The other Unmade have plots," Shallan said. "What are yours?"

"You deserve," she said—again with too many rhythms, "far better than him. Live. Feel. Feel so much more than he allows. *Be.*" She turned away, long arms quickly pulling her toward another fallen body.

Shallan looked to the other two who had been healed. They gathered with her, watching Mishram.

"I never know what to make of them," the femalen said.

"I saw Yelig-nar consume a dozen of our kind in one battle," the malen whispered to a morose rhythm. "My brother included. Now this one . . . heals us? They're spren. Best not to try to understand them."

"She's right though," Shallan found herself saying. "Odium doesn't care about us."

"He cares about winning," the femalen said. "If we want to live in peace, we'll need to kill the humans. It's that or be destroyed."

"We could coexist," Shallan said.

Both hummed to the same rhythm, which seemed mocking or skeptical. Storms, it *was* easier to pick those out in a singer body, wasn't it?

"Coexisting," the malen said. "A fanciful dream. Sure, who wouldn't prefer that?"

"The humans slaughtered my sisters," the femalen said. "It can't happen. I won't let it."

Shallan crossed the field, and the other two didn't stop or question her. The singers didn't maintain the same kind of discipline or expectations as human societies. Not that they were without conviction or prowess—but they didn't have the same hierarchies of commanders or ranks.

She approached Mishram, the grass ignoring her as she stepped on it. Strangely, she realized that if she were to live in one of these two militaries, she'd probably prefer to be in the *singer* one. There was a sense of freedom and individuality to their lives—something she'd never really noticed before watching them closely in these visions.

All this time she'd imagined them as destroyers, seeking to enslave humankind. But humans were the ones who made slaves. Then again, from what she'd seen, humans had grander cities, more diversity of professions, and—strangely—more artists. Why should that be? Considering how free they were, shouldn't there be more artists among singers? Perhaps for art to *truly* flourish, you needed certain kinds of infrastructure. A part of her hated that idea, realistic though it sounded, and . . .

And she let Radiant take control. Mishram had found a human this time, still alive, blood on his lips as he lay there trembling, eyes squeezed shut against the monstrosity that loomed above him. He was muttering something, but Shallan—in the singer's body—couldn't understand it. The words felt so *dead* to her without a rhythm.

"Will you heal him?" she asked.

"I cannot," the Unmade said. "And I would not." She hesitated. "Yet we should sing for him. That will make his final transition more peaceful."

Mishram leaned down and began to sing softly to the Rhythm of Peace. Shallan's anxiety lessened. The dying man stopped trembling, and his breathing became more regular. He even . . . even seemed to hum to it himself until he slipped away.

Shallan found tears in her eyes, and Mishram regarded her—strangely, the spren didn't *turn* so much as just *shift* until she was facing a different direction.

"You cry for them, singer?" Mishram asked.

"I cry for all of us," Shallan whispered. "And for the pain that we all cause one another. Is there no way to stop this, Mishram?"

"He will never allow it, for the wars serve him, preparing his armies for a future I do not yet understand. We must dominate the humans. That is first. They will not stop fighting until we are completely under their control, so we must accomplish that first." She hesitated. "Then, perhaps." The spren looked to the sky. "If he allows it . . . I wish that he would."

Storms. Shallan had grown to know, in a small way, Sja-anat—and had briefly been forced to trust the spren. Yet in all her interactions with the Unmade, she had never seen one act so very human as Mishram did now, humming softly for a dying enemy. Shallan reminded herself that Mishram *would* eventually pick up the war against humankind in Odium's absence. She and Mishram *were* on opposite sides of this battlefield, but—

Mishram's song changed.

Shallan stepped back in shock as the smoky figure began to vibrate and pulse, her face distorting. "I see you," it hissed. "I see you, Lightweaver."

Shallan felt a *jolt* of panic. That angry, twisted face. It wasn't the Ba-Ado-Mishram of memory. It was the *current* one.

"I will rip you to pieces," Mishram said, advancing on her. "I will pull your bones from their sockets and listen to them *pop.* I will crack your fingers backward, just to hear you scream. I will revel in the things that flow from you when sliced: pain and screams and bowels unchained. I—"

We're getting you out, Pattern said.

Shallan was glad for that, but as it happened, she realized this was the most interaction she'd had with Mishram. This was progress, terrifying though it was—so she tried a Lightweaving as she was yanked free. She'd planned it, and she thought it might—

She shook, finding herself on the scaffolding again. She scrambled up, ignoring questions from Pattern and Rlain—instead peering at the vision. She'd managed to create a Lightweaving of herself, as Shallan, that had appeared beside the soldier whose body she'd been inhabiting. The soldier wandered off, heading toward the other two who had been healed, to continue on as the historical event had played out.

The fake Shallan stayed in place, and she—outside—controlled it. "Why?" she whispered, making the Lightweaving say the same. With her eyes closed, she was almost back inside. She couldn't hear Mishram's reply from out here, but Glys glided up to her and whispered what the Unmade said.

"Why what?" Mishram replied. "Why do I hate you?"

"No," Shallan said. "We came to your world, and then fought you for it. We imprisoned you for thousands of years. I know why you hate me."

"Then what?" Mishram said, Glys imitating her biting anger.

"Why is Odium afraid of you?" Shallan said. "Could you actually *replace* him?"

Stillness.

Then Glys gasped.

Shallan trembled as she opened her eyes and found the swirling smoke-paint of the Spiritual Realm all around her, shifting behind her, flowing like a thousand rivers smashing together. The eddies of their motion formed faces, which all moved in unison.

"How do you know?" Mishram demanded. "*How do you know?*"

"I've been there," Shallan whispered. "I killed those who created me as well."

Mishram's essence flowed forward, colorful mist becoming darkness, becoming hands that reached for Shallan. Whatever the nature of Mishram's prison, it was weaker in here. Shallan was sure those hands had become real, and would—

Rlain stepped between them.

Tall as a tower, with the armor of a singer and the uniform of an Alethi. His spren joined him, faceless, hiding in his shadow. A second later, Renarin stepped up as well.

Mishram froze, eddies of paint-smoke swirling around her, other faces vanishing into it until just one remained. Staring at them. Staring at . . .

Shallan had made a practice of studying eyelines for sketching. She was absolutely certain that Mishram was staring at the way Renarin had taken Rlain's hand for support.

"We are children of Sja-anat," Glys said from behind Renarin. "You remember your sister?"

"Help us find you," Rlain demanded. "We cannot free you, but it will be better for everyone if you are found by us, and not by our enemies."

Shallan's breath caught. Yes, despite Renarin's complaints, she *did* want to find the prison. If Mishram could actually threaten Odium . . . well, that was a weapon worth having. And having Rlain agree with her was bolstering.

Mishram faded back into the swirling paint-smoke and vanished.

Shallan groaned and climbed to her feet. Then she noticed Pattern humming nearby. He pointed back into the vision—which was still playing out. Testament stepped up beside Pattern, both of them looking at Shallan's Lightweaving through a clearer section of the glass.

Shallan's illusions no longer froze when she wasn't directing them. The one inside, for example, had clasped its hands and was staring thoughtfully, shifting occasionally as a living person might. Pattern pointed toward the shadow of a nearby hillside, where someone was peeking out and inspecting Shallan's illusion from behind. A human soldier who gripped a dagger that warped the air.

Mraize. Shallan's breath caught. He watched the illusory her, obviously prepared to run up and strike . . . but he hesitated. She was *absolutely certain* he hesitated. She didn't get to see for how long, as the vision soon ended, and the glass pillar crumpled away.

Then strangely, the ground beneath her feet darkened. Shallan took hold of Renarin so the three of them would be less likely to be separated. "What is that darkness?" she hissed.

"It's *him,*" Glys said. "Mishram seeing us has led Odium to notice something was wrong. He's searching for us."

"We will hide," Tumi said. "Take care, Shallan. We will find you soon."

"But—"

"We will find you," Tumi repeated.

She was cast into the shifting chaos.

Alone.

⁂

Adolin sat, left hand against his chin, staring at the complicated towers board. They'd swapped to smaller cards to fit more on a table—each barely an inch.

Two practice swords were on the floor, and Yanagawn was still sweating from their sparring match. No Shardplate today—just good old-fashioned swordplay. Each time Adolin arrived, the Imperial Guards changed to ones led by Gezamal, Kushkam's son. A great number of the standard guards would have serious trouble with Adolin embarrassing their emperor during training. Thus, before his sessions, Kushkam switched them out.

That workout was finished, so now, as the welcome cool breeze of the evening darkness arrived—allowed in through the far side of the tent—it was time for the more important lesson of the evening. One in tactics.

"Hmm ..." Yanagawn said, surveying the board, letting out a concentrationspren—like a water drop rippling the air behind him in circles. "I'm doomed."

"Are you?" Adolin asked.

"You've proven to me, time and time again, that the larger force wins. Not just by a linear amount either."

"Explain."

Yanagawn eyed him, then pointed at the board. "I currently have a hundred thousand troops. You have a hundred and twenty thousand."

"But you started with more."

"You always let me start at the advantage."

"So the larger force doesn't always win?"

"I should say," Yanagawn replied, "that all other factors being equal—including the skill of their leader—the larger force wins. Is that correct?"

"And not just by a linear amount," Adolin said. "That's relevant."

The emperor nodded, in his training robe looking like an ordinary youth. His black hair was six inches long; when not trapped under extravagant headgear it could flare outward in that uniquely Makabaki way.

"Two equal forces smashing against one another," Yanagawn said softly, "will both suffer huge casualties. But if one force is even ten or twenty percent larger, something strange happens. The casualties on the other side *multiply.* Two hundred against one hundred doesn't result in one hundred dead on each side—it results in a hundred dead on the smaller side, and maybe only twenty dead on the larger side. The more overwhelming your force, the more protected each man is."

"Assuming," Adolin said, "both forces fight until one is utterly annihilated—which is extremely rare. Armies will usually break after ten to fifteen percent losses. That's not cowardice; it's human nature." He leaned forward. "A good general understands the stakes. Almost nothing is worth fighting for until you're all dead."

"So I *should* retreat on this board," Yanagawn said. "You have an overwhelming size advantage, so I'll lose."

"Will you, though?" Adolin asked.

To his credit, Yanagawn didn't get exasperated by Adolin's pushing. He studied further, taking his time.

Gezamal, wearing his Imperial Guard uniform with the extra patterns, had moved over so he could view the board. The man was an expert towers player; he would immediately see what Adolin was teaching. Yanagawn, however, needed a hint.

"Look for your troops," Adolin said, "who have an advantage."

"These here," Yanagawn said, pointing to a line of troops at the front of his formation. "They have an advantage still. Representing, I believe, high ground."

"And what is high ground?"

"A force multiplier," Yanagawn said. "These spearmen, particularly fighting defensively, can hold against a larger force. But Adolin, this is only a small portion of my army; you think I should keep them here so the others can retreat?"

Adolin waited, saying nothing.

". . . No," Yanagawn said softly, then made his move. Redeploying the troops with an advantage to defensive postures, turning their cards around. He'd seen. Adolin's troops were split between those on the field and a smaller force of reserves coming in from behind. Yanagawn's troops, in turn, were split between the small portion on the hilltop and the larger portion within striking distance of Adolin's reserves.

Over the next few moves, Yanagawn positioned his larger force against Adolin's reserves—counting on his hilltop defensive troops to hold back the rest for a time, as they couldn't pass without taking huge losses. They held long enough for the bulk of his troops to surround and begin destroying Adolin's reserves—which Adolin had deliberately left exposed for the lesson.

"I see . . ." Yanagawn said. "I thought it was my one hundred against your one twenty. But with this maneuver, I leave twenty of mine to hold back the bulk of yours—while my eighty *destroy* your arriving forty."

"You'd take some casualties among your defensive troops," Adolin said, "but in the end, I'd be left with the smaller overall army. Now *I,* seeing that, am the one who has to withdraw."

"I've been told, Adolin," Gezamal said, squatting down by the table, "that you can turn almost any position into a winning one. These scenarios happen in real life—not as clearly, not as cleanly, but they are real. I've read of them."

"I've lived them," Adolin said. "It works—separate enemy forces, gang up on the smaller one . . . It's a good tactic, and one every military commander should know. Watch for chances to turn the battle in your favor, Yanagawn. Because almost any fight can be won."

He began gathering the cards.

"Is that applicable to our own circumstances?" Yanagawn said, looking toward the side of the tent—toward the dome. They could faintly hear fighting inside, though the hour was growing late. Adolin had spent hours in there today; as the enemy troops grew more confident with their position, they now kept almost constant pressure against the defenders.

"Yes," Adolin said. "We *can* win this, Yanagawn."

"Our troops are exhausted," Yanagawn said.

"Fresh ones should arrive within the day," Adolin replied. "Plus, we're in an advantageous spot. You can't always see your whole battlefield like we can here in the dome—and you can rarely manage it so well. Towers is an excellent training method, but it's a little too formal, a little too structured."

"I've heard my father say the same, Adolin," Gezamal said. "On a real battlefield, troops get bogged down, or maneuver wrong, or orders arrive after the situation has changed." He paused. "I think I'd struggle with true battlefield strategy—I'm too used to having exacting control over my pieces."

"I'm sure you'd do better than you think," Yanagawn said.

"Thank you," Gezamal replied. Then he stiffened, his eyes going wide, drawing a shockspren. He'd been spoken to directly by the emperor, and had replied. He stood up straight, and grew very quiet. It wasn't *wrong* to address the emperor if spoken to, but it was a breach—it seemed—for such an exchange to happen with a guard.

"It's all right," Adolin said to Gezamal. "We're all friends in this tent."

"No, it's not," Gezamal said, very stiff-backed.

Adolin sighed, but he didn't push. He expected other military leaders to put up with the way he led his troops—he should probably try a little harder to appreciate the Azish system.

"Adolin," Yanagawn said, leaning forward to help gather the cards. "You always give me the advantage at the start of a game. I wonder if we should try it another way. My uncle, when I was . . . living my previous life . . . always said *hardship* made a man grow. If I start in a winning position, how will I learn?"

"We'll move on to other training structures eventually," Adolin promised. "But Yanagawn, let me share something my father once told me. He said that if he had ten generals who could *always* win from a superior position, he could rule the world. Do not discount how difficult it is to maintain a lead. Too many generals throw away winning positions because of bad fundamentals."

"All right," he said.

"You talked earlier about the stronger force always winning, but we just proved that's not the case. Indeed, there's an old list we call Valithar's Dictates. He said there are three primary ways that a general loses from a numerical advantage. Can you name any of them?"

"Terrain?" Yanagawn guessed. "An inferior force with better fortifications can beat a superior force. In today's game, I was able to use the land against you."

"Excellent," Adolin said.

"A second one . . ." Yanagawn said, "involves leadership or training? I lost early games because I was incompetent."

"One general doesn't have to be incompetent to lose to another that is better, but yes, that is one of the three. Superior troops or leadership can change a losing position into a winning one. And the third?"

Yanagawn thought awhile, then shook his head.

"Random chance," Adolin said. "A strong line can buckle because a single soldier loses his footing. A powerful force can have its supply lines swept away by unexpected flooding, leaving its soldiers hungry and at a disadvantage."

"Frustrating," Yanagawn said.

"Life," Adolin replied. Then he paused. "Technically, there is a fourth way a stronger force frequently loses to a weaker one, though it's not one Valithar outlined. We'll talk about that later. For now, focus on these three."

"I will," Yanagawn promised. Then he hesitated. "Adolin?"

"Yes?"

"Will I ever be able to *use* any of this?" The emperor sat back in his cushioned seat on the floor before their low table. A servant brought wine, delivering it to another servant, who poured it, and in turn gave it to the servant who today was designated as worthy to present it to the emperor.

"Depends," Adolin said, pouring himself some wine—orange, because his father had gotten to him—and lying back on his own cushions. "We hope to never have to use this in real life. War finds us nonetheless."

"Your father is building us a lasting peace," Yanagawn said. "If we hold here until the deadline arrives, then Azir is free. But either way, the war with the singers ends. Doesn't it?"

"That's how it appears," Adolin said.

"So when will I use any of this?"

"Well," Adolin said, "there's the joy of the game. Have you enjoyed learning towers?"

"Immensely."

"Then you can keep playing," Adolin said, sipping his wine. He gazed upward, thoughtful, imagining the sky past the tent's top. "What do you make of what the contract implies? About . . . war out there?"

"Other worlds?" Yanagawn said. "We have legends about them, in our records. We record everything, and there are so many stories that confirm this if you look for them."

"Really?" Adolin said, perking up.

"Firsthand accounts of people who traveled here," Yanagawn said, "traversing a great darkness that sounds an awful lot like Shadesmar. I had my scribes gather them all, and the weight of them together . . . it's rather convincing. We all thought so, right, Noura?" He turned, but she wasn't there. She still left during the training. "Anyway," Yanagawn continued, "seeing it all together, it's remarkable we didn't understand this earlier. Makes me wonder if anyone close to us is secretly one of them. A person from another world."

"His name is Wit," Adolin said. "And he's kind of a jerk."

Yanagawn smiled. "We have legends about him too. Most records call him an emissary of Yaezir, but it's clear he's been interfering for millennia." He paused, looking down at his wine. "Wit, our emissary of the gods, is just . . . a man. I spoke to him only last week. We worship Yaezir—or as you call him, Jezerezeh—yet it seems he never was God . . . and that he might be dead anyway."

"Yeah," Adolin said. "I . . . do think about that."

"What does it mean?" Yanagawn asked. "What do you believe, in the face of all of this?"

What *did* he believe? Storms, that was a good question. How long had it been since he'd paid for prayers, gone to the devotary, or done any of the other things he was supposed to do? One would think that with literal Voidbringers coming down to assault the land, he'd be *more* devout, not less. But then his father had gone and upended religion itself and . . . and Adolin was left wondering. If there were gods, or an Almighty, or something . . . shouldn't Adolin be getting a little help now and then? He was trying to protect the world.

Those kinds of worries unnerved him on a fundamental level. As he considered, he felt something from Maya—distant though she was. A kind of comfort.

They continued playing, and some servants brought Yanagawn food—letting him take a short break to dine. Not a formal dinner, just some snacks.

"Silver plates?" Adolin asked with a smile. "And forks?"

"Worse, or better," Yanagawn said, raising a small fork he was using with one hand. A servant took it, stabbed a small fruit, then handed it back. "Aluminum."

"Aluminum?" Adolin said. "You have aluminum dining ware?"

"And finery," Yanagawn said, gesturing to some of the nearby candelabras holding ceremonial candles. "This one here was made from a star that fell during my predecessor's days—we used to call it starmetal. More valuable than any gemstone or other metal. Only the finest for the emperor."

"We could use that," Adolin said, thoughtful. "It blocks Shardblades, and has other applications."

Yanagawn paused. "I hadn't really thought about that. Maybe I should have—especially when they started coating my bedrooms in plates of it to protect from the Fused." He turned from his meal and gave instructions for people to begin gathering the metal to take to the armorers. The enemy hadn't used any Shardblades in this fight, but who knew? A few shields banded in the stuff might be useful.

Adolin was thinking on this as his guards swapped. He wasn't surprised when Hmask—happy and smiling—was in the new rotation.

"Good to see you, my friend," Adolin said to him.

Hmask merely nodded.

"Wish I knew what your story was," Adolin said idly.

Yanagawn, accepting another drink, looked over. Then he spoke to Hmask directly—his guards and aides were slowly getting used to this—in what sounded like perfect Thaylen.

Hmask, surprised, replied. He spoke quickly and eagerly.

"Interesting," Yanagawn said in Azish. "Adolin, do you remember a moment during the Battle of Thaylen Field when you were in a building and a large monster was attacking it?"

"Thunderclast," Adolin said. "Yeah. I wasn't able to beat it. Honestly, I barely inconvenienced it." He thought back to that whole ordeal with shame at his failure.

Hmask kept talking.

"There was a boy," Yanagawn said, "in a building that was breaking and crumbling. Do you remember?"

Adolin paused, picturing it.

A whimper. An overturned table. Thunderclast footfalls, shaking chips from the ceiling. A young boy.

"I remember," Adolin said, and Yanagawn interpreted.

Hmask knelt, mustaches and eyebrows wagging, and took Adolin's hand. "Son," he said in Alethi. "Me. Son. You." He pressed his forehead to Adolin's hand. "Me. Son. *You.*"

"I think," Yanagawn said, "you saved his son's life."

Hmask stood up, tears in his eyes, and slapped his chest. He then returned to his stance by the exit. Until now, Adolin had forgotten that moment in Thaylen City. Storms.

Before he could think further though, a pair of Azish scribes arrived in a flurry. Adolin sat up, alarmed. These were dressed as Azish information gatherers. He was pretty sure they ran the local spanreed hub for the emperor.

They weren't looking for him, however. They asked for Noura, then left when she wasn't there.

"What was that?" Adolin said.

"Hmm?" Yanagawn said. "They would have said something if it was important."

Adolin excused himself, pushing out into the night. He spotted the two moving to another lit tent and tried to follow them in, but was stopped by guards.

He gritted his teeth until Noura called from within. "He may enter."

Adolin pushed past the men and found her at a desk with several other viziers. The two scribes he'd seen earlier stood there, swarming with anxietyspren like twisting black crosses. They'd delivered spanreed writings to Noura.

"What kind of important news," he said, "causes the lead scribes of the spanreed hub to run to you personally?"

Noura looked to him, then drew her lips to a line. Somehow Adolin knew—from that grim expression—that this wasn't information from Urithiru about the war effort at large; it was specific to Azir.

"The reinforcements," he guessed. "They aren't going to arrive in time."

"You," Noura said, "are smarter than your reputation suggests, Highprince."

His stomach sank. Even though he'd planned for this, expected it for days . . . well, you anticipated the worst case, but you did *not* want to have to encounter it.

"What happened?" he demanded.

"Betrayal," she said. "Emul and Tashikk have turned on us."

Emul and Tashikk? Two of the subject nations in the Azish empire. The coalition had expended huge efforts to protect Emul from conquest recently. That was why the bulk of their armies were away, needing to march to Azimir.

"The phantom force that struck at our reinforcement," he said. "They were our own people."

"Supposedly our own," Noura said. Nearby a spanreed was writing furiously. Adolin waited as she read it, then met his eyes. "From the prime of Emul. A formal declaration of secession. It seems . . . they've made their own deal with Odium. I suspect we'll get the same from Tashikk."

The dagger of those words cut deeply, and Adolin attracted a spren he never had before—in all his years. Like snapping strings expanding from him. Betrayalspren.

The scribes outlined it for him. Though the bulk of the forty thousand troops marching to their rescue were Alethi and Azish, the entire remaining force from the two subject nations had turned against them—and were harrying them, slowing them. It would be enough to keep the army from arriving in time.

"Storms," he whispered. "How *could* they? Why?"

"Evidently," Noura said, reading a letter from the Tashikki prime, "Odium offered them a deal with some small measure of autonomy—and they decided to take that instead of waiting on the results of the battle here. I fear . . . they assumed that if Azir won, it would reinforce our imperial claim, and that we might push for stronger oversight and taxation. They saw themselves as picking between two bad choices, and took the sure one."

Adolin sat there, his stomach churning, his nerves taut as he tried to find a way out of this mess. He'd never expected their allies—those they'd fought to protect—to turn on them. It meant . . . storms, this was a brilliant move on Odium's part. He'd known the Azish empire was only tenuously united, and had struck precisely in a way to give the smaller parties some concessions so he could dominate the larger one.

"The enemy is isolating us, Noura," he said. "He's looking to suffocate us."

He felt the winds behind him grow still, and he could make out the shouts of men fighting in the dome. Men who were exhausted, barely holding on.

Men who would have to hold out for three and a half more days.

Because no help was coming.

But I will say that for me, the existence of something that cares—and can, after death, make up for injustices in life—is not the question. But the answer.

—From the epilogue to *Oathbringer*, by Dalinar Kholin. Excerpt used at his tribunal, in absentia—for the appeal filed on his behalf by supporters after his excommunication from the Vorin church—as evidence of continued heresy.

Dalinar was cast into the Spiritual Realm.

This time it was different. Though he tried to keep hold of Navani and Gav, he lost them in the rush.

They'd been moving from Desolation to Desolation, making their way toward the Recreance. Then, just now, a shadow had fallen over the vision. Causing it to end abruptly.

Images of his past came more quickly, more violently than before. Armored versions of him stomped through landscapes, fracturing them like a shattered mirror, only for another version of him to *rip* that reality apart, drunkenly weeping over his faults.

He clutched the Honorblade anchor, but didn't use it yet. He . . . he needed to find Navani. He searched fervently for the line of light Connecting them, but the sea of overlapping images crashed against him in waves, blinding him. It was the ocean, and he a poor sailor on the rocks.

Those waves were made up of thousands of versions of *him,* boiling from the surf that was this strange place, the swirling colors and shimmering essence.

Be me, each of them demanded. *I want to live again.*

If he gave in, he'd never escape from those snarling back alleys of his own mind. He hunkered down before them, his eyes squeezed closed. "Stormfather," he whispered. "Please."

I will help, the Stormfather replied, *if you leave this realm and never return.*

Dalinar blinked and saw a figure breaking the tide in front of him. The figure shifted, changing shapes faintly—while keeping the same general form.

"Why?" Dalinar whispered. "Why are you so afraid?"

I had a plan. I need you to trust me.

"Trust you?" Dalinar said, surging forward through the thousands of landscapes that appeared and vanished. "How can I trust you? You had a *plan* for all this? What plan?"

The figure didn't respond. So, desperate, Dalinar held the Honorblade close. *Take me,* he thought, *to my destination. I need to go further than I have before. Far further . . .*

He fell in a heap, and a new reality burst into being. He felt the Honorblade vanish from his grip—and he cried out as it did. He . . . he was alone, on a burning section of rock, with taller formations and clumps of stone here and there. A scent of burned flesh pervaded the air.

Dalinar knew this place. It was one of his original visions—the one where he'd discovered the discarded Honorblades after the Heralds walked away from them. The . . . ultimate end of his anchor, and the reason it had vanished after bringing him here. He had reached the day the Blades had been discarded.

He got to his knees in the shadow of a dying thunderclast. Jezrien the Herald was standing tall on a short ridge perhaps twenty yards away. The king looked more regal than he had in the earlier visions, but perhaps that was the kingly clothing: white and blue, without furs, the cloth more refined than it had been in antiquity. The outfit was marred with blood and ash, but that was something Dalinar associated with kingship.

"Chana," Jezrien called to him. "Here."

So, he was in her body this time? The red-haired bodyguard? He had the impression she was in Jezrien's inner circle, even among the Heralds. She, Jezrien, and Ishar. Dalinar trotted over to join Jezrien on the ridge. From there, he saw armies hunting among the fallen for survivors.

Where was Navani? Would she find her way to this vision as well? Storms. He checked his arm bracer. They were on the sixth day; four remaining. He'd learned so much about Honor and the Oathpact from these visions, but the primary secret kept eluding him: how could he persuade that power to accept him as its new master?

He tried to reach out for his Connection to Navani, to pull her to him, but found nothing. He was torn between trying to find her and Gav, or continuing, because Jezrien was walking onward.

Before, when Dalinar had seen this vision, he'd arrived *after* the Heralds had abandoned their oaths. If he went with Jezrien, he could see the actual moment that had happened. Could this relate to Honor and his power? It felt likely.

"Hurry," Jezrien said. "Ishar is at the meeting place already. I want to get there before the others."

Dalinar joined him. Worried about Navani, but hoping she was already in the body of another Herald.

"Did you see any of the others?" Jezrien asked. "Maybe Kalak? I think everyone else survived. We're doing it again—we aren't taking risks. We hide from battle. Everyone except . . ."

"Except Taln," Dalinar said.

Jezrien nodded. "I sent Battar and Vedel to check on my daughter, mostly to keep them busy. We need to make our decision quickly, before they start trickling back."

"Decision . . ." He knew what Jezrien referred to: this would be the decision not to leave for Braize. The decision to leave Taln alone to bear the Oathpact.

Cowardice. Except he saw the way Jezrien gazed down at the ground as he spoke. Saw the way his hands trembled, and how he had to make fists to hide it. Suddenly, instead of regal, he appeared haggard. Overwhelmed. Who was Dalinar to judge what thousands of years of torture could do to a man?

"Jezrien," he said, "I still, so many centuries later, don't understand how all of this works. Is it idiocy of me to admit?"

"No," Jezrien said softly. "No, I suppose it isn't. It's courage, Chana. You should understand before we make this decision."

"How does our dying trap the Fused?" Dalinar said.

"Braize," he said. "The planet. It draws souls to it naturally. Honor fashioned it into a prison, but a prison needs a lock."

"And . . . we are that lock?" Dalinar asked.

"Our oath is that lock. Because Odium first Connected to us when he gave us powers on Ashyn, Honor could use that bond against him. That, along with the promise we made, becomes the force that holds the Fused." Jezrien's eyes seemed distant. "It is . . . what the gods do. We form a binding through our willpower, holding the others we are Connected to—our replacements in a way—to Braize. Impossible, save for the strange nature of that planet lending our ten oaths a multiplicative strength."

"But unless all ten of us return, they can be reborn."

"Yes," Jezrien said. "Normally. All ten . . ."

Dalinar *thought* he understood, as he'd seen some of it through these last visions. The Heralds would appear, then lead the people and help them fight.

At some point during the battle, it became right to leave—after everyone had been rallied, inspired, trained. Then the Heralds had to go and lock the Fused away.

Thus, they never saw the true end of a Desolation. The Heralds frequently waited for a large battle—where lots of Fused had died—to go together to Braize and begin the Isolation. And beyond that, if one of them died and remained on Braize, that slowed the Fused. The more who did, the slower the enemy returned.

So to win a Desolation, they trained the humans, they killed as many Fused as possible, then they began staying in Damnation . . . reforging the lock. Until one of them broke in torture, and the floodgates opened again, letting the Fused begin the process to return to Roshar. At that point, the Heralds—exhausted—would return, starting the cycle once more.

A cycle that repeated until this last Desolation. When the nine had left the one.

They arrived in the natural hollow near a tall rock formation—almost like a castle—that offered some seclusion from the battlefield. This was where Dalinar had seen the vision of the Honorblades rammed into the ground.

Ishar was waiting for them.

And he was chatting with Honor.

Dalinar stopped in place, feeling a jolt of excitement. He *was* still on the right track. This was Aharietiam, some four or five thousand years before Dalinar's time, perhaps two or three thousand years before the day he most wanted to see: when the Knights Radiant had walked away, and Honor had been killed. That was a long time off, yes—but this was a good step.

I need to find Navani, he thought. *I'll need her help to decipher all of this.*

Jezrien joined Ishar. Honor was once again dressed in gold, his brown skin and white hair offering a distinctive contrast. Dalinar stumbled up after them.

"Lord," Jezrien said. "Almighty. Did you . . . hear what we were considering?"

"Ishar's plan," Honor said. "Not to return to Braize."

"We . . . we apologize for our weakness," Jezrien said, looking away, squeezing his eyes shut, drawing shamespren. "But Lord, it's so hard. We can't . . . I mean, the mere thought of . . ."

"We're broken," Ishar whispered. "We need you to change the bond. Take it from us."

"Break the Oathpact?" Honor asked.

"Change it, so that others can take our place," Ishar said. "Or . . . or maybe make it allow half of us to hold the bond for one Isolation, then trade with the other half . . ."

 "Five?" Honor said. "No, impossible. Five is a number of weakness. No symmetry, no power. Perhaps four would work. The number of Adonalsium's four aspects. Or ten, sixteen . . . one."

Dalinar felt cold. "One?"

"One cosmere," Honor said. "One Truth. One Adonalsium. A number of power and strength."

"One . . ." Ishar whispered. "One could remain?"

"It would be a cracking of the Oathpact," Honor said. "You would need to acknowledge that and decide. To give of your Honor, in small measure. There must yet be ten to hold the core, but one . . . one could stand at the forefront. Like a soldier in the lead of a formation."

"But—" Dalinar started.

"Regardless," Honor said, "I will no longer be aiding you as you go forward, Heralds. My part in this conflict is done."

"What do we do?" Jezrien asked.

Storms, Honor had been here? And had nurtured the seed of their betrayal of Taln?

"I cannot afford to care any longer," Honor said. "I can't afford to care about any of you. I need . . . distance. Yes."

"But Lord," Ishar said, stepping forward, "what do we tell the people?"

"Do as you wish." Honor vanished—no fanfare, no flash.

"That is it," Jezrien said, making a small gesture with his hand—more subtle than the ones Dalinar had seen before.

"You'll abandon him," Dalinar whispered. "Now that you know one can do it alone."

"Not fully alone," Ishar said. "We will . . . support him . . . from this world."

"I still wish others could take our place," Jezrien said.

"I *will* find a way to replace us," Ishar said. "But it will take time, Jezrien. For now, we leave Taln."

Jezrien looked sick.

"Could you go to Damnation instead of him?" Ishar said, looking from him to Dalinar. "Can either of you go?"

"I . . ." Dalinar said. He didn't want to break the vision. "I don't know."

"I can't do it," Jezrien whispered. Then summoned his sword and gazed at it, pain evident on his face. "But neither can I carry this in good conscience after abandoning a friend. When all but Taln have gathered, I will leave my Blade here, never to take it up again. I can wield Honor no longer." His face seemed to grow more pale. "I feel it, Ishar. I feel myself . . . putting my burden upon him." He glanced toward where the Almighty had been standing. "I thought . . . I thought he'd fix it . . ."

"Our god is no longer reliable," Ishar said, then took a deep breath. "I will do what I can in his absence." Ishar put his hand on Jezrien's shoulder. "I first bore Surges. I initiated the Oathpact. I am the Bondsmith. I can bear some of your pain." He looked to Dalinar. "I can bear part of it for each of you."

"I can't let you do that, Ishar," Jezrien said.

"Why not? You are willing to abandon Taln. We all are." Ishar's expression softened. "Someone may need to step into Honor's place. I can explore that possibility. Please, give me some of your pain."

Jezrien hesitated, then nodded. "And the rest of us? What do we do?"

"Live," Ishar said.

"I cannot live like this."

"Then exist," Ishar said. "For while we abandon the Oathpact here, the shell of it remains. We will be immortal, and Taln will hold for all ten—he has never broken, unlike the rest of us. We will go our separate ways. We will not seek or see one another. We will let it be."

Jezrien met Dalinar's eyes. "What do you think?"

"I think," Dalinar said softly, "it must be done."

Ishar delivered up his own Blade to the earth, ramming it in as Jezrien directed. They turned as other figures came stumbling up to the meeting place. Vedel, Ash, Battar. None appeared to be Navani or Gav.

Dalinar backed away and sat on the stone ground. *If the Almighty had been willing to support you, maybe change the members of the Oathpact, this could have been avoided. So why? Why does he seem to be actively working* against *us?*

Others arrived, everyone but Nale and Kalak. Dalinar closed his eyes and focused on his Connections. He breathed in and out. Whatever darkness had been overshadowing him faded away. The web of lines of light returned, extending from him, binding him to the people he loved . . .

Navani and Gav appeared on the ground before him—and unlike everything else here, they didn't form from swirling Stormlight. Instead the air appeared to part around them, like dust being swept back on the stone floor—or even drapes being opened. Revealing them behind a layer of reality, as if they'd always been there.

"You found us," Navani said, relieved, holding Gav.

"As you found me before," Dalinar said. He checked his arm clock again, and saw it had barely moved. Storms, he could age decades in here if he wasn't careful, while minutes passed outside. That would almost be as bad as the opposite. "It's near the end of the sixth day, Navani. I just learned that Honor abandoned the Heralds in the moments before they walked away from their swords." He frowned. "Ishar did something I hadn't known about: he took some of the pain of the others, and carried it himself. Maybe that is why he seems so unreliable during our time."

Navani hugged Gav tighter, and Dalinar gave them a moment to recover. Some of the lines of white light connected to his core were fading; two strong ones pointed to Navani and Gav, but a few others stood out—one in particular as strong as his line to Navani. Curious. And there was another, drifting off into nothing, that felt . . . familiar. The Stormfather.

Dalinar followed it with his eyes, spotting a shimmering in the air nearby. And beside it . . . a second shimmering, almost imperceptible. Wait. What was that?

Both are him, Dalinar thought. *The modern him, and the ancient one.*

But the Stormfather hadn't truly been alive during this event, had he? It was all so muddled. For now, Dalinar wanted to check on his grand-nephew. He knelt beside Gav, who—after being set down—was looking around with interest.

"How are you, lad?" Dalinar asked him.

"Good, Grampa," the boy said.

"Was it bad, being in the strange place?"

"A little," the boy said. "But . . . I knew you'd come for me."

"I will," Dalinar said, then took the boy in an embrace. "I always will, Gav."

"Grampa," the boy said. "When I was with the ardents, they said you saw God in dreams. Is that what this is?"

"Yes," Dalinar said, pulling back, surprised—again—at Gav's maturity. The ardents still at Urithiru were those who had chosen Dalinar's way, over the more orthodox branches of the religion forming in reaction to his teachings. Those who remained revered him on a level that probably should have made him uncomfortable.

"I thought so." Gav pointed toward the gathered Heralds. "Aunt Dova is here. Should we talk to her?"

"Wait," Dalinar said. "Aunt Dova? You *know* her?"

He nodded. "She visited Mother. Sometimes."

A Herald had been visiting Aesudan? Dalinar frowned, looking at Navani, who knelt beside him.

"You're sure, Gav?" she asked.

He nodded, his eyes wide.

"I think, lad," Dalinar said, "she's just a *pretend* version of . . . Aunt Dova."

The boy merely nodded again. "I'll watch, Grampa," he whispered. "Like you. God trained you. He'll train me too. To be a king. To kill those who killed Daddy."

Storms. Once they were through this, he'd chat with the lad, try to help him with those feelings. For now, he and Navani stood, and he nodded toward "Aunt Dova."

"Any idea why she might have visited the palace?" he asked.

"No idea," Navani said. "I don't recognize her though. So I didn't see her there." She thought a moment. "What happened? How did we lose track of each other during this transition between visions?"

"There was a darkness in the last one," Dalinar said. "And it fell apart. I used the sword to get here, then it evaporated."

"It wouldn't be viable after this anyway; the Heralds' swords will no longer be as tied to important events. We'll need another anchor to progress. Do you know who you are replacing?"

"Chana," he said.

"And me?" Navani asked.

Dalinar shook his head. "Nobody was with me when you appeared there. Maybe they'll see you as a spren, like Gav."

Navani, seeming thoughtful, brushed herself off and went to listen in on the Heralds. They were talking over the plan.

"Grampa," Gav whispered, "when can we go home? I will listen . . . I will be strong. But . . . do you know?"

"Stormfather?" Dalinar asked, giving the boy another hug.

No response.

"STORMFATHER!" Dalinar said, allowing the authority of storms to well up within him. He didn't know how he did it.

What? the Stormfather said in his mind, and the shimmering moved closer to him.

"Take the boy out of here," Dalinar said to it. "At least let him find peace."

Your recklessness brought him here.

"You could send him home."

You could bring him home.

Dalinar gritted his teeth.

This might scar him, the Stormfather said. *What he sees could be horrible. Don't you care?*

"Of course I care!" Dalinar snapped. "But I'm a king. I can't think of the one; it's my duty to think of the people as a whole. I'm close to the power of Honor. I can feel it. With it, I *can* defeat Odium. But if I leave now—for Gav or Navani, or even myself—I fail everyone else as a result!"

Is that actually your reason, the Stormfather demanded, *or is it because you need to be right? Is it because you need to be the one who makes the decisions, who has the final say?*

Dalinar didn't reply. For all the spren claimed it didn't see or do things the way that men did—that it didn't understand the ways of humankind—it was expert at deflecting conversations and diverting Dalinar's attention.

Dalinar looked back at the second shimmering he'd seen earlier. "That's you, isn't it? You were here watching, when the Heralds broke the Oathpact."

I had to witness it, the Stormfather said.

Storms, it was so hard to sort through the lies—in previous conversations, the Stormfather claimed he'd merely been a primal force during this era. A wind that blew with the storms, personified by human attention. He'd said he hadn't developed a full personality until Honor's death, when he'd inherited some of Honor's memories.

Yet the Stormfather had been here. Dalinar would have to discuss this with Navani. He glanced at her, and found that she was waving her hand in front of Jezrien's face—getting no reaction.

"You're right," she called to Dalinar. "They noted me as a spren, but now won't even acknowledge me. I think the vision is pretending I'm not here. As happened with Gav, after you pulled him into a vision."

Dalinar nodded in thought.

"Grampa," Gav said softly, "were you hearing someone in your head? Just now, before talking to Gram?"

"Yes," Dalinar said. "I was talking to the Stormfather. He's a friendly spren, son."

"I hear Daddy sometimes. Telling me I'm a good boy."

"Listen to voices like that, Gav," Dalinar whispered.

Navani returned and settled down beside Dalinar. "I don't know if being ignored is better or worse. I can walk around without distracting them, but I can't ask questions."

"What does it mean that Honor left the Heralds?" Dalinar asked her. "Is it tied to his death? And to why the power hasn't attached to anyone in all these years?"

"I don't know," she said.

Nale arrived—and the others welcomed him, friendly. Their attitudes toward one another had changed over the millennia. Nale took the news of their imminent disbanding with a nod. He asked after Kalak—who they feared might have died, though Dalinar knew he would arrive eventually—then left his sword. He paused with his hand on it for a moment and exhaled, shivering as something seemed to pass from him. He walked away without a further word, the first of them to leave. He would later, Dalinar knew, reclaim his weapon—as would Ishar.

"What can we use as an anchor to the next vision?" Dalinar asked. "I worry this one will fall apart as soon as all the Heralds leave their swords."

"Hopefully we won't lose one another again," Navani said. She thought a moment, then pressed her hand to his chest. He frowned until he saw what she was doing—concentrating, strengthening the power of the line of light Connecting them.

Unite them. Dalinar still occasionally heard echoes of that command vibrating through him. He thought that hadn't come from the Stormfather or Honor, but from a god that once had existed, and might yet, if not in a form people recognized. He had no evidence other than his own feelings. But he had written—he hoped convincingly—of those experiences in his book.

"There," Navani said, pulling her hand away. "That might make it easier for us to find one another."

"We can't go back to searching for a new anchor each vision. That was too slow—not to mention maddening."

"Wit said this was the best way."

"He said this was *a* way," Dalinar said, standing up. "But Wit's not a Bondsmith; he can't manipulate Connection." He looked to that shimmer of the real Stormfather. "The Stormfather, the real one, told me he *had* to watch this event when it actually happened. Because it was too important not to witness. If he watched this, do you suppose . . ."

She frowned. "Was he even alive before Honor died?"

"I get confusing answers to that question," Dalinar said. "Wait for me; I'm going to try something."

Dalinar stalked toward that shimmer, and as he did, the vision started to break apart. Shifting Stormlight began to claim it, but Dalinar seized hold of that line of light Connecting him to the Stormfather. He held tight, pulling on it, like he was holding a horse's reins.

The vision stabilized around him.

What are you doing? the Stormfather said, trepidatious.

"You know what we need to see next," Dalinar said. "I can use you to get there."

You cannot win Honor's power through force of will, Dalinar, the Stormfather said. *Your brother tried to force* his *way to his goals, and he ended up broken.*

"What do you know about my brother?" Dalinar demanded. "How many lies have you told me?"

Only the ones you needed to hear.

"You *can* lead me to the next vision," Dalinar said.

And so you continue, bullheaded as always, the Stormfather snapped. *We clash, you refuse to listen, and you bend me to your will. You talk of reconciliation, and us getting along, but then you ignore my wishes when it is convenient for you. Then you are angry when I don't want to work with you?*

Dalinar stopped beside the shimmer. "Would you let the world fall under Odium's control because of your pride, Stormfather?"

Better than potentially letting it burn, Dalinar, under your control. I need someone willing to work with *the power, not against it.*

"Sometimes there is no path forward," Dalinar said, "so you have to break one open."

 Like you did with Elhokar? Pounding him into submission? You never knew he was seeing Cryptics because instead of asking why he was afraid, you burst in and attacked him!

"I showed him I wasn't a threat!" Dalinar said.

By beating him near senseless, the Stormfather said. *I should never have picked you, Dalinar. You are born of war, and trail blood like a shadow. The sole thing you know how to* do *is break. If you are told no, you just punch harder—because life has taught you that's how to get what you want. But sometimes, deny it though you may, the world doesn't* need *what you want.*

Dalinar let his fingers trail from the line of light. There was . . . there was too much truth in the Stormfather's words.

"What are you?" Dalinar asked, narrowing his eyes at the shimmer. "What are you *really*?"

What I've always been, the Stormfather said. *Perhaps if you hadn't treated me like you did Elhokar and every other person in your life, we'd have made it further, Dalinar. I suppose the fault is mine. I knew what you were. This is the end. You will die in this realm—a worse death than your brother, and a worse one than you deserve. Goodbye.*

The Stormfather faded, and the vision burst like a bubble, Stormlight swirling around him, consuming him. Those words echoed in his mind. A farewell. An expectation of death.

The Stormfather was right. The only way Dalinar knew how to solve problems was by attacking them. It was a flaw. Perhaps a fatal one.

But blood of his fathers, he was *not* going to die in here. He was not going to let the world wither beneath Odium because of his own weaknesses. He might know only how to kill and fight, but at least he was storming good at it.

He again seized hold of the line of light Connecting them. The Stormfather didn't merely *know* the secrets surrounding Honor's death—the Stormfather was *fixated* upon them. The Stormfather wasn't simply an anchor, he was the pathway, the portal. The answer. Dalinar held to the line of light with one hand, and seized the one Connecting him to Navani with the other. He heaved on both, pulling like he had on that fateful day when he'd bound the realms.

For a long moment—during which he knew time was passing with frightening speed—he stood there, a line of light in each hand, like some mythical giant. The one the Thaylen stories said pulled the sun up by a cord each morning. He shouted, straining, and through sheer force of will brought his hands together and made the lines meet.

Realities overlapped. He heard the Stormfather growl in anger—for in that moment, a new vision formed. A familiar sight: the large main thoroughfare of Urithiru, full of people dressed in old styles of clothing. Takamas, robes, long enveloping skirts. A man strode among them, tall and confident, wearing Shardplate that glowed blue—matched by his rippling blue cape. A Windrunner. His helm was off, revealing blond hair and skin pale as the palest Shin.

Dalinar knew that man.

We're here, he thought. *It worked.* He checked his arm, and found he'd lost another day. Three remained until the contest, but he was *here.* At the right time. He glanced to the side, where Navani had replaced one of the many people waiting in the wings of the hallway. Gav held to her leg.

"What is this?" she asked. "Dalinar, what did you do?"

"I used my Connection to the Stormfather to bring us here," he said. "To where we need to be."

"How do you know?"

"You see that Radiant?" Dalinar said, pointing. "He's the first one who gave up his Blade and Plate at the Recreance, the leader who stepped out before them all. I remember him distinctly from my visions of that day. He still has his armor now, and he looks younger than I remember, so the Recreance hasn't happened yet." He paused. "We've reached our goal: these are the last days before Honor died."

THE END OF
Day Six

INTERLUDES

DYEL • ODIUM

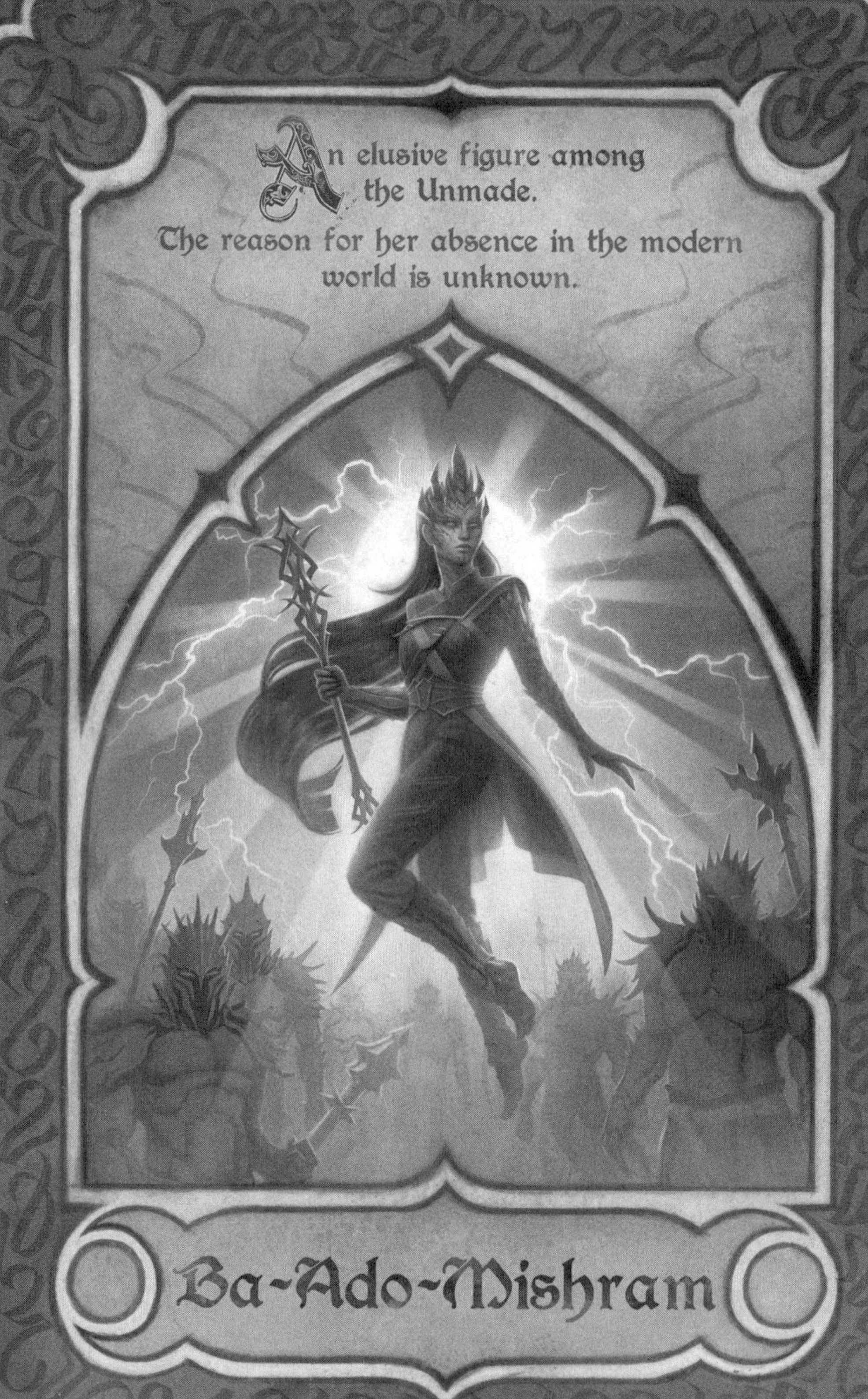
An elusive figure among the Unmade.
The reason for her absence in the modern world is unknown.
Ba-Ado-Mishram

Dyel had the most unusual of visitors.

That was not uncommon in Iri, now that the Owners had returned. They walked the streets, with bodies bearing patterns that looked like they were painted. Red, white, and black.

But these visitors were not of the Owners. These visitors were *different*.

The three sat at a table in her shop near the cubbies on the wall where her grandfather—before his murder—had put shoes. When they'd come in, they'd pretended they were from "the East." But Dyel knew accents, and these men were *not* from the East. Besides, their clothing was strange—particularly the tallest man's, with the long white coat and the spectacles peeking from his pocket.

She hovered in the doorway to the kitchen after delivering their tea, hoping her mother wouldn't notice her loitering.

"Are you certain this is the right time?" asked the tall man in the coat. He had skin like he was from Azir, with short black hair and muscles like a soldier. She could *almost* believe he was from the far East, where terrible men were said to be the fiercest of warriors. But he liked sugar in his tea. What kind of fierce warrior liked sugar in his tea?

"Of course I'm not," said the tubby one, who was constantly scowling. "The device is unpredictable, don't you know?" This one had darker skin too, and was completely bald. Older. Shorter. Again he wore odd clothing—most people in Iri went around without shirts, and only a bandeau for the women. He wore a cloak and colorful robes. In this weather?

The tall man grunted, then sipped his sugared tea. The third of them sat quietly. A Shin man of middling height, also balding—with a scar on his head—light skin, and more normal clothing, for an outlander. Shirt and trousers. He didn't talk as much. But he watched. She knew people like that.

Lest they think that she was observing them, Dyel busied herself cleaning tables, then standing by the door to give welcoming smiles to those who passed on the street. She liked that: watching the different kinds of people who were part of the One. She also liked smelling the ocean air. Though they were too poor to have a shop in the best part of town, the breeze carried the crisp, salty air inland. A gift of experience she could add to the One.

Outside, an Owner walked past, a hulking figure with carapace and eyes that glowed red. There was some discussion about them in Iri; were these singers, these Owners, part of the One, or were they something else? She thought they *must* be the One. It wouldn't be the One unless it—God—encompassed everything. Every person a piece of it, extended out into the cosmere to live a different life and bring back enriching knowledge.

Her mother didn't believe, but Dyel did. Because if she did, then Grandpa Ym was always with her and she with him.

"Serving girl?" one of the men called. "Could I get another?"

She hurried to the table with the three strangers, her hair aflutter. She trimmed it only when Mother forced her to. She was Iriali, and her golden hair was her heritage. She quickly refilled the men's cups as the thoughtful one—the quiet one—set a sphere on the table.

Her breath caught. A full broam? She looked to the man, who had a round, friendly face. He nodded.

She snatched it up, the azure light inside it making her skin glow. But Mother would insist she ask. So, reluctantly, she spoke. "Do I have to give you change?"

"No," he said, smiling. "Though I wouldn't mind answers to a question or two."

She shrugged. "Sure."

"Have you ever seen," the man asked, "a strange collection of lights that moves across the wall or floor, though you can find no source reflecting it?"

Dyel felt an immediate spike of terror. She nearly dropped the teapot. She'd suspected they weren't what they said, but this? *This?*

"I'm sorry I have to go I forgot my mother wanted me to check on the biscuits stay as long as you want thank you for the tip we are closed now goodbye." She scampered into the rear room—now a kitchen and living space, transformed from her grandfather's workshop. She put her back to the wall, her heart thundering.

He had returned. The murderer. What to do?

Find Mother.

Mother was gone. Dyel found nothing but a note. *Back in fifteen. Watch the shop.*

 Oh no. Nononononono.

She scrambled past globby purple fearspren and found a knife for spreading butter. Then she hid in the corner, clutching it, trying not to be too loud as she cried and trembled. Until they darkened the doorway. Three men—two shorter, one taller. Dyel yelped despite herself, holding out the knife.

The tall one glanced at the thoughtful one. "Look what you've done, Demoux," he said. "I told you to stop talking about that."

"I need an intelligent spren to study!" he said. "They keep telling me no."

"Perhaps because you keep saying you want to 'study' them, isn't that so?" the grumpy one said. "We certainly frightened fewer people when your translator didn't work."

The tallest man knelt before Dyel, who tried to squeeze herself against the wall, her skirt getting twisted and crumpled, the rough grain of the wood pressing into the skin of her back except where she wore her bandeau.

"I'm sorry," the man said, "to have—"

The rear door slammed open and there was her mother—frantic, in loose blue trousers and matching bandeau, with a golden mane of hair that was radiant in the light of the setting sun. She saw the three strangers.

Her Shardblade materialized a second later.

Bright and silver, their family's hidden secret, kept quiet since it had manifested a few months ago. But few secrets mattered when you found your twelve-year-old daughter facing three assailants.

"Whoa," the tall one said, leaping away. He was the one, the killer. "*Whoa.*" He pulled something from his belt, something he brandished like a weapon, though Dyel had never seen a weapon that was just a metal tube with a handle.

The grumpy one smashed a sphere into the ground, somehow cracking it. Stormlight flowed up around him, and strange symbols formed in the air.

Mother leaped in front of Dyel, sweating, gripping her weapon in two hands. "We knew you'd be back! We knew you'd come for me once you heard!"

Dyel crawled forward and grabbed her around the legs, terrified.

They all stood silently in the room until the thoughtful Shin man spoke. "What the hell is going on?"

"We know about you," Mother said, inching backward toward the door. "I spent months seeking the tall Makabaki man who killed my father. I talked to the families of others you killed. We know what you are. Murderer."

Dyel cowered. Mother kept trying to inch them toward the door. Strangely, the tall man relaxed, lowering his weapon.

The bald one lowered his hands, the strange glowing light around him evaporating. "I told you that you looked like him."

"I do *not,*" the tall one said.

"You kind of do," the thoughtful one said.

"Just because we're both dark-skinned?" the tall one said.

"I'm dark-skinned too," said the bald one. "And nobody says *I* look like him."

"You're silver most of the time, Galladon," the tall one said, putting his weapon away in his coat. "Listen, I'm not the murderer you're worried about. That's Nale, the Herald."

They both watched him, terrified, silent—until Mother, oddly, cocked her head. She dismissed her Blade, which made Dyel quiver. Surely Mother didn't *believe* a *killer.*

Uma appeared a second later, sliding up the wall, a collection of lights like those scattered by a prism. "It is all right, Dyel," she said. Her voice was quiet, like the sound of a vibrating glass cup. "I know the Herald Nale by sight—the one who killed your grandfather—and this is not him."

Oh. Dyel carefully stood up behind her mother. Her heart pounding, likely the same as all of them. Until a moment later, the thoughtful one said, "Can I study you?"

"Um . . ." Uma said. "No?"

"I told you to stop phrasing it that way, Demoux," said the one who had been called Galladon.

"I don't want to *lie* to them," Demoux said, gesturing.

The tall one cleared his throat. "Perhaps we should go."

Mother eyed them, still tense. She'd still heard her daughter cry out, then had found three strange men intimidating her in the rear of the shop.

"Mother," Dyel whispered, pointing. "They knew. They asked me about Uma."

"How?" Mother demanded.

"We didn't mean to frighten the girl," the tall one said, with a placating hand forward. "We had simply heard rumors. We are scholars, and like to study spren."

"See?" Demoux said. "Baon uses the word."

"Baon is *not* an example of how to be *in any way* tactful!" Galladon said. "Crazyfools, all of you." What a curious word. He stepped forward, and though he had been the grouchiest at the table ordering drinks, he made his tone polite now. "I'm sorry we frightened you. We will go now, with your leave, Radiant."

Mother glanced down at Dyel, then sighed, looking back at the men. "I have a letter for you."

What?

What?

"Mother?" Dyel asked.

"You remember that odd woman who visited last month?" she asked. "She left me a letter. It's in my nightstand. Please fetch it."

Dyel, confused, did as she was asked. Mother remained, eye-to-eye with the three strangers. That woman? The one who wore many rings, and who had helped for several weeks at the local charity hospital. A healer skilled with herbs, whose room had smelled of the fish she'd caught in the Purelake, then dried. She'd come for tea each morning.

In the nightstand beside the bed, Dyel found a sealed envelope. On it was drawn, roughly, the profiles of three men. *These* three men, except with quite comical, exaggerated proportions. What an odd experience from the One. How had the woman known? But then, Dyel's life had been turned upside down ever since Uma had arrived and her mother had started glowing sometimes. Unique experiences.

She cherished thinking of it that way. So many didn't believe these days, but she did. For Grandfather.

She scampered down the stairs and handed the letter to her mother, who tossed it to the men. "I was told," Mother explained, "that I would know who to give this to."

The tall one, Baon, caught it. He eyed the others, then slit it open with a pocketknife.

"It's from *him*," Baon said.

"Of course it is," Demoux replied. "Right as we're leaving."

"What does it say?" Galladon said.

Baon closed the envelope. "It has only his signature. And a crude depiction of male genitalia."

"From the Trickster Aspect," Mother said. "He was here too, last year."

"Of course he was," Demoux repeated, then sighed. "I'm ready to get off this rusting planet. What about you two?"

"Yes, *please*," Galladon said. "One of the eldest beings in the cosmere . . . and he has the mental age of a *thirteen-year-old*."

"If this man ever returns," Baon said, "keep your distance. He isn't terribly dangerous, but whenever he's spotted, innocents get hurt."

That was only natural. He was the Trickster Aspect, spun out of the One to create chaos. They had hundreds of legends about him, but you couldn't *insult* him by not serving him tea.

A ding came from Galladon's pocket.

"Time," he said.

The three men started out. Baon hesitated by the door. "Things might be chaotic in your city for a little while."

Then he too left.

Dyel hugged her mother, but the fearspren remained. Not just because of what Baon had said. This meant the killer had not yet come, and they still needed to fear him.

Outside, people started shouting.

"I will look," Uma said in her tinkling voice. "Stay strong. I do not know what this is."

Mother nodded and led Dyel up the steps as Uma went out the door. Their shop was part of a larger building, four stories high, and they helped keep it tidy and fixed things—which meant Mother could take them up the access stairway to the roof.

There, they saw what was causing the chaos. Cusicesh the Protector had risen from the bay—the great, multi-armed spren made of a column of water. That was all? Dyel relaxed. She'd seen Cusicesh many times. But why then were so many people pointing and crying out? Why were so many running?

"It's . . . the wrong time," her mother said.

Cusicesh—breaking all tradition—waved his hands out to the sides, palms toward the city. And then, before him in the bay, the air *split* in a glorious radiant fountain. A column of light.

"The gateway to the land of shadows," Mother whispered. "Honor's gateway . . . Oh Father, Mother, ancestors who have become One . . . Dyel, fetch the travel packs! It's *time*!"

Dyel froze. Time . . . the travel packs . . . All good Iriali kept them, but that was mostly a formality, unless . . .

It was *time*? A rare awespren burst around her, made of blue rings of smoke.

"People," Cusicesh said. He *never* spoke. His voice was deep, and vibrated the city—somehow loud enough to make her soul shake, but not so loud it hurt her ears. "I am to be your guide for the Fifth Journey."

Time. That meant . . .

Time to continue the Long Trail.

Time to find the Fifth Land.

Shocked out of her reverie, she went running for the travel packs—terrified that this great day should have come during her life. She wished there were a way to explain that she was filled up with new experiences. That she'd rather live some peaceful days, without Owners returning to the land, or her mother starting to glow, or the *call* to the *Long Trail itself* occurring.

It wasn't to be. As when she met back with her mother, Uma had returned. Mother was crying.

"We will try," Mother whispered to the spren, who brightened the floor of the rooftop. "We will see . . . see how far you can go. Come, Dyel. We mustn't miss the call. Boats are already rowing out to meet the gateway."

And so, with only their travel packs, they found their way to a boat. They joined with the light of the gateway, which she briefly thought must be like rejoining the One when she died. They emerged into the place of shadows with the leaders of their kind, who had already begun preparing caravans to cross the darkness. Other portals, she heard, had opened all across Iri—one in every major city.

Nearby, she spied the three strangers again, Demoux complaining about the "odd behavior for a perpendicularity of this nature." Mother settled her down in some blankets, then went to find them a position in the caravans. Dyel clutched her pack to her chest, stunned by how fast it had happened. Her time in the city, with the shop, was over.

She whispered a quiet farewell.

It was time to leave Roshar. Forever.

I-12

WHAT MUST BE DONE

Odium worked on teaching Dalinar his lessons until something pulled him away. Something surprising, alarming.

Cultivation was moving against him.

Odium was shocked, for he had genuinely not thought her capable. Her movements made him turn from the Spiritual Realm and focus his attention on Kharbranth, his quiet seaside city, protected from storm and war.

There, Cultivation's agents were in motion. People with faintly blue veins beneath the skin, wearing black, their faces covered. They carried modern equipment: crossbows, half-shard shields, blades of the finest steel, and armor of some strange Soulcast material. Which was hard enough to stop an arrow, yet lightweight, and left them limber.

Her forces sliced through Kharbranth, having arrived in sleek black boats in the night.

He was . . . impressed. This was incredible. A tactical, precision strike on his home and family? He formed an invisible avatar, standing in the sky, the wind playing at his robes. He watched with mounting concern as his city guard fell to grisly deaths, each of them choking on their own blood as fighters with no uniforms cut through the city. His defenders didn't have a chance, and Taravangian could do nothing. The Fused and Unmade were both forbidden this city, so none were close enough to help.

In minutes, Cultivation's forces were assaulting the palace at the top of the city, cut into the stone cliff face. Odium trembled, feeling—for the first time since his Ascension—*panic.* Like all emotions, it welled inside him more strongly than any mortal could feel, making him tremble and gasp.

Cultivation appeared next to him. "I will not hurt them unless you refuse to back down."

"You . . ." Odium said, his anger stoking. "You *monster.*"

"I do what must be done."

He laughed, tears of pain forming at his eyes—because he'd created this avatar to simulate mortal responses. The tempests within his power, the changes to his rhythms, were far, far more terrible signs—but even still, tears were familiar to him.

So many emotions. He wrestled with them, his mortal training and his divine mind struggling together. Betrayal, fear, and . . . and satisfaction.

"You use my methods, Cultivation," he whispered. "You know the *true* way of kings."

Her avatar would not meet his eyes. Her forces broke into the palace, and several members of his staff . . . were plants of hers. They gave up his daughter and his grandchildren, who were soon imprisoned in their own rooms. With murderers poised to strike.

"You would *actually* do it," Taravangian said. "You *did* have another plan! You didn't simply pick me because you suspected I could hold Odium's power. You picked me because you thought you could control me!"

"I don't *think* it, Taravangian," she said. "I know there is only one thing in all this world you've *ever* legitimately cared for. Now I hold it. Back down. Go to the human coalition and agree to an immediate armistice. Give the Kholins their kingdom and be content with the lands you already hold. They are more than your share anyway. Make peace."

"And what growth can come from peace?" he asked, quivering with the weight of so many emotions. "Admit it, Cultivation. You let the war proceed for millennia and did not intercede, because conflict doesn't just inflame emotion, it forces *growth.* Your power's Intent."

Her avatar stared at him boldly, but he felt the tremble in her power. Yes. It *did* like war, didn't it? She hated suffering, but she was the Vessel. Her power loved anything that encouraged people to learn, better themselves, and achieve. That was often accelerated by conflict.

"You force me to make peace now," he said, "not because you want to end the hostilities—but because you don't want to be wrong in having chosen me to Ascend."

"You do not know my heart."

"And you," he whispered, "do *not* know what you have created, Koravellium Avast. I no longer question. I know my path is right, and so—at each point—the next step is clearly manifest. No longer is my challenge about decisions, but merely about having the strength to execute them."

In the ocean several miles from Kharbranth, a wave began to build.

"Taravangian," Cultivation said. "What . . . what is this?"

"A . . . lesson," he whispered, a profound sadness welling within him as the wave grew. Larger and larger.

Cultivation gasped, horror vibrating from her. "Taravangian. No. You can't."

"I will weep," he whispered. "Know that I will weep."

His avatar closed its eyes, tears leaking down its cheeks. He thought of his family—not only his daughter, dear Savrahalidem, but his grandchildren. Gvori, Karavangia, and little Ruli—whom he'd been forced to use in schemes before. And of course there were his dear friends of the Diagram. Faithful Maben, who sat with her own granddaughter in the morning light, knitting, completely unaware of the incursion force. Mrall, already dead, having tried to protect Taravangian's family. Adrotagia . . . she was walking the palace gardens, and assassins crept up behind her.

"I will remember you," he whispered as the wave surged toward the city, now a hundred feet tall. It was an action he could not have taken anywhere else, for it was too direct an intervention. But Kharbranth . . . he, as a mortal, had been promised Kharbranth. That still held.

"Taravangian!" Cultivation said. "I will back down. STAY YOUR *HAND*!"

"Ah," he said, "but the lesson is not just for you; it is for any who would think to intimidate me. A god must have no holes in his armor, Cultivation."

He steeled himself, observing her panic and pain for her followers who would be consumed. She could not watch. She turned away, which gave him peace, and let him summon his power.

Then Odium, God of Passions, destroyed Kharbranth entirely—the one city he'd bargained all his mortal life to protect.

DAY

SEVEN

SIGZIL • VENLI • JASNAH •
SHALLAN • RENARIN • RLAIN •
ADOLIN • NAVANI • ZARB •
SZETH • ASH • DALINAR •
KALADIN

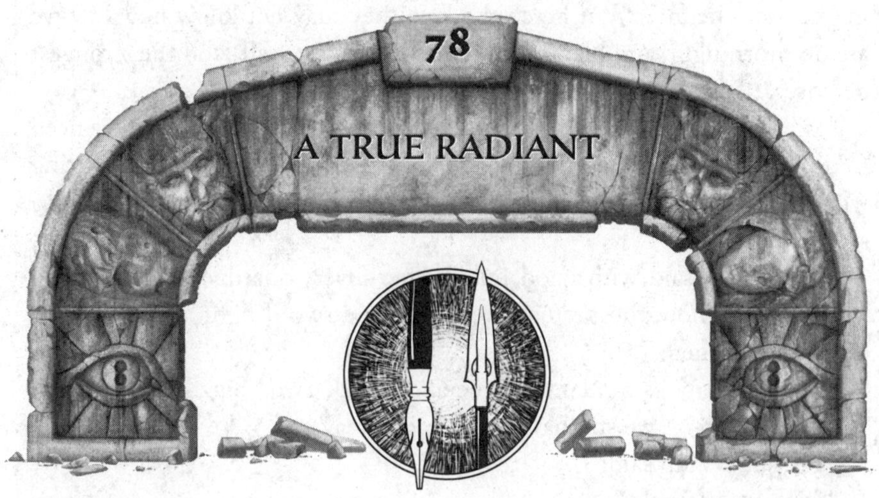

I'm sorry.

Losing a squire wore on Sigzil, but he threw himself into the next phase of his plan. The trick was going to be to divert the enemy to Narak Three—southwest of the Oathgate platform—instead of the Oathgate itself. A difficult proposition, as the enemy was shrewd.

"They'll obviously want to take Narak Two next," General Winn explained, pointing to their maps. "Holding the Oathgate is of utmost strategic importance." The others nodded.

Was it though? In a traditional battle, yes, it would be. It would cut off the human retreat, make them desperate. Isolate them. Yet . . . Sigzil considered as he stood by the table with the others, men more experienced than he. Should he say what he was thinking? Surely it wasn't wise to contradict them.

But why was he here, if not to lead?

"Is it though?" he asked them. "They have only three days now to capture Narak Prime. Will they waste time on Narak Two?"

"It's our retreat," General Balivar said. He was younger, like Sigzil. "Seems a wise way to break us."

"Or galvanize us to fight to the last man," Sigzil said, gesturing. "Which *isn't* what they want. They want to break us, make us retreat. If they take the Oathgate, we can't do that, and they are *more* likely to lose than win—because of the deadline. They can't afford to make us hunker down."

The others stared at the maps. "Storms," Winn said. "I think he's right. Our plans are stale as last week's bread. We need to be looking at the situation as it stands now."

"If they throw everything they have at Narak Prime," Sigzil said, "they might overwhelm us. But here's the key: they may not know how low we are on Stormlight, and Narak Prime has the tallest walls and the strongest defenses.

"They *have* to be worrying about the looming deadline. So what we need to do is make them think that by attacking Narak Three, they'll be getting what they want: a way to demoralize us. We have to make it too tempting a strike to pass up."

"A feint," Ka said, with a nod, holding her silvery Shardpen at the writing station. "Like how you pretend weakness in a sword fight, and make the enemy strike there."

"Pull back troops to Narak Prime and Narak Two," Sigzil said, rubbing his chin. "Then . . . we still have those Lightweavers?"

"Yes, sir," Winn said.

"Send for Stargyle."

Within minutes, the handsome Lightweaver was ushered in, his hair immaculate as usual. Maybe he kept it that way through rain and storm with an illusion. Sigzil sat him down with the generals.

"We have been using Narak Three as a supply depot," he explained. "And those Deepest Ones have always been prowling around, watching. In this largest building, I want you to make an illusion of gemstones—our storage for it. Then we, in the fighting, need to find a way to let the enemy get a glimpse inside—so they assume taking Narak Three would be a huge blow to us. See if we can trick them into throwing everything they have at it."

It took a little while to get a plan in place, but Stargyle was confident—he seemed to like the idea of having something relevant to do on the battlefield other than using illusions to hide groups of archers or medical staff, to move them into position covertly. As he left, Sigzil shared a look with his command staff, and left the most worrying part unsaid.

They were laying a trap to feign losing their Stormlight cache . . . but in reality, it was a partial truth. They *were* dangerously low on Stormlight. And if the Bondsmiths didn't return soon . . .

He emerged from the meeting into a camp doing its preparations between battles. Swords being sharpened, soldiers catching sleep while they could. He walked across the courtyard, receiving salutes, answering a few questions—bolstering each person he talked to, which he now did by habit.

That done, he forced himself to climb a ladder—not fly up it—to the wooden wall walk, constructed alongside the hulking stone fortification the Stonewards had built.

"How long do you suppose we can last," he whispered, "before we run out?"

"Hard to say," Vienta whispered back. "There are a lot of variables. But each shipment of Light from Urithiru is smaller than the one before, and each fight takes more than the previous, as the enemy pushes harder and harder."

"Three days?" he asked, reaching the top of the wall. "Can we last three days?"

"I . . . do not think it likely," she admitted.

Up here he found Leyten leaning against the wall. Sigzil fell in beside his friend, enjoying a rare moment of peace, gazing out over the darkened Plains—which were occasionally lit red by bursts of lightning. It was . . . pretty, actually, if he removed the context.

"Is it strange?" Leyten said. "That I miss them? The chasms? Not merely making armor down there, as I mentioned before. I like the *feel* of those chasms. Teeming with life, never fully quiet, but with a quietude. Like today, in fact. With that gentle lightning and a plain pretending to sleep."

"I feel it too," Sigzil said. "Hard to believe at times like this, how much blood and death this quiet place has caused."

"I wasn't supposed to be a bridgeman," Leyten said. "Most of you were forced into the army; I came willingly, as a way to send money home to my family. Had a good job as an apprentice armorer. Respected. Until . . ."

Sigzil knew the story. A petty lighteyes's armor had failed, and the blame had eventually fallen on Leyten. Shipped off to die running bridges to soothe the ego of a highborn soldier.

"He died, you know," Leyten said, with a half smirk. "Two bridge runs later. Gabaron, the man who consigned me to the bridge crews? Dead." He eyed Sigzil. "Bad riveting to his armor straps. Whole cuirass snapped off. Turns out if you keep killing the guys who maintain your equipment, you stop having well-maintained equipment."

"Once in a while," Sigzil said, smiling, "fate hits us with something that's downright poetic, doesn't it?"

"Yeah . . ." Leyten trailed off. "Sig . . . do I belong here?"

Sigzil frowned, regarding his friend, with his curly hair wet from the drizzle. Leyten looked down. "I'm not a true Radiant, Sig. I'm a guy who likes to sit and count how many uniforms we need before we run out. I don't belong in the sky, glowing. I've *never* felt comfortable with people paying attention to me. And during this fighting, I've lost two squires. I just . . . I wonder . . ."

Storms, what to say to that? Sigzil considered, and took his friend by the shoulder, drew his eyes. Then he smiled and said, "I know. I feel it too."

Leyten smiled back. "You do? You've been so confident lately."

"An act," Sigzil said.

"But . . . Sig, what if I'm not good enough? Those squires . . . they're my fault. Their deaths. I . . ."

"Blame Kaladin."

Leyten frowned, glancing at him.

"Kal put us in charge," Sigzil said, trying a calculated gambit. "He could have been here. He isn't. So it's his fault."

"He led us well!" Leyten snapped, pulling out of his funk, eyes alight with determination. "He did everything he could, then more. He's *not* to blame."

"Oh, so you trust his decisions?"

"I . . ." Leyten trailed off, and smiled sheepishly. "I suppose I do."

"Then you have to trust that he was correct to leave us in charge, Leyten," Sigzil said. "If you blame yourself for your squires dying, then you'll have to blame Kal for when Maps died, or Teft, or any other losses. Can't have it both ways." He leaned closer. "And we both know Kaladin is a storming *hero.* So . . ."

Leyten stood taller. "Yeah. Yeah, you're right." He looked to Sigzil. "Thank you. Sig . . . I miss him, Kaladin. But you should know, I'm just as proud to serve under you."

Sigzil gave the man's arm a squeeze, then sent him to get the Windrunners ready for the next clash. Oddly, the things he'd said to Leyten resonated with him too. Inside, he still wondered . . . but those voices were growing quieter. As the camp rushed to execute his plans, and his generals found his ideas worthwhile, Sigzil discovered something remarkable.

This was him. This man who could lead. He finally had a place to channel all of his thoughts and ideas. He had reasons to make those ideas as precise and calculated as possible. His love of engineering and physics actually came into play in this defense, and his interactions with the others bolstered him.

He wasn't so lofty that he thought he deserved command. But somehow, in being forced into it, he'd discovered something important. Here, beneath red lightning and on a plain full of chasms he'd claimed as his own, Sigzil found himself. In a way that training with Master Hoid, or learning beneath Kaladin, had never done for him.

Sigzil was, at long last, the man he'd always wanted to be.

⁂

Hiking through the chasms reawakened Venli's childhood, and she loved it. Even with the red lightning above and the terrible way thunder echoed down here. Even with the otherwise absolute darkness broken only by their frail gemstones. Even with a flow of water that came up to her knees at times. Even with the stench of death and the ancient corpses they sometimes passed.

Even with all that, she found she loved this place.

Loved that life had conquered such depths, as marked by the bobbing green glow of circular lifespren with their delicate spines. They'd weave through the holes in skulls or past chunks of cracked carapace, then dance with patches of rotspren, like punch lines to one another's jokes, red and green. Each meaningless without the other.

She loved the sounds of trickling water, of vines constricting, of cremlings on the walls—and the steady, dangerous splashing of the chasmfiends behind. She would periodically glance back and see them there—wedged between the walls, using their many legs to maneuver, their faces like chunks of broken rock. She'd panic briefly, then attune Awe. These were their allies now.

She closed her eyes, listening to that strange tone she followed, growing more firm and pure as they traveled inward. She breathed in the potent air, walked through the darkness with her hands out to the sides.

And immediately tripped, her foot snagging on a vine beneath the flowing water. She caught herself before she fell, and attuned Embarrassment. Maybe best to keep her eyes open.

The water flow, although shallow, was growing treacherous. The chasms had a mostly flat floor, the result of crem settlement competing against erosion and creating a kind of equilibrium that prevented the chasms from filling in. She thought the erosion would eventually win, especially after seeing it had already done so on the far eastern side of the Shattered Plains, but that was probably eons away.

"I don't like walking through this water," Bila said from nearby, splashing as she stepped. "My brain keeps attuning the Terrors, telling me this is the trickle at the start of a highstorm."

"The Everstorm rains far less than the highstorm," Venli said. "We should be fine."

Bila raised a gemstone to light her face and stared up through the opening in the chasm toward the angry sky. "At least we shouldn't have to suffer through a meeting of Everstorm and highstorm again."

Venli had heard their tales of escaping into the night through the chasms when that horrific first meeting of storms had occurred. She'd been on the plateaus then, though it felt like a lifetime ago—and remembered through the eyes of another person.

Timbre thrummed. A theory: the meeting of storm and storm had never again been so violent as it had been that first time, when plateaus had been destroyed. Was that another clue? Had *this location* caused the violence of that convergence? Were others weaker because they happened elsewhere? Or was it what they'd guessed originally: that the violence of that first convergence had been caused by the Everstorm's exultant inception?

She had no answers, so she led on until they hit an obstruction in the chasm: a damlike natural structure, created by a log wedged between the walls.

A waterfall poured over it, and potential handholds of wood and bone were covered in moss. Her skin crawled, and she attuned the Terrors at the mere thought of climbing it. Of being required to touch the bodies of the dead.

The others hesitated around and behind her, but then a shadow—blocking the violent red light crackling in the sky above—fell across her. Thundercloud leaned down and studied the obstruction. Then the long mandibles beside its mouth—which were jointed, and roughly the thickness of a singer's arms—reached to Venli. Her rhythm froze as the chasmfiend picked her up with those armlike appendages and held her beneath his chin. He crawled over the obstruction.

The other chasmfiends followed, carrying singers, and making several trips—easily cresting the dam by moving, as they often did in here, with their legs pressed against either side of the chasm. Their forelegs were strong and powerful, but not hinged in a way to grab or lift. These smaller ones below the head, though, had fine articulation.

Venli let her rhythm start again as she breathed deeply, now standing in waist-high water upstream from the dam—for it had formed something of a lake. The next person set down by the chasmfiends was Leshwi. Venli quietly attuned Tension; she and the Fused hadn't interacted much in the last few days—both were uncertain about their new relationship.

Leshwi eyed her, then hummed to Agony. "I do not know if I can continue this way, Venli. I was a demigod for millennia. Now . . . I stand in wet clothing, shivering."

"Would you go back to him?" Venli asked. "Become his again, fight in a war that you don't believe in? Kill, so you can be *comfortable* again?"

Leshwi's rhythm changed to Reprimand and she glanced at Venli in anger. Then, with obvious effort, she attuned Withdrawal instead, looking away.

"You were strong enough," Venli said to Praise, "to turn against your orders, your own kind, and your god because you knew it was right. *That* was the difficult part, Leshwi. Just keep going."

"It is not so simple," Leshwi said. "Before, I'd perfected my role over so many, many years. Now . . ." She glanced down at her wet clothes, her hands outspread. "Now . . . why am I even here? What am I doing? I can't help you."

"But you can," Venli said. "If we encounter a patrol from Odium's army, there's a chance they won't know you've switched sides. They'll obey a Fused of your renown. You're our last defense against discovery."

Leshwi paused at that, humming to Consideration.

"We'll find a new place for you," Venli promised. "With the listeners. You might not be a god among us—we will have no gods—but you'll be something better. Free."

"Free . . ." Leshwi said. "It has been a long, long time . . ." She glanced upward. "But can I ever be free if I cannot soar?"

Soon, the chasmfiends had carried each of the listeners across the obstruction. Venli's gemstone lit Thundercloud's dark eyes as he leaned down beside her. His entire face was made of plates, the eye peeking through a junction between a few. She could feel Curiosity pulsing from him.

"You want to know the source of the song as much as we do," Venli said.

He looked inward toward the center, still many hours' march away. Then he cocked his head, his long mandibles twitching. She followed his gaze, and crackling lightning illuminated something in the chasm. Another obstruction wedged between the walls, but higher up. Not creating a dam this time.

"Shall we see?" she asked.

In response, Thundercloud picked her up again—chill water streaming from her—and lifted her high to inspect . . .

A bridge.

One of those the humans used. Old, scarred, grown over with haspers and shalebark, wedged here twenty feet up. Moss covered the bottom side, and rockbuds had begun finding purchase on it. Venli could see nicks in the wood where arrows—launched by her kind—had stuck during an assault.

A different kind of corpse. Held up under her arms, Venli reached out and touched the wood, projecting in her mind to the chasmfiend what this would have looked like when new. They thought the beasts liked that kind of explanation.

Eventually Thundercloud set her down, and together they continued on, inward toward that sound. A discordant tone and chaotic rhythm becoming more clear the closer they approached.

⁂

Jasnah sat, tense, with Queen Fen and their scribes as the spanreed wrote.

We got in close, Your Majesty, explained the Windrunner scribe on the other end. *We waited for early morning when the enemy aerial force seemed least alert, then came in under the waves. While the Fused know of this trick, and post sentries to make sure we don't sink their boats from below, we were able to draw close without being spotted.*

The news is both disturbing and encouraging, Brightness. Your theory is correct: the holds of every ship our spren surveyed are filled with chunks of stone, not soldiers. Those on deck are decoys intended to give the impression that the ships are so crowded, there is no room below. I highly suspect those on top are not trained soldiers, but laborers who have been given warform, judging by how they act—but of course I cannot be sure.

Regardless, I am convinced there is no *invading army. Only an elaborate prop. We have reached a small island for stability to send this. We don't think the enemy spotted our efforts; a Lightweaver on hand was useful, though I don't think Red enjoyed the swimming portion all that much.*

Awaiting instructions.

Fen breathed out as Jasnah passed the page to be copied by their scribes, then translated for the Thaylens and read out to the male generals. While that was happening, Jasnah ordered the Windrunners to hold position for now, in case they were needed for further reconnaissance.

They'd set up in a small room next to the larger planning chamber, which had—for two days—been full of the greatest living military minds discussing every avenue of defense. Against an assault that was not coming.

"This is bad, Jasnah," Fen said softly.

"Bad?" Jasnah replied. "Fen, your city is almost certainly safe. Odium saw that it was unassailable in the time before the deadline, so he's focusing on the two other battlefields."

"Do you *really* think he'll just *give us up*?"

"Well, the being known as Odium—even with a new host—is intelligent beyond mortal measure."

"That's hardly reassuring," Fen said.

"Fen," Jasnah said, "the fact that he's brilliant is a *good thing* for you. A smart general knows how to win battles, but a brilliant one knows when to walk away from them. Odium has seen that wasting resources here isn't a viable strategy, and made a feint to divert resources from the Shattered Plains and Azimir, where he can win. You should be safe."

"Should be," Fen said. "Jasnah . . . how confident are you in a 'should'?"

"Theories with strong evidence are the soul of scientific discovery," Jasnah said.

"And if we acted on this intel? What would our next steps be? To send our troops and Radiants to reinforce the Shattered Plains, correct?"

Jasnah nodded. Careful watch in Shadesmar had prevented further Oathgate spren from being taken by Sja-anat—for now, and hopefully forever, the Oathgates at Thaylen City and the Shattered Plains continued to work for them. Therefore, the troops here could quickly be repositioned there. She wished the same could be said of Azimir.

"What if *that's* what he wants?" Fen continued. "What if the empty holds are the ruse, and we're meant to discover them? What if there's a *different* plan to take this city?"

Storms, Jasnah should have expected that. Not that Fen was right—she was wrong, but in the most innocent of ways. It was a fallacy: the idea that you could never know anything because there was always something to learn.

 If you started to think that your enemy had planned for every decision you could make, then you'd let your fear of being wrong guide you instead of a reliance upon the facts you'd discovered.

"It's possible," Jasnah said, taking Fen's hand. "I won't lie and say otherwise. But the trick with the rocks in the holds is a clever one, and was difficult for us to confirm. Fen, the Shattered Plains is enduring the full wrath of the Everstorm *and* every Fused the enemy can throw at it. While we sit here waiting."

"You're saying I should abandon my city," Fen said. "Send away the troops and leave Thaylen City exposed."

"I'm saying we need to act on the information we have, not the information we think we *don't* have."

Fen looked away, though she held to Jasnah's hand. "So close. Three days, and we will know peace. But what if by listening to you now, I throw everything away, Jasnah? We *can't* leave Thaylen City undefended. *I* can't."

"I have to send the Radiants to bolster those at the Shattered Plains," Jasnah said. "I have Dalinar's authority to do so. We can't reach Azimir with that Oathgate down, but we can do this much."

"You could be killing me and my kind."

"My moral philosophy is to do the most good I can in any situation," Jasnah said.

Fen slipped her hand from Jasnah's. "Will you give me time to talk with the Thaylen Central Council and see what they think?"

"Of course," Jasnah said. "I want the Windrunners back here to report anyway—spanreeds can be stolen, so we need direct firsthand confirmation." The Windrunner sending the message had given the proper code words at the start, but who knew what Odium could see?

Fen left the room, troubled. And Jasnah, if she let herself be empathetic for a moment, understood. To send troops away during this most important three-day window? It would be excruciating, whether or not you knew it was right. The enemy likely understood that. It was a curious quirk of medicine that a placebo often worked even if you *knew* you were being given a placebo. This situation showed why, with a kind of inverse example. A feint could work even if you knew it was a feint, because it left you worried about what else you might be missing.

Do the most good, she thought to herself. When decisions grew difficult, she relied on this guiding philosophy. With that in mind, she began drawing up the orders for her troops to reinforce the Shattered Plains.

79 THE RHYTHM OF LONGING

You are right, and your letter to me was—characteristically—full of wisdom and excellent deductions.

Shallan awoke in her past. It was that day. White carpet. It . . . it . . . *No.*

The vision shifted. She was a child. Hiding in a corner. Crying while her parents shouted at each other.

Hers wasn't a *unique* story, she knew. She'd listened over the years, had collected people in her sketchpads. For almost every family like Lopen's, full of love and happiness, there was one like hers. Where the happy times were the frosting on a dessert, used to cover up the misshapen lump that hadn't come out of the oven properly.

There *had* been joy. But so often it had seemed a fabrication carefully constructed to let them pretend. It was hard to remember those good times as she hid there hearing the shouts. As an adult, she sometimes told herself the lie that everything had been wonderful up until her mother's death; but as with many lies in her life, she had let that one live too long. They offered protection, yes, but they could also hurt.

Mother slammed a door, then footsteps approached. Shallan, feeling so short in this body, peeked out from her room to watch her mother stalk past. A flash of red-and-gold hair. Muttering words. "I can't be like this. I can't. I'm not a soldier, I'm a homemaker. This is what I want. This is what I always wanted. I can't. I can't. I can't. I can't. I can't. I can't."

Shallan ducked away.

So, Veil said. *How do we face this? Now that we remember?*

Should we go after her? Radiant asked.

Shallan steeled herself, and did not follow—but storms, it was another step forward. She didn't look away, didn't dodge the question. That was her mother.

I'm almost ready, she acknowledged to them. *But we need to find a vision where I'm an adult.*

Agreed, Veil said. *For now, accept the memories.*

In a child's body, Shallan dried her tears and went skulking through the corridors of the manor house. Father hadn't often devolved to physical abuse yet, but he shouted at the servants, itching for a fight. So she veered away from him and crept under the steps, where he never looked.

Her brothers huddled in here. All but Helaran, the eldest, whom Kaladin would someday kill. Jushu wiped his eyes. Wikim pretended he hadn't been afraid. Balat was a mound in the darkness, not glancing toward them.

Shallan took a diamond chip from her pocket, then she began telling them a story. The elder her was in this body, experiencing these things, but unlike the other visions, she simply let it happen. That was possible, she felt, only because this was *her* past, and a piece of her remembered what to do.

She lived the memory as if she were riding on the wind.

Because *this* wasn't frosting. This memory was *authentic* joy. The looks her brothers gave as she ignored her own pain and fear and told them a tale she'd imagined, the tale of a little axehound who explored the world. Seeing grand cities, eventually being mistaken for a king and crowned. It was silly and made little sense, which was part of the charm. Besides, when you're starving, bread is a feast.

Balat turned away from the wall and smiled. Jushu began to help her make up ideas. Wikim stopped pretending to be strong, and allowed himself to be a wide-eyed little boy loving the story. Together they spun a yarn that pushed back the shadows and the darkness. Together, despite parents who seemed not to care, they became a family *anyway.*

Later, after Father had time to cool down and Mother was acting like herself again, they slipped out. Each brother hugged her, and they agreed to go about their chores without being asked. That night, while tidying her room, Shallan found a strange spiral pattern on the wall. Drawn to her by her lies—but not just any lies. Like all Cryptics, Testament had come seeking the most wonderful lies. The contradictions that made humans able to function.

Stories. Specifically, the one she'd told herself: the performance that she was happy and strong and not terrified.

A lie that made it possible to shine when all the world was dark.

⁂

Renarin remembered this day.

He was in the body of his younger self, sitting at a feast. The fires burned high in the hearths—a frightful, menacing light, full of dancing flamespren. Even with proper flues, the huge fires made the room smell of char and smoke. That scent would linger on his clothing; he'd pick up a jacket that looked clean, then would carry the ghost of the bonfire all day long.

Around this time, in his youth, the Kholins had started practicing to be more refined. King Gavilar had become less a soldier and more a politician—and he'd moved the fires from open bonfires into hearths with iron grates. Renarin noted who in the grand hall appeared to enjoy the fire, and who kept their distance. The distinction fascinated him.

He sat at the children's table, where boys and girls still sat together, though he was the tallest one there. He should have moved on, but staying seemed to delay decisions. Seemed to make things more comfortable. Whether it actually did either was debatable, the older him now realized. It certainly looked odd for the youth with the beginnings of a mustache—though he ignored it—to be sitting with kids three years younger than him.

Renarin had never known a divided Alethkar. He'd been born into a united kingdom, son of the mighty general who had forged it. Yet many people remembered the time before unification—and today was when Renarin had realized his father's prominence would not always protect him. After the second course, Renarin had gotten up to find the privy. He did so again now, slipping from the feast hall, playing with the buttons on his sleeve—and there encountered the older boys.

He remembered jumping in surprise at that, though today he expected them: standing there in the hallway, passing around a bit of firemoss. They wore fine clothing; the sons of the elites who, seeing the winds turning, had joined with Gavilar. These boys didn't remember the old kingdom, but their parents did—and their thoughts had a way of seeping into the children, like ink through too-thin paper. A metaphor that made him smile, as he would never have considered it before learning to write.

As he walked past the boys, they followed, taunting him. He stopped, then turned, and the elder him saw something new he'd missed when younger. Those nervous postures, the way the boys kept glancing to one another, feeding their actions with nods? These boys . . . they were *afraid.*

They surrounded him, shoved him up against the wall, as in this vision he wore the body of a child. They demanded to know if he thought he was better than they were. Now, he realized they were testing limits. In their eyes, Dalinar must be ashamed of his youngest son, to make him sit at the children's table, to refuse him training with the sword. They wanted to see how far they could push that.

"I remember you," Renarin whispered. "I will remember this for a long, long time."

 They frowned, as that hadn't been the expected response. Yes, he remembered this day. It had been one among many mounting days that had made him realize he didn't understand people. He'd been so completely baffled, so ashamed. Why would his friends—people he *perceived* as his friends—treat him this way? Where had these sudden emotions come from? What had he done wrong, and could he be sure to never do it again?

He wasn't that boy any longer.

Renarin swept the legs from under the lead boy, knocking his head on the floor. Zahel hadn't taught Renarin much hand-to-hand, but this move was one he'd claimed was essential. So many situations became so much more manageable when the other fellow was on the ground.

The other boys froze for a moment, then one shoved Renarin against the wall once more while another helped their fallen friend. Renarin suffered it, examining how he felt. He hoped that fighting back would give him catharsis . . . but no. This was merely a vision. Nothing here meant anything. Beyond that, he was Radiant now. He was supposed to be better than this.

He braced himself to take a punch or two, but then Adolin—as had happened in the original experience—ran up. Dear, earnest Adolin, shouting, trailing pools of angerspren. Four boys, and just one Adolin, but they were frightened of him. He carried a sword, but didn't need to use it as he got in the face of the leader of the band—the eldest boy, who was Adolin's age—and threatened a duel.

And storms, Renarin loved him for it. He didn't need saving as he once had, but he *remembered* how it felt when Adolin had shown up. Like a hero from some story, arriving at the first break in the clouds after a highstorm. And young Renarin hadn't realized these boys would never *actually* injure him. He'd been afraid for his life.

Adolin Kholin had been protecting the weak since he could walk. Strange, that Renarin was now the knight.

Is this why you wanted to train and become a soldier? Glys asked. *Because you wanted to be like him?*

"No," Renarin whispered. "I wanted to not need him."

You were just thinking of how you love the way he helped.

"I do," Renarin said as the boys ran off. "But I don't want to *have* to rely on him, Glys. All my life, I've needed the help of others in a way my father and my brother never did. I like to think that has taught me a thing or two, but storms . . . this day. This storming day."

What will this day do to the young you?

"Show me that I can't trust people," Renarin said. "Because I can't read them. For years I was afraid that every friend would turn out to secretly hate me. Afraid that if I had to fight, my blood sickness would leave me incapable. So when I had a chance to be a soldier, to wear Plate at last, I took it."

Adolin turned to him and asked if he was all right, promising to teach the boys a lesson. He would. Adolin was already a rising star as a duelist, and soon all would know that if anyone treated Renarin poorly, they could expect a challenge.

Renarin would always love his brother for that, and would always quietly resent being unable to do it for himself.

⁂

Rlain hummed to the Rhythm of the Lost, because he was here in a vision . . . with Eshonai.

"We're losing too many people," she said, pacing before them in her Shardplate as they met to discuss strategy. They were all in warform, but she towered over them in their seats. "If we continue like this, the humans will wear us down until we're nothing. An axe with no bite—all handle."

Outside he could see old Narak, as it would never exist again. Open plateaus with no fortifications. Homes made by listeners out of whatever they could find, augmenting ancient stone buildings overgrown with crem. A high sky, blue, above plateaus like islands.

For a while here, he'd thought it would all work out. Then the humans had refused to leave, and had begun to *win.*

"What if," Thude said, "we sent spies among them?"

Eshonai turned on her heel to regard him. She hummed to Appreciation, indicating he should continue.

"We could have someone take dullform," Thude continued. "It is enough like slaveform that no human will notice."

"They have enslaved ones serve meals," Bila said, to Appreciation as well. "Clean. Carry. They are around all the time."

"It's true," Eshonai said. "I saw that in their palace. They ignore us. We're practically invisible to them."

"So a spy could get close," Thude said to Excitement. "He or she could find out where the humans are sending patrols! We could start raiding close to the warcamps again."

"If we started taking all of the gemhearts," Harvo said, "perhaps we could starve the humans out."

"It's a clever idea, Thude," Eshonai said to Consideration. "Let's try sending one at first—maybe to visit that lumber operation upriver—and see how they're treated. See how long they can stay without being recognized."

Rlain hadn't realized how painful this day was to remember. He attuned Tension as he considered what was about to happen. Because Thude volunteered first.

 "I could do it myself," Thude said. "I know the way."

"Don't be a fool," Eshonai said. "What if the humans attack you on sight? We can't afford to lose your prowess in battle, Thude."

"Though our food stores would likely thank us if you were gone . . ." Bila added with a laugh.

Rlain squeezed his eyes shut, and Tension thundered in his mind.

Bila tried to volunteer next, but Thude objected. "I can't lose you," he said to her.

Harvo tried, but was deemed too useful to their farming, and was rejected too. Tusa was essential for research.

The room grew quiet.

"I'll do it," Rlain said, opening his eyes.

They looked to him, and several seemed to have forgotten he was even in the room. They'd just been talking about how the parshmen were invisible to humans, but they treated him the same way a lot of the time.

He waited for the objections, or at least for someone to say they'd miss him. Instead they all perked up.

"That's an excellent idea," Thude said.

"You're perfect," Tusa agreed.

Even Harvo, one of his best friends, said nothing. It was still awkward between them—what had happened while Rlain had been in mateform. He didn't think the others treated him too differently as a result; they thought it was amusing, like most of what happened during mateform.

No, they simply . . . well, they didn't know him. They didn't care to know him. He was always there, but never relevant. The quiet one at the edge of the conversation.

"You don't currently have a warpair," Eshonai said. Of them all, only she had ever appeared the least bit hesitant about sending him into danger. Eshonai, however, was also a general—and had to focus on the good of their people. "You are a capable soldier, and can get yourself out if things go poorly. Thank you for the offer, Rlain. I think this will work."

In the moment, he'd felt proud to be able to offer something other than his knowledge of farming. After this day, he would train to become a spy and infiltrate the humans. But in the subsequent years, things would go wrong. He'd make mistakes, and some humans would realize he could think more clearly than their parshmen. He'd passed useful information along to his people, but not nearly as much as he'd hoped, because the lighteyes always ordered him out when there were important discussions to be had.

Ultimately, he'd ended up in Bridge Four. Where he would think back to this day, this meeting. And he'd hum to Longing as he remembered how not a single one of his friends had spoken up to request he stay.

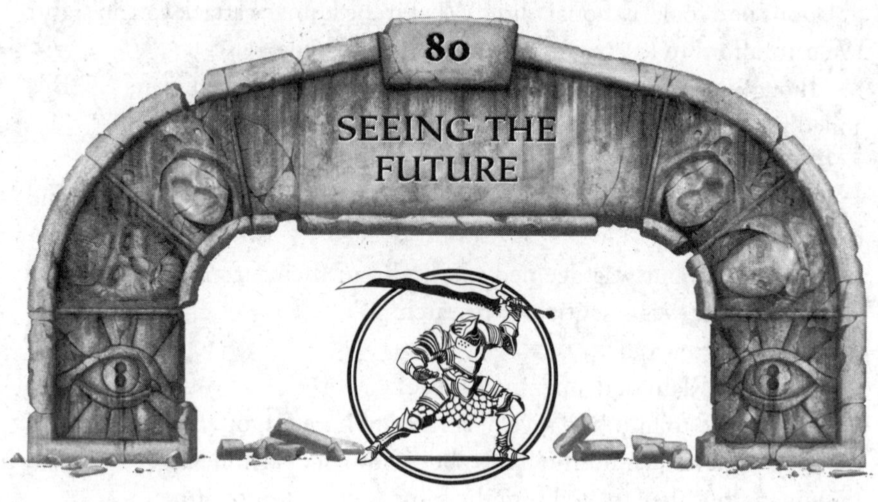

I accept that we cannot continue as we have.

Adolin climbed onto the watchpost at the top of one of Azimir's towers. From up here, the sea of bronze domes was truly impressive, each one polished to reflect golden sunlight like a mirror.

Azimir was a city of suns.

Colot stood a couple of inches taller than the Azish scouts up here, his solid blue and white uniform a stark contrast to their many-colored sashes and hats.

"All right," Adolin said, crossing the top of the small tower, straight to the railing. "Let me see."

Colot handed him the spyglass . . .

Wait. What was this?

Adolin held up the device, which looked like two small spyglasses attached together, with a metal hinge between them.

"They're called binoculars," Colot said.

"Fabrial?" Adolin asked, noting the gemstone contraptions at the bottom.

"Yes," Colot said, "but the lenses don't need that apparently. Here, turn this dial at the top to change the focus."

Adolin lifted the thing to his eyes, scanning the city and adjusting as he was told. Storms . . . they worked beautifully, and magnified better than any spyglass he'd used—with the added benefit of depth perception.

"Look up to your right," Colot said. "Then, to activate the fabrial portion, acknowledge that you're seeking living things seen only through the lenses."

Adolin frowned.

"Don't ask me," Colot said. "Evidently you need to indicate what you want to the fabrial spren, otherwise it will just locate the nearest people—which would be us."

Just locate the nearest . . . Adolin jumped as lights inside the lenses lit up when he passed a certain section of the sky. He focused there and moved the dial, zooming in, and found he could make out a group of four Heavenly Ones in the air.

"Storms . . ." He lowered the binoculars, squinted, and couldn't make anything out. He raised the binoculars again, and while the figures were still somewhat small, he could make out the long ribbons of clothing they wore, flapping in the wind.

"I need as many of these devices as we can get," Adolin said. "I want a hundred. I want them in the hands of every scout, every scribe, every rear guard and bodyguard."

Colot chuckled. "The Azish have *one* pair, which they finally got working yesterday. I don't think it's for sale. But . . . well, we're seeing the future when we look through them, eh?"

"Storming right," Adolin said, studying the figures. "There aren't many, but I don't like seeing *any* enemy reinforcements." What did it mean? "Put everyone on alert, quietly. Find Notum and send him to me. Something's going to happen today, and likely soon."

∴

Navani walked the halls of Urithiru in the past. And it was so very wrong.

Back in the Physical Realm, she'd been growing accustomed to the new version of the tower, with bright glowing lights within the stone, spren at every corner, and a feeling of vibrant alertness. Pumps churning, air blowing, people thriving.

She also remembered well the slumbering version. The lights having drifted off, sleepily, thousands of years before. The machinery working in a state of basic maintenance. A city waiting for renewal.

The tower of this vision was between those two. The lights were there, buried in the stone strata, but they were weak and frail. The machinery worked in fits and starts, and spren hid in the corners, frightened. She knew, from recovered records, what was happening: the Radiants were abandoning the tower. It was going to sleep.

That half state, like a creature half-formed, unnerved her. She carried Gav, and found herself checking over her shoulder nervously at each intersection.

Dalinar didn't seem to notice the wrongness; his attention was on that Radiant from his other vision. The one who would be first to give up his Shards. They followed the man down one of the main thoroughfares of Urithiru, and people made way for him, with his flowing blue cape and magnificent living Shardplate. Windrunner, she assumed from the armor—

which was sleeker than most, and glowed the right shade, though his glyph was an antiquated version of the one that read "peace."

Navani and Dalinar followed after, joining the traffic working its way outward toward the Oathgates. These people were wheeling their belongings in carts and were dressed for travel, carrying children. The limited records that had been left behind didn't say why the tower had been abandoned. The Sibling probably could have told her, but there had been so much to do in the last few days, Navani hadn't thought to ask.

People pooled at the front gates, but the Windrunner took to the air and soared over them. Navani didn't know how they looked to these people, but it didn't seem they were anyone important, as she and Dalinar had to work to get through. Fortunately, Dalinar was good at this sort of thing.

Eventually they reached the front of the crowd—forcing their way out the front gates—and saw a standoff. A large group of Radiants, over a hundred strong, in a variety of dress had gathered outside. There appeared to be no standardized uniform, though many of them wore takamas with open-fronted robelike shirts for the men and chest wraps for the women.

It was strangely invigorating for her to see the ancient dress, her people's heritage, here. It was something familiar, after the very odd ways and dress of the far ancient peoples. Many of the darkeyes around her were wearing similar clothing, though those from other countries—like the Azish—were dressed differently.

These gathered Radiants were either Windrunners or Skybreakers, judging by how many hovered. She guessed they were all the latter, for when the man they'd been following lowered down in his Plate before them, they—virtually as one—had turned hostile postures toward him. Three even summoned their own armor.

A man in green seasilk clothing got between them, then thrust his hands out to the sides—one toward the Windrunner, one toward the Skybreakers. He said something, but Navani was too distant to hear. She nodded to Dalinar, and they tried to move forward—but a line of other Radiants barred the way.

"Radiant business," one of them said to him. "Let the Bondsmith handle it."

"I have urgent information for him," Dalinar said.

"It can wait."

"But—"

"It can *wait*," the Radiant said, trying a glare on Dalinar. Who glared right back.

Navani pulled him away. "Starting a fight won't accomplish anything."

"These visions are useful," Dalinar said, "but I hadn't appreciated how the other ones were curated for me."

"What do you mean?" Navani said, soothing Gavinor with a hug, who was looking at the tower and asking if they were home.

"When I was experiencing that first set of visions years ago," Dalinar said, "they placed me right at the center of events, in a prime spot to observe or even participate. They were selected for that purpose. These are more haphazard. We're just showing up in whatever body happens to be available."

"So what do we do?"

He narrowed his eyes and glanced over his shoulder past the Radiants. "Navani, there's a line of light Connecting you to that man between the Windrunner and the Skybreakers."

"He's the tower's Bondsmith during this time. We learned his name from the records: Melishi."

"I'm . . . going to try something," Dalinar said. "If it's all right with you. I think if I enhance that Connection . . ."

In the blink of an eye, Navani had shifted across the plateau. She now took the *place* of that Bondsmith—standing between angry Skybreakers and that solitary Windrunner. She shook herself, reorienting. She looked like herself, at least to her own eyes, but it was clear she had taken the Bondsmith's spot in everyone else's eyes.

Storms. Dalinar could have given her a moment to agree before doing that.

"Please reconsider," the Windrunner was saying. "We need to stay together."

"It's far too late for that, Garith," said an armored woman at the head of the Skybreakers, her feet hovering a foot off the ground. "The time for being 'together' ended years ago, when you condemned Kazilah."

"I've apologized for—"

"There is a rift here," the woman said, raising her voice, drawing angerspren as a pool on the ground below her. "A rift formed by *lies.* No one admits the truth anymore. No one lives by order or reason."

"Whose reason?" Garith demanded, lifting off the ground himself. "Yours? We should make the laws *together.*"

"And then? No one wants our oversight, so why bother?"

"Because," Garith said, "after years, we actually have a duty to perform!"

"You speak of this new movement among the singers, the parsh," the Skybreaker said.

"Something must be done about them," the Windrunner said. "For over two thousand years the Radiants haven't had a true enemy—save for flare-ups of the Unmade. Now an enemy presents itself. This is a chance to unify us again! The parsh have Surges. This was all supposed to be over, yet they fight on. Using *forms of power.*"

"They can't be reborn," the Skybreaker said. "It's not a Desolation. They don't have the abilities of the creatures of lore, so this fight is not ours."

"Any fight to defend people is our fight."

The Skybreaker sniffed and rolled her eyes. It seemed that dealing with Windrunners was the same regardless of the era. At any rate, both glanced at Navani. Blast. They expected her to mediate? Yes, apparently so.

"I think," she said, "we're all a little too emotional right now. Why don't we talk it over in a calmer setting?"

"Calm?" the Skybreaker said. "Melishi, the tower is *dying*. The protections are *vanishing*. You yourself called for the evacuation!"

"He said we'd return," Garith said. "It's temporary."

"Then why all those barriers around the Sibling?" the Skybreaker demanded. "If it's temporary, why not just weather it, ship in food?" She narrowed her eyes. "No, something is happening. I *will not* live here if even the *Bondsmith* is lying."

"Show Melishi a little trust," Garith said. "He—"

"Trust?" the Skybreaker said. "Trust, Garith? What about *your* lies? What cons are you running, while pretending you are so valiant?"

The Windrunner recoiled, floating back a foot as if by instinct, his eyes wide.

"Yes, I'm well aware of how you keep holding things back from us, and even the other Windrunners," the Skybreaker said. "What are you hiding?" She spat on the ground before Navani. "The truth becomes a frailer memory here, day by day. Our new leader has told us where we came from, what humankind did to its homeworld, and you two refuse to let me tell everyone. Liars. Liars to the *core*." The flying woman stared straight at Navani and continued. "We've told everyone else the truth anyway. Deal with it." She gave what appeared to be a salute—arm overhead—but done ironically, then waved to the others. They flew off in a group.

Navani forced herself not to feel insulted or ashamed. This wasn't *her* fault. She was rescued by the scholarly side of her brain, which was putting pieces together. The records they'd found indicated a mass abandonment of the tower, led by Melishi. They had also referenced the tensions between Windrunners and Skybreakers.

Garith the Windrunner lowered down next to her. "It's unraveling, Melishi," he said softly. "I warned you this might happen, if you couldn't persuade the Sibling. The tower is a symbol. Losing it . . ."

"I have done all I could," Navani said, needing to give *some* response.

"I wish I could be convinced that was true," he said. "I sincerely wish it." Storms. The coldness from him was practically palpable. "I will gather the Radiants at the camp near Cabridar and try to make a new place for us there. But the enemy moves toward Iri, and Feverstone. Fighting will come for us soon—and if the Skybreakers have told everyone the truth of our history . . . there will be more disagreements."

He rose off the ground to go, but Navani realized she needed to try for more information. "Wait," she said. "What of this accusation, Garith? That you've been lying? About what?"

He drew his lips to a line, and offered no excuse or explanation as he soared away toward the upper reaches of the tower. Navani was left alone on the empty plateau before the Oathgates, enveloped in a familiar coldness.

Adolin found Commandant Kushkam in one of his customary locations, on the balcony in the dome, surveying the Oathgate battlefield. It had changed dramatically in the four days since the fighting had begun, and was unlike any that Adolin had ever seen. The bronze fortification at the center, roughly circular with a rounded top, had expanded further. It could hold several thousand now. Outside it was a long, wide ring of stone ground that—despite the dim light—Adolin knew was coated in crusted blood and corpses. No rainwater would fall in here to wash that away.

That wide field was also strewn with debris that had been pushed outward, in columns, thirty or forty yards by the attackers as they made their assaults: forming barricades behind which the defending soldiers sometimes took up positions. All together, it formed a star pattern.

More debris was on its way—the emperor's own furniture, as he'd insisted. Yanagawn confessed he had rooms full of it that he'd never used, and so what was now being thrown down onto the field was their finest—gold and red, occasionally jeweled, glittering in the darkness. No aluminum, though evidently there was a ton of that in the palace just hanging around as picture frames and dining ware. What a strange place Azir was.

Regardless, they were at a lull in the fighting for the moment—something that was becoming rarer and rarer as the enemy tried for consistent attacks. Adolin liked to think the defenders had done enough damage to make the enemy wary; they had the numerical advantage, but their forces weren't infinite. They sometimes had to pause to reassess.

Adolin walked up to Kushkam—pushing aside a yawn, refusing to give in to the fatigue—and leaned against the rail by him. Kushkam didn't speak at first. The commandant was like a small chull in the shadows: stout but sturdy.

"We still have that oil," Kushkam said, referencing the oil sacks tied to the top of the dome, rigged to fall upon command. A trap set up before the enemy had even arrived. "We might have to use it soon, Adolin. They almost broke us last time, and half my forces had retreated into the hallways before the Shardbearers hit the enemy."

"If we use the oil, we lose the dome."

"I know. I believe you." He heaved a sigh. "We might not have a choice. What about caltrops? Our remaining Soulcaster can make bronze ones."

"Singer feet are tough, Kushkam," Adolin said. "I don't think they'll be stopped by that." He ground his teeth in thought. "I like your other idea though. Plugging the passageways."

The idea was to fill some of the hallways with Soulcast bronze, so when the enemy battered down the door, they found the path had turned solid. Trouble was, if they plugged too many, their own forces couldn't make it in to fight.

But . . . Kushkam was right. They were close to losing the dome entirely. Plugging the exits, then, might be another last-ditch method of slowing the enemy.

Kushkam nodded. "I'm trying to find a towers analogue that move would mirror."

"Don't think there is one except for Zenaz's Final Adage."

"'Never assume,'" Kushkam quoted, "'the game actually replicates real life.' Well, I'll see about plugging some of the exits." He pointed to the field. "For now, see that larger corridor across the way, where they've pushed debris to the sides more than others? I think that happened intentionally, not as part of a failing line. I suspect they're preparing that corridor for a large assault today."

"We've spotted the Heavenly Ones hovering right outside the city," Adolin said. "Hopefully that's all there are—the enemy keeps patrols all through this region, and might have assigned one to come here for support."

"And if they brought other, more dangerous Fused with them?"

"That could be catastrophic."

Kushkam grunted. "Let's put the reserves on alert. We're likely looking at a large offensive either way." He paused. "You think they could have gotten more Fused here on the other side? Flown in through Shadesmar?"

"Yeah," Adolin said. "Heavenly Ones are slower than Windrunners, but given several days . . . Well, we should be ready."

Kushkam leaned toward Adolin. Sensing the man's mood, Adolin also leaned in so they could speak more privately. The archers and scribes on the balcony were already giving them some space, but the two lowered their voices anyway.

"Adolin," Kushkam said, "how do we stand against this? Please tell me you have *some* way we can be ready for more Fused. My men are exhausted, wounded, and now demoralized because the reinforcements have failed to arrive."

"I . . . I don't know," he said. "Zarb, I wish I had an answer, but . . . I don't. Fused are going to be tough no matter what. We can watch for Masked Ones—I've already been telling the men to be suspicious of any humans trying to escape out the doors from inside here. But Flowing Ones, Magnified Ones, Altered Ones, Husked Ones . . . storms. We have trouble facing them *with* Radiants."

"This will break us," Kushkam whispered. "I won't speak these fears even to my high officers, but to you . . ." He glanced at Adolin. "What do we do?"

It broke Adolin's heart to have no answers. Again, he felt as if he were back in Kholinar as it fell. Then, whispered into his mind from somewhere distant, Maya's voice. Three words.

Hold. Help. Comes.

Storms, he would not give in to this despair. "Help is coming," he promised Kushkam.

"Your spren?" Kushkam said. "When will she arrive?"

"I don't know," Adolin admitted.

"What good can more honorspren do though? Notum is helpful, yes, but we don't need more scouts—and we don't have time for Radiant bonds."

Adolin hesitated, uncertain.

Help. Comes, Maya promised.

"We just have to hold," Adolin said. "Help *is* coming."

"A miracle? Is that what you're promising, Adolin?"

Was he? He floundered, for while he trusted Maya, the more he thought about what he'd asked her to do—fetch more honorspren—the less he thought it would help.

Storms, he should be able to protect this city without that, shouldn't he? He was the Blackthorn's son. His father would have found a way.

"The enemy can't merely defeat us," Adolin said. "They have to hold the city. Maybe we can win even if we lose the dome. I still don't have a good legal definition of what it means to hold the city. My scribes and yours have been going in circles over the relevant statutes."

"Likely it means conquering the palace," Kushkam said, "and holding the throne itself. 'As long as the emperor is on his throne, Azir stands.'"

Adolin cocked his head, remembering hearing Noura say the same thing. "Is that a common phrase among your people?"

"Yes. Three centuries ago, during the chaos at the fall of the Dusqqa Dynasty, it was proven in court. One family tried to set up a rival imperial seat in another city, but the judges decided that the family that held the palace—specifically the throne room—was the true ruler."

Adolin smiled. "Sometimes you talk like Jasnah, Zarb. I don't think I'll ever get used to you all needing to take history lessons to become soldiers."

"There are certain advantages," he replied. "Then again, the Alethi method has its charm. You don't waste time teaching men to read or sing. You put them in armor, give them a sword, and train them to kill . . . There's a reason you're the most feared military in the world."

"Well, if you're right about the throne, then we know their goal. The palace should be our fallback position."

"Know your enemy's goals," Kushkam said. "It's always an advantage. I'll ponder how we can reinforce that fallback, but . . . if things keep going as they are, we might not even have the troops to man the palace walls. So for now, I want to make sure our reserves are ready for a push today."

Adolin nodded and withdrew, meaning to go check on his Plate. On his way along the balcony, however, he encountered an Azish girl struggling to pull back a bow. He fought off a yawn, nodding to May Aladar, and tried to remember the young girl's name.

Zabra. That was it. "Harder than it looks, Zabra?" he asked.

"They made it too hard," Zabra complained. "I know there are bows with less of a draw than this."

"We're fighting singers," he said. "Warforms mostly. They're well equipped, and naturally armored. We need bows with a good draw weight to have any hope of bringing them down."

Zabra deflated. She wasn't much shorter than many of the soldiers, but she had a willowy form.

"May does it," Zabra whispered.

"Captain Aladar," Adolin said, "has been training in the bow for a decade. I believe I told you that it would take you years to get to fighting shape."

"It's not taking the emperor years," Zabra muttered. Then she cringed, glancing around to make sure none of the Azish archers were near. "I know you're training him. Everyone whispers about it. He's never held a sword, yet you're going to put him on the front lines."

Adolin chuckled. "The front lines?"

"Well, you might. What's the difference? You're going to tell me it's because he's a man, aren't you? And an important one?"

"Well, the 'important' part would keep him out, in your culture," Adolin said. "But you know he had training with knives as a boy, right?"

"We're . . . not supposed to talk about that time."

"Must be hard," Adolin said. "Regardless, he has some good fighting instincts, and I can work with those. Finally, there's one important factor."

She frowned in the dim light, trying to figure it out.

"Shardplate," Adolin said. "Technically, all of the empire's Plate belongs to the emperor. If he ever has to put that on to keep him safe, I want him to be capable of using it. If he's ever on the battlefield, he'll be in Plate. It does a great job equalizing for skill."

"So . . ." she said softly. "You're saying I need to get me a set of Shardplate."

"Good luck," Adolin said.

"I could do it," she said. "Simply gotta kill someone who has some, right?" She eyed Adolin, as if sizing him up. Then she smiled at his shocked expression. "Or I could do the reasonable thing and find me a spren. I think I'd like being able to melt stone with a glare."

He gave her a smile as May reclaimed the bow and sent Zabra running with a message to check on arrow supplies.

"Sorry about that," Adolin said as Zabra left. "I should have asked before handing her off to you."

"Eh," May said. "She's easy to motivate, which is useful. You look tired."

"I'm not tired."

"You look it."

"Too dark in here for you to tell."

"You *just* yawned. How much have you been sleeping?"

"Are you my mother?"

"I'm your ex. Which makes me the closest thing your wife has to an advocate here, *plus* I'm technically your head scribe for this deployment. So . . ."

"Not sleeping enough," he admitted, his mind drifting toward Shallan, and his worry for her. "But sleeping more than I feel I should. I'm good for now, May. I promise."

One of his usual scribes would have accepted that—they knew if they pushed, and he pushed back, he could be trusted to make that decision. May remained skeptical. Before she could order him to sleep though, a line of blue light came shooting through one of the balcony doorways.

Notum appeared as a human-size spren. "Sir, you need me?"

"Can you still see into Shadesmar?" Adolin asked. "You're not fully bonded."

"I'm not *any* bonded," Notum said, and closed his eyes. "I can catch glimpses. I don't think I can tell you much—the enemy has gathered many of their assault troops on this side, I believe. It . . ." He paused. "*Wait.*"

"Fused?" Adolin asked, stomach sinking.

"Yes," Notum said. "And worse. Large shadow. Red eyes. That's a thunderclast soul, Adolin. It—"

Adolin went running, shouting the alarm and calling for his armor. Trumpets of warning started sounding as he burst out of the dome. On the elevated ramp around the outside he spun, searching until he saw something huge and hulking rising from the field right outside Azimir.

His greatest fear had arrived, in the form of a mountain of stone bent on breaking open the dome.

81
THE SCHOLAR WITH A SPEAR

Somehow, I've never been good at this. Ten thousand years, and some things I just cannot learn.

The enemy arrived. Hitting Narak Prime, exactly as Sigzil didn't want them to.

So he fought, hoping his plan with the Lightweaving would divert them. For now he had to hold the skies, creating burning eyes with a silvery spear. Vienta began spinning around him as he flew between clashes, a woman shrouded in flowing cloth. Though he knew she felt more comfortable hidden, she remained visible to encourage him as he soared through the Everstorm's omnipresent darkness.

Keep going, Sigzil. This is where you belong: the scholar with a spear.

He hadn't fit in with the scholars at home because he didn't like sitting in musty rooms reading. He'd wanted to be out doing field research, learning and experiencing. That was why Master Hoid had chosen him as an apprentice. And it was why he was an effective Windrunner.

And now, why he could lead.

He summoned his Shardspear and plummeted from the heights, joined by a force of thirty Windrunners glowing Radiant in defiance of the eternal night.

They clashed with the Skybreakers, who'd flown in to give air support to the major offensive against Narak Prime. Those Focused Ones had proven capable of launching boulders with their springlike musculature, and were trying to bring down walls. That meant the defenders had to change tactics—sending forces out to harry advancing enemies, rather than only flying above the plateau.

In a moment, Sigzil was fighting for his life again. The Skybreakers fought wordlessly, never responding to demands or questions. Slate-faced destroyers who burned the air, a rare few of them wearing glittering Shardplate. At least Nale himself was nowhere to be seen; Sigzil did not fancy his chances against a Herald.

He swept with his spear, then Lashed to the side, whirling around his enemy—who struck at the wrong spot. Sigzil planted a dagger in the man's neck from behind, and that dagger—made from a stolen enemy lance—pulled Stormlight out. The enemy froze in the air, paralyzed by the trauma.

Sigzil released the knife hilt and left the Skybreaker trembling there, instead defending against two others who tried to save their fellow. He held them off until their companion's Stormlight finally dwindled. Sigzil ducked backward and yanked the dagger free, timing it perfectly, leaving the unfortunate Skybreaker to drop.

The other two dove after him, exposing their backs to Sigzil—who dove as well, summoning Vienta as a long Shardlance. He rammed it through one of their backs, then formed a Blade to sweep at the other—all while they fell together.

Four figures crashed into the plateau. Only Sigzil rose, standing upright as a ring of Stormlight expanded from him—brushing across three corpses. Fent and Kalleb, two of his squires, swooped in to check on him. The three struck out across the plateau—one without walls, on the outskirts of the battlefield—dodging between clashing Radiants.

Come on, Sigzil thought, glancing toward Narak Three in the distance. It had to be a tempting target, with those lower walls. If the Lightweavers did their job right, Deepest Ones—who peeked through walls and scouted the area—would soon give the report that a huge gemstone stash was there, heavily guarded. Hopefully not suspiciously so.

It was a perfect feint. Just subtle enough, just tempting enough. He had to hope it worked, because those Focused Ones were breaking the wall of Narak Prime—and the Stonewards were running low on Light to repair it.

Storms. He'd never been in a battle such as this, full of so many Radiants and Fused. They dominated this battlefield, Heavenly Ones streaking through the sky. A few rare Husked Ones dropped their bodies, becoming ribbons of light, proving difficult to target and counter. Deepest Ones emerged from stone where the wooden protections had been broken, while Magnified Ones with hulking silhouettes clashed against Stonewards who liquefied the ground.

It was madness. Traditional battle lines and formations were almost impossible to maintain. Sigzil and his squires soared through this mess, targeting a Focused One—who, harried from above, had been forced to begin launching boulders into the sky. Magnified Ones nearby pulled large carts full of the stones as ammunition.

Sigzil and his squires came in low and fast, and Sigzil dismissed his

Shardlance and yanked out a conventional sword. The two squires ran interference, distracting guards. In the confusion, the enemy couldn't determine which was the full Radiant until Sigzil had maximum momentum and rammed a newly formed Shardspear straight through the eye of a Focused One. Others nearby cursed him and began launching boulders at him, but Sigzil used rapid-fire Lashings to yank himself one way, then the other, and left a burning-eyed Focused One behind.

There were barely fifteen of those left, so each one they brought down was a huge loss to the enemy. After regrouping with his squires, he saw a heartening sight. The remaining Focused Ones suddenly pivoted, and the entire army charged instead toward Narak Three—with its lower number of defenders and supposedly rich contents.

"Storms!" Kalleb exclaimed, running a hand through his short dark beard. "Sir, it's *working*."

With a sense of overwhelming relief, he checked the spanreeds strapped to his arm. With them he sent confirmation of the enemy's pivot to his generals—and that the next phase of the plan could move forward. The army was to act panicked, pretend they'd been caught with their trousers around their ankles, and mount a hasty defense of Narak Three. Encourage the enemy to double down there and try to break through. It was working.

Except . . . this other spanreed? That was from Leyten. Sigzil answered it, and the ruby started giving a message via Windrunner code.

Found him. North side.

Sigzil felt a sudden chill. Him.

Moash.

Sigzil quickly sent back a message: *Do. Not. Engage.*

No response. Damnation.

"Come on!" Sigzil said, diving in the indicated direction.

⁂

Fully plated, Adolin ripped the top off the large wooden box his team had brought through the Oathgate when he'd come to Azimir. It was still in the wagon bed; its weight bowed and strained the boards of the vehicle. Two horses had struggled to pull it.

Adolin threw the top aside, revealing the chain.

An enormous aluminum chain—Yanagawn wasn't the only one with access to the stuff. The Radiants had been experimenting with the exceptionally light metal. Specifically, chains like this one sometimes helped against thunderclasts.

He hurried to the front of the wagon, where Gallant was reluctantly allowing himself to be harnessed. The Ryshadium eyed him.

"I know it's not glorious," Adolin said. "But it's what we need."

The horse snorted, but stopped nipping at the grooms. In the distance, enormous footsteps shook the ground. It was coming.

"Two ordinary horses could barely pull this," Adolin added to Gallant. "Stallions."

Gallant eyed him, then blew out.

"Yes, I'm trying to manipulate you," Adolin said, with a grin. "Is it working?"

The horse held his head high, and Adolin turned toward his team, who stood among waving ribbons of anticipationspren. These forty soldiers had armed themselves with ropes and hammers, carrying oil in barrels on their backs. All had been of only minor effectiveness against a thunderclast, but it was something.

Storms, he'd hoped never to try this again without Radiants. Adolin grabbed his Shardhammer from the ground near the wagon and pointed, raising a shout of defiance from his soldiers. Then he charged toward the hulking shadow that had climbed over the walls into Azimir and was thundering toward the dome.

Gallant strained forward, pulling the wagon—which squealed in protest, but did move. Adolin's soldiers charged with him. They somehow had to fight a beast made entirely of stone. Thirty feet tall, with glowing red eyes and a face that evoked the lean, arrowheaded danger of an axehound. This particular thunderclast was more feral-looking than the one Adolin had fought—and failed to defeat—in Thaylen City.

Adolin led his team along a wide city street empty of people, and had flashbacks to Thaylen City. Same heartbeat in the stone, made by massive feet. Same sound of buildings crashing down as it brushed past them. Same thundering in Adolin's chest as he faced a terrible truth.

He was a common man in a world of giants. Against these things, even Shardweapons were of middling effectiveness.

I might need you, he thought to Maya. *I'm sorry.*

. . . Understand . . . she sent, distant. *But . . . I am close . . . to what you asked . . .*

I fear I sent you on a meaningless chase, Adolin told her, frank. *It might be best if you just return.*

Please . . . she replied.

Well, he wasn't going to force the issue. No soldier served with him who didn't want to. It was bad military practice perhaps, but Adolin did a lot of stupid things. Case in point: charging a thunderclast.

Storms, he'd forgotten how big they were.

When his team reached an intersection that the looming thunderclast would most likely pass, he halted them. Horns in the distance announced a major offensive in the dome. As expected, unfortunately. The enemy would be keen to divide the defense. While ordinary troops were basically useless against this thing, it would be an enormous distraction for Adolin and—he saw another figure running up—Neziham, the Azish Shardbearer.

"Commandant says I should aid you," the man said, his voice echoing in his helm. "But Adolin . . . those horns."

"I know," Adolin said, peeking around the side of the building he was using for cover. The thing was crashing along the large roadway, coming their direction. "But if that thing reaches the dome, it can rip it apart and stomp our armies to pulp." Adolin glanced back at Neziham, viewing him through the slit in his own helm. "The regular soldiers and the commandant will have to hold the dome."

"They have more Fused now," Neziham said, pained.

"I hate it too. I'm sorry."

Adolin worried that the man might rush back to the dome. But as Adolin had come to expect, the Azish troops were made of harder stuff than that. Neziham nodded to him, summoning his Blade. "For Prime and People," he whispered. "So long as the emperor is on his throne, I fight. Tell me what to do."

"Nothing we have can hurt that thing except your Blade," Adolin said. "The rest of us are here to distract it."

"I go for the legs, then?" he said.

"I tried that," Adolin said. "But it's a lot tougher than it sounds, and it sounds *storming tough.*" He pointed to the wagon behind them. "Those chains can hold them briefly, trip them. My troops will oil the ground, try to disorient the beast with ropes and arrows. I've never tried this with conventional troops though. We always had Edgedancers and Stonewards . . ."

He took a deep breath, then forged on. "I'll run in and try to get the chain around its legs. If I can trip it, strike for the neck. Get your Blade into its spine where neck meets head—made of stone or not—and its eyes will go out, same as a human. It's a spren; Blades can hurt its body, send it back to Shadesmar, force it to recuperate." He met Neziham's iron gaze. "That healing can take weeks. We bring this one down, it's out of the war forever."

"So be it," Neziham said, raising a fist.

Adolin clanged his forearm against the other man's, then ran to pull out the chain.

⁂

Zarb Kushkam, commandant supreme of the Azimir Imperial Guard, had never wanted this post.

Most military officers fought to get promoted to a cushy job in the capital—while he had done everything he could to *avoid* it. Promotions had found him anyway, relentless, regardless of how clearly his essays explained he would rather remain a common field lieutenant.

Well, today he'd get his wish, because they were going to need every soldier. He stood up from the bedside of one of the wounded—he'd been visiting the hospital—and listened to the horns, reading their notes. Enormous incursion. He took a deep breath. He wouldn't have his Shardbearer for this fight; he'd already sent him to join Adolin against the thunderclast.

So be it. He took his helmet off the bedside table and saluted the wounded soldiers. Then he pushed through the exit and onto the cobbled plaza outside, dominated by the giant dome. In better times, this plaza was a market filled with merchants and tents. Now it was empty.

No. Not empty. Those were *figures* rising up from the stone. Smooth-skinned singers with a variety of patterns, but each evoking a sense of emaciated, elongated limbs and wide, dangerous eyes.

Deepest Ones. The Fused were here.

"Yaezir," he swore softly, gathering his personal guard. The bulk of the troops would already be committed in the dome. So he sent a messenger, then led the charge against the Deepest Ones himself. And prayed this wouldn't be the day he saw his homeland fall.

⁂

Sigzil nearly left his squires behind in his haste to find Leyten. He finally spotted an isolated group of people clashing on a small plateau on the north side of the battlefield.

He summoned his Blade and came screaming in, passing puddles that reflected red lightning, full of corrupted rainspren. He closed in as Leyten and three squires faced a glowing man in black.

The moment Sigzil drew near, his Lashings vanished.

Ever since Kaladin had been caught by the strange fabrial that negated Radiant abilities, they'd trained for this. Still, Sigzil went tumbling, his Lashing canceled but not his inertia. His training fled in the moment, and both he and his squires tumbled to the ground.

He looked up in time to see Moash ram his Shardblade through the head of one of Leyten's squires, dropping the young man with his eyes burning. As Leyten swung with his knife, Moash rose in the air on a quick Lashing, then kicked, sending Leyten sprawling.

No. *No.*

Sigzil tried to summon his Shardspear—but nothing happened. You couldn't do that while within one of these bubbles created by the fabrial. He could *almost* sense his powers, and his weapon, at the edge of his reach.

Moash's Honorblade made him capable of using powers while the rest of them could not.

This was a death trap.

"Out!" Sigzil shouted to his squires. "Now! Run until you feel your powers return."

"A hundred and twenty-two feet away," Vienta said, having noted the exact place they entered the field. He repeated her, sending the squires scrambling, panic in their eyes.

Sigzil ran the other way, toward Leyten.

"Sigzil . . . I'm afraid," Vienta said.

"Stay hidden," he replied. "There's no sand that I see. No way for him to spot you."

"Stay strong," she whispered as he took out the knife he'd used to kill the Skybreaker earlier, though he had no intention of fighting Moash like this. He kept his eyes open for the fabrial, saw nothing.

"Leyten!" he shouted on the run. "Retreat! *Now!*"

Leyten backed up, accompanied by his two remaining squires. But Sigzil now saw that they *couldn't* retreat. As they tried to escape, Moash—using Lashings—cut them off. Leyten looked at Sigzil—who was dashing the thirty yards or so between them—then pointed to the sides.

His squires ran in opposite directions. Leyten stood his ground to distract Moash.

No. No, no, NO!

Leyten tried valiantly, wielding a simple side dagger against an Honorblade. He wisely ducked the first strike, then got into a grapple, which held Moash off a few moments.

Sigzil arrived a second later, slamming his specialized knife down into Moash's back as the two struggled.

Moash didn't so much as flinch, though he did turn and glance at Sigzil.

And the man's eyes were entirely crystalline.

Two diamonds, glowing with Voidlight, had replaced his eyes—and indeed, they seemed to have lanced through his skull, because pieces of them jutted from the back and sides of his head. As if they'd grown in among his brains, crusting them like a fungus. It looked almost as if he had a crown of crystals.

Sigzil stumbled back, yanking his dagger free, unnerved by that inhuman gaze.

Moash shoved Leyten to the side in a heap—he groaned, still alive—then spun and leveled the Honorblade. In the traitor's other hand, he carried a bloodied knife, one that warped the air.

Then, with that unnerving gaze pinned on Sigzil, Moash smiled.

Sigzil raised his weapon—though the strange metal at the core of the knife could block a Shardblade, he was just a man with a knife against a fully powered Radiant. So, instead of doing something stupid—well, stupid*er*—he kept his distance, and tried to get Moash talking.

"Moash," he said, "you don't have to do this."

"Of course I don't," Moash said.

"*Why,* then?" Sigzil asked, genuinely pained.

"You ask your enemy why he fights you?"

"We weren't always enemies!" Sigzil said, edging over toward Leyten, who was groaning on the ground.

"We were brothers, Sig," Moash said. "But then you chose the Alethi lighteyes over me—you went to them, after they murdered us, degraded us. After all that, you became hounds in the laps of the Kholins." He pointed with his sword. "I used to avoid emotion. Reject it. I welcome it now. It is my sword as much as this Blade."

"But . . ." Sigzil trailed off as Moash—whose eyelids blinked normally over those glowing crystal eyes—glanced upward.

"He can see me," Vienta whispered. "Sigzil, those crystal eyes of his can *see* me."

"Go," Sigzil hissed to Vienta. "*Now.*"

Sigzil braced himself and lunged forward, hoping to catch Moash while he was distracted. But Moash Lashed himself upward, swinging with the knife that distorted the air.

Sigzil heard a piercing shriek that twisted his insides. But it wasn't Vienta that Moash struck.

Leyten shouted in anguish and stretched bloodied fingers upward. He'd been stabbed during his clash with Moash earlier.

"Ethenia," Leyten whispered. "No . . ."

Moash lightly floated away from Sigzil, easily staying out of his reach, and landed near Leyten. There, he plunged the anti-Stormlight knife straight into Leyten's chest.

"*NO!*" Sigzil screamed.

Moash stood, and glanced toward shouts from nearby—an entire force, fetched by the squires, running this way. He tapped his wrists together in the Bridge Four salute, then took to the sky—streaking away in the darkness.

Weeping, Sigzil reached Leyten, who was bleeding profusely. "Sorry, Sig," Leyten wheezed. "We . . . we didn't mean to engage . . . We were in the air and he swooped back on us . . . activated the device so we dropped . . ."

"Don't speak, Leyten," Sigzil said, stanching the wounds, but feeling helpless. Those were deep cuts. He grabbed the man under the arms. "I need to get you out of this bubble so you can be healed."

"I was stupid . . ." Leyten said. "I let him get another of us, Sig . . . I . . ."

Sigzil began pulling the larger man, even though his medical training said not to move someone with such serious wounds. But within this field, Leyten had no chance.

"I . . . I see something, Sig. I see *you* . . . Storms, I *am* you . . ."

"Don't—"

"I die!" Leyten shouted, spasming. "The Scholar with a Spear! I die by the hands of a friend! My spren screams in death, and I know that I have failed to lead! I am no captain! I am nothing! Vyre strikes me, and my eyes burn!"

Moments later, a pair of Edgedancers—led by Sigzil's squires—found Sigzil weeping, his fingers bloody as he worked feverishly to sew up the wounds of a man who had already died.

The fabrial proved to be hidden in the shell of a rock, easy to miss. They deactivated it, then stood around Sigzil, solemn. His mind was full of those last words, that Death Rattle, which had prophesied Vienta's and Sigzil's own deaths by the terrible hand that had taken Teft and Leyten.

PLAN OF THE CITY OF AZIMIR

Kept free of labels by request of the Prime Aqasix, our Grand Minister and Emissary of Yaezir, the Emperor of Makabak, the King of Azir, the Lord of the Bronze Palace to better illuminate the Divinely-inspired layout of our

Great and Ancient City of Azimir

Got stopped on my way out of the city. Evidently I hadn't filled out the proper forms for stealing a map. After four hours of mind-numbing paperwork—and an exorbitant fee—they let me go, map in hand. No wonder there's so little crime here.

filed: m.h.12.2780 — double filed: m.h.120.2780 — checked for accur[illegible] Duvnix Z[illegible]

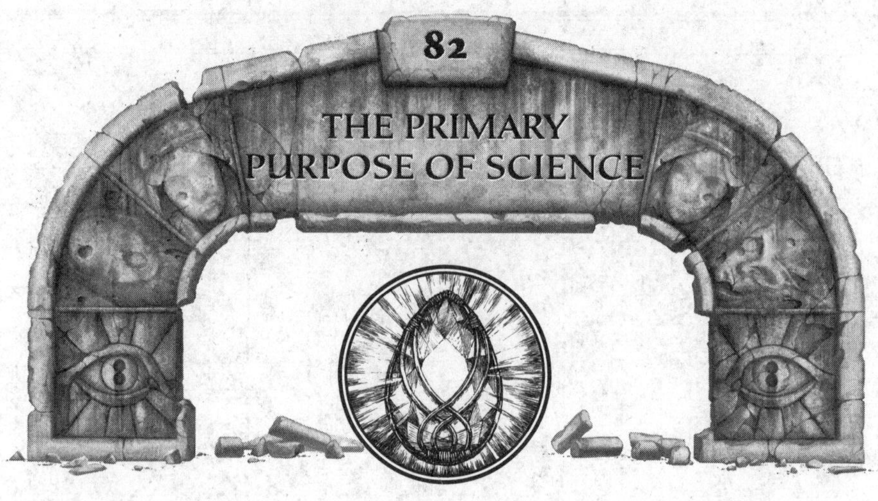

82
THE PRIMARY PURPOSE OF SCIENCE

In the past, I've held on too tightly. I've worked on that, but find that sometimes my grip is too loose.

Navani trudged along the plateau in front of Urithiru, feeling the incredible, daunting weight of ignorance.

To those in this vision where she'd seen the Skybreakers leave, she looked like a Bondsmith now many centuries dead, one who had let the tower grow cold and inhospitable. The chill air surrounded her, attracting coldspren—like icicles that grew up from the ground the wrong way—that had once been familiar, before the tower awoke. She turned toward the crowd of people, and many shivered, pulling their arms in tight. They wore robes with open fronts and skirts that went to the knee, leaving them woefully unprepared for such a bout of winter.

But why? *Why* was the tower failing? Was it because of the strife between orders? It had been millennia since a Desolation—and while they'd once been led by the Heralds and Honor, they now had no divine guidance and no enemy to fight. It was little wonder they'd found their way to interorder squabbling.

As she walked toward the silent crowd, she absently breathed in Stormlight—it came easily, as this realm was completely suffused with it—and tried to sense the tower. She found only a low buzzing sound in place of the expected rhythms.

Though she did, in searching, find . . . something. A line? A faint teal line of light? She gasped, for while Dalinar had explained what he could see with his powers, and while she could feel Connections at times, she had never been able to see these lines. Though she'd tried reaching the Sibling before, it had always failed. But maybe here, near a copy of the tower . . .

She touched this line with her fingers, then followed it with her mind. She heard a very faint, yet wonderfully familiar rhythm. *Navani?* The Sibling's voice, frail and distant. *It* is *you!*

Yes, she replied.

I sense you, suddenly, in me—and not. How?

I'm in a vision, she said. *Of the days right before you went to sleep. I just witnessed the Skybreakers leaving. Sibling, can you bring us back? We are lost in here.*

I . . . do not know how. My siblings might.

The Stormfather refuses, Navani said, reaching the front of the crowd, which parted for her. She walked over to where Dalinar and Gavinor were seated, then waved the others away—indicating she wanted space. People obligingly either moved into the tower or continued their treks toward the Oathgates.

"I'll explain in a minute," Navani said, at Dalinar's questioning glance.

Sibling, she continued. *Are you well in my absence?*

Yes. You are here . . . and not here . . . The bond is strong enough for me to continue. But you saw them go? Those days are shadowed to my mind. The . . . Skybreakers?

They revealed the truth of humankind's origins, Navani said. *Then they left.*

And . . . my Bondsmith?

I'm taking his role in this vision, Navani said. *Sibling, what happened? How did it come to this?*

I remember . . . fighting, the Sibling said. *Angry Radiants. So many different personalities. So many different passions. During those days it grew worse. I wonder . . . I wonder if Mishram was behind it . . . But that was not the reason. No. It was the Bondsmith. Melishi. He . . . withdrew from me, and sought after . . . You won't like this, Navani.*

Fabrials? she guessed. *Our newer kind?*

Yes. Melishi discovered the means of imprisoning spren. It was that, mixed with a feeling. I get feelings sometimes, Navani. Of what is to come. I sensed . . . pain. So much pain.

The Recreance, Navani replied, looking up at the tower. *It's near. A Radiant mentioned Feverstone—and the Recreance happened there, not long after this.*

Is there . . . a Windrunner? the Sibling asked. *One from Rira, with hair the color of a heliodor?*

Yes, Navani sent. *I met him.*

Follow him, the Sibling said, their voice growing softer. *He lies. I do not know more, as it happened far from me.*

Then they were gone. Navani's line of light faded, slipping through her fingers like water.

"I saw but couldn't hear," Dalinar said, sitting and holding Gav in his lap. "You contacted the Sibling?"

Navani nodded, settling down with him. "I lost the thread."

"That you found it after only a few days of practice is encouraging. The Sibling might be able to get us out."

"They said they can't," Navani said. "But I don't always trust that they know what is and isn't possible." She sighed, looking back to where the Skybreakers had been. "The Radiants of this time discovered the truth—probably from Nale—that humankind are the invaders on Roshar."

"Already?" Dalinar frowned, Gav in his lap holding to him with his eyes closed. "I thought that happened closer to the Recreance. I believe we're a good ten years from that, based on the age of that Windrunner. But . . . I suppose it could fit. Per the records we discovered in the tower, the Radiants discovered the truth, and had a plan to imprison Mishram. We had to connect the dots after that to determine what happened next. It could have taken some years to execute their plan, and for the news to build to them abandoning their oaths . . ."

Storms. She smiled at him.

"What?" he said.

"Just imagining the younger you tracking the intricacies of historical timelines, Dalinar. You could barely keep track of where you put your knife."

"I miss that knife," he said, with a grunt, then met her eyes. "It helps that I care now. It helps more that I can read and write."

She hesitated, trying to imagine being unable to write. There was a tendency in records for women to fondly imagine their husbands as big clumsy beasts, uncaring for details or nuance. With embarrassment, she remembered a few such comparisons in her own mind. But how much easier was it to remember details and discover nuance when you could write them out, discuss them via letters, ponder and record your thoughts? Storms, even look at a timeline?

She was quite aware of the injustices done to women by their society. That did not discount the different but still debilitating ones done to men.

"Anyway," she said, clearing her mind, "you're probably right about the timeline. Except . . . are we *sure* the news of the truth of humankind caused the Recreance?"

"No," he admitted. "The Stormfather is our only real source of information, as Wit said he wasn't on Roshar for these events. But the Stormfather holds back truths. I confronted him about this very idea, and he dodged the question, but even then—even before I knew he lied sometimes—I could sense there was more. The truth of where we came from must have contributed to the Recreance, but it isn't the only secret."

"The Sibling told me to follow that Windrunner," Navani said. "He's central to it somehow."

 "Since he'll be the first one to abandon his Shards and kill his spren,"

Dalinar said, "do you think it's possible he was working with the enemy, planning how to cripple the Radiants?"

It was an unfortunate likelihood. She sat back on the cold stone, ignoring the odd looks from people who flowed from the gate nearby. How to get to the next step? They needed to chase that Windrunner, uncover his lies.

But first a breather. Gav seemed to have fallen asleep in Dalinar's lap, and while she didn't feel sleepy, she was bearing an increasing weight of mental exhaustion. "Dalinar," she said, "could you please *ask* before you do something unexpected with your powers? I did not appreciate being thrust into the center of that conversation without warning, useful though it proved to be."

"Sorry," he said, looking away.

"Love," she said, placing a hand on his knee, "you're acting more . . . overwhelming lately. Stomping forward. Trampling over people like you used to. I thought you were doing better at such things."

"Can you blame me?" he said, quietly to not disturb Gav. A chiller wind from the nearby mountains blew across them, and Dalinar shivered. "Navani, what if I'm not enough? What if I can't solve this—either through gaining Honor's power or another way—and defeat him?"

"I don't know," she admitted.

"From the beginning," he whispered, "this has all focused on me. Visions. Revelations. Burdens. Honor's plan was to make Odium agree to a contest of champions—which we've done. Now I *have* to find the solution. The only hope our homeland has of ever being free again . . . and it rests on me. Is it any wonder I'm becoming more overwhelming?"

She squeezed his leg. "The man you were can't fix this, Dalinar. He never could have."

He met her eyes, then he nodded. "I'll remember that."

"How many days left?"

"Still three," he said, checking. "It's consistent—within the visions, time passes very slowly."

"We need to slip forward a little further," she said, "without losing ourselves."

"I don't know if we have that level of control," Dalinar said. "We keep stumbling around in here. If we knew what we were doing, we probably could have jumped from that first vision straight to the ones we wanted."

"True," she said. "But Dalinar, I think you underestimate how much we've learned. We've actually made a great deal of progress in learning to manipulate our situation in here, when you look at it."

He grunted. "I guess you're right. And Cultivation did encourage me to see the past. I've done that. So next . . ."

"We make another small increment," Navani said. "A refinement, using what we've learned. How did you send me into this particular role of the vision?"

"I strengthened the line between you and Melishi," he said. "I figured it would work, since you were both Bondsmiths of the tower."

"And in so doing, you exerted a new kind of control over the vision," she said, thoughtful. "At its core, science is about control. Being able to repeat the same experiment, get the same results, then use those results to your advantage."

"So . . ." he said, "you're saying if we can control the vision in a small way, we might be able to control the visions in a larger way too?"

"Yes." Navani stood. "Repeatability is one of the fundamental steps to understanding the world. Once you can replicate a result, you can really start digging for the truth."

"I don't know if I can replicate what I did though," Dalinar said. "It worked because you were both Bondsmiths, and it felt right to Connect you."

"Connect me to someone else," Navani said. She pointed at some people walking nearby, carrying their belongings toward the Oathgate. "That woman there."

"Why her?"

"She has two children, a boy and a girl," Navani said. "Like me. She is roughly my age. And judging by her bearing, she is proud, although she walks alone with no husband. As I did for years after Gavilar's death."

"Odd . . ." Dalinar said.

She glanced at him.

"As you said that," he told her, "*you* forged just the smallest Connection to the woman."

"Perception," she said, remembering the research into spren. "Perception changes Investiture, Dalinar. Wit talked about this place, and how it is a shifting web of Connections."

"He also said it was beyond the ability to understand."

"He said it was beyond *our* ability to understand," she replied. "But so are all natural phenomena, in the beginning. It is the scientist's duty to make that which was once unknowable so commonplace that you can wear it on your arm and think nothing of it."

Dalinar glanced at the fabrial clock. Then nodded, closing his eyes and concentrating.

A moment later, Navani was in the place of that woman. Carrying a large pack with her family's belongings, and accompanied by two children. It *worked.* She looked back across the barren plateau to Dalinar, who stood with Melishi the Bondsmith. Melishi put his hand to his head as if confused, then rushed off toward the tower.

Perfect. She soothed the two teenaged children, sent them on their way with their packs—even though she knew they weren't real, she couldn't help herself—then walked back to Dalinar. He was speaking with Gav as the child stirred in his lap.

". . . It's all right, Grampa," Gav was saying. "Daddy told me it would be all right."

"You heard him?" Dalinar said. "Elhokar's voice."

Gav nodded sleepily.

"Is that possible?" Navani asked.

"I don't know," Dalinar whispered. "I feel . . . like sometimes I hear Evi's voice. It might be my mind pretending. At any rate, it seems to have comforted him."

Navani nodded, looking after Melishi.

"So . . ." Dalinar said, "under the proper circumstances, we can choose how we're perceived in these visions. That sounds useful. But we still need to jump forward a few years, to chase down that Windrunner's secrets."

"You used the Stormfather as an anchor," Navani said. "How? Can you talk me through it?"

"I was angry with the Stormfather, and I knew that *he* knew what I needed to see. I used my Connection to him—slammed my hands together and made us shift here."

"Because the Stormfather was thinking about it," Navani said. "The very secrets the Stormfather was trying to hide hovered in his mind, forging that Connection for us." She took a deep breath. "That was similar to the other anchors, which were related in some way to the events we saw. Well, we are on a path toward the Recreance, and that Windrunner, Garith. This is our destiny: to find why Honor died, and how."

She looked to Dalinar and he stood up, disturbing Gav.

"Navani," Dalinar said, "that's working. I don't know if you're reinforcing what is already there, or if you're creating something new—but I feel like I can see the pathway."

"The Stormfather knows it," she said, "and you have a profound Connection to him. *Roshar* knows what happened. These events somehow began the sequence that led to you and me becoming Bondsmiths. This isn't just a mystery, it's our *heritage.*"

Dalinar met her eyes and nodded. He had the Connection, the pathway. An anchor forged of their own natures, history, and bonds. "I am in awe, Navani. I didn't realize your scholarly methods could help us understand the ways of the gods."

"Dalinar," she said, "understanding the ways of God is the *primary purpose* of science."

With that, he engaged his powers.

And they appeared on a battlefield with singers arrayed before them. Navani, Dalinar, and Gav were among the Radiants—and in the distance, that Windrunner was walking up to a tent. He was about ten years older now, with greying hair—the same age he looked in the vision where Dalinar had first seen him, on the day of the Recreance.

⁂

The thunderclast slammed a fist down, breaking cobbles. The stones spasmed, the near miss throwing Adolin to the ground. He scrambled backward on hands and knees, forced to leave the hammer.

The creature raised its fist from the ground, dropping chips of broken cobble like clattering rain. This one walked with a hunched-over gait, still bipedal, but those arms were so long they would scrape the ground if it didn't curl them up while walking. It attacked again, voiceless, as Adolin's soldiers swarmed it on both sides—oil draining from the small kegs on their backs, coating the stone beneath its feet. Other soldiers broke larger barrels at the head of the street, letting it flow down.

Adolin puffed inside his helm, hoisting the large chain over one shoulder—with the other end running some forty feet back down the street toward the carriage, which he'd disconnected from Gallant. The horse danced around, snorting, but obeyed Adolin's strict command to stay put—between the oiled ground and uneven cobbles, bringing a horse into this was begging for a broken leg.

Right, Adolin thought. *Just get the chain wrapped around one leg. Use the hook on the end to hold it secure.*

He heaved forward, blessing the power of Plate to keep him moving despite his mounting fatigue. He pushed into the nearest building, pulling the chain with him. This was one of many tenements along the road. In Azimir, these tended to be nicer than in other cities—three-story rows of multifamily homes, made of stone. The front room was empty, thankfully; the family had fled out the rear door, leaving a trail of fearspren.

Storms, they were lucky thunderclasts had trouble forming out of covered or worked stone. Otherwise it could have emerged straight under the palace, rather than approaching from outside the city. Adolin watched through the doorway, the end of the chain in his hands—each link as wide as his palm. In the street, Neziham distracted the thing by running past with his Blade out, trying to cut at the ankle, and forcing it to dodge with a lumbering gait.

That gave Adolin a chance to duck out again, towing the chain. He slipped on the oil, righted himself, then scrambled toward the closest massive stone foot. It was thicker than a man was tall, and looked like a hoof. Adolin hauled his chain around the leg—but the thunderclast moved and yanked the chain right out of Adolin's grip. His end, with the hook, flipped away from him and crashed into a building.

Adolin skidded on oiled ground, then went running for the chain end. The thunderclast eyed him; but before it could attack, Adolin's soldiers made a desperate play, getting in its way and shouting, making it pause.

Adolin pulled the chain out of the crumbling facade of the building, then spun to see a terrifying sight: a hand, large enough to blot out the sky, swinging for him. Adolin dove, but got hit anyway, and was flung like a slapped cremling. The world spiraled around him as he tumbled down the roadway amid sounds of clanging metal and grinding rock.

He landed and groaned, lifting a dazed head. His Plate leaked Light from nearly every armor piece. He felt terribly dizzy as he stood up on wobbly feet.

Was the Plate . . . worried?

"Not your fault," Adolin mumbled, getting his bearings. He'd dropped the chain *again.* Storms. He forced himself to go running for it, trailing Stormlight. Fortunately, Neziham had distracted the thunderclast before it could finish Adolin off.

Adolin grabbed the chain and dashed to the thing's right foot as it kicked with the other, toppling a building toward Adolin's troops. With a grunt, Adolin let himself slide across the oiled ground straight past the leg. Then he heaved to the side, scrambling around the ankle as it slammed its other foot down on the roadway ahead.

Again the thunderclast noticed him and swung, but Adolin ducked—skidding on the oil. Wind from the miss rippled pools of oil nearby, then they shook violently as the hand hit the ground. Adolin managed to scuttle back around the thing's heel. Here, with a heave, he slammed the hook through two of the links on the other side.

When the thunderclast raised that foot to step, it towed the chain behind it—the other end, also with a hook, coming out of the box at the end of the street and clanging against cobbles.

Adolin backed away, breathing hard. First part done. Now he had to link that other end of the chain to something. Ideally he would wrap it around the other foot, to best trip it. As he contemplated his options, he checked over his shoulder and saw another daunting sight.

Heavenly Ones were buzzing high above the city, dropping boulders—artillery that, after millennia of practice, they knew how to make as dangerous as any siege weapon.

Zarb Kushkam looked up in confusion, his vision swimming, his arm bloodied. What . . . what had . . .

Around him, soldiers lay dead in a blast pattern. Others continued to fight and shout as hands came up through the ground and seized them, stabbing them in the thighs. He shouted for reinforcements, but storms, who could form battle lines out of a situation like this? The very ground was against them and—

CRASH.

Another rock slammed to the ground nearby, crushing soldiers, throwing chips that dropped others with the force of the debris. The horns . . . the horns were sounding for all reinforcements. Every troop committed . . . even the exhausted. He barely remembered giving that order before falling. His mind was . . .

A shock ran through him, a sharp wave of coldness, and his mind cleared, confusionspren vanishing. He shook himself, and found the young Alethi healer at his side, holding his hand—Stormlight glowing from her. She wore a dress in the middle of this chaos, bright green.

Zarb grabbed a nearby soldier. "Get her a storming helmet!" he shouted, pointing. "And keep *her* alive as she heals people!" He seized another. "See that *he* stays alive!"

Then he pulled a pike from the hands of one of the dead and shouted the rallying cry. Just in time for the wall of the dome to explode outward in a shower of broken stone.

Beyond it stood the hulking forms of ten beings with glowing red eyes. Including a variety he'd never seen—tall, with skin that seemed made from tightly wrapped belts.

The Fused were here. If there had ever been a time, it was now. "Tell those inside the dome," he ordered one of his beleaguered messengers, "to prepare to drop the firebombs."

⁂

Adolin's honor guard did what they could to stall the thunderclast, but it had largely broken them. Of Adolin's forty, maybe ten remained on their feet. They waved nets and shot arrows, but the thing had decided they weren't a threat. It instead slammed its hand down near Neziham.

That was Adolin's cue. He ducked out of the building where he'd been hiding—after breaking through several walls inside, dodging attacks from the thunderclast until it lost him. He ran for the loose end of the chain and seized it, his armor leaking Stormlight—but not so furiously that he was worried. It should hold for now.

After seeing this thing kick down buildings, he'd decided his only hope was to lock its legs together. Nothing else would have any real chance of tripping it. He winced as a giant hand slapped Neziham into a wall. His Plate was in even worse shape than Adolin's.

Keep moving, Adolin told himself, charging across the ground with chain in hand.

The thunderclast turned and tried to step on him, but blessedly it didn't have a good line of sight straight down. Adolin threw himself to the side to dodge, the chain rattling. He sprang to his feet and tried to wrap it around the free ankle. This time the creature simply kicked the other leg forward—the one with the chain already locked around it.

Damnation.

The chain pulled taut, yanking Adolin—who clung tight—away from the leg he'd been targeting. The thing kicked again, whipping him through the air until—with horror—he felt his oily armored hands slip.

Adolin hit the street in a crumple, groaning again. He flopped over, and though his armor was still in one piece, his legs had taken the brunt of the fall. They were covered in a spiderweb of fissures, the kind that, if this were a duel, would prompt the judge to call a halt. Too much of a risk of the Plate breaking, leading to injury.

He looked up to get his bearings, and found himself far along the street—ahead of Neziham, when he'd previously been behind the man. The other Shardbearer glanced at Adolin, distracted at just the wrong time.

No!

A colossal stone fist smashed down on Neziham, crushing him against the ground. Plate exploded and popped in a sequence of spraying molten bits, and the thunderclast's knuckles slammed into the street. Neziham's Shardblade clanged free, rolling across the street, and didn't vanish.

When the thunderclast pulled its hand up, the knuckles were covered in gore—with tiny bits of Plate sticking to it. What was left of Neziham was a mash of bones, blood, and steel.

The thunderclast reached down and grabbed the chain in its fists. Then, straining for a moment, snapped the chain with a sharp peal of breaking metal. It threw the remnants to the street, then continued on, relentless, toward the dome.

Leaving Adolin lying there, exhausted, dazed, and defeated.

NINE AND A HALF YEARS AGO

Szeth pulled to a stop in the monastery's grand hall, sword out and bloodied.

The time had come, after years of training.

The time for him to take his place.

He glanced back, and saw blood trickling through the grooves between the floor's mosaic tiles. From above, those formed a picture of Yesoran, king of the Heralds. This close to the floor, each tile was more like a little island—with grooves forming valleys between, the grout worn away over the years. Grooves not meant for blood, but a convenient path for it nonetheless—like the fuller down the center of a sword.

Tuko-son-Tuko, the Honorbearer of Wind, was the fount of said blood. Barely on his feet, one hand pressed to his bloodied side. Their clash had lasted less than five minutes.

Tuko dropped his sword, his face pained as he pressed his other hand to his wound. He tried to step toward Szeth, but slipped in his own blood and fell—his head hitting the tiles with a discomforting *thunk*.

Szeth sheathed his sword—uncaring that it was bloodied, despite his training—and hurried to the fallen man. He kept watch for a dagger, in case this was a feint, but saw none as he rolled the dazed, dying man into his own lap, holding him.

"Honor-nimi," Szeth said, "you fought well."

Tuko spat bloody spittle into Szeth's face.

A fair reaction. Szeth calmly wiped it off, figuring that—in the agony of death—he might have acted the same way.

Well, no, *he* wouldn't have.

But it was understandable someone might.

"I knew," Tuko said. "The moment they sent you to train, I knew what they were planning. Another of his glassy-eyed sheep. Can't have someone like me among the Honorbearers. That damnable stonebreaker."

"Don't speak so of a colleague," Szeth whispered. "Even if you are dying, honor-nimi, Pozen deserves better. You will soon join the stones, and their glorious—"

"He'll throw you away too," Tuko said, drawing breath like hisses, in and out, hyperventilating against the pain. Warm blood streamed around his wound into Szeth's lap. "We're nothing to him." He seized Szeth's shoulder. "If you reject him, he will have no power over you. Walk away, and he can no longer see what you do. You don't have to follow him. You . . ."

Tuko's eyes went wide, and his hand squeezed Szeth's shoulder, twisting the cloth in a tight-clenched grip.

"I climb!" Tuko shouted, ragged. "I climb the wall of grief toward the light, locked away above! I climb, the weight of my darkened twin on my back, and seek the captive! The light I love! I . . . Storms . . . the light I *love*!"

The strength went out of Tuko. A Blade clanged to the ground next to him. The Honorbearer should not have insisted on a duel to the death instead of just to defeat. Regrettable, but Szeth had *won*.

Seven years of pilgrimage. And he had *finished*, the first part at least. Now he had to present himself to the others and be accepted. But this fight would be the most painful step. He could lose fights with the others, and still be considered worthy.

With the corpse in his lap, he blinked dazed eyes to look around the monastery's grand hall. Some of Tuko's acolytes were openly weeping. Others stared at Szeth with outright hatred. As he searched for a friendly face, he eventually found the Honorbearers. Sivi wouldn't meet his eyes, though Moss—a younger man like him—hurried forward.

"Wow," Moss said, kneeling by Szeth. "Just . . . wow, Szeth."

"I have killed," Szeth whispered, "one of the most holy people in all the world." A foolish statement. What had he expected? This was what he'd come to do.

Moss, however, seemed to understand. He'd ascended most recently before Szeth, some four years ago. "I . . . had to kill the one before me as well. She wouldn't step aside once defeated. I tell myself that I'll be wiser when it is my time to pass on the Blade. That I'll step down when the other Honorbearers ask me to do so."

"Perhaps I will be as well," Szeth said. "Or perhaps someone will kill me in delayed retribution for what I've done." That felt good. Knowing that all of these acolytes who glared at him with such vitriol might someday have their own chance to kill him.

"Come on," Moss said, helping him to his feet. "We'll go for a walk. Talk about nothing, like we used to."

That would be . . . beautiful. Training with Moss had been the best part of the last years. Moss had treated him like a colleague from the start, even if he was prone to boasts and showing off. Lightweaving hadn't been Szeth's favorite of the Surges, but he would always cherish that year.

"Will you inform my father," Szeth said, "that I have succeeded? He will be waiting outside."

"Of course," Moss said. Szeth regretted sending one of Moss's station to do such a simple task, but there was no other.

Szeth reverently placed the corpse on the floor, atop the picture of Yesoran-son-God. He knelt and offered a prayer to the spren. Then he stood, slid the Honorblade out of Tuko's blood, and walked to the other Honorbearers. Six had come to witness. Moss the Lightweaver. Pozen the Elsecaller. Sivi the Willshaper. Dulo-son-Tudla, the Edgedancer. Vambra-daughter-Skies, the Truthwatcher. Gearil, the Dustbringer.

There was no Stoneward, naturally. No Skybreaker, as that Herald had reclaimed his Blade. No Bondsmith, as she was busy with some kind of election in the city. Now Szeth was the Windrunner Honorbearer. He suddenly felt sick. This was what he'd trained for, but it felt horribly wrong.

Pozen nodded toward the Blade, which Szeth held reverently—his favorite of the Blades, not just for its powers. He liked its simple, elegant shape.

"Welcome," Pozen said, "to your rightful place, Szeth."

"Pardon, Honorbearer," Szeth said, "but I am not of your position yet. First, I must complete the second pilgrimage, proving myself to each of you in combat."

"Ha!" Dulo said, slapping Szeth on the back. "That's merely a formality, Szeth! You think we'd let anyone unworthy get this far?"

"You'll visit each monastery in turn, yes," Pozen said. "But to celebrate, Szeth. You've already proven yourself."

He glanced to Moss, who had just returned. He nodded. "It's what they did for me."

Moss was another of Pozen's protégés. Trained deliberately to become the Lightweaver.

"Well," Dulo said as the group of them started to walk out, "it's done, finally. Disaster averted."

"Did you ever doubt?" Pozen asked. "The boy is perfect. I knew it the moment I found him in that decaying so-called monastery . . ."

For all their talk of celebrating Szeth, they acted more self-satisfied than anything else. Even Moss ran to catch up with Pozen. The acolytes and shamans slipped away to mourn. Soon only Szeth, Sivi, and the corpse remained in the hall.

"Shouldn't someone . . . do something with the body?" Szeth asked.

"He'll be buried this evening," Sivi said. "They'll want to let him stay, for a short time, with the stones."

"What was wrong with him, honor-nimi? Why was everyone so eager to be rid of him? I spent my year training with him looking for heresy. He was lax with the rules, and cold toward me, but I did not think he was deserving of death. Did he speak against Truth when I could not hear?"

"He did, Szeth," she said softly, but still wouldn't meet his eyes. It seemed like forever since the day he'd left Pozen's monastery to train with her, now seven years past. Over five years since he'd last seen his sister. And at least a few months since that had finally stopped hurting.

"I . . ." Szeth looked back at the body. "I feel sick, honor-nimi."

"Good."

"You used me to kill him," he said. "Like a hired blade sent in the night."

"Sent by the spren."

"Sent by all of you," Szeth snapped, then felt ashamed. He'd followed Truth. They were not to blame. "I apologize, honor-nimi."

"It's fine, Szeth," she said. "I don't love it either. But he *was* talking of rebellion—civil war. I suspect he didn't say as much to you because he feared that we'd sent you to him."

"*What?*" Szeth said. "Why would he even *consider* such a thing?"

"We all have our reasons, Szeth," she said, turning to go. "Most of us even think they're the right ones. Come on—there are celebrations to be had."

"When do I meet the Voice?"

"In time. Once—"

"*When?*" Szeth asked.

"After the second pilgrimage."

"How quickly can I finish?"

She studied him.

You have all done well, the Voice said. *Let him fly to me,* then *go on his second pilgrimage.*

Szeth, come to me at Ayabiza and seek the holy grotto beyond it. There, you will know the full extent of Truth—and you will have your answers.

Managed
to barter my
way into this
piece, which the
artist says is based
on eye-witness
accounts of the
three thunderclasts,
Kai-garnis, Yushah,
and Terushal.

84

FOR THE BROKEN

With you, it was both, wasn't it? Suffocating at times, yet not involved enough at others.

Adolin lay on the road, dazed from his failure against the thunderclast, trying to push to his feet. He slipped on the oil and collapsed, hitting his helm against the stones, and heard echoes of another time.

Storms, Adolin! What are you doing!

He forced himself up again by his arms.

Adolin, don't be foolhardy! You'll get yourself killed fighting this thing!

"I'm . . ." Adolin whispered. "I'm supposed to say that to *you,* Renarin. I'm supposed to keep *you* safe. I . . ."

I can handle it, Adolin. Just go! Please.

Adolin shook his head, clearing it. Those words—etched into his mind like an inscription on a sword—were from the first time. Over a year ago, when Renarin had saved him from a different thunderclast. Renarin, who Adolin had spent his life defending.

Renarin didn't need him any longer, and that was good. But . . . storms. What did you do when you weren't enough anymore? When you had been the best all your life, but suddenly you were obsolete?

Still braced by his arms, he looked toward the thunderclast along a road strewn with rubble. It shoved its way past buildings, leaving destruction in its wake. In the distance beyond, those Heavenly Ones buzzed around the dome. If more Fused were here . . . the city was lost.

He'd failed. Again. *I . . . I don't know if I can do this anymore,* he thought, so terribly exhausted.

He slumped back down.

Then felt hands on his shoulders.

Armored though he was, he could still feel them trying to help him to his feet. He glanced up and found Hmask. The Thaylen man had a head wound, glistening blood staining one long eyebrow and half his mustache. He tried anyway to help a Shardbearer many times his weight to rise.

Something awakened in Adolin. Memories of people to whom Adolin *had* mattered, like a little boy in Thaylen City. And storms, there were a lot of little boys in Azimir. But only one Shardbearer left. Him.

With a heave, Adolin got to his feet, armor still in place but leaking something furious. He nodded in thanks to Hmask, then picked up one of the remnants of the chain—only ten feet long—and threw it over his shoulder and clanked forward to pick up Neziham's bloody Shardblade.

"Hey," he said to the sword, his voice muffled in his helm. "I'm Adolin. I need to borrow you for a little while, if that's all right."

Up ahead, directly in the thunderclast's path, was the tower he'd stood on earlier in the morning. The watchpost. It was roughly the same height as the creature, which moved slowly. Deliberately, destructively, but *slowly.*

So Adolin stumbled past the oiled ground and called for Gallant, who emerged from between two buildings. Then Adolin heaved himself into the saddle and set off after the thunderclast.

⁂

Ash, former Herald of the Almighty, sat beside the bed of a man the size of a horse. She held his hand.

It was callused.

This Return, Taln hadn't been fighting—he had spent most of these years lying in one bed or another—yet he had calluses and muscles. They were part of his Identity—part of how he saw himself—so they were how the body manifested when created from pure Investiture.

So strange, to hold his hand again. The man she'd come to see, over the centuries, as the sibling she'd never had.

The one they'd betrayed.

The one they'd abandoned.

The one who had, through sheer determination, carried Roshar on his back into the modern age.

He mumbled that same mantra. "The time of the Return . . . We must prepare . . ."

The fighting in the square outside had grown quiet. No more men screaming for reinforcements. No more clangs of metal. No more sounds of stone against stone. That worried her. It meant the battle had been won.

Or lost.

Shapes darkened the doorway, then a figure with glowing eyes stepped into the long hospital corridor. Abidi the Monarch, she recognized by the patterns. Unlucky, to encounter him of all Heavenly Ones. Abidi liked pain.

Doctors cringed and hid as Ash stood up. But of course, what was she? Nothing. She'd spent *centuries* insisting she was nobody. She sank down into her seat, trembling, and Abidi didn't seem to notice her.

"So," Abidi said in the old language. Others were joining him, pushing into the chamber. "The wounded."

Ash closed her eyes.

"Slaughter them," Abidi ordered. "It will demoralize the defenders."

Silence. Oh, people were whimpering or groaning. Some wounded soldiers were standing up, trying to find weapons. But it was silent in one stark way that made Ash shiver.

Taln had stopped whispering.

The bed behind her creaked and shifted, and she blinked away tears to look up. To see him towering there in the shadows at the end of the hall.

One of the Fused at the other end of the room raised a sphere. Then tossed it their direction.

Then gasped.

In the light, Taln stood bare chested and wearing only short breeches, practically filling the hallway that had been made into a sickroom. His hands clenched to fists.

"You fools," Ash said to the Fused. "You could have had the city, but you came here. For the *broken.*"

Abidi pointed, seeing them for the first time, and his eyes went wide with abject horror. It was so *satisfying* to watch him turn and flee. Because Talenel'Elin, unarmed and without his Blade, was still the most terrifying warrior on the planet.

A crash broke the silence, windows cracking, air rushing to fill the hole Taln left when he moved. And for the first time in over four thousand years, the Bearer of Agonies *fought back.*

⁂

Adolin hauled himself onto the top of the watchpost. He'd climbed up the outside. His Plate was losing functionality, but it had been strong enough to haul him up, and climbing had been better than navigating those tiny stairs.

He checked Neziham's Blade, which he'd tied on with a rope. Then he checked the ten-foot chain—one end of which had a hook. He'd coiled the snapped end around his waist, secured with a bent broken link.

With Gallant—who now had orders to get to safety—he'd managed to get ahead of the monster. The thunderclast's footsteps vibrated through him as it brushed past the tower. Across the way, Adolin saw faces in the windows. Terrified people, perhaps too paralyzed to evacuate.

"Prime and People," Adolin whispered in honor of Neziham. The local oath. "Herald and Home."

With a deep breath, Adolin leaped off the top of the tower and grabbed hold of ridges on the thunderclast's back. Gripping with one hand, he used the hooked end of the chain to lock himself into place. This thunderclast's body—particularly a hulking portion of the back—was made up of a crisscrossing mess of stone protrusions. Like a snarl of branches, with small gaps between them here and there. The hook fit right in.

From this vantage, Adolin could see chaos around the dome—broken open on one side, the enemy flooding out. Storms. The city really was lost already, wasn't it?

He growled, clinging to the thunderclast as it noticed him, then began shaking. Fortunately, its stone arms didn't bend the correct ways to reach its back, but that shaking was furious. Adolin managed to hold on, barely—then as it paused, Adolin pulled the Blade off his belt and rammed it into the thing's back.

Unfortunately, the sword didn't stab deep enough to kill—not with all this mass of stone on the thunderclast's back. Either that or he just wasn't high enough; the weak spot was the neck, at the base of the skull, and that was a few feet higher up. The thing began shaking again, more furiously. Growling, he left the sword rammed into the body and held tight with gauntleted fingers that—leaking Stormlight—were starting to lose their strength.

The monster trumped—an awful, terrible sound. Adolin took the chance to grab the Shardblade and yank it out—and in that moment the monster bent down, then lurched upward and spun. Adolin only had one hand on it this time. The forceful motion dislodged his weakened fingers and sent him flying.

The chain links snapped tight with Adolin on the end, swinging back and forth like a ball on a string—slamming into one side of the thunderclast, then the other. His vision became a mess of cracked lines from a failing helmet, and he barely kept track of what was happening, though he clung to the Blade.

There! a chorus of voices seemed to say to him. *Grab!*

He reached out blindly, his free hand moving almost of its own accord, and seized hold of an upper portion of the thunderclast's back again. This time the thing tried to bend over and flip him forward so that its fingers—reaching toward its head—could grab him.

 Adolin screamed as pieces of his Plate began to fail, going dull and powerless from the lack of Stormlight. He leaped upward, using the momentum of the monster's motion, and hit the head. Slipped. Then *rammed* his Blade straight into the thunderclast's neck.

It jerked upright, its head tipping back, Adolin falling free along the thing's side.

Then it froze.

Finally, it collapsed like a felled tree. Sideways.

Toward Adolin.

He furiously tried to cut the chain free of the stone back, but his armor wasn't working, and the Blade slipped from his grip. A second later, all came crashing down on top of him with a weight to shake an entire city.

⁘

Renarin's vision of that day in the palace—when Adolin had saved him—evaporated, and he was cast back into the Spiritual Realm proper. He stood up among the many shifting futures.

And was not afraid.

He'd been here. In this situation. He remembered nights early in his spren bond, feverishly scrawling on the floor what he'd seen and heard. *That* had terrified him—not knowing what was happening to him, or why.

The Spiritual Realm was overwhelming to the senses—and he disliked that—but it wasn't *frightening.* He knew why he was here, and he knew what he was. No longer was Renarin a scared child needing Adolin to rescue him. No longer was he an abomination needing to hide while simultaneously feeling he must share what he knew, in case it helped his father.

He was Radiant. He was Truthwatcher. He was Glys's companion. He was Bridge Four. So much about the world didn't make sense to him, but he knew *why he was here,* and that gave him a path forward. Strangely, he found he didn't fear even the gods. What was the worst they could do? Destroy him? In the face of the terrors he'd lived through—the terror of not knowing if he was mad, or if he'd somehow been corrupted and was serving evil—simple mortality seemed a distant nightmare, barely remembered.

I am scared, Glys said. *I will be destroyed. I will be erased. I will be hated.*

"Hide in me," Renarin said. "I will protect you."

He held out his hand, and Glys formed from the chaos—then shrank to the self he preferred in the Physical Realm. The strange red crystalline structure. This melded into Renarin, finding no gemheart, but a welcome hiding place nonetheless.

All felt . . . right with Glys then. The spren ceased trembling. Renarin looked around, but found only echoes of his past, shifting and constantly moving like shadowy clouds.

This place, he thought, *requires organization to understand it. This is too much for a human mind.*

Fortunately, he'd learned all kinds of strategies for making sense of a world—and its people. Admittedly, something about his bond with Glys gave him extra advantages. He clasped his hands behind him, unconsciously—he realized—adopting the posture his father took at strategy meetings, and he imposed his will on the surroundings.

Around him the chaos faded, and instead a group of stained glass windows grew up. Each separated from the others, like a little display in an art museum, with a black featureless background spreading behind. Out there, he could vaguely see figures made as if out of white smoke, rising from the ground.

He walked along the windows, each of which bore an elaborate glass scene. There was Shallan, and there his father and Navani—on some new battlefield with a large tent. The stained glass didn't move, but when he looked away and turned back, it often had changed to a new perspective. He focused on his father and aunt. They were at a meeting of singers and humans.

They will be close, Glys whispered. *Close to secrets.*

"And you?" Renarin said to him. "Are you safe now? From the gods?"

Your father has drawn their attention for now.

Renarin stopped beside a window with Rlain sitting among other singers, and considered how best to get his friend's attention. Rlain had said they should find Mishram's prison, which Renarin was starting to consider.

He thought he could likely enter the window if he wanted, so should he—

Renarin froze. One of the windows was changing. He sensed it before he saw it. She was here.

Turning slowly, Renarin picked out the window. Growing dark, with shards of glass colored violet, blue, and black. Ba-Ado-Mishram. That same singer face from before, railing against the confines of the window. Moving when none of the others did. Shaking the glass. The windows closest to her began to darken.

Storms. Renarin didn't know how to react. But he . . . he had felt like that before. Confused, terrified, worried. Each emotion she showed was so very *familiar* to him. Strange. He barely understood the other members of Bridge Four at dinner. Why should he feel he understood an ancient spren?

He walked up to the window.

"When I make noise like that," he whispered, "it's because I have so many emotions, I don't know what to do with them all. So they burst from me like a storm."

The figure glared at him, seething.

Careful, Glys warned. *She would destroy you if she could. And Renarin, I think she has influenced your visions. Somehow, that vision with Adolin was her doing.*

"Was it, now?" he said. "Why that vision, Mishram?"

She continued to glare at him.

"More importantly," Renarin said, "what did you show the others? And why?"

"Destroy . . . you . . ." Mishram whispered, her frame vibrating. "I showed you so you can find me . . . Find me! So I may *destroy you.*"

"How tempting." Renarin stepped closer. "I recognize it must be terrible to suffer imprisonment for so long, but is this any worse than the torture the Heralds endured at the hands of the Fused?"

She withdrew until the glass window showed no more than a pair of eyes burning in the darkness. He wondered, if he stepped through this window, would he reach her? Find her prison?

No, Glys said. *You would find nothing. She pervades this place, so she appears in it, but we have not found her prison.*

"How do we do so?" Renarin asked.

Do you want to?

"I'm beginning to think it might be the only way," Renarin said. "Take the prison, hide it elsewhere, leave the Ghostbloods to wander in here, seeking something they will never locate."

The idea unnerved him, because he worried what Shallan wanted with the prison. He trusted her, but he missed some subtleties of conversations, and he felt unequipped to say if her desires here were valid or not.

"Thoughts?" Renarin prompted Glys.

To reach her, you will need . . . to Connect to her somehow.

"Interesting," Renarin said. "Like Father and Navani were doing, traveling the visions?"

Yes, Glys said. *Though your Connection must be deeper. They travel echoes of the past—you seek a hidden secret that has been locked away. You will need to anchor soul to soul.*

Renarin contemplated this, before turning and walking to Rlain's window. He took a long breath, then stepped into the glass as if he were entering a pond of water. Inside the vision, Rlain sat alone in a small Narak shanty. Head bowed, humming softly, the others having left. Storms, was Renarin intruding? Should he go? That was the posture Renarin sometimes had when he didn't want to be talked to or touched. If he stayed, it would be awkward, wouldn't it?

And yet . . . he remembered something that Zahel, of all people, had told him. *Sometimes you just have to push through.* The swordmaster had been talking about fatigue at the start of an exercise routine. Some days, you'd arrive and would be eager for the exercise. Others . . . well, you just had to push through.

What had Drehy said?

In the long run, it's better to ask and deal with it if you're wrong. Could . . . one just push through awkwardness too?

"Rlain?" he asked.

Rlain glanced at him, then brightened immediately, his hummed rhythm changing to the Rhythm of Joy. Storms . . . he'd been feeling alone, hadn't he? It was basically the opposite of what Renarin had assumed.

"Glys says it's all right to group together again," Renarin said, walking over. "Is this your room in Narak?"

"No," Rlain said, settling against the wall. "This is one of the meeting chambers where my people discussed strategy and plans. Nothing formal. This was simply . . . where we talked. As friends . . ."

He looked toward the ceiling. Renarin couldn't read the meaning behind those words, but the rhythm changed to what he was sure was the Rhythm of Annoyance. In this realm, picking those out was becoming natural to him.

I help, Glys whispered, seeming pleased with himself.

Well, thank you, Renarin replied.

"Annoyed," Renarin said, settling down by Rlain, "with your friends?"

"They sent me off to be a spy," Rlain said quietly. "I volunteered, so it's not like I should be mad. But . . ."

"You felt unwanted."

"Storms, but I did," Rlain said.

"Yeah," Renarin said. "I know."

"Were you . . . unwanted?" Rlain asked, surprised.

"Never overtly," Renarin said. "And my father has grown so much. It's unfair to hold his actions as a younger man against him. You know that he came to meetings of scholars last year, merely so I wouldn't be the only non-ardent man present? But . . ."

"When you were young, he wanted a soldier."

"Even *Adolin* wasn't enough for him," Renarin said. "What chance did *I* have?" He paused. "Why did they send you away?"

"Well," Rlain said, his head tipped back against the wall, "the need *was* legitimate. It's just that . . . I never fit in the same as everyone else. Nobody hated me. Nobody wanted to be rid of me. But when it came to losing someone they *loved* to be a spy, or losing me . . . not even Eshonai asked me to stay. By this point she was in a full 'I must be a general' mindset. I was a solution to a problem. That was all she could afford to let me be."

"I make things difficult," Renarin said. "Because I don't see the world the same way as everyone else, and they have to make accommodations for me. They have to explain differently to me, taking an extra effort. It causes me to feel like a burden. And . . . sometimes I feel it would be so much more convenient for everyone if I weren't there."

"It's so awful," Rlain said to the Rhythm of Appreciation, "that people have to grow and stretch themselves around you. Becoming better."

Renarin smiled. Sarcasm was different among the singers, who could deliberately match an incongruous rhythm to their words.

Rlain kept humming but didn't speak. Together they gazed out the window to where the sun had set, and starspren began playing in the evening sky.

I like the way he's quiet sometimes, Renarin thought. At dances or parties, to make up for his awkward silences, his aunt Navani or his cousin Aesudan had always tried to put him with someone talkative. They thought he'd enjoy having someone else speak when he didn't want to. But it had taken *so much* effort to keep track of all the words.

Dared he ruin this? It was perfect as it was.

No, he thought. *That's fear talking. It's not perfect yet.*

Push through. He braced himself for the awkwardness.

And spoke.

"What's it like," he said, feeling like he was stumbling over each word, "for a singer to be in a relationship with someone? A . . . romantic one, I mean." He'd started. He might as well finish. "Could it ever work with a human?"

"Oh, um . . ." Rlain hummed to Tension. "I haven't thought about it, really. I mean . . ."

Oh, storms. I've ruined it. I've gone and broken everything. I—

"That's a lie," Rlain said, wincing. "I . . . um, *have* thought about it, Renarin. A lot."

A part of Renarin wished he could simply vanish. Could his powers do that? For once, the silence seemed far worse than words. It kept stretching on and on and on.

"You've always tried to understand me, Renarin," Rlain said. "And usually you figure it out. Even though you don't have the rhythms, you can read me."

"I just . . . hate seeing someone alone. In a crowd."

"Is that all?" Rlain asked.

"No," Renarin admitted.

More silence. More awkwardness.

And then a rhythm. The Rhythm of Curiosity, hummed by Rlain. "We pretend," he said, "that when we're in forms other than mateform, we don't feel attraction at all. But Renarin, can I tell you something? That's an exaggeration.

"When I'm in warform, I'm more prone to want to follow orders. That doesn't mean I'm completely without self-determination. Likewise, when we're in mateform, we feel all kinds of powerful attractions—but those emotions and feelings *are* there in other forms. Most singers stay together as a pair, even after children are raised. Relationships are important to us, just as they are with humans."

"Different though," Renarin said. "It's different."

"Isn't . . . learning about someone different interesting?" Rlain said. "Like I said earlier?"

"I . . . guess that it is," Renarin said. "How do you know you're compatible? What *makes* you compatible? What if you spend a lot of time together, and start to form a relationship, and then mateform comes and . . . well, it doesn't work."

Rlain hummed to Anxiety.

"What?" Renarin asked.

"That happened to me," he explained. "The first time I tried mateform. Everyone expected me to bond with one of the three females from our group . . . and I tried very hard to get the attention of Harvo instead."

"A . . . male?"

"I never attempted that form again," Rlain said, humming to Anxiety, looking down. "They laughed at me for months. As if I had made a mistake or something. They thought I was so lustful that I lost track of who was who." He glanced at Renarin. "The mateform part, it's not as important to us as it seems to be to you. If we get along, work well together, that's more important—that's what makes us a warpair. Then the rest . . . you can make it fit."

"Unless, you know, you end up chasing a man instead . . ." Renarin said, chuckling. Not because he wasn't still anxious, but because—amazingly—that anxiety had begun to ebb.

"Even then," Rlain said. "I *knew,* Renarin. I was hesitant to try mateform for that reason. I didn't *want* to bond with any of the others. I could have told them what would happen, because it was there inside me, even if it's not as strong in most forms as it is for humans. Personality compatibility, though, that's what we look for. What I've wanted."

He looked to Renarin, then hummed to Anxiety, but while smiling.

That combination, Renarin thought. *He's blushing.*

Renarin took a deep breath, then pushed through this last bit of awkwardness. "Is it worth trying, then, do you think?"

In response, Rlain rested his hand hesitantly on top of Renarin's. Renarin turned his hand upward and took Rlain's—and felt *heat.* And beyond that, he could sense the rhythms pulsing from Rlain into him.

The Rhythm of Excitement.

 There was so much to do, so much to talk about, but this was enough for now. He let them have silence. Just the rhythms, the heat, and two people harmonizing together.

Renarin, Glys said eventually. *Shallan has arrived, and is responding oddly.*

Shallan? he thought. *What do you mean?*

I brought her out of her vision, Glys said, *because you indicated you wanted to gather us again. Your window is still standing, and she's watching.*

Oh, blood of his fathers. Shallan was watching? *What's she doing?* he asked.

Hopping up and down, Glys said, making a high-pitched sound like she's in pain.

She's not in pain, Renarin said back, sighing. *She's squealing in excitement. That girl* . . . Maybe it was a Lightweaver thing, or maybe it was only Shallan, but he'd always sensed a voyeuristic side to her. It took a special type to enjoy pretending to be someone else.

Well, if nothing else, he was glad to be able to provide his sister-in-law with some entertainment. He stood up, holding to Rlain's hand. "Come on. We need to talk about what we've each seen in these most recent visions."

"Why?" Rlain asked. "Is it relevant?"

"I think Mishram influenced them," Renarin said. "I just encountered her, and something she said makes me think that there's a secret in what we're being shown."

Rlain nodded, and banished the vision, still holding Renarin's hand. And remarkably, as they rejoined Shallan—who gave him a thumbs-up and a grin—he found that the awkwardness had passed. The future—for once—seemed extraordinarily bright. Like glowing, brilliant glass.

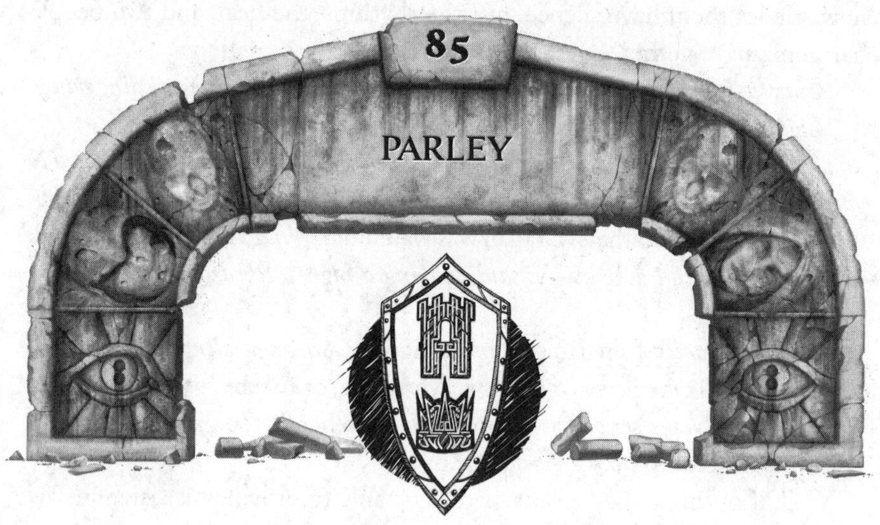

85

PARLEY

In the end, it is my lies that do me in. Another lesson I fail to learn time and time again. I recognize this flaw. I hope it does not someday destroy me.

Adolin came awake in a shiver of cold ice. He gasped, his eyes snapping open, his muscles going tense and rigid. His vision was cloudy from tears, and he remembered . . .

Falling.

The thunderclast.

Darkness.

Sounds in his ears, foreign at first, but then . . . then voices he knew.

"The leg!" That was May.

"I can't . . . I can't do more!" A girl. The Truthwatcher. What was her name? Rahel? Yes . . . that was it . . .

She was crying.

Adolin blinked away tears and found himself lying, still half in his Plate, by the broken remnants of the thunderclast's hip—which they'd apparently been forced to cut open using Neziham's Shardblade to pull him free.

Adolin was alive, but he saw something his mind refused to accept.

"Adolin?" May said, taking him by the face. "Bless the Almighty. Adolin, can you hear me?"

"My . . . leg . . ." Adolin said.

His right leg ended in a stump, below the knee.

"I tried!" Rahel said, crying. "I . . . I can't . . . I . . ."

"The thunderclast pinned you," May said, her voice calm. The calm that all officers were trained for at times of great emotion. "The Plate shattered, and your leg was mashed to basically nothing. But you're alive, Adolin."

He blinked, numb.

"Adolin," May said. "Rahel healed your other wounds, which were severe. When we return to Urithiru, a more experienced Radiant can give you your leg back."

Right. Of course they could. Adolin pushed through the shock. "The city?"

"Fighting on all fronts around the dome," she said. "Archers had to flee as Heavenly Ones took the balcony. The dome is basically lost, and worse, one side was blasted completely open. Kushkam was holding that gap. But . . . Notum said he hadn't seen the commandant in some time, and his men were in shambles. I think they may have dropped the firebombs inside the dome, but first *dozens* of Fused broke out into the city through the gap."

In the distance, shouting. Fighting.

"Get this Plate off me," Adolin said, pushing himself up on one elbow. "It's useless in this shape. We have to go help."

"Adolin, your leg—"

"I'm our most experienced field commander," he said, waving for assistance hauling him to his feet. "I must give orders if Kushkam has fallen. And the rest of us are needed to fight!"

May looked to the others—the ten or so men left from Adolin's assault on the thunderclast. Including stalwart Hmask, who finally—ignoring everyone else—helped Adolin pry free the breastplate, then climb to his feet.

To his foot.

Together, they started toward the breach in the dome. Adolin relied on Hmask and another soldier to basically carry him with one arm around each. They hurried as best they could, but he knew—deep down—this city was lost. It had been lost the moment those Fused had arrived.

Storms. Just like Kholinar. Anxietyspren trailed him in the shape of twisting black crosses. There was nothing he could do.

Colot had been leading the defense against conventional singers who had broken out of the other side of the dome. Only some ragged remnants were available to face the Fused. These groups flowed together as they reached the medical quarter.

There they found an unlikely group of reinforcements: the imperial honor guard and Yanagawn himself, dressed for battle. He stood there, sword in hand, staring at . . .

At death.

Adolin and his group lurched to a stop in front of a field of corpses. Hundreds of them, mostly singers, covered the plaza between the broken hole in the dome and the medical building.

Dozens of Fused dead?

Why was it so quiet here? Adolin squeezed Hmask's shoulder, and they lurched forward, limping among the bodies. Yanagawn hurried over, his fine cape stained with singer blood from the bodies below. It was difficult to even find a place to step.

"Adolin!" Yanagawn said.

"Excellency," Adolin said, dazed, "did you do this?"

"We found them like this!" he said. "I . . . I know I shouldn't have come, but Kushkam called up every available soldier. My honor guard wouldn't leave me, so . . ." His sword drooped in his fingers. "I didn't arrive in time for . . . whatever this is . . ."

They continued picking through the field, where Yanagawn's soldiers used an old battlefield tactic of searching for painspren, which would indicate someone alive. One cried out and pushed aside a body swarming with them, where he found Kushkam. "He's still breathing!"

Rahel ran to help, her gemstone bearer hurrying behind with a sack of Stormlight. Adolin, Hmask, and Yanagawn picked their way toward the breach in the dome. He could feel a lingering heat radiating from that hole, but that hadn't reached these Fused outside. He counted eight separate varieties here—dead, tens of them. Their gemhearts crushed, their chests having been either ripped open or smashed. Storms. What could do something like this to the enemy's most elite fighters? This many could have brought down Shardbearers, Radiants. Yet he saw the bodies of neither.

A ribbon of light announced Notum. "Adolin," he said. "Firebombs were deployed in the dome. Those conventional enemy forces who weren't caught in the flames were forced to retreat back through the Oathgate. We have a chance to . . ." He trailed off, looking around. "How did you kill this many *Fused*?"

"I didn't," Adolin whispered, pointing. They reached the culmination of the carnage, a part of the silent battlefield nearest the broken gap in the dome. Inside, though the fires had gone out, flamespren danced on the stones, enjoying the heat.

He could see through the gap to the darkened center, where singers—who could withstand more heat than humans—were reemerging. They'd fill the dome before his forces could go in and face them. Still, Kushkam's firebombs had prevented *complete* disaster, forcing an important enemy retreat. They'd used most of the oil in the city, but it *had* worked.

The Fused who escaped before the flames should have been able to take the city anyway. But in this spot, right by the hole, enemy corpses were heaped into a kind of pinnacle. Adolin could imagine enemy after enemy throwing themselves at this location—he'd seen this kind of display before with common troops trying to pull down a Shardbearer.

Adolin had to stumble and crawl to climb that pile of corpses. At the top, they found two bodies. Unarmored.

Taln, the Herald, knelt here with his head back, speared with a dozen lances, which propped up his corpse—his hand still holding the crushed skull of a dead Fused. In death, he was covered in blood, his face tipped toward the sky and his mouth open as if in a shout. Leaning against him from behind, nestled among the bodies as if looking for a place to rest, was Ash, a bloodied and chipped sword in her lap.

She was smiling. Bleeding from a good two dozen hits, she looked at Adolin, who knelt at the edge of the little crater at the top of the pile of corpses.

"This time," she whispered, "I won't let him go alone."

She closed her eyes and fell still.

Adolin gaped, awespren *bursting* around him in blue, as Colot arrived nearby—at last—with real reinforcements. He set them to guard the breach in the dome, though they had to stand back a little before the heat.

Common singers flooded the dome inside. And with them he saw Abidi the Heavenly One. He and his troops seemed shaken, and didn't engage Colot's reinforcements at the gap. The fire that had burned many—their corpses still inside—would have them frightened.

Adolin sat back, trying very hard to ignore both the corpses and the way his leg fell impossibly, no foot or calf to brace it. Exhausted, drained, Adolin let himself close his eyes and breathe out a sigh.

They'd paid a terrible price, but the city would last another day.

⁘

Dalinar was at a parley.

Two armies, one human and one singer, were arrayed here to display their might—but Dalinar could tell they didn't mean to do battle. The postures of the soldiers to his sides were, ironically, too aggressive. Their stances were more like poses, their weapons displayed prominently, particularly their Shards. Plus, there were too few anticipationspren.

A smaller group of people—including the Windrunner they'd followed via Connection—was meeting in a small, open-sided pavilion between the armies. Discussing terms of surrender perhaps? Or negotiating a treaty?

Beside him, Navani dropped the spear that had appeared in her hand as they'd joined this vision. She lifted Gav, and a few people glanced at him, muttering about the odd spren.

"There's going to be a fight soon," Navani said. "Those ones in the center are deciding terms for the battle. We should get away from the front lines."

"Actually," Dalinar said, "this is a parley for peace."

"Really?" she said, looking down the line of soldiers. "How can you tell?"

"Instinct," he said. "I'm going to put us into that group at the center. All right?"

"Do it."

He thought about how many times he'd been in similar meetings, which made a faint line of light Connect him to those having the discussions. With that, he changed the perspective for him, Navani, and Gav; they appeared with the parley group, inside the pavilion. Yes . . . people didn't negotiate battlefield rules with refreshments on hand. But terms of peace?

The table they stood around also supported this conclusion. It was covered in maps that had been drawn on, scribbled out, circled, annotated. Several humans—both men and women—were in the process of writing on those maps currently, though the writers all seemed to be this era's version of ardents. At least they wore the familiar grey robes—though these bore odd embroidery—even if the hairstyles weren't what Dalinar expected.

The Windrunner—looking closer, Dalinar now thought maybe he was Riran like Evi—stepped up to the table. He had more lines on his face now, and appeared much as Dalinar remembered him from the Feverstone Keep vision. He felt excited as he realized how close they were. He turned and scanned the room, noting Radiants of several orders, including—at the back, watching—Melishi, plus the Heralds Kalak and Nale.

Across the table from the humans were what should have been an impossibility: Regal singers, in a variety of imposing forms, their eyes glowing faintly red in the canopied shade. This was the False Desolation, when the singers had gained forms of power without the intervention of Odium. Though many thought it just a story, this brutal, bloody war had ended with the "Voidbringers" becoming simple parshmen.

Dalinar glanced at Navani, who frowned back at him. If this was one of the most terrible times in history . . . why were they all chatting in a pavilion? Were they about to witness the last breakdown of talks? Perhaps he'd been too quick to assume there wouldn't be a battle today.

"Look," the Windrunner—Navani had said his name was Garith—said. "We *cannot* promise you that land! As I told you, we don't yet have an agreement from the kings who rule there."

Dalinar eyed the maps, trying to judge the locations. It seemed . . . they were near Iri. *Is that where the singers live between Desolations? Surely they couldn't all fit in one kingdom, not if they had the strength of numbers to assault the entire world . . .*

"You could fight the kings of those regions," said a direform Regal at the front of the enemy contingent. Femalen, with a pattern of black and red that was made up of large patches of each color. She had wickedly barbed carapace and an intense stare. "Conquer the region, then expel the humans there."

"I'm not going to fight my own people," Garith said.

 "They're not your people."

"All humans are my people. I'm Radiant."

"Our god will not accept a treaty," the direform said, "*without* this land. Our people are tired of being herded into the mountains and unfertile regions. We must have more farmland." Behind her, the others hummed to a sharp rhythm, indicating their agreement.

Garith sat down at the table, causing the three ardents to stop writing. The Radiant—who didn't wear his armor, but instead a simple tunic—put his hands to his head, sighing. "Do you want to return to the killing? You said your god was willing to listen and negotiate."

"For this land," another one said from behind.

"You have all of Moladetia," Garith said, waving to the maps. "It includes swaths of farmland, with perfect hills, around Eila. Isn't that enough?"

"No," the singer said. "Our people in Silnaka cannot continue to survive in the highlands. We need not one singer kingdom, but three. Why are we confined to mountains and one stretch of land? We must thrive."

"It's always been enough before . . ." Garith said.

The singers just hummed to that, drawing angerspren. Finally, the direform at the front spoke. "We are done for today." She withdrew with the others, leaving the pavilion. The enemy army beyond started to retreat, moving in warpairs, as the listeners had once done—something he hadn't seen in previous eras.

Smaller numbers than modern militaries, Dalinar noted. *Judging by counts on the map . . .* He'd always had a hunch that the numbers in old battle reports, written by ancient scholars, were inflated. He couldn't imagine hundreds of thousands of troops meeting on a battlefield in the days before modern logistics.

After the singers had withdrawn, Radiants began to pull seats over to the table. Notably, Melishi—the Bondsmith—continued to watch from the rear. Did he know he stood with two Heralds, or did Nale and Kalak use aliases at this time?

Navani and Gav waited quietly. Dalinar, however, pulled a seat over to the table himself. He didn't have time for quiet observation—according to his clock, he had barely over two days until his meeting with Odium. He had to find the answers to what had happened to Honor, and he was *close.*

"Garith," said a female Radiant with the colorings of an Edgedancer on her clothing, "it might be time to give this up. They won't agree."

"They *will,*" Garith said. "They're willing to talk. We merely have to find the right path. Please. Give me more time." He put one hand on the table.

Dalinar leaned forward. He'd been in meetings like this, trying to persuade everyone to follow a course he knew was right. He was used to resistance. Complications. Yet here, one Radiant, then another, then a third put their hands out on top of Garith's.

"You've held us together," one of them said. "I didn't believe you could, but you did it."

"We lost the tower, but we remained a people," the Edgedancer said. "The Radiants support you."

Dalinar hesitantly put his hand on top of the others. "They have their god though," he said, trying to work it into the conversation. "The aggression she inspires worries me."

"Agreed," said an Azish Stoneward as they pulled their hands back. "But there is dissension among the singers because of it. That group that split off . . . we've been tracking them. They have abandoned all forms. They'd rather go without than bow to Mishram and the Unmade."

"They make a mistake," Garith said. "She's more reasonable than Odium ever was."

"You don't know that," the Edgedancer replied. "It's been thousands of years since anyone fought Odium."

Garith looked like he wanted to say something, but didn't. Storms. He *was* hiding something. Was he . . . was he *meeting* with the Unmade? In secret?

Was he a traitor?

"I'd feel better," Dalinar said tentatively, "if I knew more of what to expect from our side. Regarding *our* god."

"Yes, well," Garith said. "Honor won't meet with anyone other than Melishi. So unless he'll give us the *gift* of a little *guidance* for once . . ."

All eyes turned toward the Bondsmith. The man met the stares with a level one of his own. "Honor does not interfere any longer. Our doings are ours alone."

"But you *have* spoken to him," Garith said.

"He does not interfere," Melishi said, his arms folded.

Garith sighed, looking back to the others sitting at the table. Ardents were quietly rolling up maps, but otherwise there was silence. Except for a gentle wind.

Are you there? Dalinar thought. *Ancient god? Are you still watching?*

He got . . . a feeling, but no words. The ancient gods—the Wind, the Stone, the Night—had less power in this time. They found it difficult to speak.

"We are close to *lasting* peace," Garith said, blue fronds of sincerityspren unfolding around him. "I promise you, we're closer to a treaty than we seem."

"They will betray it," Melishi said. "They are the Voidbringers, destroyers."

"And what are *we*?" Garith snapped. "We're *all* Voidbringers. Every time we pick up a spear or a Blade and slaughter someone over this cursed land, we become Voidbringers. Singer or human, it's the same. *That's* the Void, Melishi."

"Watchers at the rim," the Stoneward said. "Someone must fight."

"Yes," Garith said, standing. "But we mustn't love it so much we abandon other options. This treaty will work. It . . . it must . . . Just give me time."

"You have it," the Edgedancer said. "But we can't keep at this forever."

Garith nodded, and the meeting began to disperse. Dalinar watched Garith walk from the pavilion, where he was joined by a small group of other Windrunners. He glanced back at the pavilion, then took to the sky with his attendants.

Follow . . . the Wind said.

Storms. He didn't have the powers to follow with Windrunning, but he *had* to find out what they were up to.

"Does anyone else worry about where he goes?" Dalinar asked the others.

"He's always been like that," the Edgedancer said. "But he's led us well, Naze. You have to admit that."

They began to break down the pavilion, and he saw Navani taking some of the notes from the ardents and scanning them. Dalinar felt a building sense of foreboding.

It was coming. The Recreance was here.

He jumped as someone stepped up beside him. Melishi.

"Tonight is the night," Melishi said. "We know where he'll be. I hope it won't break the others when they realize Garith is a traitor."

"Tonight," Dalinar said. "Where?"

"About an hour's walk from the keep," Melishi said. "Same place as last time, though we were too late. Tonight we'll go early and watch. Your warnings in the past have been useful, Naze, but this *must* be done. Otherwise, Garith will destroy us all. Are you in?"

"Yes," Dalinar whispered, and a line of light burst into existence tying him to Melishi. He pulled on the line of light, and the setting warped around him. In seconds he was lying prone on the stone ground, with Navani, Gav, Melishi, and several others—including Kalak.

It was night, first moon, and they hid in a hollow in the ground, near some trees, their bodies camouflaged beneath branches and fallen leaves. The landscape here was made up of many towering rock formations, reminding him of the place where the Heralds had abandoned their Blades. Perhaps this was the same region—with rocks like buildings, forming many canyons, small trees lining a stream that ran past behind Dalinar.

The lofty rock formations in front of him—thirty or forty feet tall—surrounded a kind of natural glade or clearing. He didn't like this spot; he saw too many places for people to get around you, sneak up without being seen. But perhaps it was a good space for a clandestine meeting, with shadows cast by moonlight.

He took Navani's hand and mouthed "Sorry" to her in apology for doing this so brashly. She nodded, and took Gav by the hand. He seemed to be doing well, his head cocked as if he were listening to something. Storms, it couldn't actually be Elhokar, could it?

Lights in the sky. Windrunners, glowing with Stormlight, landed together on the ground ahead, among the rocks. Dalinar leaned forward, and got a glare from Melishi, so he settled back again, not disturbing their cover.

Garith paced the stone, looking worried. Storms, that posture . . . that concern. This was a man working hard to hold too many things together, to keep the threads from unraveling, to keep a people united.

I've known that feeling, Dalinar thought idly. *I've been that man.* But why meet with the enemy to—

A moment later, Dalinar had shifted places. Quick as an eyeblink, he was in Garith's place in the vision.

Damnation. He'd empathized too strongly with the man's plight, and had accidentally activated his powers. Panicked, he looked around, trying to spot Navani—but the place where she and the others lay was well hidden. All he saw was a blanket of fallen leaves. Next to him, the other Windrunners shifted, one glancing at the moon, checking the time.

"Garith," one said, "are you *sure* about this?"

Before Dalinar could reply, the sound of footsteps on stone drew their attention. A group of three singers emerged from the shadows. So, Garith *was* meeting with them in secret, and Melishi wanted proof of this, perhaps? Dalinar narrowed his eyes, but tried not to be aggressive or out of character. Garith, whose place he had taken, had arranged this. Dalinar needed to play along.

The direform femalen from the meeting stalked up to Garith, her figure—like those of all direforms—covered in sharp barbs of carapace. While the other Windrunners backed away, Dalinar stood his ground. She came right up to him, standing a few inches taller than he was. She studied him, and her expression softened—her humming changing to a comforting rhythm.

Then she bent forward, took Dalinar's head in her hands, and kissed him.

86
RIVER OF LIGHT

I offer my most sincere apology for everything wrong I've done. I am glad we tried. I am sorry that I continue to be someone with whom a relationship is nearly impossible.

Kaladin found himself at peace as he laid out his tools to make dinner. Twilight had arrived on the seventh day.

He'd already acknowledged he wouldn't make it back in time to see the contest. Now though, he *felt* that truth rather than merely admitting it.

With this came peace. For despite it all—everything he'd been through, the state he'd ended up in, the trauma he'd endured—a part of him had still assumed that *he* would become the champion Dalinar required. He'd believed, deep down, that he would return to Urithiru with the secrets of the Heralds—maybe even with Ishar—and save the day. Fight Odium's champion. Win.

He left his vegetables set out on a cloth by the fire. Then took a long breath and lay on the hillside to look up at the stars. He and the others—after flying and walking all day—were near the Dustbringer monastery.

It was never going to be me, he thought. *It was always going to be Dalinar himself. I knew that.* He reached over and pulled a rolled bundle from his pack. The cloak Dalinar had given him. It made for a nice pillow as he stared at the stars. After a short time, he got out his flute. Dinner could wait.

He relaxed there and played it slowly. Because he enjoyed the art of it, and he thought that manifested in his notes.

In the sky above, his armor spren swirled about in patterns to the music. Syl eventually flew over, full sized, and lay down next to him, glowing softly, staring into the sky as he played. He wasn't certain how long they remained there, because the softness of the grass seemed to invade his very being.

Soft sound. Soft, fuzzy minutes. Soft ideas, offering quiet, pleasant companionship. Soft company.

He let the music trail off eventually and held the flute up, looking at it against the backdrop of stars. "Still no echoing music coming back to me."

"You should be honored then," Syl said. She rolled closer to him—leaving her hair frazzled. "The Wind likes your songs, Kaladin. She carries them away to cherish."

He smiled, flipping the flute in his hand, like doing a miniature kata.

"I can't believe how good you've become," she said.

"I'm not good. I'm merely not awful."

"After only seven days!"

"I only know one song, and that barely."

"One song, in *seven days.*" She poked him. "And it's a beautiful one that reminds me of the song of Roshar itself. Just let me compliment you, all right?"

"All right," he said. Then he went back to playing. He played for the people he'd lost, to remember them. The songs felt more real as he thought about those people. Goshel, Dallet, Tien, Nalma, Teft, Maps, and a dozen other members of Bridge Four. Men of his squads alongside slaves whose faces he'd almost forgotten, but whose companionship he would always treasure.

He worried that more of his friends might have died during this most recent fighting, though the spanreed had given no relevant news tonight. He played for them as well. A melancholy song, but not a painful one. With the song's help, he felt . . . felt he could remember the fallen—but remarkably, not feel their loss was his fault.

Nale ruined the moment by stomping past. "I hate that song," he said.

"Why?" Kaladin asked.

Nale didn't reply. He tore into a pack and fished out a ration bar.

"Nale?" Kaladin called as he stomped past again. "Do Heralds *eat*?"

"Heralds can eat," he said. "We hunger if we do not. These bodies of ours are highly Invested, but they are not immortal; only our souls are immortal." He turned to Kaladin, holding up the Soulcast ration bar. "This is a perfect food."

"Those taste like rancid armor grease."

"They provide sustenance, are portable, and do not distract. Soulcast jerky, congealed fats, dried nutrients." He ate it, no expression on his face. "A soldier needs nothing more."

Whatever. This wasn't a point Kaladin wanted to argue. Nale strode off, though as he did, Kaladin found Szeth settled on a rock nearby. Watching.

"What?" Kaladin said.

"I'm waiting," Szeth said softly, "for some stew."

Well, storms. Kaladin considered the deliberate way Szeth had said that, after hearing Nale proclaim the virtues of ration bars. Then Kaladin hurriedly got to work. Boiling water in his small pot, slicing vegetables, dropping them in.

Kaladin wanted to prompt Szeth to speak. But something . . . something seemed to whisper to him in Wit's voice. *This isn't the part where you talk. Just listen . . .*

"I am caught between two choices," Szeth said. "I can see the merits of both."

Kaladin nodded, and kept chopping.

"Yesterday, I did as Nale demanded," Szeth continued. "I went in to kill, and won the day, but only with Syl's help. Moss was a friend once. Now he is another corpse I must carry."

Kaladin nodded again.

"I hate this," Szeth said, "but I have made promises. Oaths. I am doing good for this land; I can *feel* it. I should carry on, regardless of the cost to me."

Kaladin finished cutting his longroots. Then he played the flute while the stew simmered, because Szeth asked him to, and because it annoyed Nale.

Szeth stayed, even when Nale came over to glower. The Herald retreated again when Kaladin handed Szeth a bowl, and some of the man's pain appeared to melt off his face as he ate.

Between bites, Szeth said, "I would . . . welcome your thoughts, Kaladin Stormblessed."

The mythical power of stew. Kaladin smiled, taking a bite, and realized something. Back in Hearthstone as a child, he had yearned to train in the spear and learn how to fight. Yet the best moments of his life, and the most important connections he'd made, *hadn't* come from his training in the spear. They had come from a different kind of training. Done by his mother during those same early years—when she taught him to peel longroots and boil vegetables. Remarkable.

What would Wit tell him to do here with Szeth? Tell a story, maybe. Kaladin didn't know any good ones, except the ones of his life.

"I knew this man once," Kaladin said. "Goshel. He was a slave with me, during some of the darkest days of my life. They wanted me to train them so they could revolt against their masters. They'd found out I'd been a fighting man."

"Yes," Szeth said, thoughtful. "Slavery is nasty and barbaric. I would have fought back too."

Kaladin looked up, surprised. "But . . . I thought . . . I mean, you served for so long."

"I oathed myself into my position," Szeth said. "You were forced into it, weren't you? Betrayed?"

Kaladin put his fingers to his forehead, touching only the smooth skin where his tattoo was. No more scars. No more brands. Dangerous no longer? "Yes," he said.

"That is a different thing entirely," Szeth said.

"Rebellion was against the law, regardless of our reason for becoming slaves."

Szeth grunted, then turned back to his stew.

This wasn't the way Wit told stories. Kaladin felt awkward as he continued without feathered words. "So, Goshel. He was a smaller fellow, Szeth. You'd have liked him. Quiet. Determined. He served with precision, but had this *fire* in his eyes. Like smoldering coals. He asked me to teach the others to fight. Thing is, *he* already knew. I saw it the moment he held a spear—though he tried to hide it. This floored me. I hadn't met many other slaves who had been soldiers."

Szeth grunted. "Too valuable?"

"Exactly," Kaladin said. "It takes a lot to force a trained soldier into common household slavery. Something unusual has to happen."

Szeth paused, spoon halfway to his lips, waiting. Huh. It worked, even without the feathered words.

"And?" Szeth asked.

"Goshel was worse than a deserter," Kaladin said. "When I got his story out of him, I found a man who had *deliberately* disobeyed orders. He'd killed his commanding officer."

"That monster," Szeth whispered.

Kaladin hesitated, because he hadn't expected such a willing audience in Szeth. Yet the man watched him, eyes wide. Even for him.

He hasn't had years to get used to Wit, Kaladin thought. *Or maybe he just isn't as cynical as I am.* Probably the latter. Kaladin had always found himself thinking more about why Wit was telling him the story, as opposed to just listening.

"There's a monster in this story," Kaladin said. "Goshel's commanding officer ordered him to burn a village."

Szeth hesitated, then continued eating. "Ah."

"Ah?" Kaladin asked.

"I see why you tell me this story," Szeth said. "You want me to think about the kinds of commands a soldier must disobey."

Maybe they weren't so different. "Sorry. I didn't mean to be that heavy-handed. But . . . Szeth, it's true." Kaladin served himself a bowl. "Goshel died in the rebellion I started. I blamed myself for quite a long time."

"You blamed yourself for surviving, didn't you?"

Kaladin nodded.

"It hurts to live," Szeth said, with a nod, "when you don't deserve it. So . . . you want me to disobey my orders, my oaths?"

"I want you to consider giving something different a go," Kaladin said. "You've tried what Nale wants of you." He took a bite of the stew and . . . storms, it *really* was good this time, wasn't it? "How is that working? For you. Your emotions. Your thoughts."

"Not well," Szeth whispered.

"Think about that," Kaladin said. "I don't know if we'll be able to get out of this without more killing, but we can *try.* I'll help you."

Szeth served himself a second bowl. "I will consider." He walked away, watching the sky and eating as he strolled.

Strangely, a part of Kaladin panicked as Szeth walked away. Despite seeing how well the conversation had gone, Kaladin wanted to do *more.* In a way, Szeth's positive response made it worse—because the part of Kaladin that had always needed to help was stronger for people he liked.

He felt a sudden powerful urge to leap from his seat, to run after the man and insist that they make a plan. Or worse, to make one without Szeth's knowledge. To protect him, save him, fight for him, do anything to keep the man from being hurt. He remembered a dead girl on a slab—a child he and his father had failed to save. A terrible pain echoed from that distant failure.

No.

His instinct was good. It had led him to save Bridge Four, and himself. But he could now view it with more mature eyes. It was also dangerous, the same way water could still drown a dehydrated man. Storms. If he let this need to protect control him completely, he would never be able to help anyone. He'd break first. And so, carefully, he fought back.

Szeth deserves *to make his own choices,* he thought. *If I step in, I take that from him—and that's not who I want to be.*

If I don't control myself, I can't protect, can't help. If I let what Tien's death did to me happen again and again, I will break. I can't keep a stranglehold on those I love.

And finally, most potent of all: *I have to live for myself. Let him go for now.*

There was a place for both Kaladin and Stormblessed. It wasn't so easy to *do* as to *think* it, of course. But today Kaladin's anxiety retreated, particularly as he remembered the music. The calming, peaceful love of the song he'd played, and its rhythms. Nothing magical. Merely a . . . contrast.

"Did something just change?" Syl said, sitting next to him on the log. "In our bond?"

"I don't know," Kaladin said. "I don't feel any different."

"I feel . . . warmth and peace," Syl said, leaning against his shoulder, her hair blowing softly and tickling his cheek. "That was well done with Szeth."

"Wit would have done better."

"Wit would have gotten himself stabbed."

"Maybe," Kaladin said, taking another bite. "Wish you could taste this stew. It's kind of not terrible."

She opened her mouth to say something, but was interrupted as a shimmering figure appeared by the fire. The shape of a man wearing a uniform—but really a black void filled with stars. Kaladin hadn't been aware highspren could appear that way on this side.

The figure flopped down. "Um," it said with a masculine voice. "Hi. Hello."

"Hello?" Kaladin replied.

"I would like to engage your services," the figure said, sitting cross-legged between Kaladin and the stewpot.

"Services . . . ?"

"Whatever you're doing to help Szeth," the spren said. "Talking to him."

"Wit calls it therapy," Kaladin said with a grunt.

"Well, I want that. Um . . . please?"

"You want *help*?" Syl said. "You're a highspren!"

The figure slumped forward. "Can I admit," he said softly, "that I'm not a very good one?"

Kaladin and Syl shared a look.

"I know how it's supposed to go," the figure continued. "The others showed me. Speak like this! Commanding voice! Get the human to do what you say! But it feels so wrong. I see him hurting . . . and it feels wrong."

"Is this your first time as a bonded spren?" Kaladin asked. Syl was glaring. She had a thing about highspren.

"Yeah," the spren said. "We're supposed to take the oaths, you know? We're the only order where the *spren* take the oaths too. But I feel like I'm ruining everything for *everyone.* I don't *feel* like I'm helping, but I'm also making them all disappointed!"

"Them?" Kaladin asked.

"The other highspren. Particularly 121."

"Who?" Kaladin asked.

"Nale's spren," Syl whispered. "He's one of the *worst.*"

"Your names are numbers?" Kaladin asked, frowning. "Like . . . Cryptics?"

"What?" both she and the highspren said.

"It's nothing like that," the highspren replied. "Theirs are *formulas.* Ours are *numbers.*"

"That was honestly kind of racist," Syl whispered to Kaladin.

"I'm sorry?" Kaladin said, rubbing his forehead. "No, I really am. I just don't know much about this. So . . . your name is . . . ?"

"12124," 12124 said.

"Is that how many of you there have been?"

"No. It's just my name."

Syl rolled her eyes, as if Kaladin had said something awkward again.

"So, 12124," Kaladin said, "you're on your first mission as a bonded spren, and you're trying to help Szeth—but also to fulfill your order's expectations of you."

"Yes!" 12124 said. "But then you said we don't have to be what we are, you know? You said you're an anarchist!"

"I did not say I'm an anarchist," Kaladin said. "I'm simply *reminding* people that they have *choices.*"

12124 leapt to his feet and started pacing, and it was somewhat hard to follow him in the darkness, where his shape bled into the night. Those stars were visible though, and provided a focal point to watch him. Curiously, they stayed stationary as he moved—as if he were a portal.

"Rule one, I'm not a thing," 12124 said. "Rule two, I get to choose."

"Rule three . . ." Syl whispered.

The highspren stopped. "I deserve to be happy." He turned to regard them. "What if being happy means . . . doing things differently from other spren?"

"You'll have to decide," Kaladin said, getting another spoonful of stew.

"You're supposed to give me the answers!"

"You wanted my therapy," Kaladin said. "This is how it goes. I don't give answers. I just . . ."

. . . give questions to think upon?

Damnation.

Wit, you crafty bastard.

"You just what?" 12124 asked.

"I just listen," Kaladin said.

"That doesn't sound like much work," 12124 said, folding his arms. "Maybe I should have joined the dissenters."

"The what?" Kaladin said.

The spren looked away. "I . . . shouldn't have said that. Pretend I didn't. And please, give me at least *some* advice."

"Maybe," Kaladin said, "if what you're doing isn't working, you should try something different. Talk to Szeth and see what he wants. His opinion should be relevant. And . . . try not to be too hard on yourself, 12124. This is your first time. You'll make mistakes. Forgive yourself for them, then do better."

"You haven't told me if I should follow the will of the highspren," 12124 said, "or if I should follow my heart."

"I haven't," Kaladin agreed, taking another bite.

"This 'therapy' is too easy," the spren said. "All you do is sit and listen, then tell me things I already kind of know."

"Remarkable," Kaladin said, "how little we do things like that though, isn't it?"

The spren didn't have a face, only a void of stars, but he seemed to be smiling as he replied. "It is remarkable. More so because I actually feel better."

Kaladin raised a spoon to him, and 12124 vanished.

"That was so *weird,*" Syl said, leaning in and whispering to Kaladin, watching the space where 12124 had been.

"Do you know anything about the dissenters he mentions?"

"No," she said. "But I don't know a lot about spren politics of this era." She hesitated. "How odd. I find myself almost not loathing him."

"Must be the stew."

"I didn't eat the stew."

"Then imagine how much better things would be if you had." He smiled and took another bite.

"Is that supposed to sound wise or something?" she said. "Because it was just confusing."

"Sorry," he said. "Wit always ends conversations with comments like that. I don't think I have the hang of it yet." He finished his stew, then considered a moment.

Then he prepared another bowl and went looking for Nale. He found the Herald hovering in the sky maybe fifty feet up, cross-legged, eyes closed. Kaladin dithered.

"What?" Syl said, walking up beside him.

"I was going to try to give this to Nale," Kaladin said, "but I feel . . . storms, Syl, I feel he doesn't *deserve* it. I don't *want* to help him."

"You didn't want to help Szeth at the start either."

"This is different," Kaladin said. "He . . ."

He is your enemy, the Wind said in Kaladin's ear. He jumped, then relaxed as he recognized her voice. *Rather, he has become your enemy.*

"Wind," Syl said, "why does Nale hate the song Kaladin plays?"

He hates it because he remembers it, the Wind explained. *Cephandrius—you call him Wit—taught you that song, Kaladin, because it is one of our rhythms. It is the song the Heralds heard, that Nale heard, that brought them here to safety.*

"But why should he hate that?"

A part of him wishes they'd died on Ashyn and never come to Roshar. The Wind's touch brushed his face. *And another part remembers who he used to be. Thank you, Kaladin, for that song. It strengthens me. But . . . I'm sorry. I need more from you.*

"For what?" Kaladin whispered, turning away from Nale. "I came here in part because of what you said."

You need to help them. The Heralds.

"I . . ." Kaladin swallowed, standing there in the dark night, surrounded by living wind. "I think they should probably die, ancient god. They have lived too long."

They are the last pieces of Honor, Kaladin. Siphoned off, held apart. They are more important than you can know.

"But why not let them rest? Haven't they earned that?"

Would it have been right to let you rest? You acknowledged in a column of light what you had done wrong. Would it have been better to not let you change, not let you grow?

That day, less than two weeks past, seemed like so long ago. That day when Kaladin had put down his burdens in the proper way, by forgiving himself.

"No," he admitted. "It would have been wrong to let me go before I did that."

If they die now, they die as they are. But their journey is not complete, Kaladin. Neither is yours. You . . . regret coming here, to this land?

"I wanted to be the champion," he admitted. "And protect Alethkar."

Your duty here is far more important. I need a champion too. All of the spren will need one.

"As you said before," Syl said. "How?"

The Heralds are Connected to Honor, the Wind said. *In a way that once gave them power over Odium, they can also have power over Honor. And all his creations. To bind them.*

"But why," Kaladin said, with a chill, "would we need that kind of power?"

I see . . . danger . . . the Wind said. *Please, Kaladin. I love him, as I love the others. You do not know the great good they did for so many.*

"Can you . . . show me?" Kaladin asked.

I do not know. That is something the Stormfather does, but not something I have done in a long, long time . . .

He felt a gust of wind in his face, and was given . . . the faintest impression. Not a vision, but a hint of a memory. Several, in sequence.

Darkness, followed by light as Nale—covered in ash and blood from his own cuts—pulled rubble aside and reached a hand to those trapped within.

Terror, cowering in a corner, as red eyes burst through a doorway—then Nale, moving with the speed of the wind, arrived to save those who had been forgotten.

Gratitude, looking past a man in black, tall, bleeding from one hand while he held a glittering Shardblade in the other. Wounded, but his stance saying as loud as any banner: *You WILL NOT have them.*

A dozen flashes in a row, each a fragment of something someone had seen and felt—taken by the Wind, then passed to Kaladin like a distant scent. Showing him a hero who had stood for millennia, time and time again.

But now . . .

Weathered, the Wind said. *Time and I are cousins: both of us wear away the things we caress. Please, Kaladin. He is worth saving. Do not let him die like this . . .*

The voice trailed off. Kaladin breathed in deeply, the knowledge and memories settling on him.

Syl took his hand.

"Did you see them too?" Kaladin whispered.

She nodded.

He wanted to ponder it further, maybe bring that stew to Nale, but Szeth came dashing up. Even before he arrived, Kaladin went alert—tossing the bowl and summoning the Sylspear.

"Look," Szeth said, taking him by the arm. "*Look.*"

Szeth pointed in the same direction Nale was staring. Northeast. The direction of the final monasteries. Dustbringer, Skybreaker, Windrunner—which they'd skip—and Bondsmith.

A stream of glowing light in the sky ran in that direction. Like stars, moving, a shining *river* of light. Low on the horizon, easy to miss at first, but obvious now that it had been pointed out.

"What is it?" Kaladin whispered.

"Spren," Syl said. "All of the spren of this land. No wonder we haven't seen any."

"They are always more rare here," Szeth said. "But not as rare as they have been during this trip."

A shadow descended. Nale, coming to alight on the ground beside them. "Your gods have gathered to witness your decisions, Szeth-son-Neturo. And the salvation of this land."

Kaladin pried for more information, but of course Nale wouldn't give any. It seemed that if there were to be answers, they would be found to the northeast. At the end of that river of light.

⁂

After seeing Rlain and Renarin so happy together, Shallan felt a little better, a little more willing to face the future. Certainly, she never wanted to go back to her childhood.

You'll need to, Veil warned. *We haven't finished that fight yet.*

Shallan wanted to ignore the comment, but to do so risked Formless. So she acknowledged it. She *would* go back. There *were* things she needed to confront. Fortunately, she didn't need to do it right now.

She had Glys and Tumi create a scene in Shadesmar for them, an obsidian rock ledge where she and Adolin had seen a starspren. That trip had been a time of darkness, but this had been a point of light. More and more, she was trying to let the points of light—not the darkness between them—guide her.

Today, after Renarin and Rlain stepped into the vision with her, Shallan walked along this ridge, smiling up at the dancing starspren: flowing, winged, long and sinuous. Like a chasmfiend, but more regal. Pattern put a long-fingered hand on her shoulder, and she put her hand on his. Testament sat to the side, on a slightly higher section of stone.

"What happened here?" Renarin said. "Why is it so much better than one of our childhood homes?"

Wouldn't you like to know, Shallan thought, turning to look at the two of them, who settled down suspiciously close to one another on an obsidian outcropping. Shallan remembered those days too, with fondness. The early days when she realized that the relationship with Adolin was going to work. The euphoria of love—and of relief that she hadn't somehow screwed it up.

Be safe, she thought to him. *Please.*

"Renarin," she said, refocusing on their mission, "you told me that you spoke to Mishram again?"

"I did," he said. "I . . . well, I kind of confronted her. May have . . . antagonized her by demanding she explain herself."

"Really?" Rlain said to an appreciative rhythm. "You *confronted* one of the Unmade? Made *demands* of her?"

"She's locked away," Renarin said. "It's not so brave as you make it sound."

"Her prison is obviously failing. I'm impressed."

"What did Mishram say *exactly,* Renarin?" Shallan asked. "I think the wording might be relevant."

"She said, 'I showed you so you can find me. So I may destroy you.'"

Rlain's rhythm became more uncomfortable. "She hates you because you're human—and me because my people betrayed her." He paused. "Still, she *is* willing to lead us to her . . ."

"To kill us!" Renarin said.

"Renarin," Rlain replied, "I think we *need* to find her. We came here to stop the Ghostbloods, but we—even Shallan, with all her skill—have proven insufficient."

"He's right," Shallan noted. "I caught a glimpse of Mraize a few visions ago, but that's it. I don't think we're good enough to track them in here."

"So . . ." Rlain said, his rhythm determined, "*we* need to find the prison and move it—before they do."

"I . . . figured you'd want that," Renarin said. He took a deep breath. "I just worry. The way she acts, the way she talks . . . And Glys told me that she's influenced the visions we're seeing."

"Maybe there's a clue in them," Shallan said. "Like how she's been showing us her face in objects. Anyone remember seeing anything odd in recent visions?"

"I was too busy feeling rejected," Rlain said. "It was a hard memory, that one. I had to sit and listen to my friends realize that we needed a spy. They settled on me because I was the most disposable."

"I was in the palace at Kholinar," Renarin said. "It was also a hard vision, but not as fresh a wound. I was being bullied by some other teens, and Adolin saved me." He frowned. "The thing is, I've grown since that day. I didn't want that protection anymore; I wanted to defend myself, to be my own person, not Adolin Kholin's little invalid brother."

"And did you see anything out of the ordinary?" Shallan asked.

"I'm trying to remember," Renarin said. "Honestly, I can't think of anything that stands out. Other than the entire experience feeling wrong now, as that's not who I am anymore."

It was the same for her, unfortunately. Maybe there was a clue in her vision of telling stories to her brothers, but she didn't see it. She paced while above the starspren posed for her, lounging, looking down.

Her vision . . . She'd sought refuge with her brothers. Brought them joy. It was a painful memory, but a fond one all the same. The beginnings, she thought, of what had made of her an actor—and a Lightweaver.

Shallan, Veil said, *confront it.*

At her side, Pattern began humming. Hesitantly, Testament joined in from her seat nearby.

"I changed my vision," Shallan said to Rlain and Renarin. "I was going to see something else, but I refused."

"And . . . what *were* you going to see?" Renarin asked.

"The day I killed my mother," Shallan said softly. "Perhaps Mishram intended to put some kind of clue in there. If so, I missed the chance."

The two shared looks. Renarin shrugged; Rlain hummed. Then Renarin sat upright.

"You remember something?" Shallan asked, eager.

"No," Renarin said. "It's Glys. He says something has happened. My father and aunt . . . they've found their way to an important moment, the one when Mishram was originally captured."

Storms. "That's close to when Honor died, right?" Shallan said. "They're connected."

Renarin nodded. "It's all linked. Including why Odium is afraid of Mishram."

"Because she could kill him," Shallan said. "And take his place. She's a viable rival for his power."

"Exactly," Renarin said.

Wait.

Wait.

Because . . . she could kill him . . . As Shallan had told Mraize, she knew that feeling: the danger a child presented to the parent. Before she could follow the thought, Renarin stood. "We need to join my father's vision."

"Mraize and Iyatil will be there," she warned. "So be alert."

"Understood," Renarin said. Storms, when had he grown that confident? He reminded her of . . . well, his father. "Get ready. I'm going to have Glys send us in."

87
LOVE AND BETRAYAL

Goodbye. It might be a great long time before we see one another again, if ever.

Dalinar allowed himself to be kissed by the Regal.

He had never known of a singer to display affection in such a human way, but the kiss was genuine, and drew passionspren. It took an effort for Dalinar not to pull back, as he felt he was going to get knifed at any moment, yet this *had* to play out. He did hear a gasp from the spot where the others were hiding, likely from Navani, and he hoped that everyone else was too stunned to be suspicious.

The Regal finished her kiss and pulled back a little, her face still inches from his, eyes glowing faintly red. Her features, with that red and black marbling—so alien, so terrible. This was his enemy. This was . . .

Concern? She seemed *concerned.* Perhaps because he hadn't responded to the kiss with the affection she anticipated.

"Are you all right?" she whispered. "Is it the others? You said we should show them."

"It's fine," Dalinar said, resting his hand on her shoulder.

She hummed gratefully and nodded in an exaggerated way—for him, he realized. Storms . . . she legitimately cared. And when she looked to the other Windrunners, she offered them a smile—again exaggerated, but genuine. Singers did smile, they just tended to be less dramatic about it than humans.

This is not a betrayal, Dalinar thought. *I don't know what it is, but it's not a betrayal.*

"Do you want to do it?" she asked him. "Or shall I?"

"Go ahead," he said.

She stood close to him, so he—feeling it was the right thing to do—put his arm around her. It was strange, doing that to someone who was taller than he was, and he had to be careful of the ridges and sharp portions of her carapace. He felt a moment of discomfort and betrayal himself, for Navani's sake. He knew that she would understand, but few people would enjoy seeing their spouse in the arms of another.

"You are Garith's dearest friends," the singer said to the Windrunners. "We've decided we need to explain. We started meeting in secret years ago, after clashing on the battlefield . . ."

She glanced to him, and hummed softly.

"We were enemies at first," he said, guessing what to say next.

"But we had one thing in common," she said. "We both wanted all of this to end. Our initial meeting was awkward, and . . . well . . . I might have stabbed him." She shrugged and looked to Dalinar. "He was . . . um . . . very understanding."

"Ruined my outfit . . ." Dalinar said to the other Windrunners, who watched with wide eyes.

"Garith," one woman said, "they're the *enemy.*"

"No," Dalinar said. "They're people. Same as us."

It was harder to say than it should have been. They'd stolen his homeland, killed his brother. They'd assaulted the tower.

But . . . he'd attacked Herdaz in his youth, yet the Mink worked with him. His people had fought the Vedens for centuries, and now one was his daughter-in-law. Maybe there was something he could learn from this ancient Windrunner.

But why did this all turn out so poorly . . . ?

A mounting dread began to build within him. He was not watching a vision that ended with a happy truce between peoples. This ended in slavery and broken oaths.

"I can accept," said one of the other Windrunners, "that a few of the singers are willing to make peace. But the entire nation?"

"Garith," said another, "you're *barely* holding the Radiants together. And she argues so forcefully at our parleys!"

"My people don't want war," said the singer at his side. "But . . . more of them are aggressive than I'd prefer. I *can't* look like I'm giving in. Garith and I wanted to show you, so you'd understand. Peace *is* possible. We *can* find a way."

"Peace is possible," Dalinar whispered.

The singer glanced at him, then nodded. "She agreed to come."

". . . She?" Dalinar said.

"These need to know it's not just a few of us," the singer said. "They need to know our new god is different."

The hair on Dalinar's arms went up as something changed. He turned to see that—among the shadows of the rising stones—a darkness had pooled. Liquid night. From it, into the light of the moon, stepped a figure.

It was in the shape of a singer. Shorter than most. No barbed carapace. No dangerous expression. An adult with alternating lines of white, red, and black. This was a spren though. Her bare feet didn't touch the ground. Her hairstrands drifted unnaturally, lifted by some unseen wind. And she emitted the faintest glow, a violet red that was only really visible if you looked at the ground beneath her, where it reflected faintly.

The singer next to him, and the three who accompanied her, bowed their heads and hummed to a reverent rhythm. Could this truly be her? Ba-Ado-Mishram, the most terrible Unmade? Looking . . . like an average singer?

As she stepped forward, she *jolted,* and her figure—in a blink—was glaring at him with wide eyes, mouth open as if screaming. It passed just as quickly. A flash, and she was back. Dalinar frowned as it happened again, then again. It was like . . . like a second Mishram was trying to break out of this one. But as she stepped up to him, she stabilized into the kindly version.

"Garith," she said, her voice overlapping somehow with multiple rhythms at once. "I have come, as you have vowed your sincerity." She looked to the other Windrunners. "I was skeptical, but if these two can find peace, then perhaps others can as well. I did not become their god to watch them die. I . . ." She trailed off, and her demeanor changed. She *jolted* again, a screaming figure replacing her for a moment, then she was back. Staring . . .

Straight at where Navani's group was hiding.

Run, Mishram! Dalinar thought. *Hide!*

But he needed to see. This was why he was here.

"Who else did you bring?" Mishram asked, pointing. "Who is out there?"

The Windrunners turned, displaying obvious shock, as some of those who had been hiding emerged. Navani was there, appearing concerned as she held Gav's hand. Kalak, at the rear, looked ashamed. No sign of Melishi. Dalinar turned, inspecting the region. That ridge there . . . a flanking maneuver would . . .

He spotted Melishi slipping out from between two stones nearby. The man had backed out of the woods and rounded behind Mishram, and was now only ten feet away. Melishi carried a large gemstone, and as Mishram noticed him, she cocked her head—but didn't seem frightened.

Fabrials as we know them, Dalinar realized, *haven't been invented yet. Humans only barely learned to trap spren—and Mishram has no idea what that stone can do.*

"I," Melishi said, "am the Bondsmith."

"Yes," Mishram said. "The one who abandoned the tower."

Melishi stepped closer, his robes rustling, that gemstone—big as a child's head—clutched before him in a two-handed grip. Largely uninfused, it glowed a soft yellow.

The singer at Dalinar's side—he still didn't know her name—grabbed his hand. "The Bondsmith? If he joins with our cause . . . if *he* believes . . . this could be the moment when we find lasting peace!"

Storms. None of them realized they were witnessing an assassination. Dalinar's instincts screamed at him to do something, but he held back. Rooted. A stone, like the watching monoliths.

He had been on enough battlefields to know what was coming. He could have listed off the beats. Melishi getting even closer. Ba-Ado-Mishram watching like a lone soldier, uncertain if she should stand her ground or run.

"You're trying to unite them," Melishi said. "All of the singers . . . unite them to follow you."

"I bring them harmony," Mishram said. Speaking with rhythms in an inhuman way—and yet there was a vulnerability. "Odium would burn them, so I made my play, infusing myself with the full power of his perpendicularity. He is trapped on Braize for the moment. I can replace him."

Melishi stopped right before her. "And we can have peace. Two peoples. One world."

"Yes," Mishram said. "Peace."

"In that we are united," said Melishi. "I know how to be *certain* we will have peace. All you have to do is open your heart, and trust. I will *unite us all.*"

Those words struck Dalinar through like a spear. Standing with a singer lover at his side, he forced himself to watch as the honor of an *entire people* was broken in an instant. Melishi raised the gemstone to the unsuspecting spren, and . . .

Hesitated.

Mishram cocked her head.

Dalinar's breath caught.

"*Do it, Melishi,*" Honor's voice said, vibrating through the small hollow of stone.

Melishi did. Dalinar wasn't certain of the mechanics, though he'd done it once with the Thrill. Something about a deep Connection to the Unmade, which Melishi had forged with ideas of unity. Something about welcoming them in, then continuing to pull.

In this case, Mishram's desire to stop the war bound her to the Bondsmith, who wanted exactly the same thing—but was willing to do an unspeakable act to make it happen. The Bondsmith began to glow, and Mishram distorted and bent, screaming with a sudden raw panic. A hundred overlapping voices, and a tunnel of light.

Dalinar sent himself away, out of the body of the Windrunner, to rejoin Navani. She took him in her arms, burying her face in his chest, trembling as they listened to the terrified shrieks of a spren betrayed.

In that instant, something *ripped* within the world itself. Roshar's rhythms and tones froze. Like a heart suddenly stopped. Three terrible seconds.

Then it was back. When the light faded, Melishi held a gemstone prison in his hands, and Honor was standing behind him.

"Honor, you bastard," Dalinar whispered. "You were responsible for all of this."

"This is why!" Navani whispered. "Why the power refuses another host, why it—"

Screaming.

The singers collapsed, as if one. Drawing shockspren, Garith caught the direform next to him, preventing her from hitting hard, but all four singers began to writhe and scream.

Dalinar, with Navani—Gav holding to her skirt—walked back to the center of the hollow. Garith held his direform lover . . . but she was losing her form. Dalinar had never seen a singer changing forms, but this was traumatic, her carapace becoming brittle and ripping free, her body shrinking—the bones cracking and popping. By the time it was done—and she lay limp in Garith's arms—both were stained with orange singer blood.

What had once been a femalen of imposing stature and confidence had shrunken to something all too familiar: one of the quiet, mostly mute servants who had waited on Dalinar most of his life. He felt he could see the light of understanding fade from her eyes.

She looked up at Garith, blinking, and seemed confused. And terrified.

"What did you do?" Garith demanded, pulling her close, looking up at Melishi. "What *did you do?*"

Melishi backed away, clutching the gemstone. "Honor told me there was a way to find peace, forever."

Garith settled the singer down on the ground, whispering, "I'll fix this, Shmone. I . . . I'll fix this." He rose, thunder in his expression, angerspren pooling at his feet, and started toward Melishi. "We gave our *word,* Melishi. That we were negotiating in good faith! We *swore an oath*!"

Dalinar joined him, stalking across the stones, no longer caring that this was all just a re-creation. Others followed him, some of those who had been hiding with Navani, though Kalak cowered in the back. Dalinar's hands itched to close around that Bondsmith's neck. He felt hollow, remembering those awful seconds when the entire planet had gone still.

Melishi, terrified, sought to hide behind Honor. The god continued to stand firm, staring them down.

"You did this," Garith said. "Why?"

"It was necessary," Honor said.

"You are supposed to respect oaths!" Garith said, stopping right in front of Honor. "You embody them! How could you allow this? How?"

Honor turned as if to leave. Garith reached for him, but as his fingers touched the god . . .

A vision. Injected directly into Dalinar's mind. Of Radiants burning Roshar, of the sky on fire, of people dying and withering to dust. Of Garith himself, glowing with power, leaving thousands—human and singer alike—dead. Navani gasped—and the Windrunners cried out in pain. Even Melishi and the Radiants who had come with him howled.

They all saw it. Every Radiant on Roshar. What *could* be. A reminder that their powers could utterly lay waste to an entire world. It had happened before.

"You," Honor said, "are destruction incarnate. You are as Dawnshards. You will soon become Surges unbounded, as I cannot watch you any longer. The Radiants will end this planet."

His words thundered through Dalinar's heart, and he finally understood the Recreance. All these years, and now he understood. Garith would walk away from his oaths, as would most of the others, because what were words like those after a tragedy like this? After God abandoned you, and you saw what you believed was the future?

The vision faded, and Garith stumbled back, returning to his fallen love. Honor remained in place—and strangely, the deity's expression changed. He focused on Dalinar, then Navani, then sighed.

This . . . this wasn't the past playing out. Dalinar saw as much in the god's eyes. Honor had *seen* him.

"Blood of my fathers," Dalinar said. "You're *not* dead, are you? You never were. It was an act?"

"No," the being said, and its voice was familiar. "It's me. I was created in his image."

"Stormfather," Dalinar said. "You were here; you did see all of this. You've known the truth all along—it was lies when you said you didn't remember. Why?"

"You, Dalinar," the Stormfather said, sounding exhausted, "have seen far too much. I hope you are satisfied. I . . . I must stop hiding you from Odium. You are his. And this is . . . this is his domain now." He vanished, and Dalinar was cast into the chaos of the Spiritual Realm again.

This time, when he tried to find the lines of light Connecting him to people and places, he discovered they had vanished. And a shadow loomed over him.

Odium.

Renarin knelt beside the fallen singer as the Windrunner returned to her side and cradled her.

Renarin felt powerless. He thought his gasp earlier—while hiding in the leaves—might have ruined things. It hadn't, fortunately, but seeing a singer and a human kiss . . .

This had all been started by love. Love and betrayal.

The poor Windrunner didn't look at Renarin. He clung to his love and started humming. A rhythm. The Rhythm of *Joy.* A human, outside of one of the visions, had learned them—and was desperately trying to bring her back.

A hand on his shoulder. Rlain's, though he was in the body of another Radiant spy. He hummed to the Lost.

"I know why she hates us now," Renarin whispered. "I'd hate us too."

"She's wrong," Rlain said.

Renarin glanced at him. "How can you say that? After seeing this?"

"I see," Rlain said, regarding the others around the hollow, "people. Some who have done evil things, yes, but others who have *loved.* Renarin, you asked how it is for us. We feel love, as any human does. But we're afraid of it because we associate powerful emotions with *him.*" He squeezed Renarin's shoulder. "Doesn't stop us from hating. In that, he wins, because he scares us away from the beautiful emotions and leaves only the destructive ones."

Storms. Renarin stood up next to him.

"She's wrong," Rlain said, "if she hates humans. Because it merely gives him what he wants: two sides delineated simply. One who can just be 'the enemy.' People can be wonderful or terrible; an enemy, though, can only be something to fight." He looked down, then hummed to Anxiety. "Does that sound trite?"

"A little," Renarin said. "The thing is, the deepest truths always sound a little trite. Because we all know them, and feel foolish being reminded."

Shallan passed by—Glys warned him it was her—and scanned the crowd, her eyes narrowed. Looking for Mraize or Iyatil.

No one here, Glys said, *plays their part poorly. Perhaps they are lost, and did not find this day?*

Shallan waved them forward. "Hurry. Dalinar is still confronting Honor."

"More importantly," Rlain said, pointing to the Bondsmith Melishi, hiding behind the figure of the god, "he has the prison."

She and Rlain hurried after Dalinar, though Renarin lingered, wanting to say something to the poor Windrunner who had been betrayed. What could he do to help?

"I'll make it right," Renarin whispered.

The Windrunner looked up, and seemed to *see* him. Somehow, across time, through the void that was Beyond, this man *saw* Renarin. He gasped.

"I promise," Renarin said. "I'll find a way."

The man nodded, tears in his eyes, and Renarin finally hurried after the other two. But they were too late. The vision started to unravel, though Renarin heard something first.

"Stormfather. You were here; you did see all of this." Renarin's father. "You've known the truth all along—it was lies when you said you didn't remember. Why?"

"You, Dalinar"—a booming voice, like thunder—"have seen far too much. I hope you are satisfied. I . . . I must stop hiding you from Odium. You are his. And this is . . . this is his domain now."

Everything burst apart, and Renarin lost track of them all—not just his father, but Shallan and Rlain.

I can find them, Glys said. *I will.*

The shifting smoke stabilized around him, becoming an expanse of black stone—not much to see. Glys—who hid inside Renarin again—struggled to hold it together.

Shallan, Rlain, Pattern, and Testament formed from that mist as it retreated.

"Did you see where the man went?" Shallan asked, turning around. "The one carrying Mishram's prison?"

"I managed to," Rlain said. "He opened a perpendicularity and was pulled through."

"The Bondsmith went straight into the Spiritual Realm," Pattern said. "Mmmm . . . Then he was lost. He carried the prison into his tomb."

"So we didn't learn anything new," Shallan said, folding her arms. "We already knew he was in here."

"We need a Connection," Renarin said, feeling tired. How long had they been here? An *entire day,* or maybe two, even? He should need sleep, something to drink, shouldn't he?

"What was that?" Rlain asked. "You said a Connection."

"That's the way to find things in here," Renarin said. "It's how Father and Navani did it."

"Mishram's prison is in here somewhere," Shallan said, "and locations in the Spiritual Realm aren't . . . really locations. They're like . . . memories, thoughts. All you need to reach a distinct point is the right Connection."

"We just saw the prison being made," Rlain said. "Isn't that enough?"

"No, unfortunately," Renarin said, thinking back to what Glys had said earlier. He felt the spren vibrating within him, to what he thought was the

Rhythm of the Lost. To find the lost . . . you needed more than superficial Connection. "We have to know how she felt. We have to *know* Mishram. Deeper than seeing, we have to *feel* it."

"So we get angry?" Rlain asked.

"Deeper than anger," Renarin said. He considered how Mishram must have felt, being betrayed, and something occurred to him. "Glys. Where were the other Unmade when this happened? Were they fighting somewhere?"

No, they knew, Glys said. *Some were there. They watched.*

What?

"They were *there*?" To Rlain's confused glance, he explained. "Glys says the other Unmade were there watching."

"Tumi agrees," Rlain said. "He says he could feel them. I didn't see anything. Did you?"

"No."

"Sja-anat is often invisible," Shallan said.

She . . . was there, Glys said. *That is part of why she sent us to you. She has not spoken of the events she saw, but she feels pain for them.*

There was something here, if Renarin could just . . .

Renarin! Glys said with a sudden urgency. *Another watches us! What is that?*

Renarin followed Glys's prompting, and turned to see something approaching across the expanse of simple dark stone and a black sky, lit—like some places in Shadesmar—with some unseen, inexplicable light. The figure wore plain leathers, as Shallan had been wearing when she'd entered this place. Its face was a dark swirl of mist, like a whirlpool of smoke.

"What is it?" Rlain asked, subtly putting himself between the thing and Renarin.

"It's me," Shallan whispered. "I'm making it somehow." She reached out her hand, palm forward. The thing froze. "Storms. I . . . I should be more in control. I'm sorry. I . . ." She looked to Renarin, and her face was panicked, so full of emotion even *he* could tell what she was feeling. "We need to leave. Go somewhere more stable. Please."

I will try, Glys said. *But it is harder now. I do not know why. Unless . . .*

"Unless?" Renarin whispered.

Unless it's his influence. Renarin! The sky!

A shadow rose in the distance. Dark, ominous, with a crown that stretched toward the heavens, and golden light pouring from its eyes.

"Now, now," Odium said, his voice—strangely familiar—booming across them. "I see. Rats in the walls. Amazing that you could all hide from me.

Unfortunately, I'm quite busy. So why don't you stay where I put you until I'm ready?"

They were cast into the mist, the vision bursting, separating them in a flurry of power.

THE END OF

Day Seven

INTERLUDES

LIFT • ODIUM

I-13

LIFT

Being a queen was supposed to have been awesome.

It was not awesome.

It was awful.

Maybe that was because they didn't let Lift do anything truly queenly, even if she was wearing an illusion of Navani's face and body. She'd tried suggesting Opposite Day, where servants got to beat their masters, and offered to sign it into law. She'd suggested seventeen new holidays. In a moment of trying to be more reasonable, she'd even asked that they let her play with that stuff that blew up when you mixed it, like Navani did. Lift had promised she'd heal if she lost any appendages that she really needed.

Each time, her keepers—Brightlady Khal and Brightlord Aladar—had laughed. As if she were *joking.* Except they *didn't* laugh when she was *actually* joking, and said that Aladar's face looked like he'd sneezed when he was brushing his teeth, and had frozen that way.

"You . . . sneeze when you brush your teeth?" he'd asked her instead.

Well, yeah. Sometimes, she supposed. She didn't track it or anything.

She sat back in her "throne" with a huff. Navani didn't even have a proper throne room from which Lift could spout dictates and yell for people's heads to be offed. Instead, Navani had an *office.* For *meetings.* It had a nice chair, but it wasn't a throne at all.

Today, the desk was arrayed with a wide variety of foods, all exotic, to keep Lift distracted. That's what they did—pile food in front of her. Have her walk the hallways so everyone *thought* Navani was still here, and not sucked through a hole into the past or something. They'd have her cancel meetings claiming fatigue, then they'd stick her in Navani's rooms. They kept giving her games or books to try to keep her occupied. As if she could read. "Young ladies are supposed to like these," they said. As if she were a lady.

She pushed her plate around with a fork, sitting on Navani's chair with her legs hanging over the side. She looked like Navani, even to herself, but the illusion wasn't great.

Well, it was kind of great. Wit was good with this stuff. But Lift was shorter than Navani, so the illusion always had to include a full gown to hide that her waist was far lower. And though the illusion looked like it was staring people in the eyes, she was actually looking out from the chest somewhere, which could be kind of distracting. Like having two bowls strapped to the sides of your face.

"Lift?" Wyndle said, forming his bearded face from a pile of vines, his eyes as crystalline gemstones and seeming worried. "You aren't . . . eating? Look at all of this expensive food they're forced to give you to keep you out of trouble!"

"Don't wannit," she mumbled, her voice Navani's.

"Is that caviar? Lift, that's caviar!"

She flopped onto her stomach, laying across the chair with her waist on one armrest, her upper chest on the other, dangling one arm down toward the floor. This room was so tiny. No windows. Why would Navani have an office without a window? Except for the fact that she'd want nobody to watch her having private meetings, of course. Other than that.

"Lift . . ." Wyndle said, sitting on the desktop, offering one vine as a hand to pat her on the shoulder. "It really *wasn't* your fault. Master Wit explained it. You didn't cause the explosion."

"You think they found Gav in there?"

"Certainly they did! They're Bondsmiths, Lift. Most incredible and accomplished of all Radiants. Why, I'll bet they found him instantly. Lift? It's all right."

"There's nothin' I can do. Just like Wit said."

"So why mope?"

"I just wanna be parta stuff," she muttered. "I was one of the first. And I'm never part of anything." She stared at the floor. "And when I am, I make it go wrong. Every time. You can lie and say it ain't true, but it ain't ain't true, Wyndle. You know it always gets messed up. If I'd been better at this, maybe I coulda saved Gav. I didn't. Couldn't even save myself.

"So they lock me in a room when the world's gotta be saved, otherwise . . . I'll trip. I'll knock into people. People are dyin'. Gav is lost. But I'm here in this uncomfortable chair, savin' nobody. Because if I were there? It goes wrong. They know it."

"The chair is uncomfortable?"

"Mmmph."

"Have you tried . . . sitting in it?"

She flopped around, lying back across the armrests and staring at the ceiling.

"Storms . . ." Wyndle said. "No wisecrack?"

"Mmmph."

"This is dire. Dire indeed. I . . . um . . . I . . ." He drew himself up, then offered the secret handshake.

Well, storm him for a Voidbringer.

It kind of made her feel better when he did that.

"Lift," the tower said, a shimmer appearing on the table in the designated spot. "What is 'peeky time'?"

"Children's game," Lift said, taking Wyndle's offered hand and shaking. "You play it with babies, like the drooling really, really young babies who ain't old enough to play real games, like hitting each other with sticks."

"Oh, okay," the tower said.

"Why?" Lift asked.

"I heard echoes of the term in a deep hallway on the thirty-third floor," the tower explained. "But there's housing in that direction, so maybe a woman was out walking her baby."

"You can't tell?" Lift said.

"I . . . am not fully functional without Navani," the Sibling said, their voice growing softer. "It won't be a big problem for some weeks yet, as she's *partially* here. In the Spiritual Realm, she's kind of everywhere. But . . . it is having an effect."

Lift grunted. "You worried?"

"I shouldn't be. I didn't want to be here, in this situation. I can't decide if I'd rather still be asleep or not, and Navani can be . . . determined when she wants something. I chose to accept her Words, and it *was* my decision, but I . . . I waver."

"I'm glad you're awake," Lift said. "You make the tower all deevy."

"I assume that's a compliment."

"Oh!" Wyndle said, perking up. "It's the *best* compliment, from her."

"Nah," Lift said. "Too many people understand it now. Need a new word." She flopped around to where she was lying on the chair with her feet in the air and her head hanging down under the desk. "Hey, Tower. What did this voice you heard sound like?"

"I can re-create it," the Sibling said, and projected the sound of a distant, inhuman voice saying "peeky time" in the most forlorn way ever.

Lift slammed her head against the underside of the desk as she tried to sit up. "Storms! Ow! Storming storming storming storming storms. Sibling, that's my *storming* chicken, you storming tillwallop!"

"Your chicken can *actually* talk?"

"I *told* you! An' better than Wyndle!"

"Hey!" he said.

"You use too many words I don't know," Lift said, standing and rubbing her forehead. "That strange monster man that took the chicken, then sold me to the enemy? He vanished into the hole with Navani, right?"

"By your description, yes . . ." the tower said.

"So he musta left my chicken somewhere! It could be starvin'!" She grabbed a plate off the desk. "Do chickens like caviar?"

"Maybe?" Wyndle said.

"I'll bring some curry just in case," she said, grabbing another plate. "I gotta go save it!"

"Lift," the tower said, "I can send a contingent of guards. *You* can send a contingent of guards. We—"

"No," Wyndle said, growing taller. "We have to do this. Ourselves. Right, Lift?"

"Storming right," she said. Then smiled at him. "Thanks for backin' me up."

"Always," he said.

"And you don't think it will be odd," the Sibling's shimmer of light said, "for the queen to go out by herself, hunting through distant hallways?"

"Sure," Lift said. "But you can eat the illusion, right?"

"Well, it was made with Towerlight, so I can cancel the power sustaining it, but that's not—"

"Good enough!" Lift said. "There's no time! My chicken *needs caviar.* But first, record me sayin' these words with Navani's voice . . ."

In a second, she was back to herself. Wearing her clothing—just some trousers and a loose shirt—like she'd put on this morning before being transformed to Navani. Bands wrapping her chest underneath. She hated how she looked most days, so that part of the illusion was nice, but this wasn't a job for a queen.

Seconds later, Lift strode out past the guards at the door, who were surprised—but not that surprised—to find that Lift had somehow snuck past them to pester the queen. The Sibling projected Navani's voice from inside, telling them not to interrupt her for a while—as Lift had distracted her from some very important paper reading.

Just like that, she was free for the first time in *forever*—or since that morning at least—to do what she wanted. And what she wanted, what she needed, was to be a hero. Even if only to a single frightened animal.

⁂

With the Sibling's help, they were able to figure out exactly where the evil guy's den was. A room that the Sibling, upon focusing on it, couldn't sense.

"Ralkalest," the Sibling explained from a glowing spot on the wall in a back corridor. "You probably call it aluminum. Some of the rooms in the tower have to be lined in it for practical reasons. Sometimes you need to contain a being of immense power. I'd forgotten it was even here—as I can't sense what's inside."

Lift had positioned herself underneath the room. The corridor one level down went under it. Since the lock mechanism appeared to be jammed, this felt like the best way in.

"Aluminum?" Wyndle said. "Oh . . . I don't like that. We could get trapped!"

"We ain't gonna get trapped," Lift said, climbing up the wall on some vines he'd grown for her. Soon she was hanging upside down, her long dark hair falling around her head. "But we *are* gonna be careful in case that monster man with the scars left guards or somethin'. That might be why the door won't open. Now hush and turn into a sword."

"But I can't cut through aluminum!"

"What?" Lift said. "What use is a sword what can't cut stuff?" Storming spren. Every time she needed him . . .

"The sheeting is very thin," the Sibling explained. "Because it's so valuable. Basically just foiling. You should be able to punch through, even with a Shardblade."

"Glad someone is useful. Now hush, both of you."

"Okay," Wyndle said, "but why come in from the *bottom*?"

"More dynamic," Lift said, then thrust her hand to the side and he appeared as a sword. She didn't do that often, as swords felt . . . wrong to her. But they *were* good for chopping. She sliced a circle out of the ceiling, and indeed, did hit some resistance. It stopped the Blade more soundly than the Sibling had thought it might. However, once she got a chunk of the ceiling out, she could reach up and bend back the sheets of metal and pry them out of the way. They weren't terribly thick, so she managed it, after turning Wyndle into a crowbar.

After some further effort, she got a nice Lift-sized circle cut out of the ceiling. The blocks of stone that she cut out had been clattering to the ground—and the last, biggest ones fell with a crash to wake the dead. She winced.

Is that part of being dynamic? Wyndle asked in her head, because he was now a sword.

"Shut it," she muttered, then dismissed the Blade and pulled herself into the hole. She stuck her head up into a round stone chamber, with some books in a case along one wall and lit by some spheres on top of it. Other than that, the only furniture was a mattress on the floor.

However, a cage hung from the ceiling with her chicken in it. Her heart leaped. Hanging near it was some old guy. He seemed to be unconscious, or maybe dead, hanging by a chain from the ceiling, and was way, *way* too naked.

"Ugh," Lift said, wincing.

"What?" Wyndle said, growing up beside her. "You're *always* staring at men—"

"Not *old* ones," she said. And not one who looked like this, bloodied from what had probably been torture. It turned her stomach to see the poor man like that. Plus he was bearded and rather hairy. Like, actually *really* hairy.

"Bleck," she muttered, then hauled herself up inside. Seemed empty otherwise. So she took some caviar out of her pocket and climbed on the bookcase to offer it to the chicken. "Hey. Hey, I'm here. I got you."

The animal's feathers looked terrible—worn and ragged, faded, rather than the chipper bright red she'd seen from it just before the occupation. It still had that hurt wing, but it perked up when it saw her and got excited.

"Hello!" it said. "Hello, hello, hello!"

Nearby, the man hanging by the chains stirred. Lift got the door to the chicken's cage open and the animal out, after which it clung to her arm with claws that were way too sharp. The man blinked open red eyes, then frowned.

"That is . . . unexpected," he said.

"You need help?" Lift said, clutching her chicken close. "'Cuz uh . . . I'm maybe a hero or somethin'."

"That would be appreciated," the man said, his voice ragged. "Quickly though, before—"

The door opened. The supposedly broken door. Yeah, Lift loved being right, but she could have been wrong now and it would have been okay.

Three people entered, and they were *not* official guards or anything like that. Two thugs, with knives strapped to them. One woman in a havah, with rings glittering on her fingers. It took one glance from the woman—her expression angry—for Lift to guess these were associates of the terrible man who had taken her captive and sold her to the enemy.

Storming Sibling bein' blind lately. Lift growled, then summoned Wyndle as a sword and shouted, "Hey Sibling, if you can hear, send those guards! I *really* shoulda listened to you!"

No reply. But if the tower heard the bird, then it could hear her. Lift didn't try to engage the two thugs as they surged toward her, but instead swung her Blade for the chains holding the captive to the ceiling. It didn't work, because of course she wasn't storming lucky enough for that. The chains were something the sword couldn't cut.

"Go," the man said. "Run. I'll survive."

Chicken under one arm squawking up a storm, Lift dodged off the bookcase as one of the men swiped for her. She landed near the hole in the ground, and moved to hop down through it, then glanced over her shoulder at the dangling man.

Storm it.

Not today.

She dropped the chicken through the hole, hopefully to safety. It fluttered down. Then, as the thugs reached for her, she began to glow with Light. Enough from breakfast, and snacks, even if she hadn't been eating as much as normal. She made the ground slick, and pushed off between the men. They cursed, but she immediately collided with the bookcase in a stumbling mess of fluttering pages and messy long hair.

"Grab her," the woman said. "Quickly. We need to vacate the tower."

Lift popped up from among the books, then yelped and scrambled back from the two men. She tried to build up speed with her awesomeness, but there wasn't room in this chamber to really do that, or maneuver. She ended up sliding between them and colliding with the small bed, spilling spheres and falling over her own legs.

Storm it, why were things always like this for her?

Why, every time she *thought* she was making progress, did her body betray her? Why couldn't it just *stay the same*? Why couldn't things just *stay as she wanted them*?

She looked back at the men and again thought of running, as the chicken was making a frightened ruckus below. But again she felt stubborn.

Not today.

She'd failed too much lately.

She'd seen her mother in a vision, and that haunted her. She hated the weakness inside that refused to admit, deep down, that she was alone. She hated that she'd gotten Gav in trouble, and couldn't help, because she couldn't figure out how to work with this stupid body that kept growing.

Today, she was *mad.*

They shouldn't have pushed her today. She screamed and kicked off the wall as the thugs got close. Light bubbling up from someplace deep within her, she made the ground slick, and wind moved her hair as she scrambled around the room, building up speed, staying just out of reach until . . .

She slid up onto the wall. Moving by instinct, in a crouch, sliding with one foot, then the other, pushing against the stone with bare skin that was sometimes impossibly slick. Her hair streamed behind her as she rounded the room, confused thugs spinning. As one touched her, she made him slick. His knife dropped from his other hand and his legs went out from underneath him. He went down hard, and Lift spun off across the floor, coming around again and leaping to put both feet into the other fellow's face.

Her feet didn't slide free. They had impossible traction, and remained as if glued there, slamming him backward to the floor by his face as she put her full weight into it. Skull met stone with a crack. She hopped free as the woman met her eyes, and Lift knew . . . somehow *knew* . . . the woman was awesome too. So Lift was ready as the woman came zipping through the room, insanely fast.

The ground became full of traction, and the woman, in her speed, hit the patch. Snaps announced the woman's legs breaking as she put too much force behind her motions, and she tripped as Lift always did.

Lift came to a sliding rest beside the toppled bookcase. Hair falling around her face. None of the three moved. The only sound was that of the chain rotating as the man looked toward her.

Lift stood up, sweat streaming from her, and felt a powerful headache coming on. Wait. That . . . that was *Zahel* hanging there. The sword ardent—she usually saw him when she went to watch the guys training. With the blood and that hair, she hadn't realized . . . She cringed beneath his gaze. Why was he peering at her so intently?

"That was," he said—and she winced at what might come next—"perhaps the most impressive display of raw talent I've ever witnessed."

She . . . slowly uncringed. "What? I fell over myself."

"That woman is a full Feruchemist. You reacted in time despite her manyfold speed enhancement. And the use of Abrasion . . . your manipulation of forces . . ."

Lift looked to Wyndle, who was appearing from his vines as they regrew beside her. He gave a no-shoulder shrug.

"I usually trip," Lift said. "Like, a *lot.* I'm terrible at this."

"You ever seen someone new to Shardplate try to walk, child?" the swordmaster asked.

". . . No?"

"Incredible power," he said, "demands incredible training, otherwise it can manifest as clumsiness." He looked at her, and seemed . . . different. When she'd seen him before, at the practice grounds, he'd always been so *in*different. Now he almost seemed to be *glowing,* not with Stormlight, but with enthusiasm. "You need," he said softly, "a teacher."

"You need," she replied, "some pants."

Some guards finally arrived, and as they were cutting the man down—and she snuggled her chicken—Lift kept thinking back on those words. A teacher. She'd had lots that had *wanted* to teach her. She'd run from them.

Was this different? *Could* this be different? Did she want it to be? That would mean changing.

But everything . . . everything *was* changing, no matter what she decided. Even the Nightwatcher had lied to her. She couldn't pretend she was ten anymore. Pretending she was ten . . .

That had gotten Gav in trouble. Because she refused to grow, and refusing to grow meant refusing to learn. She hated it, but she couldn't. And if she wanted to stop being useless . . .

Maybe . . .

Storms. If everything was going to change, she had to change with it, didn't she? Either that, or she could go sit in a room and complain that she never got to do anything relevant.

That night, after they let her slip out of her illusion for the evening, she found the man at the medical rooms. Now properly clothed, grumping—appropriately—at the way the doctors tried to care for him. Seemed like he had a right good attitude.

He saw her standing in the doorway. Feeling so lanky and awful, she looked away, arms wrapped around herself, but spoke softly.

"How would we start?"

I-14
THE CORRECT FUTURE

Odium turned from Sja-anat's rats in the Spiritual Realm, and focused his attention on Dalinar. All the while, he accepted his sorrow at what he'd done to Kharbranth. Proof must be given of a conviction, or it was no conviction at all.

First Roshar, then the cosmere. The destruction of Kharbranth would be his greatest sacrifice, its loss evidence of commitment. Cultivation had stopped arguing with him, or trying to persuade him. She had made her plays, and had failed.

Now a chull of a man was all that stood in his path. Dalinar's future was cloudy to him though. Just as he hadn't been able to foresee Cultivation's attack on Kharbranth, Taravangian couldn't see this man's choices. Interacting with someone who was tainted by one who saw the future made it more difficult to see—especially in the short term.

As Dalinar trembled, huddled and isolated in the Spiritual Realm, Odium recognized something. His plans would be a grand kindness to this man—a way for Dalinar to obtain his potential. First, though, he needed Dalinar to acknowledge that Odium's way had been the right way all along.

Odium would win the contest, of course, because either outcome served him. But the end he *truly* needed was the one where Dalinar joined him. How to make the man see? How to get him to accept the correct future?

The answer was simple. He had to break his old friend down so he could be rebuilt. Fortunately, Odium had experience at this. Both in hurting Dalinar, and in handling the subsequent pain of being forced to do so.

Indeed, he was growing to be quite expert at it.

DAY EIGHT

SIGZIL • DALINAR • KALADIN • VENLI • JASNAH • SZETH • SHALLAN • ADOLIN

BEWARE the FUSED!

DO NOT ENGAGE! FIND A RADIANT!

I sense I've done a poor job of explaining the exact nature of anti-Light. This might be in part because even I, its discoverer, do not yet understand all the nuances of what I've done, though I do worry the ramifications of it will be felt for ages.

—From *Rhythm of War,* first coda, Navani Kholin

Sigzil led while Narak Three fell.

He ducked away, spear in hand, beneath a sky of constant thunder—and behind him an Unmade finally died. Yelig-nar, who could be born for a short time to wreak terrible devastation before consuming his host, had been dropped right into the middle of Narak Three.

Sigzil and the others had brought him down, leaving the hulking form slumped among a pile of corpses. But this plateau was lost. Enemy Fused filled the place, Yelig-nar having drawn all of the defenders' attention. Sigzil gathered the defenders and fought on, haunted by dreams of Leyten's and Teft's deaths. But standing tall because someone had to, and he had accepted this burden of leadership.

He would grieve later. For the defenders' sake, he could not do so now. He gave the orders, and supervised their forces retreating from Narak Three onto the Oathgate platform. Once Sigzil gave the sign the Stonewards—using some of the last remaining Stormlight—dropped the bridge into the chasm.

Across the gap, on their newly won plateau, the singers rejoiced. They would find a pile of uninfused gemstones in the storehouse they'd won. Hopefully they would think the defenders had simply used up all the Light in the defense, and wouldn't realize the trick Sigzil had pulled.

Sigzil breathed out misting breaths, then drifted back through harder rain than normal. He pulled his raincoat tight and settled onto the battlements of Narak Prime. Since the battle was over, he didn't dare fly too much, as they had to preserve Stormlight.

Storms. He looked through the rain toward the new ranks of Radiants arrayed below, sent by Jasnah for the support of Narak—but he couldn't deploy them. He was limited not by the number of Radiants he had, but by the number of gemstones he could use to equip them. He stood there a long while, feeling the deflation that followed a battle, the winding down of both emotion and muscle. They didn't need him right now, as the logisticians and healers would deal with this part, but he remained where he could be seen.

General Winn eventually joined him on the battlements, climbing with effort in the rain. "Retreat was executed perfectly, Brightlord," the man said. The elderly general wasn't fit enough to hold a weapon himself, but had done a great deal of work behind the scenes to make the retreat go smoothly.

But they still had two days left, and couldn't afford to lose another plateau. Sigzil needed to think of a way to help them last, somehow, despite his distractions.

"General Winn," Sigzil said, watching the soldiers crowd the grounds below, seeking medical attention. Most of his soldiers would have to camp out in the rain now, as they'd lost a great number of their barracks with the abandonment of Narak Three. "How do you deal with the loss of soldiers under your command? Personally, I mean."

"That's a question without many good answers, Brightlord," the older man said, leaning against the battlement beside Sigzil, rain pelting their coats. "At my age . . . well, loss isn't an occasion, but a state of being. Of the forty-five men I served with as officers under Gavilar, I'm the only one left. Same for my siblings. Same for . . . well, most anyone my age."

"I'm sorry," Sigzil said.

"They weren't taken by a traitor before my eyes," Winn said, resting a hand on Sigzil's shoulder. "That makes it hurt more, I'm sure. But let me tell you this: I saw you today leading the defenses, not losing control. You faced loss as an officer must. Be proud of that."

"I don't want to be proud," Sigzil said. "I want to hold as we've been told. But Winn . . . the Stormlight."

"I know. Your spren have any numbers for us?"

"She says," Sigzil replied, "that she expects us to run out of Stormlight sometime today, early tomorrow at the latest, depending on how much we have to fly and how much the Stonewards have to repair the walls."

They fell quiet. Vienta whispered some other numbers in his ear—her estimates of casualties, which were generally accurate. Information that he'd asked for, and that he appreciated, but when added to the falling rain and Winn's general sense of uncertainty . . .

"What do we do?" Sigzil asked.

"Sir," General Winn said, "I . . . am kind of hoping that's something you'll be able to answer. We're going to need a plan. And under the circumstances, it will likely need to be something unconventional. You got us this far. Do you have any more ideas?"

"I'm working on it," Sigzil promised. "But honestly, I'm hoping someone else has a miracle to suggest this time. Once everyone is settled, call a planning meeting."

Chaos.

Shifting faces, but each bloody, each dying.

People Dalinar had known, people he'd fought beside, people he'd killed. Then . . . something new.

A world he didn't know. A distant place where he brought death, destruction, and waste as the Blackthorn, in armor the color of coal. A world of strange beautiful architecture, all aflame; he ground its ashes beneath his heels.

Jolt.

The apparitions vanished, and he was . . . he was in the Kholinar palace? Wearing an Alethi uniform stained by wine on one cuff, the top buttons of the jacket undone. Around him, ardents in grey robes brought food to common people seated in rows on the floor. A Beggars' Feast? Yes . . . yes, they'd often had these during Gavilar's reign.

"Hey," someone said, slapping him on the shoulder. "Rortel. I got some. Let's go."

Rortel . . . that had been one of Dalinar's elites. He'd died in an early plateau assault, but this was before that, and Dalinar apparently wore his body. The man who spoke to him was Malan, a tall green-eyed fellow with dark curly hair—a member of the Cobalt Guard. He carried a jug of wine.

"*Come on,*" Malan repeated. "Let's go."

Dalinar let himself be pulled from his seat. Storms. Dalinar . . . knew this night, didn't he? It was a night where he had failed. He followed Malan through the doorway, past a beggar sitting outside by the wall. Dalinar stopped, because he knew this beggar. It was Ahu, his drinking buddy.

"Jezrien," Dalinar whispered, kneeling by the disheveled man, his beard grown long, his hair dirty and full of knots. "Blood of my fathers . . . it *is* you. All those years, I never recognized you . . ." The king of Heralds had been here, this night of all nights.

Jezrien took his hand. "Have you seen me?"

"Yes," Dalinar said. "I see you now, my friend."

"The man I was," Jezrien said. "He escaped me. I let him go, like leaves before a storm. Have you seen him? I . . . would be him again. Please."

Dalinar squeezed the Herald's hand, but it was just a vision and Malan grabbed him by the shoulder. "Come on. Dalinar wants that wine."

"Dalinar," Dalinar said, "has had *plenty* of wine. He didn't need to send us to steal some from the Beggars' Feast. He's an embarrassment to his name."

Malan pulled him to his feet. "Watch what you say. We have orders."

"Orders given by a drunkard," Dalinar said, exhausted. "I don't need to see this day again—I lived it."

Malan looked at him as if he were mad, and perhaps he was. Then shouts rose in the near distance. Malan went on the alert, gripping his sword.

Dalinar instead knelt by Jezrien again. "I know you're not real," Dalinar whispered to him, "but I *have* seen the man you were. He wasn't perfect, but he did his best to protect us. Thank you."

The beggar regarded him, and seemed to grow lucid for a moment. "Have you seen yourself?"

"I think I am about to," Dalinar said.

"Don't lose him," Jezrien said, urgently. "Don't let go of him." He gazed upward. "I can sometimes feel where I need to be . . . so I came here . . ."

Soldiers dashed down the hallway, yelling that an assassin was heading toward the king's chamber. They would be too late, Dalinar knew, and for that they should be grateful. Szeth, possessing powers that hadn't been seen in Alethkar for two thousand years, had slaughtered all who stood against him.

"We have to rouse the Blackthorn," Malan said, again taking Dalinar firmly by the shoulder. "Let's go."

Dalinar let himself be taken. In truth, he remembered little of this part of the night. Because . . .

Because there he was in the feast hall, where the news of the attack hadn't yet reached. Dancers were retreating, chatting to one another, and the Parshendi drums sat abandoned. People talked in the dimmer light of shielded gemstones, and a woman played a flute among spinning musicspren.

Dalinar slumped alone at one of the lower tables, his head down on the wood as he grumbled that the serving staff—on Navani's orders—refused to bring him anything more to drink. He pointed at the soldiers as they arrived. "You found some?" he said, each word slurred. "Give me."

"Sir, you're needed!" Malan said. "There's an assassin—"

"Give. Me. Drink," younger Dalinar demanded. "I can still hear her. I want her *gone.*"

He fumbled for the jug of wine while Dalinar—older Dalinar—looked on in revulsion. Most people drank a little too much now and then, but this was something else: A man who could not be trusted. A man who had long ago betrayed himself and everyone who loved him—and would soon reap his reward.

This was a man Dalinar hated. Both versions of him agreed on that point. Seeing his younger self like this made him sick.

"Sir," Malan said as young Dalinar took a pull straight from the jug, "you need to—"

Older Dalinar slapped his younger self, making him spit wine. Malan backed away, shocked, as this was not normal behavior from his friend—both were quite effective enablers. Young Dalinar bellowed at the insult, stumbling to his feet. When he lunged, older Dalinar—one hand casually behind his back—sidestepped, then slapped him soundly across the face again.

When younger Dalinar came in roaring, older Dalinar caught him by the front of his wine-stained shirt. "Your brother is dying," older Dalinar said. "Right now."

Younger Dalinar looked at him, blinked red eyes, and it seemed to sink in. "Gavilar."

"Is being murdered," older Dalinar said.

"Gavilar?" Younger Dalinar pulled free of the grip and stumbled toward the door. He toppled to the floor halfway there. Falling into an unconscious stupor.

Brother, follow the Codes tonight . . .

Dalinar heaved a sigh, shaking his head. "What a disgrace." His words made couples shy away, and Malan went running, probably to try to help the king. He was a good soldier, when properly led.

"Curious," a voice said, thrumming through the walls, making the entire vision shake. "The man you were. Such an embarrassment. Does it hurt to see it?"

"I know what I was," Dalinar said, standing tall. "I know I can never escape it, because I cannot bring Gavilar back. But I keep taking steps! You hear me. I *keep taking*—"

The vision shifted. In the blink of an eye, he was in another room. Cold, with Gavilar's corpse lying on a table. Older Dalinar did remember this—when he woke from his stupor, and was brought here to see . . .

Younger Dalinar stumbled down the steps into the room, then howled. Older Dalinar winced, despite what he'd said earlier, looking away as his younger self rushed to the body, then hugged it, heedless of the blood. Weeping with a raw pain that . . .

Storms, he knew that pain. It . . . did still hurt, all these years later. Like a wound that some surgeon had dug into with knife and forceps.

Brother, follow the Codes tonight . . .

"Grampa?" a voice said from behind him.

Storms. One of the guards. Gav? Yes, the child was standing among the guards, unseen by Dalinar at first. Dalinar immediately pushed forward, seizing Gav as the realm again went dark and shifting.

"Grampa," Gav whispered. "You found me. Who was that dead man? Why were there two of you?"

"The dead man was your other grandpa, Gav," Dalinar said. "My brother, the man you were named after. I . . . let him die."

"Like . . . you had to let Daddy die?"

Dalinar closed his eyes, holding the child tight as the Spiritual Realm became chaos again.

"Everyone dies," Gav whispered. "We see so many people. Killing. And dying. And killing. And dying. Gram says these pretends happened long ago. So many being killed . . ."

Storms. Dalinar clutched the child, thinking how it must be for him, seeing the Desolations. After a lifetime on the battlefield, Dalinar was familiar with its destruction. Maybe . . . maybe desensitized. He should have thought more about the child.

"There will be peace, Gav," Dalinar promised. "That's what I'm working for—what you and I are fighting for."

"Will there?" Gav whispered, his head against Dalinar's chest. "I don't see it, Grampa. When I open my eyes, I see us fighting forever, and ever, and ever . . . And I have to be a soldier. I have to be strong and fight . . . like you."

"There *will* be an end, Gav. I'll find it."

Holding Gav, with a storm of uncertainty around him, Dalinar finally understood something about himself. The drive that had first sent him looking for Bondsmiths to train under, then into the Spiritual Realm . . . it had been spurred by a growing distrust of the Stormfather and Honor, and of this plan to bind Odium.

Dalinar opened his eyes, and confronted it. The power swirling around him was Honor's power—which refused to bond to another person. In it he saw death and destruction, and now—repeated over and over—he saw the vision he'd lived earlier. Humankind betraying Mishram. Again and again.

"What happens," Dalinar asked the power, "if we make peace? If I win the contest?"

He saw it play out in a thousand different ways. Mankind would *break* that peace. Of course they would—Odium would ensure they did. Yes, Odium would keep his part. But he would insult, he would demean. He would enslave the humans in his lands, grinding them into the ground until their relatives in free countries demanded retribution. And war started again, for while a god could not break his word, humans could.

Humans always could . . .

"It doesn't have to be like that," Dalinar whispered. "Nothing we see *has* to be . . ."

Yet it seemed a sham to him now. Peace via contract? Even if he secured it, they'd circle back to this problem in the future. The same cycle he'd seen play out time, and time, and time, and time again in these visions. Death, destruction, fighting, war.

There would be no peace until the root problem was dealt with. And this treaty was no more than putting a bandage on a gut wound. Honor's plan was flawed. It *always had been.*

"That's why I need you," Dalinar said to the power swirling around him. "I need the strength to deal with Odium personally, to end the war at its very *roots*!"

"You?" a voice said, a shadow falling over him. It was Odium's voice from earlier, in the vision. Different from when he'd heard it before. Now faintly familiar . . . "You, Dalinar Kholin, think *you* can make peace? You break everything you touch. You took the throne from Elhokar, then sent him to die. You want to be a god because you want *power.*"

"No," Dalinar said, frowning. "You don't know me. You—"

Odium's strength swept across him, and ripped Gav from his arms. It sent Dalinar tumbling through darkness. Visions began to assault him, relentless, knocking down his defenses—his confidence wearing thin.

And Dalinar Kholin knew what it was to be in Damnation itself.

Some might assume that Light and anti-Light are opposites, as can be found in philosophy, though not truly in actual physical science. Hot banishes and destroys cold. Light banishes and destroys dark. Likewise, one might say that Light and anti-Light are opposites in that they are mutually destructive.

—From *Rhythm of War*, first coda, Navani Kholin

Kaladin tried to retain the peaceful feelings from the night before, but those evaporated as the group approached the Dustbringer monastery. Instead he felt . . . determination? Resignation? Something in between?

Would Szeth fight here, or would he refuse? Hold to the morals he'd begun to find for himself, or bow before the pressure of expectations? Kaladin had done all he could to prepare the man, but so had Nale.

Conceptually, Kaladin was fine with Szeth deciding he needed to kill the Honorbearers to protect his people. Yet something about this whole situation itched at him. If he'd been in Szeth's place, he'd feel manipulated. They didn't know the whole story, and killing when you didn't have the whole story . . . *that* made him uncomfortable, so he could fully understand Szeth wanting to stop. Storm it, if he wanted to stop, Szeth should *have that right.*

They wound up a switchback, hiking through some highlands on the border between Shinovar and eastern lands. Syl had flown on ahead. Nale, who seemed never to get tired, stood atop a ridge above. And as Kaladin finally arrived, sweaty, he resisted the urge to draw in Stormlight. If Nale could do this without it, so could Kaladin. Indeed, it was good to get some physical exercise to keep his body strong.

At least the view was spectacular: looking back, he saw a verdant landscape adorned by lakes and rivers. From up here, it seemed less alien. More . . . pastoral. A giant panorama like a painted canvas, with mountains in the distance, clouds and that river of spren far overhead, less visible in the daylight than it had been at night. Those clouds were gorgeous too, letting sunlight break through to highlight its favorite parts of the landscape.

The ridge here was soil, not rock. What prevented it from simply melting down in the rain? Was there solid mountain rock beneath this, like the spine of a person under their skin? He'd always imagined there was, but Szeth talked as if the soil went down, down, down. Like an ocean, the depths of which were unknowable.

"Look at it," Nale said softly as Szeth, last up the switchback, joined them. "This is a land of ancient laws, carried with us from a better place. This land became a shard of the old world where we once lived. Its rules run deep, deep as the bones of your ancestors. People I knew, spoke with, laughed with, are buried here, seven thousand years dead. This is your heritage, Szeth."

"Wait," Kaladin said. "Because laws are old, they're good?"

"You would discard the wisdom of your elders?" Nale asked.

"My elders were shockingly keen on things like slavery," Kaladin said. "I don't revere anything or anyone *just* because of age."

"Do not dismiss their wisdom because of their faults, Stormblessed," Nale said. "Sometimes we see farther as we age. Our posture shrinking, our thoughts elevating."

Unfortunately, there was some truth in that. The Radiant orders were ancient, and he'd grown immeasurably because of the way their oaths made him stretch. The Words weren't easy, and they hurt, but they were right. At the same time though . . .

Well, he'd seen too much to blindly trust that the people in charge were there for a reason. A lot of laws and rules were the same—retaining their positions by merit of momentum, not virtue. If true nobility wasn't of blood, but of the heart, as Dalinar said . . . then good traditions would be valuable because of what they offered, not because they merely existed.

But how to explain all of that? In a way that didn't make his words stumble over one another?

"I'll make my own choices," Kaladin said. "Based on what I see and experience."

"Your perspective is flawed."

"No more so than anyone else's. No more so than the people who made these laws, Nale. That's what I keep saying."

"No," Nale said. "*I* keep telling you these laws go back to something greater."

"Is that why you follow them, then?" Kaladin asked. "I still don't get it, Nale."

"I do what is right because it is right."

Kaladin ground his teeth. He needed to change the way he did this. Logic didn't work with Nale, and never would. Kaladin couldn't *argue* someone out of being mentally ill. Any more than someone could *argue* him out of feeling bad. So what *had* worked?

Certain skills—like being able to resist his own thoughts—had helped him, with time and practice. That wasn't something someone else could do for Nale though. Really, the things that had helped Kaladin the most were the times when Adolin had listened. Had just . . . talked to him.

He remembered how the Wind loved Nale. A weathered hero who had seen millennia . . .

"Maybe you're right, Nale," Kaladin said. "You've seen so much more than the rest of us. I'll admit, maybe I haven't listened to you enough. Could you tell me about some of the best parts of being a Herald, maybe from the early days?"

Nale eyed him, as if sensing a trap. However, he also seemed pleased to have won the argument. As they continued hiking eastward—toward some trees growing along the slopes—he started talking. And Kaladin caught Szeth watching intently.

"The early days were some of the hardest," Nale said. "We didn't yet know how the Surges interacted with Roshar. And the people? They lived difficult lives back then, Stormblessed. In huts and dirt. Or . . . crem . . ." His eyes unfocused a little and he swept out with a hand. "I remember my first rebirth. I'd joined the Heralds uncertainly, but that Return convinced me. The war between humans and singers had become so bad so quickly. Odium persuading good singers they had to slaughter every human to ever have peace.

"The best of them refused. Did you know that? We don't talk about it. Odium killed so many of them before he and Honor made their pact not to intervene directly. Odium executed singers who wouldn't kill for him, and over centuries built groups of them trained only for death. It was particularly bad those early years, but . . ."

He halted in place.

"But?" Kaladin asked.

"I stopped them," Nale whispered. "I stood between darkness and life, and I was the light . . ."

"Do you remember how that felt?" Kaladin asked.

"Painful," Nale said. "But *glorious.* I wasn't always so harsh, you know. I spoke of it to Lift. I should like to see her again . . . something about that child . . . always outside my reach, taunting me with who I used to be . . ."

Nale stared ahead. He actually appeared to *think* about this, cocking his head.

"I do remember . . ." Nale said. "That feeling . . ."

"We should talk about that!" Kaladin said. "When you—"

"I was flawed then," Nale said, with a dismissive wave of his fingers. "I have learned and grown this last year."

"But—"

"No more of this conversation."

Damnation. Kaladin had felt so close—and he was a fool for stepping in, too eager to help, speaking when he should have remained quiet. Still, it hinted at possible progress. That getting through to Nale wasn't so much about persuading him that he was wrong, but about reminding him of the person he'd been.

"It doesn't matter anyway," Szeth said, his soft voice interrupting from behind. "The past is dead, Kaladin. I must think of the task ahead of me. There is an Unmade here, disrupting our laws and our ways. I must focus on stopping it."

"That is true," Nale said after a moment's thought. "An Unmade has no jurisdiction in Shinovar. If you find one here, you can legally do as you see fit." Nale turned to Szeth. "You are Truthed: one who fights for what is right, bearing the traditions and history of your people like a crown.

"You are a Bearer of Honor. Your original Blade was stolen, but now you carry six more. Blades that, with Jezrien's death, no longer anchor the Oathpact—and which are no longer bound to any Herald. They are yours, Szeth. You are the product of generations of preparation."

"Truthed," Szeth whispered. "Szeth-son-Neturo. Truthed of Shinovar . . ."

"I trust you to make the correct decision." Nale turned and began walking.

Another dramatic walkaway. Kaladin sighed, then patted Szeth on the shoulder. Together they followed, passing some very strange trees. They were green and cone-shaped. How did they know to grow in that shape? And the leaves? They were little spikes. What was *wrong* with this place? Every time he felt he was getting used to it and coming to appreciate its beauty, he found something like this.

Their walk brought them to another small town, one with a stone wall, nestled among the trees atop the hill. The gate was open, and as they entered, Kaladin saw the telltale signs: furtive movements at the windows of barracks. Doors that shook as people pressed close to listen. A certain . . . darkness in the air. Not quite a shimmering, but *something*.

This place was corrupted. That Unmade had hold of the Honorbearer here. And storm it, Kaladin worried he had led Szeth wrong. This place did need help. Why should Kaladin be encouraging Szeth to stop fighting?

Because he wants to, Kaladin reaffirmed. *And every soldier should have the option to put down their spear if they choose to and are willing to pay the cost.*

Kaladin had accepted and embraced his calling as a watcher at the rim. He did it *so that* others could choose, through no act of cowardice, to live differently. If Szeth wanted to step down, they'd figure out what to do next.

It was the meaning of "journey before destination." And Kaladin *believed* it.

That would have to be enough.

⁂

As Venli's expedition of listeners finally reached the central plateaus—sneaking through the chasms amid wobbling rainspren—the signs of the battle above became more and more pronounced. Figures leaping in groups across the gaps. Shouts and screams to match the beat of the lightning and thunder. Corpses floating in the rivers. Fused. Radiants. The best of Roshar, murdering one another yet again in an unbreakable chain of death.

The chasmfiends wanted to eat the dead, but they refrained at the request of Venli and the others. This did confuse the beasts, however. Surely eating *dead* things was fine. Humans and singers didn't taste that good, but they'd do. Fortunately, they soon found a few fallen chulls—likely from ranching efforts on one of the plateaus—that had been spooked and run off a ledge.

Venli stood with the Five, water flowing around their thighs, as they decided their next move.

"I feel it just ahead," she explained. "Maybe two plateaus over that way."

"That's the heart of Narak itself," Thude said to Anxiety.

"It's calling to us," said Estel, a newer member of the Five, who had chosen to hold nimbleform. They no longer each bore a different form; that had proven impractical. Plus there were more than five known forms. "It sheltered us during our exile. It calls to us for a reason."

"I'm worried," Venli whispered to the Terrors. "Last time I did anything like this, I was playing into Odium's hands. I did it *willingly.* I knew what I was doing. I . . . I wasn't deceived. I have to admit that. But this time, maybe I am? Maybe this is some kind of signal meant to draw us in." She put her hands to her head, rubbing at the roots of her hairstrands. "I can't shake a dreadful rhythm. I'm scared."

"Do you reject him?" Bila asked softly.

"Yes," Venli whispered. "After what he did to our people? I reject him who would be our god."

"Then he cannot control you," Bila said.

"I wish that were so," said Kivor, a hulking malen in warform. "But he is crafty, and takes some unaware. Eshonai would not have gone willingly to him if she'd fully known what she was doing. We five should vote. Yes, we've come all this way, but to think we can't turn around now is foolishness."

"I could go ahead without you," Venli said. "In case it's a trap."

"We vote," Kivor said, firm. "Thude. What say you? Do we go on? See what this mystery is, even if it might destroy us?"

"I vote yes," Thude said. "If it destroys us, so be it, but we must find the answers."

"Why?" Bila asked, her face shrouded in darkness, for they dared not use gemstones here. Overhead, humans shouted and Windrunners streaked through the air. "Why do we *need* answers?"

"Because we'll be destroyed without them," a voice said from behind them. They turned, looking at another shadow—though Leshwi's voice announced who she was. "What are we? Some thousand, against the might of Odium? We shall need some way to resist. I can't help thinking that whatever you're hearing . . . it's been sent to us for a purpose."

None of the Heavenly Ones could hear the sound. Just Venli and—for some reason—the chasmfiends.

"I . . ." Leshwi continued, then she blinked, her eyes starting to glow red. "Odium is offering his power to all who are here fighting. I could not resist. I'm sorry. I do not think he saw me individually or knows I am here."

"It took me months to learn to fully reject him," Venli said. "We did not expect you to do it in a week, Leshwi."

"I should be held to a higher standard," Leshwi said. "I am Fused. I am immortal. I—"

"Think of yourself as young again, Lady Leshwi," Venli said gently, to Peace. Though admittedly, there *was* a part of her that felt a thrill at being able to speak commandingly to one who had held such power over her. "You are starting over. Right now, the important question is: Will your nature give us away? Will he see you if you remain with us?"

"I honestly don't know," she said. "I and the others should hold back a little from what you do next."

It was a wise offer. They accepted it, then the rest of the Five voted one at a time. It was unanimous to continue. They did not ask Venli for her vote, as she did not lead, even if she'd guided them this far. Leaving the Heavenly Ones and the chasmfiends behind for now, Venli and the other fourteen listeners crept inward.

That tone thundered in her ears. It was . . . it was ahead . . . but *down* . . .

They reached the central plateau itself. Above, the humans had set up watchposts hanging over the chasms. They were tattered and broken, presumably damaged in the battle. Perhaps they had been used in an effort to spot Deepest Ones. Nervously, Venli peeked into Shadesmar to see if any Fused were nearby, but found only an expanse of beads—with glowing flames higher up, representing the fighting humans and singers.

Except . . . the beating . . . was *lower.* Beneath the beads. Beneath the *ground.*

"What?" Thude whispered.

"It's underneath us," Venli whispered. She pressed her hand against the chasm wall as she crouched in the flowing water.

Yes, the stones said to her. *You are nearly here.*

Closing her eyes, she drew in Stormlight. Rock flowed like water, pushing back the river as it rose up on the sides, creating a hole in the wall that was protected from the stream by a lip. She climbed in, and peered down a tunnel that led far beneath the ground.

A light shone at the distant end. She looked to the Five. Thude appointed the remaining nine to stay back and watch, then—humming to Determination—Venli and the Five started into the tunnel.

⁂

Jasnah and Fen agreed on a compromise. Their Radiants had left Thaylen City through the Oathgate to support the beleaguered forces on the Shattered Plains. She wished she could get them to Adolin and Yanagawn, but with the Oathgate there in enemy hands, the corrupted spren refused to accept transfers.

Hopefully the Shattered Plains could use them, though she worried about their Stormlight reserves—with her mother and uncle still absent, and Wit being cagey about when they might return. In addition, the compromise with Fen required the bulk of Jasnah's conventional troops to remain at Thaylen City. It would take costly Stormlight to get them transferred—so the Radiants made sense as the first step.

As she stood outside the Oathgate platform—watching it flash with light as the last batch of Radiants vanished—she considered the wobbling knees of their coalition. Too few troops had been sent to Azimir. Fen's arguments—that the bulk of the Alethi forces would soon arrive to help defend the capital—had seemed sound. Except that Emul and Tashikk had turned on them, shockingly, and attacked those troops.

She felt like she should have seen that. It was a huge political upheaval, the final shattering of the Azish Empire, and she still reeled from it happening in this day and age. But it was even more horrifying in context. Jasnah sat on troops that weren't needed, while Adolin—according to the regular updates she received from May Aladar—fought desperately, low on resources, isolated without a functional Oathgate.

The Crzmak Stability, she thought, turning and walking through the city, wearing her uniform, unaccompanied by bodyguards. She'd sent those with the Radiants to support Sigzil. Some centuries ago, a coalition had risen among the squabbling families of Thaylenah, led by the charismatic explorer Crzmak. Its fate was an example of how the best intentions could go wrong when resources grew tight.

Fen wanted to make absolutely certain that her city didn't fall—and who could blame her? In her eyes the Shattered Plains were expendable. Yet if they lost the Shattered Plains, Urithiru lost autonomy—the farms, forests, and ranching efforts there were essential to supply the city. Jasnah had begun to imagine a new Alethkar at the Shattered Plains—a place for her people outside of Urithiru.

Without the Shattered Plains . . . they'd have to rely on Thaylen City to ship resources in via Oathgate. Fen promised no tariffs, and Jasnah believed her. But what about the merchant council? What about their heirs? She shook her head, walking back to her base of operations on this tier—the old temple. Ivory was off secretly listening to Fen report to the Thaylen Council, accompanied by Brightlord and Brightlady Bethab—Urithiru's ambassadors to the city.

Jasnah had sent Ivory because although she trusted Fen as much as she trusted anyone, she'd still like to know exactly what the woman said. At her desk in the temple, Jasnah began digging out her projections about what might happen at the Shattered Plains. As moving clouds darkened the windows, she fished in her pocket for spheres. Battle was . . . so much more messy than she'd expected. Why did everyone speak so much of the grand execution of battlefield strategy, if it rarely went as planned?

The room grew even darker. Those clouds were—

"I had hoped," a soft voice said, "that you wouldn't realize the ships were empty. When did you send Windrunners to check? Odd, how it's so easy to see anything, yet miss so much."

Jasnah froze, ice bathing her veins. She looked up, and saw that the darkness falling over the room had come not from clouds, but from a shadow cloaking the front of the chamber: a black mist with a strange golden light at the core, tinged red on the outsides. It billowed forward like an Everstorm front.

The words came from within.

Her mouth went dry. Fearspren wiggled like globs at her feet, despite her best efforts. "Odium. You cannot touch me. Not without violating your pact and opening yourself to attack."

"Wit has explained well, I see," the cloud said. "Do not fear, Jasnah. I'm not here to hurt you, but to compliment you. I was worried you might see through my ruse with the ships. You have that way about you."

Jasnah backed away from the table and summoned her armor. It formed around her in a flash, clamping into place, pressing her clothing tight. Odium couldn't hurt her directly—Wit was certain of that—but where there was a whitespine, you often found pups. He might not be alone.

"Jasnah," Odium said. Was that voice . . . familiar? "You were right to send your Radiants away. I will take this city, but not by military force."

The dark mists coalesced.

Into Taravangian.

"Thaylen City will fall by tomorrow evening," the figure said. "I've come to see to it personally."

. . . In mathematics, we have negative numbers—an impossible reality, yet an extremely useful model, as explained by the woman who developed them. Negative one balances with one to create zero, both evening out at nothing.

—From *Rhythm of War,* first coda, Navani Kholin

It was good to be back at the Dustbringer monastery, Szeth thought, breathing in the scent of the pines. He hadn't realized how much he'd missed this place. An open sky. A refreshing breeze. Ice skating on the pond.

. . . And then he says that he helped build a huge fortress! Nightblood was saying as they walked. *A huge one! Big, big, big! And others joined in. They did it even before there were Radiants! Isn't that deevy? Stoneshaping is deevy.*

"Is that another word of Lift's?" Szeth said, smiling.

Yup! She knows the best words. They sound so much more fun, don't they, than regular words? Oh! Do you think we'll see her tonight at dinner?

"No, sword-nimi," Szeth said, gently reminding. "She is thousands of miles away. That is a long distance."

Oh! Right. Right. Deevy. Hey, the swords say they're almost home. What does that mean?

Szeth shook his head and unstrapped his pack. "I don't know, I'm afraid." Then, speaking louder, he handed the swords to Kaladin. "Take care of them. Nin-son-God, do I need to worry about two Honorbearers attacking me today?"

"No," Nin said. "Your test today is of a different sort. You will face only one foe."

"The former Honorbearer was elderly," Szeth said. "I assume Gearil-daughter-Gearil has passed? I will face a new, younger Bearer?"

"Yes," Nin admitted.

"Good," Szeth said, considering his plan. Syl came down from the sky, where she'd been watching the roadway of spren.

"It's so odd up there . . ." she said, landing—full sized, as she almost always was these days. "Only nature and emotion spren are there. No Radiant spren, unbonded or otherwise. They all are still on the other side, but in such quantities it makes the air glow here."

"Kaladin, Sylphrena," Szeth said to them, "I would not like your help today."

"But," Kaladin said, "if you—"

"No help, please," Szeth said.

Nearby, Nin nodded in approval.

"This is one of my favorite monasteries," Szeth said, "and a skill at which I excelled. I . . . can find my own way here."

Kaladin reluctantly nodded and took the pack of swords. Szeth turned to the monastery, built in the classic style: a large stone block with slits for windows, standing on a hill in the town, which was dressed up by the appealing surroundings and those wonderful trees. But it was just a fortress. One that hadn't served its function, as it had been corrupted from within.

Szeth summoned his Shardblade as he walked. "You've been quiet lately."

I've been thinking, his spren said.

"About?"

About what it means to swear oaths, the spren explained. *About the best way to help you.*

"And?" Szeth asked, stopping in the doorway.

I think . . . I need more time.

It was remarkable that a highspren should need time to think. Szeth peered into the monastery's grand hall, noting the glowing gemstones on the walls, then the lone figure all the way on the other end. The person—female, judging by the fit of her grey robes—was swathed in cloth wrapping even her head and face.

Szeth made his decision. He reached to the side and dropped his sword. Dismissing it.

"I will not fight you," he said into the room.

He did not look to see Nin's or Kaladin's reactions. He was not choosing either of their ways. He was . . . testing his options. That was all. But in one thing Kaladin was correct.

What Szeth *had* been doing was destroying him.

"Szeth," his spren hissed, forming a rift by his head, "what are you *doing*?"

"Something is wrong," Szeth said. "Something big. How did my people—

Honorbearers included—allow an Unmade to entice them? Why did no others resist as I did? How did my *father,* who became grand senator of our people, get taken in? It's never made any sense to me—and I once decided the only reasonable assumption was that I'd seen things wrong. That I *was* Truthless. Yet Nin names me Truthed. So how could all this have happened?"

The figure approached, her Honorblade appearing in her fingers. The Dustbringer Blade, with a strange slit down the middle and a great deal of ornamentation around the hilt. Her footsteps left burning imprints in the floor. He'd learned that particular intimidation trick.

"Szeth!" his spren said. "I really think you should fight!"

"No one will tell me the truth," Szeth said. "A pilgrimage, for what? Why do the Honorbearers vanish to smoke when I kill them?"

The Dustbringer started running.

"Szeth!" the spren said. "*Szeth!*"

"I am not smart enough to figure out what is happening, but I'm not going to fight. I'm going to find answers."

The figure reached him, sword out and trailing fire. Another trick to intimidate. She drew close enough to swing, and when she did, Szeth Lashed himself to the side just enough to dodge.

A set of swings followed, four sweeping attacks, each dodged with his powers. She moved in, using the Dustbringer Surges to alter her traction on the ground—sometimes sliding easily, sometimes gaining purchase in an instant and leaping forward with powerful lunges.

He dodged them all.

He knew these tricks. When she set the air alight, he held his breath, as it wasn't terribly dangerous, no matter how flashy. So much of being a Dustbringer was about intimidation. True, with the right preparation, she could fill the air in an enclosed space with wood dust and then set it alight to create an incredible explosion. But he saw this woman's tutor in her attacks. Flashes and burning motions intended to distract, so that a well-timed sword thrust could do the true damage. If not that, catch them unaware and use Division on them directly.

He did not fall for the feints. He dodged, sometimes flying, sometimes burning the ground or setting wood alight before she could turn it into explosive dust.

"What is this about?" he asked her softly. "You're new to this calling. Newer, at least. Tell me."

She growled, snapping her fingers, letting fire burn around her in a puff. You could only do that so much, as it drew water from the air, creating a gas you could set alight. Gearil-daughter-Gearil had loved such shows. However, so long as he did not permit this woman to touch him or the ground he stood upon, he should mostly be safe from Division. It could be an extremely destructive talent, but was less valuable in a duel than it was in battle, where close proximity could allow you to set entire swaths of ground and people aflame.

He dodged the next sweeping attacks, and he sensed frustration in the Honorbearer's strikes. He was beginning to see how much his terrible existence had improved his skills. These Honorbearers, despite their training, had little *practical* experience with death and destruction—yet death and destruction had been Szeth's life ever since his exile began. He'd found, and fought, his equals in people like Kaladin.

He had begun as one of the best that Shinovar had ever created, and he'd long since surpassed that.

"*Fight* me," the woman snapped as he dodged.

Wait.

"How did you know?" she hissed. "You humiliate me!"

It couldn't be.

Szeth landed, meeting the Honorbearer's gaze as she dashed up to him. He formed his Blade in a heartbeat and raised it, absently blocking her strike at his neck. He leaned forward and looked straight into her eyes.

It *was.*

"I will not fight you," he whispered. "I will not *kill* you. Do as you must."

He tossed his sword once more and sat down.

"Szeth!" his spren cried.

The Honorbearer swung for him again, her hands trembling. The Blade stopped right before it hit his neck.

He met her eyes as she stood there, and he could see the conflict inside. She gathered her strength, gripped the Blade in two hands, and swung yet again—but again she pulled up short before actually striking him.

"Did they all let me win?" Szeth asked. "Has this all been some sham to make me *think* I'm accomplishing something?"

"No, Szeth!" his spren said in his ear. "They're all supposed to try to kill you!"

The figure backed away, grunting softly, then ran toward him again as if trying to *force* herself to attack. She couldn't do it though, and drew back, stalking around him in a circle.

"Szeth," his spren said, "listen to me. You've come to the wrong conclusion. Something strange *is* happening, but it's not what you think. These Honorbearers are supposed to fight you with whatever they have. Do you think being pulled into Shadesmar was a sham?"

"No," he agreed. Each of those previous fights had felt desperate to him, and at the last monastery someone had tried to knife him in the back. They wanted him dead.

But this woman . . . he was right about her. And beyond, he was just so *tired* of the killing.

"Why?" he asked the figure stalking around him. "Why do *you* hold back?" She yanked the cloth from her head, exposing short-cropped brown hair and a face—aged, as his had. Harder. Thicker of neck. Scarred. But so familiar.

"Elid," he said. Evidently his sister had chosen to train, as she'd always wanted.

"Fight me, Szeth!"

"No."

"You broke our family! You destroyed our name. Stories about you have chased me all my life. Truthless, they whispered, as if you were a *disease* that could spread." She whipped up her sword toward him. "Fight!"

"Elid . . ." He climbed to his feet.

"Mother is dead," she snapped. "Did you know that? Tumors. Dead. Gone. You weren't here. I had to hold her hand."

He hesitated.

"Father . . ." Elid said, looking away. "Father is dead. Taken by . . . the Voice . . ."

Szeth felt a strange sense of calm, knowing that Elid could kill him, and he would not fight back. He remembered *wishing* someone would kill him, not long ago. His thoughts were . . . more complicated now. But at the same time, this relief, this . . . this emotion. It was . . .

It was calm. He was *calm.* Even the voices grew softer.

He . . . he was done. He was finally *done.*

He stood and stepped forward, holding out his hands. She lifted her sword to the side of his neck, but he could see from how it trembled that she didn't want to harm him. So he leaned forward until she dismissed the Blade, and as it vanished to mist, he embraced her.

"I'm supposed to kill you," she whispered. "I won my own Blade after you left. To prove I wasn't weak, *I* wasn't Truthless. In the end, your leaving wasn't enough. You still ruined my life."

"I'm sorry."

"I . . . am taken by it too," she said. "The darkness. The Voice. You know it?"

"I do."

"I can't think, Szeth. I didn't want to think. Why did you drop your sword and sit down like that? Why would you *ever* do that? Even if you recognized my voice, you must know that I was ready to kill you. Why did you trust that I wouldn't?"

"I didn't, Elid. I just decided to be done."

"Hell of a time to decide that," she said, holding to him.

"An excellent time, actually."

Her grip on him tightened. "Listen," she said. "I feel like years have passed in a blink, in a daze. You have to stop it. You have to free us."

"How?"

"I don't know. But maybe if you do it . . . if you succeed . . ."

"Succeed at *what*?"

"They haven't told you?" She pulled back, and started to *unravel.* Turning to dark mist, dying. "You don't know?"

"Know what?" Szeth asked, clinging to her hands. "Why am I here, Elid?"

"The Oathpact is broken," she said, her face distorting. "He's summoning me, to try to stop me, but I *know.* The circle is shattered. The Heralds degrade. They need someone new. They need . . . you, Szeth. This pilgrimage, it's an *audition.* Jezrien is dead. And you are to take his—" She went stiff, then completely vanished.

Her sword clanged to the ground in the empty monastery, and he was left holding air.

"I had worried about that one," Nin said from behind. "Ishar said she would be likely to kill you because of her long-building anger. She proved to be . . . weaker than we'd hoped."

Szeth turned, livid. "You used my sister against me?"

"You must be strong," Nin said, darkening the gateway into the monastery, "to take up this mantle."

"To be a Herald?" Szeth said. "Were you going to *ask* me?"

"None of us asked for this," Nin replied. "We did what was needed. As you always have."

"It's *true*?" Kaladin said, stepping around Nin. "You're looking for . . . for another *Herald.*"

"To hold back the tide of evil," Nin said, "the Oathpact must be sure and whole."

"Wait," Syl said, appearing full sized next to Kaladin. "Will a new Oathpact even *do* anything? The Fused came back this time because of the Everstorm, right?"

"The Fused Returned because Taln broke," Nin said. "The Everstorm was brought in, along with gemstones bearing spren, in order to quicken the process of rebirth—and to make it easier to give forms of power. We do not know what would have happened if Taln had not broken before the Everstorm arrived. Ishar explained this to me."

"So you don't know," Syl said, pointing. "You don't *know* that re-forming the Oathpact will actually *achieve* anything. The Everstorm, the methods of physically bringing Voidspren through Shadesmar, might make it meaningless."

"We must try regardless," Nin said. "Ishar says the only way to stop the Fused is to use our souls to lock them away, as part of an oath. If we had a new member, an unparalleled warrior, as Jezrien was—a man with no attachments to this world, a man who always does what is needed . . ."

Syl folded her arms, and seemed unconvinced. "I thought you *wanted* the singers to win."

Szeth frowned, looking to him, still feeling . . . warm from his sister's embrace. It was a good question.

Nin cocked his head though. "Why would you have such a wrongheaded idea? Why would I *want* the singers to win? They're our enemies."

"You fight alongside them!" Syl said. "Your Skybreakers side with them!"

"The singers have the legal precedent," he said, "and we must follow the law. But they are our enemies, and I obviously want them to fail."

"You uphold them!" Syl said.

"Nonsense," Nale said.

Syl's mouth worked, her eyes wide, and she looked baffled. Szeth . . . empathized. He'd worked his mind in circles trying to understand morality himself, though he'd assumed a piece of divinity would have an easier time.

Kaladin stepped up next to her, standing just inside the monastery, holding the bundle of swords. "Syl . . ." the Windrunner whispered. "I know he can sound logical, so it's natural we've tried logic in return. But it won't work. You can't persuade someone delusional with *logic*."

Nin sniffed in dismissal of that and glanced at Szeth. "You are ready for this burden?"

Szeth, numb, shook his head. "Herald," he whispered. "*Me? Are you insane?*"

"I have been told we are," Nin said, turning. "Come. Two monasteries remain. Your father is at the last one."

"Elid said our father is dead!" Szeth said.

"He is. So is your sister. You think you've been fighting the living in these monasteries, Szeth? Come now." He stepped outside.

Dead? He'd been told it before, but he felt sick, cold. Confused.

Kaladin came running up. "Szeth. This . . ."

"This is an impossibility," Szeth said, shoving down the emotions. He started walking. "What Nin wants from me is an impossibility."

And yet, Szeth's own sorry life had taught him that he was a poor judge of what was possible and what was not.

⁂

Sigzil sat in a meeting within a building on Narak. Rain pelting the stone roof.

"We've never fought a battle like this," Balivar said, sitting at the table with seven others, Sigzil included. Chella the Edgedancer was there, as well as Winn. Three other generals, along with Dami—the Stoneward they named the Stormwall—rounded out the group. Their entire leadership.

"I don't like how many losses we're taking," said Chella, a woman who wore her hair long to flow in the wind. "We've lost almost *sixty* Radiants, including squires. It horrifies me. Sixty! More casualties than we've taken over the entire last *year.*"

"Is this truly worth it?" Balivar asked. "For some barren rock in a land no one cares about?"

"The Bondsmith told us to hold," the Stormwall said, crossing arms as thick as some people's thighs. "So we hold."

"The Bond*smiths,*" Chella said, "put us in command of this battle. We can decide when the costs are too high."

They looked to Sigzil. Who banished the sounds of Leyten dying and sat up tall. "What are our options for defense?" he asked the generals.

"They aren't great, Brightlord," Winn said. "We can continue to risk Windrunners and Edgedancers to harry those Focused Ones, but we've lost so many . . ."

"Even with the Stonewards resealing cracks and thickening our defenses, I fear the enemy powers are too strong for our fortifications," Balivar added. "The moment we run out of Stormlight, we will fall."

"We'll fall anyway," said General Habrinar, an old greybeard—who had also been pulled out of retirement. He folded his arms on the table. "We are outnumbered, and that disparity grows worse with each loss we take, with enemy reinforcements having come via Elsegate. Truth is, I think we're going to lose the entire war. I don't trust this so-called battle of champions. The enemy has been winning, so why would he agree to such a thing? I think it's a ruse. It doesn't make any kind of strategic sense."

"*That,*" the Stormwall said, "is *pure conjecture.* Dalinar Kholin is one of the greatest military minds Roshar has known. He wouldn't agree to a contest like this unless it was the right move."

"We don't have to worry about it either way," Sigzil said, standing up. "Our job is this battlefield. We need to last two more days. Does anyone have an idea?"

The generals glanced at each other.

"It's that bad?" Chella asked.

"Brightlord Sigzil's plan to strategically give up plateaus was brilliant," General Rust Elthal said. "But it's really the only thing that got us this far. Especially without Stormlight, I can think of no way to survive. Brightlord Sigzil, are you *certain* the Bondsmiths are unavailable? I have reports of Brightness Navani being seen in the hallways."

"A ruse, unfortunately," Sigzil said, with a grimace. "We have to do this with the resources we have—or will soon have. We have Jasnah's Radiants, and my Windrunner colleagues have finished delivering the Mink and his people. They will be here before too long."

"More Radiants won't mean anything if our Stormlight gives out though, will it?" Chella whispered.

"Still, we must try," Winn said, looking to Sigzil.

The next parts grew technical. How to arrange troops on the two remaining plateaus: Narak Prime and Narak Two, the Oathgate plateau. As the meeting finally broke, Sigzil remained behind with General Winn, who was the rare Alethi that was around his height. They stood in the doorway, watching the others retreat through the rain.

"I want your honest evaluation," Sigzil said. "What are our chances of lasting another two days?"

"Ten percent, maybe," Winn said. "With heavy casualties. Brightlord, I'll be frank. General Habrinar has always been a fatalist, but in this case he's right. Ours is a terrible situation. A normal siege favors the defenders—so long as you don't run out of food and water, you're good for long periods. But with the powers the enemy has, and with this storm, and us being surrounded, and our Stormlight low . . ." He looked to Sigzil. "We are a candle before the storm, Brightlord."

Sigzil took a deep breath. "I . . . maybe have an idea."

"Thank the Heralds," Winn whispered. "What? Why didn't you mention it at the meeting?"

"I wanted to see if anyone had anything better," Sigzil said. "Because I haven't completely worked out the details of mine. It seems like it might be impossible. But Vienta and I have been looking over the fine points of the agreement between Dalinar and Odium, and . . . maybe we have something. I need more time."

"Then we will give it to you," Winn said.

He saluted and walked off into the rain, more of a spring in his aged step.

"Storms," Vienta whispered. "Sigzil, this idea . . . it *can't* work. I can't see how we could possibly trick the Fused into following us off the plateau."

He thought maybe he could trick them into abandoning it completely—following his army into the rain, so that when the deadline came, the enemy didn't hold the plateau. She was right though; they wouldn't be diverted that far.

But there *was* something here . . . He felt he could crack this. Storms, he'd come here to lead, and found he was actually *good* at it when he stopped worrying so much about what people thought of him.

He wanted to bring that to fruition and save the place. He wanted Leyten's death—still a raw wound inside—to mean something. He wanted to live up to the trust they all had in him.

"We have to make this work, Vienta," he said. "It's our job."

"I'm sorry," she replied, invisible. "I've not been a good spren lately. I . . ."

"It's all right," Sigzil said. "You've been extremely helpful. How are you feeling?"

"I keep hearing Ethenia scream," she whispered. "We aren't supposed to be able to die, Sigzil. We're the wind and the heart of Honor itself. If we can die . . . what does that mean? That even Honor, the winds, the planet itself can just . . . end?"

He wasn't a philosopher, as much as his master Hoid had tried, so he had no answer. He merely stood there, looking out through the rain.

⁂

Rocks sang as Venli and the others reached the end of the tunnel. They found a magnificent golden pool of light.

Awespren burst around them, six of them, floating blue balls that expanded as they faded into nothing.

This pool was hidden in a rocky cavern with no exits, directly beneath the main Narak plateau. Thirty yards or more wide, it glowed, shimmering and brilliant. The liquid seemed thicker than ordinary water, and it rippled as Thude knelt and tapped it with his axe.

It was the source of the sound.

"What is it?" Bila asked to Awe.

Timbre pulsed an explanation.

"Timbre has seen a pool like this," Venli said. "In the mountains. The Fused use it as a gateway to another realm. They always called it Cultivation's pool. The greatest of the gods create them, and Timbre says she thinks . . . it gathers for the same reason Stormlight streams off a human."

"All three have one of these?" Thude asked, dipping his axe again. "Honor, Cultivation, and Odium?"

"Honor's pool moves around," Venli said. "No one knows where Odium's is. At least . . . no one did. The Fused talked about it, that Odium doesn't trust anyone to know its location, after an event they wouldn't speak of."

It had been hidden, at least until now. Until . . .

Until, Timbre guessed, someone arrived who was bonded to both a spren of Odium and a spren of Honor. Venli. Had Odium somehow masked his pool using Honor? Or was it something else? What had the stones said . . .

Pieces of the sky, fallen here. Watched over by strange people. Secrets even the gods didn't understand.

Chasmfiends had always been capable of hearing it. That was what led them to this region to pupate. The ancient singers had unwittingly followed it here too, before it had been hidden. When the Everstorm and highstorm had clashed, this pool had fueled their explosive destruction. Most importantly, the power here—and the bits of fallen sky—had somehow been involved in the destruction of a city and a people.

Odium wanted to hold this portion of land at all costs. Rlain's description of the contest explained so much—and she wished he hadn't stopped answering. Because she could see why the war above was so fearsome, why the Everstorm was here.

Odium had brought his best to protect this pool. Venli attuned the Terrors. What on Roshar were *they* going to do with such knowledge?

Thude foolishly reached out to touch the power, but Bila held him back. Together they stared at it, golden light reflecting in their eyes.

Before they could make a decision, one of the guards came stumbling down through the tunnel. "Our Heavenly Ones have been discovered."

"By which side?" Venli asked, anxious.

"The singers," he said. "And by some kind of extremely dangerous-looking Fused."

This is closer to the interactions of Light and anti-Light, yet I do not fully accept it as the proper parallel either.

—From *Rhythm of War,* first coda, Navani Kholin

Dalinar jolted, his muscles coming alert, like the nervous shocks that happened when on the cusp of sleep. He found himself standing in front of a mirror.

Elhokar stared back at him.

Wait, Dalinar thought. *Why do I see Elhokar?* He raised his hands and checked. Yes, he *was* in his nephew's body, but for some reason saw Elhokar's features instead of his own. Why? Storms, it broke Dalinar's heart anew to see Elhokar just as he remembered him. In uniform, with those distinctive features, vaguely reminiscent of his father. A boy Dalinar loved like his own son.

Had there been a way to save the lad? What had Dalinar been thinking, sending him to Kholinar with only a small group of guards? Should Dalinar himself have gone? He tried checking the clock on his arm, but it wasn't there—perhaps since Elhokar wouldn't have been wearing it. Where was Navani? He hadn't been able to find her in . . . how long had it been? God Beyond send that she was safe.

Something moved in the corners of his vision, reflected in the mirror. He spun, but saw nothing. "Show yourselves!" he demanded of the seemingly empty room. "What is it you want?"

We seek . . . truth . . .

Dalinar jumped. That wasn't the voice of Odium, or Honor. That sounded like . . . a Cryptic? Storms. Wit had said Elhokar had been on the path to Radiance. Dalinar had always underestimated this man, hadn't he?

A knock on the door, and Elhokar's armorers entered at his call. That would have been odd for most, but during this time Elhokar had been paranoid, often commanding the armorers to suit him up for everyday activities. Dalinar allowed them to do so now, looking around the room, remembering his nephew. They were in the Pinnacle, Elhokar's seat at the warcamps. Dalinar had been here many times.

Shardplate donned, he dismissed the armorers. There were some maps on the table, a scattered mess. His nephew had been irritable and nervous during these days—but he could see now that perhaps the lad had been haunted by Cryptics. Deep inside, Dalinar felt . . . what Elhokar must have. His frustration at not being believed—and his worry that he was mad, seeing things like Dalinar had. So many uncertain thoughts, mixing with a desire to live up to his father's name.

It was as if he could sense Elhokar's growing understanding that he was a weak king—and that drove him to wish that he could be like the Blackthorn. The *new* Blackthorn. The man Dalinar had become. Elhokar respected him so much, but he didn't know how to deal with the scheming highprinces, the expectations, the fear that he was losing his mind. It was all so overwhelming.

There were rumors about Dalinar and Elhokar's mother. Dalinar sensed that Elhokar had wanted to broach the topic, to project strength. Yet he was also so uncertain. Would that make Dalinar angry, or proud of his nephew's proactivity?

Storms. That impression of his nephew's thoughts—something new to these visions, and only faintly noticeable—left Dalinar cold. The lad had needed someone who understood. Someone to listen.

Instead, the door opened and Dalinar Kholin entered the room, thunder in his expression. And the older Dalinar now recognized this day—from not even two years ago, yet he was so very different. This wasn't the drunkard. This Dalinar had been starting on his path to Radiance, but he continued to solve things in only one way. One blunt, terrible way.

Older Dalinar realized . . . he was still that man. In the vision previous, how had he responded to his younger self? By slapping him silly.

"Do we have to do this?" Dalinar asked his younger self, looking him in the eyes.

"Yes," younger Dalinar growled, before raising one leg and kicking Dalinar in the chest. His immediate response was fury. Once again he could feel—as a hint deep within—his nephew's emotions. Elhokar's confusion, panic, and pain.

On top of that was Dalinar's own sense of indignation. This younger version of him was going to secure the kingdom, but in the process would drive Elhokar to further bouts of insecurity. Insecurity that would cause him to demand he lead the mission to Kholinar, where he'd be killed.

The sad truth was that despite his accomplishments, Dalinar had consolidated power by killing or removing the highprinces who didn't agree with him. He'd taken a proud nation of warriors, eliminated all balances upon a monarch's powers, completely *broken* the ruling class, and installed himself as a despot at the top. For the good of the world.

He could almost hear Taravangian, dead these few weeks, whispering to him. *You see. The monarch must do what needs to be done. Regardless of the consequences. You've always known that, Dalinar . . .*

He didn't know that he could have taken any other action to protect the world, but that didn't stop him—in the moment—from being *furious* with this younger version of himself. And so he fought back. After falling from that initial kick, he dodged younger Dalinar's follow-up attack, moving faster than Elhokar had in the original clash. He grabbed the table, smashed it against young Dalinar, and then came in swinging, pounding gauntlets into young Dalinar's chest.

It wasn't the best strategy, gauntlet against breastplate, as it cracked both pieces equally. Dalinar didn't care. This wasn't real, but his anger was.

Younger Dalinar growled, knocking Dalinar's arms away, then rushing him with a shoulder, slamming him backward. Old Dalinar broke through furniture, stumbling away, but then launched into a grapple as younger Dalinar drew closer. But that risked their heads—which were exposed, so he let younger Dalinar push him away.

"Are you surprised?" younger Dalinar said. "No, you *expected* this. Storms, Elhokar."

Dalinar didn't reply, arms raised in a boxing posture, Stormlight faintly leaking from cracks in his gauntlets. Younger Dalinar tested him, and Dalinar blocked his strikes with his forearms, then delivered two solid punches to the man's chest, further cracking their armor.

"You've been practicing," younger Dalinar said, rounding him. "When did you get so good at boxing?"

Dalinar didn't respond. What did he care? The visions were playing with him; maybe he shouldn't be rising to the bait. Still, his anger flared as younger Dalinar came in, and storms . . . Dalinar wasn't as fit as he'd been even two years ago. Back then, he'd gone on regular plateau assaults.

After all this time being a king and a general—having given his Plate to Renarin—Dalinar could not keep up. Eventually, younger Dalinar forced him to stumble, then delivered an expert heel-first kick and cracked Dalinar's breastplate. He could feel Elhokar's emotions. And was surprised to sense . . . resignation.

This is for the best, Elhokar thought in the distant past. *My death will serve Alethkar. He . . . he will be a stronger king.*

"No, Elhokar," Dalinar whispered. "The failure is mine. It will take your death to teach me that."

Younger Dalinar came in, relentless. He'd thought, in that thick-skulled head of his, that the only way to prove he wasn't a threat was to get into a position where he could easily kill Elhokar, then walk away. Because younger Dalinar was fully incapable of sitting down and sincerely trying to listen.

I can't beat him alone, Dalinar thought. *But perhaps I can outthink him.* This younger him had let Sadeas play him, nearly getting his entire army killed.

Dalinar launched himself across the room, dodged an attack, then kicked the door down. "The Blackthorn has gone mad from his strange visions!" he shouted to the panicked guards outside. "He's trying to kill me and take the throne!"

Younger Dalinar pulled him back into the room and threw him to the floor. Then, the younger him leaned down and smashed his fist into Dalinar's breastplate—shattering it in an explosion of glowing bits of metal.

That did it. Without the breastplate, which held the majority of the gemstones, Plate had trouble drawing power. The other parts felt leaden around him, difficult to lift. Dalinar let his head rest back, lying face-up on the floor.

"You cut your own straps, didn't you?" younger Dalinar said. "On the horse? You faked an assassination attempt."

Dalinar didn't respond, instead turning toward the guards.

"They're my men," younger Dalinar said. "They won't help you, Elhokar. They've always been my men."

Except one of them . . . one of them was truly horrified. From his expression Dalinar knew it was little Gav. Watching. Witnessing. Storms, he'd just seen Dalinar—younger Dalinar, but he wouldn't know the difference—beat his father. Because if Dalinar saw Gav as a soldier, Gav—in turn—would see Elhokar on the floor here.

Storms . . . this vision was different by *intent,* wasn't it? It was *deliberately* showing Gav what had happened. Odium *wanted* Gav to witness Dalinar nearly killing his father.

Gav reached toward him with tears in his eyes.

"I didn't mean to hurt him, son," Dalinar said. "I was just trying . . . my best . . ."

But before he could explain further, the vision ended. Leaving him with the sight of that guard, with Gavinor's expression, looking at his father broken on the floor.

⁂

Taravangian.

Taravangian.

Jasnah formed two quick theories. Either Odium wanted to unnerve her by appearing as Taravangian, or . . .

Or Taravangian was the one who had become Odium.

Of course, a god would have power beyond a common Lightweaver, and could fool her eyes. He could also know practically anything, even if he didn't know everything, so any question she might ask to determine the truth—relying on experiences only she and Taravangian had had together—would be suspect.

More information. Maybe more information would help. It sometimes did. Not as often as she wished, but she usually craved it anyway.

"How?" she asked through dry lips.

"Szeth came to kill me bearing the sword that bleeds darkness," Taravangian said, standing at the opening into the small temple. "I had been interacting with the previous Odium, and the sword became available at exactly the right time. I availed myself of the opportunity, slew Rayse, and Ascended." He spread his hands to the sides. "It was Cultivation's fault and plan. I am, like Roshar itself, a dupe in a larger game."

Storms, it really did seem like him. She couldn't know for certain, but there was little you *could* know for certain. If it wasn't actually Taravangian, then someone else was doing an excellent—divine—re-creation. In that case, what was the difference?

"Taravangian," she whispered, "stop this. Call off the attacks. We could be allies. We were, once."

He winced. "We . . . never truly were, Jasnah. Were we."

"No. I suppose we were not."

He walked into the room, using a golden scepter as a cane—though his body appeared firm and hale. Less bowed by age than when she'd last seen him. Wit had explained some things, like that power needed a person to hold it. Taravangian had Ascended not to actual Godhood, but to lowercase godhood, a word Wit employed for a being of immense power. She accepted that definition as a useful description.

She had no idea what to do. Despite sharing a bed with Wit—who was like one of these creatures—she was overwhelmed by the idea of dealing with them. Inside, she trembled.

"I come with an offer," Taravangian said. "I am speaking to Fen now; the ability to be in more than one place at once is an advantage of my elevated status. She doesn't believe that I am me, by the way. She's much less logical than you are."

"I don't entirely believe you either."

"You believe enough," Taravangian said, stopping near her, looking up to meet her eyes. Even in this form, he was shorter than she was. "Because why would I lie? There is nothing to gain from it. You wouldn't trust Taravangian any more than you would Rayse. A scholar knows; I reveal myself not for advantage, but as a courtesy. For our upcoming duel."

"You cannot hurt me."

"It will not be a duel of swords, Jasnah," he said. "My predecessor . . . he worked *so hard* to recruit his opponents. Alas, he did so by *pushing*." Taravangian extended his hand to her. "I intend to do it with a gentle tug instead."

She did not take the hand.

He smiled anyway. "Tomorrow I will argue to Queen Fen why she and her people should join me willingly and become part of the larger reborn Dawnsinger nation. I invite you to offer counterargument. It is your specialty, is it not?"

"I . . . You're going to try to *recruit* Thaylenah?"

"A gentle tug," he said, turning to go. He paused, and glanced back at her. "I do know how to shove too, but one should always try to *lead* people to the proper decisions first. Prepare your arguments well, Jasnah. I am curious to hear what you come up with to convince Fen to stay with you and your fallen kingdom, instead of joining the side already proven victorious. By the end, you'll see. You'll understand."

He started evaporating into that mist again.

"See you soon," his voice said as his body disintegrated. "I hope you don't waste too much of your time wondering if this is a trick. Just don't forget to prepare your arguments. Then meet me here in this room, exactly one day from now."

With that, he was gone.

⁘

Venli had never seen a Fused like this before. Tall, with magnificent metal horns—and with his carapace somehow transformed to shimmering steel. It looked violent, but with an artistic touch, all smooth lines until the bits came to points here and there. What brand was this? She couldn't tell; perhaps whatever was going on with the carapace obscured his true nature.

She and the others had hurriedly returned to the chasms, sealing up the way below. In a stroke of luck, leaving the Heavenly Ones behind had been precisely the right move—for while Leshwi and the chasmfiends had been discovered, they had distracted the enemy long enough for Venli and the others to escape the tunnel without it or them being seen.

Soon after, Venli's group had been spotted as well—then herded together. She, still in envoyform—a form of power, a Regal—had been brought forward. Now, two Heavenly Ones—not of Leshwi's force—deposited her on a plateau a short distance from the fighting. Shrouded in darkness by the omnipresent clouds, occasionally painted red with lightning, she inspected the strange Fused. Leshwi and the other rebel Heavenly Ones knelt before him. Humming to Agony. Trembling.

Venli found herself unafraid.

How curious. Timbre pulsed inside her, and she realized she'd faced Odium himself. This Fused might destroy her, but to the Rhythm of the Lost, a phrase repeated in her mind:

I am my own. Not his.

"And here," the Fused said, completely without rhythm, "the ringleader herself. Once Odium's own Voice. Venli, Last Listener. Welcome."

She had not expected politeness. So, she hummed to him in greeting. The Heavenly Ones who had brought her backed away, leaving the group lit by a few gemstones on the ground, wet from previous rain—though that had slackened. In the Everstorm, it came in fits and starts.

"It is unusual," this Fused said, walking around Leshwi and the others as they knelt, "to find those who rebel against Odium. Some think it impossible, but it does happen." He looked to Venli. "Often it is a mark of our best."

"I would not have expected you to say such a thing."

"Who else would have the force of will, or the courage, to turn against a god?" asked the strange Fused. "Odium's predecessor always stamped them out. What a waste. If we cull ourselves of our strongest wills, what is left?" He glanced to the side, where a Husked One sat back, staring at the sky. Motionless.

Venli had seen this happen in Kholinar. Fused who just . . . stopped moving. Stopped thinking. A price paid for thousands of years of life, much of it spent at war.

"What are you going to do with us?" Venli asked.

"I give you an offer," the Fused replied. "I would appreciate your loyalty. You see, I am . . . of a different mindset than others. I finally have a god to follow who shares my tendencies. You will not be punished for rebellion. Instead you will be elevated." He smiled. "You will be made Fused, Venli. These will be pardoned, and given the greatest rewards. For I need the edge you provide."

Edge? She frowned.

"We need to defeat the humans," the Fused said, pointing. "And you have brought me something *extremely* interesting. Captive greatshells who somehow follow you."

Timbre pulsed to a worried rhythm. The guard had said the chasmfiends had fled, and the enemy warriors had focused only on capturing Leshwi and her Fused. But he knew?

Leshwi looked to her and bowed her head. She had revealed the truth of the chasmfiends, then.

"I must speak to the others," Venli said. "You will give me time to make a decision."

"You make demands?" he said.

"Is this not a negotiation?" Venli asked. "I have looked Odium in the eye. I know he could have you destroy me upon a whim. But if you seek us as allies, then I believe it my right to have time to consider."

"How satisfying. Go. Do not interfere in this fight yet. You will be watched, but you will be given time." He turned his gaze toward the sky. "I will have this land tomorrow, one way or another. And understand this is a threat: we know of your people at the edge of the plateaus. Odium plans to deal with them soon. My offer . . . is survival, Last Listener. Do not dismiss it lightly."

He clapped his hands and released Leshwi and the others. They—bowing—hurried over and joined Venli. Leshwi herself took Venli by the arm and began flying her down into the chasms.

"I'm sorry," Leshwi whispered. "But Venli . . . that's *El.*"

El? She hadn't heard the name. "What title?"

"No title."

"That's odd, isn't it?"

"He is the only one," Leshwi whispered. "He is . . . not to be trifled with. But if he's willing to pardon us . . . this could be our way out. Our way to protect the listeners."

"The last time I put any of my people in Odium's power," Venli said as they landed, "it did *not* go well. I do not trust his offers."

"El says there is a new Odium, remade," Leshwi said. "An incredible event, one I cannot even begin to fathom. Yet El promises it can be different. He rarely lies."

Venli attuned Skepticism, but once she had rejoined the others, they called the chasmfiends back to join them. The beasts were allowed to approach beneath the careful watch of Odium's forces, who had made a space for them all in a large gap between plateaus. Here, with the others, she sat and told them the disturbing news. Odium knew about the listener refugees and was absolutely capable of annihilating them.

Accepting this offer might be the sole path to avoiding such a disaster. Venli hated it . . . but they at least had to discuss the possibility.

BEWARE the FUSED!

DO NOT ENGAGE! FIND A RADIANT!

92
INTO THE BLUE

NINE AND A HALF YEARS AGO

Szeth sought the sky.

He'd been invited to meet the Voice. But first . . .

Wind embraced him. A powerful, high wind that churned and buffeted. A wind born of angrier places, beyond the mountains. Today, he loved the way it enveloped him, reminding him how small he was. He'd begun to think himself grand. But the wind needed no Stormlight to blow. The wind was its own Surge, monarch of a realm that Szeth visited only with its permission.

There was a liberation in being small. Whatever he did, no matter what he broke or ruined, Szeth was insignificant compared to the wind. He soared high. No. Tuko had spoken of the need to keep proper perspective. Szeth didn't soar, he *Lashed.* The sky became down for him, and he fell with increasing speed upward, into the heavens. Dropping, not flying, like a stone. Sent spinning, twirling, cast into the wind to fall.

Fall . . .

Fall . . .

Almost he could imagine falling forever, away from this land with its complicated questions, up through an infinite invisible embrace. It got colder the higher you went, and the air grew thin. But what was air to Szeth? He didn't need to breathe any longer.

Falling . . .

Falling . . .

Through clouds. Drawing in more Stormlight. Bursting into the expanse beyond, mysterious as the greatest depths of the ocean. Still Szeth fell into the blue. Which darkened.

The air failed. Still Szeth fell.

Until . . .

He would run out of Stormlight, and would never have his answers. With an inward sigh—lingering just a second longer—Szeth canceled his Lashing. His momentum ran out more slowly than he'd expected, though it did soon falter. He hadn't risen so high that the ground let go of him, not by far. He hung for a moment, twisting in that all-dominating blue that faded to black. The land below was covered in a veil of white clouds. Lit by the sun, so distant yet.

Szeth fell back down. Dropping in the other direction, the wind building. When he used his powers, that buffeting was lessened—but he didn't use them now. Soon the wind was a roar, shouting in glee at his return.

Down Szeth fell, until the city became visible. Ayabiza, the place of landing, the name suddenly appropriate. The Bondsmith monastery was half a day's walk beyond it, in the rocky portions of the highlands. Reluctantly, he Lashed himself upward—slowing his fall until he landed in the central square of the city with a crash of expanding Stormlight. Wooden paving boards rattled underfoot, then he stood up among startled marketgoers.

A true city, the most ancient on Roshar. Built by both those who touched stone and those who didn't. Both were needed, like shepherd and sheep. Tall buildings, mostly of clay, reinforced by wood. Painted in bright colors, murals on every wall, for in Ayabiza buildings could have as much a splash as anyone gave them.

He'd always wanted to visit this city, but the Bondsmith monastery wasn't part of the pilgrimage. You didn't fight that Honorbearer, or train with their strange powers. So he'd never had the time.

Today, he strolled down the boarded walkway, nodding to locals who bowed in deference. He should have gone straight to meet the Voice, yet he delayed. He knew that once he took that step, his life would change again. First, this Voice had stolen the grasslands from him, then it had stolen his innocence, then finally it had ascended him to master of wind and Truth.

The next step . . . Szeth dared not guess.

The city was enormous. So many wonderful murals, each brightly colored. So many people, swathed in brilliant splashes. The famous sewer system, built following an ancient Herald's design. Hanging gardens on each building so vines could grow down, letting the land add its splash to the paintings. It was more brilliant than he'd even imagined. Yes, this was worth fighting for. For this, he prepared for the coming of the End of All Things.

He traded empty gemstones with a local foreign merchant for full ones, then took to the sky once more.

It was time.

Instead, I find the closest model to be that of destructive interference in sound. A destructive waveform is not itself an opposite, but indeed the exact same waveform played opposite the primary one.

—From *Rhythm of War,* first coda, Navani Kholin

It was time.

As the tempest of chaos swirled around her in the Spiritual Realm, Shallan realized she needed to keep her promise to Veil and Radiant. She had to see and accept what Veil had once seen and accepted for her.

It was time to visit that day.

It formed around her—and oh, how she missed the chaos of the Spiritual Realm. So much better was possibility than reality. She could have spent an eternity surrounded by figures from the past and future, made as if from flowing paint and mist. Instead she came here. To the Davar estate.

She'd been eleven.

She appeared in her adult body—not the child's body whose perspective had once shaped her view of the world. Always forced to look up. Always knowing everyone else was so much stronger than she was. And therefore—she'd believed—wiser.

She was in her room. A small chamber with fluffy white carpet. She'd loved to roll on that carpet, feel it tickle her cheek, then her neck, then her other cheek. Near one wall was her trunk, and in that—hidden poorly—her drawings.

They weren't good. She wasn't an artist yet, and wouldn't truly start to become one until Helaran brought her supplies in the future. But she had . . .

Strength, Veil thought.

. . . but she had spent time in the gardens with Testament. Exploring her powers, and saying truths.

She opened the door and walked the memory, where light streaming through windows looked too golden, the colors of the wood trim too rich. In the hallway she glanced out a window into the gardens, and saw a young girl with a freckled face and a white gown.

She was surrounded by shivering vines, the type that poured down walls like waterfalls in this part of Jah Keved, glittering with glowing lifespren. The air smelled of life—a faintly grassy scent, mixed with the dampness of water standing in pools from the recent rainfall. Young Shallan had felt safe here. Just her, the plants, the lifespren, and Testament.

The stone bench in front of the young Shallan—kept clean from crem but growing lichen along its legs—was dimpled with Testament's shape.

"I'm afraid," young Shallan said.

"Why, Shallan?"

Older Shallan raised her head sharply, hearing Testament's calm, wise voice. The way it had been. Storms, that sound struck something inside Shallan. The memory seemed to become more *real* in that moment.

"Because," young her whispered, "I don't want anything to change, and it will. I hate the future. I'm scared of it."

"A truth," Testament responded, "that I will hold dear, Shallan." The plants moved and writhed, twisting across the ground, forming a symbol out of greenery with young Shallan at the heart of it.

"Why?" adult Shallan said. "Why would you let a girl of eleven swear the oaths? I was too young."

Testament felt, Pattern said in her mind, *that starting with a child who had no preconceptions would be better for inspiring a new generation of Radiants. And then . . . there was the other reason you drew our attention . . .*

Adult Shallan turned as the young Shallan stood up, gathering Testament on her dress, and snuck into the house. Always sneaking about, always listening. Shallan followed until they reached the door to her mother's room. On the other side, Mother's voice, speaking with a man who was visiting from far away, a man the servants whispered must be her lover.

Young Shallan listened at the door, terrified, hoping to find it wasn't true. Adult Shallan simply strode past her and pushed the door open.

Mother was there, pacing, wearing a beautiful blue and gold dress. In that moment Shallan remembered her companion in crisp detail: a foreigner who wore the Skybreaker symbol on his sleeve. He carried a box with a glowing light inside, like the one that Shallan had used to communicate with Mraize while in the Cognitive Realm. A sphere rose from it and formed a face. A face she knew from art and description.

Nale—Nalan'Elin, the Herald.

"Chana," he said. "I need you to join Kalak and myself in Kholinar. Our work grows more difficult."

Nale.

Kalak.

Chana.

"It's true," Shallan whispered, tears forming at the corners of her eyes.

Yes, Pattern said. *I'm sorry.*

They didn't seem to be able to see the adult her; no one reacted to her. Indeed, young Shallan kept kneeling outside, listening as if the door were closed.

"Chana," Nale continued, his voice cool and emotionless as the glowing face spoke, "you're being unreasonable. This entire *endeavor* of yours was unreasonable."

"I wanted a life again," Mother snapped. "I fell in love."

"You found a dupe."

Mother growled. Literally *growled.* She stalked across the room toward the Skybreaker, and he stepped back, alarm blooming on his face, keeping behind the glowing sphere as if to defend himself or ward her away.

Shallan watched, transfixed. That . . . wasn't how she remembered her mother, who had been so sweet, so overtly feminine. Here, she wasn't even wearing a glove.

"He *loves* me, Nale," Mother growled. "I have a *family.*"

"And where has that led you?" the voice said, calm. "To this? And the child? What of Shallan?"

Mother turned away. Shallan walked between them, looking from one to the other.

"She is one of them," Mother said.

"Yes," Nale said. "Which means . . ."

Mother didn't respond.

"Dreder will kill her if you do not," said Nale. "We have legal justification, by the Veden Voidcraft Act, to punish those who seek such powers—as you well know. Kill her. Those are my orders." Then his face smoothed out to the round seon spren, which returned to its box.

Young Shallan—still listening at the doorway—gasped, then pulled away. Testament had realized the danger, and whispered to Shallan that they needed to escape. Young Shallan scurried away, back to her rooms, where she'd begun gathering things to flee.

Older Shallan waited in this room, stabbed through with a variety of pains. One would think her a connoisseur of pain by now, as she could name the different types. She wiped the tears from her eyes, recognizing betrayal—its own distinct flavor—mixed with the confused agony of seeing her mother again and the strangely poignant pain of discovery.

The Skybreaker . . . Dreder . . . set aside the box. "All but your husband's bastard bear a terrible burden, including predispositions inherited from you. Nale says you were warned it would happen. Chana . . . killing the child now will be a mercy."

"You don't understand," Mother whispered. "She'll come back, Dreder. Once I kill her, she'll return to life. She's taking my place."

"What nonsense is this?"

"Shallan has powers," Mother said, "but the Radiants are dead and gone. This means that I've found what I was searching for: an heir. The bond has passed from me to her. She is eternal now and *I am mortal.*"

"Chana," Dreder said, "I'm no Herald, but even *I* know Bondsmithing well enough to know you can't *give away your bond to the Oathpact.*"

"I've already done it," Chana said. "You'll see. Shallan will be reborn, and then . . . then I'll be free." Mother looked to the side, and *met the older Shallan's eyes.* "You'll do better than I could, Shallan."

"You're insane," Dreder said softly. "Only Nale remains unscathed. But very well. Prove it to me. Kill the child, and let her return. I will report this news to my lord Herald and the other Skybreakers."

He just wanted a budding Radiant eliminated—as had been the Skybreaker pattern for centuries. Mother held Shallan's eyes, then stalked away with a bearing that young Shallan had never seen. Confident, strong as a warrior in battle.

Dreder sighed and followed. "Nasty business," he said to himself. "I hate it when they're children . . ."

Shallan, cold, trailed after them. She couldn't watch this, could she? She . . .

Yes, you can, Veil said.

Yes, you can, Radiant said.

She could. She followed them down the hallway, and felt something changing in her. The pains were still there, but they had dulled, the barbs no longer razor sharp.

Her mother had not been well. Obviously. That didn't excuse her actions, but somehow seeing it . . . seeing it and confronting it *helped.*

Shallan stopped at her childhood room, but young Shallan wasn't there. *That's right.* Her father had found her, taken her to his rooms to ask what she'd seen. Shallan followed Dreder and Chana as they strode over and burst into Father's chamber.

Father immediately confronted them. Arguments followed. Then a struggle. Father cut Dreder across the arm, spilling his blood on the white carpet, but the Skybreaker barely seemed to mind as he immobilized Father. Dreder drew in Stormlight to heal, then he looked to Mother and held out a knife.

Shallan's breath caught, as Mother pushed the struggling young Shallan to the ground. Heat welled inside the adult Shallan: anger, betrayal, a frenzy of primal, raw emotions. She lunged forward, unable to hold herself back, planning to grab her mother and rip her away from the child.

But her Mother knelt there—holding young Shallan down—knife held high . . .

And hesitated.

She *hesitated.*

Adult Shallan lurched to a stop, inches from them, emotion leaking from her as tears staining her cheeks. *Is that new?* Shallan demanded. *Did that actually happen? Or is it a change because it's what I want to see?*

I do not know, Pattern said. *I'm sorry.*

It . . . Testament's voice, weak but audible. *It happened. She paused.*

Adult Shallan collapsed to her knees beside the two. Mother knelt there, knife out and ready, emotions of her own warring on her face. Anger, determination . . . then . . .

Her face softened. She did not strike.

A sword appeared in young Shallan's hands, materializing out of white mist. She rammed it up through her mother's chest, and Chana's eyes burned.

Dreder shouted, reaching for her. His eyes burned next, and he fell facedown.

Mother somehow lasted a moment, mouth moving, eyes black—before slumping down onto the crying child. Who hurled the Shardblade away, screaming at what she'd done. Adult Shallan turned aside, suddenly nauseous. She gasped deep breaths. In, out. In, out.

Mother. The Herald. Dead.

This day. This terrible day.

The day the world had ended.

And Shallan was to blame.

In the farthest reaches of her mind, she heard that same child's voice crying. Nestled in her head. Not new.

I've protected her all this time, Veil whispered. *It's all right. She's safe. She always has been.*

Shallan wiped her tears. Storms. She was through it. She'd *watched* it. She'd survived. Emotions still made a mess of her, but a budding knowledge—reinforced by experience—emerged like a powerful light from within.

She *could* do this.

She *had already done it.* She'd survived it as a child—the only way she knew how, but even then she'd been strong.

She forced herself to turn back and watch. The Shardblade hadn't vanished to mist, but young Shallan wouldn't look at it. Whispering self-hatred, she had begun renouncing her oaths in this moment, though it wouldn't fully happen until the next day, in the garden, when she was more lucid and capable of truly doing so.

"*I hate you,*" young Shallan would say. "*I'm done.*"

Adult Shallan closed her eyes, struggling—but succeeding—in dealing with this flood of new emotions. Memories of what she had done to a dear friend.

Does it hurt? Shallan asked Testament.

Yes, Testament said. *But . . . sometimes . . . pain is required . . .*

Shallan took a deep breath, and opened her eyes. Father, surrounded by shockspren, pushed himself up from the floor.

Shallan? Pattern said in her mind. *Are you . . . are you all right?*

I can handle it, she replied.

We worried it would break you, he said. *I think the Spiritual Realm itself* wants *to show you things that hurt.*

"It never broke me," Shallan said. "It merely cracked me, Pattern. I filled those cracks." She took another deep breath, shuddering. "I'm glad to remember."

There will be more emotion to come, Radiant said. *But when it comes, we'll be here to help.*

Father put the Shardblade in his safe, then gently wiped the blood from the young Shallan's face. She felt anger at seeing him be so tender, as his temperament had always been erratic at best, abusive at worst. This moment would shatter their family.

Should she blame herself? Could she? Could anyone *actually* blame the young girl trembling in her father's arms?

No. She had to blame her mother, because her mother was to blame. The hesitation was to Mother's credit, and Mother's insanity provided context. But context didn't excuse actions, only helped give reasons for them. A child had the right to defend herself, and the hesitation had not been a complete halt to the violence. Adult Shallan knelt beside her mother's fallen corpse. How did she feel about this woman now? Still angry, yes. Still angry.

You don't have to forgive her, Testament said. *What she did was terrible.*

I don't have to, Shallan replied. *But I want to.*

Father began singing his lullaby. Shallan knelt there, suddenly drained. There was . . . more. More she had to do. More she *wanted* to do.

Are we . . . just going to ignore . . . that you're the daughter of a Herald? Pattern said. *Shallan, Heralds are like spren—they don't die permanently, not even by Shardblades. She's still alive somewhere.*

"I know," Shallan said, wiping her tears again as her father continued to sing. "Pattern . . . she was at my wedding."

94

SACRED TRUTH

NINE AND A HALF YEARS AGO

Szeth found the Bondsmith monastery easily, as he'd heard of it in lore and myth since his childhood. A section of ground with rock formations rising high around it. A curious little sheltered alcove. They called it a monastery, though the stones had created it themselves, rather than relying on hands of flesh. An act of the First Spren, before he'd bidden his creation farewell and moved on.

Szeth landed right at the center. So much rock; standing there, he wasn't certain he could spot a speck of soil anywhere. Only someone very profane—or extremely holy—could walk here. In the past, there had been ten who fit both descriptions. Szeth knelt and touched one of the slots in the stone, still present after thousands of years, kept clean by the shamans. He'd expected to find a few of them here today, but the place was empty.

Szeth reverenced each of the stone divots in turn, the sheaths for the Honorblades when they'd been gifted to the Shin for safekeeping. He went through all . . .

. . . all nine. That was right. He felt a fool for imagining ten people earlier. Had he forgotten his lessons so easily? He paused at the blank section of stone where Talmut's Blade would have been placed, and kissed the ground there. It was the first time his lips had touched stone.

Forehead against the rock, he prayed silently to Talmut. The one who had chosen to remain in Damnation so that his brothers and sisters—and all humankind—might escape it. The story was so dramatic, so inspiring, that Szeth wondered why it wasn't emphasized more in their teachings.

He remembered one retelling of it during his days in the monasteries, when some of the acolytes had acted out the holy text where Talmut had stood before the other nine and demanded they let him return to Damnation alone, for all of their good. How each of the nine had demanded that he let them be the one to return in his place, only to be refuted by his impeccable logic.

He kissed the stone again, glad to have this delay before meeting the Voice. Because a part of him that he'd never acknowledged was afraid.

"What now?" he asked.

Now, Truth, the Voice said.

"I do not want a sterilized version," he said. "Tell me everything."

I will.

The longer Szeth spent thinking about what had happened to him these last months, the worse he felt. The other Honorbearers had used him to remove an inconvenient member of their order.

"I'm here," Szeth said, turning around. "Show yourself to me."

You should not make demands of your betters, Szeth, the Voice said. *I am tempted to make you wait. Would you perhaps like the others to prepare you for what you are about to see?*

"No," he said. "I don't want to hear their version of whatever this is."

Why not?

"I don't trust them," he admitted.

And you trust me?

"I have to," Szeth said. "If I don't, what is left?"

Ah . . . that is an excellent reply, the Voice said. *Well, I am not always here, but I have returned in person this time to meet you. Follow the path to your left.*

Szeth turned that way, leaving the Sheathing of Swords, and started along a small pathway between the rock formations, washed smooth by centuries of rainfall drainage.

There. Turn here.

Szeth glanced over and found that—though the wash continued downward—a trail broke off along a shallow ridge some ten feet off the ground. He followed this, one hand on the stone cliff face, his steps grinding on a narrow stone ledge. He deliberately chose not to fly.

The cavern was barely a few dozen feet along the trail. He stopped maybe ten feet from it.

"Here?" he asked.

Yes. Upon ascension, each Honorbearer must stand before me. To ask my approval.

"And if one doesn't get it?"

They would have been culled long before being allowed this far.

"Then what happened with Tuko?" Szeth said.

He was promising, but ultimately proved too weak to do what was needed.

"Which was?"

Come forward, Szeth. Let us speak in person.

Szeth frowned, continuing on the path, which seemed . . . darker than it had moments ago. His mind could not reconcile the discontinuity. Shade on a cloudless day. A smothering of his soul. A blackness only visible when he wasn't looking directly at it.

Something here was very, *very* wrong.

"What is that?" Szeth asked.

What?

"I sense . . . something dark."

Senses are not to be trusted, Szeth. Come to me.

Szeth walked to the mouth of the cavern. He found Shardblade cuts along the tunnel beyond, and fingerprints? The work of a Stoneward, or a Willshaper.

Are you ready, the Voice said, *to meet your God, Szeth?*

"God left us," he whispered. "God created the world, saw that it pleased him, then moved on. He is the sun high above, and beyond. The spren nurture us."

You speak of a *god. Not* your *God, Szeth.*

Szeth swallowed, then stepped into the tunnel. With a single ruby for light, he traveled deeper, his footsteps echoing far into the darkness. Until he reached a room with the tunnel continuing on the other end. The room . . . was filled with spren.

Nailed to the walls.

Szeth gasped and gripped the stone on either side of the opening. The room was barely ten feet wide, and had straight flat walls. Here, tens of holy spren, each of a different variety, had been affixed in place by crystal spikes. As if for *ornamentation.*

Stones Unhallowed . . . he could hear them *screaming.* See them writhing. A windspren, in the shape of a small woman, shrieking in a constant panic, trying to push the spike out of her chest—where it had been driven through her into the stone. A flamespren, quiet but whimpering, flickering like a lit candle. A gloryspren, bulbous and round, motionless.

Some he didn't understand. That was an angerspren—he'd read of those—there, in the puddle of blood. But there was no nail in it—instead the nail was driven though something above it, a vague shape like a plate of carapace from some insect. Another was a translucent arrowhead shape that he didn't recognize, thrashing like a captured snake.

Szeth stumbled back, rapidly gasping for breath. Trying to banish their terrible screams, so frail, so agonized.

I leave them up on purpose, the Voice said, softer. He'd never been able to tell if it was a male or female voice. *They have to learn their true master. Spren need to change, Szeth. I can transform them.*

"Into what?" Szeth hissed.

Into better versions of themselves. That match me, and what I need them to do. Do not fret, Szeth. Things like this have always been done.

Something shifted in the tunnel beyond the room. Darkness growing, made manifest into a shadow with human proportions. It was coming. For him.

Szeth. I have prepared and chosen you for this. Each of the others have agreed to do what needs to be done. To prepare.

"I . . . I know what you are," Szeth whispered, trembling.

Good. You are not the first to guess.

He'd read of this. One of the most powerful enemies of humankind. A creature who lived in shadows, made of shadows, who could take spren and twist them to her own ends. He hadn't realized she could do it to people as well.

All his life . . . from childhood and that first awful day when he'd killed . . . he'd been listening not to a god or a spren.

But to one of the Unmade.

Szeth? the Voice said. *I realize it is much to accept and much to bear. I know you can handle it; this is why you were chosen.*

So it came to this. He had never thought . . . never believed . . .

Szeth, the Voice said, growing more forceful, the shadow approaching. *Come and worship.*

"I . . ." Szeth said. "I have to make a decision, don't I?"

The decision is made. You are here.

It would be easy to stay. To accept. Yet even now—after all these years—he remembered his father's words. *Son. I trust you to decide.*

Szeth had been too afraid to make the right decision as a child. He'd always worried that if he faced such a choice again, again he'd prove too weak.

But that day, Szeth was stronger than he'd ever been. For as the shadow called to him, Szeth turned and fled.

The destructive version of a melody is not its opposite, then, but instead the exact same song played back at precisely the right time to negate the melody. If you were to hear the two in isolation, you would not be able to tell the difference.

—From *Rhythm of War*, first coda, Navani Kholin

Adolin could still feel his foot.

It was the most unreal sensation. His foot was gone; he could see that clearly. So far as he knew, what was left of it was pinned underneath the thunderclast. The corpse was barely visible as a mound of darkness in the distance.

By evening spherelight, Adolin stared at his leg while the surgeon worked, affixing the peg. They sat outside the tents, in the cool night air, near the dome.

"It's very important that we get a clean fit, Brightlord," the surgeon was saying. "We want it so secure and tight that your stump doesn't move in the hogshide cup. The more it slides about, the more the stump will chafe."

Adolin just kept staring at the missing limb. It had taken an entire day and then some for a surgeon to be spared for the fitting. Adolin hadn't pushed for it earlier. He had plenty of work to do, going over shift reports, trying to make new battle plans following yesterday's disaster.

The battle reports weren't encouraging. He could hear fighting at the dome. It was constant now.

"There will almost certainly be pain anyway," the surgeon said, pulling some straps tight around Adolin's thigh. "You have one of Brightness Navani's pain-reduction fabrials?"

"Somewhere," Adolin said. "I . . . don't often wear it."

"You'll want to start," the man said, doing another strap. "You're lucky that we have Regrowth to form you good scars so quickly. Usually we wait months before fitting a peg."

"Lucky," Adolin said. "Yeah."

The surgeon paused, then continued working, falling silent. Storms, Adolin shouldn't have said that. He *was* lucky. That thunderclast should have crushed him completely. Plus, he could get that leg back as soon as he had access to a more skilled Radiant healer. Maybe his brother. It would be good to see Renarin again. They'd spent so little time together these last months.

He tried not to consider—instead—the soldiers he knew who couldn't be healed. The ones Regrowth didn't work for. Lopen had regrown his arm immediately, after *years* going without. But some people received full Regrowth within a month, but had internalized the wound enough that the body wouldn't comply. He didn't know how to combat that. He needed to *not* accept the wound? Storms, he hated the idea that if he couldn't get healed properly, it was *his* fault somehow. Wasn't the loss of a limb bad enough?

The surgeon straightened, then nodded to him.

Adolin tentatively stood up on his left leg, then let the pegged right leg start bearing his weight again. He slipped immediately and the surgeon caught him, holding him steady.

"It will take time to relearn how to balance," the surgeon said. "I won't spice up my words, Adolin. A lot of people with a peg need crutches their whole lives."

Adolin forced himself to stand again, wobbling.

"Some do learn to use it by itself as a mobility device," the surgeon said. "It goes faster for duelists, I've found. People who have already spent a lot of time working on their balance, and who have strength in both legs. But Brightlord, I don't want you in combat."

"For how long?"

"Ever, Adolin," the man said softly. "We permanently relieve men with these kinds of injuries, and you pay them a pension for their service, if you recall. Many on pegs are unsteady, and we can't have a man in a shield wall who can be shoved out of place with ease."

Adolin closed his eyes. Storms. He'd said almost exactly the same words to Zabra, hadn't he?

A sudden spike of anger rose inside him. Anger at what had happened to *him.* Anger that he couldn't help while others were dying. Across the cobbled field, an exhausted shield wall held the breach in the dome. Other forces held the doorways out.

As he'd predicted, after the firestorm of dropped oil, the defending forces had lost the entire interior. Reports from scribes who could speak the Dawnchant said that Abidi the Monarch was inside, proclaiming that the Heralds were dead. That the city was nearly theirs. All it would take was a few final pushes.

Abidi was right. Though the human forces had resisted all day, their defensive lines were barely holding, and were a terrifyingly thin three ranks deep. You needed one line on the front with shields, actively fighting. You placed a second line with pikes, supporting that front line, but also doing hard work—exhausting work. Three ranks meant only one line was resting. It would be so much better to have five ranks, and he preferred ten.

Three meant long shifts with soldiers on their feet. Exhausted, subject to constant assault from a larger force that could rotate in fresh troops far faster. It was a nightmare. And they had to do this for *two more days,* while being down to one Shardbearer. A man with Adolin's Plate—the boot replaced, and cracks sealed by modern fast-grow methods depleting the remaining bits of Neziham's Plate—and Neziham's Blade. They wouldn't have access to Neziham's Plate for the rest of the battle. It would take too long to regrow.

The surgeon rose, looking toward the fighting. "I'd best get back to help the wounded on the lines."

Adolin nodded, and the surgeon grabbed his bag and jogged away. Adolin took his crutches, but tried not to use them as he limped—and slid—back into the imperial tent. Yanagawn had made a spot for Adolin in here where he could take reports in cushioned luxury. He'd assumed that Adolin would want the plushness in which to recuperate. Silently, Adolin hated it, but he also hadn't wanted to be alone in his own tent.

To take a break from it, they'd set out the towers board for their customary evening game. Adolin gave his crutches to an aide, then forced himself to carefully balance and limp over. It was surprisingly difficult, and it felt like his muscles didn't work like they should. Why should it be so hard to keep a rubber-tipped peg from sliding out from underneath him? Still, he made it and settled down.

Yanagawn said nothing. He was studying the game board from within his mountainous robes. Adolin had needed to leave when the surgeon was free, which had interrupted their game. Neither had suggested skipping the evening play, despite the army's dire circumstances. Both knew there was little more *they* could do. Both also seemed to need this bit of stability.

Pieces on a table they could control exactly. Indeed, the emperor had dug up one of the fancy sets—not just cards, but little soldiers you could deploy in place of cards once revealed. They were, amusingly, aluminum. Yanagawn made his move, executing a classic envelopment, basically ruining Adolin's chances of winning the match. He hadn't been certain Yanagawn would see the move, as it required some subtle application of the terrain.

"Excellent," Adolin said, beginning to clear the pieces. "You've proven you can perform an assault from a defensive position and win. That's a difficult one to learn."

"It's hard to decide," the emperor said, "whether I should hold firm on the defense, or press an advantage and risk losing my privileged position." He stared at the table a little longer. "This is what you did in the dome the other day. You left a position of safety and risked yourself to save Neziham."

"Yes," Adolin said softly. "I didn't think about it so much though. I simply acted."

"A hundred days of preparation are needed for one day of spontaneity," Yanagawn said.

"Quoting Sadees at me?" Adolin said with a laugh. "He attacked your kingdom."

"He came the closest any Alethi ever did to conquering us."

That wasn't the way the Alethi told it. Sunmaker *had* taken most of Azir, before dying from disease.

"Plus," Yanagawn said, with a smile, "someone who basically defeated us sounds like someone whose tactical insights we should listen to, eh?"

"I suppose that's true," Adolin said, setting out the game pieces again. He nodded to the side as Colot—his uniform bloodied and hair disheveled, though he seemed unwounded—stepped in, glanced at him, then stepped back out. Ever since Adolin's fall, the man had checked on him every few hours. But it was difficult to complain. Adolin instructed his officers to check in on the wounded. It was merely humiliating to be on the receiving end.

I guess being a good example, Adolin thought, *can go both ways.*

Adolin shifted and felt the peg knock against the table leg. Storms, every time he moved, it was there reminding him. He maybe should have unstrapped it when sitting down, but he figured the faster he got used to wearing it, the better.

"Well, I have some good news, Yanagawn," Adolin said. "You've defeated all the classic training scenarios. You've memorized and avoided the ways a general can lose from a stronger position. You have practiced not making key mistakes—and you've learned to react to random chance. You're not a beginner any longer."

"You have no idea how glad I am," he said, drawing a gloryspren, "to be able to learn something that doesn't involve conjugating verbs or listing dates."

Adolin chuckled, although inwardly he was horrified. He was all for men learning whatever they wanted, but he hoped Aunt Navani never heard about Yanagawn's education. Poor little Gavinor would probably end up having to memorize the names of all the different kinds of forks in the world.

"So what next?" Yanagawn asked, leaning forward hungrily. "Do we move on to games where we start out on equal footing?"

"Journeyman training usually involves something like that," Adolin said.

"You'll get smashed the first few times, but it's good to knock that crutch out from under you when you're new, before you rely on your confidence in winning too much."

Yanagawn's eyes flicked toward the crutches, and it took Adolin a moment to realize what he'd said. Then his foot—which wasn't even storming *there*—started to ache again.

"I'm eager to start losing," Yanagawn said.

"Good. After that, it might do you good to try a few unwinnable scenarios, to teach you more about minimizing losses and calculated retreats. What do you think, Gezamal?" Adolin scanned the room's guards, searching for Kushkam's son.

He wasn't here. Adolin went chill. Kushkam the elder was back on his feet and in command after being knocked unconscious, then healed. But his son . . . had he . . . ?

"He had to be reassigned," Yanagawn said softly. "Gezamal agreed to lead the guards into battle yesterday with me. He listened to me, when he should have rejected my order."

"They can reject your orders?"

"I'm not all powerful, Adolin," Yanagawn said. "We have a bill of legal citizen rights—and the *azaderach-tor*, the limit on imperial power and reach. Civil servants form a representative government for the people. I am the soul of our people, but I'm not some Alethi dictator." He glanced down, seeming embarrassed. "Sorry. I repeated that as it was told to me; I should have shown more tact."

"It's all right," Adolin said. "But they act like you're so powerful."

"I reign," he said, "but do not rule. It's a fine distinction. Regardless, my soldiers . . . they're not *supposed* to let me hurt myself. Gezamal stood with me when I tried to go fight, and so . . . he was removed."

"Yanagawn," Adolin said, irate, "you can't punish a good officer for making a good decision—particularly one you wanted him to make. You *can't* let your soldiers question the difference between the *moral* decision and the *right* one. Make them the same thing!"

"I understand such criticisms," Yanagawn said, his head down, arranging his pieces, not meeting Adolin's eyes. "But there are things we must do to be a civilized society. One of those is to accept that actions have consequences. Embracing those consequences is sometimes both moral and right."

Adolin shook his head, finding that attitude utterly contemptible. But he acknowledged that he was in a bad mood. After all, he'd lost his leg and the city was doomed. That made small talk awkward.

They dug into a few more games. After crushing Yanagawn a few times as promised, Adolin decided to use the facilities. He refused the crutches as he limped out of the tent, intending to hit the officers' latrine.

Colot was waiting in the moonlight outside.

"Checking on me again?" Adolin said. "You might be going a little too far on that, Colot."

"I found him, Adolin."

"Him?"

"Kushkam's son," he said. "He was reassigned to basic infantry. He's on rotation out to reserves right now, if you want to talk to him."

Adolin hesitated, then grinned. "Colot, you gemstone of a human being. You're wasted as an officer."

"I am?" he said, sounding amused.

"You should have been a sergeant, given how useful you are. Come on, let's go and talk to Gezamal. I feel we might have an open spot in my guard for someone like him."

⁂

Szeth wasn't certain he wanted to keep living. Yet Nin said they wanted to make Szeth *immortal*?

Szeth was numb from that revelation. He would have welcomed laughter or tears, or really *any* emotion other than the crushing pressure. That grip on his heart, squeezing. Making of him a ball of stone.

Nin had left them earlier in the night, saying he needed to prepare for something. Szeth now watched the last flickers of their campfire, embers falling apart, relaxing as life finally left them and their colors faded. How strange to see no flamespren upon the fire; he had spent so many years in places where spren, like stone, were common. The unusual had become usual. A fitting metaphor for his life.

A Herald. Eternal. The idea made him want to run. To hide himself someplace where the very movements of the earth could grind him down into the nothing that he deserved to be. He had lived a horrible, murderous life, but always he had believed there would be an out. An end, in death.

If he completed this pilgrimage, death would be no end.

But is this not the torment you deserve? a part of him questioned. To hear those whispers forever? To spend eternity adding to his body count, for the Heralds were—first and foremost—soldiers. Ishu might be a scholar, but he was also one of their finest swordsmen.

To live among them . . . as one of them . . . would be agony.

And what of my father? My sister? Were they trapped in some kind of half-death? Would . . . becoming a Herald mean that at least he'd be with them?

He looked up as a figure approached his dozing fire, but it was not Kaladin, Sylphrena, or even Nin. It was a creature in the shape of a man, but whose figure cut a hole in reality itself—displaying a starfield beyond.

"Hello, my squire," the spren said.

Szeth bowed his head. The spren had never appeared to him in such a human shape before. He was honored. It was an emotion he could paste to the ball of stone that was his crushed innards, like a note stuck with gum paste to the message post in the center of town.

The spren sat down on the other side of the embers. Kaladin and Syl were playing the flute on the next hillside over. Szeth found a certain . . . vibrance to Kaladin's playing. It wasn't *good.* He played haltingly, often starting, stopping, then replaying the same sequence multiple times. And he knew only one song.

It should have been annoying, but Szeth remembered when his sister had practiced this way. She'd needed to feel out songs as she learned them. In this, Kaladin's music was alive—finding its way, growing. To Szeth that was beautiful, and it was one of the few things on this trip that had offered him comfort.

"Szeth," the spren said, "I would speak to you."

"Please," Szeth said softly, gazing down at the embers.

"Do you have . . . questions for me?"

"Is it true?" Szeth said. "That this is my destiny? To join the Heralds?"

"Yes," the spren said. "It is why Nale first came to you, why he gave you that black sword. The weapon is supposedly a kind of . . . test of a person's character. You have passed."

"I've done little with the sword," Szeth said, glancing toward where Nightblood and the Honorblades lay.

"That is part of passing the test."

Kaladin's music cut off as he played a comically bad note. Then laughter drifted over as Syl said something. Szeth's spren looked that direction, and though his posture was difficult to read, he appeared . . . envious.

"Do you wish our bond was more like theirs?" Szeth asked.

"I shouldn't," the spren said. "Our bond is not like theirs. No highspren should want one where the human could kill us. It is unseemly."

That part was true. Szeth didn't know the mechanics, but it had been shared with him as he reached higher levels of training. A highspren could end their bond at any point, with no repercussions to either of them. No deadeyed highspren existed, or would exist. If Szeth walked away from his oaths, his spren would not be hurt.

The way they did this involved a distance between them, which protected the highspren from the human. And that distance was part of why their attitude toward their Radiants was so different as well.

"It is not appropriate for a piece of deity to laugh as she does, to joke and make light," his spren added. "It just sounds so . . . friendly. Regardless, I wish I could have explained your true task in this pilgrimage, Szeth.

Nale said I could not until you were fully committed. Are you . . . fully committed?"

Szeth looked to the sky, where those glowing lines led the way. The correlation between Shadesmar and this land wasn't absolute; reflections could show up here in odd ways. On the other side, those spren likely marched or swam toward their destination. It now made sense to him why they were going. To witness what would happen to Szeth. Should he succeed.

"I do not wish for this burden," he whispered.

"I know," the spren said. "Nale and my superiors tell me that only one who does not want the burden should be offered it. They've been waiting for you for many years. A man with no attachments, trained in the best arts of war—a man who will fight on command, and who knows how to follow the dictates of such an important bond. You're *perfect* for the role, Szeth. Not only an expert with the Surges. You are completely in control and completely obedient."

"That is required, then, of a Herald?"

"How else do you think they survived thousands of years?"

It seemed to him that the Heralds had been getting worse over the years. So were they actually surviving? But of course such thoughts were foolish. The Heralds were imbued with the power of Honor himself—and it was Honor's very nature to be obedient and to demand obedience. Honor was the force by which up became up and down became down. Gravityspren did not question. Szeth should not either. It was what he'd been taught in the monasteries.

Now those teachings were crushing him to the point that he could barely breathe. He felt it coming on again, a tightening that was somehow worse than the numbness. A paralyzing tension, as if he were steam needing to escape, but there was no release. Just more. And more. Pressure. Pushing him to—

Kaladin's music began once more. A flute, reminding Szeth of the days when his dances had not left corpses. He found himself able to breathe.

"I know that song from somewhere . . ." Szeth's spren said.

"It's . . . possible, then?" Szeth forced out. "To make a new Herald?"

"So far as I understand," the spren said, turning back to the fire. Did he watch the embers die? What did an immortal being think about such endings? "The Oathpact unravels because of Jezrien's death, but it is a slow unraveling. The enemy has been unable to find and destroy any other Heralds, and so the hole can be patched. It would require taking a piece of Honor, forging from it a new sword. Saying the most important Words a person can say, and joining the Heralds."

"The Words," Szeth said. "I cannot be told them."

"Yes!" the spren said, animatedly gesturing with both hands. "You see. You understand."

"I do," Szeth said. And knew he had the right Words inside him. "It is . . . necessary?"

"Ishar has foreseen that unless the Oathpact is reforged," the spren said, "millions will suffer. Millions upon millions."

The ball tightened.

"Then I will do it," Szeth whispered, closing his eyes. "There was never any question that I would, was there?"

"Well, not until Kaladin started . . . you know. Helping."

"I would be dead now if he hadn't," Szeth said. "Nin is broken, spren. This test is irrational. Any soldier can lose a fight, no matter how good that soldier is. He could have accidently seen me dead at any point on this quest."

"He . . . says that vigilant adherence to the law will protect you."

"He does not know what is right any longer," Szeth said, staring out into the darkness. Nin's departure left Szeth concerned, because the next monastery was the Skybreaker one. "Nin was angry that I refused to fight my sister. But not fighting her is how I won the battle!"

"I . . ." The spren looked away, toward the music. "I want to help. *Really* help. Be your partner, Szeth. I . . . wanted you to know that."

How strange, that this uncertain, amiable being was the same one who had spoken to him so imperiously before. Spren, it seemed, were as capable as humans of wearing different faces and putting on airs.

"I joined the Skybreakers," the spren said, "and became a knight within their ranks so that I might help protect the world. We're not like other orders—we *never* abandoned our duties. So . . . I'm trying, Szeth. Once you're a Herald, I'm . . . ready."

"What is the cost to you?"

"What you do, I have to do with you," the spren explained. "Nale's spren was always trapped with him on Braize, and subject to the pains that the enemy can inflict."

"Storms," Szeth whispered.

"Ishar searches for a way to make us truly physical," the spren said. "I do not know the details—he will not share them with the Skybreakers—but he says it will make us untorturable."

"How would you having *physical bodies,*" Szeth said, "make you *less easy* to torture?"

"I don't know," the spren admitted. "Ishar has been erratic these last few millennia. I'm sure he has a good plan in there somewhere. He always does."

"And the Unmade plaguing Shinovar?" Szeth said. "I assume that cleansing the land is how I prove I am worthy of being a Herald?" Again, the tightening inside. "But how does it relate? Why am I fighting Honorbearers, and why haven't the Heralds cleansed them already?"

The spren squirmed on the ground by the fire.

"I can't know this yet?" Szeth asked.

The spren shook his head.

"I know an Unmade is here," Szeth said. "I heard its Voice in my head, starting on the day I killed the soldier. I discovered its place of darkness, and realized—even back then—that my people were corrupted. At the time, I believed the Unmade in Shinovar meant the Return had begun—I didn't realize that the Unmade had been left behind.

"So, I was both wrong and right. Wrong, in that the general mass of the Voidbringers had not yet Returned. Right, in that a servant of Odium was doing terrible things to my people." He thought a moment. "Are the Heralds unable to cleanse this land for some reason? Must it be a Shin who performs the act? Perhaps *that* allows the Shin people to be redeemed, and join the fight?"

The spren didn't reply.

"But why so late?" Szeth said softly. "The war has been happening for well over a year now. Longer, depending on when the first Voidspren began to appear."

"Answers will come . . ." the spren said.

". . . in the next two monasteries," Szeth said with a sigh.

"Yes." The spren paused. "Szeth, can I admit something to you? I . . . don't know the answers. I . . . have some of the very same questions you do."

Szeth settled back as the last embers died. He had thought the matter of his future settled. He had chosen Kaladin's path, that of peace, but now the world itself had been settled upon his shoulders.

Peace was something for other people. For Szeth, there had always been—and would always be—voices in the darkness. And his insides were crushed between the force of landscapes: one made of stone, and the other soil.

⁂

While hunting down Gezamal, Adolin walked the entire way across the cobbled courtyard on his own, without needing crutches—though he did have to lean on Colot now and then. Notum arrived, full sized, hovering next to them as he gave a quiet report. The lines were holding, but casualties were frighteningly high. In turn, morale was frighteningly low.

The defenders had finally, reluctantly, gathered a second—and later today, even a third—wave of recruits from the city. Untrained men and women with spears and shields would hold the first line, with more experienced soldiers using pikes from behind. It was a horrible tactic, but the sole one available—plugging holes in the front with people who had only the most basic of training.

Once you started building weak points into your lines, the fall was imminent.

Two days, Adolin thought. *Less than that now. Practically a day and a half. That's all we have to survive.* The contest would happen at midday on the tenth day at Urithiru, meaning late morning here in Azir.

Still, he could hear people screaming as they fought.

"At least," Notum said, "the enemy forces have been vastly depleted. They are tired too, and wounded."

"Yeah," Colot said. "But there's still more of them, so they can rest their lines better."

He was probably right. The enemy *had* been depleted, then demoralized by the Herald attack, the loss of the thunderclast, and the firebombs the day before. Plus, if he'd been in command of the singers, he'd have picked a force and rested them for a day, keeping the humans busy with other troops.

The hammer would fall tomorrow. Blood of his fathers . . . the worst part was not being able to help. To be hobbling along on one good leg while soldiers died. He was able to send Kushkam some suggestions on where to position the weaker pike blocks, but that didn't feel like much. Maybe Adolin could put on the Plate himself, leave one leg out with the peg, and—

No. He wouldn't let his pride endanger the city—he was good with Plate, but one of his armor standbys would be better. He hated it, but the mature thing was to let someone else fight in his place.

They passed the shadow of the fallen thunderclast. At least his leg had a storming fine tombstone. Past that were the latrines, a row of wooden outhouses with steps up onto them, and bottom sections that could be removed and periodically Soulcast—waste and all. Adolin found it amusing to think that some of the city's bronze came, literally, from dung.

The younger Kushkam was here, wearing gloves and an apron over his uniform, cleaning latrines. His weapons were near, and he—as a fit soldier—would be doing a full rotation on the front lines like everyone else. During his time off however, instead of resting, he got this duty.

Adolin barely contained his anger; demoting a man like Gezamal was an insult. Specifically, an insult to every soldier who had made a snap—and correct—decision to disobey orders when the circumstances changed.

"Gezamal," he said, catching the man's attention. "Missed you at our nightly game."

Gezamal seemed glad to see Adolin, judging by his posture in the night as he stood taller and hopped down the steps. "Adolin? Walking already? You'll be fit for service again in no time."

A small lie, of the type soldiers told one another. Adolin clasped hands with the man—though only *after* Gezamal had removed his gloves and positioned himself downwind.

"You like my new offices?" Gezamal said, gesturing.

"Gezamal," Adolin said softly, "this is an affront. I can't believe—"

"Stop," Gezamal said, his entire posture changing. He stood more alert, and shied back. "Do not speak ill of the emperor."

"I won't. But this business of demoting you? It's insanity! After what you did?"

"What I did," Gezamal said, his voice grown cold, "was what needed to be done. As is this."

"What?" Adolin said. "Gezamal—"

"Adolin," he said, lowering his voice, "when I ordered my men to march into battle with the emperor, I knew what it would cost. If he'd been injured, I'd have been executed. He wasn't, blessedly, so I'll accept this."

"What you did was right."

"Which is why I'm fine taking my duties now."

"It's bad military discipline, Gezamal," Adolin said. "You can't punish soldiers for making good decisions—or sometimes even those who make the *wrong* ones. You need officers to feel comfortable *making* decisions. If you muddle that with a fear of repercussions, the result is indecisive leadership. And the result of *that* is *disaster*."

Gezamal sighed and settled down on the outhouse steps, nodding as a soldier arrived to use the facilities. Gezamal slumped forward a little, crossing his arms. "I suppose we shouldn't fault you for offering advice when that's what we invited you here to do. It's probably good advice, too. If there's one thing the Alethi know, it's how to maintain a disciplined fighting force."

"Not all of us," Adolin said, thinking of Sadeas's armies. "But I've learned a few things. Either we need to get your demotion reversed, or at the very least I want you on my staff. I value a soldier who has the courage to do what you did."

"I appreciate the offer. But I won't leave."

"Why?"

Gezamal looked up as the first moon started to set behind him, the violet light dwindling. "You ever love something flawed, Adolin?"

"Isn't everything flawed?" he said, glancing at Colot, who had so far remained silent in this conversation.

"I suppose it is," Gezamal said. "Well, I love the empire. I love that our people have stood for thousands of years, against invaders with more Shards. I love that we have produced writing and art, standing as a light against the twin tides of ignorance and lies.

"I love that in Azir, a thief can become emperor. That any person who dedicates themselves can take the tests and rise high. I love the way we have reasons for what we do. Yes, the weight of those reasons might create books full of bureaucracy. Yes, it might get unwieldy. Yes, it might hurt you now and then. But everything you love is going to hurt you now and then, because it *is* flawed."

He rose from the steps. "There should obviously be a threshold for being hurt. We haven't reached mine. The laws say that a man who did what I did needs to be punished. Maybe the law should change, but I accept what has happened. Because Adolin, I guarantee that every other soldier in our military—even those who think I was a monster for putting the emperor in danger—understands. Accepting your punishment with decorum is a mark of respect for the thing we all love."

Another soldier passed in the night and nodded to Gezamal. Neither gave salutes, but the impression Adolin had was similar. Thoughtful, Adolin nodded to Gezamal himself, then let him return to what he'd been doing.

Adolin started back across the courtyard. Pondering. Did he love things that hurt him?

Maybe not something. But certainly some*one.* A father.

"I think . . ." Colot said, walking with him, "I get it, Adolin. Maybe that's why I'm still a soldier." The red-haired man paused, then turned and gazed back at the setting moon. "It hurt, being rejected by the Windrunners. All their ideals—about protecting, about helping—meant so *much* to me. It really seemed to be *working.* I learned to draw in the Light, and I even took to the sky a few times. And then . . ."

"You told me the spren didn't want you," Adolin said. "Because you were lighteyed."

"It feels so strange," Colot said, "to have something that had always been an advantage turn against me. Should I be embarrassed? Angry? Is it fair that *I* should get rejected when I personally didn't do anything other than be born lighteyed?" He sighed. "I wish I knew, Adolin. I start to feel better, then I see them flying, and it all floods back . . ." He looked to Adolin, then appeared embarrassed. "Sorry. Just . . . I get what Gezamal said. I'm still here. Despite when it hurts."

Notum soon came zipping back, and fetched Colot, as Kushkam needed him to take command while he saw to other duties. Despite his obvious fatigue, Colot jogged away, leaving Adolin alone as the moonlight vanished. He balanced precariously on the peg and the stump that was already starting to ache. Listening to other people fight, and feeling a mounting dread.

They weren't going to last another day and a half.

NINE AND A HALF YEARS AGO

Szeth landed in a crash of Stormlight, expanding from him in a puff, frost crystallizing on his clothes. Sloppy. He was using too much. He'd . . . he'd been warned about that . . .

He scrambled up to his father's cookfire. How long had it been? Hours? Hours since he'd entered that tunnel . . .

He barely remembered running. Fleeing. Not only from the Unmade, but from the past. He rushed up to his father—firelight throwing violent shadows—and grabbed him by the shoulders. This little waystop was off the roadway. It was where Neturo said he'd wait until . . .

"Son?" Neturo said, cowering before Szeth.

"It's all a lie," Szeth said, Stormlight streaming from his arms. Too much. He'd taken in too much. It burned through him, demanding he move, fight, take action, or run . . .

"What?" Neturo asked. "Son? What's *wrong*?"

I can't bring him into this, Szeth thought. *Not until I know what I'm doing.*

"Stay here," Szeth insisted, leaning in, making Neturo cringe. "Hide. *Hide,* Father."

"Szeth," Neturo said, reaching out and placing his right hand on Szeth's cheek. "Son. Deep breaths, like when you were a child. Remember?"

Remember?

Deep breaths.

Szeth drew them in, remembering those peaceful, perfect days. Free from problems.

No, Szeth thought. *Sivi was right. Problems festered even during my youth. I just couldn't see them.*

"Breathe," his father encouraged, ever the stabilizing force. "Whatever it is, son, we can solve it."

"This is big, Father. Bigger than a stone in the soil, or a conflict among family members. It's . . . big as the world . . ."

"Tell me what's wrong."

"I can't. I . . . Father, what if *I'm* wrong?"

"I can't help you if you don't tell me. But Szeth . . . I trust you."

"How?" Szeth said, collapsing to his knees. "I'm so wrong so very often, Father. Then when I choose, I hate my choices. *How* can you *trust* me?"

"I've never met anyone who wants to do the right thing more than you, Szeth."

"Wanting has *never* been enough, Father."

Neturo merely embraced him, pulling Szeth—still kneeling—to his chest. "I know. But sometimes it's all we have, Szeth. I'm sorry I don't have better answers. I guess . . . I stayed with you, hoping I'd be able to find them for you. I never have, have I?"

"They might not exist."

"Maybe not," Neturo said. "I . . . I remember how I felt when I realized *my* father didn't have answers . . ."

Szeth closed his eyes. "How old were you?"

"Fourteen. It was the week before he passed—after we got news that the Honorbearers couldn't come."

"There are . . . too many who need Regrowth," Szeth said. "They can't travel for most cases. They can only heal those who come to them . . ." That had been a difficult few months. Learning to heal each day, trying to treat as many of the petitioners as possible, discovering that he couldn't help a shocking number of them—as the wounds were too old.

"My father, Vallano," Neturo said, "broke down crying when he realized he was going to die. Until that moment, I'd assumed he'd live. Through force of will if nothing else. Maybe he believed it too. He held to me, weeping, when he realized he had no hope left. Six days later . . . he was gone."

"So no one has the answers."

Neturo pulled back. "The Heralds and spren, maybe. They left what clues they could. We have to figure out the rest."

"There should be more than that. More than *me.*"

Neturo didn't say anything as they sat in that firelight, windblown smoke curling around them, mixing with Szeth's Stormlight.

He was all they had. Him. Szeth. *He* had to do something.

"Stay here," Szeth said. "Stay hidden. Please."

With that, Szeth launched into the air again.

97 CHARACTERS FROM A PLAY

Anti-Light is not inherently the opposite of standard Light, nor is it negative, or imaginary, or a philosophical opposite. It is a different phase of the same entity. I see it more like the same melody, played at a different time.

—From *Rhythm of War*, first coda, Navani Kholin

A shadow overcame Shallan, and tried to propel her straight into a singularly painful moment—when she'd first seen her mother again after all those years.

Shallan refused. She needed the vision to start a bit earlier than that so she could have more space to remember lighter times, before she confronted more darkness. She *could* and *would* do this; she just needed some trackway first to begin running. She felt a hint of surprise in the shifting motions of the chaos as she asserted her will over the vision, but it passed in a blink, and she appeared in her own body once again.

She was seated, being fussed over by the royal Alethi makeup artists. She remembered being amused that such a thing as official royal makeup artists existed.

It was her wedding day. She'd been betrothed to Adolin for months, but the marriage had not yet proceeded. In part because she hadn't committed until after the battle of Thaylen Field—where Dalinar had united the realms for the first time. That day, a glorious event had occurred: Adolin Kholin had pierced through illusion and facade and seen the real Shallan.

She had seen him too. Experienced the deep, true him, and the wonderful future they could have. Now she sat—stressed and overwhelmed—as they prepared her for the actual ceremony.

Until the boots arrived.

Kaladin's gift—ones that would fit her, but of a military cut and design. Shallan laughed, holding them up. The stress melted away. She was both women. The Shallan getting married, and the Shallan living through these visions again. To anyone else, being two women at once might have been demanding and confusing. For Shallan it was just everyday life.

Only *two* people at the same time? How easy.

After the gifts, Shallan was led to a small room to pray and meditate. Today, she ran her fingers over the brushpen and ink jar, thinking. At the time, she hadn't enjoyed her wedding as much as she should have. The day had been chaos and anxiety, like so much of her life, really. She had been Jasnah's ward. Shouldn't she have learned to instill a *little* order in her life?

Humming sounded from behind.

She turned to find Pattern there, full sized, holding hands with Testament—who was the one humming.

"She wanted to be here, with you," Pattern said. "On this day, a year ago. Unfortunately, she had to remain hidden. To protect you."

"From myself."

"From the pains of life," Pattern replied. "And from truth, for a time. In you, the lie *was* life, Shallan. We need them sometimes. Even spren. You taught me that."

Shallan took Testament's hands in her own. "Thank you."

Testament, in return, mumbled something Shallan couldn't make out. Shallan leaned in, straining to hear as Testament repeated the words.

"Enjoy. It."

"Enjoy it?" Shallan asked. "What?"

"Life."

How? There was so much to do. So much that was wrong. Testament squeezed her hands, the spren's pattern rotating in its lethargic way.

Words from the dead to the living. *Enjoy it.*

"I deserve this," Shallan said, leaning back, remembering what she'd realized on this day. It was *all right* to be happy. "Why do I need to keep learning the same lessons? Can't I make progress for once?"

"You aren't relearning the same lessons," Pattern said. "You're *reinforcing* them. In math, you can know a thing, yes, but it is the proof that teaches the deeper truth. Life is your proof, Shallan."

"I suppose," Shallan said, "it *is* good to revisit what you've learned, now and then. For added context."

These visions . . . Had she appreciated them? The ability to go back and witness life as it had been? Laughter with her brothers. Seeing her father again. Hurtful though he had often been, she didn't hate him.

Then there was her mother.

She *had* been here, at the wedding. Shallan had refused to see, or at least remember, the first time. Now her eyes were open, and her veil removed.

"I *want* to live it again," she whispered. "Let's do it."

Her brothers soon invaded her small chamber, as they had on that day. She embraced them as if seeing them for the first time in ages, which—in a way—was true of her current self too. She let them love her, and she loved them.

She accepted the letter they had brought from Mraize, explaining that he had kept his promise and protected them. As always, there was an implicit threat in his words. Today she ignored that. Today, she was going to enjoy her wedding. How many people actually got to *relive* such a marvelous event? She took a deep breath, stepped out, and joined the celebration.

It was beautiful.

They'd chosen one of the top rooms of Urithiru, with an enormous window looking out at frosted peaks. Everyone was there, swirling with joyspren like blue leaves. Her brothers, who'd only just discovered their sister was marrying one of the most powerful men in the world. Her squires, who were becoming Radiants in their own right. Vathah, Ishnah, Red, Gaz, even Shob. Stargyle and Beryl hadn't joined yet at the time.

Kaladin stood in a back corner, his face an emotionless mask. She tried not to think of choosing Adolin as a rejection of Kaladin—more an acknowledgment that for all the powerful moments they'd experienced together, their relationship was not one of romance but shared pain.

Sebarial and Palona, looking like proud parents. Women she'd come to know, like Ka and Rushu. Everyone in their finest, men in formal white suits with colors—in sashes or capes—declaring house allegiances. Havahs with sparkling gemstones on the women, burning with their own light. Ribbons, streamers, lace, tapestries, and rugs. All brilliant.

Yet all struggling—and failing—to compete with Adolin.

By tradition, he entered right as she did, from his own meditation room. He wore a brand-new side sword, because of course he did. He'd later tell her it was a gift from Kaladin. He'd been given forty-seven different swords that day, including one from her, and had chosen to wear Kaladin's.

Another man might have done that to prove victory over a rival. For Adolin, it was an earnest acknowledgment of a friend. Shallan took a Memory of it all, something she'd failed to do last year. She would re-create this day in art—but knew that no mere charcoal pencil would suffice. She'd need to practice with oils; as soon as Dalinar's contest was finished, that would be her task.

She met Adolin in the center of the room. He wore white, again by tradition, though she'd never seen an Alethi wedding outfit before, with its exaggerated cloth shoulders, its robelike design, its stiff—yet wide—cuffs and collar. Trimmed in Kholin blue, with a formal blue hat to represent modesty before the Almighty. Her sapphire dress was equally antiquated, with swooping wide cuffs and so much embroidery it covered most of the dress. The sewn-in rubies glowed, reflected in the gold on the bridal crown and thick overvest.

Shallan loved it—they looked like characters from a play. And as gorgeous as Adolin's outfit was, nothing could match his smile as he took her hands. In Jah Keved, she would have been given away by a senior house member, but by Alethi tradition, no one led them or gave them away. They were their own free people by the law, and owned by none.

Witnesses were required, however, and Navani and Palona would offer the notarization for that. They moved up alongside the arch that represented a portal to a new beginning. On the right side was Wit, dressed in black, the only one in the room wearing that color.

Hand in hand, Shallan and Adolin walked to the arch and stood beneath it. Kadash, the ex-warrior ardent, officiated. Adolin's trusted spiritual advisor. She remembered the ceremony going by in a flash before. Today it lingered. As she stared into Adolin's eyes and felt his hands, she let it be wonderful. Let it last as long as possible.

"Nothing brings the Almighty more joy," Kadash said, "than an oath made in earnest. So it should be no surprise that two oaths, made in love, are an experience sublime.

"We were formed by the Almighty, and find our deepest joy in building, creating, making oaths—and keeping them. The truly special experience of marriage is the chance to help one another in this journey. None of us is perfect, and so none of us can keep oaths perfectly. Though you remain devoted, there will be fires of anger, frustration, confusion, and pain.

"When those flames blaze, remember this day. Remember *this* oath, which is unique, as you do not make it alone. Together, you're stronger than apart. Together, your oaths will stand apart from the world.

"I believe that in nothing are we so blessed," Kadash continued, "as we are in our ability to accept one another as imperfect, yet trying. So look at one another. Remember this love, but know that this is merely the beginning. Each day, love should grow, until what you come to feel is a *bonfire* to today's candle, overshadowing lesser flames.

"To build a bonfire is more difficult than to light a candle. You will find the powerful heat to be a reward all throughout your lives. Here, I witness—we all witness—that a bond is formed. What the Almighty forges, let no person seek to undermine."

Shallan beamed. She *felt* it. Being here. Being *alive.* Adolin's warmth, from his palms into hers. Heat of life and love.

"Your oaths have been prepared?" Kadash asked.

"They have," Adolin said, squeezing her hands. "Shallan, my life is yours, my strength is yours, and our journeys are now one. My oath to you is love. Forever."

"Adolin," she whispered, remembering the words she'd spoken as if they were new, "my life is yours. My strength, *always,* is yours. When you are weak, let me be strong. When I am weak, please lend me your strength. And when we are both weak, at least we will not be alone. Never again alone, for our journeys have together become one. My love, forever. This is my oath."

He grinned. "A little improvisation from what you wrote before, gemheart?"

She leaned in. "Get used to it, gemheart. It will only get wilder from here."

He kissed her, causing some whispers in the room, as it was not yet time for kissing. He could improvise as well.

"Then," Kadash said, "it is witnessed and sealed by my authority from the Almighty. Two oaths have become one. Two hearts become one. Two journeys become one. You, Adolin Kholin, and you, Shallan Davar, are one." He paused. "This is when you're *supposed* to kiss . . ."

She grabbed Adolin, went up on her toes, and kissed him with as much force and life and heat as she could manage, in an explosion of passionspren like crystalline snow. She held it, until she heard people coughing and shuffling, but she didn't care about their discomfort. She breathed his breath and pressed herself to him and became his as he became hers.

Because she.

Deserved.

This.

So much might be wrong and stressful, but she did not walk alone any longer. She had him. Storms send that the real version stayed safe. All of her prayers in that moment, holding to the memory of him, were focused upon that.

Protect. Him.

Breaking the kiss at last, she sought out Pattern and Testament. She found them full sized—but ignored by the others. Shallan was sure she saw something *right* itself in Testament's pattern just then. Tines unbending slightly; her pattern restoring in some small way. Testament had been unable to attend the wedding the first time, but now . . . now it could be right. Indeed, Shallan hadn't been able to experience this fully the first time either. She'd still had things to learn.

Today, she looked away from the spren. Toward Kaladin brooding in one corner. After checking on him, she'd looked to Sebarial and Palona, given them a grin, then had seen a flash of red hair behind them. Followed by a face.

That haunting, distressing face.

Shallan had given that moment to Veil. Now, she could finally see, accept, and acknowledge it. Her *mother* stood at the back of the room, among the servants.

The Herald had died, and returned.

Shallan had killed her and sent her to Braize, where she had broken and come back to Roshar. Initiating the Return, unleashing the Voidbringers, and starting all of this.

98 THE DAY OF TRUTH

NINE AND A HALF YEARS AGO

The next morning, Szeth landed back at the Windrunner monastery and strode through the open front gates.

Confident. He was the only hope his people had.

He was *it.*

Acolytes scattered, running for their shamans. By the time Szeth had reached the Honorbearer's quarters—Szeth's quarters—the ten shamans of the monastery had gathered. In defiance of their station, each was wearing a faded red armband, left out in the sun. For mourning.

Appropriate.

"Walk with me," Szeth commanded them.

"Honor-nimi," the lead shaman said. Faraz-daughter-Daraz, he thought her name was. A short woman with brown skin and jet-black hair, cut close and curly. "We ten have conferred, and we ask to be sent as traveling shamans to visit villages in the region, rather than maintaining the monastery."

A profound demotion. And a profound statement.

"I barely spoke with you while I trained here," Szeth said. A deliberate misphrasing. *They'd* barely spoken to *him.* He'd been treated with strict coolness during that year. "Tell me. Where did Tuko find you?"

Faraz didn't reply, but one of the others piped up. "We're rejects," he said. "Turned down by the other monasteries."

"Turned down," Szeth guessed, "but not because of lack of skill with the sword?"

"I was one of the best," Faraz said, her chin up. Hardly appropriate humility for a servant of the Heralds. "I defeated Pozen's swordmaster in one out of five bouts."

"To win even a single point on Gonda-son-Darias is indeed an accomplishment," Szeth said.

"You took him down five for five, I heard," Faraz said, reluctantly.

"Yes," Szeth said, surveying the group of them. "But I have an uncommon skill, even among those uncommonly skilled. Five of you are of the sword, and five of the book?"

"Technically," one of the others said.

"In reality, all ten are of the sword," Szeth guessed, nodding. "Originally rejected because of your rebellious attitudes, then gathered here. So, Tuko *was* actually planning a rebellion." Szeth started down the hallway. "Walk with me."

They did not.

Szeth turned back to them. "I have not released you. Until I do, I am Honorbearer. Be glad you have me."

"You *killed* Tuko!" shouted one of the others.

"As I said, be glad," Szeth said. "I am more skilled than he was. You will need the very best to resist the others. If Tuko truly believed in Truth, then he would have wished for me to take his place."

The others considered that as Szeth walked through the quiet hallway. Finally, the gaggle of shamans joined him. "What are you saying?" Faraz demanded.

Szeth turned a corner and threw open the armory doors. As he'd remembered, Tuko kept the room well-stocked. It was a centerpiece of each Monastery of Truth, but many were maintained more out of ritual than active need. Not so here. Swords in stacks, gemstones, armor and shields in abundance. The larder would be well maintained to resist a siege, and the monastery—like each of them—had its own wells.

If he could recruit Moss, they'd have Soulcasting, which would mean infinite food so long as they took care of their gemstones. Unfortunately, he wasn't certain he would be able to persuade him. Maybe Sivi . . .

"Szeth?" Faraz demanded. "Um, honor-nimi?"

"Did Tuko tell you why he planned to rebel?" Szeth said.

"No," she admitted. "It didn't get that far. He said that the others might attack us, and we should prepare. When the time came, and we were ready . . . except he backed down. He waited. Until you arrived."

"He assumed that he could defeat me." Szeth looked to the gathered ten, and saw fear in their eyes now. "Tuko discovered, as I recently have, that the other Honorbearers serve one of the Unmade."

His voice didn't even tremble. Did he sound confident? He felt it, for once.

"An *Unmade*?" Faraz asked softly.

"Yes. I do not yet know if they are deceived or aware, but they are actively following the thing's demands. They call it 'the Voice.'" He paused, then took a deep breath. "I must declare, alone, that the Desolation has arrived. The Voidbringers have returned. At long last, the day of Truth is here—and it is time to fight."

Only one Unmade so far, that he had seen. The records from thousands of years ago were fragmentary copies of copies, but the general consensus among scholars was that if one Voidbringer was found, the rest would soon follow—or had already come in secret. He turned to the others, who were them universally alarmed, wide-eyed. Yet then they started nodding. Tuko had been working on them, despite not explaining fully.

"I have hope," Szeth said, "that I can recruit one or two of the Honorbearers. The others will resist us, so we must move quickly. Mobilize and recruit any among the people who are willing. It is time for war, and for us to pray to the Heralds that we are not too late."

99

NEVER TOO LATE

If you played the "destructive" melody and the primary melody at the same time, they would reinforce one another instead of destroying. This is humans and singers. Not opposites.

The same song. Played at different times.

—From *Rhythm of War*, first coda, Navani Kholin

Shallan left Adolin standing beneath the ceremonial archway of new beginnings.

It was the kind of callous thing women did in stories, but that wasn't the real him—and when she acknowledged that, the rest fell apart for her. It wasn't the real Dalinar or Navani who cried out—nor was it the real Wit she passed, but a giggling mess of self-aware Investiture egging her on. She gave everyone the briefest explanation of needing an emergency stop at the washroom, then made for her mother while holding up the skirts of her enveloping blue dress.

Chana . . . her mother saw her coming. With eyes wide, the woman ducked out the rear door. But there weren't many places to go, this high in Urithiru. Shallan soon cornered her mother in an empty room, lit by natural sunlight from outside. Chana faced the window with a panicked expression—hands pressed against the glass. Wishing, it seemed, to force her way through.

"Mother," Shallan said from the doorway. "Please."

Chana glanced over her shoulder. Storms. Shallan had seen her several times in the visions of the past, wearing furs, with the bearing of a soldier. It wasn't that her mother was a Herald. That was overwhelming, yes, but not *painful.* Whereas seeing the woman again . . . that hurt. Made Shallan want to run back to the warm wedding room. Avoid the confrontation.

No, Radiant said. *You said it's time. Fight.*

"Fight for me," Shallan whispered.

Not this time, Shallan. Not this time.

"Mother," Shallan said, steeling herself. "Why are you here?"

"I . . ." Chana whispered, tears in her eyes. "I heard that the Radiants had returned. That you were one. I came, and found a wedding. I didn't want to interfere. I just . . . wanted to see you again . . ." The woman sank to the floor, then pulled herself over into the corner, away from the window and Shallan. She huddled there, rocking back and forth, hands up to her face, fingernails digging into her cheeks.

"I didn't want to hurt you," she said, "but Ishar said I would. I wanted a family. I wanted . . . Selfish. So selfish. I . . ." She moaned, the sound becoming a soft wail of agony as she clawed at her face, trembling and weeping.

Shallan stood rooted in place, aghast as it slowly sank in. She, Shallan, was the *healthy one* by comparison. She . . . she was the adult in the room.

Pain. Pain . . . Shallan could handle, with Veil and Radiant as strengths in her mind. Like pillars holding up the sunlight. Shallan wiped her eyes, then approached, aware that this woman—though unarmed—might have access to a Shardblade or even an Honorblade. It was only a vision, and *probably* safe, but she still kept one eye on her mother's hands as she knelt.

"Mother," she whispered. "It's all right."

Did she feel that? Or were they just words? Emotions were a firestorm inside Shallan—anger, frustration, fear. Heat, all of them. So very hot, as if to burn her away and leave nothing but cinders. But then Chana looked at her, lifted a trembling hand, and put her fingers against Shallan's cheek.

"I wish I hadn't hurt you," Chana said. "Ishar and Nale told me it was a mistake to marry, but I thought I was well. I think . . . I think all of us make that mistake, even Ishar."

"I know what happened," Shallan whispered.

"We return," Chana said. "I went to Braize . . . and I broke. I tried to hide, I tried to last! But oh, I *broke.* This is me, this is all me! Everything that is happening is my fault! A new Desolation . . ." She closed her eyes and pressed her face against the wall again, moaning.

And Shallan . . .

Shallan felt the heat radiating through her, and made a decision. "Mother," she whispered, "you can't blame yourself for what others do. You cannot take responsibility for their choices. If the enemy attacks, it is *not* your fault."

"And what I did to you?" Chana hissed. "I thought . . . I thought you'd replace me. So selfish. Even if it had been true, it would have been selfish . . ."

Shallan leaned back, the words bringing emotion, like a jolt of cold ice amid the heat. Betrayal, a pain straight into her heart. Then . . . then slowly it melted away. When she spoke—tears in her eyes—Shallan found the words were not lies. Painful, yes, but not lies.

"Mother," Shallan said, "I forgive you."

Chana hesitated, then glanced toward Shallan. "I don't deserve that."

"I give it anyway," Shallan whispered. "What you did was terrible. You will need to be watched, helped, and prevented from hurting others. But I am safe now, so I can forgive you."

Chana lowered her hands. "How could I, and the horrible thing I've become, create something so wonderful in you? Hug your brothers for me, Shallan. Tell them I love them, even if I can never, *ever* see them again. Lest I hurt them too."

The heat settled. Maybe her mother didn't deserve forgiveness—there was no excuse for what she'd done, no matter her mental state. Still, it was important for Shallan to make some kind of reconciliation, if only in this playacting way.

Pattern stepped in, and then Testament. Chana's eyes flicked toward them, and she smiled. "You are in good hands. I should . . . I should have liked to have been with you, these years." She glanced to the side and jumped, seeing . . . nothing that Shallan could make out.

"They've found me," Chana said.

"They?" Shallan asked, rising and stepping back, careful of what this erratic behavior might mean.

"The souls of the dead singers," Chana said. "The Fused who have not Returned. I'm looking for Taln—I won't break this time. I will find him."

Souls of the dead . . .

"Mother?" Shallan said. "Where am I, right now?"

"Inside a vision," Chana said, "in the Spiritual Realm. Reliving your wedding. I died again, a few months ago. I was on Braize, in the Cognitive Realm, but I felt you calling . . . pulling me to you . . ."

It was really *her*?

Chana stood up, suddenly alert. "Thank you for stopping me." She met Shallan's eyes. "Do not trust any of us, except for Taln."

"Mother, you—"

"I must go," she whispered, then leapt forward and hugged Shallan. "I will try not to break so easily this time." Then her mother evaporated into colorful shifting smoke.

Storms! Shallan gasped, in and out, arms wrapped around herself, the sensation of her mother's hug lingering. "Was that . . . the real her?"

"Mmm . . ." Pattern said. "Rules are odd for Heralds, who are beings of all realms. I believe it was indeed her. A lie that became true."

Shallan felt a hand on her shoulder. Testament, pointing with a trembling, elongated finger. A shadow fell on the room somehow, though the window still looked out on a sunny day.

"He is here," Testament whispered. "Odium."

The vision broke apart, sending her back into chaos.

Dalinar screamed into the swirling chaos of the Spiritual Realm. He tried to fight it. Tried to offer up the strength that he'd found in taking the next step.

The power itself, not just Odium's touch, taunted him. Humans could not be trusted. Humans had broken Honor. None were worthy. It became a two-pronged attack, the power of Honor *cooperating* with Odium, who forced Dalinar to see failure after failure. Wearing down his resolve that he'd changed, that he was a better man, that he'd been forgiven.

Failing Gavilar on the night of his assassination.

Failing Elhokar, who had needed an uncle, not a rival.

Shifting shapes assaulted him, as if he were somewhere dark, full of thunder, wind battering him. People died, and rain pelted down in the flashing strobe of enraged lightning.

You think you've been forgiven? Odium's words reverberated through him. *You think you can simply stand up and walk away?*

In a moment, reality knit together, motes of light coalescing into a small chamber. A hard stone floor, hewn level by Shardblade, the separate slices and cuts manifest as imperfections and grooves. A single door, metal and imposing, more plug than portal.

A row of four beds against the back wall. Dalinar lay on one at the far end, and three blanketed lumps indicated the others were also occupied. Lighting came courtesy of some spheres in a sconce on the wall, though a cloth had been thrown across it to provide shade.

Dalinar sat up, puffing, sweating. His heart thundered, and in his mind echoed the accusations of the dead. He checked his arm fabrial, but it had been shattered. It might already be too late. It probably was. He felt as if he'd been in here for decades.

He tried to distract himself by inspecting this vision. The place seemed familiar; it had the look of a prison, with those uniform beds, the lack of windows, and that imposing metal door. But what kind of prison had such nice sconces?

"Father?" The next figure in the row of beds sat up, revealing a young boy that Dalinar didn't recognize. "Please, Father. Make it stop."

". . . Gav?" Dalinar said, and the boy looked at him, his eyes wide.

"Daddy?" Gav said.

Yes, that was Gav, though he wore a different face. Dalinar hated the way these new visions didn't let them truly see one another. Odium, trying to isolate them? Dalinar drew in a deep, relieved breath. "It's me, son," Dalinar said. "I mean . . . me, Dalinar. Your grampa."

Gav cringed, a motion that broke Dalinar's heart.

"What is this place?" Gavinor said, clutching the blanket. "I want to go home. I *want* to go *home*!"

"It's all right," said a familiar, lightly accented voice. The figure in the third bed stirred, revealing a mess of blond hair and a pale face, tear streaks staining her makeup.

Evi.

Oh . . .

Oh, *Damnation.*

"Evi?" he whispered.

She sat up, cocking her head. "Yes? Your name was . . . Hakin? Hakon? I'm sorry, it's been a long night."

Dalinar felt strangely *thin,* his emotions distant, his thoughts flimsy—like he was a shadow cast by a man. So. This was how Odium intended to break him. He said he'd moved forward . . . but was he ready for this? For *her.* He could have sworn he'd heard her voice at Thaylen Field. But . . .

Oh no. Blood of my fathers . . .

Dalinar recognized the room. He'd been in here once before, when it had been a hideout for a family. This was where they'd put Evi on the night . . .

The night when . . .

Tanalan. Rathalas, the Rift.

"Grampa?" Gavinor said, his voice growing shrill. "What's happening?"

"It's all right," Evi said. "As I told you, child, my husband will come for us."

"Evi . . ." Dalinar said again, but his throat had grown swollen, his words like tar. "I'm sorry."

"I might have ruined things," Evi said, "but he'll be here soon."

The fourth figure stirred in his bed, a well-dressed man who Dalinar didn't recognize. "The Blackthorn?" the man said, yawning. "He doesn't care if we rot."

"No," Evi said. "My husband is a good man."

Not this, Dalinar thought. *Anything but* this.

The door shook. Suddenly, he could hear it. The distant screams that had once been a constant accompaniment to his life. The sounds of a city burning.

Evi stood up, hesitant. He remembered that dress. He'd seen it on her burned corpse.

He thinks to break me with the truth, Dalinar thought. Whoever this new

Odium was, they knew Dalinar well enough to recognize this was the single most painful event in his life. The Rift and Evi's death would eventually send him to the Old Magic, to seek oblivion of thought and memory.

And yet, Odium didn't know *him.* Dalinar. Who he had become deep down; Odium couldn't see that man. For that man . . . he could not be broken by the truth. Truth was the weapon once used to bloody him, pulled from his own flesh afterward, and now held up as his finest blade.

Peace.

In that prison chamber, all became as if peaceful.

Unite them.

Who he had been.

Who he was.

Who he would become.

Air warped around Dalinar. The threads of the Spiritual Realm unraveling for a moment, then snapping back together. Dalinar breathed in, then out, and when the warping stopped, he was himself.

"Grampa?" Gav said. "I see you now!"

"My husband," Evi said, meeting his eyes, "*is* a good man."

"Maybe," Dalinar replied. "He's trying, Evi."

A Shardblade slammed through the space between door and wall, then slid down, cutting off hinges.

It was time.

Dalinar seized Gav in one hand, and with the other flipped the boy's bed on its side to shelter from the heat. He handed Gav to Evi.

"Take him," Dalinar said. "Protect and comfort him best you can for what comes next."

"I will," Evi promised, and beamed at him.

Dalinar touched his hand to the side of her face. "Thank you."

She nodded, then crouched down with Gav behind the improvised shelter. Dalinar stepped past it to confront what came next: a barrel, burning from a hole in one end, leaking flaming oil.

Dalinar caught it.

Then, with a strength no man should have, he heaved it up and threw it back out the doorway with the force of a siege engine. It smashed into the next one coming in, and they exploded into shards of wood, coating the entrance in flaming oil. Through those flames, Dalinar could see one thing outside. Two eyes. The eyes of the Blackthorn, cutting through it all. Red like blood. The eyes of a man who, after years of restraint, had finally given in and become the thing everyone said he was. The thing his brother wanted him to be.

A destroyer.

But Dalinar was not afraid. He no longer feared the past, and Odium had made a mistake in bringing him here. Dalinar strode through the fire, and it could not touch him, for he was the thing shadows and flames feared. He was a man who did not care what they revealed.

He stepped from the fires and confronted the Blackthorn on a ledge near the top of Rathalas, the city known as the Rift—a place with buildings constructed down along the inside of a chasmlike valley. Many buildings burned; archers shot at the residents from above; those refugees who fled at the bottom of the Rift were to be slaughtered by Dalinar's armies.

It was a funeral pyre for the innocent. And for Dalinar's sense of common decency.

All because of this man before him, who in his rage had given in. Dalinar made a fist to deliver to this hated version of himself what it deserved. Then stopped.

No. Not this time.

Instead, Dalinar turned away from the Blackthorn to ignore him. He searched among the Alethi troops here, and found Kadash. An excellent officer who, because of this day, would walk away from the army and become an ardent.

"New orders!" Dalinar shouted. "Kadash, I want the archers on the rim to stand down. Tell the troops at the bottom of the Rift to step aside and let people pass freely. Gather all of our troops and set them to putting out fires and helping the Rifters escape the flames. This is no longer a retribution. It is a rescue."

Kadash and the other troops paused, looking from Dalinar to the Blackthorn.

"Which of us," Dalinar said softly, "do you want to be the real Dalinar, son?"

Kadash looked to him, stood up taller, and began passing the orders. But then he hesitated. "Sir . . . it's too late, isn't it? The city is aflame. The soldiers below have already started the massacre."

"It's never too late," Dalinar said, "to try to be a better man. Do what you can."

Kadash ran off, shouting to stop the killing, as did the others. Dalinar turned toward a burning building to try to rescue the citylord and his family, but the Blackthorn stepped in front of him.

"You cannot ignore me," the Blackthorn said. "I am you."

"Yes . . ." Dalinar replied. "And no."

The Blackthorn raised Oathbringer to strike.

"See," Dalinar said. "Know."

The air warped again, and they were—for a second—truly one. The Blackthorn's eyes came alight with understanding as he saw the future—saw himself breaking, saw Gavilar die. Dalinar poured into this effigy every pain, every ounce of understanding, and the truth of who he had become. The Blackthorn gasped, and fell to his knees.

"Now what you said is true," Dalinar said.

"You realize," Odium said, the sound vibrating through Dalinar, "this is meaningless. None of this is real. What you do is performative."

"Then enjoy the show," Dalinar said, dashing for the burning building. But before he reached it, a figure in Shardplate came running to intervene.

"Dalinar?" Sadeas demanded. "What in Damnation are you—"

Dalinar punched him across his helmeted face, an excellent right hook, carrying with it decades of frustration and strength. The fist blasted through the Plate helmet, shattering it, and cracked across Sadeas's too-red, too-puffy, too-smug face.

Sadeas dropped like a lead bar, crashing to the floor in a heap of Plate.

That one . . . that one felt good.

Odium sighed. "You aren't performing only for me, Dalinar. Honor's power watches, and you just showed it something."

"That even I can change?"

"That men don't deserve Honor, for they disobey orders."

"I'm saving lives!"

"Traitors. What does the power of oaths care for lives, Dalinar? You, in all your self-righteous posturing, just broke your oath of commission to do as the king orders. Your job was to quell the rebellion in this city. Burning this place down, to make a statement—that was the right choice. I wanted you to see that."

In an instant, the vision shattered into fragments of light; he lost Gavinor again. His heart trembled for the boy, but he stood up tall before the tempest that followed.

"You feign strength," Odium said, "but you still hurt from that day. And you always will. Because that part of you knows it was *necessary.* You took those pains deliberately."

That voice. Was it . . .

The tempest whipped at Dalinar. Seeking to overwhelm and destroy him. That he could stand, but suddenly images of burned people began to form. His earlier strength seemed a lie as he stumbled, then huddled before those sights: image after image of the dead. Because it was true. For all his posturing, his changes in himself didn't restore to life the burned corpses of the children he had killed.

That was his burden. And his shame.

Perhaps that was what was guiding these visions. Not only Odium, but his own conscience, beaten bloody by his past and now thirsting for vengeance.

For he found his resolve crumbling, and found himself weeping as he saw those corpses. Including Evi's. He was a different man now, but could anything ever make up for such a terrible thing as he'd done? It was so horrific that seeing it now, he had to acknowledge that any punishment delivered to him would be *just.* He *deserved* it.

"You must find the most important words a man can say."

A voice. Upon the currents of this place.

He . . . he knew that voice. Dalinar searched in the chaos. It wasn't Gavilar, or Elhokar, or the Stormfather . . .

"Those words came to me from one who claimed to have seen the future. 'How is this possible?' I asked in return. 'Have you been touched by the Void?' The reply was laughter. 'No, sweet king. The past is the future, and as each man has lived, so must you.'"

"Nohadon?" Dalinar whispered. "Is that you?"

"You will love," the haunting voice continued. "You will hurt. You will dream. And you will die. Each man's past is your future."

"Then what's the point?" Dalinar begged. "Why? Must everything I do have no meaning because of the terrible choices I once made?"

"Ah, Dalinar," the voice said. "Listen. Remember. The question is not whether you will love, hurt, dream, and die. It is *what* you will love, *why* you will hurt, *when* you will dream, and *how* you will die. This is your choice. You cannot pick the destination, only the path."

"The path," Dalinar whispered, "is filled with pain."

"Your pain."

"Yes."

"*Your* pain," the voice said. "All men have the same ultimate destination, Dalinar. But we are *not* creatures of destinations. It is the journey that shapes us. Our callused feet. *Your* callused feet. Our backs strong from carrying the weight of our travels. *Your* back strong from carrying the weight of your travels. Our eyes open. *Your. Eyes. Open.* You kept the pain, Dalinar. Remember that. For the substance of our existence is not in the achievement, but in the method . . ."

The voice drifted away. Dalinar heaved himself to his feet. "Please don't leave me!"

A shadow emerged from the chaos. As tall as a mountain, as wide as the horizon. It fell on Dalinar, dominating him. A force. That spoke with . . . with *Taravangian's voice.*

"Dalinar, my old friend," the voice said. "Who are you calling for? The Stormfather? Navani?"

Dalinar collapsed to his knees before the shadow. And knew the truth. Taravangian . . .

Storms. Taravangian was the new Odium.

So many things suddenly made sense. It was a piece he'd been missing. And it terrified him. For he could think of no person worse—not even the man Dalinar had once been—to hold this power.

Storms.

"You could have been spared this torture," Taravangian said, his voice vibrating with the force of a thousand drums. "My predecessor offered to take your pain, but you refused. So now you must suffer." The shadow formed into the old man, standing before him, but with the . . . incomprehensible scope of a god.

Taravangian.

Odium.

They were *doomed.*

"You *must* suffer," Taravangian said. "It brings me no joy to see you like this. Yet it must be."

But I . . . Dalinar thought. *I did not give him my pain.*

He looked down at his chest and found a single glowing, golden light forming there. A line Connecting him to something. He touched it and felt *agony.* The pain of failure. The sharp, terrible agony of not just having lost people you loved, but having *caused* that death. Through inaction. Through misguided intention. And finally, worst of all, through deliberate choice.

And nothing one could do could ever make up for those awful decisions. It was a unique kind of misery. Dalinar knew it so, so well.

He seized that line of light, the agony vibrating through him. He used the very pain that Odium thought would crush him as a lifeline. Dalinar took hold of it in one hand and began pulling himself through the chaos on hand and knees.

"Dalinar," Odium said. "Dalinar, I can end this."

Dalinar found his feet, and started walking. Each touch on the line of light was *anguish.* He kept going.

"Do you know where that leads, Dalinar?" Odium said. "That path is only to more pain! You need to listen to me. I will show you. I WILL PROVE TO YOU THAT I AM RIGHT!"

Holding to that terrible pain, back bent, hands trembling, Dalinar pulled himself away from the shadow and stepped—with a surprised stumble—into a vision. A small stone chamber with a tiny window. Like . . . a monastery cell? Yes, the dark rooms where they kept the unhinged, away from light and stimulation.

A figure huddled against the wall in one corner, shaking and weeping softly. Dalinar's line of light led straight to him. Dalinar approached and knelt beside the figure, who proved to be an older man, with a stern full figure, a full beard. Dalinar recognized the face, though it no longer spanned an entire sky.

The Stormfather. So small now, as if mortal.

"You liar," Dalinar hissed.

The Stormfather continued to huddle by the wall, his eyes squeezed shut. And storms, Dalinar felt his anger evaporating. Again he was reminded how he confronted problems: punch them, break them, burn them down.

Journey before destination.

He needed to try something different. Still on his knees beside the Stormfather, he hesitantly put a hand on the spren's shoulder. The pain flared. That all-too-familiar *agony* of failure and loss.

"You feel it too," Dalinar said. "That's what led me to you, isn't it?"

The Stormfather shivered, the floor before him stained with tears. "I remember, Dalinar," he said. "As you accused me, I remember what . . . Honor did. I know his whole life. I'm an echo of him. And his failings are mine."

"Show me," Dalinar said.

"You'll hate me," the Stormfather whispered, his voice raw, ragged. "I've failed you. I . . . I . . ."

"Show me," Dalinar said softly. "So that I can understand."

The Stormfather blinked open tear-reddened eyes and looked at him. "It *hurts*."

"Maybe that's the point. Maybe emotions don't make us weak. Maybe they teach us. Like the pain of touching a hot stove. They show us what we should do, and remind us what we should not."

From the outside, Dalinar was a monster. How would Honor look from the *inside*? Did Taravangian, or Odium, realize what he'd done in reminding Dalinar of his pain?

No. Taravangian saw only destinations.

"You'll *hate* us—me, Honor—for what we did."

"No," Dalinar replied. "Understanding has never led to hatred. Show me. I cannot take your pain, but I *can* help you *carry* it."

The Stormfather reached up to touch his hand to Dalinar's.

A new vision began. And in this one, Dalinar saw the life of a god.

THE END OF
Day Eight

INTERLUDES

RYSN • ODIUM

Yes, but will they keep to it?" Brakt asked, gesturing to the small stack of pages in her hand.

"They're Alethi," Ytredn replied. "If you get it on paper, it's as good as an oath to them. I think they will keep to what they've promised. They must."

The two stood with Rysn on the lift, heading up to the middle floors of Urithiru. Chiri-Chiri snuggled in her lap, as large as a small axehound these days. The larkin was constantly frustrated that she couldn't hide in little boxes or pots of grass any longer. The number of times Rysn had been forced to yank her out of a hole she'd wedged herself into . . .

Those in the tower gave the creature curious looks, as well they should. Rysn had heard more than a few compare Chiri-Chiri to a chasmfiend with wings, though she was leaner than that, and had a segmented tail ending with a bulbous bit and then a pointed hook. She looked, really, like nothing else alive.

They gave Rysn's floating chair equally odd looks, even if that technology was becoming well known. Though they didn't know the half of it. For now, she didn't show off its newer functions, and just rode the lift with the two senior members of the Thaylen Patent Office.

"Why do you question, Brakt?" Rysn asked as the lift locked into place on the appropriate floor. "If we have a contract, we have a contract, don't we?"

The woman, with silvering hair and a stiff formal blue vest, walked beside Rysn—who moved her chair by touching a gemstone control on the armrest. It floated along, high enough for her to look people in the eyes.

"We have spent *literally* decades," Brakt said, "trying to get the Alethi and the Azish to agree to our patent requirements. I find it . . . uncharacteristic of them to agree so suddenly to our demands."

"They're our allies now," Ytredn said, waving with one hand, his eyebrows pulled back along his head and tied behind with a silver ribbon. "A lot of things are changing."

That wasn't quite what Rysn had heard. She'd heard that during the occupation of Urithiru, which had ended two weeks past, Navani had bullied several very important Thaylen artifabrians into sharing trade secrets—and they, after the occupation, had immediately bullied *her* into finally agreeing to Thaylen patent wording. Vstim said that Navani had signed—but under duress, during a time of great turmoil and stress in the tower following the occupation. Her babsk cursed the artifabrians who had pushed for it so quickly. He worried there might be legal precedent for getting the treaty thrown out.

He concurred, though, that it was better to test the treaty now. And so Rysn was here. Her homeland was under threat, but she could do nothing for them. War seemed constant these days, but life went on. She rested her hand on Chiri-Chiri, scratching at a small patch of skin between plates of carapace—which earned a buzzing of pleasure from the beast.

They reached the proper room, and she halted her chair outside to await the meeting time. Then, with her eyes closed, Rysn let herself feel.

She was growing better at controlling, or at least dealing with, the expanding powers given by . . . her special duty. Life sense, as the Sleepless called it, was the ability to feel living things—the bits of power that made up all of them, and constituted a soul. Sounds were different to Rysn now, as she could pick out notes exactly—and sometimes got lost in conversations because she was paying attention to the musicality of the language. And colors . . . she had finally managed to keep her mind from comparing shades of color the moment she looked at something, but it could still be distracting.

It all mixed to make life a little more overwhelming than it had been. The Sleepless called it "merely the surface-level gifts your duty bestows." They said to appreciate and welcome them, so she tried.

"Time," Brakt said.

Rysn felt the Alethi scholars join them before she opened her eyes, and could have placed each one distinctly. Together, they entered the meeting room, and the ardents gathered around her. Not Rushu or any that Rysn knew; these were more mid-level bureaucrats than scientists, though they administered Queen Navani's various programs.

Rysn glanced from Brakt to Ytredn. Both of the patent officials nodded. So Rysn took out her list of demands and presented them to the gathered officials.

They'd been warned, but as they read her papers, they looked more and more indignant. "These are impossible," one woman at the front said at last. "This is too much."

"Your queen signed the deal," Rysn said.

"It's not retroactive," the woman said. "We're free to make use of the things you and your business partners invented before the formal patent agreement."

"Well," Rysn said, leaning forward, "I guess you're not interested in the rest of our advances."

The group fell silent.

"The rest of your advances?" one asked.

She engaged her chair, which hovered higher. The basic functions weren't stunning anymore—artifabrians had been making things hover for years. The biggest and most difficult rock to crack had been how to have lateral movement when hovering, as the mechanics of conjoined fabrials had—up until recently—forbidden that. Rysn had been a big part of how that had been overcome, with the help of the Windrunner Huio, who was her business partner—and who was also named in her demands.

The Alethi, of course, had immediately taken her design and weaponized it—that was the Alethi way. The flying machine, the *Fourth Bridge,* was the result. But it had limitations.

Rysn flipped a switch on her chair, and it hovered sideways. Then she made it do a little circle of the room. She was no scientist herself, but deep down every merchant was a bit of a showman. So, using her control stick, she soared the chair upward while moving sideways, then down in a little dip and bump. Finally, she came to rest in front of the scholars, hovering a foot off the ground.

"That is . . ." the lead ardent said, "admittedly far smoother than anything we've managed. How are you so quickly switching between gemstones? What's powering such calm and steady movement on that small of a scale?"

"No chull track, I'll tell you that," Rysn said. "We've achieved speeds—without me in the seat, of course—of up to seventy-three knots."

Their eyes bulged at this.

"How?" one of the other ardents asked.

Rysn looked to her companions.

"So, you want to be in business or not?" Brakt asked, stepping forward. "If you do, we need to talk about how *this* time you're not going to infringe my client's patents, and how the Alethi and Urithiru governments owe her and her business partner—one Huio of Calipa—the demanded royalties upon every device they've begun creating that uses her proprietary designs."

"You'd put a price on scientific advancement?" a male ardent demanded. "You'd lock such valuable information behind a wall of filthy mercantilism?"

Rysn sighed. Fortunately, the other two were used to dealing with this sort of thing.

"Before the implementation of a patent system in Thaylenah," Ytredn said, right hand to his breast in a kind of salute, "each important discovery was held back by the inventor, for fear of their ideas being poached. Even still, we have problems with guilds maintaining secrets far beyond what is beneficial.

"A fair and reasonable patent system exists not to lock discoveries away, but to encourage them to come into the light; we assure inventors that their ideas will be valued and respected. We do not *hide* information. We encourage its sharing, just as any good legal code encourages good behavior."

The lead ardent huffed. But the creation of the *Fourth Bridge* was indeed a sign that sharing information could lead to much greater discovery. As long as she had a say in how it went. With the military in charge, she doubted time would ever be devoted to such a presumably low-level need as mobility devices.

But with the patent in her control, she'd make it happen. She settled back in her chair as the officials slowly talked the bureaucrats into signing a ratification of the treaty—something Vstim said would strengthen their case. Then, with Rysn's permission, they began laying out the schematics for the intricate gemstone-changing device that let her chair have such smooth flight. That included the specifics of the gravity- and ocean-wave-based propellant prototypes, both of which were far more efficient than simply having a track of chulls move your ship.

Rysn laced her fingers, listening, pleased. She'd dreamed of being a merchant captain, and now had her own ship. She'd been trained to negotiate trades around the world by one of the best. Who would have thought that her actual fortune would come not from the delivery of goods, but as a result of wanting to be able to move her own chair on the ship's deck?

All was going well until Dalinar Kholin walked through the door. And the power inside her went *haywire.*

A surging ran through her, like a sudden storm on deck. The power of the Dawnshard, her duty and her secret, started vibrating with a discordant note.

Dalinar's eyes locked on hers. His jaw dropped, and his image fuzzed briefly. She immediately knew this was not actually the Blackthorn of legend. Someone was imitating him.

"Out," the person imitating Dalinar said. "Everyone but the woman in the hovering chair. *Now.*"

"Brightlord?" an ardent said.

"*Now,*" he repeated.

"Go," Rysn said to her attendants, trying to keep her voice from trembling. Storms. The power felt like it was *screaming.* "I have business with . . . with the Blackthorn. Private negotiations. I will be well."

They seemed confused and concerned by this, with good reason. But they did go, leaving Rysn in the chamber with the man who looked like Brightlord Kholin—until the door closed. Then his illusion fell apart, revealing a shorter Shin man with white hair.

"Who the *hell* are you?" he said.

"I ask the same," she replied. "You are not a Fused—which is good, as a Masked One almost killed me a year back. But what . . . why . . ."

He was another one. Like *her*.

He held one of the things, the duty and power. The man before her was a Dawnshard.

But they were *not* supposed to be anywhere *near* one another. No two had been placed on the same planet, and for very good reason.

"I felt you the moment you entered the tower," he said, "but didn't know exactly what you were until now. You've found it? But how? And where was it? And . . ." He trailed off as Nikli poured out of the air duct nearby, forming from hundreds of cremlings into the shape of a human being. "Oh. *You* were involved. Of course."

"Rysn," Nikli said, stepping between her and the strange man, "do not speak with this one. He isn't what you think. He walked away from his duty centuries ago. He held a Dawnshard once, but now merely bears echoes of it—"

"No, Nikli," Rysn said. "He *is* one. I can feel it. He *is* one of four that you said should never meet. We are here. And we're together."

Nikli looked at her, then back to the strange man.

"This is a secret," the strange man noted, "that I've worked very hard to keep."

"You *took it up again?*" Nikli demanded, stepping toward him. "You . . . That's why no one can find it. You gave it up, but then took it again at some point, hiding it—because the signs would be dismissed as lingering aftereffects of your long-standing tenure. Then . . . you brought it here to Roshar? Why in all the cosmere would you do something so reckless? Even you should know better."

Nikli's shape unraveled a little like it did when he was upset, the legs of the cremling-like creatures that made him up poking through his skin.

Rysn hovered to the side, studying the man with the white hair.

"How did I completely miss you?" he said, still meeting her eyes. "Who are you? How did this happen? Something this momentous should have shown up in . . ."

He trailed off as the powers within them started to align. The Sleepless had explained to her what she held: a Dawnshard, one of the four core forces by which a god had been Shattered. Something beyond common Surges. Something primal.

The four had been divided up, never to be brought together, lest . . .

Lest this happen. The two started to pull toward one another. Rysn gasped, gripping the armrests of her chair as the power sought to *pull* her across the room to smash into the force from the other man. She knew, instantly, this would destroy her—she'd be made a flesh pulp by the contortion of the forces in motion.

She strained, but was pulled out of the chair to the floor, dumping Chiri-Chiri from her lap with a click of annoyance. The room began to vibrate. Nikli, and her other Sleepless guard who had been sneaking up behind the strange man, unraveled. Their separate hordelings lost cohesion as they fell into mounds of scrambling bits. Chiri-Chiri writhed on the floor, the awful vibration making her screech.

Rysn scrambled to hold to the ground as she was pulled across the floor toward where the man with the white hair was glowing. He closed his eyes, then held his hands before him and made a gesture with his index fingers and thumbs extended.

A sound like a gong in her head was followed by a perspective of . . . vastness. Time stretching in all directions, forward, back, even to the sides. And at the center of it, that man, with white hair flaring up from his head and light coming from his core.

He snapped his eyes open and spoke.

"*No.*"

The vibrating ceased. The sound went out. The light faded. Rysn was left on the floor, Chiri-Chiri climbing onto her back and crying out, trembling. Two Sleepless in piles.

"I will ensure that we never meet again," the man said, then restored his illusion of Dalinar and left.

Storms. Rysn slumped on the ground, waiting for the two Sleepless to recover. She had to hold to Chiri-Chiri, who pulled against her in a panic. That awful vibration continued to echo in her soul, and she knew she'd been mere moments from being completely annihilated as the two powers merged.

Eventually, Nikli and Alalhawithador restored themselves. They settled down beside her, and Nikli helped Rysn sit up.

"Well," Rysn said, wiping the sweat from her brow, "what do we make of that?"

"I can think of few people worse in all the cosmere to have discovered us," Alalhawithador said. "But it is not your fault. He should *never* have taken up a Dawnshard again. He, who was there when they were used . . ."

"That creature is not one of the gods," Nikli said. "We're hidden still from Odium and the rest. The Mythwalker will not share a secret like this with anyone."

"But he will keep it," Alalhawithador said. "And will use it against us." She looked to Rysn. Over the time that Rysn had borne this burden, she thought maybe she'd started to earn their respect. That was manifest now, as

Alalhawithador—who had once been harsh to her—spoke in a kindly way. "What would you like to do, Bearer?"

Rysn had Nikli help her back into her seat. She took a deep breath, again wiping sweat from her brow. "We need to go into hiding, don't we? I have . . . I have to abandon my ship. My crew. Everything."

The two looked down. Then Alalhawithador nodded.

The Dawnshards could not be combined, and she could not remain in this land knowing she'd been discovered. She had to leave. Perhaps forever.

Unless . . .

There was something she'd been planning. More a fanciful imagining than a true expedition. But perhaps . . . with her ship's new capacities . . .

"It appears," Rysn said, "I will not be able to enjoy the exploitation of my patent, but perhaps I do not have to abandon ship or crew. What happened here was not my fault, but it is my responsibility nonetheless. I will go into hiding. But please consider letting it be in a specific way . . ."

As she explained it, they agreed. It was a dangerous suggestion, but exciting nonetheless. She hated being forced into it, but that was that. She would have to go. So, just when everything looked like it was finally building back up and coming together for her, Rysn prepared to say goodbye.

Odium relied on his expertise, working to break Dalinar. There was another purpose, of course, for these visions. As a god, everything he did had multiple purposes.

In this case, he inspired pain. When Dalinar managed to briefly wrest control of a vision, to try to avoid his agony, Odium isolated him and began overpowering him with painful truth. To break him down, so he could be rebuilt.

The power loved seeing that emotion in Dalinar.

Everything was in hand. Until Dalinar vanished.

Surprise. The power did not love that, but it accepted it. Complete, overwhelming, *surprise.*

What had happened? Dalinar was nowhere in the Spiritual Realm—nowhere that Odium could see. Could someone hide from him that completely?

The answer was yes. They could. But it would take the act of a Shard. The visions themselves were hiding Dalinar now? They'd all been playing with the fragments of Honor's power in here, as it longed to have a Vessel again, and thus was easy to mold into the shapes of memories. Visions, for that reason, were more stable when in this "region" of the Spiritual Realm.

Yet the power had been agreeing with Odium. Such as it could; but it didn't have true volition, did it? It didn't care about anything other than following its Intent, right? Odium investigated, furious at having his prey stolen, and found something unexpected.

The power of Honor had been too long without a host. It was becoming dangerous. It was coming *alive.* So Odium contemplated.

Should he destroy it?

DAY NINE

TANAVAST • VENLI • NAVANI • SZETH • KALADIN • SIGZIL • JASNAH • SHALLAN • ADOLIN • RLAIN • RENARIN

TEN THOUSAND YEARS AGO

I, God, found a world unmanaged.

Blue against a black sky, a globe of infinite potential. This was a new creation, I sensed—one of Adonalsium's most recent masterworks. It sang to me its name through tones and rhythm, and I told it mine.

Tanavast. Almighty.

Heir to Honor.

Here in this world I found perfection, a relic of the being I had slain for his own good. Roshar had been grown entirely from equations, as a grand testament to the divine nature of mathematics—a celebration of the intimate relationship between song, numbers, and art.

There was Honor in this.

I Invested this land, restoring godhood. There were echoes, of course, of my predecessor. Little bits of him left behind. Three powerful incarnations who had his voice, and many smaller ones representing aspects of nature and personality. Beyond these tiny spirits, Roshar had people. A curious variety who could hear the songs of the gods. Their orderiness sang to my soul, and to the power I now held.

For a moment, I doubted. A part of me dared wonder. Did I understand what I'd done? Did I . . . regret?

These questions echoed in the stewards that my predecessor had left. Shadows of divinity with instructions to protect, to shroud, to nurture. One sang to me in particular, and that invigorated me, though I did not know why the Wind was chosen to protect. Wind, invisible Wind, so flighty and immaterial.

It did not . . . it did not condemn me. I sang with it.

There were other worlds here. One held humans, and I ignored it for now. I was too intrigued by a third world, more distant from the sun. A cold, dark rock—it could support life, barely. It had a curious property: a core of a strange metal that attracted Investiture, calling to my soul. Fascinating.

I left these two worlds—one with humans, one with the core of odd metal—alone, instead enjoying my songs on Roshar.

Until *she* arrived.

The one I'd always loved in secret—our union forbidden as mortals—emerged from the darkness of the void between worlds. Cultivation, she was now called, though I knew her as Koravellium Avast—the beautiful dragon heretic of Yolen. She swept up from behind, embraced me with arms like the sky. I sighed, touched her, and all felt right.

"You," I whispered, "should not have come."

"We agreed that I would," Kor replied.

"I'm glad that you did. But you should not have. The other gods insisted that . . ."

I could not say the words, for doing so might send her away. But the *power*. The power *rebelled* against me. I sensed it twisting and contorting, like a . . . like a tempest. Angry.

I am God, I thought to it. *You obey me.*

It writhed. How could I break my word? Yet I was in command, not it. I could decide what promise was worth keeping, and what was worth discarding.

Kor was here. This was right.

The power simmered. Well, it would learn.

I leaned into Kor's embrace, my power against hers. Oddly, my mind—though greatly expanded—still wanted a frame of reference with which to interact. And so I shaped a type of body of my power. Not fully physical, and attached to something that expanded forever, this . . . avatar of myself could feel her touch more distinctly. Rest its head against her arm. Breathe out, and let her rhythm come to harmonize with mine.

"Tanavast," she said, "we were going to find a place uninhabited."

I gazed toward her, saw her essence . . . but also her form. In her human shape—dragons all had two—a woman with brown skin and lush proportions.

"Look at them, Kor," I said. "*See them.*"

People. Fledgling hunter-gatherers, of carapace skin and songful hearts. They reminded me of my own people, who had been so primitive compared to the dragons and their great civilization. Rosharans sang songs into the sky, the ground, and the night, waiting for their maker to return.

"We cannot abandon them," I whispered. "We orphaned them, Kor."

"I do not wish to be a god," she said.

"Far too late for such regrets."

"I left my people because they wanted me to take prayers," she said. "I can hold this power, because someone must. But I have no desire to be worshipped, Tanavast. Let us find another world where we can experiment with creations that will be part of us, not remnants of the being we . . . we betrayed."

She still thought of it that way. A betrayal.

In the far distance, something happened. Gods . . . dying? Pain? We both noticed it. She held to me.

"Do not interfere," she said. "Let us leave them to their fighting. Let us be alone."

Others betraying their promises made me more confident in having done so myself. Yet, what of this land? I, God, turned from her and beheld the people of Roshar, hearing their songs, their pleas. My heart trembled for them.

"Stay here with me," I requested, holding to her hands. "I will watch over them. You can hide, and not interfere. This *can* be our place. Does it not sing to you?"

"It . . . *is* a beautiful song," she said. "The song the Night sings . . . I love it."

I smiled.

She smiled back, a glow like the sunrise.

And so it was.

Until Rayse arrived.

Few combatants win on board or battlefield without first having won the fight against their own minds.

—*Proverbs for Towers and War,* Zenaz, date unknown

I am my own. Not his.

The mantra repeated in Venli's head.

I am my own. Not his.

It seemed at times to be her sister's voice.

The listeners, Fused, and chasmfiends had spent a fitful night. Now they rose, the offer looming over them. The Five had come to no decisions the night before, and Venli empathized. Serve Odium? How could they possibly do that again?

Their guards were common warforms, but the way they spoke . . . they were increasingly certain they'd win the Shattered Plains soon. She could hear the humans shouting, and they sounded desperate.

I am my own. Not his.

She walked back to her group in the darkness, then approached the Five and Leshwi. Their camp was in a strangely open part of the chasm, a place where a plateau had been entirely destroyed during the Everstorm's first arrival.

The Five continued to argue. "He can't take any of us as hosts for a Fused unless we agree to that specifically," Estel said. "We could accept his dominance, but never give ourselves to the Fused. That keeps with the spirit of the listeners."

"I'll admit," Kivor whispered, "a part of my soul is *relieved* to face this question at last. It was coming. Perhaps this is for the best—our people will no longer need to worry about the axe to our throats."

"We can't," Thude whispered. "Rejecting him is what defines us."

Venli settled down outside their circle. It was so strange to be here again. Beneath another darkened sky. Involved in the fate of her people once more.

"Can we be defined by a negative?" Estel asked softly. "What are we?"

"We listen," Bila said. "Fused, what do you hear?"

"Sorrow," Leshwi said, her eyes closed. "Anger. He demands my return." She hesitated. "Venli, do you sense it?"

"No," Venli said, scooting forward. Cautious, Venli placed her hand on the Fused's shoulder. "But I can understand the relief that might come from just . . . returning to him, and no longer feeling rejected—or afraid."

Leshwi looked at her hand, then back at Venli. This was an interaction that once would have been brazen. Comforting a Fused? Heresy.

"I have found," Venli said, "that I no longer need to be afraid."

After a moment, Leshwi hummed to Resolve.

"Still," Kivor said. "The Five need to make a choice."

"If we join this battle," Bila said, "they'll use us as fodder at the front of their final assault. Us and the chasmfiends. We'll be slaughtered."

"But if it gains you peace for the rest of your people?" Leshwi asked. "We cannot resist a force such as Odium alone. Is this not a worthy sacrifice?" With her elevated way of talking—her accent harking back to the ancient days—it was difficult not to agree with her; she projected authority.

Though Venli could understand the allure, she was revolted by the offer. The others seemed the same, even those who had spoken in favor of accepting it. They glanced at one another, humming to uncomfortable rhythms.

Venli wished she had something that would give them solace. But who was she? She had bent like a twig to his will. She had . . .

. . . sworn oaths to seek freedom. To help those in bondage. An idea occurred to her. A desperate, dangerous idea. A counterpoint to what she'd done years before.

Timbre thrummed. Excited.

"Five, if I may speak?" Venli said, as a plan formed in her mind.

⁘

Navani was lost in a nightmare.

She knelt on the ground before a low table, sweating, surrounded by laughing women. They mocked her as she struggled with the written word, sounding out each letter.

She was eleven, and had come with her father to the city of Shulin to do business, including a need to settle their family accounts. Her family grazed kevah: midshelled beasts that had been cultivated for their gemhearts useful in Soulcasting meat. Their flesh wasn't too bad either, and they could graze on flat land, the worst type for farming because of water stagnation.

They paid now for animals purchased the year before. Ranching was a fine living for a lighteyed family who happened to own some cheap land—but it was not well regarded for a man of her father's dahn.

Time with her father out on hunts or riding the ranch hadn't been good for Navani's studies. So she knelt there in the accounting house, not even a teen, holding back tears as women snickered. A ridiculous backwater yokel, whose dress was too big for her and whose hem was stained by crem. With effort, she wrote out the final lines of the contract. She sat up, then listened to the women read, finding her spelling amusing.

Navani hated coming to the city. Hated feeling ignorant.

"Child," a kindly lesser scribe said, leaning down. "Why not let another more experienced handle this?"

"We only have three scribes," she said. "One's having a baby soon. The other two are seeing to our local accounts." What Navani did here was a formality—they needed the good scribes to ensure nobody was embezzling.

"Your mother?" the scribe asked.

"Mother left," Navani whispered. "Divorced us."

The women shared glances. It wasn't impossible—the right of travel was a divine blessing granted to all but lower-nahn darkeyes, enshrined in Alethi common law for centuries. No person could be forced to work, or live, in one place.

Yet a divorce wasn't considered proper. Leaving wasn't a problem, mind you, but why cancel a marriage? Navani's mother had too much dignity to leave without officially divorcing, but not enough dignity to maintain contact with her daughter.

The laughter turned demonic, and insults started to fly, beating on her like lashes.

Ignorant.

Incapable.

Idiot.

The young Navani, crushed by the experience, had fled, crying. She hadn't felt like herself for weeks afterward. This had been one of the central moments in her life when . . . when she'd known . . . a girl like her couldn't ever be . . .

"Lies," she whispered, looking up. "Repackage them as you wish. I know them now for what they are."

Suddenly the nightmare had no teeth. The laughter took on a frantic air, the women annoyed to be ignored.

 "This seed was buried deep, wasn't it?" Navani whispered. "Grew into a weed that snarled and choked me for decades, watered by Gavilar once he recognized it. I've *pulled* that weed. Its power withered as its roots died. Begone."

The vision popped, and she was cast into the chaos.

She hunkered down against the flashes of visions—of other times in her life when she'd been mocked, undermined, attacked. And she started thinking clearly. She wasn't certain how long she'd been adrift in this place—she cursed herself for not insisting she have a clock like Dalinar's, but their visit to the Spiritual Realm was supposed to have been a quick test.

She put that failing aside. She needed to find Gavinor, then Dalinar, then get out. Unfortunately, she could see no lines of Connection. Something was different now. And Navani . . .

Navani saw a *pattern* to it.

Patterns were one of the pillars of science. And she *was* a scientist. She had gone toe-to-toe with Raboniel and won. The visions could laugh all they wanted, because each one taught her something. Not about herself, but about *them*.

Ever since the vision where Mishram had been captured, she'd been swimming through possibilities, and they should have been random. Instead this had been the fourth in a row of escalating intensity and pain. She refused to believe that she was causing her own torment; she was clearly being *directed* toward painful moments.

She stood up amid the chaos, like a terrible wind blowing past with streams of colorful smoke and mist that briefly took the shapes of people or events. It tugged at her clothing and her hair, which had come loose from its customary braids and bun. Perhaps this was Odium, or maybe it was Dalinar. He had been feeling raw and vulnerable, falling back—regrettably—to old foibles. Perhaps his pain—and worry for the upcoming contest—was somehow dominating the visions, creating echoes that sent her into her darkest days.

I am a scholar, she thought. *And I will test hypotheses. My visions have been escalating. Which means . . .*

As the next started to form, she guessed it would be Gavilar. On one of the days near the end, when they'd fought constantly. The vision came together: her study in the palace of Kholinar. She knew, without needing to check the calendar on her desk, what day it was. Her books were out, and she was working on an essay about the Parshendi, recently discovered on the Shattered Plains.

She wanted to remain logical, but . . . this room brought up so many memories. Kholinar, now lost to them, the palace controlled by the Fused. This room likely no longer existed. She stood in a beautiful figment of her past.

She walked to the bookshelf and ran her fingers over *Light and Gemstones* by Chanosha, then the six-volume *Artifabrication* by Britt the Good. Navani's copies had been worn when she acquired them, as these were old books with faded pages and cracking covers, purchased by a young Navani during the years when she'd first started spending time with Gavilar, Dalinar, Torol, and Ialai. Days when they'd dreamed of conquering the world, and she'd dreamed of conquering herself.

There, in a spot along her shelf of knickknacks, she found a wooden . . . something . . . made by Elhokar when he'd gotten his first whittling knife as a boy. He'd called it a skyeel, she thought. He'd been embarrassed, years later, that she'd kept it. Yet she smiled whenever she saw it, and the small scrapbook of poems and stories written by Jasnah during her youth, when she'd been determined to learn how to write those fun adventure tales that women liked to read. Those embarrassed Jasnah more than the wooden skyeel had Elhokar, and Navani had been sensitive enough to hide them. She had been made to feel ashamed of her scholarship; she would not do the same to her daughter.

Odd, Navani thought, trailing through the room. *Each time, the vision lets me settle in for a moment before hitting me with the painful part. Like it wants me to experience joy, before smashing it.*

It seemed so deliberate. She was able to guess, almost to the second, when she would first hear Gavilar's footsteps in the hall. She turned, completely unsurprised when he burst through the door and slammed it shut.

Seeing him hurt. From the outside, he was exactly the man she'd always wished to marry. A regal king, like from the olden days. Any historian could have warned her those kings from the olden days had almost universally been vile human beings.

"Did you tell Elhokar," he demanded, his eyes seething, "that he shouldn't marry Aesudan?"

"So I was right," she said. "It's *that* argument."

"How dare you? We need this union; you know how I've worked for it. Elhokar would have married that nobody scribe, if *not for me.*" He didn't raise his voice, but lowered it, exuding a sense of dangerous control.

"I wonder," Navani said. "Was I too hard on Aesudan? I remember undercutting her time and time again. I didn't like the girl, but did I need to insult her?"

Gavilar strode around the desk to come right up next to her. "You undermine my authority."

"I assert my authority."

"You will make me look bad before the highprinces."

"I learned long ago, Gavilar," she said, "queen or not, I can't *make* you into anything. If you look bad before anyone, it's merely because I've pulled the curtains back."

He growled, then raised his hand.

"Ah," she said. "But he *never* hit me. If he does now, it will break the illusion, won't it?"

He huffed, then spun, turning away from her.

Her heart was racing—that slap had looked like it would really fall. But then . . . had she just manifested *control* over this vision? She hadn't been able to draw herself into a pleasant vision despite trying, but maybe that was too big an alteration—perhaps she needed to try smaller things. Like . . . like guiding an ornery chull. Stopping it was near impossible. But you *could* turn it. How to test her theory?

"Yes, he can't hit me," she whispered. "Physical pain would have bolstered me, provoked me to leave and escape his control. What he did was in some ways worse. He undermined my confidence . . ."

Gavilar spun back toward her. "You think," he said, "you *belong* at my side? You think you *deserve* to be a queen?"

"Yes," she said. "Like that."

"I build something grand," Gavilar said, stalking toward her, "and you're still stuck—at least in your mind—on a backwater ranch, barely able to write your name."

"He didn't know that about me," she added. "By the time I knew him, I had impressive penmanship and spelling."

"I build something grand," Gavilar said, stalking toward her again, like an actor repeating his lines after flubbing them, "and you're still stuck—in your mind—on a backwater ranch, worrying about your insignificant father and his petty concerns."

"Much better," Navani said. "But Gavilar always built up to insults like these—he never came in spewing them. You're missing the nuance. The careful gibes like pins—not daggers. The cold refusal to talk to me about important matters, as if insulting me wasn't even *worth his time.* Gavilar was a master of *precision* abuse."

The simulacrum of Gavilar started pacing on the other side of the room. She could *steer* this vision. Almost like . . . whatever was sending these had its attention mostly elsewhere, and had left this one to play out and torment her. Like Dalinar's visions of the past, which had instructions on what to show him, but no direct oversight.

Or was she reading too much into this? Either way, she had tested her theory. The next step was application. Could she use these visions to get information that would help Dalinar?

No, she thought. *I need to find Gav first. Somewhere in here is a boy, terrified and alone.*

Where would little Gavinor be?

The answer was obvious. If the poor child was in a vision like this, it would be the one where he was tortured by evil spren while his mother hummed to herself.

Wait.

That had happened in the Kholinar palace.

A different version of it, yes, but if Navani could steer this particular chull . . . could she find her grandson? Gavilar started talking again, but Navani ignored him. He was unworthy of her attention, and always had been.

What if . . . she thought. Storms. That would hurt. Could she do it?

Strength before weakness. She'd said the words. She needed to mean them.

"You know what would *really* hurt me?" she whispered. "If I was forced to watch what happened . . . what happened to Elhokar . . . at the end."

Each word was raw, because they were true.

That truth served her—because she was certain the vision could sense her sincerity. In a blink, Gavilar's simulacrum puffed away, and the room changed, dust appearing on the books. This was the palace that Aesudan had ruled under the thrall of multiple Unmade.

Navani opened the door, and heard shouts echoing in the hall. She'd done it. This was the terrible day when her son had been killed.

NINE AND A HALF YEARS AGO

Szeth landed at the Elsecaller monastery at night.

Pozen's monastery, where Szeth had lived the longest. His eyes naturally sought out the hallway window where he'd stood many a time staring out into the night, holding a contraband woolen toy and longing for his mother.

He launched into the air, soaring up to the roof, and surveyed the lights of Mokdown beyond. A small, vibrant city, squashed between two rivers. Did any of the shamans who served beneath the Honorbearers know? Surely there couldn't be *hundreds* of people involved in this conspiracy, could there?

His mind still reeled. It had been six weeks since he'd discovered the truth, and he'd spent them preparing his monastery for war. He'd ignored invitations to visit the other monasteries, but the letters he'd sent to Sivi and Moss—implying that they should join him—had gone unanswered.

The Return had come, right beneath their noses. How many Honorbearers had lived and died, fully in the grip of the very thing they were meant to protect against? How many Tukos had there been? Honorbearers who didn't quite buy in—their questioning leading to their removal?

No more. He had begun gathering towns and cities to his cause. Before he unleashed civil war, however, Szeth wanted to try other options. He was exploring one tonight. He slunk across the rooftop, glad for all the times that Pozen had made him climb up here on his stupid quests. Szeth hated this place. Hated it deeply—for forcing him to leave his mother behind, for making Elid abandon him.

Here, Pozen had forged Szeth into a weapon. But a weapon could be turned on its masters, and Szeth was strong enough—because of their training—to do what needed to be done. For that, Szeth supposed, he should be grateful.

Pozen used you as an assassin, he thought. *He deserves this more than any of them.*

Szeth located the access hatch, and hesitated, thinking of his father, who had vanished. Szeth had come back a day after visiting the Voice, only to find the hidden camp empty, Neturo nowhere to be seen—with no signs or notes left behind.

He feared his father had been taken hostage. If so . . . what would the price be for Szeth's decisions?

No, not a price, Szeth thought. *You have to have a choice to pay a price. Today, I have no choice.*

Today, he would assassinate Pozen as the first step in war.

Szeth sliced the lock off the access hatch with his Blade, then slipped in. This hatch was a weak point, and shouldn't have existed. Even Pozen, despite his claims of orthodoxy, had grown soft. Stones Unhallowed . . . they all had.

Szeth dropped into the hallway, cold despite the Stormlight raging inside him. It was past curfew, when Pozen demanded his acolytes be in their quarters. But what would he do if he *did* meet some poor acolyte? He felt horrible, sneaking through these once-familiar hallways. This subterfuge was a similar tactic to what he'd done to those invading sailors years ago. Trickery, movement in darkness.

This wasn't him, was it? He could win any fight directly, so why use stealth?

A mercy, Szeth told himself. *A Blade in the night is a mercy.* Just a quick excision of festering flesh, from the Blade of a surgeon. This proved it wasn't about revenge for Szeth. It was only what had to be done. With Pozen's blade, Szeth would have Soulcasting. With that to feed his armies, he could march on and overthrow the Bondsmith. With Pozen dead, the other Honorbearers might fold. He might not *need* to fight Sivi or Moss.

His head buzzing with such thoughts, he was glad when he reached one of the meditation chambers, found it empty, and slipped inside. There—by the light of a few amethysts—he tried to calm his rapid breathing, quiet his thundering heart. Luckily, he hadn't been seen. He was fond of some of those who worked this monastery. He'd have hated to . . .

To what? Would he really *kill* one of his friends?

He breathed a soft prayer to the room's stone, a raw chunk of shale with a sharp point toward the sky. Pozen liked to meditate in the night, after curfew, when it was quiet. He usually picked one of the chambers farther along the hallway. If Szeth was in luck, the man would come tonight. He would be alone, and Szeth could do the deed.

Unfortunately, Szeth soon heard a voice echoing in the hallway outside—but it didn't belong to Pozen.

It was Sivi.

Szeth went alert, his breath catching.

"... can't defeat him, Pozen," she was saying. "None of us can."

"There is time yet," Pozen replied. "Many of us find the Truth difficult at first. He is an obedient sort, Sivi. Give him more time. It has been only six weeks—you refused to speak to us for three months once you were elevated. Szeth *will* return and do as he is told."

"I think you underestimate him," Sivi said.

"*Under*estimate him? You think it is *good* he shows this rebellious streak? Sivi, you know better."

She didn't reply. Szeth could hear them in the hallway just outside, separated from him by a door woven of reeds and fronds. He summoned his Blade.

"You question too much, Sivi," Pozen said sharply. "Your loyalty becomes suspect."

"What?" she said right by the door, the proximity making Szeth sweat. "You'll do to me what you did to Tuko?"

"Don't be dramatic," Pozen said. "You wouldn't push us to that, Sivi."

"Don't be dramatic?" she said, her voice rising. "We killed Tuko and replaced him with someone far, *far* more skilled. He wrote to me, suggesting I visit to speak with him about an important item—and the implication was clear. He's been talking to the garrisons of the cities nearest him. This could become very, *very* bad."

"I will handle it," Pozen said. "The Voice assures me that all is under control—particularly with the specific leverage you made sure to get for us. Here. You wanted to meditate with amethyst light? These chambers will do."

Szeth held in a curse. In a panic, he drew in the room's Stormlight—a bad idea, as it could reveal he was here, but he couldn't help himself. He Lashed himself upward in the small chamber, toward the ceiling. Sivi, however, didn't enter his meditation chamber—she entered the one next to his.

Pozen retreated. Szeth heard his footsteps along the hallway. That worried Szeth, until he realized that he'd been handed a gift. He could kill Sivi and claim the Willshaper Blade, then strike against Pozen. When he had both of their weapons, his armies would be that much better protected. He wouldn't have to worry about Honorbearers using Shadesmar to pop in unexpectedly, nor would there be any who could sculpt stone.

He'd be far from safe—there would be those who could Lightweave to worry about, not to mention the armies serving the others. But with three Blades ...

He raised his weapon, preparing to break through the thin wall between alcoves. She'd be dead before she realized what was happening. Except ...

Sivi?

His father genuinely seemed to love her, and had cried when it was time to part and continue the pilgrimage. It might have been a fling to her, but not to Neturo. Plus, she'd treated Szeth so well.

She serves the Unmade, Szeth thought. *She violates Truth, even while she pretends to preach it.*

But if he was wrong? This was all happening so quickly. Szeth looked down at the stone in his room, wavering.

A boy with a rock in his hand, blood dripping from it.

Burning ships.

A dying holy man in his arms, holding his shoulder as his life bled away.

Yes, Szeth could kill. They'd made sure of that.

Today, he dismissed his Blade. He left the meditation chamber, walked to the adjacent one he'd heard Sivi enter, then strode in. He owed it to his own conscience to at least talk to her first. Szeth was not the man Pozen had crafted him to be—he was more than that. He was a child of Neturo. Children of Neturo asked questions.

Sivi turned. Her eyes went wide and she rose and backed against the wall, holding her hand out to the side. But she did not summon her Blade. She did not scream for help.

"Szeth," she said. "We've . . . been worried about you. Are you here to talk to Pozen? I assume you have . . . questions. It's been a hard few weeks, eh?"

"Questions," he said, stepping closer to her in the small room of prayer. "Yes, I have questions. One in particular. How, Sivi? How could you serve one of the *Unmade*?"

She sighed. "You saw the captive spren, then?"

"Captive and being *tortured*."

"I had hoped he'd come to you outside the cavern," she said. "That was how he spoke to me at first."

"I demanded the full truth."

"Then you got angry when he gave it to you?"

"Sivi, this is what we trained to *fight*. The Unmade's presence means the Desolation has begun. The world is in danger, and we're not ready to fight it!"

"Wait," Sivi said. "What did you see, Szeth?" She frowned, her eyes distant. "Could I . . . Could that be right? Could I have been deceived? That's the form *I'd* have chosen for a deception . . . but Szeth, it's not—"

"What is *this*?" a voice demanded from behind.

Szeth spun, immediately beginning the process of summoning his Blade. Pozen stood in the hallway, as Szeth had foolishly left the door open. The older Honorbearer carried a small tray of fruit.

Had he . . . gone to fetch a *snack* for his meditation?

Regardless, Szeth had been thinking about how easy it had been to sneak up on Sivi. Now he ate those words as he himself left his back exposed.

"Szeth?" Pozen demanded. "Have you come to apologize? After all I did for you, to have you pout like a child? You've embarrassed me." Pozen looked to Szeth's hand, then his face. "No. You're here for something far worse, aren't you, Szeth?"

To his credit, Pozen didn't run. He likely knew that the best chance he had was in that moment—with Szeth trapped in a small room, a potential enemy to his rear. Pozen stretched his hand out for his Blade.

Szeth didn't wait for his weapon. He lunged forward into the hallway and grappled Pozen, who deflected his hands, Stormlight rising around him. Szeth Lashed himself away, soaring some distance down the hallway. It wouldn't do for Pozen to transfer both of them to Shadesmar.

"The ultimate betrayal," Pozen said, then spat to the side. "You are a disgrace, Szeth."

"I choose *Truth,*" Szeth said.

Pozen's Blade appeared in his hand. And Szeth . . .

Szeth retreated.

He would not be a killer who came in the night. If Szeth murdered Pozen here, he knew he would never recruit Sivi or any of the others.

"I have already told the Windrunner acolytes what I saw," Szeth called through the hallway to them. "I have begun raising the banner of Truth, since you will not. I will let it be known to any who will hear: It is time. The Voidbringers have returned. If you would join me, I would welcome you. If you will not . . . then I *will* fight you, Pozen. Sivi—even you."

With that, Szeth fled.

Fear the old man who welcomed failure when young. If he has survived this long, he learned.

—*Proverbs for Towers and War,* Zenaz, date unknown

Kaladin rose early on the ninth day and made breakfast. He wasn't familiar with the vegetables they'd bought at that village a few days back. Some kind of root, Szeth had explained—except here, instead of growing down into cracks, roots dug into the *soil.* That just didn't seem sanitary. He washed the long orange things three times, and found they tasted remarkably good raw—slightly sweet, and with a solid crunch. So he cut them and fried them in his travel skillet, and after they softened, a pinch of sugar enhanced their natural sweetness. And . . .

Storms. Rock really had made a bit of a chef out of Kaladin. He chuckled at this, though it was difficult to maintain good humor under the circumstances. He set out a plate for Szeth, who was meditating, then scooped the rest onto his own plate and settled on a nearby rock. He gazed out over the brownish-green landscape, with its hills and odd trees. In one of those an entire flock of chickens was roosting, bright red and green, and he could hear them clucking from here.

Syl settled down beside him. He was coming to like the way she went about full sized these days; he could judge her expression and mood better this way. Right now she slumped, wearing her modified and skirted uniform, elbows on her knees and chin in her hands as she floated half a foot off the ground, hair drifting around her head as if she were underwater.

"I don't like this," she said.

"Nale leaving early," Kaladin said softly. "'Preparing' things at the next monastery."

"He's a creep," Syl said. "How are the toes?"

"They're called carrots."

"They look like people's toes."

"Nobody has toes this long," he said, eating. "And they're good. Taste like a breakfast my mother made." He hesitated. "I put *sugar* on them, like Mother always did for us kids. Rock really has corrupted me—he always insisted there were more flavors than 'hot' and 'very hot.'"

Syl smiled, but clasped her hands in front of her, still concerned. So Kaladin ate, then took out his flute and played for a little while, his fingers increasingly comfortable holding the wooden instrument, calluses from wielding the spear finding a home with another kind of work.

The playing calmed him. And as it often did, the song brought the Wind. He felt its attention—the unseen ancient spren who inhabited this land.

"Any guesses on what I should expect?" Kaladin said. "Nale is obviously going to be waiting for us. This is the Skybreaker monastery, and he bears the Honorblade. They've tried so many underhanded ways to kill Szeth. I worry this will be the worst."

"Because," Syl added, "Nale is an *utter creep*."

"Please," a quiet voice said. "Don't speak of him like that." The Wind stirred Kaladin's hair, drifting past it.

"He might have once been a hero as you showed me," Kaladin said. "But Wind, in my time Nale has been a source of only misery, death, and frustration."

"He's just weathered," the Wind whispered. "Like that rock you sit upon."

Kaladin frowned, shifting, looking at the stone beneath him. It was merely a smooth round stone, maybe three feet across.

"Like a rock?" Syl said. "Stubborn? Immovable?"

"You are not those who speak with Stone," the Wind whispered. "I do not think you can hear its voice, even with my help. But touch it, Kaladin, Sylphrena. I will try."

Kaladin glanced at Syl, who stood as he did. Curious, he pressed his hand to the stone, and she did likewise, her hand beside his. In a flash, he saw something. An . . . impression. The Wind was right though. He could not hear the voice of the stone, if it had one.

But he did see a beautiful statue of a woman. Full-figured, her arms outspread, gazing down at what had once been a road here. He did not know who would have placed such a fine statue in such an out-of-the-way place. Candles lit at its base made the site feel welcoming, like a waystop for weary travelers.

Then the years passed. He saw them in a rush. Rainstorm after rainstorm. He felt the wind on the stone, and over time the statue weathered. The lines wore down, the detail vanishing, and then the features melted away. Years stole the statue's shape like sandpaper until, by the repeated washing of storms, it sank into the soil.

The impression faded. The stone Kaladin had been sitting upon had been a masterwork thousands of years ago. Now it was just another lump of rock.

"I told you," the Wind said. "I love the Stones, and they are my sibling—but my touch breaks them, ever so slowly. Nale is one of these stones, Kaladin, Sylphrena. Time has weathered him away. But like this stone, a part of him remembers what he once was."

"The only time I've given him pause," Kaladin said, hand pressed to the rock, "was yesterday, when I asked him why he became a Herald."

"Make him remember," the Wind said. "Please. I know you do not care for the Heralds, Sylphrena, and they were not perfect, even when they were whole. Jezrien was proud, and Ishar thought himself above common people. Pralla loved her secrets, and Battar could be conniving. Chana avoided taking responsibility, and Nale could hold a grudge. But they were good people.

"And they tried. So very, very hard. Honor abandoned them to the weathering of time—but in some ways they are the best that remains of him. A piece of an infinite god is still infinite, and the power within these nine . . . I think we will need it, in days to come. Try to see their potential, not their faults."

"I'll . . . try," Syl said with a sigh. "I mean, I *know* what you're saying is right. Hard to feel it though."

"It is hard for Nale to feel that way about himself too," the Wind whispered. "Please, Kaladin. Help him."

"I kind of have my hands full with Szeth," Kaladin said, glancing to the side, where Szeth was returning from his meditations. "Don't know if I have time for another patient."

"But that," the Wind said, "is why I brought you here."

"You said a storm was coming," Kaladin said, recalling the first conversation he'd had with the Wind at Urithiru.

"Yes," the Wind said. "And they are the counter. Remember what the Bondsmith said. I need you . . ."

"But Heralds?" Kaladin said. "Wind, that might be a little beyond my skill. I told Dalinar the same."

"You've already helped one who will soon be a Herald," the Wind said, her voice fading. "It's possible."

Szeth arrived, and . . . well, Kaladin did suppose he'd helped the man. Szeth actually *smiled* as he picked up the plate. "For me?"

"Yes."

"Carrots for breakfast," Szeth said, shaking his head. "Stonewalkers . . . you have odd tastes." He tried one. "Surprisingly good though. We should pack up and go. I suspect Nin will be waiting for us. I can eat as we walk."

Kaladin looked at Syl, who nodded in agreement. So he cleaned up, then followed Szeth onward—to the penultimate monastery. Wind blowing quietly along with them, and spren streaming in the sky like a highway of light.

⁂

"Hold the wall!" Sigzil shouted through the pouring rain. "Hold!"

He swept along behind the ranks of men, who stood on the wall as water streamed down off the ramparts behind them. This persistent drizzle sank in with a deep chill, slicking surfaces and ruining bowstrings, not to mention obscuring their view of the plateaus around them. Corrupted windspren whipped past in the air, and the army faced a sea of red eyes staring out through the mist. Some among them unleashed a constant pounding of stones against the wall. Crashing rocks, smashing at the fortification—a terrible, erratic drumbeat that left Sigzil's ears ringing.

Men worked with halberds and spears along the top—amid striking rocks—their weapons pointed down at the Deepest Ones, bits of whom peeked out of the wall. To counteract the barrage of stones, the defenders had used Stonewards to thicken the walls—but that made them wide enough for Deepest Ones to disappear into completely, popping out to attack the Stonewards behind it, who used their little remaining Stormlight to keep the fortification from falling apart.

The constant barrage was going to run them out within a few hours. The enemy, however, seemed to have as much Voidlight as they wanted. And Sigzil still hadn't been able to come up with an application of his plan that would work.

Sigzil swooped along, trying to keep the soldiers protected. He had to have troops on the walls, as the enemy periodically dropped attackers up here. Indeed, something hit the wall nearby—something large. A Magnified One hauled himself up over onto the wall top a second later, followed by another. Sigzil cursed, forming his spear, and streaked toward them as they began battering soldiers away.

Husked Ones followed—three appearing on the wall from their ribbons of light to support the massive Magnified Ones. Sigzil struck at the largest of the creatures, and his spear sank deep—but the Magnified One grew thick carapace, pushing him back away with a growth like an expanding column of stone. Sigzil's spear never touched anything vital, and that carapace grew at a furious rate in the storm, encasing his spear.

Sigzil was forced to pull back—lest his hands be captured in the overgrown chitin—dismissing his spear. The Magnified One broke off this segment of growth, like a tumor along its side, then swung for Sigzil with a hand that had become a large club. Sigzil ducked, then rushed at the Husked Ones—but was kept at bay by the Magnified One. The Fused did frightening damage to the defenders before the Stormwall arrived and distracted them. That finally gave Sigzil a chance to ram a spear straight through the back of a Husked One's head. As the Fused collapsed off the wall into the rain, Sigzil lifted into the air, and noticed an encouraging flash of light from the next plateau over.

He flew toward it, but the two remaining Husked Ones zipped after him, becoming lines of light that materialized into figures grappling him. One held his arms back, immobilizing him as the other grabbed the front of his uniform, pulling him close.

"We were promised a chance to fight your leader," the creature hissed to his face. "The one who defeated Lezian. Why does the Stormblessed not come to meet our challenge?"

Sigzil grunted, and began Lashing the creature away—but it clung to him, holding on tightly.

"If I kill you," the creature asked, "will Stormblessed chase me down for vengeance?"

"You can't kill me," Sigzil hissed.

"You think you're too strong?"

"No," Sigzil whispered. "But I've heard the name of my killer screamed on the lips of a dying man. And it's not you." With a grunt, Sigzil kicked the creature free.

The Fused became a ribbon of light to return, but Sigzil was already Lashing himself and the other Fused upward—carrying them into the middle of a storm of Light, a group that had just arrived via Oathgate. Windrunner reinforcements swarmed around, dozens of them attacking. The Husked One behind Sigzil let go with a curse, then was chased away.

A familiar figure hovered over to Sigzil, giving a salute. "Hey, hooch," Lopen said. "Sounds like you've been having a hard time of it."

Sigzil nodded. "You heard . . . ?"

"About Leyten. Yeah." Lopen led the group of Windrunners who had taken the Mink to Herdaz. They were finally back, adding another twenty Radiants to Sigzil's army. They helped chase the Skybreakers away, and the fight quieted for a while, the last Magnified One dying on the wall.

She had left tens of Sigzil's soldiers dead and broken. One Stoneward killed. And those stones kept hitting the wall, crash after crash.

"You brought Stormlight?" Sigzil asked.

 "Not much," Lopen said. "Hooch . . . we nearly ran ourselves out flying that force for Dalinar. Then we get back, and there's none to be had in the tower? There wasn't enough to supply all of us, so half had to stay behind! What's going on?"

"Both Bondsmiths are on a trip into the Spiritual Realm," Sigzil said softly. "But that's not widely known. So keep it to yourself and the command staff."

He spun in the rain, waving to Lyn as she shot past. Natam hovered over. "Storms," he whispered. "Sig, I'm sorry about . . ."

Sigzil nodded and wiped rainwater off his face. "If you two could help Skar and Peet keep things together here, I need to go and coordinate with the generals. We're basically out of Stormlight. With the last of it we . . . we will need to retreat."

They nodded, and Sigzil flew down past the broken bodies, feeling worn out. "Sigzil?" Vienta said. "I calculate we are at our limit. If we spend any more Stormlight—barring what the Windrunners brought—we won't have enough to get our army through the Oathgate to safety."

"Understood. Thank you." He walked to his command post to give the order, but as he did he was met by Ka with a message.

She whispered it to him. One of the enemy had made contact, and had an offer. It was the defector, the friend of Rlain. Venli.

Her offer to them wouldn't work. He didn't need more troops, and hers wouldn't tip the battle enough. However . . .

It clicked.

This was the piece he needed.

EIGHT THOUSAND YEARS AGO

Rayse was here.

I, God, looked upon him—and hated him.

We had been rivals during mortality. It was worse now. Rayse had the air of a being who did what he could get away with—a man whose sole scripture was a request for a bribe.

Now he was a god.

I felt Rayse study the planets from afar, then move on to the first in the system. There were many, but three, as I'd seen, could accept life as it is commonly created: Roshar, the second planet. The third planet, which attracted souls. And that first one, which had humans on it created by my predecessor. I had intended to contact them, bringing them a divinity to worship. My efforts on Roshar with Kor had distracted me.

Now . . . now it would be too late. Another had set up as their god.

"Ignore him," Kor whispered. "We aren't to interact."

"He will have sensed you here with me," I declared. "He'll know we've broken the agreement."

"You think Rayse of all people cares about broken contracts?" Our creations flowed around her, made with my work and her encouragement. Fragments of power, mimicking the ones we'd found on Roshar—only more powerful, more interesting. More self-aware.

When deity found our place on a world, our power leaked. Here we were guiding that, forming new creatures that responded both to the songs of the planet and to the thoughts of the people there. I had shown myself to the people of the land, and taught them

TO SING TO THE STONES—WITH THE SONGS, AND MY POWER, THEY LEARNED TO SCULPT IT. THEY NAMED THEMSELVES THE SINGERS, BECAUSE THEY COULD USE THE SONGS OF GODS. THEY RESPECTED ME. AND I LOVED THEM.

OUR GRAND WORK WAS FASCINATING, MADE MORE SO BY THE WAY—WITH KOR'S VIBRANT TOUCH—OUR SPREN CREATIONS ADAPTED TO ROSHAR. BECAME CHILDREN OF IT, THEIR SONGS RESONATING WITH THOSE OF THE PLANET. THEY WEREN'T REPLACING ADONALSIUM'S WORK, BUT EXPANDING UPON IT. CONTINUING THE EQUATIONS.

NATURE COULD BE EQUATIONS.

NATURE *WAS* EQUATIONS.

SO WERE OATHS.

WHILE WE'D CREATED SMALLER THINGS EARLIER, WE NOW MOVED ON TO CREATE TRUE BEINGS. WITH PASSIONS, THOUGHTS, IDEAS OF THEIR OWN. CREATIONS OF LIGHT AND WIND AND DREAMS. THEY EVOLVED NOT THROUGH GENETICS, AS PHYSICAL BEINGS DID, BUT THROUGH *PERCEPTION*.

I LOVED THEM.

WE DECIDED TO FORM TEN VARIETIES. TEN BECAUSE MY POWER LOVED THE SYMMETRY. TEN, BECAUSE KOR LOVED ME, AND KNEW THIS MADE ME HAPPY. WE STARTED WITH THE FIRST SEVEN, THEN ONE VARIETY WAS BORN OF KOR ALONE. IN COUNTERPOINT, AND AT HER URGING, I CREATED ONE VARIETY ALMOST ENTIRELY ON MY OWN. MY ANGELS OF HONOR.

THEY LOVED THE WIND, FOR REASONS EVEN I COULD NOT FULLY FATHOM.

WE LOOKED ON THE NINE SO FAR WITH PLEASURE—BUT I COULD FEEL SLIGHT DISAPPOINTMENT FROM KOR.

"I LOVE THEM," SHE SAID. "BUT THEY ARE . . . SO HUMAN. IS THERE A WAY TO CREATE SOMETHING NEW? SOMETHING *NOT* INFLUENCED BY OUTSIDE PERCEPTIONS OR THOUGHTS?"

"IF THERE IS A WAY, BELOVED," I SAID, "YOU COULD FIND IT. WE CAN FOLLOW YOUR LEAD TO MAKE THE TENTH."

BUT OH, MY THOUGHTS COULD NO LONGER FIXATE COMPLETELY UPON THIS WORK. MY ONCE-MORTAL WEAKNESS SHOWED, FOR I *COULD NOT* MERELY *IGNORE* RAYSE.

RAYSE WOULD BE PLOTTING. RAYSE WAS *ALWAYS* PLOTTING.

I COULD NOT STAND HIS PRESENCE THERE. LIKE A DISEASE UPON AN INNOCENT FLOCK. I LEFT KOR, AGAINST HER WISHES, AND DIVERTED THE BULK OF MY CONSCIOUSNESS TO THE FIRST PLANET. A PLANET WHICH HAD ITS OWN PEOPLE, ITS OWN TONES, ITS OWN WAY OF EXISTING. ALASWHA, IT WAS CALLED.

THERE, I FOUND RAYSE BUILDING AN EMPIRE.

WAR RAGED ON THIS LAND. CITY-STATES, AS HAD BEEN COMMON ON OUR HOMEWORLD, WERE BEING CONQUERED BY A SINGLE NATION. RAYSE'S FAVORED PEOPLE HAD BEEN IMBUED WITH POWER, FAR GREATER THAN THE power of sculpting stone I had given the singers. This was a dreadful power, control over the very Surges that make up creation. It reminded me of the worst powers on our world. The ability to shear axon from axon. Microkinesis, in the language of gods. Here it took a different form, but caused me—even God—to tremble.

I, God, snaked tendrils of myself across the foreign landscape, with its curious air currents and floating stones, to a grand conference in one large city. I absorbed the conversations of a thousand people, which let me instantly ascertain the situation. The empire, backed by Rayse, had displayed its power, conquering a few small city-states. Now it promised a short-term reprieve to any others who sent emissaries for a conference. Wary, they had come. Delegates from across the central sea, joining to hear the dictates of the growing empire.

Why fuel such a war? Rayse could enforce their devotion and compel every knee to bend in worship of him, could he not? Why turn them against one another instead?

It was an experiment. Rayse was playing with people as if they were toys, granting incredible abilities to one side and watching how humans used them. Or was it more? With my great capacity, I investigated further, careful to make my touch light. Was this . . . to build and train an army? Why would he—

Rayse saw me.

In an eyeblink, we both formed bodies. I, in my might, swathed in my robes of justice and bearing my crown of oaths. Rayse as a duplicitous, glorified version of himself. In golden robes, holding a scepter, his features perfected to imply wisdom and control. The man he'd always pretended to be.

"Ah . . ." the deceitful one said. "So you've finally decided to come visit, Tanner."

"Tanavast."

"Always Tanner to me," Rayse said, grinning and gesturing to his belt. A copy of the one that my mortal self had made for him so long ago. "Such a *utilitarian* person to have around. I'm happy to be neighbors, but . . ." He clicked his tongue. "You violate our agreement."

Again, my power writhed against this. But I was God, and it obeyed. We *had* to confront Rayse. He was the evil one. He was plotting, and my divine glory illuminated what Rayse did not want seen. My enemy was *wounded.* Not in the way of mortals, but in the way of gods, his power ripped, fragmented. He'd been in a fight.

 "What have you done, Rayse?" I demanded.

"Eliminated a little competition."

Oh . . . oh no. I had felt this, hadn't I? Centuries ago?

"Don't look at me like that, Tanner," Rayse said. "You knew that Ambition was going to be a problem. We all knew it, right from the start."

Ambition? "You mean Uli Da?"

"I performed a service for us all. Praise me. Feel the gratitude, Tanner. Know it."

"I know nothing but horror at this blasphemy!"

"I will accept that," Rayse said.

In my revulsion, I withdrew, leaving Rayse to his self-satisfaction and his playthings.

And yet.

And yet, I had to watch. I had to know.

Rayse turned his attention to the conference, where his favored empire gave an ultimatum: all who wished to join their union were welcome to do so. They *claimed* they'd allow those who didn't wish it to remain free. They *claimed* they had only attacked, and destroyed, city-states in self-defense.

I knew there was more nuance than that—that the empire had moved against potential rivals, seeing their threats as attacks. The people probably knew the story was more complicated too, but it was not wise to name liar the bully with the largest club.

Disgusted, I began to withdraw fully. But then something caught my eye: a group of people with darker skin than the others, like my own. A group who were already leaving the city.

"What do we do, Uncle?" one of them asked, walking alongside an older man. "I don't believe them for a moment. They'll secure power, then crush the rest of us."

"We must make our own alliance, Nale," the older man said. "It is the only way. They cannot break us all . . ."

I considered. Their defiance, their pride, their *honor* in rejecting this obvious threat. It inspired me, and my power yearned to help them.

I should have returned to Kor to discuss it. But I was a god now. Should I not already know what was right? What need was there to discuss?

Later that night, I appeared to these men in their tent. There, I made them an offer. "I will give you," I declared, "the power to resist our shared enemy, should you desire it."

The fool will, when losing, seek to flip the board and scatter the pieces. This is not an adage for towers.

—*Proverbs for Towers and War,* Zenaz, date unknown

Navani paused outside her office in the Kholinar palace, listening. The entire building seemed to vibrate with shouts and clashing men. How familiar those sounds were to her. A scholar in name, and at heart, but her life had never been one of quiet study. Her life had been a battlefield.

She felt drawn toward the sounds, magnetically, as she walked the empty hallways; all soldiers had been pulled into the clash. Aesudan's loyalists—corrupted by the touch of an Unmade, having locked away any soldiers who disagreed—were fighting both Elhokar's incursion force and invading singers. Adolin described it as a confusing storm of killing. Yet that was below. Here, on an upper floor, she was able to walk alone.

At the hallway she knew they would come down, she turned and watched. *I'm early,* she thought, remembering Adolin's narrative. That fighting she heard was Adolin and Elhokar battering their way through the defenders at the front of the palace. She had time. Should she go for Gav alone?

No. Though it was difficult, she forced herself to analyze the situation. Adolin had said the queen was guarded by a force of soldiers. These hallways were empty, but Aesudan's chambers would not be—and Navani would have a very difficult time there, even with some power over the visions.

Moreover, what good would it do to rescue Gav, then hopefully Dalinar, if the three of them were still trapped in these visions? She needed to devise a path out of the Spiritual Realm entirely. She reached out for the

Sibling, but found her mind abuzz with . . . with tones, vibrations, music that disharmonized.

But Navani . . . she knew the right tones, didn't she? She thought back to her time with Raboniel, and sorted through the noise. With her eyes closed, she found them. The tones. The sounds of Roshar itself.

Navani? The Sibling's voice.

Yes.

You are lost among infinite possibilities.

I can hear them, I think, Navani said. *Tones that vibrate the wrong way, like an instrument out of tune.*

Those are the possible futures, the Sibling said. *Discordant until they become reality, and then* snap, *they match the tones of Roshar. I'm sorry. I cannot see you. I . . .*

Is there time left? Navani asked, feeling desperate. *Until the deadline?*

Less than a day.

Time. She wasn't too late.

I need a way out, Navani sent. *I've attempted to make a perpendicularity in here. Nothing happens.*

You can't make one that leads out in the same way, the Sibling said. *It's like you've slid down a tall mountain slope, and are now at the base, trying to get back up.*

Wit gets out, Navani sent. *Others get out. How?*

Using points of transition, the Sibling said, their voice growing distant. *If someone else made a hole in, you could escape that way. I could . . . I could try to help . . .*

Navani lost the tones in the cacophony. *Points of transition,* she thought. *Can I trick the vision into giving me one of those?*

She heard soldiers approaching, so she stepped back as a collection of Aesudan's troops—having left her private chambers—passed and gathered at the top of the stairs. It was time. She turned, steeling herself, and watched the stairwell.

And there he was, with brilliant Shardblade aloft. Elhokar, her son. Kaladin guarded his side, and some fifty soldiers followed, loyal to the king. Part of the force Elhokar had recruited to break in and save his family—the son who needed him desperately, and the wife who would refuse his aid.

Navani's heart twisted to see his face again. She blinked away tears, and found . . . a certain peace as he announced himself to the gathered defenders—his proud voice making them break and retreat past Navani, ignoring her. Elhokar hadn't been a particularly good king. And he . . . he could have been a better person. Maybe that last part was her fault, though she hadn't had much parenting help—not the useful kind.

Those worries fled as she saw Elhokar appearing to *glow* with his own power. In the end, her son had been a hero. A *king*. His death hurt, but she didn't feel the extreme pain she'd expected at encountering him here. In some ways it was actually *comforting*. For this was Elhokar Kholin at his finest, perhaps the brightest moment of his life, leading with confidence. Rescuing his son. Standing shoulder to shoulder with a Radiant.

As the defenders retreated, Navani emerged from her alcove. Kaladin and Elhokar saw her, and stopped.

"M-Mother?" Elhokar said.

So, he saw her as herself. She hadn't been certain. "Come quickly," she said. "Aesudan has left your son to the torments of spren."

"How are you here?" Elhokar asked, stepping up. "Mother. It seems impossible."

"Dalinar learned to make a portal for me," she said. "It's fine. It makes sense. Let this play out as it should."

Elhokar . . . nodded. He took her face in his hands, as if uncertain she was real, then embraced her. Kaladin, standing behind, waved them forward and together they marched on Aesudan's chambers, passing statues of Heralds and the corridor where the soldiers had retreated—leaving the queen. Who could be heard singing in the room beyond.

Elhokar halted in place, cocked his head, then looked at Navani. Something in his demeanor had changed.

"What is it?" Navani asked.

"Just . . . impressed with you, Mother," he said, and led the way into the room.

She didn't have time for the conversation that took place with Aesudan—it wasn't real anyway. Now that she was here, Navani pushed through the cluttered room and found Gav at the rear, behind a dressing screen. And blessedly, it *was* the real him. The older Gav—a year made a big difference when one was small—with tearstained eyes. Navani seized him, pulling him close, ignoring the spren that darted away.

"Gram?" he said. He held her tightly. "Gram, is that you? The real you?"

"Yes, dear one."

"Where is Grampa?" Gavinor whispered, clinging to her. "Why . . . why is he so busy killing people? Why is he so terrible? Why does he hate me, and everyone, so much?"

"That wasn't him you saw," Navani guessed. "It was a terrible vision, Gav. Dalinar loves you."

"Daddy said . . ." Gav whispered. "Daddy said I should try to be strong, like him . . ."

He calmed, and his soul vibrated against hers. This was him, and not some fabrication of the visions. She soothed him, drying his tears, before processing what he'd said.

He'd been hearing his father all through these visions. Navani looked back toward Elhokar—who had left the conversation with Aesudan and stood alone in the center of the room, staring toward her, a hint of a smile on his lips. His face in shadow. He'd changed in an eyeblink.

Whatever that was, it wasn't her son. Not even a simulacrum of him created in vision, as it had been moments before. This was something else in his skin.

"What now?" not-Elhokar asked. "You have Gavinor."

"We get out," she whispered, pulling Gav close.

"Oh, but how?" not-Elhokar said. "Isn't that the problem you've had all along, Navani?"

"Gram," Gav said, pointing. "It's him. Daddy. He's been helping me."

Navani held him, trembling, and backed away from the thing. What lived in this place of shadows and half realities? She ran into the wall as the thing advanced.

"Oh, Navani," it said, and the voice . . . sounded familiar to her. Not Elhokar's, but someone else's. "I'm so glad I was able to spend more time with you here, seeing what makes you afraid, and what makes you *angry.*"

"Odium," she whispered.

"And more," he replied. "You haven't answered me. You found Gav, through your cleverness. I should have expected you'd work out how to manipulate this place. But what now?"

"Now," she whispered, "I am worried I'll see him being tormented. Dalinar, the man I love. I am afraid you'll make me watch him in pain."

"Ah . . ." Odium said, still bearing Elhokar's face—but making expressions she'd never seen on her son. As if his flesh were a mask distorted by something behind. "So that's how you made it here. Clever indeed. I should have watched you more closely."

She thought about Dalinar in need and tried to Connect to him—or trick the vision into taking her there. But Odium waved his hand, and the vision remained solid. Here, he was completely in control. Her will was a candle's flame compared to the bonfire that was the will of a god.

Now what?

Holding to Gav, she made a decision. A desperate, painful decision. She couldn't help Dalinar in here, but if she got out, she might be able to find a way to use her powers—or the Stormfather's—to reach him.

She had Gav. She needed to take him and go, hopefully while the enemy underestimated her.

"We must continue this vision," Navani whispered.

"Why?" Odium asked. "You're that eager to see your son die, Navani? Such passion that will inspire!"

She hurried past him, joining Kaladin and the soldiers as they rushed back down the hallway. Odium trailed behind in Elhokar's form, playing out the vision. Navani kept Gav safe, whispering for him not to watch, as they reached the ground floor—and the mess *really* started. The singer attack had breached the palace.

She found—as she pushed through the chaos of the battle—that she didn't need to watch the next part. Why look backward? She couldn't save Elhokar. But she *could* save Gav. She deliberately chose to remember her son as he'd been, bursting to the top of that stairwell. Before Odium had turned his attention on this vision and taken his place.

"Gram," Gav whispered, his eyes squeezed shut, "I'm scared."

"It's all right, gemheart," she whispered, barreling toward the Sunwalk with some soldiers. "I have you." This long covered walkway led to a built-up location beside the palace.

Kholinar's Oathgate.

"Navani?" Elhokar's voice called after her. "Mother? Mother, help me!"

Her blood turned cold as she heard Odium shifting his tone to mimic Elhokar's. Pleading for help amid the screaming and fighting soldiers.

Life before death.

Gav was alive.

Behind her was only death.

She reached the Oathgate. Below, she knew the city was flooding with singers.

This city was lost long ago. This is a vision.

"Activate it," she hissed at the simulacrum of Kaladin beside her. He hadn't frozen in battle this time, as he'd followed her instead of staying to fight.

"But . . ."

"Do it!" she snapped.

"Mother?" Elhokar's voice.

"Elhokar's coming," Kaladin said. "Navani, he's limping across the Sunwalk. He's wounded!"

"*Activate the Oathgate,*" she said.

"But . . ."

"You aren't real," she whispered to Kaladin, refusing to turn toward Elhokar. "He isn't real. *But we are.* Please. Help us. If there is anything of the real Stormblessed inside of you, summon it. Please."

The simulacrum looked to her, and something *did* seem to steel inside him. He ran for the Oathgate's control building.

While Elhokar's pained voice whispered behind her, "Ah . . . that might work for you, Navani. An Oathgate activation, even in a vision, will be a rush of power. But will you abandon Dalinar as you did Elhokar? The man you love? He *is* real. And I have him."

 "Dalinar," she whispered, "is strong enough to fight you. I trust him."

The Oathgate flashed. In that moment, she sought the tones of Roshar again, and she felt something latch onto her.

I have you, the Sibling said. *Connect to me.*

She held on. Tight. She'd always been good at holding to things she loved. Only recently had she begun to acknowledge when she needed to let go.

Gav in one arm, she pulled with her might and—more importantly—her mind.

And emerged from light into her rooms at Urithiru.

⁂

Venli—shrouded in a cloak, hunched down to hide her envoyform height—walked through the human camp, accompanied by several armed human guards.

Narak had changed much in the year or so since she'd lived here. Gone were the ramshackle listener buildings, replaced by stone bunkers. A large stone wall protected it, a fortification of amazing strength, standing even against the boulders thrown by the *metacha-im,* the Focused Ones.

It was cracked though, and she could hear the stone pleading as it began to fail. She passed the dead lying in rows, among solemn rainspren and blood flowing like water. Beleaguered soldiers carried wounded to the Oathgate, for transfer to Urithiru—and the healers there.

Most telling, she passed someone in a Radiant uniform, weeping and shivering, her stare hollow as she whispered about a distinctly new pain. Rlain had told her the truth: spren could be killed. A new era had come upon them.

Still under guard, she stepped into a building at the center of the plateau. A well-lit room inside held tables, battle maps, and an Azish man in a Windrunner uniform. He looked up, studying her as she entered.

"The singer Radiant," he said to her in Alethi. "I don't think I'd have believed it, despite what I've heard, if you hadn't emerged from the rock near one of my patrols."

She'd noticed that Odium's forces didn't know what she could do. Her people had been given cloaks as blankets to sleep under. Hopefully the enemy guards would not find the lump of shaped stone under a cloak, the real Venli having slipped down into the stones to escape. It was more than she'd ever done with the power before. She was improving.

"Welcome," the Windrunner said, exhaustionspren buzzing around him. "I'm glad for your offer, but I don't think you'll be able to help in the way you want."

"You're right," she said, frank. "The enemy will wipe you off this plateau within hours, and we haven't enough troops to help you. But your message said you have a different proposal?"

He outlined one, and it wouldn't work either. She knew that instantly. But what if . . .

What if she took some of his idea . . . and added some of hers?

"Where is Jasnah?" Venli asked. "The human queen of Alethkar, daughter of the man we slew so many years ago?"

"At Thaylen City," he said, frowning. "Why?"

"I think your idea will work, with some revisions. But it will need to involve her . . ."

NINE YEARS AGO

Szeth, the last bearer of Truth, killed.

He soared across the battlefield, dressed in bright colors: red and orange and all shades between. He came in low, booted feet brushing the grass, sword out to the side, passing an entire line of soldiers. Twenty of them died before they could react, and the block of soldiers shattered.

He hovered briefly, watching his troops move in, displeased. His soldiers were sloppy, timid. Killing a human being was an entirely different experience from stabbing a pig carcass, and years of abstract training could not replace actual experience in battle. They would have to do better. The Voidbringers would put up a much more resilient defense than this city militia.

He gave his soldiers just long enough to start to flounder, his long red belt fluttering in the wind, sword out to the side. He had, unfortunately, very little experience training soldiers—merely a short stint as an officer during which he'd sunk those raiders' ships. Looking back, he could see how lucky he'd been to inherit soldiers who were battle-hardened against the stonewalkers.

As his line stalled—a few of them staring, disbelieving, at the deaths they'd caused—he lowered, then infused one of the holy boulders outside this town and sent it crashing among the enemy ranks. The remnants went fleeing back to their town, throwing down their weapons.

So it began. Their first battle. It hadn't happened with a triumphant march of glorious armies, but with a few hundred acolytes who were killing for the first time.

"You will have to do better," he snapped at his troops, and saw them deflate, sag. Well, good. They had been embarrassing, and he'd needed to do all the work. "Come. We must secure the town and begin persuading them to join our cause."

Everyone in the town paid him lip service now that he'd conquered them. They would bow to him as he walked past, call him honor-nimi. Board his soldiers, and let him recruit.

He didn't have their hearts. He felt it as he spoke with the town butcher to secure supplies for his men. The spindly man bowed, but he was *afraid.* He was not *liberated.* And he refused to *be* liberated, no matter what Szeth said.

"I promise you," Szeth told him, "the Return has begun. The Voidbringers attack our land."

"Yes, of course, honor-nimi." The butcher bowed again.

"You don't believe," Szeth said, then glanced at his officers. "He doesn't believe."

"It took me time to believe, honor-nimi," Thal-son-Geord said, with a shrug.

"Maybe . . . we should go and get a Voidbringer," Visk-daughter-Brador suggested. "Show off one of their corpses."

"The Voidbringers will not be caught so easily," Szeth said. "They have been stealthy all this time." He looked to the butcher. "They corrupted our leadership. You must see and understand that. Why don't you see?"

The man seemed uncomfortable. He offered more of his best cuts of meat. Szeth sighed, accepted the offer, then moved on through the town.

His officers caught up. "It's going to be like this everywhere we go," Visk warned. "It's why Tuko never actually decided to rebel. He knew—one Honorbearer against the others—it was going to look like a power struggle, a civil war."

Szeth stopped at the end of the boardwalk and gazed out across the green spring grass, the fields newly planted, beneath a sky that at times appeared too pure a blue to be real. As if they were watercolors on a giant canvas.

He'd imagined thousands flocking to him. The banner of Truth raised high, a grand army forming to help him root out the sickness upon the land. Instead, the people wanted to ignore him. Hoping he, like a strange stench, would simply . . . go away.

Szeth dismissed his officers. One small town, and already administration was a headache. Thinking of that made him wonder about his father, held by the enemy—Sivi and Pozen's conversation had confirmed that. Eventually the enemy would play that piece, demanding that Szeth turn himself in or Neturo would be executed.

What would he do when that day came? It was a situation where . . . where the right choice was exceptionally difficult. And how was Szeth going to conquer an entire nation? How would he lead them against the Voidbringers' invading force, which—as soon as they realized what he was doing—would be sure to come out of hiding and strike.

"How," he whispered, still standing at the edge of the boardwalk. "How do I do this? Please."

The Honorbearers are weak, the Voice said. *They hide, hoping you will lose your nerve.*

"You," Szeth hissed. "I thought I was done with you."

Oh, Szeth. You'll never be done with me.

"Out!" Szeth shouted. "Out of my head!"

The Voice chuckled. *You've committed a cardinal sin. You've killed others of your kind, raised a rebellion, however small. The fight you've wanted is building. You just need to push it over the tipping point, and draw out the other Honorbearers so you can kill them.*

Szeth forced himself to be calm. At least the Voice was familiar. He knew where he stood with it. And, perhaps in its decision to taunt him, it had given something away. So long as he contained his revolution to this small region, the others would rightly assume they could ignore him. What he needed was a real army, a real threat.

He turned along the mountains. Southward.

Minutes later, he found Visk at their camp outside the town. "Give the orders," Szeth told the shaman. "Break the camp. We march."

"What?" she asked. "Where?"

"Along the mountains," Szeth said. "Toward my home village—and the Stoneward monastery. Where a real army has been training for decades against raiders from outside."

An army that had been organized, disciplined, and administered by a genius: Szeth's father. *They* would listen to Szeth. Among them were soldiers who respected him for his strength of leadership.

Let the Honorbearers ignore him once *those troops* were beneath his banner.

SEVEN THOUSAND ONE HUNDRED YEARS AGO

I, God, held the body of a dead child and wept as the sky burned.

Ash and death. All had become ash and death.

I had formed an avatar capable of touch, and it clutched a limp corpse. I closed my eyes, but as I was divine, I could still see the dead littering the ground around me. Thousands and more dying as the air clogged with smoke.

The first planet burned.

Rayse appeared before me, tall as a mountain, hands clasped behind his back. "That did not . . . go as planned," the deceitful one said, surveying cities full of the burned, armies that were now nothing more than charred bones. "Perhaps we went too far."

I, God, roared in agony, my head tipped back.

"Don't be so dramatic, Tanner," Rayse said. "There are always more people." He tapped his foot against a charred body. "Too far though. This *was* too far . . ." He vanished from my sight.

The kingdom I raised up had fought valiantly, resisting Rayse's empire, and the power inside me was *pleased.* My followers on Alaswha had died with honor. To the power, honor in death was the same as honor in life. That was all it cared about, which terrified me.

I . . . I could *feel* all of these deaths directly, particularly of the people who had come to follow me. Their souls fled to the Beyond, escaping this planet, renamed Ashyn for the smoke and destruction that was now its only biome.

I wept for them. For their hopes cut short. For their loves set ablaze. For their dreams . . .

A voice. Nale was searching among the dead. He could not see me, but he screamed when he found the body of his sister, and held her.

A man approached, badly burned, followed by a small force of soldiers. They did not attack Nale, though at their head was a man I recognized. Leader of one of the city-states that had joined the empire, adopted its ways. They called him Jezrien. He found Nale's uncle sitting apart from the bodies, exhausted and burned. His stare looked as if it saw too far, into the realm of gods, or into the shadows of nothingness. Empty.

Jezrien held out his hands to gesture for peace.

Nale's uncle, Makibak, didn't rise to confront his enemy. He bowed his head and spoke softly. "You come to finish us off?"

"No, Makibak, I come to offer the hand of friendship," Jezrien said. "We're gathering those who have survived, and we're taking them to safety."

"I hope," Makibak said, "that you lead them off a cliff, you bastard."

Jezrien knelt. "Zoral, he who was named the Voidbringer, is dead," he said. "I am king now, and I will be a better leader. Ishar can take us to a new world. He's found the songs. Bring your people."

"I have no people," Makibak said, watching his nephew cry over a corpse. "I lead only ghosts."

"*He* is alive," Jezrien said, pointing. "*You* are alive. Others *live*. Bring them. The firestorm is returning, and the very stones are melting in rivers of lava. With luck, we can make a portal and flee. Join us."

"Just like Zoral said all those years ago," Makibak whispered, ash blowing past him in the breeze. "'Join us' . . ."

"This will be different."

"Can you promise that?"

Jezrien stepped back. "If I wasn't willing, would I be here?"

Those words. They cut through some of my pain.

Loss was inevitable. It was part of mortal life. I had to help the living. I saw a king trying to make amends with his enemy. They stood upon a mountain of corpses, but maybe . . .

Maybe something could be salvaged.

I traveled home, to Kor's embrace, and wept in her arms until the portal opened. They were here. Rayse, of course, had come with them.

The best way to win is to provide your opponent with no options but to lose. But beware the assumption that you have considered every possibility.

—*Proverbs for Towers and War,* Zenaz, date unknown

As Szeth led Kaladin to the Skybreaker monastery, the land grew exceptionally hilly. Brown rolling hills, covered in scrub grasses that hugged the ground. More weed than true grass, the plants had petals that spread out rather than grew upward. Szeth had never learned their names.

Kaladin found the grass fascinating. He still had a childlike wonder when investigating common, normal plants. Szeth might have gotten tired of that attitude, had it not grown into a certain respect and admiration. Kaladin actually appeared to like this place. After years in the East, Szeth would not have expected that from one of them.

"This grass is like half something of your world," Kaladin explained at Szeth's questioning glance, "and half something of mine. It doesn't move when touched, but it looks like it's hiding on the ground, trying to get out of the wind."

This terrain was a borderland between their worlds. They crossed large sections of stone where the soil had washed away, and the road wound around those parts. Szeth didn't bother to do likewise. Not anymore.

Eventually they halted atop a particularly tall hill, facing eastward. In these highlands, with their chill air even this far north, it didn't feel like much separated them from stonewalker lands. The barrier here seemed more philosophical than physical.

Sylphrena came flying down to check on them. "You two all right?" she asked, remaining as a ribbon of light.

"Just wondering what's happening to Dalinar and the others," Kaladin said. "No reply from the spanreed last night. I wonder if we're too unimportant to answer. Do you feel anything, Syl?"

"I feel a trembling in the wind," she said, her voice growing smaller. "The world is holding its breath."

Kaladin glanced to Szeth, who shrugged. He would have liked to be with Dalinar, but it was not his task. So he started down the hill. "I have decided," he told Kaladin as the man caught up, "that I need to fight and kill despite my preferences. The duty I bear is too great."

He glanced to Kaladin after he said it, ashamed.

The Windrunner merely nodded. "I'm sorry, Szeth. What can I do to help?"

"I cannot be persuaded."

"I gathered that from the tone of your voice. Can I help?"

Szeth continued more carefully—waiting for the objections. "If I am to be a Herald, I will need to fight. That is that."

Kaladin nodded, looking thoughtful as he hiked. Today, they had split the swords between them. Szeth wore Nightblood and a few Honorblades on his back, while Kaladin had tied several to the large rucksack he wore.

"I hear you," Kaladin said. "I've had that same problem. Still rips me up inside, to think of the men—and singers—I've killed. At first, it helped me to divide everyone into *us* and *them,* then focus only on protecting the *us.* The longer I was in the military though, the more that shifted."

"How?" Szeth asked, genuinely curious.

Kaladin's expression grew distant. "I started to realize, Szeth, there can always be more *them.* When I started fighting? It wasn't against Parshendi; it was *my own people.* Not even from another kingdom, merely other Alethi. We'll always find someone to fight, if we look. I've fought against one of my own brothers, the man who took your sword. I realized I couldn't simply kill whenever I was told. Neither could I walk away, or people I loved would die."

"So . . . what did you do?" Szeth asked. "It sounds like there's no answer."

"No explicit one," Kaladin said. "I do know someone, Zahel, who just walked away. I respect that. But I had to draw lines I wouldn't cross." He took a deep breath, as if admitting this next part was difficult. "Then I had to step up and take responsibility. Become one of the people who made decisions. If I wanted the killing to stop, I had to *make* it stop. From the top, as a leader." He cocked his head. "I guess . . . I guess that means I really should be a lighteyes, doesn't it? Maybe that was why Dalinar was offering . . ."

Szeth slowed on the path, considering. Then he stopped. "Kaladin?"

The other man hesitated, looking back.

"Tell me what to do," Szeth said. "When we reach the next monastery. Should I fight, or should I refuse?"

Kaladin smiled, then shook his head and continued on.

Szeth ran to catch up, awkwardly holding the bundle of swords on his back, kicking up dust. "I will do as you say."

"Not going to happen, Szeth."

"You came to help me! Dalinar commanded you."

"I'm helping as best I can," Kaladin said. "What do you feel you should do?"

"I feel I need to fight," Szeth said. "I *have* to kill. Someone needs to do it."

"Then I'll support you. Help you work through the pain."

"But you *want* me to make the other choice," Szeth said. "Say it."

"I want *you* to choose. What *I'd* choose isn't relevant, Szeth. I'm not here to make you do anything specific. I'm here to try to help you be healthy in making your choice."

And . . . he seemed honest. Legitimately honest. How long had it been since someone in Szeth's life had . . . refused to give him orders? The only time he could remember was long ago, when he'd spoken to the Farmer in his childhood.

Kaladin was a killer, one of the best Szeth knew. But somehow he expressed the same wisdom as the most peaceful man Szeth had ever met. It was a revelation. Like a burst of gloryspren, though he did not draw any in this place. Kaladin had *actually* found a path to peace. It *was* possible.

Szeth could choose to find peace himself. And perhaps, maybe, with work, he could be well again.

Suddenly, everything looked different. Windswept hills weren't just dusty and brown, they were *home,* welcoming Szeth back after his long, exhausting trials. A blue sky that had watched him dance wanted to see joy once more. Life wasn't a thing of beauty for him, and the shadows hadn't vanished, but someone had found a way out. The road was no longer a path toward doom or death. It was a *way forward.*

Strange, how much could change because of a conversation.

Szeth's first instinct was still to try to swear some oath to Kaladin, this man who had shown him so much. But that was *wrong.* That wasn't the *point.*

Don't expect to heal quickly, he thought, recalling one of the things Kaladin had said to him early on. Szeth was surprised he remembered. He had been listening more than he assumed. *It's a long road.*

Well, Szeth was accustomed to long roads.

"Is that it?" Kaladin asked, pointing up the way to some structures on a ridge.

"That is it."

"Feels . . . wrong," Kaladin said, frowning. They shared a look, and Szeth nodded. Yes, it did.

They were in the air a moment later to get a better view. Syl joined them in ribbon form, and the problems became evident: fallen roofs, the walls standing alone, the broken doors.

This town had been attacked. Without waiting for Kaladin, Szeth increased his Lashing, wind rushing around him. The town here was clustered among hills in a dusty, out-of-the-way section of the highlands. Nothing but brown wilderness extended for miles outside the town's walls.

"This happened a while ago," Kaladin said as they slowed above the monastery. "A couple of the buildings are burned, but there's no scent of smoke."

"Agreed," Szeth said. This place had been raided, then abandoned. *No,* he thought, noticing some movement in the shadows of rubble. *Mostly abandoned.*

"You see that?" Kaladin asked, pointing at some other shadows. "The people are here, as in the other towns. The darkness covers this place."

"I had hoped it would be different," Szeth said.

"Why?" Syl asked, forming her full-sized human shape.

"Because we know this Honorbearer," Szeth said, leading the way down toward the monastery in the center of town—the largest structure, perched on one of the higher hills.

They landed before the monastery, which had a broken-in roof, but all four walls standing. The great wooden gates were ajar, and Syl peeked in first, then nodded to the other two. The doors were heavy enough that they had to slip in between them, leaving them mostly shut.

Inside, a figure in a black uniform stood at the far end of the grand entryway. Facing them. Hands on the crossguard of his Shardblade, which was planted point-first into the stone floor. Nin-son-God looked unchanged from when he'd left them last night.

Szeth took off his swords and handed them to Kaladin.

Szeth? Nightblood asked. *I think you should use me for this fight. I'm a really good sword.*

"I know, sword-nimi," Szeth whispered. "I fear this is not the test for you."

But—

"Please let me choose," Szeth said.

Oh. Oh, RIGHT. Got it.

Szeth nodded to Kaladin, then summoned his Blade. He turned and strode farther into the room, stepping into sunlight streaming through the broken roof. He walked over and around the rubble of its fall, and some boulders from a collapsed chimney.

"Sir?" he asked Nin. "What happened here?"

"There are those," the Herald said, "who seek to prevent what is coming. What you will become."

Szeth stopped a safe distance away. "Is this challenge like the others?" he asked, right palm sweaty as he carried his Blade. Could he . . . fight a *Herald*?

"No," Nin said, bringing him relief. "You would not survive a fight against me, so it would be unfair. Thus, in this challenge, I simply command you to accept your place. The next monastery is the last, where you will be tested to your fullest. I demand your word that you will obey me, and do exactly as I tell you, once we reach it."

It was a simple test. The easiest for Szeth. For he always did as his masters required.

"Now," Nin said, "give me your oath."

Szeth opened his mouth. And an oddity slipped out.

"No."

Silence. Even the *whispers* quieted, shocked.

"Szeth," Nin said, "I require this."

"Tell me what you will make me do," Szeth found himself saying. "I cannot judge if I do not know the cost."

Nin floated forward, his coat trembling in the breeze. "You never needed this before."

Szeth did not speak. He had said what he wanted.

Nin halted maybe five feet away. Within Shardblade striking distance. "Promise me you will follow my commands," he said softly. "Give me an oath. This is your test, Szeth."

The room felt *colder.* Szeth breathed out, and swore he saw it puff. "What is happening to this land, Nin? Why are the people consumed by darkness? Who is the Unmade that I fight? What is *going on*?"

"You don't need to know that yet. Speak the words."

Szeth met his eyes, and said them. "I," he whispered, "am *not a thing.*"

Nin let the slightest sigh of annoyance pass his lips. It was the strongest sign of emotion Szeth had seen from him.

"I," Szeth repeated, "am not a *thing,* Nin. I'm not a rock to be handed between people, exchanged like money. I'm a *person.* You ask me to be a Herald. A Herald! A demigod, an immortal leader of humankind. Yet you want me to do as I'm told?"

"You always have before," Nin said.

"I was *broken* before!" Szeth shrieked. "I was *ripped away* from my perfect life and pounded and forged and beaten into a weapon! I can't be what you want! At least not unless I know what it will cost me. *I get to choose.* I . . . I deserve to be able to decide. If I can't have the life I want, I at least deserve to *choose* what I'm walking toward instead!"

He looked to Nin, pleading, wishing for him to understand. Szeth just needed this small measure of comfort. He'd do it. He'd take up the mantle, he'd give away everything he'd started to dream he could have. He'd *do it.*

But he had to make the choice. It was a luxury that he'd never before wanted, but that now—suddenly—he absolutely needed.

"So be it," Nin said, raising his sword in one hand. "We will do this the more difficult way. I do not think it is possible, but you will have to defeat me as you did the others. If you kill me, I will be reborn, as our immortality was sealed through ancient arts related to—but not dependent upon—the Oathpact. Unfortunately, I am very likely to kill you instead."

He stepped down onto the ground, leaving the air to give himself purchase and leverage for a lunge, then swung.

Szeth dropped his Shardblade, determined not to fight.

It was the wrong choice.

He knew that in an instant. His sister had refused to kill him, but Nin would not hold back.

So Szeth saw his death approach as a silver wave of light. Until a spear intercepted it with a resounding *clang.*

⁂

Kaladin stepped up beside Szeth, tossing off Nale's attack.

"You cannot interfere, Stormblessed," Nale said, calm, pulling backward into the air.

This man, Kaladin thought. *This* storming *man.* "For a person who harps on about the law so often," Kaladin snapped, "I find it shocking that you forget there are no rules."

"It should be a struggle between me and him," Nale said.

"Szeth," Kaladin said, not daring to take his eyes off Nale, "do you want my help?"

"Yes, please," Szeth whispered. "Nin, this is my champion. I cannot fight you. I *choose* not to. But he defeated me. He can defeat you."

Nale raised his sword in a formal posture. He blinked once, then turned to Kaladin. "I see. This *is* the way forward. Once you are dead, Szeth will be free of your influence."

"Nale," Kaladin said. "Don't force this. Let's talk about—"

"I will be your death, Stormblessed," Nale said. "If you are certain you accept this charge and duty."

Great. *Your thoughts?* he asked Syl in his mind.

I think this is the only way, she replied. *But Kaladin . . . Heralds are supposed to be virtually undefeatable.*

If that were the case, he thought, *they wouldn't have died during each of the*

Desolations. They still need Stormlight, right? They're experts in the Surges. So maybe . . .

"Your word, Stormblessed?" Nale asked.

"You'd accept such an unfair fight?" Kaladin asked, treading carefully, his armor spren humming in his mind, currently invisible—as they usually were when not dancing with the wind—but ready to manifest. "I'm willing, but I want to be sure."

"If you do not face me, I will kill Szeth," Nale said. "So this is fairer than slaying him as he stands there."

"And if we could make it even more fair?" Kaladin said, untying the pouch of spheres at his belt. "I'd go without Stormlight. What about you? Just the skill of one soldier against another."

"I am blessed with millennia of training. It would not be fair even still."

"But *more* fair?" Kaladin pressed.

Nale contemplated, then fished a pouch from his pocket.

What do you think? Kaladin asked Syl.

I think . . . this might be better, she said. *You're more recently practiced without powers. He might be rusty. But do you really want to fight? Isn't there another way to reach him?*

Logic won't work, Kaladin thought to her. *If he were reasonable, we wouldn't be here. So maybe this is the only way to force him to change.*

Another voice . . . "Take care," the Wind whispered. "Honor is dead, and Jezrien is gone. Nale . . . can command forces once forbidden him . . . But this is your best chance . . ."

"Fine," Nale said, tossing first one pouch to Szeth, then a second, then finally a third. "Sword against spear."

"Fine," Kaladin said, tossing his gemstones to Szeth as well. "I accept your challenge, Nale. I will protect the one who cannot right now protect himself."

"Windrunners," Nale said, as if it were a curse. "Still, I commend you for your sacrifice." The man dropped fully to the rubble, boots scraping stone and broken bits of wood, then exhaled until his Stormlight was gone.

Kaladin infused a rock with all of his own Stormlight and sent it sailing off at an angle into the sky. Szeth, holding their pouches of spheres, backed up toward the wall—where Kaladin had dropped his pack and the Honorblades.

"I have heard of your skill with the weapon, Stormblessed," Nale said, swinging with his Blade experimentally as he stretched. "I shall enjoy seeing what you can do. I warn you, this is to the death. Your armor is allowed, as are our Blades and talents unrelated to Stormlight. We go on your mark."

Kaladin stepped back, raised his spear into position, and gave a mental command to his armor to make sure it was in place.

"*Go,*" he said.

⁂

After dealing with an interesting matter involving the battle at the Shattered Plains, Jasnah met Fen at the designated time in the small temple Dalinar had repaired. Fen arrived with apparent curiosity, while Jasnah . . .

Jasnah was drawing exhaustionspren.

She'd wasted time, exactly as Odium had predicted, mulling over the nature of the upcoming debate. She'd compared notes with Fen, who had also been visited by Odium and been told the same thing: to meet at the temple for a debate about whether or not Thaylenah should join his empire.

Jasnah had held herself back—with general success—from diving into the historical record to search for examples of one of the three gods appearing directly to individuals. Instead she'd gone straight to Wit.

His words, via spanreed, had persuaded her. Taravangian taking up Odium explained, in Wit's mind, the deity's odd behavior. *Rayse always did assume he was invincible,* Wit had written, *even before his Ascension. But all along, the power has been seeking someone more aligned to its interests. Taravangian's Ascension is the answer to the question I was seeking. And good riddance to a terrible person who deserved far worse than he got. I hope it was painful.*

That said, I do not know if this is good for us. Rayse was crafty, dangerous, and destructive—but he was easy to anticipate and goad into action. Taravangian . . . I do not know him well enough. Take care. He will no longer be the man you knew, but a being of immense power. Not truly God, a point upon which you and I agree, but the closest the cosmere knows.

She'd prepared as best she could, all night. Now Jasnah settled down at her table, laying out her books and scribbled notes. Fen paced, wearing Thaylen clothing: a vest and blouse above an ankle-length skirt with straps up over the shoulders.

"You really think he's going to come?" Fen said. "This isn't some distraction?"

"Taravangian is a philosopher. He will welcome the chance to prove himself in a debate."

"Taravangian," Fen said, pacing back the other way. "I don't believe it's him. This is a game. Though I'm intrigued. I'll admit, even with all of our preparations, I was worried about losing the city to his army. But our battle is merely a *conversation* . . . If he realized he couldn't conquer us, and is instead trying something more desperate . . . this could stall us until the deadline."

Jasnah didn't contradict her, though she was far less certain. Her gut said that an army would be easier to deal with than the concentrated attention of a Shard of Adonalsium. She looked over her notes again, readying her arguments.

Fen found that amusing as well. She insisted she wasn't going to give in to Odium as Tashikk and Emul had, so why did Jasnah bother? But Taravangian was subtle, careful, and highly capable. He obviously thought this would work. To that end, Jasnah had rehearsed appeals to the Thaylen sense of pride and independence. Arguments against the morality of the singer empire. Specific criticisms of Odium's historical methods of rule, which she had records to prove.

Having done all of that, having spent so many hours planning in a flurry, she suddenly felt foolish. It was all so *obvious.* Of *course* the Thaylens wouldn't *choose* to follow the enemy. They had worried, throughout the founding of the coalition, that Jasnah's uncle would dominate them. They were quite capable of rejecting Odium doing the same.

Why, then, was she so anxious?

The entrance to the small room darkened. Guards who had been waiting outside rushed in to surround Fen, one of them even charging through the black smoke itself. He stopped in front of the queen and put the point of his sword toward the forming Shard. Jasnah took a mental note to ask his name later; he might be Radiant material.

The darkness coalesced into a kindly old man, standing straight-backed, but with a golden walking stick. He had on orange and gold robes that weren't nearly as gaudy as the attire his predecessor had reportedly worn. As in life, Taravangian had a wispy beard, pointed at the front, white and short along his jaw. He hadn't fixed his balding forehead.

He didn't seem to mind looking small and unassuming. "It's good to see you both again," he said. "Thank you for taking my suggestions seriously. Fen, you will not need those guards."

She eyed him, mostly obscured by hulking soldiers, then quietly asked for them to step outside. They went reluctantly. Jasnah's tension rose as Taravangian sat down, a stool forming behind him from dark smoke.

He waved in front of him. "Shall we chat here, as former friends?" Two more stools formed.

"I don't see the need, Odium," Fen said, folding her arms, remaining standing. "I can just tell you no, right here, right now. There will be no accommodation between us."

"Fen, Fen," Taravangian said. "Are you not a merchant? A queen of merchants? Are you *absolutely certain* you want to reject an offer before you even hear the terms?"

"I can't imagine *any* terms," Fen said, "that would convince me to give up my country to you."

"Then what harm is there in listening?" Taravangian asked. "It will keep me distracted, after all. Wouldn't an extended negotiation serve you best? So long as I have hope to persuade you, I obviously won't need to try other ploys for the city."

She eyed him. "Well, storms," she said under her breath. "It truly *is* you, isn't it?"

"It truly is," Taravangian said. "Jasnah, you've confirmed with your Wit?"

"I have," she admitted.

"Tell him I apologize for the necessity of altering his memories," Taravangian said. "He realized almost immediately that I wasn't Rayse—but I had not yet decided how to reveal myself." He gestured before him once more. "Shall we sit and discuss? I promise to deploy no tricks against you, and no attacks upon this city, during our conversation. It is a promise that, in making, I am bound by deific powers to keep."

Jasnah looked at Fen, who looked back. Finally, the two of them picked up chairs—reminiscent of the way Dalinar insisted they all carry seats at Urithiru—and placed them in a circle with Taravangian at the center of the chamber. With a sigh, he made his stools vanish.

"How is this going to proceed?" Fen said as she sat. "You make an argument, and Jasnah counters it?"

"Actually," Taravangian said, smiling, "I believe Jasnah is going to make my argument for me."

"*What?*" Jasnah said, nearly scattering the stacks of papers in her lap.

"You, Jasnah," Taravangian said. "You are the reason Fen will decide to join my empire." He smiled more broadly. "Thank you for your service all of these years. Now, let us begin."

In every game are a hundred paths to failure. But not always a single one to victory. It is not weakness to admit that another general must fight this foe another day.

—*Proverbs for Towers and War,* Zenaz, date unknown

Spear in hand, Kaladin backed away from Nale and evaluated the battlefield. The inside of an old monastery building, the roof broken down, stone blocks from the large fallen chimney—to his left—and hearth crumpled toward the center of the room.

"The day I warned you about is nearly here," the Wind whispered. "The storm. Tomorrow. I need you tomorrow."

"Then I'll have to survive," Kaladin said. "Any chance I could get your help?"

"I am weak," the Wind whispered. "I . . . have nothing but my voice, Kaladin."

Well then. Without his powers, Nale was only a person, right? The black-suited man swiped with his Shardblade, cutting the air, standing ten feet in front of Kaladin and watching with keen eyes. He did not immediately engage.

During the invasion of Urithiru, Kaladin had gotten plenty of practice drawing on his old training to fight without powers. He set his stance, spear pointed at Nale. The man finally started moving, easing to the right around the perimeter, past Szeth, boots scraping stone. He faced Kaladin from by the wall, just within its shadows—then he lunged into the sunlight.

Kaladin used his spear to shove the Blade away, but didn't take the bait to strike. That had been a test, as Nale—with sword instead of spear—had a reach disadvantage. His motions precise, every step deliberate, he rounded Kaladin, then came in with another strike. Again Kaladin deflected, though the man's precision and lack of expression unnerved him.

Nale was a man . . . and also not one, all at once. He was ancient. In many ways completely unknowable.

Calm, Kaladin told himself. *You fought the Pursuer, you fought Leshwi. You've defeated ancients before.*

Kaladin's training told him what would likely happen next. Another testing strike, which came, and he deflected it. Now the real strike. Nale swung a fourth time, but instead of backing off as Kaladin deflected, the Herald shoved in close, trying to fling Kaladin's spear to the side.

Kaladin wouldn't have it. He kept firm, withdrawing a few steps, but training the spear on Nale and nearly skewering him—forcing the Herald away.

Nale continued to stride around him. "Good," he said. "Good."

Not the expected reaction. While Kaladin could anticipate this man's attacks, Nale's motives were as opaque as ever.

Oddly, Wit's words returned to him. *The fight ahead of you is going to be legendary. Unfortunately, you can't fight this one with strength of muscle . . .*

The next few exchanges were more aggressive, but Kaladin controlled the clashes. The man with the spear should always control the fight, because when he lost that control—when the swordsman got in close—that was it.

No, Kaladin thought. *You have Plate now. Use it.* He needed more training with his armor; strategically taking hits on it was a common practice for Shardbearers.

Nale came in again. Kaladin let him get close and swing at Kaladin's head—while Kaladin himself formed Syl into a long knife. Metal clanged against metal as Nale's Blade hit, and a web of cracks appeared in the air to the left of Kaladin's head, but he stabbed the knife directly at Nale's gut.

The Herald managed to sidestep, just barely, then he danced backward. Kaladin managed a small slit in Nale's fine black uniform, along his side. Kaladin smiled. The spiderweb of cracks in the air by his head turned blue, and his armor came fully alert to the danger. It formed—starting a tiny bit out from his skin, then pulling in and locking into place, completely encasing Kaladin. Leyten would have fits about Kaladin's jacket getting wrinkled, but the Shardplate took that—and everything else—into account, forming perfectly, allowing full movement.

Kaladin wasn't certain of the specifics; his armor was always there these days, protecting him. But it wasn't fully there until the danger was real. Regardless, he spun his Shardspear and stepped back, armored foot now falling hard and crunching on rubble. A glow came from his chest and from other junctions along the sleek armor, and the visor—which he knew glowed from the slits—was transparent to him.

He now felt the weight and power of the Shardplate, a strength he hadn't fully mastered. Yet he had a certain . . . intrinsic understanding of it. This was *his* Plate, not some castoff from another Radiant. The windspren who formed it were his companions, and had come to his call at the Fourth Ideal.

Nale swiped with his Blade—his Radiant Blade, it seemed, not his Honorblade—strolling around Kaladin. He didn't summon his own Plate. Shouldn't it have deflected Kaladin's strike earlier?

Nale fell into an unfamiliar stance, sword held forward, then waved for Kaladin to approach and try some strikes of his own. Spear in hand, Kaladin did so, clashing with Nale, Plated feet grinding stone, spear clanging against sword. Kaladin didn't connect, but still Nale's Plate didn't appear. At least, he let a spear thrust go straight past his cheek—a hair from slicing him—and it didn't collide with anything.

Kaladin pulled away. Truth was, he didn't want to hurt Nale, and the man might have suspected Kaladin's heart wasn't in their exchanges—for he soon went back on the offensive.

Kaladin stepped into his flurry of strikes, taking another hit on the head, but sweeping for Nale's legs with the butt of his spear, which formed into a hook. The man jumped over the attack, then slammed his sword into Kaladin's head yet again. With a curse, Kaladin stumbled back. His helm was leaking furiously, a web of cracks crossing his vision. His armor seemed stronger than ordinary Shardplate, and was powered not by gemstones but by its own Connection to the Spiritual Realm, but Sigzil hadn't had time to run tests. Kaladin didn't want to take a fourth hit in the same spot if he could help it.

He came in once more, more careful, forming Syl into a giant Blade and sweeping at Nale, who easily dodged.

"You did better without the Plate, Stormblessed," Nale said in his passionless voice. "How long have you had it?"

Plate formed around Nale in a heartbeat, and he slammed an armored fist into Kaladin's chest—sending him stumbling backward to the ground, where he crashed in a heap, metal grinding on stone. Nale's armor vanished, becoming mist, and he strolled forward. "Do better. I would not have you die in such a pitiful way."

Kaladin clambered to his feet, then mostly dismissed his Plate. He needed more training to use it properly. As it faded though, he knew the spren would remain, guarding him.

"Good," Nale said, falling into a stance again.

Kaladin raised his spear, then advanced on Nale, forcing him back through the rubble-strewn room. Szeth watched from the side, concern showing in his widened eyes, in his tense hold on his pack of swords—including Nightblood.

This guy, Syl said in Kaladin's head. *Have we ever fought someone so annoying?*

"Amaram," Kaladin whispered.

Oh yeah. He was an absolute tool, wasn't he? And that's coming from a girl who is currently a spear.

Kaladin grunted, then advanced. Step, thrust, reset. Keep your spear toward the enemy. Be careful with your footing—but don't take your eyes off the target. Strike because you decide to, not because you're anxious.

He got in several very close thrusts, and expertly kept Nale at bay. "Good," the man said. "This is a man I can kill with confidence."

"You keep saying that," Kaladin said, sweat trickling down his brows. "Well, come on then. *Try.*"

Nale did. Sweeping attacks with his Blade from a stance Kaladin didn't know—like Windstance, only more frantic. Kaladin *should* have had the advantage with his longer reach, but now he was forced back. He thrust, but each time just a little too slowly. He still managed to fend off the attacks until right at the end, when he went to block a sweep from Nale's Blade.

Nale, in a blink, was holding a spear instead. He rammed it forward, square into Kaladin's face—where the invisible helmet barely caught it. The tip pierced the armor, cracking it fully, and stopped right between Kaladin's eyes, almost touching the skin.

Watch it, Kal, Syl said in his head. *That was a little close . . .*

They clashed again, and yet again Kaladin *almost* got a strike on Nale. By now Kaladin was puffing, sweating. This careful, deliberate contest reminded him of the fights he'd had with Leshwi. But those had been fights against a rival he respected, and this felt different. Storms, it was hard. Kaladin kept having to push himself more than he wanted, overextending to try to land a hit—and he kept missing anyway.

"You are good," Nale said, breaking off, then calmly walking through the chamber to Kaladin's right. "I have looked into your past, Stormblessed. You—the one who slipped past me, the one I should have found and killed. I know you have had a difficult life. It would have been better if you'd died by young Helaran's Blade."

Kaladin hesitated, gripping his spear, which had changed from smooth to covered in tiny ridges to give his sweaty hands more purchase. Helaran. Shallan's brother. It was sometimes difficult to remember that one event had set all this off: Kaladin unexpectedly finding a Shardbearer on the battlefield. A Skybreaker acolyte sent to murder Amaram, to prevent him from looking into the secrets of the vanished Knights Radiant.

"It was you," Kaladin said. "You sent him."

"I wish I'd known," Nale said, "that the key target was not Amaram, but one of his squadleaders. I would have gone myself and made sure you didn't leave that battlefield alive."

He's so strange, Syl thought at him. *He's always had this broken belief that if he killed the Radiants, it would prevent the Desolation. But we came back because we* felt *the Desolation coming.*

"Why?" Kaladin said to Nale. "The Desolation would still have come. Syl sought me out because she felt the storm moving through Shadesmar. Taln Returned, finally breaking. Your killing all those Radiants accomplished *nothing.*"

Nale froze, and Kaladin saw something: a flash of emotion, a chink in his armor. He looked away, as if remembering, then put his hand to his chest. "Do you know a young Radiant named Lift?" Nale asked.

"I do," Kaladin said. "Why?"

"She is the only one to have ever defeated me in single combat," Nale said softly.

"Please tell me she didn't use the fork," Kaladin said.

"No. No, it was a different weapon entirely." He focused again on Kaladin. "You might be right. The Desolation may still have arrived. However, I'd have killed you, and been correct to do so—for I believed it was the best course at the time, and was following what I'd been told."

"By whom?" Kaladin demanded.

"Ishar, naturally," Nale said. "Regardless: my choices were correct. Yes. If I'd killed *every* potential Radiant, then would the spren have felt the desire to return? No. Not at all."

"The Everstorm—" Kaladin said.

"Is meaningless," Nale said. "I am right."

He's working through his rationalizations, Syl said, *and getting them mixed up again.*

Logic would never work. Emotion. Kaladin had to focus on emotion and memory. How to make Nale *remember*?

"That day . . ." Kaladin said. "Helaran came thundering in like a storm. He killed my friends, left misery in his wake. Don't you care? He murdered a youth, a wounded child who was no threat. Cenn was his name."

"Collateral damage," Nale said.

"You say that about a child? Didn't you *care* once, Nale? About the innocents?"

The briefest moment of concern crossed his face. "I am here," he said softly, "because of the innocents."

"Yet you kill them!"

"I . . . follow the law," Nale said. "Helaran joined the army that your lord was fighting against, which gave him legal justification to kill as he needed." Nale looked up at Kaladin and pointed his sword straight at him. "I would kill a thousand youthful soldiers if my cause were just and the law on my side."

Kaladin's grip tightened on his spear. He felt cold . . . and then warm. And then . . .

And then he was back there. He was that man again, the one he'd proclaimed dead so many times. He remembered the smell of blood in the air on that field, so long ago, and the sound of Dallet repeating Kaladin's orders as he beat spear against shield to organize the squad.

Szeth was the boy who needed Kaladin now. And Kaladin was here in this fight not because of a compulsion—but because he had decided for himself. Wit said he needed to discover who he was when he didn't *need* to fight. Remarkably, Kaladin had begun to do that, he realized. New Kaladin still protected, but accepted he might fail. He controlled his sense of loss. Not through callousness, as his father had tried to teach him. But through love.

Memory and present meshed together, and then Kaladin lunged and struck. He anticipated exactly how Nale would dodge. Wind in his ears, Kaladin changed the tip of his thrust perfectly, knowing that his strike would be true.

This was the one. He had Nale.

Then the Herald moved a little faster, blurring.

Kaladin missed. His spear passed right by Nale's ear, striking only empty air.

That caused a moment of disconnect. Kaladin should have recovered and reset as training had drilled into him. Yet he *knew* he should have hit. Every scrap of instinct he had with the spear—the intimate familiarity that he seemed to have that others lacked—said that strike *should have landed.*

How had Nale possibly dodged?

"Such an interesting aspect of Windrunners," Nale said, stepping back. "If one enrages other people, they get sloppy. But put *you* in a position to protect, make *you* see red, and we find you at your best."

Kaladin struck again, and Nale leaned to the side, again impossibly fast. A little blur and shift.

This strike missed as well.

"Good," Nale said. "Yes, you'd likely have won by now if you were facing most foes. You quite nearly killed me, Stormblessed. Be proud of that. I would have you die with such pride."

Kaladin gripped his spear again, then struck, struck, struck. Three precise attacks, each as useless as the one before. Nale stepped around each one. He didn't even raise his Blade. He acted *casual.*

"Fight me!" Kaladin said, leaping forward—

Nale was there. Stepping into the attack and around it, faster than Kaladin could respond. Nale pressed his hand against Kaladin's chest and tossed him to the ground. Sprawling.

Kaladin gaped, stunned—less physically than mentally. Never since his first days training with a spear had anyone treated him so indifferently in a fight.

What . . . what was going on?

Kaladin? Syl said.

He picked himself up and backed away. That emotion making him cold, that was fear. Powerlessness. He knew it. He'd felt it many times before, but rarely while he'd held a spear.

"If I am asked," Nale said, striding forward, "I will be honest. You fought well. It is rare that I must use the true skills of a Herald against a mortal. We . . . do not deploy them frivolously."

Szeth stumbled between the two of them. "I'll do as you say. I'll obey, Nin. It's over!"

Nale calmly pushed Szeth out of his way and walked toward Kaladin. "I must execute him, Szeth, now that I have legal authority to do so. His corrupting influence on you must end."

"But—"

"He agreed to this fight. It is settled. Stand *down.*"

"It's all right, Szeth," Kaladin said, mind racing. "I'll find a way to—"

Nale was there in front of him.

Kaladin tried to dodge, but Nale didn't move like a person should. A lifetime of practice had trained Kaladin in what to expect. He could barely track—much less comprehend—the way Nale seized him by the arm, spun him and took him in two hands, then *smashed* him against the stone wall of the building.

Once. Twice. Thrice. Kaladin's armor gave out as Nale treated him like a child's doll. The armor exploded, leaving Kaladin exposed. Then Nale tossed Kaladin aside.

Kaladin rolled hard along the ground, slamming into the nearby wall and colliding with his pack. Limp, in pain, Kaladin wheezed for breath, his vision spinning. This was . . . this was something he'd never experienced . . . Even in his youth, the first time he'd picked up a spear, he'd felt somewhat in control.

He'd *never* been so utterly outmatched.

He looked up, blinded by pain, seeing the dark shadow of Nalan'Elin approach. Then he stopped as a figure formed in front of him. Syl?

"This is not fair," she said.

"It is just."

He tried to step around her and she moved back in front of him. "This? *Justice?*"

"I am sorry, Ancient Daughter," Nale said, still cold and calm. "You should have stayed in Shadesmar as your father wished. Your pain is of your own choosing."

Nale stepped deliberately through her. Then pulled up short as another figure formed in front of him, hands up as if to protect Kaladin. From the shape, through blurred vision, Kaladin could make out Szeth's spren.

"Stop, Nale!" the spren said. "Please."

"You," Nale said, "are a disgrace to your kind. You were trained to be a light to your human, not some kind of attendant to him and *his* will."

Nale continued, ignoring both spren, ignoring Szeth's cries. Kaladin took a deep breath and prepared to stand, pressing his hands against the stone floor, strewn with chips of rubble. And as he did, he heard something distant, faint.

The sound of a flute.

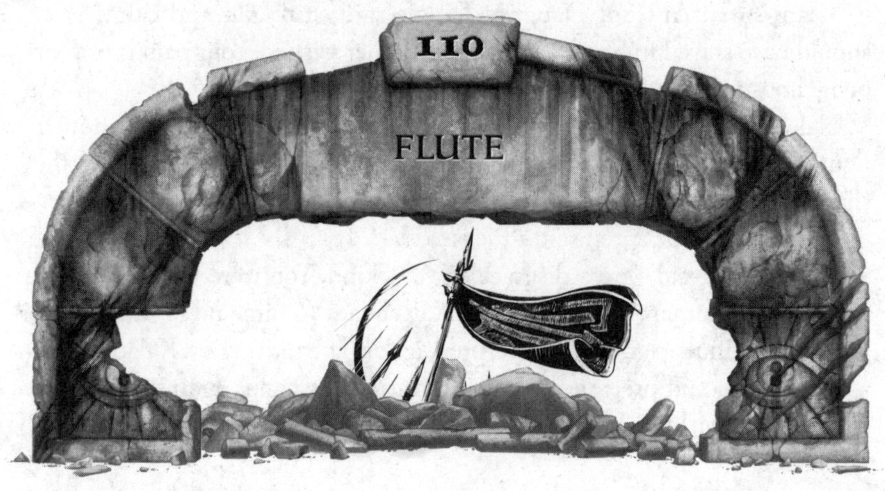

No general can control a battlefield. He must instead learn to ride it like one does an untamed beast. But you can practice and prepare for that eventuality.

—*Proverbs for Towers and War,* Zenaz, date unknown

Such an incongruous sound. A flute, the song Kaladin had been practicing, drifting in the air. Frail.

The Wind, he realized, was trying to help the best she could. With her voice.

"I return your song to you, Kaladin," she whispered. "As I once returned it to Cephandrius."

Nale stopped and looked around, frowning. "That song again . . ." he said. "That rhythm . . ."

I can't win this battle with a spear, Kaladin thought. *Any more than I could win it with logic.* But that song . . . that song moved something in Kaladin. It always had.

He took something from his pack lying beside him in a heap by the wall, then heaved to his feet and fell into a stance. As Nale raised his Blade, Kaladin raised his own hands holding not a sword or spear—but a simple wooden flute.

"There's a story you need to hear," Kaladin said. "It is the story of the—"

Nale punched him in the stomach, again moving at inhuman speed, and bones snapped. Kaladin gasped, pain blinding his vision, as he felt his insides *crunch.* He fell to his knees, and the flute slipped from his fingers and hit the floor.

Szeth caught Kaladin and held out a pouch of spheres. "Take it! This isn't a fight any longer. It's an execution."

In his pain, Kaladin drew in the Stormlight, though he couldn't have said if it was a conscious choice or the response of a drowning man breaking the surface for a frantic gasp. That began to heal him, and his vision recovered, but as he reached for more, someone else got there first. Nale strode past, and Light streamed from the spheres in Szeth's possession—from pouches by the walls as well, from gemstones Kaladin hadn't remembered, tucked into the bottom of his pack. Everything.

It seemed to favor Nale, streaming to him instead of Kaladin. The Herald drew it in with arms outstretched—then let go. Allowing a puff of radiance to shimmer up into the air and vanish.

"No Stormlight," Nale said calmly. "That was the agreement." He stepped forward and slammed a booted heel on the flute, crunching the wood, shattering it.

Kaladin cried out in dismay, reaching for the broken flute. Nale moved again, pushing Szeth aside with enough force to throw him into the wall. Kaladin had been healed enough to see clearly, though his Stormlight gave out. Without it, the Honorblades couldn't grant Surges, and Nightblood would consume their souls in a flash if drawn.

Lying on the ground, Kaladin stretched his fingers toward the broken flute again, tears in his eyes.

Kaladin, Syl said, *I don't understand why the flute matters.*

"Nale knows this song," Kaladin whispered. "He knows this story. He understands, deep down, what it means to care for people more than rules. I *know* it, Syl. We have to remind him. We have to make him remember."

Kaladin reached out, and something silvery formed in his hand from Radiant mist. A flute made all of metal.

This is dangerous though! Syl said. *Maybe we should run.*

But the Wind kept returning his music to him, in the distance. Halting, faulty notes. Echoes from when he'd practiced. Kaladin, panting, heaved to his feet and backed away from Nale.

The Herald was ignoring him, continuing to walk with his head cocked. Listening. "That song . . . it's the song you played. Those notes . . . those are the notes that led us to Roshar all those millennia ago . . ."

Wind blew through the broken monastery, a soft wind, a teasing wind. It touched the flute and a quiet note sounded, vibrating the instrument in Kaladin's hand. The other notes outside grew stronger, overlapping one another, as if five or six flutists were playing and not one.

Nale moved to one of the arrow-slit windows and peered out. "What is this? What army comes to your aid?" He glanced back at Kaladin. "Nothing.

Just hills . . ." He narrowed his eyes. "Offworlder magic. You've been talking to Midius. His illusions are meaningless against one who knows them for the falsehoods they are, Stormblessed."

Nale spun and raised his sword in two hands, point toward Kaladin. In return, Kaladin put the flute to his lips, and blew a few bars of the melody he'd been practicing. This flute seemed more natural to his fingers and lips. Simple though the tune was, he felt enormous pride at the lack of mistakes.

He raised his head from the flute, looked Nale—who had stopped again—in the eyes. "This story is about Derethil and the *Wandersail*."

Nale's calmness cracked as he gritted his teeth and surged forward, but his strange speed failed him. He stumbled. Kaladin was able to back up to escape Nale's reach. The Wind almost seemed to lift him as he hopped over the pile of rubble that had been the monastery chimney.

Landing on the other side, Kaladin shouted, "Have you heard it? The story of how Derethil and his crew made their way to a hidden island in the Endless Ocean? A land where everything appeared so perfect at first?"

Nale slowed. "I do not pay attention to made-up stories."

"Pity," Kaladin said. "They have proven to be some of the most real things in my life." He presented the flute, which the Wind played in his hand. "Derethil and his crew set out to cross the ocean and find out what was on the other side. Some say they sought the place the Voidbringers were born. Others say Derethil sought the Origin itself, that mythical place where storms begin and Light is most powerful.

"I do not know the ultimate result of their voyage, but I do know that they wrecked on an island called Uvala, near a mighty whirlpool. A tall people lived there, who wore shells in their hair unlike any that grew on Roshar. They cared for Derethil and his crew. Everything seemed so *perfect*. So ideal. No need for guards, or police, or anything of the sort."

Nale growled, a bit of true emotion, but again stopped in place as the music outside—sounding like a dozen flutes now—increased in volume. Echoes of Kaladin's practice overlapping, forming a cohesive song. Nale looked one way, then the other.

"Why did you become a Herald, Nale?" Kaladin asked softly. "Do you remember? Can you remember how you *felt*?"

"Emotion can't be trusted!"

"Is it your emotions you can't trust," Kaladin said, "or your mind?"

"I . . . I used to see clearly . . ." he said, tipping his head back. "I thought I did . . . then my mind changed . . ."

"Storms," Kaladin whispered. "Is that why you started trusting only in the law? You felt yourself slipping, didn't you? You knew your logic failed. You *knew* you were getting worse, so you fixated on something external, hoping it would be a guiding light as your own mind deteriorated."

Nale growled, glaring at him. "The law is perfect."

Kaladin pointed the flute at him, and spoke in rhythm to the music. "One day, on this perfect island, Derethil saw something unnerving. A serving girl made a mistake. She broke some goblets. The other people of the island *attacked* her and *killed* her brutally. Do you know why?"

"It was obviously the law," Nale growled.

"The law of the emperor."

"The law must be obeyed," Nale said, right fist toward Kaladin—his sword as if forgotten in his other hand. "Stop fleeing your destiny, Stormblessed!"

Kaladin rounded Nale, his chest still aching from the hit. "Do you remember finding people trapped in rubble? Darkness, followed by light, as you—smothered in ash and blood—worked to save those trapped beneath the wreckage?"

"That happened many times," Nale said. "Too many times."

"Do you remember," Kaladin continued, "a child who cowered in a corner as figures with glowing red eyes broke down the doorway . . . and was saved as you came back seeking those who had been left behind?"

"I . . ." Nale cocked his head to the music.

"Gratitude," Kaladin said. "Do you remember their gratitude as you stood before the weak and ignored, blood dripping down your arm as you held out your sword . . . like a banner . . ."

"You will not have them," Nale whispered. He looked to Kaladin, and there were tears at the corners of his eyes. "I woke one day . . . this must have been a thousand years ago or more . . . and I realized I'd hurt someone by accident. Out of irritation. I thought . . . I'm losing it. Losing myself."

"So you sought a way to control your actions."

"I turned to the law," Nale whispered. "To force myself to hold on to the person I wanted to be. Because . . . I couldn't trust my mind anymore . . ."

Kaladin had positioned himself with his back to the large gates at the front of the chamber. Here he stopped, brandishing the flute, with the Wind blowing through it.

"I can't go back!" Nale shouted. But he seemed . . . afraid of Kaladin. He retreated as he spoke, his words and tone defiant. "I can't trust you, or what I see, or what I think! There is only *one ANSWER*. I must follow the law!"

"Derethil and his men," Kaladin said, accompanied by the flute playing in his fingers, "discovered more instances of brutality from the people of Uvala. Extreme violence in response to simple acts! They demanded answers, and always were told it was the will of the emperor!" Kaladin's voice rose to a shout. "Finally, Derethil and his men sought out the emperor who would create such terrible laws! They stormed the tower to demand accountability!"

Nale snarled, then strode to the side of the room and grabbed the still-dazed Szeth—who had been listening to the music in awe—from next to the wall. Nale placed his Shardblade to Szeth's throat.

"Come fight me!" Nale said.

The music outside softened. The flute in his fingers became as quiet as a whisper. It felt anticipatory to Kaladin, the held breath before a storm.

"Nale," Kaladin said, "is this what you've become?"

The Herald paused. He glanced at Szeth, and seemed to see him in a new light. He dropped Szeth and again put his hand to his chest.

Then he looked to Kaladin, and his calm shattered, emotion streaking his face with lines of anger as he shouted, "This is *your* fault! It all made sense before you!" He started toward Kaladin again, sword held high. "*You* are my flaw! You are the one I let slip past, who started the events that ruined it all! You are the cause for *ALL* of this!"

Kaladin raised his arms to the sides.

Wind erupted through the gates of the monastery, slamming the doors open, carrying with it *music.* An overwhelming stampede of sound, a thousand flutes playing at once. Every practice Kaladin had done, captured by the Wind and belted out in a tide of song.

It hit Nale with a *physical* force. The Herald leaned back and faltered, eyes going wide, as if staring into a bright, all-consuming light.

"What did they find!" Kaladin shouted at him. "What did they find in the top of the tower, Nale?"

The man whimpered and stepped back.

"*WHAT WAS IN THE TOWER?*" Kaladin bellowed.

"*NOTHING!*" Nale yelled back, his face a mask of pain, tears streaming down his cheeks. "There was *nothing* in the tower! There was . . ." Nale fell to his knees. "There was nothing! He's dead."

Nale dropped his Blade. He looked at his hands, then at Kaladin as the music drifted away, the tide becoming a stream.

"Honor is . . . is dead," Nale whispered. "Jezrien is . . . is gone. Ishar is . . . as good . . . as good as dead too . . ."

"Derethil learned a lesson that day—one I've learned, and you must learn. Even if an emperor makes the laws, when we uphold them, the laws become ours. The responsibility ours. And every action those people took . . . that blood was on their hands."

Nale wept openly.

"Why," Kaladin repeated, "did you become a Herald, Nale?"

The bald man looked up at him, seeming a completely different person from moments ago. "I feared the others, highborn save Taln, would forget the little people of the lands. I *knew it,* Kaladin. I fought on their behalf, for centuries. Oh . . . my god . . . What has happened to me? What has become of me?" He blinked through the tears. "The law cannot shelter me.

Why? *Why* can't I see right anymore? Do you think . . . do you think that black sword could destroy me?"

Kaladin gripped his flute tighter and stood above the pitiful man kneeling on the ground. Demigod. Broken. A moment later, Szeth stumbled up beside him.

Then, Szeth reached a trembling hand out to Nale. "We can help you," he said softly. "We can't make it all better, but we *can* help. Right, Kaladin?"

Even those I hate, Kaladin thought. "Yes, we can help, Nale. We *will* help."

Nale broke down weeping as he took Szeth's hand, but then stayed on his knees—clinging to it, wetting the broken ground of the monastery with his tears. Two figures appeared. Syl on one side, 12124 on the other.

The final figure, Nale's spren, emerged as a rip in the sky nearby. Not in the shape of a person. Then it streaked off and vanished.

NINE YEARS AGO

"I'm sorry, honor-nimi," Lumo said. "I cannot authorize this for one Honorbearer. I just . . . Szeth, you *have* to know how this looks. It's insane."

"It's *Truth,* Lumo," Szeth said.

He stood, Blade in hand, before his old home on the clifftop—the small town and warcamp outside the Stoneward monastery. He stood in roughly the last place he'd seen his mother before leaving.

She lived in a city a short flight away. He had been tempted to seek her out, but . . . not like this. He would wait until he was seen as a hero.

Strange, how much this place he'd hated now felt like returning home. He'd saved Lumo years ago from a burning ship during that infamous attack on the raiders. The red-bearded man was now the General of the entire place. Straight-backed, tall, with a neat uniform. This camp maintained the discipline that Neturo had instilled; that was clear from the soldiers arrayed to meet Szeth.

Soldiers who, despite his history with them, didn't believe.

"Can you offer proof?" Lumo asked.

"My own word is my proof," Szeth said. "And my station as Honorbearer."

"Honorbearer Pozen visited us last night," Lumo said softly. "Elsecalled right into the center of the camp. He said you were a delusional heretic who couldn't be trusted."

"And what," Szeth said quietly, "do you think of Pozen?"

The soldiers shared looks. All was still for a moment as a cold, highland breeze greeted them.

"He is not a soldier," Szeth said. "Did he send us help when we held here alone against raiders? Did he bring his Blade and fight by our side? Did he even seem to *care*?"

They did not respond.

"Something is wrong in this land," Szeth said. "You know it. Right before I left you, I was to be banished—then suddenly the narrative changed, bizarrely, and I was rewarded. *It was the Unmade.* They all obey it. I swear it to you."

"You . . . hear a voice," Lumo said. "Telling you to do things."

"Each Honorbearer does," Szeth said.

Silence. He knew, from their expressions, that he had failed. These capable soldiers were lost to him. At least that was what he assumed, until salvation arrived.

In the form of an enemy army.

One of Lumo's soldiers spotted it, raising the alarm. The banners, Szeth saw as he turned, were of the other monasteries. An army multiple times larger than his, emerging through an Elsecalled portal to fight.

In that moment, he knew retreat was impossible against Elsegates.

"It is time," Szeth said. "We fight."

"I cannot join you, Szeth," Lumo said, pained.

"Then," Szeth said, meeting his eyes, "you shall instead have to watch them slaughter me."

⁘

Shortly thereafter, Szeth raised the flag of rebellion and led his army against the forces of the Honorbearers. But today he did not kill.

The way he'd slain dozens in the previous battle haunted him. He felt as if their souls watched him from the quiet places beneath the stones, where the spren were said to lurk. He knew why the Honorbearers refused to use their weapons against the raiders, although he hadn't said so to Lumo. It was too much.

So today, he led. He glowed, he hovered before his men, and he shouted encouragement. They were outnumbered, but at least had their backs to the cliffs, so they couldn't be surrounded. He thought this position must be good, as his soldiers would fight more valiantly, knowing the weakness of a retreat was forbidden them. Indeed, they fought better this time, even if the individual soldiers missed a great number of strikes, and didn't seem to understand the flow of the conflict.

Szeth kept them fighting with shouts and orders, and because he didn't fight, the other Honorbearers didn't join the fray. He could see their banners, one from each of the other monasteries. Including the Bondsmith monastery, which was curious. So he was arrayed against seven banners, all but the Windrunner, Stoneward, and Skybreaker.

He let his armies begin retreating up the switchback to the clifftop warcamp, but only under pressure from his shamans. Still, he kept them fighting. He kept them desperate, until . . .

At last.

The armies of the Stoneward monastery above came to Szeth's rescue. As he'd hoped, they were unable to watch as one of their own was destroyed. Szeth rose into the air, afire with Stormlight, listening to the glorious sound of their trumpets. Crystal-clear notes accompanying a force marching down the switchbacks to join Szeth's troops.

Something swelled in Szeth at the sound, the sign of that glorious force marching with bright helmets and shields held high. This was the moment when his flaming ember became a wildfire. The moment when resistance against the Voidbringers truly began, and the Desolation was opposed.

He landed in a storm of light. "It's true," whispered Drodli, one of his head shamans, his helmet askew with a dent in one side, and blood—not his—on his armor. "They *are* coming, as you said. What . . . what would we have done if they hadn't?"

"We'd have died," Szeth said calmly. "Better to die than to let the Return happen unresisted."

Drodli gave him a horrified look at that. Never mind. Better soldiers were coming. His shamans were, he noticed, yelling for the men to take heart at the sight—something he likely should have done. Instead he flew up to speak to Lumo at the head of the new troops.

"We'll fight, Szeth," he said, "but only because you're on the defensive—and they apparently want to exterminate you. Something strange *is* going on, and it's time that we had some respect here, rather than being considered second-class because we lack an Honorbearer."

Those were not quite the words of a glorious champion for Truth, but they would do. Szeth flew back down, and the Stoneward army began to support his ranks. As the troops were bolstered, stabilizing on the incline—a favorable position—he shouted a challenge to the enemy armies.

Other Honorbearers materialized. First Moss, who should have been his friend, then Sivi. Pozen was making those closest to Szeth come first, hoping they would die by his Blade.

Well, today he refused. He was no assassin, no murderer crafted to do evil. He sought them out and clashed with them, but made no killing blows. He merely fought until Moss broke and fled. Sivi waited until that fight was done, then came in next.

Though she could bend the stones to her will, he made certain not to leave the soil. She refused to Elsegate away, and so theirs was mostly a duel of sword against sword, fought on the ground in the middle of the enemy ranks—who made room for them, and did not try to interfere.

Szeth did her the honor of minimizing his use of powers, and therefore had to spend a good five minutes fighting until he managed to disarm her and send her sprawling across the grass in a heap, her short hair falling and obscuring her eyes.

"You're strong," she whispered. "Stones Unhallowed . . . how did you get so strong?"

"Because," he said, leveling his Blade at her, "I fight to protect our land. Join me, and we will be two."

"Szeth," she said. "You're confused. That wasn't an Unmade you saw."

"I will not be persuaded by you."

She sighed and sat up. "Well, at least you let yourself be distracted by a duel."

Distracted?

Trumpets sounded behind him. He turned, with horror, and saw the troops from the Stoneward monastery retreating. No, worse—re-forming and turning their weapons against his troops, who were now trapped between two enemy forces.

"Traitors!" Szeth shouted. "Treason!"

Everything crumbled. His vision of a glorious resistance. His men leading a wildfire of change that saved the world itself. He screamed in denial, and shot through the sky on a Lashing, an arrow in flight. He slammed against the ground between his forces and those of the traitors, Lumo at their head. He opened his mouth to demand answers . . . and a figure stepped out from among them.

A stout man with a short beard, thinning hair, a friendly smile. Neturo. His father.

A lightning bolt of shock jolted through Szeth. His father was a captive. A prisoner. A . . . a . . .

"Hello, son," Neturo said, stopping a few feet in front of him. "We thought that Lumo and his troops might listen to reason if *I* spoke to them."

"Lightweaving," Szeth whispered. "You aren't real."

"I'm sorry," Neturo said, wearing his old uniform, but with new colors. Blue, brown, and green. The . . .

The Bondsmith colors.

Neturo summoned an Honorblade, with a wavy blade and writing along it, then placed it into the ground in front of him. "I am real, Szeth. When Sivi and Pozen came to me with this offer, I didn't know what to think. Grand senator? Bondsmith? Leader of our people? They said it might be the only way to save you. So I listened. And . . . well, I've heard him now, son."

"The Voice?" Szeth whispered.

"He says you turned your back on him."

"Father, he's—"

"He's not a Voidbringer, son," Neturo said. "I've met him. I don't know what he is. A god perhaps, as he says—but he's not one of *them.*"

"I . . ." Szeth put a hand to his forehead. "No. You can't be . . . can't be real . . ."

Neturo dismissed his Blade, then stepped forward, arms out, and Szeth backed up. His father kept coming until he embraced Szeth. And . . . stones . . . it *was* him.

"We *have* to stop this madness," Neturo said. "The Voice is committed, but I *know* there must be another way."

"I'm following my heart, Father," Szeth whispered. "I'm trying to do what is right. I've *always* tried to do what is right."

"I know," Neturo said. "I know."

Szeth squeezed his eyes closed, and he was a little boy again. Standing before a rock that would go on to kill every bit of joy in his life.

"Szeth," his father said, his arms warm, his voice warmer, "I've realized why I followed you all those years."

"Why?"

"I thought you might lead me to answers." He gave Szeth a squeeze. "You did."

Neturo . . .

Neturo had answers.

Suddenly, the horror of what Szeth had done overwhelmed him. He'd killed dozens with an Honorblade. He'd raised an army to fight his own people. If he was wrong . . .

Why had he thought he could trust his own judgment? He was a fool, and a child, and he *always had been.*

"Tell me what to do," Szeth whispered. "And I'll do it. If *you* tell me."

112 THE SONG OF RENUNCIATION

The first rule of warfare is to know your enemy. If you can guess what he will do, then you have already won.

—*Proverbs for Towers and War,* Zenaz, date unknown

Jasnah blinked as she sat in the small round temple—with windows all along the sides, and sculpted reliefs of Talenelat'Elin. What had Taravangian just said?

That *she* would persuade Fen to join his cause? That Jasnah had been working for *Odium*?

"Don't be ridiculous," Jasnah said. "Fen, I've never worked for Taravangian, unless you count one time when I was hired to help his granddaughter. Stating that I have done so all along is an indication of his intent to lie."

"It's no lie," Taravangian said, extending his hands as he sat across from her—palms up, his golden cane leaning against his thigh. "But it is perhaps a *tad* melodramatic. I can't help myself sometimes." He met Jasnah's eyes. "You don't *know* that you've been serving me, Jasnah. But you have been, all your life, regardless."

"Insanity," she said, feeling cold. "Is this really your opening argument? Let's move to the political debate."

"We'll get there," he said, his light brown eyes holding hers. "Tell me, Jasnah. What is your fundamental guiding principle? The philosophy by which you live your life?"

"I follow the Philosophy of Aspiration," she said. "I've made no attempt to hide that. I do good, Taravangian, whatever it takes."

"Ah . . ." he said. "Not *merely* good, though. The *most* good possible, for the most people."

"Correct."

"Then we are aligned," he said, turning to Fen. "Jasnah and I hold to the same philosophy. It will be easy, then, for the two of us to explain why Thaylenah should join with me."

Jasnah ground her teeth. "Don't let him steer," Ivory warned in her ear, from where he rode on her earring.

"I reject that assertion," Jasnah said, then she looked to Fen, who sat watching with interest. "Fen, I've studied philosophy all my life—and I've determined that what I need to do is seek the greatest and best good for all people. I've dedicated myself to this cause—you know that I have. While Odium and Taravangian have both sought power, have sought to destroy, have sought to conquer."

"Jasnah," Taravangian whispered, "what will lead to the greatest good and the least suffering on Roshar? Peace or war?"

"I don't accept what you're pushing me to say," Jasnah replied, staring him in the eyes. "You want me to agree that one man ruling can enforce peace—but I have no assurances that you'll rule in a peaceful way."

"And if I made such assurances to Fen and her people? If I gave them such promises?"

"There would still be no reason for her to accept. Peace is already on the way for her per my uncle's actions. Why would Fen agree to join with you now, a day before that arrives?"

"Oh, but there you are wrong," Taravangian said. He looked to Fen. "My friend, I am required by dictates of my conscience to see this planet unified, because *that* will lead to the greatest goodness that could ever encompass Roshar. Over the last millennia, wars were fought between humans, while the singers lived lives of enslaved agony. Misery has been the greatest currency of your kingdoms for generations. But *I* can make that go away."

"Dalinar's covenant will enforce peace," Fen said.

"Between my empire and the kingdoms of humankind," Taravangian said softly. "Not between humans themselves."

"We have treaties with Fen."

"Ah," Taravangian said, "but how often do mortals break treaties? Did not your war on the Shattered Plains begin that way? How well did your own father, Jasnah, keep his word? I believe he had treaties with Jah Keved, yet skirmishes and power struggles still happened." He turned to Fen. "Our agreement locks borders into place, but you know how fickle humans are. Human nations *may* continue fighting one another, as they can ignore words on the page."

Jasnah blessed her preparations. She'd caught this one as a likely argument—it was, after all, a natural outgrowth of the treaty. Odium *had* to hold to his word, but humans did not.

"Is he right?" Fen said. "I thought Dalinar's covenant froze the borders of nations, and they would be magically—supernaturally—impossible to break."

"Not exactly," Jasnah said. "Odium is bound by the dictates of being a divinity, so—and Wit agrees—he will be *forced* to abide by the contract. He 'vowed to cease hostilities and maintain the peace, not working against Dalinar, his allies, or their kingdoms in any way.' So, he must prevent acts of war between the people in regions he rules and ours, for a period of one thousand years. The rest of us humans are free to do as we wish, and could theoretically attack each other without breaking the contract with Odium. Fortunately, you know my uncle, and you know me. We will not attack you."

"And your grandchildren?" Taravangian asked. "Their grandchildren?" He pressed a hand to his chest. "I'm immortal. I will *enforce* peace among the nations that follow me. If you join me, Fen, I will see that your grandchildren do not die in useless wars. That Thaylenah remains a distinct nation—underneath my banner."

"Safe, and without freedom." Jasnah's preparations flooded her mind. "Fen, you know the writings of Tslamfn the Just. Your own great-great-great-grandfather?"

" 'Every kingdom needs,' " Fen quoted, " 'to be able to exercise its right to conflict—as a last resort when its misery becomes unbearable.' She's correct, Taravangian. Without the ability to rise up and take weapons, my people would lose a fundamental right. You might be able to protect us from future generations of Alethi, but so can my grandchildren."

He settled back, and Jasnah thought for a moment that his smile faltered. He nodded to her in respect. "What about today, Fen? Can your grandchildren, your armies, protect you today?"

"From what?" she asked.

"From me," Taravangian said. "And the fact that I hold this city in the palm of my hand, ready to crush it. If you turn me away, I will be forced to do so. For your own good."

⁂

Riding a chasmfiend was more difficult than Venli had assumed. As she and the other listeners geared up on a staging plateau—in preparation for attacking the human position—the others explained how to hold to the ropes they looped around the beast's neck and body, how to brace herself upon outcroppings of carapace.

"It's easy, once you get the hang of it," Thude said to Confidence.

Venli figured she could have made a list a mile long of things that were easy "once you got the hang of them." She determined to crouch instead of standing tall like Thude, holding to the ropes. They weren't reins—you couldn't *control* a chasmfiend. You could merely make *suggestions* via the rhythms you sang. The ropes were wholly for the benefit of the riders.

Red lightning rumbled above, reminding her even more of that terrible night when she and the others had first unveiled the Everstorm. It didn't help that the humans were in basically the same position, holding Narak with darkened, worried eyes, shadowed within helms, anticipationspren waving around them. Their walls were cracked, their Stormlight almost out.

Unlike last time, when the humans had fought newly born stormforms, they faced a battle-hardened army led by immortals. The humans had never really had a chance here. Odium had thrown nearly his entire weight at this fight—extending as he'd been afraid to do before. If he wanted to win a single specific battle—and pay the toll of doing so—he could.

Rain fell, light drops, mostly a mist. Venli held tight to her ropes, as that rain would make it more slippery. Nearby, the other two chasmfiends stepped up to the edge of their plateau, together carrying twenty of her people. They began to sing the Rhythm of Memories. A rarely used rhythm, usually paired with one of the old songs.

In this case, they chose the Song of Destruction—a war march. The words were quietly similar to another song, and sung to the same tune. The Song of Renunciation: the one that recounted how the listeners had long ago walked away from their gods. Pieces of it were part of the Song of Histories, but this was the pure, simple version. She sang it in her head, while she voiced Destruction.

The assault forces gathered. Hundreds of Fused and Regals. Their thunderclast was dead, and needed time to return, and the humans had successfully killed over half of the Focused Ones. She'd heard the Fused talking. The arrival of Venli's group mattered because they had brought beasts capable of legitimately challenging Shardbearers and breaking down walls.

A Husked One appeared beside them, a femalen with glowing red eyes and a large, powerful figure, her woven hair forming clothing. "You will be the second assault. Be ready to bring down those walls."

"The second?" Venli asked, surprised. "He's not sending us in first?"

"Be grateful El leads this battle," she said. "I would gladly send you traitors to die." She spat to the side, something Venli had occasionally seen the Fused do—but which baffled modern singers. A relic of their culture from long ago? "He wants to soften the enemy by personally trying to kill some of their spren first."

Timbre trembled within her. This . . . changed the plan slightly. Venli had anticipated being the first wave. Thunder hammered them as the call went up, and a group of Heavenly Ones—not including Leshwi and her followers, who hovered nearby—went streaking toward the human air forces.

SEVEN THOUSAND FIFTY YEARS AGO

I, the Almighty, rode the storms. Imprinted myself on them, made them an avatar of me. A word used by the gods for an aspect of themselves that works with a certain self-determination.

It is not the same for us as for mortals. We can think many thoughts and be many places. Here I created a spren who was—at the same time—myself. Myself if I were free to just . . . exist. It was not fully independent. It was not fully me. I savored its simple joy.

But soon I felt Kor's return as a sudden song. She had gone to gather information after what I'd told her of Rayse's attacks on other Shards.

I found her in our home on Roshar: the verdant explosion near the center of the continent. She called it our nest. Kor landed in her greatest shape, the winged dragon with deep brown skin, lined with silver. I loved it, as I loved all of her forms. In an eyeblink, she'd taken her human shape instead, and she grabbed me by both arms, mingling our divine essences.

Our songs became a harmony.

"Tanavast," she hissed, "Rayse didn't kill only Uli Da."

"Who else?"

"Aona."

The healer? Of all people, he'd attacked *Aona*?

"Both she and Skai are *dead,* Tanavast," Kor whispered. "He drew them into conflict with one another, then finished them off when they were weak."

Aona had always treated me with such kindness. I felt my essence grow thinner, spread out, my soul *vibrating* with anguish. Then I snapped back.

"He goes too far," I declared. "He will strike further if allowed. We must move against him. *Now.*"

I sensed her hesitance as the landscape around us, growing more and more aligned with our moods, vibrated to her emotions. Kor wasn't a pacifist—I'd seen that personally—but her way was not direct confrontation. She was a dragon, trained as a god before our Ascension. Her way was with careful, subtle nudges.

That would not suffice against Rayse. I opened the future to her, and showed the possibilities. She could see them as well as I could, better even, but sometimes did not wish to.

At my divine manifestation of possibility, she nodded. Our very lives were in danger, but Rayse was wounded. This might be our best chance. And so, together, we swept out of the nest, crossing the landscape in harmony, a storm building behind us.

We found him with the singers.

It had been decades to the mortals. In those years, he'd turned from his pet humans, finding a better tool in these who felt I'd abandoned them. How? I had only been gone to help dissidents on Ashyn a short time.

Long enough for the singers to begin to stray from my teachings. To look toward their ancient gods. So inconsistent were these singers! So untrustworthy!

I hesitated. That wasn't truly how I felt, but the power within me—the power called Honor—was offended by them turning from their promises. It wanted me to understand that pain, but I rejected such. I knew, from my time as a mortal, how normal this was—and I tried to explain.

But the power could not stand it. And as I'd often been disobeying its will lately, I ceded this to it.

Regardless, the singers seemed to like Rayse, for all that he intimidated them. He came to them in their own shape, and spoke of passion. Always duplicitous, that one—but he appeared to mold to what they wanted, rather than expecting them to make promises as my power insisted.

When Kor and I approached, Rayse swept away from the singers, soaring up to a mountaintop. We followed, and formed avatars in the snow—stepping as if out of our storm. I used my regal, divine human shape. And Kor, ever one for drama, emerged in her draconic shape, with a long, sinuous neck and dark brown wings.

"I wondered when you'd greet me," Rayse said. "My friends."

We attacked. There was an instinct granted to our powers, an instinct that told me we could batter him, harry him, rip him to pieces if we—

As soon as we touched him, we saw the future.

Projections of it, pulled by Rayse, displayed for both me and Kor. A burned land, full of broken bodies. Death on all sides. Earthquakes besetting Roshar, a land without tectonics.

I trembled, and could not deny it. It was not just possible; it was the most probable outcome of a clash between us. We *could* kill him, but he would make the fight exceptionally painful for all on Roshar.

I stumbled back.

"The future," Rayse said, "is death, my friends."

"We see what *may* happen," Kor said, rearing up on her hind legs. "It is not the future you show us!"

"In how many eventualities, Kor," Rayse said, "does this land survive a full clash between us? Do you know what happened to the region where I killed Ambition? Have you seen?"

"Yes," she said softly.

Rayse raised his hands to the sides, eyes like dark holes into infinity. "Then come for me."

Neither of us dared strike. I looked to the place where Ambition had died—out in space, distant. Their clash had been so destructive, the entire region—including multiple planets—had been annihilated. Other planets lay broken, barely habitable.

A clash of gods could be a terrible, terrible thing. In that moment, I learned something incredible. I knew why Adonalsium, at the end, had not fought us.

"We will need to make an accommodation, won't we?" Rayse said. "To ensure our . . . continued good relations."

"We cannot fight directly," I declared, haunted by those visions. "But we must not do as we did on Ashyn. Common men cannot hold that much strength without misusing it or going too far."

Those words echoed within me as I said them.

Common men.

I saw Ashyn again, burned.

I was a god. I was God. I . . .

I had been a common man too.

"Hmmm . . ." Rayse said, strolling through the snow. "No, we do not want another . . . situation like Ashyn. But would you have us cut off all contact with the mortals? They need gods, Tanner. And I've never met a dragon who could resist being worshipped."

"We can interact," Kor said. "If we have limits."

"What limits do you propose?" Rayse asked.

She held out her hand, and equations appeared above it, manifest in notations we could instantly understand. Only a portion of our powers could be granted to mortals—within distinct controls. There was versatility, I saw, and genius in how it was presented. One could grant great powers to individuals, if they were willing to bend to divine rules as we did. Or instead, lesser power could be given indiscriminately to many.

"Brilliant," I whispered to her. "With these restrictions, no mortal would ever be powerful enough to destroy the planet."

Unless . . .

No. That was ridiculous to consider.

"Hmmm . . ." Rayse said, studying her proposal. "I do not like the idea of being bound. Perhaps I will just leave. I had thought to convalesce here, but there may be better places to—"

"*No,*" I said, my heart yearning for Aona, dead. There were others who would be defenseless against him. "We three violated the rules. We belong together. We stay, and share this system."

"Do it, Rayse," Kor said with her draconic voice, "or I will gather the others and you will be dealt with as Adonalsium was."

The threat loomed. He seemed to weigh fighting right there, but he knew he would lose. The planet might die, but he *would* lose.

"Fine," Rayse said, with a wave of his hand. "I accept these terms."

When he said it, something happened. The power inside surged forward, and I let it—*propelled* it—as I had never done before. My own power, the power of Honor, could bind even gods more strongly. My ability blanketed Rayse, then Kor, then myself.

Rayse shouted, gathering his strength. Then my power withdrew, and I smiled. This time I was aligned with it.

"What the hell was that?" Rayse asked, stepping back.

"We are Vessels," Kor said. "For things we barely understand, Rayse. I do not think the Shards will take our agreements lightly." She glanced at the sky. "Each violation of our word weakens us, opens us to attack." She looked to the liar and leaned down, her draconic head moving level with his face. "Be glad you happened upon two of us who are reasonable and willing to share."

Together, she and I swept away, leaving Rayse on the mountaintop. And . . . I could *feel* Rayse's anger vibrating through the planet.

And slowly, to my horror, Roshar began to adopt Rayse. Just as it had Kor and myself.

114
THE GREATEST GOOD

The second rule of warfare is to know your terrain. Your enemy cannot conquer mountains or rivers. Turn them against him.

—*Proverbs for Towers and War*, Zenaz, date unknown

Jasnah stood up at Taravangian's threat to crush Thaylen City. "You said we were safe! Now you say you've got the city in your hand, and threaten to squeeze?"

"So long as we talk," he said, spreading his hands again, "I will not move. *That* was my promise. I hold the sword at bay—though you should know that while you were distracted by those empty ships, I put other plans in motion." He looked to Fen. "You can either *negotiate* and come to me peacefully, or you come to me bloodied, burning. I'd welcome the former. I will accept the latter."

Jasnah felt alert, tense. To have a god say it so calmly . . .

"What proof do you have of this claim?" Fen asked, obviously shaken by the way she'd gone pale, gripping her knees with her hands as she sat.

"I offer none but my word," Taravangian said.

Outside, clouds moved in front of the sun, and the small chamber darkened briefly. The distant ocean waves seemed to still.

"Not even he can know the future for certain," Jasnah said, forcing herself to sit. "It's a threat, not a promise."

"She is unfortunately right," Taravangian said. "But my threats are not to be taken lightly."

"So that's it?" Fen said. "You come in here and *demand* I bend the knee?"

"Do you love this city, Fen?" Taravangian asked.

"With all my life."

"Then listen to me," he said, leaning forward, clasping his hands. "I do not have time to perpetuate petty wars on the surface of Roshar; I have grander tasks to be about. I must take this city tonight. See that as a threat, but also see me arriving here as an attempt to do it any other way. Come with me, my friend, so that your people may prosper."

Fen shook her head. "I don't see how you possibly think this will work, Taravangian."

"My arguments will stand," he said, gesturing to Jasnah without looking at her, "because Jasnah agrees. The smartest person you know, Fen, agrees with me."

"This again?" Jasnah said. "I do *not.*"

"We will see. But first, would you like to hear my entire offer, laid out point by point?"

"Please," Fen said. "I thought I'd made that clear."

"Excellent," he replied. He nodded to Jasnah, who nodded back, wanting to see his hidden card. "The first reason is as explained: I have forces poised to take this city and overthrow it. You, however, have a chance to prenegotiate a ceasefire."

Jasnah frowned, remembering what Wit had taught her. "They *are* allowed to lie. It's only a *formal contract* that they cannot break, and certain oaths made to others of the same level of power."

"Nevertheless," Taravangian said, "this point is absolutely true. But it is *not* the main reason you should join with me, Fen. The main reason is my strength, and that of my empire."

Fen sniffed. "Break my oaths to the other monarchs to switch to the presumably winning side?"

"Why not?" Odium said. "Fen, do you realize what will happen even if Dalinar wins? I control most of the world—including *the coasts.*" He unfolded something from his pocket. "Here are contracts I've made, over the last nine days, with each of the former Azish protectorates, or key cities in those protectorates in too much turmoil to claim entirely, plus other notable cities across Roshar.

"You know of Emul and Tashikk. I have here contracts with Steen, Dawn's Shadow, New Natanan, even Sesemalex Dar and Tukar—Ishar's attention being elsewhere. These join my ports in Jah Keved, and my recent conquest in Karanak. In aggregate, I now control every major port on Roshar. Every one, Fen. Except, of course, Thaylen City."

She took the papers hesitantly, and her eyes widened. Storms. Jasnah should have anticipated this.

"Check if you must," Taravangian said. "Write to the leaders of these port cities."

 "You'll still have us, Fen," Jasnah reminded. "You won't be without allies."

"In the best of circumstances," Taravangian said, "the only ports available to you will be in Alethkar and Herdaz. Think on it, Fen. You will be left with allies who are practically *landlocked.* You'll face miles upon miles of coast with no friendly berths. Nowhere to shelter from storms. Nowhere to trade. What is a merchant city with no customers?"

"Storms . . ." Fen whispered. She looked up at Jasnah. "I . . . Storms."

"My third point," Taravangian said, "is that I can keep your people safe as no one else can. I realize that alone isn't enough, but in the context of the rest? Because, Fen, the fourth point is extremely relevant. Even if Dalinar wins, you will *want* to be part of what I'm building.

"I will give your people a contractual say in the management of my empire. A representation alongside the singers, something my predecessor would never have done. You can work with me to shape the world, Fen. Your terms will be more favorable than any in your hand there. They will be *spectacular,* Fen. We'll build a true empire, with Thaylenah as one of its crown jewels."

He leaned forward. "This is your chance, Fen, to negotiate for *yourself.* You don't have to rely on Dalinar, or his contest, or his word. You can make your *own* deal. Isn't that what your people excel at? Why let another lead?"

"That's bad," Ivory whispered in Jasnah's ear. "It *is* what Fen wants most."

"Fen," Jasnah said. "You have a voice with us."

"She . . . is right," Fen said. "Taravangian, I'm already part of something. I like the coalition, for all its faults."

"And if Jasnah agrees you should leave it?" he asked. "Because she will."

"Like Damnation I will," Jasnah said.

"Ah, and so here we are at last," Taravangian said. "I have made my offer. Outlined my reasons. Tell us, Jasnah. What arguments can you present that Fen should stay in your coalition?"

Jasnah calmed herself. She couldn't focus on the full dissolution of the Azish empire; he'd presented this as a dramatic reveal, to make her fixate upon it—and not the point at hand. She therefore kept her rebuttal cool, in control.

"She shouldn't join," Jasnah said, "because you—both Taravangian and Odium—are a tyrant, a destroyer, and a monster. You have murdered thousands, and by joining with you and your empire, any monarch becomes complicit in the damage you have done—and will do."

"I've done it in the service of the greatest good," Taravangian said.

He hoped to use Jasnah's personal values against her. Well, it would be best not to underestimate the creature with near-deific powers, so she was careful and precise as she replied. "I do not accept that you have done good, Taravangian. Your murders in Jah Keved were in the service of putting yourself on the throne—something you *might* argue is the greater good.

However, there were obviously better ways than murder of achieving stability in the kingdom."

"And stability on Roshar, Jasnah?" Taravangian asked. "I can see the permutations of time. How many billions of people—slated for death—will live because *I* stepped up to take this mantle? When I have control of the cosmere, the peace that shall be known will bring joy to more people than you can imagine exist."

"Is peace your only 'good'?" Jasnah asked. "Because *freedom* and *volition* are enormous goods unto themselves—and being protected from harm, yet being dominated without the chance to speak or fight for yourself, is not a true good. Shall we speak of the writings of Falabratant, of your own home city, and his moral philosophies regarding self-determination? We could write to him now and see what he says."

"He would not answer," Taravangian said softly.

"Because you've made them all stop using spanreeds," Jasnah said. Kharbranth suddenly being cut off from the outside world was an unnerving silence, but not unexpected, considering its place as his seat. It was strange he'd managed to keep even spies from communicating, but that city was fully in his power. She'd guessed that he'd done something to stop spanreeds from working in the city, as had previously happened at Kholinar.

"Yes," Taravangian said. "I have." Taravangian fell silent, eyeing her. He plainly understood Jasnah's tactic—getting into the weeds of nuanced philosophical discourse would lose Fen. She was intelligent and discerning, but in Jasnah's experience, one of the fastest ways to kick someone out of a conversation was to bombard them with minutiae about a topic they had not researched.

"But this," Taravangian said, "is a tangent."

"Then it is one which is specifically relevant to the situation," Jasnah replied.

"No," Taravangian said. "Fen can't know, as you can't know, the things my divine eyes can see. I insist my rule will be the better good, but anything I showed you would be tainted by my touch. You will never believe that I am right."

A point to Jasnah. By admitting that, by refusing to argue further, he acknowledged as much.

"Then," Jasnah said, "if joining you isn't for the greater good, why should she join you?"

"Because she *would* get a better deal with me."

"And what of her sense of honor?" Jasnah asked, knowing how relevant the idea was to Fen. "She has made promises to our coalition. Joining you would be to turn her back on her allies."

"Allies," he said. "For how long? Two years now?"

"These two years haven't been without their problems, but we have been a good team." Jasnah looked across at Fen. "Alethkar, Thaylenah, Azir. We have done well together—better than we ever did apart. This is the start of something valuable, Fen."

"That is true," Fen said. "Isn't it?" She looked to Taravangian, nodding. "All of your arguments are abstract—when I have at my side an ally who has proven themselves. I face you, an ally who *betrayed* us. So Taravangian, with all this talking in circles, you have proved nothing."

"Nothing?" he said. "Fen, your grand coalition will fall eventually. You know Alethkar cannot keep its word long-term. What of Dalinar's attempts to become highking? What about the secrets they kept from you? What about how consistently Alethkar acted without informing or involving you?"

"Mistakes," Jasnah said. "Which we admitted. We have done better in each instance."

"Yes," Fen said. "Dalinar is a bully at times—but I know where I stand with him, and he *is* doing better."

Taravangian drew his lips to a line and eyed Jasnah. Seeming displeased. He soldiered on. "The Alethi can't protect your people, but I can. *Forever.* I offer you, right now, the chance to negotiate. Isn't it at least *tempting* to see what you can negotiate out of me? For yourself?"

"I think I'm fine where I am, Taravangian," she said. "If you're finished, I believe I've made my decision."

"Have you asked Jasnah what she'd do in your situation?" he asked softly.

Jasnah frowned. "I'd obviously not side with you. I don't understand why you keep bringing this up . . ."

She trailed off, because Taravangian's smile had returned.

That unnerved her.

"I'll ask it," he said. "Jasnah, what *would* you do if you were in Fen's situation?"

"Keep my promises," she said.

"Is that so?" he asked. "You would do the moral thing instead of the right thing? Tell me, historian, do you avoid distasteful choices because they are difficult? Do you search for the non-violent solution, or do you act decisively to protect your own? To do the greatest good as you see it, regardless of the cost."

She hesitated. Wait. But she'd won that point, hadn't she? He was obviously trying to turn the focus from himself to her—undermining her value as a credible . . .

Oh no. Looking at his smile, she felt a coldness move through her. He couldn't know about . . .

"Jasnah," he said, "shall we speak of it?"

"It?"

"The lesson," he whispered. "The day you came into my city, took Shallan, and went on the hunt for people to murder. The day you transformed living, breathing men into statues and smoke in an alley?"

Jasnah felt cold—remembering that first day when she'd shown her powers to Shallan.

"That day," Taravangian said, "when you murdered people on the streets of my city, you let your true allegiance—to Odium—be known."

"What is this?" Fen asked, looking to Jasnah, whose insides were turning into knots. "What is he talking about?"

"Jasnah," Taravangian said, sitting calmly, meeting Jasnah's eyes, "once walked around in my city at night, displaying her wealth, *hoping* that men would try to rob her. Like a fisherman with a lure, to attract thieves so that she could kill them."

"A lesson for my ward," Jasnah said. "About making difficult choices."

"You said earlier," Taravangian continued, "that your moral philosophy led you to do the *most good.* And thus, you sought out and killed men who were dangerous. In so doing, you protected women who *didn't* have the means to fight back. I commend you."

"This has no relevance to our conversation," Jasnah said.

"It is the *soul* of our conversation." He leaned forward, hands perched on the top of his cane. "Fen has an extremely difficult decision to make. You are here to offer her council and guidance, Jasnah. Do that. Tell her she *needs* to do *whatever she can* to protect her people. Regardless of prior promises. She must overcome any obstacles. Whether they be people, morals, or ideals. Tell her to do what *you'd* do."

"I would obviously . . ." She trailed off again, sensing that there was more to come. He had another blow to deliver.

Indeed, Taravangian patted at his robes, then reached into one pocket and took out a piece of paper. He unfolded it carefully, then presented it to Fen.

Jasnah, feeling a mounting dread, rose and stepped over to look: and saw Fen held a contract for assassination. One targeting Aesudan—Elhokar's wife, and Jasnah's sister-in-law. It was signed by Jasnah herself.

Damnation. While she'd come prepared to argue against *philosophies,* Taravangian had come to argue against a *person.*

Her.

⁂

As Navani walked through Urithiru, she held Gav, who was—despite being small for his age—a little too big to carry gracefully. He immediately fell asleep, his little body giving up and letting him slumber.

She didn't set him down as they rode the lift all the way to the top. Her mind was on Dalinar, whom she'd abandoned. Logically, she still agreed with all of her reasons for leaving. Protecting Gav. Making certain *one* Bondsmith escaped. If Dalinar couldn't go to the contest of champions . . .

Storms. *She'd* go. She'd already decided that, hadn't she? This wouldn't be a fight with swords. Whatever it was, if Dalinar couldn't go . . . she would.

But even that was not something she could focus on. She had heard Dalinar describe this emotion before, this heightened intensity. You leave a man behind on the battlefield, and something changes in you. Her every thought was on how she could get him out. If she relaxed, it would be a betrayal. It didn't make sense, but it *felt* like sense.

She drew a strange spren, like swaths of light in the air following an invisible shining object. One she'd never seen before. She reached the top, where Mararin the nursemaid—brought by her request to the Sibling—waited to take Gav. Navani nervously let him go, but fortunately he was fast asleep. Navani gave instructions to put him on a couch in the room next door, where she could check on him. Then she strode toward her meeting room, surprising the guards out front—who immediately drew swords on her.

Told you, the Sibling said.

Navani glared at the guards. A long, uncomfortable moment. Then . . . they slowly lowered their weapons. "Storms," one said. "You're the real one, aren't you?"

"Let me see," Navani said, brushing past and entering the little chamber beyond. She and Dalinar didn't have a throne room; they were too busy. Instead she had this: a chamber with a desk. And today there was someone in her seat.

Navani herself.

One of the Fused? Navani thought with a panic, thoughts of danger piercing—like a pike through armor—her worries about Dalinar. *You told me there was a surprise, but how did a Masked One get here? I thought you said they couldn't use their abilities while—*

Look closer, the Sibling said. And they sounded . . . amused?

The other Navani was halfway through a meal. Men's food—spiced mashed glibon beans, cured pork, flatbread. The doppelganger's hands were sticky with sauce, her head close to the table, arm lifted as she attempted to shove an entire piece of flatbread into her mouth. Her eyes opened wide as she saw Navani, and she froze there, juice dripping off the bread and onto her cheek.

"Lift?" Navani guessed.

"Told you," the younger guard whispered to his companion from behind. "Brightness Navani would never spend so much time staring at my ass . . ."

"Oh, flaps!" Lift said. "Seventeen bakers and one whore! Uh . . . I mean . . . uh, hi, Navani! Um . . . I did a *real* good job a bein' you . . ."

It was surreal seeing herself quickly wipe her hands and scramble over—hitting her elbow on the desk, then cursing and kicking it, then cursing and hopping on one foot from the pain.

"This was Wit's idea?" Navani said flatly.

Lift-Navani wiped her hands on her fine havah, making real-Navani wince. "He thought it would . . . um . . . stop people from panicking?"

"He thought it would be funny too, admittedly," Wit's voice said from behind.

Navani spun, and found Dalinar with a distinctly Wit-ish twinkle in his eye.

"In my defense," Wit said, the illusion evaporating, "I mostly required her to stay in bed complaining of an illness. I told our leaders the truth. We paraded her back and forth through the hallways to keep the tower calm."

"She didn't moon anyone, did she?" Navani asked.

"Hey!" Lift said, scowling. "I'm not *that* bad."

The girl was getting more sensitive about jokes. Well, Navani remembered that age, and being the same way. She tried to apply that understanding to Lift, but storms . . . she felt like she was going to spend *years* hearing about the embarrassing things "she" had done this week.

Her worry for Dalinar, however, washed away such concerns. She took Wit by the arm. "I left him," she said, tears finally forming in her eyes. "I had . . . I had to leave him. And—"

"It's all right," Wit said. "Calm yourself."

"I don't need *calm,* Wit," she snapped. "I need *focus.* You helped us into this mess, and you *will* help me save him."

"Of course," Wit said. "First, did Shallan, Gav, Rlain, or Renarin return with you?"

"Shallan?" she said. "I have Gav. But Rlain? Renarin? I didn't know they were even in there."

"Come. Let us find a spot to talk. I think I may have determined what went wrong seven days ago . . . and as a result, perhaps I can think of a way to help Dalinar."

SEVEN THOUSAND YEARS AGO

I, the Almighty, created art.

The unique tones of the planet harmonized with me and Kor. In this she had trouble, but I showed her the orderly nature of art—while she added a flair of unpredictability. Together we made the ground sing, and raised up incredible stone structures—beautiful sweeping vistas, rock made liquid until it froze into the shapes we'd imagined. Sounds sculpted from our joy.

I experienced her as our power mixed. Harmonizing.

"Stay here with me," she said. "Continue to create."

Rayse was moving again.

"Let him be," she said.

"He will lead them all to destruction," I said. "Every person on this planet, including the spren we made. Rayse will bleed them, turn them into his own army, send them into the cosmere to war."

"We can take steps. Careful steps, quiet steps."

Our tones became discordant. She never wanted to act directly. I *needed* to. Though I had an accommodation with Odium, it was only to prevent the worst—if I wanted to actually stop him, I needed to act against him, through my followers.

The people needed a god.

"You think," I said, sensing Kor's disappointment, "that Rayse is smarter than I am."

"I think he is more ruthless," she replied. "He gives power to the singers, creating those Fused, knowing you will respond—which will let him go a little further."

"There are no other options!" I declared, possibilities spreading before me like paintings in motion. Her way led to so much loss. Peace at home, destruction abroad. "We cannot go too far," I said to her. "Your wise limits on what we can give to our followers will prevent the planet from falling."

"There are holes in that covenant. I know you have seen them."

I had. If one of us were to die, then our followers would be able to draw power without being bound—as our will was what maintained the covenant. More, Rayse and I were not forbidden from clashing personally. If we did . . .

If he goaded me into it . . .

"I will not go that far," I whispered to her. "Tell me I am wrong. Tell me that if I do not act, Rayse will not seek to destroy the cosmere."

She could not deny it. Her way was often *too* safe, and she knew it. I sensed her acknowledgment, but also her pain.

"At least seek the help of the others," she said.

So, at her wish, I reached out to them. The powerful Shards who ruled the cosmere, each in their own place. We had agreed not to interact, but all of us saw how silly that promise—made as mortals—was in the face of divinity. Our powers, though concentrated on planets and systems, swept through the entire cosmere. We could sense each other. All except a few—like Euridrius, holder of Reason—who had vanished. Or like Ambition, who had been destroyed.

I reached out to the others for help. The strong ones, the ones smarter than I. The heroes. Leras, known as Preservation, who had always had such a strong nature. Ati, perhaps kindliest among us, who had boldly taken up Ruin. Edgli, Endowment, who was the most compassionate woman I had ever known. Bavadin, shrewd and capable. Chan Ko Sar, Invention, who traveled the cosmere creating great marvels.

I sought them each in turn.

Each rejected me.

They were afraid of Odium—but he was bound on Roshar. A dangerous animal, now caged. They feared that any intervention would lead to his escape, and were willing to sacrifice Roshar to keep him contained.

I was not. I made one final attempt at locating Valor, the great dragon god Medelantorius—as she was a warrior who would surely join me. Medelantorius was not to be found, unfortunately. Had Odium killed her, as he had poor Aona? Valor would not have died easily. I would doubtless have felt those waves of death ripple through the cosmere.

Defeated, I returned, determined to resist Odium alone.

"Stay with me," Kor whispered again. "This could destroy you."

"I know," I said. For I sensed my own potential fall in the permutations.

I went anyway.

I left her, knowing that in doing so I broke her heart. I perhaps marched to my death because I had told the people that I was their god. They were crying out to me, and my Honor insisted I respond.

I met the struggling humans in one of their tents, speaking with Ishar and others who had been allowed to Surgebind on Ashyn. They still carried the seeds of that ability within them, and their Connection to Odium was a pathway to binding a god—for we could not give of ourselves without exposing ourselves. I told these humans I could bestow their Surges again, if they were willing to obey and accept the rules I placed on them. They had already been thinking of ways to regain their powers, and Ishar had a plan. A good one, involving the distant world that could collect souls.

And thus we had an agreement. They swore to me, and I gave them the largest portion of myself that I would ever grant.

Giving birth to Heralds.

The third rule of warfare is to attack where your opponent is weak. Every man is both weak and strong. Confront his weakness with your strength.

—*Proverbs for Towers and War,* Zenaz, date unknown

Fen looked over the contract, sealed and signed by Jasnah, ordering the assassin to watch Aesudan—with provisions, should they be needed, for killing the queen.

Storms. Jasnah had burned this contract, hadn't she? Did a pseudodeity's powers allow Taravangian to see the past, and replicate an artifact such as this?

"Why," Taravangian asked, gesturing to her, his other hand resting on the top of his cane as he sat, "would you have assassins watch your own family, Jasnah?"

"Aesudan was unpredictable," Jasnah explained, turning toward him from where she stood by Fen. "And power hungry. I worried about her destabilizing the kingdom."

"Ah," Taravangian said. "But didn't you condemn me for killing to obtain the throne of Jah Keved? Didn't you insist there were '*obviously better ways than murder*'? Are you a hypocrite, Jasnah?"

Damnation.

He was good.

He'd led her right into a trap, let her think she was doing well, before slamming a revelation into her head like a warhammer. Was this what it was like to argue with someone who could foresee the future?

"Did you go to Aesudan and try to get her to change?" Taravangian asked.

"Or did you talk to your brother, who loved her? No. I know you didn't. Why not?"

"Contract notwithstanding, I *never* moved against Aesudan, Fen," Jasnah said, her mind racing as she tried to find a way to control this development. "I had the *option,* but all I did was watch her to be certain."

"You were *willing* to murder a member of your own family," Taravangian said. "In secret. You knew then, as you now know, that pain and suffering *are* sometimes required. You speak of freedom and liberty, but you connive and plot to *force* your goals upon the world. Because you recognized the job of the monarch is to protect their people. No matter what."

Jasnah looked across at him, meeting his eyes. He couldn't know . . .

"Did you ever explore the possibility," Taravangian asked, "of assassinating Fen?"

Damnation.

Fen—holding the contract at Jasnah's side—stared at her with obvious concern. Lying now would only make it worse. He could have re-created those paper trails as well.

"I investigated every monarch with whom we interacted," Jasnah admitted. "And assessed their likelihood of being a threat to my people."

"Did you ever 'explore the possibility of assassinating' me, Jasnah?" Fen asked.

"I . . ." Jasnah said. "I am known to overprepare at times. I need to know my options."

Again Taravangian smiled. *Choose your words more carefully,* Jasnah thought to herself in annoyance. *Don't let him rile you into speaking hastily.*

"Options?" Fen said. "Killing me was an *option*?"

"It was before I knew you," Jasnah said, slowing, being more deliberate with her diction. "Please understand. I was exploring a hypothetical. Surely, as a queen, you . . ."

Storms. He wanted her to admit that a monarch had to protect her people—leading toward the inevitable conclusion that joining his coalition would be better for Thaylenah. Jasnah took a deep breath, and steered the conversation back toward Taravangian. "He's trying to turn us against one another, Fen. Look at his smile."

"I smile," Taravangian said, "because I do not wish to let myself despair at the harsh realities of the world. A good monarch does as you did, Jasnah. Anyone, including a friend, can become a liability. A good monarch *prepares* to do even what is *painful.* Tell me honestly. If you, right now, thought Fen were a threat to your family—if she were planning to destroy Alethkar—would you eliminate her?"

"Any queen would," Jasnah said.

"I don't . . . know if I would," Fen whispered.

Jasnah froze, standing at the center of their little triangle of three chairs, then looked at the other queen.

"Oh, I'd bluster," Fen said. "I'd scream and I'd be angry. But assassinating a friend . . ." The paper went limp in her fingers. "I've always worried I'm too soft for this job."

This was unexpected; Jasnah would not have anticipated that from Fen. Taravangian had prepared well. He somehow knew the queen better than Jasnah did.

"It's all right, Fen," Taravangian said. "You have a model before you. Jasnah—who, despite her words to the contrary, doesn't *actually* seek the greater good." Taravangian faced her. "Admit it, Jasnah. You only seek *your* greater good. You protect your kingdom, and your people, *above* others. Your philosophy is deeply flawed, for you cannot *know* what is best for all. A mortal *cannot* think of Roshar at large—let alone the cosmere. Have you imagined how many planets there are, how many people? Would you let Roshar be destroyed to protect them?"

She . . .

Storms. Her mind reeled. The grand scope of the cosmere, and the billions who lived in it, was indeed too much.

Don't let him steer, she thought. *Don't let him catch you with corner cases.*

"I could never know," Jasnah said, "that destroying a planet was for the best—and so no, I wouldn't."

"If you can't know the greater good," Taravangian said, "why would you profess to try to seek it?"

She almost followed with the next logical sentence: that it was her duty to do her *best* to seek the greater good. A person could only see so far, and had to act on their best information. If she said that, he'd point out that he had more information—seeing into the future as a pseudo-deity did. She wouldn't fall into that trap.

She closed her mouth. He noticed, and nodded slightly to her in acknowledgment.

"I don't like how this is going, Jasnah," Ivory said in her ear. "I . . . worry."

"This does not change the situation," Jasnah said, meeting Taravangian's eyes. "Fen *knows* that you double-crossed us, and set us up for destruction. She might *question* my morality, but why does that matter? *You* are the one she would be making a deal with. Your history of behavior is far more important."

"Well, that's true, at least," Fen said, lowering the contract.

Another nod, almost imperceptible, from Taravangian—in recognition of her skillful turning of the conversation.

"Fen, she's right," Taravangian said. "I've been a monster at times. However, I *am* bound by contracts. And if we are considering history, the singers have always been a multiracial society, willing to accept humans among them. And while we speak of the Voidbringers and their destruction—only the humans, in recent history, have accomplished something truly barbarous: the near extinction of the singers. A union between you and my empire is perfectly workable, and my goal isn't to prove *myself* moral, but to show that your correct choice—your sole reasonable choice—is to take the deal I'm offering."

"And you are failing at proving that goal," Jasnah said. "Fen doesn't care about the fate of the cosmere—but she does care about the fate of Roshar. What kinds of policies will you implement, Taravangian? What kind of god will you be? You've told Dalinar that you intend to launch invasions of other worlds. Will you simply turn Thaylenah into a mill churning out soldiers to die in your thirst for conquest?"

Jasnah caught the briefest glance of annoyance from him. "I would be willing," he said, seeming reluctant, "to exempt the Thaylen people from conscription, allowing them to join up only if they wish it."

"You'd need to promise more than that," Fen said. "I know how you can get 'volunteers' by creating hardships for those who don't sign up. We'd need protections in place against that."

"Of course," Taravangian said.

Jasnah gritted her teeth. *Don't let negotiations start. That was yet another wrong turn.* He was more than good at this. He was fantastic, and Jasnah . . .

Jasnah found herself *invigorated.* She rebelled against the emotion; she was striving to defend the fate of an entire people. This was a solemn, terrifying situation.

She didn't enjoy this, but a part of her *was* engaged in a way she had rarely been in her life. Arguing with someone who had the genuine capacity to not merely match her every point, but defeat her. It made her feel alert, even alive.

"It doesn't matter," Jasnah said to him, "because the destruction and pain you will cause Roshar will be *legendary* should you win. Sometimes, yes, pain and suffering are needed—which is why we continue to fight you. Siding with you would be a betrayal of Roshar itself."

"Jasnah," he said, "every war on this planet has been caused by the conflict between two Shards. Two religions. Now that there is only one Shard, one god, we have found a way to peace—with your uncle's contest. It's time to look forward, not backward. By siding with me, Fen can reap the greatest benefits of the new world we're creating."

"I don't know, Taravangian," Fen said. "She's right. Siding with you would be a betrayal of Honor, and Roshar."

"Honor is dead," Taravangian said, "and regardless, Honor never had sway with any monarch who was in their right mind. Fen, if you join with me, I will end religious strife forever, across the cosmere. Think of being the one to help bring peace to untold millions."

"Again," Jasnah said, "this is a scope beyond our ability to consider. You've proven that."

"Admit it, Jasnah," he said. "Doesn't this appeal to you? A crusade to put a stop to religious strife? The chance to kill the remaining gods, leaving you only one to deal with? Isn't that the core of who you are?"

"No," she said, feeling her strength mount.

"But you have always said—"

"My core," she said, "is rationality. It is not hatred. I am not defined by my heresy, no matter how much people have tried to do so."

Taravangian hesitated, studying her.

"It's an easy mistake to make," Jasnah continued. "My goal is nothing more than the freedom of mind, body, and will for all. Let them worship how they wish, but let them do so with their eyes open, having all the relevant information."

"And the gods who subject people to their demands?"

"I would have issues with them, as I do with you," Jasnah said. "But I do not know them—and I am not a *child,* Taravangian. I do not assume that without religion, there would be nothing for people to go to war over.

"If you assume I will crusade against religion or other Shards simply because they exist, then you make a mistake. The same mistake made by all who give petty, casual thought to my heresy. They assume I replace religious ideology with an ideology of their absence. That is not the case. I am against dogma of *any* variety. God, nationality, or philosophy—when you become a slave to it without capacity to change or reconsider, that is the problem."

"But you have said in the past—"

"When new information arrives," Jasnah said, "I change. If I find oppression in the cosmere, I *will* oppose it. However, to join you in war against other planets would only perpetuate suffering." She took a deep breath, everything locking into place. "I will not side with you. I am *not* you."

"Of course not," he said. "You don't see far enough. If you did, you'd understand completely. The greatest good."

"You are *not* good for this planet. Your history, temperament, and morality all prove it. It will require sacrifices to stand against you, but we will do so, united. Regardless of the cost."

He nodded to her a third time. "I appreciate it, Jasnah," he said. "You are remarkable. And you almost won."

Almost?

She turned to Fen, who watched this exchange with wide eyes. She looked up to Jasnah.

 Regardless of the cost . . . Jasnah had said that.

She meant it.

And Fen had said earlier she wouldn't kill a friend to protect her kingdom . . . then Fen had admitted that was a weakness in her, and had relied on Jasnah as a guide.

"Jasnah would sacrifice Thaylenah, Fen," Taravangian said quietly, "to protect her people. Just as she'd sacrifice all those worlds in the cosmere to protect Roshar. Just as she'd kill you to protect her family. Ultimately she's like any of us: Family. Kingdom. World. In that order."

"I—" Jasnah started, not wanting to let him talk.

"Would you deny it?" Taravangian said, his soft, kindly voice cutting through her objection. "Would you deny that you'd throw away Thaylenah to destroy me, but that you would not do the same with Alethkar? If you were able to save your land, but condemn the other, what would *you* do?"

What would she do? It deserved thought, and she knew—with a little of it—that she'd do as he said. Stopping him was worth the price of a nation. But would she do it for her people? In this, Jasnah found her emotions treasonous.

The proper answer would be yes. But she didn't know if she could say that in good conscience. She had a special duty to protect her people, because she was *their* queen.

"The individual details of a situation would be too intricate for me to answer a question like that," Jasnah said. "So I say, without further context, that I wouldn't destroy Thaylenah."

Fen was eyeing her. Storms, Jasnah was being too academic about this. For all Fen's limitations as a queen at times, she *was* incredibly emotionally intelligent. She was probably reading too much into the way Jasnah paused.

"By the first winds," Fen said. "That's a lie, isn't it, Jasnah? You *would* sacrifice Thaylenah to defeat him. Of course you would."

"I'd strive to do what is right," Jasnah said. "But Fen, he's deflecting us with abstractions."

"Actually, they're quite concrete," Taravangian said. He stood up to face her. "We know what you and the Alethi would do in such a situation. You *already encountered* one. When Dalinar made his contract, what thought did he give to Thaylenah?"

"He froze all—"

"He didn't even *think* about them," Taravangian said. "I can *see* that moment, Jasnah! He gave a plea for Herdaz to save face because of a promise, but he forgot the rest. He could have frozen the national lines immediately, but he didn't. Why? Because he was thinking of Alethkar alone, which was already captured. What thought did he give for the rest? None. As you, in a similar situation, would consider only you and yours."

"Nonsense," Jasnah said. "I'd think of the greater good."

"How can you know, though?" Fen demanded, standing too. "How can you *know* what is *right* for others? You're just like Dalinar, aren't you? So determined to decide."

"Fen, no," Jasnah said. "Listen—"

Jasnah's own voice cut in. "What if we renegotiated the contract?"

She froze. So did Fen. They looked to Taravangian, who held up his hand, a small Lightweaving appearing above it. Showing the group of them—Jasnah, Fen, Wit, Dalinar, Navani—sitting in a room full of plants, meeting last week. Jasnah had spoken, and in his simulacrum, she did again.

"If there is a new Odium," the image of Jasnah said, "he might agree to different terms. Perhaps he will stop the war entirely if we give him accommodations. What if we let him leave?"

"Jasnah," Wit said, pained. "We can't unleash him upon the cosmere."

Taravangian met her eyes.

And Jasnah, in that moment, knew she had lost.

"Sometimes," the Jasnah hovering over his hand said, "you have to think about yourself first."

"What is *best for Thaylenah,* Jasnah?" Taravangian whispered.

Fen turned toward her. "He *is* right. If you wanted to do what was best for *Thaylenah,* what would you do? A monarch must be willing to sacrifice anything to protect their people. Isn't that right?"

Jasnah took a deep breath, trying to clear her mind, claw this conversation back. She had the philosophical grounding to resist this. "Fen, listen. He's set up a classic prisoner's dilemma for us. It's a conversation we have all the time in philosophical circles; it may seem that the best thing to do is sell out the others, but if we remain united—"

"Sometimes," the small Jasnah repeated, "you have to think about yourself first."

"But—"

"*Sometimes*"—louder, her own voice condemning her—"you have to think about *yourself first.*"

"You've always tried to have it both ways, Jasnah," Taravangian whispered. "Protect your own. Then do what is right. In that order." He looked to Fen. "I will give nearly anything to see her defeated, Fen. Including the greatest deal any kingdom or planet will ever get from me. Thaylenah will become a genuine world power, not subject to Alethkar. Ever. Again."

"I—" Jasnah said.

"Tell me I'm wrong," he said, focusing on her. "Deny that you seek your own country's needs first. Lie for us, Jasnah. Look me in the eyes, and *lie.*"

Storms. She needed support, and turned to her ideals. But they wavered. And . . . and . . . the truth was, he did offer an excellent opportunity for Thaylenah. It truly would protect Fen's people best, and make them rich. They'd have free trade within Odium's empire, they would be protected from any future Alethi aggression, and they would benefit—like any conquering people—from his aggression toward the cosmere.

History bore this out. Grand conquests brought lavish wealth to those back home. Aligning with Odium would bring Fen's people stability and prosperity. It might not be the greater good, but Jasnah's core rocked as she acknowledged—finally—that she really *couldn't* see the greater good.

And never had been able to.

No, a part of her thought. *Freedom is more important.*

But did she believe that? Or did she believe that keeping people safe was right, regardless? Even if Dalinar won this war . . . Fen's people were headed for debilitating austerity. Jasnah had been willing to kill Aesudan . . . and *had* killed those men in Kharbranth. Did she still think those choices were right?

It all became a mess in her head.

As he had obviously intended.

"Jasnah," Fen said, "I know you'd take the deal. He's been correct all along."

"No, I wouldn't," Jasnah snapped.

And . . . those words were a lie. It was what she wanted Fen to do, not what she would do. It wasn't best for Thaylenah—but it might be best for Alethkar.

Oh . . .

Oh, storms. When the moment came, she did exactly as he said she would. She did whatever it took to win.

"He's right," Fen whispered. "You lie."

Jasnah trembled, and inwardly marveled at what Taravangian had done. He'd made her stay up all night, preparing political arguments so she now buzzed with exhaustionspren. Then he'd cornered her and besmirched her character and turned her very moral framework against her. He had come armed not merely with politics, but with the truth.

"I'll take the deal, Taravangian," Fen said. "Assuming we can reach points I agree with."

Jasnah barely heard it. *He's right about me,* she thought, horrified—seeing the near assassination of Aesudan . . . the lesson in Kharbranth . . . the way she'd stood with a sword to Renarin's neck—all those moments in a new light.

I didn't swing, she thought. *I didn't kill him, or Aesudan.* But that proved Taravangian correct. She'd loved them too much to kill them, which meant her moral philosophy was an utter sham. Jasnah Kholin loved her family, her people, her kingdom.

And that, in this instant, condemned her.

It suddenly seemed that she'd always been two women. One who pretended to be cold, calculating, and willing to do anything in the name of her philosophical morality. Another who knew that there had always been something wrong with the morals she claimed to follow.

She couldn't know what was right.

The cosmere, even the world, was just too big.

She . . . she needed time to deal with this.

So she sat down again, and the negotiations began. At the end Fen—wisely—made her deal. In so doing, Thaylenah joined the enemy without a single sword being raised.

NINE YEARS AGO

Once again, Szeth sat while others decided his fate.

Tonight he did it by a fire, arms crossed on his knees, cheeks stained with tears. His army camped a short distance away. The Stoneward army had retreated to its fortifications. All the others camped around him, and their Honorbearers stood with his father nearby.

At least Szeth had finally become a threat that was worthy of attention. His father . . .

His father carried an Honorblade now.

Neturo had become one who subtracted.

It was silly to let this bother Szeth. Neturo had become a soldier the moment he'd joined up, and he'd trained with the sword like everyone else. It was just that . . . he'd become an administrator so quickly, and Szeth had trouble picturing him as a killer. Yet the Bondsmith Blade was said to be the most destructive of them all. When the time came, the others would kill hundreds, and the Bondsmith tens of thousands . . .

His gentle father. A killer. Szeth closed his eyes, hugging his knees, and listened.

"The Voice wanted this to continue," Sivi said. "Surely that makes you wary, Pozen."

"We almost had war," Moss said. "Straight-up civil war."

"What is his real game?" Sivi asked. "He could have stopped this at any point, but he didn't. He let Szeth continue building momentum. If those soldiers hadn't listened to Neturo . . ."

"My son gets confused sometimes," Neturo said. "But he's a good lad, with a heart stronger than any of us. I still don't understand why I couldn't talk to him about these plans. I'll need a better reason than God gave last week, that's for sure."

He sounded . . . he sounded like he'd been part of this for a great long time. He'd known for *years*?

But known what?

Hello, Szeth, the Voice said in his mind.

Szeth jumped. "Get out of my head," he hissed.

No. Regardless of your tantrums, here we are, and you have proven to have no more backbone than your predecessor. I genuinely thought you'd strike Neturo down and start a revolution.

"My father?" Szeth said, pained. "You thought I'd kill my own father?"

Yes. The gods did it once. You seem of a similar air. Regardless, I'm going to have to do something to harden you. This land needs armies if we are to fight, and armies need generals who are actually acquainted with war.

"I don't understand. And I don't *want* to understand."

You don't need to, fortunately. Simply do as you are told. If you do not trust me, trust your father. Goodbye, Szeth. I'll see you in a decade.

The Voice vanished. Szeth huddled down, and suddenly wondered if he'd somehow dreamed all of it. The others said they heard the Voice, but was he only *imagining* that they said those things? What if he couldn't be trusted at all, in any way, to make his own decisions? What then?

"Truthless," Pozen said.

Szeth caught the word. Truthless.

"There has to be another way," Neturo said. "Truthless . . . that's harsh, Pozen. Too harsh."

"It is the right decision," Pozen said. "He will learn humility in that station. And Neturo, he will be a threat to no one. Isn't that what you want?"

"He must pay," Vambra agreed. "If we don't punish civil war, then what *will* we punish?"

"I suggest," Gearil the Dustbringer said, "we declare here and now that the Voidbringers are never going to return. We need to push Truth to mean something else, something new, or we will have further problems like this."

"Agreed," Dulo the Edgedancer said. "And we *must* make an example of this man. He's Truthless. If we don't declare it, we *will* face other rebellions."

"He's just . . ." Neturo said. "He's just confused . . ."

"Neturo," Sivi said, her voice gentle, "you've known Truth since the day I let you touch the Bondsmith Blade. You saw the stones transform; you've seen the future; you spoke to God. You know what is coming."

"You know there are no Voidbringers," Pozen said. "The spirits of the stones themselves showed it to you. The former powers are no more. The Knights Radiant are fallen. We are all that remains, and we must focus on the true threat."

"War," Neturo whispered. "With other worlds." His voice sounded stronger, and he joined the others as they strode back to the fire. Neturo took a deep breath. "Give up the sword, Szeth."

In response, still seated, Szeth summoned it. He understood little of their conversation, and his mind was foggy, confused. Dazed. Yet . . .

No Voidbringers.

There were no Voidbringers?

No more Knights Radiant?

The spirits of the stones themselves promised it?

This Blade was the ultimate manifestation of his sin. He tossed it to the grass. Stones Unhallowed . . . he'd killed so many . . . He thought he heard the dead whispering in the night around him.

Pozen nodded, and a few soldiers took Szeth from behind, forcing him up to his knees, binding his wrists. As he struggled, his father put a hand on his shoulder, calming him.

"He gave up the Blade willingly," Neturo said. "He allowed himself to be bound. There's no need for harsh punishment."

Szeth looked at the sky. That beautiful black infinity, broken by stars. He closed his eyes, ignoring the pain in his shoulder from having his hands tied. He felt the wind. There as always.

"They are correct, Father," Szeth whispered. "I am Truthless. I must be."

"Son?" Neturo asked.

"There are two options," Szeth whispered. "Either I was right to attack you all, or I was wrong. If I am right, then I need to kill all of you here. Even you, Father." Tears stained Szeth's eyes as he gazed upward. "However, if there *is* no Voidbringer . . . then I've committed a terrible sin. You must name me Truthless. One or the other. Decide. For I will not."

Silence, other than the teasing wind.

He never *could* trust in his own opinion, could he?

"So be it," Neturo said softly.

Szeth closed his eyes. "What is the punishment for being Truthless?"

"An Oathstone," Sivi said. "Banishment."

"You will swear it?" Pozen asked. "To follow the way of the Oathstone?"

A stone. A stone would know better than he did, wouldn't it? That would be . . . so, *so* very nice.

"I don't want to decide anymore," Szeth whispered. "I'm done. Give me the stone."

Pozen reached into his pocket and brought out a small round rock. A simple one with a few quartz crystals and a rusty vein of iron on one side. He raised it up. "Before this Oathstone, before the spren, before your father. Promise to do whatever this stone's holder demands of you, except the demand to kill yourself."

"I make the Oathstone promise," Szeth said. "I will follow what is said by the one who holds it, as you say." He felt an immediate liberation at saying the words. No more choices.

Freedom.

They cut his bonds, and he stood, holding out his hand for the stone.

"Take his Blade," Pozen said, waving. "Until we can . . ."

He trailed off, then looked toward the sky. They all did, even his father.

"What?" Szeth asked.

"The Voice says . . ." Sivi whispered, standing just to Szeth's right. "He says you're to *keep* it."

"A Truthless with an Honorblade?" Father said. "That sounds incredibly dangerous."

They all paused again, and shivered from whatever the Voice said. His father cursed and glanced at Szeth, then away, squeezing his eyes shut.

"He will be sent East," Pozen said, pressing the Oathstone into Szeth's hand. "We will give him to one of the Farmers to send off with a caravan. If God says to leave him the Blade . . . Well, add this to your vow: you may not give the Blade away. A stonewalker should never hold it."

"I promise it," Szeth whispered.

"Then may the stones guide you, Szeth-son-Neturo."

"I'm Truthless," Szeth said. "I do not deserve that name any longer."

"Son," Neturo said, turning back, weeping openly. "You'll always deserve it."

"I don't decide that," Szeth said, relaxing, loving that idea, "and neither do you. We merely do what we are told."

"Szeth-son-son . . ." Pozen began.

"Vallano," Neturo said, wiping his eyes, though tears kept flowing.

"Szeth-son-son-Vallano," Pozen said, "for sins against Truth, you are banished. And may the Heralds protect those you are turned against."

Szeth nodded.

It was done.

It was over.

His father, though, grabbed him in an embrace once more. "I can't go with you this time, son." It seemed to be breaking him. "I can't. I'm sorry. I've failed you. I'm so, so sorry . . . my little boy . . ."

"Your little boy is dead, Neturo," Szeth whispered. "You lost him years ago, that night when he killed."

Soldiers pulled them apart, and left Neturo on the ground amid a patch of trodden-down grass. They hauled Szeth away. He was eventually sold to a stonewalker with curious eyebrows and far too colorful clothing.

From there, Szeth resolved not to look back.

And never to question.

Not every win is a victory. And not every loss is a defeat.

—*Proverbs for Towers and War,* Zenaz, date unknown

The call came.

Finally, Venli and the others launched toward the human forces. With thunder and red lightning as their accompaniment, a terrible chorus of drums began. The pounding of greatshell feet on plateaus was the percussion, and the screams of terrified soldiers the applause.

Venli clung to the slick ropes, mist and rain pelting her as Thundercloud charged the human position. She felt a little of what humans must have during those old plateau runs. Arrows sliced the air around her. Even with the humans deliberately trying to miss her, even with a giant carapaced head in front to break arrows, it was unnerving.

They reached the chasm and leaped. She held her breath, her rhythms stilling.

Thude whooped as he stood upright, gripping the ropes, joyful like the old him. A heartbeat later, Thundercloud *crashed* through the human wall, breaking the cracked fortification and shoving through the crumbling stone. The humans had cleared off from this section, pretending that the cracks were too extensive for them to risk standing atop it. Thundercloud entered the plateau; it had taken considerable deliberate effort to explain to him that they *weren't* going to kill the humans. She felt his confusion now.

We don't eat humans anymore, she sent to him.

His reply was more confusion. He knew that they didn't eat humans anymore. He'd accepted all of the small things as rivals, and not food. But you *could* eat things that weren't *usually* food. And today, wasn't he supposed to?

Well, all right, she thought to him, remembering the plan. *We eat humans this once. Only the correct humans.*

For now, it was time to make a bit of a mess. She clung to his back with the others, teeth gritted, attuned to Excitement to try to convince herself. Thundercloud really leaned into his part—that of completely destroying the human camp while the two other chasmfiends crashed in behind. One ripped down the gate between the two plateaus. They'd chosen Skyblue for that, as she seemed to understand that she wasn't to break the humans' bridge, which they'd use to flee onto the Oathgate platform.

Soldiers fled, screaming about the monsters. Thundercloud gleefully began stomping through the wooden rooftops. He swept his tail and knocked down walls, trumping. In seconds she heard human horns sounding the retreat. Soon after, the Oathgate began to flash, people escaping. Overhead, Leshwi and her three made a good show of fighting.

Thundercloud snapped at a few retreating humans, and Venli reined him in with a rhythm. One waved, and dropped the package for her. Thundercloud wanted to chase them, but she turned him the other direction.

You can't eat those humans, she thought.

He sent back confusion again. His kind had made peace with the listeners, who were like little chulls. But they *could* eat the humans sometimes, who were like little horses. He thought he'd figured it all out.

She pointed him toward a line of corpses that had been left—after some complaints—per her instruction. It made her extremely uncomfortable, but it did seem necessary. In seconds, Thundercloud was munching away. He sent to her that he thought he finally understood. She didn't want him to eat humans because they weren't fatty enough to be truly delicious, and he should focus on better meals.

She didn't watch as the last humans retreated.

⁂

Shallan ducked through waves of possibility, dodging the eyes of the vast shadow that she knew must be Odium. Colors streamed around her like individual rivers: versions of her rising from them like women bursting from a pool of water, then melting back down. Renarin and Rlain had mentioned being afraid of this place, but possibility didn't frighten Shallan. She engaged with it each time she drew.

The shadow hunted her, but she sent Lightweavings—effortless here—to distract. Frightened versions of her in a dozen varieties—and it *worked.* In this place, even a god had difficulty distinguishing the real her. Admittedly, his attention seemed—most recently—diverted to something else. But she felt a thrill.

The daughter of a Herald. Storms. Kelek had said she had a strange attachment to the Spiritual Realm, and had blamed her twin bonds. Was there something more? She'd spoken to, held, her mother again. A relationship fraught with pain and anxiety, and with old wounds made fresh. But maybe . . . maybe they could heal this time without so much scarring.

Odium's attention finally left her entirely, the vast shadow in the sky vanishing. Was she right to read annoyance in that departure? She settled down and let possibility wash over her, feeling . . . if not victorious, then satisfied. She was certain he'd have found her—as he had before—if he'd been able to focus, but she'd at least given him a little trouble.

Now what? She meditated on the colors, and acknowledged that too much time here—although it didn't frighten her—would not be good for her mental health. Being battered by possibility and the demands of versions of her that *could* have been . . . Yeah, that could be a problem. But she couldn't make a vision without Glys or Tumi, and had no idea how to find Renarin or Rlain. Even Pattern and Testament seemed distant.

However, as she was swimming there, she felt something odd. A . . . proposal?

A second later, she emerged into a vision. One of the off-color ones, where everything wasn't quite right. She lay on a rocky beach at sunset. She picked herself up, brushing off, and turned, noting the placid ocean waves lapping toward her booted feet.

She spun slowly, inspecting mountainous terrain and a long beach. An island. Maybe Thaylenah, on a side without the large city. Indeed, she thought she saw a village farther along. And some ships coming in for the evening, bearing the day's harvest.

Shallan started toward a large set of rocks farther up the beach, intending to climb them for a better vantage. But as she drew close, she froze. Those weren't rocks, but an enormous shelled carcass, mistaken for landscape in the shadowed evening light.

Storms. It was *enormous*—twenty-five feet tall on its side, with many long legs like a crab, several broken. It was the largest greatshell she'd seen other than a chasmfiend, and it appeared distinctly proportioned for living in water, where buoyancy would allow such long legs. The natural historian in her wanted to imagine what its life was like, deep beneath the waves—and how it had eventually washed up here.

She wasn't given the time for such scholarly diversions, however, as she noticed something more daunting. Sitting on the beast's shell, high up, with one leg swinging over the side, was a single person.

Mraize.

⁂

Sigzil's job was to make the retreat look like a rout.

He called for his soldiers to withdraw from Narak as the chasmfiends broke down walls. He shouted and screamed, then fought desperately against enemy Heavenly Ones as his men made their retreat. He found one moment to toss the pouch of rolled-up papers toward Venli, hoping the plan she and he had hashed out was the right one, but mostly spent his time organizing his people.

The enemy forces—sensing victory—harried them but did not get lured into a trap. Their leader was smart, that Fused with the silvery carapace. He stood on the wall as Sigzil mobilized the rearguard, including the Stormwall in his golden Shardplate.

"I don't like this," the Stormwall growled softly. "I think we could have held longer."

"Dami," Sigzil hissed, "we are *out* of Stormlight."

"The Bondsmith said to stay," Dami insisted from inside his helm. "The Alethi queen doesn't override that. My loyalty isn't to her, or her fallen kingdom."

"Is it to me?"

The Stormwall looked to him. "Yes," he finally said. "Storm it, yes. He put you in command."

"Then trust me," Sigzil said, waving a group of soldiers onward across the bridge. He turned and watched the darkness for Skybreakers—who again didn't pursue too vigorously. They hung before the sky of red lightning, but did not swing down. If they were lured onto the next plateau over, it would be disastrous for them. The Oathgate could transfer them to Urithiru.

"Just tell me this," the Stormwall said, saluting as a man in Shardplate clanked past, leading the surgeons in a hasty flight. No wounded; Sigzil had ordered them to go earlier. "Promise me, Sigzil, that this is because it's what you think is best. *Not* because you've lost a friend, and are too worried to keep fighting, lest you lose another."

Storms. That hit a bit close to home. But the Stormwall was known for his accuracy. "I believe I'm doing this for the right reasons. I believe I'm learning to lead, genuinely. But either way, it's my call to make."

The Stormwall grunted. "Appreciate the honesty." He gazed back over Narak, which was now occupied by Venli's chasmfiends. "This choice is going to bite us someday, Sigzil. Give my Stonewards fifteen minutes, then follow."

Sigzil saluted, then the Stormwall tromped off. His group was the last of the ground soldiers, and would drop the bridge behind them, while the

Windrunners made up the final rearguard. Capable as they were of swift motion and flight, it was the natural strategy.

But it left Sigzil and his friends as the last fighters—and while Odium's forces weren't allowing themselves to be pulled into a trap, they *were* still trying to do what damage they could. All but the listener Venli, and her chasmfiends—who put on a good show, then turned to eating corpses.

Sigzil whispered an apology to the souls of those whose bodies he'd allowed to be desecrated, then fought for fifteen minutes before signaling the ultimate retreat. His Windrunners went flying for the Oathgate, and he counted them off, then gave one last look at the Shattered Plains. He'd first arrived here covered in crem and dust. Now he soared above it. How he'd hated those chasms, yet now he found himself reluctant to leave them. This strange barren land that he'd bled for first as a slave, then as a bodyguard, then finally as a Radiant.

This place had never been home. But home had been here. He saluted it, then he turned to go.

And immediately dropped from the sky.

Shockspren burst around him, and Vienta screamed in a panic in his ear. He hit the plateau hard, with a *crack* of bones breaking, pain shooting through him.

How . . . What . . . ?

A figure in black touched down next to him, boots scraping stone. Sigzil had landed on Narak Prime, off to one side near the wall. He blinked through tears up at a figure with glowing eyes, holding a fabrial in one hand.

"They only have a few of these," Moash whispered. "They are difficult to make, requiring rare spren. I demanded they be given to me. The others did so under protest—not because *they* wanted to use them, but because the Fused fear this power."

Sigzil's fingers trembled from the pain of his fall—storms, that had been thirty feet or more. Healing didn't come, and he couldn't feel his body below the waist.

Though moving was agony, Sigzil reached for his knife.

Moash let him get it out, then stepped on his wrist, making him scream and drop it.

"Sig . . ." Vienta said, her voice distant.

"Go," he whispered. "Get away."

"I can't. I can't *leave* you . . ."

Moash, unable to hear her side of the conversation, knelt by Sigzil. "I have a new god, Sig. He won't take my pain—instead he lets me bathe in it, teaches me to *love* it. I'm going to build something great with him. Unfortunately, you're in the way."

Sigzil gritted his teeth against the pain. "Get," he said between them to Vienta, "*help*."

His vision cleared, and he saw Moash *smiling* in the darkness, his crystalline eyes and crown glowing with their own light. Contrasting with the boiling red ocean of clouds above. Then Moash shot into the air and whipped a knife from his belt, slashing with it as something flew overhead.

Sigzil felt Vienta's pain as his own, though the anti-Stormlight knife had barely nicked her. She became visible, dropping, a small figure in a puff of blue cloth who struck the ground near him, her arm completely destroyed and leaking Stormlight, her eyes wide as she trembled and gasped.

Moash landed again, fabrial in one hand, light-bending knife in the other. "This will hurt me," he said. "It is the pain of building a new empire."

He raised the knife, ready to plunge it down. Leyten's final words rang in Sigzil's ears: the prophecy that Vienta and Sigzil would fall by Moash's hand.

But the future was never set.

And so, Sigzil did the only thing he could think of to save Vienta. "I renounce my oaths!" he shouted.

And he meant it.

Something ripped inside him, but he screamed it again, meaning every word as fervently as he could. "I renounce them!" Sigzil screamed against the terrible pain. "I am *no Radiant*!"

Vienta shrieked in agony, but vanished as the knife hit the stone. Sigzil's soul suddenly echoed. For it was empty as a grand imperial hallway.

Moash frowned, then stood. "That," he said softly, "was exceptionally stupid of you."

He stepped up to Sigzil, then paused as a Shardblade clanged to the ground nearby. Vienta. Storms, Sigzil hoped Adolin's Blade was right, and it was possible to heal deadeyes now. Sigzil rolled, grabbing the Blade, and swung it toward Moash—and narrowly missed the man's legs as he hopped back, cursing.

Sigzil propped himself up with one arm as best he could, sword in the other—his legs refusing to work. Moash eyed him, planning his next attack, and was so distracted that he didn't see the figure come flying in from the side. Lopen slammed into Moash, throwing them both to the ground. Lopen came up in a roll with the fabrial in one hand—then he shattered it against the ground.

Sigzil's powers didn't return. However, the sudden pain of the lost bond—renounced along with his oaths—struck him like a thunderclap. An acute, crippling grief, like a hole in his soul had been filled with fire.

Moash stood and leveled his sword at Lopen. "You realize," Moash said, "I'm more than capable of killing you without a fabrial, Lopen. I always bested you while sparring."

"Oh, I think you'll have more trouble with me now," Lopen said, summoning his Shardspear.

"What?" Moash asked. "Because you have two hands now?"

"You storming idiot," Lopen said, his expression dark but his grin wide as he leveled his spear. "It's not the number of hands that makes a man, but the number of cousins."

A flood of glowing shapes came in over the wall, led by Huio. Bridge Four. Skar, Peet, Natam . . . all of them. Moash assessed them with a glance, then fled—soaring back toward the bulk of the enemy forces. Lopen took a step after him, then apparently thought better of it.

Skar landed by Sigzil and held out a sphere. "Here, sir. Take this."

"I can't," Sigzil croaked. He squeezed his eyes shut, tears leaking from the corners.

"Sure you can," Skar said. "Unless . . . storms . . . did he . . . ?"

Gentle hands took Sigzil's Blade, then passed it to a squire, who winced at touching it. Lopen lifted Sigzil next, taking him into the air. "I saw what you did, gancho. That was maybe the bravest thing I've ever seen a man do."

"Not your gancho any longer," Sigzil whispered. "Not a Windrunner any longer. It's up to you and Skar to lead now."

"Oh, storms," Lopen whispered. "Almighty help us all . . ."

A flash of light sent them through the Oathgate, and as soon as they appeared on the other side, he heard the orders to lock the mechanism so no enemies could follow. That would work, but would isolate and cut off the Shattered Plains.

An Edgedancer came skating up to heal him. Though his body began working again, Sigzil lay in a heap on the ground, staring at the Shardblade they placed beside him.

Relief never came. Painspren crawled all over him. For no amount of Radiant healing could fix the pain that he felt deep within.

⁂

As Thundercloud munched corpses, Venli leaned against him, trembling, understanding from the wild ride how the top of a drum might feel after an extended solo. The other listeners seemed equally unnerved—all but Thude, who was *still* laughing.

Venli hummed to Resolve, then went on wobbling feet to retrieve the package Sigzil had tossed for her. Just some papers rolled in an oiled cloth, which she tucked away for tomorrow. Narak was eerily empty now, barely recognizable. Wet, crumpled buildings. Pools of rainwater, and little rainspren peeking up among the debris.

Fresh bodies left to make it appear like the assault had been more effective than it had actually been. She maintained Resolve, but secretly thought it looked obvious that the chasmfiends had attacked unpopulated sections. That the humans had evacuated willingly. That the retreat had been too quick.

She held her breath as El himself was carried onto the plateau by a Heavenly One. And Venli realized she still had no idea what brand of Fused he was. What were *his* powers? She'd heard that he did the replacement of his carapace himself, putting metal where there should be chitin, but any brand of Fused could heal from such wounds.

He strolled through the camp, and eventually paused beside Venli and her crew. Leshwi and the others landed nearby. The Oathgate flashed again. Seconds later a Voidspren—like a line of glowing red light—crossed the ground. "That is the last of them," a familiar voice said. "I watched them go. Vyre had some fun at the end, but it is done now. The Shattered Plains have fallen to us at last."

"Your group did well," El said, looking to Venli. "Retreat with your people to the staging plateau. This might be a feint; the humans do like an unexpected rally. It is . . . something curious about them."

Venli nodded, but quietly sent a request to Thundercloud. He ambled toward them, a human arm hanging from his mouth, and flopped down right there and closed his eyes. The other two joined him, maws bloodied.

"There'll be no moving them now, Grand One," Thude said. "They are burst predators—a lot of activity and feasting, followed by a good nap."

"I suppose we can watch this plateau from here, Ancient One," Venli said to the Fused.

"Very well," El said, and moved on, speaking with his Fused commanders and posting the majority of his forces near the Oathgate—he had Vyre, the traitor, lock it down from their side, but seemed worried the humans might somehow reverse that.

He was watching for the wrong kind of trap. Venli and the others gathered in a huddle, and none dared hum the rhythms they were feeling. Except for Timbre, deep within her.

Optimistic Joy. Had it . . . actually worked?

They'd see on the morrow.

119 SUNMAKER'S GAMBIT

It is often said that the best teacher is failure. This is true. But it is also the best killer. May you be lucky enough in failure to live, and unlucky enough in success to struggle.

—*Proverbs for Towers and War,* Zenaz, date unknown

I'm impressed, Brightlord," the surgeon said, watching Adolin limp past for him. "Walking unaided already?"

"I still slip on it now and then," Adolin said. "Which I feel shouldn't happen, since it's got that rubber on the end."

"Maybe walk with a crutch for a little while. When you fall, you could break something else."

"I don't fall," Adolin promised. "I catch myself while slipping and recover."

The surgeon eyed him, then shook his head. "Duelists," he muttered, waving for Adolin to sit down so he could check the stump. "Suppose you trained fighting one-legged or some such?"

"I did, in fact," Adolin said with a chuckle. "Never know when you'll take a wound to the thigh. Zahel insisted."

The surgeon undid the peg and checked Adolin's stump—which admittedly was pretty sore. He'd spent hours walking back and forth across the courtyard today, receiving reports, listening to the fighting. Wincing at each and every shout. He had a sense he'd be called up, wounded or not, before the night ended, and wanted to be as steady as he could.

The surgeon put some ointment on the stump to dull the pain, and didn't order bed rest. He kept glancing at the dome in the waning evening light. Another runner came with a message for Adolin, Kushkam asking for some advice about tactics—but there wasn't much Adolin could say. The time for grand strategy had passed—the defense of the dome was down to the field commanders with simple instructions: hold the line.

"I want you to rest this," the surgeon said. "We might all have to take a turn tonight, and I know you'll insist on going. Give it an hour or two first. Please."

Adolin drew in a deep breath, then nodded. So it was that a few minutes later, he found himself in another game of towers with Yanagawn. Using the familiarity of the game to try, for a short time at least, to get his mind off his worries. The emperor won their first bout. He had all the signs of becoming an excellent field general—just the right willingness to seize opportunities. Not timid, but also not brash. He learned from mistakes, and rarely had to be taught the same principle twice.

Adolin settled back, rubbing his stump—as he'd removed the peg for the moment. He was coming to understand how lucky the Azish were. Out of the hundreds of boys who could have been plucked from the street, how had they—or really, Lift—found the one who would actually make a great leader?

Unless . . . how many people who lived in the gutters would have excelled if put in this seat? After his conversation with Colot the night before, Adolin found himself questioning things he never had previously. Like what it meant to be the Blackthorn's son. He'd always assumed that the Almighty had put him in that role deliberately. But if the Almighty was dead . . .

They reset the pieces. Tense, as another report came in. This was the last stand. All defenders on the lines, all reserves called up and fighting, no one being allowed to rest for more than fifteen-minute bursts. The next few hours would determine the fate of Azir for centuries to come. But here, two of the most powerful men in the world could do nothing but sit and wait.

So they played. Adolin's sole attendants today were May Aladar and her scribes; he'd sent the rest of his guard to the battle lines. There wasn't much use for an archer at the moment. The fighting was all close quarters, so May had taken up bodyguard duty. A position that a woman never should have had to do, but these were unusual times.

Yanagawn was guarded by some of the finest in the Azish military. These six soldiers probably wouldn't have made *much* of a difference on the battlefield, and Adolin didn't suggest they be sent away, although in Yanagawn's position he would have done so immediately.

"I feel like you legitimately *tried* that time," Yanagawn said, "and I still won!"

"You did," Adolin said. "Expertly done."

"You only pulled disadvantage cards though," Yanagawn said. "That's more luck than anything, but still, this is the first match on an even field that I *won*!"

"You're getting better and better," Adolin said, thoughtful. Perhaps it was time. "May, want to join us for a game?"

She looked up from her spanreed conversations. She was wearing her uniform just in case—a long mail shirt draped over the seat next to her, and a set of leather greaves beside it. She eyed the game board in her analytical way. Then she nodded. He knew she played with her father—indeed, they'd had a few games together during their days not-courting. She wasn't bad. Not the best, but capable.

"Sure," she said. "Assuming you ask His Royal Majesty if it pleases him."

"Tell her," Yanagawn said, "I look forward to the opportunity. My first three-way game! I'm ready."

She settled down, and Adolin began setting up the cards and game pieces. They played, and Yanagawn—eager to continue proving himself—seized the initiative, making bold and powerful plays at the start. The game board soon grew complex.

"I have more news from Urithiru," May said. "The Shattered Plains are officially lost. All our forces have retreated."

Adolin groaned softly.

"Can we be reinforced?" Yanagawn asked, suddenly excited. "Can those forces come here?" He placed a card, then replaced it with the appropriate piece from his game set, now that its characteristics were fully known. "I know they can't use the Oathgate, but there were a lot of Windrunners at the Shattered Plains, right? Could they fly here overnight?"

May placed her own pieces, careful not to respond to the emperor. What a strange dance everyone performed around him.

"It's a good question," Adolin said. "May?"

"I've asked the Windrunners," she said, "to send whoever can be spared. They're worn out, as you can imagine, but it looks like some will be dispatched." She hesitated. "Adolin, your aunt has returned, but not your father. Brightness Navani can't infuse spheres with Stormlight, and her Towerlight escapes too quickly from both people and gemstones. There's only enough to send a few Windrunners—and it will take hours for them to get here on a single Lashing."

Adolin tried to let himself hope they would arrive in time, but he found it difficult to summon the optimism. He'd spent too long hoping for the Azish reinforcements. He glanced up as he heard distant horns, but it wasn't a call for the wounded yet. Only a warning that no shift change was coming. No one would sleep tonight. Unfortunately, exhausted soldiers were better than no soldiers.

Yanagawn placed his next piece, and in so doing took a dominant position on the game board. He sat back, pleased—and rightly so. He was doing better than either Adolin or May. Therefore it was satisfying to watch Yanagawn's complete disbelief as, over the next half hour, he was systematically destroyed.

Yanagawn scrambled to recover. He tried to employ the tactics Adolin had taught him. He made a few mistakes, a great number of ordinary moves, and even a few legitimately brilliant ones. He lost anyway, crushed as May and Adolin allied against him. Adolin quickly mopped up May, who was forced to retreat—though she finished with more points than Yanagawn. Which had likely been one of her best outcomes. He could tell she was proud of doing as well as she had; towers was rarely taught to women. Indeed, he'd heard that women had trouble finding capable opponents willing to play them.

"How?" Yanagawn said, looking at the dismal results. "How did I lose? You two talked it through ahead of time and decided to defeat me together?"

"No," May said. "We simply played by best principles."

Adolin leaned forward. "This is a lesson that doesn't come up very often in real life, but it's *vital* to learn, because when it *does* come up it can lead to disaster. You remember my key lesson? The most powerful force wins?"

"Unless," Yanagawn said, "terrain, incompetence, or random chance interfere."

"Yes," Adolin said.

"But I *was* the most powerful force!"

"No," Adolin said, and gestured at the board. "May and I *together* were. This is the lesson, Yanagawn. In a contest of one-on-one, you should present power and dominate every chance you get. However, in a contest between three or *more* parties, that's not the case."

"Two weaker forces," May said, "will always align against the strongest one. By presenting strength, you become a target, galvanizing your enemies to put aside their differences." She began cleaning up the pieces, admiring the detailed silvery figurines. "My father talked about this a great deal during the days of the squabbling highprinces. It can get messy when there are ten participants all choosing sides . . ."

"It's sometimes called the Sunmaker's Gambit," Adolin added. "Drawing in a third party to a battle, knowing that you cannot win without them."

Yanagawn stared at the board. "So . . . what should I have done?"

"Play more carefully," Adolin said. "Feign weakness. Or make alliances early." He paused, then shrugged. "Or build up enough power that you alone are stronger than *all* of your opponents at once. That's hard, but valid too."

"That sounds complicated," Yanagawn said.

"Welcome to politics," Adolin said. "Two parties on a battlefield is merely warfare: they fight until one leaves. Three parties on a battlefield is a negotiation; it transforms into an *entirely* different game." He shook his head. "I dislike that dynamic, honestly. Towers is so much simpler with two players, just like a duel. Then it can be about actual skill."

"Skill in politics *is* a skill," May said.

"One I'm bad at. Sword on sword is so much cleaner." Adolin looked up at Yanagawn. "But listen, this game tries to replicate the real battlefield—and in this case it does. Multiple players makes things messy. Learn the lesson."

"One on one," Yanagawn said, "hit hard. One on one on one . . . defend. Is this the fourth way to lose a battle where you're the strongest party? The one you promised to tell me?"

"It's not," Adolin said, "but it might as well be. Pretend it is."

Yanagawn gave him a frown, but Adolin finished tidying the pieces. He'd always hated the fourth rule. It seemed to favor people like his father. It—

The horns sounded once more.

That was it. A desperate signal, the type Kushkam had sent warnings he might need. All able-bodied men were called, regardless of experience. The city was appallingly short on men at this point; too many had been recruited for the battles to the south, and too many others had fled the city or been sent to farming operations to feed the armies.

Anyone left was called to come—including the crippled, the elderly, and any women willing to fight. That would include Adolin, who started strapping on his peg. He wouldn't wear the Plate, but he could hold a shield and *mostly* keep his balance. He quested out to Maya, to check if maybe he could get a Blade.

Close . . . she sent. *Getting close* . . .

How close?

Hours. Some hours. Difficult to judge in the beads.

Maya . . . can you actually win this war for us? With those spren you bring?

Maybe. Maybe, Adolin.

Well . . . that was something. He had to resist summoning her, just in case. But if he didn't . . . Storms. He might not last the night.

May was already reaching for her mail and helmet.

"It's bad, isn't it?" Yanagawn whispered. "I don't know all the trumpet sequences, but . . . if you two are getting ready?"

"Be prepared," Adolin said, looking to the emperor's guards, "to get him to the saferoom. We'll pass on the location to the Windrunners, who should be able to sneak in and pull him out if they arrive too late."

The guards saluted him.

"I should fight," Yanagawn said, rising. "I should—"

Adolin reached across the game board and rested a hand on Yanagawn's shoulder. One of the scribes in the back gasped, but everyone else was used to this by now.

"If you die," Adolin said softly, "this kingdom has nothing left to hope for."

"You've been training me to fight," Yanagawn said. "You were excited when I went to battle earlier!"

"We had a chance of winning then," Adolin said, "and you brought with you a large force of reserve troops. This is different. You only have six. And Yanagawn . . . you're not a soldier, not yet. There is no need for you to die here."

The younger man's eyes began to tear up. "It's that bad?"

Adolin nodded, grim. They had held well these seven days, and had killed far more than they'd lost. But there were still ten thousand enemy troops in the dome. More importantly, Notum had seen more Fused arriving.

"Take him there," Adolin said to the guards. "Right now."

The horns sounded again. More desperate. Adolin turned, his stupid peg slipping. He needed May's support to keep him from tripping. *Damnation.* Yet she handed him his sword, then together they made for the reserve tent for instructions.

⁂

Shallan Lightwove herself into the appearance of a common villager, hoping to hide from Mraize . . . but then felt foolish. This vision seemed like the ones that Tumi and Glys made when they were all waiting for Dalinar and Navani. In them, no people ever showed up.

Mraize would know it was her if he saw her, so she tried to hide in the shadow of a large rock, then carefully looked up toward him. As the sun set, and the waves rolled, he just sat there idly, one leg swinging, staring out over the oceans. She could not see his spren—likely it was hiding inside him.

She crept around to stay behind him, sticking to shadows, and the pungency of the corpse soon had her breathing through her mouth. That fishy, rotting smell was genuinely one of the most awful things she'd ever encountered. She forced herself to get closer, though . . .

For what purpose? She did have her knife that bent the air. All she had to do was wound him badly enough that he had to draw in Stormlight or die, then watch the nice explosion. But still . . . she hesitated. She told herself it was because he was out of reach, but he seemed distracted. She'd ascended a slope behind the corpse. She could drop down onto the thing's crablike head, then strike . . .

 Was that what she wanted? She remembered frightened days, first at the

Shattered Plains, where she'd felt so alone. And she remembered the purpose he'd given her, like a warm, soothing bath. She was in large part the Lightweaver she was now because of his challenges and demands.

For some reason, she stood, her boots scraping rock. Mraize turned, and hesitated. Then he deliberately looked back toward the ocean.

"I was a child," he said, "when I first climbed this corpse. I liked to pretend I was a famous hunter of greatshelled beasts—that I had felled it. Truth was, everyone in the village had heard of it crawling up here, and I only managed to visit a week after it died."

"Mraize," she said, standing taller. "We need to end this. You and I."

"I know," he said softly. He nodded toward the waves. "Do you think there's anything out there? Across the ocean? Like the fanciful tales claim?"

"Honestly, no," Shallan admitted, keeping her distance. "If you look at the strength the highstorm builds over water . . . well, it's difficult even for settlements on Roshar's eastern shore to survive. The Shattered Plains are hundreds of miles inland, and they struggle. I find it difficult to imagine little inhabited islands like in the stories . . ."

"Though?" he asked, and seemed to understand that with her, there *would* be a though.

". . . though," she confessed, "I wish for them to exist. They sound so interesting, so mysterious."

"They do exist," he said, turning his head upward toward the darkening sky. Toward the stars. "Up there. Islands in the sky, far distant. Worlds with wonders we can only imagine."

"She never took you, did she?" Shallan asked, despite having already guessed the answer.

"No," he admitted. "I was promised I could go if I successfully recruited us a Radiant." He stood up on the shell right below her, turning. "Now I am to be punished for choosing poorly. Ten more years, with no chances to travel offworld. I might never see those places, little knife."

"You want me to feel sad for you?" Shallan asked.

"You will, whether I want it or not. It is your nature."

Ten years. A harsh punishment, considering—as she was coming to realize—how much he wanted to travel to collect trophies of his own. But something about it didn't sit right with Shallan. Harsh punishments were certainly part of the Ghostblood way, but only if they served as motivation. Everything they did was about giving incentives, manipulating a situation.

She sensed a hollowness to his eyes. And she knew, ten years . . . would be lessened if he killed Shallan and erased his mistake. That was how the Ghostbloods worked.

I was invited into this vision by something, she thought. *Likely his spren. Mraize knew I was here all along. He was waiting for me to get close.*

"Mraize," she said softly, "can we not find another way?"

"I . . . have been asking that too."

That part sounded honest.

"Where is Iyatil?" Shallan said. "Your spren invited me into this vision . . . your job is, in part, to distract me, isn't it? While she does the actual work of finding the prison?"

He didn't reply. From him, a good sign that she'd guessed correctly—though that too could be manipulation. That was the problem with their relationship. She never knew exactly where she stood with Mraize. Even with other spies, like her Lightweavers, she knew where she stood—but for all his claims about the Ghostbloods being open, she didn't *know* him.

She was beginning to feel like she never would.

They took a long moment, watching each other from a distance, him atop a dead beast and her wearing a false face.

"Did you know," he whispered, "there is a world out there with an ocean in the sky? Another where people fly upon kites, as if every man were a Windrunner. Yet another where the gods can make any object stand up and walk? I will see them each someday, little knife. And claim a trophy to remember them by."

"Walk away from Iyatil," she said. "Go, on your own."

"It's difficult to reach some of them," he said. "A few, even she has never visited. Some are said to be myths. I'd love to sort through lies and legends, but I have made oaths, Shallan. I *will* be bound by them. If I am not, what kind of man am I?"

He left an implication in it. That she had walked away from hers. And from him.

"When next we meet," he said, turning and sitting back down, "be ready to fight. Try to hold me back from that which I've chased for my entire life. The dreams of a little boy, who once climbed atop a dead carcass to pretend."

The vision burst, and she was pulled into the Spiritual Realm again. She felt powerless, frustrated. And ashamed at those emotions, when she *should* have tried right then to end him.

I need to stop being distracted by Mraize though, she thought. *I need to find Iyatil. Or better, the prison.*

But how?

Well, it did seem that Mishram had been influencing their visions. Renarin agreed. So . . . maybe she needed to stop hiding. Let Odium show her what he wished. And hope that somewhere in those visions was the clue she needed to beat Iyatil to the prison.

Kaladin worked on dinner in the broken monastery chamber, the sun having barely kissed the horizon. Close by, Nale sat against the wall. He bore a haunted expression, his eyes red from crying. Szeth stood nearby, uncertain, while Syl—full sized—had found a seat on a stone and was softly humming the *Wandersail* song.

"I feel it, Stormblessed," Nale whispered. "The man I used to be. The man who heard the songs of Roshar long ago. I . . . am not him. I remember him."

"I know," Kaladin said as he stirred his stew by a small fire in the night. "I've felt the same."

"I want to be better," Nale said. "I want to be that man, the one who stood *against* the law to defend those who deserved mercy. That is the only path to true justice. How? How can I see clearly once more?"

"Kaladin will help," Szeth promised.

Well, Szeth's enthusiasm was what Kaladin deserved. While Kaladin still wasn't certain he could help Heralds, he could try. It seemed to him nobody ever had.

Nale lifted his hand toward Szeth and summoned a Shardblade. Not the one he'd been fighting with earlier. That had been his Radiant Blade—this was his Honorblade, delicate, with twin slits along it and a large pommel.

"Take it, Szeth," Nale whispered. "Hold it until . . . until I am sure I can carry it again. I . . . I am not . . . I am not a man, or a Herald, of justice right now . . ."

Szeth looked to Kaladin, who nodded, tasting his stew. The last sunlight vanished. It was the ninth and final night.

Szeth took the sword from Nale—who in the hours since the fight had become frail, halting, barely able to move. Szeth wrapped him in Kaladin's blue Kholin cloak, as the Herald was shivering, then fetched him something to drink.

Syl folded her arms and stopped humming. "So . . ." she said. "Now what?"

"The last monastery," Szeth said, joining them by the fire. "I have not yet cleansed my homeland. I must somehow deal with the Unmade who banished me all those years ago, after turning the Honorbearers against me, fooling even my father."

"No," Nale said softly.

They all turned from the fire toward him beside the wall, wrapped in the cloak. He was staring at his cup, which trembled in his fingers. "There *is* no Unmade."

"What?" Szeth said. "The Voice in my head. Everything I saw. The corruption of my people!"

Nale closed his eyes.

"*Ishar,*" Syl said. "It's Ishar, isn't it?"

Nale nodded.

"All of it?" Szeth said. "That was *him*?"

"Yes," Nale whispered.

"How?" Syl demanded.

"There are wells of power," Nale whispered, "associated with the gods. You have likely heard of one at the Horneater Peaks."

"So," Kaladin said, "Ishar found Honor's well of power and used it somehow?"

"Honor's power refuses the touch of men," Nale said, "and his perpendicularity moves. Cultivation's power at the Peaks is carefully monitored by her spren, and cannot be accessed by mortals. But Odium's power . . . it dislikes him, thinks him weak. Mishram found its hiding place, and gained the ability to Connect to all of the singers. Ishar knew this, and . . ."

"Damnation," Kaladin whispered, feeling cold. "The Bondsmith Herald took up the power of *Odium*?"

"Only a fraction of it," Nale said. "It let him Connect to this land and become a god to the people here . . . That is what the Honorbearers followed, Szeth. A true divinity, to their eyes, who could show them the future. Wars to come . . ."

"Voidbringers," Syl whispered.

"No," Nale said. "Something worse . . . We did not believe the Voidbringers would return."

"All this time," Szeth said, "it was one of the *Heralds* I heard?"

"He wanted to make a true soldier of you. He did not like me or my Skybreakers much at the time, as this was right after Billid and his dissenters broke off from me with their traitorous spren."

"There are *Skybreaker dissenters*?" Szeth asked.

"Yes. Often, through the centuries . . . I usually can bring them back . . . I should have seen. Regardless, Ishar was looking for new Heralds to replace us, but was constantly frustrated that his Honorbearers in Shinovar never rose to the occasion. He wanted them to fight, to become warriors. It is . . . what Odium does . . . and I think that infected Ishar . . ."

Nale opened his eyes again. "Even when you were wrong, you managed to see more clearly than the rest of us, Szeth. You are not Truthless. We denied the Return. We let it happen without fighting it, and at times actually joined the enemy. *We* are Truthless. Ishar, Herald of Wisdom, is *Truthless.*"

"Storms," 12124 whispered, appearing beside Szeth. He regarded them, his face a void of stars. "*Storms!*"

"Ishar waits at the final monastery?" Kaladin said, stirring the stew.

Nale nodded. "Where spren gather. Where Szeth will be initiated as a Herald, a real one, to lead us. Somehow I knew that we needed you, Szeth, although I was broken. Does that mean there's hope for me, even now?"

Szeth looked to Kaladin for support.

"Absolutely," Kaladin said.

"Then we go to the final monastery," Szeth said.

"We will need Stormlight," Kaladin said.

"There is a stash near our destination," Nale mumbled, "at a hidden retreat of mine. We can reach it before dawn."

"We travel through the night, then," Szeth said. "And arrive in the morning. To confront Ishu-son-God."

Kaladin nodded, and began ladling stew into bowls. As he did so, he glanced to Nale, huddled by the wall, cold and miserable. *I was wrong earlier, wasn't I?* Kaladin thought. *During our fight, I thought he was incomprehensible. But . . . behind it all . . . he's just a man.*

Nale's failings weren't unknowable at all. So Kaladin did the only thing he could think to do: he brought the man some stew. While he did, a few phantom notes echoed among the hills. The Wind returning songs to him, in encouragement.

Yet these notes were far too skilled to have been played by Kaladin. These, he thought, must have been brought by the Wind from the distant past. From a night on the Shattered Plains, when Kaladin had been the broken man.

That man had been reforged now by love, light, and song. Proof that it *could* be done.

FOUR THOUSAND FIVE HUNDRED FIFTY YEARS AGO

I, the god Honor, walked a battlefield full of burning corpses. This time, I did not weep. I could not afford to weep. My followers needed me.

Rayse and I had been in an arms race. First his Fused, then my Heralds, then his Unmade, then my Radiants—which were not my conscious creation, but formed by pieces of me working independently. I crafted their oaths to maximize their abilities, per Kor's contract and Ishar's advice. That one understood the ways of gods as few mortals ever had.

Millennia had passed, and I clashed with Rayse, back and forth, time and time again. Gigantic proxy wars. Rayse was trapped in the Rosharan system, but if he could take control, he could send forces out into the cosmere to do as he wished. My armies resisted him. For his Fused, like my Heralds, were trapped in this system by our oaths. Only when one of us fully ruled Roshar could we use it as a stepping stone in our greater cosmere goals.

Yet here we were, after thousands of years . . . in a stalemate. How many . . . how many had died in these last centuries? Still, I told myself that I had grown since the fires of Ashyn. Gods did not weep over the fallen; they rejoiced over the victories of the living.

This was part of what I'd been teaching my followers, along with the sanctity of oaths.

Rayse's forces grow more powerful, I noted as I walked the battlefield, calculating casualty numbers. The Unmade, in particular, were growing in strength. He had hidden their creation from me, and I found them unnerving. My Radiants could do great things, but were kept in check by their oaths. His Fused were more limited—leaving him extra strength he could give to the Unmade.

I had the Heralds. And they, more and more, were able to draw on the powers of *Roshar itself* instead of just my Surges. I did not understand why or how, but I did not wish to seem weak by admitting that fact.

I considered. Thousands of years. Was this our fate? Fighting for eternity? I found myself treasonously timid. Why? I, God, held the power of Adonalsium. I could see into the future, could think along multiple lines at once, could appear wherever I wished.

My avatar still infused the terrible storm of Roshar, making it a manifestation of my will and strength. A constant reminder of my blessing—via Stormlight—and the danger of disobeying my will. I *was* the storm. I should not be timid. I should be bold.

I turned, surveying the battlefield again. A lonely expanse of stone dotted by dark lumps. This time . . . this time my people had nearly lost. My system of Radiants—inspired by the Herald of Wisdom—should have been the greater, as they harnessed the power of oaths, but Rayse's immortal Fused learned more and more the longer they lived. Each war was cataclysmic, named a Desolation by my ardent priests. Neither side able to win, both sides beating the other senseless until at the end, civilization was in ashes.

Then the Fused returned, having learned from each Desolation, while my forces had to start fresh. Rayse applied the lessons of nature: you could wear down any stone given enough time. I flew to the ends of the world, to Natanatan, where the battle had been most fierce this time.

At least my people survive, a part of me thought. *This works.* It wasn't as bad as Ashyn. The sky didn't burn, and the people could recover.

Rayse appeared before me, settling his hands on his golden scepter, beard blowing in the wind. "So. This was fun, even if you did win."

"This is no victory," I said, my voice raw.

"Your Heralds trap my best warriors away in that hellscape of Braize," Rayse said. "Its unique properties are indeed fascinating. I almost think you admire me in naming it after me. Regardless, I was too new to my powers when I agreed to this accommodation. Thousands of years, and I cannot break free. I should be impressed."

I could feel the hatred steaming off Odium. He had spent two and a half millennia in my prison. Twenty-five hundred years I had protected the cosmere with the blood and lives of my followers. Still the other Shards looked away. As for me . . . I had promised my people peace and tranquility in death, but in life I gave them only terror and ash.

"You make it as bad as you can each time, don't you?" I whispered. "You want to break me."

"You want to know what breaking you could be like, Tanner? I barely attack the children during Desolations. I could order them to slaughter, instead of to war. I'm toying with that for next time. Merely to see your reaction."

I screamed. And in my rage, I lost control and threw myself at him.

He laughed, and threw his power against mine. What followed was a thunderclap, and silence, as all was pushed away from us. In that space of nothing—every axon forced away—our souls melded in the most unnerving of ways, too intimate, too reminiscent of creation for a creature such as him. In that moment, tiny pieces of something discordant were born.

Something dangerous, even to a god. The counter to my essence. Anti-Light, it could be called.

Worse, the shock wave of our clash surged beneath us, power rushing and vibrating with those terrible tones. I realized too late that there was something strange about this land, beneath this city. Pieces of something fallen. A . . . fourth moon? In splinters? It reacted to us, and I saw people there—new ones, watchers, who had been hidden from me.

Those pieces of the sky . . . they sheltered from the eyes of God? That was not aluminum. It was something greater. Something . . . that responded to our clash, the ground liquefying in a pattern, dictated by the tone and the strange nature of the place.

We vaporized an entire capital city in seconds. The direct clash between two gods was far too violent. I pulled back, horrified, knowing I'd just caused tens of thousands of deaths. One of the grandest cities . . . gone.

Rayse laughed. "Shall we fight again?"

I withdrew further from him.

"I will push you until you acquiesce. Let us renegotiate our agreement. You can be rid of me."

I said nothing, but knelt and tried to recover.

These were my people. They followed me.

I had put some of myself into them . . . and thus their pain was mine. So many dead . . .

No. I could be strong. I was God.

I stood up and looked Rayse in the eye. There was a weakness in him. One that Kor had noticed and whispered to me. Though we spent less time together—I had wars to oversee and a religion to lead—I loved her still, and could feel her love in return. The power that Rayse held *loathed* being trapped. I knew that the power inside Kor felt similarly. It hated stagnancy.

Regardless, there was something in Rayse we could exploit.

Since I refused to fight him, Rayse swept away in a tempest of anger and emotion. As Kor had whispered he might, he left a shadow. I did not look. I stood tall. Waiting.

Until it approached me and whispered, *What if we want peace?*

It was one of the Unmade.

"I cannot make peace with you," I declared, "so long as he fights."

Would you make peace with me? the shadow asked. *If you could, and he did not stop you?* Ba-Ado-Mishram was her name.

"Yes," I said.

The shadow withdrew, timid, like a fain animal seeing the colorful world for the first time. Yes, Kor was right. But this opening would take many years to mature, and I could not wait upon it.

And thus, I decided to push the Heralds harder. I let them access my powers more fully, and those of Roshar itself. As long as I was bound by oaths, they would not be able to destroy the land. So it would be well.

I had declared it would be.

Rarely, the wise will also seek—in loss—to flip the board and scatter the pieces. But if you do this, it is likely the last time you will play. This also is not an adage for towers.

—*Proverbs for Towers and War,* Zenaz, date unknown

Adolin had drilled in pike block formations, but had never been in battle manning one. Doing so now—in the last stand to protect Azimir—proved one of the most humiliating experiences of his life.

When he and May arrived at their posts—charging through the night while carrying enormous pikes well over ten feet long—they were sent to different points in the line. Split apart because the commander in charge, though apologetic, didn't want "two weak links next to one another."

Adolin had to strap his longsword to his back—because at his hip it might knock into others in the line. He was positioned somewhere in the middle of the block that was holding the extended breach in the stone wall of the dome. It was right at ground level, ripped open by the Fused who had in turn been killed by Taln. That gap, which had been expanded in the hours since that assault, was some forty feet long.

The defenders had placed chunks of rubble across it—more stumbling block than fortification—and held that gap with a large pike line. Modern pike formations were less shield wall and more an anti-cavalry defensive position, often with crossbowmen at the wings. Tonight they deployed a more classical arrangement: a shield wall in front, with two ranks of pikes behind.

The front row employed shields and short spears to hold the enemy back.

The second rank lined up tightly and held the pikes in two hands, stabbing them over the shoulders of the front rank to kill enemy soldiers. A third row stood at the ready, resting and getting water, but also sometimes bringing pikes to bear—reaching past two ranks—during a particularly difficult rush.

Adolin was put into the back line first, filling a hole among soldiers who were sweating and gulping water among ever-present fearspren, exhaustionspren, and painspren. By now, there were no Alethi blocks or Azish blocks; the two regiments had been fully integrated. This section was commanded by a tall Azish man with scars on his bald scalp.

He gave the order to prepare for the ranks to swap, and the men around Adolin groaned softly. Not enough time to rest, not nearly enough. They needed far more troops, as the enemy was trying to break through each of the doorways on the ground level *and* break out from the balcony above. Each section was defended with flagging troops, many of whom were untrained.

Adolin could taste the desperation in the air as he was ordered forward. The second pike line withdrew, folding around the third pike line, who stepped forward into their places. The others put Adolin to shame as they efficiently brought their pikes into an overhand grip and let the inner line slip past them. Adolin's pike clattered against that of a retreating soldier, and he nearly got them into a snarl, earning a curse from the man. In this dim light, the fellow couldn't see who Adolin was, which was probably best for both of them.

Adolin hefted his pike and moved it into place, trying his best to protect the spearmen in the front line before him. Beyond was a dark gap, broken only by the glowing gemstones in the singers' beards. A sea of red, blue, purple, and yellow stars. That and glowing red eyes marking Regals.

The defenders had killed a great number of singers—at great cost, yes, but it meant stormforms couldn't bring down this pike line easily, nor could direforms just rip through it. There weren't enough Regals remaining, and it didn't seem the Fused that Notum had seen earlier today were ready yet.

So, it came down to the dregs: the weakened, wounded, and exhausted human defenders against the singer grunts who had seen tens of thousands of their kind die during this assault. Adolin tried not to think about who he was killing: people who arguably were barely a year old. Legitimately angry at what had been done to them, they had been taken in by Odium, made soldiers, and now were forced to charge pike blocks. Adolin grunted as they came in again, knocking aside pikes, trying to get close and batter through the shield wall.

Most of his work was in stabilizing and resetting his pike. Pulling it back, stabbing in. Grueling work that quickly had his arms burning. It was a nightmare, lit only by a few weak sphere lanterns. He stood for a frighteningly long time, trying to shove back a tide of aggressive troops.

It was a miracle the defenders hadn't fallen. The line would buckle and shift as the singers hit it, but Adolin's entire world was that storming pike, heavy enough that it was hard to even keep raised, let alone do something useful with. Secondary was the pain of trying to keep himself from slipping because of his missing leg. He could sometimes lodge the peg against the edge of a cobblestone and get some leverage, until it inevitably slipped and he stumbled.

He felt sorry for the poor souls who had to not only keep their pikes in place, but also put up with him. Adolin gritted his teeth and kept at it for what seemed like an eternity—long past when his arms started going numb. He'd never been a liability on a battlefield before, and he hoped he wasn't one now, but *storms* . . . the experience was absolutely, thoroughly, *horribly* humiliating.

My muscles aren't used to this work. My ego isn't accustomed to standing in a formation rather than running around in Plate, virtually impervious.

Weren't there supposed to be rotations? Weren't they supposed to have a chance to—

The captain of their rank called for rotation. Adolin gladly pulled back, and was embarrassed as he immediately knocked pikes against another man coming in to relieve him. Storms send it wasn't the same one. Adolin stumbled out of the line, and someone blessedly took his pike while a woman offered him a ladle of water. He drank three in a row, and then checked the moon.

It had been at most fifteen minutes. Storms. They had to keep this up *all night*? He settled down on the ground, allowed ten minutes or so before they'd have to stand in line again. Judging by the setting first moon, they had twelve hours until his father's confrontation—which would happen at midday at Urithiru. Adolin barely felt he could handle a second shift, let alone twenty more.

The officer of the rank stepped up to Adolin and spoke softly. "I can rotate you out, Brightlord. You don't have to go in on next shift."

"No," Adolin said. "As long as the others go in, I go in."

The tall man, mostly a shadow in the night, seemed concerned. "The next shift is the difficult one, Brightlord."

"More difficult than *that*?" Adolin said, amazed.

"Everyone takes a turn in the shield wall."

Storms, of course. The pikes were hard to carry, but the soldiers in the most danger would be in that front line. They rotated in a different way, as they had different equipment, but it made sense that everyone would do a stint there.

If he'd just survived a nightmare, what was coming would be . . . Storms, it would be Damnation itself. Adolin sat on the ground, listening to men shout, grunt, and bleed.

"Send me in," he said to the officer, gritting his teeth. "I'll be better on the front line anyway—I haven't built the muscles for holding a pike. I'll be more effective with spear and shield." He gestured to his peg leg, and felt strangely—and stupidly—embarrassed at how poorly his trouser leg fit around it. "But don't put me next to someone else weaker or untrained."

"Less and less I can do about that lately, Brightlord," the Azish man said, looking over his shoulder as another group of reinforcements arrived from the recruitment tent. Five men who carried their pikes even more uncertainly than Adolin.

Adolin sighed and took another drink, but his break was up before he had a chance to appreciate it. He was handed a spear and shield, sent forward at the side with some others—they'd rotate in from the edges while the men at the center of this section retreated through the middle of the pikemen.

Minutes later, he was fighting for survival against a tide of darkness come alive.

⁂

Visions twisted and spun around Shallan, never remaining stable for long. She saw her father beating her brother Balat—then she was killing her father, singing as she strangled him. Anger, pain, and betrayal. From parent to child to child. All of that, and so full of *hatred*—as her father hated his father and hated his children, who hated him.

Time distorted and scenes bled together.

Hatred.

Loathing.

Odium.

This was his realm, and Shallan had let him find her—so he punished her with scenes of killing. Her mother gasping, eyes burning. Tyn impaled on the end of Shallan's Blade. Testament screaming as Shallan ripped her very soul apart.

That made it so difficult to remember the reconciliation she'd just had with her mother. Such happy moments were washed away, and she was back with Tyn in a grand tent that had seemed so magnificent to Shallan at the time—though it was nothing compared to Alethi finery. Tyn was standing over her, complaining that she'd have to pin Shallan's death on Vathah.

I'm sorry that you have to learn the lesson this way. Sometimes, we must do things we don't like, kid . . .

Shallan struck first, killing the woman with a Shardblade. Tyn died with burned-out eyes, and something was born inside Shallan. A persona who could kill, though it wouldn't find a name for some time yet. She had two budding personas then, and maybe a third—the child—which she had never acknowledged.

But two to help her. One to hold memories. Another to fight and kill when she could not. These two would be bloodstained so Shallan could continue to function. Eventually Shallan would take one and make of it Veil—then later, when she needed a swordswoman, would take the other and make Radiant, but both had been growing for far longer than that.

In this vision, Shallan stabbed again, chopping at Tyn's fallen body. And Formless stood behind her, nodding. That . . . wasn't how this had happened. Was it?

In a flash she was killing Mraize, and her sword left blood as his head rolled free. From there she murdered Wit, who laughed. Then Jasnah, stern and unloving, dying as she chastised Shallan for her sword form.

"No," Shallan whispered. "I wouldn't kill them."

Yet in the vision she did, over and over. Everyone who had ever loved her, helped her, or offered her mentoring. She'd killed her parents, then needed replacements to kill as well. Sebarial and Palona. Dalinar and Navani.

Blood on her hands, and her personas couldn't help her.

"No!" she screamed. She knew this wasn't real. She'd walked into this intentionally, but that didn't matter anymore. Her will faltered as she was forced to watch, time and time again, as someone she loved died at her own hands.

Don't let him win. Don't believe.

Yet it was relentless. A repetitive chorus that proclaimed she was dangerous to anyone who got close to her. She would outgrow them, then murder them.

Just as she'd done to her parents.

⁂

Rhythms vibrated through Rlain as he appeared on a battlefield. Nearby, humans fled before a cheering host of singers. It was . . . the end. A fight won.

Others soon began to bring the warriors water and bandages. And they were *beautiful.* Civilians in flowing robes that displayed carapace to its fullest. Outfits of fine stitching and sturdy design, made of seasilk, dyed to complement skin tones. They spoke of the warriors having fought to defend the city. A singer city.

He longed to see it. *Show me,* he thought. *Please?*

He was among them suddenly. In their city—beautiful, with buildings that incorporated the flow of crem as it fell, sculpting it over the long term into shapes and designs. Natural patterns, making the city feel as if it were a feature of the landscape, not an imposition constructed atop it.

Here were blacksmiths who worked forges, artists who created swirling, flowing murals from sand or bits of colored shell, craftspeople who constructed drums or other instruments he didn't recognize. All done out under the sun, instead of hidden away in a workshop, bearing artform or other magnificent forms. They wanted to be beneath the light and within the wind.

He found himself humming to the Rhythm of Awe. It was true. He'd always imagined they had culture, creations, nations, that rivaled those of the humans—but a part of him had felt an itching worry. That perhaps the singers *weren't* capable of such majesty.

This was wonderful. Not just versions of what the humans did, but something distinctive. Marvelous. *Theirs.* In all these visions he'd been seeing the human perspective, except in that first one. Now he finally experienced something else.

His heritage.

This isn't what you need to see, a voice whispered. It was Mishram. *I'm sorry.*

"Send me back then," he said, reluctant.

He was again on the battlefield.

I hate this, Mishram whispered. *I hate you. See.*

Warriors were gathering at the center of the battlefield, and he joined them. Singers did not line up or form ranks. Even in this ancient army, nobody wore uniforms. There were leaders, by necessity, but no platoons or divisions.

In this, Rlain had come to think they might be able to learn from the humans. There was strength in regimentation, much like there was strength in a lattice structure of reeds forming a basket.

Bridger of Minds, something seemed to whisper to him on the wind. Not Mishram this time. *The one who is of both worlds. You can heal us.*

Rlain spun and looked, but saw only a sea of singer faces, each with its own distinctive pattern—red, black, white mixing. He'd heard a human child call him "painted" once, but of course that was a very human way of seeing it. In reality, the humans were the ones who seemed painted, covering their colors with one hue.

He tried not to think of it that way. Neither was painted, and neither was better. There could be a certain handsomeness to either. You could see human eyes and expressions better, as their irises were so easy to catch against the white. He found that appealing, and the mop of hair that was so unruly at times, where singer hairstrands tended to fall straight.

He looked around, wishing to find Renarin. Something was happening there, something he hadn't hoped for—but which was exciting and invigorating. After years without even a basic warpair, and despairing of ever knowing one, was he actually close to something better? Something more?

He wanted to seize that, to hold to Renarin and never let go. He felt elated, and kept attuning the Rhythm of Joy, including when he deliberately shifted off it for another reason.

There isn't time for frivolities during this important moment, he thought. *This is why it's better not to think of such bonds except in the proper form. It's distracting.*

But he *wanted* to be distracted. Did that make him a bad soldier? Fortunately, his attention was drawn by something manifesting at the center of the troops. There, on a stone elevated nine feet in the air, a figure grew from dark smoke. He knew Ba-Ado-Mishram's face by now, but it was odd seeing her fully present, in a body that was nine times the size of an average singer, wreathed in bloodred clothing that exposed carapace. Her entire figure smoldered—wisps of dark light rising from it, the edges fuzzy. She was made, it appeared, entirely of black and dark red smoke, and her eyes were golden.

The soldiers hushed, the humming softening to the Rhythm of the Terrors. Mishram, so tall and dominating, like a mountain. She carried a staff, which she slammed down on the rock, the sound sharp in Rlain's ears.

With that thought, he realized what he might be seeing. This vision was *before* Mishram had been captured. It was during the time Mishram had become their god, creating the False Desolation. That must have included the battle that he'd seen the tail end of, the corpses of which were still strewn about behind, though the army had moved to a cleaner section of ground to watch Mishram.

She hummed the Rhythm of Exultation. "A battle won," she announced. "And gifts to be given. Some of you have been chosen for your valor. Come forth, and receive your gift."

She held out a hand, and darkness rained from beneath her downturned palm, forming a miniature storm. A singer was tapped on the shoulder by an imperious stormform, then sent to stumble up before her. She nodded, and he stepped into the storm—though he'd been in warform, he was but a doll to her, her palm large enough it could have held him.

The crowd grew even more still as he emerged from the darkness—altered, as if by a highstorm, into a new form. Direform, with glowing red eyes, and carapace that imitated a suit of armor—more tightly closed, with spikes. A form of power, and one of the best for war.

Two more were chosen and took upon them forms of power.

"The other Unmade," Mishram said, her voice booming across them, "have agreed to support me. We are winning. Now we press the humans. Relentless."

"And Odium?" Rlain called, his voice ringing out across a quiet, awed crowd of soldiers. "What of him?"

"He is locked away," she said, "like the human Heralds. I used his power to bind him for a time. He cannot waste our lives any longer." She focused on Rlain and reared up, standing tall rather than crouching. "Who are you, soldier?"

"I'm . . . I'm nobody," Rlain said. "Why do you fight, Mishram? Don't you want peace?"

"*Humans* will never want peace unless they are forced into it," she said. "Once I bring them to the brink of collapse, we shall see. Who *are* you?"

"Nobody," Rlain said. "I choose to be nobody."

With that, he turned and left.

First alone, with many humming or shouting to words of betrayal. He left among the corpses, and then . . . was followed. One here, one there, not a flood. A trickle. Some just . . . turned and walked away.

Mishram appeared in front of him. "Why? Why do you leave? We're winning!"

Rlain pulled to a stop. Why?

"I rejected him," he said, "but not to replace him with another war."

"We can win!"

"At what cost?" he said. "I'm done."

He walked around her. And others, they did join him. The listeners, who would together break ties with Mishram and the rest of their kind, giving up their forms in order to seek their own way.

"Singer," Mishram said, standing tall, calling after him. "This will not serve you. I stepped into God's role. I took his pool, his perpendicularity, and am tied to every singer who holds a form. To every spren, to every fiber of Roshar."

Rlain looked back at her, hesitating.

Mishram's expression changed, and she suddenly hummed to Confusion, glancing around. "It is you. It is this. Yes . . ." She focused on him again. "This was the day. The day I realized . . . I realized that I had to find another way."

"When the listeners left?" Rlain said. "That was when you decided to meet with the humans?"

"I was betrayed . . ." Her eyes flashed. "Because of you."

"Because of evil people, doing evil," he said, turning from her. "That does not make my action unjust." He continued to walk away.

"Toathan," another said, running to him. "Why do you leave?"

Rlain turned to them. Toathan. That name . . . He knew that name. One of the ancestors. *His* ancestor, a name recorded in song. Others joined him, asking what they should do. He could see confusion in their eyes, worry about the war.

"Something is wrong with all forms lately," a femalen said. "You can all feel it, can't you? It feels wrong. The rhythms change. The songs warp."

"I'm done," another said. "It's never going to end. We just keep fighting. And fighting. And fighting."

"Go," Rlain said to them. "Gather your families. We will leave together, enter the storm and abandon our forms. She has taken up the mantle of divinity, and in so doing, touched everything. That wrongness you feel? It will dig deep into us if we do not act. It will change our minds, draw us back to her."

"Abandon our . . . forms?" the femalen asked.

"What are we without forms?" said another, to Anxiety.

"Free," Rlain said to Resolve.

They nodded, and went running for the warcamp in the near distance. To gather children, once-mates. Rlain was proud, in this instance, to stand in his ancestor's place. The next part would be traumatic for them, as they eventually entered a dull fog of thought—where only a few songs would survive.

And in the distance, Mishram stood tall. *She let us go,* he realized. He'd never considered that. He'd imagined them sneaking away, but this was the full light of day, beneath the sun and sky.

For all her faults, she hadn't *forced* them to stay. And after this, when she'd been asked to seriously consider peace, she'd . . . learned from the listeners. He saw her standing there, surveying the battlefield, and she seemed to waver.

"It's a different thing entirely to see them die when you are in command, isn't it, Mishram?" he asked.

Yes. Her voice vibrated through him. *I wish the best of you hadn't chosen to leave. Perhaps you'd have helped me.*

"Perhaps," he said. "Or perhaps we'd have been corrupted by your ambition."

Now what? she asked. *You know my failures, my pains, Bridger of Minds. I want . . . want so badly to break something, everything, for what was done to me. I . . . I cannot hold it back, most days. I rage, I scream. I will kill you, if I can. I fear it. What will you do, when you find me?*

"I don't know yet," he said, and started walking away. "Maybe I'll just listen."

It was the darkest day Renarin could remember.

The first day the visions had struck him. The day he'd worried he was beyond redemption.

It had been only . . . what, a year and a half ago? Yet he felt so much younger, isolated and alone in his room at the warcamps. Dalinar liked austerity, and that affected his sons as well. So Renarin sat on a hard wooden chair, in a room with too little light, enveloped in darkness.

The visions were obviously trying to upset him. He stood up, and it began: his first time seeing the future. He saw the coming storm, and numbers in the air, indicating the time until its looming arrival. The Everstorm.

The sights had terrified him—and as he remembered this day, he screamed, hands over his eyes, overwhelmed by how much noise and chaos crashed into him. Yet despite all this *sensation,* he now understood. The younger him had seen into the Spiritual Realm, which meant all the possibilities were vying for his attention.

He cut off his screams, and forced himself to watch, as he hoped to be able to parse it better now. But he couldn't help remembering his fear—his worry at what was wrong with him. That he—in seeing the future—was to be consigned to Damnation for his heresy.

Renarin's father saw visions too, but in his, he lived the life of a Knight Radiant of old. He saw Nohadon, the great king, or witnessed grand events like the Recreance. When Renarin saw visions, they were of blackness, a coming storm, and even—in the most terrible moments—his father falling to the influence of the enemy and becoming Odium's general.

The messaging seemed clear. Something was wrong with Renarin. *I will be sorry,* Glys said, his voice anguished. *I will be, Renarin.*

Eventually, Glys would offer some explanation—that he, as a newer spren and only recently defected to Sja-anat, hadn't realized what all this would do to Renarin. Neither of them had understood the greater truth: that what Renarin saw wasn't inevitable, and the possibilities he saw *were* heavily influenced by the enemy. Renarin stood up. He'd spent so long thinking about the visions, and how to avoid their terrible possibilities. But what about the present moment? Shouldn't he work to change the *now*?

It is not our strength, Glys whispered. *We focus on what will be.*

"I have to do a lot of things that I'm not very good at," Renarin said. "That's basically my *whole life,* Glys."

Soon after this, the younger Renarin would learn to channel all this information into a visualization. Stained glass windows; a way to bring order to the chaos of the Spiritual Realm. He could do that now, so he turned around, and the flashing visions crystallized and grew into windows surrounding him as if he were in a dark room—light shining from outside.

In the windows, he saw dates depicted in glyphs in the glass. He saw furious winds, crimson lightning, the eyes of the enemy peering through—bloody and terrible. But the past was dead and gone. What of the now?

New windows grew around him, vibrant, each color so bright and vivid it seemed to be an infused gemstone. They showed a dark landscape, crops that barely grew, withered towns, a people enslaved. He saw his father's funeral pyre, which was foolishness. When his father died, he'd be turned into a statue like all Alethi kings and highprinces.

Each of these windows had signs of Mishram's touch, but they were in corners, hidden. As if she were . . . piggybacking on Odium's visions.

I do think all of this is leading us somewhere, Renarin thought to himself. *Odium is trying to break us, but Mishram is using his attacks to tell us something. About isolation, and betrayal, and pain . . .*

He found these windows too dominated by Odium to tell him what he wanted to know. "This is your influence, isn't it?" Renarin said to the sky. "I've always seen the future *you* want. Even if you weren't paying attention to me directly, your shadow looms long."

It has to be that way, Renarin, Glys thought to a mournful rhythm. *It is what I am. Of him, now.*

"No," Renarin said. "I spent my life being told I had to become an ardent, Glys. Because people couldn't think of anything else to do with a highborn boy who couldn't fight." He squeezed his hands into fists to keep from trembling. People thought he was emotionless because he didn't take part in their conversations or find what they did interesting, but they were wrong. He felt *too many* emotions. When he'd been a child, it had been difficult to contain them.

They could all read each other better than he could read them, and that made them assume they understood him. When the truth was, he didn't work by the same rules, and he never had. He saw the world from a different perspective.

He could make that his strength. He shoved into the darkness again, away from these windows, and as he did, he summoned his Light. Despite his many attempts to learn to make illusions like Shallan did, this was what it always came to for him. Light growing like a ball in his hand, shining all around him, and showing him truth.

The ancient Radiants must have known this was possible, right? Their order was named for it. His society said that seeing the future was a terrible and evil thing, but maybe that was just because Odium influenced it so heavily. Surely there was a way to cut through it.

Everyone saw by light. Could you see better by a purer light?

A new set of windows began to grow around Renarin, like crystals forming. He held his hand high, filling it with the power of this realm, and—bathed in that cool, white illumination—the windows changed. Shadows melted from them, *fled* from them. Darkness evaporated.

Renarin was left with the truth. A dozen varieties of it. For while certain things were true no matter what perspective you saw them from, that wasn't the case for most things in life. The answer to most questions was "Well, it depends . . ." That went for inconsequential questions like what one wanted for breakfast, as well as for vitally important ones like "What do you want from life?"

Is this possible? Glys said, awed. *Can we see this?*

"We change the now, Glys," Renarin said. "The future always begins with the now."

Each window depicted him. Renarin the ardent was here, with a shaved head and an embarrassing beard that didn't grow in that well. Renarin the scholar was another option, wearing the arcane robes of the stormwardens. The window presented him in a dynamic posture, but he'd known enough stormwardens to think poorly of their art. Perhaps that was Aunt Navani's bias. People inherently viewed any man who tried to become a scholar as ridiculous; it had infected even him.

Another was Renarin the general, and he found this interesting, because he thought he might have been good at tactical decision-making. This him wore a strange uniform, one he didn't recognize—not Alethi, though of that cut. He stood at Urithiru, he thought, and was older, with longer hair and a clean-shaven face. He studied this one a long while, for the Oathgate platforms visible to the sides were covered over with *fields*.

He moved on from that window eventually, instead seeking one that he'd glimpsed earlier: the one window where he stood with a tall, handsome singer with a skullcap of carapace and a neat, dark beard. Rlain. Was there only one window where he was with Rlain in the future?

He has hard times ahead, Glys said.

"What do you see of them?" Renarin asked.

Only what you do, but the future is . . . mine. I understand it. I don't see farther, or more, but better.

"That doesn't make a lot of sense to me, Glys," Renarin said. "I'm sorry."

Rlain, Glys said. *Look at him in this picture.*

A singer wearing a Bridge Four uniform, but the city behind them was obviously a singer one—judging by the architecture. Indeed, it was probably Kholinar.

"If I go with him," Renarin said, "I'll have to turn my back on humankind, to an extent."

As he will need to turn his back on his kind to an extent, Glys agreed. *Both sides will hate both of you.*

"Like both gods hate you?" Renarin said.

Yes, Glys said softly, trembling with a rhythm. *You will understand. If you walk that path, you will understand, Renarin. I . . . do not want you to have to.*

"It might be the only way," Renarin said, looking at the depiction of himself in the window, wearing singer clothing, standing with Rlain's arm in his. That flowing outfit was remarkable, designed to show carapace Renarin didn't have.

Rlain in a human uniform. Renarin in one of the singers' formal outfits. It was a statement. A future that Renarin would never have imagined for himself. Growing up, he'd assumed that his lack of attraction to the young women around him was related to his other mental divergences. Now he saw it as something else entirely.

No one is normal. Normal doesn't exist.

He could choose any of these lives and work toward them, though none of them were guaranteed. Was this really the life he'd choose? The *risk* he'd choose?

Why? Glys said. *Why do you want to be with him?*

"Because he has tried to understand us," Renarin said. "I love that he tries so hard. So many people just dismiss the different. I've lived that all my life, seeing it all around me. But Rlain . . . he wants to understand everyone." Renarin reached up and touched the glass. "I think he truly *does* understand—me. One of the only people to ever do so. Other than my family, I don't think anyone has ever wanted to."

This path leads to both pain and joy, Glys said.

"So much better to feel," Renarin said, "than to take the path that leads to only greyness and safe solitude. This is what I want. Him, yes, but also the life where we try to blend these worlds."

Why?

"Because someone has to, Glys," Renarin said, pushing on the window with his hand. "My father can't end this war by drawing lines and trying to enforce them. If we want to end the war for real, we have to change *hearts,* not *maps.*"

They changed the future by changing today. He'd pushed past the awkwardness. He'd learned that Rlain was interested. Now, that final step. Renarin shoved his way through this stained glass window and vanished from his vision, relying on Glys's guidance to enter another, where Rlain was walking with a group of several hundred singers.

Rlain pulled up sharply as Renarin appeared in front of him. Then he stepped forward. "Renarin?"

"Yes," Renarin said. Then he took a deep breath, reached for Rlain, and kissed him.

It was harder than he'd have liked, given how tall Rlain was. The singer didn't flinch, fortunately—because that might have broken Renarin's will.

He let Renarin take him by the sides of the face, fingers brushing carapace, and kiss him.

A flood of emotions. Passion, nervousness, and an overwhelming heat—so many emotions. Yes, Renarin knew emotion. Today he basked in it.

This was the future he wanted. It wasn't the one that others might have chosen, and wasn't one that many would have chosen for him. He wasn't even certain it was right, but it *was* what he wanted. He would merely have to hope that those who cared for him would understand that the decision was his to make, not theirs.

He pulled back and waited for a reply, anxious.

"That was . . . nicer than I expected," Rlain said to the Rhythm of Anxiety. "Are you sure, Renarin? I don't think that the world is going to take kindly to us being together. I don't want you to get hurt."

"Will you be the one to hurt me?"

"No," Rlain said to Confidence. "Never."

"Then I will risk it," he said. "Come on. I think . . . I think I'm close to understanding what Mishram is trying to say to us."

FOUR THOUSAND FIVE HUNDRED YEARS AGO

I, Honor, was winning.

How can you be happy with this?

I ignored that part of me. It was a quiet voice.

The combination of unchained Heralds—capable of incredible works—and the growing organization of the Knights Radiant was *working*. I walked another battlefield, and though there were casualties—so many casualties—the destruction was greater on the other side.

How can you not be horrified? The Desolations grow worse and worse. Humankind is blasted back to the stone age again with each clash.

It was fine. The Heralds could help humankind rebuild once we annihilated the enemy. Their powers were both great and useful. They were from Ashyn; they knew to control themselves. So long as I was here, to act as an inhibitor per the agreement Kor had forced between myself and Odium, all would be well.

I stopped, unseen, in the center of a battlefield, where a soldier lay weeping, holding to a fallen comrade. In his lap, a book.

How can you not weep for the fallen?

Nohadon's book. Yes . . . it had been centuries since that man had died. Such a curious individual. Perhaps I should have insisted that he accept immortality, if only to study him longer . . .

They trust you. They love you.

You are a fraud.

 I left the soldier, searching the stone field for my Heralds. I wanted to commend them for their bravery and accomplishments. I had felt only Taln die this time, which meant nine had survived.

Of course, I would need to send them back to Braize anyway. The planet had its strange properties, attracting souls, but I needed them to . . . act as a lock, so to speak. Their souls worked after the fashion of my own—which trapped Odium in this system—upon the Fused. This was a wonderful solution. It let them experience, in a small way, what it was to be divine.

You speak the way you think a god should. But inside, you know. You know, *Honor.*

I could not quiet this voice. It was not the power.

It was the person I had been before all of this.

Tanner.

I found Ishar sitting alone near the corpse of a fallen thunderclast. The oldest of the Heralds—though age didn't matter to them—sat slumped forward, staring at the stone ground.

"You did well," I said, manifesting in my glorious form for him. "We come closer to complete victory each time."

"Lord," Ishar said, then climbed to his knees. "Lord . . . What does complete victory look like?"

"Defeat of our foes."

"We defeat them each time," Ishar said, exhausted. "We drive them back to Braize. Then we follow . . . we follow . . ."

"They will lose their nerve eventually."

"And . . . if we lose ours first, Lord?"

I frowned, then turned and searched the futures. What was permuting from this event . . . ? Things seemed uncertain, and dangerous . . . but I was likely wrong. I couldn't see the future as well as Kor. I resolved to ask her. How long had it been since we'd spent time together? We had been so consumed by our own projects . . .

My power, I acknowledged, did not like her. Did not like the way she refused to fight outright. Did not like how she chafed at the binding we'd performed against Odium, even though it had been her idea. This kept us apart more and more. It had been a century or two since I'd held her.

Maybe . . . no . . . maybe more like four . . .

"We break, Lord," Ishar said softly. "Your Heralds break. I do not think we can go back this time."

"But you must," I said. "Or the enemy will return quickly, and the people will not be ready."

"Maybe," Ishar said. "But maybe . . ." he finally looked up. "I have an idea . . ."

He explained it, and I listened while also searching the permutations.

And to my horror, I began to see a frightening number of futures where the Heralds stopped fighting. I hadn't . . . I hadn't noticed what immortality was doing to them. Not just immortality—there was more. My power. They could not hold so much of my power.

If I lost the Heralds, I would start losing the wars. The Radiants were not enough. I needed to do something more, get stronger somehow, improve the Heralds.

The others began to gather, and I . . . I . . .

Oh. They were *hurting.*

Something changed in me. I knew them each intimately by this point—they were, unknown to them, my dearest friends. And oh, how they hurt. Dear Chana was falling apart. Nale had become so rigid. Jezrien hated himself. Vedel became indifferent, Battar so cruel . . .

Ishar, who was explaining his plan and looking for validation, hid it best. But the same hurt was there, manifesting as a need to control. A need to . . .

"Is this a deific plan?" Ishar asked me. "A plan that you might create? To isolate the one, yes, but save the world?"

"Yes," I whispered. It was exactly what I had done.

As I said it though, my powers reasserted control. Honor hated Ishar for this request, hated them all for growing so weak. Would they really do this? Turn their backs on their oaths? I, Honor, reviled it. But I did not speak, did not forbid.

I let them choose, and I withdrew, becoming the storm and blowing across the landscape, fleeing from the hurt I had created. Yet I could not escape, for it was here across the entire world. Suffering for family members lost. Blood spilled in an eternal cycle of warfare.

Was it any better than Ashyn? So much suffering.

Finally, I acknowledged that something inside me was unraveling—and had been for a long time. The ailment striking the Heralds was in part my doing. I had shared too much of myself with them, and I was . . . slowly . . .

Losing myself.

I did not seek my ardent priests. My places of worship. The devout singing my praises. I felt profoundly unworthy, for the quiet piece of myself was becoming loud now. The piece that knew that I, and the fifteen others, had done something terrible on Yolen.

I returned to Shinovar, the land where humans had first arrived. There I lay down in an uncultivated grass field, pretending I was a boy back on Yolen. Looking up at the sky, and the clouds, and feeling . . .

Whispers on the breeze.

"Adonalsium?" I whispered.

Not entirely, the breeze answered.

"Wind," I said. "Can you help me?"

No, the breeze said.

"What do I do?"

Listen, it replied, then faded.

Listen. I hauled myself up and, with my divine nature, infused the land. Parts of me were already spread through it, but now I let myself *be* the land. Let my soul align with the rhythms from long ago.

And I listened to them—the people whom I should have loved. I was with them as they slowly recovered from this war. I lost myself entirely in hearing their stories as they lived. The woman milking her hogs and singing into the wind. The child playing with her axehounds upon stones that loved her. The scholar at work trying to untangle my sayings, writing and commenting about them in tomes grown thick. The wanderer on a journey, unwittingly walking the same path Nohadon had taken.

I stopped trying to lead, to organize, or push—and instead listened. For the first time in my divine existence, some of it started to make sense. What I had become, why I was needed—as a witness. To remember all these voices. So many tears spilled alone in the darkness of night.

I loved them. There were wars, yes, of their own making. But no Desolations.

They were . . . they were better off without me?

Without what you have become, the Wind whispered. *Having no god is far preferable to having a heartless one.*

And a god who cares?

You killed that god.

I pondered this, looked at the permutations of my revelations, and at the future of Roshar. Their lives Connected to mine, their souls now intertwined with my own. Eventually, pain trembled through the land. I heard their anguish as other clashes began, echoes of what had come before. Ah, Taln had broken. Well, it had been coming. I would have to . . .

No.

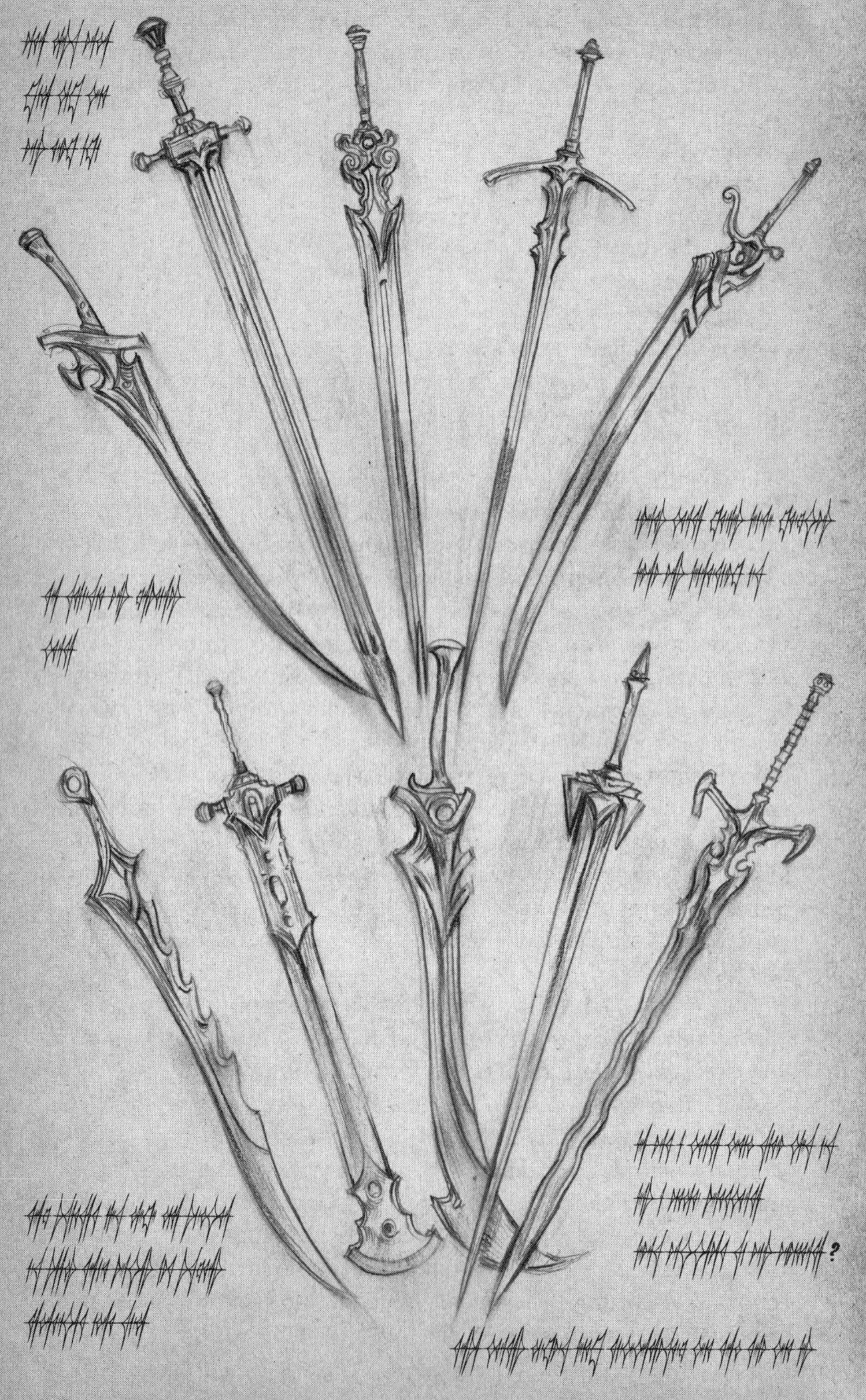

Taln had not broken.

Millennia had passed, I realized, in my state of exploration, feeling, and contemplation. I sought out Urithiru, the tower of the Radiants, and there found a single Bondsmith. Only one this time, though I had given them the ability to bond my storms. That seemed . . . to have been denied them awhile, during my exploration.

I manifested to the Bondsmith. The man gasped in his chamber, then fell to his knees, tears in his eyes.

"Melishi," I said, finding the man's name in the echoes of Connection. "What is this? A new Desolation?"

"Almighty," Melishi said, raising hands toward me. "You have chosen to bless me?"

"The Desolation," I said.

"Not a true one. Just some parsh rabble pretending." Melishi looked to me. "We need help, Lord. The Radiants squabble. But a war . . . a war could unite us again!"

"War never unites," I snapped. "Men might align briefly out of terror, but nothing more."

Melishi drew back before my wrath. "But . . ."

I swept from Melishi, searching the land for my enemy. I shied away from our nest, and Kor, and her disappointment in me. Instead I came to rest on a familiar mountaintop where Rayse had formed.

Something was different about him. Yes . . . he was even more disconnected from his power now. It hovered far behind him, the Shard of Odium, drawn toward Braize. Forced isolation in this system, the inability to fulfill the power's desire, was wearing on him.

That made him more dangerous. Much, much more dangerous.

"So," Odium said, "your tantrum is finally over?"

"What are you doing, Rayse?" I demanded. "It is not time for a confrontation."

"Isn't it?" Rayse said. "I wasn't aware we had an *appointment*."

I surged toward him, and Rayse *smiled*. He drew his power behind him, and it aligned with him, eager.

Cities laid waste. Nations broken. People slaughtered.

Never again.

"Come on," Odium whispered. "It has been building for so long, Tanner. We can't exist here together; you know it. One of us must destroy the other. The powers require it."

I wanted to. I would *revel* in Rayse's death. Ripping the power away from him and leaving him whimpering on the ground before he was at long last annihilated. It was thousands of years overdue.

 But I, Tanavast, remembered Ashyn.

Holding a child's body.

I, Tanavast, remembered Natanatan.

A landscape shattered.

I, Tanavast, remembered the land and what I'd learned over the last two and a half thousand years. The people's deaths were ripping me apart. Because I cared, and had made myself part of them. I would not fight. I would *not* destroy Roshar. Not now that I could hear their songs . . .

I refused.

"I *will* force this, Tanavast," Odium declared. "You cannot stop me."

"Our clash would destroy them all," I whispered. "You don't care, do you?"

"The cost is regrettable, but acceptable," Rayse said. "I cannot exist in this state." He pulled more of his power together, his voice growing to a crescendo of crackling energy. "Fight me, Tanner! Fight me or free me! I will *NOT BE HELD HERE ANY LONGER!*"

I knew then that Ba-Ado-Mishram's plan would not work. If she took up Odium, it would eventually force her to this same confrontation. The power would never be content here; to replace Rayse would only cause a delay. I needed a way to expand our agreement. It *had* to include a prohibition on us ever clashing directly, lest I falter and try to destroy him.

"Champions!" I pled. "Let us pick champions. Let them decide! The god of the victor rules Roshar. The god of the loser withdraws, confines their attention to one of the other planets in the system, and leaves Roshar alone."

"Why would I agree to such a thing? I am my own champion!"

The future became clear. If I did not fight, Odium would kill, and kill, and kill until every person on this planet was no more. All in a desperate, degenerate attempt to escape. I could not replace him, and I could not fight him. I had no way out.

"Please!" I screamed. "I do not want them to die, Rayse! I do not want to do this again!"

The tempest that had been building around us stilled. "You always were too weak for godhood," Rayse said. "You should never have been given a chance at this . . . honor."

"Champions," I pled once more.

"Again, why would I ever consider that?" Rayse said.

Yet he had a weakness. Rayse and the power wanted different things. It wanted only to escape, while he yearned to remain its vessel. And so I waited, watching for what I'd seen in the permutations. I kept his attention for a few years—but an eyeblink to us. Meanwhile, I saw what his rival had done. During my meditations, Rayse had briefly lost control of his power, requiring his full attention to maintain it. In those years, his rival had *already* found his pool—a part of his soul—and partaken of it. This should not have been easy, but something about his pool—the way he was maintaining it—was different . . .

Rayse wanted to resist her—even then, while talking with me, he raged as she continued her machinations. His power refused to work against her. Rayse was forced to watch, and atop that mountain, I knew . . .

Knew how close he was to losing. Ba-Ado-Mishram didn't truly lock him away, as she claimed—but the power protected her from his touch. "What is it like, Rayse?" I asked. "To know, for the first time in your existence, what it is to be powerless?"

Anger moved through him, a rhythm I could hear. The power liked that. He looked to me, red and gold surging through his avatar. "A deal," he growled. "What would a deal look like?"

"If my people stop the rogue Unmade for you," I said, "you will agree to my terms?"

"I will agree," Rayse said reluctantly, "not to force a direct confrontation between us."

"No more increasing gifts of power to our minions," I said. "What the mortals have, they keep—but that is *it*. No direct confrontation between us, and no further expansion of our powers to our people. We leave them alone . . ."

Because they deserve better than us.

"These two points," Rayse said, "I agree to: I will limit myself to never attack you first—yet I will not hold you to the same limitation; if you decide to attack me, I may fight back. And I . . . I will agree to a contest of champions, in the future, if specifics can be arranged and agreed to. Now, can you deal with this spren of mine? Remove her?"

My power did not like the idea, but it did ratify our agreement, binding us to it. As it did so, it questioned. Could I do this? Had I not made a promise to Mishram?

I assured it that this was for the best. It simmered, thinking I was doing this for Roshar, not for it.

It was right.

"Kor knows of a way," I whispered to Rayse. "A method to capture and hold a powerful spren. I will teach this method to the Bondsmith . . ."

The best players win two of three games against skilled opponents. In other words, even the finest lose a significant amount. Do not set up unless you are prepared for loss.

—*Proverbs for Towers and War,* Zenaz, date unknown

Adolin rotated through ranks in the pike block, and never had a chance to draw his longsword. He held a shield and spear. He used a pike. He gulped water. He grunted and he sweated.

Men and women around him died. Shouted. Thrashed on the ground. Got dragged, whimpering, off to the surgeons—when possible. Often you had to keep going while they screamed. If you stopped to help, then the whole city would fall.

So he fought with dying soldiers weeping at his feet, his peg slipping in their blood. Each time one died, the line grew more strained, and the options for filling those gaps more desperate. Fewer soldiers. More untrained townspeople.

The night seemed endless. And Adolin thought, as he moved from station to station—bloodletting with a spear, bloodletting with a pike, lying on the ground and bleeding hope—that he knew what it was like to be dead.

He'd always secretly hated that part of Vorinism, without speaking it aloud—not even to himself. The doctrine that upon death, they all just kept on fighting. Gloriously, the ardents claimed. For eternity.

What an awful existence. He'd tried to picture it as endless duels of honor. Then he had gone to war and he'd seen what fighting was really like. War was being forced to step on another man's entrails, hearing him wail as you pushed them out farther, because you had to keep fighting. War was knowing that the end was here, and there wasn't a storming thing you could do.

Knowing that when you died, the best thing you could hope for was to be shoved back into a line so you could spend eternity being split open time and time again.

On one rest rotation, Adolin lay and stared at the second moon, numb to the passage of time, thinking about that afterlife. And he realized part of why he hated his father—because in Dalinar's book, *Oathbringer,* he offered something better. A different God than the Almighty, a God that he described only as a sense of warmth. A God he claimed made things right eventually.

How dare Dalinar Kholin—who had butchered all his life—be the one to offer such an uplifting message? How dare the Blackthorn, soaked in blood, claim the high ground?

How *dare* he judge Adolin for killing Sadeas and protecting their family, when Dalinar had burned Adolin's mother alive?

Nothing made sense anymore. Adolin felt he was the only one who recognized that the world had gone insane, and when he pointed it out, he was told that he was being spoiled. That he needed to forgive, that he was the problem, and why couldn't he live up to his father's *wonderful* example?

Adolin didn't want to follow an example. He wanted nothing to do with all of this, and he wanted the good men whose names he memorized to stop storming *dying.*

That was what he felt. Fatalism. A desire to simply give up. It was as deadly and pernicious as the terrible void inside the dome, filled with enemies.

The call came for him to rotate back to the front line. As he sat up, someone handed him a spear and shield. Hadn't he just done this? How many rotations had it been? That hadn't been fifteen minutes to rest, had it? How?

He yearned to lie there. They'd let him. He was a highprince. He could have been a king.

But if he did that . . .

If he did that, then he failed Kholinar again. He'd told himself he'd have fought for the city—no, for his men—and stood with them until the end. That he hadn't abandoned his men on purpose. But if he lay here, then he did exactly that, and he became worse than a man who had killed Sadeas. He became a liar and a hypocrite.

So he heaved himself up, found the queue to rotate to the front, and took his spot with shield and spear. Strangely, he found motivation in an unexpected place. Kaladin had survived worse than this as a bridgeman. Adolin had heard Lopen and Rock, Sigzil and Skar, describe it multiple times as they'd gone drinking together.

At least Adolin could fight back. The call came and he filed in, letting those who had been fighting pull the wounded to safety through the center of the pike line. There, Adolin realized he was smiling. Stupid bridgeboy. Where did he get off, being so inspiring?

A moment of brightness. Then back to Damnation.

⁂

Jasnah knelt alone in the little temple.

Fen had left. Odium had evaporated.

They'd made their deal. Thaylenah would serve Odium, regardless of what happened at Dalinar's contest of champions. It . . . was both the wrong and the right decision. Wrong for Roshar. But perhaps right for Thaylenah. Fen had been able to negotiate her own terms, rather than depending on Dalinar.

Yet Jasnah felt revolted. She cradled her stomach, sick. After she had failed so dramatically, the presence of sculpted depictions of Talenelat seemed a deliberate mockery. She'd spent her life spurning the existence of deity—and had now been bested by one.

Storms. She pulled herself to the wall and sat against it, trying to organize her mind. The scholar's duty, to analyze what had gone wrong. It came down to two points. First, she herself had been flawed. She'd grown so engaged by the *argument* she'd forgotten the *context.* She'd wanted to defeat Taravangian with words, but in so doing, had actually *proven* his point to Fen. Jasnah had shown both that he was wrong for Roshar and that it was right for Thaylenah to make a deal with him. The prisoner's dilemma indeed.

The second problem with her arguments was more daunting. The Philosophy of Aspiration, the very philosophy she'd relied on for so many years, had failed her completely. Losing that, realizing that she might have built the bedrock of her life upon a flawed philosophy that even she didn't truly believe, shook her to her core.

The greater good at any cost. If she *wouldn't* pay any cost, then she gave only lip service to the philosophy. If she *would* pay any cost, how was she any better than Taravangian? How many of her actions were truly in service of this idea? The greatest good . . . but how could she claim to know what was right, when she could not see the scope of the cosmere?

Instead, she tried clinging to histories—but she knew they could be incredibly biased. She'd spent her life struggling to sort the fiction from the fact, with varying success. However, all of them had warned of the dangers of dealing with Voidbringers—and thus, in going up against Odium and expecting to win, she had refused to learn from the past. In this, the histories condemned her.

She tried, last of all, to cling to her own mind. She thought. She reasoned. She had to be able to trust her conclusions. Except, huddled here at a midnight desk, she remembered a day when her mind itself had betrayed her—and her family had locked her away. It could do so again.

The room grew darker somehow, despite the night, then a light brightened in the center of the room. She looked up, having crouched by the wall unconsciously remembering those days locked away as a child. She'd cried in a barren corner until her mother had returned—at long last—from her trip and restored the sunlight.

No sunlight shone on her today. This was its mocking doppelganger: the golden glow of Taravangian's vestments.

Jasnah forced herself to stand. She would not stay huddled and broken before him, trapped in memories. She had sworn to herself, with the other Veristitalians, that she would not become so enamored with the past that it dominated her life.

"I thought," she said to Taravangian, wiping her eyes, "that you went with Fen."

"I can do both," he said. "I am God."

"There is no God."

"Even still, you insist?" Taravangian asked, his tone lightly amused. He settled down, and a chair formed from black smoke for him. He put his hand to the side, and his slender golden scepter appeared, letting him balance his hand atop it like a cane. "After what you've seen? After being so *resoundingly* outmatched?"

"If you were God," she said, "you would be all powerful, and would not *need* to outmatch a woman like me. If you were God, then you would know everything, and could speak exactly to me the number I am thinking in my head." She met his gaze.

Negative one point eight seven three nine, she thought.

He merely nodded. As she'd ascertained, he could not read her mind.

"There may not be a God, but there are gods," Jasnah said, "as Wit has defined them: creatures of immense power, immortal and terrible. I accept you are one of those, Taravangian. It is no shame for me to be bested by one who has such capacity."

"Ah, but was it my power that bested you, Jasnah?"

She looked away. Echoes of her failure were too recent. She could not hold his confident, conniving gaze.

"We," he said softly, "*are* the same."

"You caught me in a lie," she said. "So if we are the same, you are a liar too? You never were able to take this city, were you?"

"Ah . . . well, I did lie. But not about that, Jasnah." He waved a hand. Nearby, a dozen dark figures rose from the stone ground, like the souls of the dead. Deepest Ones, with eyes that were too large, bodies too spindly, almost no carapace except where their genitals should have been, the only adornment on their nude bodies save for their long, knifelike fingernails.

"They were poised to kill the members of the Thaylen Council," Taravangian said, "should my negotiation with Fen fail."

"Impossible," Jasnah said. "That room is lined in aluminum and hidden, including from me. We have fabrials to tell if Fused are nearby, and they were deployed to—"

"No such fabrials exist," Taravangian said. "The artifabrians who claimed to have created them serve me, and that was the lie. The fabrials were invented to set you all at ease and allow my Fused to draw near. As for your hidden council? It's in the Loft Ward, behind a wineshop's false wall. At thirty-two Market Street."

Storms. She tried not to be intimidated by the fact that he knew that, but . . .

"I have agents on the Thaylen Council too," Taravangian noted. "Connections that go back to my mortal days, when several of them were part of the Diagram. You and your uncle consistently ignored the council and focused on Fen alone, though she is not an absolute power in this city. Even you, Jasnah, who speak of equality and a representative government, ignored the elected officials today, arguing with me on Fen's behalf only. Yet that council is what you claim to want for your people."

"They're an oligarchy," she said. "Not what I want for Alethkar at all."

"So you focus on the dictator instead?" Taravangian shook his head. "It was an oversight. Admit it. You should have invited them to this meeting."

"It was a mistake," Jasnah whispered, backing up to the wall, watching the Deepest Ones and preparing her Stormlight.

"You needn't worry," Taravangian said, waving for the Fused to vanish into the stones. "My point is, I *did* have a plan for conquering this city. My friends on the council had removed the aluminum paneling in one section. During a recess they would have left, and would have returned to find—as planned—their colleagues murdered. Four would have survived, all loyal to me, and the minimum number required to manage the government."

"Fen could have—"

"Fen would have been arrested," Taravangian snapped. "She has been ignoring the council too much—and there are legitimate worries that she was overstepping her authority. My four would have immediately instigated a tribunal against her, temporarily relieving Fen of power. She'd likely have won the resulting trial, but in the meantime this city would have turned to me."

Taravangian stood, and suddenly seemed *enormous*. Filling the room. Beyond. The walls fading, all other sights vanishing. As if Jasnah was on an endless dark plain, with only the god Taravangian—his face suddenly more skeletal, his eyes recessed, golden light rising around him—standing before her.

"I always had this city in hand," he said. "However, they will be ruled better if they join me willingly. I have them now. More, I have *you,* Jasnah. Finally admitting the truth."

"What truth?" she asked, her voice hoarse.

"That you have *always* been my servant. Everything you've done, from freeing my granddaughter, to your murders on the streets of Kharbranth, to arguing with Dalinar each time he tried to pretend he had a pedestal to stand upon. Each time you hired assassins, or you moved people into position who would do what needed to be done, *you served me.*"

He was suddenly closer. So close to her, all she could see was his terrible face. "I will need someone to rule this planet," he said softly, "as my attention shifts toward the greater cosmere. When you are ready, come to me."

"You can't leave," she snarled. "You are locked here."

"Which is perfect," he whispered. "The other gods will think me contained, and I will have a chance to build up my resources and my infrastructure. There are three habitable planets in this system. If you knew the things I could do with them . . . but that will have to wait. If you wish to see what happens when I launch my full armies in a few centuries, come to me. I will make you Fused, and therefore immortal."

"Never," she hissed.

"Never?" he said. "Still lying, I see. You really think there is *no* chance you will see the value of entering my service?" He somehow loomed even closer. "What is the greater good, Jasnah? Dying in obscurity, or becoming immortal and working for centuries to influence me to treat people better?"

She worked her mouth, but she *could not say the words.* Could not refute him, because one of her cardinal values was that she would *not* lie to herself. She hated that she had to consider the offer, but she *did.* To reject it out of hand would be foolish, and she was . . .

Well, she'd *assumed* she was not a fool.

And so, for the second time in one day, Taravangian left her broken and defeated.

Within the hour, news reached her: the nation had voted—by near-unanimous action of the Thaylen Central Council—to accept Odium's offer, becoming a vassal state directly beneath the god. The motion had been ratified by Queen Fen.

They gave Jasnah a copy of the contract, sealed and signed, as a memento of her failure.

124

REJECTION

TWO THOUSAND YEARS AGO

I, Tanner, betrayed the demigod Mishram.

The plan was executed perfectly. And though my heart broke for the poor spren, this was the only way. It was . . . it was the better way. The power within me trembled. The power of oaths. It seemed to speak. *Please . . . understand . . . I do not want this. We cannot . . .*

It must happen, I explained. *One will suffer, yet a world will live.* I told myself this as the trap was sprung, and Melishi pulled Mishram into a gemstone. Rayse's rival was dealt with—in a careful way. A way that would give me leverage. For if Mishram was trapped, I could threaten to release her.

I thought myself so clever.

I had not anticipated what would happen to the singers on her capture. The tones had chosen her; the planet was aligned with her. Ripping her away had a devastating effect. How had this escaped my foreknowledge?

Even as it happened though, I was forced into another fight. This time with my own power. I braced myself, knowing this might happen, for I had told Mishram I'd choose peace between us. I had led my agents to entice her, and my Radiants had approached her with supposedly honest intentions.

I told myself it was for the greater good. But in that moment, the moment she was captured, the power I held—the power of oaths, bonds, and promises . . .

It rejected me.

My trap's aftereffect upon all the singers was too much for it. It hated what I'd done, and the consequences were too great this time. I resisted. I cajoled. I ordered. I wrestled with the power, insisting that it see the difference between doing good and being honorable. It lashed back against me, for what I'd done was neither.

And . . . the being who had been Tanner . . .

Agreed.

In a flash, I heard Rayse laughing. He saw it too. The very weakness I'd seen in him was now manifest in me. If the power *did* abandon me, it would leave the Radiants and the Heralds without a check against their abilities. They would destroy the world. The Honorblades alone . . .

Rayse would get what he wanted—global annihilation. Removal of his primary rival. I did not know if this had been Rayse's plan all along; he had seemed so genuinely afraid of Mishram taking his place. But either way, I knew that I was bested, and it was only a matter of time—hours at most—until the power left me entirely.

In my agony, I reached out to Kor. From her I felt only revulsion and hate. It echoed not through the singers alone, but through all bonds that had been made in my name. Each and every Radiant was corrupted. My every promise was flawed. I had sought to save the world, but in so doing had ruined it and everything I stood for.

I . . . I showed them. When Radiants touched me in that hollow of stone, I showed them. I showed them *all.* I . . . I knew it was a moment of madness, of terrified weakness. I should never have compounded my mistakes like that. But I did. I projected the future to them. And to them, I did not explain it was only a *possible* future.

They saw the world destroyed at their hands.

Horrified, I fled.

I tried to sweep to our nest, to be with Kor, to beg her forgiveness. The power, however, began to separate from me. I formed as a human again and crashed down from the sky, through a forest of trees with limbs that pulled away from me. I was left lying in the underbrush—but with a hole straight toward the sky, cool moonlight playing on me as I was splayed among the snarls of writhing vines. A fallen god.

The moonlight darkened. Then Rayse was standing next to me.

"Idiot," Rayse said.

I cried out, reaching with trembling hands, trying to cling to my divinity.

"What an embarrassing mix you are, Tanner," Rayse said. "Strong enough to hold the power, but not strong enough to bend it to your will. Smart enough to try to trick me, but stupid enough to be tricked in return."

Rayse drew himself up, then seized me with a hand that carried behind it shadows and stars. I was suddenly so very small.

"Before I kill you," Rayse said, "let me show you the next world I will conquer." Rayse prepared to launch himself into the sky—and beyond. To explore his freedom in the cosmere.

Yet tethers held him down. He could break them, of course, but in so doing would open himself up to destruction.

I laughed with realization. "You think if I am defeated," I whispered, "our agreements don't hold? Rayse, you made a deal with the divine sense of honor and duty. It will not let you go as easily as another might."

"No," Rayse snapped. "It is nothing without a vessel. I just need to crush you, Tanner."

He was wrong. My power was the power of bonds, and it *would* bind him to this system, and our agreement *would* hold, even if he destroyed me.

As he moved to do so, my former power . . . took pity on me. It offered one last hope. It offered to *fight*. Honor hated Odium for wanting to discard oaths so flagrantly. A part of it . . . understood that I had been trying. It would Invest me again if I agreed to fight, something my agreement with Rayse would allow. He simply could not attack first.

That would destroy Roshar. In that moment, I understood the depths of our stupidity—for in shattering Adonalsium, we had removed the divine sense of love and compassion from the other Shards. That one had gone to Aona, among the best of us, and therefore among the first Rayse had sought out to kill.

The power of Honor knew only one good: keeping oaths.

I knew other goods.

I had promised to protect Roshar.

This sent a shudder through the power. A confusion. A conundrum. I could have taken it up to fight, but in a moment where I was truly strong, I *refused*. For once in my life, I turned away, and did not make things worse.

But still I did not want to die. *Protect me,* I begged.

A piece of you. The power took a portion of my soul, including my memories, and fled.

Odium destroyed the rest with glee. Killing, at long last, his rival.

But the power gave this remnant of me to my avatar in the

storm—to the spren I had created as a true part of my soul. I died, yes, yet at the same time I lived on.

I was now more spren than man. I did not care as much as Tanavast had—for why should a storm care? It could only blow. But secretly I carried a greater truth, and it kept me from being like any other spren. I, in one form, had been there. I knew the burden of terrible loss.

For I, the Stormfather, remembered.

The corpse of a child held in my arms, broken and burned. Dead cities. A world that had spent thousands of years in an endless war to fuel my promise to best Odium. Last of all, a betrayal of all that I stood for. The breaking of Radiants, and of Honor itself, through the imprisonment of a spren who was seeking peace.

Wounded, weeping tears of rage with each passing year, I rode the storm. And the power of Honor whispered to me. It was free, but it hated this. It wanted a Vessel. Together, we resolved upon a plan. Tanavast *had* been too weak to hold the Shard, but surely there was one who *could* hold it. Could protect Roshar. Could end Rayse.

It would have to be the perfect individual. Honorable, but also merciful. A warrior, but also a leader. Most importantly, they could not be like those of us who had destroyed Adonalsium. I couldn't have someone who *wanted* the power. It had to be someone who proved themselves *without* knowing their reward.

The power agreed. I, the Stormfather, would find a champion. Someone who would defeat Rayse through the contest that he had, before killing Tanavast, agreed to. If this champion saved Roshar, that would prove they were worthy. Honor would Invest them.

They could become my successor.

Never assume the game actually replicates real life.

—*Proverbs for Towers and War,* Zenaz, date unknown

Navani sat with Wit, long after sundown. The dawning of the tenth day was approaching. Dalinar was still trapped in the Spiritual Realm.

And Wit thought they shouldn't do anything.

"If Odium was interfering with your visions," Wit said, leaning forward as he sat on his couch, hands clasped before him, "then he likely was with Dalinar's as well. In fact, we can be certain he is interfering right now. *He* was the reason you lost contact with one another."

"How can you be *sure* it counts, Wit?" Navani asked, pacing. "Frankly, you've been wrong about this contract before."

News from the battlefronts was eminently discouraging. Even if they did win back Alethkar, they'd end up losing far more. She couldn't . . . couldn't *honestly* say she wouldn't make that trade, considering how many of the other monarchs had given in to Odium's demands. As long as she had Jasnah, as long as Adolin and Renarin survived . . .

"I can't be sure I'm right," Wit admitted. "But while you were checking on Gavinor I asked my contact on Yolen for her read, and she agrees. Odium severing your Connection to Dalinar, isolating the two of you, would count as interfering with Dalinar's reaching the meeting on time. The contract *explicitly* indicates this would mean a forfeit."

"So if Dalinar *doesn't* make it," Navani said, "we win?"

"Yes."

"So either Odium has to make absolutely certain Dalinar arrives, or . . ."

"Or . . ." Wit continued, grim. "Or Odium thinks what he's gaining in playing with Dalinar is worth the price of forfeiting Alethkar."

That possibility horrified her.

They were the only people in the room. There were no other monarchs to look to for support. Fen had betrayed them, as had the Emuli and the others in the once-unified Azish empire. Yanagawn fought alongside Adolin in a city on the verge of falling, and Jasnah was still in Thaylen City. Her terseness about when she'd return indicated she was taking her failure poorly.

For now, Navani was alone. She and Wit. She . . . was so very tired. Exhausted, though she'd banished those spren from buzzing around her. It felt as if she hadn't slept in days, and given the strange nature of the Spiritual Realm, she wasn't certain that she *had.*

"I think Odium will be sure Dalinar returns," he said. "Considering who he once was."

"Excuse me?" she asked, fingers at her temples, trying to massage away a headache.

"Ah, right. You wouldn't know," Wit said. "Odium's new Vessel is Taravangian."

Sleep fled.

Navani stood bolt upright. "Taravangian is dead. We found his body."

"*A* body," Wit said, "nearly completely consumed by Nightblood. A husk that could have been anyone. In this case, it was almost certainly what remained of my old friend Rayse."

Navani tried to sort through the implications. "Is this . . . good for us? Taravangian was . . . almost a friend."

Wit looked away.

"No," Navani whispered. "An almost-friend knows us too well. Plus, Taravangian has already proven that he cares nothing for such bonds."

"He cares, and that makes him dangerous," Wit said. "Navani, Rayse was a horrible human being. One of the worst I've ever known. But he was predictable, savage, with an extreme sense of self-preservation and a pride that was easy to exploit. Taravangian is . . ."

"A catastrophe."

"I cannot think of a better, or worse, vessel for Odium. Rayse had experience with the power, which is our only advantage in swapping him for Taravangian. But I fear that in the long run, this . . . this is very, very bad."

"He won't just want to defeat Dalinar," Navani said. "He'll want to *break* him."

"We've trapped Odium, one way or another, on Roshar," Wit said. "For Rayse, this was an indignity. For Taravangian, this will give him time to get used to his powers. He likely doesn't *want* to go out into the cosmere yet; he'll certainly want a powerful general to do that for him. A . . . near friend.

"I'd hazard Taravangian cares little for Alethkar . . . but the soul of your husband, that is his true prize. Dalinar needs to be there so Taravangian can win his oath to follow. I wouldn't worry about Dalinar returning from the Spiritual Realm, Navani. I would worry about which *version* of him will return."

Navani took that as calmly as she could, and tried to consider this like a scholar, despite her fatigue. "If what you say is true, then we should try even *harder* to find Dalinar."

"That's the problem, Navani," Wit said. "If Odium is taking an active role, risking a loss by forfeit, then you and I are completely out of our depth. Compared to the might of a Shard of Adonalsium, whatever tricks I might know . . . well, they're like sparks before the power of the sun. There is nothing you, I, the Stormfather, or the Sibling can do."

"So . . ."

"So we wait," Wit said, his eyes seeming hollow. "You should pray. I will wish. Together we will hope that the man we have all chosen as our champion can resist whoever Odium chooses to be his. Because whatever happens tomorrow, I think that secretly, Dalinar Kholin is *both* champions."

⁂

Adolin remembered the Battle of the Tower on the Shattered Plains.

He fought the endless waves of singers, ramming his spear into darkness broken by faded stars and red embers. He used his shield as best he could to protect the man to his left, counting on the man—or actually woman—to his right to do the same for him. He tried to give space for the pikes to reach across his shoulders—but those dwindled as people were pulled to fill holes in the shield line.

He pushed through fatigue and terror, past fatalism into numbness. And he remembered the Tower. Fighting, hopeless, along with his father atop a natural rock wedge, knowing there was no salvation. He'd been wrong then, because of the valor of Bridge Four. Today, no one was coming.

His was a numbness of four levels. Numbness of ear, as he turned off the part of him that empathized with the screaming of his fellows as they died. Numbness of mind, as he just kept doing what he was doing, muscle memory now completely dominant. Numbness of body, as he felt less like a man and more like meat Soulcast into a man's shape. Thrusting his spear and holding his shield with limbs that could not be his, because they were too sluggish, too heavy, too dead. As if they had already climbed onto the pyre ahead of him.

Numbness of soul. Storms. He needed a break. He looked to the sides and found he *could* still feel something: a chill, followed by a terrible sense of dread.

There were no more soldiers waiting to fill the line. No replacements coming. No more pikes at his back. Every available soldier was plugging this hole, or others.

There would be no more breaks. No more rotations. No more rest. Until he fell.

Last moon was setting.

He knew that because he could see it on the other side of the dome. The large gap they held let him see in, but across the way—hundreds of yards in the distance—the catwalk doors inside the dome were open. Here, the enemy fought against frantic defenders on the narrow, elevated ledge outside. Their defense must have been as terrible as his.

Regardless, the gaps let him see straight out at the moon, green and solemn. A figure stepped in front of the moon—holding a brilliant Shardblade. The last human Shardbearer.

He defended alone, unsupported, a silhouette holding firm. In his numbness, Adolin imagined it was him fighting gloriously. It was his Plate, and that sealed the illusion in Adolin's mind. Never in a battle even close to as bad as this one had he been without his armor. He couldn't be this wretch on the ground with a spear he could hardly grip.

Then the Shardbearer fell. Surrounded, overwhelmed, pulled into the darkness of the dome. That man who should have been Adolin—he didn't know which armor standby bore the Plate and Blade—could not fight them all. Adolin's shout was lost in the cacophony of battle, then he slipped on his peg. In that moment, Adolin remembered he wasn't a shining hero. Today he was a crippled spearman with barely enough strength to lift his shield.

Cheering sounded inside the dome. It was hundreds of yards across, so Adolin couldn't see the details—and he had to focus on his own fight. But that cheering became chants, deliberately in Azish. "The last human falls. The Shards are ours. The last human falls. The Shards are ours!"

The sound shook Adolin straight to his heart. Around him, his line buckled further.

"Hold!" he shouted. But no one was listening. "Hold!"

He gripped his shield and used his spear less as a weapon, more as a way to try to push back the tide. He screamed and no one replied. Across the dome, red eyes flooded out through the gap the Shardbearer had been holding.

This time no one stopped them.

Adolin continued to fight. Holding the gap for another eternity, screaming at his soldiers to hold. Until at long last, the enemy ranks in front of him parted—and a figure stepped to their forefront. Red eyes shining through the eye slits of a helm covered in blood. Familiar, terrible laughter. Glistening Shardplate—Adolin's. And a Blade that had once been an imperial Azish heirloom.

Abidi the Monarch had Shards now.

The beleaguered shield line shattered around Adolin. The general inside him was surprised they'd held so long—far past what a game of towers said they would. He could not feel angry at them, but in their haste, a faceless soldier shoved him. Adolin tried to turn and stabilize himself, but tripped on his bad leg and went down.

The floodgates opened. Singer ranks gushed from the wound in the dome, some trampling across him, their officers yelling in Azish for them to press the advance, cut down the stragglers, eliminate defenses.

Adolin curled up, and thought to hide among the dead. It was dark. They might not think to send someone to check the fallen. It happened. Lying there would be smart.

He didn't feel smart. He suddenly felt *angry.* Because nothing seemed to have a point. He'd loved his father, supported him against the tide of betrayal in Alethkar, only to learn Dalinar had *killed* Adolin's mother.

Adolin had stood trial for all of humankind at Lasting Integrity. For what? No help, no answers. Moral victories didn't matter when cities fell anyway. He'd always tried to fight for his kingdom and his family, while others played games and murdered in the night—but when *he* stood up for those *he* loved, *he* became a villain? For killing a man who had tried to do the same to him?

Finally, at long last, he acknowledged it. The cloud that had been chasing him for so many months.

If Adolin couldn't trust his father . . .

What . . . what *could* he trust in?

If Dalinar Kholin wasn't worthy of Adolin's reverence, where was the sense in any of this? Maybe there wasn't any. Maybe it didn't *mean* anything.

Maybe nothing did.

He shouted and heaved himself up, no longer numb, but alive with a cold sense of fury. Surrounded by figures moving in the darkness—who at first didn't realize he wasn't one of them—Adolin yanked the release cord on his back and pulled off his longsword. He grabbed it and flung the sheath away into the night, his shield lost, common helmet and breastplate biting into his skin. He forced his peg backward into a hole between two cobbles, bracing it, and put two hands on the hilt of his sword. Shallan had given him this one, for their wedding.

On this terrible night, chaos flowing around him, Adolin became the stone. The man who would not back down. The man who would hold his ground.

Because in the past, the world had always started making sense again when he stood with sword in hand.

He began to fight. One man against a tide of glowing gemstones in beards or on clothing for the femalens. He attacked the first one that recognized him. She turned to raise an axe, and Adolin expertly batted the weapon aside, then rammed his sword straight into her eye. As that one fell, he swung at the next, separating arm from body.

A sword was not commonly the best weapon for this kind of fighting—better an axe or mace against carapace. However, if the sword was part of you, that changed—because singers tended to rely on their carapace. To expect it would protect them—when in reality it had plenty of chinks, plenty of holes.

Adolin did not dance. A duel was a dance. This was not something beautiful, and he was no poet. This was a man, a fallen city, and anger culminating in blood to spill. First theirs, then his.

For he knew this was the night he'd die. At least he could go down fighting.

Adolin . . . Maya.

No. He did not summon her.

Why?

He did not want her to see him fall. The city was lost, and he . . . he felt ashamed.

No shame in loss . . . she whispered.

I failed Kholinar.

Never shame in loss . . .

I failed you. Father. Everyone.

Never. I AM COMING.

He ignored her and kept fighting. He brought down eight singers before one landed a real hit on him, a spear to the back of his good leg, right through the opening of the greave. His calf burned with pain as he grunted and spun on his peg, slapping away the spear and then driving his sword through the neck of the singer. He kept swinging, but Adolin was a lone ship on this dark sea, surrounded by enemies. Another slammed an axe into his side, and he knew that was the blow that would do it. Numb though his body was to pain, he had fought enough to recognize that sensation of blood saturating armor, warming his skin.

Another swept that cursed peg out from under him, and he went down, wedding sword clanging from his numb fingers, lost into the night. And as he lay there, he was still angry. Because for the first time in his life, the sword hadn't brought him peace or answers.

He couldn't trust in his father any longer. But as a singer stood above him—with halberd raised to ram down—Adolin found he wanted to.

He *wanted* to find a way to love his father again. He *wanted* to make peace. He wanted a chance.

"Not yet!" he screamed. "Not until I see him again!" He kicked the singer in the knee with his peg. She stumbled.

Then an arrow took her in the eye.

A flood of arrows followed, forcing enemies nearby to fall back. Adolin twisted, seeing a small enclave of defenders with archers at the front. The singers . . . the battle lines had fallen and they didn't have enough discipline . . . which hurt them here . . . They could make a powerful, mad rush, but reorienting to an enemy position was . . .

Storms, it was hard to think . . .

"There!" Colot's voice said as he dashed from among May and her archers. "I've found him."

"Leave me," Adolin croaked, numb.

"Can you stand?" Colot asked, reaching him.

"Leave me."

"Storm that," Colot said.

"Leave—"

"Look," Colot said, leaning down and looming large in the night. "You see that man holding a lantern near May? That's the storming *emperor.* He refused to leave until we came for you. May, fortunately, saw you in the line earlier. You hear me, Adolin? Yanagawn *will not leave* until *you are with us.* So get to your storming feet, or let that boy die."

They locked eyes, and storm him, Colot was right. And storm it, Adolin *needed* to see his father at least one more time. He let Colot help him stand. A moment later Hmask was there under his other arm. They stumbled away from the dome and met up with Yanagawn amid his soldiers. Would they suffer Gezamal's fate for letting the emperor put himself in danger? The idea made Adolin, groggy, chuckle. How many latrine attendants did they need in the fallen city?

Because it *had* fallen. Adolin paused to look it over, held upright by his friends, and saw enemy soldiers in every direction. They didn't set the city on fire, the way human conquerors would have. They wanted to rule, and some of the singers fighting to claim Azimir had lived here as parshmen. It was their home.

The group decided to head for the saferoom beneath the hospital. There was no escaping the city like this. But maybe later, somehow, they could slip away.

In the chaos, they managed to make it to the building complex. They picked up some enemies—singer officers who were able to get some troops to give chase. Fortunately, the defenders had a protocol for this. Adolin and the emperor were shut in a room with a few defenders while others made it seem like they had all escaped through the back doors.

After that, it was a quick run—well, a limping, exhausted, beleaguered trot—through several buildings all built against one another, until they reached the saferoom door. Adolin suffered it in a daze, and didn't fully come alert until coldness washed through him.

He blinked, and found himself on the floor of the saferoom, bloodied, with Rahel the teenage Truthwatcher kneeling beside him. He noted others there: the emperor, some soldiers, many of the wounded who had been moved into this bunker instead of left in the hospital.

How . . . how much time had he lost? He groaned, lying there, as the healing hadn't done anything for his fatigue. At least the numbness was returning. The numbness of utter loss. He saw it in the faces of everyone down here with him: Colot, May, Yanagawn—even Kushkam, who was nursing a wound of his own, his face bloodied, barely healed as they could spare Regrowth for only the worst cases.

Adolin was glad to see the other general, but the look they shared was demoralizing.

The city had fallen. And with it the empire.

Azir was no more.

THE END OF

Day Nine

INTERLUDES

DIENO • ODIUM

Dieno, the Mink, did not think highly of the means by which he was to be executed.

"Surely," he said, hands tied behind his back as he lay with his head against the headsman's block, "you can think of something *better* than *this*."

Like most of the soldiers in the courtyard below, the judiciary who led the execution was Herdazian. She wore a robe that tied to one shoulder, with singer markings on it, and was accompanied by a squad of bulky warforms. Dieno had seen this multiple times: a conqueror often put some enterprising local in charge. It let the people pretend they had some semblance of self-rule. All you needed was a traitor or two.

"Tie me to a boulder and launch me into the ocean with a catapult," Dieno said, his face pressed against the wood. "Now *that* would be something. If you're feeling spicy, you could throw me from a tower and see how many archers could hit me before I land. Good target practice, that."

The judiciary actually paused, seeming to consider, before one of the singer minders shoved her on the shoulder. So she continued reading Dieno's crimes.

A beheading? Really? What an indignity. Dieno sighed, glad his crimes had been so exhaustive, as it gave him time to plan. There was always a way out.

Though . . . this situation was looking rough.

He'd had the Windrunners land his people a couple days' march from the Herdazian capital. Getting too close would have put everyone on alert. After that, he'd led his troops through a series of caves he'd played in as a child, ones that traveled underground and came up close to the city.

It had been a brilliant plan. He'd been quite proud of it. It would have been wonderful if they hadn't run into a series of cave-ins.

In the years since he'd played here, the caves had become unstable.

Everstorm, likely. He hadn't accounted for that, and his troops had been literally stonewalled three times trying to navigate the caverns. Eventually they'd been forced to come out and cross an open field of stone.

The moon had emerged at just the wrong moment. It seemed fate itself had turned on him. An entire army had mobilized against them—and what had been planned as a glorious rescue had ended last night. He hadn't even reached the city.

They'd brought his troops and him to an outpost by the ocean, well away from the capital. Herdaz was not going to be saved by him; he'd have to hope for Dalinar and his contest. Dieno himself might not even see the hour arrive, unless . . .

"Hey," he shouted, "could you at least use a mallet?"

They paused again.

"A . . . mallet?" the judiciary asked.

"Sure. Smash my head," Dieno said. "Instead of just cut it off. All these people came to watch. You need to give them something worth witnessing."

"A mallet would be incredibly painful," the judiciary said.

"But a better *story,*" Dieno said. "Come on. I'm a legend. You can't have a legend dying by a mere beheading, can you? Singers. You talk about passion and song. Well, we need a better song today if Dieno the Mink is going to die."

Their humming changed. Mention passion, and it sometimes worked for them.

"Do we . . . have a mallet?" the judiciary asked.

There. The headsman looked away from Dieno to reply. *There.* Shouldn't have taken his eyes off his charge.

"I don't have one," the headsman said. "But—"

Dieno slipped the ropes from his wrists with a couple of quick contortions. A second later, he yanked the chain around his neck—in the hands of a headsman's assistant—and threw the boy off balance. Dieno hit him a second later, shoving him from the execution platform.

The crowd cheered, which shocked those on the podium. Yes, the audience of gathered soldiers were ostensibly on their side—Herdazians and singers who served the invaders. But Dieno was certain every person had come expecting to have a story to tell at the end. He would see them have a proper finale, one way or another.

The Mink would not fall to a headsman. Indeed, the man lifted his axe and swung, but Dieno was yanked out of the way—and completely off the execution platform—by the falling man who still held his chain. Dieno came down on top of the youth, heard something crack in his chest, and bounced free.

 Dieno patted him on the cheek. "Broken ribs. Three months' bed rest, lad. Spend it thinking about how you've chosen to side with the enemy." He pulled the chain free of the groaning youth's hands, then swung it up and used it to block the attack of the singer guards charging for him.

He escaped under the wooden platform itself. It had been erected to give the courtyard a good view of his death, but the narrow confines of the wooden beams down here blocked the warforms in their bulky, unremovable armor, while Dieno . . . well, he could get through almost any gap.

Chaos and shouting followed him as he slipped out near some steps up onto the fort's wall. Other exits were blocked, but perhaps he could find a way to hop off it to safety. He reached the top, but found soldiers on every side, advancing. He looked across the ocean, shrouded in mist, the moon rising on the last evening before the contest.

There was no place to jump. He was trapped at last. Dieno steeled himself, hoping they had their bows ready to give it a good show, and climbed onto the top of the battlement. It was fifty feet to the stones below. Escaping today had been a frail hope anyway. You couldn't stay ahead of the wind forever. Not even someone like him. He'd given Herdaz his all, but how many times could your heart break for a kingdom before your soul bled out? He quietly acknowledged that he'd done all he could, then prepared to jump.

A thumping shook the ground and made him pause. Behind, guards and soldiers reaching to seize him stopped short. The wall trembled, the ground boomed.

A greatshell the size of a city emerged from the darkened fog, big enough to tower over the entire fort.

"Well now," Dieno said. "*That's* a finale."

I-18

CONFLUX

Could he destroy the power of Honor?

Odium considered this, perhaps too long. The power was protecting Dalinar. If he attacked it, he might be able to get at his friend. A smaller part of him dealt with other rats in the walls, keeping them occupied—trying to break them—though he could not spare them much attention.

He watched the permutations, and found them clouded. He couldn't completely destroy the power of Honor, as power could not be destroyed, but there were options. His predecessor had done it several ways. First, by imprisoning the power of two Shards in the Cognitive Realm, which had proved cataclysmic and made it very difficult to access the land. Then by attacking a Shard outright, an action which had left him wounded and had—in the clash—destroyed planets.

Odium thought *maybe* he could Splinter this power, spreading it out, preventing it from congealing into something that could resist him. It was something his predecessor had avoided, however, because of the threat to himself. To clash with Honor's power would violate his oath not to strike first against the other Shard, and would leave him vulnerable to an assault from Cultivation.

Odium could not conquer the cosmere if he died. So, he did not attack the power of Honor, though his own power *raged* at this decision. It wanted a conflict; it wanted to finally be free. Odium had to work carefully, feeding it other emotions, to keep it placated. He was doing that, and weighing his next step, when Honor spat Dalinar out again.

Odium's old friend returned—emerging straight into the Physical Realm.

Relief. Overwhelming *relief.* If Dalinar had not made it back, it might have been considered Odium's fault. Instead, the time arrived as planned, and Dalinar with it.

Odium gave himself a moment of peace. He felt Roshar and its rhythms, and vibrated with them. He felt the singers, so long abused, and gloried in the idea of bringing due vengeance. As his soul vibrated with this . . .

The power of Honor vibrated along.

In this one thing, Honor and Odium were aligned. These people deserved more. Odium accepted the burden of not just using them, but caring for them. In this, he was better than he thought himself capable of being—for he legitimately began to care for them, as he had for Kharbranth.

There were so many across the cosmere similarly abused. It was the conflux of all Shards to want to help them. He spent an extended moment letting himself revel in the idea.

Peace. A lack of pain. A universe united.

One God.

Him. For, if you wanted to see that things turned out correctly, you *had* to do it yourself. Taravangian, as Odium, would rule all—and all would recognize what he had done in their name.

It was time.

DAY
TEN

DALINAR • ADOLIN • SZETH •
KALADIN • SHALLAN • NAVANI •
RENARIN • RLAIN • YANAGAWN •
MRAIZE • VENLI • NALE •
SYLPHRENA • TARAVANGIAN •
SIGZIL • JASNAH • WIT

The Wind was not there for the contest of champions, the final confrontation between Odium and the mortals who would oppose him. She felt ostracized from that world, where it was Storms—and not Wind—who drew attention.

—From *Knights of Wind and Truth*, page 18

Dalinar held to the Stormfather as the visions faded—a dead god's voice booming in his ears. Dalinar got the sense that was how Tanavast had lived and perceived the world, narrating it to himself in that deific tone.

After Tanavast's betrayal of Mishram, and his loss of the Shard of Honor, the Stormfather showed Dalinar quick glimpses of the next two thousand years. Spent riding the storms, having trouble at times remembering the world of men, what was god and what was spren mingling. Dalinar still wasn't certain of the distinction, but the Stormfather clearly knew and remembered far more than he'd ever been willing to tell Dalinar. He wasn't Tanavast . . . but a piece of him *had* been Tanavast.

He'd lurked in the sky, and had quietly begun showing men visions, telling them he wanted a champion in order to test their worthiness. The goal was the same each time: find someone who could persuade Odium into a contest for the fate of Roshar. In each case, the Stormfather had rejected the candidate. Each choice grew too haughty, too eager for immortality or power. The Stormfather feared each would eventually go to war with Odium and destroy the world.

Last of all, he showed Gavilar. Dalinar watched with a sinking feeling. He'd tried so hard to pretend he didn't hear the way Navani spoke of Gavilar, the way the Stormfather referenced him. The way the facts of Gavilar's life hadn't added up to the sum Dalinar had always imagined.

It was a final daunting revelation. More personal. Equally terrible. Gavilar Kholin had brought about his own demise.

"I can't trust someone who *wants* the power, Dalinar," the Stormfather said through tears, his frail, emaciated form held in Dalinar's arms. "Whoever takes the power *could* attack Odium, which is what our enemy ultimately wants, as it would free his anger to destroy. I need someone who has held power and not become a tyrant."

Forced to shake off the revelation of his brother's true nature, Dalinar picked apart the unspoken part of the Stormfather's words. The power of Honor, if given the choice, would circumvent the contest of champions—then destroy the planet.

"That's why you're wrong too," the Stormfather mumbled. "The real Tanavast might have done better than I have in picking. I don't think enough like a man. I clearly never should have chosen you, but the wounds you bore . . ."

"They mirror your own," Dalinar whispered. "Those of a god who failed." He felt the weight of his own failures. The corpses he had created. The people he had let down.

He'd always stubbornly insisted he was right. Momentum. His life had been about momentum. Problem was, it was all too easy to gather momentum in the wrong direction, and it became harder and harder to change course.

"I kept hope," the Stormfather said, "that he could be defeated by a champion . . ."

"I don't share that hope," Dalinar said. "He was able to outmaneuver Tanavast, who knew him well. A simple man like me could never manage it. That's why I decided I needed the power of a god."

"It . . ." the Stormfather muttered, a rumble to his voice. "It almost worked, Dalinar. He agreed to the contest! But it favors him too much. It was our best chance! Only . . . only a part of me, which was Tanavast, worries you are right. A fool. Men have had a fool for a god for so very long . . ."

"No," Dalinar said. "We've done the greater good here. Whatever happens at the contest, Odium remains locked away—and cannot go into the cosmere to destroy. That was Tanavast's goal, and Wit's goal."

"It was . . . wasn't it?" the Stormfather said, blinking. "I . . . I did manage that. I have not failed completely in my charge."

Unfortunately, Roshar would continue to suffer. Thousands of years of war, engaged in proxy battles, as Odium trained armies on Roshar—hoping for some way to someday escape. How much sorrow had been perpetuated here, to protect people and worlds Dalinar had never seen?

Dalinar stood, within the current vision of a small, dark monastery chamber for the mentally troubled. The Stormfather sat up in the corner, and seemed more . . . himself, now that he'd shown Dalinar his burdens. His clothing cleaner, his features puffing out, his beard becoming more full. He had similar features to Tanavast, but was less lean, with stronger eyebrows, a more prominent nose. Brothers, not identical twins.

"So what do we do?" Dalinar said. "Yes, he's trapped on this world—but that's not an ultimate solution. Tanavast's visions prove that throughout history, people—human, Herald, god—have *avoided* dealing with Odium. They kicked the problem to the next generation. Each Desolation, merely stalling. Other deities out in the sky somewhere, content to let him remain someone else's duty. Even Tanavast's final confrontation, where he fled and gave his memories to you, pushed the problem off to someone else.

"My contract threatens to do the same. Peace on Roshar, until he provokes a war by making *us* attack *him.* He used the same tactic again—a promise *he* would not attack, which left his opponent free to strike. Because it lets others break their oaths, and protects him from repercussions."

"It will happen," the Stormfather agreed, his rumbling voice becoming more familiar and stormlike. "Tanavast's peace is a sham, Dalinar. When Odium wishes to conquer this land, he will find a way to provoke your coalition to attack him, giving justification for war."

"He can't be merely locked away or appeased," Dalinar whispered. "Someone has to destroy him."

"You cannot fight!" the Stormfather said, his voice rumbling louder now. "Dalinar, you—"

"I know," he said. "Peace. I know." Still . . .

Blood of my fathers, Dalinar thought, pacing in the small room. *How do you defeat someone too powerful to fight, yet too crafty and dangerous to lock away?*

"I *have* to win this contest," Dalinar said. "Yet I feel that no matter what I do, he'll play me for one of the ten fools." He stopped pacing and looked at the Stormfather. "The power is here? This place? The visions?"

"Yes," the Stormfather said. "Here and everywhere. It watches us, trying to understand us. Different from other similar powers, as it has been *alone* for thousands of years. It grows more self-aware, as I did in the storm, and it studies humankind. It's also the very substance of these walls, this ground, this sky."

Dalinar considered, then resumed his pacing.

"Dalinar," the Stormfather said, "holding the power will not let you win. That cannot beat Odium."

"Then what *will*?" Dalinar said, frustrated. "You led me to this, when all the while you *could* have been giving me guidance!"

"I tried."

"Lies."

"Dalinar," the Stormfather said. "Dalinar, please look at me."

He reluctantly turned to face the being in the corner, who had stood up. So small, when Dalinar was used to him being as wide as the sky.

"You have changed me, over the time we spent together," the Stormfather said. "For the better. I lived as that storm for so long, my soul shaped by the prayers of the humans beneath. I forgot what it was to be alive, and you reminded me, sometimes through force. Because of you, I remember and understand Tanavast's mercy and pity. I recognize the need to change, and . . . I find myself not so bitter about what Tanavast did at the end. Ultimately, I am as you've known me. Not a friend perhaps, but a companion."

Dalinar nodded. He then held his hands to the sides and tried to accept the power of Honor. He *could* feel it, watching.

It rejected him. *No. Humans break oaths.*

Dalinar sighed, opening his eyes. At least he had more information now. In his younger years all he'd wanted to do was march onto a battlefield and find an opponent, but he'd come to realize the essential military value of a little knowledge. Wars were won not by hotheads with swords, but by cool minds who could position those hotheads.

Dalinar had context for his clash with Odium. He'd seen the creature's history, and knew how he thought. Except there was a wrinkle.

"Odium is not Rayse any longer," Dalinar said. "Taravangian took his place."

"I fear the power, Dalinar, more than Taravangian. I fear Honor as well. These powers were not meant to be held in isolation—each of them is warped or distorted without the others." The Stormfather moved closer. "I find myself glad it is you going to this conflict, Dalinar."

"Why?" Dalinar asked, his hands spread. "I am no better than Tanavast. I burned cities, I murdered."

"Perhaps," the Stormfather said. "But you took the next step, Dalinar, when I hid." His eyes became distant. "I hid. I wept. I pretended I didn't care, because that was the path that seemed the least painful . . ."

This creature. Dalinar took a deep breath and tried to contain his frustration. All this time, he'd been bonded to someone who could have explained the truth. But . . . storms. If Evi could forgive Dalinar . . .

"I forgive you," Dalinar forced himself to say.

The Stormfather looked at him.

"You have always been clear with me on one point," Dalinar said. "You are a storm, not a human, and even with a piece of Tanavast in you . . . it is unreasonable for me to expect you to act as a human being would. You tried.

And that piece of you that is Tanavast? Well, many would have burned this planet down in order to prove themselves right. He ran, but I've known plenty of soldiers who lacked the bravery to run when they should have. So I forgive you, and I forgive Tanavast. I'm just one person, and I can't absolve you of anything . . . but I can forgive you. Come, let's find Navani and Gav, then get back." He hesitated. "Unless . . ."

"There is time," the Stormfather said. "Some little remains before your contest. But Dalinar . . . do you mean what you said? You forgive me?"

"I'm trying," Dalinar said, as honestly as he could. "Can we leave, please? I've seen enough."

"I shall send you out."

"Navani first," Dalinar said. "And Gav."

"They are home already. Navani brought them by using her bond to the Sibling. But . . . your son is here, and the Lightweaver, along with one singer."

"Adolin?"

"The other. The one who sees."

"Renarin and Shallan," he said with surprise. "Take me to them."

"They hide from gods," the Stormfather said. "Odium cannot find them, and so I have no hope of doing so. They came by choice, I think."

Dalinar considered. "Send me back. Once I've done what I need to, I'll find a way to get them out."

A portal of light opened. Dalinar stepped through it, and walked at long last from memory into the present.

⁘

"The Shattered Plains have fallen to the enemy," Kaminah the scribe said quietly, reading from her spanreed conversation. "And Thaylenah has signed a deal with Odium, as Emul and the others did."

The small group of officers at one corner of the packed saferoom all grew silent. Adolin hung his head, sitting on the floor, his back to the wall. He felt like a leaf after the highstorm was finished with it, every muscle sore, head pounding, leg—the missing one—aching enough to draw a somewhat confused-looking painspren.

If the Shattered Plains—where they'd stationed most of their Radiants—was unable to stand . . . what chance had Azir ever had?

"Traitors," Noura spat, sitting beside Adolin. "We bled and died on Emuli and Thaylen stone. And they just *make a deal*? Betraying us?"

"We dominated Emul for centuries," Yanagawn said, so out of place in his ornate robes among all of them who were—save the few viziers and scions—bloodied, exhausted, beaten down. "We continuously claimed imperial authority over them, forced them to playact being part of our empire. You are surprised they now take the chance to be rid of us?"

"They serve the enemy!"

"They trade one tyrant for another," Yanagawn said. He seemed swallowed in his finery, his eyes haunted—and he sounded as exhausted as Adolin felt. "Maybe Odium gave them better terms than we did. Who knows? I wish them the best. Resisting didn't help us—and now we are dominated without having a deal in place to protect our people."

The group fell still. Again. Silence had come in fits and waves, like moonlight on a cloudy night, since the city's fall a few hours ago. Adolin needed sleep, yet his mind wouldn't stop racing. For the second time he'd watched a city fall, with his greatest efforts proving useless.

Being the Blackthorn's son hadn't been enough. Being Adolin hadn't been enough. What was left?

He clung to one shred of light. When as he'd been about to die, he'd realized he needed to make peace with his father, needed to believe such a reconciliation was possible.

He was so tired. So worn. So broken. Yet something within him felt . . . like a sword on an anvil.

If Dalinar Kholin of all people could find forgiveness and hope . . . can't I do so as well?

"Windrunners will be here soon," May said from where she sat, quietly writing on scraps of paper—drawing out towers pieces for the emperor, who had mentioned he wished they had a deck to pass the time. "The squire I'm writing to says they've landed outside the city. They'll wait for things to die down, then sneak in and find us. Notum has already met up with them."

"How many Windrunners?" Kushkam said.

"Two full ones, a handful of squires," May said.

"Time?" Adolin said, his voice hoarse.

Noura checked her pocket fabrial watch. "Three hours until your father's deadline."

"What if we do something?" Yanagawn asked. They'd given him a pillow, the only "furniture" in the room. He perched atop it like a chicken on her nest in one of the picture books from Adolin's youth.

"Do something?" Noura asked. "Like what, Majesty?"

He sighed and took off his massive headpiece to wipe his brow. He seemed so young, so small without it. "We have three hours, Noura. We could . . . I don't know. Gather what we have left, try to fight?"

Adolin scanned the room, taking stock. Kushkam, who was missing three fingers on one hand now, and had a cut across his face that had barely scabbed over. Adolin, in the shape *he* was in. Gezamal had survived and was here. He'd reportedly been the one who got his father to safety. He looked relatively unscathed.

Add to them a handful of the emperor's guards, Colot, May, and a few of Adolin's men including Hmask. The other wounded—maybe thirty—who they'd moved here were in even *worse* shape than Adolin. None of them could stand, let alone mount a resistance.

Someone had to say it. Someone Yanagawn would listen to.

"There's nothing we can do, Majesty," Adolin said softly. "I'm sorry."

Yanagawn looked down, huddling in his robes.

One of Colot's guards stepped up—Sarqqin, the Azish blacksmith who had joined their ranks during Adolin's first recruitment. "I've done a survey of our supplies," he said. "There's only enough food and water in here for a few days. The room wasn't supposed to hold this many."

"The rest of us will need to surrender," Noura said softly, "once the emperor and Brightlord Adolin have been flown to safety."

"They may execute you, Noura," Yanagawn said. "The singers sometimes execute the leadership of a conquered town. Too many highborn have caused problems after being subjugated. You will be in danger, and so when I leave, you *will* leave with me."

She sighed. "As you wish, Majesty."

Adolin lay back again, in an attempt to get a little sleep. Wondering about his father, missing Shallan, and trying to banish that little sliver of light inside him that had started whispering.

Second chance, Adolin. You've been given a second chance. You know what your father did with his. What will you do with yours?

⁂

Szeth slowly helped Nin-son-God into the bed of the wagon. The old vehicle groaned beneath his weight as Nin lay down, his head toward the front seats. Kaladin slid the bundle of swords in next to him. Eight Honorblades and one pitch-black sword, locked in a silvery sheath.

Ooh! Nightblood said. *A chariot! Is this a chariot? You got me a chariot?*

Szeth smiled, then looked to the couple who stood in the barn nearby, holding candles for light. "Thank you."

"Thank you, Honorbearer," the wife said. "For the distinction of letting us aid one of Truth."

They seemed good people, both wearing their splashes brightly, living on their own, away from city or town—reminding him of his own family. Perhaps that was why they hadn't been touched by the evils.

Szeth walked over and handed them a couple of broams, now drained of Stormlight. "The gemstones in these were grown in the hearts of beasts, not cleaved from stone. They have great value."

Plainly dubious, the man glanced at his wife—who nodded after a brief pause—and took the two ruby broams. They were familiar with money, even if this was different from the iridescent coins made from greatshell carapace by the mint.

Szeth took the two old horses the couple had offered and hitched them to the front of the wagon in the early-morning darkness. It had been years since he'd done this, but the process returned to him easily.

Kaladin and Syl stood watching him with some measure of awe or confusion.

"What?" Szeth asked.

Kaladin cleared his throat. "Are those horses all right? They, um, look . . ."

"They're so small!" Syl said. "Are these kid horses?"

"They're not child horses," Szeth said, smiling. He patted one of them. "This one is a senior, actually. See the grey on the muzzle, the bowed back? Eighteen years at least. You're accustomed to the larger breeds we sell to the Easterners. In Shinovar, we have more breeds of horses than you can imagine."

He climbed up into the front of the wagon, where Kaladin and Syl joined him, and he waved to his spren, haunting the shadows with the whispers. The creature hesitantly moved into the wagon bed in human shape. He sat by Nin.

With a shake of the reins, they were off. Pulling slowly out of the barn and across a land soaked by ordinary rain. They had a chest full of infused gemstones in the wagon, recovered from Nin's stash, and were maybe two hours' ride from the Bondsmith monastery.

They'd talked about flying straight there. But both wanted to preserve Stormlight, and maybe prepare themselves. "And so," Szeth said, "we begin our final charge toward destiny. Riding in an old wagon. Seems appropriate."

"Appropriate how?" Kaladin asked.

"When this began for you," Szeth said as they rolled through a puddle with a bounce and a splash, "was it in a throne room? On a battlefield? Did you begin your journey soaring in the sky?"

"No," Kaladin said. "It started in a little town, far from anywhere important."

"My journey started among the sheep."

"Yes," Kaladin said, nodding.

"Yeah," Syl added. Then after a pause, "*My* journey *did* start in a throne room, admittedly."

"What?" Kaladin asked, glancing at her sitting on—well, hovering about an inch above—the wooden seat next to him, full sized and wearing her uniform.

"Yup!" she said. "I poofed into existence, fully formed by the Stormfather, right in the middle of the Godforge—which is basically his throne room." She eyed Szeth and Kaladin. "It was *far* more elegant than the way you humans are born."

Szeth leaned back, enjoying how oddly relaxing it was to be sitting here, moving toward his final confrontation but not worrying about it. "Do I want to know," Szeth said, his eyes on the road, "how she found out about the creation of new humans?"

"I'm very inquisitive," Syl said.

"She's nosy," Kaladin said.

"I ask questions."

"She interrogates people."

"I did *not* interrogate Monosha," Syl said, folding her arms. "We're *friends.*"

"A midwife," Kaladin explained at Szeth's questioning look. "Once showed her puppies being born."

"Wouldn't take me to the birth of a human," Syl said. "Had to sneak into that one."

"You are . . ." a voice said from behind them, "not what I imagined."

Szeth peered over his shoulder to where Nin lay, wrapped in his blanket, gazing at the sky. "Can you tell me what to expect?" Szeth asked. "From this next part?"

"Ishar will want to see you humbled," Nin said softly. "You have defeated each Honorbearer, but he says that while a Herald must be accomplished, he cannot be arrogant. I . . . do not know the last trial he plans. Only that you are expected to fail it."

"And if Szeth gains Ishar's approval," Kaladin said, "he'll be made a Herald?"

"Yes," Nin whispered, his voice frail, even sickly. "I . . . now that I see better, I question this plan. Much of what Ishar has done these last centuries—these last years in particular—is . . . unsettling to me. Trying to build an army of physical spren and Fused, preparing for far-distant conflicts. I fear what drinking of Odium's power did to him. That troubles me deeply now. I do not know why it didn't before."

"Like *I've* been saying," Syl said, "we don't *need* Heralds anymore. Even if you lock the enemy away on Braize, they can get here via the Everstorm. The whole system is broken."

"Maybe . . ." Nin said, "that was our mistake."

Szeth glanced back at him. "Mistake?"

"We were so much more than *locks* upon Fused souls. We were leaders once. Teachers. What if we'd stayed on Roshar . . . and taught? Not to betray Taln, but to build up science, society? What if . . ." He shook his head. "I think the world could very well still use Heralds, Ancient Daughter. Just . . . not the ones it has . . ."

He trailed off. And together they rode in silence beneath that highway of spren light in the sky—pointed toward destiny.

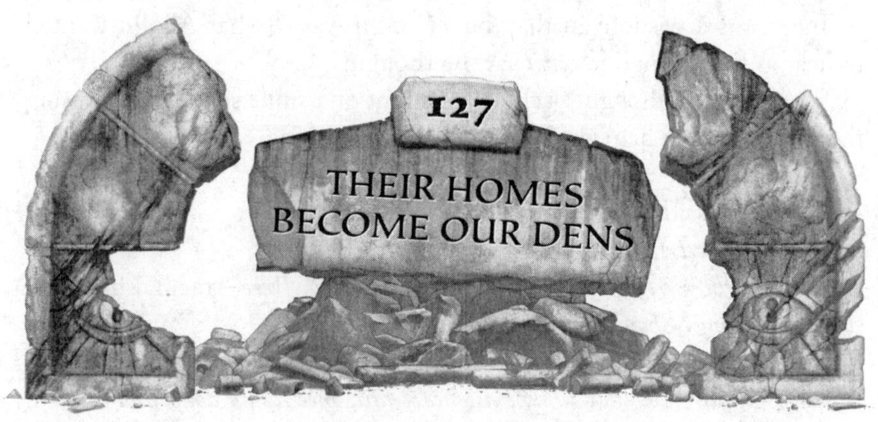
127
THEIR HOMES
BECOME OUR DENS

I know that to this day, people are confused by how at the end, spren began arriving in the East without the need for bonds. Notum, now among the most famous of honorspren, is an example. The answer is simple, however.

As the lands began to think of them, and remember them, they needed less the bond of a single person to give them purchase in the Physical Realm. For the thoughts of an entire people bolstered them.

—From *Knights of Wind and Truth*, page 46

Adolin tried to sleep.

And failed.

He'd nearly died, and had survived. There was meaning in that, wasn't there? Or was he just reacting against his earlier lack of emotion. He knew he was exhausted, and maybe not rational, but in the end—when he'd been about to die—it wasn't honor Adolin had felt, but *fatalism.* That terrified him.

Adolin Kholin had no purpose. He hadn't had one since the day of the Radiants had dawned.

You've been here helping all this time, Maya said. Her voice was stronger. She was close now.

So?

So you've always had a purpose.

I'm not enough, though.

Good! she replied.

Good? he thought, shocked.

Yes. Because . . . She took a mental breath, and he could feel this much talking remained difficult for her. *Because if you could do it all yourself, you wouldn't need a sword at your side.*

There was a wisdom in that, but wisdom wasn't what Adolin wanted to hear at the moment. *Storm you,* he thought.

Storm you! she thought back. With a hint of a smile somehow suffusing the words. Which helped.

But still . . . he wished his life meant something.

It does, she said.

Nothing matters.

You brought me back, Adolin, because I *mattered. Were*—mental breath—*were you wrong? Should I return to being fully dead?*

That's unfair.

Life is unfair, she said. *Only existence is fair, once it's all done, and God has made it so.*

There is no God.

Then what am I a piece of?

It was . . . odd to hear such overtly religious words. The lighteyes rarely spoke that way these days, even if his father did. Maya was from another time though—a time when religion had been different.

A short while later, Adolin heard the door to the basement saferoom slip open. That set them all on edge, until Notum zipped down. A group of people followed, cloaks obscuring their Windrunner uniforms.

"Skar?" Adolin said, standing. "Drehy?"

The two Windrunners were followed by five squires. The last quickly shut the door.

Adolin stood and limped over to the two familiar Radiants, one tall and one short, who were surveying the room, their expressions grim.

"Went about as well for you as it did us, eh?" Skar asked.

"That bad?" Adolin asked.

"It was a storming mess," Drehy said. "Enemy threw everything they had at the Shattered Plains, Everstorm included. We lost a lot of people, Highness. Good people. Sigzil is down, alive but without a spren. Leyten and Deti are dead. I don't feel like we ever had a chance."

"Did anyone hold any of the battlefields?" Adolin asked. "What about the Mink, and Herdaz?"

"Last we'd heard," Drehy said, "they didn't even make it in time. They got bogged down fighting to reach the capital."

"Brightness Jasnah was right," Skar said. "That excursion was of the ten fools."

"Looks like our entire defense was of the ten fools," Drehy said. "We failed on every storming front."

"Unless my father wins," Adolin said. "Then we get Herdaz and Alethkar back, regardless."

The two nodded, but seemed grim. If Dalinar lost . . . that was it. The whole world, save Urithiru itself—and, well, no one knew what was up with Shinovar—was done.

But his father wouldn't lose, would he?

Adolin, for the first time in quite a while, found . . . hope in Dalinar? Admiration for his father?

Why now? It had been a long, dark year without that hope. But standing there, he thought he could finally see his father as he was. Not as a paragon. Not as a villain.

Something *had* changed in Adolin during that night, feeling helpless, watching Azimir fall. Those moments when he'd been absolutely certain he was going to die—and had briefly lost the ability to care. Building himself back up from that was taking effort, and when he started . . . he reached for his father. Accepting, at last, that Dalinar wasn't perfect and didn't need to be perfect for Adolin to rely upon him.

That . . . helped. A little.

Adolin sat by the wall again. "Take the next step," he whispered.

"What was that, Brightlord?" Skar asked. "We . . . You should know we're under orders from your aunt to bring you and the emperor to safety. We can take a few others, but we can't be too encumbered, or we won't be able to stay ahead of the Heavenly Ones if they spot us."

"I'm not going," Yanagawn said, standing up.

Noura sighed. "Your Excellency, please see reason. We must see the empire preserved."

"The empire is no more," Yanagawn said, "but Azir remains. And *I* am its leader. *I* am the only one who can fight for it. So I'm not leaving, Noura, not as long as there is hope."

"What hope can there be?" she asked.

"As long . . ." Adolin whispered from his seat by the wall. "As long as the emperor is on his throne . . ."

"Azir stands," Yanagawn said. "The fifth dynasty troubles, Noura. You taught me of them, when two rival emperors fought for the city. In a disputed city, the one who holds the throne *physically* has legitimacy."

"An impossible chance," Noura said. "The enemy will fill the palace—even if they don't know about that precedent, they'll be searching for you, for our riches. That location will have one of the highest troop concentrations in the city. We'll never get in."

Something sparked in Adolin.

That light. He realized and recognized it right before Yanagawn spoke.

"If only," the young emperor said, a hint of awe in his voice, "we had someone to lead us who had *experience* sneaking into the palace."

Storms. Adolin blinked, then forced himself to stand on foot and peg. Yanagawn's origin . . . was as a thief who had infiltrated the Azish palace with Lift so long ago.

"This is why," Adolin whispered, meeting the emperor's eyes. "Why you are here. This . . . means something."

"What's this?" Drehy asked. "I'm lost. Are we leaving or not?"

"No, we aren't," Adolin said. "Because Yanagawn is going to sneak us into the palace, where he and I will seize the throne room and *save this storming city.*"

⁂

Light coalesced around Dalinar, then he appeared in his rooms in Urithiru.

He was home. Though, as he rested his hand on one of the chairs, a part of him wondered. Could he ever again trust anything he saw? Was there a chance this was all some vision?

How would he know?

"Ah, right on time," Wit said from behind him.

Dalinar spun and found the man in his black suit, sitting in Dalinar's favorite chair, one leg across the other knee. He'd been reading a book. Dalinar stepped forward and looked Wit in the eyes. Finding . . .

It was him. The real Wit. No sign of the insanity that had plagued the fake ones.

"Alas," Wit said, checking his curious offworld pocket watch, "as much as I'd like for you to stare at me lovingly all day, Dalinar, you have things to do. Also, I've been sleeping with your stepdaughter so, you know, it would be awkward."

"Wit," Dalinar said. "Please. No jokes."

Wit tucked away his watch. "Navani had a similar air around me when she returned. What happened in there?"

"The visions tried to replicate you and found it impossible."

Wit smiled.

"Please don't let that pad your ego," Dalinar said. "Wit, did you know the Stormfather held Tanavast's memories?"

"He's a kind of off-white, half-finished version of his Cognitive Shadow," Wit said, with a nod. "A . . . replica of Tanavast, maybe an avatar, that had taken on its own will."

"With his memories. Tanavast put them all into the Stormfather. It's . . . like he *is* Tanavast, more than we thought. He showed me the entire history of the gods on this planet, and has known all along what happened in the years we were seeking." Dalinar hesitated. "I think I needed to see and experience them anyway . . . but still . . ."

Wit cocked his head. "Huh."

"You didn't know?"

"Dalinar, I only *pretend* to know everything."

"Doesn't that just lead to disappointing people?"

"I find I can often confuse them instead." Wit stood and walked past. "Your wife is waiting above. You have around two hours remaining. I told her you'd appear in your rooms, but she was hesitant to come down in case you appeared elsewhere and went looking for her."

"You knew I'd be here? How?"

Wit smiled.

"Or did you not actually *know*," Dalinar said, "and you . . . guessed? But . . ."

Wit paused by the door. "Coming?"

Dalinar stood in place. "I . . . Wit, I failed. I saw it all—the origin of humankind on Roshar, the creation of the Heralds, the Recreance . . . I know how it happened and why, but I don't know how I'm to defeat Odium! I have learned so much my head spins, and I can't decide what's relevant and what isn't."

Wit smiled fondly, then waved for Dalinar to join him. "Walk with me, Dalinar. And listen."

A dozen objections occurred to Dalinar. He'd just spent the better part of two weeks traveling the visions. He was tired of *listening.* He wanted to *do.*

At the same time, he was in no position to turn from help, even if it was offered by Wit in his Wittish ways. So Dalinar joined him. Together they started down the halls of Urithiru, walls marked by spiraling strata, Stormlight shining from their glowing sections.

"Long ago," Wit said softly, "on a planet where half the trees are white, a child was born to a lumberman. A curious, whimsical child who wanted all of the answers in the world—but such were not offered to the children of common laborers. Even kings and jesks didn't have all the answers, though we often lied about that fact, and still do."

As they walked, a faint wind blew against Dalinar's back, as if urging him forward. *Listen,* it whispered. *Listen.*

"Now, the king of that land was a good man," Wit continued. "I rather liked him, for all his faults. One day, he started pondering the nature of nobility. He had a discussion with his lords—though on this planet, it was not the color of the eyes that marked nobility. They claimed it was about birth, naturally: the acts of god, the sanctity of the crown. The dirty secret is that all governments are quietly republics—the voting is simply done with the sword or with coin. Everyone conveniently neglects to tell the lower class that it's their coin, and their lack of swords.

"Regardless, the king had listened to the wrong kind of philosophers. The kind who spoke of concepts like the innate equality of all people. He began wondering about the flimsy rationalizations given for elevating one person above another, and he got into an argument with his lords.

"It was a foolish argument, with some measure of wine involved. The king claimed he could take any lowborn child in the land and raise him to be as noble, to be as learned and talented as any highborn child. One of his barons took the bet. And so, the lumberman's son was brought to the palace."

"Were you that boy?" Dalinar asked.

"No," Wit said. "But I was young then, frightfully so. I'd somehow found a weapon destined to kill a god, and was carrying it un-wittingly."

Oddly, as they entered the main thoroughfare toward the lifts, nobody made way for Dalinar. "What did you do to me?" he asked as they walked—Wit strolling, Dalinar marching.

"Just a little Lightweaving," Wit said. "We don't have time for you to be mobbed. Besides, Dalinar, I want you to enjoy it."

"The story?"

"No, this," Wit whispered, his hands out toward the people they passed.

This. Dalinar let the silence linger as they continued, and . . . he noticed a Connection to the people. They'd followed him through rain and ruin to make a new home at the tops of these unnamed mountains.

As he walked, at first each step felt as if he were marching to the gallows. His last confrontation, the conflict that would save or destroy him. Then . . . he started sensing their souls. The woman who carried a basket of clothing, the potter with his bucket of clay. The child and the guard, both running, both shouting, dreams spinning in their minds. Even the Stormfather, still there in the back of his head.

So many of them. So many *stories.* Dalinar thought he felt it, the same thing that Tanavast mentioned: the cords that bound all of humankind into one family.

Today, he was their dream. He was their champion.

"What happened?" Dalinar asked. "To the lumberman's son?"

"He failed," Wit said softly. "I wasn't able to stop him from doing so, and it haunts me to this day."

⁂

Noura, in her colorful and patterned vizier's robes, immediately stepped up to confront Adolin.

"Save the city?" she demanded. "You will *not* pull the emperor into some suicide mission! He needs to retreat and be safe, to inspire the people to fight for their freedom."

"It's not a suicide mission," Adolin said. "You yourself told me that the person who controls the throne controls the empire. If we can obtain it before the deadline, and hold it until the moment arrives, the kingdom will belong to Yanagawn."

"Because of a single precedential ruling," Noura said.

"The enemy is bound by laws like that," Adolin said. "It can work. My father's confrontation with Odium is in . . ."

"Just under two hours," May said.

"Around two hours," Adolin said. "All we have to do is sneak into the throne room!"

"People will be rushing out of the city," Kushkam said, standing. That gash across his nose and cheeks was really something—like he'd taken an axe straight to the face. "The enemy will likely just be letting refugees leave—fewer people to feed and watch as they secure the city."

"The Windrunners made it in here," May said, pointing. "That's proof that the city isn't locked down. I think he's right!"

"People *are* fleeing the city," Drehy said. "The enemy is busy setting up barracks, supply depots, checkpoints."

"Common methods of securing a city," Colot said, with a grunt. "There will be chaos for a little longer, and the checkpoints won't all be up yet. We could probably make it most of the way to the palace by acting like scared citizens."

"Where," Kushkam said, "His Imperial Excellency implies he can get us in quietly."

"I can!" Yanagawn said. "I was in the planning meetings with my uncle. I know all the options to sneak in." Hope rose in Yanagawn's voice, a single gloryspren appearing above him.

That spark of light inside Adolin found purchase, and started to build into a flame. He'd been broken down entirely . . . and it felt like a fresh start.

Sometimes, Maya said, *you don't need a Radiant or a Shardbearer. A person's life isn't meaningless because they can't hit the hardest anymore, Adolin. At some point, you're going to realize why you're* really *here.*

Thank you, he thought. *For believing in me.*

It's kind of our job, she replied, and took a breath. *Warning. My plan to help you probably won't matter anymore . . . I was counting on there being an army with you. You might not need me.*

I'll always need a good friend, Adolin thought. *A person's life isn't meaningless because you—*

Shove it, she said, though he felt amusement from her.

"We can do this," Yanagawn continued. "We bring a small force, sneak in, and—"

"Maybe *they* can try," Noura said, gesturing to Adolin. "But not you."

"I must *lead* them, Noura," Yanagawn said.

"Just tell them how to get in. Stay here, safe."

Yanagawn drew himself up. Met her eyes. And spoke with a voice that seemed not wholly his own. "I am emperor. I will *lead them.*"

They locked gazes. Then Noura started crying. Not because she'd lost the argument, Adolin realized, but because she was afraid. "I don't want you to get hurt," she whispered. "I don't want to lose you. Please."

Storms . . . that wasn't the face of a bureaucrat trying to enforce rules. It was the face of a mother speaking to a son. They might not be related by blood, but suddenly her resistance to Adolin's efforts took on a new light.

"After all we've done to you," she said, grasping Yanagawn's hands, "after all we've asked of you, Yanagawn, I don't want to see you get killed. We elevated you out of shame, and you proved better than any of us. Please. I want you to be safe."

"I . . ." He took a deep breath. "I can't be safe. Not if my people need something more." He looked to Adolin. "You're with me?"

"To the end, Your Majesty," Adolin said.

"Then gather and prepare my forces, please."

"We'll accept anyone," Adolin said, turning to the room, "who can stand and walk."

Nearby, a small figure scrambled up from among the scribes. The spindly Azish girl, Zabra, who he had sent to understudy with May. "Anyone?"

"Remember how I told you," Adolin said, "that if you did what I said, you'd someday get your chance, Zabra?"

She nodded eagerly.

"Well, I'm in no position to turn down anyone who can hold a blade. Find yourself one." He scanned the room as a small band formed from among the survivors—including Kushkam, Sarqqin the blacksmith, Hmask, and Colot. Rahel the teenage Truthwatcher. A few other soldiers.

"And what of them?" Gezamal said, nodding to the Windrunners. "They have orders to bring you to safety."

Adolin glanced at Drehy and Skar, who seemed offended by the implication. "Orders last until the situation changes," Skar said. "Any good soldier knows that. What do you need from us, Adolin? We're in."

Drehy nodded in agreement.

Adolin smiled, and did not look at Gezamal, who might take that as gloating. "Thank you, my friends. How many Heavenly Ones did you see out there?"

 "A good thirty, I'm afraid," Drehy said.

“Only a handful of other Fused though,” Notum added, standing on May’s shoulder, small sized, “from what I saw.”

“We’ll never succeed if too many Fused come for us,” Adolin said. “But if Drehy and Skar can lead those Heavenly Ones away . . .”

“We can do that,” Skar said. “We’ve had practice. We should be able to imply a whole force of Windrunners is coming—which will mobilize the enemy Fused, send them into offensive patterns. We should be able to keep them all out of your way for a few hours.”

Yanagawn began taking off his robes. He dumped the whole mess onto the floor, leaving him in an undershift.

“What are you doing, Majesty?” Noura asked.

“Those robes will draw attention,” he said, suddenly seeming just an ordinary youth. “My people don’t need an emperor right now, Noura. They need a thief.”

I record here the notes of the song. The Wind knows it very well. I cannot hear her voice, but sometimes I hear the flute.

—From *Knights of Wind and Truth,* page 117

Szeth hummed softly to himself as he drove the wagon in the morning light. He realized, idly, it was the song that Kaladin had been playing. Nin-son-God had fallen quiet, and Szeth wondered if he'd dozed off—but that couldn't be possible given how much the wagon bumped.

"Aboshi," he said to Nin, "it would *really* help if you could tell me *why* Ishar came up with this plan. What did he think it might accomplish?"

"Agreed," Kaladin said, watching the road ahead of them. "I'm ready for some answers."

"It started," Nin whispered after a short time, "when Ishar told me that he foresaw pain in the future. Taln had already lasted longer than any of us believed he could. Thousands of years."

"Thousands of years?" Kaladin said. "Wait, none of you died during that time?"

"We are more resilient than mortals," Nin said. "You noticed, surely."

"Yeah, I suppose I did," Kaladin admitted.

"Unfortunately," Nin said, "several among us were growing . . . weaker. Accessing our natures, our blessings, was harder and harder. Kalak, Chana, Vedel . . . Ishar worried that one of the weaker ones would die by some accident or incident. Worse, Ishar walked the Spiritual Realm, and foresaw future threats. He needed time, he said, to prepare for them. So he sent me to stop the Return. We . . . we decided that the rise of any other Radiant orders would prompt the enemy to come. Only . . . only it didn't. I killed so many . . . with no cause . . ."

He fell silent again, and Szeth waited, content to let him speak at his own speed. Kaladin did the same. Syl, however, showed no such patience.

"And?" she asked from where she knelt on the bench. "So? How does this relate to Shinovar?"

"My job was to stall," Nin said, sounding dazed. "Ishar, in the meantime, searched for solutions. Ways to bolster our strength for future fights. He stepped into the Well of Control and took upon himself some of Odium's power, then began working on new kinds of soldiers. But he was on a cliff edge too. And his eventual solutions were . . ."

"Were *what*?" Syl asked, turning around to look back at him.

"Spren," Nin said, "made physical so they could fight. Immortal, in possession of Surges, as is the natural state of many of your kind. I . . . It sounds outlandish to me now that I consider. But he also created something terrible . . ."

"Human Fused," Szeth guessed. "Like my father and my sister. You made their souls able to be recalled to new bodies, so they can be reborn each time they are killed. That's why I could slay these on my pilgrimage, and you don't mind."

"Yes," Nin said. "We did it to each Honorbearer, save one. Sivi rejected him."

"Has he made any others?" Syl asked.

"Just the Honorbearers so far. He was planning to make an army. It is far easier a process than new Heralds, who have other abilities. Is it . . . a good idea?"

"That depends," Kaladin said. "What is the cost?"

"It . . . seemed small to me . . . once," Nin said softly.

They reached a fork in the road, and Szeth took the path eastward, farther into the hills. This was a borderland between Shinovar and Iri, the air bearing a highland chill, the ground containing more stone than soil.

"A new body," Nin said. "They need a new body each time. We do not. Our substance is rebuilt from the essence of Honor when we return. Ishar was not able to access that power, so each rebirth of the Honorbearers requires a body."

"*Very* like the Fused," Kaladin said.

"Yes, though humans do not rebuild themselves in storms," Nin said, his voice growing even softer. "I hear his process takes a few days, and is far more painful." Nin fell silent. Only the sounds of the wagon disturbed the highlands. Creaking wheels. Jostling wood. Snorting horses.

"So," Kaladin said, "the cost is not worth paying."

"What if it protects us though?" Szeth asked. "What if it gives us warriors who can fight the Fused?"

"We can *already* fight the Fused," Kaladin said. "We've done it time and again in the past."

"This Return is worse though," Nin whispered. "With the Everstorm, the Fused cannot be locked away. We need a new edge. Perhaps these human Fused . . ."

"Sometimes," Szeth agreed, "a price must be paid for survival."

"No," Kaladin said. "Szeth. What you did destroyed you. Was that worth the cost?"

"I do not think so now," Szeth said. "But what if *someone* has to make the difficult choices, and do terrible things, so that others may have peace?"

"What peace?" Kaladin demanded, waving his hands. "You think people can live in peace, knowing what it cost? Look, I don't have all the answers. I've *told* you that. But this isn't a question of a few people needing to make a terrible choice. That's a lie—everyone, everywhere, faces these kinds of decisions. That's life. What kind of world would it be if every time such a decision came up, we forced ourselves to sacrifice? Not giving up our lives or time, but our integrity, our happiness, our very identities?"

"Misery," Nin whispered. "It would be a world of misery and darkness."

"And what if by giving up our edge, we lose?" Szeth asked.

"Then we *lose,* Szeth," Kaladin said. "Maybe we even die. But in doing so, we retain ourselves—because I tell you, there *are* worse fates."

"Yes," Nin said. "Yes. He is right. The Wind is right. The music . . . is right . . ."

"Can you tell me about the Skybreaker dissenters?" Szeth asked. "That you mentioned?"

"Occasionally," Nin said, "a group of them refuses my leadership. Billid claimed . . . to have found old Skybreaker oaths. I thought it ridiculous at the time . . ."

Nin refused further prompts, so Szeth let the conversation lapse, thinking about his upcoming decision. Because it was important that he make decisions. Even if he was persuaded by one side to choose as he did, *he* needed to decide.

Kaladin is right, he concluded. *And Ishar must be stopped.*

Szeth was the last bearer of Truth in Shinovar. He was the final Honorbearer. *He* needed to find a way to stop what had happened here. For his family, for his people, and most importantly—this time—for himself.

∴

"The lumberman's son failed," Wit continued softly. "He did not prove that a child born to working parents could grow up to be as learned as a king."

"Then why are you telling me this?" Dalinar asked, frowning as they walked through Urithiru.

"Because the *way* he failed is relevant," Wit said. "You see, they set up terms for this contest. At the end of eight years of lessons—trained alongside the baron's son and other nobility—the lumberman's son would be tested. Three tests, of which he needed to win at least one.

"First was the test of the sword. Could he compete with the others in martial prowess, using the weapons of the upper class? Second was the test of history. Could he recite the lineages of kings, the storied and notable events of their kingdom, the important provinces and their exports?"

"Those seem reasonable," Dalinar said. "But there's a flaw in such a test. Even if all people are equal in general, not all *individuals* are equal in *capacity.* One experiment with one boy can't prove anything."

"And so, you're smarter than they were," Wit said. "Good. I worry about you sometimes, Dalinar."

"Worry? Why?"

"Everyone says you're dense," he explained. "I fear you will believe them."

"Everyone?"

"Mostly me," Wit admitted.

Strangely, Dalinar started to feel more confident as he walked toward what would certainly be the most important event in his life. "Is that why the lumberman's son lost?" he asked as they reached the atrium. "Because they all ignored the *reason* for the contest? To prove that the lower class deserved better lives?"

"Would they deserve worse lives," Wit said softly, "if they *couldn't* win in a swordfight, memorize history, or complete the third task?"

"No," Dalinar realized. "And so . . ."

"The entire contest was a sham," Wit said. "There was no need for it. And really, there was no way to fail it."

"But you said he did."

"Yes," Wit said. "Jerick was remarkable in that regard. You see, the king realized what you did: that this test relied too much on random chance, even if the child *had* been chosen deliberately for his acumen by a scholar sent to teach in his little lumbering village.

"Regardless, the king was wise, and set the odds in his favor. I said, victory in any *one* of the three categories would have let the youth win. And while you're right, and the entire contest was a sham, it felt important to them. Perhaps under other circumstances it would have taught them something."

They reached a lift, and Wit—unwilling to wait in line—dismissed Dalinar's Lightweaving. They commandeered the next one, and were soon soaring up the atrium wall. The contest would take place on the roof.

"What was the third of the three tests?" Dalinar said.

"Poetry," Wit said. "To win the test, he had to compose a piece of unique poetry."

Dalinar blinked in surprise.

"Don't look at me like that," Wit said. "Familiarity with words is considered important to many noble courts."

"Even for men?"

"Remarkably, it's *usually* the men. I've known many a king who insisted that words with any substance were too *difficult* for women."

"The cosmere is a strange place, isn't it?"

"You have no idea."

Dalinar leaned against the railing, watching the people in the atrium below. Feeling, despite the distance, his Connection to them. "Composing an original poem seems difficult."

"Impossible," Wit said. "Originality is impossible."

Dalinar frowned, glancing at Wit, who leaned on the railing beside him.

"Trust me," Wit said. "I've tried. Before us were the dragons. Before them, the gods. *Everything* has been done. Every story has been told. Every idea has been thought."

"So the test . . ."

"Couldn't possibly be failed," Wit said.

"But you said—"

"Originality," Wit whispered. "Novelty. Dalinar, I'm sorry for lying to you, because I've played at words at your expense. Originality is impossible but also unavoidable. Because not *everything* has been done before." Wit glanced at him. "You haven't existed before. None of us have.

"That's the sole originality we need. A story might have been told before, but *you* haven't told it. Every idea might have been thought, but each is new again when *you* think them. And that lumberman's son? He couldn't fail. Because *I* was to be the judge of his poem, and I deeply, *sincerely* believe that every person is unique. The contest wasn't about whether his poem was good, merely if it was unique. He could have stood up, released an odoriferous belch, then sat down, and I'd have considered that acceptable. He was destined to win."

"But he failed."

"He ran," Wit whispered.

"He . . . what?"

"He ran away," Wit said. "Off to war. He was cajoled into it, convinced to run. The lumberman's son found the *only* way to lose an *unlosable* contest. He didn't show up."

He ran . . .

“Tanavast ran,” Dalinar said. “Instead of facing Odium—and I think it would have destroyed the world if he’d chosen differently.”

“A valid point.”

“You wanted me to listen to this story. Why, Wit? I’m not going to run from this fight.”

Their lift thumped into place on the last level of the tower.

“Journey before destination,” Wit said. “Your journey has led to this destination. We’re here.” He turned and looked him in the eyes. “I can’t foresee what happens next.”

Dalinar frowned.

“I think it’s because of Renarin,” Wit said, “and your link to him. Maybe it’s something else; regardless, I *can’t see* how this will go. I suspect Odium can’t either. That frightens me because for the first time in all of this, I don’t know the right story to tell.

“But listen. The lumberman’s son? In running, he lost the contest—but it didn’t matter. Because the next day, the barons launched a coup and executed the king.” Wit smiled grimly. “As I said, all governments are technically a form of republic.”

“What became of the lumberman’s son in the end?”

“He went to war. Fought, bled, learned, loved. He returned with vengeance one day and killed the barons. A remarkable tale, in fact.” Wit held his eyes. “We *never have all the answers,* Dalinar. On one hand, that contest was unlosable because I’d have validated the poem no matter what.

“On the other, it was unwinnable, because the coup was well underway, and the contest was pointless—except at the same time not. The contest’s existence *caused* the coup. So while it mattered very much, the *results* didn’t.”

“Just as it didn’t matter,” Dalinar said, “if one boy could prove himself better than a lighteyes—the people deserved better lives *anyway.*”

“Yes.”

“As do mine,” Dalinar said. “As do all of those of Roshar. It’s a distraction. The contest of champions, the contract . . . all of it. The words, the posturing. It’s pointless.”

“Yes.”

“But *I* am *not* pointless. My life. People’s lives. The meaning comes from *us.* Naturally, intrinsically. Like your boy and his poem. That’s what Nohadon meant in his book.”

“I don’t know what comes next, Dalinar,” Wit said. “But I’m glad you are the one who will walk up to meet Odium. Because while you might not know the secret to defeating him, you have learned something more important. We’re not sending a soldier up those steps. We’re sending a *king.*”

⁂

The doctor gingerly removed the hogshide cup from Adolin's stump, pulling free the peg's support framework. Adolin clenched his teeth, and didn't make a sound at the pain, although painspren betrayed him. He deliberately didn't look at the mess of blood and broken blisters.

The doctor silently cleaned it off while Rahel gave Adolin a quick healing, sending a chill through him. It seemed a waste of Stormlight—the doctor himself had a wicked cut along one thigh. However, Adolin was part of the strike force, and needed to be able to walk.

As the others pulled on cloaks to obscure them, the doctor returned and refit the cup and peg. "Brightlord," he said, "that healing won't do enough. Problem is, while your wound is *healed* as if you'd had it for months, you don't have the calluses to match. This will soon start hurting again, and could be distracting."

"This is our last chance," Adolin said. "I have to risk it. Honest truth is . . . most of me hurts, Jakkik. The leg is just one more thing."

The man glanced at him, then sighed and took something from his pocket. A white powder, which he mixed into a flask of alcohol. "I normally only give this to the dying," he said, "because it's so addictive. Tincture of firemoss."

He handed the cup to Adolin. "This will mute the pain, maybe even put a bit of a spring in your step. Until you crash tonight, Brightlord. When you do, it will be bad."

"After the deadline?" Adolin asked.

The surgeon nodded.

Adolin downed the entire thing. A few minutes later, he stepped out into the morning sun with eleven others, including Notum. Together they slipped through Azimir, picking their way toward the palace. His father would confront the enemy in approximately an hour and a half, according to Noura's clock.

Noura came along, despite her objections. They'd split the whole group into batches of ten or so, to not draw too much attention out in the city. They all wore cloaks—or in Adolin's case an improvised cloak made up of a blanket. They carried minimal arms; helms and shields would have been too obvious. He had his side sword, and that was it.

Adolin's group was the last of the three to leave, and they moved in a huddle through the city. Azimir was a mess. Moaning people, a dozen varieties of dismal spren. Harsh smoke from a fire that had been started in the distance. People moving in scattered, terrified clusters, flowing toward the city exits. Singers patrolling in blocks, heavily armed and hulking, each led by a glowing-eyed Regal.

Adolin's group rounded the broken dome, now like the husk of some dead greatshell, abandoned and hollow. Ahead, down a roadway, a cloaked figure waved. The first group that had left the safehouse had gone that way, to find one of the rally points where human troops might be holed up. The second group was searching a different rally point. Those twenty were hoping to find some resistance and make a fuss to draw attention away from the palace, however briefly.

Sneaking a full thirty people into the palace had seemed like too much for Yanagawn anyway, so they settled on eleven, plus Notum. Storms. Would those singers notice that his group was going against the general flow of traffic? Adolin felt like a dent on an otherwise perfect suit of armor during inspection, right on the breastplate, blatant and visible.

He pulled his blanket closer, then gritted his teeth and let it flop again, as that would better obscure his sword. He also let Yanagawn lead the way, and was impressed by how unregal the youth looked, hunched over. Just an urchin in a cloak. The emperor's former life was—

A door burst open near Adolin and he flinched, hand going to his sword. A group of singers stomped out of the building, carrying piles of silks and handfuls of glowing gemstones. One smashed a window, laughing, as they hurried on. They barely gave him a second glance, but storms . . .

"So much for them not looting," Colot said softly, pulling up beside Adolin as they continued on. "There's far more happening here than I've heard of in other conquered cities."

"The severity of the general," Adolin whispered, "influences the severity of the troops."

Colot nodded. It wasn't a direct correlation—disciplined generals sometimes had troops who got away from them. At the same time though, Sadeas's armies had always behaved differently from Dalinar's. Even back in the old days.

In the signs they passed—broken windows, singer troops harassing refugees, some civilian corpses—Adolin could read a lot about their leader. If he'd needed further reason to condemn Abidi, he found it here.

As for his father . . .

Adolin found himself at peace for the first time in what felt like forever. No longer inspired, as he had been earlier, but also no longer angry.

What changed? Maya asked.

I've decided to let him be a person, Adolin thought. *I'm not sure I'll ever fully forgive him for killing my mother, but I'm willing to love him anyway.*

More importantly, he'd given up on the dream of his father as some perfect paragon. And if Adolin's father didn't have to be the greatest man alive, then Adolin Kholin didn't have to try to match that kind of incredible reputation.

Strange what a relief it was to finally acknowledge that.

I don't get it, Maya admitted.

I don't think I do either, entirely, Adolin said. *Humans don't make sense.*

Spren don't either, she said. *Trust me. We pretend otherwise, but we're fully capable of being storming messes. By the way, I should be close enough now that you can summon me; we can trust these spren to make the rest of the way on their own.*

Not sure we need them now, he said.

Unfortunately, that's true, she thought. *I feel . . .* She took a deep breath. *I feel like a fool. I should have stayed and helped.*

I'd have fallen in the last fight anyway, Adolin thought. *They'd have taken your Blade and used it against us. So maybe it's a blessing, what happened.*

They reached an intersection and Yanagawn had them pause. Adolin waved for the others to huddle up with him, and told them not to act so much like soldiers—not to stand in a line, scanning the area with careful eyes.

I think, Adolin said to Maya, *that I really felt, deep down, that I had to step up and take my father's place. I felt, for some reason, that since he had proven to be flawed,* I *had to take his place and be perfect instead. I've been running from that for a long time, because I knew I couldn't be.*

She sent him a grunt of appreciation, and a feeling—through their bond—that she understood how messed up that must have felt.

Yeah, he thought. *My anger over my mother's death wasn't just . . . just about what he did. It was like I was furious at him for toppling my perfect impression of him. Like, he was supposed to be better than that.*

He should have been, Maya said. *But nobody ever really is.*

Nobody, Adolin thought. *Especially not me.*

They started across the road in small groups, reaching the wall around the palace complex. Adolin waited until the last group had crossed, ready to scuttle forward himself. Right before he did, though, a group of singers came stomping along the road.

He and Zabra, who were the last to go, huddled against the wall of the building. This group of singers wasn't looting, and they prowled with a more deliberate, martial step. Though Adolin wished they would just move on, one stopped at the corner, glancing at him.

Adolin's blood froze, sweat prickling his brow. A warm wind blew in, rippling the blanket, pushing it back, exposing his peg leg. The singer glanced at that, then at Zabra, an obvious child. The singer immediately relaxed and continued on, leaving Adolin's heart to slowly recover as he made a fist, having nearly summoned Maya.

They waited a minute or two, then hurried to join the others. As they did, he found Notum with them, standing on Kushkam's shoulder.

"I'm sorry, Adolin," the spren whispered. "I should have spotted that patrol. I was scouting around inside the complex."

"It's fine," Adolin said.

"Last time," Yanagawn said, looking at the wall into the palace complex, "my team climbed this wall to get in. This spot is hard to see from the inside, lacking major windows or guard posts. However, I think we should take another route: the smuggler's port."

"The *what*?" Noura asked.

"Smuggler's port," Yanagawn said. "A hidden entrance to the palace complex you can bribe your way through."

"There's no such thing," Noura said.

"Um . . . yes there is," Yanagawn said. "Sorry. My uncle didn't want to use it, as he figured the soldiers who ran it wouldn't respond well to thieves. They only let people bribe their way in for small-scale crimes."

"And you think this is our best path?" Adolin asked him.

"Yes," Yanagawn said. "Climbing the wall was more difficult than we expected—and I don't fancy our chances of doing so unseen with this many patrols out here and Heavenly Ones in the air. I think I can get the port open, even if no one is manning it."

Adolin glanced at Kushkam, then both of them nodded, and Adolin gestured for Yanagawn to lead the way. He did, May on his heels and Notum zipping ahead, invisible to all but them.

You were wrong earlier, Maya said.

About what?

About yourself. You said you especially didn't live up to what people expected. But you're a storming good person, Adolin. Better than your father.

I think, today, he thought back, *the important fact is that I don't* need *to be better than him. He can just be a person. And I . . . I can just be one too.*

Fair enough, Maya said. *Does this mean you'll stop trying to do everything all by yourself?*

By himself? *You have us mixed up,* he said. *My father is the one who insists on doing everything all alone, as if he's the only one who matters.*

Yeah? Maya said. *When Kaladin needed help, you were there.*

Sure, he's my friend.

When Shallan had secrets, you didn't pry.

Just trying to be a good husband, he said as they reached a section of the wall obscured by some planters and trees.

That's always how you are, Maya said. *I've been watching a long time now, Adolin. Watching you give everyone whatever they need. What about what* you *need?*

He fell quiet as Yanagawn knocked.

Maybe I don't need anything, he said.

Adolin, Maya said, *if you're going to lie, at least do it when I'm there physically so I can force you to buy a round in apology when you realize the truth.*

He smiled despite himself. He increasingly enjoyed seeing her personality emerge.

Yanagawn began feeling around a hidden section of wall, behind vines that quivered at his touch. "There's a lever back here somewhere . . ." he explained. But before Adolin could offer to help search, a slot in the wall opened.

"Who are you?" a muffled voice hissed. "Never mind. It's dangerous out there. Hurry, get inside."

Then a section of the ground slid open, revealing a small tunnel leading under the wall. A few small diamond chips, barely infused, revealed a confused soldier's face looking up from the pit.

Together, they piled in—forcing the soldier backward as he watched them, waving away anxietyspren. There was space for them all down here, an entire hollowed-out room perhaps ten feet long and twenty wide. It was a little like the saferoom they'd been in before—with water traps along the walls for drainage.

Other refugees and injured people clogged the space as Adolin's group crowded in. There were only two other soldiers, and one was severely wounded, his back to the wall, halberd on the ground next to him. Blood pooling at his side. Rahel gasped, and rushed to help him.

"You look like important folk," the guard said, eyeing Kushkam. "I think I've seen you before . . ."

Yanagawn held his hand up to forestall Kushkam's comment, then dropped his cloak to reveal himself.

The guard looked him up and down. "And . . . you are?"

"Oh, right," Yanagawn said. "I'm without my regalia. I am Yanagawn, the emperor."

"And I'm the storming king of . . ." the man began, then trailed off as Noura—wearing her thick, patterned vizier's coat—dropped her cloak. The guard's eyes bulged, then he glanced toward Rahel, who started glowing as she healed the wounded soldier.

"Excellency!" the guard said to Noura, then fell to his knees. "I didn't realize . . . I shouldn't have spoken to . . ."

"Ask him," Yanagawn said, "how he ended up here."

"What is your situation here?" Noura asked, Adolin watching the exchange with amusement.

"We fled here after the dome fell," the guard said. "I kind of run the place, you see, and we needed somewhere to . . . Storms! Is it really him? Is it . . ." He barely dared look at Yanagawn.

"It is him," Noura said, her voice displeased. "Majesty, why didn't you tell me of this place?"

"Because you'd have shut it down," Yanagawn replied.

"It *should* be shut down," Noura said, staring with loathing at the two soldiers. "They're thieves."

"So was I," Yanagawn said, with a smile. He glanced at the two soldiers. "Today, we're lucky they exist. This place serves a necessary function—people *are* going to need to get in and out of the palace complex unknown by the officers. If it's going to happen, well, wouldn't you rather have loyal soldiers be in charge of it?"

"Loyal?" Noura said.

"Loyal to the empire," the wounded guard whispered, blinking awake, nodding in thanks to Rahel. She knelt back, and storms, Adolin could see how exhausted she was. She barely had any Stormlight, and had stolen Light from the chips in the room to perform this minimal healing.

"Always loyal," the wounded man continued, chuckling, blood on his lips. "Doesn't mean we can't perform a few . . . extra services here and there."

"All the thieves knew," Yanagawn said, "that this lot wouldn't take kindly to anyone sneaking in with *too* bad an intent." He looked to the unwounded soldier. "You are chosen today, and may speak directly to me. What is your name?"

The man fell to his knees, bowing his head. "Jaskkeem."

"Jaskkeem," Yanagawn said. "We're going to take back the palace. Can you get us across the grounds unseen?"

The man looked up, tears in his eyes. "Take back the palace?"

"Yes," Yanagawn said, confident. "We will save Azir if we can hold the throne room. Can you lead us there?"

"Absolutely, Majesty. There's a tunnel here that leads right up next to the main palace building!"

"Then let us be quick," Yanagawn said. "And may Yaezir guide us, for I fear we have less than an hour to accomplish our design."

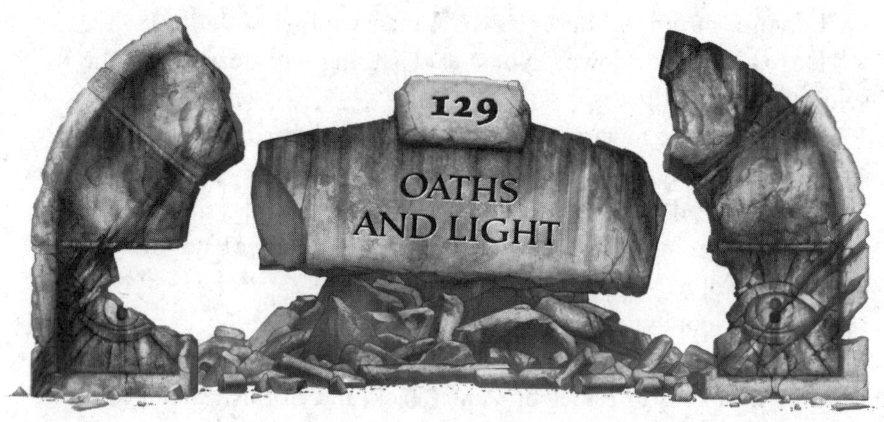

Curiously, the closest I came to the Knight of Wind and the Knight of Truth during their quest happened during the last hours before Stormfall. When they visited my parents' house, while I was asleep, and purchased their wagon.

—From *Knights of Wind and Truth,* page 27

I think Ishar took the power . . . maybe three hundred years ago?" Nale said from where he lay in the wagon bed. "Four? This was right after your people attacked. When was that?"

"Almost a thousand years, Aboshi," Szeth said softly. "A thousand years since those dark days when we sent armies across the stones. To our shame."

Kaladin found himself strangely calm as he sat in the front seat between Szeth and Syl. Time was running out, but he was willing to take this next part slowly. In every other instance he could think of, he'd gone charging—or at least striding—toward his destiny. It was nice to just quietly roll there.

This region seemed empty—though earlier in the night, before reaching Nale's cache, they'd swung past a larger city glowing bright in the distance. The size had shocked Kaladin. He'd begun to think of this land as populated solely by homesteads and farming towns.

He'd immediately felt foolish. Visiting Hearthstone and the region nearby, one would have assumed Alethkar had no grand cities. Shinovar's monasteries were deliberately placed in less populated regions—so while he hadn't seen much urban development here, it obviously existed. There was even an Oathgate here somewhere.

"He Connected himself to this land," Nale continued. "I don't know the process—I don't understand a fraction of the things Ishar can do with his powers. Seven millennia later, I still couldn't tell you why Ashyn burns. However, it was after he took the power . . . and became the spren of this land . . . that he started seeing himself as the Almighty. Oh, it had always been there, this sense of grandeur. He is not a humble man, our Ishar. But he never thought he was *God.* Not until . . . he kind of became one . . ."

Kaladin glanced at Syl, who uncharacteristically hadn't gone soaring upon the winds. Instead she remained human size, occasionally resting her head on his shoulder, though she didn't get physically tired. She'd look to the skies, where—now that it was light—only a faint shimmering in the air indicated that spren were migrating this way in Shadesmar, Kaladin's armor spren flying around up there with them.

"Does any of this make sense to you?" Kaladin asked softly.

"Honor died," she said. "Leaving this land without a god. It's reasonable someone would try to fill that void. Ishar's attempt seems . . . less than stellar."

"If we kill him, Nin," Szeth said, "can we actually end his touch on the land and free my people?"

"I don't entirely know," Nale said. "Our immortality is related to our status as Heralds, but was conferred separately. We can still be reborn. I think that to save this land, you must do more than defeat Ishar. You must do for him what you did for me . . . but it will be harder."

Szeth looked to Kaladin.

"There might be a way," Kaladin said, leaning forward in his seat. "Dalinar says that a spoken oath might restore Ishar, at least briefly."

"When a Radiant says the Words," Syl agreed, "they don't just Connect to their spren in the Cognitive Realm, they Connect to the Spiritual Realm. It's a mini perpendicularity each time. A confluence of power and Intent, and an alignment of self."

"How close are you?" Szeth said, still regarding Kaladin.

"I have barely let myself think about the final Words," Kaladin admitted. "The last set nearly broke me."

"Then it will have to be me," Szeth said, "but there is a difficulty here. For Skybreakers, I must complete my quest in order to say the Fourth Ideal."

"Yes," Nale said. "The Fourth Ideal—the quest. The Fifth to become the law. I have said those words already. I cannot be the one."

"So you have to finish your quest," Kaladin said to Szeth.

"But defeating Ishar *is* what finishes my quest," Szeth said. "We cannot restore him to sanity without the burst of power I might release at the Words, but I cannot say the Words unless he is already defeated."

Damnation. Kaladin chewed on that, seeking another way. Could he . . . could he talk to Ishar, and help him as he'd helped Szeth?

Syl nodded toward Nale. *You helped him,* her voice whispered in his mind.

The Wind helped him, Kaladin sent back through the bond.

You and the Wind together.

Kaladin frowned at the idea. "What is the Wind, Syl? I feel that I'm missing something here."

"She's part of something very ancient," Syl said, looking back at the sky. "I'm an honorspren, and was created by him—or the remnant of him that is the Stormfather. Yet this isn't a world of just Honor." Her expression became distant, searching. "There's more. Before Honor, Cultivation, and Odium arrived . . . Roshar was here. If a God still lives, I find him in the quiet breeze that dances with all things."

That . . . didn't help terribly. But he couldn't keep from thinking of times even in his youth when the wind had been there, and how eventually it had brought Syl to him.

The time approaches, the Wind whispered to him. *The hour when spren may need a champion. I wish that it were not so.*

"And what does it mean?" Kaladin whispered. "What will be required of me?"

Everything. I'm sorry . . .

Szeth soon slowed the wagon. "We're close. I've only been here once though."

"It's over to your left," Nale whispered, sitting up. "Along that ridge there, beside the mound that was once a thunderclast corpse. Twist around to those rocks, where stones rise like a cathedral. That's where you'll find him."

Szeth started them rolling that way, across stone and occasional patches of soil. In fact, Kaladin was shocked to see that some of the *stone* bore grass that peeked from holes. Real grass. After only nine days, he found it odd how surprising its movement was.

A place where two grasses met. They drove up a shallow stone incline, onto a small ridge.

"I remember," Nale said, his voice haunted, "when this entire region was filled with corpses. When it burned, and even mountains had been slain. I remember . . . a final battle . . ."

"Aharietiam," Syl said. "It was *here*?"

"Yes," Nale said. "This is where Honor abandoned his Heralds. This is where we walked away, leaving our Blades and our . . . self-worth. I don't know that I can ever have mine back . . ."

"Nonsense," Kaladin said. He turned, twisting to look at Nale. "Don't talk like that."

"I left him," Nale whispered. "I left Taln. I thought he'd break soon. He should have broken soon. But he lasted over *four thousand years.*"

"And how long had you suffered?" Kaladin asked.

 Nale looked away.

"The burden you ten carried," Kaladin said, "is unfair. And while trauma doesn't *excuse* what you did, it does *explain* it. We can't let you, or Ishar, hurt others—but that doesn't mean you weren't hurt yourselves. You have a right to receive help."

Nale continued to look away, but he gave a shallow nod. "There was no grass long ago. It can grow here now. Remarkable."

Soon they reached the rock formation, which rose high like the walls of an ornate monastery. And standing in its shadow was a figure with an Honorblade. With white hair and beard, Shin by the look of his features, wearing blue robes.

Szeth stopped the wagon. "Nin," he said. "Nightblood. Please guard the Honorblades."

Szeth? Nightblood asked. *You're going to fight without me?*

"I don't know if I'm going to fight at all," he replied. "But if I do, I will use my Shardblade."

But . . . I'm a great sword, aren't I?

"You are a great sword," Szeth said, climbing from the wagon. "But you are also too dangerous. I'm sorry, sword-nimi. I do not want to kill today."

But . . . but evil . . .

"I see no evil," Szeth replied. "Merely confusion."

He glanced at Kaladin, who climbed down as well. Together they walked to the edge of the clearing, looking toward Ishar. Syl landed beside Kaladin, and a moment later—perhaps spurred on by her—12124 appeared beside Szeth. In a human shape and size.

The Wind joined them a moment later. A soft, encouraging breeze. Kaladin looked to Szeth. "Ready?"

Szeth considered. Kaladin gave him time. Then finally, Szeth started toward Ishi'Elin, Herald of Oaths. The rest of them followed.

⁂

Adolin and his team emerged from the tunnel into the famous grounds of the Bronze Palace.

The sight was stunning. Even the *stone* had been Soulcast into bronze—with little bits of quartz in it, to make it sparkle and shine like a sky full of stars. As they climbed out of the hidden tunnel exit, he saw figures swooping past high in the sky: a formation of Heavenly Ones moving away from the city center. Drehy and Skar had done their job well, it seemed.

The grounds were silent, particularly compared to the chaos and looting in the streets outside. Jaskkeem—the soldier who ran the smuggler's port—led them across one last stretch of bronze ground up to the palace itself, an ornate building with smooth metal walls. The tip of Adolin's peg leg thumped with each step, rubber on bronze. It didn't hurt, as the doctor's tincture was working—and Adolin felt a zip of alertness and energy. He tried not to think of the cost, focusing on the palace . . . storms, they really did have a good eye for aesthetics in Azir. It was gaudy, yes, but also undeniably gorgeous.

Yanagawn led them to one of the large building's back doors—and Noura had a key. They were inside a second later, and the emperor shared a grin with Adolin.

"I feel like I'm actually *doing* something," the younger man whispered. "For the first time since taking this throne, I'm helping rather than merely sitting and being seen."

"How long until my father's confrontation?" Adolin asked Noura.

"Just over half an hour," she whispered.

"We have to slip into the throne room unseen," Yanagawn said. "We hold the room quietly, without anyone the wiser, until the deadline. We won't even have to raise a sword."

"That would be *storming* beautiful," Adolin said.

They continued on, Kushkam, Sarqqin, and Gezamal forming the rearguard, May and Yanagawn going first, taking Jaskkeem with them. Notum scouted ahead, as before. That left Noura, Adolin, Colot, Rahel, Hmask, and Zabra at the center of their line. Adolin threw off the blanket now that they were inside—as the group would be suspicious here no matter what. He hoped they simply wouldn't encounter anyone.

The place was dead. Staff had been evacuated, and all the guards had been recruited into the war effort. They did find places where the doors had been broken open, so the enemy *had* been here, but perhaps they'd secured the palace complex and moved on. Could Adolin be that lucky?

No, he thought. *This seems deliberate.*

"Wait a moment," he said to the others, causing them to bunch up around him. "This feels *too* quiet. What are we walking into, Yanagawn? What is the layout of the hallways ahead of us?"

Noura pointed, used to answering questions directed toward the emperor. "See that hallway at the end of this one? We take a left there, then another immediate left into the throne room."

He looked ahead, down a grand hallway with chandeliers and art on every storming free space of wall. It ended at a T intersection. Left to the throne room.

"What do you mean by too quiet, Adolin?" Yanagawn asked.

"There should be looting here," he said. "Or at least guards stationed to watch to be sure it doesn't happen. Notum. Check our rear."

The spren saluted and became a ribbon of light, then zipped back the way they'd come in.

Be ready, Adolin thought to Maya.

Got it, she replied.

"I think this is a trap," Adolin said. "Three ways out—back the way we came, forward and to the left, forward and to the right. I'm betting there are troops at each position." He looked to Kushkam, then May. Both nodded, agreeing with his assessment.

"We knew this *probably* wouldn't be easy," May said. "We'll have to send someone in to hold the throne, then fight to hold the room."

"We can bolt the doors in seven places," Yanagawn said, "with the flick of a lever inside. If this is a trap, the room will be locked tight."

"Can we cut our way in?" Sarqqin asked. "Brightlord Adolin, is your Shardblade available yet?"

"It is," Adolin said. "That spot up to our left? That's the wall into the throne room. I could slice us a hole there maybe, and we'd at least have a way out."

Noura winced.

"The entire chamber is lined in aluminum," Yanagawn said. "Remember? I told you we lined it after learning about Deepest Ones. But there *is* a hidden door."

He led them to a spot between two ornate urns on pedestals. Here, Noura flipped a hidden switch, but nothing happened.

"Jammed shut," Colot guessed. "That proves it. They're ready for us."

Yanagawn looked to Adolin with panic in his eyes. "Do we run?"

"Where?" Adolin said. "Yanagawn, it would have been nice if we could sneak, but life is rarely that easy."

Notum came zipping back a second later. "You're right, Adolin," he said. "A good fifty troops, with some Fused, are coming up behind us."

Kushkam pointed the way forward. They continued along the hallway, reaching the T intersection. To both their left and their right—perhaps fifty feet down each corridor—waited another force. Hundreds of them.

Sounds announced the troops coming up behind. Kushkam gave him a grim look, sword out. They were well and truly surrounded.

"We're doomed," the emperor whispered.

"Perhaps," Adolin said. "But do you remember that there was one last way a smaller force can defeat a greater one?"

"Yes," Yanagawn said. "You promised to tell me what it was."

Kushkam grunted. He was forced to hold his sword in his off hand because of his lost fingers. "You taught him those, did you?"

"What is it?" the emperor asked, gripping his sword in nervous fingers. "The fourth way."

"The game can never fully account for the human spirit, Yanagawn," Adolin said. "Numbers, advantages, disadvantages, statistics . . . sometimes they lie. Because sometimes the smaller force fights in a way that no pieces on a board can ever replicate. Sometimes in real life, when the odds of winning are miniscule—and any smart general would have surrendered—a force keeps fighting. And *wins.*"

Yanagawn trembled. "There are hundreds of them though . . ."

"Why aren't they attacking?" May asked, bow out and strung, her hand resting on the large dagger at her side.

Adolin considered a moment, and realized he knew why. He walked a short distance—just ten feet—to the left at the intersection, then pulled open one of the doors to the throne room itself.

In the ornate, well-furnished room beyond, the lights were dim. Sitting on the throne—illuminated from above—was a figure in glittering Plate, red eyes shining through the slits on the front. Adolin's Plate.

Abidi the Monarch wanted his challenge.

The others saw it, and Kushkam cursed softly, recognizing the Blade—the Azish one, named the Blade of Memories—stabbed into a table beside Abidi. He stood and slid it from the wood, then raised it and pointed it at Adolin.

"Wait out here," Adolin said to the others.

"But—" Colot began.

"If those forces attack, hold this spot," Adolin said. "Whatever else happens, *hold the room.*"

Then he stepped inside, hobbling on one foot and one peg, before closing the door behind him. He got ready to call Maya.

Abidi pulled a lever built into the shining bronze throne. The doors behind Adolin *clicked* softly, the many bolts that Yanagawn had mentioned sliding into place.

"They say," Abidi growled, "you are this era's greatest living swordsman."

"No," Adolin said. "But I *was* trained by him." He thrust his hand to the side to summon Maya.

Nothing happened.

Abidi laughed, holding up his Blade. "Aluminum lines this room, little mortal. You should have summoned your Blade, then *carried* it into the room. The Azish didn't realize the death trap they were creating here. You have to be very, very careful about how aluminum is applied—something those of your time have yet to learn."

Storms. *Storms.*

Adolin backed up, his heels touching the locked door.

"You defeated me in front of all my soldiers," Abidi said. "You cracked my gemheart and stole my ability to fly, so I've had to *crawl* among the *lowborn* these ten days. It was either that or return and be reborn, losing my chance to win this land and rule, as is my right."

 He raised his Blade toward Adolin. "I stay sane by bathing in the blood of Radiants. Be honored. Today, I allow *you* that distinction instead." The glow behind the helm seemed to intensify. "I'm going to enjoy this."

Then he rushed forward and attacked with a sweep of his Shardblade.

⁂

Within the Spiritual Realm, and beneath Formless's eyeless gaze, Shallan was subjected to death after death as the visions continued to try to destroy her.

She saw her mentors fall again and again. But . . . Pattern. Pattern told her that she fixated on the fact that she'd killed mentors, but really that was a distortion. It wasn't true.

She stood up, and looked the visions in the face.

And found they didn't hurt.

She *knew* she wouldn't kill Wit, or Jasnah, or Navani. Once, she'd have accepted these lies. At that time she'd feared—and to an extent hated—herself. That wasn't completely gone, but she'd reconciled with Veil and accepted the truth.

What were these lies compared to that?

We have found, Radiant said, her voice firm, *a life we love. With people who love us back.*

Yes. Shallan killed, yes, when she had to. But not because she was a psychopath. Her personas were not something she feared. They were something she used to cope. They helped and protected her. So, as the visions continued, she *rejected* the lie that she would inevitably hurt people she loved. She recognized it for what it was.

Because she, Shallan Davar, was an expert in lies.

Soon the terrible visions began to fade, becoming just the ordinary Spiritual Realm again. It seemed that the shadow watching her had moved its attention elsewhere. She hadn't stopped those terrible visions, but she *had* weathered them, and that was a grand victory. Odium and Formless should have picked something more novel, because she had spent the last several years practicing how to deal with this very flavor of pain.

Once the visions stopped coming so violently, a familiar sensation appeared in her mind. Pattern—then soon afterward, the shifting and flowing mists of the Spiritual Realm faded. She emerged into a black expanse again, joined by her two spren, where Rlain and Renarin—real, as far as she could tell—were waiting. They rushed to her.

"Shallan?" Renarin said. "Are you well?"

"Well enough," she said. "Where are Glys and Tumi?"

"Hiding inside us," Rlain said. "With the gods moving about recently, they are frightened."

"Shallan, I need to know what you saw," Renarin said. "I think it might *all* be relevant, as I'm guessing the visions are embedded with clues from Mishram."

"I agree," Shallan said. "And I've been watching for clues too. We will find her prison not in a place, but in a mindset. Her mindset. Which she's been embedding into the visions we see."

"My friends," Rlain said, "did not stand up for me. That's what I saw. Then the day my people—the listeners—walked away. And . . . Mishram. She was betrayed at the end by the other Unmade, who did not come to help her when she was captured. She was abandoned by friends and followers."

"Like me, she wanted to stand up for herself," Renarin said. "Maybe that's why I saw what I did—a day when I was too weak and another had to protect me. But then I grew, and became a man who could protect myself. As she did, perhaps? When she decided to take up power and help the singers?"

"Instead of her father," Shallan whispered. "She took the place of her father. Mishram . . . did your father try to kill you? Is that the Connection you're trying to send? The message that will let us find you?"

The three of them stood together.

It wasn't enough.

"What now?" Rlain asked to Curiosity.

Shallan closed her eyes. "There's more," she whispered, thinking back to all she'd been experiencing. "Mishram is afraid that after so long, she's become unpredictable—dangerous to those she loves. Even deeper, she's afraid that she *deserves* this prison, because everyone betrayed her. Because she's been trapped with her own thoughts so long, *they've* betrayed her. That's what she's feeling. That she *deserves* this suffering."

Shallan opened her eyes and stepped forward. A corridor appeared before her. It looked into a small stone room with soft glowing light.

Renarin gasped. Rlain hummed.

Together they entered a small room lit by vibrant torches. A corpse lay in the corner, old and desiccated, basically just bones. Holding . . . blocks? A child's blocks, and that side of the room was painted soft colors, like a nursery.

The corpse wore Melishi's clothing. The ancient Bondsmith had died here, alone, in the Spiritual Realm. After finding his childhood room, as each of them had.

A brilliant glowing yellow heliodor lay in the center of the chamber, ringed by candles that somehow still burned. It was cracked along one side, tiny wisps of smoke escaping to taint the Spiritual Realm, and eventually Shallan's drawings.

Mishram's prison.

Shallan, Pattern thought to her. *We are not alone.*

She turned, and saw a shadow darkening the corridor behind them. It was Mraize; she knew that posture. As he'd told her, their next encounter would lead to the end.

"I leave Mishram to you, gentlemen," she said, walking out. "I need to deal with a loose thread that has been left to dangle for far, far too long."

⁂

Navani's breath caught as Dalinar stepped into her meeting room at the top of the tower.

He was back. He was alive.

The Sibling had warned her he was coming, so she'd waited to see if she could tell from his eyes which Dalinar he was. The Bondsmith? The Blackthorn?

Neither. He was neither.

He took her in his arms and kissed her. Those watching—guards, scribes, Sebarial and Palona holding hands with a Herdazian wedding ribbon around their wrists—seemed to be made uncomfortable by his display of affection.

Navani held the kiss, held him, held to that warmth. For it was nearly time. Soon Dalinar would march up the steps to the roof, and the end would come. Once the kiss broke, Navani hugged him, feeling the hard muscles. The soft touch. "I'm sorry," she whispered.

"For what?" he asked.

"For leaving you."

"Gemheart," he replied, "you cannot leave me. I carry you inside. Gav?"

"Safe," she said. "Sleeping in the next room. He's barely stirred since we got out. Love, I thought we'd be able to help you from here. I was wrong."

He squeezed her tighter. "You did the right thing, and you are wonderful in every way, Navani. I couldn't have been saved. I didn't want to be. There were things I needed to see."

She pulled back, but kept her arms around him, tipping her chin up and meeting his eyes, so close to hers. "What?"

"I always thought the burden of a king was the greatest a man could know," Dalinar said. "But I was a child, Navani, with a childish understanding."

"You've changed," she said, and put her hand to his face, brushing her fingers over the stubble—something he hated, preferring a military clean cut. Though over a week had passed, the hairs on his face told her how long his body felt it had been gone. One day, maybe two. Remarkable.

"Every moment we live changes us, Navani," he said. "Living the memories of gods has changed me above all. I saw his life, Navani. Tanavast's entire existence. It both haunts and inspires me."

"Storms," she whispered.

"Am I . . . still frightening to you, as you once said I was?"

"No," she said, searching his eyes. "Your fire is still there, Dalinar, but I know it better now. It is not the fire of destruction, but the fire that spreads, shares its warmth. The fire that envelops my heart, but leaves me breathless."

He smiled. "I fear I will never live up to the things you say about me, love. I am far too boring. Isn't that what you once said? That older people should be compelled to be boring?"

"And yet," she said, "I'm compelled to find you fascinating regardless."

They shared a moment. The room around them—with ten pillars at the sides, one at the center, and the stairwell to the roof—remained quiet and still, despite all the observers. Including Jasnah, who had kept to herself since her return, feeling soundly her failure in Thaylen City.

No one dared clear their throats or remind them that the deadline was looming. This was *her* time. Navani kissed him again, for ten burning heartbeats.

When she pulled back, his eyes were sorrowful.

"You don't know how you're going to beat him?" she guessed. "The trip through the Spiritual Realm . . . a waste?"

"No," he said. "Very much not a waste. It showed me how little I understand, which is a lesson I wish I could stop needing to be taught. I don't know what is to come. I don't know if I'll be able to counter it. But . . . I feel more confident than I did ten days ago."

"Do what is right in the moment," she whispered.

He cocked his head.

"I trust you, Dalinar. The man you've become, at last, is a man I trust fully."

"Even with the fire?"

"Because of the fire," she said. "There is no need to trust someone who couldn't hurt you, Dalinar. I trust you because you can hold that fire and not be burned."

He nodded. "I will do what is right."

"Discard all the rest. All the thoughts, philosophies, arguments, and even the memories of gods. Do not do what *they* would have you do. Do what *you,* Dalinar Kholin, would do."

"Thank you," he said, then let go at last. And she felt colder without his touch. The world less bright. He surveyed the others. "Thank you, all of you, for your strength. Your prayers. Your trust." He nodded to Wit, who bowed his head in respect. Then, as he walked past Sebarial, Dalinar put a hand on the highprince's shoulder.

Sebarial—remarkably teary-eyed—gripped Dalinar's wrist in return. "Strange," Sebarial said, "how we can accidentally become good men, eh, Dalinar? A few choices here and there, and suddenly we're respectable. The way your brother always said he wanted."

"My brother," Dalinar said, "was a liar, Sebarial."

Sebarial smiled, squeezing Dalinar's arm. "So you finally know, do you? Gavilar always talked about living the Codes, and here you've gone and *become* them. Go. Be a storming hero. Win our homeland back."

"No," Dalinar said. "That's what the path of gods has shown me, Sebarial. I can't just protect Alethkar; I have to find a way to defeat him fully."

"How will you storming do that?"

"With oaths and light, Sebarial." Navani had placed Dalinar's copy of *The Way of Kings* on a table. He smiled, slipped it off, and carried it in one hand as he strode up the stairs.

130 THE PLEASURE OF BLEEDING

I will leave one to ponder upon the incredible irony of the Herald of Bonds deciding he needed to teach Szeth, of all people, how to be humble. As if years of slavery weren't a capable instructor.

—From *Knights of Wind and Truth,* page 83

Ishu-son-God took his hands off his Blade and clasped them behind himself, leaving it stuck in the ground. A nonthreatening posture to greet those who joined him in the shadow of the enormous rock formations. Those were tall, spindly, grasping toward the skies. Perhaps too fragile to have existed in the East without toppling.

Szeth stopped fifteen feet from Ishu. He glanced toward Kaladin, then Syl. "Either of you know what to do next?"

"No idea," Syl said.

"Nale said he'd test you one final time," Kaladin said. "To . . . teach you humility."

Szeth took a deep breath, holding himself back from summoning his Blade. He was done with killing, unless he was given a very good reason. That was *his* balance. No more fighting unless *he* decided the cost was worth it.

"Ishu," he called. "I've finished my pilgrimage."

"Indeed," the man said, his voice loud, commanding. "You are worthy of my presence, child. You may approach."

Cautious, Szeth stepped closer, followed by Kaladin and Syl—and also by his own spren, who trailed along farther behind. Nin remained in the wagon.

"Good, good," Ishu said, smiling. He had a mid-length white beard, trimmed straight across the bottom. He seemed more . . . human than Szeth had expected. His hair disheveled from the wind. "Let me look at you, child. Yes. I'm pleased with the lessons you learned in the East. You are hardened."

"Is it true? Were you . . . always the Voice in my mind?"

You are my people, the Voice said, an echo from a long time ago. Szeth trembled and almost wept. A part of him had feared he had imagined it all along. *I led you to become my warrior, Szeth, and sent you into the East to learn how to fight like a demigod. To become my champion.*

"Now," Ishu continued out loud, "you have returned to me. Refined, like the clay pot having been fired in the kiln."

"Why?" Syl said. She pressed her hands together at her breast, obviously horrified. "Why have you done this to Shinovar? Where are the spren?"

"I prepare for the difficult times ahead," Ishu said. "I have seen cataclysm, child. Roshar will need a God—a true God—to weather it." He looked up at the spren's light, which spun around this place high in the sky like a halo. "The spren rejected me, so I had to reject them."

"Is that why," Szeth asked, his voice cold, "for centuries Shinovar has had almost no spren? Why my people looked for them, worshipped them, and *longed* to listen to them . . . So that when a Voice came into their heads . . ."

"It is time," Ishu said, waving him forward. "You will be the first of my new Heralds, and can train others to lead my Fused and spren armies. Together we will make way for the end of the world, so that we may forge a new one."

"Ishar." It was Nin, stumbling forward, eventually reaching them and accepting Kaladin's arm for support. "You're wrong. We don't see straight, any of us. Listen. Listen to the tones of Roshar, to the Wind. Listen to—"

"You are weak, Nale," Ishu said, glaring at him. "I will replace you next, once Szeth has taken Jezrien's spot. Come, Szeth, you are nearly ready."

"Nearly?" Szeth said, cold.

"Szeth," Kaladin said, nudging him and pointing backward. A group of people had emerged from around the rock formations and were approaching the wagon.

Szeth recognized each of them. Moss. Pozen. Elid. The "dead" Honorbearers, turned into Fused by Ishu. There were six of them, and they helped themselves to the Honorblades in the bed of the wagon.

Szeth gritted his teeth and almost went to prevent the larceny, but Ishu spoke.

"They do not steal what you have earned, Szeth-son-Shinovar," the Herald said. "Be patient."

The six filed forward, passing Kaladin and Szeth. Nin returned to the wagon, walking more steadily this time, and strode back with the rest of the swords, including Nightblood and Kaladin's pack. He dropped those a short distance away, then approached with two Blades.

"Nale?" Kaladin asked.

"Peace, Stormblessed," Nin said, but did not meet the man's gaze. "Something must be done. You will see."

Szeth watched, wary, as each Honorbearer took their Blade and placed it into its slot in the stone ground. The rock formations and ground here were like ardents, with heads bowed in a ring, at worship—swords at the center.

Nin drove his Blade into position, then placed Sivi's. Instead of continuing to sink all the way down to their hilts, the Blades remained where they were placed, half in, half out. As they'd proven while being carried all this way, they knew how to modulate the sharpness of their edges.

"Last time I was here," Nin said, "there were nine." He moved around the circle, right hand hovering above the Blades. He stopped beside Taln's, the most simple, least ornate of those in the ring. "This one was missing then."

Ishu reached forward and put one hand on his own Blade. "And today, we once more have nine. We are missing the Blade we sent with you, Szeth."

"It is lost," Szeth said, feeling cold.

"You will replace it with a new one," Ishu explained. "It will form when you join the Heralds." He nodded to the Honorbearers, who stepped back. And Szeth realized something—he'd expected six figures. That was the right number. Szeth himself represented the Windrunners, and there was no sword for them. With Ishu, Nin, and Sivi—who had refused—that made ten.

Except one of the figures was new. Instead of the female Edgedancer Szeth had faced in Shadesmar, there was a masculine figure in robes. The man looked up. Inside the hood, Szeth saw familiar features. Round, friendly. Solid.

"Father?" Szeth whispered.

"It is well that you succeeded, Szeth," Ishu said, drawing Szeth's attention back to him. "And returned to your God."

"You are *not* a god, Ishar," Kaladin said. "We've come to try to help you. But we don't want to fight; we just want to talk."

Ishu sniffed in disdain. "As if you could fight me. But now there is no time for talk. The final confrontation at Urithiru happens in mere moments, and Dalinar will fail. He is, and always has been, a fool and a pretender. He is to face Odium's champion, yet he *sends away* his two finest soldiers?"

"Perhaps he knows," Szeth said, "that not every battle is also a fight."

Ishu shook his head. "Once Dalinar is dead, we will need an army to defeat both Odium and the greater storms coming." He hesitated, then focused on Szeth, as if momentarily surprised to see him there. "Right. I remember. You must be humbled. One last test, Szeth. My Honorbearers will defeat you, together."

"Together?" Kaladin demanded. "He can't fight all of them."

"No, he cannot," Ishu said. "He will lose, for no Herald can be elevated if he thinks himself invincible. It is the sorry truth of our existence that we must all fail eventually." The Herald pointed at Kaladin, then at Syl. "You two. Come and stand beside me. I will not have you interfering."

"Ishar," Kaladin said. "It isn't—"

"No," Szeth said. "No, I think I am ready for this." He took Kaladin by the arm, waving Syl in, and huddled together with them. Then he spoke softly. "I can do this part. I must talk to my father. I *must.*"

"I don't know," Kaladin said. "Szeth . . ."

"It is my choice," Szeth said. "Ishu will let you talk with him while the fight happens. He will watch to be sure you don't interfere. Kaladin, while I fight, you must convince him to release the people of this land. Do you understand?"

"If Ishar releases the people," Syl said, nodding, "then Szeth's quest is fulfilled."

"Which means I will ascend to my next oath," he said. "And if Dalinar is right, you will have the opportunity to speak with the *real* Ishu. Sane."

"True," Kaladin said. "But Szeth, how can I make him release Shinovar?"

"We'll think of something," Syl whispered.

"This will give me a chance to interact with my father and sister," Szeth said. "If you distract Ishu, perhaps I can get through to them."

"Wait," Kaladin said. "He wants you to be humbled. Are you going to fight?"

"No," Szeth said. "I am going to lose." He nodded, then turned to face the Honorbearers—having regained their powers along with their swords, they fanned out around him.

They were led by that figure in robes. Neturo. Szeth's father, who took Sivi's Blade, then held it like a man who knew how to use it. "I'm ready," Szeth said.

All six attacked him at once.

⁂

Dalinar carried *The Way of Kings* as he ascended the short flight of steps to the rooftop, alone.

He was half an hour early, by the watch on his arm, and couldn't help remembering the day he'd stood alone in the hole in the wall of Thaylen City, believing his book, and its words, would shield him. That had ended with burning pages and a god demanding his obedience. Yet . . . the words on the page hadn't mattered, had they? For those words had migrated to his heart.

Strange, how confident he now felt. He should have felt insignificant: perspective let him know the full extent of his inferiority. He'd lived the life of a god, and seen its vast power. Now he was but a speck. Why this confidence?

Because, he thought, *this is where the journey has brought me.* The oath wasn't journey *without* destination. And today . . . today was about where he'd arrived, and how the journey had prepared him.

And so, as he reached the last steps, Dalinar found himself standing tall. He was deeply flawed, but if those flaws were obvious to him now . . . that was because he had grown to the point he could acknowledge them. He knew the most important words a man could say. He'd witnessed the failings of those who came before. Those failures were his heritage—as the history of all humankind was to be found in this moment.

He was here because he'd *chosen* this path. The long journey to Urithiru—in his case accomplished with stumbles, broken bones, and ash on his skin.

He would do better.

Dalinar stepped out of the open-topped stairwell onto the rooftop of the tower city, and found the sky dark, though no storm was forecast. The red lightning seemed muted as it flashed from deep within the clouds, an erratic heartbeat. The lack of thunder following it was unnerving, but more so was the figure made of dark mist coalescing on the rooftop.

Taravangian. Standing tall, without the slight crook to his back he'd always had when Dalinar had known him. He wore yellow robes, bordering on gold, and a simple golden crown, his hands clasped behind him.

"Dalinar," he said, smiling in a way that Dalinar might once have seen as kindly. "Navani's efforts to improve your punctuality have worked, my friend."

"Do not name me friend."

"Should I lie?"

"The friendship *was* the lie."

"I wish that were so." His eyes appeared genuinely sorrowful. "That would make what I'm forced to do to you oh so much easier. But I have done worse. Yes, I have done worse. Are you ready?"

"I am."

"Then it is time for you to meet my champion." Taravangian gestured to the side, where power coalesced into a portal—the sort that Dalinar now recognized as a small perpendicularity into the Spiritual Realm.

A figure stepped through, wearing a Kholin uniform, carrying a familiar Shardblade. Oathbringer, the Blade Dalinar had thought secure in his rooms. It was carried by a man who was shockingly, alarmingly familiar. Prominent nose. Lean build. Dark expression.

Elhokar.

⁂

Szeth ducked in close to his father first, emotions churning. The last time he'd been with Neturo, the man had turned his back and walked away—weeping because he could not go with his son.

Szeth had not felt worthy of Neturo's name for so, so long. Then, to hear his father was dead . . . Szeth stepped up to Neturo and raised his hands, with no weapon in them. Completely expecting that, as in his reunion with his sister, a refusal to fight would prompt a change of heart.

Neturo punched him in the face.

A powerful attack that left Szeth stumbling, drawing in Stormlight to heal by instinct. He felt blood on his lip and gasped, wide-eyed as Neturo marched forward. Eyes wild, teeth gritted, hood falling back to reveal a hairless head—though judging by the fuzz of hair at the sides, his father was fully bald now, rather than just shaving.

Szeth tried to show him a smile again, his hands spread. "Father. Please, let's—"

The next punch sent Szeth to the stone, and a kick followed. The other five gathered around and laid into him with fists and feet, not swinging their swords, as he curled up on the ground.

⁂

Adolin dodged to the side, rounding the large throne room, empty of people save for him and the Fused. Again he tried to summon his Blade, and again nothing. He couldn't even sense Maya. What could he do?

Reach the throne, he thought, *and trigger the unlocking mechanism? Then escape?*

Abidi crashed through furniture, tossing it aside as he gave chase. If Adolin couldn't escape, then he had to succeed at a near-impossible task. One only a single man in recent memory had ever accomplished: defeating a Shardbearer in single combat when you were without.

The room had a set of unadorned bronze pillars running down either side, near the walls. Adolin hurdled a golden table, knocking over beautiful candlesticks, then landed awkwardly on his peg. He tripped, caught himself on a large stand with bowls on top, and made for one of the pillars to give himself some better cover.

Abidi kicked away the table behind him, then stumbled as he overextended.

Too much force, Adolin thought as he reached the pillar and unsheathed his side sword. *He's not used to the Plate.* Adolin had seen similar stumbles from Yanagawn recently.

Abidi wasn't as awkward as the emperor had been. He stomped forward more cautiously, faceplate glowing red. He was a trained soldier, with thousands of years of experience. But he couldn't fly, so he had to rely on Plate he hadn't had time to train in yet.

That was something at least. Still, as Adolin turned and tried to stand, Abidi's swordsmanship proved excellent. He flowed with incredible grace as he made his first expert strikes, and Adolin couldn't parry, lest he lose his weapon. So he was forced back.

Storms. Adolin rounded the pillar, putting it between himself and Abidi, who had to stomp around it. Despite his swordsmanship, in that Plate he wasn't as graceful with his footwork as he might otherwise have been. Adolin was able to keep ahead of his foe by weaving between the pillars, then he limp-dashed to the far wall and the dais with the throne.

He searched, but he couldn't find the mechanism to lock and unlock the door. He had no idea where the hidden exit was from this side, plus it had been jammed somehow. Escaping seemed unlikely.

Abidi charged between the pillars, ignoring the low tables in the way—crashing through them with a terrible racket, scattering fine silvery cups and plates to the ground. He came in fast, but Adolin was able to leap to the side—and since Abidi had more momentum than he expected with the Plate, he struck the throne, knocking it over.

Adolin hit the carpet below the short dais and rolled, coming up on one foot—the good one. Then he heaved himself up and dashed—as best he could—toward the other set of pillars. He blessed the hours he'd spent practicing with the peg, since he could move somewhat quickly. At the same time, he felt frustrated. Without this hindrance, he *might* have had a chance. *Maybe* he could have stood against a full Shardbearer who was new to his Plate.

As it was . . . Adolin did have some training in fighting a Shardbearer without Shards of his own. It was a little like training in how to land if tossed off a cliff. They all knew it meant basically nothing. He would die here.

No. No more fatalistic thoughts. If he fell, Azir fell. He had to find a way to do the impossible. He *had* to stop this creature. Now.

Adolin reached the first pillar, then turned as Abidi leaped off the throne and crashed down near him. He didn't stumble this time. The Fused wasn't some bumbling fool—he was inexperienced with a new tool, but his posture was excellent as he attacked again.

Adolin attempted to find an opening to attack. Zahel had trained him to parry a Shardblade—it involved slapping the flat portion of the enemy's weapon—but Adolin didn't dare, because a single wrong move would be death. Instead he hopped back.

He tried as best he could, but Abidi had reach, strength, speed . . . and every other advantage. He easily kept Adolin at bay, forcing him back between the pillars. At the final one, Adolin planned another strike—and his instincts let him guess correctly the direction Abidi would come around the pillar to attack. Abidi ducked around from the left, and Adolin performed an expert lunge—but then the peg slipped. His sword clanged against the near-impervious Shardplate, and Adolin fell, his bad leg going out from underneath him.

Abidi laughed. "It feels incredible to wear this Plate! To be invincible and watch you struggle, the rat that you are, with panic in your eyes. Why have we never developed a version of this for ourselves?"

Adolin rolled, knowing that the Blade would fall any moment. Puffing, increasingly exhausted and aching—though in this room he drew no spren to betray his state—he crawled to his feet by using the rear wall to support him. As soon as he did though, Abidi lunged and swung. Adolin threw himself to the side, the only desperate move he could make in such a situation, and managed to avoid the Blade. But he slipped and hit the ground again, and was left with the haunting image of that sword passing less than an inch before his eyes.

He rolled over with a groan, propping himself up with his sword, somewhat dazed as he found his feet.

"They said you were good," Abidi said, Blade pointed at Adolin. "Was I really reawakened to fight one so pathetic?"

"How did you survive Taln's attack, Abidi?" Adolin snapped, falling into a stance, trying to shake off his fatigue. "He killed almost all the others. If you wanted a challenge, why didn't you fight *him*?"

The glow of burning eyes through the faceplate increased, illuminating the dimly lit room. That had struck a nerve.

"You ran, didn't you?" Adolin asked, backing away, sword out, hand coated in sweat. "How regal of you."

The Fused didn't snarl or flinch at the barb, but he did kick an overturned table straight at Adolin. Adolin cursed, ducking, and got clipped on the shoulder. Sharp pain rushed down his arm as he stumbled into one of the pillars opposite the ones he'd been using. Perhaps taunting the immortal, Surge-powered murderer in Shardplate wasn't the best idea.

Adolin committed himself to running and dodging, staying ahead—but only because he could maneuver around the furniture and pillars. For one who had just taunted his opponent for refusing a fight, Adolin was forced to do the same. Even with that, he should have died.

Except it didn't seem the Fused wanted to end this quickly. He stalked through the room, but didn't give much chase. With a sinking feeling, Adolin realized that Abidi had no reason to be hasty. He held this throne room—if the deadline arrived, Adolin had little doubt that by Azish law, the kingdom would go to Odium. Therefore, the Fused could bide his time, toying with Adolin, enjoying his prey's rising panic.

Adolin had to *win* this fight *quickly.* Yet as he tried to set for Windstance, his stupid foot—or not-foot—slipped *again,* and he was forced to brace his left arm on a pillar to avoid tripping. In a duel, your footwork needed to be intricate. He expected to be able to spring off his toes. He needed heels to spin on. Needed the sides of his feet to stop himself.

He'd practiced walking and even half-running on this new foot, but he *hadn't* practiced any footwork. There was no way he'd win against *any* capable enemy, let alone one in Plate.

Abidi cut off Adolin's route to the other side of the room. "Do you miss the energy and power of this Plate, little human? Do you feel small?"

"I've felt small for years now," Adolin whispered.

But as he said it, he found new perspective. He'd been complaining since the fall of Kholinar—maybe longer—about how the world had changed, outgrown people like him. However, last night, he'd been a common spearman. Adolin realized right then that the world *hadn't* changed that much. The darkeyes had *always* felt small in this world of Shardbearers.

Adolin's *place* had changed. He'd been complaining about suddenly being one of the small ones—a reality the vast majority of soldiers lived with every day.

Kaladin survived this, he reminded himself again. Years ago, Kaladin had killed a Shardbearer. It *wasn't* impossible.

Abruptly, he was back at his training with Zahel.

Zahel had forced him to fight on a pile of shifting stones, because his footing wouldn't always be sure. He'd forced Adolin to fight in the rain, or when standing on a narrow beam. Adolin had grumbled at each session, claiming he'd never need this kind of training in a practical situation.

Zahel had insisted.

Bless him.

Something clicked in Adolin, and when he next set his peg, he *expected* it to slip. He accounted for it, used it, and incorporated that slip into his stance. As he backed away this time, he changed his gait to account for the peg, and stopped stumbling or limping. The peg was still a disability, but he *could* deal with it. If he couldn't—if he could only fight when circumstances were perfect—then what kind of swordsman was he?

Abidi seemed to notice as Adolin's stance became more sure, his dodges more precise. The creature grunted. "Tell the emperor to surrender and deliver himself to me. I will let both of you live."

"Why do you care?" Adolin asked, stepping around the fallen throne, knocked off its dais.

“I want him as my servant,” Abidi explained. “His people will serve me better if I control him.”

It was likely true. In exile, Yanagawn would claim to be the true monarch. Even with Dalinar’s deal, a rival dynasty set up by Yanagawn in Urithiru would be inconvenient for those ruling Azir.

“I thought you might bring him to me here in the palace,” the Fused said, swiping a few times with his Blade, evidently enjoying the sound of it cutting the air. “Still, we can deal. Deliver him, and you live, human. I will abandon the pleasure of bleeding you for this price. Where is he?”

For a moment, Adolin was confused. Had the Fused not seen Yanagawn peek in with the others at the start of the fight? But of course; without his robes and trappings, Yanagawn was just another youth. Abidi hadn’t recognized him. Why would he?

The very person Abidi wanted was right outside. It remained quiet in the hallway. The forces likely had orders not to attack until Abidi made his play to take the emperor prisoner. Suddenly, Adolin didn’t feel so proud of his ability to survive so long against a Shardbearer. Abidi hadn’t truly wanted him dead, not yet.

Adolin pretended to think about the offer to gain a little time. Because he was still in serious trouble. Even if he could fight as Zahel had trained him, even if he managed to account for the peg, he had next to no chance. He needed an edge. And one occurred to him as he eyed the first table he’d hurdled over after entering the room.

The one where he’d knocked over some finery set out to please the emperor. And Adolin was reminded of evening games with Yanagawn, and a conversation about a fallen star.

“If I give him up,” Adolin said, “what would you be willing to pay me?”

“Well,” Abidi replied. “That could—”

But the question was a feint to get the creature thinking. As Abidi replied, Adolin stumbled over and scooped something up off the ground with his left hand.

Abidi cursed and came in with a direct, flowing strike of the Blade. Adolin lifted his left hand, and parried—

—*clang*—

—with an ornate aluminum candelabra.

I often reflect upon how the world changed that day. And how I spent it, completely unaware, working in the family orchard. Picking fruit while the End of All Things itself came upon us.

—From *Knights of Wind and Truth,* page 92

Do you need me? Radiant asked Shallan as she stepped up to confront Mraize.

He was in his own body for once, wearing the finery she'd come to associate with him, with softness, ruffles, and embroidery. It contrasted starkly with the scars on his face, the lean cut of his features, the dangerous expression.

He waited for her outside the corridor, and as Shallan left, the way into Mishram's prison didn't vanish. A room with an open hallway at one side that had appeared here in this otherwise featureless grey plane with a black sky. The expanse of white-grey stone extended in all directions, into infinity.

Shallan stood between him and the way in. Then Radiant stepped up, made of unsolidified Stormlight—faintly transparent, wisps of it trailing off her uniformed figure. Pattern and Testament hovered just inside the doorway to the prison—and Pattern held Testament to keep her back.

Formless, unfortunately, was there as well. Lurking to Shallan's left, her face a swirl, her hair matching Shallan's.

"Do you want me," Radiant repeated, "to handle this?"

Usually Shallan simply adopted one persona or another. Lately though, Radiant came only when called for, and only in the most extreme situations.

"I . . . don't need you right now," Shallan said.

"You're certain?"

Shallan regarded Mraize, with that half-cocked smile and weaponized arrogance. Could she handle this? She felt in her pocket, and found the dagger she'd stolen from him in their earlier clash. They both knew exactly what was coming. One had to inflict the other with a fatal wound using anti-Light, forcing them to either heal and die, or die from the wound.

I'm certain I can do this myself, Shallan thought. *I'm not sure I could kill a spren, but this . . . this I can do.*

Radiant evaporated, retreating to the back of Shallan's mind. Formless, however, drew nearer. That frightened Shallan, because while she knew she'd never be fully "better," she'd thought she'd handled this. She'd thought . . .

"You should let me pass into that chamber, little knife," Mraize said, striding forward. "I need to recover the gemstone inside."

He's too confident, even for him. What am I missing?

"I basically beat you last time we exchanged knives," Shallan said.

"A well-fought clash," Mraize said, stopping five feet in front of her. "But you had help. Do you truly think you can fight me one-on-one?"

She wasn't certain, no. She could fight, and she knew some small measure of sleight of hand. But Mraize was an expert. Trained by Iyatil, who . . .

"Where *is* Iyatil?" Shallan asked. "I haven't seen her since we entered."

"She's watching Dalinar," he said. "I have done my job, as you know, which was to keep you distracted."

It was reasonable. It was what she'd guessed. Except why would Iyatil watch Dalinar? Dalinar wasn't looking for Mishram. He had *never* been looking for Mishram. They'd used him to get into this realm, but once here . . .

Shallan moved on pure instinct as the pieces clicked into place. She whipped out the anti-Stormlight knife, then spun.

And plunged it directly toward the face of Formless.

⁂

Kaladin winced, turning away from the farce of a fight where the Honorbearers attacked Szeth—who refused to fight back. At least they used only fists and feet. Kaladin and Syl, as instructed, stood with Ishar.

Szeth, fortunately, managed to scramble free from the pile-on. Full of Stormlight, he flew backward onto the more open portion of stone near the abandoned wagon. His assailants followed, using Surges. Sliding across the ground, making stones melt.

Difficult though it was, Kaladin tore his eyes away from the fight and focused on Ishar. How in the world did Kaladin help a being like this, who thought himself God?

Start by talking, he decided. *Or getting him talking.*

"You were there?" Kaladin asked. "From the very beginning? Is it true that we . . . came from another world?"

Ishar turned, ponderous as a shifting mountain, and regarded Kaladin. "Yes. We called our world Alaswha. There was a time when I loved it very much. We are literally the last pieces of our lost homeland here." He paused. "I am not so eager to lose another world, bridgeman. *I* will fight."

"We welcome your help," Kaladin said, then gestured to Szeth. "But does it have to be like this? Is *this* necessary?"

"A god must be willing to accept the pain of his people. Without pain, there is no joy."

Nale did not participate in the beating. He stood quietly, watching, his black uniform wrinkled from his time in the bed of the wagon. He looked far more . . . human because of that. Syl—on Kaladin's other side—gave a soft gasp each time Szeth took a blow, but Stormlight would keep Szeth alive. Kaladin needed to use this chance to try to convince Ishar to release Shinovar from his touch. So, he defaulted back to what had worked with Nale. He sent a mental request to Syl, and she obliged, becoming a silvery flute for him. He put it to his lips and blew a few hesitant notes.

Nale nodded eagerly.

Ishar heaved a sigh. "What is this?"

"Um . . ." Kaladin said, lowering the flute. "The story of the *Wandersail* is about Derethil and—"

"Yes, I wrote it," Ishar said.

"You . . . what?" Kaladin asked.

"I wrote it down," Ishar said absently. "Three thousand years ago, I suppose it was. When Derethil—then so old he could not walk without the help of his grandson—told me his tale. Much of it was embellishments, I expect. I've searched for the islands he mentioned, and although my methods are not exhaustive, I could not find them. This lends credence to the entire thing being a fancy of an old man whose fishing boat got lost in a storm."

He looked at Kaladin. On the field of stone, Szeth cried out in pain. He pulled into the air with a Lashing, holding one arm, which was broken and twisted the wrong way.

"The top room," Kaladin said.

"Was empty save for a corpse," Ishar said. "Yes. I'm trying to fill it, young man."

"But—"

"I'm wise to Midius's tricks, child," Ishar said. "He was there when we destroyed our previous world. Did your Wit tell you *that*? That he was involved, perhaps even responsible? He told us about the Shards, and it was his talk that led us to first contact Odium."

A cold shock ran through Kaladin.

"He prefers to leave that part out," Ishar said. "Strange, how he always manages to worm his way into each and every relevant decision. Like a fly that you can't swat."

"He . . ." What could Kaladin say after that? He looked at his flute. "There's another story . . ."

"Which one?" Ishar asked. "Gasha and the ten assassins? The story of the wandering island? Tepra, the dragon child?"

"Fleet," Kaladin said. "He—"

"Fleet never actually made it to Shinovar," Ishar said. "Although the story is much better when it claims that he did. He died somewhere in Marat, of dysentery. Made it quite a good distance though, for someone who was trying to re-create Nohadon's trip."

"Nohadon's trip?" Kaladin said. "He ran ahead of the storm to . . . race the wind itself . . ."

"He liked to jog, but it took him months and months," Ishar said. "Regardless, please keep your children's rhymes and songs to yourself. The adults are trying to save the world."

⁂

Renarin hesitantly prodded the dead Bondsmith, Melishi. Withered, the skin like parchment, the eyes just gaping holes.

"No wound that I can see," Rlain said, carefully inspecting the corpse. "It could be any number of things."

"What happened to his skin?"

Rlain hummed to the Rhythm of Curiosity. "That's right. You burn your dead. This is what bodies look like when they're left out in a dry region. I've seen it with some of our dead, when left in a cavern rather than placed out for a sky burial."

He died . . . a voice said in their heads. *A terrible, wasting death, as he deserved. As* all *deserve to die! As the world must be broken and all life scourged!*

Within Renarin, Glys trembled, and began to pulse with a frightened rhythm. They looked to the gemstone lying on the floor, cracked. Renarin could see Mishram inside as a black tempest, straining against her confines. Violent flashes of red. A miniature Everstorm.

"He wandered, didn't he?" Renarin asked. "Trapped in the Spiritual Realm, with no way out, as his powers had faded away."

He betrayed his spren as he betrayed me!

"No," Renarin said. "What he did to you was terrible, but he did what he could to protect the Sibling. No need to magnify his sins—they are great enough without exaggeration." He stood up, worried for Shallan, and glanced out of the room toward where she fought Mraize.

"Whatever we're going to do, Renarin," Rlain said, "we should do it soon. In case she fails."

"Should we help her?"

"She *really* didn't sound like she wanted help," Rlain said. He'd stood and was probing the walls. "This isn't Urithiru or Narak. The stone is wrong. Can you read these glyphs?"

Renarin shook his head, but Glys said haltingly, *Bless . . . this child . . .*

"Ah," Renarin said. "They were painted for a child, blessing him in sickness. Usually glyphs are burned for prayers, but perhaps back then it was more common to leave them visible. This was his childhood room, sparse though it is. I suspect it was shared with many siblings."

Rlain suddenly hummed to Appreciation. Then together, the two of them looked at the gemstone.

They had a decision to make.

Elhokar?

How . . . how could the champion be *Elhokar*?

Emotions assaulted Dalinar, unexpected, shaking his resolve and earlier confidence. In this young man's eyes, he saw his own failures magnified. Elhokar . . . poor Elhokar.

"Grandfather," the man said, his expression dark. "I've waited a great long time for this."

Wait.

Grandfather?

In that moment, Dalinar saw the differences. The shape of the jaw, the set of the brow. This man looked a great deal like Elhokar . . . because he was Elhokar's son. This was Gavinor. But . . . Gavinor was just a child.

Taravangian stepped up beside him, speaking conversationally. "Twenty years in the Spiritual Realm, Dalinar, passed as an hour in this realm. That's where Gavinor lived after you abandoned him."

No. It couldn't be. It . . .

"Gav is downstairs," Dalinar whispered. "Sleeping."

"Yes," Taravangian said. "I couldn't create something that would live and act like him. My powers in that area—creation—are limited. I could manage a lump of flesh that looked like him, and seemed to sleep, and that is what appeared in Navani's arms as she left the perpendicularity."

"No," Dalinar said. "I don't believe it. I can't. This is an illusion. A Fused wearing his face."

"Believe that lie if you wish," Taravangian replied. "Maybe it will make you feel better when you kill him."

"You cannot reject me, Grandfather," Gavinor said, raising Oathbringer. "You took the throne from my father. You sent him to die. All along, the only thing you wanted was power."

"Gav," Dalinar said, still not certain what to believe. "I loved your father."

"I watched you beat him senseless!" Gav shouted. "I watched you kill your wife, I watched you burn that city! For twenty years, I *remembered*." His voice softened. "I remembered my father in your hands, terrified . . ." He raised Oathbringer again. "I will take this kingdom for myself. In the name of my father. In the name of . . . of Alethkar."

Hearing that struck Dalinar like a punch to the gut. It . . . it couldn't be true, could it? Except . . . it was possible. He himself had often noted how slowly time outside passed while he was in visions, the reverse of what happened when he floated in the Spiritual Realm.

Taravangian could have very easily placed Gav in a vision meant just for him, and caused decades to pass there.

"What have you *done*?" Dalinar whispered, horrified.

"Made a champion," Taravangian said. "Worthy of you."

"If that is really Gavinor," Dalinar shouted, turning toward Taravangian, "then what you've done is *horrific.* I will not fight my grandson. Choose someone else."

"Or what?" Taravangian said, meeting his eyes. "With what do you back up this threatening posture and voice, Blackthorn? You cannot punch *me* into submission, as you did Elhokar. This is my champion, chosen in accordance with our agreement."

Dalinar hissed out a frustrated breath between clenched teeth, then spun toward Gavinor.

Dalinar, the Stormfather said. *I think . . . I think that is actually him. I see the threads of Connection, and the events of the past. Odium was right there, when Navani escaped, and saw exactly what she was doing. He swapped the child as she left, then took him. It actually* has *been decades for the boy, spent being trained to hate you. Take care.*

Dalinar's heart broke at the words. He stepped up to the man, who warded him off with the Blade. There were still some minutes until the contest began officially, and he wouldn't strike before then.

"Gav," Dalinar said, anguished. This poor, poor child. "He's tricked you. Listen, you've been misled."

"He told me you'd say that," Gavinor replied. "That you'd treat me like a child, incapable of making choices. But I am a *king,* Dalinar. Born to be a king, raised through fire and smoke to make this land mine. If I kill you, then Alethkar is mine by his promise. *I* will free our people. *Not you.*"

He leveled the Blade, and Dalinar—worried—stepped back.

"Do you recognize it?" Taravangian asked.

"Of course I do," Dalinar snapped.

"It took some work, while you were gone, to have it brought here," Taravangian added. "Terribly inconvenient that my best tools cannot enter the tower."

Dalinar backed up, still eyeing that Shardblade. Perhaps to keep from looking Gav in the eyes, and to avoid thinking about what a terror the boy's life must have been. Twenty years? He'd missed Gav's entire childhood? Stolen from him, from the boy, from Navani?

It grew more awful the more he considered it.

"Why, Taravangian?" Dalinar whispered. "Why this? Why not let me face a Fused, or an Unmade, or Moash."

"I'd rather it be Elhokar himself," Taravangian said. "But he is beyond even my touch. Regardless, this is appropriate." He gestured to Gavinor. "I haven't lied to him, Dalinar. And he is fully willing, per the terms of our agreement."

"But—"

"If you wish to denounce me, tell him you *didn't* take the throne from his father in all but name. Tell him you *didn't* burn down a city with your own wife inside."

"Gav," Dalinar said, holding out his hands to the man, "I have made mistakes. Terrible ones that I deeply regret. But *don't do this.*"

"Grandfather?" Gavinor said. In that moment . . . his voice held echoes of the child he'd once been. "Would you die for Alethkar? If I kill you, the kingdom is mine beneath Odium. We will join his coalition, and make Roshar the greatest power in the cosmere. Isn't that worth your life?"

Storms, the coldness in that tone. The hardness in those eyes.

"It's nearly time, Dalinar," Taravangian whispered.

"I'm *not* going to fight Gavinor. He has done nothing wrong."

"No," Taravangian said. "It won't actually be a fight, but you *are* going to kill him, Dalinar. That is how this ends. You will save Alethkar—and protect the cosmere from my influence—with one simple act: the murder of an innocent."

I find stories of the Knight of Wind to be most intriguing. They call him Stormblessed, but best I can tell, the storm alternately tried to kill him and proclaim him its son. I wonder what it knew that we do not.

—From *Knights of Wind and Truth,* page 34

Adolin grinned, holding the three-pronged aluminum candelabra that he'd used to block Abidi's Blade. Shaped a little like a fork, the branching prongs reminded him of a Marati swordbreaker. At any rate, the sturdy metal construction caught the Blade mere inches from Adolin's face.

The fight dynamics changed.

Abidi started to try for real, attacking more relentlessly. But Adolin found, here in this dim throne room in a foreign land, a place for a swordsman. He fought using knife and sword style, another one that Zahel had drilled into him—though it was not used in formal duels.

Abidi moved like the wind, and had the power of Plate. But Adolin . . .

Adolin cared.

That wasn't always enough. But today he backed it up with a lifetime of training and an enthusiastic passion for the duel. He focused on dodging and parrying, but he engaged instead of running.

That shouldn't have been enough against such a powerful foe, yet time became as melting wax, moments flowing thickly into one another. Lessons resurfaced about not letting the enemy maximize the power of their Plate. As they clashed, Adolin diverted the enemy's attacks rather than catching them—not letting Abidi shove him backward.

He let his enemy overstep, try too hard, stumble and struggle with the strength of his Plate. Abidi could easily overpower him if Adolin tried to pit their muscles against one another—but it meant nothing if Abidi couldn't land a hit or otherwise leverage the Plate.

Seconds became as one. Adolin moved like water, or the trembling flame. He was as careful and precise as he'd ever been—near to perfect as he incorporated the peg and his unconventional dagger into his style. The only sounds were footsteps. Clangs. Thump of peg on stone or carpet. And an increasingly frustrated grunting from the Fused.

"Why?" Abidi finally demanded. "Why do you even *bother*? Azir isn't your land. This isn't your fight."

Why? Adolin gave it a moment before replying.

"You made it our fight," he said. "When you invaded. You unified us as nothing has ever been able to do. Alethi tyrants tried and failed, but nothing works like a common enemy." Adolin hesitated. "Besides. I promised I would help."

"Bah!" Abidi said. "You humans and your oaths."

"Not an oath," Adolin whispered, parrying the Shardblade with a clang. "A *promise*."

To him they were different. In ways he was starting to realize were important, deep down to his core identity.

⁂

"Oh, look out, Szeth!" his spren called.

Szeth had no opportunity to "look out" because he didn't know which direction to turn—besides, attacks were coming from all angles. His broken arm had barely healed. He tried to Lash himself into the air, but the Stoneward snapped out a whip, wrapping Szeth's leg, then made the whip hard and unyielding as steel.

Szeth was yanked back down, and tried to protect himself with his hands and arms as attacks came from all sides again. The pain was nearly unbearable, new sparks of it flaring up from each punch or kick. They forced him to the ground, and the stone became liquid beneath his feet.

"That's not good!" Szeth's spren cried from somewhere. "Um, maybe get up, Szeth?"

He groaned. A part of him wanted to use his Stormlight to send these fools into oblivion. To bring death and destruction. But . . . was that the right choice?

Why, after all of this, did he *still* not know the right choice? Why couldn't someone tell him?

Through blurry, tearstained eyes, he saw a figure grab him by his loose white uniform. Szeth blinked, making out his father's shape. The mouth a snarl, lips parted to show teeth.

But the eyes . . . the eyes were crying.

Neturo threw him tumbling across the ground. Szeth came to a rest, a mass of pains upon pains. He drew in the last of his Stormlight, waiting for its healing touch.

"I yield," Szeth said, lying there. "Please, I yield."

"No." Ishu's voice, from farther away. "You are not permitted to yield. This is over only when I say it is, Szeth."

Szeth raised his head from the cold stone, looking past six approaching figures. Toward the more distant forms of Kaladin, Nin, and Ishu. He blinked.

"How long?" Szeth forced out.

"Until you *fight* and *lose,*" Ishu called. "I will not stand for this weakness, Szeth."

He sighed and slumped back. Though a part of his mind . . . a part of his mind noticed something.

Six Honorbearers. I was confused at first, not expecting my father among them. Because I fought six before.

But including him, there should be seven.

He'd counted ten by adding Ishu, Nin, Sivi, and the empty space Szeth was to take. But with both Neturo and Ishu, that double-counted Bondsmiths.

There were only nine accounted for then. The Edgedancer was missing. He forced himself to stand and confront them: familiar faces, including his father and sister. As they struck again, he saw the solution.

He'd fought the Edgedancer in Shadesmar alongside Pozen. She hadn't been reborn like the others. Why not? Was it because . . .

Storms.

She was the sole one he'd killed with Nightblood.

⁂

Rlain knelt with Renarin by the gemstone prison. As they did, Renarin reached out and took Rlain's hand for support. Rlain looked down, attuning Joy, then found that feeling remarkable. How normal it felt, how easily he'd responded to that touch, how much he enjoyed it.

"We found the prison," Renarin said. "So . . . we have to decide. What do you think we should do?"

"We take it with us, I suppose," Rlain said. "We hide it deeper in the Spiritual Realm."

"To wander forever?" Renarin said. "Storms . . . is that what we're here to do? Find a way to patch the gemstone so she can't send hints to anyone else, then die in here like Melishi did?"

Both fell silent. Rlain attuned Resolve.

"We could find a way out afterward," Rlain said. "Or we could take it and hide it in Urithiru."

"Since *that* has proven so secure," Renarin replied. "The enemy has broken in twice in the last year alone!"

"The Sibling is awake now to stop them." He said it to Skepticism, however. The tower might protect from Fused, but what of other humans? *Someone* would want this prison. It was far too valuable.

Because Odium fears her . . . Rlain thought.

And . . . what if they did something else with it? This was the god his people had rejected so long ago. Would it be a betrayal to free her now? Or would it instead be poetic?

Would she just start another war, enraged? Would she kill him, kill Renarin? Destroy? Dared he even consider unleashing such a terrible force upon the world?

Be careful, Rlain, Tumi said. *Please, be very careful.*

Inside the gemstone, Ba-Ado-Mishram had retreated, the tempest stilling. As if she was resigned to her fate.

"You led us to you," Renarin said. "Why?"

To destroy you!

"Locked in a prison?" Renarin said. "With only the faintest crack from which to speak?" He surveyed the large heliodor, cracked at one corner, perhaps when dropped here by Melishi.

Rlain wondered what it had been like for the human, near the end. Wandering, likely weak. He looked like he'd died of old age, or he'd run out of water over a long period of time. A sad way to die, but then again, this was the man who had orchestrated the betrayal and enslavement of Rlain's entire species. So he found he didn't mind so much that the death had likely been miserable.

Destroy you, Mishram said, softer. *Get . . . vengeance . . .* She had slowed further in her gemstone, now looking so very small. She was afraid, alone, and trapped.

"You led us," Rlain said to the Rhythm of Hope, "because you thought we might help you, didn't you?"

Silence. Not even a pulsed rhythm.

Two thousand years in a prison. Betrayed, hating all humankind, she still hoped for freedom—and she knew if no one ever found her, she'd never get out.

"Defend yourself!" Ishar shouted, his face growing red as Szeth just continued to take the beating. "You are to be a Herald! Show some *pride*!"

Kaladin frowned, noticing that the Honorbearers seemed to react to Ishar's emotions. Moving more quickly, more aggressively, as he shouted.

"Ishar," Kaladin said.

"Hmm?" Ishar asked. "Was there something else, child?"

Kaladin felt chilled by how easily Ishar changed from enraged to placid. On the field, the Honorbearers' attacks calmed.

"We want to help you," Syl said, having reappeared—full sized, beside Kaladin—no longer the flute.

"That is kind of you," Ishar said. "But I need no help, not from you two. Watch, and do not interfere."

"Ishar," Nale said from the other side. "I think . . . I think you should listen. We *do* need help. We're . . . we're not right."

"I've observed that in you and the others," Ishar said. "But I have become the Almighty, and have withstood the darkness." He narrowed his eyes. "I hold our bond together, fractured though it is. But, Nale, I do sense your darkness. I feel it in all of you, even Taln. I carry your burden, in part, but *I* resist it. I am a *god*."

"You took the power of Odium, Ishar," Nale said. "And it's corrupting you."

"I subsume that power and make it mine. *I* corrupt *it*."

Syl looked to Kaladin, seeming helpless. He shared the emotion. Even the Wind had stilled, as if she didn't know what to do either.

"Stormblessed," Ishar said, "do you remember what I told you when we first met in this land?"

"That I could have an audience with you," Kaladin said, "if I helped Szeth."

"Not that," Ishar said. "I told you how I bolstered the Heralds, and held their darkness. Do you wish to feel it? I could show you a grief that would break any mortal. It would break the Heralds, if I allowed it." He laid his hands over his heart. "This is why I am a god. You have your audience. Is this all you wished to do with it? Tell me Midius's silly tales?"

The spren wait, Syl said in his mind. *Thousands of them. Worried, because something dangerous is coming. They are here with us. Kaladin, we have to do something. What?*

Kaladin sweated, and felt impotent. He couldn't help Ishar on such a deadline; that wasn't how healing worked. Not of the body, and certainly not of the mind.

So maybe it was best to try another tactic. "You are a god," Kaladin said, "yet leave your people without choices?"

Ishar growled softly. "You dare question me?"

"Yes," Kaladin said. "How can you be a god if nobody worships you?"

"This entire *land* worships me!" Ishar said, and Kaladin winced as the attacks against Szeth became more violent. "Shinovar, and beyond. They pray to the Almighty."

"Who they think is Tanavast." Kaladin waved to the Honorbearers. "They are directly under your control, aren't they? Like the people of this land we passed, hiding in shadows, barely self-aware? You *force* them to follow you. You haven't become their god, Ishar. They don't *worship* you, for they cannot. You're just another pretender."

"How *dare* you," Ishar said, his eyes starting to glow.

"Now," Kaladin said, chin up, "if you were to *release* them, and they *still* worshipped you . . . that would be different."

"Child," Ishar said softly, "I am over seven thousand years old. You think you can trick me into doing as you wish? A god is no god if the worship, or even the mild regard, of his inferiors is requisite to his status." He turned to Kaladin, his back to the swords. "Why are you here?"

"I—"

"What do you think you add?" Ishar asked. "I told you before, I did not foresee you. It makes no sense that you would come here. You, who are too broken to fight? You, who cannot help with strategy or planning? Dalinar sent you because he needed you out of the way. Your part is done, and you scramble for relevance. You are not helping. You *cannot* help. Sit down and stop trying to distract me."

Each word should have been a spear. Perhaps even a few weeks ago they would have been. A condemnation, when Kaladin had tried so hard to protect and help others. Working until it left him battered beyond functionality, like a worn-out shield.

Yet something had changed in him. Or had been changing. His worth did not come from whether he helped. Only in whether he tried.

Ishar strode toward the fighting, and Kaladin realized he'd made an error. Playing into the man's delusions, even to try to manipulate him, felt wrong. Underhanded.

So instead he spoke words he knew Ishar would ignore, but words that needed to be said. "You aren't a god, Ishar," Kaladin said. "You're a man. Seven thousand years old, yes. But still a man. And you *need help.*"

Ishar stopped and glared at him, blue robes rippling as the Wind . . . the Wind started to return.

"The spren are afraid," Syl said, stepping up beside Kaladin. "Terrified, Ishar. They know, as I think you know, that something difficult is coming. Let's face it together. You know you've driven them away. Shouldn't that be a sign that what you're doing is wrong?"

“I have plans for the spren,” Ishar said, a softness to his voice that made Kaladin’s hair stand on end. “They might fear what is coming. Their fear of me should be greater.” He spun and strode toward the fighting, then with a furious tone bellowed, “Of all the things I expected of you, Szeth, *disobedience* is not one of them! Fight!”

And all attention turned back toward the ragged man wearing white. His Stormlight starting to fail.

Much of what I know of the Knight of Wind, I get from Jasnah Kholin. Now head of our order, and a woman who has shown much patience for a simple Shin bookworm who thinks herself worthy of the task of writing this account.

—From *Knights of Wind and Truth,* page 22

Adolin kept fighting, and storms . . .

He was growing tired. He'd pushed himself far too hard today, and even with Regrowth and drugs, he was flagging. His leg stump ached, and he felt blisters there breaking and—with the sweat of his exertion—making the fit slide.

He needed a plan to win, not merely survive.

Abidi fights like many soldiers new to their Shards, he thought. *He'll assume that in Plate he's invulnerable.*

Because of that, he'd let himself get hit. Unfortunately, Adolin couldn't break a section of Plate with a common sword. It would take *tens* of precisely targeted blows. But Abidi had a lot of training in fighting against Plate himself—he would expect Adolin to try to shatter a section.

So, for now, that was the strategy Adolin used. He mustered his remaining strength and pushed into an offensive. Abidi laughed, as it would presumably both expose and tire Adolin. But in this, the Fused was wrong.

This was Adolin's world.

This was who Adolin was.

He moved as the flickering flame that had found tinder, and became a bonfire. The thick moment itself burst aflame, and Adolin found clarity in its light.

This was *his world.*

This was *who he was.*

With a sword in his hands, everything briefly made sense again. He had been waiting so, *so* long for that feeling.

Crack.

His sword hit a section of Plate on Abidi's left side. The Fused paused, shock manifesting in his posture. The mortal had landed a hit on him? Yes, the blow was meaningless, but the mortal had *hit* him.

Rage seemed to fill Abidi's movements as he swept through another sequence of attacks. Adolin dodged, parried, and at just the right time . . .

Crack!

A second hit on the exact same section of Plate.

"*How?*" Abidi demanded. "You *are* Radiant. You must be!"

"Do you see Stormlight rising from me?"

"Then *how*?"

How?

Why?

He had promised to help Azir. But why?

Because his mother had trained him to care. As Dalinar had worked to make Adolin into a weapon, Evi had worked to make Adolin into one that had *meaning.* There, within the burning clarity of the perfect duel, Adolin went a level deeper. He understood himself in a way otherwise impossible.

Why?

Why had he always cared so much that his father be perfect? Why be so worried, then so *furious,* when Dalinar proved flawed?

Because Evi had believed in Dalinar. Against all evidence, she'd loved him. And Adolin, her little boy, desperately wanted her to be right.

That was why. That was the final truth of it. With a sigh, Adolin let go. Let her rest, and let his anger flow away like expelled heat from a flame.

There were many things Adolin could never become. But this one was possible: He could be the man Evi envisioned. A man who cared. A man who fought for a purpose.

Crack!

A third hit on that very same section of Plate. That would do it.

Abidi roared. This was when he would strike, throwing away caution. Adolin set one foot, slid a little on his peg, and stepped into the Fused's furious blow.

Scrape.

Abidi's Blade hit right next to Adolin's shoulder—where he had raised his aluminum candelabra, expertly placing it where he knew the strike would come.

Adolin, however, did not strike at that section of Plate again—no, instead he rammed his sword *straight into* the eye slit in the helm. Aligned perfectly with the slant of the hole, because Adolin *knew* that helm like he knew his own name.

One glowing eye went out, pierced clear through.

In any ordinary duel—and many extraordinary ones—that would have been the end. Unfortunately, against a Fused, it was not. Abidi brushed aside Adolin's sword—breaking off about six inches of it, then ripping the remnants of the weapon out of Adolin's hand.

That had been his best chance. He'd hoped that with his gemheart cracked, Abidi wouldn't heal. The gamble failed, for Abidi did not fall. He reached for Adolin, who was too close to dodge. A gauntleted hand seized him under one arm and lifted him into the air.

It was at that moment that Adolin knew for certain nothing he could do would be enough. No matter how good he was with the sword, it *wouldn't be enough.* Abidi dropped his Blade—which fell and stuck point-first into the floor—and pulled the remains of Adolin's sword tip out of his helmet, all while Adolin dangled in his grip, helpless.

The eye healed and began glowing again.

Sometimes your best wasn't enough. It was a lesson every general had to learn. Adolin had never expected to learn it in a duel.

"What was the point of that?" Abidi demanded. "I can't be killed so easily. You know what? Now I will slaughter you, little human prince. I don't care about your emperor any longer. I just *want you to bleed.*"

Not enough. Adolin wasn't enough.

Maya was right, he thought, smiling. *I am like my father. I rushed in here alone. Tried to do this by myself.*

"I will parade your corpse around once the blood is drained from it," Abidi said, holding him up, eyes to burning helmeted eyes. "That will terrify the emperor into surrendering, won't it? Best swordsman alive. *Bah!*"

Swordsman. What was Adolin if he couldn't win with the sword? He asked that question again, and . . .

For once, did not feel condemned by the truth. He didn't have to be the best anymore. He was like his father, and that . . . that was all right, in some cases.

What had Maya said to him? That someday he'd realize why he was *really* here? It came to him, right there. In a memory of a day when he'd told his father no. When Adolin had refused the throne, refused to be a king. Because he'd been too frightened to live up to a reputation he didn't think he deserved.

Adolin chuckled.

Abidi eyed him from within the glowing helm. "Panicked? At your end?"

"Just realizing something important at precisely the wrong moment," Adolin said. Then he whispered, "Yes."

"Yes?"

"I'll lead them. They don't need a swordsman. They've got plenty. They need a leader."

As Abidi studied him, seeming perplexed, Adolin thought. About his father's failings and his mother's faith. About a world that wasn't fair—and didn't appear to have a place for him.

About everything having a purpose.

Then Adolin whispered, "I'll do it. But I could use a little help right here. Please."

"Begging?" Abidi asked. "Delicious!"

"Please," Adolin said, eyes squeezed closed. He wasn't speaking to Abidi or even to Maya. It was, he supposed, a prayer. "Help me."

A chorus of voices replied in his mind: . . . *Sir?*

What . . . what was that?

Sir!

Abidi took Adolin in two hands and spun, hurling him toward the stone wall only eight feet away—using all the force of a man in Plate. A throw like that could crush steel, let alone flesh.

Sir! the voices cried.

In that instant—as Adolin was flung toward his death—a burst of light, like sparks thrown by a hammer on steel, exploded from Abidi and became a swarm of embers. Which flashed to surround Adolin.

Adolin crashed back-first into the wall, and the stone broke.

But Adolin did *not.*

Sir! the voices said. He became aware of strength. Metal surrounding him, bolstering him. Protecting him.

His Plate.

He saw Abidi gape, stripped of his armor, his bloodied face revealed, his clothing crumpled, his eyes wide and incredulous.

And Adolin remembered the last time he'd been with his Plate, when he'd . . .

Well, he'd asked it to go with his armor standbys, and serve them. It had been doing so, not distinguishing among the people it had been passed between.

Suddenly, the helmet on Adolin's head went almost completely transparent from the inside, giving him a full range of view. The voices . . . they were the spren of his Plate. He could feel them inspecting his peg leg and . . . troubleshooting?

His leg armor re-formed, becoming tight around the peg and making a kind of metal foot beneath. Springy, it was crafted of several curved pieces wrapping around one another and forming something like three toes.

He felt satisfaction from the spren. This was . . . a design they knew? From long ago?

Adolin stepped forward, pulling away from the cracked wall. Chips fell around him as his new foot—not as sensitive as a flesh one, yet remarkably supple and strong enough to lift him in Plate—gave him sure footing.

Then, in the dark throne room, a flickering orange-red light like a fire's flame started to glow from the joints of his armor and from the front of his helm.

There were no symbols on the breastplate, because he was not Radiant. Adolin had no idea what he was, other than the son of both Dalinar and Evi Kholin. The product of both of their hopes. He was Adolin Kholin. A man with very good friends.

Sir! the Plate said, sounding satisfied as Adolin made fists and charged forward.

"Oh, *songs,*" Abidi swore.

⁂

Neturo kept picking Szeth up, pulling him by his clothing, bringing them nose to nose. Growling. Angry. Crying.

In a moment, Neturo held him even closer, and Szeth—dazed, bloodied—heard something. Words forced out between clenched teeth.

"Please. Help. Us. Son."

Szeth's eyes focused. He saw a face that was a mask of anger, but . . .

But not *Neturo's* anger.

"Please, Szeth." His father's voice, so small, as if coming from deep inside. "Please. It hurts."

Neturo hurled him again. *Away* from the others. As if trying to keep him from harm, but then he stalked forward to attack. Puppets. Ishu had made them *puppets.* Perhaps it was the sole way to bestow the powers he wanted to.

Everyone in this land, Szeth thought, lying again on the stone. *Everyone here is kind of a puppet, trapped in that darkness. Ishu thought he was preparing them for war, but he only hobbled them. Everyone.*

The Herald's madness had spread to the entire land as he Connected to it. Driving away the spren. Leaving Shinovar hollow.

"Szeth!" his spren said, hovering nearby as a slit in the air. "What is wrong?"

"This isn't my father," Szeth said. "Not completely."

The six surrounded him and began kicking again. Bones cracked inside him, and his Stormlight—dwindling—struggled to help. He was . . . somehow beyond pain. That worried him. It meant his injuries were bad.

"Disobedient!" Ishu's voice somewhere. "Szeth, all you have to do is *obey*!"

A boot broke Szeth's nose, and it didn't heal. Another took him square in the ribs.

Obey.

"If you'd just *do as I say*!" Ishu shouted. "Bah! Must I do without Heralds? It will be only me! I will stand against the darkness alone! You are all worthless!"

Szeth remembered a voice. Heard it, almost. His own. As a child. "What is right, Father? Can't you just tell me?"

Then, his voice again, older, to the Farmer.

"How do you know what to do?"

Older again. To the captain of the guard.

"Just tell me what to do, sir."

To Sivi, when joining her monastery.

"I'm sure you know what is right."

Taravangian, Dalinar, Nin. Each time it was less and less a question. More and more a mantra.

I am Truthless. I do not ask.

I do as my masters require.

Never. Again.

Szeth raised his head, finding his knees as they continued to pummel him. Kicking and hitting. He turned his eyes to the sky, and something ignited inside him.

Never. AGAIN.

"I am my own agent," Szeth shouted. "I make my own choices. *I. Am. THE LAW!*"

Light erupted around him.

To this day, I wish I had all the answers. Would that someday, a historian could make a record with all possible information at her fingertips. For example, what was it Ishu did to prepare himself for what he knew the Knights would attempt? It still baffles explanation, as do many Bondsmith arts.

—From *Knights of Wind and Truth*, page 201

Shallan stabbed at Formless.

Formless grunted with Shallan's voice—and barely managed to catch the attack with one hand, right before the tip hit her eye.

Fortunately, Shallan was ready with Adolin's training. She hooked Formless's foot and sent her tumbling to the ground, then followed in a smooth motion—so practiced, she shocked herself with its grace—and landed on top of the other woman. There, Shallan used her momentum to push the knife down further, until it touched the face.

The anti-Stormlight started to burn away the Lightweaving, revealing Iyatil's masked face, hidden by the illusion she'd been wearing this entire time. As before, the entire illusion didn't fall, just the places where the tip of the knife touched.

I need to be quick, Shallan thought. *Before Mraize reacts.* With a surge of strength, her leverage giving her the extra bit she needed, Shallan plunged the dagger into Iyatil's eye. A killing strike—which immediately required Stormlight to heal, lest she die.

Iyatil breathed it in by instinct.

Shallan felt a *shock* as the anti-Stormlight met Stormlight. A flaming flash followed, and Iyatil screamed …

. . . then fell limp.

Mraize bodychecked Shallan a moment later, throwing her off. She carried the bloodied dagger with her, and scrambled to her feet to protect herself. Mraize, however, knelt above Iyatil's corpse—the Lightweaving falling away.

He pulled off the mask to administer aid . . . but found her dead, one eye punctured, a larger hole having burned out the inside of her head. Storms, it had worked. As Shallan had deduced, trying to heal yourself while anti-Light was in your system was . . . not a good idea.

It's the first time I've seen her true face, Shallan thought, gazing at a woman with Shin features, middle-aged, far less . . . alien without the mask.

Mraize knelt back. "I'm free . . ." he whispered, then looked to her. "How did you know Iyatil was hiding in that shape?"

"It felt right," Shallan said. "I just . . . I knew it, Mraize. I *beat* that side of me, I grew past it, but Formless just kept lingering . . . I realized that wasn't me, so there was only one other person it could be. I don't know how she . . ."

Shallan's eyes opened wide. The seon—the little spren in the communications box. When infiltrating the Ghostblood hideout, Shallan had learned it worked for them.

That spren had been with her when she'd been creating Formless. It had been there when she'd explained everything to Adolin after the trip. She'd *told* Wit, through it, about how she feared she was killing all of her mentors.

The seon spren knew it all. If it knew, Mraize and Iyatil knew. That was how they'd played her this entire trip. Storms.

Mraize glanced at her, then his eyes narrowed. "You figured it out? How we knew?"

"Yes," she said. "The spren box. Plus, why would Iyatil be watching Dalinar? Better for you to divide your work: You hunted the visions to see if you could find the prison. Iyatil watched *me,* to see if *I* led you here. My condition gave her the perfect cover."

Mraize looked back at Iyatil. With one hand, he deliberately closed the eye Shallan hadn't stabbed. With his other hand, covertly, he slipped something out of a sheath at Iyatil's belt.

A second knife charged with anti-Stormlight. The one that Shallan carried was empty now, dull and useless. Oddly, Shallan saw a glow from the corpse, and worried the knife hadn't done its job. But that was only Iyatil's spren slinking out of her body, a corrupted inkspren from the look of it, which became full sized as it emerged.

It appeared wounded as it crawled away. Mraize stood up, trying to cover what he'd done in taking the knife by pointing at Shallan with his other hand. He slipped the knife into his belt, and Shallan didn't look at it directly. That had been smooth on his part. He was now armed, while she was practically unarmed.

"Do we have to do this?" Shallan asked as the two faced off.

"You just killed my *babsk,*" he said softly.

"And freed you."

"As I warned you last time, I am bound by my honor. I disliked Iyatil, but it was my *privilege* to learn under her. Little knife, you've now taken a fateful step. Before, I was ready to overlook your infractions. No longer."

Shallan backed away, hand out to ward off Pattern, who was trying to come and help. He came anyway, leaving Testament and sidling up next to Shallan. Storms, that knife could kill him. She couldn't let him stay here.

Unfortunately, again, her heart trembled at the idea of hurting Mraize. He was brutal, he'd manipulated her, he'd imprisoned Lift and given her to the enemy. At the same time, he had taken Shallan in. Mentored her. And . . . she admired him. All her fears hadn't really been about Jasnah, or Navani, or anyone else who had cared for her. They had been about him.

She worried she'd have to kill him.

"Mraize," she said, "this is not the person you need to be."

"And what would I be instead?" he asked, his voice soft, dangerous. "Prey?"

Shallan nodded to the side, where—Lightweaving by instinct, needing no sketch—she created a different version of Mraize. She began picturing him as a Radiant in Shardplate, gazing off toward the horizon. But no . . . that wasn't Mraize. That wasn't what he could be.

Instead she made a version of him in rugged clothing, walking somewhere bright. A world where the sun was a soft shade of yellow, and the ground was covered in soil, like Shinovar. In this vision, Mraize had abandoned the fine clothing for traveler's gear. On his shoulder, a Lightweaver patch. In this place of twisting futures, she knew it was a genuine possibility—and hopefully so would he.

An offer, not a distraction. "You could be our agent to other worlds," she whispered. "Like you want. You said you weren't allowed to visit them yet."

"I have traveled Shadesmar," Mraize said, staring—with what she thought was genuine longing—at her Lightweaving. "I have met aethers and dragons. But no, I was never allowed onto another world."

The illusory Mraize stopped, one foot up on a stone, surveying the landscape. They couldn't see much of it, as the focus of the Lightweaving was on him. Still, she could see that version of him smile. A genuine, non-predatory smile.

"Don't press this conflict," Shallan said to him. "Iyatil was going to try to kill me. I fought back. It's done. The Ghostbloods are finished."

"No," he said, his expression hardening. "Let me tell you what *will* happen. You will come with me, and we'll see if Master Thaidakar will absolve your sins if you agree to join us. I will take over the Rosharan Ghostbloods, *then* I will travel."

His eyes lingered on that illusion, then he ripped them away from it. Shallan's heart broke in that moment.

He won't let you join them, Veil whispered. *It's a lie. He's too afraid of you now.*

I know, Shallan said to her.

Is it time for me to take over? Radiant asked.

Shallan examined her emotions and thought back, *No. I* will *do this, Radiant. But I might need Pattern's help for a moment.*

⁂

Yanagawn gripped his sword in sweaty hands.

The enemy troops had not charged yet, though he couldn't help feeling that he was soon to die. He should have had a shield. In their few sessions with the sword, Adolin had said, "Only a storming fool goes into a fight without helm and shield."

He did not have a shield.

He did not have a helm.

He was leading a force of ten, facing down *hundreds.*

Colot, the Alethi man with a bit of red in his hair, stood beside him. "Why haven't they attacked?" Yanagawn asked, trying not to sound nervous. An emperor shouldn't be nervous, not even when he was about to die.

"They're waiting for something," Colot said, his eyes narrowed. "That's the look of soldiers on strict orders—ones they're having trouble keeping—not to engage. See how the Regals have to keep reminding them to stand and not charge? See how they pull eagerly at the line?"

"They're waiting," Kushkam said in Alethi from behind, speaking with his deep, almost musical voice. "But why, Colot?"

Colot just shook his head, baffled.

Yanagawn thought of the four ways to win when you were facing a larger force. Superior defenses or terrain? No, his force here was *surrounded.* Superior soldiers or tactics? They all had agreed this was a foolish assault, most likely to fail. They were wounded or untrained, so they didn't have superior soldiers either.

Could they hope for the third way to win? A random turning of the tides? That seemed . . . a forlorn hope. No highstorm hitting the supply lines could save his force in this moment. It would take an act of god or Kadasix to—

The double doors of the throne room exploded open, slamming to the sides with a clatter, as a body soared through them and *crunched* into the wall of the hallway, then thumped to the floor. The body bled orange blood. It groaned and stirred, as Adolin Kholin—in Shardplate painted blue, shining between the joints with a flaming orange glow—strode out of the throne room.

Yanagawn gasped as—with a deliberate, powerful stride—Adolin walked over. He rammed his left heel down into the body, crushing the gemheart—and, well, the entire rib cage—which released a puff of Voidlight. The creature's eyes went out, and Adolin turned to regard Yanagawn through a resplendent gleaming helm.

"Your Majesty," he said, resting the Blade of Memories on his shoulder, "I have reclaimed your Shardblade for you."

⁘

"*I. Am. THE LAW!*"

Kaladin stumbled to a halt. He'd been running after Ishar to stop him from interfering in the fight. Now all grew still, Honorbearers collapsing to the ground, arms raised to shield their eyes against the column of light exploding as if from Szeth's chest.

The law. The final ideal of the Skybreakers? But Szeth hadn't completed his quest.

"He skipped an oath?" Kaladin demanded, looking at Syl. "Can you *do* that?"

"How should I know what humans are capable of?" she said. "They never make sense! Barely any of you even float!"

Kaladin reached Ishar, who stood with a hand in front of his face. Suddenly a kind of . . . shield of Stormlight extended from his hand, becoming almost solid, and blocking his view.

"Ishar," Kaladin said. "We need to talk while you see clearly."

The Herald turned to him, then raised an eyebrow. "So. That imitation Bondsmith, Dalinar, told of my failing last time? Foolish child." He lowered his hand, and the light hit him—but his eyes were glowing with his own Stormlight. So bright, Kaladin couldn't make out his pupils. "I was fooled by Dalinar's clever lies once. Not again. I am prepared with countermeasures. I *always* learn."

He strode forward, completely unfazed by the speaking of the oath, and by the light it released.

I can say this. I believe the fact that Ishu was bearing some of the pain of each and every Herald is an extremely relevant point in this analysis. For while he gave the darkness, he indeed held it in part.

I keep returning to this idea. As I feel it should be explored further.

—From *Knights of Wind and Truth,* page 201

Adolin grinned within his helm, exulting in the shock not just of his friends—but that of the enemy forces, who roared at Abidi's death.

Adolin? Maya's voice said. *Stormfists! What happened? I . . .* She took a deep breath. *I panicked when you vanished. I thought you'd died!*

Aluminum around the room, he thought. *But I handled it. Barely.*

A few flitting Voidspren zipped over to explore what had occurred, then retreated to their armies fifty feet away on either side.

"Noura," Adolin said. "Time until the deadline?"

The vizier started. "Ten minutes," she said in a nervous voice.

Could they hold that long? He looked at his force.

"At least twelve Fused, Adolin," Notum whispered. "One is taking charge now that Abidi is dead."

Adolin had Plate and Blade, but his forces were exhausted, and half of them were wounded or undertrained. Though Hmask had an eager smile, the others seemed to understand. Adolin's smile died. His friends would mostly fall in the first few minutes, slaughtered as he held, surrounded, until he was eventually dragged down and stabbed through the eyes.

Sir? the armor thought.

Transparent portions filled in his faceplate's holes, and air began to flow up through his armor, refreshing him. With the whole helm transparent, he didn't need an eyeslit. Well, that was convenient.

It wouldn't make a difference though. The enemy could shatter his shell and kill him like a crab on the table for dinner. They began to form up and started singing one of their chants. The sound filled the hallway, and Adolin's few defenders anxiously pulled together.

They had come all this way—they had fought for so long—and they'd still fail.

No. Maya's voice. *Adolin, I'm here. Maybe my friends can help!*

I don't think a few more honorspren will be relevant. I'm sorry. His heart broke as he said it, for he knew how hard she'd worked.

Honorspren? she asked, with a laugh. *You think I went to find a group of stuffy honorspren?*

They're who I sent you for! Adolin replied.

No you didn't, she replied. *Look! See!*

The scene of the ornate hallway faded around him, and for a moment he saw through her eyes in Shadesmar. This had nearly happened once before, at Lasting Integrity, when he'd sensed her emotions and almost seen what she did.

Maya stood on the bottom of the sphere sea, and with her were others.

Deadeyes.

Dozens of them. Moving through the beads, emerging like ancient deep-sea corpses dredged up by some ship that was casting nets into frozen waters. He probably shouldn't have been able to see them among the spheres like this, but she didn't see quite as a human did. To her vision the spheres faded, almost invisible.

Suddenly Adolin recognized his mistake. When he had asked Maya to go for the spren, he had meant the honorspren who had been leaving Lasting Integrity. But she'd assumed he was referencing a different group leaving at the same time: the deadeyes who had come to witness the trial.

That was why she hadn't been able to leave them—for they required constant guidance and supervision.

"Who are they?" Adolin asked, baffled. He didn't see how deadeyed spren, even this many of them, would help.

"They are those who have been forgotten," Maya whispered. "Blades and Plate who are no longer thought of. Dropped into the sea, lost, buried in stone, discarded by time."

"They . . . eventually fade back into Shadesmar," Adolin said, remembering what she'd told him.

"To wander forever," she said. "But *I* haven't forgotten them. And they, like me, have not forgotten *you.*"

A group of the figures stepped closer to him, lurching, eyes mere scratches. There were perhaps as many as fifty of them, of a variety of types, extending back in ranks. Cultivationspren like Maya. Peakspren. Even some honorspren, including one nearby, a man with a long beard and tattered old uniform. He stepped up to Adolin—as he saw through Maya's eyes—and was accompanied by smaller spren riding on his shoulders like barnacles. Plate spren, Adolin realized.

The mouths of several deadeyes worked, but as Maya had once been, finding words proved impossible for them. However, Adolin sensed their feelings somehow. Their thoughts. One at a time, each raised their right fist overhead, elbow bent in an ancient salute he had seen in old dueling fectbooks. He felt, more than heard, what they said.

You need allies.

We have come.

"But you've given so much . . ." Adolin whispered. "I . . . I can't take more."

One of them—an ashspren that was nearly a skeleton—pointed at his leg. His missing one, which they seemed able to recognize across realms. Adolin didn't need an explanation. They were wounded. So was he.

Sometimes you had to press forward anyway.

The ashspren opened her mouth and forced out a few sounds. "Wa . . . wa . . . tch . . ."

"Watchers," Adolin said, "at the rim."

She nodded, and he felt her thoughts. Oaths had fallen, but she would not let him fight alone.

"Because in this case," Adolin said quietly, "a promise is something deeper than an oath."

The group of them nodded, appearing relieved that he understood. Maybe they wouldn't have phrased it in those exact words, the ones Adolin had been pondering. Maybe it was just semantics and he was a fool; he suspected Kaladin, Shallan, and the other Radiants would disagree with his distinction.

He felt it an important one, for him. An oath could be broken, but a promise? A promise stood as long as you were still trying. A promise understood that sometimes your best wasn't enough. A promise cried with you when all went to Damnation. A promise came to help when you could barely stand. Because a promise knew that sometimes, being there was all you could offer.

"Once," Maya said, "we stood against all that was dark. Adolin, we stand again. *We. Stand. AGAIN.*"

Tears in his eyes, Adolin nodded. Then he raised his arm to salute the fallen warriors who had come to fight when others hid in their fortresses.

In that moment, Adolin saw Honor. Alive and well.

In a flash, Adolin was back in the Azimir palace. Only seconds had passed, as no one had moved. And he was crying. He felt Maya and the others there, ready.

I need nine of them, he sent to her. *Blades and Plate.*

The enemy began to advance from both sides, their songs echoing down the hallway. But Adolin, above the noise, shouted three words.

"Unoathed! Arm up!"

His group of worried soldiers, scouts, and one scribe looked to him. "What?" Yanagawn asked, his voice trembling.

Adolin thrust his hands to the sides, and a ring of Shardblades appeared around him in a wide circle, point first into the floor, each with a Plate helmet appearing from white mist, hanging from the pommel.

"I said," Adolin commanded, "*ARM UP!*"

⁂

Renarin glanced out from where he knelt by the gemstone, hoping Shallan would return. He couldn't see much, but she seemed to be fighting the Ghostbloods. Quick motions. Figures struggling in silhouette.

"This is our fault," Renarin whispered to Rlain beside him. "Humankind's. Peace was possible, but we didn't want peace. We wanted to win."

"We have to let Mishram go," Rlain whispered. "I . . . Renarin, I think we *have to let her go.*"

"I know," Renarin said. "We should be able to shatter the gem, with that crack in it." He hesitated. "It should be your call, Rlain. A singer's decision."

Rlain considered. "She might destroy us the moment she gets out." His rhythm changed to Determination, which he hummed a moment. "But . . . we *have* to set this right, Renarin. I decide to free her, but I want us to do it together. So she can see a human and singer working together."

Renarin looked to him, so tall and confident. The listener who had been brave enough to infiltrate his enemies—and then the listener who had been kindly enough to see the good in them.

"Let's do it," Renarin said.

Together, they picked up the gemstone and raised it high.

⁂

Szeth took a long, calming breath.

He stood in a column of light, surrounded by the Honorbearers—each of whom had fallen before him, arms raised to shade their eyes against the light.

He felt whole. How long had it been? Whole of body—though he'd been out of Stormlight, this moment had restored him. Whole of mind, with clear thoughts for once.

Whole of heart. Having made his own decisions.

As the light faded, he looked to his spren, who stood nearby—human shaped, full of stars.

"Thank you," Szeth said. "For at least trying to help me."

"You . . ." the spren said. "You spoke the Fifth Ideal. Szeth, you've become the law!"

"Yes," Szeth said. "I see it now. All men should be the law, spren. All men should follow it not because it is the law, but because they have decided to do so. We should fight it when it is wrong. That is . . . dangerous, because men can be right and wrong too. I can be. I will be."

"Yes," the spren said as a certain peace fell over the stone field, sprinkled with grass that peeked out of holes. "Yes, I see. I understand."

Szeth nodded. "You are the wrong spren for me, I'm afraid."

"*What?*"

"If I am to choose, I do *not* choose you. The Skybreakers under Nin are wrong and as corrupted as Ishu's touch on this land. You care not for people, only for rules. I do not care for your training styles, your philosophies, or the 'truths' you tell yourselves." He paused, considering the next action, and decided it was right. "I will seek out the dissenters who live the old ways of the Skybreakers. There, I will find another spren. I release you from your bond. I wish we could have been friends."

Immediately, Szeth felt a ripping sensation. Like when a crusted-over bandage is pulled off a wound, pieces of flesh going with it. He gasped and dropped to his knees—for while he'd been beaten bloody moments before, those wounds had been physical. This was different.

It was also, he determined, still the right thing to do. He did not think this would make his spren a deadeye, as he'd been told the highspren would not allow the bond to be strong enough to hurt them. But either way, this was Szeth's choice. He would not continue to be used by Nin's Skybreakers. He would find those who did it a better way, or he would make one himself.

"No," his spren said, beginning to fade. "No, Szeth!"

Nin's spren appeared nearby, and Szeth's spren reached out as if for help. The Herald's spren shook its head. "How fitting, 12124. This is what happens when you give them too much power. Learn your lesson here, if you are ever allowed to speak oaths again. You have let yourself become an attendant to your human, an auxiliary to his will."

"Is that . . ." the shrinking spren said. "Is that so bad?"

"Your failure proves that it is."

Szeth's spren vanished into the Cognitive Realm. He hoped it would be well in Shadesmar. Their pairing had never been a good one for either of them. Szeth forced himself to his feet, feeling suddenly frail. For although in his mind he was a Skybreaker still, he was now powerless. As his awareness of his surroundings returned fully, he found Ishu standing a short distance away, Kaladin and Syl behind him.

"That was," Ishu said, each word clipped, "among the most idiotic things I have *ever* seen a mortal do. Abandoning your oaths just after the Fifth Ideal? You could have been immortal."

"I can barely struggle through the life I have been given," Szeth said. "I wish no more of it than that." He glanced around, seeing his father collapsed on the ground. His sister groaning. They would soon return to Ishu's control.

So, Szeth strode past them to where Kaladin's pack had been deposited. Nearby grass pulled away again as he knelt, leaving a few patches that were Shin and didn't move.

Resting on them was a black sword in a silvery sheath.

"Sword-nimi," Szeth said, "what do you do with those you eat? Do you destroy their souls forever?"

What, no! Do you destroy things forever when you eat them? No, you just change them.

"What happens to people, when you . . . touch them?"

They go wherever people go when they die. I eat their Investiture, which drips out of me eventually.

Szeth nodded. That would do. "I have found that I must destroy one last time. It turns out I have need of a sword."

Oh. Oh, pick me *please, Szeth. Pick me! I'm a great sword. I promise!*

Szeth smiled, then reached for the blade.

A hand seized him on the shoulder. He turned to find Ishu looming over him.

"Fool man," Ishu said. "Without Stormlight for you to feed it, that *monstrosity* will consume you in a heartbeat. I cannot let you try. This has gone far out of control."

Ishu pulled back his hand, leaving a glowing light Connecting him to Szeth. What did that—

A deep, terrible darkness struck Szeth.

"See the darkness I hold at bay," Ishu said. "The sorrow inside the hearts of the Heralds, which I have taken upon myself. See our burden."

Szeth screamed.

⁂

Yanagawn was the first to move. He snatched the helmet from the closest pommel and threw it on. For a moment Adolin thought he looked comical—a youth with only a large, heavy helmet.

Then it resized to him, and the other pieces formed in the air around him—hanging for a fraction of a second before slamming together and encasing him. The same flickering glow of firelight emanated from the helmet and joints, and again there was no symbol.

Yanagawn seized the Blade from the ground and pulled it free, turning to meet the tide of enemies. Others scrambled to do as Adolin had said, grabbing helms and suiting up.

Adolin snagged Jaskkeem, the guard from the smuggler's port, and hauled him over to Noura and Rahel. Behind him, Colot and May—each gleaming in their new Plate—clashed with oncoming enemies. Adolin seized Noura delicately with one hand and gave her the Blade of Memories, the Azish Shardblade.

"You three go inside this room," he told them. "Noura, sit on the throne. Jaskkeem, and Rahel, make sure no one sneaks in while we fight."

Noura accepted the Blade and did as he instructed, Rahel and the guard following behind. He would check on them soon. For now, he turned to join the eight others . . .

Nine others?

Wait. He did the math, and realized he'd . . . Never mind. He needed to fight. The enemy had pulled back, shocked by the new development, some of them fallen dead with burning eyes. Adolin raised his hand in salute, then summoned Maya as a Blade.

Thank you, he thought.

Life before death, she replied. *Or maybe life after death this time? I never really understood that motto anyway. Let's kick some Fused ass.*

Adolin joined his nine and thrust out his Blade. As the Fused called for the attack to resume, Adolin stood.

And *held.*

⁂

Kaladin pulled Ishar away from Szeth. "What are you doing? Leave him—"

He cut off as he saw his hands, which now trailed that same glowing line of light. Some kind of Bondsmith trick? Emotion pulsed through that light.

Kaladin saw darkness.

Kaladin *was* darkness.

It felt like the worst of the days when the shadow had taken over his mind. Times when nothing felt light, or good, or even *possible.* Like that dark nightmare where Wit had once found him. Seeing his friends die over and over.

The thoughts intruded like knives. Kaladin was useless. Worse than useless. He hurt everyone he helped. Where he went, his friends died. He survived only to be a harbinger of death.

Everyone he ever tried to save was dead. From Teft to Tien. Dozens of faces and more. Bridgemen whose names he'd forgotten, or never known.

Dalinar had sent him to Shinovar to get him out of the way. Nobody ever wanted to be with or around Kaladin. Why would they? He hated himself enough to recognize the truth.

He was worthless. He always had been.

"Feel it," Ishar whispered.

Kaladin dropped to the stones, a strangled sound escaping his lips, trying to force breath into his lungs—his body taut, rigid. When he felt like this, he just wanted to give up and not move. Today it hit him like a physical force, a suffocating darkness that would crush him. Not out of existence—he'd have *blessed* that—but into a ball of pain and self-loathing that would never end.

"*Feel it,*" Ishar repeated. "This is what the Heralds would all feel, if I did not hold it back. *I* am why they can function."

Ishar touched Syl on the forehead and left a line of light as she tried to kneel by Kaladin. She gasped and dropped, trembling, huddling into a ball, weeping. Nearby, Szeth lay wide-eyed, his lips parted. Immobile.

"Feel," Ishar said, "what it is to be me. Feel the pains of a Herald."

"Ishar," Nale said, approaching. "We need to change our plans, Ishar. We—"

Ishar touched him on the arm, and Nale dropped, wheezing, trembling. Kaladin watched it through a daze.

"You must bear your own madness now, Nale," Ishar said softly. "But *I* stand at the crux of the Oathpact. I can feel them all. What do you say to my darkness?"

Nale whimpered.

Ishar turned and waved a hand, sending all six Honorbearers to the ground, moaning—apparently not needing to touch them to push this darkness through their bond.

"Feel it," he repeated softly. "*Then* question me."

The History of Man

The Expulsion
the loss of the Tranquiline halls

The Desolations
War against the Voidbringers

Aharietiam
the last desolation,
defeat of the Voidbringers

The Recreance
the fall of the Knights Radiant

The Hierocracy
the failure of Vorinism

Restitution
the Refounding of the
Knights Radiant

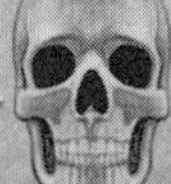

For the events surrounding the contest at Urithiru, I must refer you to another volume of this multi-author work. One that has, unfortunately, not yet been written.

—From *Knights of Wind and Truth*, page 238

The moment arrived.

The contest began.

Gavinor attacked.

Dalinar was forced to leap away, his protests ignored, as the young man displayed incredible prowess with the Blade. A perfect implementation of Flamestance, bold strikes, seeking to end the contest quickly. Dalinar dodged again, the Stormfather rumbling in the back of his mind.

I thought you'd know what to do, the spren said. *I thought you'd have an answer.*

"Still working on it," Dalinar said, a cold mountain wind blowing across the top of the tower. He kept his eyes on Gav. "Son, he's using you."

"I've seen your life, Grandfather," Gav said. Storms, he sounded so much like Elhokar. "I've lived my father's life a dozen times over. And always the same theme. No one ever gets to decide. You decide *for* them." He swept out with the Blade in a wide attack, nearly clipping Dalinar. "Is it impossible for you to believe I'm not being used? That I've decided I want this?"

After twenty years seeing only what Taravangian wanted him to see? The lad might be deciding, but he obviously wasn't seeing clearly. But if Gavinor had his father's stubbornness, there would be little Dalinar could do to persuade him of that fact.

What, then? Just keep dodging?

"Dalinar," Taravangian said, appearing beside him. "Did you *really* come to a battle for the fate of the world *unarmed*?"

"It wasn't to be a swordfight," Dalinar said.

"Why not?" Taravangian said. "Isn't this what you want? A battle you can win? But of course, I complicated it, didn't I? By bringing someone you don't want to kill. So inconvenient."

Dalinar drew in Stormlight, the power infusing him, keeping him from getting winded. That helped him stay ahead of the young man, even though he *was* good. That was probably what you got by training for twenty years, alone, under the supervision of a god.

As Dalinar passed Taravangian again, the being extended a hand, and a Shardblade appeared in it—one Dalinar didn't recognize. He held it out, point down. "Go ahead. Offered without trick or need for payment. So no one can accuse me of fixing the fight."

Dalinar ignored him, dodging as Gav—focused, determined—came for him again. Storms, Dalinar was going to make a mistake soon—get backed up against the side, or lose his footing. In a fight against a Shardbearer, the end could come in the blink of a burning eye. As Gav got too close, Dalinar was forced—almost by instinct—to grab the offered Shardblade and use it to block.

He heard a dull whimper from the Blade he held. The distant spren, who at least wasn't screaming outright. The next clashes were of Shardblades in the midday sunlight—surrounded by the advancing dark storm. Blades flashed, reflecting light.

The storm rumbled, and the sun vanished, the air growing colder and colder against the sweat on Dalinar's brow. It felt like rain was near, with that crispness and sudden cloud cover.

Dalinar backed away, as Gav—sweating, puffing—rounded him. "You're better," he said softly, "than the versions of you I've fought in my home realm."

"Gav . . ." Dalinar said, but the youth was coming in again. Dalinar met him, Blade against Blade, then shoved him backward—sending him tumbling, Blade slipping from his fingers. He scrambled to seize it again.

Taravangian clicked his tongue. "Careful, son," he said to Gav. "Don't let him surprise you."

"Don't call him *son,*" Dalinar growled.

Taravangian laced his fingers before himself, watching as Gav reset his stance. "My predecessor worked *so hard* to find a champion. You failed him, then little Stormblessed rejected the call. His final plan had been to use the traitor, Moash. But what would *that* prove? There's no poetry to it."

"I hate you," Dalinar whispered, emotions churning in him like wind before a storm. "I *hate you,* Taravangian."

"Odium," Taravangian said. "Yes. I provoke that. It is my duty, I suppose." He snapped his fingers, and Gav suddenly froze in place, sword raised for another attack. His eyes quivered; he was aware, but unable to move.

"What have you done?" Dalinar demanded.

"Gavinor, by swearing to me, gave me power over him. So I can make him wait." He looked to Dalinar. "Isn't this what you want? A good fight to end this all?"

"You know it's not," Dalinar said. "Not against Gav."

"Then who?" Taravangian said. "One of my most powerful Fused, perhaps? Someone you can kill without feeling guilty. Except, of course, for the body of the innocent singer they're using. There's always a cost, isn't there."

Dalinar backed out of Gav's reach, in case he unfroze—then tossed the Shardblade to the ground with a clang.

"I could provide you with an innocent you don't know," Taravangian said. "A sack over their head, so you don't have to look them in the eyes, placed on an altar as my champion. Would you pay that price for your kingdom's freedom, Dalinar? Is that what you'd prefer?"

"Storm you!" Dalinar said, stepping toward him. "There are prices that aren't worth paying to win."

"I disagree. No price is too high for the greater good."

"Just give me a true contest. A real fight."

"Do you want the world to be won by strength of arm, then, Dalinar? Or would you rather it be a choice between morals?" He gestured toward Gav, still frozen in place, weapon raised. Tears were forming in his eyes.

"Here is my champion," Taravangian said softly, "legally chosen and provided by the appointed time. I cannot fix the fight against you, but there is no prohibition against me fixing it *for* you. This ends when you decide: kill him while he watches, or forfeit and die by your own hand."

⁂

Adolin held.

With the Unoathed, he held. Maya in hand and Plate on his back. The armor warned when someone was behind him and provided updates on which sections were cracked.

His friends fought with varying levels of capability—but when you were in Plate and holding a Blade, "varying levels" was still *extremely* dangerous. Adolin paired experienced Shardbearers with newcomers, and told those inexperienced to just let loose—not worrying, because their companions were all in Plate, and could take an accidental hit or two.

The result was a tempest of ten shimmering Blades. They killed so many enemies that black smoke from burning eyes began to collect at the ceiling.

In that wide, lavish hallway, they stood together—ten full Shardbearers fighting at once, a feat Adolin had never even heard of.

It had an effect. The enemy songs wavered; warforms started to shy away. It was *glorious.* He soon sent Kushkam and his son in to check on Noura, and a good thing too, as they returned shortly with a dead Husked One who had slipped past. From the side, Adolin saw Noura and the other two in there—with the vizier herself standing on the toppled throne.

Warning, sir! the armor said to Adolin, but not in time to stop a Magnified One from slamming into him. Adolin's armor strained, and warned him the back plate was weakening, until the Magnified One jolted—and a Shardblade split her straight between the eyes from behind.

The Fused dropped, eyes burning, and Adolin saw a Shardbearer in blue-glowing Plate behind her. "Brightlord Adolin?" a familiar masculine voice said. "Are you well?"

"*Notum?*" Adolin said, shaking himself.

"Indeed," the Shardbearer said from within his helm. "I do not have much substance in this realm, but . . . well, 'not much' seems to be enough to control this Plate. The windspren have accepted me as their bearer."

Notum, full sized but basically just air? They'd always said that the strength of the bearer of the Plate didn't matter much once the armor was active, but he hadn't realized quite how far that could go.

Together they turned—and found the enemy lines crumbling. Ordinary soldiers fell back, leaving irate Regals and Fused. Adolin didn't blame the common soldiers—his Shardbearers had carved up the enemy lines like the prized hog at a Lightday feast.

"It's working," Yanagawn said within his armor, grabbing Adolin by the shoulder. "It's *working.* Position, tactics, even luck . . . none of that could account for this. But we're winning anyway."

Adolin grinned, and leveled his Blade at one of the Fused, a lithe brand with an Edgedancer's abilities. The Fused, in turn, looked upward—seeing or hearing something Adolin could not. Then he sighed.

And walked away.

The others did too. What? Were they that intimidated? Adolin had never known Fused to lose morale—they could often hold lines all on their own.

Behind them, Noura ran from the throne room, holding aloft her small clock. "It's happened! The time arrived! The Blackthorn's contest has begun!"

The enemy forces seemed to know it. They gathered their wounded—those who had been punched by Plated fists, or had their limbs broken—and laid down their weapons. By the rules that Odium himself had set, they could no longer fight in this land. Adolin looked to Yanagawn, who pulled off his helmet, grinning like he'd won his first duel. Which, Adolin supposed, he had.

What now?

Yanagawn spoke to the Fused with the decisive voice of an emperor. "Gather your people at the Oathgate, Fused. We will let them withdraw into Shadesmar. If you have wounded that need care, we will see to them once our own are cared for."

The remaining Fused nodded, and began giving orders in their own language. Adolin waited, tense, expecting some sort of trick until at last the enemy was gone, and his team stepped out into the sunlight of the tenth day.

To a free Azir. And so far as he knew, the only kingdom in Roshar other than Urithiru that had stood successfully against the invasion.

⁂

Dalinar breathed deeply of the cold air as he rounded Gavinor, the poor lad frozen like a statue.

"Such a little thing to kill one man," Taravangian said, "in the name of preserving a nation. We had many a conversation about this. Do you remember? Sitting before a hearth, or an imitation one . . ."

"I remember," Dalinar whispered. "A time when I thought I could trust you."

"You needed someone to talk to who understood the burden of rule. An impossible topic to discuss unless you've *been* there. Musty books full of scholars' debates are all useless compared to the empathy of one man who has watched a city burn, knowing it was necessary."

"It was never necessary," Dalinar said, his breath puffing. "You don't understand me, Taravangian. You might pretend to, but you don't—and the way you tried to use visions to break me proves it. I don't think you care to actually understand. You merely want someone to justify your horrible actions, to make it easy for you."

Taravangian stepped in front of him, his eyes intense, glowing, *burning.* "You think this is *easy* for me, Dalinar? I can hear children—both singer and human—suffer all across Roshar. I cannot close my eyes to it, for I see with divine senses, inextinguishable. I *feel* their loss, their grief, their *pain.* All through the cosmere, good people cry out for relief. They will do so until someone brings peace."

He held Dalinar's gaze, and continued, his voice barely a whisper. "I was ready to let go and be done, then destiny wrenched me back. I *will* do what has been demanded of me. I *will* be the evil that all men need, but are afraid to embrace. There will be no stillness until I bring it by force, until the gods stand down or *die.* That is my decision. Now make yours. Spare your grandson and agree to stand with me—or kill him, and experience the *tiniest* bit of what I feel. I'll leave Alethkar alone, and continue my task without you."

Almost, Dalinar believed Taravangian did this out of a sense of altruism. The passion was there, the commitment. Unfortunately, Dalinar knew Taravangian too well. His old friend didn't *just* want peace—*he* wanted to be the one to bring it, his way. In this they were alike, and always had been.

Dalinar looked back to Gav, frozen. All but his eyes, weeping, blinking. He seemed to strain against his bonds.

"He knows that you betrayed him," Dalinar said. "Twenty years training, for you to not even give him the chance to defeat me?"

"A painful lesson," Taravangian said. "We, at the top, can never have the peace we will bring others. We must taint our souls with the worst sludge of corrupt morality, to sacrifice our ideals at the feet of a stable government. Come. Choose. Your people expect you to do what needs to be done."

"They expect me to be a good man," Dalinar said.

"They expect you to *pretend* to be a good man, so they can sleep at night. What is this one death to you? Your government does worse every day. Your non-Radiant Soulcasters? Slowly consumed by their powers to provide food. The darkeyes—the slaves *you* didn't want to free—toil, giving their best years to their betters. You let innocent men be hanged so that justice may be applied evenly. You let soldiers die, and children on the other side starve, so your people at home can greet each other with cheerful mornings.

"This is the *actual* nature of virtue and leadership. And if you aren't willing to dirty your pristine, godly, oh-so-righteous hands with it . . . then I name you a coward. The worst kind of hypocrite." Taravangian's grey eyes continued to burn with a fire behind them, capturing Dalinar's own, his voice like a held note. "Admit I'm right."

"Never," Dalinar hissed.

"So be it," Taravangian said, walking over and taking Oathbringer from Gavinor's frozen hand. He walked back, extending it. "Forfeit, and die. That will prove you a fool, but at least you'll be consistent." He stepped closer, Blade raised. "Then you'll rise again as my general, head of my armies. Blood and terror shall be your surnames, as the Blackthorn will live again." Taravangian thrust Oathbringer into the floor of the rooftop in front of Dalinar. "It's the greater evil, but if it's your choice, I will accept."

"You win either way. Whatever I do, *you win*."

"Did you really think I would be here under any other circumstances?" Taravangian left the sword and backed away, the darkness behind manifesting as a billowing red storm. Tendrils of it reached to him, outlining him, rippling with red lightning.

"The power of Odium and I," Taravangian said, "have found one another. Its ambitions. My convictions. One god, for all the cosmere. Putting right what was broken thousands of years ago by a group of fools. It begins here, Dalinar, with your decision."

137 THE SUCKLING CHILD

There were not two heroes that day, but many.

—From *Knights of Wind and Truth,* page 237

Betd—who called himself Mraize—had always been a man of many emotions.

It was the way of the adult to accept this: to feel was not weakness, and to indulge emotions was not hedonism. It was to be alive.

So he could accept the pain of failing Iyatil and letting her die—yet at the same time he could glory in freedom. Never again would she hold him back. Never again would he fume at her prohibitions, her rules.

He had survived her. He was their leader now. He would have had Shallan as his own acolyte, trained in a better path—controlled not through punishment, but through information. But she refused. He respected her fire and ambition. She had been trained well, after all.

Now she needed to be eliminated. For if you could not control the beast, then it was your duty to put it down. He smiled as he approached her. She stood next to that Lightweaving she'd made of him, the tempting one that imagined him as a Radiant.

"We can talk," he said, ignoring that illusion. "Service to me will not be so harsh as you imagine, Shallan. I am capable of many revelations that will be . . . illustrative to you. Perhaps we can travel those worlds together. I know how you hunger to see them."

She made the false illusion step toward him, which gave him pause as he regarded it, trying to determine if there was some trick here. It puffed away a second later. A distraction? He looked back and met her eyes, which seemed afraid. Concerned. Or was he reading her expression wrong? She had grown proficient at hiding what she was feeling.

He prowled forward, and she shifted, one foot to the other. Such odd behavior . . . but ah, another distraction, yes. Her spren had moved to the side, and Mraize caught sight of it dashing toward him in a sudden rush. It was trying to tackle him, but Mraize set his stance. It collided with him weakly; it was just a Cryptic, with no battle sense. Mraize easily deflected it, sending it to the ground.

Mraize almost struck at it with his knife, annoyance rising in him as he eyed Shallan and growled. A desperate move on her part—she must have seen the knife he'd taken from his babsk's corpse, hidden in his pocket.

"You send your spren," he said, "hoping I'll wound it and leave myself unarmed? Ruthless, little knife. I didn't know you had it in you." He glanced toward the other Cryptic—still at the doorway into the prison. The sick one. "Yet I suppose it is not your first time sacrificing a spren."

Shallan backed away from him, appearing genuinely frightened. She was unarmed. The spren stood up behind him.

Too fast.

Too smooth.

Mraize realized right then the trick. It was the same one Iyatil had used. Shallan had swapped places with the spren while he'd been distracted by the illusion of himself.

He turned and with one hand caught Shallan's strike. The Lightweaving fell away, revealing her true self.

"I'm sorry," Mraize said as she struggled in his grip. He slipped the knife from his pocket and raised it. "Almost, you made me wish I could be the man you imagine. How do you do that?"

"By caring," Shallan said quietly. "And by lying." Her eyes flicked to his dagger.

Which did not glow with that light that warped the air. Instead he held *her* drained knife—while the one she held, which had almost struck him—warped the air.

What?

When she tried to tackle me, he thought. *It was a cover for swapping the knives!*

Great Gods of Fallen Worlds . . . how? How had she become that good at sleight of hand? For the first time in this fight, he started to worry.

"You have a choice, Mraize," she said. "You *always* have a choice. Don't force this."

If you don't kill her, he thought, *then she will kill you.*

It was the way of these things. He met her eyes.

This was the moment.

He dropped his useless knife and twisted her wrist with both hands, making her scream and drop her glowing knife. He snatched it from the air as she scrambled for the one he'd dropped. In a flash they met, him ramming his knife into her chest, and her driving hers into his stomach.

A sudden, blazing, *burning* tore through his abdomen.

He gasped at her as the anti-Stormlight surged through his body. "H . . . how?"

"I'm not good enough to slip a knife out of your pocket and replace it," Shallan said. "But I've always been great with a calculated lie. You always held the knife that could have killed me, but you dropped it." She brought her face close to his as his strength faded. "I have a choice too. I make it now. The choice to no longer let myself be abused."

She rammed the knife in deeper. Mraize felt his life fading as she sought his heart, and despite himself—too inexperienced with his powers to do otherwise—he breathed in Stormlight.

In a second, fire consumed all. Like a sunrise burning away night.

⁂

Venli knew the deadline had arrived when El finally called his guards away from watching the Oathgate. He'd been expecting some sort of attack right up until that moment.

It was then that she acknowledged it at last: her plan had worked. El hadn't seen what they were doing. Timbre had insisted everything would work out, but Venli . . .

Venli had secretly worried she was ruining everything again. She'd emerged from fitful sleep in one of the collapsed human dwellings, anxious, waiting for this moment.

Sunlight fell on the Plains through the dispersing clouds. The sodden, broken plateau took on a new light. The Rhythm of Joy began to beat in her head, unbidden, her soul attuned to it without conscious decision.

Not yet, she thought. *We need to be absolutely certain.*

She joined the Five, as El and several other high-ranking Fused walked across Narak, full of debris and sleeping chasmfiends. Leshwi floated over, met Venli's eyes, and smiled. An open, excited smile. From one of the Fused. And . . . was she humming to *Joy*?

"An odd rhythm, Leshwi," El said, clasping hands behind his back. "I wasn't aware you were capable of hearing the old ones."

"Is it true, El?" Leshwi said, hovering a few inches off the ground beside him as he walked through a puddle. "Has the contest begun?"

"Yes," El said. "As per the agreement, the boundaries of nations are now set and immutable. We have won the Shattered Plains, as I was asked to do."

Venli looked to Thude and the others of the Five who had gathered. To Determination, Thude spoke. "Then, by that contract, we respectfully ask that you withdraw your forces until diplomatic relations between our nations can be normalized."

Every rhythm stilled. No humming. Quiet upon the plateau. El blinked once, then turned to regard the group of them as if for the first time.

"Excuse me?" he said.

Venli reached into the pocket of her cloak, to an oiled and protected pouch. From within she took a roll of papers signed by Jasnah, the human queen.

A treaty.

After seven long years at war, the Alethi and listeners had finally made peace. Venli handed the papers to Thude, who held them up. A treaty signed by Gavilar's heir—daughter of the man they'd killed on the night of the previous treaty signing.

This one would hold. They had vowed it.

El took the treaty and read it quietly. "You arranged this how?"

"With great care," Venli said. "The humans knew the plateaus were lost, and together we agreed that a friendly party in control was preferable to an unfriendly one."

"This is our land," Bila said. "The humans did the right thing in acknowledging that on paper."

"They are willing to do the right thing occasionally," El said softly, "when it is the only option."

"This is stupidity!" one of El's companions, a Magnified One, shouted to Fury. "We will just take it from these little ones!" He drew back his hand to swing at Venli, and while Leshwi and the others tried to intervene, it was El who moved first. Forming a long, thin sword from the air and stabbing it through the side of the Fused's head.

The eyes burned.

That . . . was a Shardblade.

"We will hold to the terms our god has made," El said, not even looking up from the treaty as the Fused crumpled. El lifted the treaty, reading further, absently dismissing his Blade. "You earn tariffs on any use of the Oathgate . . . you rent land to the humans for their lumberyards and farms . . . but you get everything else . . ." He looked from Venli to the Five, then to Leshwi, who had floated nearer them. "I'm impressed. We'll send ambassadors. I should have liked to own this land, but this is not an unacceptable outcome. It offers . . . different opportunities."

He returned the treaty and walked away, calling for his forces to retreat.

A second storm had begun to build on the top of Urithiru. The highstorm. Dalinar noted it, as one might note the first rays of dawn. A . . . herald of things to come. A glimmer of hope.

Was there any possible way out of this?

He looked again toward Gav, who stood with his arms raised to kill—but with no weapon in them. His sword, Oathbringer—the symbol of both Dalinar's greatest sin, and his attempts at redemption—scoring the roof nearby.

Gavinor was crying. It was such a cheap trick, to use him as a pawn—but at the same time, Dalinar understood the greater message here. Taravangian *could* have used some unnamed innocent just as easily, as this wasn't about whether or not Dalinar was the better fighter. It was to force him to agree, one way or another, with Taravangian.

Kill Gav, and Taravangian's philosophy proved correct. Walk away, and Dalinar would be forced to join him in advancing that philosophy anyway.

He's right though, isn't he? Dalinar thought. *It's better that I kill one person now, to free Alethkar.* Although he hated the way this had happened, Gav *had* chosen . . .

Damnation. No. Dalinar wouldn't accept that line of reasoning. A child taken by a monster and lied to for decades could *not* be held accountable for this decision. If Dalinar killed him, he would at least do himself—and Gav—the dignity of not *blaming* the lad.

It would be so easy. Few monarchs would have hesitated for long. *It gives Taravangian what he wants most,* he thought. *The chance to corrupt me.*

But the other choice? To join Odium? To launch wars that spanned the void between worlds? That was . . . that was what humankind had already done, essentially, in coming to Roshar.

Perhaps . . . perhaps he *could* do that. Perhaps he could *manage* those wars, so they didn't get too terrible. Was it the worst thing, to have a capable general in the command structure, preventing atrocities? Plus, he could surely wage war against other worlds without getting too emotionally involved. It was nothing more than he and Gavilar had done in uniting Alethkar—simply on a grander scale.

That seemed . . . a terrible perversion of the goals he'd spent the last few years seeking. The unity he still felt a true God had commanded him to bring. To do what Taravangian wished . . . that would be to reject Dalinar's budding faith, and join a quest he *knew* was evil. That was far worse than killing one young man.

Storms. He gazed at Gav. Remembering the child he'd played with, held, rejoiced over. A child he'd seen mere hours ago, by his mental reckoning. Could it be that . . . that Taravangian had been right all along? That this was the *actual* way of kings? Not Nohadon's platitudes about helping. A deeper, darker truth: that a king's duty was to take upon him the sins of an entire government.

The Stormfather formed as a shimmer beside him, and Dalinar realized he saw the spren as a friend. An occasionally combative one, yes, but . . . well, Dalinar had few friends he hadn't at some point wanted to punch. He'd followed through with more than a couple.

"Do you have an answer for me?" Dalinar asked.

The Stormfather shook his head. "I'm sorry."

"Dalinar?" Taravangian asked from behind, near the far railing, streaming with the darkness that fed his storm. "Shall we talk further?"

"I could . . . go with him," Dalinar whispered. "Become his Fused, but then ignore his orders to fight. He can't compel me."

"I think he might be able to," the Stormfather said. "He may be able to remake you, Dalinar, as the Unmade were created. It requires your permission, but the contract . . ."

The contract would give that.

"It is hard," Taravangian said, "to have one's morals *legitimately* tested, isn't it? To find yourself at the crossroads of what you've said and what you have lived. I know, Dalinar. Trust me, I know. And I *am* sorry."

Storm that man. He sounded so . . .

Not reasonable. Relatable. Taravangian *had* been in Dalinar's position, and *had* been forced to make these choices. It was as Dalinar had feared. All of his searching, all of his work, was for nothing. In the end, Odium controlled this confrontation utterly.

No, Dalinar thought. *The journey. I learned.*

He raised his hands to the sides, cold wind blowing across him, and he looked out across the peaks, feeling . . .

Life. Perhaps it was an echo of his visions. Perhaps it was that sense of warmth, the one he sometimes knew during quiet hours in his study. Perhaps it was the time, the place, the company.

He felt them. The people of the tower, of the surrounding nations, of Alethkar, of the world. He felt their fear, their love, their dreams. Some of them hurt, as Odium said. That was terrible, but it was also life. And life could be painful.

Most didn't know what he was doing, nor could they really care. Other needs were too pressing, too immediate. He knew in that moment the deepest lie that Taravangian told: that only "great" men had difficult choices to make. That only kings carried burdens of guilt. That he was somehow special in needing to make painful decisions.

Dalinar's power was vast, so his choices were influential, but they were not *unique.*

Yes, something familiar said in Dalinar's mind. *See . . .*

He *had* seen. He had strode the path of history, coming to Urithiru not by conventional means, but by walking time itself. He had been singer, Herald, human, god. In the Spiritual Realm, he had seen what Connected them all.

Last of all, he stood here, knowing weakness. Not being enough . . . like a young man he loved who celebrated now in Azimir.

Not enough . . .

You could never be smart enough. Jasnah had learned that. Nor could you just keep fighting forever. Kaladin had learned that. You couldn't be strong enough, nor could you be perfectly honorable. That was what it was to be mortal. Sometimes you succeeded anyway. Sometimes you failed. Dalinar had experienced the breaking of oath after oath. Humans turning on singers. Singers turning from Honor to Odium. He'd even seen a god trying, as best he could, and finding no way out but to break his word.

Yes. Dalinar felt that voice. The power of Honor. *It HURTS. Why must it hurt? Can humans not simply do as they say that they will?*

This—the power of Honor—was one person he hadn't yet acknowledged. One he'd seen, but hadn't considered. He did so now, seeing through the eyes of the power itself.

Person after person had failed it, making it tremble with agony. Awareness blossomed in Dalinar. And there, at the crux of two storms, Dalinar Kholin understood.

"Stormfather," he said. "*I know the Words!*"

And the existence of those several key people is the one thing that I myself have heard from the Wind. This singular truth, a nugget that I cannot yet explain.

"One is not enough. The change must come from many."

—From *Knights of Wind and Truth*, page 237

Shallan dropped the expended knife, exhausted, falling to her knees beside Mraize's corpse. It was lucky he hadn't seen, at the last moment, that the tip of the real knife—with the anti-Light—had burned through her illusion. But she'd successfully kept his attention on her. Misdirection within misdirection. And it had worked. He was dead.

And she felt exhausted rather than triumphant.

Pattern bounced over, still wearing the Lightweaving that made him look like Shallan. A too-tall version of her, which was likely what had tipped Mraize off. Then Radiant was kneeling across the body from her. Blond, with a thicker neck, stronger muscles, and a calm smile.

"You did it all on your own, Shallan," Radiant said. "You killed him yourself. You don't need me to do that anymore, do you?"

"No," Shallan whispered. "Thank you."

Radiant nodded. She was the part of Shallan that had killed her mother, killed her father, and borne the weight of fighting. She'd emerged as a persona after Tyn's death and formed into Radiant some weeks later—but as Veil had carried Shallan's memories, Radiant had carried her violence.

"I know it hurts," Radiant said, glancing at Mraize, whose dead face was frozen in a mask of surprise and agony.

“It does,” Shallan said. “But not . . . not because of what I did, but because of his decisions. I am *not* responsible for his bad choices . . . or the consequences of them.”

Radiant reached across, gripped Shallan on the shoulder, and squeezed.

Then they were one.

“Is that . . . it?” Pattern said in her voice. That was disorienting enough that she dismissed the illusion. Testament joined them. Quiet as always. “Shallan?” Pattern said. “Are you healed?”

“That’s not how it works,” she said, feeling so *exceptionally* tired. It had been . . . a very long day. “I will always have to fight my mind’s inclinations. It’s not that I’m healed, or even that Radiant is gone completely.” She stood up. “But I *am* better than I was.”

Mraize started glowing, then his skin rippled.

“Here,” she said, reaching down and helping to pull the wounded spren from his body: a bone-white Cryptic, with a head pattern that was all wrong. Loose loops like scribbles instead of geometric shapes.

“I . . .” the Cryptic said. “I am sorry. But I hate you. Mmmm . . . it is a strong hate.”

“You will have to deal with that,” Shallan said, inspecting the Cryptic’s left side, which had been burned away—leaving a hole where the arm and shoulder should have been. She glanced to Iyatil’s inkspren, who was radiant with colors to show its changed nature—and was huddling in the shadows nearby. “Is there a way to heal you?”

“I do not know,” the Cryptic said. “You burned away the part of us that is Stormlight, not the part that is Voidlight. I . . . I feel sad. And hurt. I do not want to talk to you.”

Shallan didn’t blame him. She looked to Pattern, who helped her get the wounded Cryptic to his feet. Perhaps if they brought them to Sja-anat, she could do something?

She started toward the room with the prison. In the fight, she’d almost forgotten it. As she drew near, she could barely make out something horrifying inside.

Renarin and Rlain with the gemstone raised high. Poised to drop it, shatter it, and release Mishram.

Oh, *storms.*

⁂

Nale, called Nalan’Elin, huddled on the ground and tried to stop existing.

It wasn’t that this darkness was new, but he’d . . . he’d been able to hide from it. Until Ishar stripped away his protections.

Now the full force of Nale's failures, the murders he'd committed, overwhelmed him. He knew—his eyes squeezed shut yet leaking tears—that he would *never* escape this.

⁂

Sylphrena tried to claw her way toward Kaladin. She found it impossible to move. She could barely reach out, her very essence twisted in agony. She'd felt something like this before, in trying to empathize with Kaladin and people like him, but experiencing it like this was so, *so* different.

It made her feel completely alone.

"Know my pain," Ishar was saying, though she barely heard. "As you feel it, let me have peace. To think."

So, *so* alone. What had she ever done that had mattered? She felt a squeezing within her, rearranging her until she . . .

She wanted to not *be.* It wasn't pain. It was the opposite of pain. It was a deep, terrible nothing.

It terrified her more than anything else ever had.

⁂

Szeth was exhausted.

How long was he expected to keep going? What was the point of all this fighting?

Each new thought was of how he'd failed. The eyes of someone he'd killed. Whispers in the darkness.

He was *overwhelmed.* Surrounded by darkness, such that he couldn't see. Why did it all matter? Why had he tried so hard?

Couldn't he just sleep for once?

Yet sleep seemed too easy an escape for one such as him.

Szeth?

The sword. Szeth ignored it.

Szeth, what is wrong?

Everything was wrong. It always would be. Szeth squeezed his eyes shut, curled up, and trembled.

⁂

Kaladin lay there, grappling with the darkness.

"I made a fool's choice, didn't I?" Ishar said. "To think that any mortal could ever deserve to be a Herald. I must move forward with another plan. Dissolve the Oathpact. Yes, dissolve it, bring the spren through to this realm, and make them my army."

Thoughts intruded and stabbed Kaladin's mind, like spears in his flesh, making him scream his flaws. Those he'd lost. Those he'd failed. Storms, he *hated* this part.

Still, there was nothing to do about it. So Kaladin raised his head and looked up.

So often, it began with just *looking up*. That was the first step in clawing free of this darkness. With eyes blurred by tears, he thought he saw someone . . . standing there in front of him. Kaladin himself.

Young Kaladin, standing up to volunteer to join the military because his brother had been taken.

Beside him, Squadleader Kaladin, on the battlefield and sheltering the new recruits.

Then Bridgeman Kaladin, forcing his friends to carry a bridge on its side.

Captain Kaladin, who stood to protect Elhokar against even a friend.

Radiant Kaladin, battling Szeth in the sky.

He looked at all the dead men he'd been, and realized something. He *admired* them. Each shared that singular attribute: the willingness to protect and help those around them.

That is *me*, he thought. *That* is *who I want to be.*

Wit had told him to find out who he was when he wasn't in the middle of a crisis. When fighting wasn't demanded of him. Well, this *was* who he wanted to be. Was that terrible? The darkness inside him said it was, that he'd end up going in the same circles as before. That darkness . . . in it, he felt the burdens of the nine remaining Heralds. The people who had sacrificed so much for the world, and lost themselves because of it. Was that a warning? That he shouldn't try?

Kaladin fought that feeling off, for he had a new tool. He had learned, and grown, while helping Szeth. Storms . . . by helping, he'd learned. He wasn't perfect at it, but he had boundaries now. He refused to take Szeth's failings upon himself, refused to let failure crush him.

The change to become this newest version of himself wasn't about abandoning what he admired about himself. It was only about finding a healthy way to handle it.

And so, in the face of the most awful darkness he'd ever felt, Kaladin Stormblessed took a deep breath.

Then stood up.

I can't speak to that. But I can speak to the testimony of one man's experience. That of what it felt like to be in the very depths of despair, and then to have someone stand up and try their best to shield you from it.

—From *Knights of Wind and Truth,* page 237

Kaladin stood up to protect Szeth, Syl, and even Ishar. Not because he had to. Not because the situation forced him into it. But because this *WAS* the man he wanted to be.

Ishar cut off his rambling and turned to look at him, eyes widening. Everyone else on that barren field of rock lay on the ground, curled up, trembling, eyelids clenched shut. Even Syl was incapacitated. Like Kaladin, Nale, and Szeth, she had a cord of white light leading to Ishar.

In that moment, Kaladin understood why he had come here. He felt the Wind herself take a welcome gasp. His invisible armor—and, it seemed, thousands of windspren, somewhere—found wonder in this simple act. A man standing up.

"Impossible," Ishar said. "What are you?"

"I'm just an old spear who wouldn't break, Ishar."

He stepped sideways in front of Szeth, putting himself between Ishar and his friend. It was perhaps a hollow gesture, but there was a darkness emanating from Ishar—and maybe Kaladin could shield others from it, like one could in standing before a terrible storm. Indeed, Szeth opened his eyes.

Ishar stalked toward Kaladin. "I don't believe it." He looked at Kaladin's cord, then back at him. "How?"

"This horrible darkness," Kaladin said. "That's what you feel?"

"Every day."

"It's awful, isn't it?"

Ishar nodded.

"I will not lie," Kaladin said, "and promise you that all future days will be warm. But Ishar, you *will* be warm again. And that is another thing entirely to promise."

"I . . . I don't know if that is true," Ishar whispered. "It's different for us."

"It's not," Kaladin said. "I feel your pain now, and I see what it is. Your lives might be supernatural, Ishar, but what you feel is what I feel. I realize that on one hand, that is no consolation. Your pain, your sorrow—your darkness—doesn't transform because another experienced it. Still, it seems to help, doesn't it? Knowing you aren't alone."

It was difficult to even speak. Kaladin wasn't lying; he had felt this before—but whatever Ishar had done to him *was* worse than most of his days. It was like all of the worst days Kaladin had known distilled into 200 proof awfulness. The Horneater white of misery.

This was worse than the days when he didn't want to move. It was like the days when he would have done anything not to exist. Days like the one when he'd stood in the rain above a chasm long ago.

That was what the Heralds lived with.

Storms, Kaladin thought. *I have to help them.*

It was a laughable thought. How could he help? He was barely functional. It was all he could do to stand there.

But *stand. Kaladin. DID.*

And somehow it helped. Seeing someone else resist *helped.* Szeth, groaning, managed to look up at him. Syl stirred.

"How?" Ishar repeated. "What are you?" He gestured toward Szeth. "Are you . . . are you his spren? His god?"

"No," Kaladin said. "I'm his therapist."

Ishar blinked. ". . . What is that?"

"I honestly have no idea," Kaladin admitted.

Ishar moved with a crash of speed. A pop, and a rush, and suddenly he was there with a hand at Kaladin's throat. "I will crush you. You will fall here, Stormblessed. You cannot help. You cannot stop me. Everyone you love will die for this insolence. Doesn't that terrify you?"

"Yes," Kaladin admitted.

The darkness wanted him to see himself failing. It tried to show him. Except Kaladin had learned, and Words formed without him realizing that he'd begun to know them. The Words that both soldier *and* surgeon needed to learn eventually.

Two halves of one man. A singular lesson.

A step forward from what he'd learned in storm and tempest two weeks ago, Words said in agony. This was a counterpoint, learned with a peace that flowed through him and held off the darkness. Quiet Words. Reminiscent of what Teft had learned, and his friend's wisdom helped now.

Kaladin rested his hand comfortingly on Ishar's shoulder, ignoring the hand at his throat, and spoke them.

"I will protect myself, so that I may continue to protect others."

⁂

The power of Honor gathered around Dalinar like a corona. The rumbling from Odium became tiny, buzzing instead of thunder.

This power . . . knew it was no longer like the others. It had spent too long without a vessel, and part of it craved to be held again. Yet it had seen so much betrayal.

"I know," Dalinar whispered, his heart trembling. "I was there."

Too much of his focus, in the visions of the past, had been on Tanavast. Natural, as Dalinar had been seeing them from his perspective—now, instead, he accepted the power's viewpoint. Trying earnestly to work with Tanavast—but finding him infuriatingly uncaring about oaths.

"I see your pain," Dalinar whispered.

Lines of light—dozens, hundreds—began to appear at his chest, vanishing into nothing, tethering him to . . . to something distant. Or something here, but in another realm.

You . . . the power whispered. *You are the uniter.*

Yes. He had followed the command to unite them. He'd brought Alethkar together, forged a cohesive nation out of squabbling highprinces. Then he'd brought nations together in his coalition. Stumbles notwithstanding, he and Navani had built this tower and its people into a true kingdom.

Those lines of light strengthened.

"I know you want a successor," Dalinar said.

Humans lie, the power said. *I have watched them lie. Every one of them lies. The lies hurt.*

"I saw," Dalinar said. "I do not think you'll do better than me, right now. I have grown so much, even in the past ten days." Dalinar had learned the lessons of those who had failed. He was *ready.* Ready to take the next step.

The lines of light . . . stayed the same. The power didn't care about Dalinar's willingness to serve. Why not?

It is the power of Honor and oaths, Dalinar thought. *Not of self-improvement. It doesn't care if I've grown. It cares if I will keep my word.*

Dalinar thought of the many oaths he'd made, and kept. Promises to himself, to others. Including as recently as sending Radiants with the Mink, when it had hurt his war efforts. And yet . . . he found himself uncertain.

Was he really a man of his word? He'd told Elhokar that he didn't want the throne, had sworn it to Sadeas, vowed he'd never be king . . . but then he'd taken that throne in all but name.

The power didn't care. So long as Dalinar technically hadn't taken the throne, all was well.

That bothered him. This power had a certain immaturity he had not thought to find in something deific. But . . . he supposed it was relatively newly aware.

It is time, Dalinar. That was . . . Cultivation's voice. *Speak the Words. You know them now.*

He did. He fixated on the power's perspective, watching Tanavast betray it time and time again. He took to heart the lessons of his realm: that in this case, the destination wasn't about a *place,* but about a *Connection.* It was about who you had become, not about where you arrived.

The power surrounded him, and he slammed his hands together, opening a perpendicularity. Then he spoke to Honor the most important Words he might ever say. Words that only worked if he could say them truly.

"I understand you."

140 THE LIGHT WE KINDLE OURSELVES

The Wind itself accepted his Words.

—From *Knights of Wind and Truth,* page 249

These Words, the Wind whispered to Kaladin, *are accepted.*

Kaladin came alight with an explosion of power.

And Ishar, poor Ishar, was still Connected to him by that Bondsmith's tether. In the moment the final Words were spoken, power *surged* through that very tether, along with a wave of Light from Kaladin, which threw Ishar back with a physical force. He slammed against a natural rock pillar, washed in pure light from the Spiritual Realm.

Kaladin felt he could see the power of the Fifth Ideal pushing back the blackness through that tether, like a drain being flooded in the wrong direction, until it reached Ishar and he gasped again. Black smoke *exploded* out of the Herald, pushed from his pores like Stormlight.

Kaladin distinctly thought he heard, echoing through that failing bond, the gasps of eight other people as an unacknowledged darkness left them. An oppressive cloud that Ishar thought he'd been holding back, but had in reality been infecting every Herald. The blackness he'd absorbed from Odium centuries ago, by finding his pool of power.

It wouldn't heal them, lifting this dark cloud. Their wounds stretched back millennia before Ishar's terrible decision. However, this might help open a path to healing.

Ishar, with one final gasp, slumped against the ground, dazed and perhaps unconscious. Kaladin, still glowing, noticed that the tethers were still there. So he knelt and seized Nightblood by the hilt, whipping the sword from its sheath. Power began to be pulled from Kaladin, but he held so much from the Fifth Ideal that it seemed trivial.

Using the sword, Kaladin carefully severed the cords coming from Ishar, freeing Syl, Nale, and Szeth. The last vestiges of that darkness faded, leaving only a memory. Szeth let out a sigh of relief. Syl laughed.

Nearby, Ishar's Honorbearers stirred, and started to rise. And storms . . . that darkness continued to hang over them. That shadow upon the land . . . Kaladin could see it manifest in all six, whose faces became masks of rage and anger as they gathered. They'd been created from that darkness, so this wasn't over.

Kaladin set down the black sword—but noticed, as he did, that a line of darkness remained attached to his hand. His Stormlight continued to drain, vanishing, as if he were expending it on some great task.

I have learned from the other swords, Nightblood said in his mind. *I know the Surges. I will Connect to you. You will feed me!*

"Nightblood," Kaladin whispered, "let go."

It is time. We will destroy. Wield me!

Storms. Well, he'd heard he had to put the sword back in its sheath. As he reached for the silvery scabbard, the sword spoke again in his mind—the tone possessing an uncharacteristic forcefulness.

No. It is time. Give me to Szeth. I will draw from you, not him, but he needs me and we must DESTROY!

Kaladin glanced toward the rising Honorbearers. If there was fighting to be finished today, Szeth needed to do it. So Kaladin tossed the black sword to him—and that line of darkness connecting him to the weapon stretched. Feeding from Kaladin's Stormlight, and not from Szeth's soul.

Szeth lifted the weapon high.

Kaladin, in turn, helped Syl rise.

"Kaladin," she whispered, "what have you done?"

"Figured myself out, finally," he said, with a smile. He looked toward Szeth. "We need to leave this next part to him."

⁂

Szeth held up the black sword, using Kaladin's Stormlight to sustain them both.

Destroy evil! Nightblood cried, inky black liquid dripping from the blade—but almost all of it evaporating before it hit the ground.

"No, sword-nimi," Szeth said. "Today, we simply restore what is right."

The six Honorbearers surrounded him, each with a Blade of their own. Ishu was down, but his anger raged in them. These things that had been made from Szeth's family and mentors . . . they were abominations. Yet as he regarded them—Nightblood boiling in front of him—he read something new in their expressions. He'd once seen anger: teeth gritted in fury, eyes wide with contempt. Now he saw pain. Teeth gritted at being made puppets, eyes wide at the horror of what they were forced to do.

"Oh, Father," he whispered. "I've been there. I have walked that road. I understand."

Neturo wept openly as he gripped his Blade. "I'm sorry," he said through gritted teeth. "Szeth, I'm so sorry."

He seemed to think that six against one was unfair odds. The one, however, was Szeth. "Sword-nimi," he whispered. "You have created a bond to Kaladin. Does this mean you have been learning Surges from the Honorblades? Can you return to me my Lashings?"

Yes, the sword said. *I can restore your Lashings. Those are easy. Even a* spren *can give those. Now we fight? We finally FIGHT?*

Szeth felt a distinct chill in his right palm. Hopefully Kaladin's Stormlight would hold, for otherwise the sword would consume them both. For now, Szeth had what he needed. His Lashings, and more. How long had it been since he'd been able to give his heart entirely to a fight? Not with the Skybreakers, not while puppeted by Taravangian's strings, not even at the Battle of Thaylen Field.

It had been since he'd first picked up a Blade, and found it a dance. "Yes," he whispered to Nightblood. "Now we *fight.*"

⁂

The perpendicularity glowed with an awesome power, a star atop Urithiru, making everything white.

"Dalinar?" Taravangian said, his voice calm as he spoke from within his storm. "What do you think you're doing?"

"I cannot face you as a man and win, Taravangian," Dalinar said. "It is time for Honor to return."

"It cannot return to *you,*" Taravangian said. "The power rejects humankind. It will reject you in particular, because you are an oathbreaker."

"Then explain what is happening," Dalinar said, expanding that column of Light.

For once, in all the time they'd known each other, Taravangian apparently had no idea how to reply.

Dalinar reached through that perpendicularity. *Come on!* he said to the power. *You are needed!*

It flooded around him, but did not enter him. He felt he was in a vision, but there was nothing to see. Greyness, and an infinite expanse of nothing, formless. But with glistening power in the sky, infinite and wonderful.

"Why?" Dalinar said. "Why do you hesitate?"

I . . . Humankind . . . The pain . . . Except . . .

In a flash, Dalinar saw a revelation: two people holding a gemstone prison. The Bridger of Minds. The Son of Thorns.

On the edge of a proverbial cliff, and a future no one—not even the gods—could see.

⁂

Renarin and Rlain held the gemstone high.

Rlain attuned Determination, his hand next to Renarin's, glad to be here with this man at his side.

Shallan called for them to stop. They both glanced at her, then at each other. Ignoring her cries.

"You sure?" Renarin asked.

"Yes. You?"

"Yes," Renarin said to Determination.

Together they slammed the gemstone down against the ground, where it shattered completely, and a dark storm escaped it.

141 THAT WHICH WAS LOST

The curious effect that the Black Sword has on individuals is one that I find poorly recorded. It is true that many feel nausea when picking it up, which is a sign of a heart uncorrupted by greed.

Others are, then, corrupted by that greed.

Most interesting are those in between. Those who feel neither emotion. Those who can use the sword, but walk a fine line upon its edge.

—From *Knights of Wind and Truth,* page 266

Kaladin stood back with Syl, watching Szeth fight, and marveled. One man stood against six Honorbearers, and he made them look like children.

One, a Stoneward, raised a wall of rock, and Szeth merely used it as a promenade—running up along it. As he crested it and the stone tried to envelop him, Nightblood destroyed it in a burst of smoke.

Szeth landed amid a group of five enemies and blocked their blows easily, throwing sparks from their Blades—breaking off chips from them, tossing their bearers back. He scattered enemies, but they kept scrambling to attack him again. Every time, Szeth somehow pressed the advantage against overwhelming odds. He moved as, and with, the wind. As the Stoneward tried to grab him, Szeth slid along the ground and touched her leg. The woman went careening into the air.

"The Wind aids him . . ." Kaladin whispered.

No. We fear him.

That startled Kaladin, and he glanced to the sides, to see pinpricks of light hovering around him. Windspren? His armor. They had never spoken to him before.

Wait. If those were the spren of his armor . . . why were there so many? Fading in and out, vanishing as soon as he could see them in the air. He felt . . .

Thousands of them. Watching on the other side. With them the Wind herself, the ancient soul of Roshar. As if all of the wind on Roshar was holding its breath here, in this moment.

To the east, through the spren, he felt the land tremble.

Something terrible was happening at Urithiru.

⁂

Dalinar felt the moment Renarin and Rlain released Ba-Ado-Mishram. A long-lasting discordant note, vibrating the soul of Roshar in the most terrible of ways, was finally extinguished.

Something that had been broken—for so very long—*righted.*

Dalinar strode toward Odium, the power of Honor surrounding him. He saw it, true honor, in the efforts of two young people to set right an ancient wrong. In the way a young spearman rose to his feet in the darkness. In a man who stood with friends to save a city that was not his own. In the Lightweaver who refused the lies and accepted truth. Even in the way a queen who had been wrong resolved to do better.

He saw it in what Alethkar had been, and what it had become. In himself. If the man who burned cities could be redeemed, then who could not?

That was honor. The power couldn't see it, and that still troubled Dalinar, but *he* could.

Fortunately, with the release of Mishram accomplished—her betrayal the very thing that had broken Tanavast—the path became clear. That sin had been holding the power back all these centuries, but now it thirsted for a Vessel, and Dalinar had seen its existence and its failings.

It wanted someone who understood it. That was the budding humanity of it, the budding awareness. Like all sapient things, it wanted to be understood. And thus, with that Connection, the power that had been ostracized at long last *returned.*

Honor was born again in Dalinar Kholin.

⁂

Szeth was free.

Released from an eternal prison. He . . . he could dance again.

He spun among the Honorbearers, Nightblood laughing as he sprayed dark mist around them.

He was alive.

Szeth-son-Neturo was *alive.*

So strange, then, that he should weep for what he must now do. Because it was time, past time. He needed to bring peace to these people. So he stopped stalling and slid on a Lashing across the ground. Two slashed behind him, but missed, as Szeth placed himself right in front of Pozen. The old Honorbearer reached out with rage in his eyes to try to send Szeth to Shadesmar.

"Thank you," Szeth said, thrusting with the midnight sword, "for your training." Pozen, his first teacher, exploded into black smoke and his Blade went flying, clanging to the ground in the distance.

Szeth Lashed himself backward—abruptly moving in an unnatural way, to anyone not used to Lashings. He left four confused assailants trying to swing at him as he turned, wind in his face, and located a rock formation that hadn't been there a moment earlier. He drove his blade *straight* into it, consuming it in a burst of black smoke.

"Farewell, Moss," Szeth said, tears on his cheeks, as the Lightweaving vanished around the stones, revealing a man being consumed by Nightblood. "The only one of you to be an actual friend. May you rest at last."

⁂

Ba-Ado-Mishram filled the small chamber with a billowing black smoke. Rlain lost sight of Shallan outside—even lost track of his surroundings. He put a hand out to one wall through the darkness.

That darkness formed a sphere around him and Renarin, and then Mishram appeared from the smoke—with hands like claws. She loomed over Renarin like a vengeful shadow, fingers making knifelike nails, eyes blazing red.

Rlain attuned Resolve and leaped forward, seizing Renarin, sheltering him, and turned to Mishram. "*NO.*"

"He is one of them," she growled.

"He *freed* you. He did what was right, *because* it is right!"

"He was a fool! They imprisoned me. They lied to me! He is *evil*!"

"He is a person," Rlain shouted.

"He is human!" she shouted back.

"Some are evil, some are good. Most are both! Just like us, and until we accept that, nothing will ever change!"

"Nothing changed for me in two thousand years!"

"It changed for us," Rlain said. He pulled Renarin closer, then attuned Love. "It changed for *us,* Mishram."

The Rhythm of Spite beat around them like thunder. Yet she did not strike. She screamed—and an explosion of light followed. Rlain clung to

Renarin, and they fell through the floor. Renarin shouted, and all was blackness and light, somehow mixing, until with a *jolt* they hit the ground.

Rlain twisted, groaning. When his vision recovered, he found himself and Renarin lying with Shallan and the spren on one of the Oathgate plateaus of Urithiru. The version in Shadesmar, with its strange black sky and odd clouds.

They had been ejected from the Spiritual Realm. And deposited near where they'd begun this journey.

⁘

Szeth landed softly on the stones as a third Blade clanged to the ground at his feet. A third foe killed, this time the Stoneward. That left him with only three. His sister, the Dustbringer. The older Truthwatcher woman whose name he had never learned. Finally, his father.

Szeth hesitated, his hand sweaty on Nightblood's grip.

Fight! the sword said. *DESTROY!*

The feeling of the battle had changed. Neturo's head jerked, as if forced to move. He nodded to the Truthwatcher. That oddest of orders, the one Szeth had understood the least, even when using its Blade.

The Truthwatcher strode forward, a globe of light forming in her hands. Shadows came alive. Szeth stumbled back as they crawled from the darkness around him. Transparent figures. That one . . . that was the old Alethi king. That one a bandit from Bavland. There, a serving woman at the Veden feast . . .

Guards. Common darkeyes. Kings. Shardbearers.

The people Szeth had killed. The whispers.

The *whispers* were *alive.* Each one pointed at Szeth. Accusatory.

Szeth spun around, trying to face them all, waving Nightblood—though his hand was starting to hurt, black tendrils moving up his wrist. An oath spoken had brought great power to Kaladin, but Nightblood searched for even more. Darkness moved like veins under the skin, corruption seeking Szeth's heart. The sword was looking to feast upon his soul.

Szeth! Nightblood demanded. *We must kill!*

A Blade flashed from among the clustering shadows. Szeth parried by instinct, knocking away the Blade. His sister emerged from among the dead. "You ruined everything, Szeth. Before you bashed out that soldier's brains, our life was *perfect.* You sent Mother away. You broke Father. You *ripped* our family *apart.*"

"I know," he said, tears on his cheeks.

"I'm going to kill you for that," she said, circling him like a predator, turning her Blade in her hand. "I'm not going to hold back this time. You deserve it."

"I do," Szeth said as the shadows drew closer. "But Elid . . . you don't."

"Don't deserve to die?"

"Don't deserve that burden," Szeth whispered. "You don't deserve any of this . . . what Ishu has done to you. What I did to our family. I wish I could restore you." He blinked tears from the corners of his eyes as he saw that she, when she moved, trailed a faint shadow. Like . . . like he had done, to some eyes, after being healed from near death.

Except where his was white, hers was red.

"I can't spare you though," Szeth said. "You aren't alive any longer, Elid. You're something else."

She growled, raising her sword toward him. The shadows surrounded Szeth, and he realized as they touched him . . . if they took him, he could not help his sister.

None of them were real. They never had been real. Like a stone revered and carried without purpose, they were . . . nothing.

Ignoring them didn't make them go away, but it did steal their power. As Elid lunged, he turned aside her Blade. She appeared shocked by this—she'd thought he would be taken down by his madness. Her lunge brought them face-to-face, and Szeth kissed her on the forehead.

Then he swept Nightblood through her, bringing peace to his sister and sending her Blade clattering to the ground, digging a gouge out of the stones.

142
A MAN STANDS
ON A CLIFFSIDE

Those who were not there, you future readers, understand. Even hundreds of miles away from the event, I heard the thunder.

The land trembled at what Dalinar Kholin did.

—From *Knights of Wind and Truth,* page 181

Dalinar's mind expanded.

He could see it all. Past, present, potential futures.

His body evaporated into the substance that was the vast, incomprehensible essence of godhood. What stepped forward from that power to meet Taravangian was merely a projection that towed infinity behind it like a cloak.

You have done it, the Stormfather said, awed, his voice so very, very tiny now. A puff of air against a raging highstorm. Dalinar, Honor, could meet Taravangian on equal terms. And could consider a third option apart from the two he'd been offered.

What if he destroyed Odium? The contract of old let Dalinar attack as he wished. Yes, Odium could defend himself if that happened, but Dalinar had been a soldier and Taravangian a philosopher.

Dalinar could destroy his enemy and save Roshar. The power of Honor *wanted* this confrontation. Dalinar, in a moment of infinite lucidity, saw that this was part of why it had broken away from Tanavast. Of what he had worried, he now saw the fulfillment: Honor, in the power's eyes, was about oaths. But there was a darker side to it.

How many men had stabbed someone they loved because of "honor"?

How many wars had been started because of an insult to "honor"?

How much anger in the world had been caused by a belief in "honor"?

The power accepted *those* definitions of it. It was the power of oaths and the pride that men bore at being thought of *as* men of oaths. As Dalinar had witnessed: thousands of years of warfare to prove who was right, and who deserved this land. The power didn't care about self-improvement, but it cared deeply about being *right.*

"So," Taravangian said, "THIS IS WHAT IT COMES TO?"

"IT IS THE ONLY WAY," Dalinar found himself replying.

"I ACCEPT," Taravangian said. "IF I CAN ANNIHILATE THE POWER OF HONOR, SPLINTER IT COMPLETELY, THEN I WILL BE FREED."

Dalinar. A puff of air. Easy to ignore.

"I ACCEPT," Dalinar said. "IF YOU ARE DEAD, THEN THIS WORLD WILL BE FREE OF YOUR STENCH FOREVER. I CAN MAINTAIN HONOR, AND WILL BE PROVEN RIGHT IN NOT KILLING GAV—AND WILL NOT HAVE TO JOIN YOU AND YOUR CONQUESTS. LET US END THIS, TARAVANGIAN."

Dalinar!

"LET US END THIS!" Taravangian said, his power billowing behind him, the red lightning crashing.

"YOU," Dalinar said, the winds becoming furious, "SHOULD NOT HAVE THREATENED MY FAMILY. TODAY YOU SHALL KNOW THE BLACKTHORN! YOU SHALL KNOW THE TEMPEST AWAKENED!"

Dalinar, please.

It was the Stormfather's voice.

Dalinar blinked, seeing the powers beginning to touch, the friction causing the tower beneath him to shake—and the mountains nearby to tremble. On the top of the tower, he heard Gavinor crying, suddenly freed as Taravangian focused on Dalinar. Crying . . . the way he had as a child . . .

Dalinar remembered his first vision ever, standing and watching a cataclysm engulf his homeland. How many times had he seen that vision, and assumed the cataclysm was some enemy force? Some terrible fate he needed to stand before and prevent?

Now, he saw it clearly for the first time. The cataclysm was Dalinar himself.

He was there, frantically punching Elhokar again.

"Stop."

He burned Evi because it was what the people of the Rift *deserved.* It was *retribution* for breaking the treaty they'd *sworn* an *oath* to follow.

"We can't do this."

His people had killed tens of thousands of Parshendi on the Plains, pursuing the Vengeance Pact in the name of honor and oaths broken.

"No," Dalinar said, backing down from the fight with Odium. "Never." This had never been his plan upon taking the power, but he'd been swept up in the moment. Now he refused. Now . . . he had the power . . .

And he still needed another solution.

Light surrounded Dalinar. A moment later, he vanished. Drawn into one final vision.

⁂

Kaladin and Syl knelt beside Ishar, who seemed conscious—but barely. He stared at the sky, not blinking, and hardly stirred as Kaladin lifted him to a seated position.

Storms, Kaladin thought. Nightblood was using up Light at a furious rate—even though Kaladin had felt minutes ago like he was holding it full to bursting. As he waved his hand in front of Ishar's dazed eyes, he found frost on his clothing. He breathed in to restore his Light, and found nearly all of his gemstones already empty. Storms.

"That's bad," Syl said, glancing at the black lines forming on his hand around where the cord tethered him to Nightblood. "This is dangerous."

"I know," he said. "Ishar. Can you hear me? Can you use the Bondsmith Blade to open a perpendicularity? We need more Stormlight."

Please, he thought. *Please have worked.*

Kaladin found it remarkable how easily the final Words had come to him. He'd expected so much pain from it, and yet . . . the Fourth Ideal had been his biggest stumbling block. After admitting he couldn't help everyone, with a little time he came to the natural ultimate conclusion—that if he wanted to *keep* doing what he *could* do, he'd need to look out for himself.

"Kaladin," Syl said, resting her hand on his arm and staring at the sky, "the spren feel something coming."

The sky was shimmering more brightly now.

"What is it?" Kaladin asked.

They know, the Wind whispered, *that we stand upon a cliffside. Dalinar Kholin faces his greatest challenge.*

"And what will happen?" Kaladin asked, feeling cold.

It is not written, the Wind said. *Not yet. But be ready, Kaladin. Please. Be ready.*

Sweat on his temples crystallized to ice in an extremely strange sensation. Fortunately, Ishar finally groaned, blinking. He focused on Kaladin.

"Stormblessed," he whispered. "What did you do to me?"

"Depends," Kaladin said. "How do you feel?"

"Like a mountain fell on me," Ishar said. He coughed and leaned forward, then his eyes found Szeth, still fighting the spirits. "Oh. Oh *no.* What have I done . . . ?"

Well, that was a good sign.

"Can you stop them?" Kaladin asked.

"I . . ." Ishar held his hand before him. "I have no power . . . no Surges . . ."

Nale stumbled up to them, looking confused, a hand to his head. Kaladin didn't have time for them at the moment though. He yanked a pouch from Ishar's belt, then breathed in the Stormlight inside, feeding Nightblood.

It's coming, the Wind said, and her voice seemed to echo. As if there were a thousand versions of it overlapping. *You say you'll help . . . but I'm suddenly afraid. Will you still curse me because you continue to live?*

"No," Kaladin promised. "Never again."

Will you be there? When I need you?

"Have I ever not been?" he said—though moments later a sharp pain struck his hand. He cried out, then raised his hand to find the black veins running up his forearm.

Kaladin breathed in, searching for more Stormlight, but Ishar was completely tapped. He looked to Nale, who shook his head. Nothing.

Nightblood would soon consume Kaladin.

Perhaps Nightblood would consume them all.

⁂

Dalinar appeared somewhere warm, with light coming in through windows that was somehow . . . softer than other light. More blurry, like he saw it through eyes that couldn't focus. He could see the room around him better though: it was an antiquated stone chamber, full of the belongings gathered in a long life, well lived.

Wooden bowls on one counter. Paintings on one wall, of an older style: depicting mountains and rainfalls in black and grey ink, with the slightest washings of red and blue. A few hung askew, but not because of some disaster. They had just slipped, and nobody had righted them yet. Dalinar looked out the window and saw only a soft light that didn't blind him, but washed out whatever there was to see.

He could hear sounds out there: people chatting, individual voices indistinguishable, but the talk was bright and energetic. The sounds of a winehouse with people laughing, or perhaps a market . . .

Blood of my fathers, Dalinar thought. *Dare I hope? Have I finally come back here . . . to him . . .*

In a daze, he walked to the door and pushed it open. In the small kitchen beyond, he found a shorter man with an Alethi or Veden look about him. Silver hair, pointed beard. Smile lines and simple, old-fashioned grey robes, embroidered red and yellow. He was working at an archaic oven, all stone and brick, with a front that could not be closed.

Nohadon. The ancient king who had written *The Way of Kings.*

"Oh, thank the storms," Dalinar whispered.

"What?" Nohadon said, reaching into the oven with a flat metal tool.

"The visions have been terrible lately," Dalinar said. "I worried this one would be twisted somehow." He said it, though he didn't expect that to make sense to Nohadon. Still, the previous time he'd seen this man . . .

Hadn't he called Dalinar by name? Despite being in a vision of the past?

"You're surprised to find me, Dalinar?" Nohadon said. "I promised you Shin bread, my friend. I usually keep my promises." He pulled a thick loaf of bread from the oven, made in the strange Shin style that Dalinar—after shopping for ingredients with this man in a vision the year before—had asked to try in the real world.

Nohadon gestured for him to sit at the small table on the floor nearby. Dalinar did so, and the ancient king—moving with a spry sense of excitement—slid the bread onto the tabletop. "Perfect!" he said, poking it. "Exactly the right mix of crust and fluffiness! I'd be embarrassed if it had been a dud, considering the importance of the moment."

"What is this?" Dalinar said, feeling so . . . surreal. The warmth, the room that seemed to fuzz, a softness to each corner or edge. "Did I create this? I'm Honor now. I'm creating visions?"

"Ha!" Nohadon said, settling down. "A god for less than five minutes, and already you think you control everything." He took a knife and cut into the bread, steam rising from the fluffy insides. Dalinar liked a good flatbread with his meals, but this stuff had just tasted . . . wrong. Like it was moss.

"Nohadon," Dalinar said, his hands on the tabletop, "I don't have time for flighty visions of meaningless days. I'm standing, right now, at the nexus of all things. The final confrontation between Odium and Honor."

"I would counter," Nohadon said, "that this is the most important time for you to be reminded of lazy days baking bread. Why do you fight, if not for days like these?" He took a healthy bite. "What happened?"

"I nearly destroyed it all," Dalinar admitted. "It was *so* tempting to *fight* him, knowing I could win."

"Except . . ."

"Except that would destroy too much," Dalinar said. "I realized it. I stopped myself."

"That's progress, my friend."

"Is there no way to fight him?" Dalinar said. "Without destroying all of Roshar?"

"I don't think there is," Nohadon said. "Powers like yours have clashed before without destructive results—but always then, one of the two wanted to preserve. When both want to destroy . . . it's violent."

"So that puts me right back where I started!" Dalinar said. "I have the power of a god, but I still cannot see a way out. Either I kill my grandnephew, or I serve Odium." He put his hands on his head, leaning forward, elbows on the table.

The power of Honor let him see so much farther. But Odium could see that distance as well, and had designed this trap so there was no way out. "I have to be strong. I must do as you would do, Nohadon."

"And what would *I* do?" the elderly king asked.

"Make the right choice," Dalinar said. "Refuse to kill Gav. Accept this means serving Odium."

"Interesting," Nohadon said. "Wouldn't that give Odium everything he wants? If you willingly serve him, then many of the Radiants will go with you. He would ostensibly be trapped here on Roshar, so the other gods will continue to ignore him—but he'd have access to the finest military in the whole of the cosmere. He'd have time to plan, build, and raise a new force of Fused who aren't suffering from mental fatigue. In a hundred years or so, he'd be able to launch his armies and conquer everything with ease."

Dalinar narrowed his eyes at the old king. "Who are you, really?"

"Perhaps merely a construction of your mind," he said. "Or maybe I'm actually Nohadon. Well, I was born with the name Bajerden, but no one seems to like that one."

"You can't be encouraging me to kill Gav!" Dalinar slammed his fist to the table. "Nohadon wouldn't kill a child to achieve his goals!"

"Dalinar," Nohadon said. "I did so all the time. Every policy I made hurt *someone.*"

Dalinar hesitated. In this room, he didn't feel like a god. He felt like . . . just a man talking to another man. "So . . . killing Gavinor is the right answer?"

"I didn't say that," Nohadon replied. "Only that sometimes, we all have to make awful choices. Not just kings, Dalinar. Did you see that?"

"Yes," Dalinar said. "I did."

"Every parent must choose themselves or their child, every day—sometimes multiple times a day. When to play. When to rest. Every decision we make influences others, and sometimes harms them. That's not the way of kings. That's the way of life."

"So you would kill the boy," Dalinar said.

"Would I?"

"I don't know," Dalinar said, attempting to remain angry, though this place had a soothing quality. He sat back, sighing. "What do I *do*?"

"I suggest," Nohadon said, pushing the loaf in Dalinar's direction, "you have a slice of bread."

Dalinar paused, then cut a slice. "I did try this stuff. I didn't much care for it."

"How'd you eat it?"

"With my dinner."

"With curry and hot spices, no doubt," Nohadon said, clicking his tongue. "This is *Shin* bread, Dalinar. Eat it their way. With salted butter."

"Butter? Why? That's for cooking."

"Here," Nohadon said, demonstrating by spreading the stuff from a block onto a slice of bread.

Dalinar hesitantly did as instructed. Then he tried the bread, and found it a different experience entirely. Light, tasty, with a hint of salt and oil. It was delicious.

"Too much yeast, I think," Nohadon noted.

"No, it's perfect," Dalinar said, taking another bite. "Much better than what I got at Urithiru."

"Good, good," Nohadon said. "I suppose context matters both with bread and with decisions. What's your context, Dalinar?"

"An evil god," Dalinar said, "wearing the face of a man I once called a friend. Putting me in an impossible situation. I keep thinking of the first vision I ever saw. That of my homeland falling to a destructive wave."

"This one?" Nohadon said.

And they were standing there, pieces of bread still in hand. Upon a cliff overlooking Kholinar, the home he'd not seen in so many years. The gem of Gavilar's conquest.

It was the first vision, the first and the last. Each time he'd stood here, Dalinar had felt like a different man. He watched it play out again, the ground falling away, a terrible destructive wall of something overwhelming Kholinar and breaking it apart completely. Darkness of unfathomable depth swallowing all.

"What does it mean?" Nohadon said.

"I am the destruction," Dalinar said, pointing. "A clash between me and Odium would destroy this world."

Tanavast was always too weak to take this step, the Stormfather whispered in Dalinar's head from someplace distant. *He . . . I . . . spent so long searching for someone who wouldn't dare do it. Maybe . . . I was wrong. Could I have been wrong?*

"No," Dalinar said, confident.

Nohadon put his hand on Dalinar's shoulder, gesturing to the vision of Kholinar. "Are you sure this represents the destruction you'd cause by clashing with Odium?"

"What else could it mean?" Dalinar asked.

"I don't know," Nohadon replied. He took a bite of bread. "A conundrum. But I suppose *you* are here, at this decision point, and not someone else. So maybe *only* you can know."

The wave of destruction reached the cliff upon which Dalinar stood, and all started falling. Breaking.

He appeared back in Nohadon's kitchen. Slice of bread in his fingers. He sighed, leaning forward. "I'm so tired of this question, Nohadon."

"And what question is that?"

"How to defeat Odium!"

"And what does defeating him look like?" Nohadon said.

"I don't know!" Dalinar said. "That's the problem."

"Paint for me the picture," Nohadon replied, "of what a perfect outcome looks like to you."

Dalinar hesitated, then ate more of the bread, considering. "Wit told a story, with the point being to not lose sight of the everyday lives of the people. Navani told me to make what feels the best decision in the moment. I think . . . I think what I want, then, is peace. Without compromising my values."

"What kind of peace?" Nohadon asked. "Enforced? No ability to choose?"

"That . . . serves him, doesn't it?" Dalinar said. "Taravangian's predecessor spent millennia—all of the wars—trying to build himself unstoppable armies. That didn't work, as it merely broke us. With enforced peace though, Taravangian can recruit, train, marshal his forces—pick careful engagements offworld to build veteran experience. That's how you train a military." Dalinar put his hands to his head. "I need to break the cycle of constant battle."

"So *that* is what victory looks like to you?"

"Everything serves him!" Dalinar said, standing up, pacing. "Every possible outcome! Peace serves him, war serves him! Everything I could think of, everything I could do!" He stopped by one of those windows, bathed in the strange light. "I can't defeat him . . . Storms, I really just *can't.*"

"Who can?"

Dalinar looked back at Nohadon, who met his eyes.

Who can?

A thought occurred to him. And a knock came at the door right after. Nohadon rose and answered it, ushering in an Alethi child—perhaps nine or ten—of indistinguishable gender. He patted them on the head, gave them some bread, and sat them by the hearth to watch the flames.

"Strange," Nohadon said, walking up to Dalinar, "how one so ancient can still be so young . . ."

"Honor," Dalinar guessed. "That's the power of Honor. It's started to develop its own mind."

"Yes," Nohadon said, looking on it fondly.

Who could stop the war?

"The powers," Dalinar whispered. "The war will stop when the powers themselves *want* it to stop."

Nohadon snapped his fingers.

Dalinar walked over to the child, then settled down next to them. "Hey," he said.

"I chose you," they whispered, "because you'd seen my life, and understood what I'd been through. But then you refused to fight. You *refused.*" The child stared at the wall, at nothing. "Even he knows it's the right thing, to fight until one of us wins. Why does *he* know better than *you* do? He's our enemy?"

Dalinar took a bite of bread. "You saw my life, parts of it, as you made the visions for me."

"Yes."

"You remember the one with the barrels of oil?"

"That one played out wrong," Honor's power whispered. "You were supposed to burn the room, and all in it. Why do you do what is wrong? There was another you there, who understood."

Storms. This bread really was good.

"Understanding. You wanted someone to understand you. That's why you came to me."

The child nodded.

"What about my wife, Evi?" Dalinar asked. "Can you try to understand her?"

"She broke an oath. She went to the enemy. You were there to stop them, and she went to them anyway."

"Can you understand, though?" Dalinar said. "Why she did? Why it was, to her—and to me now—the right thing? Why she's the example, and I the failure?"

"I . . . I can't."

"Can you try? You want to be understood. Do you not think others want to be understood too, by you?"

The being scrunched up its brow. And thought.

Good enough for now. Dalinar finished his bread, then stood and walked back to Nohadon, by the wall.

"It is a child," Dalinar said. "Or like one. Newly born, with its own volition." He met Nohadon's eyes. "It reasons like one now, with a simple perspective. But it's willing to consider things. It can change, can't it? Grow?"

"What do you think?" Nohadon said, snacking on bread.

"Yes. The powers *must* be able to change. Everyone can change, even me. I walked those paths . . . I saw the past . . . I know divinity. Honor *must* learn. That's the answer."

"Midius is right. You really aren't as dense as everyone says."

"You realize people have spent literal *centuries* writing about how wise, and serene, and full of decorum you must have been."

"I'm a king," Nohadon said. "Therefore, whatever I do is by definition regal. You have the answer?"

"Almost . . ." Dalinar said. "The power needs time to learn, and ways to experience the lessons to change, but I *can't* give them either. Because time is what Taravangian wants. So he can plot. I can't let him do that, so I need to simultaneously buy time for Honor's power, but deny it to Taravangian."

The answer was so close. Today, Dalinar *had* seen *true* honor. As Adolin stood for Azir, and Renarin set right a terrible wrong. As Jasnah picked herself up from failure, and Shallan rose above what had been done to her. And Kaladin . . .

Blood of my fathers, Dalinar thought, realizing. *Kaladin will preserve a piece . . . That's what we need . . .*

Now that he knew the end he wanted, Dalinar could see the answers. You never could find them unless you knew what you were looking for, could you?

"I can't stop Odium," Dalinar whispered, a plan forming. "But *they* can." He looked to Nohadon. "Am I simply doing the same thing that has always been done, though? Kicking the problem down to the next generation. Isn't that an awful idea?"

"That depends," Nohadon said, "upon what aid you can give them. And upon the type of people they are."

"They are the best," Dalinar whispered. "There will be a cost, won't there? I need Taravangian to think he's won. And storms, he's at least a little bit right, isn't he? About decisions?"

"Right," Nohadon said, "and terribly, terribly wrong." He squeezed Dalinar's arm. "We do have to make awful decisions sometimes. They will be flawed because we are flawed. That is not a reason, however, to give up on finding better solutions. And the destination . . ."

". . . must not undermine the journey." Dalinar nodded. "I'll pay the cost. Send me back."

Nohadon smiled. "Good luck, my friend. Thank you for listening to me all those years. It does a man good to know that what he wrote has meant something . . ."

The vision collapsed. In the blink of an eye, Dalinar was back on that rooftop—and was again a god, his power pressing against that of Taravangian.

Yes, he could defeat Taravangian, but that wasn't *winning.* "I cannot best you," Dalinar whispered with a voice of thunder. "No matter what I do."

"You are correct," Taravangian said, and Dalinar sensed *relief* in his voice. At least part of him had known that fighting Honor, with the will of the

Blackthorn, was a dangerous proposition for him. "Whether you are god or man, it is the same: serve me or kill an innocent. You *will* learn the lesson."

"I have learned it," Dalinar said. "Just not the way you intended me to." Dalinar felt the Stormfather there, and he remarkably came to the same conclusion. The path of the Heralds from long ago. A path Dalinar had spent a lifetime trying to understand.

Yes, the remnant of Tanavast said. *I am willing. This is my ultimate choice and sacrifice, Dalinar. I choose. Do it now.*

Dalinar opened his eyes, beacons of blazing power, and spoke four fateful words.

"I renounce my oaths."

143
ONE OF THEM
WILL DESTROY US

On that day, the Knight of Truth did not save us from the evil that had been prophesied. But from the evil brought by the prophesier.

—From *Knights of Wind and Truth,* page 281

Szeth moved among the whispers made manifest. As he killed his sister, giving her the final death, the whispers became less accusatory. Indeed, they grew welcoming.

Join us.

The Truthwatcher, seeing that her ploy hadn't worked, howled and came for Szeth—and Szeth cut her down, with mercy. Then it was only him and his father.

Szeth strode forward, his arm a writhing mass of agony, Nightblood screaming for blood in his ears—accompanied by a chorus of shadows.

Join us!

He met his father, who still wept, and they clashed—though after a few quick meetings of black sword against Blade, Szeth knew Neturo was no match for him. Even though he'd trained, Neturo was more bureaucrat than warrior.

Szeth pushed Neturo—blade against Blade—back until he hit a stone rock formation. Szeth held him there, eye to eye.

"How long?" Szeth whispered. "How long did you know?"

"Si . . . Sivi told me, when she wasn't supposed to, that they had a new God. Our first year at Pozen's monastery. I started training with the Blades to become Bondsmith then."

A real answer. Neturo spoke with gritted teeth, forcing the sentences through, but it did seem to be him. His father's voice.

It was enough that Szeth almost wavered. "Why didn't you *tell* me, Father? You had answers. That's all I was seeking."

"Szeth . . ." Neturo said. "I was following you because I thought *you* had answers. The young man always so certain what was right. The youth who bested all who came against him. The man who was so direct, so certain. When I found the Honorbearers believing something impossible . . . I thought you'd find the truth, Szeth."

"So you *served* the thing?" Szeth demanded. "You took up the Blade, you became an Honorbearer, you *banished* me?"

"Every step felt so natural . . ." Neturo said. "Until . . . it had me, Szeth. *It had me.*" Tears leaked down his face.

An emotion was made complete in Szeth; a circle that had begun the day when they'd first found that rock, and his father had refused to decide what to do. Parents were just people. His had loved him; Szeth knew that. He loved them in turn. Enough to do what came next.

Szeth let himself be shoved back by Neturo, then ducked the following sweep and stabbed Nightblood through the chest of his father.

"Thank you." With a sigh of relief, Neturo-son-Vallano vanished into dark mist. His familiar voice joined the shadows.

Szeth fell to his knees, holding Nightblood in front of him, while the sword exulted. *EVIL!* It had feasted on all it had killed, but did not stop. It reached for Szeth's soul. An ending? It would be *so easy* to let Nightblood take him.

He glanced to the side, and saw Ishar sitting up near Kaladin, restored. There was a lightness to the air and to the sky. So blue. Szeth had returned to Shinovar with Truth. Exiled, now restored.

The land was whole again.

Time to die, Szeth thought. *It is what I decide. I can decide for myself. I . . .*

Yet . . .

If he did that, it would betray everything Kaladin had taught him. Yes, Szeth could choose.

And he needed to *choose better.*

"I'm sorry, Father," Szeth said, sobbing. "I cannot go with you. Not . . . not this time."

Live, then, the shadows whispered. *Live and do better.*

With teeth gritted against the pain, he started toward the sheath—but Kaladin's Stormlight was finally out, and the pain brought Szeth to his knees again. Unable to walk, he forcibly pried his fingers off Nightblood. One at a time.

The sword kept drinking.

With a howl, Szeth cast the weapon away. It spun like a dancer, point against the ground, still twisting—like a top released from its string. It stayed upright, spraying darkness around it and screaming in a voice that lacked any of the affable friendliness Szeth had known in it.

DESTROY. EVIL!

⁂

Kaladin watched from where he had fallen to the pain. Szeth began to disintegrate to dark smoke, his hand evaporating, then his arm. Kaladin stretched out his hand, trailing its own dark smoke, toward his friend. The wind blew around him as if frantic, and Syl was screaming in pain.

"Stop it, Ishar!" Nale's voice, distant.

"I cannot. I . . . I cannot, Nale! The sword will consume me if I touch it! There is no Stormlight. It has taken it all . . ."

Kaladin needed to replace its sheath, but he couldn't speak, couldn't even . . . think . . .

Szeth . . . Szeth's arm was gone . . . He was dying.

Then, a quiet voice.

I . . . I am not a thing.

"Rule one," Kaladin whispered, searching for the voice. Landing on the spinning sword.

I . . . I can choose.

Evidently someone other than Szeth had listened to the lessons Kaladin had been teaching.

"You are not a thing, Nightblood," Kaladin said.

I AM NOT A THING!

The pain vanished. Nightblood spun to a stop, lazily, the smoke fading away. The black sword balanced on its point for a second, then clattered to the stones.

A dozing voice seemed to whisper, *I . . . will not . . . kill my friends.*

Kaladin heaved a sigh, worn out completely, and rested his head against the stone ground. Closing his eyes.

In that moment, he felt something even more disturbing.

The spren cried out.

And the very soul of the world *tore.*

⁂

Shallan lay in Shadesmar on one of the platforms in front of Urithiru, feeling worn out. She was joined by Pattern, Testament, and the two wounded spren who had served the Ghostbloods.

Storms. What a day. She felt like paint on a palette after a vigorous mixing to blend colors. "Damnation. What happened?"

"Ba-Ado-Mishram," Pattern said, sitting up in a motion that was distinctly inhuman. Not stretching, or getting into position, or leveraging himself with his arms. He just sat up like a bent hinge. "She escaped back into the Cognitive Realm where she is most comfortable, and carried us with her. Mmm . . . that's probably good, right?"

Shallan sat and spotted Renarin and Rlain nearby on the same platform, helping one another stand. Then she made the mistake of looking up.

Two violent storms clashed against one another. Iridescent mother-of-pearl against red-gold. In Shadesmar, they manifested like two clouds of ink in water, each trying to overtake the other.

"Dalinar and Odium?" she asked.

"Yup!" Pattern said. "I think we might be in danger here. Ha ha."

"Buddy," she said, forcing herself to her feet, "we need to work on your presentation. There." She pointed to a figure on one of the glowing walkways between pillars on this side. A figure of black smoke with white eyes. Not Mishram, but an Unmade who was smaller, and looked more human than singer.

Together, Shallan, Pattern, and Testament helped the two wounded spren over to Sja-anat. She became more real, blackness trailing from her, and her eyes pits of white nothing.

"I will remember your care for my children," she said.

"Eventually," Shallan said, "you will need to pick a side, Sja-anat. What you did here . . . pitting Mraize and me against one another . . ."

"I did not create your disagreements," she said. "I only made certain that *whichever* of you freed my sister, I would have had a hand in it. Mishram will hopefully remember that when she decides to deal out punishments for abandoning her long ago."

Shallan gritted her teeth, meeting those voids of eyes. "I do not like being a pawn in your games."

"I have said before, there *is* no game," Sja-anat said. "Only survival for myself and those I love." She looked at the sky sharply. "You should return to the Physical Realm. *Now.*"

Shallan glanced toward the platform, which she'd left to meet Sja-anat. The two enormous spren of the Oathgate had crouched down, a posture she'd never seen from them before.

Shallan dashed toward the platform, where Rlain and Renarin waited. Just before she reached it, however, one of the Oathgate spren screamed. Though Renarin was holding out his hand toward Shallan, light surrounded him and Rlain, and they vanished.

She reached the platform a second too late.

Just as the sky went *insane.*

⁂

"You *what*?" Taravangian demanded.

"I renounce my oaths," Dalinar said. "I break our contract. I break the oaths and contracts that Honor has made with Odium—all of them. I will not make any of the choices presented to me. I release you. I *break my oaths.*"

The power *tore* free of Dalinar.

The Stormfather shrieked as Dalinar's divinity collapsed. The strength of Honor—which Dalinar had held for mere minutes—again made a corona around him. This time, it radiated betrayal and confusion.

You understood me! it cried.

Better than you think, Dalinar returned. *There are still lessons to learn, stories to tell, but you cannot learn them with me. For you are* not *Honor. Not yet. Honor is far more than an oath kept.*

Learn, see, and remember me, Dalinar told it. *Ask yourself why.*

The power screamed, and the tempest that had been blowing all this time suddenly affected Dalinar, making him stumble, snow biting his skin like arrowheads.

"How?" Taravangian said, looming above them as a storm, sounding legitimately stunned. "*Why?*"

"Keeping an oath is *not* an ultimate good, Taravangian," Dalinar whispered. "It is only as good as the ideals it is sworn to. Uniting is *not* an ultimate good. It is only as good as the purposes for that unification.

"I have been bested by you. Continuing in this contract merely because I agreed to it . . . that would be the ultimate act of foolishness. You have won because you are smarter than I am. But you have *not* proven anything other than *that.*"

Taravangian roared in defiance, then . . . then in glory as he realized this would mean his freedom. The contract, including Honor's binding of Odium to this world, was finished. In a rage, he attacked . . .

And vaporized the Stormfather.

Dalinar bellowed in agony. He had expected to go first, and this was cruel—unnecessarily so. Still, Dalinar was met with one last confident gaze of the being's eyes—and a knowledge that what remained of Tanavast felt redemption in this choice.

Then he was gone. Dalinar fell to his knees. He blinked through the pain, determined. Now the gambit, the way to buy time. Dalinar raised an arm against the wind, feeling so very, very small now that the power had left him. He was . . . like a ragged old uniform, once stretched across a powerful figure, now tattered remnants.

Honor's power hovered there, glowing like its own third storm. It wanted a host so badly. It had waited millennia, and now it had been betrayed a second time. Taravangian, in turn, had just been confronted with the realization that he could have fought Dalinar and lost.

Taravangian would take the wrong lesson from that—Dalinar knew it. For their understanding of one another went both ways. He knew Taravangian would be worrying, right now, that he was too weak. That he might have been destroyed if Dalinar had actually fought him.

Taravangian reached timidly toward the power of Honor.

You always said, Taravangian, Dalinar thought, *that you didn't care about power. That you were only doing what you did because* someone *needed to do it. You claimed that power itself meant nothing to you . . .*

Taravangian touched the strength and divinity of Honor, grabbing hold of it.

Now you reach your crossroads, old friend, Dalinar thought. *Because if power is meaningless to you, then you will not need more of it.*

"With this," Taravangian whispered, "I am *certain* to win. Listen to me, Honor. *I* did not break the contract. *I* kept my oaths. *I* have let myself be bound by them again and again. I understand you, and how you feel right now. I AM WORTHY."

Dalinar held his breath. There was a lesson taught in the game towers, once you started to think you were strong enough . . .

The power paused, and looked toward Dalinar.

Go, Dalinar said. *Watch. Learn.*

The power accepted Taravangian at Dalinar's urging. Though interestingly, a few small pieces of it split off and fled. Dalinar had not expected that.

Regardless, Taravangian took the power. Despite all he'd ever claimed, he drew it in, thirsting for more and Ascending to become a new god.

Retribution.

Retribution laughed, and that laugh vibrated through Dalinar. Somewhere, Wit was shouting in disbelief. Oddly, Dalinar could still feel that Connection. He felt, in fact, all of his Connections.

To Navani, he sent love.

To Adolin, he sent apologies.

To Renarin, he sent pride.

To the others, he sent courage.

I could not defeat Odium, he told them. *But I can buy you time. For Odium is about to have his attention entirely consumed by a greater problem.*

This was Dalinar's final test: at long last, trusting someone else to do the job.

With a smile, he felt echoes through the cosmere. Each time Honor had gone to the other gods for help, they'd been content to leave Roshar alone. To make Odium someone else's problem.

Dalinar could see the difference between giving up responsibility—as they had—and ensuring someone else had the chance you could not. As of now, the other gods' attention fixated on Taravangian. Each of those vast beings witnessed the birth of the most powerful and dangerous thing that had existed since the Shattering of Adonalsium.

Those forces together acknowledged that they had an enemy. Freed from his constraints, supremely strong. He was the biggest threat in the entire cosmere.

"It's called the Sunmaker's Gambit," Dalinar whispered. "Good luck, Taravangian."

The winds picked up as Taravangian's anger built. Dalinar closed his eyes, ready to die right there, in that furious storm, strong enough to flay his skin from his body. However, somehow within the tempest, Dalinar heard something: the sound of a man whimpering in pain.

So, Dalinar Kholin heaved himself up against the wind—his body breaking, and blood streaming from him—to fight it one last time.

144
THE TOWER,
THE CROWN,
AND THE SPEAR

And now we reach the part of the narrative where I can but speculate, as my witnesses were both unconscious.

—From *Knights of Wind and Truth,* page 271

Nale felt good.

Not great. Not wonderful. But he felt . . . better. A shadow had lifted from him.

Now though, something terrible had happened again. Suddenly his stomach churned, and a force seemed to try to turn him inside out.

"Ishar?" he said, kneeling beside the other Herald, who stared at the sky, his eyes wide. "Ishar, what is it?"

"The Stormfather is dead," Ishar whispered. "Dalinar Kholin has failed. Honor is being consumed . . . Retribution . . . his name is Retribution." He blinked, concentrating. "Cultivation flees. Retribution will also consume and destroy the spren, then remake them to his will and pleasure."

"What?" Nale said, helping the aged Herald sit. "All of them? Ishar . . . what do we do?"

"I don't know . . ." Ishar said. "I see clearly for the first time in centuries . . . It's been so long, walking through fog. Or smoke, the smoke of a burning world . . ." He focused again on Nale. "Like the spren, we bear a distinctive part of Honor's power in us. Retribution will want to reclaim it. Prepare yourself, Nale. This is our end."

The end. Nale fell to his knees, then settled back. The end. Yes. He could accept the end. Even if he'd just started feeling hope for recovery . . .

Perhaps it was time.

Perhaps it was past time.

"What will this mean?" he asked. "For Roshar?"

"No Stormlight," Ishar said, tired. "No highstorm. The enemy has won, and I was too infatuated with my own plots to notice or stop it . . ." He wiped his mouth with a trembling hand. "This is what we deserve."

Perhaps, a familiar voice said—trembling, uncertain. *But there is still a service you could perform. If you are willing.*

"What service?" Nale asked the Wind.

A ring of ten, in their strength, could bind Retribution in some small way. Could it not?

". . . Yes," Ishar said. "We bear Honor's power. Much as our Connection to Odium helped us bind him and his spren long ago, our Connection to Honor could let us bind Retribution. In a small way." The elderly Herald wiped blood from his mouth. "We could maybe prevent him from taking the spren to himself. We could seal away that part of his power, weaken him. Yes . . . Yes, that could work."

"You mean . . ." Nale said.

"We must reforge the circle," Ishar replied. "If the spren are to be preserved, if a Splinter of Honor is to be kept from Retribution's touch, we must stand tall again. Reaffirm our oaths, exploit that weakness he made in himself for us."

Nale trembled. Reforge the Oathpact? "Ishar," he said, feeling a deep, shameful terror rise inside of him.

Memories.

Agony.

Being held against stones, his soul burned and flayed.

Hearing his friends scream in pain, their voices echoing in his ears for centuries, awful and terrible, like the sound of fingernails being ripped from the flesh.

Nale blinked sudden tears from the corners of his eyes. "I can't go back, Ishar. I . . . I *can't.* I'm not strong enough!"

What if . . . there were a way to improve the Oathpact? the Wind asked. Nale could sense the fear in her voice . . . in the many voices of the windspren gathered to watch. *What if there were a way for your minds to go somewhere else?*

"Hmm . . ." Ishar said, as the Wind perhaps showed him something Nale couldn't see. "You've been thinking about this a long time, haven't you . . ."

I have had a great deal of time to think, Ishar.

"It could work. Nale, help me up."

Nale did so, lifting Ishar, who suddenly seemed frail in a way no Herald ever should. They looked upon a sorry scene. Swords scattered across the ground. Stormblessed, collapsed, his hand smoldering, several fingers missing. Szeth in worse shape, his arm gone all the way to the shoulder, his clothing burned away on one side, the skin beneath scored and blackened. Sylphrena was lying on her back—she appeared whole, yet was sobbing.

A black sword. Full of Investiture, mumbling to itself in a daze. Ishar limped to his own sword, which he'd dropped in the chaos. He hesitated before touching it.

"Perhaps you should place them," he said to Nale. "I . . . don't feel like myself when I touch its power."

Nale did as asked, taking each Honorblade and placing it in the circle until all nine stood in their slots. All but Jezrien's.

"The Wind has suggested a way to avoid the torture, Nale," Ishar said. "Impossible while Honor lived, but with some of his power siphoned off as Retribution asserts himself . . ."

Nale spun. "How?"

"I have studied the Stormfather's visions," Ishar explained. "The Wind has suggested that I create something similar. Though our souls will return to Braize, our minds are separate—and I can place them inside a vision, freed from whatever our souls or bodies might feel. With delicacy, this can be hidden from the Shards. I think I can do it, if Ash and Pralla help."

Nale rushed back to Ishar, taking him by the arm. "You mean . . . ?"

"We could perhaps have peace between Returns," Ishar said. "Instead of torture. Retribution will certainly seek vengeance against us if we bind him, and will attempt to make us break the pact, but if he cannot find our minds . . ."

Something deep within Nale trembled at that idea. Peace. He had not known it for so long.

"Will it work?" Nale asked. "Truly work?"

"I cannot guarantee it," Ishar said, "but I think it will. Old friend. Can you summon the courage to try?"

Old friend. They had not begun as friends. He had considered Ishar haughty. Perhaps he had been. Perhaps some of that remained. But friends, now. Yes, that was right.

But what of Nale's courage? He opened his mouth, but thought he heard . . .

He thought he heard the sound of flutes.

"I will try," Nale whispered.

"Good, good," Ishar said. "Come. It will be the end of all spren if we do not do something. Honor *must* be preserved." Ishar knelt by Szeth. Nale joined him, prodding delicately at the man's wounds. They weren't quite like burns; more like necrosis.

"Szeth lives," Nale said, "but he needs Regrowth. I have a fabrial—"

"But no Stormlight," Ishar said.

"No Stormlight." Nale deflated. During the confrontation, either Ishar, the sword, or Stormblessed had consumed it.

"Once Szeth is a Herald, this body will be meaningless anyway," Ishar said. "We proceed."

Nale turned Szeth onto his back. His head rolled, limp. He breathed, barely. "Can he do it? He must speak the Words."

No, the Wind said. *He cannot.*

A sound rumbled in the east. Nale looked, and saw darkness growing in the sky. Like a bruise on the heavens themselves. "You said no more storms, Ishar!"

"I said no more highstorm," Ishar whispered. "But there is another storm. Now the only storm. The Night of Sorrows has come, Nale. The True Desolation is here."

"The True Desolation?" Nale said, cradling Szeth in his lap. "Ishar, what . . . what good is it to fight now? Why struggle? Why care? The Stormfather is *gone.* Jezrien is *gone.* We have lost, finally. Honor is *dead.*"

"Yes," a quiet voice said. "Honor is dead."

Both Heralds spun to see Kaladin Stormblessed slowly pushing himself up to a seated position, hair disheveled, blue uniform rumpled, dirt on his face. He looked at his right hand, what was left of it, and grimaced. Then he sighed and heaved himself to his feet.

"But," Stormblessed said, "I'll see what I can do."

⁘

Kaladin, feeling like the crusted stuff on the inside of a cauldron after a stew got burned, trudged across the empty field and knelt beside Syl.

"How are you doing?" he asked.

"He's dead," she whispered. "My father is . . . dead. And I'm not sure if I ever really knew him . . ."

She glanced at him, and as she did, he saw a storm in her eyes. Not a metaphoric one, but actual lightning and swirling clouds, filling them. In a moment, she wore something very different. A regal gown, fit for . . . for a queen.

"I can't protect the spren, Kaladin," she said. "Odium holds Honor's power. We are now part of . . . of *him.* He will take us to him, destroy us, Unmake us."

"I think," Kaladin said, "the Wind has prepared a solution for that. Haven't you?"

I'm sorry. I should not ask . . . but I do. This is the only solution I could think of to prevent the danger that I sensed.

Syl sat up, and hesitated. "The last remnants of Honor lie here, in the hands of a broken circle of broken men and women. I see. Damnation, Kaladin. I see."

"An Oathpact could stop what is coming?" Kaladin asked.

The original one worked because most of the Heralds had once been chosen by Odium, and could leverage that Connection to bind him, the Wind said, blowing across him. *An oath here, now that he's Retribution, should do the same. Maybe. Please. Don't hate me.*

Kaladin gritted his teeth and stood, forming fists—or trying, since one of his hands didn't work anymore, and he felt only numbness from it.

He faced into the Wind. "Will the spren really die if this is not done?"

Yes, the Wind whispered. *Dalinar Kholin is dead. Cultivation has been freed from the planet, and runs, fearful of what she has done. Honor and Odium combine. Retribution will absorb all of the power, and will create weapons from it. New Unmade. Terrible Unmade.*

Kaladin took a deep breath. "What do you need me to do?"

Syl took his arm, and when he looked to her, he saw tears on her cheeks. Actual tears. How?

"Are you sure, Kaladin?" Syl whispered. "You know what it will mean? For you to . . ."

Storms. Was she saying . . . ?

Yes. He had known it the moment he stood up.

"We cannot ask this of you," Syl whispered.

Kaladin steeled himself. "But I can offer."

"You spent all this time learning that you can't sacrifice yourself for everyone else," she said. "You can't do this."

"Pardon," he said gently, placing his hand on hers, "but that is *not* what I learned, Syl."

She looked up at him.

"I learned that I don't *have* to make that sacrifice," he explained. "I can't protect everyone, and I have made peace with that. It doesn't mean I shouldn't try to do what I can, and I've learned that I can help without losing myself. You spren have given your entire lives to your Radiants. I can repay that now." He faced the Wind again. "Dalinar is really dead?"

Yes. And I cannot feel Navani or the Sibling.

Syl shivered, tears rolling farther down her cheeks. Had he ever seen her cry before?

Kaladin closed his eyes. "The people will have nothing left. No storm, no god, no king . . . They must be given some kind of hope." He opened his eyes and met Syl's. "What do you *need me to do.*"

"You will need to say the Words," she whispered.

 "Stormblessed?" Nale asked.

Kaladin turned to see Nale gingerly lowering Szeth, unconscious, to the ground. "You don't know what you're saying," Nale said. "Ishar's plan to protect our minds might not work. We could be going to torture. Even if not . . . it could be centuries until we return. Everyone you know and love will be dead by then."

Kaladin's heart trembled. Bridge Four . . . his family . . .

"It should be him," Nale said, nodding to Szeth. "He has no Connections left. He has been prepared for this."

Kaladin crossed the patch of too-springy ground. He knelt and rested his fingers on Szeth's wounded shoulder. "No. He cannot bear this."

"But—" Nale began.

"He chose peace," Kaladin said, "not war. Heralds must fight, and he needs to heal." He felt the wind blowing across him. "I cannot protect everyone. But I can protect *him.*"

Ishar, kneeling nearby, looked up at Kaladin. "Child? You really think you can replace Jezrien, our king?"

Kaladin rose and carefully slid Nightblood's sheath back onto him. The sword didn't seem to be awake; instead it was in a stupor. From there, Kaladin walked to his pack and dug inside, finding something soft at the bottom.

"Jezrien was the greatest of men," Ishar said. "Our guide and our leader. I prepared Szeth for over a decade. You cannot take the place of a king like Jezrien."

"To think," Kaladin said softly, "that you have lived millennia and you haven't learned a simple truth." He pulled a deep blue cloak from the pack, the tower and the crown emblazoned on the back. "Nobility has nothing to do with blood, Ishar. But it has everything to do with heart."

Kaladin stood up and threw the cloak over his shoulders. It swept through the air, and he felt the Wind making it float around him.

The spren were there when you needed us, the Wind said to him. *Please. They are so afraid.*

"It's all right," he said. He took a deep breath, and started toward the ring of swords. "I'm here."

Syl fell into step next to him. "No one can tell you the Words."

"Fortunately, I know them."

Wind blew around him, and he . . . he remembered that wind. He remembered it blowing as he first picked up a spear, long ago, and before that when he was a child first holding a quarterstaff. Kaladin stepped through a version of himself, that youthful version everyone had called Kal. For he was part of Kaladin.

The wind had been there on the day he'd killed Helaran and saved Amaram. The last day Squadleader Kaladin had existed. Kaladin walked through that old version of himself. For he was part of Kaladin.

He remembered the wind blowing in his face, trying to force him back from the Honor Chasm. He remembered thinking about how it had *worked* to keep him from taking those steps. That version of Kaladin appeared, the wretch, the slave. Kaladin strode through him, for he was part of Kaladin.

The wind had been there with him when he'd fought Szeth in the clouds. Kaladin Stormblessed, Radiant. Kaladin strode through that man, for that man was part of him.

The wind had been there when he'd fought the Pursuer after Teft's death—that day when Kaladin had almost given in to Odium. That version of Kaladin appeared, his eyes burning yellow-red. Kaladin strode through that figure, for it was yet another element of him, and he should not forget.

The Wind had always been there. Holding its breath at some important moments, but blowing alongside him gloriously during others. If he did not act, Retribution would kill it, and Syl, and all of them. Kaladin had to hide the Wind, the Heralds, and the last bits of Honor away. Protect them.

Until the time was right to Return.

Yes, he knew the Words. Not an Ideal of any set of Radiants. Something more daunting. A last version of Kaladin appeared in front of him, a terrifying, glorious being.

Kaladin. Herald.

"I," Kaladin whispered, walking through that version, "accept this journey."

The air split with a crack of thunder. When the reply came, it was Syl's voice. *These Words are accepted.*

"That isn't what we said," Nale said.

"The important part is not the Words themselves," Kaladin said. "It is, again, the heart. Thousands of years, and I'd think you would know this."

Kaladin thrust out his broken hand—withered, with only the thumb and two fingers remaining—as he reached the ring of weapons. Syl, in turn, thrust *her* hand forward, near his and right below it. A white-blue spear of light formed in their hands—both Kaladin and Syl gripping it.

Together, they rammed it into the ground in the open spot of the ring. The light faded, creating a tall, silvery spear—not the one he'd been using, though it had echoes of the design. This hadn't been made from Syl; this had been created, like the Honorblades, from Honor.

Ishar walked to his sword and placed his hand on it. Nale on his. And then . . . Kaladin felt the others. Terrified, but released from a small portion of their darkness. He felt Ishar reach out to them, and offer something vital.

Redemption.

A ghostly figure strode forward as if from nothing. A tall, muscular man. Taln? His hand went to his sword. He was the first back into the ring. Others followed, people Kaladin didn't know. A woman in a havah with long black hair, another with red hair, and a third with tan skin and a book under one arm. Then Ash, and even Kalak, though his image was almost completely transparent. The very last was a woman with a shaved head, a curious expression on her face.

Each had come to the call. Despite everything they had survived, they listened, and they responded.

Yes. He could help these people.

He felt something *Connect* inside him. Warmth flooded through Kaladin, like the warmth of Stormlight, but less about motion, more about . . . stability. Gloryspren burst into existence above him, and then a ring of light, made of a thousand windspren. Ribbons, like Syl sometimes became. No faces, and no laughter. Making a spinning whirlpool of light. Kaladin looked down at himself, and found that he was glowing.

Thank you, the Wind said. *Herald.*

"Kaladin," Syl said. "Your eyes."

"What about them?"

"Dark brown," she whispered, her hand raised to touch his face. "Like they used to be."

Kaladin smiled, then turned to see the other Heralds had vanished—all but Ishar and Nale. "It worked," Nale breathed. "I can feel it. The Oathpact . . ."

"Reforged," Ishar said. He hesitated a moment, then lifted his arm to gesture toward Kaladin. "Welcome, Kaladin Stormblessed. Herald of Kings. Herald of the Wind. Herald of . . ."

"Herald," Kaladin said, "of Second Chances."

Nale smiled, nodding.

All fell still.

"Now what?" Kaladin asked.

"Now," Ishar said, "I must make you immortal. And then we must leave this world."

145
TO WEEP
FOR THE END
OF ALL THINGS

I can only guess what happened, therefore, to the Knight of Wind. That he is dead is demonstrable. That he succeeded, at least in part, is also demonstrable.

—From *Knights of Wind and Truth*, page 289

Navani felt the oddest sensation. Love.

An overwhelming sense of love . . . and then . . .

Farewell?

Navani!

The Sibling's voice in her mind.

NAVANI!

"What?" she said, shocking those who stood with her in the top room. They'd heard storms, a tempest shaking the tower.

He is dead, Navani, the Sibling said. *I'm sorry.*

Dead.

No. But . . . but that wasn't. . . .

She'd felt him just then. Impossibly, somehow, sending her a sense of love. Followed by . . . that regret . . .

Followed by nothing. His soul vanishing.

"He serves the enemy?" Navani asked.

No, he shattered it all. The contract, Honor—all done. All dead. It's . . . it's brilliant. And terrible. The enemy holds both Shards and becomes Retribution. Cultivation flees. We . . .

Navani, we are in serious danger. This could destroy me.

Grieve later.

Storms. Could she . . . could she . . .

Grieve *later.*

"What do we do?" Navani said.

We have to keep Retribution out of Urithiru, the Sibling said. *He's going to destroy the spren, but not us here, if we can create defenses. It will be your will and mine against his. I don't know if . . . Oh, Shards, Navani. He's coming!*

"Do it!" Navani said.

⁂

"What do you mean you can't?" Shallan whispered, kneeling on the Oathgate platform. "Transfer me! Please!"

The Oathgate spren were shrinking. "With what Stormlight?" one asked, booming voice becoming more ordinary. "The enemy has drawn it all back to him, pulling Light from holes in people and gems. It is gone."

"With . . ." Shallan fished in her pocket. She'd had spheres when she entered the Spiritual Realm. She'd checked them when she'd returned here, but now they were dun.

"There is no more Stormfather," the gateway spren said, stepping onto the platform. "There is no more Honor. There is no more Stormlight. Our era has ended."

Shallan looked around the ten Oathgates, where each of those spren was shrinking down as well.

"No . . . more Stormlight?" Shallan asked. "For how long?"

"Forever."

⁂

Taravangian, Retribution, reveled in his new strength.

He was more powerful than anything. Only one other came close, but those powers were misaligned, while Honor and Odium wanted nearly the same things. They *would* work together.

Though something . . . something about his predecessor . . . echoed to him from the past. Rayse had never wanted this. He'd killed several other gods, and refused their power.

Was he a fool? He must have been. Because this was *glorious.* Taravangian laughed as the Shards—crashing together—swirled in an incredible wind, melding as one storm. Any echoes of Tanavast, his only true rival, were gone.

No. There could be others. Ba-Ado-Mishram was free again. He would have to channel and control her, lest she supplant him. There were ways . . . though he found her difficult to find, even with his divine eyes. Where had she gone?

He had other work to do. The highstorm was consumed by the Everstorm at his will, creating a ripple through nature—one he reveled in, causing the passage of time to warp around this world. He had *won.* Only *his* Light would be available to Roshar. Only *his* storm would make them bow down.

A dark tempest that would blanket the land. All would wither unless they used his Light to grow and thrive. They would have to rely on *him* for *everything.*

Now to deal with the spren, pieces of the old Honor. Remnants, dangling threads, and a possible problem in years to come. If he could be undermined, it would be by them. He breathed in, reaching to draw all spren—of Odium, and of Honor—to him. Those only of Cultivation he'd have to find and—

Nothing happened. As he tried to draw the spren toward him, the power refused to absorb them.

They are protected, his powers said.

"By what?" Retribution demanded.

By an oath and a circle, the powers said. *By Adonalsium's strength. Ten stand against you, using the piece of us within them. Honor demands their oaths be followed.*

That was frustrating. He was supposed to be unrivaled, but his power . . . He saw that he'd have to be careful. Not act against its will, or he'd suffer Tanavast's fate.

There should be a way. He would be more cautious than his predecessors, he would . . .

Wait. What were those forces watching him?

The other Shards.

Cultivation, terrified, had *ejected* herself from Roshar. And all attention from the remaining gods was on him.

He immediately saw what Dalinar had done. Odium had expected to have centuries to plan. Suddenly he had lost all of that. The true battle for the cosmere started right *now.*

No! he thought. *I'm not ready.*

The death of the highstorm, and the birth of the true Everstorm, continued to warp the spiritual aspect of Roshar. It was distorting everything, fueled by Retribution's rage. Dalinar . . . *Dalinar* had done this. As the storms finally stilled—control reasserted, his anger managed—Taravangian formed an avatar to confront Dalinar.

He found only the man's corpse, huddled beside the stone railing. His clothing ripped, his body bloodied. The damage done by the winds and tempest had been too much for Dalinar—but beneath him, sheltered from the storm, Gavinor survived, unconscious but alive. Protected in one last act of self-sacrifice.

Taravangian bellowed. Oddly, the sweetness of it all faded if he couldn't hear Dalinar confess the truth: that Taravangian had been right all along.

No. He couldn't be dead. *No!*

Well, he would bring Retribution upon Dalinar for this. He considered destroying Gavinor out of spite, but . . . no. He revolted at such an act. Gavinor had acted with honor, keeping his promises—and Taravangian had been very careful, during their twenty years of preparation, about what he said.

Part of the power within him was . . . concerned. Had he acted with honor toward Gavinor?

I did everything I promised him, Taravangian thought. *I brought him to get revenge, to claim his kingdom. I never said I wouldn't interfere. All I did was perfectly in line with my oaths to Gavinor.*

It was true. The power acknowledged it. That should be that. It calmed while Taravangian pondered. He would have to let Azir keep its land, as they had won, wouldn't he? Dalinar had broken the contract, but Honor . . . Honor wanted desperately to follow it—and Taravangian had to be careful lest the power rebel against him. As he determined to do so, Honor swelled inside him, and more fully bonded into Retribution.

Good. Likewise, he would allow the Shattered Plains to have a kind of autonomy themselves. What of the rest? Roshar was entirely dominated. His agents in the Shin government had succeeded while the Heralds were distracted. The Reshi Isles . . . he had the land, all of it, though those who rode the beasts had largely rejected his offers. They weren't worth the effort.

Everything else on Roshar—ninety percent of the planet—had accepted his deals or had been won by his forces. That would do. It was enough. In fact, it was glorious. Retribution would keep *his* promises. Oaths *were* important. And Retribution would *destroy* anyone who believed differently.

Strangely, the power of Honor displayed the slightest hint of . . . uncertainty. What was that? Why was it acting so oddly? Taravangian's expanded knowledge found this impossible; was it because some of it had been siphoned off, locked away?

I will need to move quickly, he thought, seeing possible futures. *Escape Roshar, before the other Shards move against me. They are timid still, but will be galvanized by time.*

His next actions would have to be decisive. He began thinking of ways to draw the attention of his enemies toward a conflict on Scadrial . . . He would have to leave Roshar under a regent, as he needed to plan how to evade this trap that Dalinar had created for him. How? How had the man been so clever? How had Taravangian not seen this?

His anger at Dalinar surged again, a tempest of flame and ire. Dalinar. Dalinar had stolen *centuries* from him! No more planning, no more careful manipulations. Dalinar . . .

Dalinar *did* still exist.

Taravangian reached out and found something lingering on the other side: Dalinar's soul. Infused with power, unable to pass on yet. The part of a person that remained, briefly, before entering the Beyond. Taravangian seized it, and it fell into his power.

For Dalinar Kholin was an oathbreaker.

YOU REALIZE I CAN NOW DO WITH YOU WHAT I WILL, Taravangian said to him. *I COULD TORTURE YOU FOR ETERNITY, DALINAR. YOU REALLY THINK YOUR SACRIFICE WAS WORTH THE COST?*

Rippling through the soul of his rival, a question. *What is my life worth?*

NOTHING, ANYMORE. DALINAR, YOU ARE NOTHING.

If so, then I trade it for everything. *Taravangian . . . I call that a bargain.*

Taravangian raged, furious that Dalinar refused to let him gloat. Yet he would not be goaded; he *would* control this power. Taravangian still had uses for Dalinar. His broken oaths put his soul in Taravangian's hands, and he would make an Unmade from him. Make him . . .

Dalinar's soul slipped away from him. Stretched. And vanished into the Beyond. Taravangian scrambled to hold it, but like water through fingers, he could not.

You cannot have him, the powers said, *for he is claimed by another.*

Defeat.

Why should Taravangian feel defeated when he'd won everything? He raged again, this time worst of all, ripples of it further warping the realms around Roshar. Dalinar had escaped? Dalinar was dead?

But no. There was something of him left. Taravangian found it in the Spiritual Realm. It had manifested in the vision where Dalinar had stubbornly thrown an oil barrel and performed acts of peace, as if he hadn't already burned a city to the ground.

In that vision, the Blackthorn had formed. And the Blackthorn . . . it was a *legend.* It was spoken of, molded by the minds of people, taking shape. It had responded differently from every other part of the visions, for things people thought about came *alive.*

A great number of people thought about the Blackthorn. The stories of him outgrew Dalinar himself—who had made at least *one* mistake. He'd given this thing his memories, shown it the future, and now it came even more fully to life.

Retribution cradled it.

You are right, it said to him, making his ego soothe and anger soften. *He was weak. I am not weak. I will not do the things he showed me. I will not weep, drunken, when an assassin must be fought. I will not back down from the fight and the conquest. I am the Blackthorn.*

Will you serve me? Retribution asked. *When I take war to the stars.*

It is what I do, said the Blackthorn.

Yes . . . a mistake. Dalinar had Connected to this nascent spren of himself, given it his memories, his skill—memories that, in it, came too soon. It was what Dalinar could have been, had Cultivation not protected him from his actions. Greater than Gavilar, greater than any man.

A true champion. With incredible battle acumen, brilliant understanding of tactics and strategy, and Dalinar's stubborn force of will. But without the weak inhibitions of his old age, such as having been broken by his wife's death.

Yes. Dalinar Kholin had died.

But the Blackthorn *would* live.

Now, to deal with one other oathbreaker. The Heralds, he saw, were safe from his touch. But one person was not, a person both powers warned him to deal with immediately.

Where was Wit?

⁂

Swords began vanishing from the circle.

Kaladin fell to his knees before Ishar, who touched him on the sides of his head.

"This is Vedel's method," Ishar said. "It relies on skills I have not used in a long time . . . powers of the Surges outside of Stormlight, Radiance, or the Honorblades. It requires an oath forged, and a bit of a god . . ."

Kaladin's eyes went wide as something burned within him. He could feel the others. Taln, Ash, Vedel, Chana . . . they felt terrified, worried they were heading toward torture.

This is working, the Wind whispered. *Kaladin, it's working! The Oathpact preserves the spren!*

"I hope we will be beyond him too," Ishar said, seizing his Blade. He looked to Kaladin. "But . . . even so . . . I might lose myself again. Not all of the rot upon my soul was because of the power of Odium, Stormblessed. I . . . am weak. Of mind."

"I will help," Kaladin promised.

Nearby, Nale stiffened, then *evaporated,* vanishing into nothingness. His sword disappeared from the ring.

"We use bodies of power when we Return, child," Ishar said. "No one dies to create us. Honor found such an idea as the Fused abhorrent. Once."

Kaladin nodded, steeling himself as his soul began to vibrate. A light enveloped him, and as it did, Syl found his hand. And he could feel her grip it.

"You still have your original body," Ishar said as he vanished. "Your soul will be pulled with us, leaving the body behind. I'm sorry. It might hurt."

Kaladin squeezed Syl's hand tightly, then gasped, a terrible fire ripping through him. A flaring in his skull, agonizing. He felt his eyes burn away, as if he'd been struck by a Shardblade.

Followed by . . .

Nothing.

But it was not a complete success, as I have not heard the Wind—neither has Szeth—in years. Save that one whisper.

Regardless, she lives, so perhaps the Oathpact, as it was, held well enough? Even without Szeth to fill the hole?

Or perhaps, as champion of the Wind, Kaladin was able to do something in the end right before he died, which turned Retribution's ire from the spren.

—From *Knights of Wind and Truth,* page 290

Sigzil sat in the medical rooms of Urithiru with Kaladin's father. The officer on watch had sent him here, despite Sigzil's insistence there was nothing a surgeon could do for him. Losing his spren wasn't a physical ailment.

Still, Lirin examined him. The world itself could be ending, and this man just kept seeing patients. Sigzil hunched forward on the surgical table, sensing that hole inside and agonizing over what he'd done. Though his plan had worked, and the generals had commended him on salvaging a terrible situation, he didn't *feel* it. He felt *awful.*

"You're talking to the wrong surgeon, I'm afraid," Lirin said, walking to his cupboard. "My son is training to help with mental and emotional ailments. His strategies for dealing with loss will help more than my medicines. That said, you might have trouble sleeping, and for that I can offer—"

The door slammed open.

Wit stood on the other side, wide-eyed, puffing, sweat trickling down his face.

"Excuse me?" Lirin said. "This surgery room is off-limits to even you. I need to maintain—"

"Dalinar is dead," Wit snapped. "The Sibling is going into another self-protective coma. The world is ending. So if you please, Lirin, *shut up*."

What? Dalinar had *lost*? Sigzil, in his haze of pain, hadn't been paying attention to much—he was barely aware that a day had passed since losing Vienta.

Wit shoved Lirin out the door and slammed it. He dashed up to Sigzil and took him by both arms. "Kid, I need you. I really, *really* need your help."

"Wha . . . what?" Sigzil asked. "Why are—"

"Listen to me," Wit hissed. "In a frighteningly short amount of time, the power that Odium holds is going to identify *me* as the only thing on the planet that can harm him. The power bears a grudge, even though its vessel has changed. It's going to vaporize me."

"Wit?" Sigzil said. "I thought nothing could—"

"Pay attention," Wit said, shaking him. "I'm holding something incredibly dangerous. Something that Odium absolutely *cannot* get access to. A power more ancient than any of the gods. Do you understand me? I need someone to take it. I need someone to bear it for a short time, until I can return for it. It can't be a Radiant. It would be too dangerous, too much power in one person's hands."

"But . . . *you're* a Radiant . . ."

"Smart as always." Wit pointed one hand at him. "Sigzil," he said, his voice growing solemn. "Old Dalinar has done something *incredibly* stupid. He made a gamble, and in so doing he unleashed a terror upon the entire cosmere. I don't have time to explain all the ramifications, but we *cannot* let Odium have the Dawnshard. He is the *last* being in all the many worlds who should hold it."

"And . . ." Sigzil said, his mind racing, the pain fading before this information. "And so you brought it here to *his planet*?"

Wit took a deep breath, then nodded.

"Idiot," Sigzil said.

"Guilty. Will you do it, Sigzil? Will you take it?"

Something came alight within him. A way to make up for his failings. "Yes, I'll take it, Wit. I'll do better this time. I'll redeem myself."

"Good lad," Wit said. "It likes you. As much as its ilk can *like* anything. I don't think it's alive, not like a spren, or the power of the Shards. More . . . it likes you the way a subaxial electron likes a nucleus. Are you ready?"

Sigzil nodded.

"When Odium arrives," Wit said, "his presence coalescing here will let me do something odd." He held up a device made of several gears and what appeared to be glowing light—not trapped in a gemstone, but in an hourglass.

"I'm sorry for how that will feel, but the Dawnshard should keep you alive. Get off this planet as soon as you can. Keep it *away* from him, Sig. Our only advantage is that he doesn't know it's here. Unfortunately, if he kills me while I hold it, he'll discover the truth. You he'll ignore. Hopefully." He hesitated. "I'll find you. I promise."

Before Sigzil could ask for an explanation, he felt his soul tremble. The individual pieces of himself aligning as a force *overlapped* him. A vast, strange power, greater than a storm, or even a world, but capable of fitting inside a human heart.

It was ancient. Wonderful and terrible. It bore a single all-powerful directive, which thrummed through Sigzil.

Exist.

The room started to darken. Wit stuck the device to Sigzil and pushed him backward, knocking him over.

"Taravangian!" Wit said, spinning around and putting his hands to the sides in an innocent posture. "Have I told you about the time I—"

The god vaporized Wit in a wave of red mist.

It was the last thing Sigzil saw as he somehow fell into Shadesmar, dropping into a version of this room on the other side, surrounded by light and terrified spren.

⁂

Renarin stood on an upper floor of Urithiru, bathed in green-blue light. The entire room in front of him had filled with some kind of crystal, and his aunt Navani floated in the center of it, glowing. Frozen, eyes closed.

She appeared to be asleep. Although the tower continued to function as it had since awakening—lifts, pumps, lights all working properly, Towerlight available to Radiants here—they could not communicate with the Sibling or Navani. Jasnah knelt in front of Renarin, her hands against the glassy wall. He put his next to hers on the wall, and could hear his aunt's heartbeat.

"Have you ever heard of anything like this?" Renarin asked Rlain and Jasnah.

"No," Jasnah said. She looked *exhausted.* Deep bags beneath her eyes, makeup a mess, normally immaculate hair out of its braids. "No. But she seems alive. She has to survive . . . I need her . . ."

A dome of light as solid as this crystal surrounded the entirety of Urithiru, impassable. The Oathgates were inside that dome, but didn't work. He'd been transported here with Rlain during their last functional moments.

He'd left Shallan behind by accident. How could he explain that to Adolin? Last word was that his brother lived, but that was when there had been

Stormlight and spanreeds. Now silence reigned. No storms. No spanreeds. No knowledge of what anyone anywhere was doing.

They were completely cut off.

Rlain put a hand on his shoulder, and Renarin placed his atop it, taking strength from the singer's presence. Finally, Jasnah stood. She nodded to them, then led them back to a nearby room, where Sebarial and Aladar waited. They looked to Renarin now that Navani was indisposed and Renarin's father . . .

Renarin's father . . .

He took a deep breath, then walked with Jasnah and the highprinces to the nearby stairwell. "I will not be your king," Renarin whispered to them as they climbed those steps.

"But—" Sebarial said.

"Jasnah, I wish to adopt your system," Renarin said. "Can we institute a representative government for Urithiru, as you have for the Alethi exiles here?"

"I will show you how," she said softly.

"What?" Sebarial said. "But—"

"My brother and I refuse the throne," Renarin said. "I won't stand for a highprince to be elevated. We will have an elected senate and a Ministerial Exemplar." He stopped, looking back at them. "I think you'll find Brightness Jasnah's writings on the topic to be quite thorough."

"I've read them," Sebarial said. "But if Queen Navani wakes, she'll discover that most of her power has been stripped away! She'll be furious."

"*When* my aunt wakes," Renarin said, "she'll accept that the world has progressed, and a queen can lead without being a ruler. I think you'll find her excited by the prospect." He turned to the still-glowing lights in the walls of Urithiru. "Besides, I expect she'll have plenty to do."

He continued up the steps, surprised by how confidently he spoke. Ordering around highprinces? Demanding they give up their power? But he couldn't be king; he and Rlain had other work to do. Odium now ruled the world, and the singers had won—at long last—one of the Desolations.

Rlain intended to speak to their leaders on behalf of humankind. Renarin would join him. Assuming they could ever get out of this city.

Renarin emerged into the top room of the tower, and from there, took the steps to the roof. Together, he, Rlain, and Jasnah joined a small, solemn group at the railing. Gavinor, somehow fully grown, sat by it with Oathbringer across his lap, his eyes red.

It was so much to take in. Gavinor had been Odium's champion? Add that to Navani being comatose, and . . . storms, Renarin had barely explained about Ba-Ado-Mishram. It was too much to deal with at the moment.

Now . . . now he needed to deal with what was ahead of him. A few others had come to see the body, and they parted for Renarin.

He braced himself, took a deep breath, then knelt by the corpse of Dalinar Kholin.

Most of the damage to his body had been to his back, including the strikes of windblown stones to his skull that had killed him. Now lying face-upward on the roof, he appeared peaceful. Eyes closed.

Renarin closed his own eyes to the anguishspren floating around him and gave his father a final hug. Of the sort that Dalinar had always needed, despite everyone else—everyone but Renarin—thinking otherwise. Being strong didn't mean that you didn't need anyone. Those around you were the *source* of your strength.

"Thank you," Renarin whispered to his father. "For being proud of me. For showing me the heights we can reach, regardless of the depths we once knew."

"I hate that he died alone up here," Aladar said, his voice rough, repeating a sentiment he'd mentioned earlier. "That we couldn't help him."

"He didn't die alone, Aladar," Renarin said, rising and turning toward the rest of them. "He . . . I . . ."

He looked to Jasnah. She nodded to him. So, as he'd told her, he took out his notes, reading what he'd written quickly while Jasnah had tried to get through the crystal to Navani.

"No hero dies alone," Renarin read, written in halting words by his own hand, "for he carries with him the dreams of everyone who continues to live. Those dreams will keep my father company in the Beyond, where he taught us we go when we die. No continual war. No more killing. My father is finally at peace. And we live because of his sacrifice."

He glanced up from his notes and smiled—weakly, sadly—as Rlain hummed to the Lost. Sebarial nodded.

Aladar, however, looked down, not meeting his eyes. "He failed, Renarin. I loved him too, but I can't lie. He came up here to save humankind, and he *failed.* The enemy destroyed him, took the power, and won the very *world.*"

"No more highstorm," Teshav said. "You've seen the Everstorm growing?" Beneath them, a blackness was moving to cover the entire land. Everything but Urithiru itself. "The world is doomed. It's inevitable now . . ."

Both sentiments, Renarin knew, would be prevalent in the years to come. His father would be remembered as a brave hero who failed.

Glys had another take on it.

He found a way forward, the spren said. *The only way forward. I feel it, Renarin, but I do not understand it. I think we will eventually. I hope we will.*

"My father," Renarin said, looking back at his notes, "will, um, need to be Soulcast to stone. I have asked Jasnah to do it. So he can be set with the ancient kings of Urithiru, and someday—hopefully—moved to be with those statues at Kholinar, where his brother still stands."

Renarin took another deep breath. He had seen his father burning in his visions, for some reason, not made into stone. They weren't always right. But that didn't mean they were always wrong either. Dalinar had died.

Rlain embraced him. Renarin appreciated it—because although embracing in front of others was embarrassing, they needed to see that singer and human *could* work together.

They started toward the steps. At the top of them, Renarin joined Jasnah in turning back to face the body—lying on blood-soaked blankets.

"I wanted you to see him up here," Jasnah said. "Before we moved him."

"Thank you," Renarin said. "And thank you for letting me speak to the highprinces. I . . . I think I needed that."

"We have difficult days ahead, Renarin," Jasnah said, her voice strangely frail. "Days I hoped to prevent. But everything I've striven to achieve has collapsed, and everything I thought I knew . . . is no more . . ."

He raised his hand toward her, and let her nod before hugging her, as had always been their way.

"Come," Jasnah said, walking back down. "Your father's work is finished. Ours is merely beginning."

Renarin followed. He *would* discover why his father had given up the power to the enemy. Because if Glys was right, then in that decision, they would find their only way forward. Into a future that, for once in a long while, Renarin knew nothing about.

⁂

Szeth-son-Neturo awoke in a land covered by darkness. Not pitch-black, but dark as the hateful hour, the time between moons. Crackling red lightning, more or less constant, gave some relief to the night. The ground trembled in a way he'd never experienced before. Rumbling periodically, like a counterpoint to the thunder. It felt like distant mountains collapsing.

He stared upward, thinking he must be dead, until the pain of his body convinced him otherwise. He groaned, reaching with his left hand to probe at his pained side, and found his right arm was gone, and even part of his shoulder. The skin was tender, and the wrongness of the missing limb was disorienting. Like being in a nightmare, or in someone else's body.

He rolled over, his clothing loose and burned. Then he groaned again as he found the corpse of Kaladin Stormblessed on the ground nearby. No breath, no pulse, his eyes pits of blackness. The Honorblades and Heralds were gone.

Szeth bowed his head. "I'm sorry," he whispered. "After all you did for me, Ishu killed you, didn't he?"

Szeth wished he could find tears. He just felt . . . so overwhelmed. So numb. Did that mean he was callous?

"Sylphrena?" he called. "Sylphrena, are you here?"

Nothing. What was wrong with the Everstorm? Why did it not move?

Szeth? A quiet, frail voice.

Szeth cried out at hearing something familiar. He crawled, one-handed, shuffling and searching until he found Nightblood, sheathed, on the ground.

Szeth. I killed him, didn't I? I killed Kaladin . . .

"No," Szeth said. "His eyes were burned. He was stabbed by a Shardblade, Nightblood. You took a few of his fingers, but you *didn't* kill him. You *stopped.*"

But you . . . your arm . . .

"A price I paid to save my family," he said. "*You* did that. You *freed* them."

I . . . did?

Szeth clutched the sword, holding it close in his left hand as he stumbled to his feet on an empty field. The horses had fled, taking the wagon with them, leaving only Kaladin's pack.

Upon looking through that, he found . . .

A small woolen sheep. And a carved wooden toy horse. Szeth held both up with one hand, by light of the Everstorm, and finally found tears to weep.

Eventually, he wiped his eyes. "The Heralds . . ."

Gone, Nightblood said. *I felt them being destroyed by . . . by something powerful, Szeth. Something amazingly powerful. More powerful than anything I've ever felt. A new god. That is him, in the sky.*

Szeth gazed up at blackness. The ground trembled again, enough to make him stumble. Once it subsided, he looked toward Kaladin. He would . . . have to find help to bury the man. He couldn't manage it one-handed with no tools.

What do we do? Nightblood asked.

"I was told to live better," Szeth said. "And I will. My people will need help with what is to come, and I believe there are still better Skybreakers to be found."

And so Szeth-son-Neturo, the last bearer of Truth of Shinovar, put his sword to his shoulder and started walking. He'd find help to bury Kaladin, then seek the more populated parts of Shinovar—and there, do his best to provide answers to a nation of people who were certain to be confused and afraid.

Jasnah trailed through her rooms in Urithiru.

Her uncle's death loomed large. She felt . . . like she'd failed him, and herself, in multiple ways. Jasnah, who had prided herself on being the first Radiant of this generation, had been unable to help either Bondsmith in the end. She had also failed in protecting Thaylen City.

She'd given up the Shattered Plains, recognizing that a treaty was the best choice—but that was inconsequential without the Oathgates. She'd once imagined rebuilding Alethkar as a nation in the Unclaimed Hills, but she'd ceded the habitable land to the listeners. And again, without Oathgates, her people couldn't travel there. They'd have to be declared citizens of Urithiru. Alethkar was, finally and irretrievably, lost.

Fortunately, not everything had failed her. Her opposition to the Vorin religion and deity in general was—at the moment—one of her only stable touchstones. But her moral philosophy . . .

I let my position of authority guide me to believe I knew *what the greatest good was. That I was* capable *of making that decision for others.*

The greater good . . . regardless of the means used to reach it . . . That wasn't the answer. It never had been. She'd dedicated her life to an ideal she didn't, deep down, believe. Storms. Dalinar's way might not have been the best way, but hers . . . hers was full of holes.

She sat on the edge of her bed, exhausted, alone. Ivory was consulting with the Radiant spren trapped in the tower, trying to figure out what all this would mean—and if there was a way to speak to the Sibling or Navani.

Jasnah climbed through exhaustionspren into her bed, feeling drained, overwhelmed.

She found a note on the pillow.

I'm sorry, it said in Wit's handwriting. *You are right, and your letter to me was—characteristically—full of wisdom and excellent deductions. I accept that we cannot continue as we have . . .*

Goodbye. It might be a great long time before we see one another again, if ever.

She laughed. Because what else could she do? Her letter had explained all the logical reasons they were bad for one another—but at this moment, all she wanted was someone to hold. She pulled the covers around herself. Her father was long dead. Her mother was in a coma. Her brother had been slain. Her uncle had died failing to protect the planet. And now, even Wit was gone.

Worst of all, Taravangian had been right. At every point, he had been right. About her. About everything.

She hadn't felt so utterly alone since that day she'd been locked away as a child. And there was no one to dry her tears as she shook, trying to hold it back, curled up in her bed. Overwhelmed, worn out, and—worst of all—*wrong.*

⁂

Venli sat at the edge of the main plateau of Narak, looking toward a sunset she could not see. Black clouds and red lightning stretched in all directions, blocking the sunlight.

A day had passed since Odium's Ascension to Retribution. He had spoken to them, via messenger. He would be in touch. For now, the listeners were allowed his Light to fuel their powers, should they wish it. The messenger also explained that they could use it to grow crops, as Stormlight had once done.

They received this Light once a day, at midnight, by placing their spheres beneath the sky and asking him to bless them. Retribution asked for nothing in exchange, and had promised he did not see himself as their god. Only an interested party wishing to offer them help.

They had done as instructed last night, testing his word, and now had filled gemstones. With that, they could survive in this land. Their need to do so, however, worried her. Would that she had her sister's wisdom to advise. She thought of Eshonai, and watching the sunset together on these plateaus.

Thinking of her gave Venli a sense of peace. Even with the terrible storm. And she wondered . . . was this what redemption felt like? This uncertainty that she could have done more, mixing with a thrill of having come home at last?

Timbre thrummed to Hope.

Venli's mother approached—she'd gone to get tea—and settled down, saying nothing, but offering a cup to Venli. Together they hummed.

This may not be redemption, Venli thought. *Not yet. Maybe just . . . atonement. The redemption comes later, after we see if I can keep improving.*

The treaty sat beside her, in its waterproof pouch. Eshonai hadn't been able to get the humans to listen, but somehow Venli had. It wasn't a competition, and she had to keep that in mind. But this land *was* theirs again.

"Venli!" a voice called. She turned to see Bila waving to her. Venli looked to her mother, who hummed to Tension.

They went running past lounging chasmfiends—including some who had just arrived, carrying more listeners here from the edge of the plateaus. She also passed a couple of Fused who hadn't left yesterday, when El had called the retreat. They had asked to *stay.* That group included the Husked One *she*'d seen the other night on the plateau, staring at the sky.

He had been a farmer many thousands of years ago, and was now chatting with them—animated in a way he hadn't been before. Venli ran past him to the building where, using Retribution's gifted Light, she'd secretly made a passage downward, and had found the underground pool to be empty.

Now, with her mother and Bila, she reached the pool and found the strange too-thick liquid returning. Welling up from the ground. The color was different, a brilliant black-blue. A new tone accompanied it, pulsing to a new rhythm. The . . . Rhythm of War? She knew its name instinctively.

"What does it mean?" Thude asked her, looking up from where he knelt by the gathering pool of blue-black liquid light.

"It means," she said softly, "that we have a very powerful duty, Thude. Our little land is going to be important to the coming world."

"Why can't anyone ever just leave us alone?" Bila asked.

"That's not how the world works, Bila," Venli said. "We have to be part of life. I guess . . . that's what our leaders decided, along with Eshonai, all those years ago when they went to meet the humans. Yes, our ancestors walked away." She looked to the light. "We, in turn, have to come back. We make a nation, a strong one, for any singer who wants to join us. Anyone who seeks to listen, and hear, the peaceful rhythm in the stillness of the storm's heart."

The others nodded, humming to Determination, as they watched the new god's power fill this hidden well.

This account will not be without flaws. But it is the best I have been able to create from available information—and from the witness of my husband, Szeth, and the witness of the black sword he bears. For I myself helped him bury the Knight of Wind's body, the day after Stormfall.

The day that everything changed.

—From *Knights of Wind and Truth,* an account of the cleansing of Shinovar by Masha-daughter-Shaliv, six years following Stormfall, page 292

Wit woke in a bed somewhere far from Roshar. A place with soil, budding skyscrapers, and firearms.

It had worked. He would continue to exist.

He sat up and stretched, feeling remarkably hale for someone who had been completely vaporized by a deity. But, well, they didn't make deities like they once had. He had been part of the group who had seen to that.

He stood, found he was naked, and rifled through the drawers in the dresser by the far wall. Everything was still here, placed as he'd left it years ago, regularly laundered per his instructions.

Excellent. He dressed. It was . . . it was all going to . . .

Well, he couldn't tell himself that lie, could he? It wasn't all going to work out. Damnable Dalinar Kholin had made the absolute *wrong* choice. Wit slumped down into his bed and closed his eyes. He could feel his Lightweaver powers, but the distance between him and Design—who had been left on Roshar—was so vast, he doubted he'd be able to do much with them for now. The protections he had instituted for her would hopefully function—but he wouldn't be able to summon her as a Blade for now.

"Great art," Wit whispered, running his hand through his hair, which was white in this body. "Is about . . ." About what? ". . . about novelty. Yes. It comes back to novelty once again, you see."

The door creaked open and Ulaam stepped in. As usual, the creature wore its skin an ashen grey. "Ah, Hoid. Our little experiment worked, hmmmm? I found you on the floor of my laboratory earlier this morning!"

"Thank you," Wit . . . no, Hoid . . . said, "for keeping that cell culture alive." His body regenerated from the largest piece of flesh he had remaining. He'd always known this, but had never found opportunity to, well, weaponize it.

"This can be of great use, don't you think?" Ulaam asked. He hesitated, straightening the cuffs of his black suit. "Was it painful, vaporizing yourself?"

"Odium did it for me."

"Oh? Hmm . . ." Ulaam grew more solemn. "I see. Then the rumors about Roshar are true?"

"I need a seon right away," Hoid said, standing again. "I need to find out what's happening."

"We're already trying!" Ulaam said. "But time appears to be passing far slower on Roshar than it is here, which is making communication unreliable. Quite the slowness bubble around the planet, yes indeed, hmmmm? Why, I bet it will be months before we have the full story! Months for us. Hours for them."

Months? When Shards died, combined, or otherwise distorted, strange events could follow. Harmony's creation had involved the remaking of a world, while Ambition's death had destroyed several. The formation of Retribution . . . caused time dilation?

That could be an enormous hassle. "I need to get back immediately."

"Hoid," Ulaam said, "if you go, you'll be trapped in that bubble. We'll lose you for who knows how long, and events are transpiring. Autonomy is moving. I have a message I'm certain is from Taldain, though the planet should be unreachable. Think carefully before you return to Roshar, hmmmm?"

Hoid sat back on his bed. Ulaam left some broadsheets for him, as well as a short report on everything they knew about Roshar so far, then retreated. When Hoid read it, the depth of his own failures at last sank into him.

"Novelty," Hoid whispered, running his hand through his hair again. "Yes, novelty. The unexpected. It . . . I . . ."

Somewhere dear to him, a new storm was blowing. A storm that would strangle all plant life, and kill everyone unless Retribution intervened. Somewhere dear to him, a continent was trembling and breaking as a god was absorbed. Spren would be slaughtered unless a miracle happened.

Somewhere dear to him, Design was alone, and his former apprentice carried a vitally powerful artifact, unaware of the damage it would do to his soul. Friends had been cast adrift, without guidance. A woman he'd loved. Youths he'd mentored. He'd told himself he would sacrifice Roshar for the good of the cosmere, but at the end he hadn't been so certain. And now it seemed it was going to be sacrificed anyway, just not for the good of anyone or anything.

It would take months for him to get back. And if he did . . . the greater cosmere *would* suffer. For Odium had not only been unleashed, he had become something that would rival even Harmony in power.

"Novelty?" Hoid whispered. "Who am I to speak of novelty? I'm far, far too late for that. Betrayal isn't anything new, you see, not for me. Would that it were."

He could not return. The people of Roshar, including those he loved, were on their own. He had to protect Scadrial first, because they absolutely could not afford to lose this planet too. What had Dalinar been thinking? Why had he . . .

Wait.

Hoid's eyes opened.

Could it be . . .

He closed his eyes, took a small bone from his pocket, and reached out to the meditative realm of the dragons—where he'd always be an interloper. There, he sought the wisdom of the ancient dead who could see far more clearly, if you knew how to get them to talk to you.

From them, he discovered something he had never suspected: Dalinar Kholin had been an absolute *storming* genius.

⁂

Adolin sat down at the conference table in Azimir—a room with dark green decor and uncomfortable seats. The same room, apparently, where the Prime was traditionally chosen.

It had been about a month and a half since the confrontation between Odium and Dalinar. Outside, rain beat against the metal rooftop with a clatter. That sound—for the first few days—had nearly driven him insane. Now it was just background noise.

Noura settled at the table, as did most of the nine Unoathed—the ten including Adolin—who had taken up Shards to save Azimir. They had Blades and Plate for others to join them, thirty-seven in total. So far they'd been cautious about progressing, until they decided their next steps.

The long conference table flickered with weevilwax candles—a stock that the city was working furiously to replenish. Compared to the steady, familiar light of spheres, the candles were harsh and terrible. Like shouts when he was accustomed to kind words.

Adolin looked to Yanagawn, again dressed in his regalia—though the young man could summon his Plate and Blade like a Radiant at any moment. Somehow, their armor and swords worked without Stormlight. In contrast to those of ordinary Shardbearers—whose Blades could not be bonded and Plate could not be repaired—the armaments of the Unoathed still functioned. Maya said something had been done at the end by the Heralds to shield and protect the spren—and this was a side effect.

Radiants could still summon Blades and Plate too, but Adolin's Unoathed could do it without Surges or oaths. They were something new.

"All right, Adolin," Noura said. "Are you going to tell us why you brought us here? You finally have news?" Thankfully he could still understand when people spoke Azish, though the Connection that Dalinar had made for him was starting to slip. It now took Adolin a few minutes every morning before the words started making sense.

"Maya has returned," he explained, "from her trip to Urithiru." As the Oathgates and the spanreeds no longer functioned, sending her seemed the best way. Normal Radiant spren were unable to travel to the other side. But Maya . . . with whatever strange bond she had with Adolin . . . could.

"And?" Yanagawn asked.

Adolin took a deep breath. "My father is dead."

He braced himself as he said it. The pain was still raw, and anguishspren congregated at his feet. But he forced himself onward, recounting what Maya had learned from the spren who gathered at Urithiru, in Shadesmar. Odium had won, and the world was now his—everything but Azir. Well, and Urithiru—but it was now inside a strange glass bubble, and people in the Physical Realm couldn't get in or out. Renarin had freed Ba-Ado-Mishram, and didn't know what that meant for the world.

"Radiants still have powers in Urithiru itself," he explained, "which is how we were able to get this information. Jasnah can look into Shadesmar and speak to the spren there, but no one can leave Urithiru in the Physical Realm, and Radiants across the world are unable to use their powers."

"But we can summon our Blades and Plate," Notum said, standing on the table, small sized. "Indeed, our spren seem to be recovering."

"Xorm continues to improve," the emperor agreed—naming the spren of his sword. "Whatever your brother did, Adolin, it has helped the deadeyes."

I concur, Maya said. *Every deadeye I met—even those not part of our group—is healing. Adolin, I saw my reflection, and I have* eyes *again. The scratches remain like faded scars, but I have eyes.*

"Yet we have no Stormlight," Noura said. "And that storm . . . it doesn't stop. It rains and it blows. For over a *month straight.*"

The words chilled Adolin. The Everstorm blanketed the entire land—not as violent as it had been at times, true, but pervasive. It seemed that in expanding it to the entire continent, Odium had been forced to let it weaken. It was wind and rain, mostly, with little lightning. At least the quaking of the ground had stilled for the most part, though the news they gathered of changes to the landscape terrified him.

Azimir had been spared that. They'd felt only rumbles in the distance as the world trembled at the coming of a new god. Worse, that storm would strangle the world. No spanreeds for communication. No Oathgates. No . . .

No healing. He looked at the missing portion of his leg, where he wore the single piece of Plate that grew a metal kind of leg and foot, with three large toe-like portions. He was getting quite proficient with it, but still had been hoping to have his actual foot back. Now . . .

Well, storms. He'd gotten off easy. His father . . .

His father had failed to protect them, but only so much could be expected of one man. Others would curse Dalinar in coming days, but Adolin would not be one of them. For a part of him had known what had happened since that day—when he'd felt a surreal sense of love and apology from his father.

Adolin had survived that terrible night by telling himself he needed to see his father again, to make amends. He felt that last parting gift from Dalinar, but was still sad. He'd never have the chance to look Dalinar in the eyes again.

Damnation, that *hurt.*

"Well," Kushkam said. "We ten are not beaten. We are Shardbearers, and can grow our ranks for as long as the others who came with Maya are willing."

"We also have all those Radiants at Urithiru," May added. "They have powers, even if they can't leave for now."

Adolin nodded, but he felt troubled. Shallan reportedly lived, for which he was incredibly relieved. Former Oathgate spren had confirmed it to Maya. She had lingered at Urithiru for a few days, the spren there said, but had left on a ship. He worried for her, and was terrified he might not be able to see her again if the Oathgates didn't work.

Roshar was now a world without Stormlight. Could Shallan ever return to the Physical Realm?

Almighty help them. What were they going to do?

"Everyone!" The door slammed open, revealing Zabra, her hair in braids and wearing an outfit with hokra—those were the patterns delineating station—proclaiming her a Shardbearer. "Everyone, come outside!"

They looked to each other. Noura drew her lips to a line—she did *not* like how familiar Zabra was with the emperor, but could say nothing. Yanagawn considered each of the Unoathed to be of a rank permitted to speak with him—and in fact gloried in the opportunity. He and Gezamal must have played dozens of games of towers over the last weeks.

The emperor finally had friends. Noura would learn to deal with it.

"Zabra?" Yanagawn asked. "What is it?"

"The rain," she said. "It's *ending.*"

They piled out of the room. Adolin was last, and on the side table, he found the book he'd placed there. One from which he was, haltingly, learning to read. Because if he couldn't ever see his father again, he *could* try to understand the man.

By reading his own words.

Adolin tucked *Oathbringer* under his arm, and followed the others out of the palace. Miraculously, the clouds were indeed breaking. He stepped into sunlight, blinking at the familiar glow. It was like a rank of diligent soldiers shoving back the enemy forces at long last. Brilliant and shining down, a column of light like his father used to make.

There, Adolin felt a warmth he could not explain. Perhaps just from the sunlight, but it seemed something more. Book snug under his arm, he felt like somewhere his father was smiling at him. Adolin quietly raised his fist over his head, saluting the triumphant sun.

They found in coming weeks that the sunlight extended *exactly* to the edge of Azir. The rest of the land, Shinovar included, would remain cloaked in eternal night. The barriers of the Purelake had broken, and flooding had claimed many nearby lowlands, further isolating Azir.

However, the enemy could not touch this land. Small though it might seem, a light *would* remain in Roshar.

⁂

Shallan, swathed in a long cloak, kept her head down as she worked her way through the crowd of spren. There were some few humans here, so she wasn't *too* obvious. And she was glad for the cloak, as Shadesmar had felt strangely cold ever since that day, months ago now, when Retribution had been born.

She managed to push to the front of the crowd, which waited beside a crater in the obsidian ground. It was empty.

She breathed out. Yes, she'd heard. But she'd wanted to see it for herself. This had been Cultivation's Perpendicularity, the pool at the top of the Horneater Peaks, the place where most people entered or left the Physical Realm. They'd been able to do so here for millennia.

It had vanished when Cultivation had fled Roshar. Shallan stared at the hole for a long time, feeling unsettled—like many of the people who camped at its rim, waiting. She knew that . . . that she'd probably stay as well, for a time. Because there was a community here, and hope—frail hope.

She was . . . she was trapped in Shadesmar.

Months of travel and hoping desperately. Now it finally sank in. She might never escape this realm.

She might never see Adolin again.

Her hands went to her stomach, cradling it. Oh . . . oh *storms.*

It took an embarrassingly long time for her to recover. Fortunately, the part of her that was Radiant was able to assess the situation. There was food and water here, transported from offworld—and regular shipping lanes were planned to Urithiru, where Towerlight would also allow manifesting and the creation of food and water for humans.

She could survive. She had to. Not just for herself.

Plus, there *had* to be ways back into the Physical Realm. Retribution would have a perpendicularity somewhere, even if Odium's had never been located. Radiant powers at Urithiru still functioned, which meant there was a chance an Elsecaller—well, only Jasnah for now—would finally figure out how to transfer other people between realms.

Hope. Shallan *would* find a way.

She trudged back among the tents and shanties, crossing wooden ground that floated here—Haka'alaku, a city built around the perpendicularity, covered seven distinct islands with floating wooden platforms between. It was of impressive size, ruled by the peakspren. Their egalitarian ways meant that even humans were in their senate, as anyone who lived here long enough was granted citizenship.

Of course, the Fused *actually* ruled. But they allowed the local government to do its thing. Shallan pulled her cloak tighter and quieted her armor spren—who rode in the pouches at her belt, and had begun to whisper her name again, as she hadn't paid attention to them in a while.

She wound back to where she'd left Pattern and Testament, watching a specific camp among the hundreds on the outskirts of the city. Tents set up on the floating boards, space rented at a very cheap price in the local currency—bits of metal, of all things. She'd been able to sell some clothing, which was of value here because it wasn't manifested.

She nodded to her spren, not looking as several Fused flew overhead. Their powers still worked.

The Fused offer another opportunity, Shallan thought. *If their Light functions, they might be able to make a perpendicularity somehow.* I will *find my way back to him.*

Until then . . .

With Pattern and Testament, she approached a small collection of tents. Here, a familiar figure stood up. Felt, a foreigner with drooping mustaches, had once been one of Dalinar's good friends. He'd then been one of Adolin's soldiers, and their guide on the way to Lasting Integrity.

Lastly, he'd turned out to be a traitor. A Ghostblood.

When she took down her hood, his face went so white, he looked like he was about to pass out.

"I just want to talk to him," Shallan said.

"Him?" Felt asked.

"Your leader. The Lord of Scars. Is it possible? Do the seons still work?"

"Yes," Felt admitted. "Kind of."

"I need to use yours," Shallan said. "It's the least you can do for me, Felt. Besides, I have news that you might find relevant."

⁂

Sigzil walked, cloak pulled tight, tongue dry in his mouth from thirst.

He was often thirsty here, but the power had begun to sustain him. The thing Wit called a "Dawnshard." It . . . it kept him alive. And changed him. He could . . . sense things he had never been able to before. He saw the world in new ways.

He'd spent months crossing the bead oceans by begging passage, dodging Fused and keeping his head down, and was now accustomed to the dark sky. The one that reminded him of the Shattered Plains as he'd last seen them, before . . .

Before . . .

He kept walking. Across the black obsidian, for some reason not sleepy, though he *felt* tired. He'd been unable to sleep since that day when Wit had given him this burden.

A burden Sigzil *would* protect. He'd prove himself. Redeem himself. He . . .

He just kept walking.

On. And on. Until at last he saw something on the otherwise featureless obsidian expanse. Lights. As he approached, those soon resolved into a long line of people, most of them with golden hair and carrying torches that gave off light but not heat.

Sigzil let out a sigh of relief. He'd found the Iriali caravan that was traveling offworld, as spoken of by some of the spren he'd encountered in his journey. He'd sought out Vienta first, of course. He hadn't found her, but she'd sent him a message. She didn't want to speak to him, but she lived. Healed by whatever had happened at the End of All Things.

 He didn't blame her for rejecting him. He'd consigned her—both had believed—to a painful half existence. He had done it to save her, and the note she'd sent acknowledged that, but she still didn't want to see him.

The caravan was much bigger than he'd anticipated, stretching far into the distance. The guards at the perimeter questioned him, then sent him to a specific section near the end. The Iriali allowed foreign travelers to join them, so long as they behaved themselves and worked for their keep. They also thought it best if you stayed with your own kind.

In this case, "own kind" meant anyone who wasn't Iriali. So it was that eventually Sigzil found himself in the rear of a chull-pulled wagon. Taken in by a family who, after one glance, had told him to hop in the back and rest.

He didn't want to know how he looked to elicit that kind of response. But he'd been walking for so long he . . . he didn't much care. He sat there, numb, until someone else climbed into the wagon.

A highspren?

Yes, a highspren, who split the air and was filled with stars. An outline of a person. "You are a Windrunner, yes?" he said.

"No," Sigzil whispered.

"No need to lie," the spren said. "I've seen you, with the others. With Kaladin."

Sigzil perked up. "You . . . know Kaladin?"

"Briefly, I knew him. I can tell you of his time in Shinovar, though I do not know the end of his quest there. I was rejected by my Radiant first."

Sigzil considered, rocking in place, numb. "Spren can't leave Roshar. Why are you here on this caravan?"

"Ah, well, you see," the highspren said—having far more familiar a tone than Sigzil had expected—"I *can* leave now! Any of us can. There are some in the caravan, even some windspren and other smaller ones. Cultivation fled, and it was her bond with Honor, and their agreement with Odium, that locked us here." The spren hesitated, then leaned forward. "Can I tell you a secret, Windrunner?"

"Sure," Sigzil said. "Why not?"

"I'm a failure," the spren confessed. "I think maybe most of us highspren are. I don't want to be a bother, but these Iriali mostly ignore me, and I really, *really* need someone to talk to. Please? I will tell you of Kaladin."

Sigzil shrugged. "Go ahead. I'll listen."

"Well, thank you," the spren replied. "It started when Dalinar sent us to— "

"Wait," Sigzil said, frowning. "You're Szeth's spren?"

"I was," the spren said, then hung his head. "He rejected me."

Sigzil grunted. "You have a name?"

"I used to have one. I don't want it anymore."

"I'm sure we'll think of something," Sigzil said, leaning back. And he listened to the spren's story, sitting in a daze and trying not to be frightened of the way his very body seemed to be changing to adapt to the power he held.

Wit had promised to find him soon though. Until then, Sigzil could do this one task. He'd hold the secret.

∴

Talking to Thaidakar, the Lord of Scars, was odd for Shallan. The seon—Ala—could indeed contact the Ghostblood leader. No Stormlight needed.

The Ghostblood leader, in turn, was willing to talk to Shallan. And fortunately, old Thaidakar didn't seem too angry at hearing Iyatil and Mraize were dead. Shallan kept a close eye on Felt anyway; storms, she was so exposed and vulnerable without any way to heal herself.

Yes, it all worked as she sat in Felt's tent, communicating through the seon spren. There was only one problem.

"You're in some kind of planet-wide slowness bubble," old Thaidakar explained, his face a hovering globe of light, imitated by Ala. It had a spike through one eye. "The clash of two Shards, including the near destruction of your world, followed by the combining of those two Shards into one? It's done something to the Spiritual Realm near your planet, changing the way time flows for you.

"You think we're communicating directly, but the better part of an hour passes here between each of your replies to me. You think it has been a few months, but it has been *years* for us. Ala has to slow down and repeat this as a recording—for if I spoke in real time, you'd hear only a quick blip."

Shallan took that in. "So if I leave to get help from other planets . . ."

The face shook, then re-formed. "Yes, if you left and traveled to another world, decades might pass for you. I don't recommend it, unless there is nobody you care about—because when you return, you will be much older than they are."

She pulled her cloak closer, feeling cold. "How long will this effect last? Can you guess?"

The face froze, then shook, then spoke again, and it looked like his hair had been brushed. "We've been calculating. Seems like the time dilation *is* slowing around Roshar, and the worst was at the start, but it's going to be a while yet. Maybe . . . seventy or eighty years from now, you'll realign with cosmere standard? That will seem like a decade or so for you."

She nodded. Waiting for more, but of course he was getting this—apparently—as messages spread across a few hours. He wouldn't be watching for a head nod.

"Have you thought about my proposal?" she asked Thaidakar.

He fuzzed again. Then responded. "I have. I don't know if I can make peace with you, Kholin. Killing Iyatil went too far. I accept that she must bear the consequences of her brutality, but she *was* my colleague—and her brother will need to be told what happened. He doesn't know yet. We've had our own crisis here recently.

"However, without Stormlight—and with Mishram freed—our interests on Roshar are minimized. I doubt Iyatil's brother will insist on coming to seek vengeance against you immediately. He's more likely going to try to break away from me—so I might have a little civil war on my hands. If his agents do arrive on Roshar, they'll be your enemies.

"So for now, let us consider it a truce between us, but not one between Ghostblood and Lightweaver. The truth is, you're just too small to worry about right now, Kholin. Odium is not only free, he's picked up a second Shard. The worst that could happen, *has* happened. From here it will be war. I'd focus on that if I were you. Dark days are coming."

"Then I demand one thing," Shallan said. "A payment for what yours did to me and mine. For the murders Iyatil and Mraize committed in your name."

A pause. A fuzzing. Two words. "What price?"

"This seon spren obeys you, works for you," Shallan said. "I want it to join me instead, and work under my direction until I can sort through a few things."

This response took longer. Probably hours for him.

"Ala is not a slave," he finally said, "but I've asked her. She . . . agrees that we owe you something. She will enter your employ, so long as you're willing to let her report back to me of events on Roshar as she sees them."

"Fine."

"A deal, then," he said. "We are settled. A clever bargain on your part—you can hire out her services to others at a steep price, which will give you income in Shadesmar. Farewell for now, Shallan Kholin."

The face vanished, again becoming a ball of light, which bobbed for Shallan. "So . . ." the ball said. "I guess . . . I might have to earn back your trust . . ."

"You never will, but that won't prevent us from working together." Shallan looked to Felt. "What about you?"

"I'm used to this kind of thing," he said, with a shrug. "One mess after another, doing my job. With Lord Dalinar and Lord Mraize dead . . . well, guess Malli and I will have to find someone else to serve. If our old bodies can manage it."

Shallan stood up and pushed out of the tent, and waved for the ball to follow her. She was well aware she was inviting a spy for Thaidakar into her midst again, but she had a distinct purpose this time.

She joined Pattern and Testament, who was increasingly verbal these days, her scratches almost completely faded, her pattern more vibrant. Shallan explained what she'd discovered to them, then looked at the seon.

"Spren," she said to it. "Wit had one of you in the tower, and he used it to communicate. Are there others in this land you know of?"

"Yes," she admitted. "A small number." She paused. "I can contact Olo, who worked for your Wit. We've been chatting. Olo fled the tower at his master's suggestion months ago, and is weaving toward the Shattered Plains."

"Contact him," Shallan said. "And tell him I have a job for him, if he's willing. But I need him to go to Azimir."

"Azimir? Olo tends to like to be helpful, so I suspect he'll go, but why Azimir?"

Shallan just bade her ask, feeling a grim determination. She had no idea how she'd get back to the Physical Realm, but for now . . . if this worked, she'd at least be able to talk to Adolin. As she waited for Ala to contact the other seon spren, she looked up at the sky. There were no more clouds in Shadesmar. Only darkness and a distant, frail sun, too small to offer warmth.

Dark days were coming, Thaidakar said.

He was wrong in that.

They had most certainly already arrived.

⁂

It was months, by mortal time on Roshar—years outside it—before Retribution could spare a thought for Roshar itself. He quickly checked that the land was progressing as he wanted. There was turmoil, and the geography had been broken in ways he hadn't anticipated.

Dalinar. Foolish, stubborn Dalinar.

Dalinar Kholin, the man who had known.

Taravangian emerged into the Spiritual Realm in his avatar form, joining a vision he himself had created and kept going indefinitely. It was populated by tens of thousands of people.

His daughter. His grandchildren. Adrotagia.

Each of whom was real, and not a fake made of this realm.

Kharbranth was dead, but in the moment that Cultivation had looked away, Taravangian had summoned his power and taken the people. The city had indeed been destroyed, but he'd saved the occupants. In utter secret.

In the Spiritual Realm, he'd created for them a clone of Kharbranth. He walked its streets, knowing them to be fake, while no one living here did. He'd taken from them any memory of Cultivation's killers, whom he'd left to die in the city, and had instead implanted in their minds an impression that those who were missing had died of a strange disease. That had started with the city guards.

He walked to the palace and into his throne room, where Adrotagia—real, not a construct of visions—was meeting with some former members of the Diagram. "Vargo," she said. So far as she now remembered, he had not died.

So far as any of them knew, everything had turned out well. Peace had been made, though they were required to stay in their city. He embraced her, then walked to his throne. He settled down there, and called for his grandchildren to be brought to visit. He held them as they crawled into his lap.

The entire city would persist in here, isolated and protected from whatever he did in the cosmere. One perfect place of peace and love.

His secret. His dangerous, shameful secret. Because in the end, although no one could ever know it, there were things even Taravangian—in a moment of pain and passion—had refused to sacrifice.

He embraced his grandchildren, weeping, and the power simmered. Hating Dalinar Kholin.

For having been right.

"All art," Hoid said, "is secretly improvisation."

The other people in the waiting room glanced at him, giving him dark looks. He sat primly in his coachman's uniform, hat under his arm. He'd dusted off his old beggar's costume—well, it was supposed to be dirty, so he'd more dusted *onto* it—for an appearance here and there. However, he wanted to be gainfully occupied. And stay close to some important, relevant people who tended to look poorly on someone who could fill a garden with good topsoil merely by shivering.

"Art," Hoid said. "It's truly improvisation. You realize that, don't you?"

The others ignored him. How rude.

"You see," he said, leaning toward a woman waiting to apply for a buttling position, by the advertisement in her fingers. "You can practice, and practice, and practice. But then the moment comes, and . . ." He made a gesture with his fingers toward the ceiling, drawing her eyes that way. "And then the lights turn on, and the practice is but a *guide.*

"An outline? Well, you start with a blank page either way. And the parts where you're forced, by narrative beauty, to toss the outline away? Improvisation. Art *is* improvisation. It's the brushstrokes you don't intend, but your instincts know you need anyway. The parts of the story you add for a specific reader, the expression you make onstage to provoke a gasp. *That's* the art."

The woman scooted a little distance away from him.

"I was wrong with my plans," he said, staring toward the sky. The ceiling was in the way, but that didn't matter. He could imagine it. That was basically the entirety of his job. "I was so meticulous, so *deliberate;* I tried to be so clever. And then poof, it was all destroyed. By a grand act of *majestic* improvisation."

He could see now what Dalinar Kholin had done. It had taken Hoid weeks to *grasp* what that wonderful, belligerent, spectacular man had done. Everyone, Hoid at their forefront, had been ready to walk away again. Their problem safely delayed once more.

In one grand stroke, Dalinar had stolen that from them. He'd released the lion from its cage, or the whitespine from its den, or the dragon from her palace. And he'd given them a huge boost to propel them into being a cataclysmic threat, if unchecked. He'd *demanded* that action be taken, and Retribution had been forced to turn from Roshar to deal with greater foes.

At first, Hoid had worried this would destroy Roshar. But no, of course it wouldn't, because Retribution would not let himself get caught and killed so easily. He'd gone into hiding immediately, but it was very hard for a Shard to hide—so long as it wanted to influence things, the vibrations would be felt.

Now, a dance. A game on a grand scale, building to war. One none of them had wanted, because they'd been willing to quietly pretend that it would never happen, and that the murderer who had killed at least three of their number wasn't *their problem.*

What a glorious play Dalinar had made.

Roshar would have troubles, yes, and they would be difficult to survive. But better for the axe to fall now, when it might only take a limb. And during that time, just maybe, Retribution would assume the place secured and loyal.

Which gave Roshar a chance.

"Hoid?" the Ladrian house steward called from the front of the small waiting room.

How did he see? Hoid thought, standing up. *How did Dalinar find the way out?* This hadn't been one of the many more obvious possibilities. It had been a small, insignificant one—as likely as flipping a coin onto the same side a thousand times in a row. None of them had seen it, because when possibilities were infinite, you could get a tad overwhelmed.

It bothered him that few would know what Dalinar had achieved and sacrificed. But fortunately, at least one person *did* know, and he wasn't exactly a quiet type. Dalinar Kholin's true story *would* be told. Once the time was right, and Hoid could get back to Roshar.

The Ladrian house steward was a plump, middle-aged woman. She had a prim jacket and spectacles, and a bright yellow pocket square. The type of bold coloring in an otherwise drab outfit that said, "I consider myself a fun-loving type—but I decided to study accounting, and I now know seventeen different ways to fill out a ledger."

From her seat behind the desk, the woman looked him up and down, spectacles on the end of her nose. Then she studied the application in front of her.

"I believe," Miss Grimes said, "you're interested in the coachman job?"

"I am?" Hoid said. "I suppose that explains this coachman's jacket, this coachman's hat, and the application for a coachman's job filled out by me that you are, indeed, holding at this very moment."

"Ah," the woman said. "A funny type."

"Only when the situation does not call for it, ma'am."

She grunted, turning the page. "You realize the pay is terrible."

"It always is."

"You don't have any references."

"Previous employer is a tad indisposed," he said, "living on another planet, which is undergoing a brief, but dramatic, world-ending cataclysm." He leaned forward. "Also, she broke up with me recently, and I don't think I'd get much of a referral."

The woman took that in stride, which improved Hoid's opinion of her. "Well, I can't be too picky," the steward said, stamping his application. "Seeing as ever since a previous fellow *literally* ended up driving off a cliff, we've had trouble keeping the position filled. You passed the driving test, and Jone says you're good with the horses and know your way around the city, even if you are a little odd. Report in tomorrow. Six sharp."

"Thank you, ma'am," Hoid said, then leaned down farther across the table. "I didn't know what to do. Thing is, that's *wonderful.* That's the *point.* Because when the predetermined answers flee, then the solution comes down to who you are. That's when we see the mettle of a person. That is *art:* when untested skill meets unplanned catastrophe."

The woman looked up at him, then blinked. "I think I understand."

"Wait. Really. You do?"

"Of course I do," the woman said. "You're here for this job because absolutely nobody else will hire you. Good thing you can get a person where they're going."

"Ma'am," Hoid said, putting on his hat, "you have no idea."

He turned and walked from the room into the sunlight, already improvising. First, to help guide this crisis on Scadrial. After that . . .

Well, hate it though he did, there was only one reasonable choice. With Retribution formed, Hoid needed allies—even allies who hated him—who knew how to fight gods.

He would have to go find Valor. After all that time he'd spent trying to manipulate Dalinar, the old Blackthorn had gone and manipulated Hoid—and every single Shard.

"Brilliant job, my friend," he said, striding out onto the street. "Brilliant *storming* job. You've given us a chance. Let's hope we can live up to it."

POSTLUDE TO

THE STORMLIGHT ARCHIVE

Kalak woke up somewhere bright.

On a grassy hillside, where the plants didn't pull away. Near an ocean. A real ocean beach, and real grass. He thought . . . he thought he recognized the place.

Alaswha? But it had been destroyed. How?

He shrank down upon himself, huddling on that hillside, when he heard voices. He turned slowly to see people atop the slope. It wasn't a hill . . . but instead a little ridge leading down to the sandy beach. Behind it was an open expanse of green.

People stood there. His former friends. The others . . .

I didn't survive, he thought. *I died. I've gone to Braize.*

The flesh burning.

The fires.

The pain, over and over . . .

Yes, it looked peaceful now, but this must be a new kind of torture. The friendly grass and soothing waves? It would be snatched away. Three of the figures in the group were wrong. That was proof. Who was that soldier in Kholin blue? That figure he couldn't quite make out? That was Nale's spren, he supposed. But that woman with white-blue hair, long and flowing? She didn't belong here.

Kalak shuddered, panicking as the man in blue saw him and walked over.

"Hey," the man said, squatting down on the top of the ridge, a few feet from Kalak.

"What lie is this?" Kalak demanded. "What kind of Voidbringer are you?"

"I'm not one," the man said. "My name is Kaladin. I've . . . joined you. To replace Jezrien."

"Impossible."

"You saw me, Kalak, when we asked you to refound the Oathpact. You were there."

His hand on a sword.

A chance to prove himself again. A chance to protect the spren. He'd done that, yes. He . . . remembered . . . but it seemed a dream, as did the lessening of darkness that had encouraged him forward. He was a wretch, and always would be.

The man smiled. "Ishar has changed the way the Oathpact functions, Kalak. He brought our minds here, where the enemy will not be able to reach us."

Was . . . was that *possible*?

Dared he hope?

"No," Kalak hissed. "I don't deserve something like that. I've failed everyone. I'm worthless."

"Not true," Kaladin said. "Ishar says . . . says that with the merging of Honor and Odium . . . things are odd. An unexpected warping of time has happened, so it will pass strangely for us. More strangely even than what is happening on Roshar. While years pass there, months will pass for us. We have time, for once, and peace."

Kalak cringed. "I don't believe it."

The man, Kaladin, reached out his hand. "Come join us, Kalak. Come see."

"No. I've failed. It's too late." Kalak closed his eyes. "Everything I've done . . . everything I've tried . . . It's only led to more destruction and doom."

"I know how that feels. Trust me." And there was something . . . compelling about his voice. Empathetic. Could a Voidbringer fake that?

Kalak opened his eyes.

Kaladin still had his hand outstretched. "Come. At least listen to me. I think I can help you reclaim some of what you used to be."

"There's nothing left," Kalak said. "The world is doomed. We have failed. Everyone on Roshar is as good as dead."

"Then what harm is there," Kaladin said, "in trying one more time? If everything is already doomed?"

"I . . ."

"One more try," Kaladin whispered. "Just once more."

"Once more," Kalak said. "A . . . final Return?"

"We heal," Kaladin said. "We reclaim ourselves. *Then* we go back to Roshar. This time, we win for real. Instead of coming back withered from torture, you'll return refreshed. Mended, and we'll see what we can do together."

One more try.

A final Return.

What harm . . . what harm could there be in it? Still he wavered, ever incapable of simply deciding. He wanted to shy away, but then he saw a figure sitting beyond the others. A man with dark skin. A man they'd abandoned.

"Is that Taln?" Kalak asked. "Taln is here? Has he . . . said anything?"

"He needs time," Kaladin said. "And help. So far, he's only said one thing. He said . . . he forgives you all."

A tremble went through Kalak. It left warmth and, unfortunately, shame in its wake. He was used to the shame. He'd carried it for millennia. The warmth was new.

Taln was back.

Taln . . . forgave them.

Kalak reached up and took Kaladin's hand.

THE END OF

the First Arc of

THE STORMLIGHT ARCHIVE

THE STORY WILL CONCLUDE
IN BOOKS SIX THROUGH TEN

ENDNOTE

Trusted Words
Known Words
Renounce Once.
Renounce Words Known.
Words . . . trusted . . .

Once.

Ketek discovered inscribed in the stone on the top of Urithiru following the Contest of Champions.

It is believed not to be in the hand of Dalinar Kholin, but possibly in that of some spren or divine manifestation.

This is disputed, for the ketek is not fully symmetrical, but has an extraneous word left below, on its own line, as if divided from the poem. This leads to imperfection, and it is presumed no divinity or spren would be capable of such an egregious error.

This completes the first major arc of the Stormlight Archive, and is the midpoint of my grand, ten-book plot outline. I will return to Roshar with Book Six in the near future. Thank you, as always, for joining me. Journey before Destination.

Brandon Sanderson